OXFORD WORLD'S CLASSICS

ANNA KARENINA

COUNT LEO NIKOLAEVICH TOLSTOY was born in 1828 into an aristocratic family at Yasnaya Polyana, his father's estate in Tula province, about 200 miles from Moscow. His mother died before he was two, and his father when he was nine. He studied Oriental languages and law at the University of Kazan, before leading a somewhat dissolute life until 1851, when he joined an artillery regiment in the Caucasus. It was here that he wrote his first stories. He then served as an artillery officer at the siege of Sevastopol during the Crimean War. A period in St Petersburg and abroad followed during which he studied educational methods he used for the benefit of peasant children at Yasnaya Polyana. In 1862 he married Sofya Behrs, and for some years led a secluded life as a country gentleman and author. *War and Peace* was finished in 1869 and *Anna Karenina* in 1877. He fathered thirteen children. In 1879, after undergoing a severe spiritual crisis, he wrote the autobiographical *Confession*, and from then on he renounced his earlier literary works, seeking to promote his views on religion, morality, pacifism, and sexuality. A champion of religious freedom and enemy of church dogma, Tolstoy assigned the royalties from his late novel *Resurrection* (1899) to a pacifist Christian sect. *The Death of Ivan Ilyich* (1886) is most characteristic of his later work in its intense philosophical scrutiny of life and death. *The Kreutzer Sonata* (1889), a novella about adultery and sexual jealousy, is a masterpiece of disturbed narration. In 1901 Tolstoy was excommunicated by the Russian Orthodox Church for heresy. His life as a sage put his marital and family life under increasing emotional and financial strain. He died in 1910 of pneumonia at the railway station of Astapovo after fleeing his home.

ROSAMUND BARTLETT is a writer, scholar, and translator whose books include *Wagner and Russia* (1995) and *Shostakovich in Context* (2000), as well as biographies of Chekhov (2004) and Tolstoy (2010). As a translator she has produced the first unexpurgated edition of Chekhov's letters, as well as an anthology, *About Love and Other Stories*, published by Oxford World's Classics.

OXFORD WORLD'S CLASSICS

*For over 100 years Oxford World's Classics have brought
readers closer to the world's great literature. Now with over 700
titles—from the 4,000-year-old myths of Mesopotamia to the
twentieth century's greatest novels—the series makes available
lesser-known as well as celebrated writing.*

*The pocket-sized hardbacks of the early years contained
introductions by Virginia Woolf, T. S. Eliot, Graham Greene,
and other literary figures which enriched the experience of reading.
Today the series is recognized for its fine scholarship and
reliability in texts that span world literature, drama and poetry,
religion, philosophy, and politics. Each edition includes perceptive
commentary and essential background information to meet the
changing needs of readers.*

OXFORD WORLD'S CLASSICS

LEO TOLSTOY

Anna Karenina

Translated with an Introduction and Notes by
ROSAMUND BARTLETT

OXFORD
UNIVERSITY PRESS

OXFORD

UNIVERSITY PRESS

Great Clarendon Street, Oxford, ox2 6DP
United Kingdom

Oxford University Press is a department of the University of Oxford.
It furthers the University's objective of excellence in research, scholarship,
and education by publishing worldwide. Oxford is a registered trade mark of
Oxford University Press in the UK and in certain other countries

First published 2014
First published as an Oxford World's Classics paperback 2016
Impression: 6

Published in the United States of America by Oxford University Press
198 Madison Avenue, New York, NY 10016, United States of America

British Library Cataloguing in Publication Data

Data available

Library of Congress Control Number: 2015943753

ISBN 978-0-19-874884-7

Printed in Great Britain by
Clays Ltd, Elcograf S.p.A.

CONTENTS

ANNA KARENINA

INTRODUCTION

Readers who do not wish to learn details of the plot will prefer to treat the Introduction as an Afterword.

ANNA KARENINA, one of the world's greatest novels, and with justification regarded by many as Tolstoy's finest artistic work, also marks the culmination of his career as a professional writer. Begun in 1873, when the author was 45 years old, it resumes and develops themes explored in previous works, most notably the epic *War and Peace*, which he had embarked on ten years earlier. These themes, which may be subsumed under the central question 'how to live?', are explored with a pressing urgency in *Anna Karenina*, for Tolstoy was increasingly overcome during the novel's protracted composition by an existential despair which is reflected in its closing pages. While *Anna Karenina* represents the summation of the literary journey that Tolstoy had completed thus far, all the way from *Childhood*, his first work of published fiction of 1852, the novel also looks forward to what he would write over the next three decades of his life.

Tolstoy emerged from the spiritual crisis which engulfed him upon completion of *Anna Karenina* no longer as a novelist, but as a crusader for his own brand of ethics-based Christianity. He did not completely forswear the writing of literature, indeed some of his best fiction dates from this next period, but he resolutely turned his back on publishing novels for what he regarded as the pampered educated classes. Having been the most highly paid author in Russia, he also now relinquished the earning of fees and royalties for personal enrichment, and channelled his creative energies into proselytizing his new-found religious beliefs. Many of their central precepts are adumbrated in embryonic form in *Anna Karenina*, and also underpin the enthralling love story which lies at the heart of its narrative, thus making it a truly pivotal novel in Tolstoy's oeuvre. As a work passionately bound up with questions of national destiny, *Anna Karenina* also belongs firmly to the great Russian literary tradition, which reached its fullest flowering during Tolstoy's lifetime.

Russian literature had developed along very different lines to those of Western Europe by virtue of the simple fact that there was no tradition of *belles lettres* until Peter the Great launched Russia on an accelerated Westernization programme at the beginning of the eighteenth century, secularizing the arts in the process. The first Russian novel, Pushkin's *Eugene Onegin*, was not published until 1831 (so the old Countess who expresses surprise in his story 'The Queen of Spades', written and set in 1833, that there are any novels written in Russian, is not far from the mark). The belated start, coupled with the imposition of censorship by the end of the eighteenth century and the general lack of political freedom in the Tsarist state, ensured that artists in Russia inevitably practised their craft with a greater seriousness of purpose than elsewhere in Europe. There is, then, a fundamental difference from Western literature, memorably described by John Bayley as being so 'swaddled in the inertia of its accomplishment, the complacency of its prolongation', that even at its 'most urgent' it still sounds literary, with Chaucer's tone 'already professional'. By contrast, he writes, the 'critical dicta of the Russians seem like telegrams exchanged by revolutionaries after a *coup d'état* has begun, but before it is known whether it will succeed'.[1]

The nominally liberal era of Alexander I was replaced in 1825 by the reactionary regime of his martinet younger brother, Nicholas I, who immediately put his stamp on national life by dealing brutally with the idealistic young officers who staged the abortive Decembrist Uprising just as he was coming to power. As time went on, and Nicholas's reign grew more repressive, Russian writers increasingly came to be seen as bearers of the truth, and as moral leaders, particularly by those young members of the intelligentsia from a lowly social background who had benefited from a university education. Figures such as Vissarion Belinsky, Russia's first professional critic, saw literature first and foremost as a weapon for social reform, and believed writers had a vital role to play in helping to arouse in the Russian people a sense of their human dignity and bringing the barbaric institution of serfdom to an end. In 1847, as he lay dying in Germany, Belinsky penned a vituperative letter to Nikolay Gogol, in which he lambasted him for defending serfdom and absolutist government. Russia did not need sermons and prayers or an encouragement in the shameless trafficking of human beings, he thundered, but rights and laws compatible with good sense and justice. The fresh forces trying to break through in Russian society, he argued, were crushed by the weight of oppression, and so produced only despondency, anguish, and apathy. Only in literature, he declared, was there life and forward movement, despite the Tatar censorship.[2]

---

[1] John Bayley, *Tolstoy and the Novel* (London, 1966), 10.

[2] Vissarion Belinsky, *Letter to Gogol*. See Thomas Riha (ed.), *Readings in Russian Civilization*, vol. 2 (Chicago, 1969), 315–20.

Tolstoy was 21 when Belinsky's incendiary letter was smuggled into Russia and circulated secretly in manuscript two years later in St Petersburg. Unlike the earnest and impoverished Dostoevsky, who was imprisoned and exiled to Siberia for having been present at a reading of Belinsky's letter, Tolstoy was leading a dissolute life of gambling, carousing with gypsies, and going into society, to which his aristocratic pedigree gave him an automatic entrée. Within a few years, however, he had joined the army, developed a sense of responsibility, and discovered his vocation: to be a writer. Tolstoy's first work of fiction, the semi-autobiographical *Childhood*, was published in 1852 while he was serving in the Caucasus, and was immediately acclaimed for its acute powers of pyschological analysis, and what the critic Nikolay Chernyshevsky defined as 'purity of moral feeling'. By the time Tolstoy arrived in St Petersburg in November 1855, straight from the siege of Sebastopol, where he had penned several outstanding pieces of reportage about the realities of the Crimean War (and become a pacifist in the process), he was greeted as a conquering hero. He met Turgenev and other luminaries in the literary community for the first time, but soon fell out with them all and retreated back to his beloved country estate of Yasnaya Polyana. It was here, as an archetypal 'repentant nobleman', that he would write *War and Peace* and *Anna Karenina*, both works in which peasants are ultimately the sources of the greatest wisdom.

Tolstoy re-entered civilian life at an exciting time in Russian history. After Nicholas I died in February 1855, the new Tsar, his son Alexander II, allowed scores of political exiles to return from Siberia, amongst them surviving Decembrists and Dostoevsky, and it became easier for Russians to travel abroad. The censorship was relaxed, paving the way for the foundation of new journals such as the *Russian Messenger* in 1856, and books and articles by Western thinkers suddenly became accessible. A number of important new cultural institutions opened, amongst them public libraries, the Mariinsky Theatre, the Moscow School of Painting, Sculpture, and Architecture, and the St Petersburg and Moscow Conservatoires. To accompany Russia's belated embrace of industrialization, an extensive national railway network was finally inaugurated, with lines converging on the emerging business metropolis of Moscow. In 1867 a station on the main line to Kursk opened at Yasenki, a few miles from Yasnaya Polyana, enabling Tolstoy to make the two-hundred-mile journey north to Moscow in half the time it had previously taken. And, most importantly, the great 'Tsar Liberator', as Alexander II came to be known, also introduced a number of far-reaching political reforms at the beginning of his reign, chief of which was the long-awaited Abolition of Serfdom in 1861. These new developments naturally exerted an impact on all the Russian arts, including Russian literature, which in the 1860s entered a glorious decade.

The era of the great Russian realist novel began in the dynamic early years of Alexander II's reign with the publication of Turgenev's *Rudin* in 1856. His masterpiece, *Fathers and Sons* (1862), provides a vivid depiction of the social ferment in Russia in the immediate aftermath of the abolition of serfdom, but sparked controversy by presenting an ambivalent portrait of a nihilist from the new revolutionary generation. Incensed on behalf of this new generation, Chernyshevsky responded with his novel *What Is To Be Done?* (1863), in which he creates a wholly positive revolutionary hero, and advocates woman's liberation and free love. Dostoevsky also concerned himself with contemporary Russia in his new, post-Siberian fiction, but diverged dramatically from both the urbane Westernizer Turgenev and the radical atheist Chernyshevsky. Beginning with *Notes from Underground* (1864), he launched a sustained assault on the Western political and philosophical ideas of utopian socialism he believed were contaminating Russian youth. In 1866 *Crime and Punishment* appeared in the *Russian Messenger* alongside the first chapters of *War and Peace*. Tolstoy shared his fellow writers' preoccupation with Russia, and their strong moral impulse, but was highly unusual in choosing to deal with an earlier historical period in his fiction during such a turbulent time.

By 1875, when Tolstoy began publishing *Anna Karenina* in monthly instalments (also in the *Russian Messenger*), Alexander II had been on the throne for twenty years, and much of the optimism which had greeted his accession had subsided. The terms of the emancipation proved to be so unsatisfactory that the radical intelligentsia began immediately to contemplate revolution, and the first assassination attempt was made on the Tsar's life in 1866. Even those of a more liberal persuasion were disconcerted when their peaceful attempts to inculcate the peasantry with a desire to embrace socialism failed in 1874. Amidst waves of arrests and a rapid deceleration in the progress of reform, hardened Populists turned to terrorism. The new mood of uncertainty and unease pervading Russian society is reflected in *Anna Karenina*. 'Everything was confusion in the Oblonskys' house', we read in the opening lines of the novel. Everything was also confusion in Russia. It is thus understandable why, at a time of such social and political upheaval, some of Tolstoy's more progressive readers were nonplussed by the idea of a novel about an aristocratic woman who has an affair with an army officer. It seemed out of date to them, and their author out of kilter with his age. But of course *Anna Karenina* is very much more than a society novel. Through his characters Levin and Kitty, who embrace traditional values, Tolstoy constructs his own response to Chernyshevsky's inflammatory text and its utilitarian ideas, and the extensive sections in *Anna Karenina* devoted to agrarian issues engage in a very practical way with the seemingly intractable problems facing Russian rural inhabitants (who made up most of the population) as they struggled to survive in conditions which proved to be barely viable and highly unstable.

There was, however, nothing premeditated about the way in which Tolstoy began writing *Anna Karenina*. He first conceived the idea of writing about a high-society woman who has committed adultery a year after completing *War and Peace* in 1870, when his imagination was briefly struck by the idea of making her character pitiable but not guilty. At the same time, he began drafting an article about the 'woman question', a topic debated as hotly in Russia as elsewhere in Europe during this period. John Stuart Mill's influential *The Subjection of Women* had just been published, but the conservative Tolstoy rejected his call for equality between the sexes, and agreed with an article on the subject by Nikolay Strakhov, who argued that a woman's place was in the home. No doubt Tolstoy had also found much to concur with in Schopenhauer's article 'On Women' (1851), which he would have devoured along with all the German philosopher's other works in 1869, and which negated the idea of women's independence.

Tolstoy next proceeded to throw his energies into compiling a 700-page ABC book designed to help teach millions of illiterate Russian children how to read and write, and into trying to write a novel about Peter the Great. Two years later, however, a concatenation of chance occurrences served to bring the idea about the adulterous woman back into Tolstoy's mind. In January 1872 he was shaken after attending the autopsy of a young woman of his acquaintance called Anna Pirogova. Spurned by her lover, she had thrown herself under a goods-train at Yasenki, the railway station close to Yasnaya Polyana which had opened only five years earlier. Then, in the spring of 1873, Tolstoy was very taken with the analysis of marriage he read in a much-discussed article by Alexandre Dumas fils, for whom the struggle between man and woman was the central conflict in life. Prompted by reactions in the press to a controversial trial in which a husband was given a light prison sentence for murdering his unfaithful but estranged wife (divorce being illegal in France between 1816 and 1884), Dumas argued in

L'Homme-femme (1872) that a husband ultimately had the right to kill an unfaithful wife. Finally, in March 1873 Tolstoy also stumbled across an unfinished sketch for a story by Pushkin, the immediacy of whose narrative style launched him straight into the first draft of the opening of *Anna Karenina*.

Chance also plays an important role within *Anna Karenina*, which in its revelation of the often unconscious motivation behind human behaviour is a strikingly modern novel for its time, which was the high-water mark of Russian realism. Tolstoy depicts everyday life in an unidealized, objective way, indeed his dissection of the shifting states of emotional experience is often executed with a surgical precision, but a key element of his realism is also to depict his characters, Anna and Vronsky in particular, doing or saying things they had not intended. This technique certainly illustrates Tolstoy's acute powers of psychological analysis, and his frequent use of the word 'involuntary' when describing behaviour betrays his debt to Schopenhauer's concept of the 'Will'—that blind force driving the futile engine of human striving, and which can only lead to suffering. Along with the introduction of many random details, however, which appear to have no apparent function in the plot, symbolic or otherwise, this technique also provides us with a reminder of the contingency of being, thereby demonstrating a sensibility more readily associated with twentieth-century modernism. While Tolstoy never consciously allied himself with the artistic avant-garde, or indeed with any artistic group at all (although he was a modernist *avant-la-lettre* in his pioneering use of stream of consciousness), he did nevertheless set out to write a novel about modernity. While *War and Peace* is a retrospective work extolling the golden age of the Russian nobility and its patriarchal values in the era of the Napoleonic Wars, *Anna Karenina* is quite deliberately set in what Tolstoy shows us to be the much more disturbing present of 1870s Russia, in which those values are in the process of being eroded by the repercussions of very recent political reform.

The composition of *Anna Karenina* was in fact so contemporaneous with the times that events such as the Serbo-Turkish War, which broke out in June 1876, are not merely woven into the backdrop but inform the narrative: in the last part of the novel, completed in the spring of 1877, Vronsky enlists as a volunteer. By this time four years had passed since Tolstoy had started writing the novel, a challenging period during which he had begun to call into question his entire belief-system and, as a consequence, his attitude towards his fictional characters, who develop in sometimes unexpected ways and are rarely static. A sign of what was to come can be found in the stridency of the anti-militarist views Tolstoy puts forward in the final part of *Anna Karenina*, which he submitted for publication in April 1877, just as Russia declared war on Turkey. Like most Russian novels, *Anna Karenina* had been appearing in serial form as each part was completed, and when the patriotic editor of the *Russian Messenger* took issue with Tolstoy's pacifism and refused to include the book's conclusion in his May issue, a scandal ensued which naturally only increased its popularity with the public. St Petersburg's leading bookshop sold an unprecedented five hundred copies on the day *Anna Karenina* first became available as a separate work in early 1878.[3]

Tolstoy confided in his wife that whereas in *War and Peace* he had loved the 'national idea as a result of the war of 1812', in *Anna Karenina* he loved the 'family idea'. While the tumultuous story of Anna's adulterous liaison with Vronsky takes centre-stage, it is important to recognize that, being the kind of writer he was, Tolstoy could not have proceeded very far without a counterweight. In fact, we have two: the troubled marriage of Stiva and Dolly Oblonsky, and the far happier one of Levin and Kitty. It is by telling their stories side by side, at times interweaving them, and by touching on many other stories of family life in *Anna Karenina* that Tolstoy is able to write a peerless work of fiction which is also an investigation of the institution of marriage, the nature of love, the destiny of Russia, and ultimately the meaning of life. It may be tempting to view the many chapters devoted to such pursuits as mowing, portrait-painting, mushroom-gathering, and participating in local elections as extraneous to the main story, and nothing more than a pleasant diversion. Film adaptations of the novel understandably tend to focus almost exclusively on Anna and Vronsky's passionate love affair, which is characterized by high drama and romance, but this is to illuminate just one layer of what is an extraordinarily complex work of art in which not one word is extraneous. Closer acquaintance with the novel's intricate structure reveals that everything in the novel is interconnected and contributes in some way to its central theme.

Chekhov famously said about *Anna Karenina* that not a single problem was resolved, but it was a novel which nevertheless fully satisfied, as all the problems were correctly stated.[4] The central problem, of

---

[3] N. N. Apostolov, *Zhivoi Tolstoi: zhizn' L'va Nikolaevicha Tolstogo v vospominaniyakh i perepiske*, first published 1928 (Moscow, 2001), 207.

[4] Letter to Alexey Suvorin, 27 Oct. 1888, in *Anton Chekhov's Life and Thought: Selected Letters and Commentary*, tr. Michael Henry Heim, ed. Simon Karlinsky (Berkeley, 1973), 117.

course, relates to the fate of Tolstoy's captivating heroine Anna. Much of the attention of the considerable body of critical literature devoted to *Anna Karenina* is directed at exploring the cause of Anna's tragedy, particularly with respect to the novel's epigraph: *Vengeance is mine; I will repay*. If it is God taking revenge on Anna for committing adultery, it has reasonably been asked, then why are all the other adulterous characters in the novel not punished too? Why do Anna's philandering brother Stiva Oblonsky and her depraved friend Betsy Tverskaya escape divine justice? Or are we meant to understand that it is Anna who wreaks vengeance on Vronsky? Or that it is Tolstoy wreaking vengeance on Anna for the crime of being a beautiful and intelligent woman who dares to break the mould, and seek a fulfilling life, free from the constraints imposed on her gender by a hypocritical, patriarchal society? That was certainly the view of D. H. Lawrence, who was indignant that Anna had apparently fallen victim to Tolstoy's didactic urge. There is, in fact, no agreement amongst critics on whether Anna is a victim or not, and whether or not she is responsible for her own destiny. Tolstoy complicates matters considerably by not completing the epigraph: the words 'saith the Lord' are missing. So who *is* speaking?

What is successful about Tolstoy's characterization of Anna is her complexity. We are drawn to Anna when we first meet her for her warmth and generosity, and we are sympathetic to her desire to follow her heart and live life to the full after the sterility of her marriage to a dry bureaucrat of a husband to whom she has been married off at a young age. We admire her for wanting to live truthfully and openly, and suffer with her when she is forced into a new life of sterility when society closes its doors to her, while still welcoming Vronsky. And yet is it not also true that she rejects her role as wife and mother and becomes increasingly narcissistic? So much of her behaviour with Vronsky is taken up with the attention he pays to her, yet there is little evidence of what she gives to him. Dolly notices Anna's new habit of screwing up her eyes when she goes to visit her, as if she is unable to face reality.

Rather than take responsibility for her own actions, Anna alights on omens—the accident at the railway station, her recurrent dreams—and prefers to blame fate. Just as there are times when Karenin is not an unsympathetic character (as when he is filled with compassion after the birth of Anna's daughter, for whom he feels a tender affection), there are times when the reader's identification with Anna is challenged by her wilful and egotistical behaviour. If Tolstoy's characters change during the course of the novel, it was because his attitude towards them changed as his own thinking developed. It is, therefore, not wholly surprising that *Anna Karenina* can be seen 'as an array of readings that contradict and diverge from each other, and that cluster around an opposition between personal truths and universal truth', as Vladimir Alexandrov has shown in his examination of the novel's many possible meanings.[5]

Levin similarly is a complex character, whose path to personal fulfilment and happiness is far from smooth. But it is as if he and Kitty inhabit a different novel. Anna seems to want to live like a romantic heroine, inspired by all the English fiction she reads, and the story of her love affair with Vronsky is full not just of drama, but melodrama. Ultimately, Anna's fate bears witness to her inability to gravitate from romance, which by its nature is not reality, to love, which is a far more prosaic and demanding proposition, as Levin and Kitty discover in the first months of their marriage. As Gary Saul Morson observes, the novel explicitly 'tries to redirect our attention to aspects of everyday living: love and the family, moral decisions, the process of self-improvement, and, ultimately, all that makes a life feel meaningful or leads us to contemplate suicide'.[6] Can we really see Anna's fate, then, in tragic terms? Tolstoy seems to invite us to subscribe to conventional views of romance because his Olympian narrator remains impersonal. It is easy, for example, to succumb to the idea that the horse race is an allegory of Vronsky's relationship with Anna, and that he is to blame for its failure, just as he is to blame for breaking his horse's back. But to some scholars this interpretation now seems a little too pat.

Tolstoy was naturally well aware of works such as Flaubert's *Madame Bovary* (1857) and Zola's *Thérèse Raquin* (1867), but he wanted to write more than just another novel of adultery. He was also very fond of what his son Sergey called 'English family novels', whose faint shadow can be discerned behind the plot-lines and characterization of *Anna Karenina*. The stiff, aristocratic statesman Plantagenet Palliser, from Anthony Trollope's six 'Parliamentary Novels' (1864–79), seems in certain respects like a benign Karenin (with elements of Lady Glencora and Burgo Fitzgerald in Anna and Vronsky), while Anna shares certain physical traits with Hetty Sorel in George Eliot's *Adam Bede* (1859), to name just a few examples. Tolstoy had little interest, however, in emulating what he saw as a favoured plot-line of English novels, in which the hero 'puts his arm around her waist, then they get married, and

[5] Vladimir Alexandrov, *Limits to Interpretation: The Meanings of* Anna Karenina (Madison, Wisc., 2004), 297.

[6] Gary Saul Morson, *'Anna Karenina' in Our Time: Seeing More Wisely* (New Haven, 2007), 31.

he inherits an estate and a baronetcy'.[7] He was much more interested in what happens *after* his characters get married. The high incidence of marital discord Tolstoy depicts in *Anna Karenina* conveys a rather bleak vision of family life, but there were compelling artistic and moral reasons for why he ended his novel not with the melodramatic death of his adulterous heroine, but with a mundane conversation his hero Levin has with his wife on the veranda on a summer night after contemplating the stars. They have everything to do with the literary tradition in which Tolstoy was nurtured.

   If Russian novelists trod a different path with regard to the content of their works, they also saw no reason to capitulate to the Western model in terms of form. As Tolstoy put it himself in one of the draft prefaces to *War and Peace*, 'in the modern period of Russian literature there is not one work of art in prose even slightly better than average that could fully fit into the form of a novel, epic, or story'.[8] Tolstoy was doing more than making a statement of fact by pointedly calling *Anna Karenina* a 'novel', for he had never previously used the term to describe anything he had written. There is also a possible degree of hidden provocation contained in this appellation, because deeper familiarity with the text of *Anna Karenina* encourages the interpretation of the Anna and Vronsky plot-line, partnered as it is by far less romantic stories, as almost a parody of the European novelistic tradition and the expectations engendered by it in the reader. Certainly it is important to resist the temptation to view *Anna Karenina* as exemplary of the European nineteenth-century realist novel, with which it is often identified, despite the many valid areas of correspondence. Its scope is far wider, and its richly symbolic structure, replete with recurring dreams and careful juxtaposition of contrasting stories and themes (such as Levin and Kitty's lawful wedding, followed by Vronsky and Anna's cohabitation abroad; and Nikolay Levin's death, followed by discovery of Kitty's pregnancy), is too much at odds with any perceived objectivity of depiction.

   Even before Tolstoy self-consciously became a religious crusader, he was a religious artist who claimed that his real hero was the truth. With the Russian Orthodox Church in an increasingly moribund state after Peter the Great subordinated it to the state by abolishing the Patriarchate in 1721, it is possible to argue, as Richard Gustafson has

---

   [7] Sergey Tolstoy, 'Ob otrazhenii zhizni v "Anne Kareninoi": iz vospominanii', *Literaturnoe nasledstvo*, 37/38, vol. 2 (Moscow, 1939), 567.

   [8] L. N. Tolstoi, *Polnoe sobranie sochinenii*, ed. V. Chertkov, 90 vols. (Moscow, 1928–58), vol. 16, p. 7.

done, that in the nineteenth century literature became a kind of substitute for the icon, which had traditionally fulfilled the role of theology and was now in decline. Seen in this perspective, Tolstoy's fictional works function as 'verbal icons' of his religious world-view, which is why his realism is inherently 'emblematic'.[9] This certainly offers us a way of understanding Tolstoy's characteristic use of repetition, a cornerstone of his literary style, as well as the proliferation of important symbols embedded in the structure of *Anna Karenina*, which are both fundamental attributes of Russian religious art.

Tolstoy was not interested in preaching Russian Orthodox dogma, as he was a non-believer like Levin while he was writing *Anna Karenina*, and Levin's painfully articulated spiritual journey mirrors the trajectory of his own thought (and was one of the reasons he did not keep a diary at this time). Having been raised in the Orthodox Church, however, Tolstoy could not help emulating its artistic methods while conducting his quest in *Anna Karenina* for a divine love which might provide solace when even love within an essentially happy marriage fails to be enough. He felt compelled to propose a positive alternative to the ultimately one-dimensional, self-centred love which Anna and Vronsky's story represents. This is why Tolstoy follows Levin and Kitty past their marriage (at the exact halfway point of the novel), past their first painful months together as man and wife, and even past the birth of their first child (an event seen unusually through the eyes of the father). It is also why he was so meticulous with the novel's construction, as his meditations on love and marriage, the nature of artistic creation, and the meaning of life itself are communicated as much obliquely through the myriad connections he forges between characters, themes, and situations as they are openly articulated by means of dialogue and description.

The text of *Anna Karenina* is like a Persian carpet of intricate symmetrical design, whose workmanship can only be appreciated by seeing the reverse side. Tolstoy found this novel immensely difficult to write, but he was nevertheless proud of his skill as an architect, seeing his novel as a building whose arches had been joined in such a way that it was impossible to see the keystone. Naturally, identification of this 'keystone' has dominated much of the research into the novel. Some regard Oblonsky's dinner party as the key to the whole, or Mikhailov's portrait of Anna as the essential link, while others see as the crux Anna's meeting with Levin, when the two storylines of the novel

[9] Richard Gustafson, *Leo Tolstoy: Resident and Stranger* (Princeton, 1986), p. xii.

finally converge through the agency of the ever-emollient Oblonsky. Certainly Tolstoy takes pains to align these two central characters who, as Donna Tussing Orwin has commented, are 'in touch both physically and spiritually with the illogical forces that govern life from minute to minute'.[10] By contrast, both Vronsky and Karenin, who share the same first name, have a carapace of rules to buffer themselves against the storms of life.

The networks of connections in *Anna Karenina* are wide-ranging. On the one hand there is a persistent association of trains with death and adultery. Anna and Vronsky meet at a railway station, where they are witness to a tragic accident which later gives rise to recurring nightmares. Vronsky confesses his love for Anna during a stop at a railway station in the middle of the night, and after she has committed suicide by falling under a train, he himself travels to certain death on a train headed for the Serbian front. But there are other, more subtle ways in which Tolstoy conveys his idea that trains are a pernicious symbol of modernity, an evil innovation imported from the West which threatens to destroy what is best about Russian life. Both the Oblonsky children and Anna's son play games with trains, and danger is present as an element in both cases. Oblonsky finds himself, towards the end of the novel, negotiating for a job connected with the new railways in order to pay off his debts. Trains are nowhere portrayed positively in *Anna Karenina*, because Tolstoy's personal attitude to them was supremely negative. When travelling, Tolstoy himself regularly but reluctantly used the 'iron road' (the Russian *zheleznaya doroga* is a straight translation of the French *chemin de fer*), but he abhorred this intrusion of modern technology into rural Russia. It is striking that a vital moment of epiphany for Levin concerning his love for Kitty takes place when he catches sight of her travelling, at dawn, not at night, and in a horse-drawn carriage rather than a train.

At the other remove are the many tiny connections which may serve to deepen and illuminate Tolstoy's themes, even contradicting those lying on the surface, or which simply invite the reader to see new patterns in the weft of his design. Kitty's friend Varenka, for example, first appears at the beginning of Part Two wearing a toadstool hat. In Part Six it is while gathering mushrooms that Koznyshev fails to propose to her. In Part One Kitty imagines Anna wearing a lilac dress to the ball, and in Part Seven, just before she dies, Anna notices that the young girl who has come on an errand, and of whom she is jealous, is wearing

---

[10] Donna Tussing Orwin, *Tolstoy's Art and Thought, 1847–1880* (Princeton, 1993), 177.

a lilac hat. Similarly, the red bag which Anna has with her on her return journey to Petersburg at the beginning of the novel reappears when she undertakes her last rail journey. Words and phrases are repeated in an almost musical way. As well as the idea of not casting stones, drawn from St John's Gospel, which occurs three times in the novel, associated with three different characters, two characters at separate points in the novel give voice to the idea of giving up one's cloak to the man who takes your coat, which comes from the gospels of St Luke and St Matthew. Crucial to the artist Mikhailov's creative process is the notion of removing veils in order to see more clearly, and a similar analogy is made when Levin looks at his wife shortly before she is about to give birth and feels that the veils have been removed. There are also extensive networks of symbols running through the narrative linked to light and darkness, bears and bear hunting, stars and constellations. Attentive readers will be able to thread together for themselves other subtle chains of reference in the novel relating, for example, to French and English themes, or Tolstoy's dialogue with Plato's *Symposium*.

It is when we consider how Tolstoy paces *Anna Karenina* that we can further appreciate his consummate skill in constructing his narrative. By comparison with the progress of Levin's and Kitty's romance, Anna's and Vronsky's story seems to hurtle along at breakneck speed, almost like a runaway train. Their association with trains is appropriate, for they seem to be travelling on a fixed track with a single destination. Levin and Kitty, by contrast, embark on a journey which is open-ended. It seems after he is married that Levin has discovered what can give his life meaning, but his disappointment at not being able to share his insights with his wife, who intrudes into his stargazing with a mundane, practical question, suggests no simple endpoint can ever be reached. Time seems to go by with Levin and Kitty much more slowly—witness the long chapters devoted to Levin's thoughts while mowing or the many chapters describing his wedding to Kitty. Tolstoy's technique is at other times almost cinematic. We see the horse race from many different angles, for example, and in different time-frames, prompting the great film director Sergey Eisenstein to view this scene as an example of audio-visual counterpoint par excellence, and as prime material for his technique of montage.[11] Tolstoy's own technique of montage, which has him compare, contrast, and mesh at least two different storylines in a seamless way, is unparalleled.

---

[11] Sergey Eisenstein, *Towards a Theory of Montage*, in Michael Glenny and Richard Taylor (eds.), *Selected Works*, vol. 2 (London, 1991), 281–95.

Tolstoy's methods of narration are also richly varied and boldly innovative, moving unobtrusively from a voice of lofty omniscience to one that is far more intimate, and seemingly coloured with the thoughts and feelings of a particular character, or, in the case of the novel's contentious final chapters, unmistakably those of the author himself. We see Anna for the first time, for example, through Vronsky's eyes, and with equal skill Tolstoy filters the events of the fateful ball in Part One through the prism of Kitty's consciousness. In Part Six the reader experiences the visceral excitement of hunting for snipe in the marshes from the point of view of Levin's dog, Laska. And we perceive the emptiness and falsity of Anna's new life because we see it through Dolly's eyes when she goes to visit her at Vronsky's country estate; it is a typically Tolstoyan touch that we follow the complex but lucid progression of Dolly's thoughts as they evolve from a feeling of envy when she is first setting out on her journey to Vozdvizhenskoye, to one of relief and gratitude when she returns home the following day.

In some instances, such as the early chapters describing Oblonsky's personality or Vronsky's habits, we can detect a very faint trace of irony in the narration, while a deliberate tone of sardonic humour or satire is perceptible in those sections of the novel dealing with Karenin's visit to the lawyer and the hypocrisy and pietism of a character like Countess Lydia Ivanovna. The chapters detailing Karenin's thought-processes abound with an inflexible and lifeless bureaucratic lexicon consonant with his general character, and they form a sharp contrast to the gentle, lyrical language used to depict the scene at the skating rink, for example, or Levin's unorthodox proposal to Kitty, in which Tolstoy drew on his own experiences of writing the initial letters of words in chalk on a card-table for Sofya Behrs to decipher. The subsequent scene in the church in which Levin is betrothed to Kitty is very moving in its simplicity, but lyricism in this novel is not always where one would expect to find it. It is absent when the narrator describes the consummation of Vronsky's and Anna's love, which is likened to an act of brutal murder, but often present when Levin experiences a feeling of being one with nature, such as when he spends a day mowing with his peasants.

'Between the lines as you read, you see a soaring eagle who is little concerned with the beauty of his feathers. Thought and beauty, like hurricanes and waves, should not pander to usual, conventional forms.'[12]

---

[12] A. P. Chekhov, *Polnoe sobranie sochinenii*, ed. N. F. Bel'chikov, vol. 7 (Moscow, 1977), 511.

Tolstoy is not named in this unfinished fictional fragment Chekhov worked on in the late 1880s, but it is clear which writer his narrator has in mind. Because Tolstoy paid such scant regard to the 'beauty of his feathers', it took a long time for critics to perceive the full extent of his artistry in *Anna Karenina*. And both conservative and radical critics found fault with the ideology of the novel when it was first published in Russia. Dostoevsky, for example, may have been initially generous with his praise of *Anna Karenina*, which he described as 'perfection as a work of art' in the February 1877 issue of his journal *Diary of a Writer*. After he read the epilogue, however, he excoriated Tolstoy for voicing through Levin the unpatriotic view that the Russian people shared his lack of concern for the Balkan Slavs, and Levin's unwillingness to kill, even for the sake of preventing atrocities (this embryonic non-resistance to violence would, of course, lie at the heart of the new religious outlook Tolstoy was about to develop). The proto-Bolshevik critic Peter Tkachev, meanwhile, naturally fulminated against the novel's aristocratic focus.

The views of critics did nothing to dent the popularity of *Anna Karenina* with all sections of the Russian reading public, and persistent rumours about Tolstoy being embroiled in a fracas with his editor (which ultimately proved to have substance) only served to increase their interest. Due to its depiction of both old- and new-world nobility and its contemporary setting, this was the very first Russian novel certain members of the aristocracy deigned to read, having previously only considered French literature worth their trouble. So great, indeed, was the enthusiasm for *Anna Karenina* amongst St Petersburg high-society salons that some ladies with connections to the court even contrived ingenious measures to obtain the proofs of instalments before their publication. But the novel made an even greater impact on ladies without connections, who, like Anna Karenina, had fallen foul of society's strictures, or longed for love. Tolstoy struck a chord with thousands of female readers suffering unhappy marriages when he wrote *Anna Karenina*. Few had the bravery of Anna Arkadyevna, but they all identified with her.

The paradox of Tolstoy writing with such sympathy about Anna while at the same time writing a novel which clearly condemns adultery is perhaps partly explained by the fate of his younger sister Maria, whose unhappy experience of marriage was one of the many life stories which served as the raw material for his 'family' novel. In the early 1860s, after fleeing abroad from her abusive husband, she had given birth to an illegitimate daughter, but she was ashamed to bring her back to Russia and face the opprobrium of society. In a particularly desperate letter she sent to her brother in March 1876 (by which time she was a widowed single mother), she spoke of the bitter life lessons she had learned, and directly identified with his literary heroine. 'If all those Anna Kareninas knew what awaited them,' she wrote, 'how they would run from ephemeral pleasures, which are never, and cannot be pleasures, because nothing that is *unlawful* can ever constitute happiness.'[13] This was essentially Tolstoy's own view, but it was complicated by the realities of the relationships of his own family, many of which were highly unorthodox. His brother Dmitry lived for several years with a former prostitute (as does Levin's brother Nikolay in *Anna Karenina*), his brother Sergey had several illegitimate children with his gypsy mistress before he married her, and even his wife's mother was illegitimate.

Russian society began to change rapidly in the 1860s, but the patriarchal structures enshrined in law by the Tsarist government remained in place. Divorce became possible in the English court of civil law in 1857, but in Russia, where it lay under the jurisdiction of the Orthodox Church, marital separation remained extremely difficult. In the eyes of the Church, not only was marriage a holy sacrament which could not be dissolved, but illegitimate children had no rights, and the Russian law-code specifically upheld male authority and female subservience. The Tsarist government had a particular interest in supporting such patriarchal structures, as it equated domestic stability with political stability. Nevertheless, despite the stigma attached to it, the number of divorces in Russia rose steadily during the 1860s and 1870s. Tolstoy could have picked no better way of portraying the disintegration of late imperial Russian society than by writing a novel with the theme of the 'family'.

The Great Reforms, urban growth, and the expansion of education inevitably stimulated new attitudes towards marriage, divorce, and the position of women—issues which lie at the heart of *Anna Karenina*. While it is easy to dismiss Tolstoy's views on these topics as misogynist, perceptive feminist critics have shown why they deserve much more careful consideration. That Tolstoy was deeply exercised by the nature of beauty and the objectification of women can be seen by the scrupulous attention he devotes in *Anna Karenina* to the way in which his heroine is viewed or 'framed', not just in the flesh, but in the three different portraits of her, one painted by a 'famous artist' in St Petersburg, one by Vronsky, and one by the artist Mikhailov

[13] R. Bartlett, *Tolstoy: A Russian Life* (London, 2010), 241.

(the last of which we see again towards the end of the novel through Levin's eyes). For Tolstoy, these issues are intimately bound up with the perils of romantic convention, both in art and in real life. As Amy Mandelker puts it, in *Anna Karenina*: 'Tolstoy conflates the aesthetic question—what is the beautiful and can it be represented? What is its nature? What can it show us?—with the woman question—what is woman and what is her proper role in life?—to interrogate the literary conventions of realism and the social conventions of romantic love and marriage.'[14] In true Tolstoyan style, his novel poses a formidable challenge to conventional assumptions on every level.

[14] Amy Mandelker, *Framing Anna Karenina: Tolstoy, the Woman Question and the Victorian Novel* (Columbus, Ohio, 1993), 4.

NOTE ON THE TEXT AND TRANSLATION

THE text of *Anna Karenina* has a complicated history. During the course of the novel's protracted composition between 1873 and 1877, Tolstoy changed not only the names of the major characters, in some cases several times, but also many key elements in the storyline, and indeed the title itself. And it was always his habit to make further changes at proof-stage. In addition to authorial amendments, the final text of the novel was also affected by minor changes made by Tolstoy's wife Sofya, who made fair copies, and his friend Nikolay Strakhov, who assisted in revising the text for publication in book form. Ultimately, the final text of the novel proceeded from five separate drafts filling two and a half thousand manuscript pages.

As in the Pushkin fragment which first sparked Tolstoy's creative imagination, the characters who open his first draft have all just been to the theatre in St Petersburg to attend a performance of *Don Giovanni*, Mozart's opera about seduction and adultery. In a scene slightly reminiscent of the soirée at Princess Betsy's in Part Two of *Anna Karenina*, we meet guests arriving at an aristocratic salon, where they discuss the civil servant Mikhail Mikhailovich Stavrovich (the future Karenin) and his wife Tatyana Sergeyevna (the future Anna). It transpires that she has been unfaithful to him, and he seems ignorant of the fact. The couple then arrive in person, followed later on by Ivan Balashov (the future Vronsky), who proceeds to have an intimate and animated conversation with Tatyana, scandalizing those present. Stavrovich finally realizes the misfortune that has befallen him, and his wife is henceforth no longer to be invited to society events.

In this first draft Tolstoy sketched out a further eleven chapters. Tatyana becomes pregnant and Balashov loses a horse race when his mare falls at the last fence. Stavrovich then leaves Tatyana and moves to Moscow; she gives birth and her husband agrees to a divorce. Tanya's second marriage is no happier, however, and after Stavrovich informs her that their marriage bonds can never be sundered, and that everyone has suffered, she drowns herself in the Neva. Balashov goes off to join the Khiva campaign, echoing real-life events, as Russian troops attacked the city and seized control of the Khanate of Khiva in 1873, just when Tolstoy was writing. Tatyana has a brother in the first sketch (a prototype of Oblonsky), while her husband has a sister called Kitty, but there is no trace of Levin and his brothers at this early stage, nor any members of the Shcherbatsky family. Stavrovich is portrayed sympathetically, while his beautiful wife is intriguingly described as both 'provocative' and 'meek', and also 'demonic' at certain points.

Tolstoy had never before sketched a synopsis of a fictional work in advance, but this initial raw material soon changed significantly. He developed and dramatically expanded every part of this storyline in future drafts. By the time Tolstoy began his third opening draft Tanya had become Anastasia ('Nana'), her husband is now firmly Alexey Alexandrovich, and Balashov is named Gagin. Tolstoy was beginning to shift attention away from the tragedy of Stavrovich's predicament to that of Anastasia, who has fallen in love with someone to whom she is not married. She becomes increasingly sympathetic as a character, while the reverse happens with Stavrovich. With a few exceptions (Stavrovich, for example, has a conversation with a nihilist on a train), Tolstoy's social radius was at first stiflingly small, and he therefore decided to introduce in his third draft Kostya Neradov, a prototype of Levin, who becomes an increasingly important character. Neradov is a rural landowner, and both a friend of Gagin (the future Vronsky) and his rival for the hand of Kitty Shcherbatskaya, who also makes her first appearance in the third draft. The action, moreover, now moves from St Petersburg to Moscow.

Tolstoy's fourth draft received the title 'Anna Karenina', followed by 'Vengeance is Mine' as an epigraph. This draft begins with the familiar scene of a husband waking up after a dreadful quarrel the previous evening with his wife, who has discovered his infidelity. 'Stepan Arkadyich Alabin' is the prototype of Oblonsky. Anna comes to Moscow as peacemaker, and she meets Gagin at the ball. But Tolstoy was still not satisfied: there was no tension in the relationship between the Levin and Vronsky prototypes, as they were friends. He decided to change their names to Ordyntsev and Udashev, and now made them rivals for Kitty's hand rather than friends.

Tolstoy had now constructed solid foundations for his novel by creating the 'Levin' storyline to act as a counterpoint to the Karenin plot, with the 'Oblonskys' as the arch joining them together. Tolstoy reworked the crucial opening scenes four times to get them exactly right, and these were the first chapters he gave Sofya to make fair copies. Everything else stayed in draft form.

In all, Tolstoy produced ten versions of the first part of *Anna Karenina*, and he changed his mind several times about how his new novel should begin. At one point he crossed out 'Anna Karenina' as a title and wrote in 'Two Marriages', and inserted titles for each chapter, such as 'Family Quarrel', 'Meeting at the Railway Station', 'The Ball'. The modern Russian words of the earlier epigraph ('Mine is the Vengeance') were now replaced with the Church Slavonic equivalent taken from the Bible, and Stepan Arkadyich was given the surname of Oblonsky (now relegating Alabin to his dream). Tolstoy initially planned to publish his novel in book-form rather than follow the more customary practice of initial publication via instalments in a literary journal. Accordingly, in March 1874 he delivered to his Moscow printer the first thirty-one chapters of Part One for typesetting, by which time the novel once again bore the title *Anna Karenina* and Levin was Tolstoy's new and final name for Ordyntsev. In this draft Vronsky is a more attractive character than he is in the final version of the novel, and his intentions towards Kitty are much more serious.

Tolstoy had intended to press on with *Anna Karenina*, but by the summer of 1874 he had, for various reasons, lost momentum, and now referred to his novel as 'vile' and 'disgusting'. He returned to it that autumn, however, not least because he needed money. One money-raising tactic was to chop down some forest and sell the wood (which is something that happens in *Anna Karenina*), but his main potential source of revenue was royalties. Tolstoy now changed his mind in favour of printing *Anna Karenina* in instalments in a monthly journal. He had sold *War and Peace* for 300 roubles per printer's sheet, but for *Anna Karenina* he demanded 500 roubles, with an advance of 10,000 roubles (the sum he needed). No other writer in Russia could hope to earn what would be a total of 20,000 roubles for a novel, and after protracted negotiations, in November 1874, Tolstoy finally agreed to publish in Mikhail Katkov's journal the *Russian Messenger*. When he finally picked up the proofs of the chapters that had already been typeset, he proceeded to rewrite the opening one last time.

Parts One and Two and the first twelve chapters of Part Three of *Anna Karenina* were published in the first four issues of the *Russian Messenger* in 1875, between January and April. After an eight-month gap, the rest of Part Three was published in the January 1876 issue of the journal, followed by Part Four and the first twenty chapters of Part Five in the February, March, and April issues. Another long hiatus followed. Chapters 20 to 33 of Part Five appeared in December 1876, Part Six was published in the January and February 1877 issues of the journal, and Part Seven appeared in the March and April issues. Katkov refused to print the novel's eighth and final part for political reasons (see Introduction, p. xiii), and it was eventually published separately by Tolstoy. In early 1878 *Anna Karenina* was published for the first time as a complete novel. This was the standard edition until its appearance in the ninety-volume 'Jubilee Edition' of Tolstoy's complete works, which was launched in 1928, the centenary of the writer's birth. The respective volumes, 18, 19, and 20, were published in 1934, 1935, and 1939. A new, authoritative edition of *Anna Karenina* was published by the Academy of Sciences 'Literary Monuments' series in 1970, however, and it is this edition which has been used for the present translation.

The editors of the Jubilee Edition sought to correct misprints and remove the changes made by Tolstoy's friend Nikolay Strakhov, who had helped him prepare the novel for its first publication as a separate edition in 1878. By the time work began on the Literary Monuments edition, it was possible to make further changes to the text due to all the work that had been done on the manuscripts and drafts for the novel since the 1930s. The editors now removed further stylistic changes made by Strakhov, as well as about seventy changes made by Tolstoy's wife when she was making fair copies of his illegible drafts, and more than eight hundred changes made during the production process. While most of the changes would appear to be small, they nevertheless reveal important idiosyncrasies of Tolstoy's style, and amount to an important new reading when taken together. C. J. G. Turner has compiled a valuable list of the changes, detailing the discrepancies between the Literary Monuments and the Jubilee Edition.[1]

The Literary Monuments edition cannot claim to be definitive, as work on Tolstoy's manuscripts and drafts has been ongoing, and that imprimatur is most likely to be given to the version being prepared for the new, hundred-volume edition of Tolstoy's Collected Works. Until its publication, however, we can rely on the Literary Monuments edition as the version closest to what Tolstoy actually wrote. As Nikolay Strakhov discovered when helping to prepare the text for its first publication in book form in 1878, Tolstoy set great store by what he had actually written, no matter how unconventional or clumsy it might initially appear. As he later recalled: 'Lev Nikolayevich firmly defended his slightest expression and would not agree to the most, one would have thought, innocuous changes. From his explanations I was convinced that, in spite of all the apparent carelessness and unevenness of his style, he thought over every word, every turn of speech no less than the most fastidious poet.'

As with *War and Peace*, the Louise and Aylmer Maude translation

---

[1] C. J. G. Turner, *A Karenina Companion* (Waterloo, Ont., 1993), 53–97.

of *Anna Karenina*, first published by World's Classics in 1918, has long been considered one of the very best English versions of the novel. The Maudes lived in Moscow, were personal friends of Tolstoy, and were devoted to studying and disseminating his work. Nevertheless, they did not come from a literary background—Aylmer Maude ran a carpet business in Moscow before acquaintance with Tolstoy and his radical Christian ideas led him to abandon the world of commerce. Careful study of their translation shows a large number of discrepancies with Tolstoy's original text, as well as what Henry Gifford defined as an absence of the 'creative sense of language' needed to render the nuances of Tolstoy's style.[2] They also make the regrettable decision to anglicize all first names, to the detriment of the reader's appreciation of this aspect of Tolstoy's sophisticated technique of characterization (as briefly outlined in the note on 'Principal Characters' below).

This translation seeks to preserve all the idiosyncrasies of Tolstoy's inimitable style, as far as that is possible, including the majority of his signature repetitions, so often smoothed over by previous translators, his occasional use of specialized vocabulary, particularly in those chapters concerning rural life, and his subtle changes of register, as in those instances where the introduction of an almost imperceptible but unmistakable note of irony is concerned. At the same time, it is a mistake to render Tolstoy too literally. He was often a clumsy and occasionally ungrammatical writer, but there is a majesty and elegance to his prose which needs to be emulated in translation wherever possible. Tolstoy loved the particular properties of the Russian language, but he would not have expected them to be reproduced exactly in translation, and would have surely expected his translators to draw on the particular strengths of their own languages. The aim here, therefore, is to produce a translation which is idiomatic as well as faithful to the original, and one which ideally reads as if it was written in one's own language.

Russian, where one word can convey many meanings, each dependent on the context, functions in a very different way to English, which tends to have many different words for a phenomenon, all with precise shades of meaning. Thus, while this translation retains most of Tolstoy's repetitions, in those instances where identical translation of the same word would fail to convey the richness of meaning implied in the original, nuance has been sought by finding equivalents in English. This is the case with the Russian word *veselo* and its variants, for

[2] Henry Gifford, 'On Translating Tolstoy', in Malcolm Jones (ed.), *New Essays on Tolstoy* (Cambridge, 1978), 22.

example, a word which in general means 'jolly' or 'cheerful'. It occurs three hundred and eighteen times in the text of *Anna Karenina*, and nine times in the space of a few paragraphs in Part Two, chapter 35. Seven different English words or expressions have been used in this translation to convey what is implied in the original Russian single root-word: 'high spirits', 'merrily', 'jolly', 'livelier', 'amusing', 'light-hearted', 'gleeful'.

Tolstoy's congested sentences, brimming with gerunds, participles, and relative clauses, pose a particular challenge to the translator wishing to render them into English. Not only is word-order more rigid in English, due to the fact that words do not decline, as in Russian, but some sentences are extremely long (some contain over a hundred words). 'Have you ever paid attention to Tolstoy's language?' Chekhov once said to a friend; 'enormous sentences, one clause piled on top of another. Do not think this is accidental, that it is a flaw. It is art, and it is achieved through hard work. These sentences produce an impression of strength.'[3] Russian writers marvelled at Tolstoy's ability to write so simply, using non-bookish, everyday speech, eschewing rhetorical devices and trite turns of phrase, but also so powerfully. As the Soviet writer Yury Olesha perceptively observed in 1950 in his notebooks, Tolstoy's style was of a piece with the anarchic position he took on nearly everything in his life:

It's strange that, existing in plain view, so to speak, of everyone, Tolstoy's style with its piling up of coordinating subordinate clauses [several 'thats' ensuing from a single 'that'; several subsequent 'whiches' from a single 'which'] is, in essence, the only style in Russian literature characterized by freedom and by a distinctive incorrectness, and up to the present time, despite the demand that young writers write in a so-called correct way, no one has yet given an explanation of just why Tolstoy wrote incorrectly. It would be necessary (and it's odd that up to the present time it hasn't been done) to write a dissertation about the distinctive 'ungrammaticalness of Tolstoy'. Someone observed that Tolstoy knew about his violation of syntactic rules (he spoke constantly of having a 'bad style') but that he felt no need whatsoever to avoid these violations—he wrote, it's said in this observation, as if no one had ever written before him, as if he were writing for the first time. Thus, even Tolstoy's style is an expression of his rebellion against all norms and conventions.[4]

[3] S. N. Shchukin, 'Iz vospominanii ob A. P. Chekhove', *Russkaya mysl'*, 10 (1911), 45, reprinted in N. I. Gitovich *et al.* (eds.), *A. P. Chekhov v vospominaniyakh sovremennikov* (Moscow, 1960), 463–4.

[4] Yury Olesha, *Povesti i rasskazy* (Moscow, 1965), 492–3, cited in Natasha Sankovitch, *Creating and Recovering Experience: Repetition in Tolstoy* (Stanford, 1998), 20.

Transliteration

A simplified version of the British Standard transliteration system has been chosen for ease and accuracy of pronunciation, with a final '-y' used for proper nouns ending in й, ий and ый, as in 'Tolstoy', and 'ye' replacing 'e' in place-names and proper names, so that 'Pokrovskoe' becomes 'Pokrovskoye' and 'Arkadevna' becomes 'Arkadyevna'. Proper names with 'ks' have also been spelled with an 'x', thus 'Alexandrovna' has been preferred to the more accurate Aleksandrovna. In the case of 'ë', confusion often results since it is invariably printed as 'e'. This has led to a long-standing debate about whether the name of Tolstoy's hero Levin should be pronounced 'Lyovin', in accordance with the writer's own family nickname of 'Lyova' and his habit of projecting his own thoughts and ideas into his central characters. In this translation 'yo' replaces 'ë' (so that 'Fedorovna', for example, becomes 'Fyodorovna', and 'Matrena' becomes 'Matryona'), but Levin has been preferred to Lyovin. This is both in accordance with recent scholarly consensus,[5] and because 'ë' in Russian phonology is generally only followed by a hard consonant—the 'v' is softened by 'i' in 'Levin', but not by 'a' in 'Lyova'. Finally, the spelling of the novel's English names and nicknames has been retained, so that 'Kitty' is preferred to an accurate transliterated Russian version ('Kiti' or 'Kity') and 'Lydia' preferred to 'Lidiya'.

A few Russian words known internationally, including 'zemstvo' and 'dacha', are transliterated, rather than translated. Proper names are reproduced exactly as they are in the original. This translation largely preserves Tolstoy's punctuation, but diverges from his practice of never capitalizing the names of biblical figures or institutions.

This translation has benefited immensely from painstaking comments made by Amy Mandelker, to whom thanks are gratefully expressed.

[5] See Alexis Klimov, 'Is it "Levin" or "Lëvin"?', *Tolstoy Studies Journal*, 11 (1999), 108–11.

SELECT BIBLIOGRAPHY

Critical Studies

Adelman, Gary, *Anna Karenina: The Bitterness of Ecstasy* (Boston, 1990).

Alexandrov, Vladimir E., *Limits to Interpretation: The Meanings of 'Anna Karenina'* (Madison, Wisc., 2004).

Armstrong, Judith, *The Unsaid Anna Karenina* (New York, 1988).

Blackmur, R. P., 'The Dialectic of Incarnation: Tolstoy's *Anna Karenina*', in Ralph E. Matlaw (ed.), *Tolstoy: A Collection of Critical Essays* (Englewood Cliffs, NJ, 1967), 127–45.

Browning, Gary L., *A 'Labyrinth of Linkages' in Tolstoy's Anna Karenina* (Brighton, Mass., 2010).

Cruise, Edwina, 'Tracking the English Novel in *Anna Karenina*: Who Wrote the English Novel that Anna Reads?', in Donna Tussing Orwin (ed.), *Anniversary Essays on Tolstoy* (Cambridge, 2010), 159–82.

Evans, Mary, *Reflecting on Anna Karenina* (London, 1989).

Feuer, Kathryn B., 'Stiva', in K. N. Brostrom (ed.), *Russian Literature and American Critics: In Honor of Demig B. Brown* (Ann Arbor, Mich., 1984), 347–56.

Grossman, Joan, 'Tolstoy's Portrait of Anna: Keystone in the Arch', *Criticism*, 18 (1976), 1–14.

Grossman, Joan, 'Words, Idle Words: Discourse and Communication in *Anna Karenina*', in Hugh McLean (ed.), *In the Shade of the Giant: Essays on Tolstoy*, California Slavic Studies, 13 (Berkeley, 1989), 115–29.

Gutkin, Irina, 'The Dichotomy Between Flesh and Spirit: Plato's *Symposium* in *Anna Karenina*', in Hugh McLean (ed.), *In the Shade of the Giant: Essays on Tolstoy*, California Slavic Studies, 13 (Berkeley, 1989), 84–99.

Hardy, Barbara, 'Form and Freedom: Tolstoy's *Anna Karenina*', in *The Appropriate Form* (London, 1964), 174–211.

Heldt, Barbara, 'Tolstoy's Path to Feminism', in *Terrible Perfection: Women and Russian Literature* (Bloomington, Ind., 1987), 38–48.

Jackson, Robert Louis, 'Chance and Design in *Anna Karenina*', in Peter Demetz *et al.* (eds.), *The Disciplines of Criticism: Essays in Literary Theory, Interpretation and History* (New Haven, 1968), 315–29.

Jahn, Gary, 'The Image of the Railroad in *Anna Karenina*', *Slavic and East European Journal*, 25 (1981), 8–12.

Jones, W. Gareth, 'George Eliot's *Adam Bede* and Tolstoy's Conception of *Anna Karenina*', in W. Gareth Jones (ed.), *Tolstoi and Britain* (Oxford, 1995), 79–92.

Knapp, Liza, 'The Estates of Pokrovskoe and Vozdvizhenskoe: Tolstoy's Labyrinth of Linkings in *Anna Karenina*', *Tolstoy Studies Journal*, 8 (1995–6), 81–98.

Knapp, Liza, and Amy Mandelker (eds.), *Approaches to Teaching Tolstoy's Anna Karenina* (New York, 2003).

Lönnqvist, Barbara, '*Anna Karenina*', in Donna Tussing Orwin (ed.), *The Cambridge Companion to Tolstoy* (Cambridge, 2002), 80–95.

Mandelker, Amy, *Framing Anna Karenina: Tolstoy, the Woman Question and the Victorian Novel* (Columbus, Ohio, 1993).

Meyer, Priscilla, 'Anna Karenina', in *How the Russians Read the French: Lermontov, Dostoevsky, Tolstoy* (Madison, Wisc., 2008), 152–209.

Morson, Gary Saul, *'Anna Karenina' in our Time: Seeing More Wisely* (New Haven, 2007).

Nabokov, Vladimir, 'Anna Karenin', in *Lectures on Russian Literature* (London, 1982), 137–235.

Orwin, Donna Tussing, 'Drama in *Anna Karenina*', in *Tolstoy's Art and Thought, 1847–1880* (Princeton, 1993), 171–87.

Osborne, Suzanne, '*Effi Briest* and *Anna Karenina*', *Tolstoy Studies Journal*, 5 (1992), 67–77.

Schultze, Sydney, *The Structure of Anna Karenina*' (Ann Arbor, Mich., 1982).

Stenbock-Fermor, Elizabeth, *The Architecture of Anna Karenina: A History of Its Writing, Structure and Message* (Lisse, 1975).

Stern, J. P. M., '*Effi Briest; Madame Bovary; Anna Karenina*', in Henry Gifford (ed.), *Leo Tolstoy: A Critical Anthology* (Harmondsworth, 1971), 281–7.

Thorlby, Anthony, *Leo Tolstoy: Anna Karenina* (Cambridge, 1997).

Turner, C. J. G., *A Karenina Companion* (Waterloo, Ont., 1993).

Wachtel, Andrew, 'Death and Resurrection in *Anna Karenina*', in Hugh McLean (ed.), *In the Shade of the Giant: Essays on Tolstoy*, California Slavic Studies, 13 (Berkeley, 1989), 100–14.

Criticism and Reception

Gifford, Henry (ed.), *Leo Tolstoy: A Critical Anthology* (Harmondsworth, 1971).

Knowles, A. V. (ed.), *Tolstoy: The Critical Heritage* (London, 1978).

Sorokin, Boris (ed.), *Tolstoy in Prerevolutionary Russian Criticism* (Miami, 1979).

Wasiolek, Edward (ed.), *Critical Essays on Tolstoy* (Boston, 1986).

General Critical Studies

Bayley, John, *Tolstoy and the Novel* (London, 1966).

Christian, R. F., *Tolstoy: A Critical Introduction* (Cambridge, 1969).

Eikhenbaum, *Tolstoy in the Seventies*, trans. Albert Kaspin (Ann Arbor, Mich., 1982).

Gifford, Henry, *Tolstoy* (Oxford, 1982).

Gustafson, Richard, *Leo Tolstoy: Resident and Stranger* (Princeton, 1986).

Medzhibovskaya, Inessa, *Tolstoy and the Religious Culture of His Time: A Biography of a Long Conversion, 1845–1887* (Lanham, Md., 2008).

Orwin, Donna Tussing, *Tolstoy's Art and Thought: 1847–1889* (Princeton, 1993).

Orwin, Donna Tussing (ed.), *The Cambridge Companion to Tolstoy* (Cambridge, 2002).

Sankovitch, Natasha, *Creating and Recovering Experience: Repetition in Tolstoy* (Stanford, 1998).

Silbajoris, Rimvydas, *Tolstoy's Aesthetics and His Art* (Columbus, Ohio, 1991).

Steiner, George, *Tolstoy or Dostoevsky: An Essay in the Old Criticism* (New York, 1959).

Wasiolek, Edward, *Tolstoy's Major Fiction* (Chicago, 1978).

Weir, Justin, *Tolstoy and the Alibi of Narrative* (New Haven, 2010).

Biography

Bartlett, Rosamund, *Tolstoy: A Russian Life* (London, 2010).

Christian, R. F. (ed.), *Tolstoy's Letters*, 2 vols. (London, 1978).

Christian, R. F. (ed.), *Tolstoy's Diaries* (London, 1985).

Maude, Aylmer, *The Life of Tolstoy* (Oxford, 1929).

Nickell, William, *The Death of Tolstoy. Russia on the Eve, Astapovo Station, 1910* (Ithaca, 2010).

Paperno, Irina, *'Who, What Am I?': Tolstoy Struggles to Narrate the Self* (Ithaca, 2014).

Porter, Cathy (ed.), *The Diaries of Sophia Tolstoy*, rev. edn. (London, 2009).

Simmons, Ernest J., *Leo Tolstoy* (Boston, 1945–6).

Wilson, A. N., *Tolstoy* (London, 1988).

A CHRONOLOGY OF LEO TOLSTOY

Tolstoy's works are dated, unless otherwise indicated, according to the year of publication. Dates marked 'OS' (Old Style) refer to the Julian calendar.

1828   28 August (os): born at Yasnaya Polyana, province of Tula, fourth son of Count Nikolay Tolstoy. Mother dies 1830, father 1837.

1844–7   Studies at University of Kazan (Oriental Languages, then Law). Leaves without graduating.

1851   Goes to Caucasus with elder brother. Participates in army raid on local village. Begins to write *Childhood* (publ. 1852).

1854   Commissioned. *Boyhood*. Active service on Danube; gets posting to Sevastopol.

1855   After its fall returns to Petersburg, already famous for his first two *Sevastopol Sketches*. Literary and social life in the capital.

1856   Leaves army. *A Landlord's Morning*.

1857   Visits Western Europe. (August) returns to Yasnaya Polyana.

1859   His interest and success in literature wane. Founds on his estate a school for peasant children. *Three Deaths*; *Family Happiness*.

1860–1   Second visit to Western Europe, in order to study educational methods.

1861   Serves as Arbiter of the Peace, to negotiate land settlements after Emancipation of Serfs.

1862   Death of two brothers. Marries Sofya Behrs, daughter of a Moscow physician. There were to be thirteen children of the marriage, only eight surviving to adulthood. Publishes educational magazine *Yasnaya Polyana*.

1863   *The Cossacks*; *Polikushka*. Begins *War and Peace*.

1865–6   *1805* (first part of *War and Peace*).

1866   Unsuccessfully defends at court-martial soldier who had struck officer.

1869   *War and Peace* completed; final volumes published.

1870   Studies drama and Greek.

1871–2   Working on *Primer* for children.

1872   *A Prisoner in the Caucasus*.

1873   Goes with family to visit new estate in Samara. Publicizes Samara famine. Begins *Anna Karenina* (completed 1877).

1877   His growing religious crisis. Dismay over Russo–Turkish War.

1879   Begins *A Confession* (completed 1882).

1881 Letter to new Tsar begging clemency for assassins of Alexander II.

1882 *What Men Live By.* Begins *Death of Ivan Ilyich* and *What Then Must We Do?* (completed 1886).

1883 Meets Chertkov, afterwards his leading disciple.

1885 Founds with Chertkov's help the *Intermediary,* to publish edifying popular works, including his own stories. Becomes vegetarian, gives up hunting.

1886 *The Death of Ivan Ilyich.* Writes play *The Power of Darkness.*

1889 *The Kreutzer Sonata* completed. Begins *Resurrection.*

1891–2 Organizes famine relief.

1893 *The Kingdom of God Is Within You* published abroad.

1897 Begins *What is Art?* (publ. 1898) and *Hadji Murat.*

1899 *Resurrection.*

1901 Excommunicated from Orthodox Church. Seriously ill. In Crimea meets Chekhov and Gorky.

1902 *What is Religion?* completed. Working on play, *The Light Shineth in Darkness.*

1903 Denounces pogroms against Jews.

1904 *Shakespeare and the Drama* completed. Also *Hadji Murat* (publ. after his death). Pamphlet on Russo-Japanese War, *Bethink Yourselves!*

1906 Death of favourite daughter, Masha. Increasing tension with wife.

1908 *I Cannot Be Silent,* opposing capital punishment. 28 August: celebrations for eightieth birthday.

1909 Frequent disputes with wife. Draws up will relinquishing copyrights. His secretary Gusev arrested and exiled.

1910 Flight from home, followed by death at Astapovo railway station, 7 November (os).

PRINCIPAL CHARACTERS AND
GUIDE TO PRONUNCIATION

Russian Names

EACH Russian person has, in addition to a surname, a patronymic. This is a middle name ending either in '-ovich' or '-evich', meaning 'son of' (e.g. Sergey Ivanovich, Stepan Arkadyevich), or in '-ovna' or '-evna', meaning 'daughter of' (e.g. Darya Alexandrovna, Anna Arkadyevna). The first name with patronymic is used as the most common polite form of address, in contrast to the practice of combining title with surname which is customary in English-speaking countries. And when speaking or thinking about a third person, Russians commonly use only the surname, which appears brusque if translated directly. When the narrator describes Vronsky first seeing Anna at the railway station before he has been introduced to her, for example, we read: 'Vronsky remembered now that this was Karenina.' In these cases 'Madame' has to be interpolated. Surnames decline according to gender, thus Konstantin Levin is married to Kitty Levina.

First names on their own are used only between family and friends, and an additional level of intimacy or familiarity is introduced by diminutives. Konstantin, for example, becomes 'Kostya', Ekaterina becomes 'Katya' or 'Katenka', and Sergey becomes 'Seryozha'. Patronymics can also have diminutives, and they are used for many of Tolstoy's male characters, so that 'Arkadyevich' becomes 'Arkadyich' and 'Kirillovich' becomes 'Kirillich'. Russians can even address each other by their patronymics alone, so that at the peak of early Soviet adulation of Lenin, the Soviet leader was referred to in an officially affectionate and familiar way as 'Ilych' in certain particular circumstances. In *Anna Karenina*, the Karenins' doorman is known familiarly as 'Kapitonich', a diminutive of 'Kapitonovich'. It is notable that neither Anna nor Vronsky use diminutives with each other, nor do their friends use diminutives to address them; Vronsky is invariably referred to by his surname only, and only his mother calls him by the affectionate 'Alyosha'. Karenin, however, is usually referred to by his name and patronymic. This is all deliberate practice on Tolstoy's part, as manner of address is an intrinsic part of his characterization.[1] A case in point is the comic character of Vasenka Veslovsky, who not only is always referred to by the diminutive of his name (short for 'Vasily'), but by the diminutive of the diminutive ('Vasenka' rather than 'Vasya'). We never learn his patronymic. Conversely, we never learn Countess Lydia Ivanovna's surname, but the repeated refrain throughout the narration of 'Countess Lydia Ivanovna' is also telling in its own way. The

---

[1] See Liza Knapp, 'The Names', in Liza Knapp and Amy Mandelker (eds.), *Approaches to Teaching Tolstoy's Anna Karenina* (New York, 2003), 8–34.

proliferation of English nicknames (Stiva, for example, which is a Russian version of 'Steve') is unusual, but denotes a particular fashion. The previous French vogue is reflected in old Prince Shcherbatsky being known as 'Alexandre'.

Names *In* Anna Karenina

Names are therefore important in Tolstoy. It was clearly not carelessness on his part that he chose to give Karenin and Vronsky the same first name, or that Anna, her daughter Annie, her maid Annushka, and her ward Hannah all share the same name (Anna being derived from the Hebrew 'Hannah'). There is also the original meaning of names to consider, many of which are of Greek origin and arrived in Russia along with the adoption of Christianity ('Platon', the name of the wise peasant Levin hears about, for example, naturally means wisdom). Many of the invented surnames in the novel have symbolic meanings or associations, some of which are humorous. The surname of the waspish Princess Myagkaya, for example, means 'soft'. The new passion which Tolstoy developed for learning Greek in the early 1870s is reflected in the etymology of 'Karenin' (derived from the Greek word for head: κάρηνον). Tolstoy's known enthusiasm for Xenophon, meanwhile, may have generated the name of Levin's friend Katavasov, which would seem to be derived from the Greek 'katabasis' (κατάβαίνω), defined in the *Oxford English Dictionary* as: 'A going down; a military retreat, in allusion to that of the ten thousand Greeks under Xenophon, related by him in his *Anabasis*.' Katavasov, of course, as an incisive polemicist, does not like to retreat. Other names in *Anna Karenina* follow Tolstoy's practice of adapting familiar Russian ones, such as his invented 'Oblonsky', which is close to 'Obolensky'.

The following list of principal characters has been organized into families, households, and groups. To assist the reader, stressed syllables are marked with an acute accent wherever there might be lack of clarity.

THE OBLONSKYS

Prince Stepán Arkádyevich Oblónsky (Stepan Arkádyich, Stiva)

Princess Dárya Alexándrovna Oblónskaya, née Shcherbatskaya (Dáshenka, Dolly, Dóllinka)

Their six children are Tánya (diminutive of Tatyana), who is also known as Tanechka and Tanchúrochka, Grísha (diminutive of Grigóry), Masha (Maria), Lily (diminutive of Elizavéta), Alyosha (Alexey or Alexander), and Vasya (Vasily).

Matvey, Oblonsky's valet

Matryona Filimonovna, the family housekeeper (Matryosha)

THE SHCHERBATSKYS

Shcherbátsky, Prince Alexander Dmítrievich (Alexandre)

Princess Shcherbátskaya (her other names are not given)

Princess Ekaterína Alexándrovna Shcherbátskaya, later Levina (Kitty, Katerína, Kátya, Kátenka)

Prince Nikolay Shcherbátsky, a cousin

Vásenka Veslóvsky (diminutive of Vasíly; we do not know his patronymic), second cousin of the Shcherbatskys

THE KARENINS

Anna Arkádyevna Karénina, née Oblónskaya

Alexey Alexandrovich Karénin

Sergéy Alexéyevich Karénin (Sergey Alexéyich, Seryózha)

Anna Alexéyevna Karénina (Annie), Anna's daughter by Vronsky (who shares a first name with Karenin, so the patronymic is correct)

Ánnushka (diminutive of Anna), Anna's maid

Hannah, English ward of Anna

Kornéy Vasílyevich, servant

Kapitónich Petrov, doorman

Vasily Lúkich Vunic, tutor to Seryozha

Countess Lydia Ivánovna (we never learn her surname), Karenin's friend

THE LEVINS

Konstantín Dmítrievich Lévin (Konstantin Dmítrich, Kóstya).

Nikoláy Dmítrievich Lévin (Nikólenka)

Márya Nikoláyevna (Másha), Nikolay's partner (surname not given)

Sergey Ivánovich Koznyshév (Sergey Ivánich), Levin's half-brother

Dmitry Konstantínovich Lévin, Levin and Kitty's son

Agáfya Mikháilovna, Levin's housekeeper

THE VRONSKYS

Countess Vrónskaya (we never learn her name or patronymic), Vronsky's mother

Count Alexéy Kiríllovich Vronsky (Alexey Kiríllich, Alyosha)

Count Alexander Kiríllovich Vronsky, Vronsky's brother, married to Varya (diminutive of Varvára)

Princess Betsy Tverskáya, Vronsky's cousin, married to Anna's first cousin (she is addressed by her full first name and patronymic, Elizaveta Fyodorovna, only once)

THE LVOVS

Prince Arsény Lvov (patronymic not known)

Princess Natálya Alexándrovna Lvóva, née Shcherbatskaya

OTHER CHARACTERS

Várenka (diminutive of Varya, itself a diminutive of Varvára), Kitty's friend, who is addressed by her full first name and patronymic, Varvara Andreyevna, only once

Princess Varvára, Anna's aunt
Katavásov, Fyodor Vasílievich, Levin's friend
Sviyázhsky, Nikolay Ivánovich, Levin's friend
Yáshvin, Captain Prince, Vronsky's friend (we do not learn his name and
   patronymic)

ANNA KARENINA

Vengeance is mine; I will repay*

PART ONE

I

ALL happy families are alike, each unhappy family is unhappy in its own way.

Everything was confusion in the Oblonskys' house.* The wife had found out that the husband was having an affair with the French governess formerly in their house, and had announced to the husband that she could not live with him in the same house. This situation had been going on now for three days, and was acutely felt by the couple themselves, as well as by the members of the family and the household. The members of the family and the household all felt there was no point in their living together and that people meeting by chance at any coaching inn had more connection to each other than they did, the members of the family and the Oblonsky household. The wife had not left her rooms, the husband had not been at home for three days. The children were running about the house as if lost; the English governess had quarrelled with the housekeeper and written a note to a friend, asking her to find her a new position; the cook had walked out the day before, right in the middle of dinner; the scullery-maid and the coachman had given notice.

On the third day after the quarrel, Prince Stepan Arkadyich Oblonsky—Stiva, as he was called in society—woke up at the usual time, that is to say, at eight o'clock in the morning, not in his wife's bedroom but in his study, on the morocco leather sofa. He turned over his plump, well-groomed body on the springs of the sofa as if wanting to go back to sleep for a long time, clasped the pillow tightly from the other side, and nestled his cheek against it; then suddenly he leapt up, sat down on the sofa, and opened his eyes.

'Yes, yes, what was going on?' he thought, remembering his dream. 'Yes, what was going on? Yes! Alabin was giving a dinner in Darmstadt;* no, it wasn't Darmstadt but something American. Yes, but Darmstadt was in America there. Yes, Alabin was giving a dinner on glass tables, yes—and the tables were singing *Il mio tesoro*,* except it wasn't *Il mio* *tesoro* but something better, and there were some little decanters and they were women,' he remembered.

Stepan Arkadyich's eyes twinkled merrily, and he smiled as he became lost in thought. 'Yes, it was good, very good. There was a lot of other excellent stuff in it too, but you couldn't put it into words or express it in thoughts even if you were awake.' And noticing the shaft of light seeping in at the side of one of the cloth blinds, he jauntily threw his feet down from the sofa, felt about with them for the gold morocco slippers which his wife had embroidered (a birthday present the previous year), and from an old habit of nine years' duration stretched out his hand without getting up towards the place where his dressing-gown hung in the bedroom. And that was when he suddenly remembered how and why he came to be sleeping in his study rather than his wife's bedroom; the smile vanished from his face and his brow became furrowed.

'Oh, oh, oh! O-o-oh! . . .' he groaned, as he remembered everything that had happened. And once again all the details of the quarrel with his wife, the utter hopelessness of his situation, and, most agonizing of all, his own guilt, loomed into his imagination.

'Yes! She won't forgive me and can't forgive me. And the worst thing of all is that the blame is all mine, all mine, and yet I'm not to blame. That's the whole tragedy of it,' he thought. 'Oh, oh, oh!' he kept repeating in despair as he remembered what for him were the most painful impressions from this quarrel.

Most unpleasant of all had been that first moment when, after returning happy and contented from the theatre, with an enormous pear in his hand for his wife, he had not found her in the drawing room; to his surprise he had not found his wife in the study either, and had finally caught sight of her in the bedroom, with the unfortunate note which revealed everything in her hand.

Dolly, the eternally anxious, bustling, and, as he thought, not very bright Dolly, was sitting motionless with the note in her hand, and looking at him with an expression of horror, despair, and anger.

'What is this? This?' she asked, pointing to the note.

And as often happens, it was not the event itself which mortified Stepan Arkadyich when he remembered this so much as the way in which he had responded to what his wife had said.

What happened to him at that moment was what happens to people when they are unexpectedly caught out doing something thoroughly shameful. He had not managed to compose his face to suit the situation in which he now found himself in front of his wife after the revelation of his guilt. Instead of taking offence, denying everything, asking for forgiveness, or even remaining impassive—anything would have been better than what he did!—his face had suddenly broken quite involuntarily ('reflexes of the brain,'* thought Stepan Arkadyich, who loved physiology) into his usual, good-natured and therefore stupid smile.

He could not forgive himself that stupid smile. When she saw that smile, Dolly had flinched as if from physical pain, exploded with her usual hot temper into a torrent of harsh words, and run out of the room. Since then she had not wanted to see her husband.

'That stupid smile is to blame for everything,' thought Stepan Arkadyich. 'But what is to be done? What is to be done?' he asked himself in despair, and could find no answer.

2

STEPAN ARKADYICH was a truthful person where his relationship to himself was concerned. He could not deceive himself and persuade himself that he repented of his actions. He could not now repent of something he had repented of some six years earlier, when he had first been unfaithful to his wife. He could not repent that he, a thirty-four-year-old, handsome, amorous man, was not in love with his wife, the mother of five living and two deceased children, who was only one year younger than he was. He only repented that he had not managed to hide things better from his wife. But he did feel the full gravity of his position, and felt sorry for his wife, his children, and himself. Maybe he could have managed to hide his misdemeanours better from his wife if he could have anticipated that this news would have such an effect on her. He had never thought this matter through clearly, but dimly imagined his wife had guessed a long time ago that he was not faithful to her, and was turning a blind eye. He had even thought that, as a worn-out, ageing, no longer pretty woman, wholly unremarkable, ordinary, simply the good mother of a family, she ought by rights to be indulgent. But it had turned out quite the opposite.

'Ah, this is awful! Oh dear, oh dear! It's awful!' Stepan Arkadyich kept repeating to himself, unable to come up with anything. 'And how good it all was before this, what a good life we had! She was contented and happy with the children, I didn't ever get in her way, and let her take care of the children and the household as she wanted. It's true that it was not good *she* was a governess in our house. Not good at all! There is something tawdry and vulgar about chasing after your own governess.

But what a governess! (He vividly remembered Mademoiselle Roland's mischievous black eyes and her smile.) But I didn't take any liberties while she was living in our house, after all. And the worst thing of all is that she is already . . . It's just my luck! Oh dear, oh dear! Oh-oh-oh! But what can be done, what on earth can be done?'

There was no answer, except the general answer which life gives to all the most complicated and unanswerable questions. This answer was: one must live by satisfying immediate needs, that is, by seeking oblivion. Seeking oblivion in dreams was no longer possible, at least until night-time; it was no longer possible to go back to the music which the little decanter women had been singing; consequently he had to seek oblivion in the dream of life.

'We'll see what transpires,' Stepan Arkadyich said to himself, and getting up, he put on his grey dressing-gown with the blue silk lining, knotted the tassels, took an ample amount of air into his broad ribcage, and with the usual sprightly step of his turned-out feet, which so nimbly carried his plump frame, walked over to the window, raised the blind, and rang loudly. At the sound of the bell, his old friend the valet Matvey immediately came in, carrying his clothes, his boots, and a telegram. Matvey was followed by the barber with shaving implements.

'Are there any papers from the office?' asked Stepan Arkadyich, taking the telegram and sitting down in front of the mirror.

'They're on the table,' replied Matvey. He looked enquiringly and with sympathy at his master, then after a pause added with a sly smile: 'Someone came from the owner of the livery stable.'

Stepan Arkadyich did not reply and just glanced at Matvey in the mirror; from the look they exchanged in the mirror it was clear how well they understood each other. Stepan Arkadyich's look seemed to be asking: 'Why are you saying that? Don't you know?'

Matvey put his hands into the pockets of his jacket, stuck one foot out slightly, and gazed silently and kind-heartedly at his master with a barely perceptible smile.

'I told him to come back next Sunday, and not to trouble you or himself needlessly until then,' he said in an obviously prepared phrase.

Stepan Arkadyich realized that Matvey wanted to joke and draw attention to himself. Tearing open the telegram, he read it, using guesswork to correct the words which were garbled as usual, and his face lit up.

'Matvey, my sister Anna Arkadyevna is arriving tomorrow,' he said, stopping for a moment the shiny, chubby hand of the barber, which was clearing a pink path between his long curling whiskers.

'Thank goodness,' said Matvey, showing with this answer that he understood as well as his master what this arrival meant, namely that Anna Arkadyevna, Stepan Arkadyich's beloved sister, might be able to assist in the reconciliation of husband and wife.

'Alone or with her husband?' asked Matvey.

Stepan Arkadyich could not speak, as the barber was busy with his upper lip, so he raised one finger. Matvey nodded to him in the mirror.

'Alone. Should we get a room ready upstairs?'

'Tell Darya Alexandrovna, wherever she decides.'

'Darya Alexandrovna?' Matvey repeated, as if in doubt.

'Yes, tell her. Here, take the telegram, and let me know what she says.'

'You want to test the waters,' Matvey understood, but he said only: 'Very good, sir.'

Stepan Arkadyich was already washed and combed and about to get dressed when Matvey came back into the room with the telegram in his hand, treading gingerly with his squeaky boots on the soft carpet. The barber had already gone.

'Darya Alexandrovna told me to inform you that she is going away. Let him, that is you, do as he likes,' he said, laughing with just his eyes, and putting his hands in his pockets, with his head tilted to one side, he gazed at his master.

Stepan Arkadyich was silent for a moment. Then a kind and rather pathetic smile appeared on his handsome face.

'Well? Matvey?' he said, shaking his head.

'Don't worry, sir, things will shape up,' said Matvey.

'Shape up?'

'Exactly, sir.'

'You think so? Who is that?' asked Stepan Arkadyich, hearing the rustle of a woman's dress behind the door.

'It's me, sir,' said a firm and pleasant female voice, and the stern, pockmarked face of Matryona Filimonovna the nanny peeped round the door.

'Well, what is it, Matryosha?' asked Stepan Arkadyich, going up to the door to speak to her.

Despite the fact that Stepan Arkadyich was completely in the wrong with regards to his wife and was conscious of it himself, almost everyone in the house, even the nanny, Darya Alexandrovna's main ally, was on his side.

'Well, what is it?' he said despondently.

'Go and say sorry again, sir. Maybe God will help. She is suffering ever so much, it's pitiful to see, and everything in the house is turned upside down. You must take pity on the children, sir. Say sorry, sir. Can't be helped! After the feast . . .'*

'But she won't see me . . .'

'You just do your bit. God is merciful, pray to God, sir, pray to God.'

'Well, all right, off you go,' said Stepan Arkadyich, suddenly going red. 'Well now, let's get dressed,' he said, turning to Matvey, and he resolutely threw off his dressing-gown.

Matvey was already holding up the prepared shirt like a yoke, blowing away some invisible speck, and he enveloped his master's well-groomed body in it with obvious pleasure.

3

ONCE dressed, Stepan Arkadyich sprayed himself with cologne, straightened the sleeves of his shirt, distributed cigarettes, wallet, matches, and watch with two chains and seals* amongst his pockets with a practised gesture, and, after shaking out his handkerchief and feeling clean, fragrant, healthy, and physically spry in spite of his misfortune, walked with a spring in every step into the dining room, where his coffee was ready waiting for him, and next to the coffee, letters and papers from the office.

Stepan Arkadyich sat down and read the letters. One of them was very unpleasant—from the merchant who was buying a wood on his wife's estate. This wood had to be sold; but there could be no question of that now until there was a reconciliation with his wife. The most unpleasant thing about this was that it introduced a financial consideration into the impending matter of reconciliation with his wife. And the thought that he might be guided by this consideration, that he would seek a reconciliation with his wife so he could sell this wood—this thought offended him.

After finishing the letters, Stepan Arkadyich drew towards him the papers from the office, quickly leafed through two files, made a few notes with a big pencil, then shunted the papers to one side and started on his coffee; while he was drinking he unfolded the still-damp morning paper and started reading it.

Stepan Arkadyich subscribed to and read a liberal newspaper,* which was not extreme, but represented the views of the majority. And despite the fact that neither science, nor art, nor politics actually interested him, he clung to the views on all these subjects held by the majority and by his newspaper, and only changed them when the majority changed them, or to be more precise, he did not change them, as they themselves imperceptibly changed within him.

Stepan Arkadyich did not choose either his tendency or his views, as these tendencies and views came to him by themselves, in just the same way that he did not choose a style of hat or frock-coat, but plumped for the ones which other people wore. And as someone frequenting a certain section of society and in need of a modicum of mental activity, such as usually develops in maturity, it was just as indispensable for him to have views as it was to have a hat. If there was a reason why he preferred the liberal tendency over the conservative one, as did many others in his circle, it was not because he found the liberal tendency made more sense, but because it more closely suited his lifestyle. The liberal party said that everything in Russia was bad, and Stepan Arkadyich did indeed have many debts, and was decidedly short of money. The liberal party said that marriage was an outdated institution, and that it was necessary to reform it, and indeed, family life brought Stepan Arkadyich little pleasure, and obliged him to lie and dissemble, which went so much against his nature. The liberal party said, or rather implied, that religion was simply a means to rein in the barbaric section of the population, and indeed, Stepan Arkadyich could not endure even a short service without his feet aching, nor could he understand the point of all those daunting and high-flown words about the next world, when living in this one could be very jolly. At the same time, Stepan Arkadyich, who was fond of a good joke, also enjoyed taxing the occasional meek soul with the idea that if one is seriously going to take pride in one's lineage, one shouldn't stop at Ryurik* and repudiate our original ancestor—the ape.* The liberal tendency thus became a habit for Stepan Arkadyich, and he liked his newspaper, like his after-dinner cigar, for the mild fog it produced in his head. He read the leading article, which explained that it was nowadays completely pointless to raise a commotion about the radicalism supposedly threatening to swallow up all the conservative elements, and the government supposedly needing to take measures to crush the hydra of revolution, and that, on the contrary, 'in our opinion, the danger lies not in the imaginary hydra of revolution, but in the stubborn traditionalism which holds up progress', etc. He also read another article, in the financial section, which mentioned Bentham and Mill* and levelled subtle barbs at the Ministry. With his characteristically quick powers of perception he understood the meaning of every barb:

by whom, at whom, and the reason it had been launched, and this, as always, afforded him a certain amount of pleasure. But today this pleasure was spoilt by the memory of Matryona Filimonovna's advice, and the fact that things were so miserable at home. He also read that Count Beust* was rumoured to have travelled to Wiesbaden, that grey hair was a thing of the past, that a light carriage was for sale, and that a young lady offered her services; but these pieces of information did not afford him the same quiet ironic pleasure as before.

After finishing the newspaper, a second cup of coffee, and a roll* and butter, he got up, shook the crumbs from his waistcoat, and, expanding his broad chest, smiled happily, not because he was harbouring anything particularly pleasant in his soul—the happy smile was brought on by good digestion.

But that happy smile now reminded him of everything, and he became pensive.

Two children's voices (Stepan Arkadyich recognized the voices of Grisha, his youngest boy, and Tanya, his eldest girl) could be heard behind the doors. They were carrying something, which they dropped.

'I said we couldn't put passengers on the roof,' shouted the girl in English, 'so you pick everything up!'

'Everything is confusion,' thought Stepan Arkadyich; 'the children are running about on their own out there.' And going up to the doors, he called out to them. They abandoned the box which was supposed to be a train, and ran in to their father.

The girl, her father's favourite, charged in boldly, put her arms around him and giggled as she hung on to his neck, revelling as always in the familiar scent of cologne emanating from his whiskers. After she had finally kissed him on his face, which had turned red from his crouched position and radiated affection, the girl unclasped her hands and was about to run back; but her father held on to her.

'How is Mama?' her father asked, running his hand down his daughter's smooth, tender little neck. 'Hello,' he said, smiling at the boy who was greeting him.

He was aware that he was less fond of the boy, and always tried to be fair; but the boy sensed this and did not respond to his father's cold smile with a smile.

'Mama? She's up,' the girl answered.

Stepan Arkadyich sighed. 'That means she was awake all night again,' he thought.

'And is she cheerful?'

The girl knew that there had been a quarrel between her father and mother, that her mother could not be cheerful, that her father ought to know this, and that he was putting on an act in asking about it so breezily. And she blushed for her father. He immediately understood this and blushed as well.

'I don't know,' she said. 'She didn't tell us to study, but she did tell us to go for a walk with Miss Hull to Grandmamma's.'

'Well, off you go then, my darling Tanchurochka. Oh yes, wait a minute,' he said, still holding on to her, and stroking her soft little hand.

He fetched from the mantelpiece the box of sweets he had put there the day before and gave her a couple, picking out her favourites, a chocolate and a fondant.

'Is this for Grisha?' the girl asked, pointing to the chocolate one.

'Yes, yes.' And after stroking her little shoulder once more, he kissed the roots of her hair, and her neck, and let her go.

'The carriage is ready,' said Matvey. 'And there is a woman with a petition,' he added.

'Has she been here long?' asked Stepan Arkadyich.

'About half an hour.'

'How many times have you been told to let me know straight away!'

'But I have to let you at least finish drinking your coffee,' said Matvey in that gruff but friendly tone with which it was impossible to get angry.

'Well, ask her to come in without delay,' said Oblonsky, frowning with annoyance.

The petitioner, the widow of a staff-captain Kalinin, was asking for something which was impossible and absurd; but Stepan Arkadyich sat her down in accordance with his usual custom, heard her out dutifully without interrupting, gave her detailed advice about whom she should approach and how to go about it, and even dashed off a brisk little note in his large, expansive, beautiful, and clear handwriting for her to take to the person who could provide assistance. After dismissing the staff-captain's wife, Stepan Arkadyich picked up his hat and paused as he considered whether he had forgotten anything. It turned out that he had forgotten nothing apart from the one thing he wanted to forget—his wife.

'Oh yes!' He hung his head, and his handsome face took on a mournful expression. 'Should I go or not?' he said to himself. And an inner voice told him that he should not go, that it could produce nothing but falsity, and that it was impossible to restore or mend their relationship, because it was impossible to make her attractive and physically desirable again or to turn him into an old man incapable of love. Nothing could come out of it now except falsity and lies; but falsity and lies were inimical to his nature.

'But I'll have to sooner or later; after all, it can't go on like this,' he said, trying to muster some courage. He drew himself up, got out a cigarette, lit it, took a couple of puffs, threw it into the mother-of-pearl shell ashtray, walked briskly through the sombre drawing room, and opened the other door, into his wife's bedroom.

4

DARYA ALEXANDROVNA, wearing a dressing-jacket, with the braids of her once thick and beautiful but already wispy hair pinned to the nape of her neck, and a haggard, drawn face and large, frightened eyes made prominent by the gauntness of her face, was standing amongst things scattered about the room in front of an open chest of drawers, from which she was removing something. At the sound of her husband's footsteps, she stopped, vainly trying to give her face a stern and disdainful expression as she looked at the door. She felt that she was afraid of him, and afraid of their imminent encounter. She had just been trying to do something she had already tried to do ten times during the past three days: sort out which of the children's and her own things she would take to her mother's—and she had again been unable to bring herself to do it; but as on the previous occasions, she was now telling herself that this situation could not continue, that she had to do something to punish him, shame him, and take revenge on him for at least a small part of the pain he had caused her. She was still saying that she would leave him, but she felt it was impossible; it was impossible because she could not get out of the habit of regarding him as her husband and loving him. Apart from that, she felt that if she could barely manage to look after her five children here in her own house, it would be even worse for them wherever she took them all. As it was, during these three days the youngest had fallen ill because he had been given some broth that was bad, and the others had almost gone without dinner the previous day. She felt that it was impossible to leave; but deluding herself, she was still sorting things and pretending that she was going to leave.

When she saw her husband, she lowered her hands into a drawer as if she was searching for something, and turned to look at him only when he had come right up close. But her face, to which she had wanted to impart a stern and resolute expression, was a picture of bewilderment and suffering.

'Dolly!' he said in a quiet, timid voice. He drew his head into his shoulders in an attempt to look pitiful and meek, but he still radiated health and vigour.

She ran a quick eye from top to toe over this figure radiant with health and vigour. 'Yes, he is happy and contented!' she thought, 'but what about me? . . . And that ghastly kind-heartedness which everyone loves and admires about him; I hate that kind-heartedness of his,' she thought. She pursed her lips, and a muscle in her cheek began to twitch on the right side of her pale, tense face.

'What do you want?*' she asked in an abrupt, rasping voice that was not hers.

'Dolly!' he repeated with a trembling in his voice. 'Anna is arriving today.'

'Well, what has that got to do with me? I can't receive her!' she cried.

'But we must nevertheless, Dolly . . .'

'Go away, go away, go away!' she cried without looking at him, as if her cry was prompted by physical pain.

Stepan Arkadyich could be calm when he thought about his wife, he could hope that everything would *shape up*, as Matvey had put it, and he could calmly read his newspaper and drink his coffee; but when he saw her worn-out, suffering face and heard that submissive, despairing sound in her voice, he gasped, a lump came into his throat, and his eyes glistened with tears.

'Heavens, what have I done! Dolly! For God's sake! . . . After all . . .' He could not continue, as his throat was choked with sobs.

She slammed the drawer shut and glanced at him.

'Dolly, what can I say? . . . Only one thing: forgive me, forgive me . . . Think back: surely nine years can atone for moments, moments . . .'

She stood listening with her eyes cast down, waiting to hear what he had to say, as if entreating him to dissuade her somehow . . .

'Moments . . . moments of infatuation . . .' he managed to utter, and was about to go on, but her lips pursed at the mention of that word as if in physical pain, and the muscle in her cheek on the right side of her face started twitching again.

'Go away, go away from here!' she cried even more shrilly, 'and don't talk to me about your infatuations, about your vile behaviour!'

She wanted to walk away but was unsteady on her feet, and gripped the back of a chair for support. His face expanded, his lips swelled, and his eyes filled with tears.

'Dolly!' he said, sobbing. 'For God's sake, think about the children; they are not to blame. I'm the one to blame, so punish me, order me to atone for my sin. I am ready to do whatever I can! I am guilty, there are no words to express how guilty I am! But forgive me, Dolly!'

She sat down. He heard her loud, heavy breathing, and felt unbelievably sorry for her. She tried to begin saying something several times, but could not. He waited.

'You think about the children* when you want to play with them, Stiva, but I always think about them, and know they are ruined now,' she said, clearly producing one of the phrases she had been saying to herself over the last three days.

She had reverted to the familiar form of address with him, and he looked at her with gratitude and made a move to take her hand, but she shrank from him in disgust.

'I do think about the children, and therefore I would do anything in the world to save them; but I do not know myself how to save them: whether by taking them away from their father, or leaving them with a father who is depraved—yes, a father who is depraved . . . Well, you tell me, after . . . what has happened, is it really possible for us to live together? Is it really possible? Tell me, do you think it is really possible?' she repeated, raising her voice. 'After my husband, the father of my children, has had an affair with the governess of his children . . .'

'Well what . . . Well what is to be done then?' he said in a pitiful voice, not knowing himself what he was saying, hanging his head lower and lower.

'You are loathsome and disgusting to me!' she shouted, growing more and more angry. 'Your tears are just water! You never loved me; you have no heart, no sense of honour! You are a vile, loathsome stranger to me, yes, a stranger!' She pronounced this word *stranger* she found so terrible with pain and fury.

He looked at her, and the fury expressed on her face frightened and surprised him. He did not understand that his pity for her irritated her. She could see he had pity for her, but not love. 'No, she hates me. She won't forgive me,' he thought.

'This is awful! Awful!' he said.

A child cried out at that moment in another room, probably after falling down; Darya Alexandrovna listened out and her face suddenly softened.

It clearly took her several seconds to collect herself, as if she did not know where she was or what she should do, and then she got up quickly and headed for the door.

'She does love my child, though,' he thought, noticing how her face had changed when the child cried out, '*my* child; so how can she hate me?'

'Dolly, just one more word,' he said, following her.

'If you come after me, I will call the servants and the children! Let everyone know that you are a scoundrel! I am leaving today, and you can live here with your mistress!'

And she went out, slamming the door.

Stepan Arkadyich sighed, wiped his face, and walked slowly out of the room. 'Matvey says: things will shape up, but how? I can't even see any possibility. Oh, oh, what a nightmare! And her shouting was so tawdry,' he said to himself, remembering her screaming and the words: scoundrel and mistress. 'And maybe the maids heard! It was awfully tawdry, it really was.' Stepan Arkadyich stood alone for a few seconds, wiped his eyes and sighed, then straightened himself up and left the room.

It was Friday, and the German clockmaker was winding up the clock in the dining room. Stepan Arkadyich remembered his joke about this punctilious bald clockmaker, which was that the German 'had himself been wound up his whole life so that he could wind up clocks', and he smiled. Stepan Arkadyich loved a good joke. 'Well, maybe things will shape up! That's a good little phrase: *shape up*,' he thought. 'I'll have to tell people that one.'

'Matvey!' he shouted. 'If you and Marya could get everything ready in the sitting room for Anna Arkadyevna,' he said when Matvey appeared.

'Very good, sir.'

Stepan Arkadyich put on his fur coat and went out on to the porch.

'You won't be dining at home?' said Matvey as he saw him out.

'We'll see. Look, take this for expenses,' he said, pulling ten roubles from his wallet. 'Will that be enough?'

'Whether it is enough or not, we'll have to make do,' said Matvey as he banged the carriage door shut and stepped back on to the porch.

Darya Alexandrovna, meanwhile, after comforting the child and realizing from the sound of the carriage that he had left, retreated back into the bedroom. It was her only refuge from the domestic worries which besieged her as soon as she set foot outside. Even during the short time when she had come out to go into the nursery, the English governess and Matryona Filimonovna had managed to ask her several questions which could not be put off, and which she alone could answer: what should the children wear for their walk? Should they be given milk? Should another cook be sent for?

'Oh, leave me, leave me alone!' she said, and after coming back into the bedroom she sat down again in the same place where she had been talking to her husband, clenched her thin hands with the rings which kept slipping down her bony fingers, and started going over the whole of their previous conversation in her mind. 'He has gone! But how has he left things with *her*?' she thought. 'Surely he can't still be seeing her? Why didn't I ask him? No, no, we can't become intimate again. Even if we stay in the same house, we will be strangers. Forever strangers!' she said, repeating that word she found so terrible with particular emphasis. 'And how I loved him, Heavens, how I loved him! . . . How I loved him! And don't I love him now? Don't I love him even more than before? What is terrible, what is the main thing, is that . . .' she began, but she did not finish her thought, because Matryona Filimonovna had poked her head round the door.

'You should send for my brother,' she said. 'He will prepare dinner; otherwise the children won't eat anything until six, like yesterday.'

'Well, all right, I will come out in a minute and see to things. And has someone been sent for fresh milk?'

And Darya Alexandrovna immersed herself in the day's chores and drowned her sorrows in them for a while.

5

STEPAN ARKADYICH had done well at school due to his natural abilities, but he was lazy and disobedient so had ended up near the bottom of his year, yet despite his always dissolute life, modest rank, and young age, he occupied a venerable and well-paid post as head of department in one of the Moscow government institutions.* He had obtained this post through his sister Anna's husband, Alexey Alexandrovich Karenin, who occupied one of the key posts in the ministry to which the institution belonged; but if Karenin had not appointed his brother-in-law to this position, then a hundred other individuals, brothers, sisters, relatives, cousins, uncles, and aunts, would have helped Stiva Oblonsky obtain either this post or something similar, with a salary of about six thousand roubles, which he needed, since despite his wife's ample means, his affairs were in a bad way.

Half of Moscow and Petersburg were Stepan Arkadyich's relatives and friends. He had been born into the circle of people who were, or would become, the powerful of this world. One third were government figures, old men, and friends of his father, who had known him in baby clothes; another third were on intimate terms with him, while the third third were good acquaintances; consequently the purveyors of earthly blessings in the form of appointments, leases, concessions, and so forth were all friends of his and could not pass over one of their own; so Oblonsky did not need to exert himself too much in order to obtain a well-paid post; all he needed to do was not refuse, not be envious, not quarrel, and not take offence, which he would never have done anyway owing to his innate good nature. He would have found it ridiculous if he had been told that he would not obtain a post with the salary he needed, not least since he was not asking for anything excessive; he only wanted what his peers were getting, and he could perform the duties of that sort of position no worse than anyone else.

Stepan Arkadyich was not only loved by everyone who knew him for his kind, cheery disposition and undoubted honesty, but there was something in him, in his handsome, bright appearance, his shining eyes, his black brows, his hair, and his pink-and-white complexion, which had the physical effect of instilling friendliness and jollity in the people who met him. 'Aha! Stiva! Oblonsky! Here he is!' people would say almost invariably with a delighted smile when they met him. And even if it turned out after talking to him that nothing particularly delightful had taken place, as sometimes happened, they were just as delighted to run into him the following day, and the one after that.

Now into his third year as head of one of the institution's offices in Moscow, Stepan Arkadyich had won not just the affection but also the respect of his colleagues, subordinates, superiors, and all those who came into contact with him. The principal qualities which had won Stepan Arkadyich this universal respect at work consisted firstly of his extraordinary forbearance towards people, which was based on an awareness of his own faults; secondly, his supremely liberal views, which were not of the kind he found in the newspapers but the kind he had in his blood, and led him to treat all people, whatever their position and rank, completely equally and in the same way; and thirdly— and most importantly—his complete indifference to whatever he was engaged in, as a result of which he never got carried away or made mistakes.

Once he had arrived at his place of work, Stepan Arkadyich proceeded with his portfolio to his small office, accompanied by a deferential porter, then put on his uniform and went into the main chamber. The copyists and clerks all stood up and bowed cheerily and respectfully. Stepan Arkadyich walked over to his place as briskly as always, shook hands with the members, and sat down. He cracked jokes and chatted for as long as was seemly, then got on with the proceedings. No one could do a better job than Stepan Arkadyich in setting the limits of the simplicity and formality necessary for the pleasant conduct of business. The secretary came up with some documents in that cheery and respectful manner shared by everyone in Stepan Arkadyich's office, and said in the familiar liberal tone which Stepan Arkadyich had introduced:

'We did after all manage to get the information from the Penza* regional government. Here it is, if you would care . . .'

'You got it finally?' said Stepan Arkadyich, marking a page with his finger; 'Well, gentlemen . . .' And the proceedings began.

'If they only knew what a guilty boy their chairman was half an hour ago!' he thought, inclining his head meaningfully as he listened to the report. And his eyes twinkled while the report was being read. Until two o'clock the proceedings were supposed to continue without a break, but at two o'clock there would be a break and lunch.

It was not yet two o'clock when the large glass doors of the chamber suddenly opened and someone entered. All the members sitting under the Tsar's portrait and behind the symbol of imperial justice* looked round to the door, glad of the distraction; but the caretaker standing by the door immediately expelled the intruder and closed the glass door behind him.

When the case had been read, Stepan Arkadyich stretched as he stood up and, in deference to the liberality of the times, took out a cigarette in the chamber before proceeding to his office. Two of his comrades, the old campaigner Nikitin and the Gentleman of the Bedchamber* Grinevich, went out with him.

'We will manage to finish after lunch,' said Stepan Arkadyich.

'We certainly will!' said Nikitin.

'That Fomin must be an utter rogue,' said Grinevich about one of the people involved in the case which they were examining.

Stepan Arkadyich scowled at Grinevich's words, thus letting him know that it was improper to make a premature judgement, and said nothing in reply.

'Who was that who came in?' he asked the caretaker.

'Someone who sneaked in without permission the moment my back was turned, Your Excellency. He was asking for you. I told him: when the members come out, then . . .'

'Where is he?'

'He must have gone into the lobby, but he was walking up and down here just now. That's him,' said the custodian, pointing to a well-built, broad-shouldered man with a curly beard running quickly and lightly up the worn steps of the stone staircase with his sheepskin hat still on. A lanky official with a portfolio who was amongst those coming downstairs paused and looked disapprovingly at the feet of the person running past, and then glanced quizzically at Oblonsky.

Stepan Arkadyich stood on the stairs. His face, which was beaming good-naturedly from behind the embroidered collar of his uniform, beamed even more when he recognized who it was running up.

'So it is you! Levin, at last!' he said, looking Levin over with a friendly, wry smile as he approached. 'How is it you weren't too squeamish about coming to find me in this notorious den?' said Stepan Arkadyich, not content with a shaking of hands and kissing his friend. 'Have you been here long?'

'I've just arrived, and I really wanted to see you,' replied Levin, looking round shyly, but at the same time crossly and anxiously.

'Well, let's go into my office,' said Stepan Arkadyich, knowing his friend's prickly and petulant diffidence; and taking hold of his arm, he ushered him along, as if steering him between dangers.

Stepan Arkadyich was on intimate terms with nearly all of his acquaintances: old men of sixty, boys of twenty, actors, ministers, merchants, and adjutant-generals, so that a great many of those who were intimate with him were at opposite ends of the social ladder, and would have been extremely surprised to discover they had something in common through Oblonsky. He was intimate with everyone with whom he drank champagne, and he drank champagne with everyone, so for that reason, whenever he met any of his 'disreputable chums', as he jokingly called many of his friends, in the presence of his subordinates, he was able to diminish the unpleasantness of this impression for his subordinates with his inborn tact. Levin was not a 'disreputable chum', but Oblonsky sensed with his tact that Levin thought he would not want to display his closeness with him in front of his subordinates, and therefore was in a hurry to whisk him away to his office.

Levin was almost the same age as Oblonsky and was not intimate with him just because of the champagne. Levin had been his comrade and friend from early youth. Despite their different characters and tastes, they were very fond of each other, as people who have been friends since childhood tend to be. But despite that, as often happens with people who choose different kinds of occupations, while each could rationally justify the other's occupation, deep down they despised it. Each felt that the life he was leading was the only real life, while the one his friend was leading was just an illusion. Oblonsky

could not suppress a slightly sardonic smile whenever he saw
Levin. He had seen him umpteen times arrive in Moscow from
the country, where he did something, but what exactly Stepan
Arkadyich could never quite figure out, nor was he interested.
Levin always arrived in Moscow agitated, frantic, slightly awkward,
and annoyed by this awkwardness, and, more often than not, with
some completely new and unexpected approach to things. Stepan
Arkadyich laughed at this and loved it. Similarly, Levin inwardly
despised the urban lifestyle of his friend, and his office job, which
he considered trivial, and laughed at that. The difference was that
Oblonsky, doing what everyone else did, laughed in a confident and
good-natured way, while Levin did so unconfidently and sometimes
angrily.

'We've been expecting you for a long time,' said Stepan Arkadyich,
going into his office and letting go of Levin's arm, as if to show that
they were out of danger now. 'I'm very, very glad to see you,' he continued. 'Well, what's new? How are things? When did you arrive?'

Levin remained silent, looking at the unfamiliar faces of Oblonsky's
two colleagues, and in particular at the hand of the elegant Grinevich,
who had such slender white fingers, such long yellow nails curling at
the ends, and such huge shiny cuff-links on his shirt, that his hands
clearly consumed all his attention and allowed him no freedom of
thought. Oblonsky immediately noticed this and smiled.

'Ah yes, allow me to introduce you,' he said. 'My colleagues: Filipp
Ivanich Nikitin, Mikhail Stanislavich Grinevich,' and turning to
Levin: 'zemstvo* activist, new generation zemstvo man, gymnast, lifts
a hundred and fifty pounds with one hand, cattle-breeder, hunter, and
my friend, Konstantin Dmitrich Levin, brother of Sergey Ivanich
Koznyshev.'

'Pleased to meet you,' said the old man.

'I have the honour of knowing your brother, Sergey Ivanich,' said
Grinevich, holding out his slender hand with the long nails.

Levin frowned, shook hands coldly, and immediately turned to
Oblonsky. Although he had great respect for his maternal half-brother,
a writer known throughout Russia, he could not stand it when people
addressed him not as Konstantin Levin but as the brother of the
famous Koznyshev.

'No, I'm no longer a zemstvo activist. I fell out with them all and
don't go to meetings any more,' he said, turning to Oblonsky.

'That was quick work!' said Oblonsky with a smile. 'But how come?
What happened?'

'It's a long story. I'll tell it to you some time,' said Levin, but he started telling it straight away. 'Well, to put it bluntly, I became convinced that there is no zemstvo activity, nor can there be,' he began, speaking as if someone had just offended him; 'on the one hand, it's a plaything, people playing at parliament, and I am neither sufficiently young nor sufficiently old to amuse myself with playthings; but,' he stammered, 'on the other hand, it is a way for the local *coterie* to make a bit of money. It used to be trustees and courts, and now we have the zemstvo . . . not in the form of bribes, but unearned salaries,' he said, speaking as vehemently as if one of those present had challenged his point of view.

'Aha! I see you are in a new phase again, a conservative one,' said Stepan Arkadyich. 'Anyway, we'll talk about that later.'

'Yes, later. But I had to see you,' said Levin, looking with loathing at Grinevich's hand.

Stepan Arkadyich smiled almost imperceptibly.

'What was it you used to say about never wearing European clothes again?' he said, looking over his new clothes, clearly from a French tailor. 'So! I see: it's a new phase.'

Levin suddenly blushed, but not in the way that grown-up people blush—faintly, without noticing it themselves—but in the way that boys who feel their shyness is ridiculous are prone to blush, and as a result become embarrassed and blush even more profusely, almost to the point of tears. And it was so strange to see this clever, manly face in such a childish state that Oblonsky stopped looking at him.

'Yes, but where shall we meet? You know, I do really need to talk to you,' said Levin.

Oblonsky seemed to be deliberating.

'I tell you what: let's go to Gurin's for lunch, and talk there. I am free until three.'

'No,' replied Levin, after pondering this, 'there's somewhere else I have to go.'

'Well, all right, let's have dinner together.'

'Dinner? But it's nothing special, just a couple of words I want to say and ask you about, and we could have a talk later.'

'Well, say your couple of words now, and we can chat over dinner.'

'The couple of words are these,' said Levin; 'actually, it's nothing important.'

His face suddenly acquired a surly expression which came from his efforts to overcome his shyness.

'What are the Shcherbatskys up to? Same as usual?' he asked.

Stepan Arkadyich, who had known for a long time that Levin was in love with his sister-in-law Kitty, smiled almost imperceptibly and his eyes began to twinkle merrily.

'You said a couple of words, but I cannot answer in a couple of words, because . . . Excuse me for a moment . . .'

The secretary entered with unceremonious deference and a certain modest awareness, common to all secretaries, of his superiority to his chief in his knowledge of matters, came up to Oblonsky with some papers, and under the guise of a question started to explain some difficulty. Without hearing him out, Stepan Arkadyich gently placed his hand on the secretary's sleeve.

'No, you just do as I have told you,' he said, softening the remark with a smile, and after briefly explaining to him how he understood the matter, he pushed the papers aside and said: 'Just do as I have told you, please. If you wouldn't mind, Zakhar Nikitich.'

The flustered secretary departed. Having completely recovered from his embarrassment during the consultation with the secretary, Levin stood leaning both his elbows on a chair, and there was an expression of scornful attention on his face.

'I don't understand, I don't understand,' he said.

'What don't you understand?' said Oblonsky, smiling just as merrily as he reached for a cigarette. He was expecting some strange outburst from Levin.

'I don't understand what you are all doing,' said Levin, shrugging his shoulders. 'How can you seriously do this?'

'What makes you say that?'

'Because there is nothing to do.'

'You might think that, but we are overwhelmed with work.'

'Paperwork. Well, yes, you have a gift for that,' added Levin.

'You mean you think I am lacking in something?'

'Maybe you are,' said Levin. 'All the same, I am in awe of your eminence and am proud to count such an eminent man as my friend. However, you haven't answered my question,' he added, with a desperate effort looking Oblonsky straight in the eye.

'Well, all right, all right. Wait a bit and you'll come round. All right, you might have eight thousand acres in the Karazin district,* and all those muscles, and the freshness of a twelve-year-old girl, but you will come round to our way of thinking. Now, about what you were asking: no change, but it is a shame you haven't been here for such a long time.'

'What do you mean?' asked Levin in alarm.

'Oh, nothing,' answered Oblonsky. 'We will talk about it. But why actually have you come this time?'

'Oh, we will talk about that later too,' said Levin, blushing to his roots again.

'Well, all right. I understand,' said Stepan Arkadyich. 'The thing is: I would invite you home, but my wife's not terribly well. Here's what I suggest, though: if you want to see them, they are bound to be in the Zoological Gardens today from four to five. Kitty goes skating. You go there, I'll drop by, and then we will go off and have dinner together somewhere.'

'Excellent. I'll see you later then.'

'But look, I know you, you are bound to forget, or you'll suddenly go off back to the country!' Stepan Arkadyich exclaimed with a laugh.

'No, I won't, really.'

And Levin left the office, remembering that he had forgotten to bow to Oblonsky's colleagues only when he was already in the doorway.

'He must be a very energetic person,' said Grinevich, after Levin had left.

'Oh yes indeed, my friend,' said Stepan Arkadyich, shaking his head. 'He's a lucky man! Three thousand acres in the Karazin district, everything ahead of him, and such vigour! Not like yours truly.'

'What have you got to complain of, Stepan Arkadyich?'

'Oh, things are grim, not good at all,' said Stepan Arkadyich with a heavy sigh.

6

WHEN Oblonsky had asked Levin the real reason for his visit, Levin had blushed and been angry with himself for blushing, because he could not reply: 'I have come to propose to your sister-in-law,' although this was the only reason for his visit.

The Levin and Shcherbatsky families belonged to the old Moscow nobility, and there had always been close and friendly relations between them. The tie had been further strengthened during Levin's student days. He had prepared for and entered university alongside the young Prince Shcherbatsky, Dolly and Kitty's brother. Levin had been a frequent visitor to the Shcherbatsky household at that time, and had fallen in love with the Shcherbatsky family. However strange it may seem, Konstantin Levin really had fallen in love with the household, with the family, and particularly its female half.

Levin could not remember his own mother, and his only sister was older than him, so it was in the Shcherbatsky household that he encountered for the first time the old noble, educated, and honest family milieu that had been denied him by the death of his father and mother. All the members of this family, particularly its female half, seemed to him to be enveloped in some mysterious, poetic veil, and not only did he fail to see any faults in them, but presumed the most elevated feelings and every possible perfection behind this poetic veil enveloping them. Why these three young ladies had to speak French one day and English the next; why at certain times they took turns in playing the piano, the sounds of which always could be heard in their brother's room upstairs, where the students were working; why all those French literature, music, drawing, and dancing teachers came to the house; why at certain times all three young ladies drove off in a carriage with Mademoiselle Linon to Tverskoy Boulevard wearing their satin pelisses—Dolly in a long one, Natalie in a half-length one, and Kitty in one that was so short that her shapely young legs in their tightly pulled-up red stockings were on full display; why they had to walk along Tverskoy Boulevard accompanied by a footman with a gold cockade on his hat—none of this, nor many other things which went on in their mysterious world, did he understand, but he knew that everything that went on was wonderful, and he was in love with precisely the mysteriousness of what was taking place.

During his student years he had almost fallen in love with Dolly, the eldest, but she was soon married off to Oblonsky. Then he was on the verge of falling in love with the second. He somehow felt he had to fall in love with one of the sisters, but could not work out exactly which one. But Natalie went and married the diplomat Lvov as soon as she came out. Kitty was still a child when Levin left university. The young Shcherbatsky, who joined the navy, drowned in the Baltic, and Levin's contacts with the family became fewer, despite his friendship with Oblonsky. But at the beginning of that winter, when Levin came to Moscow after a year in the country and saw the Shcherbatskys, he realized which of the three he was really destined to fall in love with.

It would seem nothing could be simpler than for him, a wealthy rather than poor man from a good family, thirty-two years old, to propose to Princess Shcherbatskaya; in all probability he would immediately be accepted as a good match. But Levin was in love, and therefore it seemed to him that Kitty was such perfection in every respect, and a being so far above everything ordinary, while he himself was such an ordinary, lowly being, that there could not be even the remotest thought that either she herself or others could acknowledge him as being worthy of her.

After spending two months in Moscow as if in a daze, seeing Kitty almost every day in society, which he had started to frequent in order to meet her, Levin had suddenly decided it could never happen, and so he had left for the country.

Levin's conviction that it could never happen rested on the notion that in the eyes of her family he was an unsuitable, unworthy match for the lovely Kitty, and that Kitty herself could never love him. In the eyes of her family he had no regular fixed occupation or position in society, while his contemporaries, now that he was thirty-two years old, had already become colonels and aides-de-camp, professors and respected leaders—directors of banks or railways, or chairmen of government institutions, like Oblonsky; whereas he (and he knew very well how he must seem to others) was a landowner who bred cattle, shot snipe, and put up buildings, in other words, a talentless fellow who had not come to anything, and who, in the eyes of society, was doing exactly what good-for-nothing people do.

The mysterious and lovely Kitty herself, meanwhile, could not possibly love such an unattractive man, as he considered himself to be, and, above all, such an ordinary, undistinguished man. Moreover, his previous relationship with Kitty—that of an adult and child, emanating from his friendship with her brother—seemed to him yet one more obstacle to love. He supposed that an unattractive, good man, as he considered himself to be, could be loved as a friend, but in order to be loved with the kind of love he had for Kitty, a man needed to be handsome, but most importantly, exceptional.

He had heard that women often love unattractive, ordinary men, but because of his own experience he did not believe it, since he himself could only love beautiful, mysterious, and exceptional women.

But having spent two months alone in the country, he came to the conclusion that this was not one of those infatuations he had experienced in his early youth, that these feelings were not giving him a moment's peace, that he could not live without resolving the question as to whether or not she would become his wife, that his despair was only a product of his imagination, and that he had no proof that he would be refused. So he had now come to Moscow with the firm intention of proposing and getting married if accepted. Or . . . he could not imagine what would happen to him if he were to be refused.

7

AFTER arriving in Moscow on the morning train, Levin went to stay with his elder maternal half-brother Koznyshev and, after a change of clothes, he went into his study, intending to tell him straight away the reason for his visit, and to ask his advice: but his brother was not alone. Sitting in his study was a famous professor of philosophy who had come expressly from Kharkov* to clear up a misunderstanding which had arisen between them on an extremely important philosophical question. The professor was conducting a heated polemic with the materialists, and Sergey Koznyshev had been following this polemic with interest. After reading the professor's latest article, he had written him a letter stating his objections, in which he reproached the professor for making too many concessions to the materialists. And the professor had come straight away so they could iron out their differences. They were discussing a fashionable topic: is there a boundary between psychological and physiological phenomena* in human activity, and, if so, where does it lie?

Sergey Ivanovich greeted his brother with the kindly but cold smile he usually bestowed on everyone and, after introducing him to the professor, carried on the conversation.

The sallow, bespectacled little man with the narrow forehead broke off the conversation for a moment to say hello, then carried on talking, not paying any attention to Levin. Levin sat down to wait for the professor to go, but soon became interested in the subject of the conversation.

Levin had come across the journal articles they were discussing and read them, interested in them as a development of the principles of natural science familiar from his university studies as a natural scientist, but he had never allied all these scholarly conclusions about the origins of man as an animal, and about reflexes, biology, and sociology with those questions about what life and death meant for him personally, which lately had been coming into his mind with increasing frequency.

As he listened to his brother's conversation with the professor, he noticed that they aligned scientific questions with emotional ones and came close on several occasions to broaching these questions, but as soon as they approached what seemed to him to be the nub of the matter, they each time instantly veered off swiftly and immersed themselves again in the sphere of subtle distinctions, reservations, quotations, allusions, and references to authorities, and he found it difficult to understand what they were talking about.

'I cannot allow,' said Sergey Ivanovich with his usual clarity and precision of expression and elegant articulation; 'I cannot on any account agree with Keiss that my perception of the external world derives entirely from impressions. The most fundamental concept of *being* has not been received by me via the senses, as there is no special organ to transmit this concept.'

'Yes, but Wurst, and Knaust, and Pripasov* will reply by saying that your consciousness of being is a product of a combination of every sensation, that this consciousness of being is the result of sensations. Wurst even says straight out that once there is no sensation, there can be no concept of being.'

'I would say the opposite,' began Sergey Ivanovich . . .

But at this point it again seemed to Levin that, having come close to the most important thing, they were meandering off again, so he decided to pose the professor a question.

'Therefore, if my feelings are destroyed, if my body dies, there can be no further existence of any kind?' he asked.

The professor glanced with irritation and almost mental pain at the strange person posing the question, who looked more like a barge-hauler than a philosopher, then transferred his gaze to Sergey Ivanovich as if to ask: what is there to say? But Sergey Ivanovich, who was not nearly as assertive and as one-sided as the professor, and was sufficiently broad-minded to be able to answer the professor and also understand the simple and natural point of view from which the question had emerged, smiled and said:

'We do not yet have the right to answer that question . . .'

'We do not have the data,' confirmed the professor, before continuing with his arguments. 'No,' he said; 'I should like to point out that if, as Pripasov directly states, sensation is based on impressions, then we must draw a clear distinction between these two concepts.'

Levin stopped listening, and waited for the professor to go.

8

WHEN the professor had gone, Sergey Ivanovich turned to his brother: 'I'm very glad you've come. Are you here for long? How is the estate?'

Levin knew that his elder brother had little interest in the estate and was only making a concession in asking him about it, so he only responded about the sale of wheat and about money.

Levin had wanted to tell his brother of his intention to marry and ask his advice, and had even firmly resolved to do so; but when he saw his brother and listened to his conversation with the professor, and when he heard the unconsciously patronizing tone with which his brother asked him how the estate was prospering (their mother's property had not been divided, and Levin managed both parts), Levin felt he could not, for some reason, launch into a discussion with his brother about his decision to marry. He felt his brother would not look at it in the way he would have wished.

'Well, what is going on at your zemstvo?' asked Sergey Ivanovich, who was very interested in the zemstvo and attached great significance to it.

'I really don't know . . .'

'How can that be? Aren't you a member of the board?'

'No, not any longer; I stepped down,' Konstantin Levin replied. 'And I don't go to meetings any more.'

'A pity!' said Sergey Ivanovich, frowning.

Levin started to tell him what had been going on at the meetings in his district by way of justification.

'Oh, it's always like that!' interrupted Sergey Ivanovich. 'We Russians are always like that. Maybe it's one of our good points, this ability to see our faults, but we overdo it—we console ourselves with irony, which is always ready to come tripping off our tongues. All I will say to you is that if another European nation was given the same rights as our zemstvo institutions, the Germans and the English would have secured freedom with them, but we just laugh.'

'But what can be done?' said Levin guiltily. 'That was my last attempt. And I put heart and soul into it. I can't do it. Not up to it.'

'It's not that you are not up to it,' said Sergey Ivanovich, 'you're just not looking at things the right way.'

'Maybe,' answered Levin gloomily.

'Our brother Nikolay is here again, you know.'

Brother Nikolay was Konstantin Levin's elder brother, and Sergey Ivanovich's maternal half-brother, a ruined man who had squandered the greater part of his inheritance, kept the strangest, most disreputable company, and had quarrelled with his brothers.

'What did you say?' exclaimed Levin in horror. 'How do you know?'

'Prokofy saw him in the street.'

'Here, in Moscow? Where is he? Do you know?' Levin got up from his chair, as if about to go at once.

'I'm sorry I told you about it,' said Sergey Ivanovich, shaking his head at his younger brother's agitation. 'I made enquiries to find out where he is living and sent him his promissory note to Trubin, which I've paid. Here is what he replied.'

And Sergey Ivanovich handed his brother a note he retrieved from under a paperweight.

Levin read what was written in the strange, familiar handwriting: 'I humbly request to be left in peace. That is all that I require from my dear brothers. Nikolay Levin.'

Levin read this and stood before Sergey Ivanovich with the note in his hands, his head bowed.

A battle was going on in his heart between the desire to forget now about his unfortunate brother and the recognition that this would be wrong.

'He obviously wants to insult me,' continued Sergey Ivanovich, 'but he cannot insult me, and I wish with all my heart that I could help him, but I know it's impossible.'

'Yes, yes,' repeated Levin. 'I do understand and appreciate your attitude to him; but I'm going to go and see him.'

'Go if you like, but I wouldn't advise it,' said Sergey Ivanovich. 'I mean, I'm not afraid on my own account, as he won't sow dissension between us; but I advise you not to go for your own sake. He can't be helped. However, you must do what you want.'

'Maybe he can't be helped, but I feel, particularly just now—well yes, that's something different—I feel I cannot be at ease.'

'Well, I don't understand that,' said Sergey Ivanovich. 'One thing I do understand, though,' he added, 'is that it is a lesson in humility. I've begun seeing what is regarded as contemptible in a different light, and with greater acceptance since our brother Nikolay became what he is now . . . You know what he has done . . .'

'Oh it's awful, awful!' repeated Levin.

After obtaining his brother's address from Sergey Ivanovich's servant, Levin was about to go and see him at once, but after thinking it over he decided to postpone his visit until evening. First of all, in order to have some peace of mind, he needed to resolve the matter that had brought him to Moscow. From his brother's, Levin drove to Oblonsky's office, and after enquiring about the Shcherbatskys, he drove off to the place where he had been told he might find Kitty.

9

At four o'clock, feeling his heart beating, Levin stepped out of his cab at the Zoological Gardens, and set off along the path towards the toboggan runs and the skating-rink, knowing he was bound to see her there, because he had seen the Shcherbatskys' carriage at the entrance.

It was a clear, frosty day. By the entrance stood ranks of carriages, sleighs, cabbies, and police. Smart people, their hats shining in the bright sun, were milling about the entrance and on the paths cleared between the Russian-style huts with carved eaves; the garden's curly old birches, their branches all heavy with snow, seemed to have been adorned with festive new vestments.

He walked along the path towards the skating-rink, saying to himself: 'You mustn't be nervous, you must calm down. What's the matter with you? Be quiet, stupid!' he told his heart. But the more he tried to calm down, the more breathless he became. An acquaintance he encountered called out to him, but Levin did not even recognize who it was. He walked up to the slopes, with the clanking of chains hauling toboggans up and down mingled with the thunder of speeding toboggans and the sound of merry voices. He took a few more steps, the rink opened out before him, and amongst all the other skaters he immediately recognized her.

He could tell she was there from the joy and fear gripping his heart. She was standing talking to a lady at the other end of the rink. There did not seem to be anything special about either her clothes or the way she held herself, but it was as easy for Levin to recognize her in the crowd as a rose among nettles. Everything was lit up by her. She was a smile illuminating everything all around. 'Can I really step on to the ice and go up to her over there?' he wondered. The place where she was standing seemed like an inaccessible, sacred shrine, and there was a moment when he almost left, so terrified had he become. He had to make a concerted effort to persuade himself that all kinds of people were walking near her, and that he too might have come there to go skating himself. He walked down, trying to avoid looking at her for too long, as if she were the sun, but like the sun, he could still see her even when he was not looking at her.

The people gathering on the ice on that day of the week, at that time, were from the same circle, and they all knew each other. They included expert skaters showing off their skill, beginners pushing chairs along with timid, awkward movements, boys, and elderly people who were skating for health reasons; to Levin they all seemed like the lucky chosen few, because they were there, close to her. The skaters all seemed to be blithely overtaking her, going up to her, and even talking to her and enjoying themselves completely independently of her, making the most of the excellent ice and the fine weather.

Nikolay Shcherbatsky, Kitty's cousin, dressed in a short jacket and narrow trousers, was sitting on a bench with his skates on, and when he caught sight of Levin, he called out to him:

'Hey, it's Russia's number-one skater! Have you been here long? The ice is excellent, put your skates on.'

'I don't have skates,' replied Levin, surprised by this boldness and overfamiliarity in her presence, and not letting her out of his sight for a minute, even though he was not looking at her. He felt the sun coming near him. She was at a corner, and, with her slender little feet in their high boots placed at an obtuse angle, was skating towards him with evident timidity. A boy in Russian dress overtook her, bending down low and recklessly flinging his arms about. She was not skating very steadily; having removed her hands from the little muff hanging on a cord, she was holding them out in readiness, and as she looked at Levin, whom she had recognized, she smiled at him and at her fear. When she had completed the turn, she pushed off with a supple foot and skated straight over to Shcherbatsky, and catching hold of him with her hand, she nodded to Levin with a smile. She was even lovelier than in his imagination.

When he thought about her, he could vividly imagine all of her, in particular the charm of that small blonde head with its expression of childlike candour and goodness, so lightly poised on those graceful, girlish shoulders. The childlike expression of her face combined with the beauty of her slender figure constituted her particular charm, which he remembered well; but what was always so astonishing and unexpected about her was the expression of her gentle, calm, and truthful eyes, and in particular her smile, which always transported Levin into a magical world where he felt tender-hearted and soothed, as he could remember being on rare days in his early childhood.

'Have you been here long?' she asked, holding out her hand to him. 'Oh, thank you,' she added when he picked up the handkerchief which had fallen out of her muff.

'Here? No, not long, I arrived yesterday . . . I mean today,' replied Levin, his nerves preventing him from immediately understanding her question. 'I was going to call on you,' he said, and then immediately became embarrassed and went red when he remembered why he was seeking her out. 'I did not know that you skated, and so well too.'

She studied him carefully, as if wanting to understand the cause of his embarrassment.

'From you that is praise indeed. Legend has it that you are a first-class skater,' she said as she brushed off with her small black-gloved hand the needles of hoarfrost which had fallen on to her muff.

'Yes, I was passionate about skating at one time; I wanted to do it perfectly.'

'You seem to do everything passionately,' she said with a smile. 'I would so like to see you skate. Do put on some skates and let's skate together.'

'Skate together! Could that really be possible?' thought Levin, looking at her.

'I'll put some on right away,' he said.

And he went off to put on some skates.

'We haven't seen you here in a long while, sir,' said the attendant, holding his foot as he tightened the screw on his heel. 'None of the other gentlemen can hold a candle to you. Will it be all right like that?' he said, tightening the strap.

'It's fine, it's fine, please hurry up,' replied Levin, struggling to repress the smile of happiness spontaneously appearing on his face. 'Yes,' he thought, 'this is life, this is happiness! *Together*, she said, *let's skate together*. Should I tell her now? But after all, it's precisely because I'm afraid to say anything that I am happy now, happy at least in having hope . . . But then? . . . No, I must, I must! No more weakness!'

Levin got to his feet, took off his coat, and after taking a run-up on the rough ice by the hut, sprinted on to the smooth ice and glided off without effort, as if he could increase his speed, slow down, and change direction through willpower alone. He approached her diffidently, but once again her smile reassured him.

She gave him her hand and they set off together, picking up speed, and the faster they went, the tighter she clasped his hand.

'I'm sure I would learn faster with you, I feel more confident with you somehow,' she said to him.

'And I have confidence in myself when you lean on me,' he said, but immediately took fright at what he said and blushed. In fact, as soon as he uttered those words, her face lost all its warmth, like the sun going behind a cloud, and Levin recognized the familiar movement of her face which indicated concentrated thought; a tiny wrinkle puckered her smooth forehead.

'Is anything the matter? Not that I have any right to ask,' he said quickly.

'What do you mean? . . . No, there is nothing the matter,' she replied coldly, and added immediately: 'Have you seen Mademoiselle Linon?'

'Not yet.'

'Do go over to her, she's so fond of you.'

'What is this? I've upset her. Oh Lord, help me!' thought Levin as he skated over to the old Frenchwoman with grey ringlets sitting on a bench. Smiling and showing her false teeth, she greeted him like an old friend.

'We're growing up, as you can see,' she said, indicating Kitty with her eyes, 'and growing older. *Tiny bear*[1] has already become big!' the Frenchwoman went on, chuckling, and she reminded him of his joke about the three young ladies, whom he had called the three bears after the English fairy-tale. 'Do you remember how you used to say that?'

He had absolutely no recollection of it, but she had been laughing at the joke for ten years now, and was very fond of it.

'Well, you go off and skate now, off you go. Our Kitty has begun to skate rather well, don't you think?'

When Levin went over to Kitty again, her face was no longer stern, and her eyes looked as truthful and warm-hearted as ever, but it seemed to Levin that there was a particular, deliberately calm tone to her warm-heartedness. And he felt sad. After talking about her old governess and her eccentricities, she asked him about his life.

'Isn't it boring for you being in the country during the winter?' she said.

'Oh no, it's not boring, I'm very busy,' he replied, feeling that she was subjecting him to her calm tone, from which he would be incapable of freeing himself, just as it had been at the beginning of winter.

'Have you come for long?' Kitty asked him.

'I don't know,' he replied, not thinking about what he was saying. The thought occurred to him that if he yielded to her tone of calm friendship, then he would leave again without having resolved anything, so he decided to put up some resistance.

'Why don't you know?'

'I don't know. It depends on you,' he said, immediately horrified at his words.

Whether she heard what he said, or just did not want to hear, she seemed to stumble after striking her foot twice, and hurriedly skated away from him. She skated up to Mademoiselle Linon, said something to her, then headed off towards the hut where ladies took off their skates.

'Heavens, what have I done! Dear God, help me, teach me,' said Levin, praying, and at the same time feeling a need for strong physical exertion as he picked up speed and started carving large and small circles.

[1] [English in the original.]

Just then, one of the young men, the best of the new skaters, happened to come out of the café on his skates with a cigarette in his mouth, and after building up speed, he hurled himself down the steps on his skates with a bounce and a clatter. He flew down and glided across the ice without even bothering to alter the casual position of his arms.

'Ah, that's a new trick!' said Levin, and he immediately ran up to try this new trick out for himself.

'Don't kill yourself, it needs practice!' Nikolay Shcherbatsky shouted out to him.

Levin went to the top of the steps, gathered as much speed as he could and hurtled downwards, keeping balance with his arms as he executed this strange movement. He tripped on the last step, but he managed to right himself with a forceful movement after his hand just grazed the ice, and skated off with a laugh.

'He's nice, he really is,' thought Kitty at that moment as she came out of the hut with Mademoiselle Linon and looked at him with a smile of quiet affection, as if he were a favourite brother. 'And it's not my fault, surely; I haven't done anything bad, have I? They say it's flirting. I know that it's not him I love; but I still enjoy being with him, and he's so nice. But why did he have to say that? . . .' she wondered.

When he saw Kitty leaving with her mother, who had met her on the steps, Levin stopped and thought for a moment, his face red after all the exertion. He took off his skates and caught up with mother and daughter as they were leaving the garden.

'I'm very glad to see you,' said the Princess. 'We're at home on Thursdays, as always.'

'Today, then?'

'We will be very glad to see you,' said the Princess stiffly.

Kitty was upset by this stiffness, and she could not repress her desire to smooth over her mother's coldness. She turned her head and said with a smile:

'Goodbye.'

It was just then that Stepan Arkadyich entered the Gardens like a conquering hero, his hat set at an angle and his face and eyes shining. But when he went up to his mother-in-law, he answered her questions about Dolly's health with a sad and guilty expression. After exchanging a few quiet and despondent words with his mother-in-law, he drew himself up and took Levin's arm.

'Well, shall we go?' he asked. 'I've been thinking about you all the time, and I'm very, very glad you have come,' he said, looking straight at him with a significant expression.

'Yes, let's go,' said the happy Levin, who was still hearing the sound of the voice which had said: 'Goodbye,' and seeing the smile with which it was uttered.

'To the Angleterre or the Hermitage?'*

'I don't mind.'

'Well, let's go to the Angleterre then,' said Stepan Arkadyich, choosing the Angleterre because he owed more there than he did at the Hermitage. He therefore felt it would be bad form to avoid that hotel. 'Do you have a cab? Well, that's grand, as I let my carriage go.'

The friends were silent all the way there. Levin was thinking about what the change in expression on Kitty's face meant, one minute assuring himself that there was hope, and the next succumbing to despair and seeing clearly that it was madness to hope, but meanwhile he felt like a completely different person, and utterly unlike how he had been before her smile and that *Goodbye*.

Stepan Arkadyich was composing the menu during the journey.

'You do like turbot, don't you?' he said to Levin as they pulled up.

'What?' asked Levin. 'Turbot? Oh yes, I'm *awfully* fond of turbot.'

10

WHEN Levin entered the hotel with Oblonsky, he could not help noticing a certain particular expression of a kind of suppressed elation on Stepan Arkadyich's face and about his whole person. Oblonsky took off his coat, and with his hat set at a jaunty angle he proceeded into the dining room, giving out orders to the obsequious Tatars* carrying napkins who were dressed in tails. Bowing right and left to acquaintances who were as happy to see him there as everywhere else, he went up to the bar, had a bit of fish to accompany his vodka, and said something to the painted Frenchwoman in ribbons, lace, and ringlets sitting at the counter which had even this Frenchwoman bursting out in genuine laughter. Levin refused a vodka only because he was offended by the sight of this Frenchwoman, who seemed to consist entirely of false hair, *poudre de riz*, and *vinaigre de toilette*.[1] He swiftly moved away from her, as if from some dirty place. His soul was overflowing with memories of Kitty, and a smile of triumph and happiness shone in his eyes.

'This way please, Your Eminence, you won't be disturbed here,

---

[1] Rice powder, aromatic vinegar.

Your Eminence,' said a particularly obsequious and chalky old Tatar, whose coat-tails parted over his wide haunches. 'Your hat please, Your Eminence,' he said to Levin, attending to Stepan Arkadyich's guest as a token of respect to him.

After instantly spreading a fresh tablecloth over the tablecloth already covering a round table under a bronze wall-lamp, he pulled out the velvet-covered chairs and stopped in front of Stepan Arkadyich with a napkin and the menu in his hands, awaiting instructions.

'If you would like a private room, Your Eminence, one will become available shortly: it's Prince Golitsyn with a lady. We have some fresh oysters in.'

'Ah! Oysters.'

Stepan Arkadyich stopped to think.

'Should we change our plan, Levin?' he said, placing a finger on the menu. His face expressed serious confusion. 'Are they good oysters? Tell the truth!'

'They're Flensburg oysters, Your Eminence, there weren't any from Ostend.'

'That's all very well, but are they fresh?'

'Came in yesterday, sir.'

'So in that case, how about beginning with oysters, and then changing our plan completely? Eh?'

'I don't mind. I like cabbage soup and buckwheat kasha best; but they don't have that here, obviously.'

'You would like to order kasha *à la russe*?'* said the Tatar, bending over Levin like a nanny administering to a child.

'No, seriously, I'll be happy with whatever you order. I've been skating, and I'm hungry. And don't think', he added, noticing the disgruntled expression on Oblonsky's face, 'that I won't appreciate your choice. I will enjoy having a good meal.'

'I'll say! Whatever you say, it is one of life's pleasures,' said Stepan Arkadyich. 'So, my good fellow, we'll have two-dozen oysters, or maybe that's not enough—let's say three-dozen, some vegetable soup . . .'

'*Printanière*,' prompted the Tatar. But Stepan Arkadyich clearly did not want to give him the pleasure of naming the dishes in French.

'Vegetable soup, you know? Then turbot with a thick sauce, then . . . roast beef; but make sure it is good. And capons, I think, and some fruit salad too.'

Remembering Stepan Arkadyich's practice of not naming dishes according to the French menu, the Tatar did not repeat what he said, but gave himself the pleasure of repeating the whole order from the menu: '*Soupe printanière, turbot sauce Beaumarchais, poularde à l'estragon, macédoine de fruits . . .*'—and then, as if on springs, he managed in the blink of an eye to put down one bound menu, pick up another, the wine menu, and present it to Stepan Arkadyich.

'And what shall we have to drink?'

'I'll have whatever you want, but not too much, maybe some champagne,' said Levin.

'What do you mean? To begin with? Actually, maybe you're right. Do you like the one with the white seal?'

'*Cachet blanc*,' prompted the Tatar.

'Well, give us some of that with the oysters, and then we will see.'

'Certainly, sir. What table wine would you like?'

'Let's have some *Nuits*. No, a classic *Chablis* would be even better.'

'Certainly, sir. Would you like *your* cheese?'*

'Oh yes, Parmesan. Or is there another that you like?'

'No, I don't mind what we have,' said Levin, unable to repress a smile.

And the Tatar hurried off with his coat-tails billowing out over his wide haunches, only to sprint back five minutes later with a plate of shucked oysters in their pearly shells, and a bottle between his fingers.

Stepan Arkadyich crumpled up his starched napkin, tucked it into his waistcoat, rested his arms comfortably, and made a start on the oysters.

'They're not bad,' he said, prising the slippery oysters from their pearly shells with a small silver fork, and swallowing one after another. 'Not bad,' he repeated, looking up with moist and shining eyes, first at Levin and then the Tatar. Levin ate the oysters too, although the white bread and cheese was more to his liking. But he was in awe of Oblonsky. Even the Tatar, after uncorking the bottle and pouring the sparkling wine into shallow, slender glasses, was looking at Stepan Arkadyich with a distinct smile of pleasure as he straightened his white tie.

'You don't like oysters that much?' said Stepan Arkadyich, downing his glass; 'Or is there something on your mind? Eh?'

He wanted Levin to be in good spirits. But it was not that Levin was not in good spirits, he felt uncomfortable. With everything that was going on in his soul, it was ghastly and awkward for him to be in a restaurant sandwiched between private rooms where ladies were being wined and dined, in the midst of this hustle and bustle; this whole environment of bronzes, mirrors, gas, and Tatars was offensive to him. He was afraid of contaminating what was overflowing in his heart.

'On my mind? Yes, there is something, but all this also makes me feel uncomfortable,' he said. 'You cannot imagine how peculiar this all is to a country-dweller like me; like the fingernails on that gentleman I saw in your office . . .'

'Yes, I saw how riveted you were by poor old Grinevich's nails,' said Stepan Arkadyich laughing.

'I can't help it,' said Levin. 'Try and put yourself in my shoes, and see things from the point of view of someone who lives in the country. In the country we try to bring our hands into a condition so that we can work with them easily; so we cut our nails and sometimes roll up our sleeves. But here people deliberately grow their nails as long as possible and put on cuff-links as big as saucers, so you definitely can't do anything with your hands.'

Stepan Arkadyich smiled merrily.

'Yes, it's a sign that he does not need to do rough labour. His mind does the work . . .'

'Maybe. But I still find it peculiar, just as I find it peculiar now that whereas we country-people try and finish our meal quickly so we can get on with our work, you and I are trying to spin it out as long as possible, and that's why we are eating oysters . . .'

'Well, of course,' broke in Stepan Arkadyich. 'But that is the aim of education: to turn everything into a pleasure.'

'Well, if that is the aim, I would rather be peculiar.'

'You are peculiar already. You Levins are all peculiar.'* Levin sighed. He remembered his brother Nikolay and began to feel ashamed and troubled, and he frowned; but Oblonsky started discussing a topic which immediately distracted him.

'So, are you going over this evening to visit the family, the Shcherbatskys, I mean?' he asked, pushing away the empty rough shells and drawing the cheese towards him with a significant twinkle in his eyes.

'Yes, I will definitely be going,' answered Levin. 'Although it didn't seem to me that the Princess was particularly keen to invite me.'

'Oh no! What nonsense! That's her manner . . . Now come on, my good fellow, let's have the soup! That's her manner, she is a *grande dame*,' said Stepan Arkadyich. 'I'm also coming, but I have choir practice at Countess Banina's. But how can you not be seen as peculiar? What else was the reason for your sudden disappearance from Moscow? The Shcherbatskys kept asking me about you as if I ought to know. But I only know one thing: you always do what no one else does.'

'Yes,' said Levin slowly and nervously. 'You are right, I am peculiar. But it was not my departure which was peculiar, but the fact that I have come now. I have come now . . .'

'You are a lucky man!' Stepan Arkadyich broke in, looking Levin in the eye.

'Why?'

'Spirited steeds I recognize by their something-or-other brands, and love-sick youths by their eyes,'* declaimed Stepan Arkadyich. 'You have got everything ahead of you.'

'Surely you don't have everything behind you?'

'No, not exactly behind me, but you have a future, while I have a present, and it's a bit of a mixed bag, to be honest.'

'What do you mean?'

'Not good. Well, actually I don't want to talk about myself, and it would be impossible to explain everything anyway,' said Stepan Arkadyich. 'So why have you really come to Moscow? . . . Hey, take this away!' he shouted to the Tatar.

'Can you guess?' answered Levin without taking his intensely shining eyes off Stepan Arkadyich.

'I can guess, but I can't be the one to broach the subject. Which should already be enough for you to see whether I have guessed correctly or not,' said Stepan Arkadyich, looking at Levin with a subtle smile.

'Well, what can you tell me?' said Levin in a trembling voice, feeling all the muscles on his face also tremble. 'What do you think about it?'

Stepan Arkadyich drank his glass of Chablis slowly, not taking his eyes off Levin.

'What do I think?' said Stepan Arkadyich. 'There is nothing I would like more than this, nothing. It would be the best thing that could possibly happen.'

'You're sure you are not mistaken? You do know what we are talking about?' said Levin, his eyes glued to his friend. 'Do you think it's possible?'

'I do think it's possible. Why shouldn't it be?'

'No, do you really think it's possible? Come on, tell me everything you think! And what, what if I am refused? . . . I am even sure . . .'

'Why should you think that?' said Stepan Arkadyich, smiling at his agitation.

'That is how it sometimes seems to me. After all, it would be awful for her and for me.'

'Well, there is nothing awful about it for a girl at any rate. Any girl would be proud to receive a proposal.'

'Yes, any girl, but not her.'

Stepan Arkadyich smiled. He knew this feeling of Levin's so well; he knew that for him all the girls in the world were divided into two sorts: one sort was all the girls in the world except for her, and they had every conceivable human frailty, and were very ordinary girls, while the other sort consisted of her alone, devoid of all weaknesses and superior to all humanity.

'Wait, have some sauce,' he said, stopping Levin's hand as he tried to push away the sauce.

Levin meekly poured himself some sauce, but would not let Stepan Arkadyich eat.

'No, you must wait—wait,' he said. 'You have to understand that this is a matter of life and death for me. I have never talked to anyone about this. And there is no one I can talk to about this except you. We are poles apart in everything, you and I—different tastes, different views, everything; but I know that you care for me and understand me, and you mean the world to me for that. But for God's sake, please be completely frank with me.'

'I am telling you what I think,' said Stepan Arkadyich, smiling. 'But I will tell you something else: my wife is an extraordinary woman, you know . . .' Stepan Arkadyich sighed as he remembered his relations with his wife, and after a moment's pause he continued: 'she has the gift of prophecy. She can see right through people, but not just that— she knows what is going to happen, especially where marriages are concerned. She predicted that Shakhovskaya would marry Brenteln, for example. No one was prepared to believe it, but that is what happened. And she is on your side.'

'What do you mean?'

'I mean that not only is she very fond of you, but she says that Kitty will definitely be your wife.'

On hearing those words Levin's face suddenly lit up with a smile, the sort of smile when one is nearly moved to tears.

'She actually says that!' exclaimed Levin. 'I always said she was wonderful, your wife. Well, anyway, enough of that, let's not talk about it any more,' he said, getting up from the table.

'All right, but do sit down, the soup has arrived.'

But Levin could not sit down. He walked round the cage-like room twice with his firm step, blinking so that his tears should not be seen, and only then did he sit down again at the table.

'You must understand,' he said, 'this is not love. I've been in love, but this is different. This is not my feeling, but some kind of external force which has taken possession of me. I had to leave, you see, because I decided that it could never be, like the sort of happiness that doesn't exist on earth; but I battled with myself, and can see that there is no life without it. And I have to resolve . . .'

'Then why did you go away?'

'Ah, wait! Ah, so many thoughts! So much I have to ask! Listen. After all, you can't imagine what you have done for me by saying what you did. I am so happy that I have even become despicable; I have forgotten everything . . . I learned today that my brother Nikolay . . . he's here, you know . . . and I just forgot all about him. I feel he is happy too. It's a sort of madness. But there is one awful thing . . . You got married, so you will know this feeling . . . What is awful is when we—older men, who already have a past history . . . of sinning, not of love . . . suddenly become close to a pure, innocent creature; it's loathsome, and for that reason one can't help but feel unworthy.'

'Well, you don't have many sins.'

'Oh, all the same,' said Levin, 'all the same, "as I with loathing behold my life, I tremble and curse, and bitterly lament . . ."* Yes.'

'Nothing to be done about it, that is how the world is,' said Stepan Arkadyich.

'The only consolation, like in that prayer I have always loved, is to be forgiven not according to my deserts, but according to God's mercy.* That is the only way she can forgive . . .'

11

LEVIN drained his glass and they fell silent.

'There is just one other thing I must tell you. Do you know Vronsky?' Stepan Arkadyich asked Levin.

'No, I don't. Why do you ask?'

'Bring us another,' said Stepan Arkadyich to the Tatar who was filling the glasses, and hovering around them just when he did not need to be.

'Why do I need to know Vronsky?'

'You need to know Vronsky because he is one of your competitors.'

'Who is this Vronsky?' asked Levin, and his face suddenly switched its expression from the child-like rapture which Oblonsky had just been admiring to one which was ill-humoured and disagreeable.

'Vronsky is one of Kirill Ivanovich Vronsky's sons, and one of the best examples of Petersburg's gilded youth. I got to know him in Tver,* when I had a post there, and he came to be enlisted. Terribly rich, handsome, excellent connections, aide-de-camp, and at the same time a very pleasant, decent fellow. But he's more than just a decent fellow. As I have discovered here, he is also educated and very clever; he is a person who will go far.'

Levin glowered and remained silent.

'Anyway, he turned up here soon after you left, and as I understand it, is head over heels in love with Kitty, and her mother, you understand . . .'

'Excuse me, but I don't understand anything,' said Levin, scowling gloomily. And he immediately remembered his brother Nikolay, and how loathsome he was to have forgotten about him.

'Just wait, wait,' said Stepan Arkadyich, smiling and touching his arm. 'I've told you what I know, and I repeat that the odds seem to be in your favour in this subtle and delicate affair, as far as one can judge.'

Levin leaned back in his chair; his face was pale.

'But I would advise you to settle the matter as quickly as you can,' continued Oblonsky, filling up his glass.

'No, thank you, I can't drink any more,' said Levin, pushing away the glass. 'I'll be drunk . . . Well, how are things with you?' he continued, clearly wanting to change the subject.

'One word more: I do advise you to settle the matter soon in any case. I don't advise you to say anything today,' said Stepan Arkadyich. 'Go over tomorrow morning, propose in the time-honoured way, and may God bless you . . .'

'You know you've always wanted to come to my place for some shooting? You should come in spring, when the woodcock are roding,'* said Levin.

He now regretted with all his heart starting that conversation with Stepan Arkadyich. His *special* feeling had been tarnished by the conversation about some Petersburg officer being a rival, and by Stepan Arkadyich's speculations and pieces of advice.

Stepan Arkadyich smiled. He understood what was going on in Levin's heart.

'I will come some time,' he said. 'Yes, my friend, women are the pivot on which everything turns. I'm in a bad way too, very bad. And all because of women. Be frank with me,' he continued, picking up a cigar and holding his glass with the same hand. 'Give me some advice.'

'But about what?'

'Well, it's like this. Let us suppose you are married, and you love your wife, but you are attracted to another woman . . .'

'I'm sorry, but I really do not understand this, it's as if . . . like I would not understand it if I now went past a bakery after having had a good meal and stole a roll.'

Stepan Arkadyich's eyes twinkled more than usual.

'But why not? Sometimes rolls smell so good you can't resist.

> *Himmlisch ist's, wenn ich bezwungen*
> *Meine irdische Begier;*
> *Aber noch wenn's nicht gelungen,*
> *Hatt' ich auch recht hübsch Plaisir.'*[1]

As he said this, Stepan Arkadyich smiled artfully. Levin also could not stop himself from smiling.

'Yes, but joking aside,' continued Oblonsky. 'You have to understand that the woman is a sweet, gentle, affectionate creature who is poor and lonely, and has sacrificed everything. Now that the deed is done, you understand, I can hardly abandon her, can I? I'm presuming we will have to separate so as not to destroy family life, but how can I not feel sorry for her, make arrangements for her, and soften the blow?'

'Well, you must forgive me. For me, as you know, all women are divided into two sorts . . . no, what I mean is . . . to put it better: there are women and there are . . . I have never ever seen any lovely fallen creatures,* nor will I, and the ones like that painted Frenchwoman at the desk with the ringlets are vermin, and all fallen women are the same.'

'But what about the one in the Gospels?'

'Oh, stop it! Christ would have never said those words if he had known how they would be misused.* Out of the entire Gospels, those are the only words people remember. Anyway, I am not saying what I think, but what I feel. I have an aversion to fallen women. You are afraid of spiders but I'm afraid of these vile creatures. You probably haven't studied spiders, after all, and don't know their manners and customs: it's the same for me.'

'It's all very well for you to say that; you're just like that gentleman in Dickens who throws all troublesome questions over his right shoulder with his left hand.* But denying a fact is not an answer. Just what am I to do, please tell me, what am I to do? Your wife is getting old, but you are full of life. You've barely had time to turn around and you are already feeling that you can't love your wife with love, however much you respect her. And then suddenly love comes along, and you're lost—lost!' said Stepan Arkadyich in grim despair.

---

[1] 'It is heavenly when I have mastered my earthly desires; but even when I have not succeeded, I have also had right good pleasure!'

Levin chuckled.

'Yes, I'm lost,' continued Oblonsky. 'But what am I to do?'

'Don't steal rolls.'

Stepan Arkadyich burst out laughing.

'You're such a moralist! But you have to understand, we have two women here: one insists only on her rights, and these rights are your love, which you cannot give her; while the other sacrifices everything for you, and asks for nothing. What are you to do? How should you behave? It's a terrible drama.'

'If you want my frank opinion about this, then I have to tell you that I do not believe there is any drama going on. And here is why. As far as I see it, love . . . both kinds of love, which you remember Plato defines in his *Symposium**—both loves serve as a touchstone for people. Some people understand only the first kind, and others only the second. And those who only understand non-Platonic love should not be talking about drama. There cannot be any drama with this kind of love. "Thanking you humbly for the pleasure, my compliments," and that is all the drama. And there cannot be any drama in Platonic love, because in that kind of love everything is clear and pure, because . . .'

At that moment Levin remembered his own misdemeanours, and the inner struggle he had gone through. And he added unexpectedly:

'However, maybe you are right. Maybe indeed . . . But I don't know, I really don't.'

'The thing is,' said Stepan Arkadyich, 'you are a very integrated person. It's both your strength and your weakness. You yourself are integrated, and you want all of life to consist of integrated phenomena, but that cannot happen. You despise the activities of civil servants, for example, because you want the work to correspond to the goal, and that cannot happen. You also want the activities of each individual to always have a goal, and for love and family life always to be one. But that cannot happen either. All the variety, all the wonder and beauty of life is made up of light and shade.'

Levin sighed and did not reply. He was thinking his own thoughts and was not listening to Oblonsky.

And suddenly they both felt that although they were friends, and had dined together and drunk wine, which ought to have brought them even closer, each was thinking his own thoughts and had no common ground with the other. Oblonsky had experienced this acute alienation happening after a dinner instead of intimacy several times before, and knew what to do in these circumstances.

'The bill!' he shouted, and went into the next room, where he immediately ran into an aide-de-camp he knew and started having a conversation with him about an actress and the man who kept her. Talking to the aide-de-camp, Oblonsky immediately experienced a feeling of relief and respite after speaking to Levin, who always caused him too much mental and emotional strain.

When the Tatar appeared with the bill for twenty-six roubles and a number of kopecks, plus tip, Levin, who as a country-dweller would have been appalled at any other time to have to pay fourteen roubles as his share, now took no notice of it, paid up, and set off home, so that he could change before going to the Shcherbatskys, where his fate would be decided.

12

PRINCESS KITTY SHCHERBATSKY was eighteen years old. She had come out for her first season that winter.* Her success in society was greater than that of both her elder sisters, and even greater than her mother had expected. Not only were almost all the young men who danced at the Moscow balls in love with Kitty, but two serious suitors had already presented themselves in her first season: Levin and, immediately after his departure, Count Vronsky.

Levin's appearance at the beginning of winter, his frequent visits, and his obvious love for Kitty had prompted the first serious conversations between Kitty's parents about her future, and also arguments between the Prince and Princess. The Prince was on Levin's side, and said that he could wish for nothing better for Kitty. The Princess, however, with that habit women have of sidestepping the issue, said that Kitty was too young, that Levin had done nothing to show he had serious intentions, that Kitty was not attached to him, and there were other arguments; but she did not cite the most important one, which was that she was expecting a better match for her daughter, that she did not like Levin, and did not understand him. When Levin had suddenly left, the Princess was glad, and told her husband triumphantly: 'You see, I was right.' And then when Vronsky appeared, she was gladder still, since it confirmed her opinion that Kitty should make not just a good but a brilliant match.

For the mother there could be no comparison between Vronsky and Levin. The mother did not like Levin's unconventional and strident opinions, his awkwardness in society, which she supposed was based on pride, and what to her was a peculiar kind of life in the country, involving cattle and peasants; she also greatly disliked the fact that he was in love with her daughter and had paid visits for a month and a half, as if he were waiting for something or scouting things out, or as if he were afraid he would be bestowing too great an honour if he proposed, and did not understand that paying frequent visits to a house where there was a marriageable girl obliged him to make his intentions clear. And then he had suddenly left without any explanation. 'It's a good thing he is so unattractive, and that Kitty did not fall in love with him,' the mother thought.

Vronsky satisfied all the mother's desires. He was very rich, clever, high-born, on his way to making a brilliant career in the army and at court, and completely charming. One could not hope for better.

Vronsky was clearly courting Kitty at balls, he danced with her and called on her at home, so it was impossible to doubt the seriousness of his intentions. Despite that, however, the mother had been in a terrible state of anxiety and agitation all winter.

The Princess herself had married thirty years before, following her aunt's matchmaking. The fiancé, about whom everything was known in advance, had arrived, inspected his future bride, and been inspected in turn; the matchmaking aunt* had ascertained and communicated the impression produced by both parties; the impression had been favourable; then on the appointed day the expected proposal was made to her parents and accepted. Everything had been very easy and simple. At least that is how it had seemed to the Princess. But with her own daughters she had experienced how the apparently ordinary business of giving away a daughter in marriage was neither easy nor simple. How many fears had been experienced, how many changes of heart there had been, how much money had been spent, and how many disagreements there had been with her husband over the betrothals of her two eldest, Darya and Natalya! Now that her youngest had come out, she was experiencing the same fears, the same doubts, and even more arguments with her husband than there had been over the two eldest. Like all fathers, the old Prince was particularly sensitive where the honour and purity of his daughters was concerned; he was inordinately protective of his daughters and particularly Kitty, who was his favourite, and he harangued the Princess every step of the way for compromising their daughter. The Princess had grown accustomed to this with their first two daughters, but she now felt that the Prince had more justification for being so fastidious. She saw that the mores of society had changed a good deal in recent times, and that a mother's responsibilities had become even more difficult. She saw that girls of Kitty's age now formed various kinds of associations, enrolled in courses,* consorted freely with men, drove about the city alone; she saw that many did not curtsey, and above all, all were firmly convinced that choosing a husband was their business and not their parents'. 'Girls aren't married off nowadays like they used to be,' was what all these young girls and even all old people thought and said. But how girls were married off these days the Princess could not find out from anyone. The French custom for parents to decide the fate of their children was not accepted and was condemned. The English custom of giving girls complete freedom was also not accepted and was impossible in Russian society. The Russian custom of matchmaking was considered abominable in some way, and was laughed at by everyone, including the Princess herself. But how a girl should marry or be given in marriage no one knew. Everyone whom the Princess happened to talk to about this told her the same thing: 'Good gracious, it is high time we left that old stuff behind. It is the young people who are getting married, after all, not the parents, and we must leave young people to arrange things as they see fit.' But it was all very well for those who did not have daughters to say such things; and the Princess realized that if her daughter became close to someone, she might fall in love, and fall in love with someone who did not want to marry, or someone not suitable as a husband. And no matter how much it was impressed upon the Princess that these days young people should decide their own fates, she could no more believe this than she could believe that loaded pistols could ever be the best toys for five-year-old children. And for that reason the Princess worried more about Kitty than she had about her elder daughters.

Now she was afraid that Vronsky would limit himself to merely courting her daughter. She could see that her daughter was already in love with him, but she comforted herself with the idea that he was an honest man and would not do something like that. But she also knew how easy it was to turn a girl's head with the current freedom of address, and how men generally made light of this misdeed. The previous week Kitty had recounted to her mother her conversation with Vronsky during the mazurka. The Princess was partly reassured by this conversation, but still she could not be completely calm. Vronsky had told Kitty that he and his brother were so used to submitting to their mother in all things that they would never decide to undertake anything important without consulting her. 'And I'm now looking forward to my dear mother's arrival from Petersburg with particular happiness,' he had said.

Kitty had relayed this without attaching any significance to these words. But her mother understood them differently. She knew that the old lady was expected any day, and that the old woman would be happy about her son's choice, and she found it strange that he did not propose through fear of offending his mother; but she so longed for the marriage itself, and above all for her fears to be allayed, that she believed this. However painful it was now for the Princess to witness the unhappiness of her eldest daughter Dolly, who was intending to leave her husband, all her feelings were absorbed by the anxiety over her youngest daughter's fate, which was now being decided. Levin's appearance that afternoon had added a new worry. She was afraid lest her daughter, who she believed had at one point nurtured feelings for Levin, would refuse Vronsky out of excessive honesty, and generally that Levin's arrival would complicate and delay the matter which was so close to being concluded.

'So has he been here long?' the Princess asked about Levin when they returned home.

'He arrived today, *Maman*.'

'There is one thing I want to say . . .' the Princess began, and from her eager but concerned expression Kitty guessed what it would be about.

'Mama,' she said, blushing and turning quickly towards her, 'please don't say anything about it, please. I know, I know everything.'

She wanted the same thing as her mother, but was offended by her mother's motives for wanting it.

'I just want to say that after giving one person hope . . .'

'Mama, dearest, please don't say anything, for heaven's sake. It's so awful to talk about that.'

'All right, I won't,' said her mother, seeing tears in her daughter's eyes. 'But there is just one thing, my darling: you promised me you won't keep any secrets from me. You won't, will you?'

'No, Mama, none,' replied Kitty, blushing and looking directly at her mother. 'But I don't have anything to say now. I . . . I . . . if I wanted to, I don't know what I would say, and how . . . I don't know . . .'

'No, with those eyes she cannot tell a lie,' her mother thought, smiling at her excitement and happiness. The Princess was smiling at how immense and significant what was now going on in the poor girl's heart must seem to her.

13

AFTER dinner and before the evening commenced, Kitty experienced a feeling similar to what a young man experiences before going into battle. Her heart was beating fast, and she could not keep her mind focused on anything.

She felt that this evening, when the two of them would meet for the first time, was bound to be decisive in her fate. And she kept imagining them, first on their own and then both together. Whenever she thought about the past, she would dwell with pleasure and tenderness on the memories of her relationship with Levin. Memories of her childhood as well as memories of Levin's friendship with her late brother lent her relationship with him a particular poetic charm. His love for her, of which she was certain, was flattering and pleasing to her. And it was easy for her to remember Levin. By contrast, there was something awkward mixed in with her memories of Vronsky, although he was an extremely urbane and poised person; it was as if there was some kind of falsity—not in him, as he was very straightforward and nice—but in herself, whereas she felt completely natural and at ease with Levin. But then as soon as she thought about her future with Vronsky, a vision of dazzling happiness arose before her; with Levin, however, the future seemed unclear.

As she went upstairs to dress for the evening and glanced in the mirror, she noted with delight that she was having one of her good days and was in full possession of all her powers, and this was so vital to her for what lay ahead; she sensed in herself an outer serenity and a supple gracefulness in her movements.

At half-past seven, just after she had come down into the drawing room, the footman announced: 'Konstantin Dmitrich Levin.' The Princess was still in her room, and the Prince had not emerged. 'So be it,' thought Kitty, and all the blood rushed to her heart. She was horrified to see how pale she was when she glanced at the mirror.

Now she knew for certain that he had made a point of coming early in order to find her alone and propose to her. And only now for the first time did the whole matter appear to her from a new and different angle. Only now did she understand that the issue—with whom she would be happy and whom she loved—did not concern her alone, but that any minute now she would have to hurt someone she cared for. And hurt him dreadfully . . . And why? Because he, this nice man, loved her, was in love with her. But there was nothing to be done, this is the way it had and ought to be.

'Goodness, do I really have to tell him this myself?' she thought. 'Well, what am I going to say to him? Will I really tell him that I do not love him? That would not be true. What will I say to him then? Tell him that I love someone else? No, it's impossible. I'm going to go, I'm going to go.'

She was already approaching the door when she heard his steps. 'No! It would be dishonest. What have I got to fear? I have not done anything bad. What will be, will be! I shall tell the truth. It's impossible to feel awkward with him anyway. Here he is,' she said to herself, seeing the whole of his strong and hesitant figure, with shining eyes trained on her. She looked straight into his eyes, as if begging him for mercy, and held out her hand.

'It seems I have not come at the right time, I'm too early,' he said, scanning the empty drawing room. When he saw that his expectations had been fulfilled, and that nothing prevented him from speaking out, his face darkened.

'Oh no,' said Kitty, and she sat down at a table.

'But actually I wanted to find you alone,' he began, not sitting down or looking at her, for fear of losing his nerve.

'Mama will be down in a minute. She was very tired yesterday. Yesterday . . .'

She spoke not knowing herself what her lips were saying, and not taking her entreating, gentle eyes off him.

He glanced at her; she blushed and fell silent.

'I told you that I don't know how long I will be here . . . that it depends on you . . .'

She dropped her head lower and lower, not knowing herself how she would reply to what was coming.

'That it depends on you,' he repeated. 'What I meant . . . What I meant . . . That is why I came . . . is that . . . to be my wife!' he blurted out, not knowing himself what he was saying; but feeling that the most terrifying thing had been said, he stopped and looked at her.

She was breathing heavily, not looking at him. She felt exultant. Her soul was overflowing with happiness. She had in no way expected his declaration of love to make such a powerful impact on her. But that lasted for only a second. She remembered Vronsky. She raised her bright, truthful eyes to Levin, and, seeing his despairing face, hurriedly answered:

'That cannot be . . . forgive me . . .'

How close she had been to him a moment ago, and how important to his life! And how foreign and remote from him she had become now!

'It could not have been otherwise,' he said, without looking at her.

He bowed and prepared to leave.

14

BUT at that very moment the Princess made her appearance. Her face was a picture of horror when she found them alone and saw their distressed faces. Levin bowed to her and said nothing. Kitty remained silent, not lifting her eyes. 'Thank goodness, she's refused him,' thought her mother, and her face beamed with the usual smile with which she greeted guests on Thursdays. She sat down and began to question Levin about his life in the countryside. He sat down again, awaiting the arrival of other guests, so that he could slip away unnoticed.

Kitty's friend Countess Nordston, who had married the previous winter, came in five minutes later.

She was a brittle, sickly-looking, nervous woman with a sallow complexion and shining black eyes. She was very fond of Kitty, and her affection for her, in keeping with the affection of all married women for young girls, expressed itself in the wish to marry Kitty off according to her own ideal of happiness, so she wished to marry her off to Vronsky. Levin, whom she had often met at the Shcherbatskys' at the beginning of winter, had never appealed to her. Her perennial and favourite pastime when meeting consisted of poking fun at him.

'I do like it when he looks down at me from his magisterial height: either he breaks off his clever conversation with me because I am stupid, or he is condescending to me. I love that: *condescending* to me! I am delighted he cannot stand me,' she would say about him.

She was right, because Levin really could not stand her, and despised her for what she took pride in and identified as a virtue in herself—her high-strung nature, and her refined contempt and disregard for everything crude and mundane.

Countess Nordston and Levin had established the kind of relationship often encountered in society between two people who outwardly remain on friendly terms, but loathe each other to such an extent that they cannot even address each other seriously and cannot even be insulted by each other.

Countess Nordston immediately pounced on Levin.

'Ah! Konstantin Dmitrich! You have come to visit our depraved Babylon again,' she said, offering him her dainty yellow hand and remembering what he had said at some point earlier in the winter, that Moscow was a Babylon. 'So, has Babylon improved, or have you deteriorated?' she asked, looking at Kitty with an arch smile.

'I'm very flattered, Countess, that you should remember my words so well,' replied Levin, who had managed to recover, and from habit slipped straight away into his jocular but hostile mode of addressing Countess Nordston. 'They seem to have made a strong impression on you.'

'Absolutely! I write everything down. So tell me, Kitty, you have been skating again? . . .'

And she started talking to Kitty. However much of a blunder it would be for Levin to go now, it was nevertheless easier for him to commit that blunder than stay for the whole evening and see Kitty, who was throwing him the occasional glance and avoiding his gaze. He was about to get up, but the Princess, noticing his silence, turned to him.

'Have you come to Moscow for long? But you are involved in the zemstvo I believe, so you cannot stay for long.'

'No, Princess, I am no longer involved in the zemstvo,' he said. 'I have come for a few days.'

'There is something odd about him tonight,' thought Countess Nordston as she peered at his stern, serious face; 'he is not getting embroiled in one of his diatribes. But I will definitely draw him out. I adore making a fool of him in front of Kitty, and that's what I am going to do.'

'Konstantin Dmitrich,' she said to him, 'could you explain something to me, please, since you know all about this sort of thing—at our estate in Kaluga,* the peasants and their womenfolk have all spent everything they possess on drink, and now they are not paying us anything. What does this mean? You have always had a good word to say about the peasants.'

Another lady came into the room at that moment, and Levin got up.

'Forgive me, Countess, but I really don't know anything about this, and can't tell you anything,' he said, and then looked round at the officer who had followed the lady in.

'That must be Vronsky,' thought Levin, and he glanced at Kitty to make sure. She had already managed to steal a glance at Vronsky, and she looked round at Levin. And from that one glance of her involuntarily shining eyes, Levin realized that she loved this man, realized it as surely as if she had told him so in words. But what sort of a man was he?

Now—for better or for worse—Levin had no option but to stay; he needed to find out what sort of a person this man was whom she loved.

There are people who, when meeting their victorious rival in whatever sphere, are immediately ready to turn their back on all that is good about him and see only bad things; and then there are people who, on the contrary, take pains to find in this victorious rival the qualities with which he defeated them, and who, with an aching heart, look only for good things about him. Levin belonged to the latter category. But it was not difficult for him to see what was good and attractive about Vronsky. It was immediately apparent. Vronsky was a dark-haired, sturdily built man of medium height, with a good-natured, handsome face which was exceedingly calm and composed. Everything about his face and figure, from his close-cropped black hair and freshly shaven chin to his loose-fitting, brand-new uniform, was simple but also elegant. After making way for the lady who was coming in, Vronsky went up to the Princess, and then to Kitty.

As he approached her, his handsome eyes began to shine with a particular tenderness, and with a barely perceptible, happy smile of modest triumph (so it seemed to Levin), he respectfully and solicitously bent over her and held out to her his small but broad hand.

Once he had greeted everybody and said a few words, he sat down, without once glancing at Levin, who had not taken his eyes off him.

'Allow me to introduce you,' said the Princess, indicating Levin. 'Konstantin Dmitrich Levin. Count Alexey Kirillovich Vronsky.'

Vronsky stood up, looked Levin affably in the eye, and shook hands with him.

'I believe I was to have dined with you earlier this winter,' he said, smiling his simple and ingenuous smile; 'but you unexpectedly had to leave for the country.'

'Konstantin Dmitrich despises and hates the city and us townfolk,' said Countess Nordston.

'My words must have made a strong impression on you for you to have remembered them so well,' said Levin, and realizing he had already said that earlier, he blushed.

Vronsky looked at Levin and at Countess Nordston, and smiled.

'Are you always in the country?' he asked. 'I suppose it's dull in winter?'

'It's not dull if you have things to do, and being on your own isn't dull,' snapped Levin.

'I love the country,' said Vronsky, noticing and pretending not to notice Levin's tone.

'But I hope, Count, that you would not consent to live permanently in the country,' said Countess Nordston.

'I don't know, I've never tried it for long. I did once experience a strange feeling,' he continued. 'I have never missed the countryside, the Russian countryside with bast shoes* and peasants, so much as I did when I spent a winter in Nice with my mother. Nice is dull in itself you know. And Naples and Sorrento are only all right for a short time. And it is precisely there that one remembers Russia particularly vividly, and precisely the countryside . . . They are just like . . .'

He addressed both Kitty and Levin as he spoke, transferring his calm and friendly gaze from one to the other, and clearly saying whatever came into his head.

Noticing that the Countess Nordston wanted to say something, he broke off without finishing his sentence, and listened attentively to her.

Not for one moment did the conversation flag, so that the old Princess, who always kept two heavy weapons in reserve in case of lacking a topic—classical and modern education and universal military service*—had no occasion to deploy them, and Countess Nordston had no occasion to tease Levin.

Levin wanted and was unable to enter the general conversation; constantly telling himself 'I should leave now,' he kept not leaving, and waiting for something.

The conversation touched on table-turning and spirits,* and Countess Nordston, who believed in spiritualism, started recounting the wonders she had seen.

'Ah, Countess, do take me next time, please, I beg you! I have never ever seen anything unusual, although I have been looking everywhere,' said Vronsky with a smile.

'All right, next Saturday then,' replied Countess Nordston. 'But what about you, Konstantin Dmitrich, do you believe?'

'Why are you asking me? You know what I will say.'

'But I want to hear your opinion.'

'My opinion', replied Levin, 'is only that this table-turning proves that the so-called educated class is in no way superior to the peasants. They believe in the evil eye, curses, and magic spells, while we . . .'

'So you do not believe then?'

'I cannot believe, Countess.'

'But if I have seen it with my own eyes?'

'Peasant women say they have seen house-spirits* with their own eyes too.'

'So you think I am not telling the truth?'

And she started laughing mirthlessly.

'No, Masha, Konstantin Dmitrich is just saying that he cannot believe,' said Kitty, blushing on Levin's behalf, and Levin understood this and, becoming ever more irritated, was about to respond, but Vronsky, with his candid, open smile, immediately came to the rescue of the conversation, which was threatening to become unpleasant.

'You do not admit even the possibility?' he asked. 'After all, if we admit the existence of electricity, which we do not understand, why should there not be some new force, still unknown to us, which . . .'

'When electricity was discovered,' Levin interrupted quickly, 'it was just a phenomenon which had been uncovered, and it was not known where it came from and what it could produce, and centuries went by before people thought of harnessing it. The spiritualists, on the other hand, started with tables writing to them and spirits visiting them, and it was only then that they started to say it was an unknown force.'

Vronsky listened attentively to Levin, as he always listened, clearly interested in what he was saying.

'Yes, but the spiritualists say: we do not know what this force is right now, but it exists, and these are the conditions in which it operates. So let scientists work out what this force consists of. No, I do not see why this cannot be a new force, if it . . .'

'Because with electricity,' Levin interrupted again, 'every time you rub resin against wool it produces a known phenomenon, but it doesn't happen every time with this, so therefore it is not a natural phenomenon.'

No doubt feeling that the conversation was taking on too serious a tone for the drawing room, Vronsky did not object, but in an attempt to change the topic of conversation and, smiling jovially, he turned to the ladies.

'Let's try now, Countess,' he began, but Levin wanted to finish saying what he thought.

'I think', he continued, 'that this attempt on the part of the spiritualists to interpret their wonders as some kind of new force is most unfortunate. They talk explicitly about it being a spiritual force and want to submit it to material experiment.'

Everyone was waiting for him to finish, and he could feel that.

'Well, I think you would be an excellent medium,' said Countess Nordston. 'There is something ecstatic about you.'

Levin opened his mouth and was about to say something, but he blushed and said nothing.

'Please, Princess, do let us try the tables now,' said Vronsky to Kitty. 'Would you permit it, Princess?' he asked her mother.

And Vronsky stood up, looking round for a little table.

Kitty got up to find a table, and her eyes met Levin's as she walked past. She pitied him with all her heart, not least because she was pitying him for an unhappiness she herself had caused. 'If you can forgive me, then do,' her look said, 'I'm so happy.'

'I hate everyone, and you, and myself,' his look replied, and he reached for his hat. But he was destined not to leave. They were just about to arrange themselves around the little table, and Levin was at the point of going, when the old Prince came in, and after greeting the ladies, he turned to Levin.

'Ah!' he began delightedly. 'Have you been here long? I did not know you were here. I'm very glad to see you.'*

The old Prince vacillated between the informal and formal forms of address with Levin. He embraced Levin, and while he was talking to him did not notice Vronsky, who had got up and was patiently waiting for the Prince to speak to him.

Kitty felt that her father's friendliness was bound to be painful for Levin after what had happened. She also saw how coldly her father eventually responded to Vronsky's bow, and how Vronsky looked at her father with friendly bewilderment, trying and failing to understand how and why anyone could be unfavourably disposed towards him, and she blushed.

'Prince, let Konstantin Dmitrich come and join us,' said Countess Nordston. 'We want to conduct an experiment.'

'What experiment? Table-turning? Well, excuse me, ladies and gentlemen, but in my opinion playing hide the ring* is a lot more fun,' said the old Prince looking at Vronsky and guessing it was his idea. 'There is a point to playing hide the ring too.'

Vronsky turned his firm gaze on to the Prince in surprise, and with a slight smile immediately started talking to Countess Nordston about the big ball taking place the following week.

'I hope you will be there?' he said, addressing Kitty.

As soon as the old Prince turned away from him, Levin left without being noticed, and the last impression he took away from that evening was that of Kitty's smiling, happy face as she answered Vronsky's question about the ball.

15

When the evening was at an end, Kitty told her mother about her conversation with Levin, and despite all the pity she felt for Levin, she was thrilled by the thought that someone had *proposed* to her. She was in no doubt that she had acted correctly. But once in bed she found it difficult to fall asleep. One impression pursued her remorselessly. It was of Levin's face, with furrowed brows, and kind eyes looking grimly and forlornly out from under them as he stood listening to her father and looking at her and Vronsky. And she began to feel so sorry for him that her eyes welled up with tears. But then she immediately thought about whom she had exchanged him for. She vividly recalled that strong, manly face, that dignified composure, and the kindness he radiated and imparted to everyone; she remembered the love for her shown by the one she loved, and she felt joy in her heart again and lay back on her pillow with a smile of happiness. 'It's a pity, it's a pity, but what can be done? It's not my fault,' she kept telling herself; but an inner voice was telling her otherwise. Whether she felt remorse for having led Levin on, or for having refused him, she did not know. But her happiness was poisoned by doubts. 'Lord have mercy, Lord have mercy, Lord have mercy!' she repeated to herself until she fell asleep.

Downstairs, meanwhile, in the Prince's small study, the parents were having another of their frequently recurring quarrels over their favourite daughter.

'What? I'll tell you what!' shouted the Prince, waving his arms about then immediately wrapping his squirrel-lined dressing-gown around him. 'It's that you have no pride, no dignity, that you are compromising and ruining our daughter with this abominable, idiotic matchmaking!'

'Mercy, Prince, what in heaven's name have I done?' said the Princess, almost in tears.

Happy and contented after her conversation with her daughter, she had come to say goodnight to the Prince as usual, and although she had not intended to tell him about Levin's proposal and Kitty's rejection, she had hinted to her husband that she thought the matter with Vronsky quite settled, and that it would be concluded as soon as his mother arrived. And it was then, at these words, that the Prince had suddenly flared up and started shouting rude things.

'What have you done? I'll tell you what: firstly, you are out to trap a husband, so all of Moscow is going to talk, and with good reason. If you are going to hold soirées, then invite everybody, not just hand-picked little suitors. Invite all those *young pups* (as the Prince called young Muscovites), invite a pianist and let them dance, but not like tonight—little suitors and brokering. It's vile for me to watch, quite vile, and you have succeeded, as the poor girl's head has been turned. Levin is a thousand times the better man. And as for that little Petersburg fop, they turn them out on a machine, all from the same mould, and they are all worthless. Even if he was a prince of the blood, my daughter doesn't need anyone!'

'But what on earth have I done?'

'Oh, you've . . .' shouted the Prince furiously.

'I know full well that if I listened to you,' interrupted the Princess, 'we would never give our daughter away in marriage. And if that's the case, we should just go to the country.'

'It would be better if we did.'

'Now wait a moment. Do you think I am trying curry favour? I am not doing that at all. A fine young man has fallen in love, and she, it seems . . .'

'Yes, that is how it seems to you! But what if she really does fall in love, and he has as much thought of marrying as I do? . . . Ugh! I wish I could have turned away my eyes! . . . "Ah, spiritualism, ah, Nice, ah, at the ball . . ."' And the Prince curtseyed at each word, imagining he was portraying his wife. 'You'll see what misfortune we will bring to Katenka if she should really take it into her head . . .'

'But why do you think that?'

'I don't think that, I know; we are the ones with eyes for that, not you womenfolk. I see a man who has serious intentions, and that is Levin; and I see a popinjay, like this time-waster, who is just having fun.'

'Well, if you are really going to take it into your head . . .'

'And you'll remember, when it's too late, like with our Dashenka.'

'Well, all right, all right, let's not talk about it.' The Princess stopped him when she remembered poor, unfortunate Dolly.

'Fine, and goodnight!'

And after making the sign of the cross over each other and kissing, but sensing that each other's opinion had not changed, the couple parted.

The Princess had at first been firmly convinced that this evening had decided Kitty's fate and that there could be no doubts about Vronsky's intentions; but her husband's words troubled her. And after returning to her room, terrified by the uncertainty of what the future held, she repeated several times in her heart, just like Kitty: 'Lord have mercy, Lord have mercy, Lord have mercy!'

16

VRONSKY had never known family life. In her youth his mother had been a brilliant society woman who had a great many affairs during her marriage, and particularly after it, which all of society knew about. He barely remembered his father, and had been educated in the Corps of Pages.*

Leaving school as a very young and brilliant officer, he had straight away fallen into the lifestyle of rich military men in Petersburg. Although he occasionally went into Petersburg society, all his love interests lay outside society.

In Moscow, after his extravagant and coarse Petersburg life, he had for the first time experienced the delight of getting to know a sweet, innocent society girl who had fallen in love with him. It did not occur to him that there might be anything wrong with the way he behaved towards Kitty. At balls he danced mostly with her; he called on her family at home. He spouted the sort of nonsense to her which is usually spouted in society, but it was nonsense which he unintentionally endowed with a special meaning for her. Despite the fact that he had not said anything to her which could not have been said in front of everybody, he felt that she was becoming more and more dependent on him, and the more he felt this, the more pleasant it was for him and the more tender his feelings for her became. He did not know that his pattern of behaviour with regard to Kitty had a specific name, that it was the leading on of young girls without the intention of marrying them, and that this leading on was an example of the bad conduct commonly encountered amongst brilliant young men like himself. He thought he was the first person to have discovered this pleasure, and he was enjoying his discovery.

If he could have heard what her parents said that evening, if he could have seen things from her family's point of view and discovered that Kitty would be unhappy if he did not marry her, he would have been very surprised and would not have believed it. He could not believe that something which gave him, and above all her, such great and sincere pleasure could be bad. Still less could he have believed that he should get married.

Marriage had never seemed a possibility to him. He not only did not like family life, but in keeping with the general outlook of the bachelor world in which he lived, he saw something alien, hostile, and above all ridiculous in families, and particularly husbands. But although Vronsky had no inkling of what her parents were saying, as he left the Shcherbatskys that evening he felt the secret spiritual bond existing between him and Kitty had become so firmly established that some action was called for. But what that action could or ought to be he could not imagine.

'What is delightful,' he thought as he returned from the Shcherbatskys, bringing away from them, as always, an agreeable feeling of purity and freshness emanating partly from his not having smoked all evening, and also a new feeling of tenderness engendered by her love for him, 'what is delightful is that nothing has been said by me or by her, but we understood each other so well in that invisible conversation of looks and intonations that she told me tonight that she loves me more clearly than ever before. And how sweetly, simply, and above all, trustingly! I myself feel better, purer. I feel I have a heart, and that there is a lot of good in me. Those sweet, loving eyes! When she said: *and very much . . .*'

'So what then? So nothing. I'm having a good time, and so is she.' And he started pondering where to round off the evening.

He weighed up the places he could go to in his mind. 'The club? A game of bezique,* champagne with Ignatov? No, I'm not going there. The Château des Fleurs, where I'll find Oblonsky, songs, the can-can?* No, I'm bored with that. That is exactly why I love the Shcherbatskys, because I am improving myself. I'll go home.' He went straight to his room at Dusseaux's,* ordered supper, and after getting undressed had barely managed to place his head on the pillow before he had fallen, as always, into a deep and peaceful sleep.

17

THE next day, at eleven o'clock in the morning, Vronsky drove out to the Petersburg railway station to meet his mother, and the first person he ran into on the steps of the main staircase was Oblonsky, who was expecting his sister on the same train.

'Ah! Your Eminence!' shouted Oblonsky. 'Who are you meeting?'

'My Mama,' replied Vronsky, smiling like everyone else who met Oblonsky as he shook his hand and went up the steps with him. 'She is due to arrive from Petersburg today.'

'You know, I waited for you until two o'clock. Where did you go from the Shcherbatskys?'

'Home,' answered Vronsky. 'I have to confess, I felt so good after the Shcherbatskys yesterday that I did not feel like going anywhere.'

'Spirited steeds I recognize by their something-or-other brands, and love-sick youths by their eyes,' declaimed Stepan Arkadyich, just as he had to Levin before.

Vronsky smiled in a way which suggested he did not deny this, but he immediately changed the topic of conversation.

'And who are you meeting?' he asked.

'Me? A pretty woman,' said Oblonsky.

'I see!'

'*Honi soit qui mal y pense*![1] My sister Anna.'

'Karenina, you mean?' said Vronsky.

'You know her, I expect?'

'I think I do. Or maybe not . . . I really don't remember,' Vronsky replied absent-mindedly, the name Karenina dimly conjuring up something stuffy and dull in his mind.

'But you must surely know Alexey Alexandrovich, my famous brother-in-law. The whole world knows him.'

'Well, I know him by reputation and by sight. I know he is clever, learned, pious in some way . . . But you know, that's not in my . . . *not in my line*,'[2] said Vronsky.

'Yes, he is a very remarkable man; a bit conservative, but a very good man,' observed Stepan Arkadyich, 'a very good man.'

'Well, so much the better for him,' said Vronsky with a smile. 'Ah, you're here,' he said, turning to his mother's tall, elderly footman standing by the door. 'Come in here.'

Apart from Stepan Arkadyich's general appeal, to which everyone was susceptible, Vronsky had also felt attached to him lately because in his imagination he was connected to Kitty.

'So, shall we hold a dinner for the *diva* on Sunday?' he said to him, smiling as he took him by the arm.

'Absolutely. I will start collecting contributions. Oh, and did you meet my friend Levin last night?' asked Stepan Arkadyich.

'Of course. But he left early for some reason.'

'He's a good fellow,' continued Oblonsky. 'Don't you think?'

'What I don't understand,' answered Vronsky, 'is why all Muscovites, present company excepted, of course, have something brusque about them,' he added jokingly. 'They always seem to get so prickly and hot under the collar, as if there is something they keep wanting you to feel . . .'

'Yes, there is a degree of that, you're right . . .' said Stepan Arkadyich, laughing merrily.

'Will it be in soon?' Vronsky asked an attendant.

'Just left the last station,' answered the attendant.

The approach of the train was made increasingly apparent by the flurry of preparations at the station, porters bustling about, the appearance of policemen and attendants, and the arrival of people coming to meet it. Through the steam caused by the frost, workmen in sheepskin

---

[1] 'Shame on him who thinks evil of it!'   [2] [English in the original.]

jackets and soft felt boots could be seen crossing the rails of the curving tracks. The whistle of a locomotive and the shunting of something heavy could be heard down the line.

'No,' said Stepan Arkadyich, who was anxious to tell Vronsky about Levin's intentions towards Kitty. 'No, you have got the wrong idea about my Levin. It's true that he is a very tense person and can be disagreeable, but then at other times he can be very amiable. He's such an honest, trustworthy sort, and he's got a heart of gold. But yesterday there were particular reasons,' continued Stepan Arkadyich with a significant smile, completely forgetting the sincere sympathy he had felt the day before for his friend, and now feeling it again, but for Vronsky. 'Yes, there was a reason why he might have been either extremely happy or extremely unhappy.'

Vronsky stopped and asked directly:

'What do you mean? Or did he propose to your *belle-soeur*[1] yesterday? . . .'

'He may have done,' said Stepan Arkadyich. 'There was something like that in the air yesterday. But if he left early, and was also not in good spirits, then it must have been that . . . He has been in love for so long, and I feel very sorry for him.'

'I see! . . . I think she can count on a better match, though,' said Vronsky, and straightening up, he started walking again. 'However, I don't know him,' he added. 'Yes, it's a painful situation! That is why the majority prefer associating with the Claras of this world. Failure with them only demonstrates that you don't have enough money, but here it is your dignity which is on the line. Anyway, here's the train.'

Indeed, a locomotive was already whistling in the distance. A few minutes later the platform started to shake and, puffing steam that was being forced downwards by the icy cold, the locomotive rolled past, with the connecting rod of the central wheel drawing back and extending slowly and evenly, and the muffled, hoarfrost-covered driver bent over; and behind the tender, going slower and slower, and making the platform shake more and more, came the wagon with the luggage and a yelping dog, and then finally the passenger carriages, shuddering before they came to a halt.

The smart-looking guard blew a whistle as he jumped down, and following him, the impatient passengers started to get off one by one: a guards officer, holding himself erect and looking round sternly;

---

[1] 'sister-in-law'.

a twitchy merchant fellow with a bag, who was smiling brightly; a peasant with a sack over his shoulder.

Vronsky was studying the carriages and the people getting off while standing next to Oblonsky, and he completely forgot about his mother. What he had just learned about Kitty excited and gratified him. His chest involuntarily swelled and his eyes shone. He felt like a victor.

'Countess Vronskaya is in this compartment,' said the smart-looking guard, coming up to Vronsky.

The conductor's words roused him and forced him to remember his mother and his imminent encounter with her. In his soul, he did not respect his mother, and, without being conscious of it, did not love her, although in keeping with the convictions of the circle in which he lived and his upbringing, he could not imagine his attitude to his mother being anything other than extremely obedient and deferential, and the more obedient and deferential he was outwardly, the less he respected and loved her in his soul.

18

VRONSKY followed the conductor to the carriage and paused at the door of the compartment to make way for a lady coming out. With the customary tact of a society man, Vronsky ascertained with one glance at this lady's appearance that she belonged to the highest echelons of society. He apologized and was about to go into the carriage, but felt the need to glance at her again—not because she was very beautiful, and not because of the elegance and unassuming grace evident in her whole figure, but because there was something particularly gentle and tender in the expression of her pretty face when she walked past him. When he looked round, she also turned her head. Her shining grey eyes, made dark by her thick lashes, focused intently on his face for a moment in a friendly fashion, as if she recognized him, then immediately transferred to the approaching crowd, as if looking for someone. In that brief glance Vronsky had time to notice the suppressed animation which sparkled in her face and flitted between her shining eyes and the barely perceptible smile curving her rosy lips. It was as if an abundance of something so overflowed her being that it expressed itself independently of her will, now in the radiance of her glance, now in her smile. She had deliberately extinguished the light in her eyes, but it shone against her will in her barely perceptible smile.

Vronsky went into the carriage. His mother, a dried-up old lady with black eyes and ringlets, narrowed her eyes as she peered at her son, and a faint smile appeared on her thin lips. Getting up from the seat and handing her handbag to the maid, she proffered her small, withered hand to her son then lifted up his head in order to kiss him on the face.

'You got the telegram? You're well? Thank heavens.'

'You had a good journey?' asked her son, sitting down next to her and involuntarily listening to a woman's voice outside the door. He knew it was the voice of the lady he had encountered when he was coming in.

'All the same, I don't agree with you,' said the lady's voice.

'That's a Petersburg view, madam.'

'Not a Petersburg view, just a woman's view,' she replied.

'Well, allow me to kiss your hand.'

'Goodbye, Ivan Petrovich. Have a look, will you, and see if my brother is here, and send him to me,' said the lady just outside the door, then she came back into the compartment.

'So, have you found your brother?' asked Countess Vronskaya, turning to the lady.

Vronsky remembered now that this was Madame Karenina.

'Your brother is here,' he said, getting up. 'Excuse me, I did not recognize you, and our acquaintance was also so brief,' said Vronsky, bowing, 'that you're bound not to remember me.'

'Oh no,' she said, 'I would have recognized you, because your mother and I seem to have spent the entire journey talking only about you,' she said, finally allowing the exuberance clamouring to be let out express itself in a smile. 'But my brother still isn't here.'

'Go and call him, Alyosha,' said the old Countess.

Vronsky went out on to the platform and shouted:

'Oblonsky! Here!'

But Madame Karenina did not wait for her brother; instead, when she caught sight of him, she left the carriage with a decisive, light step. And as soon as her brother came up to her, she encircled his neck with her left arm in a movement which astonished Vronsky by its decisiveness and grace, quickly drew him to her, and kissed him warmly. Vronsky looked at her without lowering his gaze and smiled without knowing why. But then he remembered that his mother was waiting for him, and went back into the carriage.

'Very nice, isn't she?' the Countess said about Anna Karenina. 'Her husband seated her next to me, and I was very glad. We talked for the whole journey. Well now, you, I hear . . . *vous filez le parfait amour. Tant mieux, mon cher, tant mieux.*[1]

'I do not know to what you are referring, *Maman*,' her son replied crisply.

'Well, *Maman*, let's go.'

Madame Karenina came back into the carriage to say goodbye to the Countess.

'Well, there we are, Countess, you have met your son and I've met my brother,' she said merrily. 'And I've run out of stories; there wouldn't have been anything else to tell you.'

'Oh no, my dear,' said the Countess, taking her by the hand. 'I could travel the world with you and not be bored. You are one of those delightful women with whom it is a pleasure to talk and also be silent. And please don't worry about your son; it's impossible for you never to be separated from him.'

Anna Karenina stood motionless, holding herself ramrod straight, her eyes smiling.

'Anna Arkadyevna has a little boy of about eight, I believe,' said the Countess, explaining to her son, 'and she has never been separated from him and keeps agonizing about having left him.'

'Yes, the Countess and I talked the whole time, I about my son and she about hers,' said Anna Karenina, and again a smile lit up her face, a gentle smile directed at him.

'That must have been very boring for you,' he said, deftly catching this ball of flirtation she had thrown to him straight away. But she evidently did not want to continue the conversation in this tone, and turned to the old Countess.

'Thank you so much. I did not even notice the time going by yesterday. Goodbye, Countess.'

'Goodbye my dear,' answered the Countess. 'Let me kiss your pretty little face. Since I'm an old woman I can be frank and tell you that I have become quite smitten with you.'

However trite this phrase was, it was clear Anna Karenina sincerely believed it, and was pleased by it. She blushed, leant over slightly, offered her face to the Countess's lips, straightened up again, and, with the same smile hovering between her lips and her eyes, held out her hand to Vronsky. He pressed the small hand offered to him, and savoured as something special the vigorous grip with which she boldly

---

[1] 'You are living love's dream. So much the better, my dear, so much the better.'

and firmly shook his hand. She went out with a rapid step which bore her rather full frame with a strange lightness.

'Very nice,' said the old lady.

Her son thought the same. He followed her with his eyes until her graceful figure disappeared from view, and a smile remained on his face. Through the window he saw her go up to her brother, place her hand on his arm, and start talking to him animatedly about something which clearly had nothing to do with him, Vronsky, and he found that irksome.

'So, *Maman*, you are completely well?' he repeated, turning to his mother.

'I'm fine, perfectly well. Alexandre was very sweet. And Marie has become very pretty. She is very interesting.'

And she began telling him again about what most interested her, about her grandson's christening, the reason for her journey to Petersburg, and the special favour the Tsar had showed to her eldest son.

'Here's Lavrenty,' said Vronsky, looking through the window. 'Now let's go, if you don't mind.'

The old butler who had travelled with the Countess appeared in the carriage to announce that everything was ready, and the Countess stood up in order to leave.

'Let's go, it's not crowded now,' said Vronsky.

The maid took her handbag and little dog, and the butler and a porter took care of the other bags. Vronsky took his mother's arm; but just as they were getting out of the carriage, several people with frightened faces suddenly ran past. The station-master in his unusually coloured cap also ran past. Clearly something unusual had happened. The people from the train were rushing back.

'What? . . . What? . . . Where? . . . Threw himself! . . . Crushed! . . .' could be heard amongst the people going past.

Stepan Arkadyich, with his sister on his arm, had also turned back, and with frightened faces they stopped by the door of the carriage to avoid the crowd.

The ladies got into the carriage, while Vronsky and Stepan Arkadyich followed the crowd in order to obtain details of the accident.

A watchman, who was either drunk or wrapped up too tightly against the freezing cold, had not heard the train being shunted backwards and had been crushed.

The ladies had found out these details from the butler before Vronsky and Oblonsky had even returned.

Oblonsky and Vronsky had both seen the mutilated corpse. Oblonsky was clearly very upset. His face had creased up and he seemed to be on the verge of tears.

'Oh, what an awful thing! Oh Anna, if you had seen it! Oh, what an awful thing!' he said.

Vronsky was silent, and his handsome face was serious but completely unruffled.

'Oh, if you had seen it, Countess,' said Stepan Arkadyich. 'And his wife is here . . . It was terrible to see her . . . She threw herself on the body. They say he was the only person feeding an enormous family. What a nightmare!'

'Couldn't we do something for her?' said Karenina in an agitated whisper.

Vronsky glanced at her and immediately left the carriage.

'I'll be back shortly, *Maman*,' he added, turning round at the door.

When he returned a few minutes later, Stepan Arkadyich was already talking to the Countess about a new singer, while the Countess kept glancing impatiently at the door, waiting for her son.

'Let's go now,' said Vronsky as he arrived. They left together. Vronsky went ahead with his mother. Karenina followed with her brother. Having chased after Vronsky, the station-master came up to him at the exit.

'You gave my assistant two hundred roubles. Would you be so kind as to indicate for whom this sum is intended?'

'The widow,' said Vronsky, shrugging his shoulders. 'I don't see the need to ask.'

'You gave that?' Oblonsky shouted out from behind, and, squeezing his sister's hand, he added: 'That's so nice of him, it really is! He's a wonderful fellow, don't you think? My respects, Countess.'

And he and his sister stopped to look for her maid.

When they came out of the station, the Vronskys' carriage had already departed. People coming out of the station were still talking about what had happened.

'What a terrible way to die!' said a gentleman walking past. 'He was sliced in two, they say.'

'On the contrary, I think it was the easiest, as it was instantaneous,' said another.

'They ought to take precautions,' said a third.

Karenina settled into the carriage, and Stepan Arkadyich saw with surprise that her lips were trembling, and that she was finding it difficult to hold back her tears.

'What's the matter, Anna?' he asked when they had travelled a few hundred yards.

'It's a bad omen,' she said.

'What nonsense!' said Stepan Arkadyich. 'You have come, that's the main thing. You can't imagine how much I am counting on you.'

'So have you known Vronsky long?'

'Yes. We are hoping he is going to marry Kitty, you know.'

'Really?' said Anna quietly. 'Well, let's talk about you now,' she added, shaking her head as if she wanted physically to banish something extraneous which was bothering her. 'Let's talk about your affairs. I received your letter, and here I am.'

'Yes, all my hopes are pinned on you,' said Stepan Arkadyich.

'Well, come on then, tell me everything.'

And Stepan Arkadyich started recounting what had happened.

When they arrived at the house, Oblonsky helped his sister out, sighed, pressed her hand, and set off to go to work.

19

WHEN Anna came in, Dolly was sitting in the small drawing room with a fair-haired, chubby little boy who already resembled his father, listening to his French reading lesson. As he was reading, the boy was twisting a button hanging from his jacket and trying to pull it off. His mother had pulled his hand away several times, but the chubby little hand kept reaching for the button. His mother tore off the button and put it in her pocket.

'Keep your hands still, Grisha,' she said, and went back to her blanket, an old piece of work she always took up at difficult moments and now was knitting nervously, her finger thrust out as she counted stitches. Although the previous day she had instructed her husband to be told that it was no concern of hers whether his sister came or not, she had still prepared everything for her arrival, and had been awaiting her sister-in-law with trepidation.

Dolly was shattered by her grief, utterly consumed by it. But she remembered that her sister-in-law Anna was the wife of one of the most prominent figures in Petersburg and a Petersburg *grande dame*. As a result of this circumstance she had not gone through with what she had told her husband, that is, she had not forgotten that her sister-in-law was coming. 'Well, after all, Anna is not to blame for anything,' thought Dolly. 'I have no reason to think anything other than the very best about her, and I have only seen her show kindness and friendship towards me.' It was true that, from what she could remember of her impression of visiting the Karenins in Petersburg, she had not liked their house itself; there was something false in the whole cast of their family life. 'But why should I not receive her? Just as long as she doesn't try and console me!' thought Dolly. 'All those consolations and admonitions and acts of Christian forgiveness—I have gone over it all a thousand times, and none of it's any good.'

Dolly had been alone with the children these last days. She did not want to talk about her grief, but she could not talk about anything else with that grief in her heart. She knew that she would end up telling Anna everything, one way or another, and while she relished the prospect of being able to tell her, she was also angry about having to discuss her humiliation with her, his sister, and hear from her the stock phrases of admonition and consolation.

As often happens, she had kept glancing at the clock, awaiting her arrival every minute, but then missed the actual moment of her guest's arrival, so did not hear the bell.

When she heard the rustle of a dress and light footsteps already in the doorway, she looked round, and her careworn face could not help expressing surprise rather than joy. She rose and embraced her sister-in-law.

'What, you're here already?' she said, kissing her.

'Dolly, how glad I am to see you!'

'I am glad too,' said Dolly, smiling wanly as she tried to work out from the expression on Anna's face whether she knew. 'She must know,' she thought, noticing the sympathy on Anna's face. 'Come on, I'll show you to your room,' she continued, trying to put off as long as possible the moment of explanation.

'Is this Grisha? Goodness me, how he's grown!' said Anna, and after kissing him, with her eyes still fastened on Dolly, she stopped and blushed. 'No, let's not go anywhere.'

She took off her scarf, and her hat, and shook her head to disentangle a lock of her abundantly curly black hair which had got caught in it.

'Well, you are glowing with happiness and health!' said Dolly, almost with envy.

'I am? . . . Yes,' said Anna. 'Goodness me. Tanya! She's the same age as my Seryozha,' she added, turning to the little girl who had come running in. She took her in her arms and kissed her. 'A lovely girl, lovely! Show them all to me.'

She identified them all, and remembered not just their names, but the year and month in which they were born, their characters, and their various ailments, and Dolly could not but appreciate this.

'Well, let's go and see them,' she said. 'Vasya is asleep at the moment, which is a pity.'

After they had inspected the children, they sat down to coffee in the drawing room, alone now. Anna took hold of the tray and then moved it to one side.

'Dolly,' she said, 'he told me.'

Dolly looked coldly at Anna. She was waiting now for the phrases of feigned compassion, but Anna said nothing of the kind.

'Dolly, my dear!' she said, 'I don't want to speak to you on his behalf, or console you; that's impossible. But I'm just sorry for you, darling, sorry with all my heart!'

Tears suddenly started from behind the thick lashes of her shining eyes. She sat down closer to her sister-in-law and took her hand in her own energetic small hand. Dolly did not move away, but her face did not change its stiff expression. She said:

'Nothing can console me. Everything is finished after what has gone on, everything is ruined!'

And as soon as she said this, the expression on her face suddenly softened. Anna lifted up Dolly's dry thin hand, kissed it, and said:

'But Dolly, what is to be done, what is to be done? What is the best thing to do in this terrible situation? That's what we need to think about.'

'It is all over, and there is nothing that can be done,' said Dolly. 'And the worst thing of all, you understand, is that I cannot leave him; there's the children, I'm tied. But I cannot live with him, it's torture for me to see him.'

'Dolly, sweetheart, he has talked to me, but I want to hear from you, tell me everything.'

Dolly looked at her quizzically.

Anna's face showed unfeigned concern and love.

'All right,' she said suddenly. 'But I'll have to start at the beginning. You know how I got married. With the upbringing I had from *Maman*, I was not only innocent, but stupid too. I didn't know anything. They say that men tell their wives about their previous lives, I know, but Stiva . . .' she corrected herself, 'Stepan Arkadyich did not tell me anything. You won't believe this, but up until now I had thought that I was the only woman he had known. I lived like that for eight years. I not only did not suspect him of being unfaithful, you understand, but I considered it inconceivable, and then, just imagine me having those ideas and suddenly discovering all the horror, all the filth . . . You have to understand. To be completely secure in my happiness, and suddenly . . .' Dolly continued, trying to stop herself sobbing, 'to stumble across a letter . . . A letter he wrote to his lover, to my governess. No, it's just too awful!' She hurriedly took out a handkerchief and covered her face with it. 'I can even understand an infatuation,' she continued after a pause, 'but to deceive me deliberately, cunningly . . . and with whom? . . . To go on being my husband together with her . . . it's awful! You can't understand . . .'

'Oh no, I do understand! I do understand, dearest Dolly, I do,' said Anna, squeezing her hand.

'And do you think he understands the full horror of my position?' Dolly continued. 'Not at all! He's happy and contented.'

'Oh no,' Anna interrupted quickly. 'He's pitiful, he's consumed with remorse . . .'

'Is he capable of remorse?' interrupted Dolly as she scrutinized her sister-in-law's face.

'Yes, I know him. I couldn't look at him without feeling pity. We both know him. He is a good person, but he is proud, and now he is so humiliated. What touched me most (and here Anna guessed what could touch Dolly the most)—there are two things tormenting him: firstly shame before the children, and secondly the fact that while loving you . . . yes, yes, more than anything else in the world,' she hastily interrupted Dolly who was about to object, 'he has hurt you, crushed you. "No, no, she won't forgive me," he keeps saying.'

Dolly gazed pensively past her sister-in-law as she listened to her words.

'Yes, I understand that his position is terrible; it's worse for the guilty party than for the innocent one,' she said, 'if he feels he is to blame for this whole misfortune. But how can I forgive him, how can I be his wife again, after her? It will be agony living with him now, precisely because I loved him as I did, because I love my past love for him . . .'

And her words were halted by sobbing.

But as if intentionally, each time she softened, she again began to talk about what annoyed her.

'She is young, she is beautiful after all,' she continued. 'And do you realize who my youth and beauty were taken by, Anna? By him and his children. I have outlived my usefulness to him, I gave it my all, and of course he finds a young, vulgar creature more attractive now. They must have talked about me, or even worse, didn't say anything—you understand?' Her eyes blazed with hatred again. 'And after this, he is going to tell me . . . So, am I to believe him? Never. No, everything that was a consolation and a reward for all that hard work and suffering is completely over, all of it . . . Can you believe it? I was just teaching Grisha: it used to be a joy, and now it's torture. Why do I bother, why do I toil away? Why have children? What is awful is that my heart has suddenly been turned upside down, and instead of love and tenderness, all I feel for him is anger, yes, anger. I could kill him and . . .'

'Dolly dearest, I understand, but don't torment yourself. You have been so hurt, and you are so worked up that there is a lot you can't see clearly.'

Dolly quietened down, and they were both silent for a couple of minutes.

'Think about what I should do, Anna, help me. I have thought everything over and cannot see any solution.'

Anna could not think of anything, but her heart responded directly to every word and every expression on her sister-in-law's face.

'There's one thing I will say,' began Anna, 'I'm his sister, I know his character, that capacity he has of forgetting absolutely everything'— she made a gesture in front of her forehead—'that capacity he has of complete infatuation but then complete repentance. He cannot believe or understand now how he could have done what he did.'

'No, he does understand, he did understand!' interrupted Dolly. 'But I . . . you're forgetting me . . . do you think it's easier for me?'

'Wait. When he told me, I must confess that I did not yet understand the full horror of your situation. I only saw his position and the fact that the family was upset; I felt sorry for him, but now that I have talked to you, and being a woman, I see things differently; I see your suffering, and I can't tell you how sorry I feel for you! But, Dolly, darling, although I completely understand what you are going through, there is one thing I don't know: I don't know . . . I don't know how much love there still is for him in your soul. Only you know whether there is enough to allow you to forgive. If there is, then forgive him!'

'No,' began Dolly; but Anna interrupted her, kissing her hand again.

'I know society better than you do,' she said. 'I know these sorts of people, people like Stiva, and how they view this. You say that he talked to *her* about you. That won't have happened. These people may commit infidelities, but their home and their wife—they are sacrosanct to them. Somehow these women remain objects of contempt for them and don't get in the way of family life. They draw some kind of invisible line between their family and them. I do not understand it, but that's how it is.'

'Yes, but he kissed her . . .'

'Dolly, wait, darling. I saw Stiva when he was in love with you. I remember the time when he used to come and see me and how he used to cry when he talked about you, and what a poetic and exalted being you were for him, and I know that the longer he has lived with you, the higher you have risen in his eyes. We used to laugh at him you know, because he would tack on "Dolly is a remarkable woman" to everything he said. You were always a goddess for him and still are, whereas this infatuation is not from his soul . . .'

'But what if the infatuation happens again?'

'It can't, as far as I understand it . . .'

'Yes, but would you forgive?'

'I don't know, I cannot judge . . . No, actually I can,' said Anna upon reflection; and after pondering the situation and weighing it up in her mind, she added: 'No, I can, I definitely can. Yes, I would forgive. It is true I would not be the same, but I would forgive, and would forgive as if it had never happened, as if it had never ever happened.'

'Well, of course,' interrupted Dolly quickly, as if she was saying something she had often thought herself, 'otherwise it would not be forgiveness. If you forgive, you have to forgive completely. Well, let us go, I'll show you to your room,' she said, getting up, and on the way there Dolly embraced Anna. 'I'm so glad that you have come, my dear, I really am. I feel better, so much better.'

20

ANNA spent the whole of that day at home, that is, at the Oblonskys, and did not receive anyone, since some of her acquaintances, having already managed to learn of her arrival, came to call that same day. Anna spent all morning with Dolly and the children. She only sent a note to her brother telling him he should without fail dine at home. 'Come, God is merciful,' she wrote.

Oblonsky dined at home; the conversation was general, and his wife talked to him using the familiar form of address, which she had not done earlier. The frostiness in the relations between husband and wife remained, but there was no longer any talk of separation, and Stepan Arkadyich saw the possibility of dialogue and reconciliation.

Kitty arrived immediately after dinner. She knew Anna Arkadyevna, but only very slightly, and had driven now to her sister's with some trepidation as to how she would be received by this Petersburg society lady, about whom everyone sang such praises. But Anna Arkadyevna liked her—she saw that straight away. Anna clearly admired her beauty and youth, and before Kitty could collect herself, she not only felt she was under her spell, but was in love with her, as young girls are capable of falling in love with older married ladies. Anna was not like a society lady or the mother of an eight-year-old son, but would have more closely resembled a twenty-year-old girl in the lissom movements, vitality, and constant animation in her face, one minute breaking out into a smile and into a glance the next, were it not for the serious and sometimes sad expression of her eyes, which struck Kitty and drew her to Anna. Kitty felt that Anna was completely straightforward and was not hiding anything, but that there was some kind of other, higher world of complex and romantic interests within her, to which she had no access.

After dinner, when Dolly left to go to her room, Anna quickly stood up and went over to her brother, who was lighting a cigar.

'Stiva,' she said to him with a merry wink, making the sign of the cross over him and indicating the door with her eyes. 'Off you go, and may God help you.'

Understanding her, he put down his cigar and disappeared behind the door.

When Stepan Arkadyich went out, she returned to the sofa, where she had been sitting surrounded by children. Either because the children could see that their Mama was fond of this aunt, or because they themselves felt she had some special charm, the eldest two, followed by the younger ones, as often happens with children, had attached themselves to the new aunt even before dinner and would not leave her alone. And between them they had made up a kind of game, which consisted of sitting as close as possible to their aunt, touching her, holding her small hand, kissing it, and playing with her ring, or at least touching the ruffle on her dress.

'Come along now, as we were sitting before,' said Anna Arkadyevna, resuming her place.

And Grisha tucked his head under her arm again, leant it against her dress, and beamed with pride and happiness.

'So when is the ball, then?' she asked Kitty.

'Next week, and it will be a wonderful ball. One of those balls which are always jolly.'

'Are there any balls which are always jolly?' said Anna with gentle mockery.

'Strangely enough, there are. It's always jolly at the Bobrishchevs, and at the Nikitins, but it's always boring at the Meshkovs. Haven't you noticed?'

'No, my dear, there are no longer any balls which are jolly for me,' said Anna, and Kitty glimpsed in her eyes that special world which was not open to her. 'For me there are those which are less taxing and boring to attend . . .'

'How can *you* be bored at a ball?'

'Why should I not be bored at a ball?' asked Anna.

Kitty noticed that Anna knew what answer would follow.

'Because you are always the best person there.'

Anna had a capacity for blushing. She blushed and said:

'Firstly, I never am, and secondly, even if that were the case, what difference would that make to me?'

'Will you go to this ball?' asked Kitty.

'I think it will be impossible not to go. Here, take this,' she said to Tanya, who was pulling off a loose-fitting ring from her white, tapering finger.

'I'll be very glad if you go. I would so like to see you at a ball.'

'Well, if I have to go, I will at least comfort myself with the thought that it will give you pleasure . . . Grisha, don't tug, please, my hair is already messy enough as it is,' she said, adjusting a stray lock which Grisha had been playing with.

'I can picture you at the ball in lilac.'

'Why lilac in particular? asked Anna, smiling. 'Now, children, off you go, off you go. Listen, Miss Hull is calling you in to tea,' she said, pulling the children off her and sending them into the dining room.

'But I know why you want me to go to the ball. You have great expectations of this ball, and you want everyone to be there, to be part of it.'

'How do you know? Yes.'

'Oh, it's wonderful to be your age,' continued Anna. 'I know and remember that blue haze, like you see on the mountains in Switzerland. The haze covering everything at that blessed point when your childhood is coming to an end, and the path leading from that huge, carefree, happy circle becomes narrower and narrower, and it is both jolly and terrifying entering that *enfilade*,* even though it is bright and beautiful . . . Who has not been through that?'

Kitty smiled silently. 'But how can she have been through that? I would so like to know her whole love story,' thought Kitty, remembering the unromantic appearance of Alexey Alexandrovich, her husband.

'I know a bit about it. Stiva told me, and I congratulate you, I like him very much,' Anna continued, 'I met Vronsky at the railway station.'

'Oh, was he there?' asked Kitty, blushing. 'What did Stiva tell you?'

'Stiva gave the game away to me. And I would be very happy. I travelled yesterday with Vronsky's mother,' she continued, 'and his mother couldn't stop talking to me about him; he's her favourite; I know that mothers are biased, but . . .'

'So what did his mother tell you?'

'Oh, a lot! I know he is her favourite, but you can still see that he is very gallant . . . Well, for example, she told me that he wanted to give his entire inheritance away to his brother, that he did something remarkable when he was still a child, saved a woman from drowning. In a word, he's a hero,' said Anna, smiling and remembering the two hundred roubles which he had given at the station.

But she did not mention those two hundred roubles. For some reason she found it distasteful to remember that. She felt there was something about it which related to her, something which should not have been there.

'She was very keen that I go and visit her,' continued Anna, 'and I'll be glad to see the old lady, so I'll go and see her tomorrow. Well, Stiva has been in Dolly's room a long time, thank goodness,' added Anna, changing the subject and getting up, as it seemed to Kitty, displeased with something.

'No, I was first! No, I was!' shrieked the children as they raced in to their Aunt Anna after finishing their tea.

'Everyone together!' said Anna, laughing as she ran to hug them, bringing the whole heap of wriggling, rapturously squealing children tumbling to the floor.

21

DOLLY came out of her room for the grown-ups' tea. Stepan Arkadyich did not appear. He had evidently left his wife's room through the back door.

'I'm worried you are going to be cold upstairs,' remarked Dolly, turning to Anna. 'I'd like to move you downstairs, then we'll be nearer each other.'

'Oh, please don't worry about me,' replied Anna, examining Dolly's face and trying to work out whether there had been a reconciliation.

'You'll have light here,' answered her sister-in-law.

'I assure you, I always sleep like a dormouse wherever I am.'

'What's this about?' Stepan Arkadyich asked his wife as he came out of his study.

From his tone, Kitty and Anna immediately realized a reconciliation had taken place.

'I want to move Anna downstairs, but I've got to re-hang the curtains. I suppose I'll have to do it myself, as no one else will manage to do it,' replied Dolly, turning to him.

'Heaven knows, are they really reconciled?' thought Anna hearing her tone, which was cold and impassive.

'Come on now, Dolly, don't keep creating difficulties. I'll see to it if you like . . .'

'Yes, they must be reconciled,' thought Anna.

'I know how you'll see to things,' answered Dolly. 'You'll tell Matvey to do something which can't be done, then you'll go off and he will get everything muddled,' and Dolly's usual wry smile wrinkled the corners of her mouth as she said this.

'Complete, complete reconciliation,' thought Anna, 'thank God!' And jubilant that she had brought this about, she went up to Dolly and gave her a kiss.

'Of course not; what have Matvey and I done to deserve such contempt?' said Stepan Arkadyich to his wife with a barely perceptible smile.

Dolly subjected her husband to her usual faint mockery all evening, and Stepan Arkadyich was good-humoured and jolly, but not excessively so, as he did not want to show that he had forgotten his guilt after being forgiven.

At half-past nine the family chatter round the Oblonskys' tea table, which happened to be particularly happy and convivial that evening, was broken up by what seemed to be the simplest of events, but this simple event for some reason seemed strange to everybody. While they were talking about mutual Petersburg acquaintances, Anna quickly rose.

'She's in my album,' she said, 'and I'll also be able to show you my Seryozha, by the way,' she added with a proud maternal smile.

Towards ten o'clock, which was when she usually said goodnight to her son, and often put him to bed herself before she went to a ball, she began to feel sad that she was so far away from him; and no matter what they talked about, her thoughts kept coming back to her curly-headed Seryozha. She yearned to look at his picture and talk about him. Seizing the first opportunity, she got up and set off with her light, determined step to fetch the album. The stairs leading up to her room began at the landing of the heated main staircase in the hall.

Just as she was leaving the drawing room a bell rang in the lobby.

'Who can that be?' said Dolly.

'It's early for me, and late for anyone else,' remarked Kitty.

'Probably someone with papers,' added Stepan Arkadyich, and while Anna was walking past the staircase, a servant ran upstairs to announce the arrival of the visitor, who was standing by the lamp. Glancing downwards, Anna immediately recognized Vronsky, and a strange feeling of pleasure mixed with an amorphous fear suddenly stirred in her heart. He was standing there without removing his coat, and taking something out of his pocket. Just as she came level with the middle of the staircase he raised his eyes, saw her, and his face took on a frightened, sheepish expression. She went on, with her head slightly inclined, and next came the booming voice of Stepan Arkadyich, asking him to come in, and the quiet, soft, and calm voice of Vronsky refusing.

When Anna returned with the album, he was no longer there, and Stepan Arkadyich was recounting how he had dropped by to find out about the dinner they were giving for a visiting celebrity.

Kitty blushed. She thought she was the only one who realized why he had stopped by, and why he had not come in. 'He was at our house,' she thought, 'and did not find me there, so thought I might be here; but he did not come in, because he thought it was late, and because Anna is here.'

They all exchanged glances without saying anything, and started looking at Anna'a album.

There was nothing unusual or strange about someone calling on a friend at half-past nine to find out the details of a dinner that was being planned, and not coming in; but it did seem strange to everyone. It seemed strange and wrong most of all to Anna.

22

THE ball had just begun when Kitty and her mother stepped on to the central staircase, which was bathed in light and embellished with flowers and powdered footmen in red livery. From the interior came a steady rustle of movement which filled the rooms like bees buzzing in a hive, and while they adjusted their hair in front of a mirror between the potted plants on the landing, the delicately clear sounds of the violins in the orchestra could be heard striking up the first waltz in the ballroom. An old gentleman in civilian dress who had been adjusting his grey whiskers in front of another mirror, and exuded the smell of cologne, bumped into them on the staircase and stood aside, clearly admiring Kitty, whom he did not know. A clean-shaven youth, one of those society youths whom old Prince Shcherbatsky called *young pups*, wearing an extremely open-cut waistcoat and straightening his white tie as he went, bowed to them, and after dashing past came back in order to invite Kitty for the quadrille. The first quadrille had already been given to Vronsky, so she had to give this youth the second. An officer who was buttoning his glove stepped aside at the door, stroking his moustache as he admired the pink Kitty.

Despite the fact that her dress, her hair, and all her preparations for the ball caused Kitty a great deal of trouble and thought, she now entered the ball so effortlessly and simply in her intricate tulle gown over a pink slip that it was as if none of the rosettes and lace, or any details of her dress had caused her or her servants a moment's thought, as if she had been born in all this tulle and lace and with this tall hair-style, crowned by a rose and two leaves.

When the old princess wanted to put the twisted ribbon of her sash in order before they entered the ballroom, Kitty gently demurred. She felt that everything on her should look good and graceful on its own and that nothing needed to be adjusted.

This was one of Kitty's happy days. Her dress was not too tight, her lace collar was not drooping anywhere, the rosettes had not crumpled or been torn off, and her pink slippers with the high, curved heels did not pinch, but energized her slender feet. The thick braids of blonde hair clung to her small head as if they were her own. All three buttons on the long glove which encased her arm without changing its shape had fastened without breaking. The black velvet ribbon of her locket encircled her neck to particular gentle effect. The velvet ribbon was enchanting, and as she gazed at her neck in the mirror at home, Kitty felt this velvet ribbon was speaking. There might be some doubt about everything else, but the velvet ribbon was enchanting. Kitty had also smiled here at the ball when she had looked at it in the mirror. Her bare shoulders and arms felt as cool as marble, which was a feeling Kitty particularly liked. Her eyes shone, and her rosy lips could not but smile from an awareness of her attractiveness. No sooner had she entered the ballroom and approached the crowd of ladies in brightly coloured tulle, ribbons, and lace, awaiting invitations to dance (Kitty never lingered long in this crowd) than she was invited for the waltz, and by the best dancer, the top dancer in the ball hierarchy, famous as a director of balls and master of ceremonies, the handsome, portly, married man Yegorushka Korsunsky. Having just left Countess Banina, with whom he had danced the first round of the waltz, and surveyed his charges, that is, the handful of couples already on the dance-floor, he saw Kitty entering, made a beeline for her in that relaxed saunter which is the preserve of ball directors, bowed, and held out his arm so he could clasp her slender waist without even asking for her consent. She looked around for someone to whom she could hand her fan, and the hostess took it from her with a smile.

'How good that you have come on time,' he said to her, putting his arm round her waist. 'I don't understand this habit of arriving late.'

She bent her left arm in order to place it on his shoulder, and her little feet in their pink slippers began moving quickly, lightly, and evenly in time to the music across the slippery parquet.

'One relaxes waltzing with you,' he said to her as they launched into the first slow steps of the waltz. 'Your lightness and *précision* are sheer delight,' he told her, which is what he said to almost all his close acquaintances.

She smiled at his praise, and continued to survey the ballroom over his shoulder. She was not one of those girls who had just come out, for whom all the faces at a ball merge into one magical impression; nor was she one of those girls dragged to balls for whom the faces are all so familiar they become boring; she was somewhere in the middle—she was excited, but at the same time she had enough self-possession to observe her surroundings. She could see that the cream of society had gathered in the left-hand corner of the ballroom. The beautiful and audaciously naked Lydia, Korsunsky's wife, was there, the hostess was there, as was Krivin, always to be found with the cream of society, his bald head shining; that is where the youths were looking, not daring to go over; her eyes picked out Stiva there, and then she saw the lovely figure and head of Anna in a black velvet dress. And *he* was there. Kitty had not seen him since the evening when she had refused Levin. She immediately recognized him with her far-sighted eyes, and even noticed that he was looking at her.

'So, how about another round? You are not tired?' said Korsunsky, slightly out of breath.

'No, thank you.'

'Where shall I take you?'

'Madame Karenina is here, I believe . . . take me to her.'

'Wherever you command.'

Slowing his step now, Korsunsky waltzed directly over to the crowd in the left corner of the ballroom, repeating '*Pardon, mesdames, pardon, pardon, mesdames,*' and after navigating through the sea of lace, tulle, and ribbons without catching on a single feather, he spun his partner round sharply, exposing her slender legs in their lacy stockings, and causing her train to spread out like a fan and cover Krivin's knees. Korsunsky bowed, straightened out his shirt-front, and proffered his arm in order to escort her to Anna Arkadyevna. Blushing deeply, Kitty removed her train from Krivin's lap and looked round for Anna, her head spinning a little. Anna was standing talking, surrounded by ladies and men. She was not in lilac, which Kitty had so set her heart on, but in a low-cut black velvet dress, revealing her curvaceous shoulders and bosom like old chiselled ivory, rounded arms, and tiny slender hands. The entire dress was trimmed with Venetian lace. On her head, in her black hair, which was not augmented by any extension, was a small garland of pansies, and there was another on the black ribbon of her sash, between pieces of white lace. Her hair arrangement was inconspicuous. Only those obstinate little locks of curly hair constantly escaping at the nape of her neck and on her temples were conspicuous, and they enhanced her beauty. There was a string of pearls around her strong, chiselled neck.

Kitty had seen Anna every day, was in love with her, and had pictured her definitely in lilac. But now that she had seen her in black, she felt she had not understood the full extent of her charm. She now saw her in a completely new and unexpected light. She realized now that Anna could not have worn lilac, and that her charm consisted precisely in the fact that she always stood out from what she wore, that what she wore could never be noticeable on her. The black dress with its sumptuous lace was indeed not noticeable on her; it was just a frame, and all that was visible was her simple, natural, elegant, and yet also light-hearted and vivacious self.

She was standing holding herself extremely straight as always and, when Kitty went over to that cluster of people, talking to the host with her head turned slightly towards him.

'No, I will not cast the first stone,'* she was replying to him about something, 'although I do not understand it,' she continued, shrugging her shoulders, and then she immediately turned to Kitty with an affectionate, protective smile. Running a swift female eye over her dress, she made a barely perceptible gesture with her head, but which Kitty understood as approval of her dress and her beauty. 'You even come into the ballroom dancing,' she added.

'This is one of my most faithful assistants,' said Korsunsky, bowing to Anna Arkadyevna, whom he had not yet seen. 'The princess is helping to make the ball jolly and beautiful. Anna Arkadyevna, a waltz,' he said, bowing low.

'So you know each other?' asked their host.

'Whom do we not know? My wife and I are like white wolves; everyone knows us,' Korsunsky answered. 'A waltz, Anna Arkadyevna.'

'I don't dance when it is possible not to,' she said.

'But tonight it's impossible,' replied Korsunsky.

Vronsky approached at that moment.

'Well, if it is impossible not to dance tonight, come along then,' she said, not acknowledging Vronsky's bow and quickly placing her hand on Korsunsky's shoulder.

'Why is she cross with him?' thought Kitty, noticing that Anna deliberately not responded to Vronsky's bow. Vronsky came up to Kitty to remind her of the first quadrille and express his regret that he had not had the pleasure of seeing her all this time. Kitty looked admiringly at Anna waltzing as she listened to him. She was expecting him to invite her for the waltz, but he did not, and she glanced at him in surprise. He blushed and hurriedly invited her to waltz, but barely had he put his arm around her slender waist and taken the first step when the music abruptly stopped. Kitty looked at his face, which was such a short distance from hers, and years later that look full of love which she gave him, and which he did not reciprocate, would still tear at her heart with an agonizing sense of shame.

'*Pardon, pardon*! The waltz, the waltz!' Korsunsky shouted out from the other end of the ballroom, and, taking hold of the first available young lady, he started dancing himself.

23

VRONSKY and Kitty danced several waltzes together. After the waltzing had finished, Kitty went over to her mother, and she had barely managed to say a few words to Countess Nordston before Vronsky arrived to collect her for the first quadrille. Nothing significant was said during the quadrille; they had a desultory conversation, ranging from the Korsunskys, husband and wife, whom he described very amusingly as endearing forty-year-old children, to the projected public theatre,* and only once did the conversation touch a raw nerve with her, when he asked whether Levin was there, and added that he had liked him very much. But Kitty had not expected more from the quadrille. She was waiting for the mazurka with her heart in her mouth. She thought that everything would be decided during the mazurka. She was not perturbed that he had not asked her for the mazurka during the quadrille. She was sure she would dance the mazurka with him, as she had at previous balls, and had turned down five invitations for it, saying she was already engaged. Up until the last quadrille, the whole ball was a magical reverie of joyous colours, sounds, and movements for Kitty. She only stopped dancing when she felt too tired and asked for a rest. But as she danced the last quadrille with one of the dull youths she was unable to refuse, she happened to come face to face with Vronsky and Anna. She had not encountered Anna since her arrival, and she now once again saw her in a completely new and unexpected light. She recognized in her a quality with which she was so familiar herself, of exhilaration with one's success. She saw that Anna was drunk on the wine of the admiration she was inspiring. She knew that feeling, knew its tell-tale signs, and she saw them in Anna—she saw the dazzling sparkle shimmering in her eyes, the smile of happiness and excitement involuntarily curving her lips, and the precise grace, assurance, and lightness of her movements.

'Who is it?' she wondered. 'Everyone or just one person?' While she was failing to help the hapless youth with whom she was danc-ing keep up the conversation, the thread of which he had dropped and could not retrieve, and outwardly following the commands that Korsunsky was barking out merrily, which one minute had everyone forming a *grand rond* and the next a *chaîne*, she was observing, and her heart constricted more and more. 'No, it is not the admiration of the crowd intoxicating her, but the adoration of one person. And that one person? Can it really be him?' Every time he spoke to Anna, a joyous sparkle twinkled in her eyes, and a radiant smile curved her rosy lips. It was as if she was making a conscious effort not to show these signs of joy, but they appeared on her face by themselves. 'But what about him?' Kitty looked at him and was horrified. Everything Kitty saw so clearly depicted in the mirror of Anna's face was reflected in his. What had happened to his perennially calm, steady manner and blithely calm expression? No, every time he spoke to her now, he bent his head slightly, as if wanting to throw himself down before her, and his look expressed pure submission and fear. 'I do not want to hurt you,' his glance seemed to say each time, 'but I want to save myself, and do not know how.' On his face was an expression she had never seen before.

They were talking about mutual acquaintances, and conducting the most trivial of conversations, but it seemed to Kitty that every word they spoke was deciding their destiny, and hers. And strangely enough, although they really were talking about how funny Ivan Ivanovich was when he spoke French, and how a better match could have been found for that Eletskaya girl, these words had a special meaning for them, and they were aware of that, just as Kitty was. The whole ball, the whole world, everything in Kitty's soul disappeared into a fog. Only her strict upbringing kept her going and forced her to do what was required of her, namely dance, answer questions, talk, and even smile. But before the beginning of the mazurka, when they were already beginning to arrange the chairs, and some couples had moved from the small rooms into the main ballroom, Kitty succumbed to a moment of despair and horror. She had declined five invitations, and now she was not dancing the mazurka. There was not even any hope that she would be invited, precisely because she had scored too great a success in society, and it would simply never occur to anyone that she had not been invited earlier. She would have to tell her mother she was unwell and go home, but she did not have the strength for that. She felt crushed.

She went to the back of a small drawing room and sank into an armchair. The diaphanous skirt of her dress billowed up around her thin frame like a cloud; one thin, bare, delicate girlish arm, hanging limply, had disappeared into the folds of her pink *tunique*; with the other she was holding her fan and waving it in front of her hot face with short, rapid movements. But despite looking like a butterfly which has just landed on a blade of grass and is ready any second to take flight and unfold its rainbow wings, a terrible despair gripped her heart.

'But perhaps I'm mistaken, perhaps it didn't happen?'

And she again remembered everything she had seen.

'Kitty, what is all this?' said Countess Nordston, stealing up to her noiselessly on the carpet. 'I don't understand it.'

Kitty's lower lip trembled; she stood up quickly.

'Kitty, aren't you dancing the mazurka?'

'No, no,' said Kitty in a voice trembling with tears.

'He asked her for the mazurka in front of me,' said Countess Nordston, knowing that Kitty would understand who he and she were. 'She said: are you not dancing with Princess Shcherbatskaya?'

'Oh, I don't care!' answered Kitty.

No one except Kitty herself understood her situation, and no one knew that the day before she had refused a man whom she perhaps loved, and refused him because she had put her faith in someone else.

Countess Nordston found Korsunsky, with whom she was to dance the mazurka, and ordered him to invite Kitty.

Kitty danced in the first pair, and fortunately she did not have to speak, because Korsunsky was running about the whole time, managing everything. Vronsky and Anna were sitting almost opposite her. She saw them with her far-sighted eyes, and she also saw them up close when they came together in pairs, and the more she saw of them, the more she was convinced of the calamity which had befallen her. She could see they felt they were on their own in the crowded ballroom. And on Vronsky's face, always so resolute and detached, she was startled to see a distracted and submissive expression, like that of a clever dog when it has misbehaved.

Anna smiled, and her smile transferred to him. She became thoughtful, and he became serious. Some kind of supernatural force drew Kitty's eyes to Anna's face. She was lovely in that simple black dress, her rounded arms with bracelets were lovely, her firm neck with its string of pearls was lovely, the straying curls of her dishevelled hair arrangement were lovely, the graceful, light movements of her small feet and hands were lovely, that beautiful face was lovely in all its liveliness; but there was something terrible and cruel in her loveliness.

Kitty was more admiring of her than before, and she was suffering more and more. She felt crushed, and her face expressed this. When Vronsky caught sight of her as they brushed up against each other in the mazurka, he did not recognize her straight away, so greatly had she changed.

'Wonderful ball!' he said to her, in order to say something.

'Yes,' she replied.

In the middle of the mazurka, as they repeated the complicated steps which Korsunsky had just thought up, Anna went into the middle of the circle, took two partners and beckoned one lady and Kitty to her. As she came up, Kitty looked at her in fright. Anna narrowed her eyes as she looked at her, and smiled as she pressed her hand. But when she noticed that Kitty's face only responded to her smile with an expression of despair and incredulity, she turned away from her and started talking merrily to the other lady.

'Yes, there is something alien, demonic, and lovely about her,' Kitty said to herself.

Anna did not want to stay for supper, but her host tried to persuade her.

'Come on now, Anna Arkadyevna,' Korsunsky said, tucking her bare arm under the sleeve of his tail-coat. 'I have such a good idea for the cotillion! *Un bijou!*'

And he performed a few movements in an attempt to enthuse her. Their host smiled approvingly.

'No, I won't stay,' answered Anna, smiling; but despite her smile, both Korsunsky and their host realized from the resolute tone in which she answered that she would not stay.

'No, as it is I've danced more at your one ball in Moscow than during the whole winter in Petersburg,' Anna said, glancing at Vronsky, who was standing nearby. 'I need to rest before my journey.'

'And are you definitely leaving tomorrow?' asked Vronsky.

'Yes, I think so,' replied Anna, as if surprised by the boldness of his question; but the irrepressible, lustrous sparkle of her eyes and smile set him ablaze when she said this.

Anna Arkadyevna did not stay for supper and left.

24

'YES, there is something loathsome and repellent about me,' thought Levin as he left the Shcherbatskys and set off on foot to see his brother. 'And I don't fit in with other people. Pride, they say. No, I don't have any pride. If I did, I wouldn't have put myself in such a position.' And he imagined the happy, kind, clever, and calm Vronsky, who had probably never been in the awful situation he found himself in that evening. 'Yes, she was bound to choose him. That's the way it has to be, and I can't blame anyone or anything. It's my fault. What right did I have to think that she would want to join her life to mine? Who am I? And what am I? An insignificant person, who is no earthly use to anyone.' And he remembered his brother Nikolay, and it made him happy to linger on this memory. 'Isn't he right about everything in the world being rotten and vile? And we are hardly judging brother Nikolay fairly, nor have we judged him fairly in the past. Obviously he is a contemptible person from the point of view of someone like Prokofy, who saw him in a tattered fur coat, and drunk; but I know another side to him. I know his soul, and I know we are similar. But instead of going off to find him, I went out to dinner and came here.' Levin went up to a streetlamp, read his brother's address, which he had in his wallet, and hailed a cab. Levin spent the whole of the long journey over to his brother's vividly recalling all the events of Nikolay's life that he knew about. He remembered how, despite the taunts of his comrades, his brother had lived like a monk at university and the year after university, strictly observing all the religious rites, the services, and the fasts, and abstaining from all pleasures, especially women; and then how he had suddenly cracked, consorted with the vilest people and launched into the most licentious debauchery. Then he remembered the story about the boy he had taken from the country in order to educate, and in a fit of rage had beaten so badly that proceedings were started against him for causing grievous bodily harm. Then he remembered the story concerning the card-sharp to whom he had lost money and given a promissory note, and about whom he had himself issued a complaint, claiming he had been cheated. (That was the money Sergey Ivanich had paid out.) Then he remembered the night he had spent in the lock-up for disorderly conduct. He remembered the shameful court case he had brought against his brother Sergey Ivanich, for allegedly not paying him his share from their mother's estate; and the most recent incident, when he had taken up a post in the Western Territory* and was taken to court there for assaulting his superior . . . All this was unspeakably vile, but it did not seem nearly as vile to Levin as it was bound to have seemed to those who did not know Nikolay Levin, did not know his whole story, did not know his heart.

Levin remembered that during the time when Nikolay was going through his phase of piety, fasts, monks, and church services, when he sought help in religion, and a way of curbing his passionate nature, not only had no one supported him but everyone had laughed at him, himself included. They had all teased him and called him Noah, or 'the monk';* but when he had cracked, no one helped him; instead, everyone had turned their backs on him in horror and disgust.

Levin felt that in his soul, in the very depths of his soul, his brother Nikolay was no more in the wrong than those people who despised him, despite all the depravity of his life. It was not his fault that he had been born with his unruly character and a mind that was constrained by something. But he had always wanted to be good. 'I'll tell him everything, I'll make him tell me everything, and I'll show him that I love him and therefore understand him,' Levin resolved while driving up to the hotel indicated in the address, some time after ten.

'Twelve and thirteen are upstairs,' said the porter in answer to Levin's question.

'Is he there?'

'He ought to be.'

The door of room twelve was half-open, and from it, in a shaft of light, came the thick smoke of low-grade, weak tobacco and the sound of a voice which Levin did not recognize; but Levin immediately knew his brother was there, as he heard his intermittent coughing.

When he walked in, the unfamiliar voice was saying:

'Everything depends on how intelligently and conscientiously it's managed.'

Konstantin Levin looked through the doorway and saw that the speaker was a young man with a great shock of hair, dressed in a short kaftan, while a young, slightly pockmarked woman in a woollen dress without cuffs or collar* was sitting on a sofa. His brother was not visible. Konstantin's heart froze at the thought of his brother living amongst such alien people. No one had heard him, and while he took off his galoshes, Konstantin listened to what the gentleman in the short kaftan was saying. He was talking about some kind of venture.

'Well, to hell with the privileged classes,' said the voice of his brother, coughing. 'Masha! Get us some supper and let us have wine, if there is any left, otherwise send for some.'

The woman stood up, stepped out from behind the screen and saw Konstantin.

'There's some gentleman here, Nikolay Dmitrich,' she said.

'Who does he want?' Nikolay Levin's voice asked angrily.

'It's me,' answered Konstantin Levin, coming into the light.

'Who's *me*?' repeated Nikolay's voice even more angrily. He could be heard quickly getting up and stumbling against something, and then Levin saw before him in the doorway the huge, thin, stooping figure of his brother with his large, frightened eyes, a figure so familiar yet nevertheless shocking in its savage and unhealthy demeanour.

He was even thinner than he had been three years earlier, when Konstantin Levin had seen him last. He was wearing a short frock-coat. And his hands and broad bones seemed even more enormous. His hair had thinned, the same straight moustache hung over his upper lips, and the same eyes looked strangely and naively at the person who had come in.

'Ah, Kostya!' he exclaimed suddenly when he recognized his brother, and his eyes lit up with happiness. But the very next second he looked round to the young man and made the convulsive movement with his head and neck which Konstantin knew so well, as if his tie was too tight; and then a completely different, savage, anguished, and cruel expression settled on his emaciated face.

'I wrote to both you and Sergey Ivanyich that I neither know you or want to know you. What is it you're after, what do you both want?'

He was not at all as Konstantin had imagined. The toughest and worst side of his character, which was what made being with him so difficult, had been forgotten by Konstantin Levin when he was thinking about him; and now, when he saw his face, particularly that convulsive jerking of his head, it all came flooding back.

'There isn't anything I want,' he answered timidly. 'I've just come to see you.'

Nikolay was clearly mollified by his brother's timidity. His lips twitched.

'Ah, you're just stopping by?' he asked. 'Well, come in, sit down. Do you want some supper? Masha, bring three portions. No, wait. Do you know who this is?' he said, turning to his brother and indicating the gentleman in the short kaftan. 'This is Mr Kritsky, who I have been friends with from my Kiev days, a very remarkable person. He is being hounded by the police, of course, because he is not a scoundrel.'

And he eyed everyone in the room, as was his custom. When he saw that the woman standing in the doorway was making a move to go, he shouted to her: 'I told you to wait.' And with that awkwardness and conversational clumsiness which Konstantin knew so well, he eyed everyone again and proceeded to tell his brother Kritsky's story: how he was thrown out of university for starting Sunday schools* and a society to help poor students, and how he had then gone to work as a teacher in a peasant school, and how they had thrown him out there too, and how he had been taken to court for something.

'You were at Kiev university?' Konstantin Levin asked Kritsky, in order to break the awkward silence which ensued.

'Kiev, yes,' Kritsky said with an angry frown.

'And this woman,' Nikolay Levin interrupted him, pointing to her, 'is my life partner, Marya Nikolayevna. I took her from the brothel,' and his neck jerked as he said this. 'But I love her and respect her, and I ask that everyone who wants to know me,' he added, raising his voice and glowering, 'loves and respects her. She is just the same as my wife, just the same. So now you know who you are dealing with. And if you think you are demeaning yourself, goodbye and good riddance.'*

And again he ran his eyes over them all searchingly.

'I don't understand why I should be demeaning myself.'

'Well then, Masha, ask them to bring supper: three portions, vodka and wine . . . No, wait . . . No, never mind . . . Off you go.'

25

'So you see,' Nikolay Levin continued, wrinkling his brow with effort and twitching. He clearly found it difficult to work out what to say and do. 'You see now . . .' He pointed to some kind of iron bars tied up with twine in the corner of the room. 'You see this? It's the beginning of a new project we are launching. It's a manufacturing co-operative . . .'

Konstantin was barely listening. He was peering into his brother's unhealthy, consumptive face and feeling more and more sorry for him, so he was unable to make himself listen to what his brother was telling him about the co-operative. He could see that this co-operative was merely an anchor saving him from despising himself. Nikolay Levin carried on talking:

'You know that capital oppresses the worker—our workers, the peasants, bear all the burden of labour, and they are placed so that however hard they work, they cannot escape their brutish situation. All the profits from their wages, which they could have used to improve their situation, obtain some leisure time and, as a consequence, some education—all their surplus earnings are taken from them by the capitalists. And the way society has evolved, the more they work, the more the merchants and the landowners will make, and they will be beasts of burden for ever. And this state of affairs has to be changed,' he concluded, looking enquiringly at his brother.

'Yes, of course,' said Konstantin, contemplating the red blotches which had appeared under his brother's prominent cheekbones.

'So we are organizing a metalworkers' co-operative, in which everything we produce, and the profits, and, most importantly, the tools, will all be shared.'

'And where is this co-operative going to be?' asked Konstantin Levin.

'In the village of Vozdremo, in Kazan province.'*

'But why in a village? There is already enough to do in the villages, it seems to me. Why set up a metalworkers' co-operative in a village?'

'Because the peasants are just as much slaves now as they were before, and that is why you and Sergey Ivanich don't like the idea of people wanting to take them out of this state of slavery,' said Nikolay Levin, irritated by the objection.

Konstantin Levin sighed as he looked round the room, which was gloomy and dirty. This sigh appeared to irritate Nikolay even more.

'I know the aristocratic views you and Sergey Ivanich have. I know that he uses all his mental faculties to justify the existing evil.'

'No, but why are you talking about Sergey Ivanich?' said Levin with a smile.

'Sergey Ivanich? I'll tell you!' Nikolay Levin cried out suddenly at the mention of Sergey Ivanich. 'I'll tell you why . . . But what is there to say? There's just one thing . . . Why have you come to see me? You despise all this, and that's fine, so you can be on your way now, off you go!' he shouted, getting up from his chair. 'Go on, off you go!'

'I don't despise it at all,' said Konstantin Levin timidly. 'I am not even arguing.'

Just then Marya Nikolayevna came back. Nikolay Levin looked at her angrily. She went up to him quickly and whispered something.

'I am not well, I've become irritable,' Nikolay Levin said, calming down and breathing heavily, 'and then you have to talk to me about Sergey Ivanich and his article. It's such rubbish, such lies, such self-deception. What can a man write about justice when he does not know what it is? Have you read his article?' he asked Kritsky, sitting back down at the table and moving some half-filled cigarettes off it to clear some space.

'No, I haven't,' said Kritsky gloomily, clearly not wanting to enter into conversation.

'Why not?' Nikolay Levin now turned with irritation to Kritsky.

'Because I don't consider it necessary to waste time on it.'

'Forgive me for asking, but how do you know you would be wasting time? That article is inaccessible to many people, I mean it's above their heads. But with me it's a different matter, I can see through his thinking, and I know why it is unconvincing.'

Everyone fell silent. Kritsky got up slowly and reached for his hat.

'You don't want supper? Well, goodbye then. Come by tomorrow with the metalworker.'

As soon as Kritsky left, Nikolay Levin smiled and winked.

'He's no good either,' he said. 'You know, I can see . . .'

But just then Kritsky called him from the door.

'What else do you want?' he said and went out to him in the corridor. When he was alone with Marya Nikolayevna, Levin turned to her.

'Have you been with my brother long?' he asked her.

'This is the second year now. His health has got very bad. He drinks a lot,' she said.

'What exactly is he drinking?'

'Vodka, and it's bad for him.'

'Does he really drink a lot?' whispered Levin.

'Yes,' she said, looking round apprehensively at the doorway in which Nikolay Levin had appeared.

'What have you been talking about?' he said, frowning and transferring his frightened eyes from one to the other. 'Tell me!'

'Nothing,' answered Konstantin in embarrassment.

'Well, if you don't want to talk, that's up to you. But there is nothing for you to talk to her about. She is a common wench, and you are a gentleman,' he said, his neck jerking.

'But I can see that you have understood and considered everything, and are taking pity on the error of my ways,' he began again, raising his voice.

'Nikolay Dmitrich, Nikolay Dmitrich,' Marya Nikolayevna whispered again as she went up to him.

'Oh, all right, all right! . . . But what about supper? Ah, here it is,' he said, seeing a servant with a tray. 'Here, put it here,' he said angrily, and promptly took the vodka, poured a glass, and drank it greedily. 'Want a drink?' he asked his brother, having immediately brightened up. 'Well, that's enough about Sergey Ivanich. I'm glad to see you anyway. When all is said and done, you're still family. Come on, drink up. Tell me, what are you doing these days?' he continued, greedily chomping on a piece of bread and pouring another glass. 'How are you getting on?'

'I'm living on my own in the country, as before, managing the estate,' Konstantin answered, observing with horror the greediness with which his brother was drinking and eating, and trying to conceal the fact of his having noticed.

'Why don't you get married?'

'Hasn't happened,' answered Konstantin, blushing.

'Why not? As for me, it's all over! I have ruined my life. I've said it before and I'll say it again; if I had been given my inheritance when I needed it, my whole life would have been different.'

Konstantin Dmitrich hurriedly changed subject.

'Did you know that I've got your Vanyushka working for me in the office at Pokrovskoye?' he said.

Nikolay's neck jerked and he became pensive.

'So tell me, what is going on at Pokrovskoye? Is the house still standing, and what about the birches, and our classroom? Filipp the gardener, he can't still be alive, can he? I remember the summer-house and the sofa so well! Make sure you don't change anything in the house, but hurry up and get married, and set things up again the way they used to be. Then I'll come and visit you, if your wife is nice.'

'You should come and visit me now,' said Levin. 'We'd settle in together very cosily!'

'I would come and visit you if I knew I wouldn't find Sergey Ivanich there.'

'You won't find him there. I live completely independently from him.'

'Yes, but you have still got to choose between me and him, whatever you say,' he said, looking timidly into his brother's eyes. Konstantin found this timidity touching.

'If you want to know my true feelings on that matter, let me tell you that I don't side with either you or Sergey Ivanich in your argument with him. You are both wrong. You are more outwardly wrong, and he is more inwardly wrong.'

'Aha! You've understood that, you really have?' exclaimed Nikolay jubilantly.

'But if you want to know, I personally cherish my friendship with you more, because . . .'

'Why do you, why?'

Konstantin could not say that he cherished it more because Nikolay was unhappy and in need of friendship. But Nikolay realized this was exactly what he wanted to say, and, frowning, he reached for the vodka again.

'That's enough, Nikolay Dmitrich!' said Marya Nikolayevna, stretching her plump, bare arm towards the decanter.

'Leave it! Don't nag me! I'll hit you!' he said.

Marya Nikolayevna's meek and kind smile transferred to Nikolay, and she took the vodka.

'Do you think she doesn't understand?' he said. 'She understands all this better than any of us. There is something kind and good about her, don't you think?'

'You haven't been to Moscow before?' Konstantin asked her in order to say something, using the polite form of address.

'Don't address her formally. She's scared of that. No one has addressed her formally except the magistrate when she was taken to court for wanting to leave the house of sin. Good gracious, there is so much nonsense in the world!' he suddenly exclaimed. 'All these new institutions, the magistrates, the zemstvo, it's all appalling!'

And he started to talk about his altercations with the new institutions.

Konstantin Levin listened to him, and the denial of sense in all the public institutions, a view he shared and often articulated, now sounded unpleasant coming from his brother's mouth.

'We'll understand it all in the next world,' he said jokingly.

'In the next world? Oh, I'm not fond of the next world! Not fond at all,' he said, fastening his frightened eyes on to his brother's face. 'You'd think it would be good to leave behind all this mess and mis-understanding, both other people's and your own, but I am afraid of death, I'm very afraid of death.' He shuddered. 'Come on, you must drink something. Do you want some champagne? Or maybe we should go somewhere. Let's go to the gypsies! You know, I've taken a great liking to gypsies and Russian songs.'

His speech was becoming slurred, and he started jumping from one subject to another. With Masha's assistance, Konstantin persuaded him not to go out anywhere, and put him to bed, completely drunk.

Masha promised to write to Konstantin in case of need, and to try and persuade Nikolay Levin to go and live with his brother.

26

IN the morning Konstantin Levin left Moscow, and by evening he had arrived home. During the journey he talked to the other passengers in his compartment about politics, about the new railways, and just as in Moscow, he was overwhelmed by a confusion of concepts, dissatisfaction with himself, and shame about something; but when he got out at his station and recognized his one-eyed coachman Ignat with the collar of his kaftan turned up, when he saw his upholstered sleigh in the dim light cast by the station windows, his horses with braided tails, and the rings and tassels on their harness, and when Ignat the coachman started telling him the village news while they were loading up, about the contractor arriving and Pava calving, he felt the confusion slowly unravelling, and the shame and dissatisfaction with himself beginning to recede. He felt that at the mere sight of Ignat and the horses; but when he put on the sheepskin coat brought for him, sat down in the sleigh, all bundled up, and set off, mulling over the instructions that needed to be given once he was home, and keeping an eye on the outrunner, a broken-winded but still lively former saddle-horse from the Don, he began to understand what had happened to him in a completely different way. He felt himself again, and did not want to be different. He now just wanted to be better than he was before. Firstly, he decided from that day on that he would no longer pin his hopes on the exceptional happiness which marriage was supposed to bring him, and as a result of that would not be so dismissive of the present. Secondly, he would never again allow himself to be carried away by vile passion, memory of which had so tormented him when he was about to propose. Next, remembering his brother Nikolay, he made a pact with himself that he would never again allow himself to forget him, but would keep track of him and not let him out of his sight, so he would be ready to help out when things became difficult for him. And that would be soon, he could feel that. Then what his brother had said about communism, which he had been so flippant about, was also now causing him to reflect.

He thought the idea of altering economic conditions was nonsense, but he had always been conscious of his wealth in comparison to the poverty of the people, and he now resolved that in order to feel he was being completely just, although he had worked hard before and did not live extravagantly, he would now work even harder, and would allow himself even fewer luxuries. And all this seemed so easy to take on that he spent the entire journey lost in the most pleasant daydreams. He arrived home some time after eight in the evening with a buoyant feeling of hope for a new and better life.

Light from the windows of the room of his old nanny, Agafya Mikhailovna, who acted as his housekeeper, was falling on to the snow in the courtyard in front of the house. She was not yet asleep. After being woken by her, Kuzma ran barefoot and sleepy out on to the porch. Laska, his setter bitch, almost knocked Kuzma down as she raced out too, yelping; she rubbed herself against his knees, and jumped up, wanting but not daring to put her front paws on his chest.

'You've come back quickly, sir,' said Agafya Mikhailovna.

'Got homesick, Agafya Mikhailovna. Nice to be away, but it's nicer at home,' he replied and went into his study.

The study was slowly lit up by the candle that was brought in. Familiar details emerged: deer antlers, bookshelves, the shiny stove with the vent that had long been in need of repair, his father's sofa, the big desk, an open book on the desk, a broken ashtray, a notebook with his handwriting. When he saw all this, he surrendered to a moment of doubt about whether he could create that new life he had been dreaming about during his journey home. It was as if all these traces of his life had grabbed hold of him and were saying: 'No, you'll never get away from us or be any different, but you'll be just the same as you have always been: with your doubts and eternal dissatisfaction with yourself, your vain attempts to improve and your failures, and your eternal expectation of a happiness which can never possibly be granted to you.'

But that was just his possessions talking, while another voice in his heart was saying that he should not give in to the past, and could make whatever he wished of himself. And heeding this voice, he went over to the corner where he had two heavy dumb-bells, and started doing lifting exercises, trying to instil some vigour into himself. Footsteps creaked outside the door. He hurriedly put down the dumb-bells.

The steward came in and said that everything, thank goodness, was fine, but reported that the buckwheat had got slightly burnt in the new kiln. This news annoyed Levin. The new dryer had been built and partly invented by Levin. The steward had always been against this kiln, and was now announcing with hidden triumph that the buckwheat had burned. Levin was firmly convinced that if it had burned, it was only because the instructions he had given a hundred times had not been carried out. He became cross, and he reprimanded the steward. But there had been one important and joyous event: Pava, his best and most valuable cow, who had been bought at a show, had calved.

'Kuzma, hand me my sheepskin. And get them to bring a lantern, I'm going to take a look,' he said to the steward.

The cattle-shed for the most valuable cows was right behind the house. Going across the yard past the snowdrift by the lilac, he walked up to the shed. When the frozen door was opened there was a warm, steamy smell of manure, and the cows, startled by the unfamiliar light from the lantern, stirred on the fresh straw. There was a brief glimpse of the smooth, broad, black-and-white back of a Friesian. Berkut, the bull, was lying with his ring in his nose and seemed to want to get up, but had second thoughts, and only snorted a couple of times as they walked past. Pava, the red beauty, huge as a hippopotamus, her back turned, was protecting her calf from the intruders and nuzzling it.

Levin entered the stall, looked Pava over, and lifted the red-and-white calf on to its spindly long legs. The anxious Pava began to low, but calmed down when Levin moved the calf over to her, and after sighing deeply, she started licking it with her rough tongue. The calf pushed its nose under its mother's groin, looking for her udder, and twirled its little tail.

'Shine the light here, Fyodor, bring the lantern here,' said Levin, looking over the calf. 'Just like its mother! But she's got her father's coat. Very good-looking. Long and deep-flanked. Don't you think she's good-looking, Vasily Fyodorovich?' he said turning to the steward, completely reconciled with him about the buckwheat thanks to his joy about the calf.

'How could she be ugly coming from that stock? Semyon the contractor came the day after you left, by the way. You'll have to settle up with him, Konstantin Dmitrich,' said the steward. 'I told you before about the machine.'

This one question plunged Levin into all the details of managing his estate, which was large and complicated, so from the cowshed he went straight to the office, and after talking to the steward and Semyon the contractor, he returned to his house and went straight upstairs into the drawing room.

27

THE house was large and old, and although Levin lived on his own, he heated and occupied all of it. He knew this was stupid, and that it was even quite bad and flew in the face of his current new plans, but this house was a whole world for Levin. It was a world in which his father and mother had lived and died. They had lived a life which to Levin seemed the acme of perfection, and which he dreamed of reviving with his own wife and with his family.

Levin could hardly remember his mother. The idea of her was a sacred memory for him, and in his imagination his future wife had to be a replica of that enchanting, holy ideal of womanhood which his mother had been for him.

Not only could he not imagine loving a woman outside marriage, but first and foremost imagined having a family, and only then the woman who would give him a family. His ideas about marriage were therefore not like those of the majority of his acquaintances, for whom marriage was one of many routine undertakings; for Levin it was the main undertaking in life, on which depended all happiness. And now he had to renounce it!

After he had come into the small drawing room where he always drank tea, and had settled into his armchair with a book, and Agafya Mikhailovna had brought him his tea with her usual 'I'll just sit down for a minute, sir,' and had sat down on the chair by the window, he felt that, however strange it was, he had not parted from his dreams and indeed could not live without them. Whether it be with her or someone else, it was going to happen. He read his book and thought about what he was reading, stopping in order to listen to Agafya Mikhailovna, who was chattering away incessantly; and at the same time various disconnected pictures of the estate and his future family life came into his mind. He felt that deep within his soul something was taking shape, settling down, and falling into place.

He listened to Agafya Mikhailovna talking about how Prokhor had forgotten God and was drinking round the clock on the money Levin had given him to buy a horse, and had almost beaten his wife to death; he listened and read his book, and retraced his whole sequence of thoughts stimulated by what he was reading. This was Tyndall's book about heat.* He was recalling his censure of Tyndall for being so smug about conducting such clever experiments, and lacking a philosophical approach. And then suddenly a joyous thought came bobbing into his mind: 'In two years I will have two Friesians, Pava herself may still be alive, and with twelve of Berkut's young daughters, plus these three to put on show—wonderful!' He picked up his book again.

'Well, all right, electricity and heat are one and the same thing; but is it possible to substitute one quantity for another in order to solve a problem in an equation? No. So what does that mean? The connection between all forces of nature is felt instinctively anyway . . . It is particularly nice that Pava's daughter is going to be a red-and-white cow, and the whole herd, to which these three will be added . . . It's excellent! I can see myself going out with my wife and our guests to greet the herd . . . My wife will say: "Kostya and I reared this little calf like a child." "How can you find this so interesting?" a guest will ask her. "I'm interested in everything that interests him." But who is she?' And he remembered what happened in Moscow . . . 'Well, what can I do? It's not my fault. But now everything will proceed differently. It's nonsense to think that life won't allow it, that the past won't allow it. I must do my utmost to live a better life, a much better life . . .' He lifted his head and became pensive. Old Laska, who had still not fully digested the joyous event of his arrival and had run off to go and bark in the yard, came back wagging her tail and bringing in with her the smell of fresh air, and she now went up to him and pushed her head under his hand, whimpering plaintively and demanding that he pet her.

'She can almost talk,' said Agafya Mikhailovna. 'Not bad for a dog . . . After all, she does understand her master has come home and is sad.'

'Why do you say that?'

'Do you think I can't see, sir? Ought to know the gentry by now. Grew up with them since I was a mite. Not to worry, sir. The main thing is to be healthy and have a pure heart.'

Levin stared at her, amazed that she could read his thoughts.

'Well, how about another nice cup of tea?' she said, and she picked up the cup and went out.

Laska was still pushing her head under his hand. He stroked her, and she immediately curled up into a ball by his feet, resting her head on her outstretched back paw. And as a sign that everything was now all right in the world, she opened her mouth a fraction, and after arranging her sticky lips better around her old teeth, smacked them and settled down into a state of blissful rest. Levin watched these last movements of hers closely.

'I'm just the same!' he said to himself. 'Just the same! Never mind . . . All is well.'

28

EARLY in the morning after the ball, Anna Arkadyevna sent her husband a telegram to say she was leaving Moscow that same day.

'No, I must go, I really must,' she said, explaining her change of plan to her sister-in-law, in a tone implying she had remembered so many things to do there were too many to count. 'No, it's best if I go today!'

Stepan Arkadyich was not dining at home, but had promised to come home so he could see his sister off at seven o'clock.

Kitty also did not come over, having sent a note to say she had a headache. Dolly and Anna ate on their own, with the children and the English governess. Whether it was because the children were fickle or very sensitive, and felt that Anna on this day was not at all like how she had been on the one when they had so fallen in love with her, and was no longer interested in them, they abruptly put a halt to their game with their aunt and their fondness for her, and were completely unconcerned about her leaving. Anna was busy all morning with preparations for her departure. She wrote notes to her Moscow acquaintances, settled her accounts, and packed. Dolly had the general impression she was not in a calm frame of mind, but in that state of unease Dolly knew well from her own experience, and which does not materialize without cause and is more often than not a mask for dissatisfaction with oneself. After dinner Anna went to her room to get dressed, and Dolly followed her.

'How strange you are today!' Dolly said to her.

'Strange? You think so? I'm not strange, but I don't feel right. It happens to me sometimes. I keep wanting to cry. It's very silly, but it does pass,' said Anna quickly, and she bent her flushed face over the miniature bag into which she was packing a nightcap and some lawn handkerchiefs. Her eyes were shining with a particular sparkle and they kept filling with tears. 'I so didn't want to leave Petersburg, and now I don't want to leave here.'

'You came here and did a good deed,' said Dolly, examining her closely.

Anna looked at her with eyes wet with tears.

'Don't say that, Dolly. I didn't do anything, and I couldn't have done anything. I often wonder why people have conspired to spoil me with flattery. What did I do, and what could I have done? You found enough love in your heart to forgive . . .'

'Heaven knows what would have happened without you! You are so lucky, Anna!' said Dolly. 'Everything in your soul is so clear and good.'

'Everyone has *skeletons*[1] in their soul, as the English say.'

'What *skeletons* do you have? Everything is so clear with you.'

'Oh, I have them!' Anna said suddenly, and unexpectedly after her tears, a sly, humorous smile wrinkled her lips.

'So your *skeletons* are funny, not grim,' said Dolly, smiling.

'No, they are grim. Do you know why I am going today and not tomorrow? It's a confession which has been weighing on me, and I want to make it to you,' said Anna, leaning back decisively into her armchair and looking straight into Dolly's eyes.

And to her amazement Dolly saw that Anna had blushed to her ears, to the curly black ringlets of hair on her neck.

'Yes,' continued Anna. 'Do you know why Kitty did not come to dinner? She is jealous of me. I have spoiled . . . I was the reason why that ball was a torment rather than a joy for her. But it's not my fault, it really isn't, or maybe just slightly,' she said, drawing out the word 'slightly' in a high-pitched voice.

'Oh, you sounded just like Stiva when you said that!' said Dolly, laughing.

Anna was offended.

'Oh, no, no! I am not like Stiva,' she said, frowning. 'That is why I am telling you this, because I will not allow myself even for a moment to doubt myself,' said Anna.

But the moment she uttered those words, she felt they were untrue; she not only did doubt herself, but the thought of Vronsky gave her a thrill, and she was leaving earlier than she had wanted purely to avoid meeting him again.

'Yes, Stiva told me that you danced the mazurka with him, and that he . . .'

'You cannot imagine how absurdly it turned out. I was only thinking about matchmaking, and then suddenly it was something quite different. Maybe against my will, I . . .'

She blushed and broke off.

'Oh, they feel that immediately!' said Dolly.

'But I would be in despair if there was anything serious in it on his part,' said Anna, interrupting her. 'And I am sure that it will all be forgotten and Kitty will stop hating me.'

'Actually, Anna, to tell you the truth, I do not really want this marriage for Kitty. And it's better that it should not work out, if he, Vronsky, can fall in love with you in one day.'

---

[1] [English in the original.]

'Oh, heavens, that would be too silly!' said Anna, and a deep flush of pleasure appeared on her face again when she heard the thought absorbing her uttered out loud. 'So, there you are, I am leaving, having made an enemy of Kitty, whom I have come to love. Oh, how lovely she is! But Dolly, you will put things right, won't you?'

Dolly could barely suppress a smile. She loved Anna, but it was nice for her to see that she too had weaknesses.

'An enemy? That's not possible.'

'I would so like you all to love me as I love you; and now I love you all even more,' she said with tears in her eyes. 'Ah, how foolish I am being today!'

She dabbed her face with a handkerchief, and started to get dressed.

Just as she was about to depart, Stepan Arkadyich arrived, late, with a red, cheery face and a smell of wine and cigars.

Anna's emotional state communicated itself also to Dolly, and as she embraced her sister-in-law for the last time, she whispered:

'Anna, remember: I will never forget what you have done for me. And remember that I love you, and will always love you as my best friend!'

'I don't understand why,' said Anna, kissing her and trying to hide her tears.

'You do understand, I know you do. Farewell, my dearest!'

29

'WELL, it's all over, and thank heavens for that!' was the first thought which occurred to Anna Arkadyevna when she said goodbye for the last time to her brother, who stood blocking the way into the carriage until the third bell.* She sat down on her seat, next to Annushka, and looked around her in the half-light of the sleeping-compartment. 'Thank goodness, tomorrow I will see Seryozha and Alexey Alexandrovich, and my nice, ordinary life will go on as before.'

Still in the same preoccupied state she had been in all that day, Anna took pleasure and particular care settling herself for the journey; with her small, deft hands she fastened and unfastened her little red bag, took a small cushion and placed it on her knees, neatly wrapped up her legs, and sat back calmly. A lady in poor health was already getting ready to go to sleep. Two other ladies started talking to her, and a fat old woman was wrapping up her legs and passing comment on the heating. Anna said a few words in reply to the ladies, but not foreseeing any interest in the conversation, asked Annushka to get out a small lamp, attached it to the arm of her seat, and took out a paper-knife and an English novel from her bag. At first she found it hard to read. First she was hindered by the noise and bustle; then, when the train departed, she could not help listening to the various sounds; then her attention was distracted by the snow driving against the left-hand window and sticking to the glass, by the sight of the muffled conductor going by, one side of him covered with snow, and by conversations about the terrible snowstorm now raging outside. After that everything repeated itself endlessly; the same jolting and banging, the same snow on the window, the same rapid transitions from steaming heat to cold, and back to heat, the same people flitting past in the semi-darkness, and the same voices, and Anna started to read and understand what she was reading. Annushka had already dozed off, holding the little red bag on her lap with her broad hands in gloves, one of which was torn. Anna Arkadyevna read and understood, but it was unpleasant for her to read, that is, to follow the reflection of other people's lives. She had too great a longing to live herself. If she read about the heroine of the novel caring for a sick man, she wanted to tiptoe with silent steps about the sick man's room; if she read about a Member of Parliament giving a speech, she wanted to give that speech; if she read about Lady Mary riding to hounds, teasing her sister-in-law and amazing everybody with her daring, she wanted to do all that herself. But there was nothing she could do and, running her small hands over the smooth paper-knife, she returned to her reading with greater concentration.

The hero of the novel had already begun to attain his English fortune, a baronetcy and an estate, and Anna was experiencing a desire to go with him to this estate, when she suddenly felt that he ought to feel ashamed and that she was ashamed for the same reason. But what should he be ashamed of? 'And what exactly am I ashamed of?' she asked herself in aggrieved surprise. She put down her book and leaned back in her seat, gripping the paper-knife tightly in both hands. There had been nothing shameful. She sifted through all her Moscow memories. They were all good, all pleasant. She remembered the ball, she remembered Vronsky and his love-stricken, submissive face, and she remembered all her interactions with him; there had been nothing shameful. But it was also at this particular stage in her recollections that her feeling of shame increased, as if some kind of inner voice was saying to her right at the moment when she remembered Vronsky: 'Warm, very warm, hot.' 'Well, then?' she said to herself resolutely as she shuffled in her seat. 'What can it mean? Am I really afraid to look at this directly? Well, then? Can there really be, and could there ever be any kind of relations between me and that officer boy which might be different to those with every other acquaintance?' She smiled contemptuously and picked up her book again, but now she definitely could not understand what she was reading. She ran her paper-knife over the window, then pressed its smooth and cold surface against her cheek, and almost laughed out loud from the joy suddenly overcoming her for no apparent reason. She felt that her nerves were being stretched ever more tautly, like strings on some kind of twisting pegs. She felt her eyes opening wider and wider, her fingers and toes twitching nervously, something in her chest constricting her breathing, and every image and sound in this flickering half-light striking her with exceptional sharpness. She kept being visited by moments of doubt as to whether the carriage was moving forwards, or backwards, or standing stock-still. Was that Annushka beside her or a stranger? 'Over there on the armrest, is that a fur coat or an animal? And what am I doing here? Is this me or someone else?' She was afraid of surrendering to this oblivion. But something was luring her into it, and she could surrender to it or resist it at will. In order to try and come to her senses, she stood up, threw aside her rug, and removed the cape from her warm dress. For a moment she did come to her senses, and realized that the emaciated peasant in the long nankeen coat with a missing button who had come in was the stoker, that he was looking at the thermometer, and that the wind and the snow had burst in through the door after him, but then everything became confused again . . . The long-waisted peasant started gnawing at something in the wall, the old lady started stretching her legs out the whole length of the carriage, filling it with a black cloud; then there was a terrible screeching and banging sound, as if someone were being torn to pieces; then there was a blinding red light, and then everything was shut out by a wall. Anna felt she had vanished. But all this was enjoyable, not frightening. The voice of the muffled, snow-covered man shouted out something above her ear. She stood up and collected herself; she realized they had arrived at a station, and that this was the conductor. She asked Annushka to hand her back the cape she had taken off, and her scarf, put them on, and headed for the door.

'Would you like to get out?' asked Annushka.

'Yes, I'd like some fresh air. It's very hot in here.'

And she opened the door. The blizzard and the wind hurled themselves at her and jostled with her for the door. And she found this enjoyable too. She opened the door and stepped outside. As if it had

been waiting expressly for her, the wind whistled gleefully and tried
to snatch her and carry her off, but she took hold of the cold doorpost
with a strong hand, stepped down on to the platform, holding on to her
dress, and went behind the carriage. The wind had been strong on the
steps, but on the platform behind the carriages it was calm. She took
pleasure in inhaling the snowy, frosty air deep into her chest, and as
she stood beside the carriage she surveyed the platform and the lit-up
station.

30

THE terrible storm was tearing and whistling around the corner of the
station between the wheels of the carriages and along the posts. Carriages,
posts, people—everything that was visible was covered on one side with
snow, and being continually covered with more. The storm would die
down for a moment, but then it would blow up again in such gusts it
seemed impossible to withstand it. Meanwhile there were some people
running about, talking cheerfully, making the boards of the platform
creak, and endlessly opening and closing the main doors. The hunched
shadow of a man slipped past beneath her feet, and there were sounds
of a hammer striking iron. 'Let's have the telegram!' an angry voice
rang out of the stormy darkness on the other side. 'This way, please! No.
28!' shouted various other voices, and people ran past, all wrapped-up
and covered in snow. Two gentlemen with cigarettes burning in their
mouths walked past her. She took another breath in order to get her fill
of fresh air, and had already taken her hand out of her muff in order
to grasp the post and proceed into the carriage when another man in
a military greatcoat just beside her blocked out the flickering light of
the lamp. She looked round and immediately recognized Vronsky's
face. Putting his hand to the peak of his cap, he bowed to her and asked
if there was anything she needed, and could he be of service to her?
She gazed at him intently for quite a long time without replying, and
despite the shadow in which he stood, she saw, or imagined she saw,
the expression both on his face and in his eyes. It was once again that
same expression of reverent admiration which had so affected her the
previous evening. She had told herself more than once these last days
and just now, that to her Vronsky was simply one of the hundreds of
endlessly indistinguishable young men who were to be encountered
everywhere, and that she would never allow herself even to think about
him; but now, from the first moment she set eyes on him, she was

overcome with a feeling of jubilant pride. She did not need to ask why he was there. She knew, just as surely as if he had told her, that he was there to be where she was.

'I didn't know you were travelling. Why are you travelling?' she asked, lowering the hand which had been about to take hold of the post. Her face radiated irrepressible joy and excitement.

'Why am I travelling?' he replied, looking straight into her eyes. 'You know that I am travelling to be where you are,' he said. 'I can't do otherwise.'

And right at that moment, as if it had overcome some obstacle, the wind hurled down snow from the roof of the carriage and rattled a loose sheet of iron, while up in front, the locomotive's low whistle started to wail mournfully and gloomily. The full horror of the snowstorm seemed even more splendid to her now. He had said precisely what her soul desired, but which she feared with her reason. She did not answer, and he saw a struggle in her face.

'Forgive me if what I said displeased you,' he said meekly.

He spoke courteously and respectfully, but so firmly and insistently that for a long time she could not say anything in reply.

'What you are saying is wrong, and I must ask you, if you are a good man, to forget what you have said, as I will,' she said finally.

'I will never ever forget a single word or gesture of yours, nor can I . . .'

'That's enough, enough!' she cried out, vainly trying to impart a severe expression to her face, which he was eagerly scrutinizing. And taking the cold post in her hand, she went up the steps and quickly stepped into the vestibule of the carriage. But she paused in this small vestibule while she went over in her mind what had happened. Without being able to remember what either of them had said, she understood through her feelings that this brief exchange had brought them terribly close; and she was both frightened and overjoyed by this. After standing there for a few seconds, she went into the compartment and sat down in her seat. That magical, tense state which had tormented her before had not only returned but had intensified, and had reached the point where she feared something too taut inside her might snap at any moment. She did not sleep all night. But there was nothing unpleasant or gloomy in the tension or the dreams which filled her imagination; on the contrary, there was something joyous, searing, and exciting. Towards morning Anna dozed off as she sat in her seat, and when she woke up it was already broad daylight and the train was approaching Petersburg. She was immediately inundated with thoughts of home, her husband, her son, and the concerns of the coming day and those to follow.

In Petersburg, as soon as the train stopped and she stepped out, the first face which caught her attention was that of her husband. 'Oh goodness! How did he come to have ears like that?' she thought, looking at his cold and imposing figure, and particularly at the cartilages of his ears propping up the brim of his round hat, which now startled her. When he caught sight of her he came towards her, pursing his lips into his usual ironic smile and looking straight at her with his large, tired eyes. An unpleasant kind of feeling gripped her heart when she met his obdurate and weary gaze, as if she had expected him to look different. She was particularly struck by the feeling of dissatisfaction with herself which she experienced on meeting him. That feeling was a familiar one, of long-standing, which was similar to the state of pretence she experienced in her relationship with her husband; but whereas she had not noticed this feeling before, she was clearly and painfully aware of it now.

'Yes, as you see, your devoted husband, as devoted as in the first year of marriage, has been burning with desire to see you,' he said in his languid, high-pitched voice, and in the tone he almost always used with her, full of scorn for anyone who might actually speak like that.

'Is Seryozha well?' she asked.

'And this is the only reward for my ardour?' he said. 'He's well, quite well . . .'

31

VRONSKY did not even try to fall asleep at all that night. He sat in his seat, either staring straight ahead of him or inspecting the people coming in and going out, and if previously he surprised and unnerved people he did not know with his appearance of unshakeable composure, he now seemed even more haughty and aloof. He looked at people as if they were objects. The nervous young man who worked in the district court sitting opposite him took a violent dislike to him on account of that look. The young man had asked him for a light, and tried striking up a conversation with him, and had even given him a nudge to make him feel he was a person, not an object, but Vronsky continued to look at him in just the same way, as if he was a lamp-post, and the young man scowled, feeling he was losing his self-possession under the stress of not being acknowledged as a person, and could not fall asleep because of it.

Vronsky was not able to see anything or anyone. He felt like a tsar, not because he believed he had made an impression on Anna—he did not believe that yet—but because the impression she had made on him inspired him with happiness and pride.

What would come of all this he did not know, and did not even consider. He felt that all his previously dissipated, disparate energies had converged, and were now being directed with a terrifying force towards one blessed goal. And he was happy about that. He only knew that he had told her the truth, that he was travelling to be where she was, and that he now derived all his happiness in life, the only meaning in his life, from seeing and hearing her. And when he got out of the carriage at Bologovo* to drink some seltzer-water, and caught sight of Anna, his first words to her involuntarily told her exactly what he was thinking. And he was glad he had said that to her, that she now knew it, and was thinking about it. He did not sleep all night. After he had returned to his compartment, he endlessly went over in his mind all the situations in which he had seen her, everything she had said, and pictures of a possible future floated through his imagination, causing his heart to skip a beat.

When he got out of the carriage in Petersburg, he felt as invigorated and fresh after his sleepless night as after taking a cold bath. He stopped by his carriage to wait for her to get out. 'I'll see her again,' he said to himself, unable to stop himself smiling, 'I'll see her walk, her face; she will say something, turn her head, cast a glance, maybe smile.' But before he caught sight of her, he caught sight of her husband, whom the station-master was courteously escorting through the crowd. 'Oh yes! The husband!' Only now did Vronsky clearly understand for the first time that her husband was a person connected to her. He knew she had a husband, but he had not believed in his existence, and only truly believed in him when he saw him, with his head, his shoulders, and his legs in black trousers; especially when he saw this husband calmly take her arm with a proprietary air.

After seeing Alexey Alexandrovich, with his Petersburg-fresh complexion and his austerely self-assured figure, in a round hat and with a slightly protruding back, he believed in him and experienced an unpleasant feeling, like that which would be experienced by a person dying of thirst who finally reaches a spring only to find a dog, a sheep, or a pig there which has drunk from it and fouled the water. The way Alexey Alexandrovich walked, twisting his whole pelvis and splaying his feet, particularly offended Vronsky's sensibilities. He believed only he had the incontestable right to love her. But she was just the same, and the sight of her had just the same effect on him, rejuvenating him physically, exciting him, and filling his soul with happiness. He instructed his German valet, who had come running up from second-class, to take his things and go on ahead, while he himself went over to her. He witnessed the first encounter between husband and wife, and with the perceptiveness of someone in love noticed the signs of slight uneasiness with which she spoke to her husband. 'No, she does not and cannot love him,' he decided to himself.

As he approached Anna Arkadyevna from behind, he noticed with delight that she could sense his approach and wanted to turn round, and having recognized him, she turned to her husband again.

'Did you have a good night?' he asked, bowing to her and her husband together, and leaving Alexey Alexandrovich to assume this bow as intended for him, and to recognize him or not, as he saw fit.

'Very good, thank you,' she answered.

Her face seemed tired, and lacked that sparkle of animation that before had clamoured to express itself either in her smile or her eyes; but something gleamed in her eyes for a brief moment as she glanced at him, and despite the fact that this light was immediately extinguished, he was happy to have had that moment. She glanced at her husband to ascertain whether he knew Vronsky. Alexey Alexandrovich looked at Vronsky with distaste, vaguely remembering who he was. Vronsky's composure and self-confidence now came up against the glacial self-confidence of Alexey Alexandrovich like a scythe on stone.

'Count Vronsky,' said Anna.

'Ah! We are acquainted, I believe,' said Alexey Alexandrovich indifferently, holding out his hand. 'You set off with the mother and returned with the son,' he said, enunciating distinctly, as if each word was worth its weight in gold. 'You must be returning from leave, I suppose?' he asked, and without waiting for an answer, asked his wife in his jocular tone: 'So, were there many tears shed in Moscow at your parting?'

By addressing these words to his wife, he let Vronsky perceive that he wished to be left alone, and he turned to him and touched his hat; but Vronsky addressed Anna Arkadyevna:

'I hope I may have the honour of calling on you,' he said.

Alexey Alexandrovich glanced at Vronsky with weary eyes.

'Delighted,' he said coldly. 'We are at home on Mondays.' Having dismissed Vronsky altogether, he then said to his wife: 'And how wonderful that I had precisely half an hour to spare so I could come and meet you, and could show you my devotion,' he continued in the same jocular tone.

'You place too much emphasis on your devotion for me to appreciate it fully,' she said in the same jocular tone, unable to stop herself listening to the sounds of Vronsky's footsteps as he walked behind them. 'But what is that to me?' she thought, and she started to ask her husband how Seryozha had spent his time without her.

'Oh, splendidly! Mariette says that he was very sweet and . . . I have to disappoint you . . . he did not miss you, not like your husband did. But *merci* once again, my dear, for making me the present of a day. Our dear samovar will be delighted . . .' (Samovar was what he called the famous Countess Lydia Ivanovna, because she was always becoming heated about everything and bubbling over.) She has been asking about you. And you know, if I may be so bold as to make a suggestion, you should go and see her today. You know how she takes everything to heart. At the moment she is concerned with the Oblonskys' reconciliation, apart from all her other worries.'

Countess Lydia Ivanovna was a friend of her husband's, and the centre of the circle in Petersburg society with which Anna was most closely connected through her husband.

'But I wrote to her.'

'But she needs to know all the details. Do go over if you are not too tired, my dear. Well, Kondraty will give you the carriage, as I have a committee to go to. I won't be dining alone any more,' Alexey Alexandrovich continued, no longer in his jocular tone. 'You won't believe how accustomed I have become . . .'

And pressing her hand for a long time, he helped her into the carriage with a special smile.

32

THE first person to meet Anna at home was her son. He leapt down the stairs, despite the cries of his governess, and with a wild delight shrieked: 'Mama, Mama!' He ran up to her and hung on her neck.

'I told you it was Mama!' he shouted to the governess. 'I knew!'

Her son, just like her husband, also produced in Anna a feeling akin to disappointment. She had imagined him to be better than he was in reality. She had to descend to reality in order to enjoy him as he was. But he was also adorable as he was, with his blond curly hair, blue eyes, and plump, shapely little legs in tightly pulled-up stockings.

Anna experienced an almost physical pleasure in feeling his closeness and his affection, as well as a moral serenity when she encountered his ingenuous, trusting, and loving gaze, and heard his naive questions. Anna got out the presents which Dolly's children had sent, and told her son about how there was a girl in Moscow called Tanya, and how this Tanya could read, and was even teaching the other children.

'So am I worse than her?' asked Seryozha.

'To me, you're better than anyone else in the world.'

'I know that,' said Seryozha, smiling.

Anna had not managed to finish drinking her coffee before Countess Lydia Ivanovna was announced. Countess Lydia Ivanovna was a tall, plump woman with an unhealthy, sallow complexion and lovely, dreamy black eyes. Anna was fond of her, but today it was as if she saw her with all her flaws for the first time.

'Well, my friend, did you take the olive branch?' asked Countess Lydia Ivanovna as soon as she entered the room.

'Yes, that's all over, but none of it was quite as grave as we thought,' answered Anna. 'My *belle soeur* is generally a bit too intransigent.'

But Countess Lydia Ivanovna, who took an interest in everything which did not concern her, and had a habit of never listening to what did interest her, interrupted Anna: 'Yes, there is much sorrow and evil in the world, and I am so worn out today.'

'What's happened?' asked Anna, trying to restrain a smile.

'I am beginning to tire of all this pointless clashing of swords in the name of truth, and sometimes I feel quite undone. The project with the Little Sisters' (this was a philanthropic, religious, and patriotic institution) 'ought to have gone splendidly, but you can never do anything with these gentlemen,' added Countess Lydia Ivanovna, in mock resignation to fate. 'They seized on the idea, distorted it, and are now discussing it in such a superficial, trivial way. A handful of people, including your husband, understand the full importance of this mission, but the others are just abandoning it. Pravdin wrote to me yesterday . . .'

Pravdin was a famous Pan-Slavist,* who lived abroad, and Countess Lydia Ivanovna relayed the contents of his letter.

Then the Countess recounted other obstacles and intrigues against the plan to unite the churches, and left in a hurry, since that day she still had to attend a meeting of a society and be at the Slavic Committee.

'But all this was there before; so why didn't I notice it before?' Anna said to herself. 'Or was she particularly irritated today? It really is quite funny: her aim is to do good works and she is a Christian, but she is always getting cross, she always has enemies, and the disputes are always about Christianity and good works.'

After Countess Lydia Ivanovna left, an acquaintance who was the wife of a director arrived, and she relayed all the Petersburg news. At three o'clock she also left, promising to come for dinner. Alexey Alexandrovich was at the ministry. Left alone, Anna used the time before dinner to sit with her son while he ate (he dined separately), put her things into order, and read and answer the notes and letters which had piled up on her desk.

The feeling of groundless shame she had experienced during the journey, as well as the anxiety, had completely disappeared. Back in her usual routine, she once more felt steadfast and beyond reproach.

She recalled her state of mind the previous day with amazement. 'What exactly happened? Nothing. Vronsky said something foolish, which was easy to put a stop to, and I answered as I should have done. There is no need to tell my husband, nor should I. Talking about it would mean attaching importance to something which has none.' She remembered recounting to her husband how one of his subordinates in Petersburg had once almost made a confession of love to her, and how Alexey Alexandrovich had replied that every woman in society was liable to encounter this sort of thing, but that he had complete faith in her discretion, and would never allow himself to demean either of them by being jealous. 'So there's no reason to tell him? No, and thank goodness there is nothing to tell anyway,' she said to herself.

33

ALEXEY ALEXANDROVICH returned from the ministry at four o'clock, but as often happened, he did not have time to go in and see her. He went straight to his study to receive the petitioners who were waiting for him, and to sign some papers brought by his secretary. Coming to dinner that evening (there were always about three people dining with the Karenins) were an old lady who was Alexey Alexandrovich's cousin, the department director and his wife, and a young man who had been recommended to Alexey Alexandrovich for a post. Anna went into the drawing room to entertain them. At five o'clock, before the bronze Peter-the-Great clock had finished striking five times, Alexey Alexandrovich appeared wearing white tie and tails with his two stars,* as he needed to leave straight after dinner. Every minute of Alexey

Alexandrovich's life was allotted and accounted for. And he maintained the strictest punctuality so that he could manage to achieve everything on his agenda each day. 'No haste and no rest,' was his motto. He came into the room wiping his brow, bowed to everyone, and hurriedly sat down, smiling at his wife.

'Yes, my solitude has ended. You wouldn't believe how awkward'— he stressed the word *awkward*—'one feels dining alone.'

During dinner he talked to his wife about Moscow affairs, and enquired after Stepan Arkadyich with an ironic smile; but the conversation was mostly a general one, about Petersburg official and public affairs. After dinner he spent half an hour with the guests, then pressed his wife's hand again with a smile, left, and went off to the Council. On this occasion Anna went neither to see Princess Betsy Tverskaya, who had heard of her arrival and invited her over that evening, nor to the theatre, where she had a box for that evening. The principal reason she did not go out was because the dress she had been counting on was not ready. Having occupied herself with her wardrobe after the guests had left, Anna had in fact become very angry. Generally expert in dressing inexpensively, before leaving for Moscow she had given three dresses to the seamstress for altering. The dresses needed to be altered in such a way that they would not be recognized, and were supposed to have been ready three days earlier. It turned out that two dresses were nowhere near finished, while the third had been altered, but not in the way Anna wanted. The seamstress came to explain, maintaining it would be better that way, and Anna flew into such a rage that she was ashamed to recall it later on. In order to calm down completely, she went into the nursery and spent the whole evening with her son; she put him to bed herself, made the sign of the cross over him, and covered him up with his blanket. She was glad she had not gone out anywhere and had spent the evening in such a pleasant way. She felt so light-hearted and calm, and saw so clearly that what had seemed so meaningful to her on the train was just another of those typically insignificant events in one's social life, and that she had no reason to feel ashamed, either on her own account or in respect of anyone else. Anna sat down by the fire with her English novel, and waited for her husband. At precisely half-past nine she heard him ring, and he came into the room.

'Here you are at last,' she said, holding out her hand to him.

He kissed her hand and sat down next to her.

'I can see that, on the whole, your trip was a success,' he said to her.

'Yes, very much so,' she replied, and started to tell him everything from the beginning: her journey with Countess Vronskaya, her arrival, and the incident at the railway station. Then she told him about her feelings of pity, first for her brother, and then for Dolly.

'I do not believe a person like that can be excused, even if he is your brother,' said Alexey Alexandrovich sternly.

Anna smiled. She realized that he had said that precisely to show that family considerations could not prevent him from expressing his sincere opinion. She knew this quality of her husband's, and she liked it.

'I am glad that everything ended happily and that you have come home,' he continued. 'Well, what are they saying there about the new statute I passed in the Council?'

Anna had not heard anything about this statute, and felt contrite to have so easily forgotten something which was so important to him.

'It's caused quite a stir here, however,' he said with a self-satisfied smile.

She could see that Alexey Alexandrovich wanted to tell her something about this matter which gratified him, and she drew the story out with questions. With the same self-satisfied smile he told her about the ovations he had received as a result of this statute being passed.

'I was very, very pleased. It shows that finally we are beginning to establish a sensible and robust view on this matter.'

After finishing a second glass of tea with cream and bread, Alexey Alexandrovich got up and went into his study.

'But you didn't go out anywhere; I expect you were bored?' he asked.

'Oh no!' she replied, getting up after him to escort him through the drawing room to his study. 'What are you reading at the moment?'

'I'm reading Duc de Lille's *Poésie des enfers** at the moment,' he replied. 'A very remarkable book.'

Anna smiled, as people do smile at the weaknesses of people they love, and putting her arm under his, she escorted him to the doors of his study. She knew his habit, which had become a necessity, of reading in the evening. She knew that, despite his official duties consuming almost all of his time, he considered it his duty to keep abreast of everything noteworthy appearing in the intellectual sphere. She also knew that books on politics, philosophy, and theology really did interest him, and that art was completely alien to his nature, but that despite this, or rather because of this, Alexey Alexandrovich never missed anything that created a stir in this area, and considered it his duty to read everything. She knew that in politics, philosophy, and theology, Alexey Alexandrovich either had doubts or was still searching; but where art

and poetry were concerned, and particularly music, which he had not
the first idea about, he had the most definite and firm opinions. He
liked talking about Shakespeare, Raphael, Beethoven, and the significance of the new schools in poetry and music, which were all classified
by him into a very clear sequence of development.

'Well, God bless you,' she said at the door of his study, where
a shaded candle and a carafe of water had already been prepared for
him next to his armchair. 'And I'm going to write to Moscow.'

He pressed her hand and kissed it again.

'All the same, he is a good man, trustworthy and kind, and remarkable in his own sphere,' said Anna to herself as she went back to her
room, as if defending him to someone who was accusing him and saying
he was impossible to love. 'But why do his ears stick out so strangely?
Or has he had his hair cut?'

On the dot of midnight, when Anna was still sitting at her desk,
finishing her letter to Dolly, she heard the sound of measured steps in
slippers, and Alexey Alexandrovich, washed and combed, came up to
her with a book under his arm.

'Come along now, it's time,' he said with a special smile, and proceeded into the bedroom.

'And what right did he have to look at him like that?' thought Anna,
remembering the glance Vronsky had given Alexey Alexandrovich.

After she had undressed, she went into the bedroom, but not only
was there none of that liveliness in her face which had sparkled in
her eyes and smile during her stay in Moscow, but on the contrary,
the light now seemed to have been extinguished in her or was hidden
somewhere far away.

34

WHEN he was departing from Petersburg, Vronsky had left his large
apartment on Morskaya Street* to his friend and favourite comrade
Petritsky.

Petritsky was a young lieutenant, not particularly distinguished, and
not only not rich but mired in debt, always drunk by evening, frequently
in the guard-house for various exploits both amusing and seedy, but
loved by his comrades and his superiors alike. When he drove up to his
apartment from the railway station towards noon, Vronsky saw a familiar hired carriage by the entrance. Even as he was ringing the bell, he
could hear behind the door men laughing, a woman's voice babbling in

French, and Petritsky shouting: 'If it's one of those scoundrels, don't let him in!' Vronsky told the batman not to announce him, and went quietly into the front room. Petritsky's lady-friend, Baroness Shilton, resplendent in her lilac satin dress, blonde hair, and pink-cheeked little face, was sitting at the round table making coffee and filling the whole room with her Parisian chatter, like a canary. Petritsky, in a greatcoat, and Captain Kamerovsky, in full uniform, probably just off duty, were sitting on either side of her.

'Bravo! Vronsky!' shouted out Petritsky, his chair clattering as he jumped up. 'The host himself! Baroness, some coffee for him from the new coffee-pot. We weren't expecting you! I hope you're pleased with the decoration of your study,' he said, indicating the Baroness. 'You do know each other, don't you?'

'I'll say!' said Vronsky, smiling happily, and pressing the Baroness's dainty little hand. 'Of course we do. Old friends.'

'You've just arrived home from a journey,' said the Baroness, 'so I must be off. Oh, I'll leave this very minute if I am in the way.'

'You are at home wherever you are, Baroness,' said Vronsky. 'Hello Kamerovsky,' he added, shaking Kamerovsky's hand coldly.

'Now you never seem to be able to say such nice things,' said the Baroness to Petritsky.

'You don't think so? After dinner I'll say no worse.'

'But it's not worth anything after dinner! Well, I'll make you some coffee, but in the meantime you go and wash and tidy up,' said the Baroness, sitting down again and carefully turning the screw in the new coffee-pot. 'Pierre, give me the coffee,' she said, turning to Petritsky, whom she called Pierre because of his surname, making no secret of her relations with him. 'I'll put in some more.'

'You will ruin it.'

'No, I won't! Well, what about your wife?' said the Baroness suddenly, interrupting Vronsky's conversation with his comrade. 'Haven't you brought your wife? We've married you off here.'

'No, Baroness. I was born a gypsy and will die a gypsy.'

'So much the better, so much the better. Give me your hand.'

And without letting Vronsky go, the Baroness, in between jokes, started telling him the latest plans for her life and asking his advice.

'He still doesn't want to grant me a divorce! So what am I to do?' (*He* was her husband.) 'I want to begin proceedings now. How would you advise me? Kamerovsky, keep an eye on the coffee—it's boiled over; you can see I am occupied with serious business! I want to start proceedings, because I need my assets. You see how ridiculous this is—because I am supposedly unfaithful to him,' she said contemptuously, 'he thinks he can have the use of my estate.'

Vronsky enjoyed listening to this pretty woman babble away merrily; he humoured her, gave her advice half in jest, and more or less immediately adopted his usual manner of talking to women of this kind. All people were divided into two completely contrasting categories in his Petersburg world. One was the inferior category: common, stupid, and above all ridiculous people, who believed that one man should live with one wife, to whom he should be married, that girls should be innocent, women modest, and men virile, abstemious, and steadfast, that one should raise children, earn one's daily bread, pay off debts—and other such nonsense. This was the old-fashioned, ridiculous category of people. But there was another category of real people, to which they all belonged, which required one to be above all elegant, attractive, generous, intrepid, good-humoured, ready to surrender to any passion without a blush and laugh at everything else.

Vronsky was stunned only for the first moment after the impressions of the completely different world he had brought back from Moscow; but just as if he had stuck his feet into a pair of old slippers, he immediately slipped back into his enjoyably comfortable old world.

The coffee never did get brewed, but splattered everybody, boiled over, and did precisely what was required of it, which was to provoke noise and laughter and spill on to the expensive carpet and the Baroness's dress.

'Well, I'll say goodbye now, otherwise you will never have your wash, and I will have slovenliness on my conscience, which is the respectable person's most heinous crime. So you recommend a knife to the throat?'

'Definitely, and positioned so your little hand is as close as possible to his lips. He will kiss your hand and all will end well,' replied Vronsky.

'See you tonight at the French Theatre!'* And with a rustle of her dress, she disappeared.

Kamerovsky also stood up, and Vronsky shook hands with him and headed for the bathroom without waiting for him to leave. While he was washing, Petritsky gave him a brief account of his situation, insofar as it had changed since Vronsky's departure. He had no money. His father had said he would not give him any, nor would he pay his debts. One tailor wanted him behind bars, and another was threatening the same thing. The commander of his regiment had declared that if these scandals did not stop, he would have to resign. He was heartily sick of the Baroness, particularly since she always wanted to give him money; but there was this one girl, he would point her out to Vronsky, who was wonderful, entrancing, in that strictly oriental style, the 'Rebecca-the-slave-girl genre,* you know'. He had also come to blows with Berkoshev the day before, and wanted to send his seconds, but of course nothing would come of it. Generally, everything was marvellous, and exceedingly jolly. And not letting his comrade enquire further about the details of his situation, Petritsky embarked on telling him all the interesting news. As he listened to Petritsky's so familiar stories in the so familiar surroundings of his apartment of three years, Vronsky experienced the pleasant sensation of returning to his customary, carefree Petersburg life.

'That's incredible!' he shouted, releasing the pedal of the basin, from which he was splashing water on to his healthy red neck. 'I don't believe it!' he shouted at the news that Laura had taken up with Mileyev, and had dropped Fertinhof. 'And is he just as stupid and smug as before? Well, what about Buzulukov?'

'Ah, there's a story about Buzulukov—it's superb!' exclaimed Petritsky. 'You know his passion is balls, and that he never misses a court ball. Well, he set off for some grand ball in a new helmet. Have you seen the new helmets? They are very good, much lighter. He was just standing there . . . No, listen.'

'Yes, I am listening,' answered Vronsky, drying himself with a fluffy towel.

'The Grand Duchess passes by with some ambassador or other, and unfortunately for him, they start talking about the new helmets. The Grand Duchess naturally wants to show off the new helmet . . . The next thing they see is our good friend standing there.' (Petritsky demonstrated how he stood there with his helmet.) 'The Grand Duchess asks him to give her the helmet and he refuses. Whatever next? Everyone is winking at him, nodding, frowning. Hand it over. He won't. He's rooted to the spot. Can you imagine! . . . It's then that this . . . whatever his name is . . . tries to take the helmet from him . . . he won't budge! . . . The next thing, he rips it off and hands it to the Grand Duchess. "This is the new helmet," says the Grand Duchess. She turns it over, and can you imagine, out of it plops a pear, some sweets—two pounds of sweets! . . . Our dear friend had swiped it all!'

Vronsky rocked with laughter. And for a long time afterwards, whenever he remembered the helmet, by which time they were already talking about something else, he started shaking with his hearty laughter, showing his strong, solid teeth.

Having heard all the news, Vronsky put on his uniform with the help of his valet, and went to report for duty. After that, he intended going to see his brother, and Betsy, and paying a few calls so he could begin moving in the circles where he might meet Anna Karenina. As always in Petersburg, he left home expecting not to return until late at night.

PART TWO

I

AT the end of the winter, a consultation took place at the Shcherbatsky home to determine the state of Kitty's health and the measures needed to restore her diminishing strength. She was ill, and with the approach of spring her health had worsened. The family doctor had given her cod-liver oil, then iron, then silver nitrate, but since neither the first of these, nor the second, nor the third had helped, and since his advice was to go abroad in the spring, a famous doctor was called in. The famous doctor, who was still relatively young, and an extremely handsome man, demanded to examine the patient. He seemed to take a particular pleasure in insisting that a maidenly shamefacedness was merely a remnant of barbarism, and that nothing could be more natural than for a still relatively young man to be prodding a naked young girl all over. He considered this to be natural because he did it every day, did not feel or think anything bad while doing it, or so it seemed to him, and therefore regarded shamefacedness in a girl not only to be a remnant of barbarism, but also a personal insult.

It was necessary to submit, since despite the fact that all doctors studied at the same medical school, from exactly the same books, and had the same scientific knowledge, and despite the fact that some people said that this famous doctor was a bad doctor, it was for some reason accepted in the Princess's household and in her circle that this famous doctor had some unique special knowledge, and was uniquely capable of saving Kitty. After carefully examining and sounding the bewildered patient, who was dying of embarrassment, the famous doctor diligently washed his hands and stood in the drawing room talking to the Prince. The Prince frowned as he listened to the doctor, coughing every now and then. As someone with some life experience behind him, who was neither stupid nor infirm, he did not believe in medicine, and was secretly infuriated by the whole charade, especially since he was probably the only one who fully understood the cause of Kitty's illness. 'What a babbler,'* he thought, mentally applying this term

from hunting vocabulary to the famous doctor as he listened to him
prattle on about his daughter's symptoms. The doctor, meanwhile, was
finding it difficult to restrain his contempt for this old grandee, and
equally difficult to descend to his low level of intelligence. He understood that it was pointless talking to the old man, and that the head
of this household was the mother. It was before her that he intended
scattering his pearls of wisdom. Just then the Princess came into the
drawing room with the family doctor. The Prince withdrew, trying not
to show how ludicrous he found this whole charade. The Princess was
confused and did not know what to do. She felt guilty about Kitty.

'Well, doctor, decide our fate,' said the Princess. 'Tell me everything.' 'Is there any hope?' is what she wanted to say, but her lips had
started trembling, and she could not manage to utter the question.
'Well, doctor?'

'I will now consult with my colleague, Princess, and then I will have
the honour of presenting my opinion to you.'

'So we should leave you?'

'If you please.'

The Princess sighed and went out.

When the doctors were left alone, the family doctor began timidly to
expound his opinion, which was that there were symptoms of incipient
tuberculosis, but . . . and so on. The famous doctor listened to him,
and halfway through his deliberations looked at his large gold watch.

'I see,' said he. 'But . . .'

The family doctor respectfully fell silent halfway through his
deliberations.

'As you know, we are not in a position to diagnose incipient tuberculosis; until there are cavities, nothing is definite. But we may suspect
it. And there are indications: malnutrition, nervous excitement, and
so on. The question is this: with a case of suspected tuberculosis, what
should be done to maintain nutrition?'

'But there are always hidden moral and spiritual causes in such
cases, as you know,' the family doctor permitted himself to interject
with a subtle smile.

'Yes, that goes without saying,' replied the famous doctor, looking
again at his watch. 'Forgive me, is the Yauza bridge* in place, or do you
still have to drive round?' he asked. 'Ah, it is in place! Oh, well then,
I can do it in twenty minutes. So as we were saying, the question is
to maintain good nutrition and to restore the nerves. The one is connected to the other, so the problem must be tackled from both sides.'

'But what about a trip abroad?' asked the family doctor.

'I'm against trips abroad. And please note: if we are dealing with a case of incipient tuberculosis, of which we cannot be certain, a trip abroad will not help. What is needed is a means of sustaining nutrition, and not damaging it.'

And the famous doctor set out his plan for a course of treatment with Soden waters,* the main aim of prescribing them clearly being that they could do no harm.

The family doctor listened attentively and respectfully.

'But in favour of a trip abroad I would propose a change of routine, and removal from conditions liable to provoke memories. And then the mother is keen,' he said.

'Ah! Well, in that case, why not, let them go; but those German charlatans will do harm, I warn you . . . They must listen to advice . . . Well, let them go then.'

He glanced at his watch again.

'Oh! It's already time I went,' he said, and made for the door.

The famous doctor announced to the Princess (a sense of propriety prompted this) that he needed to see the patient again.

'What? Another examination!' exclaimed the mother in horror.

'Oh no, I just need a few details, Princess.'

'By all means.'

And accompanied by the doctor, the mother went into the drawing room to find Kitty. Emaciated and crimson-faced, with a particular glitter in her eyes as a result of the shame she had endured, Kitty was standing in the middle of the room. When the doctor came in, she blushed deeply and her eyes filled with tears. Her illness and treatment all seemed so stupid and even ridiculous to her! The idea of treating her seemed as absurd to her as putting together the pieces of a broken vase. Her heart was broken. Why did they want to treat her with pills and powders? But she could not hurt her mother, especially since her mother considered herself to blame.

'If you would be good enough to sit down, Princess,' the famous doctor said to her.

He sat down opposite her with a smile, felt her pulse, and again started asking tedious questions. She answered him, then suddenly lost her temper and got to her feet.

'Excuse me, doctor, but this really is not going to lead anywhere, and you've asked me the same thing three times.'

The famous doctor was not offended.

'Morbid irritation,' he said to the Princess when Kitty had left the room. 'I was just finishing, in any case . . .'

And the doctor set out his diagnosis of Kitty's condition in scientific terms to the Princess as if she were an exceptionally intelligent woman, and concluded with instructions about how to drink the waters which were not needed. On the question of whether they should go abroad, the doctor was plunged into reflection, as if trying to solve a difficult problem. Finally he presented his decision: they were to go and not trust any charlatans, but refer to him on all matters.

It was as if something light-hearted happened after the doctor left. The mother cheered up when she went back to her daughter, and Kitty pretended that she had cheered up. These days she often, in fact almost always, had to pretend.

'I'm well, really, *Maman*. But if you want to go, let's go!' she said, and trying to show interest in the forthcoming trip, she started talking about preparations for their departure.

2

AFTER the doctor left, Dolly arrived. She knew a consultation was to have taken place that day, and although she had only recently risen from her confinement (she had given birth to a girl at the end of winter), and although she had enough misery and trouble of her own, she had left her newborn baby and a sick daughter and driven over in order to learn Kitty's fate, which was being decided that day.

'Well?' she said, coming into the drawing room without taking off her hat. 'You're all very jolly. Must be good news, then?'

They tried to tell her what the doctor had said, but it turned out that although the doctor had talked eloquently and at great length, it was utterly impossible to relay what he had said. The only interesting thing was the decision to go abroad.

Dolly could not help sighing. Her best friend, her sister, was going away. And her life was not at all jolly. Relations with Stepan Arkadyich had become humiliating following their reconciliation. The welding carried out by Anna had not proved durable, and domestic harmony had suffered another fracture in the same place. There was nothing specific, but Stepan Arkadyich was almost never at home, there was also almost never any money at home, and Dolly was constantly plagued by suspicions of infidelity, which she was already driving away, dreading the agonies of jealousy she had experienced before. The first attack of jealousy, once experienced, could not come back again, and even the discovery of infidelity could not affect her so much as it had the first time. Such a discovery now would only mean a disruption to her normal domestic routine, so she allowed herself to be deceived, while despising him and most of all herself for this weakness. On top of all this, caring for a large family was a constant worry to her: either her newborn baby was not feeding properly, or the nanny had left, or, as now, one of the children had fallen ill.

'Well, how are you all?' asked her mother.

'Oh, *Maman*, you have enough troubles of your own. Lily is ill, and I'm worried it's scarlet fever. I have come out now to find out how things are, because I'm not going to be able to leave the house, if, God forbid, it is scarlet fever.'

The old Prince had also come out of his study following the doctor's departure, and after offering his cheek to Dolly and exchanging a few words with her, he turned to his wife:

'So what's your decision—are you going? Well, and what do you want to do with me?'

'I think, Alexander Andreyich,* you had better stay here,' said his wife.

'As you wish.'

'*Maman*, why shouldn't Papa come with us?' said Kitty. 'It would be more fun for him, and for us.'

The old Prince got up and stroked Kitty's hair. She raised her face and looked at him, forcing herself to smile. It always seemed to her that he understood her better than anyone else in the family, even though he did not talk to her much. Being the youngest, she was her father's favourite, and she felt that his love for her made him particularly perceptive. Now, as she met his kind blue eyes gazing at her intently from his wrinkled face, she felt he could see right through her, and understood all the difficulties she was enduring. Blushing, she leaned towards him, expecting a kiss, but he only patted her hair and said:

'These stupid chignons! You never even get to your real daughter, you're just stroking the hair of poor wenches. Well, Dollinka, my love,' he said, turning to his eldest daughter, 'what's that young card of yours up to?'

'Nothing much, Papa,' answered Dolly, realizing he was talking about her husband. 'He's always out, I hardly ever see him,' she could not help adding with a mocking smile.

'What, he still hasn't gone off to the country to sell the wood?'

'No, he is still getting ready to go.'

'I see!' said the Prince. 'I suppose I should be getting ready to go too? I'm at your command,' he said to his wife, sitting down. 'And as for you, Katya,' he added, addressing his youngest daughter, 'there will come a time when one fine day you will wake up and say to yourself: I'm actually feeling completely well and cheerful, so Papa and I should go for a walk again in the early morning frost. Hmm?'

It seemed what her father said was very simple, but these words made Kitty feel as flustered and embarrassed as a criminal caught in the act. 'Yes, he knows everything, he understands everything, and by saying this, he is telling me that although I am ashamed, I have to get over my shame.' She could not pluck up the courage to say anything in reply. She tried, then suddenly burst into tears and ran out of the room.

'You and your jokes!' the Princess flew at her husband. 'You always . . .' and she launched into one of her tirades.

The Prince listened to the Princess's reproaches for quite a long time and remained tight-lipped, but his face grew more and more downcast.

'She's so miserable, the poor thing, so miserable, and you do not sense how any reference to the cause of it all is painful to her. Ah, to be so mistaken about people!' said the Princess, and from the change in her tone, both Dolly and the Prince realized she was talking about Vronsky. 'I don't understand why there aren't laws against such vile, dishonourable people.'

'Oh, I can't listen to this!' said the Prince darkly, getting up from his armchair and appearing to want to leave, but stopping in the doorway. 'There are laws, my good woman, and since you've challenged me on this, I'll tell you who's to blame for everything: you, you, and you alone. There have always been laws against such rogues, and there still are! Yes, and even if there hadn't been anything untoward, I may be an old man, but I'd have had that fop face me across the barrier. And now you're trying to find a cure and bringing in all these charlatans.'

The Prince seemed to have plenty more to say, but as soon as the Princess heard his tone, she backed down and became remorseful, as she always did in serious matters.

'*Alexandre, Alexandre*,' she murmured, going towards him, and she burst into tears.

As soon as she began to cry, the Prince calmed down too. He went up to her.

'Now, now, that's enough! It's hard for you too, I know. What can be done? There's been no great misfortune. God is merciful . . . be thankful . . .' he said, no longer knowing himself what he was saying and responding to the Princess's wet kiss, which he felt on his hand, before leaving the room.

As soon as Kitty had left the room in tears, Dolly had immediately seen, with her maternal, family instincts, that there was woman's work to be done, and she prepared herself for it. Mentally rolling up her sleeves, she took off her hat and prepared for action. While her mother was attacking her father, she had tried to restrain her mother as far as filial deference permitted. During the Prince's outburst she was silent; she felt shame on her mother's behalf and affection towards her father for so quickly becoming kind again, but when her father went out, she girded herself to do the main thing which was needed, which was to go and comfort Kitty.

'I've been meaning to tell you for a long time, *Maman*: did you know that Levin was planning to propose to Kitty when he was here last? He told Stiva.'

'What of it? I don't understand . . .'

'Well, maybe Kitty refused him? . . . She didn't tell you?'

'No, she said nothing to me about either of them; she's too proud. But I know it's all because of that . . .'

'Yes, but suppose she refused Levin—she wouldn't have refused him if that other one had not been on the scene, I know . . . and he deceived her so horribly too.'

It was too awful for the Princess to contemplate how much she was to blame for her daughter's plight, and she became angry.

'Oh, I don't understand anything any more! These days they all want to follow their own minds, they don't tell their mothers anything, and then look what . . .'

'*Maman*, I'll go to her.'

'Do. It's not as if I am stopping you, am I?' said her mother.

3

WHEN she went into Kitty's small boudoir, a pretty, pink room full of *vieux Saxe** figurines which was as young, pink, and light-hearted as Kitty herself had been only two months earlier, Dolly remembered how they had decorated the room together the year before, with such merriment and love. Her heart froze when she saw Kitty sitting on a low chair near the door, her eyes riveted on a corner of the carpet. Kitty glanced at her sister, and the cold and rather severe expression on her face did not change.

'I'm about to leave, and will be shut up at home, and you won't be able to come and see me,' said Dolly, sitting down beside her. 'I want to talk to you.'

'What about?' Kitty asked quickly, lifting her head in fear.

'What else but your grief?'

'I don't have any grief.'

'Come on, Kitty. Do you really think I don't know? I know everything. And believe me, it's so unimportant . . . We've all been through it.'

Kitty remained silent, and her face bore a stern expression.

'He's not worth you suffering over him,' continued Darya Alexandrovna, coming straight to the point.

'No, because he scorned me,' said Kitty in a trembling voice. 'Don't say anything! Please, don't say anything!'

'But who told you that? No one said that. I'm sure he was in love with you, and was still in love, but . . .'

'Oh, I find all this commiseration worse than anything else!' Kitty cried out, suddenly becoming angry. She turned round on her chair, blushed, and started moving her fingers rapidly as she gripped the buckle of a belt she was holding, first with one hand and then with the other. Dolly was familiar with her sister's habit of switching from one hand to the other when she lost her temper; she knew that Kitty was capable of forgetting herself and saying many unnecessary and unpleasant things in the heat of the moment, so Dolly wanted to calm her down; but it was too late.

'Just what is it you want to make me feel—what?' said Kitty rapidly. 'That I was in love with someone who did not want to know me, and that I'm dying of love for him? And it is my own sister telling me this, who thinks that . . . that . . . that she's commiserating with me! . . . I don't want all this pity and pretence!'

'Kitty, you're being unfair.'

'Why are you tormenting me?'

'But on the contrary, I . . . I can see you're grieving . . .'

But in her frenzied state Kitty did not hear her.

'There's nothing for me to be distressed or comforted about. I have sufficient pride that I would never allow myself to love a man who does not love me.'

'But I'm not saying that . . . There's just one thing, and you must tell me the truth,' said Darya Alexandrovna, taking her by the hand: 'Tell me, did Levin speak to you? . . .'

Mention of Levin seemed to deprive Kitty of the last vestiges of self-control; she leapt up from her chair, threw the buckle on the floor, and making rapid gestures with her hands, she burst out:

'Why do you have to bring Levin into this too? I don't understand, why do you have to torment me? I've said it once, and I'll say it again, that I have my pride, and I will never, *ever* do what you are doing—go back to a man who has been unfaithful to you, who has fallen for another woman. I don't understand it, I just don't understand it! You might be able to, but I can't!'

She glanced at her sister after saying these words, and when she saw that Dolly was silent, her head bowed in sadness, Kitty sat down by the door instead of leaving the room as she had intended, buried her face in her handkerchief, and bowed her head.

The silence lasted for a couple of minutes. Dolly was thinking about herself. The pain of her humiliation, of which she was always conscious, became particularly acute when her sister reminded her of it. She had not expected such cruelty from her sister, and she was angry with her. But suddenly she heard the rustle of a dress and with it the sound of muffled sobbing, then someone's arms embraced her neck from below. Kitty was on her knees before her.

'Dollinka, I am so, so unhappy!' she whispered contritely.

And the dear, tear-stained face buried itself in the skirt of Darya Alexandrovna's dress.

It was as if tears were the essential lubricant without which the machinery of mutual relations between the two sisters could not operate effectively—after the tears the sisters did not talk about what preoccupied them, but they understood each other even though they were talking about other things. Kitty understood that she had deeply wounded her poor sister with those words she had uttered in a fit of pique about her husband's infidelity and her humiliation, but that she was forgiven. For her part, Dolly understood all that she had wanted to know; she confirmed that her suppositions were correct, that Kitty's grief, her inconsolable grief, was due precisely to the fact that Levin had proposed to her and she had refused him, while Vronsky had deceived her, and that she was ready to love Levin and hate Vronsky. Kitty did not say a word of this; she talked only about her state of mind.

'I'm not grieving,' she said after she had calmed down, 'but I wonder if you can understand how horrible, disgusting, and coarse everything has become for me, and above all how disgusting I have become to myself. You can't imagine what horrible thoughts I have about everything.'

'But what horrible thoughts can you possibly have?' asked Dolly, smiling.

'The most utterly horrible, crude ones; I can't tell you. It's not sadness or boredom, but something much worse. It's as if everything that was good in me has been hidden away, and only the most horrible things have remained. Well, how can I put it?' she continued, seeing the look of bewilderment in her sister's eyes. 'Papa started talking to me just now . . . It feels to me that he just thinks I need to get married. Mama takes me to a ball: it feels to me that she is only taking me so she can marry me off as soon as possible and get rid of me. I know that's not true, but I can't drive out these thoughts. I can't bear to see those so-called eligible bachelors. It feels like they're sizing me up. Going somewhere in a ball–gown was sheer pleasure for me before, and I used to admire myself, but now I feel ashamed and awkward. Well, what do you expect! The doctor . . . Well . . .'

Kitty faltered; she wanted to go on to say that ever since this change had taken place in her, she had found Stepan Arkadyich completely odious, and that she could not see him without having the most crude and hideous thoughts.

'Well, yes, I see everything in the coarsest, most loathsome light,' she went on. 'That's my illness. Maybe it will pass.'

'But you shouldn't think . . .'

'I can't help it. I only feel all right when I am with the children, only at your house.'

'It's a pity you can't spend time with me.'

'No, I'm going to come. I've had scarlet fever, and I'll persuade *Maman* to let me.'

Kitty insisted on having her way and went to stay at her sister's, and she looked after the children throughout the entire bout of scarlet fever, which it indeed turned out to be. The two sisters brought all six children successfully through it, but Kitty's health did not improve, and in Lent* the Shcherbatskys went abroad.

4

THERE is essentially just one circle in Petersburg high society; everybody knows one another and even calls on one another. But this large circle has its subdivisions. Anna Arkadyevna Karenina had friends and close ties in three different circles. One circle was the official circle associated with her husband's work, consisting of his colleagues and subordinates, who in the social environment were connected and divided in the most varied and arbitrary way. Anna found it difficult now to recall the feeling of almost pious reverence she initially had towards these individuals. She now knew them all in the way that people know each another in a provincial town; she knew their habits and their weaknesses, and whose shoe pinched which foot; she knew their relations with one another and with the powers that be; she knew who sided with whom, and how and why, and who agreed and disagreed with whom, and why; but this male, government circle could never have interested her, despite Countess Lydia Ivanovna's inducements, and she avoided it.

Another little circle close to Anna was the one through which Alexey Alexandrovich had built his career. At the centre of this little circle was the Countess Lydia Ivanovna. This was a little circle of elderly, unattractive, virtuous, and pious women and clever, learned, ambitious men. One of the clever men who belonged to this little circle called it 'the conscience of Petersburg society'. Alexey Alexandrovich greatly valued this little circle, and Anna, who was so good at getting on with everyone, had also found friends in this little circle during the early days of her Petersburg life. But now, after returning from Moscow, she found this little circle unbearable. It seemed to her that they and she were all putting on a show, and she started to feel so bored and ill at ease in their company that she called on Countess Lydia Ivanovna as little as possible.

The third circle, finally, where she had connections, was essentially *le beau monde*—a world of balls, dinners, and dazzling gowns, and a world which kept one hand on the court, so as not to descend to the *demi-monde*, which the members of this circle affected to despise, although their tastes were not only similar, but identical. Her connection with this circle was maintained through Princess Betsy Tverskaya, her cousin's wife, who had an income of a hundred and twenty thousand roubles, and who from the moment of Anna's first appearance in society had become greatly attached to her, taking her under her wing and luring her into her circle, while scoffing at Countess Lydia Ivanovna's circle.

'When I'm old and ugly I'll be just like them,' Betsy used to say, 'but it's too early for a pretty young woman like you to go into that almshouse.'

Anna had initially steered clear of Princess Tverskaya's circle as much as she could, since it required expenditure beyond her means, and her natural inclination was anyway to prefer the other set; but after her trip to Moscow the reverse happened. She avoided her virtuous friends and went into high society. There she would encounter Vronsky, and she experienced a joyous thrill during those encounters. She encountered Vronsky particularly often when she visited Betsy, who had been born Vronskaya and was his cousin. Wherever there might be a possibility of meeting Anna, Vronsky was there, and he spoke to her of his love whenever he could. She gave him no encouragement, but every time she met him, her soul lit up with that same feeling of animation which had taken hold of her that day in the railway carriage when she saw him for the first time. She herself could feel the joy shining in her eyes and pursing her lips into a smile when she saw him, and she could not suppress this joy from manifesting itself.

At first Anna sincerely believed that she was displeased with him for taking the liberty of pursuing her, but when, soon after her return from Moscow, she arrived at a soirée where she thought she would find him but did not, she clearly realized from the sadness which overcame her that she was deceiving herself, and that not only was his pursuit of her not unpleasant to her, but that it constituted the whole interest of her life.

The famous prima donna* was singing for the second time, and all of high society was at the theatre. When Vronsky caught sight of his cousin from his seat in the front row, he went into her box without waiting for the interval.

'Why didn't you come to dinner?' she said to him. 'I'm amazed at the clairvoyance of people in love,' she added with a smile, so that only he could hear: '*She wasn't there*. But come round after the opera.'

Vronsky looked at her quizzically. She inclined her head. He thanked her with a smile, and sat down behind her.

'And when I remember how dismissive you were!' continued Princess Betsy, who took a particular pleasure in following the course of this love affair. 'What's become of all that? You're caught, my dear boy.'

'My only desire is to be caught,' answered Vronsky with his serene, good-natured smile. 'If I do have a complaint, it's only that I haven't been quite caught yet, to tell the truth. I'm beginning to lose hope.'

'And what hope can you possibly have?' said Betsy, offended on behalf of her friend; '*entendons nous . . .*'[1] But her eyes were twinkling with a look which suggested that she understood very well, and in just the same way he did, the sort of hope he might cherish.

'None whatsoever,' said Vronsky, laughing and showing his solid row of teeth. 'Excuse me,' he added, taking the opera-glasses from her hand, and proceeding to look over her bare shoulder at the row of boxes facing them. 'I'm afraid I'm becoming ridiculous.'

He knew very well that he ran no risk of looking ridiculous in the

[1] 'let us understand each other'.

eyes of Betsy or anyone else in society. He knew very well that the role of the unsuccessful lover of a young girl or generally unattached woman might be ridiculous in their eyes; but the role of a man pursuing a married woman, and staking his life at all costs on luring her into adultery—that role had something attractive and illustrious about it, and could never be ridiculous, so with a proud and mischievous smile hovering under his moustache he lowered the opera-glasses and looked at his cousin.

'But why didn't you come to dinner?' she said, looking at him admiringly.

'I must tell you about that. I was busy, and do you know what I was doing? I'll give you a hundred guesses, a thousand . . . but you'll never guess. I was making peace between a husband and a man who insulted his wife. Yes, really!'

'Well, did you succeed?'

'Almost.'

'You must tell me all about it,' she said, getting up. 'Come in the next interval.'

'I can't; I'm going to the French Theatre.'*

'After hearing Nilsson?' asked Betsy in horror, despite being unable to distinguish Nilsson from any chorus girl.

'Can't help it. I've an appointment there, to do with this peacemaking still.'

'Blessed are the peacemakers, for they shall be saved,'* said Betsy, vaguely remembering that she had heard someone saying something similar. 'Well sit down then, and tell me, what is this all about?'

And she sat down again.

5

'It's rather indiscreet, but so charming I'm dying to tell the story,' said Vronsky, looking at her with laughing eyes. 'I won't mention any names.'

'But I will guess—so much the better.'

'So listen: two cheery young men are on their way . . .'

'Officers from your regiment, I presume?'

'I didn't say they were officers, simply two young men who have had lunch. . . .'

'Which translates as drinking.'

'Possibly. They are on their way to dinner with a comrade, and are in the best of spirits. And they see this pretty woman overtaking them in a cab, looking round and, so it seems to them at least, beckoning them and laughing. They follow her, of course. They gallop off at full speed. To their amazement, the beautiful woman stops at the entrance of the very same building they are going to. The beautiful woman runs up to the top floor. All they can see are some little crimson lips under a short veil, and lovely little feet.'

'You're telling this story with such feeling that I think you must be one of these two young men.'

'And what were you telling me just now? Well, the young men go in to their comrade's apartment where he is having a farewell dinner. They certainly drink at this point, perhaps too much, as one always does at farewell dinners. And during the dinner they ask who lives on the top floor of the building. No one knows, and when they ask whether there are any *mam'selles* living upstairs, only their host's servant answers and says that there are lots of them up there. After dinner the young men go to their host's study and write a letter to the unknown woman. They write a truly passionate letter, a declaration of love, and they take the letter upstairs themselves, so that they can explain anything that might not be quite clear.'

'Why do you tell me such horrible things? Well?'

'They ring. A maid opens the door, they hand over the letter, and assure the maid that they are both so in love that they are about to die right then and there by the door. The bewildered maid tries to arbitrate. Suddenly a gentleman with whiskers like little sausages appears, red as a lobster, and declares that no one lives there except his wife, and throws them both out.'

'But how do you know his whiskers were, as you say, like little sausages?'

'Now listen. I went to make peace between them today.'

'So what happened?'

'That's the most interesting bit. It turns out that this happy couple consists of a Titular Councillor* and his wife. The Titular Councillor issues a complaint, and I become a peacemaker, and what a peacemaker! . . . I assure you, Talleyrand* is nothing compared to me.'

'But what was so difficult?'

'Well, just listen . . . We apologized in the proper way: "We are in despair, and ask you to forgive us for the unfortunate misunderstanding." The Titular Councillor with the little sausages begins to loosen up, but he also wants to express his feelings, and as soon as he begins to express them, he starts losing his temper and saying rude things, and again I have to exercise all my diplomatic talents. "I agree that their behaviour was bad, but I ask you to take into consideration that this was a misunderstanding, and their youth; and then the young men had only just been at luncheon. You understand. They regret this with all their hearts, and ask you to forgive their misdemeanour." The Titular Councillor relents again: "I give my consent, Count, and am ready to forgive, but you understand that my wife, my wife, an honourable woman, has had to endure harassment, rudeness, and impudence from some young pipsqueaks, scoundr . . ." Well, I've got one of the pipsqueaks right there, you understand, and I have to make peace between them. I call on my diplomatic skills again, and again, just as we are about to settle the matter, my Titular Councillor loses his temper, goes red in the face, his little sausages bristle, and again I am gushing diplomatic subtleties.'

'Ah, I must tell you this story!' exclaimed Betsy, laughing, to a lady coming into her box. 'He has made me laugh so much.'

'Well, *bonne chance*!'[1] she added, holding out to Vronsky the spare finger on the hand holding her fan, and moving her shoulders in order to lower the bodice of her gown which had risen up, so as to be properly and completely bare when she leaned out towards the stage, into the glare of the gaslights and everyone's eyes.

Vronsky went off to the French Theatre, where he really did have to see the colonel of his regiment, who never missed a single performance at that establishment, in order to tell him about his peacemaking, which had kept him occupied and amused for the last three days. Implicated in the affair were Petritsky, of whom he was fond, and the young Prince Kedrov, another fine young fellow who had recently joined the regiment and was an excellent comrade. But most importantly, the interests of the regiment were implicated.

Both young men were in Vronsky's squadron. The official, Titular Councillor Venden, had come to see the colonel with a complaint about his officers, who had insulted his wife. Venden related that his young wife—he had been married for six months—had been in church with her mother when she had suddenly felt unwell as a result of a certain condition, could no longer remain on her feet, and had set off home in the first available fast cab.* At this point the officers started pursuing her, she took fright, and ran home up the stairs, by this stage feeling even more unwell. Venden himself, after returning from his office, heard the bell and some voices, had gone to the door and seen

---

[1] 'good luck!'

the drunken officers with the letter, and had pushed them out. He had requested severe punishment.

'No, however you look at it,' said the colonel to Vronsky, having asked him to come and see him, 'Petritsky's becoming impossible. Not a week goes by without some scandal. This official won't let it drop, he'll pursue it.'

Vronsky saw all the impropriety of the affair, that there could be no question of a duel in this case, and that everything needed to be done to placate this Titular Councillor and hush the matter up. The colonel had summoned Vronsky precisely because he knew him to be an upstanding and intelligent man, and, above all, a man who cared about the honour of the regiment. They talked it over, and decided that Petritsky and Kedrov should go with Vronsky to see the Titular Councillor and apologize. Both the colonel and Vronsky realized that Vronsky's name and his imperial aide-de-camp's insignia would be of great assistance in placating the Titular Councillor. And these two measures were indeed partially effective; but the outcome of the reconciliation remained in doubt, as Vronsky had recounted.

After arriving at the French Theatre, Vronsky withdrew with the colonel to the foyer, and told him about his success, or lack thereof. After thinking it all over, the colonel decided not to take any further action, but then for his own amusement proceeded to question Vronsky on the details of the meeting, and for a long time could not stop laughing as he listened to Vronsky describe how the appeased Titular Councillor had suddenly lost his temper again when he remembered details of the incident, and how Vronsky had beaten a hasty retreat, pushing Petritsky in front of him, right when they were on the verge of reconciliation.

'It's a shameful story, but quite hilarious. There is no way Kedrov could fight a duel with this gentleman! So he really lost his temper, did he?' he asked, laughing. 'But what do you think of Claire tonight? She's wonderful!' he said about a new French actress. 'No matter how often you see her, she's different every time. Only the French can do that.'

6

PRINCESS Betsy left the theatre without waiting for the end of the last act. She had just enough time to go into her dressing room, sprinkle her long, pale face with powder, dab it off, adjust her hair, and order tea in the large drawing room, before carriages began arriving at her enormous mansion on Bolshaya Morskaya Street, one after the other.

The guests stepped into the wide porch, and the corpulent porter, who in the mornings read the newspapers behind the glass door for the edification of passers-by, noiselessly opened this enormous door, letting those who had just arrived come in past him.

The hostess, with her freshened-up hair and freshened-up face, entered through one door at almost exactly the same moment as the guests passed through another into the large drawing room with its dark walls, plush carpets, and brightly lit table, the snow-white table-cloth, silver samovar, and translucent china tea service all gleaming in the candlelight.

The hostess seated herself next to the samovar and removed her gloves. Drawing up chairs and armchairs with the assistance of discreet footmen, the assembled party settled into their seats, having divided into two groups—one by the samovar with the hostess, and the other at the opposite end of the drawing room, near a beautiful ambassador's wife with arched black brows, who was dressed in black velvet. As always in the first few minutes, the conversation in both groups wavered while it was interrupted by introductions, greetings, and offers of tea, as if searching for something to alight on.

'She's exceptionally good as an actress; one can see she's studied Kaulbach,'* said a diplomat in the ambassador's wife's circle. 'Did you notice how she fell? . . .'

'Oh, please, let's not talk about Nilsson! It's impossible to say anything new about her,' said a stout, red-faced, fair-haired lady in an old silk dress, who had neither eyebrows nor a chignon. This was Princess Myagkaya,* nicknamed the *enfant terrible*,[1] and renowned for her straightforwardness and brusque manner of speaking. Princess Myagkaya was sitting with her ears pricked between the two groups, taking part in first one and then the other. 'Three people have said that same phrase about Kaulbach to me today, as if by some prior arrangement. And I don't know why they liked the phrase so much.'

The conversation was cut short by this observation, and it was necessary to think up a new subject again.

'Tell us something amusing but not malicious,' said the ambassador's wife, a past master in the art of the refined conversation the English call *small talk*,[2] turning to the diplomat, who was also at a loss to know what subject to raise next.

---

[1] [Lit. 'terrible child', French term also used to denote an unconventional, outspoken person.]

[2] [English in the original.]

'They say that's very difficult, and that only malicious things are amusing,' he began with a smile. 'But I'll try. Give me a topic. The topic is what counts. Once you have a theme, it's easy to embroider upon it. I often think that the famous conversationalists of the last century would be hard pressed to talk cleverly now. People are so bored with everything clever . . .'

'That has been said long ago,' said the ambassador's wife interrupting him with a laugh.

The conversation began amiably, but precisely because it was a bit too amiable, it came to a halt again. They had to resort to the tried-and-trusted remedy—malicious gossip.

'Don't you think there's something Louis Quinze* about Tushkevich?' he said, indicating with his eyes a handsome, fair-haired young man standing by the table.

'Oh, yes! He matches the drawing room, and that's why he's here so often.'

This conversation was sustained, since they talked by means of insinuation about the one thing which could not be discussed in this drawing room, namely Tushkevich's relationship to their hostess.

The conversation near the samovar and the hostess, meanwhile, after wavering in just the same way between the three inevitable topics—the latest social news, the theatre, and criticism of one's neighbour—also settled, once it had stumbled on to it, on the last of these, that is to say, malicious gossip.

'Have you heard, Maltishcheva—not the daughter, the mother—is making herself a *diable rose* outfit* now.'

'I don't believe it! No, that's priceless!'

'I'm surprised that with her brains, she can't see how ridiculous she will look—she's not a fool, after all.'

Everyone had something critical or withering to say about the unfortunate Maltishcheva, and the conversation started crackling away merrily, like a well-stoked bonfire.

Princess Betsy's husband, a good-natured, portly fellow who was a passionate collector of engravings, dropped by the drawing room before going to his club when he found out his wife had guests. Treading silently on the soft carpet, he walked over to Princess Myagkaya.

'How did you like Nilsson, Princess?' he asked.

'Oh, heavens, do you have to steal up on people like that? You gave me such a fright!' she responded. 'Please don't talk to me about the opera, you don't know anything about music. It's better if I descend to your level and talk about your majolica and your engravings. Well, what treasure have you bought recently at the flea market?'

'Do you want me to show you? But you don't understand these things.'

'Do show me! I've been learning about them from those, what are they called . . . bankers . . . they have some splendid engravings. They showed them to us.'

'What, have you been at the Schützburgs?' asked the hostess from the samovar.

'We have, *ma chère*. They asked me and my husband to dinner, and told me the sauce at the dinner cost a thousand roubles,' Princess Myagkaya said loudly, aware that everyone was listening; 'and it was a revolting sauce too, something green. We then had to invite them over, and I made sauce for eighty-five kopecks, and everybody was very pleased with it. I can't make thousand-rouble sauces.'

'There's no one like her!' said the ambassador's wife.

'She's amazing!' said someone.

The effect produced by Princess Myagkaya's pronouncements was always the same, and the secret of the effect she produced lay in the fact that she said simple things which made sense, even if they were not quite to the point, as on this occasion. In the circles in which she moved, such pronouncements produced the effect of an extremely witty joke. Princess Myagkaya could not understand why they had that effect, but she knew they did, and made the most of it.

As everyone had listened to Princess Myagkaya while she was talking and the conversation around the ambassador's wife had stopped, the hostess wanted to bring the whole party together, and she turned to the ambassador's wife:

'Are you sure you don't want some tea? You should come over and join us.'

'No, we're very happy here,' the ambassador's wife responded with a smile, and resumed the conversation that had been begun earlier.

It was a very enjoyable conversation. They were criticizing the Karenins, husband and wife.

'Anna has changed a great deal since her Moscow trip. There's something odd about her,' said one of her friends.

'The main change is that she has brought back with her the shadow of Alexey Vronsky,' said the ambassador's wife.

'Well, what of it? Grimm has a tale: the man without a shadow, about a man who is deprived of his shadow.* It is a punishment he is given for something or other. I never could understand why it was a punishment. But it must be unpleasant for a woman not to have a shadow.'

'Yes, but women with shadows usually come to a bad end,' said Anna's friend.

'Button your lip!' said Princess Myagkaya abruptly when she heard these words. 'Anna Karenina is a fine woman. I don't care for her husband, but I am very fond of her.'

'Why don't you like her husband? He's such a remarkable man,' said the ambassador's wife. 'My husband says there are few statesmen like him in Europe.'

'And my husband tells me the same thing, but I don't believe it,' said Princess Myagkaya. 'If our husbands didn't talk, we would see things as they really are, and in my opinion Alexey Alexandrovich is just stupid. I say this in a whisper . . . but doesn't it explain everything? Before, when I was instructed to find him clever, I kept looking for his intelligence, and I thought I myself must be stupid for not seeing it; but as soon as I said *he's stupid* in a whisper, it all becomes quite clear, don't you think?'

'How malicious you are today!'

'Not at all. I didn't have any other option. One of the two of us is stupid. And well, as you know, it's impossible to say that about yourself.'

'No one is ever happy with his fortune, but every person is happy with his wits,' said the diplomat, quoting a French saying.*

'Exactly so,' said Princess Myagkaya, quickly turning to him. 'But the fact is that I won't surrender Anna to you. She's such a sweet, lovely person. What is she to do if everybody is in love with her, and follows her about like shadows?'

'But I have no intention of criticizing her,' Anna's friend said, trying to justify herself.

'Just because no one follows us about like a shadow, it doesn't mean that we have any right to criticize her.'

And having berated Anna's friend as she deserved, Princess Myagkaya got up, and she and the ambassador's wife joined the group at the table, where the conversation was about the king of Prussia.

'Who were you gossiping about over there?' asked Betsy.

'About the Karenins. The Princess was giving us an appraisal of Alexey Alexandrovich,' the ambassador's wife replied, sitting down at the table with a smile.

'A pity we didn't hear it,' said Princess Betsy, glancing towards the door. 'Ah, here you are at last!' she said, turning with a smile to Vronsky who was coming in.

Vronsky was not only acquainted with everyone he met here, but he saw them every day, and so he came in with the relaxed air of someone coming into a room to join people he has only just left.

'Where have I just come from?' he replied to the ambassador's wife's question. 'Nothing for it, I'll have to confess. From the Opera Bouffe. I must have been about a hundred times, but there is always something new to enjoy. It's wonderful! I know I should be ashamed of myself, but I sleep through the opera, whereas at the Opera Bouffe I'm glued to my seat until the very end, and it's fun. This evening . . .'

He named a French actress, and was about to tell some story about her, but the ambassador's wife interrupted him in mock outrage:

'Please don't tell us about this horror.'

'All right then, I won't, especially since everyone is familiar with these horrors.'

'And everyone would go if it were as acceptable as going to the opera,' chimed in Princess Myagkaya.

7

STEPS could be heard at the door, and Princess Betsy glanced at Vronsky, knowing this was Karenina. He was staring at the door, and his face had acquired a strange new expression. He was looking intently, joyfully, and also shyly at the woman coming in, and slowly getting to his feet. Anna entered the drawing room. Holding herself as always extremely erect, and not changing the direction of her gaze, she took the few steps separating her from her hostess with that brisk, firm, and light step which distinguished her from other society women, pressed her hand, smiled, and looked round at Vronsky with the same smile. Vronsky made a low bow and drew up a chair for her.

She responded with a mere inclination of her head, blushed, and frowned. But she turned straight away to her hostess, nodding quickly to her acquaintances and shaking the hands held out to her as she did so:

'I was at Countess Lydia's, and meant to come earlier, but I could not get away. She had Sir John* there. He's very interesting.'

'Ah, is he that missionary?'

'Yes, he was recounting some very interesting things about life in India.'

After being interrupted by her arrival, the conversation started flickering again, like the light of a lamp that is going out.

'Sir John! Yes, Sir John. I've seen him. He speaks well. Vlasieva* is completely in love with him.'

'And is it true her younger sister is marrying Topov?'

'Yes, they say it's quite settled.'

'I'm surprised at the parents. They say it's a match based on passion.'

'Passion? What antediluvian ideas you have! Who talks of passion in this day and age?' said the ambassador's wife.

'What's to be done? This quaint old fashion has not died out yet,' said Vronsky.

'So much the worse for those who follow that fashion. The only happy marriages I know are marriages of convenience.'

'Yes, but on the other hand, think how often the happiness of marriages of convenience crumbles like dust, precisely because of the emergence of that very passion which had not been acknowledged,' said Vronsky.

'But we call them marriages of convenience because both parties have already put their wild period behind them. It's like scarlet fever—something you have to go through.'

'Then we need to learn how to inoculate ourselves against love artificially, like with smallpox.'

'I was in love with a sexton when I was young,' said the Princess Myagkaya. 'I don't know if it did me any good.'

'No, joking apart, I think that to know what love is, one must make mistakes and learn from them,' said Princess Betsy.

'Even after marriage?' said the ambassador's wife playfully.

'It's never too late to repent,' said the diplomat, quoting an English saying.

'Exactly,' chimed in Betsy, 'one must make mistakes and learn from them. What do you think about all this?' she said, turning to Anna, who had been listening silently to the conversation with a faint but definite smile on her lips.

'I think,' said Anna, toying with the glove she had just taken off, 'I think . . . if there are as many heads as there are minds, then there must be as many kinds of love as there are hearts.'

Vronsky had been looking at Anna, waiting to hear what she would say with bated breath. He sighed as if some danger had passed when she said these words.

Anna suddenly turned to him.

'Now, I have had a letter from Moscow. They've written to tell me that Kitty Shcherbatskaya's very ill.'

'Really?' said Vronsky, frowning.

Anna looked at him sternly.

'Does that not interest you?'

'On the contrary, very much. Might I enquire as to exactly what was said in the letter?' he asked.

Anna got up and went over to Betsy.

'May I have a cup of tea, please,' she said, coming to stand behind her chair.

While Betsy was pouring out the tea, Vronsky went up to Anna.

'What was said in the letter?' he repeated.

'I often think men do not understand what's honourable and what's dishonourable, although they are always talking about it,' said Anna, without answering him. 'I've been meaning to tell you this for a long time,' she added, and moving away a few steps, she sat down at a table in the corner with albums on it.

'I don't quite understand the meaning of your words,' he said, handing her the cup.

She eyed the sofa beside her, and he instantly sat down.

'Yes, I have been meaning to tell you,' she said, not looking at him. 'You behaved badly, very, very badly.'

'Do you think I don't know that I behaved badly? But who caused me to behave like that?'

'Why are you telling me this?' she said, looking at him severely.

'You know why,' he answered boldly and joyously, meeting her gaze and not lowering his eyes.

It was she, not he, who was embarrassed.

'That only proves that you have no heart,' she said. But her eyes said that she knew he had a heart, and that was why she was afraid of him.

'What you were talking about just now was a mistake, and not love.'

'You will remember that I have forbidden you to pronounce that word, that ghastly word,' said Anna with a shudder; but she sensed straight away that with just that one word *forbidden* she was showing that she was claiming certain rights over him, and thus actually encouraging him to speak about love. 'I have long been meaning to tell you,' she went on, looking at him straight in the eye, her flushed face burning, 'and I made a point of coming tonight, knowing I would meet you here. I have come to tell you that this must end. No one has ever made me blush before, but you make me feel guilty about something.'

He looked at her and was struck by a new spiritual beauty in her face.

'What do you want from me?' he asked, simply and seriously.

'I want you to go to Moscow and ask Kitty's forgiveness,' she said, and a tiny flame began to flicker in her eyes.

'You don't want that,' he said.

He saw that she was saying what she was forcing herself to say, not what she wanted to say.

'If you love me, as you say you do,' she whispered, 'do it so that I may be at peace.'

His face lit up.

'You must surely know that you are my whole life; but I don't know peace, so I can't give you that. All of me, love . . . yes. I can't think about you and me separately. To me, you and I are one. And I cannot foresee any possibility of peace for either me or you. I can see the possibility of despair and unhappiness . . . or I can see the possibility of happiness, and what happiness! . . . Is that really not possible?' he added with just his lips; but she heard him.

She did her utmost to focus her mind in order to say what ought to be said, but in place of that she brought her love-filled gaze to rest on him and did not answer.

'There it is!' he thought jubilantly. 'Just when I was beginning to despair, and thought there was no end in sight—there we are! She loves me! She is admitting it!'

'So do this for me, never say those words to me, and let us be good friends,' were the words she spoke; but her eyes said something quite different.

'We shall never be friends, you know that yourself. As to whether we shall be the happiest or the unhappiest of people—that is in your power.'

She was about to say something, but he interrupted her.

'There is only one thing I am asking for, after all, and that is the right to hope and to suffer as I am doing now; but if even that is not possible, command me to disappear, and I will disappear. You will not see me if you find my presence difficult.'

'I don't want to banish you anywhere.'

'Only don't change anything. Leave everything as it is,' he said in a trembling voice. 'Here's your husband.'

Indeed, at that very moment Alexey Alexandrovich was coming into the drawing room with his plodding, awkward gait.

Casting a glance at his wife and Vronsky, he went up to the hostess, sat down with a cup of tea, and started talking in his unhurried, always audible voice, mocking someone in his usual jocular way.

'Your Rambouillet has a full complement,' he said, looking round at everyone there; 'the graces and the muses.'*

But Princess Betsy could not bear that tone of his—his *sneering*[1] as she called it, and being a smart hostess, she immediately led him into a serious conversation on the subject of universal conscription. Alexey Alexandrovich immediately became engrossed in the conversation and started to mount a serious defence of the new decree to Princess Betsy, who had attacked it.

Vronsky and Anna continued to sit at the little table.

'This is becoming indecorous,' whispered one lady, indicating Karenina, Vronsky, and her husband with her eyes.

'What did I tell you?' answered Anna's friend.

But not only these ladies, but almost everyone in the drawing room, even Princess Myagkaya and Betsy herself, glanced several times over towards the couple who had withdrawn from the main party, as if it inconvenienced them. Alexey Alexandrovich was the sole person not to look once in their direction or be distracted from the interesting conversation that had started up.

Taking note of the disagreeable impression made on everyone, Princess Betsy deposited another person in her place to listen to Alexey Alexandrovich, and went over to Anna.

'I'm always amazed at the clarity and precision with which your husband expresses himself,' she said. 'I can grasp the most transcendental ideas when he's speaking.'

'Oh, yes!' said Anna with a radiant smile of happiness, and not understanding a word of what Betsy was saying to her. She went over to the big table and took part in the general conversation.

After staying for half an hour, Alexey Alexandrovich went up to his wife and suggested that they go home together; but without looking at him, she replied that she was staying to supper. Alexey Alexandrovich made his bows and left.

The Karenins' coachman, a rotund old Tatar in a shiny leather coat, was having difficulty restraining the grey horse on the left, which, frozen with cold, was rearing up by the porch. The footman stood holding open the carriage door. The porter stood holding on to the front door. Anna Arkadyevna was detaching the lace on her sleeve from a hook on her fur coat with her small deft hand, and with her head bowed, was listening raptly to what Vronsky was saying as he escorted her out.

'You haven't said anything; and let us suppose I ask for nothing,' he was saying; 'but you know that it's not friendship I want, as there's only

[1] [English in the original.]

one possible happiness in life for me, and it is that word you dislike so much . . . yes, love . . .'

'Love . . .' she repeated slowly to herself, and just at the moment when she managed to unhook the lace, she suddenly added: 'The reason I don't like that word is because it means too much to me, far more than you can understand,' and she looked into his face. 'Goodbye!'

She held out her hand, walked past the porter with her brisk, jaunty step, and disappeared into the carriage.

Her glance, and the touch of her hand, set him on fire. He kissed his palm in the place where she had touched it and set off home, happy in the knowledge that he had come closer to reaching his goal that evening than during the whole of the last two months.

8

ALEXEY ALEXANDROVICH saw nothing unusual or improper about his wife sitting with Vronsky at a separate table and talking animatedly about something; but he did notice that it seemed unusual and improper to everyone else in the drawing room, and for that reason it seemed improper to him too. He decided he needed to speak to his wife about it.

On arriving home, Alexey Alexandrovich proceeded to his study, as he usually did, sat down in his armchair, opened his book on the Papacy at the place marked by his paper-knife, and read until one o'clock, as he usually did; just occasionally, he rubbed his high forehead and gave his head a shake, as if trying to expel something. At the usual time he got up and prepared for bed. Anna Arkadyevna was still not back. He went upstairs with the book under his arm; but this evening, instead of his usual thoughts and reflections about office matters, his thoughts were filled by his wife and something unpleasant which was happening to her. Contrary to his usual habit, he did not get into bed, but started walking up and down the rooms of the house with his hands clasped behind his back. He could not go to bed, as he felt it was vital for him first to ponder the newly arisen circumstance.

When Alexey Alexandrovich had decided to himself that he needed to have a talk with his wife, it had seemed very easy and simple to him; but now, when he began to ponder this newly arisen circumstance, it seemed very complicated and difficult to him.

Alexey Alexandrovich was not jealous. Jealousy, according to his conviction, was insulting to a wife, and it was necessary to trust one's wife. Why he should trust her, that is to say, have complete confidence that his young wife would always love him, he did not stop to consider; but he did not experience a feeling of distrust, because he trusted her, and told himself it was necessary to do so. Now, however, although his conviction that jealousy was a despicable feeling and that one should have trust had not been destroyed, he felt he was standing face to face with something illogical and nonsensical, and he did not know what he should do. Alexey Alexandrovich was standing face to face with life, with the possibility of his wife loving someone other than himself, and this seemed to him very nonsensical and incomprehensible because it was life itself. Alexey Alexandrovich had spent his entire life living and working in official spheres which had to do with the reflections of life. And every time he had bumped into life itself he had shied away from it. He was now experiencing a feeling similar to that which would be felt by someone who, calmly crossing a bridge over a precipice, suddenly discovers that this bridge has been taken down, revealing an abyss. This abyss was life itself, while the bridge was the artificial life Alexey Alexandrovich had been leading. For the first time conjectures occurred to him about the possibility of his wife falling in love with somebody, and he was horrified by the idea.

Without undressing, he paced with his even step up and down the echoing parquet of the dining room, lit by a single lamp, then across the carpet of the dark drawing room, where light was reflected only on the large, recently completed portrait of himself hanging above the sofa, and across her boudoir, where there were two candles burning, illuminating the portraits of her relatives and female friends and the beautiful curios on her writing desk he had come to know so well. He walked through her boudoir to the bedroom door and turned round again.

On each stretch of his walk, and mostly on the parquet of the lit dining room, he would stop and say to himself, 'Yes, it is essential to sort this out and stop it, give my opinion about it and my decision.' And he would turn back. 'But give my view on what? What decision?' he would say to himself in the drawing room and find no answer. 'And what has actually happened anyway?' he would ask himself before turning to go into her boudoir. 'Nothing. She spent a long time talking to him. And what of it? Surely a woman in society can talk to whom she pleases. And then jealousy would mean humiliating both myself and her,' he would tell himself as he went into her boudoir; but this reasoning, which had always carried so much weight with him before, now carried no weight and meant nothing. And from the bedroom door he would turn round and head towards the drawing room again; but as soon as he went back into the darkened room, there would be some voice telling him it was not so, and that if others had noticed it, there had to be something in it. And he would tell himself again in the dining room: 'Yes, it is essential to sort this out and stop it, and give my view on it . . .' And he would ask himself again in the drawing room before turning round: 'how do I resolve this?' Then he would ask himself: 'What has happened?' And he would answer: 'Nothing', and remember that jealousy was a feeling demeaning to his wife; but in the drawing room he would again be persuaded that something had happened. His thoughts, like his body, had come full circle without stumbling across anything new. He noticed this, wiped his brow, and sat down in her boudoir.

Here, looking at her bureau, with the malachite blotter and a note she had begun sitting on top of it, his thoughts suddenly changed. He began to think about her, and about what she was thinking and feeling. For the first time he conjured up a vivid picture of her personal life, her thoughts and her desires, but the idea that she could and should have her own private life was so alarming to him that he hastened to drive it away. This was the abyss he was afraid of peering into. Putting himself into the thoughts and feelings of another person was a mental activity alien to Alexey Alexandrovich. He regarded this mental activity as pernicious, dangerous daydreaming.

'And the worst thing of all', he thought, 'is that this pointless worry should befall me precisely now, when my work is nearing completion'— he was thinking of the project he was trying to launch just then—'and when I need all the peace and inner strength I can muster. But what is to be done? I'm not one of those people who suffer anxiety and worry and lack the strength to confront them.'

'I must think it over, come to a decision, and put it out of my mind,' he said aloud.

'Questions regarding her feelings, about what has gone on and might be going on in her soul are not my concern; they are a concern for her conscience, and appertain to religion,' he told himself, feeling relief in the awareness that he had found the point in the statutes which covered the newly arisen circumstance.

'And so questions about her feelings and so on,' Alexey Alexandrovich said to himself, 'are essentially questions for her conscience, which can be no concern of mine. But my duty is clearly defined. As the head of the family, I am the person whose duty it is to guide her, and therefore I am a person with a certain amount of responsibility; I must point out the danger I can see, caution her, and even exert my authority. I must be frank with her.'

And everything Alexey Alexandrovich planned to say to his wife now took clear shape in his head. As he thought over what he would say, he regretted that he would have to use his time and mental energy for domestic purposes, with so little to show for it; nevertheless, the form and sequence of the things he was going to say clearly and distinctly assembled themselves in his head, like a memorandum. 'I must say and clearly articulate the following: firstly, explain the significance of public opinion and decorum; secondly, explain the religious significance of marriage; thirdly, if necessary, indicate the possible unhappiness for our son; fourthly, indicate her own unhappiness.' And, interlocking his fingers, palms downwards, Alexey Alexandrovich stretched them, and the knuckles of his fingers cracked.

This gesture—the bad habit of joining his hands together and making his fingers crack—always soothed him and introduced a semblance of order, which he now so badly needed. A carriage could be heard driving up to the front door. Alexey Alexandrovich stood still in the middle of the drawing room.

A woman's footsteps came up the stairs. Ready with his speech, Alexey Alexandrovich stood clenching his interlocked fingers to see if there would be another crack somewhere. Another knuckle did crack.

He could already feel her approaching from the sound of her light steps on the stairs, and although he was satisfied with his speech, he began to dread the impending discussion . . .

9

ANNA was playing with the tassels of her hood as she walked, her head bent. Her face radiated a bright glow, but it was not a merry glow—it was reminiscent of the terrible glow of a conflagration in the middle of a dark night. Seeing her husband, Anna lifted her head and smiled, as though she was waking up.

'You're not in bed? That's a miracle!' she said, throwing off her hood and proceeding, without stopping, into the dressing room. 'It's time to turn in, Alexey Alexandrovich,' she called out from behind the door.

'Anna, I need to talk to you.'

'To me?' she said in surprise before emerging from behind the door and looking at him.

'Yes.'

'What is going on? What is this about?' she asked, sitting down. 'Well, let's talk, if we need to. But it would be better to go to sleep.'

Anna was saying whatever came to her lips, and as she listened to herself, she was surprised at her capacity for lying. How simple and natural her words were, and how convincing it seemed that she was just sleepy! She felt she was clad in the impenetrable armour of falsehood. She felt that some kind of unseen force was helping her and supporting her.

'Anna, I must caution you,' he said.

'Caution me?' she said. 'About what?'

She looked at him so ingenuously and merrily that anyone who did not know her as her husband knew her would have been unable to notice anything unnatural, either in the sound or the meaning of her words. But it meant a great deal to him, knowing her as he did—knowing that she would always notice whenever he went to bed five minutes later than usual and ask the reason why, knowing that she would immediately share with him all her joys, amusements, and sorrows—to see now that she did not want to notice his state of mind, or say a single word about herself. He saw that the recesses of her soul, which had been open to him before, were now closed to him. Moreover, he realized from her tone that she was not even perturbed by this, and it was as if she were telling him directly: 'Yes, closed, that's how it should be, and will be from now on.' The sensation he was experiencing now was like that which might be experienced by someone who has returned home and found his house locked. 'But perhaps the key may yet be found,' thought Alexey Alexandrovich.

'I want to caution you,' he said in a quiet voice, 'that through imprudence and a lack of responsibility you may give society reason to talk about you. Your excessively lively conversation this evening with Count Vronsky'—he pronounced this name with slow, clear deliberation—'attracted attention.'

While he was talking, he looked at her laughing eyes, whose impenetrability now frightened him, and felt the sheer futility and pointlessness of his words as he was speaking them.

'You're always like this,' she answered, as though completely failing to understand him, and wilfully only understanding the last thing he said. 'You don't like it when I am glum, and you don't like it when I am in high spirits. I wasn't bored. Does that offend you?'

Alexey Alexandrovich shuddered, and he bent his hands back to make the knuckles crack.

'Oh, please, don't make your fingers crack, I so dislike it,' she said.

'Anna, is this you?' said Alexey Alexandrovich quietly, making an effort to restrain himself from moving his hands.

'But what is this all about?' she said, with apparently genuine and comic surprise. 'What do you want from me?'

Alexey Alexandrovich fell silent and rubbed his forehead and his eyes. He saw that instead of doing what he had intended—that is, caution his wife from making a mistake in the eyes of society—he was unwittingly brooding on what was a matter for her conscience, and was battling against some imaginary wall.

'Here is what I want to say,' he went on coldly and calmly, 'and I ask you to hear me out. As you know, I consider jealousy to be an offensive and degrading feeling, and I will never allow myself to be governed by this feeling; but there are certain rules of decorum which cannot be breached with impunity. This evening it was not I who noticed, but to judge from the impression made on people there, everyone else noticed that your conduct and deportment were not altogether what could be desired.'

'I really don't understand this,' said Anna, shrugging her shoulders. 'He doesn't care,' she thought, 'but people noticed, and that worries him.' 'You're not well, Alexey Alexandrovich,' she added, standing up and making for the door, but he moved forward as if to bar her way.

His face was ugly and baleful, like Anna had never seen before. She stopped, and leaning her head back and to one side, began taking out her hairpins with her agile hand.

'Well, I'm ready to hear what is next,' she said coolly and derisively. 'Indeed I'm looking forward to hearing it, as I should like to understand what this is all about.'

She was astounded at the calm and natural tone in which she was speaking, and the selection of words she used.

'I do not have the right to enter into the intricacies of your feelings, and generally regard it as a fruitless and even detrimental activity,' began Alexey Alexandrovich. 'When we start digging around in our souls, we often unearth something that might have lain undetected. Your feelings are a matter for your own conscience; but I have a duty to you, to myself, and to God, to point out your duties. Our lives have been joined, and joined not by man, but by God. This union can only be severed by a crime, and a crime of this nature carries a heavy punishment.'

'I don't understand a thing. Oh, goodness, and being so sleepy doesn't help!' she said, rapidly running her hand through her hair, and feeling for the remaining hairpins.

'Anna, for heaven's sake, don't speak like that,' he said meekly. 'Perhaps I am mistaken, but believe me, what I am saying I am saying as much for my own benefit as for yours. I am your husband, and I love you.'

Her face softened for a moment, and the derisive spark in her look
went out; but the word 'love' aggravated her again. She thought:
'Love? Is he capable of love? If he hadn't heard that there was such
a thing as love, he would never have used this word. He doesn't even
know what love is.'

'Alexey Alexandrovich, really, I don't understand,' she said. 'Explain
what it is you find . . .'

'Please allow me to finish. I love you. But I am not speaking of
myself; the main people here are our son and you yourself. It may very
well be, I repeat, that what I am saying will seem completely unnecessary and inappropriate to you; it may be that it is occasioned by my
error. If that is the case, I ask you to forgive me. But if you yourself feel
it is in the slightest way justified, then I ask you to reflect, and, if your
heart moves you, to tell me . . .'

Without noticing it himself, what Alexey Alexandrovich was saying
was completely different to what he had rehearsed.

'I have nothing to say. And anyway . . .' she suddenly said hurriedly,
barely repressing a smile, 'really, it's time to go to bed.'

Alexey Alexandrovich sighed, and headed into the bedroom without
saying more.

When she came into the bedroom, he was already in bed. His lips
were tightly pursed, and his eyes did not look at her. Anna got into her
bed, expecting any minute that he would start talking to her again. She
both feared he would start talking, and she also wanted him to. But he
was silent. She waited for a long while without moving, and then forgot about him. She was thinking about someone else, whom she could
picture, and she felt her heart fill with excitement and illicit joy at the
thought of him. Suddenly she heard a calm, steady whistling through
the nose. At first Alexey Alexandrovich seemed to be frightened by this
whistle he was producing, and stopped; but after two intakes of breath
the whistling started up again with a calm, new regularity.

'It's late, late, so late,' she whispered with a smile. For a long time
she lay still with her eyes open, and it seemed to her that she could
herself see their sparkle in the darkness.

10

FROM that evening a new life began for Alexey Alexandrovich and for
his wife. Nothing particular happened as such. As always, Anna went
into society, visiting Princess Betsy particularly often, and meeting

Vronsky everywhere. Alexey Alexandrovich saw this, but there was nothing he could do. She countered all his efforts to draw her into a frank discussion by putting up an impenetrable wall of a sort of baffled amusement. Outwardly everything was the same, but on the inside their relationship was utterly changed. Alexey Alexandrovich, who was such a formidable person in affairs of state, felt powerless in this situation. Like a bull submissively bowing its head, he awaited the axe which he felt was raised above him. Every time he began to think about it, he felt he should try again, and that by dint of kindness, affection, and persuasion there was still hope of saving her, and making her come to her senses, so every day he prepared himself to talk to her. But every time he did begin talking to her, he felt that the spirit of evil and deception which had taken hold of her was taking hold of him too, and he could never say to her what he wanted to say, nor in the right tone. He could not help talking to her in that habitual tone of his which seemed to mock anyone who might really talk like that. But it was impossible to say what needed to be said to her using that tone.

11

THAT which had been the single supreme desire of Vronsky's life for almost a whole year, replacing all his previous desires, and that which for Anna had been an impossible, frightful, and hence all the more alluring dream of happiness—that desire had now been satisfied. Pale, his lower jaw trembling, he stood over her and implored her to be calm, not knowing himself how or why.

'Anna! Anna!' he said in a trembling voice. 'Anna, I beg you! . . .' But the louder he spoke, the lower she bowed her once proud, lively head in shame, and she crumpled up and started to slip off the sofa on which she was sitting on to the floor, towards his feet; she would have fallen on to the carpet if he had not held her.

'My God! Forgive me!' she said, sobbing, pressing his hands to her breast.

She felt so sinful and guilty that all that remained for her was to stoop and ask for forgiveness; but there was no one in her life now apart from him, so she addressed her plea for forgiveness to him. As she looked at him, she felt physically humiliated and could say nothing more. He meanwhile was feeling what a murderer must feel when he looks at the body he has robbed of life. That body he had robbed of life was their love, the first period of their love. There was something terrible and loathsome in the memories of what this terrible price of shame had bought. Shame at her spiritual nakedness oppressed her and communicated itself to him. But in spite of the murderer's deep horror before the body of his victim, the body must be hacked to pieces and hidden, and the murderer must take advantage of what he has gained by murder.

And so the murderer falls on this body with a malevolence which is almost like passion, drags it away, and cuts it up; and this is how he covered her face and shoulders with kisses. She held his hand, and did not move a muscle. Yes, these kisses are what have been bought with this shame. Yes, and this one hand, which will always be mine, is the hand of my accomplice. She lifted this hand and kissed it. He sank to his knees and wanted to see her face; but she hid it, and said nothing. Finally, as if she had to force herself, she got up and pushed him away. Her face was still as beautiful as before, but all the more pitiful for it.

'It is all over,' she said. 'I have nothing but you. Remember that.'

'I can never forget that which is my whole life. For a minute of this happiness . . .'

'What happiness!' she said with loathing and horror, and the horror was ineluctably transmitted to him. 'I beg you, not a word, not a word more.'

She quickly got up and moved away from him.

'Not a word more,' she repeated, and she left him with a look of cold despair on her face which he found strange. She felt unable at that moment to put into words the shame, joy, and horror she felt standing at this threshold into a new life, and she did not want to talk about it and trivialize this feeling with inexact words. But not only could she not find the words to express all the complexity of these feelings later, either the next day or the one after, but she also could not find the thoughts with which to reflect on what was going on in her soul.

She said to herself: 'No, I can't think about this now; later, when I am feeling calmer.' But the calmness she required for thinking never arrived; whenever the thought of what she had done, what would happen to her, and what she ought to do arose in her mind, she was overcome with horror and drove those thoughts away.

'Later, later,' she said; 'when I am calmer.'

But in her dreams, when she had no control over her thoughts, her position presented itself to her in all its hideous nakedness. One dream haunted her almost every night. She dreamed that both of them were her husbands at the same time, and that both were lavishing caresses on her. Alexey Alexandrovich would weep, kiss her hands, and say, 'How good things are now!' And Alexey Vronsky was there too, and he was also her husband. And surprised by something which had seemed impossible to her before, she would explain to them, laughing, that this was much simpler, and that both of them were now happy and contented. But this dream weighed on her like a nightmare, and she always awoke from it in horror.

12

IN the first days and weeks after his return from Moscow, whenever Levin cringed and blushed as he remembered the ignominy of being rejected, he would say to himself: 'I used to blush and cringe in just the same way, thinking my life was over, when I did badly in physics and had to repeat my second year; and I also thought my life was over when I made a mess of that business of my sister's I was entrusted with. And would you believe—now that the years have gone by, I look back and am amazed that it could have upset me. It will be the same with this heartache. Time will pass, and I will cease to care.'

But three months went by and he had not ceased caring, and it was just as painful for him to remember it as it had been in the first few days. He could not put his mind at rest, because after having dreamed about family life for such a long time, and having felt so ready for it, he was still not married, indeed he was further away from marriage than ever. He was himself acutely aware, as was everyone around him, that it was not good for a man of his age to be on his own. He remembered how, before he had left for Moscow, he had at one point said to his cowherd Nikolay, a naive peasant whom he liked talking to: 'You know, Nikolay, I want to get married!', and Nikolay had promptly answered, as if there could be no possible doubt in the matter: 'And about time too, Konstantin Dmitrich.' But marriage had now become a more remote prospect than ever. The place was taken, and whenever he imagined putting one of the girls he knew in that place, he felt it was a complete impossibility. Moreover, the memory of being rejected and the part he had played in it caused him excruciating embarrassment. However much he told himself that he was in no way to blame, that memory, together with other such embarrassing memories, still made him cringe and blush. He was conscious of having done bad things in his past, as every person had, for which his conscience should have tormented him; but the memory of those bad things did not torment him half as much as those trivial but embarrassing memories. Those wounds never healed. And on a level with those memories there was now his rejection and the pathetic situation in which he must have appeared to others that evening. But time and work did their part. The painful memories were gradually blotted out by the unremarkable but important events of country life. With each week that went by he thought less about Kitty. He looked forward to hearing that she had already got married, or was about to get married, hoping that such news, like having a tooth out, would completely cure him.

Meanwhile spring arrived—a beautiful, kind-hearted spring, without spring's usual promises and deceptions, and one of those rare springs which plants, animals, and people rejoice in together. This beautiful spring energized Levin even more, and hardened his resolve to make a complete break with the past, in order to put his solitary life on a firm and independent footing. Although he had not carried out many of the plans with which he had returned to the country, he had nonetheless stayed true to the most important of his resolutions, which was to live a pure life. He did not experience that sense of shame which usually afflicted him after a lapse, and he could look people boldly in the eye. In February he had received a letter from Marya Nikolayevna telling him that his brother Nikolay's health was getting worse, but that he did not want to receive treatment, and as a result of this letter Levin had gone to see his brother in Moscow and managed to persuade him to consult a doctor and go abroad to take the waters. He was so successful in persuading his brother, and lending him money for the journey without irritating him, that he was satisfied with himself in this respect. Apart from managing the estate, which demanded special attention in the spring, and getting on with his reading, that winter Levin had begun writing an agricultural treatise, which argued that the character of the agricultural worker should be taken as an absolute given, like the climate and the soil, and that scientific theories about agriculture should consequently not just be based on data about the soil and the climate, but on data about the soil, the climate, and the known, invariable character of the worker. Thus in spite of his solitude, or because of it, his life was extremely full, and it was only occasionally that he experienced an unsatisfied desire to communicate the ideas wandering round his head to someone other than Agafya Mikhailovna, although he often ended up discussing physics, agricultural theory, and especially philosophy with her; philosophy was Agafya Mikhailovna's favourite subject.

Spring was a long time coming. During the last weeks of Lent the weather was clear and frosty. In the daytime everything thawed in the sun, but at night it went down to minus nine;* the snow was frozen so hard that carts were able to travel off-road. Easter was snowbound. Then all of a sudden, on Easter Monday, a warm wind began to blow, the clouds gathered, and warm, heavy rain poured down for three days and three nights. On the Thursday the wind dropped, and a thick grey fog descended, as if to hide the mysteries of the changes being wrought in nature. Inside the fog, waters began to flow, blocks of ice cracked and moved, turbid and foaming torrents started flowing faster, and then right on Thomas Sunday*, in the evening, the fog lifted, the clouds dispersed into fleecy wisps, the sky cleared, and real spring arrived. The following morning a bright sun rose and quickly devoured the thin layer of ice coating the waters, and everywhere the warm air shimmered as it was suffused with the steam rising from the worn earth. The old grass and the emerging needles of young grass turned green, buds swelled on the guelder-rose, and on currant bushes and birch trees sticky with sap, and bees on the first spring flight from their new home* started buzzing about the gold-flecked willows. Invisible larks burst into song above the velvety green shoots and the ice-covered stubble, peewits sent up plaintive calls over wetlands and marshes still sodden with murky, stagnant water, and up on high cranes and geese flew past with their spring cackle. The cattle, still showing patches of their winter coats, started lowing in the pastures, lambs started frisking on their crooked legs round their bleating mothers, who were shedding their fleeces, fleet-footed children started running along paths that were beginning to dry, leaving behind prints of their bare feet, women washing linen at the pond started chattering merrily, and axes started falling in the yards, where peasants were repairing their ploughs and harrows. Real spring had arrived.

13

LEVIN put on big boots and a cloth coat for the first time instead of his sheepskin, and walked round the farm, treading on ice one minute and into sticky mud the next, and stepping over streams which sparkled so brightly in the sunshine they hurt his eyes.

Spring is the season for plans and proposals. And like a tree in spring that does not yet know how and in which direction the young shoots and branches imprisoned in their swollen buds will grow, Levin did not really have much of an idea himself what project he should tackle now on his beloved estate as he came out into the yard, but he felt full of the most admirable plans and proposals. First of all he went off to see the cattle. The cows had been let out into the pen, and having been basking in the sun, their glossy new spring coats shining, they were mooing to be taken to pasture. After admiring the cows, with whose every detail he was familiar, Levin ordered them to be driven to pasture, and the calves to be let into the pen. The herdsman ran off cheerfully to get ready for the pasture. Hitching up their skirts and splashing barefoot through the mud, their white legs not yet suntanned, the dairymaids ran with switches after the calves, who were lowing, crazed with spring joy, and drove them into the yard.

After admiring that year's offspring, who were particularly fine— the early calves were the size of peasants' cows, and Pava's daughter at three months was as big as a yearling—Levin ordered a trough to be brought out for them, and for hay to be put in the racks. But the racks, which had been made in autumn for the pen and not used during the winter, turned out to be broken. He sent for the carpenter, who by rights should have been working on the threshing machine. But it turned out that the carpenter was repairing the harrows, which were supposed to have been mended back in Shrovetide. This annoyed Levin a great deal. It was annoying that the endlessly sloppy farm-work he had been valiantly fighting against for so many years was happening again. He discovered that the racks had been taken to the carthorses' stable since they were not needed in winter, and had got broken there, having been made from light materials for the calves. This led to the discovery, moreover, that the harrows and all the agricultural tools which he had ordered to be inspected and repaired back in the winter, for which express purpose three carpenters had been taken on, had not in fact been repaired, and that the harrows were being repaired now when it was time to be using them in the fields. Levin sent for the steward, but then immediately went off himself to look for him. The steward, beaming like everything else that day, was coming out of the barn in a short sheepskin coat trimmed with fleece, breaking a piece of straw in his hands.

'Why isn't the carpenter at the threshing machine?'

'Oh, I meant to tell you yesterday: the harrows need repairing. It's the time for ploughing, after all.'

'But what was he doing during the winter, then?'

'But what do you want the carpenter for?'

'Where are the racks from the calves' yard?'

'I instructed them to be put in place. What can you do with these people?' said the steward, with a wave of his hand.

'These people? What can you do with this steward more to the point!' said Levin, flaring up. 'Why do you think I employ you?' he shouted. But remembering that this would not help, he stopped mid-flow and just sighed. 'So, can we begin sowing?' he asked, after a pause.

'Should be possible beyond Turkino tomorrow or the day after.'

'And what about the clover?'

'I've sent Vasily and Mishka; they're out sowing. Only I don't know if they'll get through; it's soggy.'

'How many acres?'

'Sixteen.'

'Why not the whole lot?' Levin yelled.

That they were only sowing sixteen acres of clover and not fifty was even more annoying. From his own experience he knew that clover, both in theory and in practice, only did well when it was sown as early as possible, almost while the snow was still around. And Levin could never manage this.

'There's no one to send. What can you do with these people? Three haven't turned up. And then Semyon . . .'

'Well, you could have let the straw wait.'

'That's exactly what I did.'

'Where is everybody then?'

'There are five of them making compote' (which meant compost). 'And four are turning over the oats; lest they start sprouting, Konstantin Dmitrich.'

Levin knew very well that 'lest they start sprouting' meant that his English seed oats were already spoiled—yet again they had not done what he had ordered.

'But I told you back in Lent about the ventilation chimneys! . . .' he exclaimed.

'Don't worry; we will do everything in good time.'

Levin waved his hand angrily, went off to the barns to look at the oats, and returned to the stable. The oats were not spoiled yet. But the labourers were scattering them with shovels, when they could simply be let straight down into the lower barn; and after arranging for this to be done, and extracting two of the labourers there to go and sow clover, Levin recovered from his annoyance with the steward. Besides, on such a nice day it was impossible to get angry.

'Ignat!' he shouted to the coachman, who was washing the carriage with his sleeves rolled up by the well. 'Saddle up for me . . .'

'Which horse, sir?'

'Oh, I'll take Kolpik.'

'Right, sir.'

While they were saddling his horse, Levin once again called over the steward, who was hovering about in view, so he could mend fences with him, and he began telling him about the spring tasks that lay ahead, and his plans for the estate.

The manure was to be carted earlier, so that would all be finished before the first haymaking. And the far field had to be ploughed continually to keep it fallow. The hay was to be brought in by hired labourers, and not split fifty-fifty with their peasants.

The steward listened closely, and was clearly making an effort to approve his master's proposals, but he still had that hopeless and despondent look that Levin knew so well and which always irritated him. It was a look that said: 'That's all very well, but it will be as God wills.'

Nothing dismayed Levin so much as that tone. But it was a tone common to all the stewards who had ever worked for him. They all had the same attitude towards his proposals, so he no longer got angry now, but he was discouraged, and felt all the more fired up to do battle with this odd elemental force he constantly found himself coming up against, and for which he could find no other name than 'as God wills'.

'We'll see if we can manage it, Konstantin Dmitrich,' said the steward.

'Why shouldn't you manage it?'

'We've absolutely got to take on about fifteen more labourers. But they don't turn up. There were some here today who were asking for seventy roubles for the summer.'

Levin was silent. He had come up against this force once again. He knew that, however hard they tried, they would not be able to take on more than thirty-seven or thirty-eight men at the going rate—forty at most; and once they had taken on forty, there was no one else. All the same, he could not give up fighting.

'If they don't turn up, send word to Sury and to Chefirovka. We'll have to start looking.'

'I'll send word,' said Vasily Fyodorovich despondently. 'But the horses aren't up to much either.'

'We'll buy some more. I know you,' Levin added laughing; 'you're always scrimping and cutting corners; but this year I'm not going to let you have your own way. I'll see to everything myself.'

'Seems like you're wide awake as it is. We enjoy working more when the master keeps an eye on us . . .'

'So they're sowing clover on the other side of Birch Dale? I'll go and take a look,' he said, mounting the small dun Kolpik, who had been brought round by the coachman.

'You won't get across the stream, Konstantin Dmitrich,' the coachman shouted.

'Well, I'll go through the wood then.'

And setting out at a brisk pace on his trusty little horse, who snorted at the puddles and tugged at the reins after long inactivity, Levin rode across the muddy yard, through the gates, and into the open country.

If Levin was happy in the cattle-pens and in the farmyard, he became happier still in the open country. Swaying rhythmically along with the ambling pace of his trusty little horse, drinking in the warm, fresh scent of the snow and air as he rode through the wood, over soft, fast-disappearing snow that was covered with tracks, he rejoiced in every one of his trees, with their swelling buds and the moss reviving on their bark. When he came out of the wood, an unbroken, velvety carpet of green without a single bare or wet patch stretched out before him in the immense open space, with only occasional patches of melting snow dotting the hollows. He was angered neither by the sight of a peasant's horse and colt trampling his young crop (he ordered another peasant he encountered to drive them out), nor by the insolent and stupid reply which came from the peasant Ipat, whom he asked when he ran into him: 'Well, Ipat, do you think we will be sowing soon?' 'We must plough first, Konstantin Dmitrich,' was Ipat's answer. The further on he rode, the higher his spirits soared as he conjured up plans for his estate, each one better than the last; he would plant willows in all his fields along the southern edges, so that the snow below them should not linger too long; he would divide the fields up into six arable and three pasture as reserve; he would build a cattle-yard at the far end of the field and dig a pond, and construct movable pens for the cattle to provide manure. And then he would have eight hundred acres of wheat, two hundred and fifty of potatoes, four hundred of clover, and not a single one wasted.

And it was with such dreams, as he carefully led his horse along the ridges between the furrows so as not to trample his young crops, that he rode up to the labourers sowing clover. The cart with the seed was standing not at the edge but in the middle of the ploughed field, and the winter wheat had been churned up by its wheels and trampled by the horse. Both the labourers were sitting on a ridge, probably sharing a pipe together. The soil in the cart, with which the seed had been mixed, had not been broken up, but had either caked together or frozen into clods. When they saw the master, Vasily the labourer went over to the cart, and Mishka started sowing. This was not good, but Levin seldom lost his temper with labourers. When Vasily came over, Levin told him to take the horse out of the field.

'Don't worry, sir, it'll grow over,' Vasily replied.

'Don't argue, please,' said Levin, 'just do as you're told.'

'Yes, sir,' answered Vasily, and he took hold of the horse's head. 'The sowing is going first-rate, Konstantin Dmitrich,' he said ingratiatingly. 'It's just the walking that's terrible! You're dragging a ton of mud along with every step.'

'Why haven't you sifted the soil?' said Levin.

'But we are breaking it up,' answered Vasily, taking some seed and rubbing the earth between his palms.

It was not Vasily's fault that his cart had been filled with unsifted soil, but it was still annoying.

Having already successfully tried and tested a technique for suppressing his irritation and putting everything that seemed negative back into a positive light, Levin employed it now. He watched Mishka striding along, dragging huge clods of earth that had stuck to each of his feet, then got off his horse, took the sieve from Vasily, and set off to start sowing.

'Where have you got to?'

Vasily pointed to a mark with his foot, and Levin proceeded as best he could, scattering the earth and seeds. Walking was as difficult as wading through a bog, and by the time Levin got to the end of the row he had broken out in a sweat, and so he stopped and gave the basket of seeds back to Vasily.

'Well, sir, mind you don't scold me for this row when summer's here,' said Vasily.

'Why should I?' said Levin cheerily, already feeling the benefits of his technique.

'Well, you'll see when summer comes around. It'll look different. Have a look at where I sowed last spring. I did a good job! You know, I think I try as hard for you as I would for my own father, Konstantin Dmitrich. I don't like doing a bad job myself, and won't let others do badly. What's good for the master's good for us too. When you look over there,' said Vasily, pointing to the field, 'it just gladdens the heart.'

'It's a good spring, Vasily.'

'Yes, even the old folk don't remember a spring like this. I've been home, and our old man has been sowing wheat too, about two acres. He says you can't tell it from rye.'

'And did you start sowing wheat a long time ago?'

'No, it was you who taught us the year before last; and you gave me two bushels. We sold about a quarter and sowed about two acres with the rest.'

'Well, make sure you break up those lumps,' said Levin, going towards his horse, 'and keep an eye on Mishka. If it comes up well, you'll get fifty kopecks an acre.'

'Thank you kindly. Seems we already have a lot to thank you for.'

Levin got on his horse and rode off towards the field with last year's clover, and also the one that had been ploughed in preparation for the spring wheat.

The clover was coming up splendidly in between the stubble. It had already fully renewed itself, its green colour clearly visible through the broken stalks of last year's wheat. The horse stepped into mud up to its forelocks, each hoof making a squelching sound as it broke free from the half-thawed earth. Getting across the ploughed field was completely impossible: ice provided the only footholds, and the horse's legs sank into the thawing furrows over its fetlocks. The ploughed field was in superb condition; in a couple of days they would be able to harrow and sow. Everything was wonderful, everything was rosy. Levin rode back across the stream, hoping the water might have gone down. He did indeed get across, and startled two ducks in the process. 'There must be woodcock around too,' he thought, and just at the turning to his house he happened to meet the forester, who confirmed his hunch about the woodcock.

Levin rode home at a trot, so as to have time to eat his lunch and get his gun ready before evening.

14

ARRIVING home in the best of spirits, Levin heard the sound of sleigh-bells coming from the main entrance of the house.

'Yes, that's someone coming from the station,' he thought, 'it's just the right time for the Moscow train . . . Who could it be? What if it's my brother Nikolay? He did say: "Maybe I'll go to a spa, or maybe I'll come to you."' For a brief, unpleasant moment he feared his brother Nikolay's presence would ruin his happy spring mood. But he felt ashamed for experiencing that feeling, and immediately opened his heart in an embrace, as it were, anticipating with joy and affection, and now hoping with all his heart, that it was his brother. He nudged his horse on, and as he emerged from behind the acacia he saw the hired troika from the railway station and a gentleman in a fur coat driving up. It was not his brother. 'Oh, if only it could be someone nice, who I could talk to,' he thought.

'Ah!' Levin shouted out joyfully, raising both his hands. 'Here's a most welcome guest! Oh, how glad I am to see you!' he exclaimed when he recognized Stepan Arkadyich.

'I'm bound to find out if she's married, or when she will be,' he thought.

And on that wonderful spring day he noticed it was not at all painful to remember her.

'You mean you weren't expecting me?' said Stepan Arkadyich as he got out of the sleigh, the bridge of his nose, his cheek, and his eyebrows all splattered with mud, but radiating health and good cheer. 'I've come first of all to see you,' he said, embracing and kissing him, 'secondly to do some shooting, and thirdly to sell the wood at Ergushovo.'

'Splendid! What about this spring we're having? How did you manage to get here in a sleigh?'

'It's even worse in a cart, Konstantin Dmitrich,' answered the driver, whom he knew.

'Well, I'm very, very glad to see you,' said Levin, beaming ingenuously with a smile of childish delight.

Levin took his guest to the spare room, where Stepan Arkadyich's things were also brought—a bag, a gun in a case, and a pouch for cigars— and then left him to wash and change his clothes, while he went over to the office to issue instructions about the ploughing and the clover. Agafya Mikhailovna, always very mindful about the honour of the house, met him in the hall with questions about dinner.

'Do whatever you like, just get it ready as soon as you can,' he said, and went off to see the steward.

When he returned, Stepan Arkadyich, all washed and combed and smiling from ear to ear, was just coming out of his room, and they went upstairs together.

'Well, I am so glad I've made it all the way out here to visit you! Now I shall understand what is behind all the mysterious things you do here. No, really, I envy you. What a house, how splendid everything is! So bright and cheerful!' said Stepan Arkadyich, forgetting that it was not always spring and clear skies as on that day. 'And your old nanny is a treasure! I'd rather see a pretty maid in a little apron, but she fits in very well with your austere monastic habits.'

Stepan Arkadyich told him many interesting pieces of news, including one of particular interest to Levin, which was that his brother Sergey Ivanovich was intending to come and visit in the summer.

Stepan Arkadyich did not utter a single word about Kitty or about the Shcherbatskys generally, but merely passed on greetings from his wife. Levin appreciated his sensitivity and was very glad to have him as a guest. As always, during his period of solitude he had accumulated a mass of thoughts and feelings which he could not communicate to those around him, and now he poured out to Stepan Arkadyich the poetic joys of spring, his failures and plans for the estate, his thoughts and observations about the books he had been reading, and above all the idea for his treatise, which was grounded, although he himself had not noticed it, in a critique of all previous books on agriculture. Stepan Arkadyich, who was always genial, and picked things up at the merest hint, was being particularly genial during this visit, and Levin noticed in him a new note of respect and tenderness, which he found flattering.

The efforts made by Agafya Mikhailovna and the cook to ensure that the dinner was particularly good simply resulted in the two famished friends sitting down to appetizers and stuffing themselves on bread and butter, smoked goose, and pickled mushrooms, and also in Levin ordering the soup to be served without the little pies with which the cook had particularly hoped to impress the guest. But Stepan Arkadyich, even though he was used to very different kinds of dinners, thought everything was superb: the herb liqueur, the bread, the butter, and especially the smoked goose, and the mushrooms, and the nettle soup, and the chicken in white sauce, and the white Crimean wine—everything was superb and delicious.

'Splendid, splendid!' he said as he lit up a fat cigarette after the roast. 'Coming to you is just like getting off a steamer after all that noise and juddering, and stepping on to a quiet shore. So you're saying that the labourer himself needs to be studied as a factor in the equation, and taken into account when choosing agricultural methods. I'm a layman in this, of course, but I would imagine that this theory and its application will make an impact on the labourer too.'

'Yes, but wait: I'm not talking about political economy, I'm talking about the science of agriculture. It ought to be like natural science, and observe given phenomena and the labourer in his economic, ethnographical . . .'

At that moment Agafya Mikhailovna came in with jam.

'Well, Agafya Mikhailovna,' said Stepan Arkadyich to her, kissing the tips of his plump fingers, 'your smoked goose, your herb liqueur! . . . Now, don't you think it's time we were off, Kostya?' he added.

Levin looked out of the window at the sun sinking behind the bare treetops in the forest.

'Yes, it's time we went,' he said. 'Kuzma, get the trap ready!' And he ran downstairs.

When Stepan Arkadyich went downstairs, he carefully removed the canvas cover from the lacquered case himself, then opened it and began assembling his expensive, newfangled shotgun. Already sensing a big tip in the offing, Kuzma did not leave Stepan Arkadyich's side, putting on both his stockings and boots for him, which Stepan Arkadyich willingly let him do.

'Kostya, if that merchant Ryabinin turns up—I told him to come today—could you make sure he is let in and asked to wait . . .'

'Are you really selling the wood to Ryabinin?'

'Yes. Do you know him then?'

'I certainly do. I have had dealings with him, "positively and finally".'

Stepan Arkadyich laughed. 'Positively and finally' were the merchant's favourite words.

'Yes, it's hilarious the way he talks. She's understood where her master's going!' he added, patting Laska, who was prancing around Levin, yelping and licking his hands, his boots, and his gun.

The trap was standing ready by the porch when they went out.

'I told them to harness it up, although it's not far; but what about walking?'

'No, best to drive,' said Stepan Arkadyich, going up to the trap. He sat down, tucked the tiger-skin rug round his legs, and lit a cigar. 'How is it you don't smoke? A cigar is not so much a pleasure in itself, but the badge and hallmark of pleasure. This is the life! How splendid! This is how I'd like to live!'

'And what's stopping you?' said Levin, smiling.

'No, you're a lucky man. You've got everything you love. You love horses—you've got them; dogs—got them; shooting—got that; farming—got that.'

'Maybe it's because I enjoy what I have, and don't grieve over what I don't have,' said Levin, remembering Kitty.

Stepan Arkadyich understood and cast a glance at him, but said nothing.

Levin was grateful to Oblonsky for noticing with his usual tact that he was reluctant to talk about the Shcherbatskys, and for not saying anything about them; but Levin did now want to find out about the matter tormenting him, except he did not have the courage to raise the subject.

'So, how are things with you?' said Levin, thinking how poor it was on his part to think only about himself.

Stepan Arkadyich's eyes sparkled merrily.

'I know you'll never acknowledge that one can like rolls when you already have your daily bread—it's a crime in your eyes; while I won't acknowledge a life without love,' he said, understanding Levin's question in his own way. 'What am I to do? That's the way I'm made. And really, it brings so little harm to anyone, but so much pleasure for one-self . . .'

'I see—or is there something new?' asked Levin.

'There is, my friend! Now, you know Ossian's type of woman* . . . the kind of woman you see in your dreams . . . Well, these women exist in reality . . . and these women are terrible. The subject of woman, you see, will always be completely new, however much you study it.'

'So better not to study it then.'

'Oh no. Some mathematician or other said that pleasure comes from the search for truth, not in finding it.'

Levin listened in silence, but in spite of his best efforts he could not find any way of entering into his friend's soul and understanding his feelings and the charms of studying such women.

15

THE place where the woodcock would be roding was not far beyond the stream, in a little aspen grove. When they arrived at the wood, Levin got out and led Oblonsky to a corner of a mossy, swampy glade which was already free from snow. He himself returned to a double birch on the other side, and leaning his gun on the fork of a dead lower branch, he took off his coat, tightened his belt, and made sure he could move his arms freely.

Old, grey-haired Laska, who had followed them, sat down warily opposite him and pricked her ears. The sun was setting behind the big forest, and the little birch trees dotted about the aspen copse stood out clearly in the twilight, with their drooping branches and swollen buds ready to burst.

Water could just be heard trickling along the narrow, winding streams in the thicket, where there was still snow. Small birds were twittering and occasionally flitting from tree to tree.

In the spells of complete silence one could hear the rustle of last year's leaves, stirred by the thawing earth and growing grass.

'How about that! You can see and hear the grass growing!' Levin said to himself, noticing a wet, slate-coloured aspen leaf stirring beside a blade of young grass. He stood there, listening and gazing down at the wet mossy ground, at the attentive Laska, at the sea of bare treetops which stretched out before him at the foot of the hill, and at the darkening sky, which was covered with strips of white cloud. High above the distant forest a hawk flew over, flapping its wings slowly; another one just like it flew in the same direction and disappeared. The birds were twittering more and more loudly and busily in the thicket. Not far off an eagle-owl hooted, and Laska gave a start, took a few cautious steps, and put her head on one side, listening intently. A cuckoo could be heard on the other side of the stream. It uttered its usual cuckoo call twice, then began making an increasingly hurried rasping sound and became confused.

'How about that! A cuckoo already!' said Stepan Arkadyich, coming out from behind a bush.

'Yes, I can hear it,' answered Levin, disgruntled about having to disturb the silence of the forest with his voice, which he himself found jarring. 'Won't be long now!'

The figure of Stepan Arkadyich disappeared again behind the bush, and Levin saw only the bright flame of a match, which was then replaced by the red glow of a cigarette and a wisp of blue smoke.

'Click! Click!' came the sound of Stepan Arkadyich cocking his gun.

'What's that cry?' asked Oblonsky, drawing Levin's attention to a drawn-out squealing, like the high-pitched whinny of a frisky foal.

'You don't know what that is? It's a buck hare. But enough talking! Listen, it's on the wing!' Levin almost shouted, cocking his gun.

They heard a distant, shrill whistle, and precisely two seconds later, at that regular interval so familiar to hunters, another, then a third, and after the third whistle came a croaking sound.*

Levin cast a glance to the right and the left, and there in front of him against the dusky blue sky, above the mass of tender shoots at the top of the aspen trees, was the airborne bird. It was flying straight at him: the close croaking sounds, which were like the measured tearing of taut fabric, rang out right above his ear; the bird's long beak and neck were already becoming visible, and just at the moment when Levin took aim there was a flash of red lightning behind the bush where Oblonsky was standing; the bird swooped down as fast as an arrow and then soared up again. There was another flash of lightning and the sound of something being hit, then, fluttering its wings as though trying to stay up in the air, the bird stopped, hovered for an instant, and fell with a heavy thud on to the marshy ground.

'Surely I didn't miss it?' shouted Stepan Arkadyich, who could not see through the smoke.

'Here it is!' said Levin, pointing to Laska, who, with one ear raised and wagging the tip of her upright shaggy tail, was taking her time in bringing the dead bird to her master, as if wanting to prolong the pleasure and almost smiling. 'Well, I'm glad you got it,' said Levin, at the same time already experiencing a twinge of envy that he had not managed to bag that woodcock.

'Missed badly with the right barrel,' Stepan Arkadyich replied as he loaded his gun. 'Ssh . . . there's one coming!'

Indeed, a rapid succession of shrill whistles could be heard. Two woodcock, playing and chasing one another, and only whistling rather than croaking, flew right over the hunters' heads. Four shots rang out, and like swallows, the woodcock took a sharp turn and vanished from sight.

. . . .

The shooting was excellent. Stepan Arkadyich shot another brace, and Levin got two, one of which could not be found. It began to get dark. Low in the west, bright, silvery Venus was already shining from behind the birch trees with her soft light, and the red glow of sombre Arcturus was already shimmering high up in the east. Levin kept finding and losing the stars of the Great Bear above his head. The woodcock had already stopped flying, but Levin decided to wait a little longer, until Venus rose above the birch branch beneath which it was currently visible, and the stars of the Great Bear were clear everywhere. Venus had already risen above the branch, and the chariot of the Great Bear with its shaft was now clearly visible against the dark blue sky, but still he waited.

'Isn't it time to head home?' said Stepan Arkadyich.

It was quite still now in the forest, and not a single bird stirred.

'Let's stay a bit longer,' answered Levin.

'As you like.'

They were now standing about fifteen paces from one another.

'Stiva!' said Levin suddenly out of the blue. 'How come you won't tell me whether your sister-in-law has got married yet, or when she will be?'

Levin felt so secure and calm that he thought no answer could possibly upset him. But he certainly did not expect what Stepan Arkadyich said in reply.

'She has not thought of getting married, nor is she thinking of it now; she's actually very ill, and the doctors have sent her abroad. They even fear for her life.'

'I don't believe it!' cried Levin. 'Very ill? What is wrong with her? How did she . . . ?'

As they were speaking, Laska had pricked up her ears and was gazing both up at the sky and also reproachfully at them.

'A fine time to talk,' she was thinking. 'There's one on the way . . . Sure enough, here it is. They'll miss it . . .' thought Laska.

But at that very moment they both suddenly heard a shrill whistle that seemed to lash their ears and they both suddenly seized their guns; there were two flashes of lightning, and two shots sounded at the very same moment. The woodcock that had been flying high above instantly folded its wings and fell into the thicket, bending the delicate shoots.

'Excellent! Joint effort!' cried Levin, and he ran off with Laska to look for the woodcock in the thicket. 'Oh, yes, what was that unpleasant thing?' he thought, trying to remember. 'Yes, Kitty's ill . . . Well, it can't be helped, and I'm very sorry,' he thought.

'Ah, she's found it! Clever dog,' he said, taking the warm bird out of Laska's mouth and putting it into the game bag, which was almost full. 'I've found it, Stiva!' he shouted.

16

ON the way home Levin asked for all the details of Kitty's illness and the Shcherbatskys' plans, and although he would have been ashamed to admit it, he was pleased by what he found out. He was pleased that there was still hope, and even more pleased that the person who had made him suffer so much was suffering herself. But when Stepan Arkadyich began to discuss the causes of Kitty's illness, and mentioned Vronsky's name, Levin cut him short:

'I have no right whatever to know about these family matters, and, to tell the truth, I've no interest in them either.'

Stepan Arkadyich broke into an almost imperceptible smile as he noticed the sudden and so familiar change in Levin's expression, which was now as gloomy as it had been cheerful a moment earlier.

'Have you sewn up the deal with Ryabinin about the wood?' asked Levin.

'I have, yes. It's an excellent price, thirty-eight thousand. Eight up front, and the rest over six years. I spent a long time negotiating. No one would offer any more.'

'You've virtually given away your wood for free,' said Levin despondently.

'What do you mean, given it away for free?' said Stepan Arkadyich with a good-natured smile, knowing that nothing would be right in Levin's eyes now.

'Because that wood is worth at least two hundred roubles an acre,' answered Levin.

'Ah, you country gents!' said Stepan Arkadyich jokingly. 'That tone of contempt you have for us townsfolk! . . . But when it comes to business, we always have the upper hand. I assure you, I have worked it all out,' he said; 'the wood is fetching a very good price, so I'm even afraid the man will back out. It's not *young-growth*,* you know,' said Stepan Arkadyich, hoping this distinction would persuade Levin of the unfairness of his doubts, 'but more suited for firewood. It won't yield more than thirty yards' worth per acre, and he's giving me a rate of seventy-two roubles per acre.'

Levin smiled scornfully. 'I know that habit,' he thought, 'and it's not just him, but all city people who come to the country a couple of times in ten years, pick up two or three rural terms, and use them appropriately and inappropriately, completely convinced that they know everything there is to know. *Young-growth, yield thirty yards per acre.* He uses the words, but he does not have the faintest idea what they all mean.'

'I wouldn't try to teach you whatever it is you write about in your office,' he said, 'but if there is something I need to know, I will ask you. But you're so positive you know everything about forestry. It's difficult. Have you counted the trees?'

'What do you mean, count the trees?' said Stepan Arkadyich with a laugh, still keen to lift his friend out of his bad mood. 'Although a lofty mind might count the grains of sand, and the planets' rays . . .'*

'Well, the lofty mind of Ryabinin certainly can. And no merchant will buy without counting, unless someone is giving it away for nothing, like you are. I know your wood. I shoot there every year, and can tell you your wood is worth two hundred roubles an acre in cash, while he's giving you seventy-five in instalments. That means you're making him a present of about thirty thousand.'

'Come on now, don't get carried away,' said Stepan Arkadyich pitifully. 'Why would no one make me a better offer then?'

'Because he has a racket going with the merchants; he's bought them off. I've had dealings with all of them, and I know them. They're not merchants, you know, they're profiteers. He will never do any business that will make him ten or fifteen per cent, because he is waiting until he gets a rouble for twenty kopecks.'

'Come on now, that's enough! You're in a bad mood.'

'Not in the least,' said Levin despondently as they drove up to the house.

A trap tightly upholstered in leather and iron, with a sleek horse tightly harnessed to wide traces, was already standing by the porch. Sitting in the trap was the ruddy, tight-skinned, tightly belted clerk who served as Ryabinin's driver. Ryabinin himself had already gone into the house, and he met the friends in the hall. Ryabinin was a tall, lean, middle-aged man with a moustache, a prominent, clean-shaven chin, and protuberant, dull eyes. He was dressed in a long-skirted, blue frock-coat with buttons below the waist at the back, tall boots which wrinkled at the ankles but straightened out over the calves, and large galoshes on top of them. He rubbed his face all over with his handker-chief, did up his coat, which already was very snug on him, and greeted the arrivals with a smile, holding out his hand to Stepan Arkadyich as though wanting to catch something.

'So you've arrived,' said Stepan Arkadyich, extending his hand to him. 'Marvellous.'

'I did not take the liberty of disobeying Your Eminence's orders, although the road was really too bad. I positively had to come the whole way on foot, but I got here on time. My respects, Konstantin Dmitrich,' he said turning to Levin, and trying to grasp his hand too. But the scowling Levin, pretending he had not noticed his hand, was taking out the woodcock. 'Your Eminences have been enjoying some shooting? What sort of birds might they be?' added Ryabinin, looking disdainfully at the woodcock. 'They must taste good, I suppose.' And he shook his head disapprovingly, as if he had grave doubts that this game was worth powder and shot.

'Do you want to go into my study?' said Levin in French to Stepan Arkadyich with a baleful glare. 'Do go through into my study; you can talk there.'

'Very fine, wherever you please, sir,' said Ryabinin with dignified disdain, as if wishing to make them realize that while some people might find it difficult to know how to behave with others, there could never be any difficulties about anything where he was concerned.

When he entered the study, Ryabinin looked round from habit, as if searching for the icon,* but when he found it, he did not cross himself.

He cast his eyes over the cabinets and bookshelves, and with the same doubts that he had about the woodcock, he smiled disdainfully and shook his head disapprovingly, by no means willing to allow that this game could be worth the powder and shot.

'So, have you brought the money?' asked Oblonsky. 'Do sit down.'

'The money won't be a problem. I've come to meet you and talk it over.'

'What is there to talk over? Please do sit down.'

'Very well,' said Ryabinin, sitting down and leaning his elbows against the back of the chair, in the most uncomfortable manner. 'You'll have to knock it down a bit, Prince. It's not right. But the money is absolutely ready, down to the last kopeck. There won't be any hitches with the money.'

Levin had meanwhile been putting his gun away in the cabinet and was just going out of the door, but he stopped when he heard the merchant's words.

'You've got the forest for next to nothing,' he said. 'He came to me too late, otherwise I'd have set a price.'

Ryabinin got up, and smiled as he silently looked Levin up and down.

'Very tight-fisted is Konstantin Dmitrich,' he said with a smile, turning to Stepan Arkadyich. 'There's absolutely nothing you can buy off him. I was trading with him over some wheat, and offering good money.'

'Why should I give what is mine to you for nothing? I didn't pick it up off the ground or steal it, after all.'

'Good gracious, stealing is positively impossible nowadays. There are open legal proceedings for absolutely everything nowadays,* everything is proper these days; there's no question of stealing. We're doing honest business. The price for the wood is too dear, the sums don't add up. I'm asking you to come down a bit.'

'So have you concluded your deal or not? If you have, it's useless haggling; but if not,' said Levin, 'I'll buy the wood.'

The smile suddenly vanished from Ryabinin's face. A hawk-like, rapacious, and cruel expression settled on it. He unbuttoned his frock-coat with rapid, bony fingers, revealing a loose shirt, a waistcoat with brass buttons, and a watch-chain, and quickly pulled out a fat old wallet.

'The wood is mine, please,' he said, crossing himself quickly and holding out his hand. 'Take the money, it's my wood. That's how Ryabinin does business, no counting of coppers,' he added, brandishing the wallet with a frown.

'I wouldn't be in a hurry if I were you,' said Levin.

'Gracious,' said Oblonsky in surprise. 'I did give him my word.'

Levin went out of the room, slamming the door. Ryabinin shook his head with a smile as he looked at the door.

'There's youth for you, absolutely nothing but childishness. Believe me, I'm buying it after all just for the glory of it being Ryabinin who bought Oblonsky's copse rather than anyone else. And it's God's will as to whether the sums work out. You have to trust God. Now if you please, there's this little agreement to sign . . .'

An hour later, after wrapping himself up neatly in his kaftan and doing up the hooks of his frock-coat, with the agreement in his pocket, the merchant seated himself in his tightly bound trap and set off home.

'Ugh, these gentry!' he said to the clerk, 'all the same.'

'It's true,' replied the clerk, handing him the reins and fastening the leather apron. 'But I can congratulate you on your little purchase, Mikhail Ignatich?'

'Well, I suppose . . .'

17

STEPAN ARKADYICH went upstairs, his pocket bulging with the banknotes the merchant had paid him for three months in advance. The business with the wood was over, the money was in his pocket, the shooting had been marvellous, and Stepan Arkadyich was in the happiest frame of mind, so he was especially keen to dispel the bad mood that had descended on Levin. He wanted to finish the day over supper as pleasantly as it had begun.

Levin really was in low spirits, and despite his wholehearted desire to be kind and hospitable to his cherished guest, he could not get the better of his feelings. The intoxication of the news that Kitty was not married had gradually begun to overwhelm him.

Kitty was not married and was ill—ill from her love for a man who had scorned her. This insult somehow reflected on him. Vronsky had scorned her, and she had scorned him, Levin. Consequently, Vronsky had the right to despise Levin and was therefore his enemy. But Levin did not think all those things. He had a vague feeling there was something personally offensive about it, and was not angry about the thing that had upset him, but instead found fault with everything around him. The stupid sale of the wood and the swindle to which Oblonsky had succumbed, which had taken place in his house, were irritating him.

'So, all done?' he said, meeting Stepan Arkadyich upstairs. 'Would you like some supper?'

'Oh, I wouldn't say no. I have such an appetite in the country, it's unbelievable! Why didn't you offer Ryabinin something to eat?'

'Oh, to hell with him!'

'The way you treated him!' said Oblonsky. 'You didn't even shake hands with him. Why not shake hands with him?'

'Because I don't shake hands with my footman, and my footman's a hundred times better than he is.'

'Really, what a reactionary you are! What about the merging of classes?' said Oblonsky.

'The best of luck to those who enjoy merging, but I loathe the idea.'

'I can see you're definitely a reactionary.'

'I have really never thought about what I am. I am Konstantin Levin, and that's all.'

'And a Konstantin Levin who is very much out of sorts,' said Stepan Arkadyich, smiling.

'Yes, I am out of sorts, and do you know why? Forgive me, but it's because of your stupid sale . . .'

Stepan Arkadyich good-naturedly pulled a wry face, like someone who has been insulted and upset without just cause.

'Come on, enough of that!' he said. 'When did anybody ever sell anything without being told immediately after the sale: "It was worth much more"? When you want to sell, no one makes an offer . . . No, I can see you've got a grudge against the unfortunate Ryabinin.'

'Maybe I have. And do you know why? You'll tell me again that I'm a reactionary, or some other terrible word; but nevertheless it does anger and annoy me to see going on around me everywhere this impoverishment of the nobility to which I belong, and am glad to belong, despite the merging of classes. And this impoverishment is not down to extravagance—that's the least of it; living the high life is the gentry's prerogative, and only the gentry know how to do it. The peasants around us are buying up land now, and I don't mind that. The landowner does nothing, the peasant works and forces out someone idle. That's how it should be. And I'm very glad for the peasant. But I do mind seeing this impoverishment happening because of some sort of naivety, for want of a better word. First you have the Polish tenant who buys a magnificent estate from a lady who lives in Nice at half-price. And then three acres of land are rented out to a merchant for a rouble, when it's worth ten. And now you've made that swindler a present of thirty thousand roubles for no reason at all.'

'So what should I have done? Counted every tree?'

'Certainly you should have counted them. You didn't count them, but Ryabinin did. Ryabinin's children will have the means to live well and be educated, while yours maybe will not!'

'Well, forgive me, but there's something petty about this counting. We have our business and they have theirs, and they need to make a profit. Anyway, the deal's done, and let there be an end to it. Ah, here come the fried eggs, my favourite way of cooking them. And Agafya Mikhailovna will give us that wonderful herb liqueur . . .'

Stepan Arkadyich sat down at the table and began joking with Agafya Mikhailovna, assuring her it was a long time since he had eaten such a dinner or supper.

'Well, at least you appreciate it,' said Agafya Mikhailovna, 'whereas Konstantin Dmitrich, whatever you give him, even if it's a crust of bread, he has a bite to eat and then he's off.'

No matter how hard Levin tried to conquer his feelings, he remained gloomy and silent. There was one question he needed to put to Stepan Arkadyich, but he could not bring himself to ask it, and could find neither the right way nor the right moment to broach the topic. Stepan Arkadyich had already gone downstairs to his room, undressed, washed again, attired himself in a crimped nightshirt, and climbed into bed, but Levin was still lingering in his room, talking about various trivial matters and unable to summon up the courage to pose the question he wanted to ask.

'It's wonderful how they make this soap,' he said, examining and unwrapping a fragrant bar of soap which Agafya Mikhailovna had put out for his guest, but which Oblonsky had not used. 'Just look, it's a real work of art.'

'Yes, everything's brought to such a state of perfection nowadays,' said Stepan Arkadyich, with a moist-eyed and blissful yawn. 'Theatres, for instance, and those entertainment . . . ah—ah—ah!' he yawned. 'Electric light everywhere* . . . ah—ah—ah!'

'Yes, electric light,' said Levin. 'Yes. Well, where's Vronsky these days?' he asked suddenly, putting down the soap.

'Vronsky?' said Stepan Arkadyich, stopping his yawn. 'He's in Petersburg. He left soon after you did, and hasn't been seen in Moscow since. And you know, Kostya, I'll tell you the truth,' he went on, leaning his elbow on the table and resting on his hand his handsome, florid face, from which his sensuous, kind, and sleepy eyes shone like stars. 'It's your own fault. You were frightened off by your rival. But as I told you back then, I don't know who had the better chance. Why didn't you go for it? I told you at the time that . . .' He yawned with just his jaws, without opening his mouth.

'Does he or doesn't he know that I proposed?' Levin wondered, looking at him. 'Yes, there's something crafty and diplomatic going on inside him,' and feeling that he was blushing, he looked Stepan Arkadyich straight in the eye without saying a word.

'If there was anything on her side at the time, it was just a superficial attraction,' continued Oblonsky. 'And it was her mother's head which was turned by his perfect aristocratic qualities and his future prospects in society, you know, not hers.'

Levin glowered. The humiliation of the rejection he had undergone blazed in his heart, as though it were a wound he had only just received. But he was at home, and even the walls help when you are at home.*

'Just a minute,' he began, interrupting Oblonsky. 'You say he's an aristocrat. But I'd like to know what exactly is so aristocratic about Vronsky, or anyone else for that matter, that I am to be looked down upon? You consider Vronsky an aristocrat, but I don't. A man whose father came up from nowhere purely through intrigue, and whose mother had liaisons with goodness knows whom . . . No, excuse me, but I consider myself and other people like me to be aristocrats, who can point to three or four honest generations going back in their family, who are in the highest degree educated (talent and intellect are another matter), who have never demeaned themselves before anyone, and never depended on anyone for anything, which is how my father and my grandfather lived. And I know many such people. You consider it beneath me to count the trees in a wood, while you give away thirty thousand to Ryabinin; but you will receive rent and heaven knows what else, whereas I won't, and therefore I value what I've inherited and worked for . . . It is we who are the aristocrats, and not those who owe their existence to favours from the high and mighty of this world, and who can be bought for a few kopecks.'

'Who are you railing against? I agree with you,' said Stepan Arkadyich with cheerful sincerity, although he felt that Levin was bracketing him with those who could be bought for a few kopecks. Levin's fervour genuinely pleased him. 'Who are you railing against? Although there is a good deal of untruth in what you say about Vronsky, that's not what I am talking about. I'm telling you this frankly, that if I were you, I would come to Moscow with me, and . . .'

'No, I don't know whether you know or not, but I don't care. So I'll tell you—I did propose and I was rejected, and Katerina Alexandrovna is now just a painful and humiliating memory for me.'

'Why? That's just nonsense!'

'Let's not talk about it. Please forgive me if I've been rude to you,' said Levin. Now that he had got everything off his chest, he again became how he had been in the morning. 'You're not angry with me, Stiva? Please don't be angry,' he said, and took his hand with a smile.

'Oh no, not in the slightest, there's no reason to be. I'm glad we've had all this out. Woodcock roding in the morning can be good,* you know. Shouldn't we go? I wouldn't sleep afterwards, but would go straight from shooting to the station.'

'Splendid idea.'

18

DESPITE the fact that Vronsky's inner life was completely taken up with his passion, his outer life continued to roll inalterably and inexorably along its usual old rails of social and regimental connections and interests. Regimental interests occupied an important place in Vronsky's life, both because he liked the regiment, and even more because his regiment liked him. They not only liked Vronsky in his regiment, but they respected and were proud of him, proud that this immensely wealthy man, with his superlative education and abilities, and the road open to every kind of success, ambition, and vainglory, had turned his back on all that, and out of all the interests in his life had chosen to keep those of his regiment and his comrades closest to his heart. Vronsky was aware that his comrades had this view of him, and apart from the fact that he liked this life, he felt obliged to maintain this established view of himself.

It goes without saying that he did not speak about his love to any of his comrades, nor did he blurt anything out even in the wildest drinking bouts (although he was never so drunk that he lost control of himself), and he would silence any of his more frivolous comrades who attempted to allude to his liaison. But in spite of the fact that people all over the city knew about his love—everyone guessed more or less correctly about his relations with Karenina—the majority of young men envied him the most difficult aspect of his affair, which was Karenin's high position, and hence the high profile of this liaison in society.

The majority of young women envious of Anna, who had long tired of her being described as *principled*, rejoiced at something they had surmised, and were just waiting for confirmation that the tide of public opinion had turned so they could unleash on her the full weight of their scorn. They were already gathering their little lumps of mud to sling at her when the time came. The majority of elderly and highly ranked people were unhappy about the impending social scandal.

Vronsky's mother was initially happy when she heard about his liaison, both because, in her view, nothing gave the finishing touch to a brilliant young man quite like a high-society liaison, and also because it turned out that Karenina, whom she had liked so much, and who had talked so much about her son, was, in the view of Countess Vronskaya, just like every other beautiful and respectable woman after all. But she had recently found out that her son had turned down a position offered to him which was important for his career, just so he could stay in his regiment and be able to see Karenina, and she found out that his superiors were displeased with him about that, so she changed her mind. She also did not like the fact that, from what she could gather about this liaison, it was not a brilliant, stylish society liaison, such as she would have approved, but a kind of Werther-like,* desperate passion, so she was told, which might well lead him into doing something foolish. She had not seen him since the time of his unexpected departure from Moscow, and was insisting, via her eldest son, that he come and see her.

The elder brother was also displeased with his younger sibling. He did not investigate what sort of love affair this was, grand or modest, passionate or passionless, immoral or moral (he had children himself but kept a ballet dancer, so he was indulgent in these matters); but he knew it was a love affair which did not please those whom one needed to please, and therefore he did not approve of his brother's conduct.

Besides his military and social pursuits, Vronsky had another— horses—of which he was a passionate devotee.

A steeplechase had been arranged for the officers that year. Vronsky had entered the race, bought an English thoroughbred mare, and, in spite of his love affair, was passionately, albeit quietly, enthralled with the forthcoming race . . .

These two passions did not interfere with one another. On the contrary, he needed a pursuit and an enthusiasm independent of his love affair, so that he could refresh himself and recuperate from the excessively strong feelings coursing through him.

19

ON the day of the Krasnoye Selo races,* Vronsky arrived earlier than usual to eat his steak in the officers' mess. He did not need to be particularly strict with himself, as he happened to weigh the regulation eleven and a half stone; but neither could he afford to put on weight, so he avoided starchy food and sweets. He sat with his frock-coat unbuttoned over a white waistcoat, resting both his elbows on the table and staring at a French novel on his plate while he waited for the steak he had ordered. He was only looking at the book so as to avoid having to talk to the officers coming in and out while he was thinking.

He was thinking about the fact that Anna had promised to see him that day after the race. But he had not seen her for three days, and since her husband had returned from a trip abroad, he did not know whether it would be possible, nor did he know how to find out. He had seen her last at his cousin Betsy's dacha.* The Karenins' dacha, by contrast, he visited as rarely as possible. Now he did want to go there, and was pondering how to go about it.

'Of course, I'll say that Betsy sent me to ask whether she's coming to the races. Of course, I'll go,' he decided, lifting his head from the book. And his face lit up as he vividly imagined the happiness of seeing her.

'Send to my lodgings, and tell them to get the troika ready as quick as they can,' he said to the servant who served him the steak on a hot silver platter, and he drew the platter towards him and began eating.

From the billiard room next door came the sound of balls clattering, talk, and laughter. Two officers appeared in the doorway: one young, with a weak, delicate face, who had recently joined their regiment from the Corps of Pages,* and the other a portly old officer, with a bracelet on his wrist and small, puffy eyes.

Vronsky glanced at them, frowned, and looking sidelong at his book, as if he had not noticed them, proceeded to eat and read at the same time.

'What's this? Beefing yourself up for the work ahead?' said the portly officer as he sat down beside him.

'As you see,' responded Vronsky, frowning and wiping his mouth without looking at him.

'So you're not afraid of putting on weight?' he said, turning a chair round for the young officer.

'What?' said Vronsky angrily, with a grimace of disgust, showing his even teeth.

'You're not afraid of putting on weight?'

'Waiter, sherry!' said Vronsky without replying, and moving his book to the other side, he went on reading.

The portly officer picked up the wine menu and turned to the young officer.

'You choose what we're going to drink,' he said, handing him the menu and looking at him.

'Maybe some Rhine wine,' said the young officer, looking shyly at Vronsky out of the corner of his eye, and trying to catch the wisps of his incipient moustache with his fingers. Seeing that Vronsky did not turn round, the young officer got up.

'Let's go into the billiard room,' he said.

The portly officer got up meekly, and they walked towards the door.

At that moment the tall, well-built Captain Yashvin walked into the room, and jerking his head into a contemptuous nod to the two officers, he went up to Vronsky.

'Ah! Here he is!' he cried, giving him a hard slap on the epaulette with his large hand. Vronsky looked round angrily, but then his face immediately lit up with the calm, steady affection which was characteristic of him.

'Good idea, Alyosha,' said the captain in his loud baritone. 'Have something to eat now, and just one drink.'

'But I don't feel like eating.'

'There go the inseparables,' Yashvin added, looking witheringly at the two officers who were just then leaving the room. And he sat down next to Vronsky, contorting into acute angles his thighs and shins in their tight riding-breeches, which were too long for the height of the chair. 'Why didn't you turn up at the Krasnoye Theatre* yesterday? Numerova wasn't at all bad. Where were you?'

'I stayed too long at the Tverskoys,' said Vronsky.

'Ah!' responded Yashvin.

Yashvin, a gambler, a rake, and a man who not only had no principles but had immoral principles—Yashvin was Vronsky's best friend in the regiment. Vronsky liked him both for his exceptional physical strength, which he for the most part demonstrated by being able to drink like a fish and dispense with sleep without suffering any ill effects, and also for the great strength of character he displayed in his relations with his superiors and comrades, in whom he inspired fear and respect, and at the card table, where he would play for tens of thousands, and always with such skill and conviction, despite the wine he had drunk, that he was regarded as the top player at the English Club. Vronsky particularly liked and respected him because he felt

Yashvin liked him for who he was, rather than for his name and his wealth. Out of everyone, he was the only one with whom Vronsky would have wished to talk about his love affair. He felt that Yashvin, despite appearing to despise all emotion, could alone comprehend the fierce passion that now filled his whole life, or so it seemed to Vronsky. Moreover, he was certain that Yashvin definitely took no pleasure in gossip and scandal, and understood these feelings in the right way, that is to say, he knew and believed that this love affair was not a joke, or an amusement, but something more serious and important.

Vronsky had never spoken to him about his affair, but he knew that he knew everything, understood everything in the right way, and was pleased to see that in his eyes.

'Ah, yes!' he said, on hearing that Vronsky had been at the Tverskoys, and with his black eyes twinkling, he grasped his left moustache and started twisting it into his mouth, which was a bad habit of his.

'And what did you do yesterday? Did you win?' asked Vronsky.

'Eight thousand. But three of them are no good, as he's not likely to cough up.'

'Well, so you can afford to lose over me,' said Vronsky, laughing. (Yashvin had placed a large bet on Vronsky.)

'There is no way I am going to lose.'

'Makhotin's the only danger.'

And the conversation turned to their forecasts for the race that day, which was the only thing Vronsky could think about now.

'Let's go, I've finished,' said Vronsky, and he got up and headed for the door. Yashvin got up too, stretching his huge legs and long back.

'It's too early for me to dine, but I need a drink. I'll come along in a minute. Hey, some wine!' he shouted in his gravelly voice, which was famous for making the windows rattle during drill. 'Actually, no, I don't need one,' he shouted immediately afterwards. 'You're going home, so I'll go with you.'

And he went off with Vronsky.

20

VRONSKY was billeted in a spacious and clean Finnish log cabin, divided into two. Petritsky also lived with him in camp. Petritsky was asleep when Vronsky and Yashvin came into the cabin.

'Get up, that's enough sleep,' said Yashvin, going behind the partition and giving the dishevelled Petritsky, whose nose was buried in the pillow, a prod in the shoulder.

Petritsky suddenly sprang to his knees and looked round.

'Your brother's been here,' he said to Vronsky. 'He woke me up, damn him, and said he'd come by again.' And pulling up the blanket, he flung himself back on the pillow. 'Leave me alone, Yashvin!' he said angrily to Yashvin, who was pulling the blanket off him. 'Leave me alone!' He turned over and opened his eyes. 'You can tell me what to drink though; I've got such a nasty taste in my mouth that . . .'

'Vodka's better than anything else,' boomed Yashvin. 'Tereshchenko! Vodka for the master, and pickles,' he shouted, obviously enjoying the sound of his own voice.

'You think vodka, eh?' asked Petritsky, blinking and rubbing his eyes. 'Will you have a drink? Let's have a drink together! Vronsky, are you going to have a drink?' said Petritsky, getting up and wrapping a tiger-skin rug round his midriff.

He went to the door of the partition, raised his hands, and began to sing in French, 'There was a king in Th-u-u-le'.* 'Vronsky, will you have a drink?'

'Clear off,' said Vronsky, putting on the frock-coat his valet was handing him.

'Where are you going?' asked Yashvin. 'Here's the troika,' he added, seeing the carriage drive up.

'To the stables, and I need to see Bryansky about the horses as well,' said Vronsky.

Vronsky actually had promised to call on Bryansky, who was about seven miles from Peterhof,* and bring him the money for the horses; he hoped he would manage to get there too. But his comrades immediately realized that was not the only place he was going.

Petritsky, continuing to sing, winked and pouted, as if to say: 'We know who Bryansky is all right.'

Yashvin merely said, 'Make sure you're not late!' then asked, in order to change the subject: 'How's my roan? Is he doing all right?' while looking out of the window at the middle horse, which he had sold to Vronsky.

'Wait!' shouted Petritsky to Vronsky as he was walking out. 'Your brother left a letter and a note for you. Now, where are they?'

Vronsky stopped.

'Well, where are they?'

'Where are they? Good question!' said Petritsky solemnly, moving his forefinger up from his nose.

'Come on, tell me, this is silly!' said Vronsky smiling.

'Well, I didn't stoke the fire. They must be here somewhere.'

'All right, that's enough nonsense! Where is the letter?'

'No, really, I've forgotten. Or did I dream about it? Wait, wait! No point getting cross! If you had drunk four bottles a head yesterday like we did, you'd forget where you ended up. Wait, I'll remember in a minute!'

Petritsky went behind the partition and lay down on his bed.

'Wait! I was lying down like this, and he was standing there. Yes—yes—yes—yes . . . Here it is!' Petritsky pulled a letter out from under the mattress, where he had hidden it.

Vronsky took the letter and his brother's note. It was what he was expecting—a letter from his mother reproaching him for not having gone to see her, and a note from his brother saying they needed to have a talk. Vronsky knew that it was about the same thing. 'What business is it of theirs?' thought Vronsky, and crumpling up the letters, he tucked them between the buttons of his coat so he could read them carefully on the road. Going into the porch he ran into two officers: one from his own and the other from another regiment.

Vronsky's billet was always the officers' favourite hangout.

'Where are you off to?'

'I need to go to Peterhof.'

'Has your horse come from Tsarskoye?'*

'Yes, but I haven't seen her yet.'

'Apparently Makhotin's Gladiator is lame.'

'Nonsense! But how are you going to race in all this mud?' said the other.

'Here are my saviours!' cried Petritsky, seeing the new arrivals. Before him stood his batman with vodka and pickled cucumbers on a tray. 'Yashvin has just ordered me to have a drink as a pick-me-up.'

'You really did us in yesterday,' said one of the new arrivals; 'you wouldn't let us sleep all night.'

'And what about the way we ended up!' recounted Petritsky. 'Volkov climbs on to the roof and says he is sad. So I say: "Bring on the music, let's have the funeral march!" And he goes and falls asleep to the funeral march on the roof.'

'So what should I be drinking?'

'You must definitely knock back a vodka, and then drink some seltzer water with lots of lemon,' said Yashvin, standing over Petritsky like a mother making her child take medicine, 'then you can have a tiny bit of champagne—just a little bottle.'

'That makes sense. Vronsky, wait, let's have a drink.'

'No, goodbye gentlemen, I'm not drinking today.'

'What, are you putting on weight? Well, we'll have to drink on our own. Let's have the seltzer water and a lemon.'

'Vronsky!' someone called out when he had already gone out into the porch.

'What?'

'You'd better get your hair cut, as it's a bit heavy, especially where you're bald.'

Vronsky really was beginning to go prematurely bald. He laughed merrily, showing his even teeth and, pulling his cap down over his bald patch, went out and got into the carriage.

'To the stables!' he said, and was about to get out the letters so he could read them, but then he changed his mind, so he would not be distracted before inspecting his horse. 'Later! . . .'

21

A TEMPORARY stable, a shed made out of wooden planks, had been put up near the racecourse, and his horse was supposed to have been brought there the previous day. He had not seen her yet. These last few days he had not ridden her himself, but had entrusted her to the trainer, and now he had no idea what condition his horse had arrived in, or was in now. He had scarcely got out of his carriage when his stable-hand, or *groom*, as the boy was called in English, called over the trainer, having recognized his carriage from far off. A stiff-looking Englishman, in high boots and a short jacket, with just a tuft of hair left below his chin, came out to meet him, walking with the unwieldy gait of a jockey, sticking his elbows out and rocking from side to side.

'Well, how's Frou-Frou?'* Vronsky asked in English.

'*All right, sir*,'[1] the Englishman's voice came from somewhere inside his throat. 'Better not go in,' he added, raising his hat. 'I've put a muzzle on, and the horse is excited. Best not go in, as it'll agitate her.'

'No, I'm going in. I want to have a look.'

'Come along, then,' said the Englishman, frowning and still not opening his mouth; he went on ahead with his lurching gait, swinging his elbows.

They went into the little yard in front of the shed. The stable-boy

---

[1] [English in the original.]

on duty, a spruce, smartly dressed lad in a clean jacket, with a broom
in his hand, met them as they came in and followed them. In the shed
there were five horses standing in stalls, and Vronsky knew that his
chief rival, Makhotin's sixteen-hand chestnut Gladiator, was to have
been brought that day and should be standing there. Vronsky wanted to
see Gladiator, whom he had never set eyes on, even more than his own
horse; but Vronsky also knew that, according to the laws of horse-racing
etiquette, it was not only impossible for him to see him but improper
even to ask about him. While he was walking along the passage, the boy
opened the door into the second stall on the left, and Vronsky caught
a glimpse of a big chestnut horse with white legs. He knew this was
Gladiator, but, feeling like a person averting their eyes from someone
else's unfolded letter, he turned away and went into Frou-Frou's stall.

'This horse here belongs to Mak . . . Mak . . . I never can pronounce that name,' said the Englishman over his shoulder, indicating
Gladiator's stall with the grimy nail of his thumb.

'Makhotin? Yes, he's my only serious rival,' said Vronsky.

'If you were riding him,' said the Englishman, 'I'd bet on you.'

'Frou-Frou's more spirited; while he's stronger,' said Vronsky, smiling at the compliment paid to his riding skills.

'In a steeplechase it all depends on riding skills and *pluck*,'[1] said the
Englishman.

Vronsky not only felt that he had enough *pluck*, that is to say dash
and daring, but far more importantly, he was firmly convinced that no
one in the world could have more *pluck* than he had.

'And you're sure she didn't need a serious sweating?'*

'No, she didn't,' answered the Englishman. 'Don't speak loudly,
please. The horse is nervous,' he added, nodding towards the closed
stall they were standing in front of, and from which came the sound of
hooves moving about on the straw.

He opened the door and Vronsky went into the stall, which was
dimly lit by one small window. In the stall stood a dark bay mare in
a muzzle, shifting from one foot to the other in the fresh straw. After
looking round in the half-light of the stall, Vronsky could not then help
but take in at a glance all the attributes of his favourite horse. Frou-
Frou was an average-sized horse, and not altogether free from blem-
ish. She was narrow-boned throughout; although her breast-bone was
extremely prominent, she was narrow in the chest. Her hindquarters
hung a little, and her front legs, and particularly her hind legs, were

---

[1] [English in the original.]

noticeably pigeon-toed. The muscles in her hind and front legs were not particularly developed; but she had an unusually broad girth, which was now particularly striking with her lean stomach and racing form. Her cannon bones seemed no thicker than a finger seen from the front, but were unusually broad seen from the side. Except for her ribs, she seemed compressed at the sides and elongated vertically. But she possessed one supreme quality that made one forget all her defects: that quality was *breeding*, the breeding that *tells*, according to the English expression. Her muscles, standing out sharply under the network of veins stretched over her delicate, mobile skin, which was as smooth as satin, seemed as solid as bone. Her slender head, with its prominent, bright, shining eyes, broadened at the muzzle into flared nostrils lined with a bloodshot membrane. There was a distinctly strong-willed but also gentle expression to her whole figure, and especially her head. She was one of those animals who, it seems, do not talk only because the mechanical apparatus of their mouths does not allow them to.

To Vronsky, at least, it seemed that she understood everything he was feeling as he looked at her now.

As soon as Vronsky went up to her, she drew in a deep breath, and rolling her prominent eye till the white became bloodshot, she looked from the other side at the people who had come in, shaking her muzzle, and springing from one foot to the other.

'Well, you can see how excited she is now,' said the Englishman.

'There, there, darling!' said Vronsky, going up to the horse to quieten her.

But the nearer he came, the more excited she grew. Only when he got close to her head did she suddenly calm down, and the muscles started quivering under her delicate, soft coat. Vronsky patted her strong neck, straightened out a strand of her mane that had fallen on the wrong side of her bony withers, and brought his face close to her dilated nostrils, which were as fine and as elongated as a bat's wing. She breathed in and out noisily through her tensed nostrils, shuddered, pinned back her pointed ear, and extended her strong black lip towards Vronsky, as if wanting to catch hold of his sleeve. But remembering the muzzle, she shook it and again began shifting from one finely chiselled foot to the other.

'Quiet, darling, quiet!' he said, patting her also on her hindquarters; and he left the stall with the joyful realization that his horse was in peak condition.

The horse's excitement communicated itself to Vronsky; he felt the blood rushing to his heart, and he wanted to prance about and bite like the horse; he felt both scared and in high spirits.

'Well, I'm counting on you to be here at half-past six,' he said to the Englishman.

'All right,' said the Englishman. 'But where are you going, my Lord?' he asked, unexpectedly using the title *my Lord* which he had almost never done before.

Taken aback by the impertinence of his question, Vronsky lifted his head in surprise and glared, as he knew how to glare, not into the Englishman's eyes but at his forehead. But when he realized the Englishman was putting this question to him as a jockey, not as his employer, he answered:

'I've got to go to Bryansky's, but I'll be home in an hour.'

'How often I've been asked that question today!' he said to himself, and blushed, which he rarely did. The Englishman looked at him closely. And as if he knew where Vronsky was going, he added:

'The main thing is to be calm before a race,' he said; 'don't be in a bad mood or get upset about anything.'

'*All right*,'[1] answered Vronsky with a smile; and he jumped into his carriage and asked to be driven to Peterhof.

He had only driven a few yards when the dark clouds that had been threatening rain since morning gathered overhead, and there was a torrential downpour.

'That's bad!' thought Vronsky as he pulled the hood up. 'It was muddy before, but now it will be a complete swamp.' As he sat in solitude in the closed carriage, he took out his mother's letter and his brother's note, and read them.

Yes, it was just more of the same. Everyone, including his mother, his brother, and absolutely everyone, found it necessary to interfere in his romantic life. This interference aroused anger in him, which was a feeling he rarely experienced. 'What business is it of theirs? Why does everyone feel it their duty to be concerned about me? And why do they have to pester me? It's because they can see this is something they can't understand. If this were the usual trivial society liaison, they would have left me alone. But they sense this is something different, that it's not a diversion, that this woman is dearer to me than life itself. And that's what they don't understand, and it irritates them. Whatever our destiny is or will be, we have made it ourselves, and we are not complaining about it,' he said, linking himself with Anna in the word *we*. 'No, they have to teach us how to live. They have no idea what happiness is, and they don't know that without this

---

[1] [English in the original.]

love, there can be neither happiness nor unhappiness for us—or life,' he thought.

He was angry with everyone for interfering, precisely because in his soul he felt that they, all of these people, were right. He felt that the love which joined him to Anna was not a brief infatuation which would come to an end as society liaisons do, leaving no traces in the life of either party except pleasant or unpleasant memories. He felt all the wretchedness of his and her situation, all the difficulty of concealing their love, of lying and deceiving while being exposed to the gaze of the whole of society, and of lying, deceiving, scheming, and continually thinking of others, when the passion that united them was so intense that they both forgot about everything but their love.

He vividly recalled all the frequently recurring occasions when there was a need for lies and deceit, which were so contrary to his nature; he recalled particularly vividly the feeling of shame he had often noticed in her due to that need for deceit and lies. And he experienced a strange feeling that had sometimes come over him since the beginning of his relationship with Anna. It was a feeling of loathing for something: whether it was for Alexey Alexandrovich, for himself, or the whole of society, he really did not know. But he would always drive this strange feeling away. And now, after shaking himself out of it, he continued his train of thought.

'Yes, she was unhappy before, but proud and serene; whereas now she cannot be serene and dignified, though she does not show it. Yes, this must end,' he decided to himself.

And it occurred to him clearly for the first time that it was vital to put an end to this lie, and the sooner the better. 'She and I should give everything up and hide away on our own somewhere with our love,' he said to himself.

22

THE downpour did not last long, and by the time Vronsky drove up at a full trot, the shaft horse pulling the trace horses as they galloped through the mud without reins, the sun had come out again, the dacha roofs and the old lime trees in the gardens on both sides of the main street shone with a wet gleam, and water was dripping merrily from the branches and running down the roofs. He was no longer thinking about how this downpour would ruin the racecourse, but was rejoicing now that he would probably find her at home and alone thanks to the rain, as he knew that Alexey Alexandrovich, who had recently returned from taking the waters, had not moved from Petersburg.

Hoping to find her alone, Vronsky got out before crossing the little bridge, as he always did to avoid attracting attention to himself, and continued on foot. He did not go up to the porch from the street, but went into the courtyard.

'Has the master arrived?' he asked the gardener.

'No, sir. The mistress is at home. But if you would care to go to the porch, there are people there who will let you in,' the gardener answered.

'No, I'll go in from the garden.'

And having made sure she was alone, and wanting to take her by surprise, since he had not made any promise about coming that day and she most probably was not thinking he would come before the races, he set off for the terrace that overlooked the garden, keeping a hand on his sword, and treading cautiously on the sandy path that was bordered with flower-beds. Vronsky had by now forgotten everything that he had thought during the journey about the gravity and difficulty of his situation. He was thinking about one thing, that he was about to see her, not just in his imagination, but in the flesh, all of her, as she was in reality. He was already going up the raked steps of the terrace, taking full-length strides so as not to make a noise, when he suddenly remembered the thing he always forgot, and which constituted the most agonizing aspect of his relationship with her—her son, with his inquisitive and, to his mind, hostile look.

This boy got in the way of their relationship more frequently than anyone else. When he was present, not only would neither Vronsky nor Anna allow themselves to speak about anything they could not have repeated in front of everyone else, but they also would not allow themselves even to hint at anything the boy would not have understood. They had not arranged this, but it had naturally evolved that way. They would have considered it a personal insult to deceive this child. They talked to each other like acquaintances in front of him. But in spite of this caution, Vronsky often noticed the child's attentive and confused gaze fixed on him, and a strange shyness and unevenness in his attitude to him, which alternated between affection and a coldness and reserve. It was as though the child sensed that between his mother and this man there was an important relationship, the significance of which he could not fathom.

The boy did indeed feel that he could not understand this relationship, and try as he might, he could not work out what feelings he ought to have towards this man. With a child's sensitivity to the feelings of others, he could clearly see that his father, his governess, and his nanny did not merely dislike Vronsky, but regarded him with aversion and fear, although they never said anything about him, while his mother regarded him as her best friend.

'What does it mean? Who is he? How am I supposed to like him? If I don't understand, it's my fault, either I'm stupid or I'm a bad boy,' thought the child; and this was what lay behind his searching, inquisitive, and partly hostile expression, and the shyness and inconstancy which made Vronsky feel so uncomfortable. The presence of this child always and without exception aroused in Vronsky that strange feeling of inexplicable loathing which he had been experiencing lately. The presence of this child aroused in both Vronsky and Anna a feeling akin to that experienced by a seafarer, who sees from the compass that the direction he is swiftly heading in is far from the proper one, but is incapable of stopping the momentum, is with every minute carried off further and further off his course, and knows that to admit this to himself would be tantamount to admitting certain ruin.

This child, with his innocent outlook on life, was the compass showing them how far they had diverged from what they knew, but did not want to know.

This time Seryozha was not at home, and she was completely alone, sitting on the terrace waiting for the return of her son, who had gone out for a walk and been caught in the rain. She had sent a manservant and a maid out to look for him, and was sitting waiting. Wearing a white dress with wide embroidery, she was sitting in a corner of the terrace behind some flowers, and did not hear him. Inclining her head of black curls, she had pressed her forehead against a cool watering-can that stood on the parapet, and had clasped it with both her lovely hands, on which were the rings he knew so well. The beauty of her whole figure, her head, her neck, and her hands struck Vronsky every time with renewed surprise. He stopped to gaze at her in adoration. But just when he was about to take a step nearer to her, she became aware of his approach, and she pushed aside the watering-can and turned her flushed face towards him.

'What's the matter? Are you unwell?' he said to her in French as he walked up to her. He had wanted to run up to her, but remembering that there might be other people about, he glanced round at the balcony door and blushed, as he always did, feeling that he should be apprehensive and on his guard.

'No, I'm fine,' she said, getting up and squeezing his outstretched hand tightly. 'I did not expect . . . you.'*

'Goodness! What cold hands!' he said.

'You gave me a fright,' she said. 'I'm on my own, waiting for Seryozha; he went off for a walk. They'll come in this way.'

But in spite of her efforts to be calm, her lips were trembling.

'Forgive me for coming, but I couldn't let the day go by without seeing you,' he went on, speaking in French as he always did, so as to avoid using with her the impossibly cold polite form of address in Russian, and also the far more dangerous, familiar one.

'But what is there to forgive? I'm so glad!'

'But you're unwell or upset,' he continued, not letting go of her hands and bending over her. 'What was it you were thinking about?'

'Always the same thing,' she said with a smile.

She was speaking the truth. Whenever she was asked what she was thinking about, at whatever time of day, she could answer unerringly: about the same thing, her happiness and her unhappiness. And this is what she was thinking about when he came up to her just now: she was wondering why for others, for Betsy, for example (she knew about her relationship with Tushkevich, which was concealed from society), all this was easy, while it was so agonizing for her? For certain particular reasons, this thought was causing her particular agony today. She asked him about the race. He answered her questions, and seeing that she was anxious, tried to distract her by telling her all about his race preparations in the simplest manner possible.

'Should I tell him or not?' she thought, looking into his quiet, affectionate eyes. 'He is so happy and absorbed with his race that he won't understand it in the right way, he won't understand the full significance of what this event means for us.'

'But you haven't told me what you were thinking about when I arrived,' he said, breaking off in mid-flow; 'please, tell me!'

She did not answer, but inclined her head slightly to steal a furtive and enquiring glance at him, her eyes sparkling under their long lashes. Her hand shook as it toyed with a leaf she had broken off. He saw this, and his face took on that expression of submissive, slavish devotion which had so captivated her.

'I can see something has happened. Do you think I can have a moment's rest, knowing you have some sorrow that I cannot share? Tell me, I beg you!' he repeated imploringly.

'No, I really won't forgive him if he does not realize the full significance of this. It's better not to tell him; why put him to the test?' she thought, still looking at him in the same way, and aware that the hand holding the leaf was shaking more and more.

'I beg you!' he repeated, taking her hand.

'Shall I tell you?'

'Yes, yes, yes . . .'

'I'm pregnant,' she said, quietly and slowly.

The leaf in her hand started to shake even more violently, but she did not take her eyes off him, in order to see how he would receive this. He went pale, was on the verge of saying something, but stopped; he let go of her hand and lowered his head. 'Yes, he does understand the full significance of what has happened,' she thought, and gratefully squeezed his hand.

But she was mistaken in thinking that he understood the full significance of the news in the way that she, a woman, understood it. Hearing this news caused him to experience with ten-fold force an attack of that strange feeling of loathing for someone he was susceptible to; but at the same time, he realized that the crisis he had wished for had now arrived, that it was impossible to go on concealing things from her husband, and that somehow or other they had to sever this unnatural situation as soon as possible. But apart from that, her agitation also communicated itself physically to him. He cast a tender, submissive glance at her, kissed her hand, got up, and proceeded to pace up and down the terrace in silence.

'Yes,' he said decisively, going up to her. 'Neither you nor I have looked on our relationship as a trivial amusement, and now our fate is decided. It is essential to put an end', he said, looking round, 'to the lie we are living.'

'Put an end? What do you mean, put an end, Alexey?' she said quietly. She was calmer now, and her face shone with a tender smile.

'To leave your husband and join our lives together.'

'They are already joined,' she answered in a scarcely audible voice.

'Yes, but completely, completely.'

'But how, Alexey, teach me, how?' she said in sad mockery of the hopelessness of her situation. 'Is there a way out of a situation like this? Am I not the wife of my husband?'

'There is a way out of every situation. We have to make our minds up,' he said. 'Anything's better than the situation in which you're living. I do see how you agonize about everything—society, your son, your husband.'

'Oh, not my husband,' she said, with a wry smile. 'I don't know, I don't think of him. He doesn't exist.'

'You're not speaking truthfully. I know you. You agonize about him too.'

'Oh, he doesn't even know,' she said, and suddenly a bright colour suffused her face; her cheeks, her forehead, and her neck turned red, and tears of shame sprang into her eyes. 'Anyway, let's not talk about him.'

23

VRONSKY had already made several attempts, albeit none as concerted as this one, to steer her into a discussion of her situation, and every time he had come up against the same superficial and facile reasoning with which she was now responding to his challenge. It was as if there were something about it which she could not or did not want to comprehend; it was as if the minute she began to speak about it, she, the real Anna, withdrew somewhere inside herself, and another strange woman emerged, alien to him, whom he did not love, and feared, and who resisted him. But today he had resolved to speak his mind.

'Whether he knows or not,' said Vronsky, in his usual calm and steady voice, 'whether he knows or not is of no concern to us. We cannot . . . you cannot continue like this, especially now.'

'What should I do then, in your opinion?' she asked with the same slightly mocking tone. Having been so afraid that he would not take her pregnancy seriously, she was now vexed with him for drawing the conclusion that it was necessary to do something about it.

'Tell him everything, and leave him.'

'Very well, suppose I do that,' she said. 'Do you know what will happen then? I can tell you everything in advance,' and a malevolent gleam lit up her eyes, which had been so tender a minute earlier. 'So, you love another man, and have entered into a criminal relationship with him?' (In imitating her husband, she emphasized the word *criminal*, just as Alexey Alexandrovich would have done.) 'I warned you of the consequences from the religious, civil, and family point of view. You have not listened to me. Now I cannot let you bring disgrace on my name . . .'—'and on my son,' she wanted to say, but she could not joke about her son—'disgrace on my name—and other things in the same vein,' she added. 'He'll generally say in his official manner, with his clarity and precision, that he cannot let me go, but will use whatever means are in his power to prevent a scandal. And he will do what he says, calmly and to the letter. That's what will happen. He's not a man, he's a machine, and a vicious machine when he's angry,' she added, recalling Alexey Alexandrovich as she spoke, together with every detail of his figure, manner of speaking, and character, blaming him for every bad thing she could find in him, and not forgiving him anything on account of the terrible misconduct she was guilty of before him.

'But, Anna,' said Vronsky, in a quiet, persuasive voice, trying to calm her, 'it is nevertheless essential to tell him, and then be guided by whatever he undertakes.'

'So, should we run away?'

'Why not run away? I don't see how we can keep on like this. And not on my account—I can see that you are suffering.'

'Yes, so I'm to run away and become your mistress?' she said bitterly.

'Anna!' he said in affectionate reproach.

'Yes,' she went on, 'become your mistress, and destroy everything . . .'

She had again wanted to say 'my son', but she could not utter the words.

Vronsky could not understand how, with her forceful, honest nature, she could endure this state of deceit and not want to leave it; but he had not grasped that the main reason for this was that word *son*, which she could not utter. When she thought about her son, and his future relationship to a mother who had abandoned his father, she felt so appalled at what she had done that she could not think rationally, and, like a woman, she was simply trying to reassure herself with false arguments and words so that everything could remain as before and it would be possible to forget the terrible question of what would happen to her son.

'I beg you, I beseech you,' she said suddenly, taking his hand, and speaking in quite a different, sincere and tender voice, 'never speak to me about this!'

'But, Anna . . .'

'Never. Leave it to me. I am aware of all the ignominy and all the horror of my position, but it is not as easy to resolve as you think. So leave it to me, and do as I say. Never speak to me about it. Do you promise? . . . No, no, you must promise! . . .'

'I promise everything, but I cannot be calm, especially after what you have just said. I cannot be calm, when you cannot be calm . . .'

'I?' she repeated. 'Yes, I do agonize sometimes; but that will pass, if you never talk about it to me. It is only when you talk about it that I agonize about it.'

'I don't understand,' he said.

'I know', she said, interrupting him, 'how hard it is for someone of your truthful nature to lie, and I feel sorry for you. I often wonder how you could have ruined your life for me.'

'And I was wondering the same thing just now,' he said; 'how you could sacrifice everything for me? I can't forgive myself that you're unhappy.'

'You think I'm unhappy?' she said, coming closer to him, and looking at him with a rapturous, loving smile. 'I am like a hungry man who has been given something to eat. He might be cold, and his clothes in tatters, and he might feel ashamed, but he is not unhappy. You think I'm unhappy? No, this is my happiness . . .'

She heard the voice of her son, who was returning and, casting a swift glance at the terrace, she abruptly got to her feet. Her eyes blazed with the fire he knew so well, and with a rapid movement she lifted her beautiful, ring-covered hands, took hold of his head, gave him a long look, brought her face and her smiling, parted lips close, quickly kissed his mouth and both his eyes, and pushed him away. She was about to go, but he held her back.

'When?' he said in a whisper, gazing at her rapturously.

'Tonight, at one o'clock,' she whispered, and after a heavy sigh, she set off with her brisk, light step to greet her son.

Seryozha had been caught by the rain in the large garden, and he and his nurse had sat it out in the summer-house.

'Well, goodbye,' she said to Vronsky. 'I must leave for the races soon. Betsy promised to stop by for me.'

Vronsky glanced at his watch and hurried away.

24

WHEN Vronsky looked at his watch on the Karenins' balcony, he was so agitated and wrapped up in his own thoughts that he saw the hands on the face, but could not work out what time it was. He went out on to the road and headed for his carriage, treading carefully through the mud. He felt so overwhelmed by his feelings for Anna that he did not even think about the time, and whether he would manage to get to Bryansky's. As often happens, he was left with only a minimal memory function, indicating what came next in his schedule. He went up to his coachman, who was dozing on the box in the already lengthening shadow of a dense lime tree, admired the shimmering columns of midges that were hovering above the sweating horses,

woke his coachman up, jumped into the carriage, and gave orders to be
driven to Bryansky's. It was only after driving nearly five miles that he
came to his senses sufficiently to look at his watch, realize that it was
half-past five, and that he was late.

There were several races that day: the Cossack Horse Guards' race,*
then the officers' mile-and-a-half, the three-mile, and the race in which
he was competing. He could still be in time for his race, but if he went
to Bryansky's he would not have a minute to spare, and would arrive
when the whole court would be already there. That was not good. But
he had given his word to Bryansky that he would come, and so he
decided to drive on, telling the coachman not to spare the horses.

He arrived at Bryansky's, spent five minutes with him, then galloped
back. The fast drive calmed him down. All the difficulties in his relationship with Anna, all the uncertainties which remained after their
conversation, everything flew out of his mind; he was now thinking
with pleasure and excitement about the race, about how he would get
there in time after all, and every now and then a happy anticipation of
that night's meeting blazed up in his imagination like a bright light.

The thrill of the coming race took ever greater hold of him as he
plunged ever deeper into the atmosphere of the races, and overtook
carriages making their way from dachas and from Petersburg to the
racetrack.

At his quarters there was no longer anyone at home: everyone was
at the races, and his valet was waiting for him at the gate. While he was
changing, his valet told him that the second race had already started,
that many gentlemen had come asking for him, and that a boy had
twice run over from the stables.

After taking his time changing (he never hurried or lost his composure), Vronsky gave orders to be driven to the stables. From the
stables he could already catch a glimpse of the sea of carriages, pedestrians, and soldiers surrounding the racecourse, and also the pavilions
swarming with people. The second race must have been in progress,
for he heard the bell just as he went into the stables. As he was walking
over to the stables, he encountered Makhotin's white-legged chestnut
Gladiator, who was being taken to the racecourse in an orange and blue
blanket, the blue-trim making his ears seem huge.

'Where's Cord?' he asked the stable boy.

'In the stable, saddling up.'

Frou-Frou was standing already saddled in the open stall. They were
about to lead her out.

'I'm not late?'

'*All right! All right!*'[1] said the Englishman. 'Everything is in order, keep calm!'

Vronsky cast one more glance at the exquisite lines of his beloved horse, whose body was quivering all over, and finding it hard to tear himself away from the spectacle, he left the stables. He drove up to the pavilions at the most propitious time to avoid attracting attention to himself. The mile-and-a-half race was just finishing, and all eyes were fixed on the Horse Guards officer in front and the Life Guard Hussar behind, urging their horses on with one last effort towards the winning post. Everyone was converging on the winning post from the middle of the circuit and outside it, and a group of Horse Guards soldiers and officers was celebrating the expected victory of their officer and comrade with loud whoops. Vronsky slipped unnoticed into the middle of the crowd almost at the very moment when the bell rang to mark the end of the race, and the tall, mud-spattered Horse Guard who had come in first lowered himself into his saddle and started to slacken the reins of his panting grey stallion, which had become dark with sweat.

Digging its hooves in with effort, the stallion shortened the fast pace of its large frame, and the Horse Guards officer looked round him and just managed a smile, like a man waking from a heavy sleep. A crowd of friends and strangers thronged round him.

Vronsky consciously avoided the select, high-society crowd which was circulating and chatting freely yet with restraint in front of the pavilions. He had found out that Karenina and Betsy and his brother's wife were there, and purposely did not go over to them so as not to be distracted. But he kept running into acquaintances who stopped him to tell him all about the previous races and ask him why he was late.

When the riders were called to the pavilion to receive prizes, and everyone headed off there, Vronsky was approached by his elder brother Alexander, a colonel with aiguillettes, of middling height, just as heavily built as Alexey, but more handsome and pink-cheeked, with a red nose and a drunk, open expression.

'Did you get my note?' he said. 'One can never track you down.'

Despite his dissipated and, in particular, drunken life, for which he was notorious, Alexander Vronsky was very much the courtier.

As he tackled his brother on a matter he found highly distasteful, knowing that many people's eyes might be fastened on them, he

---

[1] [English in the original.]

maintained a jovial expression, as if he was joking with his brother about something of little importance.

'I did get it, and I really can't understand what *you* are so worried about,' said Alexey.

'I'm worried because it's just been pointed out to me that you weren't here, and you were seen in Peterhof on Monday.'

'There are some matters which may only be discussed by those directly involved, and the matter you are so worried about happens to be one of those . . .'

'Yes, but not by serving officers, not . . .'

'I must ask you not to interfere, that's all.'

Alexey Vronsky's scowling face went pale and his prominent lower jaw quivered, which happened rarely with him. Being a very kind-hearted man, he was seldom angry, but, as Alexander Vronsky well knew, when he became angry and when his chin quivered, he was dangerous. Alexander Vronsky smiled merrily.

'I just wanted to pass on our dear mother's letter. Do reply to her, and don't get upset before the race. *Bonne chance*,'[1] he added with a smile, and walked off.

But hard on his heels came another friendly greeting bringing Vronsky to a halt.

'So you don't want to acknowledge your friends! Hello, *mon cher*!' said Stepan Arkadyich, his pink-cheeked face and shiny, combed whiskers no less lustrous amongst all that Petersburg glamour than in Moscow. 'I arrived yesterday, and I'm very glad I will be able to see you triumph. When can we meet?'

'Stop by the mess tomorrow,' said Vronsky, and squeezing the sleeve of his coat as he apologized, he walked off into the middle of the racecourse, where the horses were already being led in for the great steeplechase.

The sweat-laden, exhausted horses which had raced were being led home by the grooms, and one by one fresh, new, mostly English horses were appearing for the coming race, looking like strange, huge birds with their hoods and tightly girthed bellies. On the right they were leading in the lean and beautiful Frou-Frou, who was prancing on her elastic and rather long pasterns as if she was on springs. Not far from her they were taking the blanket off lop-eared Gladiator. Vronsky could not help his attention being drawn to the stallion's strong, lovely, completely regular lines, to his superb hindquarters and unusually short pasterns

---

[1] 'Good luck.'

that sat squarely on his hooves. He wanted to go up to his horse, but was again detained by an acquaintance.

'Ah, there's Karenin!' said the acquaintance to whom he was talking. 'He's looking for his wife, and she's in the central pavilion. Have you seen her?'

'No, I haven't,' answered Vronsky, and he walked over to his horse without even glancing round at the pavilion where he had been told Karenina was.

Vronsky barely had time to look at his saddle, which required some adjustments, when the competitors were summoned to the pavilion to draw numbers and starting positions. Seventeen officers with serious, stern, and in many cases pale faces, converged on the pavilion and sorted out the numbers. Vronsky drew the number seven. 'Mount your horses!' came the call.

Conscious that he and the other competitors were the focal point on which all eyes were trained, Vronsky walked up to his horse in that state of tension which usually made him become calm and deliberate in his movements. In honour of the races, Cord had put on his smartest outfit: a buttoned-up black frock-coat, a stiffly starched collar propping up his cheeks, a black bowler hat, and tall boots. He was calm and dignified as always, and was standing in front of the horse, holding both reins himself. Frou-Frou continued to tremble as though she was in a fever. Her eye was full of fire while stealing a sideways glance at Vronsky as he approached. Vronsky slipped a finger under the saddle-girth. The mare rolled her eye even more, bared her teeth, and pinned back an ear. The Englishman wrinkled his lips into a smile, as if to scoff at the idea that his saddling was being checked.

'If you mount you won't be so nervous.'

Vronsky took one last look at his rivals. He knew that he would not see them during the race. Two were already riding on ahead to the starting line. Galtsin, a dangerous rival and a friend of Vronsky's, was dancing around a bay stallion that would not let him mount. Curled up like a cat on the saddle, in a desire to imitate the English, a small Life Hussar in tight breeches galloped past. Prince Kuzovlev sat pale-faced on his thoroughbred mare from the Grabovsky stud, while an English groom led her by the bridle. Vronsky and all his comrades knew Kuzovlev and his particular condition of 'weak' nerves and terrible vanity. They knew that he was afraid of everything, and afraid of riding a battle horse; but precisely because it was frightening, because people broke their necks, and because at each obstacle there was a doctor positioned with a field ambulance with a cross sewn on it, and a nurse, he had decided to race. Their eyes met, and Vronsky gave him an affectionate and approving wink. The only person he did not see was his chief rival, Makhotin on Gladiator.

'Don't be in a hurry,' said Cord to Vronsky, 'and remember one thing: don't hold her back at the obstacles, and don't urge her on; let her choose how she tackles them.'

'Very well, very well,' said Vronsky, taking the reins.

'Lead the race if you can; but even if you're behind, don't lose heart till the very last minute.'

Before the horse had time to move, Vronsky stepped into the notched steel stirrup with an agile, strong motion, and lightly and firmly lowered his stocky body on to the squeaky leather saddle. Taking hold of the other stirrup with his right foot, he then evened out the double reins between his fingers in a practised movement, and Cord let go. As if not knowing which foot to put first, Frou-Frou moved off as though on springs, pulling on the reins with her long neck, and making her rider sway from side to side on her supple back. Cord quickened his step and followed him. The excited horse tried to mislead her rider by pulling on the reins first on one side and then on the other, and Vronsky tried vainly to calm her with his voice and hand.

They were already nearing the dammed-up stream on their way to the starting line. There were many riders in front and many behind, when Vronsky suddenly heard the sound of a horse galloping along the muddy path behind him, and Makhotin overtook him on his white-legged, lop-eared Gladiator. Makhotin smiled, showing his long teeth, but Vronsky looked at him angrily. He did not like him generally, regarded him now as his most dangerous rival, and was annoyed with him for galloping past and agitating his horse. Frou-Frou threw out her left leg into a canter, made two leaps, and then, angered by the tightened reins, transferred to a bumpy trot which jolted her rider about. Cord also frowned, and almost broke into a run as he walked behind Vronsky.

25

THERE were seventeen officers competing in all. The race was to take place on the big three-mile, elliptical circuit in front of the pavilion. Nine obstacles had been set up on this ring: a stream, a large, solid five-foot barrier right in front of the pavilion, a dry ditch, a ditch with water, a slope, and an Irish bank (one of the most difficult obstacles), consisting of a bank with brushwood stuck in it, beyond which, invisible to the horse, was another ditch, so that the horse had to clear both obstacles or injure itself; then there were two more ditches, one with water, one without—and the race finished opposite the pavilion. The race did not actually begin on the circuit but two hundred yards away, and the first obstacle—the dammed-up stream, seven-feet wide, which the racers could jump over or wade across as they preferred—was located on this stretch.

The riders lined up three times, but each time someone's horse thrust itself forward, and they had to start all over again. Colonel Sestrin, an expert starter, was beginning to lose his temper when finally, at the fourth attempt, he shouted 'Go!' and the riders were off.

All eyes, all binoculars, were trained on the brightly coloured bunch of riders when they lined up.

'They're off! They're racing!' could be heard on all sides after the hush of anticipation.

And little groups and solitary figures amongst the spectators began to run from one place to another to get a better view. Within the very first minute the tight bunch of riders had spread out, and they could be seen approaching the stream in groups of two or three, one after the other. It looked to the spectators as though they had all started off together, but for the riders there were a few seconds of difference, which were of huge significance to them.

The excited and overly nervous Frou-Frou squandered the first moment, and several horses started in front of her, but by holding in his horse with all his might as she pulled on the reins, Vronsky easily overtook three of them before reaching the stream, so that ahead of him now remained only Makhotin's chestnut Gladiator, whose hind-quarters were beating a light, even rhythm right in front of Vronsky, and, leading them all, the lovely Diana, carrying Kuzovlev, who was more dead than alive.

For the first few minutes Vronsky was not in control of either himself or his horse. And up until the first obstacle, the stream, he could not control his horse's movements.

Gladiator and Diana approached it together and almost at the same moment: one-two, they rose up over the stream and flew across to the other side; inconspicuously, Frou-Frou soared after them, as if on wings; but just at the moment when Vronsky felt he was airborne, he suddenly saw, almost under his horse's hooves, Kuzovlev floundering with Diana on the other side of the stream (Kuzovlev had let go of the reins after the jump, and both he and the horse had gone flying, head-first). These details Vronsky learned later; right now he saw only that Diana's head or leg might end up right under him, just where

Frou-Frou was going to land. But Frou-Frou made a calculated movement with her legs and her back when she jumped, the way a cat lands,
and sped on, missing the horse.

'Oh, you darling!' thought Vronsky.

After the stream Vronsky had complete control of his horse, and
he began reining her in, intending to cross the big barrier behind
Makhotin, and then try to overtake him on the next five-hundred-yard
stretch, which was without obstacles.

The big barrier stood right in front of the imperial pavilion. The Tsar
and the entire court and crowds of people were all looking at them—at
him and Makhotin, who was a length ahead as they approached the
devil (as the solid barrier was called). Vronsky could feel those eyes
fastened upon him from all sides, but he saw nothing except the ears
and neck of his horse, the ground racing to meet him, and Gladiator's
croup and white legs beating time rapidly in front of him, still at the
same distance in front. Gladiator flicked his short tail, rose up without
hitting anything, and disappeared from Vronsky's sight.

'Bravo!' cried a voice.

At that moment the planks of the barrier loomed into Vronsky's
vision, and next they were before him. Without the slightest change of
movement, his horse reared up beneath him; the planks disappeared,
and he could just hear a knock behind him. Excited by Gladiator, who
was ahead, his horse had risen too early in front of the barrier, and
had clipped it with her hind hoof. But her pace did not change, and
after receiving a clump of mud in the face, Vronsky realized that he
was again the same distance from Gladiator. Once again he could see in
front of him his croup and short tail, and once again those fast-moving
white legs were firmly within view.

At the very moment when Vronsky thought that it was imperative
for him to overtake Makhotin, Frou-Frou herself markedly quickened
her pace without any encouragement, having already understood what
he was thinking, and she started closing in on Makhotin on the most
favourable side, next to the perimeter rope. Makhotin would not give
way. As soon as Vronsky began to think about perhaps overtaking on
the outside, Frou-Frou changed leads and began doing just that. Frou-
Frou's shoulder, which was now starting to darken with sweat, came
level with Gladiator's croup. For a few lengths they raced side by side.
But Vronsky began working the reins before they got to the obstacle
they were approaching, so as not to have to go wide, and quickly overtook Makhotin on the slope itself. He caught a glimpse of his mud-
splattered face. It even seemed to him that he was smiling. Vronsky had

overtaken Makhotin, but now he was aware of him being behind him, and behind his back could hear Gladiator's relentless, even gallop and the staccato and still very lively breathing of his nostrils.

The next two obstacles, the ditch and the barrier, were negotiated easily, but Vronsky began to hear the sound of Gladiator's gallop and his snorting coming closer. He urged his horse on, and was delighted to feel she was accelerating with ease, and the sound of Gladiator's hooves could again be heard at the same distance as before.

Vronsky was leading the race, exactly as he had wanted and as Cord had advised, and he was now confident of success. His excitement, his joy, and his affection for Frou-Frou kept mounting. He wanted to look round, but he did not dare do this, and tried instead to keep calm and not urge on his horse, so as to maintain in her the same reserves he felt were left in Gladiator. There was one obstacle left, and the most difficult one; if he could clear it ahead of the others he would win. He was racing towards the Irish bank. He and Frou-Frou had both seen the bank from far away, and both he and his horse had experienced a joint moment of doubt. He saw the uncertainty in his horse's ears and raised the whip, but then immediately felt that his fears were groundless: the horse knew what was needed. She increased her speed and rose up smoothly, just as he had thought she would, pushing off from the ground and letting herself be carried by the momentum, which took her far beyond the ditch; Frou-Frou then effortlessly continued on with the race at the same pace, without changing lead.

'Bravo, Vronsky!' The voices of a cluster of people standing by this obstacle who he knew were from his regiment, and his friends, resounded in his ears; he could not fail to recognize Yashvin's voice, but he did not see him.

'Come on, my precious!' was the thought he directed at Frou-Frou as he listened closely to what was going on behind him. 'He's cleared it!' he thought as he heard the sound of Gladiator's hooves behind him. There remained that one last five-foot wide ditch, filled with water. Vronsky did not even look at it, but his desire to win by a clear margin led him to raise and lower his horse's head in time to her gallop by working the reins in a circular fashion. He felt that his horse was running on her last reserves; not only were her neck and shoulders damp, but beads of sweat had appeared on her mane, her head, and her pointed ears, and her breath was coming in short, sharp gasps. But he knew those reserves would be more than enough to cover the last five hundred yards. It was only from feeling closer to the ground and from the particularly smooth way they were moving that Vronsky could tell how much the horse had increased her speed. She flew over the ditch as though not noticing it. She flew over it like a bird; but at the same instant Vronsky felt to his horror that he had not kept pace with his horse, and that without understanding how, he had done something terrible and unforgivable by dropping back into the saddle. All at once his position changed, and he realized that something awful had happened. Before he could work out what it was that had happened, the white legs of the chestnut stallion had come up very close to him, and Makhotin sped past at a swift gallop. Vronsky was touching the ground with one leg, and his horse now began to collapse on to that leg. He barely had time to free his leg before she fell on one side with heavy gasps, and after making vain efforts with her slender, perspiring neck to stand up, she lay there at his feet, trembling on the ground like a wounded bird. Vronsky's clumsy movement had broken her back. But he only realized that much later. Now all he could see was that Makhotin was rapidly getting away, he was staggering about alone on the muddy, unmoving ground, and Frou-Frou was lying there before him panting, with her head bent back, gazing at him with her lovely eye. Still not understanding what had happened, Vronsky tugged at his horse's reins. She again started quivering all over like a fish, making the saddle-flaps creak, and managed to free her front legs, but since she was unable to lift her back, she immediately keeled over and fell again on to her side. Pale, with his face contorted with passion and his lower jaw trembling, Vronsky kicked her in the stomach with his heel, and started pulling on the reins again. But she did not budge, and with her nose buried in the ground, she just gazed at her master with her expressive eyes.

'A-a-ah!' groaned Vronsky, clutching at his head. 'A-a-ah! what have I done!' he cried. 'And the race lost! And it's my own shameful, unpardonable fault! And this poor, beloved, doomed horse! A-a-ah! What have I done!'

All kinds of people, a doctor and his assistant, and officers from his regiment came running up to him. To his great dismay he felt completely safe and sound. The horse had broken her back, and the decision was taken to shoot her. Vronsky could neither answer questions nor talk to anyone. Without picking up the cap that had flown off his head, he turned and walked away from the racecourse, not knowing where he was going. He felt desolate. For the first time in his life he was experiencing the bitterest of misfortunes, and it was a misfortune which was irreparable, and which he himself had caused.

Yashvin caught up with him with his cap, and took him home, and

half an hour later Vronsky had come to his senses. But the memory of
that race remained for a long time in his heart as the worst and most
painful memory of his life.

26

ALEXEY ALEXANDROVICH's relationship with his wife was outwardly
the same as before. The only difference was that he was even busier
than before. As in previous years, with the onset of spring he had gone
abroad to a spa to restore his health, which every year suffered from
his increased industry over the winter, and as usual he had returned in
July and immediately taken up his usual work with a renewed energy.
As usual, his wife had moved out to the dacha, while he remained in
Petersburg.

Since the time of that conversation after Princess Tverskaya's
soirée, he had never spoken to Anna about his suspicions and jealousy,
and his usual tone of mimicking someone had never been more convenient than for his current relationship with his wife. He was a little colder towards his wife. It was just as if he was slightly displeased
with her on account of that first nocturnal conversation which she had
brushed aside. There was a touch of vexation in his relationship with
her, but nothing more. 'You did not want a frank discussion with me,'
he seemed to be saying, mentally addressing her, 'and so much the
worse for you. You will have to be the one to ask me now, because *I'm*
not going to initiate a frank discussion. So much the worse for you,' he
said to himself, like a person who, after vainly attempting to extinguish
a fire, might become frustrated with his vain efforts and say, 'Go on
then! Go ahead and burn for all I care!'

This man who was so intelligent and subtle in his professional affairs
simply could not grasp the sheer madness of such an attitude towards
his wife. He could not grasp this, because it was too frightening for him
to come to terms with his current situation, and he had shut, locked,
and sealed the box in his heart containing his feelings for his family,
that is to say, for his wife and son. Having been an attentive father,
he had become particularly cold towards his son from the end of this
winter, and had adopted with him the same bantering tone he used
with his wife. 'Ah, young man!' was how he addressed him.

Alexey Alexandrovich believed and maintained that he had never
in any other year had so much official business as he had in this one,
but he did not admit that he had actually been thinking up work for

himself this year, and that it was a way of not having to open that box containing his thoughts and feelings about his wife and family, which became more frightening the longer they lay there. If anyone had possessed the right to ask Alexey Alexandrovich what he thought of his wife's behaviour, the meek, docile Alexey Alexandrovich would not have answered, but he would have become very angry with the person asking him about it. This is why there was something supercilious and stern in Alexey Alexandrovich's expression whenever anyone enquired after his wife's health. Alexey Alexandrovich did not want to think anything about his wife's conduct or her feelings and, indeed, he did not think anything about them.

Alexey Alexandrovich's permanent dacha was in Peterhof, and the Countess Lydia Ivanovna usually spent her summers there too, close by and in constant contact with Anna. Countess Lydia Ivanovna declined to stay in Peterhof this summer, did not once call on Anna Arkadyevna, and hinted to Alexey Alexandrovich about the awkwardness of Anna's intimacy with Betsy and Vronsky. Alexey Alexandrovich sternly cut her short by declaring his wife to be above suspicion, and since then he had begun to avoid Countess Lydia Ivanovna. He did not want to see, and so did not see, that many people in society already looked askance at his wife, nor did he want to understand, and so did not understand, why his wife had so particularly insisted on moving to Tsarskoye, where Betsy was living, not far from where Vronsky's regiment was camped. He did not allow himself to think about it, and so did not think about it; but at the same time, in the depths of his soul, while never voicing this to himself, and having neither evidence nor proof, he knew beyond all doubt that he was a deceived husband, and he was deeply unhappy about it.

How many times during the eight years of his happy marriage to his wife had Alexey Alexandrovich looked at other people's unfaithful wives and deceived husbands, and asked himself: 'How can they let it happen? Why don't they put an end to such a hideous situation?' But now, when this misfortune had befallen him, he not only did not think of how to put an end to this situation, but did not want to confront it at all, and did not want to confront it precisely because it was too awful and too unnatural to contemplate.

Since the time he had returned from abroad, Alexey Alexandrovich had been to the dacha twice. On one occasion he had dined there, and on the other he spent the evening with guests, but he had not once stayed the night, which it had been his custom to do in previous years. The day of the races was a very busy one for Alexey Alexandrovich;

but having drawn up a schedule for himself that morning, he decided he would go straight to the dacha to see his wife after an early lunch, and from there go on to the races, which the entire court would attend, and which he also needed to attend. He was going to call on his wife, because he had resolved to see her once a week to keep up appearances. Besides, he needed that day to give his wife money for expenses so she would have it by the fifteenth day of the month, according to their prior agreement.

With his usual control over his thoughts, having pondered all this about his wife, he did not allow his thoughts to stray further into anything concerning her.

It was a very busy morning for Alexey Alexandrovich. The day before, Countess Lydia Ivanovna had sent him a pamphlet by a celebrated traveller to China, now in Petersburg, along with a letter asking him to receive the traveller himself, who for a number of reasons was a highly interesting and indispensable person. Alexey Alexandrovich had not managed to read the pamphlet the previous evening, but had finished it that morning. Then people with petitions started appearing, followed by the usual round of reports, consultations, appointments, dismissals, allocations of awards, pensions, salaries, correspondence—all the humdrum business, as Alexey Alexandrovich called it, which took up so much time. Then came personal business—a visit from the doctor and his steward. The steward did not take up much time. He just gave Alexey Alexandrovich the money he needed, and a brief report on the state of his finances, which were not completely healthy, as more had been spent that year as a result of frequent trips, and there was a deficit. But the doctor, a celebrated Petersburg doctor, who was on friendly terms with Alexey Alexandrovich, took up a great deal of time. Alexey Alexandrovich had not expected him that day, and was surprised by his visit, even more so when the doctor questioned him carefully about his health, listened to his chest, and tapped and prodded his liver. Alexey Alexandrovich did not know that his friend Lydia Ivanovna had asked the doctor to go and examine his patient after noticing that he had not been well that year. 'Do it for me,' the Countess Lydia Ivanovna had said to him.

'I will do it for Russia, Countess,' replied the doctor.

'He's an incomparable man!' said the Countess Lydia Ivanovna.

The doctor was very unhappy with Alexey Alexandrovich. He found his liver significantly enlarged, his nutrition impaired, and no evidence at all that taking the waters had done him any good. He prescribed as much physical exercise as possible, and as little mental exertion as possible, and above all, no stress—in other words, precisely what was as impossible for Alexey Alexandrovich as not breathing; then he went away, leaving Alexey Alexandrovich with the unpleasant feeling that something in him was amiss that could not be put right.

In the porch, as he was leaving Alexey Alexandrovich, the doctor bumped into Slyudin, Alexey Alexandrovich's private secretary, whom he knew well. They had been comrades at university, and although they rarely met, they respected each other and were good friends, and so to no one but Slyudin would the doctor have been prepared to volunteer such a frank opinion of his patient.

'How glad I am you've been to see him!' said Slyudin. 'He's not well, and it seems to me . . . Well, what do you think?'

'It's like this,' said the doctor, waving over Slyudin's head to his coachman to bring the carriage round. 'It's like this,' said the doctor, grasping a finger of his kid gloves with his white hands and pulling it. 'It's very difficult to try and break a string if you don't stretch it, but stretch it to its limit, and press just one finger on that taut string, and it will snap. And with all his diligence, and his conscientious approach to his work, he is stretched to the limit; plus he has some outside pressure, of a grave kind,' concluded the doctor, raising his eyebrows significantly. 'Will you be at the races?' he added, as he sat down in the carriage that had come round. 'Yes, yes, of course, it takes a lot of time,' replied the doctor in response to something Slyudin said, which he had not fully heard.

After the doctor, who had taken up so much time, came the celebrated traveller, and drawing on the pamphlet he had just finished reading and his previous knowledge of this subject, Alexey Alexandrovich amazed the traveller with the depth of his knowledge on the subject and the breadth of his enlightened outlook.

The traveller's arrival was announced together with that of a Marshal of the Nobility* from the provinces who had turned up in Petersburg, and with whom there were things to discuss. After his departure, it was necessary to complete all the routine matters with his private secretary, and he still had to pay a visit to a certain important individual about a serious and pressing matter. Alexey Alexandrovich only managed to return towards five o'clock, the time he dined, and after dining with his secretary, he invited him to drive out with him to the dacha and on to the races.

Without being aware of it, Alexey Alexandrovich now sought opportunities to have a third person present during his meetings with his wife.

27

ANNA was standing upstairs in front of the mirror, pinning the last bow on to her dress with help from Annushka, when she heard the sound of carriage wheels crunching on the gravel outside the front door.

'It's too early for Betsy,' she thought, and glancing out of the window she saw a carriage, a black hat sticking out of it, and Alexey Alexandrovich's familiar ears. 'That's inconvenient; surely he is not going to stay the night, is he?' she wondered. And the possible consequences of that seemed so awful and frightening to her that, without a moment's thought, she went down to meet him with a bright and happy face, and feeling within her the presence of that already familiar spirit of dishonesty and deception, she surrendered to it and began talking, not knowing herself what she would say.

'Ah, how nice this is!' she said, giving her husband her hand, and smiling when she greeted Slyudin as a member of the household. 'You're staying the night, I hope?' came the first utterance prompted by the spirit of deception. 'And we can go together now. It's just a shame that I promised Betsy. She's coming to pick me up.'

Alexey Alexandrovich frowned at Betsy's name.

'Oh, I wouldn't want to separate the inseparables,' he said in his usual jocular tone. 'I'll go with Mikhail Vasilievich. The doctors have ordered me to take some exercise. I'll walk along the road, and imagine I'm at the spa.'

'There's no hurry,' said Anna. 'Would you like some tea?' She rang.

'Bring us some tea, and tell Seryozha that Alexey Alexandrovich is here. So, how have you been feeling? Mikhail Vasilievich, you've not been here before; look how lovely it is out on my balcony,' she said, addressing first one and then the other.

She was speaking very simply and naturally, but too much and too quickly. She was herself aware of this, not least because she noticed, from the inquisitive way in which Mikhail Vasilievich was looking at her, that he seemed to be observing her.

Mikhail Vasilievich went straight out on to the terrace.

She sat down beside her husband.

'You don't look completely well,' she said.

'I know,' he said, 'the doctor came to see me today and took up an hour of my time. I have the feeling that one of my friends sent him: my health's so precious . . .'

'But what did he say?'

She asked him about his health, and what he had been doing, and tried to persuade him to take a rest and come and stay with her at the dacha.

She said all this brightly and rapidly, with a particular gleam in her eyes; but Alexey Alexandrovich did not attach any meaning to this tone of hers now. He heard only her words and ascribed to them only their direct meaning. And so he answered her simply, but glibly. There was nothing special about any part of this conversation, but afterwards Anna could never recall this brief scene without an excruciating feeling of shame.

Seryozha came in, preceded by his governess. If Alexey Alexandrovich had allowed himself to be observant, he would have noticed the timid, bewildered glance which Seryozha directed first at his father and then at his mother. But he did not want to see anything, and so saw nothing.

'Ah, the young man! He's grown. He's really becoming quite adult now. Hello, young man.'

And he gave his hand to the terrified child.

Seryozha had been shy of his father before, but ever since Alexey Alexandrovich had taken to calling him young man, and ever since he had begun to puzzle over whether Vronsky was a friend or an enemy, he had avoided his father. He looked round to his mother as if seeking protection. It was only with his mother that he felt comfortable. Alexey Alexandrovich had meanwhile been holding on to his son's shoulder while he talked to the governess, and Seryozha felt so painfully ill at ease that Anna saw he was on the verge of tears.

Anna had blushed slightly when her son came in, and when she noticed that Seryozha was feeling uncomfortable, she quickly got up, lifted Alexey Alexandrovich's hand from her son's shoulder, kissed her son, took him out on to the terrace, and immediately returned.

'Ah, I see it's time to go already,' she said, glancing at her watch. 'I wonder what has happened to Betsy! . . .'

'Yes,' said Alexey Alexandrovich, and he got up, folded his hands, and cracked his fingers. 'I've also stopped by to bring you some money, as we all know that nightingales don't live on fables,'* he said. 'I'm sure you need it.'

'No, I don't . . . actually, yes, I do,' she said, not looking at him, and blushing to her roots. 'But you'll be coming back here after the races, won't you?'

'Oh, yes!' answered Alexey Alexandrovich. 'Here's the pride of Peterhof, Princess Tverskaya,' he added, looking out of the window at the English carriage drawn by blinkered horses which was driving up, its tiny body perched exceedingly high. 'What style! How charming! Well, we should be off too.'

Princess Tverskaya did not get out of her carriage, but her servant, in laced-up boots, cape, and black hat, leapt out by the front door.

'I'm going, goodbye!' said Anna, and after kissing her son, she went up to Alexey Alexandrovich and held out her hand to him. 'It was sweet of you to come.'

Alexey Alexandrovich kissed her hand.

'Well, goodbye. You'll come back for tea, and that will be lovely!' she said, and went out in radiant high spirits. But as soon as she could no longer see him, she was aware of the spot on her hand which his lips had touched, and she shuddered with disgust.

28

By the time Alexey Alexandrovich arrived at the races, Anna was already sitting next to Betsy, in the pavilion where all the high-society people had gathered. She caught sight of her husband from afar. There were two people who were the focal points of her life, her husband and her lover, and she had no need of external stimuli to be aware of their proximity. She could feel her husband approaching from afar, and could not stop herself from watching him as he navigated his way through the crowds. She saw him coming towards the pavilion, and then watched him responding haughtily to ingratiating bows, exchanging friendly, distracted greetings with his equals, trying diligently to catch the eye of the great and the good, and removing his large, round hat, which pinched the tips of his ears. She knew all these patterns of behaviour, and she found them all repugnant. 'Nothing but pure ambition and a desire to succeed—that's all there is in his heart,' she thought, 'and those lofty ideals, such as his love of learning and religion, are just a means to achieve success.'

From the glances he was casting towards the ladies' pavilion (he was staring straight at her, but did not recognize his wife in the sea of muslin, lace, ribbons, hair, and parasols), she realized he was looking for her; but she deliberately failed to notice him.

'Alexey Alexandrovich!' Princess Betsy shouted out to him. 'You probably can't see your wife: she is here!'

He smiled his chilly smile.

'There's so much splendour here I feel quite dazzled,' he said, and he went into the pavilion. He smiled to his wife in the way a husband should smile on meeting a wife he has just seen, and greeted the Princess and other acquaintances, giving each their due, that is to say, joking with the ladies and exchanging greetings with the men. Below, next to the pavilion, stood the Tsar's adjutant-general, whom Alexey Alexandrovich respected for his intelligence and education. Alexey Alexandrovich entered into conversation with him.

There was an interval between the races, and so nothing hindered their conversation. The adjutant-general was condemning the races. Alexey Alexandrovich was defending them. Anna listened to his monotonous, high-pitched voice without missing a word that he said; every word struck her as false, and jarred painfully on her ear.

When the three-mile steeplechase was about to start, she leaned forward and fixed her gaze on Vronsky as he went up to his horse and mounted, and at the same time she could hear her husband's loathsome, relentless voice. She was suffering agonies about Vronsky's safety, but a far greater torture for her was the seemingly relentless sound of her husband's shrill voice with its familiar intonations.

'I'm a bad woman, a doomed woman,' she thought, 'but I don't like lies, I can't stand lies, but *he*'—her husband—'subsists on lies. He knows everything, he sees everything; so what can he be feeling if he can speak so calmly? If he were to kill me, or kill Vronsky, I would respect him. No, all he wants are lies and propriety,' Anna said to herself, not knowing exactly what she wanted from her husband, or how she wanted to see him behave. She also did not understand that Alexey Alexandrovich's peculiar loquacity that day, which she found so irritating, was merely the expression of his inner anxiety and distress. As a child who has been hurt will leap about and flex his muscles in order to stifle the pain, so Alexey Alexandrovich needed mental activity to stifle the thoughts of his wife which claimed his attention in her presence, and in the presence of Vronsky, whose name was on everybody's lips. And it was as natural for him to speak cleverly and well as it is natural for a child to leap about. He was saying:

'Danger in officers' and cavalry races is a necessary criterion of racing. If England can point to the most brilliant cavalry exploits in military history, it is only because she has historically cultivated this strength in her animals and in her men. Sport, in my opinion, has great significance, and as always, we are seeing only the most superficial side.'

'Hardly superficial,' said Princess Tverskaya. 'Apparently, one officer has broken two ribs.'

Alexey Alexandrovich smiled his smile, revealing only his teeth, but not expressing anything else.

'Let's say then, Princess, that it's not the surface but the essence,' he said, 'but that's not the point,' and he turned again to the general with whom he was having a serious conversation. 'Don't forget that the people racing are soldiers, who have chosen to engage in this activity, and you must agree that there is another side to the coin in every occupation. It's part and parcel of a soldier's duties. Gruesome sports such as fist-fighting or Spanish bullfights are a sign of barbarism. But specialized sport is a sign of sophistication.'

'No, I won't come again; I find it too upsetting,' said Princess Betsy. 'Don't you agree, Anna?'

'It is upsetting, but one can't tear oneself away,' said another lady. 'If I lived in ancient Rome, I wouldn't miss a single circus.'

Anna said nothing and, without lowering her binoculars, kept her eyes glued on one spot.

A tall general walked through the pavilion at that moment. Stopping in the middle of what he was saying, Alexey Alexandrovich stood up hastily but with dignity, and bowed low to the general as he walked past.

'You're not racing?' the officer asked him jokingly.

'My race is harder,' Alexey Alexandrovich responded deferentially.

And although the answer did not mean anything, the general pretended he had received a pearl of wisdom from a wise man and fully grasped *la pointe de la sauce*.[1]

'There are two sides,' continued Alexey Alexandrovich, as he sat down again, 'the participants and the onlookers; and a love of these spectacles is the surest sign of low development in the onlookers, I agree, but . . .'

'Time to place your bets, Princess!' sounded Stepan Arkadyich's voice, addressing Betsy from below. 'Who is your money on?'

'Anna and I are for Prince Kuzovlev,' replied Betsy.

'I'm for Vronsky. A pair of gloves?'

'Done!'

'It's wonderful, isn't it?'

Alexey Alexandrovich was quiet while all this talking was going on around him, but he then immediately resumed.

'I agree that sports requiring courage . . .' he began.

But at that moment the race started, and all conversations ceased. Alexey Alexandrovich fell silent, and everyone stood up and turned

---

[1] 'the flavour of the sauce'.

their attention towards the stream. Alexey Alexandrovich was not interested in the races, and so he did not look at the jockeys, but started scanning the spectators with his tired eyes. His gaze rested upon Anna.

Her face was pale and rigid. She clearly only had eyes for one person and could see nothing else. Her hand was gripping her fan convulsively, and she was holding her breath. He looked at her, then quickly turned aside to examine other faces.

'But this lady and others are also very worked up; it's quite natural,' Alexey Alexandrovich told himself. He did not want to look at her, but his gaze was instinctively drawn to her. He studied her face again, trying not to read what was so plainly written on it, and was aghast to find himself reading what he did not want to know, against his will.

Everyone was shaken when Kuzovlev was the first to fall at the stream, but Alexey Alexandrovich could clearly see on Anna's pale, triumphant face that the man she was watching had not fallen. When, after Makhotin and Vronsky had cleared the big barrier, the next officer was thrown head-first and knocked unconscious, and horrified whispers ran through the assembled spectators, Alexey Alexandrovich saw that Anna had not even noticed, and could scarcely understand what people around her had started talking about. His gaze kept returning to her ever more frequently, and he began to watch her even more persistently. Anna was completely absorbed in watching Vronsky race, but she nevertheless felt her husband's cold eyes fixed on her from the side.

She glanced round for an instant, looked enquiringly at him, then turned back again with a slight frown.

'Ah, I don't care!' she seemed to be saying to him, and she did not look at him again.

The race was ill-starred, and out of seventeen competitors more than half were thrown and injured. By the end of the race everyone was in a state of agitation, which was intensified still further by the fact that the Tsar was displeased.

29

EVERYONE was loudly expressing their disapproval, everyone kept repeating a phrase someone had said: 'It will be lions and gladiators next,' and the horror was felt by everyone, so when Vronsky fell and Anna gave a loud gasp, it was nothing out of the ordinary. But a change then came over Anna's face that was decidedly improper. She completely lost her composure. She began flapping about like a caged bird; first she wanted to get up and go somewhere, next she turned to Betsy.

'Let's go, let's go!' she said.

But Betsy did not hear her. She was leaning over to talk to a general down below who had come up to her.

Alexey Alexandrovich went up to Anna and courteously offered her his arm.

'Let us go, if you please,' he said in French, but Anna was listening to the general and did not notice her husband.

'Apparently he's broken his leg too,' the general was saying. 'There hasn't been anything like it.'

Without answering her husband, Anna raised her binoculars and looked towards the place where Vronsky had fallen; but it was so far off, and there was such a crowd of people there, that it was impossible to make anything out. She lowered her binoculars and was about to go; but at that moment an officer galloped up and delivered a report to the Tsar. Anna craned forward to listen.

'Stiva! Stiva!' she shouted out to her brother.

But her brother did not hear her. She again prepared to leave.

'Once again I offer you my arm if you wish to leave,' said Alexey Alexandrovich, touching her arm.

She recoiled from him in disgust, and answered without looking at him:

'No, no, let me be, I'm going to stay.'

She now saw an officer running across the racetrack from the place where Vronsky had fallen towards the pavilion. Betsy waved her handkerchief to him.

The officer brought the news that the rider was not injured, but the horse had broken its back.

When she heard this, Anna quickly sat down and buried her face in her fan. Alexey Alexandrovich saw that she was weeping, and that not only could she not control her tears, but that the sobs were making her bosom heave. Alexey Alexandrovich stood over her like a shield, giving her time to recover.

'For the third time, I offer you my arm,' he said to her after some time had passed. Anna looked at him and did not know what to say. Princess Betsy came to her rescue.

'No, Alexey Alexandrovich, I brought Anna and I promised to take her home,' Betsy said, intervening.

'Forgive me, Princess,' he said, smiling courteously but looking her very firmly in the eye, 'but I can see that Anna is not very well, and I would like her to come home with me.'

Anna looked about her anxiously, then got up meekly and laid her hand on her husband's arm.

'I'll send someone over to find out about him, and will let you know,' Betsy whispered to her.

As they left the pavilion, Alexey Alexandrovich talked to the people they ran into as always, and as always, Anna had to answer and converse; but she was not herself, and she walked along holding her husband's arm as though in a dream.

'Is he injured or not? Is it true? Will he come or not? Will I see him tonight?' she was wondering.

She sat down silently in her husband's carriage and remained in silence as they departed from the mass of vehicles. Despite everything he had seen, Alexey Alexandrovich still was not permitting himself to think about the reality of his wife's situation. He merely saw the external signs. He saw that she had behaved improperly, and considered it his duty to tell her so. But it was very difficult for him not to say more, and to say only that. He opened his mouth to tell her she had behaved improperly, but could not help saying something completely different.

'It is strange how we are all drawn to these cruel spectacles,' he said. 'I notice . . .'

'What? I don't understand,' said Anna contemptuously.

He was offended, and at once began to say what was on his mind.

'I have to tell you,' he began.

'This is it, we're going to have things out,' she thought, and she became frightened.

'I have to tell you that you behaved improperly today,' he said to her in French.

'How did I behave improperly?' she said loudly, turning her head swiftly towards him, and looking him straight in the eye, no longer with the previous jollity that concealed something, but with a determined look, behind which she could barely conceal the fear she was experiencing.

'Don't forget,' he said to her, indicating the open window behind the coachman. He got up and raised the window.

'What did you find improper?' she repeated.

'The despair you were unable to conceal when one of the riders fell.'

He waited for her to object; but she remained silent, her eyes looking straight ahead.

'I have already asked you to comport yourself in society in a manner such that even malicious tongues can find nothing to say against you. There was a time when I spoke about our internal relations, but I am not speaking of that now. I'm speaking about external relations. You have behaved improperly, and I would not like this to be repeated.'

She did not hear half of what he was saying, she was feeling frightened of him, and wondering whether it was true that Vronsky had not been injured. Were they talking about him when they said he was unhurt, but the horse had broken its back? She simply feigned a sarcastic smile when he finished speaking, and did not reply, because she had not heard what he said. Alexey Alexandrovich had begun by speaking boldly, but when he properly understood what he was talking about, the fear she was experiencing transferred to him too. He saw that smile, and he succumbed to a strange delusion.

'She is smiling at my suspicions. Yes, she is about to tell me what she told me before; that there are no grounds for my suspicions, that it's absurd.'

Now, with the revelation of everything hanging over him, there was nothing he wished for more than for her to answer mockingly, like she had done the last time, that his suspicions were absurd and had no foundation. What he knew deep down was so awful that he was now ready to believe anything. But the frightened and gloomy expression on her face did not promise even deception now.

'Maybe I am mistaken,' he said. 'In which case, I beg your forgiveness.'

'No, you are not mistaken,' she said slowly, glancing in desperation at his cold face. 'You are not mistaken. I was, and cannot help being in despair. I hear you, but I am thinking about him. I love him, I am his mistress, I can't stand you, I'm afraid of you, I hate you . . . Do what you like with me.'

And she retreated into the corner of the carriage and started sobbing, covering her face with her hands. Alexey Alexandrovich did not move a muscle, and he continued to look straight ahead. But his whole face suddenly acquired the imposing immobility of a corpse, and this expression did not change during the entire drive back to the dacha. When they arrived home, he turned his head to her, still wearing the same expression.

'I see! But I demand that the formal requirements of propriety are observed until such time'—his voice started to shake—'as I have taken measures to safeguard my honour, which I will communicate to you in due course.'

He got out first and helped her out of the carriage. He pressed her hand in front of the servants, got into the carriage, and left for

Petersburg. Immediately afterwards a footman came from Princess Betsy and brought Anna a note.

'I sent someone over to Alexey to find out how he is, and he wrote to me that he is safe and sound, but in despair.'

'So *he* will be here!' Anna thought. 'What a good thing I told him everything!'

She glanced at her watch. There were still three hours to go, and the memory of the details of their last meeting set her blood aflame.

'Heavens, how light it is! It's dreadful, but I love to see his face, and I love this fantastic light . . . My husband! Ah, yes . . . Well, thank heavens everything is over with him.'

30

As in all places where people gather, so too in the small German spa to which the Shcherbatskys had come there occurred the usual kind of crystallization of society that determines a specific and immutable place for each of its members. As specifically and as immutably as a particle of water in cold weather takes on the well-known form of a snow crystal, so each new person arriving at the spa was precisely and immediately established in their appropriate place.

Fürst Shcherbatsky, *sammt Gemahlin und Tochter*,[1] as a result of the accommodation they occupied, their name, and the acquaintances they made, immediately crystallized into their specific and predestined place.

There was a real German Fürstin[2] visiting the spa that year, and consequently the crystallization of society proceeded with even greater energy. Princess Shcherbatskaya wanted without fail to present her daughter to the German Princess, and she performed this rite on their very second day. Kitty made a low and graceful curtsey in her *very simple*, that is to say, very elegant summer frock that had been ordered from Paris. The Princess said, 'I hope the roses will soon return to this pretty little face,' and immediately certain specific paths of life were firmly established for the Shcherbatskys, from which there now could be no deviation. The Shcherbatskys also became acquainted with the family of an English *Lady*, a German countess and her son, who had been wounded in the last war, a Swedish scholar, and with a Monsieur Canut and his sister. But the Shcherbatskys inevitably spent most time

---

[1] Prince Shcherbatsky with his wife and daughter.   [2] Princess.

with a Moscow lady, Marya Evgenievna Rtishcheva, and her daughter, whom Kitty did not warm to, because she had fallen ill over a love affair, like she had, and also a Moscow colonel whom Kitty had known from childhood and had always seen in uniform and epaulettes, and who here, with his small eyes, open neck, and colourful cravat, was unbelievably ridiculous and also tedious, because there was no getting rid of him. When all this became firmly established, Kitty grew very bored, especially as the Prince had gone off to Carlsbad* and she was left alone with her mother. She was not interested in the people she knew, feeling that nothing new could come from them now. What stimulated her imagination at the spa most of all now was observing and making guesses about the people she did not know. It was in keeping with Kitty's character that she always saw the best in people, particularly those she did not know. And now as she made guesses about who was who, what sort of relationships they had with each other, and what kind of people they were, Kitty conjured up the most astounding and admirable qualities for them, and found confirmation in her observations.

Among such people, she was particularly captivated by a Russian girl who had come to the spa with an invalid Russian lady—Madame Stahl, as everyone called her. Madame Stahl belonged to the highest society, but she was so ill that she could not walk, and only on exceptionally fine days made an appearance at the springs in a wheelchair. But it was not so much down to ill-health as pride, Princess Shcherbatskaya explained, that Madame Stahl was not acquainted with any of the Russians there. The Russian girl looked after Madame Stahl and, as Kitty noted, she was also friendly with all the people who were seriously ill, of whom there were many at the springs, and she looked after them in the most natural way. This Russian girl, as Kitty observed, was not related to Madame Stahl, but neither was she a paid companion. Madame Stahl called her Varenka, while the others called her '*Mademoiselle Varenka*'. Apart from the fact that Kitty was intrigued by what she saw of this girl's relations with Madame Stahl and other people she did not know, Kitty felt an inexplicable liking for this Mademoiselle Varenka and, as often happens, she felt her feelings were reciprocated whenever their eyes met.

This Mademoiselle Varenka was not so much past her first youth as a kind of creature without youth: she could have been taken for nineteen or thirty. Analysing her features, one would have said she was more attractive than plain, despite her wan complexion. She would also have had a good figure had she not been excessively thin and did not have a head incommensurate with her medium height; but she could not have been attractive to men. She was like a beautiful flower which has already lost its bloom, despite having a full head of petals, and has no scent. Apart from that, she could not have been attractive to men because she also lacked what Kitty had in excess—a repressed spark of vitality, and an awareness of her own attractiveness.

She always appeared to be busy with something about which there could be no doubt, and for that reason it seemed she could not be interested in anything else. It was this contrast with herself that Kitty found particularly attractive. Kitty felt that she might find in her, and in her way of life, a model of what she was now painfully seeking: interests in life, virtues in life, beyond a girl's relations with men in society, which Kitty found odious, and which for her now resembled the shameful parading of goods awaiting purchasers. The longer Kitty observed her unknown friend, the more convinced she became that this girl was the perfect creature she had imagined her to be, and the more eager she was to make her acquaintance.

The two girls encountered each other several times a day, and every time they met, Kitty's eyes would say: 'Who are you? What are you? Are you really the lovely creature I imagine you to be? But please don't think', her eyes would add, 'that I would take the liberty of thrusting myself on you. I just admire you and like you.' 'I like you too, you're very, very nice. And I would like you even more, if I had the time,' answered the eyes of the unknown girl. And Kitty did indeed see that she was always busy: she was either taking the children of a Russian family home from the springs, or fetching a shawl for a sick lady and wrapping her up in it, or trying to entertain some grumpy invalid, or choosing and buying biscuits for someone to have with coffee.

Soon after the arrival of the Shcherbatskys, two other people started coming to take the waters in the morning who attracted general unfriendly attention. They were a tall, stooping man dressed in an old coat, too short for him, who had huge hands and black eyes which were at once naive and frightening, and a pockmarked, attractive woman, who was very badly and tastelessly dressed. Recognizing these people as Russians, Kitty had already begun in her imagination to compose a wonderful and heart-rending romantic story about them. But when the Princess found out from the *Kurliste*[1] that they were Nikolay Levin and Marya Nikolayevna, and explained to Kitty what a bad man this

[1] List of visitors at the spa.

Levin was, all her daydreams about these two people evaporated. It was not so much what her mother told her as the fact that this was Konstantin's brother, but these individuals suddenly seemed highly disagreeable to Kitty. This Levin, with his habit of jerking his head, now aroused in her an insurmountable feeling of disgust.

It seemed to her that his large, frightening eyes, which pursued her doggedly, expressed a feeling of hatred and contempt, and she tried to avoid meeting him.

31

IT was a wet day, rain had been falling all morning, and the invalids had crowded into the arcade with their umbrellas.

Kitty was walking with her mother and the Moscow colonel, who was proudly showing off his European jacket, bought off the peg in Frankfurt. They were walking on one side of the arcade, trying to avoid Levin, who was walking on the other side. Varenka, in her dark dress and black hat with the brim turned down, was walking up and down the whole length of the arcade with a blind French lady, and every time she met Kitty, they exchanged friendly glances.

'Mama, may I speak to her?' said Kitty, who had been watching her unknown friend, and noticing that she was walking towards the spring, where they might meet.

'Well, if you are really that keen, I'll find out about her first and approach her myself,' answered her mother. 'What do you see in her that is so special? She must be a companion. If you like, I'll become acquainted with Madame Stahl. I used to know her *belle-soeur*,[1] added the Princess, tossing back her head haughtily.

Kitty knew the Princess was offended that Madame Stahl seemed to be avoiding making her acquaintance. Kitty did not insist.

'She's so incredibly nice!' she said, watching Varenka proffer a glass to the French lady. 'Look how natural and nice it all is.'

'I find your *engouements*[2] quite hilarious,' said the Princess. 'No, we'd better turn back,' she added, noticing Levin coming towards them with his lady and a German doctor, to whom he was speaking loudly and angrily. They were just turning round to walk back when suddenly they started hearing not just raised voices but shouting. Levin had stopped and was shouting, and the doctor was also irate.

---

[1] 'sister-in-law'.   [2] 'infatuations'.

A crowd gathered round them. The Princess and Kitty walked swiftly away, while the colonel joined the crowd to find out what was going on.

A few minutes later the colonel caught up with them.

'What was that all about?' asked the Princess.

'It's an outright disgrace!' answered the colonel. 'If there's one thing you fear, it's meeting Russians abroad. That tall gentleman was abusing the doctor, throwing insults at him for not treating him in the right way, and then he began waving his stick about. It's simply disgraceful!'

'Oh, how unpleasant!' said the Princess. 'Well, how did it end?'

'It was lucky that girl—the one in the toadstool hat—intervened at that point. She is Russian, I think,' said the colonel.

'Mademoiselle Varenka?' asked Kitty joyfully.

'Yes, that's the one. She appeared on the scene before anyone else, took the man by the arm, and led him away.'

'There, Mama,' said Kitty; 'and you wonder that I admire her.'

As she observed her unknown friend at the spring the next day, Kitty noticed that Mademoiselle Varenka was already on the same terms with Levin and his companion as she was with her other protégés. She went up to them, engaged them in conversation, and acted as interpreter for the woman, who could not speak any foreign language.

Kitty started to press her mother even more insistently for permission to make Varenka's acquaintance. And, however distasteful it was for the Princess to appear to be taking the first step in wishing to become acquainted with Madame Stahl, who seemed to be giving herself certain airs and graces, she made enquiries about Varenka, and after ascertaining certain facts about her which made it possible to conclude that no harm, although also little good, could come of the acquaintance, she herself took the first step in approaching Varenka and introducing herself.

Choosing a moment when her daughter had gone to the spring, and Varenka had stopped outside the baker's, the Princess went up to her.

'Allow me to make your acquaintance,' she said, with her dignified smile. 'My daughter has lost her heart to you,' she said. 'You perhaps do not know me. I am . . .'

'The feeling is more than mutual, Princess,' Varenka answered quickly.

'What a good deed you performed yesterday for our poor compatriot!' said the Princess.

Varenka blushed. 'I don't remember, I don't think I did anything,' she said.

'Yes you did—you saved that Levin from getting into trouble.'

'Yes, *sa compagne*[1] asked me to help, and I was trying to calm him down: he is very ill, and he is unhappy with the doctor. But I'm used to looking after these invalids.'

'Yes, I've heard you live at Menton with your aunt, Madame Stahl, I believe: I used to know her *belle-soeur*.'

'No, she's not my aunt. I call her *Maman*, but I am not related to her; I was brought up by her,' answered Varenka, blushing again.

This was said so simply, and the sincere and open expression on her face was so endearing, that the Princess understood why Kitty had taken such a liking to this Varenka.

'Well, and what's going to happen to this Levin?' asked the Princess.

'He's leaving,' answered Varenka.

Meanwhile, Kitty had come over from the spring, and was beaming with happiness that her mother had become acquainted with her unknown friend.

'Well, Kitty, your great desire to become acquainted with Mademoiselle . . .'

'Varenka,' prompted Varenka with a smile, 'everyone calls me that.'

Kitty blushed with happiness, and silently and slowly pressed her new friend's hand, which did not respond to her pressure, but lay motionless in her hand. The hand did not respond to her pressure, but Mademoiselle Varenka's face shone with a quiet, happy, although also slightly sad smile, revealing large but beautiful teeth.

'I have long wanted to meet you too,' she said.

'But you have so much to do . . .'

'On the contrary, I don't have anything to do,' answered Varenka, but at that moment she had to leave her new acquaintances, because two little Russian girls, the children of an invalid, had run up to her.

'Varenka, Mamma is calling for you!' they shouted.

And Varenka followed them.

32

THE details that the Princess had found out about Varenka's past and her relationship with Madame Stahl were as follows.

Madame Stahl, about whom some said that she had persecuted her husband, and others that he had persecuted her with his depraved behaviour, had always been a sickly and emotional woman. After

---

[1] 'his companion'.

giving birth to her first child, when she was already divorced from her husband, the child immediately died, and Madame Stahl's relatives, knowing how sensitive she was and fearing this news might kill her, substituted another child, a baby born the same night and in the same house in Petersburg, who was the daughter of a court chef.* This was Varenka. Madame Stahl learned later on that Varenka was not her daughter, but she continued to bring her up, which was just as well, since very soon after that Varenka was left with no relatives at all.

For more than ten years Madame Stahl had been living permanently abroad, in the south, and never rising from her bed. And while there were some who said that Madame Stahl had carved out a social niche for herself as a virtuous, extremely religious woman, others said she really was at heart the extremely righteous creature she made herself out to be, living only for the good of others. No one knew what her faith was—Catholic, Protestant, or Orthodox; but one thing was certain—she was on friendly terms with the most senior figures of all faiths and denominations.

Varenka lived permanently with her abroad, and everyone who knew Madame Stahl knew and liked Mademoiselle Varenka, as she was universally called.

Having uncovered all these details, the Princess found nothing to object to in her daughter becoming friends with Varenka, particularly since Varenka's manners and education were exemplary: she spoke excellent French and English, and—most importantly—she conveyed Madame Stahl's regret that she was prevented by ill-health from making the acquaintance of the Princess.

After meeting Varenka, Kitty became more and more enchanted by her friend, and every day discovered new virtues in her.

The Princess asked her to come and sing to them one evening, after hearing that Varenka had a good voice.

'Kitty plays, and we have a piano, not a good one, it's true, but you will give us great pleasure,' said the Princess with her feigned smile, which Kitty found particularly unpleasant now, because she had noticed that Varenka did not want to sing. Varenka came over in the evening, however, and brought a music album with her. The Princess invited Marya Evgenievna and her daughter, and the colonel.

Varenka seemed quite unperturbed by the presence of people she did not know, and she went straight over to the piano. She could not accompany herself, but she could sing music at sight marvellously. Kitty, who played well, accompanied her.

'You have an exceptional talent,' the Princess said to her after Varenka had sung the first song very beautifully.

Marya Evgenievna and her daughter thanked her and paid her compliments.

'Come and see what an audience has gathered to listen to you,' said the colonel, looking out of the window. A sizeable crowd had indeed gathered beneath the windows.

'I am very glad it gives you pleasure,' Varenka answered simply.

Kitty looked at her friend with pride. She was in awe of her artistry, her voice, and her face, but most of all she was in awe of her manner, and the fact that Varenka clearly thought nothing of her singing, and was quite indifferent to praise; she seemed only to be asking: 'Do I need to sing again, or is that enough?'

'If it had been me,' Kitty thought to herself, 'how proud I'd be! How thrilled I would be to see that crowd under the windows! But it's all the same to her. She is only driven by a desire not to refuse, and to give pleasure to *Maman*. What is it about her? What gives her this power to spurn everything, and be so calmly independent? I would so like to know, and to acquire it from her!' thought Kitty, gazing at her calm face. The Princess asked Varenka to sing again, and Varenka sang another song, just as smoothly, crisply, and proficiently, standing up straight next to the piano and beating time to it with her thin, dark hand.

The next song in the album was Italian. Kitty played the opening bars, and looked up at Varenka.

'Let's skip this one,' said Varenka, blushing.

Kitty's startled, inquisitive eyes rested on Varenka's face.

'Well, something else, then,' she said hurriedly, turning the pages, having immediately realized that there was an association with that song.

'No,' answered Varenka, laying her hand on the music and smiling, 'no, let's sing this one.' And she sang it just as calmly, as coolly, and as proficiently as the others.

When she had finished, everyone thanked her again and went off to drink tea. Kitty and Varenka went out into the little garden next to the house.

'Am I right in thinking you have some memory connected with that song?' said Kitty. 'Don't tell me,' she added quickly, 'just tell me, am I right?'

'No, why shouldn't I? I'll tell you,' Varenka said simply, and, without waiting for a reply, she went on: 'Yes, there is a memory, and it used once to be painful. There was someone I loved. And I used to sing that song to him.'

Kitty gazed silently and tenderly at Varenka with her big, wide-open eyes.

'I loved him and he loved me; but his mother was not keen, and he married someone else. He is living not far from us now, and I see him sometimes. You didn't think I had a love story too?' she said, and in her lovely face there was a faint glimmer of the fire which, Kitty felt, had once lit her whole being from within.

'Why would I have thought that? If I were a man, I could never love anyone else after knowing you. I simply can't understand how, to please his mother, he could forget you and make you unhappy; he had no heart.'

'Oh no, he's a very good person, and I'm not unhappy; quite the opposite, I'm very happy. So, you don't think we'll be singing again today?' she added, setting off towards the house.

'How nice you are, how nice you are!' cried Kitty, stopping her so she could kiss her. 'If only I could be just a little bit like you!'

'Why do you need to be like anyone else? You're nice as you are,' said Varenka, smiling her meek, tired smile.

'No, I'm not nice at all. So, tell me . . . Wait, let's sit down,' said Kitty, sitting her down on the bench again next to her. 'Tell me, isn't it humiliating to think that a man spurned your love, that he did not want? . . .'

'But he didn't spurn it; I believe he did love me, but he was a dutiful son . . .'

'Yes, but what if he hadn't been obeying his mother and he was just . . . ?' said Kitty, feeling she was giving away her secret, and that her face, burning red with shame, had already betrayed her.

'Then he would have behaved badly, and I would not have regretted losing him,' answered Varenka, clearly realizing that they were now talking about Kitty, not herself.

'But what about the insult?' said Kitty. 'One can never, ever forget an insult,' she said, remembering her expression at the last ball, when the music stopped.

'What insult? You haven't behaved badly, have you?'

'Worse than badly—shamefully.'

Varenka shook her head and laid her hand on Kitty's arm.

'But what is so shameful?' she said. 'You couldn't have told a man who was indifferent to you that you loved him, could you?'

'Of course not; I never said a word, but he knew it. No, no, there are looks, there are ways. I won't forget it in a hundred years.'

'So what then? I don't understand. The most important thing is whether you love him now or not,' said Varenka, who called everything by its name.

'I hate him; I can't forgive myself.'

'So what then?'

'It's the shame, the insult.'

'Oh, if everyone was as sensitive as you are,' said Varenka. 'There isn't a girl who hasn't gone through this. And it's all so unimportant.'

'So what is important?' asked Kitty, looking into her face with an expression of intrigued surprise.

'Oh, there are a lot of things which are important,' Varenka replied, not knowing what to say. But just then the Princess's voice could be heard from the window:

'Kitty, it's chilly! Either get a shawl, or come indoors.'

'Yes, it really is time to go!' said Varenka, getting up. 'I still have to look in on Madame Berthe; she asked me to.'

Kitty held her hand, while her eyes asked with an avid curiosity and entreating look: 'What is the important thing which imparts such serenity, what is it? You know, so please tell me!' But Varenka did not even understand what Kitty's eyes were asking her. She was just remembering that she still had to call in on Madame Berthe and arrive home by midnight, in time for *Maman*'s tea. She went indoors, collected her music, said goodbye to everyone, and prepared to leave.

'Allow me to see you home,' said the colonel.

'Yes, how can you go out alone at night?' the Princess agreed. 'At least let me send Parasha.'

Kitty saw that Varenka could barely repress a smile at the notion that she needed an escort.

'No, I always walk alone and nothing ever happens to me,' she said, taking her hat. And after kissing Kitty once again, but still not saying what was important, she set off briskly with her music under her arm and vanished into the dusk of the summer night, taking away with her the secret of what was important, and what gave her that enviable calmness and dignity.

33

KITTY also made the acquaintance of Madame Stahl, and together with her friendship with Varenka, this acquaintance not only had a great influence on her, but also was a source of great comfort to her while she grieved. This comfort came from the fact that this new acquaintance revealed a completely new world to her, which had nothing in common with her past, and was a beautiful, lofty world from whose heights she could look down calmly on this past. Kitty discovered that besides the instinctive life to which she had hitherto been in thrall, there was a spiritual life. It was religion which revealed this life to her, but one which had nothing in common with the religion Kitty had known from childhood, which found expression in the liturgy and all-night vigil at the Widows' Home,* where one could meet friends, and in learning Old Church Slavonic texts by heart with a priest; this was a lofty, mysterious religion, connected to an array of noble thoughts and feelings, which was not only possible to believe in because one was told to, but also possible to love.

It was not from words that Kitty learned all this. Madame Stahl talked to Kitty as if she were an adorable child, to be looked on fondly as a reminder of one's youth, and only once did she mention that love and faith alone can provide comfort for all human sorrows, and that there is no sorrow too trifling when it comes to Christ's compassion for us, and then she promptly changed the subject. But in every one of her gestures, in every word she spoke, in every one of what Kitty called her heavenly looks, and in the whole story of her life, which she heard about from Varenka, she found out 'what was important', which was something she had never encountered before.

But however lofty Madame Stahl's nature, however touching the whole story of her life, however loftily and tenderly she might speak, Kitty could not help perceiving certain traits in her which bothered her. She noticed that Madame Stahl had smiled disdainfully when enquiring about her family, which was at odds with Christian kindness. She also noticed that when she had found a Catholic priest with her one day, Madame Stahl had studiously kept her face in the shadow of the lampshade, and smiled in a particular way. However trivial these two observations were, they bothered her, and she began to have doubts about Madame Stahl. Varenka, on the other hand, solitary, without family, without friends, with her sad disappointment, wanting nothing, regretting nothing, was that acme of perfection about which Kitty only allowed herself to dream. Through Varenka she learned that one just had to forget oneself and love others in order to become a calm, happy, and worthy person. And that was what Kitty wanted to be. Having now clearly grasped what *the most important thing* was, Kitty was not content to revel in this knowledge, but threw herself wholeheartedly into this new life that had opened up to her. From Varenka's accounts of the activities of Madame Stahl and other people she named, Kitty started mapping out her future life. Like Madame Stahl's niece Aline, about whom Varenka had told her a great deal, she would seek out those who were in need, wherever she might be living, and help them as much as she could, by distributing the Gospel and reading the Gospel to the sick, to criminals, and the dying. Kitty was particularly captivated by the idea of reading the Gospel to criminals, as Aline did. But these were all secret dreams, which Kitty did not divulge either to her mother or Varenka.

For the moment, while she awaited the time when she could carry out her plans on a large scale, Kitty easily found the opportunity of applying her new principles in imitation of Varenka even now while she was at the spa, where there were so many sick and unfortunate people.

At first the Princess only noticed that Kitty was strongly under the influence of her *engouement*, as she called it, for Madame Stahl, and especially for Varenka. She saw that Kitty was not only imitating what Varenka did, but unconsciously imitating the way she walked, spoke, and blinked her eyes. But the Princess then noticed that some kind of serious spiritual transformation was taking place in her daughter independently of this fascination.

The Princess saw that Kitty was spending her evenings reading a French edition of the Gospels which Madame Stahl had given her, which she had never done before; that she was avoiding society acquaintances and associating with the sick people under Varenka's care, and especially with the impoverished family of the sick painter Petrov. Kitty was clearly proud to be performing the duties of a sister of mercy in that family. All this was fine, and the Princess had nothing against it, particularly since Petrov's wife was a perfectly respectable woman, and the German Princess, noticing Kitty's activities, had praised her, calling her a ministering angel. All this would have been fine and good, if it had not been excessive. But the Princess saw that her daughter was going to extremes, and told her so.

'*Il ne faut jamais rien outrer*,'[1] she said to her.

But her daughter did not reply; she only thought in her soul that one could never be excessive where Christianity was concerned. What could possibly be excessive about following a teaching which commands that when you are struck on one cheek, you should turn the other, and give up your tunic if someone takes your cloak?* But the Princess disliked this excess, and disliked even more Kitty's apparent unwillingness to open up her soul to her. Kitty was indeed concealing

---

[1] 'You should never go to extremes in anything.'

her new views and feelings from her mother. She was concealing them not because she did not respect or love her mother, but simply because she was her mother. She would have revealed them to anyone sooner than to her mother.

'Anna Pavlovna hasn't been to see us for quite a long time,' the Princess said one day about Petrov's wife. 'I've invited her, but she seems rather disgruntled about something.'

'No, I've not noticed anything, *Maman*,' Kitty said with a sudden blush.

'You haven't been to see them recently?'

'We're planning to take a walk in the hills tomorrow,' answered Kitty.

'Well, you should go then,' answered the Princess, peering into her daughter's embarrassed face and trying to work out the reason for her embarrassment.

That day Varenka came to dinner and told them that Anna Pavlovna had changed her mind about going up into the hills the next day. And the Princess noticed that Kitty blushed again.

'Kitty, have you had some disagreement with the Petrovs?' said the Princess when they were alone. 'Why has she stopped sending her children over and coming to see us?'

Kitty answered that nothing had happened between them, and that she really did not understand why Anna Pavlovna seemed to be upset with her. Kitty's answer was perfectly truthful. She did not know why Anna Pavlovna had changed towards her, but she could guess. She guessed something which she could not tell her mother, and which she could not say to herself. It was one of those things which you know, but which you cannot articulate even to yourself; it would be so awful and shameful to be wrong.

Again and again she went over in her memory all her relations with this family. She remembered the naive joy on Anna Pavlovna's round, friendly face when they met; she remembered their secret discussions about the sick man, their plots to distract him from his work, which he had been forbidden to do, and to take him off for walks; the attachment of the youngest boy, who called her 'my Kitty' and would not go to bed without her. It was all so nice! Then she recalled Petrov's painfully thin figure, his long neck, his brown frock-coat, his sparse curly hair, his penetrating blue eyes which Kitty had found so frightening at first, and his painful attempts to seem cheerful and lively in her presence. She remembered the effort she had made at first to overcome the revulsion she felt for him, as for any consumptive person, and her concerted efforts to think of what to say to him. She remembered that bashful, tender look he had given her, and the strange feeling of compassion and awkwardness she had experienced as a result, followed by a consciousness of her own virtue. It was all so good! But all that had been at the beginning. A few days ago, however, everything had suddenly gone wrong. Anna Pavlovna had greeted Kitty stiffly, and not once taken her eyes off her and her husband.

Could that touching joy of his when she approached really have been the cause of Anna Pavlovna's coolness?

'Yes,' she recalled, 'there was something unnatural about Anna Pavlovna, and quite unlike her usual kindness, when she had said crossly two days earlier: "Yes, he's been waiting and waiting for you, wouldn't drink his coffee without you, even though he's become terribly weak."'

'Yes, and perhaps she didn't like it when I gave him that rug. It was all so simple, but he accepted it so awkwardly, and he spent such a long time thanking me that I ended up feeling awkward too. And then there was that wonderful portrait he did of me. But the main thing was that embarrassed, tender look! Yes, yes, that was it!' Kitty repeated to herself in horror. 'But no, it can't be, it mustn't be! He's so pitiful!' was the next thing she said to herself.

This doubt poisoned the charm of her new life.

34

BEFORE the end of his course of treatment, Prince Shcherbatsky, who had gone on from Carlsbad to see Russian friends in Baden and Kissingen in order to stock up on Russian spirit, as he put it, returned to his family.

The views of the Prince and of the Princess about life abroad were diametrically opposed. The Princess thought everything was wonderful, and despite her secure position in Russian society, tried whenever she was abroad to be like a European lady, which she was not—because she was a Russian noblewoman—and therefore she had to pretend, which she found slightly awkward. The Prince, on the other hand, thought everything abroad was ghastly, found European life tedious, kept to his Russian habits, and went out of his way whenever he was abroad to show he was less European than he was in reality.

The Prince came back thinner, with drooping bags of skin on his cheeks, but in the very best of spirits. His spirits soared even higher when he saw that Kitty had completely recovered. The news of Kitty's friendship with Madame Stahl and Varenka, and the observations which the Princess relayed about some kind of change going on in Kitty, troubled the Prince, arousing in him his usual feeling of jealousy towards anything which took his daughter away from him, and fear that his daughter might escape from his influence into spheres which were inaccessible to him. But this unpleasant news drowned in the sea of warm-heartedness and jollity which was always inside him, and which had been intensified by the Carlsbad waters.

Dressed in his long coat, with his Russian wrinkles and puffy cheeks propped up by a starched collar, the Prince set off with his daughter to the springs the day after his arrival in the very best of spirits.

It was a lovely morning; the neat, cheerful houses with their little gardens, the sight of beer-filled German servant girls with their red faces and red hands, working away merrily, and the bright sunshine gladdened the heart; but as they approached the springs they started to meet more and more sick people, and their appearance seemed all the more abject amongst the ordinary surroundings of comfortable German life. Kitty was no longer struck by this contrast. The bright sun, the sparkling lustre of all the greenery, and the sound of music were for her a natural frame for all these familiar faces and the changes for the better or worse which she was following; but to the Prince, the brightness and splendour of a June morning, the sound of the orchestra playing a fashionable merry waltz, and particularly the appearance of those robust servant girls seemed somehow indecent and grotesque when juxtaposed with the sight of those corpses who had gathered from every corner of Europe, forlornly shuffling along.

In spite of feeling proud and somehow rejuvenated walking along with his beloved daughter on his arm, he was now almost awkward and embarrassed by his vigorous step and his burly, fat-encased limbs. He felt rather like a man who was undressed in public.

'Come along now, introduce me to your new friends,' he said to his daughter, pressing her arm with his elbow. 'I've even taken a liking to your horrid Soden for doing you so much good. Only it's sad, this place of yours, very sad. Who's that?'

Kitty told him the names of both the acquaintances and strangers whom they met. Right by the entrance to the gardens they met the blind Madame Berthe with her guide, and the Prince was delighted by the tender expression on the old Frenchwoman's face when she heard Kitty's voice. She at once began talking to him with exaggerated French courtesy, complimenting him on having such a wonderful daughter, praising Kitty to the skies in front of her, and calling her a treasure, a pearl, and a ministering angel.

'Well, she has to be the angel number two then,' said the Prince, smiling. 'She calls Mademoiselle Varenka angel number one.'

'Oh! Mademoiselle Varenka, she's a real angel, *allez*,'[1] Madame Berthe agreed.

In the arcade they met Varenka herself. She was walking quickly towards them and carrying an elegant red handbag.

'Look, Papa has arrived!' Kitty said to her.

Varenka made a movement between a bow and a curtsey which was as simple and as natural as everything she did, and immediately began talking to the Prince simply and freely, as she did to everyone.

'It goes without saying that I know you, very well,' the Prince said to her with a smile, from which Kitty was delighted to see that her father liked her friend. 'Where are you off to in such a hurry?'

'*Maman* is here,' she said, turning to Kitty. 'She did not sleep all night, and the doctor advised her to go out. I'm bringing her work.'

'So that's angel number one!' said the Prince when Varenka had gone.

Kitty saw that her father had meant to make fun of Varenka but was simply unable to, because he liked her.

'Well, it seems we shall see all your friends,' he added, 'even Madame Stahl, if she deigns to recognize me.'

'Why, did you used to know her, Papa?' Kitty asked apprehensively, noticing the gleam of mockery that had lit up in the Prince's eyes at the mention of Madame Stahl.

'I used to know her husband, and her too a little, in the days before she joined the Pietists.'*

'What is a Pietist, Papa?' asked Kitty, already alarmed to discover that what she valued so highly in Madame Stahl had a name.

'I don't quite know myself. I only know that she thanks God for everything, for every misfortune, and she thanks God that her husband died too. And that's rather funny, as they led a bad life.'

'Who's that? What a pitiful face!' he asked, noticing a sick man of medium height sitting on a bench, who was dressed in a brown coat and white trousers that fell in strange folds on the fleshless bones of his legs.

The gentleman raised his straw hat from his thin curly hair to reveal a high forehead on which the hat had left an unhealthy red mark.

---

[1] 'it goes without saying'.

'That's the artist Petrov,' answered Kitty, blushing. 'And that's his wife,' she added, indicating Anna Pavlovna, who seemed to have deliberately gone after a child which had run off down a path just as they were approaching.

'How pathetic he looks, but such a nice face!' said the Prince. 'Why didn't you go up to him? Didn't he want to say something to you?'

'Well, let us go over, then,' said Kitty, turning round decisively. 'How are you feeling today?' she asked Petrov.

Petrov got up, leaning on his stick, and looked shyly at the Prince.

'This is my daughter,' said the Prince. 'Allow me to introduce myself.'

The painter bowed and smiled, showing strangely dazzling white teeth.

'We were expecting to see you yesterday, Princess,' he said to Kitty.

He lurched as he said this, and then repeated the movement, trying to show it had been intentional.

'I wanted to come, but Varenka said Anna Pavlovna had sent word that you were not going.'

'What do you mean, not going?' said Petrov, going red, and immediately beginning to cough as he looked around for his wife. 'Annetta! Annetta!' he said loudly, and the thick veins stretched along his thin white neck like cords.

Anna Pavlovna approached.

'How could you have sent word to the Princess that we weren't going?' he whispered to her angrily, having lost his voice.

'Good morning, Princess!' said Anna Pavlovna, with a feigned smile that was so unlike her former manner. 'Delighted to meet you,' she said to the Prince. 'You've long been expected, Prince.'

'How could you have sent word to the Princess that we weren't going?' the artist whispered hoarsely again, even more angrily, and clearly irritated still further that his voice had failed him and he could not give his words the expression he would have liked.

'Oh, good heavens! I thought we weren't going,' his wife answered with annoyance.

'How come, when . . .' he started coughing and waved his hand.

The Prince raised his hat and walked away with his daughter.

'Oh dear!' he said with a deep sigh. 'The poor things!'

'Yes, Papa,' answered Kitty. 'But you have to know that they have three children, no servants, and scarcely any means. He receives something from the Academy,' she went on animatedly, trying to suppress the anxiety that had arisen in her as a result of the peculiar change in Anna Pavlovna's attitude to her.

'And here's Madame Stahl,' said Kitty, indicating a bath-chair in which there lay something in blue and grey under a parasol, propped up by pillows.

This was Madame Stahl. Behind her stood the sullen-faced, strapping German hired hand who wheeled her about. Standing close by was the fair-haired Swedish count, whom Kitty knew by name. Several invalids were dallying about the bath-chair, looking at this lady as if they were seeing something extraordinary.

The Prince went up to her. And Kitty immediately detected that disconcerting glint of mockery in his eyes. He went up to Madame Stahl and started speaking to her extremely politely and affably in that excellent French which already so few people spoke nowadays.

'I don't know if you remember me, but I need to remind you of who I am so I may thank you for your kindness to my daughter,' he said, taking off his hat and not putting it on again.

'Prince Alexander Shcherbatsky,' said Madame Stahl, looking up at him with her heavenly eyes, in whose expression Kitty discerned displeasure. 'How lovely! I have become so fond of your daughter.'

'You are still in poor health?'

'Oh, I'm used to it now,' said Madame Stahl, and she introduced the Prince to the Swedish count.

'But you've hardly changed,' the Prince said to her. 'I have not had the honour of seeing you for ten or eleven years.'

'Yes, God gives us the cross and the strength to carry it. One often wonders why this life has to drag on . . . From the other side!' she said, turning with irritation to Varenka, who had not wrapped the rug round her legs the right way.

'Probably so we can do good,' said the Prince with a twinkle in his eye.

'That is not for us to judge,' said Madame Stahl, noticing the subtle nuance in the expression on the Prince's face. 'So will you send me that book, dear Count? Thank you very much,' she said to the young Swede.

'Ah!' exclaimed the Prince, catching sight of the Moscow colonel standing nearby, and after bowing to Madame Stahl he walked on with his daughter and the Moscow colonel, who joined them.

'That's our aristocracy, Prince!' said the Moscow colonel with sarcastic intention, as he bore a grudge against Madame Stahl for not wishing to be acquainted with him.

'She's just the same,' replied the Prince.

'So did you know her before her illness, Prince, I mean before she took to her bed?'

'Yes. She took to her bed while I knew her,' said the Prince.

'They say she hasn't got up for ten years.'

'She won't get up because her legs are short. She has a very bad figure . . .'

'Papa, it's not possible!' cried Kitty.

'That's what wicked tongues say, my dear. But your Varenka certainly comes in for some stick,' he added. 'Ah, these invalid noblewomen!'

'Oh no, Papa!' Kitty objected hotly. 'Varenka adores her. And then she does so much good! Ask anyone! Everyone knows her and Aline Stahl.'

'Maybe,' said the Prince, squeezing her arm with his elbow. 'But it's better to do things in such a way that no one knows, no matter whom you ask.'

Kitty fell silent, not because she had nothing to say, but because she did not want to reveal her secret thoughts even to her father. Curiously, however, despite having girded herself not to succumb to her father's views, nor give him access to what she held sacred, she felt that the divine image of Madame Stahl, which for a whole month she had carried in her heart, had vanished irrevocably, as the figure created by discarded clothes will vanish as soon as you realize it is only clothes lying there. All that was left was a woman with short legs, who stayed in bed because she had a bad figure, and tormented the hapless Varenka for not tucking in her rug the right way. And no effort of the imagination could succeed now in bringing back the former Madame Stahl.

35

THE Prince transmitted his high spirits to his family, to his acquaintances, and even to the German landlord in whose accommodation the Shcherbatskys were staying.

After returning from the springs with Kitty, and having invited the colonel, Marya Evgenievna, and Varenka to come for coffee, the Prince ordered a table and chairs to be taken out into the little garden, and for breakfast to be served there under the chestnut tree. The landlord and the servants all perked up under the influence of his high spirits. They were familiar with his warm-hearted ways, and within half an hour the invalid doctor from Hamburg who lived upstairs was looking enviously out of the window at the jolly Russian party of healthy people who had gathered under the chestnut tree. Beneath the shimmering circles of shadow cast by the leaves, at a table covered with a white cloth, laid with coffee-pots, bread, butter, cheese, and cold game, sat the Princess in a cap with lilac ribbons, handing out cups and slices of bread and butter. At the other end sat the Prince, tucking in heartily, and talking loudly and merrily. The Prince had spread out his purchases next to him—carved boxes, knick-knacks, and paper knives of all kinds, which he had bought quantities of at every spa, and was giving them away to everyone, including Lieschen, the servant girl, and the landlord, with whom he joked in his comically bad German, assuring him that it was not the waters that had cured Kitty but his excellent food, especially his plum soup. The Princess laughed at her husband for his Russian ways, but she was livelier and jollier than she had been during their entire stay at the spa. The colonel smiled, as he always did, at the Prince's jokes, but he took the Princess's side when it came to Europe, which he believed he had studied meticulously. The good-natured Marya Evgenievna rocked with laughter at every funny thing the Prince said, and Varenka subsided into mild but infectious laughter, which Kitty had never seen before.

Kitty found all this amusing, but she could not help being preoccupied. She could not solve the problem her father had unconsciously set her by taking such an insouciant view of her friends and the life to which she had become so drawn. To this problem was also added the change in her relations with the Petrovs, which had so conspicuously and unpleasantly been made manifest that morning. Everyone was light-hearted, but Kitty could not be light-hearted, and that troubled her even more. She was experiencing a feeling similar to the one she had experienced in childhood when she was locked in her room as a punishment and could hear her sisters' gleeful laughter.

'Now why did you go and buy this clutter?' said the Princess, smiling as she handed her husband a cup of coffee.

'Well, you're out walking, you go over to a shop, and they ask you to buy something: "*Erlaucht, Excellenz, Durchlaucht.*"[1] Well, the minute they say "*Durchlaucht*," I can't resist, and there's ten thalers gone.'

'It's just boredom,' said the Princess.

'Of course it is. Such boredom, my dear, that you don't know what to do with yourself.'

'How can you be bored, Prince? There's so much that is interesting in Germany these days,' said Marya Evgenievna.

'But I know all the interesting things: I know the plum soup, and I know the pea sausage. I know everything.'

[1] 'Eminence, Excellency, Serene Highness.'

'No, but you must admit, Prince, that their institutions are interesting,' said the colonel.

'What exactly is interesting about them? They're all as pleased as brass farthings: they've conquered everybody.* What have I got to be pleased about? I haven't conquered anyone; but you have to take off your boots yourself here, and go and put them outside the door yourself too. And then in the morning, you have to get up, get dressed straight away, and go to the dining room, and drink horrible tea. Not like at home! Where you can wake up slowly, get cross about something, have a grumble, pull yourself together properly, and have a good think about everything without any pressure.'

'But time is money, you forget that,' said the colonel.

'Depends which time! Sometimes you could hand over a whole month for a few kopecks, but there are other times when you wouldn't give up half an hour for love or money. Isn't that so, Katenka? Why are you so glum all of a sudden?'

'I'm fine.'

'Where are you off to? Stay a little longer,' he said to Varenka.

'I have to go home,' said Varenka, getting up and dissolving into giggles again.

When she had recovered, she said goodbye and went into the house to get her hat.

Kitty followed her. Even Varenka seemed different to her now. She was not worse, just different from how she had imagined her to be before.

'Oh, I haven't laughed so much in ages!' said Varenka as she picked up her parasol and her bag. 'How nice your Papa is!'

Kitty was silent.

'When are we going to see each other?' asked Varenka.

'*Maman* wanted to call on the Petrovs. Might you be there?' said Kitty, testing Varenka.

'Yes, I will be,' answered Varenka. 'They're about to leave, so I promised to help them pack.'

'Well, I'll come too, then.'

'No, why should you?'

'Why not, why not, why not?' said Kitty with wide eyes, taking hold of Varenka's parasol so as not to let her go. 'No, wait, tell me why not?'

'Because your Papa has arrived, and then they feel uncomfortable with you.'

'No, you have to tell me why you don't want me to see the Petrovs so often. You don't, do you? Why not?'

'I didn't say that,' said Varenka quietly.

'No, please tell me!'

'Tell you everything?' asked Varenka.

'Everything, everything!' Kitty echoed.

'Well there's not very much to tell, it's just that Mikhail Alexeyevich'—that was the artist's name—'had wanted to leave earlier before, and now he doesn't want to leave,' said Varenka, smiling.

'Well? Well?' said Kitty, looking darkly at Varenka, and urging her on.

'Well, and for some reason Anna Pavlovna said that he didn't want to go because you are here. Of course, that was irrelevant, but an argument broke out because of it, because of you. You know how irritable these sick people are.'

Kitty was frowning more and more, and Varenka, seeing an imminent outburst, she did not know whether of tears or words, went on talking on her own, trying to placate her and calm her down.

'So it's best if you don't go . . . You understand, you won't be offended . . .'

'And it serves me right, it just serves me right!' Kitty said quickly, snatching the parasol out of Varenka's hand, and looking past her friend's face.

Varenka wanted to smile, observing her friend's childish rage, but she was afraid of offending her.

'How does it serve you right? I don't understand,' she said.

'It serves me right, because it was all a pretence, because it was all contrived, and not from the heart. Why was I interfering with a stranger? And now it turns out that I've caused an argument, and have been doing something no one asked me to do. Because it was all a pretence! a pretence! a pretence! . . .'

'But why was there a need for pretence?' said Varenka quietly.

'Oh, how stupid, how horrible! There was no need for me . . . It's all a pretence!' she said, opening and shutting the parasol.

'Yes, but what was the need for it?'

'To seem better to people, to myself, to God, and deceive everyone. No, I'm not going to fall for that any more! I may be bad, but at least I won't be a liar, a deceiver.'

'But who is being a deceiver?' said Varenka reproachfully. 'You speak as if . . .'

But Kitty was having one of her tantrums. She would not let her finish.

'I'm not talking about you, not at all. You are perfection. Yes, yes, I know you are complete perfection; but what can I do if I'm bad? This would never have happened if I hadn't been bad. So let me be what I am, but at least I won't be pretending. What have I got to do with Anna Pavlovna? Let them live as they want, and let me live as I want. I can't be any other way . . . and all this is wrong, it's wrong!'

'What is wrong?' asked Varenka in bewilderment.

'Everything. I can only live by following my heart, but you live according to rules. I just liked you, as simple as that, but you probably only liked me because you wanted to save me, to teach me!'

'That's unfair,' said Varenka.

'But I'm not talking about other people, I'm talking about myself.'

'Kitty!' came her mother's voice. 'Come here and show Papa your corals.'

Kitty picked up the corals in their little box from the table with a haughty look, and went out to her mother without making peace with her friend.

'What's the matter? Why the red face?' her mother and father said to her with one voice.

'It's nothing,' she answered. 'I'll just be a minute,' and she ran back.

'She's still here!' she thought. 'Goodness, what should I say to her? What have I done, what have I said? Why did I have to offend her? What should I do? What should I say to her?' thought Kitty, and she stopped in the doorway.

Sitting at the table in her hat, and with the parasol in her hands, Varenka was examining the spring Kitty had broken. She lifted her head.

'Varenka, forgive me, forgive me!' whispered Kitty, going up to her. 'I didn't know what I was saying. I . . .'

'I really didn't mean to upset you,' said Varenka, smiling.

Peace was made. But with her father's arrival, the world in which Kitty had been living changed utterly. She did not renounce everything that she had discovered, but she realized that she had deceived herself in thinking she could be what she wanted to be. It was as if she had woken up; she now felt all the difficulty of maintaining the high standards to which she had aspired without hypocrisy and conceit; she also now felt the full weight of this world of pain, sickness, and dying people in which she lived; the efforts she had made to force herself to like it now seemed excruciating, and she now longed to get as quickly as possible into the fresh air, to go to Russia, to Ergushovo, where, as she learned from a letter, her sister Dolly and the children had already moved for the summer.

But her affection for Varenka had not diminished. When they said goodbye, Kitty begged her to visit them in Russia.

'I'll come when you get married,' said Varenka.

'I'm never going to get married.'

'Well, I'll never come then.'

'In that case I will get married just so you will. Make sure you remember your promise!' said Kitty.

The doctor's predictions were fulfilled. Kitty returned home to Russia cured. She was not as blithe or as high-spirited as before, but she was calm, and her Moscow sorrows became a memory.

PART THREE

I

SERGEY IVANOVICH KOZNYSHEV wanted to take a rest from intellectual work, and at the end of May, instead of going abroad as he usually did, he went to stay with his brother in the country. According to his convictions, country life was the very best kind of life. He had now come to enjoy this life at his brother's. Konstantin Levin was very glad, especially as he was no longer expecting his brother Nikolay that summer. But despite his love and respect for Sergey Ivanovich, Levin felt uncomfortable with his brother in the country. He felt uncomfortable and even unhappy observing his brother's attitude to the country. For Konstantin Levin the country was a place where one encountered the stuff of life, that is to say, joy, suffering, and toil; for Sergey Ivanovich the country was on the one hand a rest from work, and on the other a pleasant antidote to dissipation, which he took with enjoyment and an awareness of its benefits. For Konstantin Levin the country was good because it was the location for unquestionably useful work; for Sergey Ivanovich what was particularly good about the country was that one could and should do nothing there. Sergey Ivanovich's attitude to the peasantry* also rather grated on Konstantin. Sergey Ivanovich would say that he loved and knew the peasantry, and often chatted to the peasants, which he was capable of doing well, without pretence or affectation, drawing from every such conversation general facts in favour of the peasants, and as proof that he knew these people. Konstantin Levin did not like this kind of attitude to the peasantry. For Konstantin, the peasantry was simply the main partner in their shared work, and despite all the respect and almost familial love he had for the peasants, which, as he said himself, he had probably imbibed with his peasant wet-nurse's milk, and while he was sometimes in awe of these people's strength, humility, and fairness, he very often, as a partner in their common work, was infuriated by their negligence, slovenliness, drunkenness, and lying when their common work called for other qualities. If Konstantin Levin had been asked whether he loved the peasantry, he would have been at a loss to know what to reply. He loved and did not love the peasantry, as he loved and did not love people in general. As a good man, he naturally loved people more than he did not love them, and that went for the peasantry too. But it was impossible for him to love or not love the peasantry as a separate entity, because not only did he live with the peasantry, and not only were all his interests bound up with the peasantry, but he regarded himself as part of the peasantry, could not see any particular qualities or defects in either himself or the peasantry, and could not contrast himself to the peasantry. Moreover, although he had long lived cheek by jowl with the peasants as master and mediator, but mainly as adviser (the peasants trusted him, and would walk twenty-five miles to come and consult him), he had no definite views about the peasantry, and if asked whether he knew the people, he would have been placed in the same quandary as if he were asked whether he loved them. To say that he knew the peasantry was for him tantamount to saying he knew people. He was continually observing and getting to know all kinds of people, including peasants, whom he regarded as good and interesting people, and he was constantly observing new things about them, changing his previous views or forming new ones. It was the opposite with Sergey Ivanovich. Just as he loved and praised country life as a contrast to the life he did not love, he also loved the peasantry as a contrast to the class of people he did not love, and it was just the same with his knowledge of the peasants, whom he saw as the opposite of people generally. Certain ideas about peasant life had taken clear shape in his methodical mind, which were partly drawn from peasant life itself, but mostly from its contrast. He never altered his opinion about the peasants or his sympathetic attitude towards them.

In the disagreements that arose between the brothers when discussing the peasantry, Sergey Ivanovich always had the better of his brother, for the simple reason that Sergey Ivanovich had definite ideas about the peasantry with regard to its character, qualities, and tastes, whereas Konstantin Levin had no definite or fixed views, so in their arguments Konstantin was always caught contradicting himself.

In Sergey Ivanovich's eyes, his younger brother was a thoroughly nice fellow, with a heart that was *well placed* (as he put it in French), but with a mind which, although quick enough, was subject to transient influences, and therefore full of contradictions. With the condescension of an elder brother, he sometimes explained to him the meaning of things, but he did not derive any pleasure from arguing with him because he defeated him too easily.

Konstantin Levin regarded his brother as a man of immense intellect and education, who was noble in the highest sense of that word, and endowed with an ability to work for the common good. But in the depths of his soul, the older he became, and the better he got to know his brother, the more frequently it occurred to him that this ability to work for the common good, which he felt he lacked totally, was perhaps not a virtue but, on the contrary, a deficiency of something—not a deficiency of good, honest, noble desires and tastes, but a deficiency of life force, the thing which is called heart, the impulse which drives a person to choose one of the innumerable life paths open to him and stick to it. The more he discovered about his brother, the more he noticed that Sergey Ivanovich, and many other people who worked for the common good, were not drawn with their hearts to this love of the common good, but had worked out in their minds that this was a good cause, and took it up for that reason alone. The observation that his brother did not take the question of the common good or the immortality of the soul any more to heart than he did a game of chess or the ingenious construction of a new machine only served to confirm Levin's hypothesis.

Apart from that, Konstantin Levin also felt uncomfortable being with his brother in the country because he was constantly busy with the estate in the country, particularly in the summer, and the long summer days were never long enough for him to get through everything that needed to be done, and Sergey Ivanovich was on holiday. But although he was on holiday now, that is, he was not writing his book, he was so used to intellectual activity that he liked to articulate the ideas that occurred to him in a beautifully concise form, and he liked having someone to listen to him. His most regular and natural audience was, of course, his brother. And so, despite the amicable simplicity of their relationship, Konstantin felt uncomfortable about leaving him on his own. Sergey Ivanovich liked to lie down on the grass in the sun, and chat idly while he lay there basking.

'You wouldn't believe how much I'm enjoying this rustic idleness,' he would say to his brother. 'There's not a single thought in my head, you could roll a ball in it!'

But it was tedious for Konstantin Levin to sit and listen to him, especially when he knew that without his oversight the peasants would cart manure to an unploughed field and dump it heaven knows where; or they would take the shares off the ploughs rather than screw them in, and then say that steel ploughs were a stupid invention and not a patch on the old wooden ploughs, and so on.

'Come on, you've done enough tramping around in the heat,' Sergey Ivanovich would say to him.

'No, I've just got to drop by the office for a minute,' Levin would answer, and run off to the fields.

2

IN early June, when the old nanny and housekeeper Agafya Mikhailovna was taking a jar of mushrooms she had just pickled down to the cellar, she happened to slip, fall, and sprain her wrist. The zemstvo doctor,* a talkative young student who had just come to the end of his course, came on a visit. He examined the wrist, said it was not dislocated, applied compresses, and, having stayed for dinner, clearly enjoyed talking to the famous Sergey Ivanovich Koznyshev, to whom, in order to show off his progressive views on things, he related all the district gossip, complaining about the poor state of zemstvo affairs. Sergey Ivanovich listened attentively, asked questions, and, stimulated by having a new audience, became loquacious and made some perceptive and compelling observations which were reverently admired by the young doctor, and he entered into that lively state of mind, familiar to his brother, which he usually entered into after brilliant and lively conversation. After the doctor left, he decided he wanted to go down to the river with a fishing-rod. He liked fishing, and seemed to be almost proud of liking such an inane activity.

Konstantin Levin offered to take his brother in the trap, since he needed to go to the ploughed field and to the meadow.

It was that time of the year, the turning-point of summer, when the harvest of the current year can already be counted on, when thoughts turn to the sowing of next year's crops and mowing is at hand, when the rye has come into ear and its grey-green, unripe and still light ears are swaying in the breeze, when green oats are shooting up unevenly in late-sown fields amongst odd clumps of yellow grass, when the leaves of early buckwheat are already spreading out and covering the soil, when the fallow fields, trampled hard as rock by the cattle, with tracks too deep for the plough, have been turned over to the midway point; when the dried-out clumps of carted manure and sweet honey leaf give off a scent at dawn and the protected lowland meadows, with their blackened heaps of weeded sorrel stalks, stand like an unbroken sea, awaiting the scythe.

It was that time of year when there is a short breathing-space in farm-work before the start of reaping, which comes around every year, and every year demands every ounce of the peasantry's energy. There was a splendid crop, and there had been a long spell of clear, hot summer days and short, dewy nights.

The brothers had to drive through a wood to reach the meadows. Sergey Ivanovich kept admiring the beauty of the wood, which was overgrown with foliage, one moment pointing out to his brother an old lime tree, dark on its shady side but with bright yellow stipules about to burst into flower, and next the sparkling emerald colour of this year's young shoots on the trees. Konstantin Levin did not like talking and hearing about the beauty of nature. Words for him removed the beauty of what he was seeing. He agreed with what his brother was saying, but could not stop thinking about other matters. When they came out of the wood, he became engrossed by the sight of a fallow field on the hillside which was a mixture of yellowing grass, trodden-down patches, clustered heaps, and untilled soil. A string of carts was moving across the field. Levin counted the carts and was pleased that they were taking out everything they needed, and at the sight of the meadows his thoughts turned to mowing. Haymaking always struck a particularly deep chord with him. When they reached the meadow, Levin pulled up the horse.

The morning dew still clung to the thick young shoots of grass down below, and in order to avoid getting his feet wet, Sergey Ivanovich asked his brother to drive him in the trap across the meadow, over to the willow where the perch always bit. Much as Konstantin Levin regretted having to flatten his grass, he drove into the meadow. The tall grass wrapped itself softly round the wheels and the horse's legs, leaving its seeds on the wet spokes and hubs.

After sorting out his rods, his brother sat down under the willow, and Levin led the horse away, tied it up, and walked into the huge grey-green sea of the meadow, which was untouched by the breeze. The silky grass with its ripening seeds was waist-high in parts where there had been flooding.

After cutting across the meadow, Konstantin Levin came out onto the road and met an old man with a swollen eye who was carrying a skep* full of bees.

'You've captured them, Fomich?' he asked.

'Captured, Konstantin Dmitrich! It's a job keeping hold of our bees. This is the second time they've swarmed . . . Luckily the lads galloped after them. They're ploughing your field. They unharnessed a horse and galloped after them . . .'

'So, what do you think, Fomich, should we start mowing or wait a bit?'

'Goodness me! We always wait till St Peter's Day.* But you always mow sooner. God willing, the grass will be good, so it should be all right. The cattle will have more room.'

'And the weather, what do you think?'

'In God's hands. It might stay fair.'

Levin went over to his brother. Sergey Ivanovich had not caught anything, but he was not bored, and seemed in fact to be in the best of spirits. Levin could see that he had been fired up by his conversation with the doctor and wanted to talk. Levin, on the other hand, wanted to get home as soon as possible so he could make arrangements to have mowers ready to go out the next day, and also make up his mind about the mowing, which was causing him a great deal of thought.

'Well, let's be going,' he said.

'What's the hurry? Let's sit for a while. Goodness, you're sopping wet! It's good being here, even without catching anything. The great thing about all field-sports is that you have contact with nature. Isn't this steely water wonderful!' he said. 'The banks of this meadow always remind me of that riddle—do you know it? The grass says to the water: we will sway and sway.'*

'No, I don't know that riddle,' answered Levin glumly.

3

'You know, I've been thinking about you,' said Sergey Ivanovich. 'The things that are going on in your district are quite appalling, so that doctor was telling me; he's a bright fellow. I've told you before and I'll tell you again: it's not good that you don't go to the meetings, and have generally stopped being involved with the zemstvo. If decent people stop being involved, God knows how it will all turn out. We allocate money which goes on salaries, and yet there are no schools, no medical assistants, no midwives, no dispensaries—nothing.'

'I did try, you know,' Levin said in a quiet, hesitant voice, 'but I just can't! So what is there to be done about it?'

'But what is it you can't do? I must confess, I don't understand. It can't be indifference or inability; it's not just laziness, is it?'

'It's none of those things. I've tried, but I can see that there is nothing I can do,' said Levin.

He was not really concentrating on what his brother was saying.

As he gazed across the river at the ploughed field, he could make out something black, but he could not work out whether it was a horse, or his steward on a horse.

'Why can't you do anything? You tried, and you felt you didn't succeed, so you're giving up. Where's your self-respect?'

'Self-respect,' said Levin, stung by his brother's words; 'I don't understand. If they had told me at university that some people understood integral calculus, and I didn't, that would be a matter of self-respect. But with this you have to be convinced first of all that you have a certain ability in these matters, and most importantly that all these matters are of great importance.'

'What? You don't think they are important?' said Sergey Ivanovich, hurt both by the fact that his brother found what concerned him insignificant, and particularly that he was clearly hardly listening to him.

'They don't seem important to me, they don't grip me, what can I say?' answered Levin, having worked out that what he was looking at was the steward, and that the steward had probably told the peasants to stop ploughing. They were turning the ploughs over. 'Can they really be finished with ploughing?' he wondered.

'But listen,' said his brother with a frown on his handsome, clever face, 'there are limits to everything. It's all very well to be eccentric and sincere and dislike hypocrisy—I know all about that; but what you're saying either makes no sense or makes very bad sense, after all. How can you consider it unimportant that the peasants, whom you assure me you love . . .'

'I've never said that,' thought Konstantin Levin.

'. . . die without help? We've got primitive midwives killing off children, peasants wallowing in ignorance and remaining under the thumb of any old clerk, and you're given a means to help; but you don't help because it's not important.'

And Sergey Ivanovich confronted him with a dilemma: 'Either you are so dim-witted that you can't see everything you could do, or you don't want to forgo your peace of mind, or your vanity, or I don't know what, by getting involved.'

Konstantin Levin felt that he had no option but to capitulate, or confess that he had insufficient love for the common good. And that offended and upset him.

'It's both,' he said firmly. 'I don't see how one could . . .'

'What? You mean it's not possible to provide medical care if the money is distributed properly?'

'Well, it doesn't seem so to me . . . I can't see how one could provide medical care across the three thousand square miles of our district, with our mud, blizzards, and our seasonal work. And I don't really believe in medicine anyway.'

'Come on; that's unfair . . . I can give you thousands of examples . . . Well, what about schools?'

'Why do we need schools?'

'What are you saying? Can there be any doubt about the benefits of education? If it's good for you, it's good for everyone.'

Konstantin Levin felt he had been morally pinned against a wall, and so he lost his temper and blurted out the main reason for his indifference to the common good.

'Maybe all this is indeed good; but why should I concern myself with the establishment of clinics I shall never use, and schools to which I will not send my children, to which even the peasants don't want to send their children, and to which I am still not convinced they ought to send them?' he said.

Sergey Ivanovich was momentarily taken aback by this unexpected view of things; but he straight away devised a new plan of attack.

He paused for a minute, lifted one of his rods, cast it again, and turned to his brother with a smile.

'Well, if you will allow me . . . Firstly, the clinic is needed. We've just sent for the zemstvo doctor for Agafya Mikhailovna.'

'Well, I think her hand will stay crooked.'

'That's another issue . . . And then a peasant or a labourer who can read and write is going to be more useful and valuable to you.'

'No, you can ask anyone you like,' Konstantin Levin answered firmly, 'a man who is literate is much worse as a labourer. You can't get the roads repaired; and as soon as a bridge is put up it's stolen.'

'However,' said Sergey Ivanovich, frowning because he disliked being contradicted, and especially by those who continually jumped from one subject to another and introduced new and unconnected arguments, making it impossible to know which to answer, 'however, that's not the point. Allow me to ask: do you acknowledge that education is a public good?'

'I do,' said Levin inadvertently, and he immediately realized he had said something he did not think. He felt that if he admitted this it would be proved to him that he was spouting nonsense which had no meaning at all. How it would be proved to him he did not know, but he did know it would undoubtedly be proved to him logically, so he now awaited this proof.

The argument turned out to be far simpler than he had expected.

'If you acknowledge that it is a public good,' said Sergey Ivanovich, 'then, as an honest man, you cannot help caring about and sympathizing with this cause, and therefore wishing to work for it.'

'But I'm not ready to acknowledge that it is a good cause,' said Konstantin Levin, going red.

'What? But you just said . . .'

'I mean, I don't acknowledge it to be either good or possible.'

'But you can't know that if you haven't made any effort.'

'Well, let's suppose,' said Levin, although he did not suppose anything of the kind, 'let us suppose that this is so, but I still don't see why I should have to bother about it.'

'What do you mean?'

'No, since we have got talking about this, you explain it to me from a philosophical angle,' said Levin.

'I don't understand what philosophy has to do with it,' said Sergey Ivanovich in a tone which seemed to imply to Levin that he did not acknowledge his brother's right to discuss philosophy. And that annoyed Levin.

'Then let me tell you!' he said, becoming angry. 'I believe that the impetus behind all our actions is still personal happiness. As a nobleman, I cannot see anything in any of the zemstvo institutions that might enhance my well-being. The roads are not better and cannot be any better; my horses carry me just as well on bad ones. I don't need doctors and clinics. I don't need a magistrate—I never have any reason to approach one, and never will. I not only have no need for schools, but even find them harmful, as I've told you. For me, the zemstvo institutions are just an obligation to cough up six kopecks an acre, drive to town, sleep with bedbugs, and listen to all kinds of nonsense and filth, and self-interest does not prompt me to do that.'

'Excuse me,' Sergey Ivanovich interrupted with a smile, 'self-interest did not prompt us to work for the emancipation of the serfs,* but we worked for it.'

'No!' Konstantin interrupted, becoming even angrier. 'The emancipation of the serfs was a different matter. There was self-interest there. There was a desire to throw off that yoke which oppressed us and all good people. But to be a councillor and discuss how many privy-cleaners are needed and how to put drains in a town in which I don't live; to serve on a jury and try a peasant who's stolen some ham, and listen for six hours to all kinds of rubbish churned out by the defence and the prosecution, and the chairman of the jury asking my

old Alyoshka-the-fool: "Do you, the accused, sir, admit to the misap-
propriation of the ham?" "Huh?" '

Konstantin Levin had already digressed, and was starting to imitate
the chairman and Alyoshka-the-fool; he thought it was all to the point.

But Sergey Ivanovich shrugged his shoulders.

'So what are you trying to say?'

'I am just trying to say that I shall always defend to the hilt those
rights which affect me . . . my interests; that when the police made
raids on us students and read our letters, I was ready to defend to the
hilt those rights, and my rights to education and freedom. I understand
military conscription, which affects the destinies of my children, my
brothers, and myself; I am ready to discuss that which concerns me;
but judging how best to dispense forty thousand roubles of zemstvo
money, or judging Alyoshka-the-fool—that is something I do not
understand and cannot do.'

Konstantin Levin spoke as if the dam holding back his words had
burst. Sergey Ivanovich smiled.

'But tomorrow you might be on trial: would you rather be tried in
the old criminal courts?'

'I won't be going to court. I won't cut anybody's throat, and I have
no need of it. And another thing . . .' he continued, again jumping
to a subject which was completely beside the point, 'our institutions
and all of that are just like the little birch trees we stick in the ground
on Trinity Sunday,* so they look like a wood which in Europe would
have grown naturally, but I can't put my heart into watering these little
birches and believing in them!'

Sergey Ivanovich just shrugged his shoulders, this gesture expressing his bewilderment at how these little birch trees could have suddenly
come into their argument, although he had immediately understood
what his brother had meant by them.

'I'm sorry, but this is no way to conduct an argument,' he remarked.

But Konstantin Levin wanted to justify the failing he knew he had,
of indifference to the common good, and he went on.

'I think', he said, 'that no activity can be sound if it is not based on
self-interest. It's a general, philosophical truth,' he said, emphatic in
his repetition of the word *philosophical*, as though wishing to show he
had as much right as anyone else to talk about philosophy.

Sergey Ivanovich smiled again. 'He also has some kind of philosophy of his own at the service of his inclinations,' he thought.

'Well, I think you'd better leave philosophy out of it,' he said. 'The
main task of philosophy down the ages has been precisely to find that

essential link which exists between personal and public interest. But that is beside the point; what is to the point is that I just need to correct your comparison. The little birch trees are not stuck in, but are either planted or sown, and they need careful nurturing. Only those nations which have a sense of what is important and significant in their institutions, and value them, have a future and can be called historic.'

And Sergey Ivanovich transferred the issue into the realm of philosophy and history, impenetrable to Konstantin Levin, and showed him the full injustice of his point of view.

'As far as your not liking all this is concerned, well, forgive me— that is our Russian laziness and snobbery, but I'm sure it's a temporary error in your case, and will pass.'

Konstantin was silent. He felt well and truly crushed, but he also felt that his brother had not understood what he wanted to say. He just did not know why he had not been understood: whether it was because he was not capable of expressing himself clearly, whether it was because his brother did not want to understand him, or because he could not understand him. But he did not pursue this line of thought any further, and without answering his brother back, began thinking about a quite different, personal matter.

Sergey Ivanovich reeled in his last line, Konstantin untied the horse, and they drove off.

4

THE personal matter occupying Levin's thoughts during the conversation with his brother was the following: after turning up at the mowing one day the previous year and losing his temper with the steward, Levin had used his own method of calming down—he took a scythe from a peasant and started mowing.

He had so enjoyed this work that he had gone out mowing several times; he mowed the entire meadow in front of the house, and since the onset of spring this year had been hatching a plan to spend whole days mowing with the peasants. From the time his brother arrived, however, he had been in two minds: should he mow or not? He felt bad about leaving his brother on his own for days on end, and he was also afraid his brother would laugh at him. But after walking across the meadow and remembering the impression the mowing had made on him, he had almost made up his mind that he would go and mow. And after the annoying conversation with his brother, he remembered that intention again.

'I need physical exercise, otherwise my character definitely suffers,' he thought, and resolved that he would go and mow, however awkward it would be for him with his brother and the peasants.

That evening Konstantin Levin went to the office, gave orders about the work to be done, and sent to the villages to summon mowers for the following day to mow the Kalina meadow, which was the biggest and the best.

'And send my scythe to Titus, please, so he can sharpen it and bring it tomorrow; I might do some mowing myself,' he said, trying not to be embarrassed.

The steward smiled and said:

'Yes, sir.'

That evening over tea, Levin also told his brother.

'The weather seems to have settled,' he said. 'I'm going to start mowing tomorrow.'

'I like that work very much,' said Sergey Ivanovich.

'I really like it. I've mowed with the peasants myself on occasion, and I want to spend the whole day mowing tomorrow.'

Sergey Ivanovich lifted his head and looked at his brother with curiosity.

'What do you mean exactly? Mow alongside the peasants, all day?'

'Yes, it's very agreeable.'

'It's marvellous as physical exercise, but you are hardly going to be able to keep going,' said Sergey Ivanovich without a hint of mockery.

'I've tried it. It's hard to begin with, but then you get used to it. I think I will keep up . . .'

'I see! But tell me, how do the peasants look at it? They must be sniggering about how odd their master is.'

'I don't think so; but it's such jolly and, at the same time, hard work that there is no time to think.'

'Well, how are you going to have lunch with them? It'll be a bit tricky having roast turkey and a bottle of Lafite sent out to you.'

'No, I'll just come home when they take their break.'

The next morning Konstantin Levin got up earlier than usual, but he was delayed by estate matters, and when he arrived at the meadow, the mowers were already on the second row.

From the top of the hill he could see the shady, freshly mown section of the meadow down below, with its greying rows and black heaps of kaftans, taken off by the mowers at the place where they had started on the first row.

As he was riding up, he saw a long-drawn-out line of peasants walking one after the other and swinging their scythes in different ways, some in kaftans, some just in shirtsleeves. He counted forty-two men.

They were moving slowly along the uneven bottom part of the meadow, where there was an old dam. Levin recognized some of his own men. There was old Yermil, in a very long white shirt, his back bent as he swung his scythe; there was the young lad Vaska, Levin's former coachman, who was taking each swathe in one swing. And there was Titus, Levin's tutor in mowing, who was a small, skinny fellow. Walking in front without bending over, he seemed to be playing with his scythe as he cut wide swathes.

Levin got off his horse and, after tethering it by the road, he went over to Titus, who got out a second scythe from the bushes and held it out.

'It's all ready, sir; like a razor, mows by itself,' said Titus, taking his hat off and handing him the scythe with a smile.

Levin took the scythe and began trying it out. As they finished their rows, the sweaty and cheerful mowers came out on to the road one by one, chuckling as they greeted the master. They all looked at him, but no one said anything until a tall old man with a wrinkled and beardless face in a sheepskin jacket came out on to the road and addressed him.

'Watch you don't fall behind, sir—can't give up once you've started!' he said, and Levin heard titters amongst the mowers.

'I'll do my best not to fall behind,' he said, standing behind Titus and waiting to begin.

'Watch out,' the old man repeated.

Titus cleared a place, and Levin followed him. The grass was low and close to the road, and Levin mowed badly for the first few minutes, even though he was taking strong swings, because he had not mowed for a long time and was embarrassed by the looks directed at him. He could hear voices behind him:

'It's not fixed right, the handle's too high, look how he has to bend over,' said one.

'Dig in more with the heel,' said another.

'He is doing all right, he'll sort himself out,' the old man continued. 'See, there he goes . . . If you take a wide swathe, you get tired . . . The master's working for himself, there's no telling him! But look at the edge of that swathe! Our lot would get it in the neck for that.'

The grass became softer, and Levin, listening but not answering and trying to mow as well as he could, followed Titus. They covered about a hundred paces. Titus kept going without stopping or showing the slightest sign of fatigue; but Levin had got so tired he was beginning to fear he would not hold out.

He felt as if he was mowing with his last ounce of energy, and he made up his mind to ask Titus to stop. But just then Titus himself stopped, bent down to pick some grass, then wiped his blade and began whetting it. Levin straightened up, caught his breath, and looked around. The peasant walking behind him was also clearly tired, because he immediately stopped and started whetting his scythe without catching up with Levin. Titus whetted his scythe and Levin's, and they carried on.

It was the same with the second patch. Titus went on swinging his scythe without stopping or getting tired. Levin walked behind him, trying not to fall behind, and he found it harder and harder: there was a point when he felt he had no more strength, but just at that moment Titus would stop and whet his scythe.

And so they completed the first row. Levin found that long row particularly hard; but when the row was finished, and Titus began slowly to retrace his steps along the track left by his heels in the mown grass, with his scythe thrown over his shoulder, and Levin also went back along the grass he had mown, he felt very good, despite the fact that the sweat was pouring down his face and dripping from his nose, and his back was all wet, as if drenched in water. He was particularly happy because he knew now that he would last the course.

The only thing that spoiled his pleasure was the fact that his row was not good. 'I'll swing less with my arm and more with my whole body,' he thought, comparing the row Titus had cut in a dead-straight line with his haphazard and uneven row.

Levin noticed that Titus had gone along the first row especially quickly, probably because he wanted to test his master, and it turned out to be a long row. The next rows were easier, but Levin still had to expend all his energy so as not to fall behind the peasants.

He thought of nothing, and wanted nothing except to keep up with the peasants and to do the best job he could. All he could hear was the clanking of the scythes, and all he could see in front of him was the erect, receding figure of Titus, the curved semicircle of the swathe, the slow ripples of the grass and the flower tops as they bent over near the blade of his scythe, and ahead of him the end of the row, where there would be a rest.

Not understanding what it was, or where it came from, in the middle of his work he suddenly experienced a pleasant sensation of coldness on his hot, sweaty shoulders. He looked up at the sky while the scythes were being whetted. A low, heavy cloud had blown over, and large drops of rain were falling. Some peasants went to put their kaftans on, while others, like Levin, just shook their shoulders gleefully at being so pleasantly refreshed.

They did row after row. They did long rows and short rows, and rows with good and bad grass. Levin lost all awareness of time and had absolutely no idea whether it was late or early. A change had begun to take place in his work now which brought him immense pleasure. There were moments in the middle of his work when he forgot what he was doing and it became easy, and in those moments his row came out almost as evenly and as well as Titus's. But as soon as he remembered what he was doing, and began trying to do it better, he immediately felt the full difficulty of the work, and his row came out badly.

As they completed another row, he wanted to go back over it again, but Titus had stopped and gone across to the old man and was quietly saying something to him. They both looked at the sun. 'What are they talking about, and why isn't he going back over the row?' thought Levin, not realizing that the peasants had been mowing now for over four hours, and that it was time for them to have breakfast.

'Breakfast, sir,' said the old man.

'Already? Well, breakfast it is then.'

Levin gave his scythe to Titus and, accompanying the peasants as they went to fetch the bread from their kaftans, he walked over to his horse across the rows of the long area of mown grass, which were lightly sprinkled with rain. Only now did he realize that he had misjudged the weather, and that the rain was making his hay wet.

'The hay will be spoiled,' he said.

'Don't worry, sir, mow in the rain and rake when it's fine!' said the old man.

Levin untied his horse and went home for coffee.

Sergey Ivanovich had only just got up. Levin had drunk his coffee and gone back to the mowing before Sergey Ivanovich had managed to get dressed and go into the dining room.

5

AFTER breakfast Levin ended up not in his previous place in the row, but between an old joker who invited him to be his neighbour and a young peasant, married only since autumn, who had come to do his first summer's mowing.

Holding himself very erect, the old man went in front, taking broad, even strides with his turned-out feet, and, with a precise and even movement which clearly cost him no more effort than swinging his arms while walking, brought down a uniform, tall swathe as if it were a game. It was as if the sharp scythe was whistling through the moist grass by itself.

Behind Levin came young Mishka. His attractive young face, with a twist of fresh grass tying back his hair, was under continuous strain from the effort, but as soon as anyone looked at him, he smiled. He would clearly have sooner died than admit he found it hard.

Levin walked between them. The mowing did not seem so difficult during the hottest part of the day. The sweat pouring off him cooled him down, while the sun burning his back, his head, and his arms, which were bare to the elbow, gave him the strength and stamina to keep going; those moments of being in an unconscious state when he did not have to think about what he was doing, meanwhile, had started to come more and more often. The scythe cut by itself. Those were happy moments. Even more joyous were the moments when they got to the river at the end of the rows, where the old man would wipe his scythe with thick, wet grass, rinse its steel blade in the cool river-water, then dip his whetstone tin into it and offer it to Levin.

'So what do you think of my kvass?* It's pretty good!' he would say, winking.

And indeed, Levin never had drunk anything like this warm water, which had greenery floating in it and a rusty taste from the tin. And straight afterwards came the blissful slow walk with his hand on his scythe, when he could wipe away the sweat pouring down him, inhale air deep into his chest, and look at the long line of mowers, and at what was going on in the woods and fields around him.

The longer Levin mowed, the more often he experienced moments of oblivion, when it was no longer his arms swinging the scythe, but the scythe itself bringing his fully self-aware, dynamic body into motion, and the work did itself correctly and neatly as if by magic, without it being given any thought. Those were the most blissful moments.

It was only difficult when he had to stop this now unconscious movement and think, when he had to mow around a tussock or some sorrel which had not been weeded out. The old man did this easily. When he came to a tussock, he changed his movement and used the heel or the tip of the scythe to cut down the tussock from both sides with short strokes. And while he was doing this, he examined and observed everything that appeared before him; he might pull up a wild gladiolus, nibble it or offer it to Levin, or brush aside a twig with the tip of his scythe, or peer into a quail's nest, from which the hen would fly out, right from under the scythe, or catch a snake crossing his path, lift it up on his scythe like on a fork, show it to Levin, and toss it aside.

Levin and the young lad behind him found these changes of movement difficult. Having got to grips with one kind of strenuous movement, they had now got into a rhythm with their work, and were incapable of changing movements and observing what was in front of them at the same time.

Levin did not notice the time going by. If he had been asked how long he had been mowing, he would have said half an hour—yet it was getting on for dinner-time already. As they walked back along a swathe, the old man drew Levin's attention to the barely visible figures of girls and boys coming along the road and through the tall grass towards the mowers from different directions, their small arms weighed down by bundles of bread and jugs of kvass stoppered with rags.

'See, they're like little insects crawling along!' he said, pointing to them, and he looked up at the sun from under his hand.

They did two more rows and then the old man stopped.

'Time for lunch, sir!' he said firmly. And after going down to the river, the mowers walked across the swathes towards their kaftans, where the children who had brought their lunch sat waiting for them. The peasants gathered together—those from far away in the shadow of their cart, and the locals under a willow bush, on which they had thrown some grass.

Levin sat down with them. He did not want to leave.

Any embarrassment about being with their master had long ago disappeared. The peasants were getting ready for lunch. Some were washing, the young lads were taking a dip in the river, and others were fixing up a place for a nap or undoing the bundles of bread and unstopping the jugs of kvass. The old man crumbled some bread into a cup, kneaded it with a spoon handle, poured in some water from his whetstone tin, cut up some more bread, sprinkled it with salt, and turned to the east to pray.

'Here, sir, try my soup,' he said, squatting down in front of the cup.

The soup was so good that Levin changed his mind about going home for lunch. He had lunch with the old man, and got talking to him about his family affairs, showing the keenest interest in them, and he also told him about everything he was doing, and about other things he felt might be of interest to the old man. He felt closer to him than to his brother, and could not help smiling at the affection he felt for this man. When the old man stood up again to pray, and then lay down right there under the bush, putting some grass under his head, Levin did the same, and despite the flies and midges which would not leave him alone and tickled his sweaty face and body in the sun, he fell asleep at once, and only woke up when the sun passed over to the other side of the bush and began to shine on him. The old man had been awake a long time, and was sitting there whetting the young lads' scythes.

Levin looked around and hardly recognized the place, it had changed so much. An immense expanse of the meadow had been mown, and, with its already fragrant swathes, it shone with a special new gleam in the slanting rays of the evening sun. The bushes they had mowed around by the river, and the river itself, not visible before, but now sparkling like steel where it curved, the peasants moving about and getting up, the sheer wall of grass in the unmown part of the meadow, and the hawks circling above the stripped meadow—all this was completely new. When he had woken up properly, Levin began working out how much had been mown, and how much more could be done that day.

It was an extraordinary amount of work for forty-two men. They had already mown all of the big meadow, which thirty scythes used to take two days to mow back in the days of corvée.* The only bits left to mow were the corners, where the rows were short. But Levin wanted to get as much mowing as possible done that day, and was irritated with the sun for setting so fast. He did not feel at all tired; he just wanted to do as much work as possible, and to get on with it as quickly as possible.

'What do you think—do you think we could mow Mashkin Hill as well?' he said to the old man.

'As God wills, but the sun isn't high. Maybe some vodka for the lads?'

At teatime, when they sat down again, and the smokers lit up, the old man told the lads: 'If we mow Mashkin Hill, there'll be vodka.'

'Can't say no to that! Come on, Titus! We'll get it done as quick as a flash! We can eat our fill tonight. Come on!' came the cries, and the mowers finished their bread and got going.

'Come on, lads, keep up!' said Titus, running on ahead almost at a trot.

'Go on, go on!' said the old man, hurrying after him and catching him up easily, 'Watch out or I'll mow you down!'

And young and old threw themselves into the mowing as if they were in competition. But they did not spoil the grass, however much they hurried, and the swathes fell just as neatly and precisely as before. The little patch left in the corner was mown in five minutes. The last mowers were just ending their rows when those in front were already slinging their kaftans over their shoulders and crossing the road to go to Mashkin Hill.

The sun was already low over the trees when they entered the small wooded ravine of Mashkin Hill, their whetstone tins rattling. The soft, tender, feathery grass was up to their waists in the middle of the hollow, and dotted with brightly coloured wood cow-wheat* under the trees.

After briefly deliberating whether to go lengthwise or across, a huge, swarthy peasant called Prokhor Yermilin, another famous mower, set off first. He did one row, then turned back and started mowing again, and they all proceeded to fall into line behind him, going downhill through the hollow and then uphill, right up to the edge of the wood. The sun set behind the wood. Dew was already falling, and the mowers were in the sun only on the top of the hill, but down below, where a mist was rising, and on the other side, they were walking in cool, dewy shade. The work was in full swing.

Lopped down with a luscious sound, and giving off a heady fragrance, the grass was laid in tall rows. Converging on each other from all sides in the short rows, their tins rattling, the mowers urged each other on to the sound of scythes clashing together, the whistle of a whetstone along a blade being sharpened, and merry cries.

Levin kept his place between the young peasant and the old man. The old man, wearing his sheepskin jacket now, was just as light-hearted and jovial and just as lithe in his movements as before. In the wood they kept coming across birch mushrooms that had swelled in the succulent grass and which they cut with their scythes. But every time the old man saw a mushroom he would bend down, pick it up, and put it under his shirt. 'Another treat for my old woman,' he would say.

However easy it was to mow the wet, soft grass, it was hard work going up and down the steep slopes of the ravine. But this did not bother the old man. Swinging his scythe, and taking short, firm steps with his feet in their big bast shoes, he climbed slowly up the steep slope, and though his whole body shook, as did his breeches hanging below his shirt, he did not miss a single blade of grass on his way, nor a single mushroom, and he continually cracked jokes with Levin and the peasants. Levin walked behind him and often thought he was bound to fall, going up such a steep hill with a scythe, when it would have been hard even without a scythe; but he made it, and he did what was needed. He felt some external force pushing him on.

6

THEY mowed Mashkin Hill, finished the last rows, put on their kaftans, and merrily set off for home. Levin got on his horse, said a wistful goodbye to the peasants, and rode home. He looked back from the hill; they could not be seen in the mist rising from below; he could just hear cheery, rough voices, laughter, and the sound of scythes clanking.

Sergey Ivanovich had finished dinner long ago, and was drinking water with ice and lemon in his room while he looked through the newspapers and journals which had just arrived in the post when Levin burst in full of merry chatter, his tangled hair sticking to his sweaty forehead, and his back and chest all damp and grimy.

'We did the whole meadow! Ah, it was so good, it was amazing! And how have you been?' Levin said, completely forgetting the unpleasant conversation the day before.

'Heavens, whatever do you look like!' said Sergey Ivanovich, looking at his brother testily to begin with. 'The door, shut the door!' he cried. 'You must have let in at least a dozen of them.'

Sergey Ivanovich could not stand flies, only opened the windows in his room at night, and made a point of shutting doors.

'Not one, I swear to God. But if I did, I'll catch them. You won't believe how enjoyable it was! How did you spend the day?'

'It was good. But have you really been mowing all day? You must be ravenous. Kuzma has got everything ready for you.'

'No, I don't even feel hungry. I had something to eat there. But I will go and have a wash.'

'Yes, you do that, and I'll come and join you shortly,' said Sergey Ivanovich, shaking his head as he looked at his brother. 'Go on, off you go,' he added with a smile, and gathered up his books in order to go. He felt suddenly in high spirits himself, and did not want to part from his brother. 'So where were you when it was raining?'

'What rain? There were just a few drops. I'll come up in a minute. So you had a good day? Well, that's excellent.' And Levin went off to change.

Five minutes later the brothers gathered in the dining room. Although Levin thought he was not hungry, and he only sat down to dinner so as not to hurt Kuzma's feelings, when he started to eat he found the dinner extraordinarily delicious. Sergey Ivanovich watched him with a smile.

'Oh yes, there's a letter for you,' he said. 'Go down and get it please, Kuzma. And make sure you shut the door.'

The letter was from Oblonsky. Levin read it aloud. Oblonsky wrote from Petersburg: 'I have had a letter from Dolly, she's at Ergushovo, and nothing is going quite right for her. Do go over and see her, please, and give her some advice; you know about everything. She will be so glad to see you. She's all alone, poor thing. My mother-in-law and the others are still abroad.'

'That's excellent! Of course I will go over to see them,' said Levin. 'Or we could go together. She's a lovely person. Don't you think?'

'So they're not far from here?'

'About twenty miles. Maybe twenty-five. But the road is excellent. We will have an excellent trip.'

'Sounds delightful,' said Sergey Ivanovich, still smiling.

The sight of his younger brother immediately put him in a good mood.

'Well, you've got an appetite!' he said, looking at his ruddy-brown, sun-tanned face and neck bent over the plate.

'Excellent! You can't imagine how effective this regime is for all kinds of idiocy. I want to enrich medicine with a new term: *Arbeitskur*.'[1]

'Well, you don't seem to need it.'

'No, but people suffering from nervous illnesses might.'

'Yes, it ought to be tried. I was going to come and watch you mowing, you know, but it was so unbearably hot that I got no further than the wood. I sat down for a bit, went through the wood to the village, ran into your old wet-nurse, and sounded her out as to how the peasants see you. As far as I can see, they don't approve of all this. She said: "It's not work for the gentry." It seems to me generally that the peasants have a very fixed idea of the criteria for what they call "gentry" activities. And they are not prepared for the gentry to step outside the boundary of their fixed idea.'

'That may be; but it's brought me a pleasure I've never had in my whole life. And there's nothing wrong with it after all. Is there?' answered Levin. 'It can't be helped if they don't like it. However, I think it's fine. Hmm?'

'All in all,' continued Sergey Ivanovich, 'I can see you're pleased with your day.'

'Very pleased. We mowed the whole meadow. And then there was this old man I made friends with there! You can't imagine what a marvellous person he is!'

'So you're pleased with your day. And so am I. First, I solved two

[1] 'Work-cure.'

chess problems, and one of them is very ingenious—it opens with a pawn. I'll show it to you. And then I thought about our conversation yesterday.'

'About what? Our conversation yesterday?' said Levin, half-shutting his eyes blissfully and exhaling loudly after finishing his dinner, and decidedly not in a state to recall what their conversation yesterday was about.

'I think you are partly right. Our difference of opinion lies in the fact that you put self-interest as the main motivation, while my argument is that every person with a certain level of education is bound to have an interest in the common good. Maybe you are right that it would be more desirable to have activity which offers some material benefit. You're generally a bit too *prime-sautière*,[1] as the French say; you want passionate, energetic activity or nothing.'

Levin listened to his brother and understood absolutely nothing, and did not want to understand. He was only afraid his brother might ask him a question that would make it clear he had not been listening.

'So there you are, my friend,' said Sergey Ivanovich, touching him on the shoulder.

'Yes, of course. Anyway, it doesn't matter! I'm not going to stand my ground,' answered Levin, with a childlike, guilty smile. 'What on earth was I arguing about?' he wondered. 'Of course, I'm right, and he's right, and everything is fine. I've just got to go over to the office and make arrangements.' He got up, stretching and smiling.

Sergey Ivanovich smiled too.

'If you want to go for a walk, let's go together,' he said, not wanting to be parted from his brother, who was simply oozing vitality and energy. 'Let's go, and we can stop by the office, if you need to.'

'Oh, heavens!' exclaimed Levin so loudly that Sergey Ivanovich was startled.

'What is it, what is the matter?'

'How's Agafya Mikhailovna's hand?' said Levin, slapping his head. 'I clean forgot about her.'

'It's much better.'

'Well, I'll run over and see her anyway. I'll be back before you've had time to put your hat on.'

And he raced down the stairs, his heels clacking away like a wooden rattle.*

---

[1] 'impulsive'.

7

WHILE Stepan Arkadyich had gone to Petersburg to perform a most natural and most essential duty, an indispensable rite of passage familiar to all civil servants, albeit baffling to non-civil servants—reminding the ministry of his existence—and, after taking nearly all the money in the house, was having a jolly and agreeable time at the races and at dachas while performing this duty, Dolly and the children had moved to the country in order to cut down on expenses as much as possible. She had gone to Ergushovo, the village that had been her dowry, the very one where the forest had been sold in spring, and which was about thirty-five miles from Levin's Pokrovskoye.

The large old house in Ergushovo had been pulled down long ago, and it was then that the annexe* had been redecorated and extended by the Prince. The annexe had been spacious and comfortable about twenty years ago when Dolly was a child, although, like all annexes, it stood sideways to the main drive and the south. But this annexe was now old and dilapidated. When Stepan Arkadyich came down in the spring to sell the forest, Dolly had asked him to look over the house and see to whatever repairs might be necessary. Like all guilty husbands, Stepan Arkadyich was very solicitous about his wife's comfort, so he looked over the house himself, and made arrangements to have everything he considered necessary carried out. What he considered necessary was to reupholster all the furniture in cretonne, put up curtains, clear the garden, put up a little bridge by the pond, and plant some flowers; but he forgot to do many other vital things, the absence of which later made Darya Alexandrovna's life a misery.

As hard as Stepan Arkadyich tried to be an attentive father and husband, he could never quite keep in mind the fact that he had a wife and children. He had bachelor tastes, and he only ever took them into consideration. When he returned to Moscow, he proudly informed his wife that everything was ready, and that everything in the house would run like clockwork, and he strongly urged her to go. For Stepan Arkadyich, his wife's departure for the country was very appealing in all respects: it was good for the children, there were fewer expenses, and he had more freedom. For her part, Darya Alexandrovna regarded moving to the country for the summer to be essential for the children, especially the little girl, who had not fully recovered after the bout of scarlet fever, and, finally, to escape from all the petty humiliations, the petty sums owed to the wood-merchant, the fishmonger, and the shoe-maker, which made her life a misery. On top of that, she was also happy about the move because she was dreaming of luring her sister Kitty to the country, as she was due to return from abroad in the middle of the summer and had been prescribed bathing. Kitty wrote from the spa that nothing appealed to her more than the idea of spending the summer with Dolly at Ergushovo, which was full of childhood memories for them both.

Life in the country was very difficult for Dolly at first. She had lived in the country as a child, and had retained the impression that the country was a salvation from all city ills, and that while life there might not be refined (Dolly could easily reconcile herself to that), it was cheap and comfortable: everything was on hand, everything was cheap, everything was easy to get, and it was good for the children. But coming to the country now as mistress of the house, she saw that it was all quite unlike what she had thought.

The day after their arrival there was torrential rain, and during the night water flooded the landing and the nursery so that the cots had to be carried into the drawing room. There was no cook amongst the servants; of the nine cows, it turned out, as the dairy-woman put it, that some were about to calve, some had calved for the first time, some were old, and some had hard udders; there was not enough butter or milk even for the children. There were no eggs. It was impossible to get a chicken; they had to roast and boil sinewy, old, purple roosters. It was impossible to find women to scrub the floors—they were all in the potato fields. Driving anywhere was impossible, because one of the horses was restive, and tugged at the shaft. It was impossible to go bathing because the entire riverbank had been trampled by cattle and was open to the road; it was even impossible to go for a walk, because the cattle strayed into the garden through the broken fence, and there was one terrible bull who bellowed, and therefore was liable to charge. There were no decent wardrobes. The ones already there would either not close or would open by themselves when people walked past. There were no pots and pans; there was no copper for the laundry, and not even an ironing-board in the maids' room.

Darya Alexandrovna was at first in despair when she encountered what from her point of view were terrible calamities instead of tranquillity and rest: she worked her fingers to the bone trying to sort things out, felt the hopelessness of the situation, and constantly had to fight back the tears springing into her eyes. The steward, a former cavalry sergeant to whom Stepan Arkadyich had taken a liking and had elevated from being a hall porter on account of his handsome and deferential appearance, did not concern himself at all with Darya

Alexandrovna's calamities, merely saying respectfully: 'The peasants are such a rotten lot, they're quite impossible,' and did nothing to help.

The situation seemed hopeless. But in the Oblonsky household, as in all family households, there was one inconspicuous but most important and useful person: Matryona Filimonovna. She calmed her mistress down, assured her that everything would *shape up* (that was her expression, and Matvey had appropriated it from her), and calmly and coolly took action herself.

She immediately made friends with the steward's wife, and on the very first day drank tea with her and the steward under the acacias and talked everything over. Soon a Matryona Filimonovna club had established itself under the acacias, and it was here, with the help of this club, consisting of the steward's wife, the village elder, and the clerk, that life's difficulties gradually began to be ironed out, and within a week everything really had begun to shape up. They mended the roof and found a woman who was a friend of the village elder to come in and cook, they bought hens, they started getting milk, they fenced in the garden with stakes, the carpenter made a mangle, hooks were attached to the wardrobes so they no longer opened at will, an ironing-board covered with army cloth lay between the arm of a chair and a chest of drawers, and the maids' room began to smell of ironing.

'There we are then! And to think you were in despair,' said Matryona Filimonovna, pointing to the ironing-board.

They even built a bathing-hut out of straw matting. Lily started bathing, and Darya Alexandrovna's expectations of a comfortable, if not tranquil, life in the country were at least partially fulfilled. With six children, Darya Alexandrovna could not be tranquil. One would be ill, another might be ill, a third would need something, a fourth would show signs of a bad character, and so on and so forth. Rare indeed were the brief periods of tranquillity. But these concerns and worries were the only possible happiness for Darya Alexandrovna. Without them, she would have been left alone to brood about her husband who did not love her. Besides, however difficult it was for a mother to deal with the fear of illnesses, the illnesses themselves, and the pain of seeing signs of bad tendencies in her children, the children themselves were now rewarding her pains with small joys. These joys were so small that they were as unnoticeable as specks of gold in sand, and during the bad moments she could see only the pain and only the sand, but there were also good moments when she could see only the joy and only the gold.

Now, in the solitude of the country, she began to become more and more aware of those joys. Often, as she looked at them, she would make every possible effort to persuade herself that she was mistaken, that she was partial to her children since she was their mother; nevertheless, she could not help telling herself that she had delightful children, all six of them, each in their own way, each one of a kind, and she was happy with them and proud of them.

8

AT the end of May, when everything had more or less been sorted out, she received her husband's reply to her complaints about the disarray in the country. He wrote to ask her forgiveness for not having thought about everything, and promised to come at the first opportunity. This opportunity did not present itself, and Darya Alexandrovna lived on her own in the country until the beginning of June.

On the Sunday of St Peter's Fast, Darya Alexandrovna drove over to church so that her children could take communion. In her intimate, philosophical conversations with her sister, mother, and friends, Darya Alexandrovna very often surprised them with her freethinking views regarding religion. She had her own strange religion of metempsychosis,* in which she firmly believed, caring little about Church dogma. But within her own family she followed all the Church's admonitions to the letter—not just to set an example, but with all her heart—and the fact that the children had not taken communion for about a year worried her greatly, so with Matryona Filimonovna's full approval and support, she decided that it should happen now in the summer.

Several days ahead of time, Darya Alexandrovna mulled over how to dress all the children. Clothes were made, altered, and washed, hems and flounces were let down, buttons were sewn on, and ribbons got ready. Only Tanya's dress, which the English governess had undertaken to make, caused Darya Alexandrovna a great deal of distress. When she altered it, the governess put the tucks in the wrong place, made the armholes too big, and nearly ruined the dress. It was so tight around Tanya's shoulders it was painful to see. But Matryona Filimonovna improvised a way of putting in gussets, and adding a little pelerine. That solved the problem, but there was almost a row with the governess in the process. By morning, however, everything had been sorted out, and shortly before nine o'clock—the time until which they had asked the priest to delay starting the liturgy—the smartly dressed children were standing in front of the carriage by the porch, beaming with happiness as they waited for their mother.

Through the offices of Matryona Filimonovna, the steward's Brownie had been harnessed to the carriage instead of the frisky Raven, and Darya Alexandrovna, delayed by the care she had taken with her attire, came out in a white muslin dress and took her seat.

Darya Alexandrovna had arranged her hair and dress with care and excitement. She used to dress for herself before, to look beautiful and be admired; but the older she became, the less she had enjoyed dressing up; she could see how she had lost her looks. But now she dressed with pleasure and excitement again. She was not dressing for her own sake, or to look beautiful, but so that she, as the mother of these delightful children, would not spoil the general impression. And as she looked at herself in the mirror one last time, she was pleased with herself. She did look pretty. Not as pretty as she once had been, when she wanted to look pretty for a ball, but pretty enough for the object she now had in mind.

There was no one in church except the peasants, the servants, and their womenfolk. But Darya Alexandrovna saw, or thought she saw, the admiration she and her children aroused. The children not only looked beautiful in their smart little outfits, but their good behaviour was endearing as well. Alyosha, it has to be said, did not stand still properly: he kept turning round, trying to see his jacket from behind; but he was still utterly adorable. Tanya stood there like a grown-up, keeping an eye on the little ones. The smallest, Lily, was charming, with her naive amazement at everything, and it was difficult not to smile when she said after taking communion, '*Please, some more.*'[1]

During the journey home, the children felt that something solemn had happened, and were very well-behaved.

Everything went well at home too; but at lunch Grisha began whistling, and worst of all, disobeyed the governess, so he had to go without any tart. If she had been there, Darya Alexandrovna would not have resorted to punishment on such a day; but she had to support the governess's orders, and she confirmed her decision that Grisha should have no tart. This slightly spoiled the general happy mood.

Grisha cried, saying that Nikolenka had whistled too but was not being punished, and that he wasn't crying about the tart—he didn't care about that—but at the unfairness of it all. This really was too sad, and Darya Alexandrovna resolved to have a word with the English governess and get her to forgive Grisha, so she went off to find her. But as she walked through the drawing room, she encountered a scene

---

[1] [English in the original.]

that filled her heart with such joy that tears sprang to her eyes, and she forgave the delinquent herself.

The punished boy was sitting on the windowsill in the corner of the room; Tanya was standing next to him with a plate. Pretending she wanted to give her dolls lunch, she had asked the governess's permission to take her portion of the tart into the nursery, but had brought it instead to her brother. Still crying about the injustice of the punishment meted out to him, he was eating the tart, and saying between sobs, 'You have some; let's eat it together . . . together.'

Tanya was affected first by pity for Grisha, then by an awareness of her good deed, and there were tears in her eyes too; but she did not refuse, and was eating her share.

They were scared when they saw their mother, but when they looked at her face more closely, they realized they were doing something good and started giggling, and, with their mouths full of tart, they began wiping their smiling lips with their hands, and smearing tears and jam all over their shining faces.

'Heavens! Your new white dress! Tanya! Grisha!' said their mother as she tried to rescue the dress, but with a beatific, ecstatic smile on her face and tears in her eyes.

The new clothes were taken off, orders were given for the girls to be dressed in blouses and the boys in their old jackets, and orders were also given for the trap to be harnessed with Brownie again—much to the steward's chagrin—so they could drive out to pick mushrooms and go bathing. A roar of delighted shrieking went up in the nursery, which did not stop until they set off for the bathing-place.

They gathered a whole basketful of mushrooms, and even Lily found a birch mushroom.* Before it was Miss Hoole who found them and pointed them out to her; but now she found a big birch toadstool all by herself, and there was a general scream of delight, 'Lily has found a toadstool!'

Then they drove to the river, put the horses under the birch trees, and walked down to the bathing-place. After Terenty the coachman had tied the horses to a tree, where they stood swishing away gadflies, he lay down, flattening some grass in the shade of a birch, and smoked his shag tobacco, while the children's incessant squeals of delight carried across to him from the bathing-place.

Although it was hard work looking after all the children and stopping them from getting into mischief, and although it was difficult to remember and not muddle up all those little stockings, drawers, and shoes from various feet, and untie, unbutton, and then do up again all those laces and buttons, Darya Alexandrovna liked nothing better than to go bathing with all the children, having always enjoyed bathing herself, and considering it to be good for the children. Sorting out all those plump little legs and pulling stockings on them, taking those naked little bodies in her arms, dipping them in the water and hearing their mingled shrieks of delight and fear, and seeing the breathless faces of her little splashing cherubs with their wide-open, frightened, and happy eyes, gave her great pleasure.

When half the children were already dressed, some peasant women in their Sunday best who were out gathering angelica and milkwort came over to the bathing-place and lingered shyly. Matryona Filimonovna called out to one of them to give her a towel and a shirt that had fallen into the water so she could dry them, and Darya Alexandrovna got into conversation with the women. At first they laughed behind their hands and did not understand her questions, but soon they grew bolder and found their tongues, immediately winning Darya Alexandrovna over with the sincere admiration they showed for her children.

'Look what a beauty she is, as white as sugar,' said one, admiring Tanechka and shaking her head; 'she's thin though . . .'

'Yes, she has been ill.'

'Look, you seem to have been bathed too,' said another to the baby.

'No, he's only three months,' answered Darya Alexandrovna with pride.

'You don't say!'

'Do you have children?'

'I've had four, two left: a boy and a girl. I weaned her before Lent.'

'How old is she?'

'She'll be getting on for two now.'

'Why did you nurse her so long?'

'That's how we do it here: through three fasts . . .'

And the conversation turned to what most interested Darya Alexandrovna: how was her delivery? What illnesses had there been? Where was her husband? Did he visit often?

Darya Alexandrovna did not want to leave the peasant women, so interesting was their conversation, and so completely identical were their interests. Nicest of all for Darya Alexandrovna was that she could clearly see these women admired her more than anything else for having so many children, and such attractive ones at that. The peasant women amused Darya Alexandrovna and offended the English governess because she was the cause of laughter she did not understand. One of the young women could not take her eyes off the Englishwoman, who was getting dressed after everybody else, and when she put on a third petticoat* she could not help passing comment. 'Look at that, she's been twirling and twirling, she'll be twirling for ever!' she said, and they all collapsed into giggles.

9

SURROUNDED by all the bathed, wet-haired children, and with a kerchief on her head, Darya Alexandrovna was just approaching the house when the coachman said:

'There's a gentleman coming, from Pokrovskoye it looks like.'

Darya Alexandrovna looked ahead and was delighted to see the familiar figure of Levin coming towards them in his grey hat and grey coat. She was always glad to see him, but she was particularly glad that he should see her now in all her glory. No one could understand her true splendour, and what it comprised, better than Levin.

When he saw her, he found himself looking at a picture of the family life he had once imagined for himself.

'You're just like a mother hen, Darya Alexandrovna.'

'I am so glad to see you!' she said, holding out her hand to him.

'Glad to see me, but you didn't get in touch. I've got my brother staying with me. It was Stiva who sent me a note to say that you were here.'

'Stiva?' Darya Alexandrovna asked with surprise.

'Yes, he wrote to say you had moved here, and thought you might allow me to be of assistance in some way,' said Levin, and after saying this he suddenly became embarrassed, and, clamming up, he continued walking beside the trap in silence, breaking off shoots from the lime trees and nibbling on them. His embarrassment stemmed from the presumption that Darya Alexandrovna would dislike the idea of being helped by an outsider with things that should have been done by her husband. Darya Alexandrovna did indeed not like this habit Stepan Arkadyich had of foisting his family affairs on to strangers. And she immediately realized that Levin understood that. It was precisely for this sensitivity of understanding, this tact, that Darya Alexandrovna liked Levin.

'I realized, of course,' said Levin, 'that this just meant that you wanted to see me, and I'm very glad. But I can imagine, of course, that after running a household in the city things must seem rather primitive here, so I am totally at your service if there is anything you need.'

'Oh no!' said Dolly. 'It was uncomfortable at first, but everything has been sorted out wonderfully now, thanks to my old nanny,' she said, indicating Matryona Filimonovna, who was directing a merry, friendly smile at Levin, aware they were talking about her. She knew him, and knew he would be a good match for the young lady, so was keen to see the matter settled.

'Do please sit down, we'll squeeze up here,' she said to him.

'No, I'm happy to walk. Children, who wants to race the horses with me?'

The children scarcely knew Levin, and could not remember when they had seen him before, but they displayed towards him none of that strange feeling of shyness and aversion which children so often experience when with hypocritical adults, and for which they are so often severely punished. Hypocrisy in whatever guise can deceive the cleverest and most perceptive person, but the dullest of children will recognize it, however artfully it may be concealed, and be repelled. Whatever Levin's faults, there was not a shred of hypocrisy in him, and so the children displayed to him the same friendliness they found reflected in their mother's face. The two elder ones immediately jumped down in response to his invitation, and ran off with him as simply as they would have done with their nanny, Miss Hoole, or their mother. Lily also started begging to join him, so her mother handed her to him, he sat her on his shoulders, and started running with her.

'Don't worry, Darya Alexandrovna, don't worry!' he said, beaming happily to the mother, 'I would never hurt her or let her fall.'

And as she watched his agile, strong, carefully attentive and ultra-cautious movements, the mother calmed down and looked on with a merry, approving smile.

Here, in the country, in the company of the children and the con-genial Darya Alexandrovna, Levin relaxed, as he often did, into that state of childish merriment which Darya Alexandrovna particularly liked about him. As he was running around with the children, he taught them gymnastics, made Miss Hoole laugh with his bad English, and told Darya Alexandrovna about what he got up to in the country.

After dinnner, while she was sitting alone with him on the balcony, Darya Alexandrovna began talking about Kitty.

'Did you know? Kitty's coming here to spend the summer with me.'

'Really?' he said, blushing, and in order to change the subject he said immediately: 'So shall I send two cows over to you? If you want to put a figure on it, you could pay me five roubles a month, if you are not too embarrassed.'

'Thank you, but no. We've got everything sorted out.'

'Well, I could have a look at your cows, and if you will allow me, I will give some instructions on how to feed them. The feeding is crucial.'

And solely to steer the conversation away, Levin expounded to Darya Alexandrovna the theory of dairy farming, which is based on the idea that the cow is simply a machine for turning fodder into milk and so on.

While he was saying this, he was dying to hear all the details about Kitty, but he was also frightened at the prospect. He was scared that his hard-won peace of mind would be destroyed.

'Yes, but all that needs to be managed, however, and who is going to do that?' Darya Alexandrovna replied reluctantly.

She had got the household running so well now with the help of Matryona Filimonovna that she did not want to change anything; besides, she did not believe in Levin's knowledge of agriculture. Theories about cows being milk-making machines seemed suspicious to her. She felt such theories could only hinder the whole process. She felt, indeed, that it was all much more straightforward: all you needed, as Matryona Filimonovna had explained, was to give Brindle and Whiteflank more food and drink, and not let the cook take away all the kitchen scraps for the washerwoman's cow. It was obvious. But these theories about meal and grass fodder were dubious and vague. Most of all, though, she just wanted to talk about Kitty.

10

'KITTY writes that there is nothing she wants so much as peace and quiet,' Dolly said after the silence that ensued.

'So, has her health improved?' Levin asked nervously.

'She's completely recovered, thank goodness. I never believed it was anything to do with her chest.'

'Oh, I'm very glad!' said Levin, and Dolly felt there was something touching and helpless in his face as he said this and looked at her silently.

'Listen, Konstantin Dmitrich,' said Darya Alexandrovna, smiling her kind and slightly ironic smile, 'why are you angry with Kitty?'

'Me? I'm not angry,' said Levin.

'Yes, you are. Why did you not call on us, or on them, when you were in Moscow?'

'Darya Alexandrovna,' he said, blushing to his roots, 'I'm actually surprised that you, with your kind heart, cannot feel what the answer is. How is it you aren't simply sorry for me, when you know . . .'

'What do I know?'

'You know that I proposed and was refused,' said Levin, and all the tenderness he had been feeling for Kitty a minute earlier was replaced in his soul by a feeling of rancour at the insult he had received.

'But why did you think I knew?'

'Because everybody knows.'

'Well, that's where you are very much mistaken; I did not know about it, although I guessed.'

'Oh! Well, you know now.'

'All I knew was that something happened, but I could never find out what it was from Kitty. I could only see that something had happened, that it tormented her dreadfully, and that she was adamant I never talk about it. But if she did not tell me, then she did not tell anyone. But what did happen between you? Tell me.'

'I've told you what happened.'

'When was it?'

'When I last visited your family.'

'You know, I have to tell you,' said Darya Alexandrovna, 'I feel terribly, terribly sorry for her, I really do. You only suffer from pride . . .'

'That may be so,' said Levin, 'but . . .'

She interrupted him:

'But I feel terribly, terribly sorry for her, poor thing. Now I understand everything.'

'Well, Darya Alexandrovna, you must excuse me,' he said, getting up. 'I must be going! Goodbye, Darya Alexandrovna.'

'No, wait a minute,' she said, grabbing him by the sleeve. 'Wait a minute, sit down.'

'Please, I beg you, let us not talk about this,' he said, sitting down and at the same time feeling that the hope he thought he had buried was stirring and rising up in his heart.

'If I did not care for you,' she said, her eyes welling with tears; 'if I did not know you as I do . . .'

The supposedly dead feeling was steadily coming back to life, rising up and taking possession of Levin's heart.

'Yes, I've understood everything now,' Darya Alexandrovna continued. 'You can't understand this; for you men, who are free and able to make your own choice, it's always clear whom you love. But a young girl in a state of expectation, with that feminine, girlish modesty, a young girl who sees you men from afar, and takes everything on trust—a young girl can and may well feel that she does not know whom she loves, and does not know what to say.'

'Well, if her heart does not tell her . . .'

'No, her heart does tell her, but you just think about it: you men set your sights on a girl, you visit her at home, you become friends, you keep watching and waiting to see if what you have found is love, and only then, when you are sure you are in love, do you propose . . .'

'Well, it's not quite like that.'

'All the same, you propose when your feelings of love have matured, or when the scales between two choices tip one way. But a girl is not consulted. People are keen that she choose for herself, but she is not in a position to choose and can only answer: yes or no.'

'Yes, the choice was between me and Vronsky,' thought Levin, and the cadaver that had come back to life in his soul died again and weighed just as heavily on his heart.

'Darya Alexandrovna,' he said, 'that's how people choose clothes or whatever else they want to buy, but not love. The choice has been made, and so much the better . . . It can't be repeated.'

'Ah, pride, pride!' said Darya Alexandrovna, as if despising him for the meanness of this feeling in comparison with that other feeling, which only women know. 'When you proposed to Kitty, she was precisely in that situation when she was unable to give an answer. She was hesitating. The hesitation was between you and Vronsky. She was seeing him every day, but you she had not seen for a long time. Let us suppose she had been older . . . If I had been in her shoes, for example, I wouldn't have had a moment's hesitation. I have always found him odious, and so it has turned out.'

Levin recalled Kitty's answer. She had said: '*No, that cannot be . . .*'

'Darya Alexandrovna,' he said drily, 'I appreciate your confidence in me; I think you are mistaken. But whether I am right or wrong, this pride which you so despise makes any thought of Katerina Alexandrovna impossible for me—you must understand, quite impossible.'

'I will say only one more thing: you do realize that I am speaking about my sister, whom I love like my own children. I am not saying she loves you, I simply want to say that her refusal at that moment proves nothing.'

'I don't know!' said Levin, jumping up. 'If you only knew how painful you are making this for me! It would be just the same if one of your children died, and people said to you: well, he might have been like this or like that, and he might have lived, and you would have rejoiced over him. But he's dead, dead, dead . . .'

'How funny you are!' said Darya Alexandrovna with a sad, wry smile, despite Levin's agitation. 'Yes, I understand everything now,' she continued. 'So you won't be coming over to see us when Kitty's here?'

'No, I won't. Obviously I won't go out of my way to avoid Katerina Alexandrovna, but I will endeavour to spare her the displeasure of my presence wherever possible.'

'You really are very funny,' repeated Darya Alexandrovna, looking affectionately into his face. 'All right then, let it be as if we had never spoken about it. Why have you come in, Tanya?' Darya Alexandrovna said in French to the girl who had just entered.

'Where's my spade, Mama?'

'I'm speaking in French, and so should you be.'

The girl tried, but could not remember the French for spade, so her mother told her what it was, and then told her in French where to look for the spade. And Levin did not like that.

Nothing about Darya Alexandrovna's house and her children now seemed quite as appealing as before.

'Why does she have to talk French with the children?' he thought. 'How unnatural and false! And the children feel that. Learning French and unlearning sincerity,' he thought to himself, unaware that Darya Alexandrovna had already turned this over in her mind twenty times, and still believed it necessary to teach her children French that way, even if it was at the cost of sincerity.

'But where do you have to go to? Stay a while.'

Levin stayed until tea, but his high spirits had completely vanished, and he felt ill at ease.

After tea he went out into the hall to order his horses to be brought round, and when he returned, he found Darya Alexandrovna agitated, and looking upset and teary-eyed. While Levin had been out of the room, something awful had happened for Darya Alexandrovna, which had destroyed at one stroke all that day's happiness and pride in her children. Grisha and Tanya had been fighting over a ball. Darya Alexandrovna had run out when she heard screaming in the nursery and had found them in a shocking state. Tanya was holding Grisha by the hair, while he was punching her with his fists wherever he could, his face distorted with rage. Something snapped in Darya Alexandrovna's heart when she saw this. It was as if darkness had descended on her life: she realized that those children in whom she took such pride were not just thoroughly ordinary children, but actually bad, poorly brought-up children, wicked children with coarse, brutal proclivities.

She could not talk or think about anything else, and she could not help telling Levin her woes.

Levin saw she was unhappy and tried to console her, saying that it was not proof of anything bad, and that all children fought; but as he said this, Levin was thinking in his soul: 'No, I'm not going to put on airs and talk French to my children, but my children won't be like that anyway: you just have to make sure you don't spoil or warp children, and they will be delightful. No, my children won't be like that.'

He said goodbye and left, and she did not try to detain him.

11

IN the middle of July, Levin received a visit from the elder in his sister's village, fifteen miles from Pokrovskoye, who came to report on the general state of affairs and on the haymaking. The main income on his sister's estate came from the water meadows. In previous years the peasants had bought the hay for eight roubles an acre. When Levin took over managing the estate, and went over to inspect the hay that had been gathered, he found it was worth more, and so set the price at ten roubles. The peasants refused to pay that price, and, as Levin suspected, were also discouraging other buyers. Levin then rode over himself, and arranged for the hay-gathering in the meadows to be done partly by hired labour and partly on a share basis. The peasants resisted this innovation in every way possible, but it went ahead, and in the very first year the income from the meadows almost doubled. The peasants continued to put up the same resistance the following year and last year, and the haymaking proceeded in the same way. This year the peasants were doing all the mowing for a one-third share, and now the village elder had come to announce that the hay had all been gathered, and that, fearing rain, he had invited the clerk to come over, divided the crop in front of him, and already set aside eleven stacks as the master's share. From the vague answers he received to his question about how much hay the main meadow had produced, the elder's haste in dividing it up without asking permission, and the peasant's general tone, Levin realized that there was something suspicious about the way the hay had been divided up, and he resolved to go over himself and investigate.

Arriving at the village at dinner-time, and leaving his horse at the home of an old man with whom he was friendly, the husband of his brother's wet-nurse, Levin went to find him in his apiary, hoping to glean from him some more details about the haymaking. Parmenych, a garrulous, good-looking old man, greeted Levin very warmly, showed him round his apiary, and told him all about his bees and the swarms that year; but he was vague and reluctant when answering Levin's questions about the haymaking. This gave Levin even more confirmation of his suspicions. He went across to the meadow and looked over the haystacks. The haystacks could not possibly have produced fifty cartloads each, and to catch the peasants out, Levin ordered the carts that had transported the hay to be brought back immediately, and for one stack to be loaded up and transferred to the barn. The haystack produced only thirty-two cartloads. Despite the elder's assurances about the hay being all fluffed up and then settling down in the stacks, and despite his swearing that everything had been done fairly, Levin insisted that the hay had been divided up without his orders, and he was therefore not accepting this hay as fifty loads per stack. After lengthy arguments, it was decided that the peasants would take those eleven stacks to be their share, reckoning them at fifty loads each, while the master's share would be measured out again. The negotiations and the division of the haystacks lasted until late afternoon. When the last of the hay had been divided up, Levin entrusted the clerk with the rest of the supervision, sat down on a haystack marked by a willow branch, and admired the sight of the meadow swarming with people.

In front of him there was a brightly coloured chain of women moving in the bend of the river behind the marsh, their sonorous voices prattling away merrily, while the scattered hay was swiftly distributed into grey, winding ridges along the pale green stubble. The women were followed by men with pitchforks, and out of the ridges grew tall, wide, fluffy haystacks. Carts were rumbling across the meadow over to the left where the hay had already been gathered, and one after another the haystacks vanished as they were lifted up in huge forkfuls and replaced by heavy loads of fragrant hay hanging over the horses' hindquarters.

'Fine weather for gathering in! It'll be good hay!' said the old man, who had sat down beside Levin. 'It's like tea-leaves, not hay! Just like scattering grain to the ducks, the way they pick it up!' he added, pointing to the haystacks being loaded up. 'They've taken a good half of it since dinner.'

'Is that the last then?' he shouted to a young lad who was standing on the box of an empty cart and flicking the ends of the hempen reins as he drove past.

'It is, Pa!' the lad shouted as he reined in the horse, and looking round with a smile at the cheerful, rosy-cheeked girl sitting on the box, who was also smiling, he drove on.

'Who's that? Your son?' asked Levin.

'My youngest,' said the old man with an affectionate smile.

'What a fine young fellow!'

'He's all right.'

'Married already?'

'Yes, it was two years last St Philip's Day.'*

'Well, well—any children?'

'Hardly! For a whole year he didn't understand a thing, and he was shy too,' answered the old man. 'What hay! Just like tea!' he repeated, wishing to change the subject.

Levin looked more closely at young Ivan Parmenov and his wife. They were loading a haystack not far from him. Ivan Parmenov was standing on the cart, receiving, then levelling out and stamping down, the huge bundles of hay which his pretty young wife was deftly giving him, first in armfuls, and then on a pitchfork. The young woman was working easily, cheerfully, and deftly. The massive bundles of compressed hay would not go straight away on to the fork. First she smoothed it out and stuck the fork in, then she leaned the whole weight of her body on it with a quick, supple movement and, arching her back, which was encircled by a red belt, she immediately straightened up, displaying her full bosom beneath her white smock as she deftly changed her grip and tossed the bundle of hay on to the top of the load. Clearly trying to save her every minute of unnecessary labour, Ivan quickly caught each load in his outstretched arms and smoothed it out in the cart. After passing up what was left of the hay with a rake, the young wife shook off the wisps that had fallen on to her neck and straightening the red kerchief that had slipped on to her white, untanned forehead, she crawled under the cart to fasten the load. Ivan was teaching her how to tie the rope to the cross-piece, and burst into peals of laughter at something she said. In the expressions on both their faces could be seen an intense, young, newly awakened love.

12

THE load was tied. Ivan jumped down and led the docile, well-fed horse by the bridle. The young wife tossed the rake up on to the cart and, swinging her arms, marched off briskly to join the women who had gathered in a circle. Ivan drove out on to the road and joined the string of carts. Eye-catching in their bright colours, the women were walking behind the carts with rakes over their shoulders, chattering with merry, ringing voices. One coarse, wild, female voice struck up a song and sang it through to the refrain, then fifty different, coarse, high-pitched, healthy voices all joined in harmoniously together to sing the same song from the beginning again.

The women were approaching Levin with their singing, and he felt as if a thundercloud of merriment was bearing down on him. The cloud advanced and enveloped him, and the haystack on which he was lying, and the other haystacks, and the carts, and the whole meadow and the distant fields—everything started vibrating and shaking in time to this wild, rollicking song with its cries, whistles, and hollering. Levin started to feel envious of this healthy merriment, and he wanted to take part in expressing this joy of being alive. But he could do nothing, and had to lie there, look, and listen. When the peasants and their song disappeared both from his sight and his hearing, Levin was overcome by a feeling of deep melancholy on account of his loneliness, his physical indolence, and his resentment of this world.

Some of those very peasants who had argued with him the most over the hay, those whom he had offended, or who had tried to cheat him, those very peasants had bowed to him cheerfully, and clearly did not and could not bear him any grudge or feel remorse, or indeed any memory of having tried to deceive him. All that had been drowned in the sea of good-humoured, common labour. God had given the day, and God had given the energy. The day and the energy had been devoted to labour, and therein lay the reward. But whom was this labour for? What would be the fruits of this labour? These considerations were irrelevant and trivial.

Levin had often admired this life, and often felt envious of the people who lived this life, but today for the first time, and particularly under the impact of what he had seen of Ivan Parmenov's relationship with his young wife, it dawned on him clearly for the first time that it was up to him to exchange the oppressive, idle, artificial, and personal life he had been leading for this hard-working, pure, and delightful shared life.

The old man who had been sitting beside him had long since set off home; the peasants had gone their separate ways. Those who lived nearby had gone home, while those who came from afar had gathered to have supper and spend the night in the meadow. Unnoticed by the peasants, Levin continued to lie on the haystack, looking, listening, and thinking. The peasants who had stayed to spend the night in the meadow were awake for almost the entire short summer night. First came the sound of them all talking and laughing over supper, then more songs and laughter.

The long working day had left no other mark on them except merriment. Before sunrise everything fell silent. All that could be heard were the unbroken nocturnal sounds of the frogs in the marsh, and the horses snorting in the mist that rose over the meadow before daylight. Awakening, Levin got up from the haystack, looked at the stars, and realized the night was over.

'So what am I going to do? How am I going to do it?' he said to himself, trying to articulate for his own benefit everything he had been pondering and feeling during this brief night. What he had been pondering and feeling could all be divided into three separate trains of thought. One was the renunciation of his old life, his pointless knowledge, and his utterly useless education. Renouncing all this gave him pleasure, and he found it easy and straightforward. Other thoughts and ideas concerned the life he wished to live now. He had a clear sense of the simplicity, the purity, and the validity of this life, and he was convinced he would find in it the fulfilment, the peace of mind, and the dignity he so painfully lacked. But a third series of thoughts revolved around the question of how to make the transition from the old to the new life. And he had no clear-cut ideas about this. 'Should I have a wife? Should I have a job, and the necessity of work? Should I leave Pokrovskoye? Buy land? Join a peasant commune? Marry a peasant girl? How am I to go about it?' he asked himself again, without finding an answer. 'However, I haven't slept all night, and I can't see straight,' he said to himself. 'I'll work it all out later. One thing is certain: this night has decided my fate. My old dreams about family life were all nonsense, and wrong,' he said to himself. 'All this is much simpler and better . . .'

'How beautiful!' he thought, gazing at a strange, mother-of-pearl-like shell of white, fleecy clouds that was suspended right above his head in the middle of the sky. 'How lovely everything has been on this lovely night! And when did that shell manage to materialize? I looked at the sky a short while ago, and there was nothing there except for two white streaks. But then my views of life have changed just as imperceptibly!'

He left the meadow and walked along the highway towards the village. A slight breeze had picked up, and the weather turned grey and gloomy. This was that brief overcast moment which usually precedes dawn, and the complete victory of light over darkness.

Shivering from the cold, Levin walked quickly, looking at the ground. 'What's that? Someone is coming,' he thought as he heard the sound of bells, and he lifted his head. Forty paces away there was a coach-and-four with luggage on top travelling towards him on the grassy highway he was walking along. The ruts were making the shaft-horses press against the shaft, but the skilful driver sitting sideways on the box was managing to ensure the shaft went over the ruts, so that the wheels could run on smooth ground.

That was all Levin noticed, and without thinking who might be making the journey, he glanced absent-mindedly into the carriage.

There was an old lady dozing in the corner of the carriage, but by the window sat a young girl who had clearly just woken up and was holding the ribbons of a white cap in both hands. Bright and pensive, brimming over with a refined and complex inner life to which Levin was a stranger, she was gazing out beyond him towards the sunrise.

At the very moment when this vision was about to disappear, the candid eyes came to rest on him. She recognized him, and an expression of joy and surprise lit up her face.

He could not have been mistaken. There was only one pair of eyes like that in the world. There was only one being in the world capable of concentrating the whole world and the meaning of life for him. It was her. It was Kitty. He realized that she was driving to Ergushovo from the railway station. Everything that had disturbed Levin during that sleepless night, and all the decisions he had taken suddenly vanished. He recalled his dreams of marrying a peasant girl with disgust. It was only there, only there in that rapidly receding carriage which had crossed over to the other side of the road, that there was a possibility of solving the riddle of his life, which had been preying on him so heavily of late.

She did not look out again. The sound of the carriage springs was no longer audible, and the harness bells became only just audible. The barking of dogs indicated that the carriage had driven through the village, leaving behind the empty fields on either side, the village ahead, and he himself, alone and a stranger to everything, walking alone along the deserted highway.

He glanced up at the sky, hoping to find the shell he had admired earlier, which had embodied for him the whole progression of his thoughts and feelings that night. There was no longer anything resembling a shell in the sky. A mysterious change had already taken place up in the unattainable heights above. There was not a trace of the shell, and a smooth carpet of ever smaller fleecy clouds had spread out across half the sky. The sky had turned blue and brightened, and was responding to his questioning look as gently but also as unattainably as before.

'No,' he said to himself, 'however good that simple, working life is, I cannot go back to it. I love *her*.'

13

NO ONE except those closest to Alexey Alexandrovich knew that this apparently most cold and calculating of men had one weakness which went against the grain of his general character. Alexey Alexandrovich was unable to hear and see a child or a woman crying with detachment. The sight of tears confounded him, and he completely lost his powers of reasoning. His chief secretary and clerk knew this, and they forewarned female petitioners on no account to cry if they did not want to ruin their case. 'He will get angry and not listen to you,' they would say. And indeed, the emotional distress wrought in Alexey Alexandrovich by tears on such occasions would find expression in a rapid loss of temper. 'There is nothing, nothing that I can do. Kindly leave!' he would usually shout on these occasions.

When, as they returned from the races, Anna told him about her relationship with Vronsky and then immediately hid her face in her hands and burst into tears, Alexey Alexandrovich, despite the anger towards her that this provoked, also felt a surge of the emotional distress which tears always aroused in him. Aware of this, and aware that expressing his feelings at this particular juncture would be inappropriate to the occasion, he tried to suppress within himself every manifestation of life, and so remained completely still and did not look at her. This was the cause of that strangely lifeless expression on his face which had so astonished Anna.

When they arrived at the house he helped her out of the carriage, and making a supreme effort, took leave of her with his customary chivalry and uttered words which did not bind him to anything; he said he would inform her of his decision the following day.

His wife's words, which confirmed his worst suspicions, induced a cruel pain in Alexey Alexandrovich's heart. This pain was intensified by the strange feeling of physical pity for her which her tears had aroused in him. But once he was alone in the carriage, Alexey Alexandrovich to his surprise and joy felt a complete liberation, from both this pity and the doubts and agonies of jealousy which had been troubling him of late.

He experienced the sensations of a person whose aching tooth is finally extracted, when, after excruciating pain and the feeling of something huge being pulled from his jaw that is bigger than his head, the patient does not yet believe his luck but suddenly feels that what has poisoned his existence for so long, and claimed all his attention, is no longer there, and he can once again live, think, and be interested in other things apart from his tooth. This is the feeling Alexey Alexandrovich was experiencing. The pain had been strange and ghastly, but now it was gone, and he felt that he could live again, and think about something other than his wife.

'A depraved woman, without honour, without a heart, without religion! I always knew it and always saw it, though I tried to deceive myself because I felt sorry for her,' he said to himself. And it really did seem to him that he always had seen it; he remembered details from their past life, which had never seemed bad to him before—these details now showed clearly that she had always been depraved. 'I made a mistake in joining my life to hers; but there was nothing bad about my mistake, and so I cannot be unhappy. I am not the guilty party,' he told himself, 'she is. But she is nothing to do with me. She does not exist for me . . .'

He ceased to have any interest in what would happen to her and her son, towards whom his feelings had changed as much as they had towards her. The only thing that interested him now was the question of how to shake off the mud she had spattered on him during her fall in the best, most decorous, most convenient, and therefore most just way for him, and continue on his path of leading an active, honest, and useful life.

'I cannot be unhappy because a contemptible woman has committed a crime; I only have to find the optimum way out of the difficult position in which she has placed me. And I shall find it,' he said to himself with an ever deeper frown on his face. 'I'm not the first, nor am I the last.' And to say nothing of historical precedents starting with Menelaus, fresh in everyone's memory thanks to *La Belle Hélène*,* a whole number of contemporary incidences of women being unfaithful to their husbands in high society came into Alexey Alexandrovich's mind. 'Daryalov, Poltavsky, Prince Karibanov, Count Paskudin, Dram. . . . Yes, even Dram, such an honest, sensible man . . . Semyonov, Chagin, Sigonin,' Alexey Alexandrovich recalled. 'I suppose these men are subject to a certain amount of foolish *ridicule*,[1] but I have never seen

---

[1] [French in the original.]

anything but misfortune in their predicament, and have always sympathized,' Alexey Alexandrovich said to himself, although this was untrue, and he had never sympathized with misfortunes of this kind, as the higher his self-regard, the more frequent were the examples of wives betraying their husbands. 'It is a misfortune which can befall anyone. And this misfortune has befallen me. It is just a matter of knowing how best to cope with this situation.' And he began going over the actions undertaken by men who found themselves in the same position he was in.

'Daryalov fought a duel. . . .'

Duelling had particularly beguiled Alexey Alexandrovich in his youth, precisely because he was physically timid, and well aware of it. Alexey Alexandrovich could not contemplate the idea of a pistol aimed at him without a feeling of horror, and had never in his life used a weapon. When he was young, this feeling of horror had often forced him to think about duels and imagine himself being in a situation where he would have to expose his life to danger. Having attained success and an established position in life, he had long ago forgotten this feeling, but the habit had become ingrained, and the fear of being a coward proved to be so intense even now that Alexey Alexandrovich spent a long time entertaining the thought of a duel and contemplating it from every angle, although he knew in advance that he would never under any circumstance fight one.

'There is no doubt our society is still so uncivilized (unlike in England) that there are many people'—including those whose opinion Alexey Alexandrovich particularly valued—'who would look favourably on a duel; but what would be achieved? Suppose I do challenge him to a duel,' Alexey Alexandrovich went on thinking to himself, and vividly picturing the night he would spend after the challenge, and the pistol aimed at him, he shuddered and realized he could never go through with it. 'Suppose I do challenge him. Suppose I get taught how to shoot,' his thoughts continued, 'and I'm put in position, and I press the trigger,' he said to himself, closing his eyes, 'and it turns out I have killed him,' Alexey Alexandrovich said to himself, and he shook his head to dispel these foolish thoughts. 'What is the point of murdering a man in order to define my attitude to my criminal wife and to my son? I will still have to decide what to do with her. But what is far more probable and what indeed would doubtless happen, is that I would be killed or wounded. It would be me, the innocent party, the victim, who would be killed or wounded. Even more pointless. Besides, it would be dishonest on my part to issue a challenge. Don't I know already that my friends would never allow me to fight a duel, as they would never allow the life of a statesman needed by Russia to be placed in jeopardy? What would it really be about? It would be about me, knowing in advance that it would never get out of hand, just wanting to give myself some false lustre with this duel. It would be dishonest, it would be false, it would mean deceiving others, and myself. A duel is quite inconceivable, and no one expects it of me. My aim is to safeguard my reputation, so that I can carry on with my work without interruption.' Alexey Alexandrovich's work as a civil servant had always been of great importance in his eyes, but now it assumed a particular importance.

Having considered and rejected the idea of a duel, Alexey Alexandrovich turned to divorce, which was another solution chosen by some of the husbands he could recall. Going over in his memory all the incidences of divorce he knew about (there were a great many of them in the elite society he knew well), Alexey Alexandrovich could not find a single one where the purpose of the divorce was that which he had in mind. In all these cases, the husband had relinquished or sold his unfaithful wife, and the very party whose guilt deprived her of the right to enter into marriage had entered into a fictitious and pseudo-lawful relationship with a new partner. Alexey Alexandrovich saw that obtaining a legal divorce in his case—that is to say, one in which only the guilty wife was disowned—would be impossible. He saw that the complex life circumstances in which he found himself did not allow the possibility of providing the crude proof the law required* in order to expose his wife's guilt; he saw that the recognized gentility of this life also did not allow the application of such proof, if it existed, and that applying this proof would damage his standing in public opinion more than hers.

An attempt at divorce could lead only to a scandalous court case, which would be a godsend for his enemies, for slander, and the undermining of his high position in society. And a divorce would not help him attain his chief objective, which was to define the situation with a minimum of upset. Besides, a divorce, even an attempt at divorce, made it obvious that a wife was breaking off relations with her husband and taking up with her lover. And in Alexey Alexandrovich's soul, despite the utterly contemptuous indifference he believed he felt for his wife now, there was still one feeling which lingered with regard to her—an unwillingness to let her take up freely with Vronsky, and so be able to turn her crime to her own advantage. This one thought so annoyed Alexey Alexandrovich that the mere thought of it made him groan in inner agony and get up and change places in the carriage, and, frowning, he spent a long time after that wrapping the fleecy rug round his chilly, bony legs.

'Apart from a formal divorce, one could also do what Karibanov, Paskudin, and good old Dram did, that is, separate from one's wife,' he went on thinking once he had calmed down; but this course of action also brought with it the same embarrassment of a scandal as a divorce did, and the main thing was that it would fling his wife into Vronsky's arms just as with a formal divorce. 'No, it's impossible, quite impossible!' he said loudly, rearranging his rug again. 'I cannot be unhappy, but neither should she and he be happy.'

The feeling of jealousy which had tortured him when he was in a state of ignorance had ceased the instant the tooth had been painfully extracted by his wife's words. But that feeling had now been replaced by another: the desire that she should not only not emerge triumphant, but that she should receive retribution for her crime. He did not acknowledge this feeling, but deep in his soul he wanted her to suffer for having destroyed his equilibrium and his honour. And having once again ruminated over the implications of a duel, a divorce, and separation, and once again rejected them, Alexey Alexandrovich became convinced that there was only one solution: to keep her with him, concealing what had happened from society, and to use every means in his power to sever the relationship and above all—and this was something he would not admit even to himself—to punish her. 'I must announce my decision, which is that, after reflecting on the difficult position in which she has placed her family, all other solutions would be worse for both sides than outwardly maintaining the *status quo*[1], which I agree to maintain on the strict condition that she does my bidding, that is to say, breaks off her relationship with her lover.' Another important consideration occurred to Alexey Alexandrovich in vindication of this decision once it had already been definitively taken. 'Only by taking this decision am I acting in accordance with religion,' he said to himself, 'only by taking this decision am I not casting off a guilty wife, but giving her a chance to reform, and even—however difficult it will be for me—devoting some of my energies to her reform and salvation.' Although Alexey Alexandrovich knew he could not exert any moral influence on his wife, and that nothing would come of this attempt to reform her except lies; although he had not once thought about seeking guidance in religion while living through these difficult moments, now that his decision coincided with the dictates of religion,

---

[1] [Latin in the original.]

or so it seemed to him, this religious sanction of his decision gave him complete satisfaction and partial comfort. He was pleased to think that even in a matter of such life importance, no one would be able to say that he had not acted in accordance with the dictates of the religion whose banner he had always held aloft amid general apathy and indifference. As he reflected on subsequent details, Alexey Alexandrovich could not see even why his relations with his wife should not remain almost the same as before. Certainly, he would never be able to recover his respect for her, but there was no reason, nor could there be, why he should disrupt his life or suffer because she was a bad and unfaithful wife. 'Yes, time will pass, that great healer time, and our old relations will be restored,' Alexey Alexandrovich said to himself, 'restored, that is, to the extent that I won't feel the course of my life is disrupted. She is bound to be unhappy, but I am not guilty of anything, so I cannot be unhappy.'

14

As he approached Petersburg, Alexey Alexandrovich not only settled firmly on this decision, but also composed in his head the letter he would write to his wife. Going into the porter's office, Alexey Alexandrovich glanced at the letters and papers brought from the ministry, and ordered them to be taken into his study.

'Unharness the horses and admit no one,' he said in answer to the porter's question, emphasizing the words 'admit no one' with a certain amount of pleasure, which was an indication he was in a good mood.

Alexey Alexandrovich completed two circuits of his study, stopped in front of the enormous desk on which six candles had already been lit by the valet who had preceded him, cracked his fingers, then sat down and sorted out his writing implements. Placing his elbows on the desk, he cocked his head to one side, thought for a minute, then began to write, without pausing for a second. He wrote without addressing her, and in French, using 'vous' as a pronoun, which does not have the same cold character it does in Russian.

'At the time of our last conversation, I expressed to you my intention of informing you of my decision regarding the subject of that conversation. Having carefully thought everything over, I am writing now with the object of fulfilling that promise. My decision is as follows: however you might have behaved, I do not consider I have the right to

sunder the ties with which we have been bound by a higher power. The
family cannot be broken up by the whim, caprice, or even transgression
of one spouse, and our life must go on as before. This is essential for
me, for you, and for our son. I am quite sure that you have repented,
and are repenting that which is the cause of the present letter, and that
you will co-operate with me in eradicating the cause of our discord and
forgetting the past. If not, you can yourself surmise what will await you
and your son. I hope to talk this over in more detail in person. Since
the dacha season is drawing to a close, I would ask you to return to
Petersburg as quickly as possible, no later than Tuesday. All the necessary arrangements will be made for your arrival. I ask you to take note
that I attach particular significance to my request being carried out.

                                                                    A. Karenin.
P.S.—Enclosed with this letter is the money you may need for expenses.'

He read the letter through and was pleased with it, especially for
remembering to enclose money; there was not a single harsh word or
reproach, but nor was there any lenience either. Above all, there was
a golden bridge for her return. After folding the letter, smoothing it
out with a massive ivory paper-knife, and putting it in an envelope
with the money, he rang, feeling the pleasure he always derived from
handling his neatly organized writing implements.

'Give this to the courier for delivery to Anna Arkadyevna tomorrow
at the dacha,' he said, and stood up.

'Certainly, Your Excellency; will you take tea in the study?'

Alexey Alexandrovich ordered tea to be served in his study and,
toying with the massive paper-knife, he went over to the armchair,
by which a lamp had been prepared, together with the French book
he had begun reading on the Eugubine Tables.* Above the armchair
hung an oval portrait of Anna in a gold frame, which had been finely
executed by a famous artist. Alexey Alexandrovich glanced at it.
Her inscrutable eyes fixed him with a mocking, brazen stare as they
had on the evening of their altercation. The sight of the black lace
on her head, her black hair, and beautiful white hand with its fourth
finger covered with rings, superbly painted by the artist, also struck
Alexey Alexandrovich as unbearably brazen and defiant. After looking at the portrait for a minute, such a shudder ran through Alexey
Alexandrovich that his lips quivered and uttered the sound 'brr', and
he turned away. He sat down quickly in his armchair and opened his
book. He tried to read, but was quite unable to revive his previously
extremely lively interest in the Eugubine Tables. He was looking at

the book but his thoughts lay elsewhere. He was not thinking about his wife, but about a complication that had arisen in his government duties which just then constituted the main focus of his work. He felt he was now penetrating this complication more deeply than ever before, and had conceived in his mind a fundamental idea—he could say this without false modesty—which he believed would unravel the whole business, advance him in his career, discredit his enemies, and thus bring enormous benefit to the government. As soon as the servant laying out the tea had left the room, Alexey Alexandrovich got up and went over to his desk. Moving into the middle of it a portfolio containing current business, he took a pencil from the stand with a barely perceptible smile of self-satisfaction and immersed himself in reading the complex file relating to the present problem. The complication was as follows. Alexey Alexandrovich's distinguishing quality as a statesman, that characteristic feature peculiar to him alone, which every aspiring civil servant possesses, and which, together with his dogged ambition, prudence, honesty, and self-confidence, had made his career, consisted in his tendency to scorn red tape, reduce correspondence, engage in direct contact with real facts insofar as it was possible, and practise economy. It so happened that the famous Commission of the 2nd of June had been presented with the case about the irrigation of lands in Zaraisk province, which came under Alexey Alexandrovich's ministry, and was a glaring example of wasteful expense and needless paperwork. Alexey Alexandrovich knew this to be true. The enquiry into the irrigation of the lands in Zaraisk province had been initiated by Alexey Alexandrovich's predecessor's predecessor. And a great deal of money had indeed been spent and was still being spent on this case, completely unproductively, while the whole case was obviously leading nowhere. Alexey Alexandrovich had immediately realized this when he took up office, and wanted to get his hands on the case; but at first, when he still felt insecure, he knew it touched on too many interests and was not feasible; then later on he got caught up with other matters, and had simply forgotten about this case. Like all such cases, it carried on by itself, through inertia. (Many people were making their living out of this case, in particular one very respectable, musical family: all the daughters played stringed instruments. Alexey Alexandrovich knew this family and had given one of the elder daughters away at her wedding.) The raising of this case by a hostile ministry was dishonest, in Alexey Alexandrovich's opinion, because there were even worse cases in every ministry that no one ever brought up for well-known reasons

of professional etiquette. Now that the gauntlet was being thrown
down to him, however, he was boldly picking it up and demanding
the appointment of a special commission to investigate and inspect
the work being carried out by the commission for the irrigation of
the lands in Zaraisk province; but he was not going to let those gentlemen get away lightly. He was also demanding the appointment of
another special commission to investigate the case of the settlement of
minorities.* The case about the settlement of minorities happened to
have been brought up at the 2nd of June committee meeting, and had
been vigorously supported by Alexey Alexandrovich as one that could
brook no delay owing to the minorities' deplorable situation. This
case had served as the pretext for a dispute between several ministries
at the committee. The ministry opposed to Alexey Alexandrovich
had attempted to show that the minorities' situation was extremely
healthy, and that the proposed restructuring could be injurious to
their prosperity, and that if there was anything wrong, this was solely
due to the failure of Alexey Alexandrovich's ministry in carrying out
measures prescribed by law. Alexey Alexandrovich now intended to
demand: firstly, that a new commission be formed, which would be
charged with investigating the situation of the minorities on the spot;
secondly, that if it should turn out to be the case that the situation of
the minorities really was as it appeared from the official data which
the committee had to hand, another new scientific commission should
be appointed to investigate the reasons for the deplorable situation
of the minorities from the following points of view: (a) political, (b)
administrative, (c) economic, (d) ethnographic, (e) material, and (f)
religious; thirdly, that the hostile ministry should be asked to provide
evidence of the measures taken during the last ten years by this ministry to prevent the disadvantageous conditions in which the minorities
now found themselves; and finally, fourthly, that the ministry should
explain why, as could be seen from the evidence brought before the
committee in documents Nos. 17015 and 18038, of 5 December 1863
and 7 June 1864, it had acted in direct contravention of the spirit
of the fundamental and organic law, vol. . . ., article 18, article note
36. A flush of exhilaration suffused Alexey Alexandrovich's face as he
quickly wrote out a synopsis of these thoughts for himself. Having
covered a sheet of paper, he got up, rang, and sent a note to his chief
secretary requesting the necessary information. Getting up and walking around the room, he glanced again at the portrait, frowned, and
smiled contemptuously. After reading a little more of the book on
the Eugubine Tables, and resuscitating his interest in them, at eleven

o'clock Alexey Alexandrovich went to bed, and when he remembered
what had happened with his wife when he was lying in bed, it did not
now seem nearly so gloomy.

15

ALTHOUGH Anna had stubbornly and bitterly contradicted Vronsky
when he told her that her position was impossible and urged her to
tell her husband everything, in the depths of her soul she regarded
her position as false and dishonest, and longed with all her heart to
change it. Returning with her husband from the races, she had told
him everything in the heat of the moment; despite the agony it had
cost her, she was glad she had done so. After her husband left her, she
told herself that she was glad everything would now be clarified, and
that at least there would be no lies and deception. She felt certain her
position would now be clarified once and for all. It might be bad, this
new position, but it would be clear, and there would be nothing vague
or deceitful about it. The pain she had caused herself and her husband
by uttering those words would now be rewarded by everything being
clarified, she thought. That same evening she saw Vronsky, but she
did not tell him what had happened between her and her husband,
although for the position to be clarified he needed to have been told.

When she woke up next morning, the first thing that came into her
mind were the words she had spoken to her husband, and these words
now seemed so terrible to her that she could not understand how she
could have brought herself to say such strange, coarse things, and she
could not imagine what would happen next. But the words had been
said, and Alexey Alexandrovich had gone away without having said
anything. 'I saw Vronsky and did not tell him. Right at the point when
he was leaving, I wanted to call him back and tell him, but I changed
my mind, because it was odd that I had not told him at the outset.
Why didn't I tell him if I wanted to?' And in answer to this question
a hot flush of shame spread over her face. She realized what had held
her back; she realized that she was ashamed. Her position, which the
previous evening appeared lucid, now suddenly seemed not only not
lucid, but hopeless. She started to dread the disgrace, which she had
not even considered before. The most dreadful ideas came into her
mind at the mere thought of what her husband would do. It occurred
to her that the steward would turn up any minute to turn her out of
the house, and that her disgrace would be made public. She wondered

where she would go when she was turned out of the house, and could find no answer.

When she thought of Vronsky, she imagined that he did not love her, that he was already beginning to find her a burden, that she could not offer herself to him, and she resented him because of it. It felt to her as if the words she had spoken to her husband, which she repeated endlessly in her mind, had been said to everyone, and that everyone had heard them. She could not bring herself to meet the gaze of the people with whom she lived. She could not bring herself to call her maid, let alone go downstairs where she would see her son and the governess.

The maid, who had been listening at the door for a long time, came into the room herself. Anna looked her quizzically in the eye and blushed with fright. The maid apologized for coming in, and said she thought she had heard the bell. She brought her clothes and a note. The note was from Betsy. Betsy reminded her that Liza Merkalova and Baroness Stolz were coming over to play a game of croquet that morning with their admirers, Kaluzhsky and old Stremov. 'Do come at least to watch, as a study in behaviour. I will expect you,' she finished.

Anna read the note and heaved a deep sigh.

'There is nothing I need, nothing,' she said to Annushka, who was rearranging the bottles and brushes on the dressing-table. 'You may go. I'll dress and come down straight away. There's nothing I need, nothing.'

Annushka went out, but instead of getting dressed, Anna went on sitting there in the same position, her head and arms drooping; occasionally she would shudder all over, as if wanting to make some gesture or say something, but then she would become rigid again. She kept repeating, 'My God! My God!' But neither 'my' nor 'God' had any meaning for her. The idea of seeking help for her predicament in religion, despite never having experienced doubt in the religion in which she had been raised, was as alien to her as seeking help from Alexey Alexandrovich himself. She knew in advance that the help which religion could provide was only possible on the condition that she renounce what constituted the whole meaning of her life. Not only did she feel wretched, but she began to experience fear in the face of this new emotional state which she had never experienced before. She felt that everything was beginning to double in her soul, just as objects sometimes appear double to tired eyes. At times she did not know what it was she feared, what she wanted. Whether she feared or wanted what had happened or was going to happen, and what exactly she wanted, she did not know.

'Ah, what am I doing!' she said to herself, suddenly feeling pain in both sides of her head. When she came to her senses, she saw she was holding her hair on either side of her temples with both hands, and pulling it. She jumped up and began pacing about.

'The coffee is ready, and Mam'selle and Seryozha are waiting,' said Annushka, coming in again, and again finding Anna in the same position.

'Seryozha? What about Seryozha?' Anna asked, suddenly reviving and remembering her son's existence for the first time that morning.

'He's been naughty, I think,' answered Annushka with a smile.

'What has he done?'

'You had some peaches in the corner room; it seems he crept in and ate one.'

The reminder of her son suddenly brought Anna out of the hopeless situation she had been in. She remembered the partly genuine, although much exaggerated, role of the mother living for her child which she had taken on in recent years, and with joy became aware of having a realm in this plight in which she found herself that was independent of her position with regard to her husband or to Vronsky. This realm was her son. She could not leave her son, no matter what position she might be in. Let her husband bring disgrace on her and turn her out, let Vronsky cool towards her and resume his independent life (she again thought of him with bitterness and reproach), but she could not leave her son. Her life had a purpose. And she needed to act, and act quickly, to secure this position with her son before he was taken away from her. She needed to take her son and go away. This was the one thing she needed to do now. She had to calm down and find a way out of this harrowing situation. The thought of a practical activity connected with her son, and of going away somewhere with him, was what calmed her down.

She dressed quickly, went downstairs, and walked decisively into the drawing room, where her coffee, Seryozha, and the governess were waiting for her as usual. Seryozha, dressed all in white, was standing by the table under the mirror and, his back and head bent over, with that expression of rapt attention she recognized in him, and in which he resembled his father, and was doing something to the flowers he had brought in.

The governess had a particularly stern look. Seryozha cried out, 'Oh, Mama!' in a piercing voice as he often did, then stopped, unsure as to whether he should go and greet his mother and put down the flowers, or finish making the garland and go up to her with the flowers.

After saying good morning, the governess embarked on a long and detailed account of Seryozha's misdemeanour, but Anna did not listen to her; she was thinking about whether she would take her along with them or not. 'No, I won't take her,' she decided. 'I'll go away with my son on my own.'

'Yes, that was very bad,' said Anna, and taking her son by the shoulder, she gave him a timid rather than stern look, much to the boy's bewilderment and delight, then kissed him. 'Leave him with me,' she said to the astonished governess, and without letting go of her son's hand sat down at the table, where coffee was laid out for her.

'Mama! I . . . I . . . didn't . . .' he said, trying to work out from her expression what was in store for him for eating the peach.

'Seryozha,' she said as soon as the governess had left the room, 'that was bad, but you won't do it again, will you? . . . Do you love me?'

She could feel tears welling in her eyes. 'How can I not love him?' she said to herself, looking deep into his frightened but also delighted face. 'Will he really side with his father in order to punish me? Will he not feel sorry for me?' The tears were already running down her face, and to hide them she got up abruptly and almost ran out on to the terrace.

After the thundery showers of the last few days, the weather was now cold and clear. There was a chill in the air, despite the bright sun shining through the rain-washed leaves.

She shuddered, both from the cold and the inner horror that gripped her with renewed force in the open air.

'Go, go to Mariette,' she said to Seryozha, who had followed her out, and she began walking up and down on the straw matting of the terrace. 'Will they really not forgive me, not understand that all this could not have happened any other way?' she said to herself.

Stopping to look at the top of an aspen tree swaying in the wind, its washed leaves sparkling brightly in the cold sunshine, she realized that they would not forgive, that everyone and everything would now treat her as pitilessly as this sky and this foliage. And she again felt things beginning to double in her soul. 'I mustn't, mustn't think,' she said to herself. 'I must get ready. Where will I go? When? Who will I take with me? Yes, to Moscow on the evening train. Annushka and Seryozha, and only the most necessary things. But first I must write to them both.' She went quickly indoors, to her boudoir, sat down at the desk, and wrote to her husband:

'After what has happened, I can no longer remain in your house. I am going away, and taking my son with me. I do not know the law, and therefore do not know which parent the son should be with;

but I am taking him with me because I cannot live without him. Be generous, leave him with me.'

Up to this point she wrote quickly and naturally, but the appeal to his generosity, a quality she did not believe he possessed, and the need to conclude the letter with something poignant made her pause.

'I cannot talk about my guilt and remorse because . . .'

She paused again, unable to find any coherence in her thoughts. 'No,' she said to herself, 'I don't need any of that,' and after tearing up the letter, she wrote it out again, leaving out any mention of generosity, and sealed it.

The other letter had to be written to Vronsky. 'I have told my husband,' she wrote, and she sat a long while, unable to write anything more. It was so crude, so unfeminine. 'Anyway, what on earth can I write to him?' she said to herself. A flush of shame spread over her face again as she recalled his composure, and a feeling of annoyance with him made her tear the sheet with the phrase written on it into shreds. 'I don't need to do anything,' she said to herself, and she closed her blotting-pad, went upstairs, told the governess and the servants that she was going that night to Moscow, and immediately started packing her things.

16

PORTERS, gardeners, and servants were going in and out of every room of the country house, carrying things out. Wardrobes and chests of drawers were opened; twice they had to run over to the shop for twine; the floor was littered with newspaper. Two trunks and some bags and tied-up rugs had been taken out into the hall. The carriage and two hired cabs were standing by the porch. Anna, having forgotten her inner anxiety with all the packing she had to do, was standing in front of the dressing-table in her boudoir packing her travel bag when Annushka drew her attention to the sound of a vehicle drawing up. Anna looked out of the window and saw Alexey Alexandrovich's courier at the porch, ringing at the front door.

'Go and see what it is,' she said, and calmly prepared for anything, she sat down in the armchair, her hands folded in her lap. A servant brought a thick package addressed in Alexey Alexandrovich's hand.

'The courier has orders to bring back a reply,' he said.

'Very well,' she said, and as soon as the man left, she tore open the letter with trembling fingers. A wad of unfolded banknotes in a wrapper fell out of it. She pulled out the letter and began reading at the end. 'I have made preparations for your arrival here, I attach particular significance to my request being carried out,' she read. She read on, then went back, read it all through, and then read the whole letter once again from the beginning. When she finished, she felt cold and that a terrible calamity had befallen her, the likes of which she had never expected.

That morning she had regretted what she had said to her husband, and wished only that those words could be, as it were, unsaid. And here was this letter treating them as unspoken, and giving her what she wanted. But now this letter seemed to her more awful than anything she could possibly imagine.

'He's right, he's right!' she said. 'Of course, he's always right, he's a Christian, he's magnanimous! Yes, he is a vile, odious man! And no one except me understands that or ever will understand that; and I can't explain it. They say he's a devout, principled, honest, clever man; but they don't see what I've seen. They don't know how he has suffocated my life for eight years, suffocated everything alive in me, never once thinking about the fact that I'm a woman who is alive and who needs love. They don't know that he has insulted me at every step, and remained pleased with himself. Have I not tried, tried with all my might to find some justification for my life? Have I not endeavoured to love him, and to love my son when it was no longer possible to love my husband? But the time has come to realize that I can no longer deceive myself, that I am alive, that I am not to blame, and that God created me as a person who needs to love and to live. And now what? If he had killed me, if he had killed him, I could have endured everything, I could have forgiven everything, but no, he . . .

'How did I not guess what he was going to do? He'll do what is in keeping with his mean character. He'll remain in the right, but will plunge me, when I am already ruined, into deeper and worse ruin . . .' She recalled the words from the letter: 'You can yourself surmise what will await you and your son.' 'That's a threat to take away my son, and according to their stupid laws he probably can. But don't I know why he is saying this? He doesn't even believe in my love for my son, or else he despises my feelings (just as he has always scoffed at them), but he knows that I won't abandon my son, that I cannot abandon my son, that there can be no life for me without my son, even with the man I love, and that by abandoning my son and running away from him, I would be behaving like the most shameless, vile woman—he knows that, and he knows that I am not capable of doing that.'

'Our life must go on as before'—she recalled another sentence in the letter. 'That life was wretched even before, and lately it has been dreadful. What will it be like now? And he knows all that; he knows that I can't repent breathing, or loving; he knows that it can lead to nothing but lies and deceit; but he has to go on torturing me. I know him! I know that he exults in lies and swims about in them like a fish in water. But no, I will not give him that pleasure, I'll tear apart the web of lies in which he wants to entangle me; what will be, will be. Anything is better than lies and deceit!

'But how? My God! My God! Was there ever a woman as unhappy as I am? . . .

'No, I will break it off, I will break it off!' she cried out, jumping up and fighting back her tears. And she went over to her desk to write him another letter. But in the depths of her soul she already sensed that she did not have the strength to break anything off, nor did she have the strength to extricate herself from her old situation, however false and dishonest it might be.

She sat down at the desk, but instead of writing she folded her arms on the desk, lay her head on them, and burst into tears, her whole chest racked with sobs, like a child cries. She was crying because her dream of clarifying and defining her position was shattered for ever. She knew beforehand that everything would stay as it was before, and would actually be far worse than before. She realized that the position she enjoyed in society, which that morning had seemed of so little consequence to her, was in fact something she cherished, and that she would not have the strength to exchange it for the shameful position of a woman who has abandoned her husband and son and gone to join her lover; that however hard she tried, she could not be stronger than she actually was. She would never experience the freedom of love, but would always remain under constant threat of exposure as the guilty wife who had betrayed her husband for a shameful liaison with a stranger, an unattached man whose life she could not share. She knew that this was how it would be, and at the same time it was so awful that she could not even imagine how it would all end. And she sobbed uncontrollably, as children do when they have been punished.

The sound of the servant's footsteps forced her to rally herself, and she hid her face from him by pretending to be writing.

'The courier is asking for a reply,' the servant announced.

'A reply? Yes,' said Anna. 'Let him wait. I'll ring.'

'What can I write?' she thought. 'What can I decide on my own? What do I know? What do I want? What do I love?' She again felt things beginning to double in her soul. She was again terrifed by this feeling, and seized the first pretext for activity which presented itself, and which might distract her from thinking about herself. 'I ought to see Alexey,'—as she referred to Vronsky in her thoughts—'as only he can tell me what I should do. I'll go over to Betsy's: perhaps I shall see him there,' she said to herself, completely forgetting that when she had told him the day before that she was not going to Princess Tverskaya's, he had said in that case neither would he go. She went over to the desk and wrote to her husband: 'I have received your letter. A.', then rang and gave it to the servant.

'We are not going,' she said to Annushka who had just come in.

'We're not going at all?'

'No, don't unpack until tomorrow, and leave the carriage. I'm going over to visit the Princess.'

'Which dress should I get ready then?'

17

THE game of croquet* to which Princess Tverskaya had invited Anna was to be played by two ladies and their admirers. The two ladies were the main representatives of a select new Petersburg set called *les sept merveilles du monde*,[1] in imitation of some other imitation. These ladies belonged to a set that was certainly upper-class, but it was totally at odds with the one Anna frequented. Old Stremov, moreover, one of the influential people of Petersburg, and Liza Merkalova's admirer, was Alexey Alexandrovich's enemy in the professional sphere. For all these reasons Anna had not wanted to go, and the hints in Princess Tverskaya's note alluded to her probable refusal. But Anna was now keen to go, in the hope of seeing Vronsky.

Anna arrived at Princess Tverskaya's before the other guests.

As she was going in, Vronsky's servant, who had the combed side-whiskers of a Gentleman of the Bedchamber, was also going in. He stopped at the door, doffed his cap, and let her pass. Anna recognized him, and only now remembered that Vronsky had said the day before that he was not coming. He was probably sending a note to say that.

As she took off her coat in the hall, she heard the servant even rolling his 'r's like a Gentleman of the Bedchamber when he said: 'From Count Vronsky for the Princess,' and handed over the note.

---

[1] the seven wonders of the world.

She wanted to ask him where his master was. She wanted to go back home and send Vronsky a letter asking him to come and see her, or else go over and see him herself. But neither the first nor the second nor the third of these options was possible: she could already hear the bells announcing her arrival ahead of her, and Princess Tverskaya's servant was already standing sideways by the open door, waiting for her to pass through into the interior rooms.

'The Princess is in the garden, and will be informed straight away. Would you care to go into the garden?' said another servant in another room.

The situation of indecision and uncertainty was the same as it was at home, in fact even worse, because it was impossible to do anything about it, it was impossible to see Vronsky, and she had to stay there, in uncongenial company that was in stark contrast to her state of mind; but she was wearing a dress that she knew suited her; she was not alone, she was surrounded by all the usual grand trappings of idleness, and it was easier for her to be there than at home, as she did not have to think about what to do. Everything would happen by itself. As she met Betsy coming towards her in a white dress whose elegance amazed her, Anna smiled at her, as always. Princess Tverskaya was walking with Tushkevich and a young female relative who was spending the summer with the famous princess, to the great delight of her provincial parents.

There must have been something particular about Anna, because Betsy noticed it at once.

'I slept badly,' answered Anna, looking intently at the servant who was coming towards them and, she presumed, bringing Vronsky's note.

'I'm so glad you've come!' said Betsy. 'I'm feeling weary, and was about to have a cup of tea before they arrive. You and Masha', she said, turning to Tushkevich, 'should go and try out the croquet lawn where they've cut the edges. And you and I will have time for a heart-to-heart over tea, *we'll have a cosy chat*,[1] won't we?' she said, turning to Anna with a smile and pressing the hand in which she held her parasol.

'Yes, especially as I can't stay with you long, I have to visit old Wrede. I promised her ages ago,' said Anna, for whom lying, which was alien to her nature, had become not only simple and natural in society, but even brought her pleasure.

Why she said something she had not thought of a moment before, she could not possibly have explained. The only reason she said it was that since Vronsky would not be coming, she had to secure her

---

[1] [English in the original.]

freedom and try to see him somehow. But why she had mentioned
the old Lady-in-Waiting Wrede, to whom she owed a visit, as she did
many other people, she could not have explained, and yet, as it turned
out later, if she had been trying to come up with the most ingenious
schemes for seeing Vronsky, she could not have thought of anything
better.

'No, I won't let you go on any account,' answered Betsy, looking
intently into Anna's face. 'Really, if I were not so fond of you, I would
feel hurt. It's as if you were afraid my society might compromise you.
Please bring us tea in the small drawing room,' she said, narrowing her
eyes as she always did when speaking to a servant. She took the note
from him and read it. 'Alexey is letting us down,' she said in French;
'he writes that he cannot come,' she added in a natural, simple tone as
if it could never enter her head that Vronsky had any other significance
for Anna than as a croquet player.

Anna knew that Betsy knew everything, but whenever she heard her
talk about Vronsky in her presence, she always managed to persuade
herself for a brief moment that she knew nothing.

'Ah!' said Anna indifferently, as if this was of little interest to her, and
she continued with a smile: 'How could your company compromise
anyone?' This play of words, this concealment of a secret, held a great
fascination for Anna, as for all women. And it was not the need for
concealment, nor the reason for the concealment, but the process of
the concealment itself which enthralled her. 'I can't be more Catholic
than the pope,' she said. 'Stremov and Liza Merkalova are the cream
of the cream of society. They are also received everywhere, and *I*—she
laid great emphasis on the *I*—'have never been rigid and intolerant.
I just don't have the time.'

'No, but perhaps you don't want to meet Stremov? Let him and
Alexey Alexandrovich clash swords at their committee, it does not
concern us. But in society he's the most amiable man I know, and
a passionate croquet player. You'll see. And, in spite of his ridiculous
position as Liza's elderly suitor, you have to see how he carries it off.
He's very nice. You don't know Sappho Stolz? She's set a completely
new tone.'

While Betsy was saying all this, Anna sensed from her bright, intelligent look that she partially understood her predicament, and was
planning something. They were in the small drawing room.

'Anyway, I must write to Alexey,' and Betsy sat down at the table,
wrote a few lines, and put the note in an envelope. 'I'm writing that he
should come for lunch. I've got one lady at lunch who will be without

a man. Have a look and see if you think it's convincing. Excuse me, I must leave you for a minute. Please seal it and send it,' she said from the door, 'I need to give some instructions.'

Without a moment's thought, Anna sat down at the table with Betsy's letter, and, without reading it added at the bottom: 'I have to see you. Come to Wrede's garden. I will be there at six o'clock.' She sealed it, and Betsy came back and sent the note off in her presence.

Over tea, which was brought to them on a little tray-table in the cool, small drawing room, the two women really did have the *cosy chat* Princess Tverskaya promised before the arrival of her guests. They discussed the people who were expected, and the conversation came to alight on Liza Merkalova.

'She's very nice and I've always liked her,' said Anna.

'You ought to like her very much. She is mad about you. Yesterday she came up to me after the races and was in despair at having missed you. She says you're a real heroine out of a novel, and that if she were a man she would commit a thousand follies for your sake. Stremov tells her she does that already.'

'But tell me please, I've never been able to work it out,' said Anna, after a pause, and in a tone that clearly showed she was not putting an idle question, but was asking about something that was more important to her than it should have been. 'Tell me, please, what are her relations with Prince Kaluzhsky, the so-called Mishka? I've not met them very often. What is that all about?'

Betsy smiled with her eyes and looked intently at Anna.

'It's the new style,' she said. 'They've all adopted this style. They've thrown their caps over the windmill,* so to speak. But there are ways and ways of doing that.'

'Yes, but what exactly are her relations with Kaluzhsky?'

Betsy unexpectedly burst into a fit of merry, irrepressible laughter, which rarely happened with her.

'You're encroaching on Princess Myagkaya's territory now. That's the question of an *enfant terrible*,' and Betsy clearly tried but failed to restrain herself, and dissolved into the kind of infectious laughter peculiar to those who seldom laugh. 'You'll have to ask them,' she managed to say through tears of laughter.

'You may well laugh,' said Anna, also unable to prevent herself from laughing, 'but I have never been able to work it out. I can't understand what role the husband plays in it all.'

'The husband? Liza Merkalova's husband carries her rugs, and is always ready to do her bidding. But as to what else actually goes on, no one wants to know. You know, in polite society there are certain details of one's appearance that are not talked or even thought about. It's the same with this.'

'Will you be at the Rolandaki party?' asked Anna, to change the subject.

'I don't think so,' answered Betsy, and she began carefully filling the small, transparent cups with fragrant tea without looking at her friend. Moving a cup towards Anna, she took out a cigarette, placed it into a silver holder, and lit it.

'You see, I'm in a fortunate position,' she began, no longer laughing now as she picked up her cup. 'I understand you, and I understand Liza. Liza is one of those naive creatures, like children, who do not understand what is good and what is bad. At least she didn't understand when she was very young. And now she knows that this inability to understand suits her. Now she perhaps deliberately does not understand,' said Betsy, with a subtle smile. 'But it still suits her. You see, you can look at something tragically and turn it into a source of misery, and you can look at the very same thing in a simple and even carefree way. Maybe you have a tendency to look at things too tragically.'

'How I would like to know others as I know myself,' said Anna seriously and thoughtfully. 'Am I worse than others or better? I think I'm worse.'

'*Enfant terrible, enfant terrible!*' repeated Betsy. 'But here they are.'

18

THERE was the sound of footsteps and a man's voice, then a woman's voice and laughter, followed by the appearance of the awaited guests: Sappho Stolz and the so-called Vaska, a young man glowing with an over-abundance of vitality. It was evident that he flourished on a diet of underdone beef, truffles, and Burgundy. Vaska bowed to the two ladies and glanced at them, but only for a second. He came into the drawing room behind Sappho, followed her across the room as if he was attached to her, and kept his shining eyes fixed on her as if he wanted to eat her. Sappho Stolz was a blonde with dark eyes. She came in taking brisk little steps on her high-heeled shoes, and shook hands vigorously with the ladies, like a man.

Anna had never met this new celebrity before, and was struck by her beauty, the sheer extravagance of her outfit, and the boldness of her manners. Her own and others' soft, gold-coloured hair had been piled up on her head into such a scaffolding of coiffure that her head was equal in size to her shapely, rounded, and very exposed bosom. Her forward precipitation was such that the shape of her knees and the upper part of her legs were discernible under her dress with every step she took, and the question involuntarily arose as to where exactly at the back of that wobbling built-up mountain was the endpoint of her small and slender body, which was so naked at the top and so hidden at the back and down below.

Betsy hastened to introduce her to Anna.

'Can you imagine, we nearly ran over two soldiers,' she began telling them at once, winking, smiling, and pulling back her train, which she had tossed too far in one direction. 'I was travelling with Vaska . . . Oh yes, you don't know each other.' And she introduced the young man by his surname, blushing and laughing loudly at her mistake, that is, speaking of him as Vaska to a stranger.

Vaska bowed again to Anna, but said nothing to her. He turned to Sappho:

'You've lost the bet. We arrived first. Pay up,' he said, smiling.

Sappho chortled even more merrily.

'Not now surely,' she said.

'It doesn't matter, I'll get it later.'

'All right, all right. Oh, yes!' she said, turning suddenly to her hostess: 'I am a fine one . . . I completely forgot . . . I've brought you a guest. Here he is.'

The unexpected young guest whom Sappho had brought, and whom she had forgotten, was, however, such an important guest that, in spite of his youth, both ladies rose to greet him.

This was Sappho's new admirer. He now hung on her heels, just like Vaska.

Soon Prince Kaluzhsky arrived, and Liza Merkalova with Stremov. Liza Merkalova was a thin brunette, with a languid, oriental type of face, and exquisite eyes which everyone said were enigmatic. The character of her dark dress (Anna immediately noticed and appreciated this) corresponded perfectly with her beauty. Liza was as soft and loose as Sappho was angular and shapely.

But Liza appealed far more to Anna's taste. Betsy had said about her to Anna that she had adopted the pose of an artless child, but when Anna saw her, she felt that this was untrue. She was indeed artless and corrupt, but also an amiable and unassuming woman. It is true she had the same style as Sappho; just like Sappho, she had two admirers, one young, one old, who followed her around as if sewn on to her, devouring her with their eyes; but there was something in her which was superior to her surroundings—she had the sparkle of a diamond of the first water amongst pieces of glass. This sparkle shone out from her exquisite, truly enigmatic eyes. The weary but also passionate gaze of those eyes, ringed by dark circles, was striking for its complete sincerity. Every person looking into those eyes felt they knew her fully, and once they knew her could not help but warm to her. When she saw Anna, her whole face at once lit up in a joyous smile.

'Oh, how glad I am to see you!' she said, going up to her. 'Yesterday at the races I was just about to come over to you, but you had left. I did so want to see you yesterday in particular. Wasn't it awful?' she said, looking at Anna with eyes that seemed to lay bare her entire soul.

'Yes, I did not expect it to be so upsetting,' said Anna, blushing.

The company got up at this moment to go into the garden.

'I'm not going,' said Liza, smiling and sitting down next to Anna. 'You're not going either? Who wants to play croquet!'

'No, I like it,' said Anna.

'But how do you manage not to be bored? Just looking at you raises one's spirits. You live, but I am bored.'

'How can you be bored? Yours is the most lively set in Petersburg,' said Anna.

'Maybe the people who aren't in our set are even more bored; but we—or rather, I—don't feel lively, we're just terribly, terribly bored.'

Sappho lit a cigarette and went out into the garden with the two young men. Betsy and Stremov remained drinking tea.

'What do you mean, bored?' said Betsy. 'Sappho says they had a very lively time with you last night.'

'Ah, it was so tedious!' said Liza Merkalova. 'We all drove back to my house after the races. And it's always the same people, always the same! Endlessly the same thing. We spent the whole evening lolling on sofas. What is lively about that? No, how ever do you manage not to be bored?' she said, addressing Anna again. 'It's enough to look at you and you can see that here is a woman who might be happy or unhappy, but not bored. Tell me, how do you do it?'

'I don't do anything,' answered Anna, blushing at these persistent questions.

'Now that's the best way,' said Stremov, butting into the conversation.

Stremov was a man of about fifty, going grey, still sprightly, very unattractive, but with a distinctive, intelligent face. Liza Merkalova was his wife's niece, and he spent all his free time with her. He was Alexey Alexandrovich's enemy in the professional sphere, but as a sophisticated and intelligent man, upon meeting his enemy's wife Anna Karenina, he tried to be particularly cordial with her.

'"Don't do anything",' he repeated with a subtle smile, 'that's the best way. I've been telling you for ages,' he said, turning to Liza Merkalova, 'that in order not to be bored, you mustn't think that you will be bored. Just as you shouldn't be afraid that you won't fall asleep if you're afraid of insomnia. That's exactly what Anna Arkadyevna has told you.'

'I would be very glad if I had said that, because it's not only clever but true,' said Anna, smiling.

'No, but tell me, why it is impossible to fall asleep, and impossible not to be bored?'

'To be able to fall asleep one has to work, and one has to work in order to enjoy oneself too.'

'Why on earth should I work when no one needs me to work? And I don't know how to try and pretend, nor do I want to.'

'You're incorrigible,' said Stremov, not looking at her, and he turned back to Anna.

As he rarely met Anna, he could say nothing but banalities to her, but he uttered these banalities, about when she was returning to Petersburg and about how fond Countess Lydia Ivanovna was of her, with an expression which showed his wholehearted desire to please her and show his respect and even more than that.

Tushkevich came in to announce that everyone was waiting for the croquet players.

'No, please don't leave,' begged Liza Merkalova when she heard that Anna was leaving. Stremov echoed her.

'It's too great a contrast,' he said, 'after this company, to go to the old lady Wrede. And besides, you will only give her an opportunity in indulge in malicious gossip, whereas here you will arouse other feelings, the best kind, and the opposite of malicious gossip,' he said to her.

Anna was lost for a moment in a state of indecision. This clever man's flattering words, the naive, childlike affection shown her by Liza Merkalova, and this familiar social setting was all so easy, and what awaited her was so difficult, that she spent a minute hesitating as to whether she should stay and put off the painful moment of explanation. But remembering what awaited her alone at home if she did not make any decision, and remembering that gesture she had made of clutching her hair in both hands, which was frightening for her to recollect, she said goodbye, and left.

19

DESPITE Vronsky's apparently irresponsible social life, he was a man who hated disorder. When he was younger, while still in the Corps, he had experienced the humiliation of a refusal when he asked for a loan after getting into difficulties, and since then he had never put himself in the same position again.

So that he could always keep his affairs in order, depending on the circumstances, but more or less frequently, about five times a year, he would shut himself away and bring all his affairs into a state of clarity. He called it doing the reckoning, or *faire la lessive*.[1]

After waking late on the day after the races, Vronsky put on his tunic without shaving or taking a bath, spread out on the table all his money, bills, and letters, and set to work. Petritsky, when he awoke and saw his comrade sitting at the table, knowing he was bad-tempered on such occasions, dressed quietly and went out without disturbing him.

Every person who knows the full complexity of the circumstances surrounding him down to the last detail will be bound to presume that the complexity of those circumstances and the difficulty of sorting them out happen to be unique to him, and it will not occur to him that others might be surrounded by a similar complexity in their own personal circumstances. So it seemed to Vronsky. And it was not without inner pride and good reason that he reckoned any other man finding himself in such difficult circumstances would long ago have got into difficulties and been forced to act badly. But Vronsky felt that it was precisely now that he had to take stock and clarify his position in order to avoid getting into difficulties.

The first thing Vronsky tackled, since it was the easiest, was his financial affairs. After writing out on a sheet of notepaper in his small handwriting everything he owed, he totted it all up and found that he owed seventeen thousand, plus a few hundred roubles which he discarded for the sake of clarity. After counting up his money and examining his bank book, he found that he had one thousand eight hundred roubles left, with no prospect of further funds before the New Year. As he went over his list of debts, Vronsky copied it out, dividing it into three categories. To the first category belonged debts he needed to pay straight away, or for which he at least needed to have the money ready so he could pay on demand without a moment's delay. Such debts amounted to about four thousand: fifteen hundred for the

---

[1] do the laundry.

horse, and two thousand five hundred as surety for his young comrade Venevsky, who had lost that sum to a card-sharper in Vronsky's presence. Vronsky had wanted to hand over the money there and then (he had it on him), but Venevsky and Yashvin had insisted they should be the ones to pay and not Vronsky, who had not played. That was all very well, but Vronsky knew that in this sordid business, even though his only involvement was to have provided a verbal guarantee for Venevsky, it was vital for him to have those two and a half thousand to throw at the swindler and be shot of him. So he needed to have four thousand roubles for this first and most important category. In the second category, which amounted to eight thousand roubles, were less important debts. For the most part these were debts to the racing stables, the oats- and hay-supplier, the Englishman, the saddler, and so on. Of these debts he also needed to pay out some two thousand, in order to put his mind at ease. The last category of debts—to shops, hotels, and the tailor—were ones he did not need to bother about. So he needed at least six thousand, and he only had eighteen hundred roubles for current expenses. For a man with an income of one hundred thousand roubles, which everyone reckoned to be the extent of Vronsky's fortune, one would not have thought that such debts could present any difficulties; but the fact was he had nowhere near one hundred thousand. His father's enormous fortune, which alone brought in an income of up to two hundred thousand a year, was left undivided between the brothers. When his elder brother, who was mired in debt, married Princess Varya Chirkova, the daughter of a Decembrist* with no fortune whatsoever, Alexey had ceded to his elder brother almost the whole income from his father's estate, reserving for himself only twenty-five thousand a year. Alexey had told his brother back then that this sum would be sufficient until he married, which would probably never happen. And his brother, commander of one of the most expensive regiments and newly married, was not in a position to turn this gift down. His mother, who had her own fortune, gave him every year another twenty thousand in addition to the twenty-five thousand he had reserved for himself, and Alexey had spent it all. After arguing with him about his affair and his departure from Moscow, his mother had recently stopped sending him money. And as a result of that, having developed a habit of living on forty-five thousand, but only having received twenty-five thousand that year, Vronsky now found himself in difficulties. He could not ask his mother for money to get out of these difficulties. What had particularly annoyed him in her last letter, which he had received the day before, were the hints it contained that she was ready to help him succeed in society and in the army, but not to lead a life which was scandalizing all of polite society. His mother's desire to buy him off offended him to the very depths of his being and further increased his cold feelings towards her. But he could not go back on the generous pledge he had made, even though he felt now, dimly foreseeing certain eventualities of his relationship with Karenina, that this generous pledge had been made thoughtlessly, and that he might indeed need all of that one-hundred-thousand-rouble income while still unmarried. But it was impossible to go back on his word. He had only to remember his brother's wife, and remember how dear, sweet Varya reminded him at every opportunity how conscious she was of his generosity and appreciated it, to realize the impossibility of reneging on his gift. It was as inconceivable as striking a woman, stealing, or lying. There was one thing he could and should do, and Vronsky opted for it without a moment's hesitation: he would borrow money from a moneylender, ten thousand roubles, which would not present any problem, generally cut down on his expenses, and sell his racehorses. Having made this decision, he wrote a note straight away to Rolandaki, who had made him several offers to buy his horses. Then he sent for the Englishman and the moneylender, and distributed what money he had amongst the various accounts. After finishing this business, he wrote a cold and brusque reply to his mother. Then he took three notes from Anna out of his wallet, reread them, burned them, and remembering his conversation with her the previous day, became lost in thought.

20

VRONSKY'S life was particularly fortunate in that he had a code of rules which unequivocally defined everything that should and should not be done. This code of rules encompassed a very small set of conditions, but the rules were unequivocal, and since Vronsky never ventured beyond these conditions, he never had a moment's hesitation about what he ought to do. These rules determined unequivocally that one must pay a card-sharper but need not pay a tailor; that one must not lie to men, but to women one may; that one must never deceive anyone, but a husband one may; that an insult can never be pardoned, but one may insult others, and so on. These rules may all have been senseless and bad, but they were unequivocal, and by adhering to them Vronsky felt that he was in control and could hold his head up high.

It was only very recently with respect to his relationship with Anna that Vronsky had begun to feel that his code of rules did not quite define all conditions, and that the future presented difficulties and areas of doubt through which Vronsky could no longer find a guiding thread.

His present attitude to Anna and to her husband was straightforward and clear to him. It was clearly and precisely defined in the code of rules by which he was guided.

She was a respectable woman who had given him her love, and he loved her, and therefore she was a woman worthy of as much or even more respect than a lawful wife. He would have let his hand be cut off before allowing himself to insult her with a word or a hint, let alone fail to show her the respect a woman should be able to count on.

His attitude to society was also clear. Everyone might know or have suspicions, but no one must dare speak of them. Otherwise he was prepared to force anyone who spoke to be silent and show respect for the non-existent honour of the woman he loved.

His attitude to her husband was the clearest of all. From the moment that Anna had fallen in love with Vronsky, he considered that only he had an inalienable right to her. Her husband was merely a superfluous person who was in the way. He was without doubt in a pitiable position, but what could be done? The one thing the husband had a right to do was to demand satisfaction with a weapon in his hand, and Vronsky had been ready for that from the outset.

But new, intimate relations had lately surfaced between them which frightened Vronsky with their lack of definition. Only yesterday she had told him she was pregnant. And he felt that this news, and what she expected of him, called for something that was not fully defined in the code of rules that governed his life. He had been in fact caught off-guard, and when she first told him about her situation, his heart prompted him to demand she leave her husband. He had said that, but thinking things over now, he saw clearly that it would be better to avoid that, although while he was saying this to himself he was also afraid, wondering if it was wrong.

'If I have told her to leave her husband, that means uniting her life with mine. Am I ready for that? How can I take her away now, when I don't have any money? Supposing I could arrange that . . . But how can I take her away while I'm in the army? If that is what I have said, I have to be ready for it, that is, find the money and resign my commission.'

And he stopped to think. The question of whether or not to resign led him to another secret matter, which was practically the main interest of his whole life, although concealed, and known only to himself.

Ambition was the old dream of his childhood and youth, a dream he did not admit even to himself, but a dream so powerful that it was doing battle with his love even now. His first steps in society and in the service had been successful, but two years ago he had committed a gross blunder. Anxious to show his independence and advance himself, he had turned down a post offered to him, hoping this refusal would raise his stock; but it turned out that he had been too bold and was passed over; and having of necessity carved out a position for himself as an independent man, he lived up to it, comporting himself with a great deal of shrewdness and intelligence, as if he was not angry with anyone, did not feel offended by anyone, and only wanted to be left in peace because he was enjoying himself. In reality, however, he had already stopped enjoying himself when he went to Moscow the year before. He felt that this stance of an independent man who could do anything but wanted nothing was already beginning to pall, and that many people were beginning to think he could not do anything but be an honest, good-natured fellow anyway. His affair with Karenina, which had caused such a stir, attracting everyone's attention and giving him a new lustre, had suppressed the worm of ambition for a while, but a week ago the worm had revived with new vigour. His childhood friend Serpukhovskoy, from the same set, the same wealthy background, and his comrade in the Page Corps, who had graduated with him and been his rival in class, in gymnastics, in pranks and ambitious dreams, had recently come back from Central Asia,* where he had received two promotions and a decoration rarely bestowed upon generals that young.

As soon as he arrived in Petersburg, people began to speak of him as a newly rising star of the first magnitude. The same age as Vronsky and his classmate, he was a general, and expecting an appointment which might influence the course of state affairs, while Vronsky, although he was independent and brilliant and loved by an enchanting woman, was just a cavalry captain in a regiment where he was allowed to be as independent as he liked. 'Of course I don't envy Serpukhovskoy, nor could I; but his advancement shows me that one has only to bide one's time, and the career of a man like me can be made very rapidly. Three years ago he was in the same position I'm in. If I retire, I'll burn my boats. I lose nothing by staying in the army. She said herself she did not wish to change her situation. And with her love I cannot feel envious of Serpukhovskoy.' And slowly twirling his moustache, he got up from his desk and walked around the room. His eyes shone particularly brightly, and he felt that lucid, calm, and happy frame of mind which always descended on him after he sorted out his affairs. Everything was immaculate and clear, like after his previous reckonings. He shaved, took a cold bath, dressed, and went out.

21

'I've come to get you. Your laundry took a long time today,' said Petritsky. 'Well, is it done?'

'It is,' answered Vronsky, smiling with just his eyes, and twirling the tips of his moustaches cautiously, as though too bold or rapid a movement might destroy the order he had brought to his affairs.

'You always look as if you're just out of the bath-house when you're done,' said Petritsky. 'I've come from Gritska' (as they called the colonel in their regiment), 'you're expected.'

Vronsky looked at his comrade without replying, his mind elsewhere.

'So that's where the music is coming from?' he said, listening to the familiar sounds reaching him of a brass band playing polkas and waltzes. 'What are they celebrating?'

'Serpukhovskoy's arrived.'

'Ah!' said Vronsky. 'I didn't even know.'

The smile in his eyes shone even more brightly.

Having made up his mind that he was happy in his love, and had sacrificed his ambition to it, or at least taken on that role, Vronsky could no longer feel either envious of Serpukhovskoy or disappointed with him for not coming to see him first when he arrived at the regiment. Serpukhovskoy was a good friend, and he was glad he had come.

'Well, I'm very glad.'

Demin, the colonel, had taken a large country house. The whole party was on the spacious lower balcony. In the courtyard, what first caught Vronsky's eye were the singers in tunics standing near a barrel of vodka, and the robust, jovial figure of the colonel surrounded by officers; having come out on to the top step of the balcony, he was shouting loudly over the music of an Offenbach quadrille as he gave orders and gesticulated to some soldiers standing to one side. A group of soldiers, a sergeant-major, and several non-commissioned officers came up to the balcony at the same time as Vronsky. After returning to the table, the colonel came back out on to the steps with a glass, and proposed a toast: 'To the health of our former comrade and gallant general, Prince Serpukhovskoy. Hurrah!'

Smiling, with a glass in his hand, Serpukhovskoy also came out after the colonel.

'You still seem to be getting younger, Bondarenko,' he said to the rather dashing, red-cheeked sergeant-major standing right in front of him, who was doing his second term of service.

Vronsky had not seen Serpukhovskoy for three years. He looked more grown-up, now that he had let his whiskers grow, but was still just as trim, and striking more for the delicacy and nobility of his face and bearing than for his good looks. One change Vronsky noticed in him was that constant, tranquil glow which establishes itself on the faces of people who have achieved success, and know their success has been acknowledged by everyone. Vronsky was familiar with this glow, and immediately noticed it in Serpukhovskoy.

As Serpukhovskoy came down the steps, he saw Vronsky. A smile of joy lit up Serpukhovskoy's face. He threw his head up and raised his glass in greeting to Vronsky, showing with this gesture that he first had to go over to the sergeant-major, who had drawn himself up and was already puckering his lips for a kiss.

'Ah, here he is!' exclaimed the colonel. 'And Yashvin told me you were in one of your dark moods.'

Serpukhovskoy kissed the dashing sergeant-major on his moist, fresh lips, and, wiping his mouth with his handkerchief, went over to Vronsky.

'I am so glad to see you!' he said, shaking his hand and drawing him aside.

'Look after him!' the colonel shouted to Yashvin, pointing to Vronsky, before going down to join the soldiers.

'Why weren't you at the races yesterday? I thought I would see you there,' said Vronsky, looking Serpukhovskoy over.

'I did come, but late. I'm sorry,' he added, and he turned to his adjutant: 'Please have this distributed amongst the men on my behalf.'

And he hurriedly took a three-hundred-rouble note from his wallet and blushed.

'Vronsky! Do you want anything to eat or drink?' asked Yashvin. 'Hey, bring the Count something to eat! Here, drink this.'

The carousing at the colonel's went on for a long time.

They drank a great deal. They swung and threw Serpukhovskoy up in the air. Then they swung the colonel. Then the colonel himself danced with Petritsky in front of the singers. Then the colonel,

by now somewhat worse for wear, sat down on a bench in the courtyard and began offering Yashvin proof of Russia's superiority over
Prussia, especially in the cavalry charge, and the carousing subsided
for a moment. Serpukhovskoy went into the house to wash his hands
in the dressing room, and found Vronsky there; Vronsky was dousing
himself with water. Having taken off his tunic, he had put his hairy red
neck under the tap in the basin, and was rubbing it, and his head, with
his hands. When he had finished washing, Vronsky sat down next to
Serpukhovskoy. They both sat there on a little couch, and a conversation began between them that was of interest to them both.

'I've found out all about you from my wife,' said Serpukhovskoy.
'I'm glad you've been seeing her often.'

'She's friendly with Varya, and they're the only Petersburg women
I like seeing,' answered Vronsky, smiling. He was smiling because he
foresaw which subject the conversation would move on to, and was
pleased about this.

'The only ones?' Serpukhovskoy queried, smiling.

'Yes, and I've been finding out about you, but not only from your
wife,' said Vronsky, forbidding this insinuation with the stern expression on his face. 'I was delighted to hear of your success, but not at all
surprised. I was expecting even more.'

Serpukhovskoy smiled. He was clearly pleased with this opinion of
himself, and did not find it necessary to hide it.

'I on the contrary expected less, to be honest. But I'm pleased, very
pleased. I'm ambitious, it's my weakness, and I own up to it.'

'Perhaps you would not have confessed to it if you hadn't been successful,' said Vronsky.

'I don't think so,' said Serpukhovskoy, smiling again. 'I wouldn't say
life is not worth living without it, but it would be boring. Obviously
I may be mistaken, but I think I have a certain ability for the sphere
of activity I have chosen, and that whatever power I am given will be
better in my hands than in the hands of many other people I know,' said
Serpukhovskoy, with a radiant awareness of his success. 'And for that
reason, the closer I get to it, the more pleased I am.'

'That may be so for you, but not for everyone. I thought the same,
but as life goes on, I've found it's not worth living just for that.'

'Now we are getting to the heart of the matter!' said Serpukhovskoy,
laughing. 'I was going to say that I'd heard about you, about your
refusal . . . I approved, of course. But there is a right way to do everything. And while I think what you did was good, you didn't go about it
in the best way.'

'What's done is done, and you know I never forswear what I've done. And besides, I'm doing very well.'

'Very well for the time being. But you won't be satisfied in the long term. I wouldn't say this to your brother. He's a dear child, just like our host here. There he goes!' he added, hearing a shout of 'Hurrah!'— 'and he's happy, but that won't satisfy you.'

'I'm not saying it will.'

'Yes, but that's not all. Men like you are needed.'

'By whom?'

'By whom? By society. Russia needs men, she needs a party, otherwise everything goes to the dogs, and will continue to do so.'

'What do you mean? Bertenev's party against Russian communists?'*

'No,' said Serpukhovskoy, frowning with annoyance at being suspected of something so silly. '*Tout ça est une blague.*[1] It always has been and always will be. There are no communists. But scheming men always have to invent a harmful, dangerous party. It's an old trick. No, what's needed is a party of authority made up of independent men like you and me.'

'But why?' Vronsky named a few people who had authority. 'Why aren't they independent men?'

'For the simple reason that they do not have or were not born with independent means, they don't have a name, and weren't born close to the sun like we were. They can be bought with money or sweet-talking. And they have to find a cause in order to maintain their position. So they bring forward some idea, some cause they themselves don't believe in, which does harm; and this cause is just a means to have an official residence and a certain salary. *Cela n'est pas plus fin que ça,*[2] when you get to see their cards. Maybe I'm inferior to them, and more stupid than they are, although I don't see why I should be inferior to them. But you and I definitely have one important advantage in that we are more difficult to buy. And such men are needed more than ever.'

Vronsky listened attentively, but it was not so much the content of what he was saying that interested him so much as Serpukhovsky's attitude to it, having already thought about challenging the authorities, and already having his own sympathies and antipathies in those quarters, while his own interest in the army was limited to his squadron. Vronsky also realized how powerful Serpukhovskoy could be, with his undoubted ability to think through and understand things, together

---

[1] 'All that's humbug.'   [2] 'That's all there is in it'.

with his intellect and eloquence, so rarely encountered in the milieu he inhabited. And ashamed though he was, he was envious.

'All the same, I lack the one key thing for it,' he answered; 'I lack the desire for power. I did have it, but it's gone.'

'Excuse me, that's not true,' said Serpukhovskoy, smiling.

'No, it is true, it is! . . . now,' Vronsky added, in order to be honest.

'Yes, it's true *now*, this is another matter; but this *now* won't last for ever.'

'Perhaps,' answered Vronsky.

'You say *perhaps*,' Serpukhovskoy went on, as though guessing his thoughts, 'but I'm telling you *definitely*. And that's why I wanted to see you. You acted as you should have done. I understand that, but you mustn't persevere with it. I only ask you to give me *carte blanche*. I'm not patronizing you . . . Although why shouldn't I patronize you? You've patronized me often enough! I hope our friendship is above that. Yes,' he said, smiling at him tenderly, like a woman. 'Give me *carte blanche*, leave the regiment, and I'll draw you in imperceptibly.'

'But you must understand that I don't want anything,' said Vronsky, 'except for everything to stay as it is.'

Serpukhovskoy got up and stood facing him.

'You say everything should stay as it is. I understand what that means. But listen: we're the same age; maybe you've known a greater number of women than I have.' Serpukhovskoy's smile and gestures told Vronsky that he need have no fear, and that he would be gentle and careful when he got to the painful area. 'But I'm married, and believe me, getting to know only your wife (as someone wrote), whom you love, you get to know all women much better than if you knew thousands of them.'

'We're just coming!' Vronsky shouted to an officer who had put his head round the door and called them to go and join the colonel.

Vronsky now wanted to hear the rest of what Serpukhovskoy had to say to him.

'And here's my opinion. Women are the chief stumbling-block in a man's career. It's hard to love a woman and achieve something. There's only one comfortable way of doing that and loving without any stumbling-blocks, and that's marriage. I'm wondering how to put my thoughts into words,' said Serpukhovskoy, who liked similes. 'Wait, wait! Yes, it's like this: you can only carry a *fardeau*[1] and do something with your hands when the *fardeau* is strapped to your back—that's

[1] 'burden'.

what marriage is like. And I felt that when I got married. My hands were suddenly free. But if you drag that *fardeau* about with you without being married, your hands will be so full you won't be able to do anything. Look at Mazankov and Krupov. They've ruined their careers for the sake of women.'

'But what women!' said Vronsky, recalling the Frenchwoman and the actress with whom the two men were involved.

'So much the worse—the more established the woman's position in society, the worse it is. In that case you are not only lugging the *fardeau* around in your arms but snatching it away from someone else.'

'You have never loved,' Vronsky said softly, looking straight ahead and thinking of Anna.

'Perhaps. But you remember what I've told you. And another thing, women are always more materialistic than men. We make something immense out of love, but they are always *terre-à-terre*.'[1]

'We're coming!' he said to a servant who had come in. But the footman had not come to call them again, as he supposed. The servant brought Vronsky a note.

'A servant brought this from Princess Tverskaya.'

Vronsky unsealed the letter and flushed.

'My head has started to ache, I'm going to go home,' he said to Serpukhovskoy.

'Well, goodbye then. Do you give me *carte blanche*?'

'We'll talk about it later. I'll look you up in Petersburg.'

22

IT was already after five, and in order to arrive on time and also not use his own horses, which everyone knew, Vronsky got into Yashvin's hired carriage and told the coachman to drive as fast as possible. The old four-seated hired carriage was roomy. He sat in the corner, stretched out his legs on the front seat, and sank into thought.

A vague sense of the clarity into which his affairs had been brought, a vague recollection of Serpukhovskoy's friendship and flattery in considering him to be a man who was needed, and, above all, excitement about the assignation—everything merged into a general impression of the joyous feeling of being alive. This feeling was so strong that he could not help smiling. He put his feet down, placed one leg over the

---

[1] 'down to earth'.

knee of the other, took it in his hand, felt the firm calf of the leg which had been hurt when he had fallen the day before, then threw himself back and drew several deep breaths into his chest.

'Very, very good!' he said to himself. He had often experienced a joyous sense of his body before, but he had never loved himself, his body, as he did now. He enjoyed feeling that slight ache in his strong leg, and he enjoyed the sensation of the muscles moving in his chest as he breathed. The same clear, cold August day which had made Anna feel so hopeless seemed invigorating and exhilarating to him, and refreshed his face and neck, which were glowing from the dousing he had given them. The scent of the brilliantine from his moustache seemed particularly pleasant in this fresh air. Everything he saw through the carriage window, everything in that cold, pure air, in the pale light of the sunset, was as fresh and as bright and as vigorous as himself: the rooftops of houses shining in the rays of the setting sun, the sharp outlines of fences and corners of buildings, the shapes of the occasional pedestrians and carriages, the motionless greenery of the trees and the grass and the fields with their regular furrows of potatoes, and the slanting shadows falling from the houses, from the trees, from the bushes and even the potato furrows. Everything was beautiful, like a pretty landscape that has just been finished and coated with varnish.

'Come on, get a move on!' he said to the driver after putting his head out of the window and, taking a three-rouble note out of his pocket, he handed it to the coachman when he looked round. The driver's hand fumbled with something next to the lamp, the whip could be heard cracking, and the carriage bowled rapidly along the smooth highway.

'I don't want anything, anything at all but this happiness,' he thought as he gazed at the ivory knob of the bell in the space between the windows and conjured up in his mind a picture of Anna as she was the last time he saw her. 'And the more time goes on, the more I love her. Here's the garden of Wrede's state dacha. Where can she be? Where? How? Why did she arrange for us to meet here and write in that letter from Betsy?' he started wondering only now; but there was no longer any time to think. He ordered the cab to stop before they reached the drive, opened the door, jumped out of the carriage while it was still moving, and set off down the drive leading to the house. There was no one in the drive, but when he looked round to the right he caught sight of her. Her face was hidden by a veil, but with a joyous gaze he took in the particular way she walked, peculiar to her alone, the slope of her shoulders and the poise of her head, and immediately it was as if an electric current ran through his body. The surge of energy brought a new awareness of himself, from the supple movements of his legs to the movements of his lungs as he breathed, and there was something tickling his lips.

When she came up to him, she pressed his hand firmly.

'You're not angry that I told you to come? I absolutely had to see you,' she said; and the serious and stern way her lips were set, which he could see under the veil, immediately changed the state of his emotions.

'Me? Angry? But how did you get here, where are you going?'

'Never mind,' she said, laying her hand on his, 'let's go, I must talk to you.'

He realized something had happened, and that the meeting would not be a happy one. In her presence he had no will of his own: without knowing the reason for her anxiety, he could already feel the same anxiety automatically transferring itself to him.

'What is it? What?' he asked her, squeezing her arm with his elbow, and trying to read her thoughts from her face.

She walked on a few steps in silence as she plucked up courage, then suddenly stopped.

'I did not tell you yesterday,' she began, breathing quickly and heavily, 'that when I was coming home with Alexey Alexandrovich, I told him everything . . . I told him I could not be his wife, that . . . And I told him everything.'

He listened to her, unconsciously leaning over with his whole body, as if wanting to ease the difficulty of her position by doing this. But as soon as she had said that, he suddenly straightened up, and his face took on a proud and stern expression.

'Yes, yes, this is better, a thousand times better! I realize how hard it was,' he said.

But she was not listening to what he was saying, she was reading his thoughts from the expression on his face. She could not know that the expression on his face related to the first thought that had occurred to Vronsky—the inevitability of a duel. The idea of a duel had never even entered her head, and therefore she interpreted this fleeting expression of sternness in a different way.

When she received her husband's letter, she already knew in the depths of her soul that everything would stay the same, that she would not have the strength to spurn her position, abandon her son, and join her lover. The morning spent at Princess Tverskaya's had provided her with even more confirmation of that. But this meeting was still exceptionally important for her. She hoped this meeting would change this situation and save her. If, on hearing this news, he were to say to her decisively, passionately, and without a moment's hesitation: 'Throw up everything and run away with me!' she would abandon her son and go away with him. But this news did not have the effect on him she was expecting: he only seemed to be offended by something.

'It was not hard at all for me. It happened by itself,' she said irritably; 'and here . . .' she took her husband's letter from her glove.

'I understand, I understand,' he interrupted her, taking the letter but not reading it and trying to calm her. 'The one thing I wanted, the one thing I asked, was to put an end to this situation, so I can devote my life to your happiness.'

'Why are you telling me this?' she said. 'Can I possibly doubt it? If I had doubts . . .'

'Who's that coming?' said Vronsky suddenly, indicating two ladies walking towards them. 'Maybe they know us,' and he hurriedly headed for a side path, drawing her with him.

'Oh, I don't care!' she said. Her lips started to tremble. And he felt her eyes were looking at him with a strange malevolence from behind the veil. 'As I was saying, that's not the point, I can't doubt that, but look what he has written to me. Read it.' She stopped again.

Just as in the first moment when he learned she had broken with her husband, as he read the letter Vronsky once again could not help surrendering to the natural reaction provoked by his stance towards the insulted husband. Now that he was holding his letter in his hands, he could not help imagining the challenge he would probably find at home that day or the following one, and also the duel itself, when he would stand waiting for the insulted husband to shoot after firing into the air, with the same cold and proud expression that his face bore now. And immediately through his mind flashed the thought of what Serpukhovskoy had just said to him, and which he himself had been thinking that morning—that it was better not to tie himself down—and he knew he could not convey this thought to her.

After reading the letter, he raised his eyes to her, and there was no firmness in his look. She immediately realized that he had already thought about this earlier on his own. She knew that whatever he might tell her, he would not tell her everything he was thinking. And she realized that her last hope had been betrayed. It was not what she was expecting.

'You see the sort of man he is,' she said in a shaking voice, 'he . . .'

'Forgive me, but I am glad about this,' Vronsky interrupted. 'Hear me out, I beg you,' he added, imploring her with his eyes to give him the time to explain himself. 'I am glad, because it is impossible, quite impossible for things to remain the same, as he proposes.'

'Why is it impossible?' Anna said, fighting back tears, and clearly no longer attaching any significance to what he might say. She felt that her fate was sealed.

Vronsky meant to say that after the duel, which he regarded as inevitable, things could not go on as before, but he said something else.

'It can't go on. I hope you will leave him now. I hope'—he became embarrassed and blushed—'that you will allow me to arrange our life and think it through. Tomorrow . . .' he began.

She would not let him finish.

'What about my son?' she exclaimed. 'You see what he writes! I would have to leave him, and I can't and don't want to do that.'

'But for heaven's sake, which is better? Leave your son, or continue with this humiliating situation?'

'Humiliating situation for whom?'

'For everyone, and most of all for you.'

'You say humiliating . . . don't say that. Those words have no meaning for me,' she said in a trembling voice. She did not want him now to say something that was not true. She had nothing left but his love, and she wanted to love him. 'You must understand that from the day I fell in love with you everything changed for me. The one single thing I have is your love. If I have it, I feel so exalted, so secure, that nothing can be humiliating for me. I am proud of my position, because . . . I am proud of . . . proud . . .' She could not manage to say what she was proud of. Tears of shame and despair choked her voice. She stopped and burst out sobbing.

He also felt something rising in his throat and tickling his nose, and for the first time in his life he felt he was on the verge of tears. He could not have said exactly what it was that had so touched him; he felt sorry for her, and he felt he could not help her, and yet he knew that he was the cause of her misfortune, that he had done something bad.

'Is a divorce not possible?' he said feebly. She shook her head without answering. 'Could you not take your son, and still leave him?'

'Yes; but it all depends on him. Now I must go to him,' she said drily. Her presentiment that everything would stay the same had not deceived her.

'On Tuesday I shall be in Petersburg, and everything will be decided.'

'Yes,' she said. 'But let us not talk about it any more.'

Anna's carriage, which she had sent away and ordered to come to the railings of Wrede's garden, had just drawn up. Anna said goodbye to him, and drove home.

23

ON Monday there was the usual meeting of the 2nd of June Commission. Alexey Alexandrovich walked into the meeting room, greeted the members and the chairman as usual, and sat down in his place, putting his hand on the papers lying ready before him. Among these papers lay the references he needed and a rough outline of the statement he intended to make. He did not actually need the references. He remembered everything, and did not think it necessary to go over in his mind what he was going to say. He knew that when the time came, and he saw the face of his opponent trying vainly to assume an expression of indifference, his speech would flow more naturally than if he prepared it now. He felt that the contents of his speech were so momentous that each word would carry weight. Meanwhile, as he listened to the usual report, his face bore the most innocent and innocuous look. No one thought, looking at his white hands with their swollen veins, his long fingers so delicately touching both edges of the sheet of white paper lying before him, and his head with its weary expression inclined to one side, that words were about to pour from his lips which would create a frightful furore, cause the members to shout as they interrupted each other, and the chairman to call for order. When the report was finished, Alexey Alexandrovich announced in his quiet, reedy voice that he had certain observations of his own to communicate regarding the settlement of the ethnic minorities. Attention turned to him. Alexey Alexandrovich cleared his throat, and without looking at his opponent, but selecting, as he always did when delivering his speeches, the person directly in front of him—a timid little old man, who never expressed any opinion at the Commission—he began to expound his views. When he got to the discussion of fundamental and organic law, his opponent jumped up and began to raise objections. Stremov, who was also a member of the Commission, and also very thin-skinned when it came to this issue, began to justify himself, and the meeting became generally very stormy; but Alexey Alexandrovich emerged victorious, and his proposal was accepted; three new commissions were appointed, and in a certain Petersburg set the following day the talk was of nothing but this meeting. Alexey Alexandrovich's success was even greater than he had expected.

When he woke the next morning, on the Tuesday, Alexey Alexandrovich looked back with pleasure to his victory of the previous day, and could not help smiling, although he tried to appear indifferent when his chief secretary, wishing to flatter him, told him about the rumours that had reached him about what had happened at the Commission.

While he was busy with his chief secretary, Alexey Alexandrovich completely forgot that it was Tuesday, the day he had set for Anna Arkadyevna's return, and he was surprised and unpleasantly taken aback when a servant came to inform him of her arrival.

Anna had arrived in Petersburg early in the morning; the carriage had been sent for her following her telegram, so Alexey Alexandrovich might have known about her arrival. But he did not come and greet her when she arrived. She was told that he was still in his study, and was busy with his chief secretary. She sent word to her husband that she had arrived, went to her boudoir, and started sorting out her things, expecting he would come to her. But an hour went by and he had not come. She went into the dining room under the pretext of giving some instructions, and deliberately spoke loudly, expecting him to come in; but he did not appear, although she heard him going to the doors of his study to usher out his chief secretary. She knew that he would soon leave for work, as usual, and she wanted to see him before that, so their relations might be defined.

She walked through the ballroom then proceeded with determination to go and find him. When she entered his study he was sitting in his uniform, obviously ready to leave, at the small desk on which he had rested his elbows, staring forlornly in front of him. She saw him before he saw her, and realized he was thinking about her.

When he saw her he made to get up, changed his mind, and went bright red in the face, which Anna had never seen before, then he got up quickly and came towards her, looking not into her eyes but higher up, at her forehead and hair. He came up to her, took her hand, and asked her to sit down.

'I am very glad you have come,' he said, sitting down next to her and obviously wanting to say something, but faltering. He made several attempts to start speaking, but kept stopping. Despite teaching herself to despise and blame him while preparing for this meeting, she did not know what to say to him, and she felt sorry for him. And so the silence lasted for some time. 'Is Seryozha well?' he said, and without waiting for an answer added: 'I won't be dining at home today, and I have to go now.'

'I wanted to go to Moscow,' she said.

'No, you did very well to come, very well,' he said, and fell silent again.

Seeing that he was incapable of beginning the conversation, she began it herself.

'Alexey Alexandrovich,' she said, looking at him and not lowering her eyes beneath his gaze, which was fixed on her hair, 'I'm a guilty woman, I'm a bad woman, but I am the same as I was, as I told you then, and I have come to tell you that I can't change anything.'

'I have not asked you about that,' he said suddenly, looking at her unflinchingly and with hatred straight in the eye; 'I had assumed that.' Under the impact of anger, he had clearly regained complete possession of all his faculties. 'But as I said then and wrote to you,' he said in his harsh, shrill voice, 'I will say once again, that I am not obliged to know this. I ignore it. Not all wives are as kind as you in wanting to impart such *agreeable* news to their husbands.' He laid special emphasis on the word 'agreeable'. 'I will ignore it as long as society knows nothing of it, and my name is not dishonoured. And so I will simply warn you that our relations must be the same as they have always been, and that only if you *compromise* yourself will I have to take steps to safeguard my honour.'

'But our relations cannot be the same as they always were,' Anna began in a timid voice, looking at him in fright.

When she saw those calm gestures again, and heard that piercing, childish, and sarcastic voice, her aversion for him obliterated the pity she had felt, and she wanted at all costs to clarify her position.

'I cannot be your wife when I . . .' she began.

He let out a spiteful, cold laugh.

'The kind of life you have chosen must have affected your ideas. I respect and despise the one and the other so much . . . I respect your past and despise your present . . . that I was far from the interpretation you have given my words.'

Anna sighed and bowed her head.

'I actually do not understand, how with all the independence you have,' he went on, becoming irate, 'after telling your husband bluntly about your infidelity and finding nothing reprehensible in it, or so it appears, you can find it reprehensible to perform a wife's duties with respect to her husband.'

'Alexey Alexandrovich! What do you want from me?'

'What I want is not to meet that man here and for you to conduct yourself so that neither *society* nor the *servants* can accuse you . . . And for you not to see him. That is not too much, I think. And in return you will have all the rights of an honest wife without fulfilling her duties. That is all I have to say to you. Now I have to go. I'm not dining at home.'

He stood up and headed for the door. Anna also stood up. Bowing silently, he let her pass.

24

THE night which Levin spent on the haystack had not passed without leaving its mark on him: he became disgusted with the agricultural work he had been doing and lost all interest in it. Despite the magnificent harvest, there had never been, or at least he thought there had never been, quite so many failures and so much hostility between him and the peasants as there had been that year, and the reason for these failures and this hostility was now perfectly plain to him. The delight he had experienced in the work itself, the friendship with the peasants which resulted from it, the envy he felt towards them and their life, the desire to cross over to that life, which that night had no longer been a dream but an intention, the practicalities of whose realization he had been mulling over in his mind—all this had so transformed his view of agriculture that he could no longer find any of his former interest in it or be blinded to the unpleasant way in which he treated his labourers, which was at the root of it all. Herds of improved cows like Pava, the land all fertilized and ploughed, nine level fields bordered with willows, three hundred acres heavily manured, seed-drills, and so on—all that would have been splendid if he had brought it about himself, or had worked with associates, people who shared his views. But he saw clearly now (working on his book about agriculture, in which the labourer would emerge as the linchpin in farming, had helped him a lot with this)—he saw clearly now that the agriculture he had been administering was just a bitter and intractable struggle between him and the labourers, in which on the one side, his side, there was a constant, fervent striving to alter everything according to what was considered the best model, while on the other side there was the natural order of things. And in this struggle he saw that, amid the utmost exertion on his part, and the complete absence of effort or even commitment on the other, all that was achieved was unproductive work, while fine tools, and fine cattle and land were going to rack and ruin for nothing. And worst of all, not only was the energy expended on this work completely wasted, but he could not help feeling, now that the true nature of his work had been exposed, that the purpose of his endeavours was most unworthy. What was the struggle about fundamentally? He fought for every last penny (and could not do otherwise, for if he slackened off he would not have enough money to pay his labourers), while they only fought for their work to be untroubled and pleasant, that is, what they were used to. It was in his interest for each of his labourers to work as hard as possible and at the same time remain alert, trying not to break the winnowing-machines, the horse-rakes, or the threshers, and also think about what he was doing; but the labourer wanted his work to be as pleasant as possible, with breaks, and above all, carefree and instinctive, not requiring thought. That summer Levin had seen this at every step. He would send them to go and mow clover for hay, picking out the worst acres which were overgrown with grass and artemisia, and no good for seed—and they would go and mow the best-sown acres, arguing that the steward had instructed them to, and reassuring him that the hay would be excellent; but he knew that it was because these acres were easier to mow. He would send a hay-tedder* to turn over the hay, and they would break it after the first rows because the peasant found it boring to sit on the box under the waving arms. And they would tell him: 'Don't worry sir, the women will shake it up in no time.' The steel ploughs turned out to be useless, because it never occurred to the labourer to lower the raised ploughshare, so when he forced it round he overstrained the horses and ruined the soil; meanwhile he was told not to worry. The horses were let into the wheat field, because not one of the labourers was willing to be night-watchman, and so the labourers took it in turns to guard at night, in spite of the order not to, and Vanka fell asleep after working all day and confessed his guilt, saying, 'Do what you like with me.' They overfed the three best heifers by letting them graze in the replenished clover field without watering them, and refused to believe that it was the clover which made them bloated, but told him by way of consolation that one of his neighbours had lost a hundred and twelve head of cattle in three days. None of this happened because anyone wished Levin or his farming ill; on the contrary, he knew that they liked him and saw him as a down-to-earth gentleman (which was the highest praise); it happened simply because they wanted their work to be enjoyable and carefree, and his interests were not only alien and incomprehensible to them, but fatally opposed to their own entirely legitimate interests. Levin had long been dissatisfied with his attitude to farming. He could see that his boat was leaking, but he had not located or looked for the leak, perhaps deliberately deceiving himself. But now he could no longer deceive himself. The farm-work he managed had not only lost its interest for him but had become repugnant, and he could no longer carry on with it.

To this was now added the presence, twenty miles away, of Kitty Shcherbatskaya, whom he wanted to see but could not. Darya Alexandrovna Oblonskaya had invited him to come and visit when he had seen her last: to come and visit with the object of renewing his proposal to her sister, who, she gave him to understand, would now accept him. Levin himself had realized he had never stopped loving Kitty Shcherbatskaya when he had caught sight of her; but he could not go over to the Oblonskys, knowing she was there. The fact that he had proposed to her and she had refused him placed an insurmountable barrier between them. 'I can't ask her to be my wife just because she cannot be the wife of the man she wanted,' he said to himself. The thought of this made him feel cold and hostile towards her. 'I won't be capable of speaking to her without a feeling of reproach, or looking at her without resentment, and she will only hate me all the more, as she should. And anyway, how can I go and see them now, after what Darya Alexandrovna told me? How can I possibly avoid showing that I know what she told me? I'm supposed to arrive full of magnanimity, so I can forgive and show her mercy. I'll be standing before her as the one forgiving her and bestowing his love on her! . . . Why did Darya Alexandrovna tell me that? I could have seen her by chance, and then everything would have happened naturally; but now it's impossible, quite impossible!'

Darya Alexandrovna sent a note asking to borrow a side-saddle for Kitty. 'I was told you have a saddle,' she wrote to him. 'I hope you will bring it over yourself.'

This was more than he could stand. How could an intelligent, sensitive woman so deeply humiliate her sister! He wrote ten notes and tore them all up and sent the saddle without any reply. To write that he was going to come and visit was impossible, because he could not come; to write that he could not come because he was unable to, or because he was going away, was even worse. He sent the saddle without a reply, conscious he had done something shameful, and the next day, after handing over all the abhorrent farm-work to the steward, went off to a remote district to visit his friend Sviyazhsky, who had marvellous snipe marshes nearby, and who had recently written, asking him to carry out his long-standing intention of going to stay with him. The snipe marshes in the Surovsky district had been tempting Levin for a long time, but he had kept putting off this trip because of his farm-work. He was glad to get away now, though, both from the proximity of the Shcherbatskys, and above all from the farm-work, and he was particularly keen to do some shooting, which was the best solace for all his woes.

25

THERE was no railway or post road to the Surov district and Levin went in the *tarantass** with his own horses.

At the halfway point on his journey he stopped to feed his horses at a wealthy peasant's house. A bald, sprightly looking old man with an expansive red beard, greying at the cheeks, opened the gates, pinning himself against the post to make room for the troika* to pass. After showing the coachman a place under an awning in the large, clean, and tidy new yard where there were a few charred wooden ploughs, the old man invited Levin into the house. A cleanly dressed young woman, galoshes on her bare feet, was bent over in the new entrance-way, scrubbing the floor. She took fright at Levin's dog which came running in after him, and cried out, but immediately began laughing at her fears once she found out the dog would not touch her. After showing Levin the door into the front room with her bare arm, she bent over again, hiding her beautiful face, and carried on scrubbing.

'Do you want the samovar?' she asked.

'Yes, please.'

The room was large, and had a Dutch stove and a partition. Beneath the icons stood a table decorated with a painted pattern, a bench, and two chairs. Near the entrance there was a small dresser with crockery. The shutters were closed, there were very few flies, and it was so clean that Levin wanted to make sure that Laska, who had been running along the road and bathing in puddles, would not leave footprints on the floor, so he showed her a place in the corner by the door. After looking round the room, Levin went out into the backyard. The good-looking young woman in galoshes, with empty pails swinging from a yoke, ran down in front of him to fetch water from the well.

'Look lively!' the old man shouted after her merrily, and he went up to Levin. 'So you are on your way to Nikolay Ivanovich Sviyazhsky, sir? He drops in on us too,' he began chattily, resting his elbows on the railing of the porch.

In the middle of the old man's story about his acquaintance with Sviyazhsky, the gates creaked again and labourers from the fields came into the yard, with wooden ploughs and harrows. The horses harnessed to the ploughs and harrows were sleek and sturdy. The labourers were obviously part of the household: two were young men in cotton shirts and caps, and the other two were hired labourers in hempen shirts— one was an old man, the other a young lad. The old man left the porch, went up to the horses, and began unharnessing them.

'What have you been ploughing?' asked Levin.

'We've been earthing up the potatoes. We've got a bit of land too. Fedot, don't let the gelding out, take him to the trough, and we'll harness another one.'

'Those ploughshares I ordered, Pa—have you brought them?' asked a tall, strapping lad, who was obviously the old man's son.

'Over there . . . in the sleigh,' answered the old man as he coiled up the unhitched reins and threw them on the ground. 'You can adjust them while they are having their dinner.'

The good-looking young woman went into the house, her shoulders weighed down by the full pails. More women appeared from somewhere—young and attractive, middle-aged, old and unattractive, with and without children.

The chimney of the samovar began to whistle; after attending to the horses, the labourers and the family went off to have dinner. Levin got his provisions out of the carriage and invited the old man to have tea with him.

'Well, we've already had our tea today,' said the old man, clearly pleased to receive this invitation. 'But I'll keep you company.'

Over tea Levin heard the whole history of the old man's farm. Ten years ago the old man had rented three hundred and twenty acres from a lady landowner, and last year he had bought them and rented another eight hundred from a neighbouring landowner. A small part of the land, the worst part, he was renting out, while he was cultivating about a hundred acres himself with his family and two hired labourers. The old man complained that things were not going well. But Levin realized he was only complaining to observe proprieties, and that his farm was flourishing. If things had been going badly, he would not have bought land at forty roubles an acre, married off three sons and a nephew, and rebuilt twice after fires, each time better than before. Despite the old man's complaints, it was clear that he was justly proud of his prosperity, his sons, his nephew, his daughters-in-law, his horses, and his cows, and especially of the fact that the farming sustained all this. From his conversation with the old man, Levin found out that he was also not averse to innovations. He had planted a lot of potatoes, and his potatoes, which Levin had seen as he was driving up, had already flowered and were beginning to set, while Levin's were only just coming into flower. He was earthing up his potatoes with a plougher, as he called the plough he had borrowed from a landowner. He had sown wheat. Levin was particularly impressed with one small detail: after thinning out the rye, the old man fed his horses with the thinnings. There had been countless times when Levin had seen this excellent fodder going to waste and wanted to collect it; but it had always proved impossible. This peasant managed it, however, and he could not praise this fodder too highly.

'What is there for the womenfolk to do? They bring the heaps up to the road, and the cart comes to pick them up.'

'We landowners don't seem to get on too well with our labourers,' said Levin, handing him a glass of tea.

'Thank you,' said the old man, and he took the glass, but refused sugar, indicating a lump he was still nibbling. 'When can you ever get things done with labourers?' he said. 'It's a disaster. Take Sviyazhsky, for instance. We know what his soil is like, it's as black as poppy-seed, but he doesn't have much of a crop to boast about either. It's just lack of care!'

'But you do your farming with labourers, don't you?'

'But it's peasant work. We can do everything ourselves. If a man is no good, he's out, and we'll manage on our own.'

'Pa, Finogen wants some tar fetched,' said the young woman in galoshes, coming in.

'That's how it is, sir!' said the old man, and after getting up and taking his time to cross himself, he thanked Levin and went out.

When Levin went into the back room to call his coachman, he saw all the men of the family sitting at table. The women were serving standing up. The young, strapping son, with his mouth full of *kasha*, was saying something funny, and they were all laughing, and the woman in the galoshes was chortling with particular glee as she ladled cabbage soup into bowls.

It could well be that the good-looking face of the young woman in galoshes had a great deal to do with the impression of well-being that this peasant household made on Levin, but the impression was so strong that Levin could not expel it from his mind. And all the way to Sviyazhsky's after leaving the old man, he kept harking back to the household as though there were something in this impression that demanded his special attention.

26

SVIYAZHSKY was Marshal of the Nobility in his district. He was five years older than Levin, and had been married a long time. His young sister-in-law, a girl towards whom Levin was very well disposed, lived in his house. And Levin knew that Sviyazhsky and his wife were very keen to marry this girl off to him. He knew this without a shadow of a doubt, in the way that young men, so-called eligible bachelors, always know such things, although he would not have dared tell anyone that, and he also knew that despite the fact that he wanted to get married, and despite the fact that this very attractive girl would by all accounts make an excellent wife, he could no sooner marry her, even if he had not been in love with Kitty Shcherbatskaya, than he could fly up into the heavens. And this knowledge spoilt the pleasure he hoped to derive from his visit to Sviyazhsky.

Levin had immediately thought of this when he received Sviyazhsky's letter inviting him to go shooting, but he had nevertheless decided that Sviyazhsky's designs on him were only based on his own groundless conjecture, and therefore he would go anyway. Besides, in the depths of his soul he had a desire to put himself to the test and have another go at measuring himself up against this girl. Life at the Sviyazhskys' house was also extremely pleasant, and Sviyazhsky himself, the best type of zemstvo activist Levin had ever known, was someone he had always found exceptionally interesting.

Sviyazhsky was one of those people who never ceased to amaze Levin, whose very logical, albeit never independent, thought processes go one way, while their lives, rigidly defined and fixed in their course, go in another direction which is completely independent and almost always in blatant contradiction of their thought processes. Sviyazhsky was an extreme liberal. He despised the nobility and believed most nobles to be secret supporters of serfdom who were just too timid to be open about it. He regarded Russia to be a doomed country, like Turkey, and the Russian government to be so bad that he never even deigned to criticize its policies seriously, and yet he served as an exemplary Marshal of the Nobility, and always put on his cap with the red band and cockade* when travelling. He believed that human existence was only possible abroad, where he would go and stay at the first opportunity, but at the same time he ran a very complex and sophisticated farming operation in Russia, and with an avid interest followed everything and knew about everything going on in Russia. He considered that the Russian peasant was at the intermediate stage between ape and man in terms of development, and yet at the zemstvo elections he was the first to shake hands with the peasants and hear their opinions. He believed in neither God nor the devil, but was very concerned with the issue of improving conditions for the clergy and reducing the number of parishes, and he went out of his way, moreover, to ensure that there continued to be a church in his village.

On the woman question he sided with the extreme advocates of complete freedom for women, and especially their right to work, but he lived with his wife in a manner which aroused universal admiration for their affectionate, childless family life, and he arranged his wife's life so that she did and could do nothing except share her husband's concern to pass the time in the best and most enjoyable way possible.

If it had not been Levin's habit always to see the best in people, Sviyazhsky's character would not have been a difficulty or an issue for him; he would have said to himself: a fool or a knave, and that would have been that. But he could not say *fool*, because Sviyazhsky was undoubtedly not only very clever, but very educated, and a man who wore his learning extremely lightly. There was no subject of which he was ignorant; but he only ever displayed his knowledge when compelled to do so. Still less could Levin say that he was a knave, because Sviyazhsky was undoubtedly an honest, kind, clever man, who cheerfully, energetically, and constantly did things which were highly valued by everyone around him, and it was highly probable he had never consciously done, or was capable of doing, anything bad.

Levin had tried but failed to understand him, and always looked at him and his life as a living enigma.

He and Levin were on friendly terms, so Levin would take the liberty of questioning Sviyazhsky closely, to try and get to the heart of his attitude to life; but it was always in vain. Every time Levin tried to penetrate beyond the doors of the reception rooms of Sviyazhsky's mind, which were open to everyone, he noticed that Sviyazhsky became slightly uncomfortable; a barely noticeable alarm would appear in his eyes, as though he were afraid Levin would figure him out, and he would put up a good-humoured, amiable resistance.

Levin was particularly happy to be spending time with Sviyazhsky now, after his disenchantment with the farm-work. Apart from the fact that just the sight of these happy turtledoves in their cosy nest, pleased with themselves and everyone else, had a salutary effect on Levin, now that he felt so dissatisfied with his own life, he wanted to unlock the secret which gave Sviyazhsky such clarity, certainty, and cheerfulness in his life. Levin knew, moreover, that he would meet neighbouring landowners at Sviyazhsky's, and he was now particularly keen to talk and to hear all those conversations about the harvest, hiring labourers, and so on, which Levin knew were regarded as being very unsavoury, but which he felt were now the only important issues. 'Maybe this was unimportant when we had serfdom or may be unimportant in England. In both cases the conditions themselves are clearly defined; but in our country, where everything has been turned upside down and is only just beginning to settle, the question of what form these conditions will take is the only important question in Russia,' thought Levin.

The shooting turned out to be worse than Levin had expected. The marsh had dried up, and there were no snipe at all. He walked all day and only brought back three birds, but on the other hand he did bring back, as he always did from shooting, an excellent appetite, excellent spirits, and that feeling of intellectual exhilaration which vigorous physical exercise always aroused in him. And while he was out shooting, when it did not seem he was thinking about anything at all, he persistently kept harking back to the old man and his family, and this impression seemed to demand not only his attention, but the resolution of something that was connected with it.

That evening at tea, the very interesting conversation Levin had been looking forward to sprang up in the presence of two landowners who had come over on some trusteeship business.

Levin was sitting beside his hostess at the tea table and had to make conversation with her and her sister-in-law, who was sitting opposite him. His hostess was a round-faced, fair-haired, rather small woman, wreathed in dimples and smiles. Levin was trying through her to find a solution to the important puzzle her husband represented; but he did not have complete freedom of thought because he felt acutely uncomfortable. He felt acutely uncomfortable because the sister-in-law was sitting opposite to him in a dress he believed she had put on specially for him, which had a special neckline on her white bosom cut in the shape of a trapezium; despite her bosom being very white, or precisely because it was very white, this quadrangular neckline deprived Levin of his freedom of thought. He imagined, probably mistakenly, that this neckline had been cut that way for his benefit, and he felt he had no right to look at it, so he tried not to look at it; but he felt guilty that the neckline had been cut that way in the first place. Levin felt he was deceiving someone and that there was something he ought to explain, but that there was no way of explaining it, and so he continually blushed, and was ill at ease and awkward. His awkwardness communicated itself to the pretty sister-in-law. Their hostess did not appear to have noticed this, however, and kept making a point of drawing her into the conversation.

'You say', the hostess said, continuing the conversation they had started, 'Russian things cannot be of interest to my husband. On the contrary, he may be happy abroad, but never so much as when he is here. He feels he is in his element here. He has so much to do, and he has the gift of being interested in everything. Oh, you haven't been to our school, have you?'

'I've seen it . . . It's the little house covered with ivy?'

'Yes, that's Nastya's work,' she said, indicating her sister-in-law.

'Do you teach yourself?' asked Levin, trying to look past the neck-line, but feeling that he was going to see the neckline no matter where he looked in that direction.

'Yes, I've been teaching myself, and I still do, but we have a marvel-lous teacher now. And we've introduced gymnastics.'

'No, thank you, I won't have any more tea,' said Levin, and he got up, blushing, conscious of being impolite, but unable to continue this conversation any longer. 'I can hear a very interesting conversation,' he added, and went to the other end of the table, where the host was sitting with the two landowners. Sviyazhsky was sitting sideways-on with his elbow on the table, twirling a cup round with one hand, and with the other continually gathering his beard into his fist, bringing it to his nose as if he was sniffing it, and releasing it. He had his sparkling black eyes fixed on the impassioned landowner with the grey moustache, and was clearly finding what he was saying amusing. The landowner was complaining about the peasants. It was obvious to Levin that Sviyazhsky had an answer to the landowner's complaint which would immediately demolish the whole point of his argument, but which he could not articulate by virtue of his position, and so was listening, not without pleasure, to the landowner's comic tirade.

The landowner with the grey moustache was obviously an invete-rate defender of serfdom, a long-time country-dweller, and a passion-ate farmer. Levin saw the signs of this in his dress—an old-fashioned, shabby frock-coat he was clearly not used to wearing—but also in his intelligent, scowling eyes, his flowing Russian, his imperious tone, clearly acquired through long experience, and the vigorous gestures of his large, attractive, sunburnt hands, with one old wedding ring on his third finger.

27

'IF it weren't such a shame to abandon something up and running . . .
so much effort put into it . . . I'd wave goodbye to it all, sell up, and go
off like Nikolay Ivanich . . . to hear *La Belle Hélène*,' said the landowner,
a pleasant smile lighting up his intelligent old face.

'But you don't abandon it,' said Nikolay Ivanovich Sviyazhsky, 'so
there must be some reward.'

'The only reward is that I live at home, so nothing to buy or rent.
And I keep on hoping the peasants will come to their senses. Because
it's all drunkenness and debauchery at the moment, believe me!
They've divided everything up again, down to the last horse and cow.
He might be starving to death, but take him on and give him some
work and he'll contrive to foul things up for you, and he'll have you up
before the magistrate to boot.'

'But you can complain to the magistrate too,' said Sviyazhsky.

'Do you think I would complain? Not for anything in the world!
There would be so much talk about it I'd soon regret complaining!
Down at the mill they took their advance and left. And what did the
magistrate do? Acquitted them. Everything is held together these days
by the village tribunal and the village elder—he'd give them a good
old-fashioned flogging. Without that you might as well give it all up!
Run away to the ends of the earth!'

The landowner was obviously teasing Sviyazhsky, but Sviyazhsky
not only was not getting angry but evidently finding it amusing.

'But we seem to be able to farm without resorting to such measures,
you know,' he said, smiling, 'Levin, and I, and him.'

He indicated the other landowner.

'Yes, things function at Mikhail Petrovich's, but have you asked him
how? Could you call it a rational way to farm?' said the landowner,
clearly wanting to show off the word 'rational'.

'My farming is simple,' said Mikhail Petrovich. 'Thank God. My
farming is all about getting the money ready for the autumn taxes. And
then the peasants turn up: "Be a father to us, sir, help us out!" Well,
they're our neighbours, all these peasants—you feel sorry for them.
So you give them a third in advance, but you say: "Remember I helped
you, lads, so you help me when the time comes—with sowing the oats,
the haymaking, or the harvesting,"—well, you sort it out according to
the level of their tax. There are some dishonest ones amongst them
though, it's true.'

Levin, who had long been familiar with these patriarchal methods, exchanged glances with Sviyazhsky and interrupted Mikhail Petrovich by turning to the gentleman with the grey moustache again.

'So what do you think?' he asked. 'How should one farm nowadays?'

'The way Mikhail Petrovich does: either let the land in return for half the crop, or rent it to the peasants; it's possible, but that's how you wipe out the country's general wealth. My land yielded ninefold with serf labour and good management, but when it is let for half the crop, it's threefold. Emancipation has ruined Russia!'

Sviyazhsky looked with twinkling eyes at Levin, and even made a barely perceptible gesture of mockery at him; but Levin did not find the landowner's words ridiculous—he understood them better than he understood Sviyazhsky. Much of what the landowner went on to say as proof of why Russia was ruined by the emancipation even seemed very true to him, and was new and indisputable. The landowner was clearly expressing his own idea, which so rarely happens, and the idea he had arrived at was not born of a desire to occupy an idle mind, but an idea which had emerged from the conditions of his life, conceived in his rural solitude, and considered from every point of view.

'The point is, you see, that progress is only ever brought about by the exercise of power,' he said, evidently wishing to show he was no stranger to education. 'Take the reforms of Peter, Catherine, and Alexander. Take European history. Not to mention progress in agriculture. Even the potato—that was introduced here by force too. After all, we haven't even always used the wooden plough either. That had to be introduced too, maybe in the days of old Rus, but probably by force. Now in our own day, we landowners used to run our farms under serfdom with improvements; the dryers and the threshing-machines and the carting of manure, and all the equipment—we introduced it all by exerting our authority, and the peasants resisted at first, but then copied us. Now, gentlemen, with the abolition of serfdom, they have taken away our power, and our farming, wherever it was raised to a high level, is bound to collapse into the most savage, primitive state. That's how I understand it.'

'But why? If it's rational, you can farm with hired labour,' said Sviyazhsky.

'We've no power. Who am I going to farm with, may I ask?'

'There you are—the workforce, the main element in farming,' thought Levin.

'Labourers.'

'Labourers don't want to work well, or work with good tools. Our labourer only knows one thing: how to get as drunk as a pig, and while he's drunk he will ruin everything you give him. He'll give the horses too much water, shear off a perfectly good harness, change a wheel with an iron tyre for one without and sell it for drink, drop a bolt into the threshing-machine in order to break it. He loathes the sight of anything that doesn't suit him. That's why farming standards have generally gone down. Land is neglected and overgrown with wormwood or divided among the peasants, and wherever it yielded millions of bushels before, it's a few hundred thousand now; the general level of wealth has decreased. Had the same thing been done, but with proper calculation . . .'

And he proceeded to develop his plan for emancipation, which would have avoided these drawbacks.

This did not interest Levin, but when he finished, Levin went back to his first argument, and turned to Sviyazhsky in order to try and provoke him into expressing a serious opinion on the matter:

'The idea that farming standards are in decline, and that there is no possibility of any rational farming making a profit with our current attitude to labourers, is perfectly true,' he said.

'I don't think so,' Sviyazhsky countered, in earnest now. 'All I see is that we don't know how to farm, and that what farming we did do during serfdom, far from being at too high a level, was at one which was too low. We have no machinery, no decent livestock, no proper management, and we don't even know how to keep accounts. Ask any landowner—he doesn't know what is profitable and what's not.'

'Double-entry book-keeping,' said the landowner sardonically. 'It doesn't matter how you do your accounting, because if they are going to ruin everything you have, there won't be any profit.'

'Why would they ruin everything? They might break a shoddy threshing-machine, or your Russian treadmill, but not my steam thresher. They might ruin a poor Russian nag of the—what do you call that breed?—dray-horse variety, because you have to draw it along by the tail, but if you keep Percherons,* or at least good Russian cart-horses, they won't ruin them. And so it is with everything. We must raise our farming standards.'

'If only one had the means, Nikolay Ivanich! It's all right for you, but I've got to keep my son at university, and put the young ones through high school—I can't afford any Percherons.'

'That's what banks are for.'

'And end up with the last of my possessions coming under the hammer? No, thank you!'

'I don't agree that it's necessary or possible to raise farming standards any higher,' said Levin. 'This is what I am occupied with, and I have means, but I haven't been able to do anything. I don't know who finds banks useful. At any rate, I always make a loss, whatever I spend money on in my farming: livestock—a loss, machinery—a loss.'

'That's certainly true,' confirmed the landowner with the grey moustache, who had even started chuckling with delight.

'And I'm not the only one,' continued Levin. 'I'm speaking for all the landowners running their farms on a rational basis; with a few exceptions, they all make a loss. Now, you tell us, is your farming profitable?' said Levin, and he immediately noticed in Sviyazhsky's eyes that fleeting expression of alarm that he noticed whenever he wanted to penetrate beyond the reception rooms of Sviyazhsky's mind.

Levin was not being completely ingenuous in asking this question. His hostess had just told him at tea that in the summer they had engaged a German from Moscow, an expert in book-keeping, who for a fee of five hundred roubles had audited their farming accounts and found that they were making a loss of three thousand-odd roubles. She did not remember the precise sum, but it seems the German had worked it out down to the last quarter of a kopeck.

The landowner smiled at the mention of Sviyazhsky's farming being profitable, obviously aware of the gains his neighbour and a Marshal of the Nobility stood to make.

'It may not be profitable,' answered Sviyazhsky. 'That just proves that either I'm a bad farmer, or I'm spending capital to increase the rental value.'

'Oh, rental value!' Levin exclaimed in horror. 'There may be rental value in Europe, where the land has been improved by the labour invested in it, but the land here is deteriorating from the labour invested in it, or from being ploughed up, in other words, so there can't be any rental value.'

'What do you mean, no rental value? It's a law.'

'Then we're outside the law: rental value can explain nothing to us, but simply confuses the issue. No, you tell me how the theory of rent can be . . .'

'Would you like some yoghurt? Masha, pass us the yoghurt or the raspberries,' he said, turning to his wife. 'The raspberries have had a wonderfully long season this year.'

And Sviyazhsky got up in ebullient spirits and walked away, evidently assuming the conversation had ended precisely at the point where Levin thought it was just beginning.

Deprived of his interlocutor, Levin continued the conversation with the landowner, trying to prove to him that the whole problem stemmed from the fact that we did not want to know the characteristics and habits of our labourers; but the landowner, like all people who think independently and in isolation, was slow in getting to grips with someone else's ideas, and was particularly partial to his own. He insisted that the Russian peasant was a swine and liked swinishness, and that power was needed to rid him of his swinish ways, but there was none, the stick was what was needed, but we had become so liberal that the thousand-year-old stick had suddenly been replaced by some kind of lawyers and prisons where the worthless, putrid peasants were fed on good soup and allotted so many cubic feet of air.

'Why do you think', said Levin, trying to get back to the question, 'that it is impossible to establish a relationship with the workforce whereby the work would be productive?'

'That will never happen with Russian peasants without the stick! There is no power,' answered the landowner.

'But what new conditions could possibly be established?' said Sviyazhsky, who had eaten some yoghurt, lit a cigarette, and come back to the discussion. 'All possible relations with the workforce have been defined and studied,' he said. 'That relic of barbarism, the primitive commune* with its principle of mutual responsibility, is falling apart by itself, serfdom has been abolished, free labour is what remains, and its forms are defined and ready, and we must accept them. The hired-worker, the day-labourer, the farmhand—you can't get away from that.'

'But Europe is not satisfied with these forms.'

'No, and it is looking for new ones. And it will probably find them.'

'That's exactly what I am talking about,' answered Levin. 'Why shouldn't we look too?'

'Because it would be like inventing methods for building the railways all over again. They already exist, they've been invented.'

'But what if they don't suit us, or if they're stupid?' said Levin.

And again he noticed the expression of alarm in Sviyazhsky's eyes.

'Yes, I know: we'll leave them standing, we've found what Europe is looking for! I know all that; but, excuse me, do you know everything that's been done in Europe on the question of working conditions?'

'No, I don't.'

'This question is now taxing the best minds in Europe. There is the Schulze-Delitzsch movement . . . And then all that vast literature on the labour question from the ultra-liberal Lassalle movement . . . the Mulhausen system*—that's already a fact, as you must know.'

'I have some idea of it, but only a very vague one.'

'No, you're only saying that; you probably know as much about it as I do. I'm not a professor of sociology, of course, but it has interested me, and really, if it interests you, you should study it.'

'But what conclusion have they come to?'

'Excuse me . . .'

The landowners got up and Sviyazhsky went to see his guests out, once again impeding Levin in his unpleasant habit of prying beyond the reception rooms of his mind.

28

LEVIN was insufferably bored with the ladies that evening: more than ever before, he was excited by the thought that the dissatisfaction he was now experiencing with his farming was not exclusive to him, but symptomatic of the general state of agriculture in Russia, and that establishing the kind of relations with labourers whereby they would work as they did for the peasant he had met at the halfway point on his journey was not a dream, but a task which needed to be solved. And he felt that this task could be solved, and that he ought to try and do so.

After saying good-night to the ladies, and promising to stay the whole of the next day so they could ride over together to look at an interesting landslide in the state forest, Levin stopped by his host's study before going to bed in order to collect the books on the labour question which Sviyazhsky had recommended to him. Sviyazhsky's study was a huge room lined with bookcases, and it had two tables—one a massive desk standing in the middle of the room, and the other a round table spread with the latest issues of newspapers and journals in different languages, all arranged in a star-shape around a lamp. By the desk was a cabinet divided into drawers marked with gold labels which contained files of various sorts.

Sviyazhsky fetched the books and sat down in a rocking-chair.

'What are you looking at?' he said to Levin, who was standing by the round table leafing through the journals.

'Oh yes, there's a very interesting article in there,' Sviyazhsky said about the journal Levin was holding in his hands. 'It turns out', he added, 'that the chief culprit in the partition of Poland was not Frederick at all.* It turns out . . .'

And with his characteristic clarity, he gave a brief account of these new, very important and interesting revelations. Although Levin was now mostly preoccupied with thoughts about farming, he wondered as he listened to Sviyazhsky: 'What goes on inside his head? And why on earth is he interested in the partition of Poland?' When Sviyazhsky finished, Levin could not help asking: 'So what does all this mean?' Nothing, it transpired. It was just the 'it turns out that' which was interesting. But Sviyazhsky did not explain, and did not deem it necessary to explain why he found it interesting.

'Yes, but I found the angry landowner very interesting,' said Levin with a sigh. 'He's clever, and said a lot of true things.'

'Oh, come on now! He's a diehard secret supporter of serfdom, like they all are!' said Sviyazhsky.

'And you're their Marshal . . .'

'Yes, except I marshal them in the other direction,' said Sviyazhsky, laughing.

'I'll tell you what interests me,' said Levin. 'He's right that our project, rational farming I mean, isn't working, and that the only farming which works is either usurious, like with that quiet fellow, or completely basic. Who's to blame?'

'We are, of course. But it's not true that it is not working. It works at Vassilchikov's.'

'But that's a mill . . .'

'But I still don't see what you find so surprising. The peasants are at such a low level of material and moral development that they're obviously bound to oppose anything they are not familiar with. Rational farming works in Europe because the peasantry are educated; therefore we need to educate the peasantry here—pure and simple.'

'But how can we educate the peasantry?'

'Three things are needed to educate the peasantry: schools, schools, and schools.'

'But you said yourself that the peasantry is at a low level of material development. What help will schools be?'

'You know, you've reminded me of the joke about advice to an invalid: "You should try laxatives." "Did: made things worse." "Try leeches." "Did: made things worse." "Well, there's nothing left but to pray to God." "Did: made things worse." That's how it is with you and me. I say political economy, you say: worse. I say socialism: worse. Education: worse.'

'But what help will schools be?'

'They'll give the peasantry other needs.'

'Now that's something I've never understood,' Levin retorted vehemently. 'How are schools going to help the peasants improve their material position? You say schools and education will give them new needs. So much the worse, because they won't be capable of satisfying them. How a knowledge of addition and subtraction and the catechism is going to improve their material position I've never been able to figure out. The other evening I met a peasant woman with a baby in her arms, and I asked her where she was going. She said: "I've been to the midwife, as my little boy had screaming-fits, and I took him to be cured." I asked how the midwife cured screaming-fits. "She puts the baby in with the chickens on the hen roost, and says something . . ."'

'There you are, you're saying it yourself! To prevent her from taking her child to the hen-roost to cure it of screaming-fits, we need . . .' Sviyazhsky said, smiling good-humouredly.

'Oh, no!' said Levin with annoyance; 'I just wanted to compare it to curing people with schools. The peasants are poor and ignorant—we can see that just as plainly as the woman can see it's a screaming-fit because her baby is screaming. But why schools might be able to help with poverty and ignorance is just as incomprehensible as why chickens on a roost might help with screaming-fits. What must be helped is the cause of the poverty.'

'Well, there at least you're in agreement with Spencer,* whom you dislike so much; he also says that education can be the consequence of enhanced prosperity and living standards, of frequent ablutions, as he puts it, but not of the ability to read and write . . .'

'Well, then, I'm very glad, or rather very sorry that I'm in agreement with Spencer; only I've known this a long time. Schools will not help; what will help is an economic structure which will enable people to be better off and have more leisure—then there will be schools.'

'But schools are obligatory now across Europe.'

'But what about you yourself, do you agree with Spencer yourself about this?' asked Levin.

But an expression of alarm flashed in Sviyazhsky's eyes, and he said with a smile:

'Yes, that story about the screaming-fits is superb! Did you really hear it yourself?'

Levin saw that he never was going to find the connection between this man's life and his thoughts. He was clearly not in the least bit concerned where thought-processes would lead; he was only concerned with the thought-process itself. And he did not like it when his thought-process led him up a blind alley. That was the only thing he disliked and tried to avoid, by changing the conversation to something pleasant and amusing.

All the impressions of that day, beginning with the one made by the peasant halfway on his journey, which served as a kind of touchstone for all of the day's impressions and thoughts, had an intensely stimulating effect on Levin. The affable Sviyazhsky, who kept a stock of ideas just for public use but clearly had some other kinds of life principles, hidden from Levin, and was at the same time, along with that crowd whose name is legion, guiding public opinion with ideas that were alien to him; the resentful landowner, perfectly correct in the reasoning to which he had been led by bitter experience, but wrong in his resentment towards a whole class which happened to be the best class in Russia; his own dissatisfaction with what he had been doing, and the vague hope of finding a remedy for it all—all this merged into a feeling of inner disquiet, and a presentiment that a solution was round the corner.

Lying alone in the room assigned to him, on a spring mattress that unexpectedly bounced whenever he moved his arm or his leg, Levin lay awake for a long time. Not a single conversation with Sviyazhsky had interested Levin, although he had said a great many clever things; but the landowner's arguments demanded scrutiny. Levin could not help recalling everything he had said, and he started correcting in his head what he had said in reply to him.

'Yes, I ought to have said to him: you say that our farming does not work because the peasants hate all improvements, so they must be introduced by force; and if our farming did not work at all without these improvements, you would be right; but it does work, although it only works where the labourer works in accordance with his habits, like for that peasant at the halfway point. Our mutual dissatisfaction with farming shows that either we or the labourers are to blame. We have been trying to impose our ideas, European ideas, for a long time now, without stopping to consider the characteristics of our workforce. Let's try to recognize the workforce not as an ideal work-*force*, but as the *Russian peasant* with his instincts, and try to organize our farming accordingly. Just imagine, I ought to have said to him, that you organize your farming like the old man does, that you have found a way for your labourers to have a vested interest in the work being successful, and have found the happy medium with improvements that they will accept—and you will get two or three times what you got before, without exhausting the soil. Divide it equally in two and give half to the workforce; the share left to you will be bigger, and the workforce will get more. But to do this you need to lower the standard of farming and involve the labourers in the success of the farming. How to do that is a question of detail, but there is no doubt that it is possible.'

This idea brought Levin into a state of great excitement. He was awake half the night thinking over the details of how to put his ideas into practice. He had not planned to leave the next day, but now he decided he would go home early in the morning. Besides, that sister-in-law with her low-cut dress aroused in him a feeling of shame and remorse, as if he had done something thoroughly bad. But mainly he had to get back without delay: he needed to present his new project to the peasants before the winter crops were sown, so the sowing could be done on a new foundation. He had decided to overhaul all his old farming methods.

29

THE execution of Levin's plan presented many difficulties; but he put his heart and soul into it, and although what he achieved was not what he wanted, it was enough to enable him to believe without any self-deception that it was worth the effort. One of the main difficulties was that the farming was already in full swing, and it was impossible to stop everything and start all over from the beginning, so the machine had to be retuned while it was running.

When he told the steward of his plans the same evening he arrived home, the steward took evident pleasure in agreeing with the part which showed that everything done up to then was idiotic and unprofitable. The steward said that he had been saying that for a long time, but no one had wanted to listen to him. As for Levin's proposal that he participate in the whole farming enterprise as a shareholder along with the labourers, the steward reacted to this with great despondency and expressed no definite opinion, but immediately started talking about the need to cart the remaining sheaves of rye the next day, and get on with the second ploughing, so Levin sensed this was not the best time to broach the matter.

When he talked to the peasants about it and offered them the land on new terms, he also came up against the major difficulty that they were so busy with the day's work that they did not have the time to consider the advantages and disadvantages of the enterprise.

It did seem that one naive peasant, Ivan the cowherd, fully understood Levin's proposal that he and his family take a share of the profits of the dairy farm, and fully approved of this scheme. But whenever Levin tried to inspire him with talk of the benefits it would bring, Ivan's face expressed alarm and regret that he could not hear to the end, and he would hurriedly find some activity that could not be put off: he would pick up a fork to toss hay out of the stalls, fetch water, or clear out the manure.

Another difficulty lay in the peasants' unshakeable distrust in the idea of a landowner's goal being anything other than a desire to fleece them as much as possible. They were firmly convinced that his real goal (whatever he might say to them) would always be something he would not tell them. And although they themselves said a great deal when they expressed their opinions, they never said what their real goal was. Moreover (Levin felt the bilious landowner was right), the peasants stipulated that they should not be forced into any new farming methods or into using new tools as the first and unalterable condition of any agreement. They agreed that the iron plough did a better job, and that the scarifier was more efficient, but they found thousands of reasons as to why they could not use either, and although he was convinced of the necessity of lowering the standard of farming, he felt sorry to give up improvements which had such obvious benefits. But in spite of all these difficulties he got his way, and by autumn it was all up and running, or so it seemed to him at least.

At first Levin had thought of leasing the whole farm as it was to the peasants, the labourers, and the steward on the new partnership terms, but he very quickly realized this was impossible, so he decided to divide it up. The cattle-yard, the orchard, the vegetable garden, the meadows, and the fields, all divided into several parts, would constitute separate lots. The naive cowherd Ivan, who Levin felt understood the plan better than anyone else, formed a co-operative mostly with members from his family, and became a partner in the dairy farm. The distant field which had lain fallow for eight years was taken on under the new partnership terms by six peasant families with the help of the clever carpenter Fyodor Rezunov, and the peasant Shurayev took over all the vegetable gardens on those same terms. The rest remained as before, but these three lots were the beginning of a new system, and they took up all Levin's time.

True, things at the dairy farm went no better than before, and Ivan vigorously opposed heating the cowshed and making butter from cream, maintaining that cows would want less fodder if kept in the cold, and that butter made from sour cream was more economical, and he demanded wages as before, and was not remotely interested in the fact that the money he received was not wages but an advance on his future share of the profits.

True, Fyodor Rezunov's group did not plough the ground twice before sowing as had been agreed, giving as their excuse that time was short. True, the peasants in this group, despite having agreed to run operations on the new principles, described this land as rented not on a shared but sharecropping basis, and more than once the peasants from the co-operative and also Rezunov himself said to Levin, 'If you took money for the land, it would save you trouble, and be easier for us.' Moreover, these peasants kept coming up with various pretexts to put off building a cattle-yard and threshing barn on the land, as had been agreed, and they procrastinated until the winter.

True, Shurayev would have liked to have sublet the kitchen gardens he was renting to the peasants in small lots. He had evidently completely misunderstood, and apparently deliberately misunderstood the terms on which the land had been let to him.

True, Levin often felt when he was talking to the peasants and explaining all the advantages of the enterprise to them that they were just listening to the sound of his voice and were positive that, whatever he might say, they would not be taken in by him. He particularly felt this when he talked to Rezunov, the smartest of the peasants, and noticed that glint in Rezunov's eyes, which clearly showed both scorn for Levin and the firm conviction that if anybody was to be hoodwinked, he, Rezunov, was not going to be the one.

But in spite of all this, Levin thought it was a going concern, and that by keeping strict accounts and standing his ground, in the future he would be able to show them the advantages of the new arrangement, and then things would take their own course.

These matters, together with the rest of the farming left in his hands, and the desk work on his book, kept Levin so busy throughout the summer that he barely did any shooting. At the end of August he heard from the servant who brought back the saddle that the Oblonskys had returned to Moscow. He felt that with his rudeness in not answering Darya Alexandrovna's letter, which he could not remember without a flush of shame, he had burned his boats and would never visit them again. He had behaved in just the same way with Sviyazhsky, by leaving without saying goodbye. But he would never visit them again either. He did not care now. The reorganization of his farming absorbed him as nothing had ever done in his life before. He read the books Sviyazhsky had given him, and after ordering up those he did not have, read books on this subject in the sphere of political economy and socialism, and, as he expected, found nothing that had any bearing on what he was undertaking. In the political-economy books, in Mill for example, whom he studied first, and with great fervour, hoping any moment to find a solution to the problems which occupied him, he found laws derived from the European agricultural situation; but he simply failed to see why these laws, which were not applicable to Russia, had to be universal. He saw the same thing in the books on socialism: they were either beautiful but unrealizable fantasies which had fascinated him when he was a student, or modifications and adjustments to the situation Europe was placed in, with which agriculture in Russia had nothing in common. Political economy said that the laws according to which Europe's wealth had grown, and was still growing, were universal and unquestionable. Socialist doctrine said that growth along these lines would lead to ruin. And neither of them gave an answer, or even the slightest hint, as to what he, Levin, and all Russian peasants and landowners should do with their millions of hands and acres to make them as productive as possible for the general prosperity of all.

Having taken this matter up, he conscientiously read everything relevant to his subject and resolved to go abroad in the autumn to pursue it further on the spot, so that what had happened to him so often with other issues would not happen to him with this one. He would often just be on the point of grasping his interlocutor's idea and expounding his own when he would suddenly be told: 'But what about Kauffmann, and Jones, and Dubois, and Micelli?* You haven't read them. Read them; they have unravelled this issue.'

He saw clearly now that Kauffmann and Micelli had nothing to tell him. He knew what he wanted. He saw that Russia had fine land, fine labourers, and that, in certain cases, as at that peasant's at the halfway point on his journey, labourers and the land could produce a great deal, but that in the majority of cases, when capital was applied in the European way, they produced little, and this was simply because the labourers wanted to work and worked well in the one way natural to them, so their resistance was not accidental, but something constant which had its roots in the national spirit. He thought that the Russian people, whose vocation was to populate and cultivate vast tracts of unoccupied land, would consciously adhere to the methods necessary for this until all the land was occupied, and that these methods were by no means as bad as was commonly thought. And he wanted to prove this theoretically in his book and in practice in his farming.

30

AT the end of September the timber to build the cattle-yard on the land allotted to the peasants' co-operative was delivered, the butter from the cows was sold, and the profits were shared out. The farming system was working splendidly in practice, or at least so it seemed to Levin. But in order to explain it all theoretically and finish his book, which Levin dreamed would not merely revolutionize political economy, but completely destroy it as a discipline and lay the foundation of a new discipline, dealing with the relation of people to the land, he just needed to take a trip abroad, so he could study on the spot everything that had been done in this connection, and find conclusive evidence that everything that had been done there was not what was needed. Levin was just waiting for the delivery of his wheat, so that he could get the money and go abroad. But rain set in, preventing the grain and potatoes left in the field from being harvested and stopping all work, even the delivery of the wheat. The roads were made impassable by mud; two mills were carried away by floods, and the weather got steadily worse and worse.

On the morning of 30 September the sun came out and, banking on good weather, Levin began making serious preparations for his journey. He ordered the wheat to be bagged up, sent the steward over to the merchant to get the money, while he himself went round the estate to give final instructions before leaving.

Having got everything done, Levin returned home in the late afternoon, sopping wet from the rivulets trickling down his neck and into the tops of his boots from his leather coat, but in a thoroughly buoyant and exhilarated state of mind. The weather by late afternoon had become even worse, and the sleet was lashing his drenched horse so painfully it was walking sideways, shaking its head and ears; but Levin felt all right under his hood, and enjoyed looking round at the muddy streams running along the ruts, at the drops hanging from every bare twig, the whiteness of the patch of unthawed sleet on the planks of the bridge, and at the succulent, still fleshy elm leaves which had fallen in a thick layer around the denuded tree. In spite of nature being so dank all around him, he was feeling particularly exhilarated. Conversations with the peasants in the far village had shown that they were beginning to get used to their changed relations. The old innkeeper whom he called on so he could dry off clearly approved of Levin's plan, and had himself suggested joining the association for buying cattle.

'I just have to keep stubbornly working towards my goal, and I will get there in the end,' thought Levin, 'but at least there is something worth working and plodding away for. This is not my own personal project, it's about the common good. Agriculture and, above all, the situation of the peasantry, must completely change in all respects. Instead of poverty there should be general prosperity and contentment; instead of enmity there should be harmony and shared interests. In short, a bloodless revolution, but a mighty revolution, at first in the small confines of our district, then the province, Russia, and the whole world. Because a valid idea cannot fail to bear fruit. Yes, it is a goal worth working towards. And the fact that it is I, Kostya Levin, who went to a ball in a black tie and was refused by Kitty Shcherbatskaya, and who perceives himself as pathetic and worthless, proves nothing. I am sure Franklin* felt just as worthless, and also had no faith in himself when he thought about himself in general terms. It means nothing. And no doubt he also had his Agafya Mikhailovna to whom he confided his plans.'

Immersed in such thoughts, Levin rode up, already in darkness, to his house.

The steward, who had been to see the merchant, came back bringing part of the money for the wheat. An agreement had been made with the old innkeeper, and on the way the steward discovered that the corn was still standing in the fields everywhere, so their one hundred and sixty uncarted stacks were nothing compared to other people's situations.

After dinner Levin sat down in an armchair with a book as usual, and as he read, he went on thinking about his forthcoming trip in connection with his book. Today he had perceived the full significance of his work with particular clarity, and whole paragraphs illustrating his theories were forming in his mind. 'I must write that down,' he thought. 'That should be the brief introduction, which I thought was unnecessary before.' He got up to go over to his desk, and Laska, who had been lying at his feet, also got up, stretching herself, and looked at him as if asking where to go. But there was no time to write anything down, as the foremen had come for their roster, and Levin went out into the hall to meet them.

After sorting out the roster, that is, the instructions for the following day's work, and receiving all the peasants who had business to discuss with him, Levin went into his study and sat down to work. Laska lay under the desk; Agafya Mikhailovna settled in her place with a stocking.

After writing for a while, Levin with unusual vividness suddenly remembered Kitty, her refusal, and their last encounter. He got up and started pacing about the room.

'There's no point moping,' said Agafya Mikhailovna. 'What are you doing sitting at home? You ought to get off to those warm springs, now you're all ready.'

'But I am going the day after tomorrow, Agafya Mikhailovna. I've got work to finish.'

'You and your work! As if you hadn't already done enough for the peasants! They're already saying, "Your master will be rewarded by the Tsar for it." It's odd: why should you bother so much about the peasants?'

'I'm not bothering about them, I'm doing it for myself.'

Agafya Mikhailovna knew all the details of Levin's agricultural plans. Levin often explained his ideas to her in all their subtlety and often argued with her and did not agree with her explanations. But now she understood what he told her in a completely different way.

'Of course, you do need to think about your soul above all else,' she said with a sigh. 'Parfen Denisych now, he couldn't read and write, but God grant everyone a death like he had,' she said, referring to a servant who had recently died. 'They gave him communion and last rites.'

'That's not what I mean,' said he. 'I mean that I'm working for my own benefit. I benefit if the peasants work better.'

'It doesn't matter what you do, as if he's an idler, he'll always be slipshod. If he has a conscience, he'll work, but if not, there's nothing you can do.'

'Well, yes, but you have been saying yourself that Ivan has begun looking after the cattle better.'

'All I'm saying,' answered Agafya Mikhailovna, clearly not speaking randomly, but with a strict logic in her thinking, 'is that you ought to get married, that's what!'

Agafya Mikhailovna's mentioning of the very thing he had just been thinking about distressed and offended him. Levin frowned and sat down again at his work without answering her, rehearsing to himself everything he had been thinking about the significance of his work. Occasionally he listened in the silence to the sound of Agafya Mikhailovna's needles, and frowned again as he remembered what he did not want to remember.

At nine o'clock he heard the tinkle of harness bells and the muffled sound of a carriage squelching through the mud.

'Well, you've got visitors now, so you won't be able to mope,' said

Agafya Mikhailovna, getting up and going to the door. But Levin overtook her. His work was not going well now, and he was happy to have
any visitor, whoever it might be.

31

AFTER running halfway down the stairs, Levin heard a familiar sound
of coughing in the hall; but he heard it indistinctly because of the
sound of his footsteps and hoped he was mistaken; then he saw all
of the lanky, angular, familiar figure, and it seemed it was no longer
possible to be deceived, but he still hoped that he was mistaken and that
this lanky man taking off his fur coat and coughing was not his brother
Nikolay.

Levin loved his brother, but being with him was always agonizing.
And now, when Levin was in an unsettled, confused state of mind due
to the thoughts which had come to him and Agafya Mikhailovna's
reminder, the prospect of meeting his brother seemed particularly
onerous. Instead of a guest who was a cheerful, healthy stranger who,
he hoped, might divert him in his emotionally unsettled state, he had
to spend time with his brother, who knew him inside out, and who
would provoke in him the most intimate thoughts and force him to
unburden himself completely. And he did not want to do that.

Angry at himself for this despicable feeling, Levin ran into the hall.
As soon as he saw his brother up close, his feeling of disappointment
immediately disappeared and was replaced by pity. As terrible as his
brother Nikolay's gauntness and frailty had been before, he was now
even thinner, and even more wasted. He was a skeleton covered with
skin.

He stood in the hall, jerking his long, thin neck and pulling his scarf
from it, with a strange and pitiful smile. When he saw that meek, submissive smile, Levin felt a lump in his throat.

'See, I've come to stay with you,' said Nikolay in a hollow voice, not
taking his eyes off his brother's face for a second. 'I've been meaning to
for a long time, but I kept being unwell. I'm much better now though,'
he said, rubbing his beard with his large, thin palms.

'Yes, yes!' answered Levin. And he felt even more scared when, as
he kissed him, he felt the dryness of his brother's skin with his lips and
saw his large, strangely shining eyes close up.

A few weeks earlier, Konstantin Levin had written to tell his
brother that after the sale of the small part of their property which had

remained undivided, his brother stood to receive his share, which was about two thousand roubles.

Nikolay said that he had come now to receive this money and, above all, to spend some time in the family nest and touch the soil, like the warriors in ancient legends,* in order to build up his strength for the tasks that lay ahead. Despite his increased stoop, and despite being shockingly thin for his height, his movements were as swift and abrupt as ever. Levin led him into his study.

His brother changed his clothes with particular care, which he had never done before, combed his sparse, lank hair, and came upstairs smiling.

He was in the most affectionate and light-hearted of moods, as Levin remembered him often being in their childhood. He even mentioned Sergey Ivanovich without any rancour. When he saw Agafya Mikhailovna, he joked with her and asked after the old servants. The news of Parfen Denisych's death made a disagreeable impression on him. Fear appeared in his face; but he pulled himself together immediately.

'He was old, after all,' he said, and changed the subject. 'So I'll spend a month or two with you, and then go to Moscow. You know, Myagkov has promised me a position, I'm going to start a regular job. I'm going to organize my life quite differently now,' he went on. 'You know, I got rid of that woman.'

'Marya Nikolayevna? Why, whatever for?'

'Oh, she is a vile woman! Caused me a lot of trouble.' But he did not say what the trouble had been. He could not say that he had driven Marya Nikolayevna away because the tea was weak, but mainly because she had looked after him as though he were an invalid. 'And then I generally want to change my life completely now. I've done some stupid things, of course, like everyone else, but money is least important, and I don't miss it. Just as long as there's health, and my health, thank God, has improved.'

Levin listened and tried, but failed, to think of something to say. Nikolay probably felt the same; he began asking his brother about his affairs; and Levin was glad to talk about himself, because he could speak without pretending. He told his brother about his plans and the things he had been doing.

His brother listened, but was clearly not interested.

These two men were so alike and close to each other that the slightest gesture or inflection in their voices communicated more to each of them than anything that could have been said in words.

They both now had only one thought on their minds: Nikolay's illness and approaching death, suppressing everything else. But neither of them dared talk about it, and so everything they said, since they did not express the one thought that occupied them, was a lie. Levin had never been so glad when the evening was over and it was time to go to bed. Never with any stranger or on any formal visit had he been as unnatural and false as he had been that evening. And his awareness of this unnatural behaviour, and the self-reproach it caused, made him even more unnatural. He wanted to weep over his beloved, dying brother, and he had to listen and keep up a conversation about how he was going to live.

As the house was damp, and only one room was heated, Levin put his brother to sleep in his own bedroom, behind a screen.

His brother went to bed, and whether he was sleeping or not, being a sick man he tossed about and coughed, and when he could not clear his throat he muttered something. Sometimes, when he was finding it hard to breathe, he would say: 'Oh, my God!' And at other times, when he was choking on phlegm, he would exclaim angrily: 'Ah, the devil!' Levin lay awake for a long time listening to him. His thoughts were disparate in the extreme, but they all ended with the same thing: death.

Death, the inevitable end of everything, confronted him for the first time with irresistible force. And this death, which was there, in this beloved brother, groaning in his sleep and from force of habit indiscriminately invoking first God then the devil, was not nearly as remote as it had seemed to him before. It was in him too—he could feel it. If not today, then tomorrow, and if not tomorrow, then in thirty years—did it really matter when? But what this inevitable death was, he not only did not know and had never thought about, but also did not feel competent or bold enough to think about.

'I'm working, I want to achieve something, but I forgot that it will all end, that there is—death.'

He sat hunched up on his bed in the darkness, with his arms around his knees, and thought, holding his breath from all the concentration. But the more he concentrated, the more apparent it became to him that this was unmistakably the case, that he really had forgotten, overlooked, one small factor in life—that death would come along and everything would end, that it was not worth even starting anything, and there was no way this could be helped. Yes, it was awful, but that is how it was.

'But I am still alive. So what should I do now, what exactly should I do?' he said with desperation. He lit a candle, got up carefully, went over to the mirror, and started looking at his face and hair. Yes, there

were grey hairs about his temples. He opened his mouth. His back
teeth were beginning to decay. He bared his muscular arms. Yes, he
had a lot of strength. But Nikolenka, who was lying there breathing
with what remained of his lungs, also used to have a healthy body once.
And all of a sudden he remembered how they would go to bed when
they were children, waiting for Fyodor Bogdanich to leave the room
so they could start throwing pillows at each other and laugh, laugh so
uncontrollably that even their fear of Fyodor Bogdanich could not stop
that overflowing, effervescent sense of the happiness of life. 'And now
there is this lop-sided, hollow chest . . . And I, not knowing what will
become of me and why . . .'

'*Cough! Cough!* Ah, the devil! What are you fidgeting about for, why
aren't you asleep?' his brother's voice called to him.

'Oh, I don't know, I can't sleep.'

'Well, I've slept well, I don't sweat any more. Look, feel my nightshirt. Is there any sweat?'

Levin felt it, went behind the screen and put out the candle, but still
could not sleep for a long time. The question of how to live had only
just become a little clearer to him when he was confronted with a new,
insoluble problem—death.

'So he's dying, so he'll die before spring, so how can I help him?
What can I say to him? What do I know about it? I had forgotten it
even existed.'

32

LEVIN had long ago observed that whenever it is uncomfortable being
with people who are excessively accommodating and humble, it will
very soon become unbearable due to their being excessively demanding
and captious. He felt this would happen with his brother. And indeed,
his brother Nikolay's meekness did not last long. He became irritable
the very next morning and did his best to find fault with his brother,
touching his sorest points.

Levin felt guilty and could not rectify things. He felt that if they had
both not put on an act, but had spoken from the heart, as it is called,
that is, said only what they were really thinking and feeling, they would
simply have looked into each other's eyes, and Konstantin would have
simply said, 'You're going to die, you're doing to die, you're going to
die!' and Nikolay would have simply answered, 'I know I'm going to
die, but I'm afraid, I'm afraid, I'm afraid, I'm afraid!' And they would

not have said anything else if they had spoken from the heart. But it was impossible to live like that, and so Konstantin tried to do what he had been trying to do all his life and was not able to do, and what he noticed many people were able to do so well, and without which it was impossible to live: he tried to avoid saying what he was thinking, and he continually felt that it sounded false, that his brother saw through it, and was irritated by it.

On the third day of his stay, Nikolay got his brother to explain his plan to him again, and began not only disparaging it, but deliberately confusing it with communism.

'You've just taken someone else's idea, but you've distorted it and want to apply it to that which is inapplicable.'

'But I am telling you, it's completely different. They reject the legitimacy of property, capital, and inheritance, while I, without denying this chief *stimulus*'—Levin felt disgusted with himself for using such words, but since he had become engrossed in his work he had unconsciously started using foreign words more and more frequently—'just want to regulate labour.'

'Exactly—you've taken someone else's idea, cut out everything that gives it its power, and are trying to make out that it's something new,' said Nikolay, jerking his neck angrily.

'But my idea has nothing in common with . . .'

'The other,' said Nikolay Levin with a sarcastic smile, his eyes flashing angrily. 'The other at least has, how can one put it, the geometrical appeal of clarity and certitude. Maybe it's a utopia. But suppose one could turn the whole of the past into a *tabula rasa*[1]—no property, no family—then labour would also sort itself out. But you've got nothing . . .'

'Why are you confusing things? I've never been a communist.'

'But I have, and I think it's premature, but it's rational and has a future, just like Christianity during its first centuries.'

'All I am proposing is that the workforce should be examined from the natural scientist's point of view, that is, we should study it, take note of its characteristics, and . . .'

'But that is a complete waste of time. The workforce will find a form of activity appropriate to its level of development by itself. There were slaves everywhere, then *métayers*,* and in Russia we have sharecropping, we have rent, we have hired labour—what are you looking for?'

Levin suddenly lost his temper at these words, because in the depths

---

[1] 'blank canvas' [Latin in the original].

of his soul he feared that it was true—true that he wanted to find a compromise between communism and established forms, and that this was hardly possible.

'I am looking for ways of working productively, both for myself and the labourer. I want to organize . . .' he answered hotly.

'You don't want to organize anything; you just want to be original, just like you have been your whole life, and show that you are not just exploiting the peasants, but have an idea.'

'Well, if you think that you can leave!' answered Levin, feeling a muscle in his left cheek twitching uncontrollably.

'You've never had any convictions, and you don't have any now; you just want to flatter your ego.'

'Fine, so please leave!'

'I am going to leave! It's high time too, and you can go to hell! And I'm very sorry I came!'

In spite of all Levin's subsequent efforts to appease his brother, Nikolay was not prepared to listen, saying it was better for them to part, and Konstantin saw that life had simply become unbearable for his brother.

Nikolay was just getting ready to leave when Konstantin went up to him again and asked him in an unnatural way to forgive him if he had offended him in any way.

'Ah, magnanimity!' said Nikolay and smiled. 'If you want to be right, I can give you that pleasure. You're right, but I'm still going to leave!'

Just before his departure, Nikolay kissed him and said, suddenly looking with a strange seriousness at his brother:

'Anyway, don't think ill of me, Kostya!' And his voice trembled.

These were the only words that were spoken sincerely. Levin knew that these words meant: 'You see and you know that I'm in a bad way, and maybe we will not see each other again.' Levin knew this, and tears spurted from his eyes. He kissed his brother again, but he could not say anything, and was indeed incapable of saying anything to him.

Three days after his brother's departure, Levin also left to go abroad. At the railway station he ran into Shcherbatsky, Kitty's cousin, who was greatly surprised by Levin's despondency.

'What's the matter with you?' Shcherbatsky asked him.

'Oh, nothing, only there's not much reason to be jolly in this world.'

'What do you mean, not much? Come with me to Paris instead of Mulhouse or wherever it is you're going. You'll see how jolly it is!'

'No, I've finished with all that. It's time for me to die.'

'Good heavens!' said Shcherbatsky, laughing. 'I'm just getting ready to begin.'

'Yes, I thought the same not long ago, but now I know I shall die soon.'

Levin said what he had genuinely been thinking of late. He saw nothing but death or its approach in everything. But the work he had started absorbed him even more as a result. He had to get through life somehow until death arrived. Darkness smothered everything for him; but precisely because of this darkness he felt that the only guiding thread in the darkness was his work, and he grasped it and held on to it with all his might.

PART FOUR

I

THE Karenins, husband and wife, continued to live in the same house and meet every day, but they were complete strangers to one another. Alexey Alexandrovich made it a rule to see his wife every day so that the servants had no grounds for making conjectures, but he avoided dining at home. Vronsky never came to Alexey Alexandrovich's house, but Anna saw him elsewhere, and her husband knew it.

The situation was agonizing for all three, and not one of them would have been capable of enduring this situation for a single day had it not been for the expectation that it would change, and that this was just a temporary painful difficulty which would pass. Alexey Alexandrovich expected this passion would pass, like everything else, that people would forget about it and his name would remain unsullied. Anna, who was responsible for this situation, and for whom it was more agonizing than for the others, endured it not only because she expected, but was firmly convinced that very soon it would all be sorted out and resolved. She had no idea what was going to sort the situation out, but she was firmly convinced that whatever it was would materialize very soon. Vronsky, automatically following her lead, was also expecting something that would resolve all the difficulties independently of him.

In the middle of the winter Vronsky spent a very dull week. He was attached to a foreign prince who had arrived in Petersburg, and had to show him the sights of Petersburg. Vronsky himself was distinguished-looking, moreover he possessed the art of comporting himself with dignity and respect and was used to dealing with such people; that was why he was attached to the Prince. But he found his duty very irksome. The prince did not want to miss anything he might be asked if he had seen in Russia once he returned home; and he himself wanted to make the most of the Russian pleasures on offer. Vronsky was obliged to be his guide to both the former and the latter. In the mornings they went sightseeing, and in the evenings they partook of national pastimes. The prince enjoyed exceptionally good health, even among princes; through gymnastics and good care of his body he had developed such stamina that, despite indulging in the pleasures to excess, he was as fresh as a large, green, glossy Dutch cucumber. The prince travelled a lot, and considered that one of the main benefits of the current-day ease of communications was the accessibility of national pastimes. He had been to Spain, sung serenades, and become intimate with a Spanish girl who played the mandolin. In Switzerland he had shot a *Gemse*.[1] In England he had galloped over fences in a red coat and shot two hundred pheasants for a bet. In Turkey he had been in a harem; in India he had ridden an elephant; and now in Russia he wished to partake of all the exclusively Russian pastimes.

As his chief master of ceremonies, so to speak, Vronsky went to considerable trouble to fit in all the Russian pastimes that various people offered to the Prince. There were trotting races, and *bliny*,* and bear hunts, and troikas, and gypsies, and revelries with Russian-style smashing of crockery. And the Prince entered into the Russian spirit with astonishing ease, smashed trays of plates and glasses, sat a gypsy girl on his knee, and seemed to be asking: what else is there, or is the whole of the Russian spirit summed up in this?

Essentially, what the Prince liked best out of all the Russian pastimes were French actresses, a ballet dancer, and white-seal champagne. Vronsky was used to foreign princes, but either because he himself had changed of late or was in too close proximity to this prince, he found this week awfully taxing. Throughout the week he persistently experienced what a man might feel if attached to a dangerous lunatic, namely fearful of the lunatic, and at the same time fearful for his own sanity through proximity to him. Vronsky constantly felt the necessity never to relax for a second the strict tone of official respect, to avoid being insulted. The prince's manner with the very people who, to Vronsky's surprise, were bending over backwards to furnish him with Russian pleasures was contemptuous. His opinions about Russian women, whom he wished to study, frequently made Vronsky flush with indignation. But the main reason why Vronsky found being with the Prince so difficult was that he could not help seeing himself in him. And what he saw in this mirror did not flatter his self-esteem. The prince was a very stupid, very self-assured, very healthy, and very decent man, and nothing more. He was a gentleman—that was true, and Vronsky could not deny it. He was easy-going and not sycophantic with his superiors, free and easy in his relations with his equals, and

---

[1] chamois [German].

contemptuously good-natured with his inferiors. Vronsky was the same himself, and regarded it as a great merit; but he was an inferior with regard to the Prince, and that contemptuously good-natured attitude infuriated him.

'Stupid lump of beef! Am I really like that?' he thought.

In any case, when on the seventh day he said goodbye to the Prince before his departure for Moscow, and received thanks, he was happy to be rid of this awkward situation and unpleasant mirror. He said goodbye to him at the station after returning from a bear hunt, where they had been entertained all night by a display of reckless Russian bravado.

2

WHEN he returned home, Vronsky found a note from Anna. She wrote: 'I am ill and unhappy. I can't go out, but I can't go any longer without seeing you. Come over this evening. Alexey Alexandrovich goes to the council at seven and will be there until ten.' After pondering for a minute the strangeness of her inviting him to come directly to her house, despite her husband's demand that she not receive him, he decided to go.

Vronsky had been promoted to colonel that winter, had left regimental quarters, and was living alone. After having lunch, he immediately lay down on the sofa, and within five minutes his memories of the outrageous scenes he had witnessed over the previous few days had become confused and mixed up with images of Anna and the peasant stalker* who had played an important part in the bear hunt; and Vronsky fell asleep. He woke up in the dark, trembling with fear, and hurriedly lit a candle. 'What was that? What? What was the awful thing I dreamed about? Oh, yes. That peasant stalker, I think, who was small and dirty, with a dishevelled beard, was bent over doing something, and suddenly he started saying some strange words in French. No, there was nothing else in the dream,' he said to himself. 'But why was it so awful then?' He vividly recalled the peasant again and the incomprehensible French words the peasant had been uttering, and a chill of horror ran down his spine.

'What nonsense!' thought Vronsky, and he glanced at his watch.

It was already half-past eight. He rang for his servant, dressed hurriedly, and went out on to the porch, completely forgetting his dream and fretting only about being late. As he drove up to the Karenins' porch, he looked at his watch and saw that it was ten minutes to nine.

A tall, quite narrow carriage harnessed to a pair of greys was standing at the front door. He recognized it as Anna's carriage. 'She is coming to me,' thought Vronsky, 'and that would be better. I don't like going into that house. But it doesn't matter; I can't hide,' he said to himself, and with the air, acquired in childhood, of a man who has nothing to be ashamed of, Vronsky got out of his sleigh and went up to the door. The door opened and the hall porter, with a rug over his arm, called the carriage. Although he was not in the habit of noticing details, Vronsky now did notice the startled expression with which the porter glanced at him. In the doorway Vronsky almost bumped into Alexey Alexandrovich. The gas-jet shone a direct light on the bloodless, haggard face under the black hat, and on the white tie gleaming behind the beaver collar of his coat. Karenin's lacklustre, staring eyes turned towards Vronsky's face. Vronsky bowed, and Alexey Alexandrovich, chewing his lip, raised his hand to his hat and walked past. Vronsky saw him get into the carriage without looking round, take the rug and opera glasses through the window, and disappear. Vronsky went into the hall. His brows were furrowed, and his eyes shone with an angry, proud glitter.

'This is a tricky situation!' he thought. 'If he was prepared to fight and defend his honour, I could act, express my feelings; but this weakness or underhandedness . . . He puts me in the position of being the deceiver, which I never wanted and now do not want to be.'

Since the time of his frank discussion with Anna in Wrede's garden, Vronsky's ideas had changed a great deal. Unconsciously submitting to Anna's weakness, since she had given herself to him totally, expecting him alone to decide her fate, and submitting to everything in advance, he had long ago stopped thinking that their relationship might end as he had thought back then. His ambitious plans had again retreated into the background and, feeling that he had left that sphere of activity in which everything was definite, he had surrendered totally to his feelings, and those feelings were binding him ever more closely to her.

He heard her receding footsteps while he was still in the hall. He realized she had been expecting him and had been listening out, and had now returned to the drawing room.

'No!' she cried when she saw him, and tears sprang into her eyes at the first sound of her voice. 'No, if things carry on like this, it will happen much, much sooner!'

'What, my love?'

'What? I've waited in agony for an hour, two hours . . . No, I won't . . . I can't quarrel with you. No doubt you couldn't come. No, I won't!'

She placed both her hands on his shoulders and fixed him for a long

time with an intense and rapturous yet searching gaze. She was studying his face to make up for the time she had not seen him. As at every
one of their meetings, she was bringing together the picture she had
of him in her imagination (incomparably better, impossible in reality)
with him as he really was.

3

'You met him?' she asked, when they had sat down at a table under
a lamp. 'That's your punishment for being late.'

'Yes, but what happened? Wasn't he supposed to be at the council?'

'He was there, and he came back, and now he has gone off again
somewhere else. But it doesn't matter. Don't talk about it. Where have
you been? With the Prince still?'

She knew all the details of his life. He was about to say that he had
been up all night and had fallen asleep, but as he looked at her excited
and happy face he felt ashamed. And he said that he had needed to go
to report that the Prince had left.

'But that's all over now? He is gone?'

'Yes, thank goodness. You wouldn't believe how unbearable it was.'

'But why? It's the kind of life all you young men lead, after all,' she
said with a frown, and picking up the crochet-work that was lying on
the table, she began disentangling the hook without looking at Vronsky.

'I left that life a long time ago,' he said, surprised at the change in
the expression on her face and trying to penetrate its meaning. 'And
I have to confess,' he said, showing his solid white teeth as he smiled,
'that it was as if I was seeing myself in a mirror this week, looking at
that life, and I didn't enjoy it.'

She was holding her crochet-work in her hands, but was looking at
him with strange, glittering, unfriendly eyes instead of crocheting.

'This morning Liza came to see me—they're not afraid to call on
me yet, despite Countess Lydia Ivanovna,' she added, 'and she told me
about your Athenian evening. How disgusting!'

'I just wanted to say that . . .'

She interrupted him.

'It was Thérèse, wasn't it—the one you used to know?'

'I wanted to say . . .'

'How vile you men are! How can you not see that a woman can
never forget that,' she said, becoming more and more heated, thereby
revealing to him the cause of her irritation. 'Particularly a woman who

cannot know your life? What do I know? What did I know?' she said. 'Only what you tell me. And how would I know whether you've been telling me the truth . . .'

'Anna! That offends me. Do you not believe me? Haven't I told you that I don't have a single thought that I wouldn't reveal to you?'

'Yes, yes,' she said, clearly trying to expel her jealous thoughts. 'But if you only knew how hard it is for me! I believe you, I believe you . . . So what were you saying?'

But he could not immediately remember what he had wanted to say. These fits of jealousy which lately had been overcoming her with increasing frequency horrified him, and no matter how much he tried to conceal it, they cooled his feelings for her, despite his knowing that the cause of her jealousy was her love for him. How often had he told himself that her love was happiness; and now she loved him as a woman for whom love has outweighed all the good things in life— and he was much further from happiness than when he had followed her from Moscow. Back then he had thought he was unhappy, but happiness was in prospect; now he felt that his greatest happiness was already behind him. She was completely different to how she had been when he had first set eyes on her. She had changed for the worse, both morally and physically. She had filled out all over, and there was a bitterness in her expression when she spoke about the actress which distorted her features. He looked at her as a man looks at a faded flower he has picked, in which he can scarcely recognize the beauty for which he picked and destroyed it. And in spite of that, he felt that if he had really wanted, he could have torn this love from his heart when his love had been stronger, but that now, when it seemed to him he felt no love for her, as at this moment, he knew that the bond with her could not be broken.

'Well now, what was it you were going to tell me about the Prince? I have driven away the demon, I promise,' she added. The demon was what they called her jealousy. 'What was it you were going to tell me about the Prince? Why did you find it so difficult?'

'Oh, it was unbearable!' he said, trying to pick up the lost thread of his thought. 'He does not improve on closer acquaintance. If I were to define him, I would say he is the sort of well-fed animal that wins top medals at agricultural shows, and nothing more,' he said with a note of irritation that intrigued her.

'But how can that be?' she replied. 'He's seen a great deal, after all, and he's educated, isn't he?'

'But their education is a completely different kind of education. It's clear he's only been educated in order to have the right to despise education, like they despise everything except animal pleasures.'

'But you all love these animal pleasures,' she said, and he once again noticed the gloomy look which avoided his gaze.

'Why are you defending him?' he said, smiling.

'I'm not defending him, it's all the same to me; but I think that if you didn't care for those pleasures yourself, you could have refused. But you do get pleasure from looking at Thérèse dressed up as Eve . . .'

'There's that devil again!' Vronsky said, taking the hand she had laid on the table and kissing it.

'Yes, but I can't help it! You don't know the agonies I went through waiting for you! I don't think I'm jealous. I'm not jealous; I believe you when you're here with me; but when you're off on your own, leading a life which is incomprehensible to me . . .'

She turned away from him, finally disentangled the hook from her crochet-work, and, with the help of her forefinger, started swiftly producing one loop after another from the white wool shining in the lamplight, her slender wrist rotating rapidly and nervously in its embroidered cuff.

'So what happened? Where did you meet Alexey Alexandrovich?' her voice suddenly rang out in a stilted way.

'We bumped into each other in the doorway.'

'And did he bow to you like this?'

Pulling a long face and half-closing her eyes, she quickly changed the expression on her face and folded her hands, and Vronsky suddenly saw in her beautiful face the very expression with which Alexey Alexandrovich had bowed to him. He smiled, while she let out a merry peal of that endearing, chesty laughter which was one of her main charms.

'I don't understand him at all,' said Vronsky. 'If he had severed relations with you after what you told him at the dacha, if he had challenged me to a duel . . . but this I don't understand: how can he put up with a situation like this? He is suffering, that's plain to see.'

'You think he's suffering?' she said scornfully. 'He's perfectly happy.'

'Why do we all have to be so miserable, when everything could be so good?'

'Only he's not miserable. Do you think I don't know him, and all the falsehood he is saturated with? . . . Is it possible for a person with feelings to lead the life he lives with me? He doesn't understand anything, he doesn't feel anything. Can a person capable of feeling something really live in the same house as his *lawbreaking* wife? Could he talk to her? Call her "my dear"?'

And again she could not help mimicking him: ' "Anna, *ma chère*, my dear!" '

'He's not a man, he's not a human being, he's a puppet! No one knows, but I do. Oh, if I'd been in his place, if anyone else had been in his place, I'd have killed a long time ago, I'd have torn to shreds a wife like me, and I wouldn't have said, "Anna, *ma chère*"! He's not a man, he's a ministerial machine. He doesn't understand that I am your wife, that he's an outsider, that he's superfluous . . . We're not going to talk about him, we're not! . . .'

'You're being unfair, very unfair, my love,' said Vronsky, trying to soothe her. 'But never mind, let's not talk about him. Tell me, what have you been doing? What is the matter? What is this illness, and what did the doctor say?'

She looked at him with a scornful glee. She had obviously found other ridiculous and unattractive aspects in her husband, and was waiting for the opportunity to name them.

He continued:

'I imagine it's not illness, but your condition. When will it be?'

The scornful gleam in her eyes was extinguished, but another smile—of knowledge of something he did not know and quiet sadness—replaced her previous expression.

'Soon, soon. You were saying that our situation is miserable, that it needs to be sorted out. If you only knew how hard it is for me, and what I would give to be able to love you freely and fearlessly! I wouldn't torment myself and I wouldn't torment you with my jealousy . . . And that will happen soon, but not in the way we think.'

And at the thought of how it would happen, she seemed so pitiful to herself that tears sprang into her eyes, and she could not continue. She laid her hand, whose rings and whiteness sparkled in the lamplight, on his sleeve.

'It won't happen the way we think. I didn't want to tell you this, but you've forced me to. Soon, soon, everything will be sorted out, and we shall all be at peace, all of us, and we will not suffer any more.'

'I don't understand,' he said, but he did.

'You were asking when? Soon. And I won't survive it. Don't interrupt me!' And she continued hastily. 'I know this, I know it for certain. I'm going to die, and I'm very glad I will die and save myself and you both.'

Tears began to run from her eyes; he bent down over her hand and started to kiss it, trying to hide the anxiety which he knew had no foundation, but which he could not overcome.

'There, that's better,' she said, tightly gripping his hand. 'That's the one last thing we have left to us.'

He recovered and lifted his head.

'What nonsense! What absurd nonsense you are talking!'

'No, it's the truth.'

'What, what is the truth?'

'That I shall die. I had a dream.'

'A dream?' Vronsky repeated and instantly remembered the peasant in his dream.

'Yes, a dream,' she said. 'I had this dream a long time ago. I dreamed that I ran into my bedroom because I needed to get something or find something out; you know what it is like when you are dreaming,' she said, opening her eyes wide in horror; 'and in the bedroom, in the corner, there was something standing there.'

'Oh, what nonsense! How can you believe . . .'

But she would not let him interrupt her. What she was saying was too important to her.

'And this something turned round, and I saw it was a small peasant with a dishevelled beard and very frightening. I wanted to run away, but he was bent over a sack, and was rummaging about in it with his hands . . .'

She showed how he had rummaged in the sack. There was horror in her face. And Vronsky felt the same horror filling his soul as he remembered his dream.

'He was rummaging and saying in French, very quickly, and, you know, rolling his *r*'s like the French: *Il faut le battre le fer, le broyer, le pétrir . . .*[1] And I was so scared I wanted to wake up, and I did wake up . . . but I woke up in a dream. And I began asking myself what it meant. And Korney tells me: "You'll die in childbirth, ma'am, in childbirth . . ." And I woke up. . . .'

'What nonsense, what nonsense!' said Vronsky, but he himself was aware that his voice lacked all conviction.

'But let's not talk about it. Ring the bell, and I'll ask for tea. But wait, it won't be long before I . . .'

But suddenly she stopped. The expression on her face instantly changed. Horror and anxiety were suddenly replaced by an expression of quiet, serious, and blissful attention. He could not understand the meaning of this change. She was feeling the stirring of new life inside her.

---

[1] 'the iron must be beaten, pounded, shaped, . . .'

4

AFTER meeting Vronsky on his own doorstep, Alexey Alexandrovich drove, as he had intended, to the Italian Opera.* He sat through two acts and saw everyone he needed to see. Upon returning home, he carefully inspected the coat-stand and, perceiving no military coat, went as usual to his rooms. Unusually for him, however, he did not go to bed, but paced up and down in his study until three in the morning. The anger he felt towards his wife, who would not observe propriety and adhere to the one condition he had imposed on her—not to receive her lover at home—gave him no rest. She had not complied with his demands, and he was obliged to punish her and carry out his threat—to insist on a divorce and take her son from her. He knew all the difficulties this entailed, but he had said he would do it, and now he must carry out his threat. Countess Lydia Ivanovna had intimated to him that this was the best way out of his situation, and divorce procedures had lately been honed to such perfection that Alexey Alexandrovich saw the possibility of overcoming the formal difficulties. Moreover, misfortunes never come singly, and the affairs concerning the settlement of minorities and the irrigation of lands in Zaraisk province had embroiled Alexey Alexandrovich in such unpleasantness at work that lately he had constantly been in a state of extreme irritation.

He lay awake all night, and his anger, increasing in a kind of huge progression, had reached extreme limits by morning. He dressed hurriedly and, as if carrying a full cup of fury and fearing to spill any of it, lest he should lose along with his fury the energy he needed for the confrontation with his wife, he went to her room as soon as he heard she was up.

Anna, who thought she knew her husband so well, was astonished by the sight of him when he came in. His brow was furrowed, and his eyes were staring grimly straight ahead, avoiding her gaze; his lips were tightly and disdainfully pursed. In his gait, in his gestures, and in the sound of his voice, there was a determination and firmness that his wife had never seen in him. He came into the room, and without greeting her, went straight over to her writing-desk, took the keys, and opened the drawer.

'What do you want?' she exclaimed.

'Your lover's letters,' he said.

'They're not here,' she said, shutting the drawer; but he realized from this gesture that he had guessed correctly and, roughly brushing her hand aside, he quickly seized the folder in which he knew she put her most important papers. She tried to wrench the folder from him, but he pushed her away.

'Sit down! I need to speak to you,' he said, putting the folder under his arm, and squeezing it so tightly with his elbow that his shoulder rose.

She looked at him silently, in surprise and trepidation.

'I told you that I would not allow you to receive your lover here.'

'I had to see him, to . . .'

She stopped, unable to think of an excuse.

'I am not going into the details of why a woman needs to see her lover.'

'I meant, I just . . .' she said, flushing. His coarseness nettled her, and gave her courage. 'Can you not feel how easy it is for you to insult me?' she said.

'One may insult an honest man and an honest woman, but to tell a thief that he is a thief is simply *la constatation d'un fait*.'[1]

'I have not seen this new trait of cruelty in you before.'

'You call it cruelty that a husband grants his wife freedom, giving her the honourable protection of his name, with the sole condition that she observes propriety. That is cruelty?'

'It's worse than cruelty, it's despicable, if you really want to know!' exclaimed Anna in an outburst of rage, and got up to leave.

'No!' he shouted in his squeaky voice, which had now risen one note higher than usual and, gripping her arm so tightly with his large fingers that red marks were left from the bracelet he was pressing on, he forced her to sit back down. 'Despicable? If you want to use that word, it is despicable to abandon a husband and son for a lover and go on eating the husband's bread!'

She hung her head. Not only did she not say what she had said the previous evening to her lover, that *he* was her husband, and her husband was superfluous; she did not even think this. She felt the full justice of his words, and merely said quietly:

'You cannot describe my situation as being worse than I know it to be myself, but why are you saying all this?'

'Why am I saying this? Why?' he continued just as angrily. 'So you know that, since you have not carried out my wishes in regard to observing propriety, I am going to take steps to put an end to this situation.'

'It will come to an end soon enough anyway,' she said, and tears

---

[1] 'the statement of a fact'.

sprang into her eyes again at the thought of her approaching and now longed-for death.

'It will end sooner than you and your lover have planned! You need to satisfy animal passions . . .'

'Alexey Alexandrovich! I won't say it's unkind, but it's unseemly to strike someone when they are down.'

'Yes, you only think of yourself, but the sufferings of the man who was your husband are of no interest to you. You don't care that his whole life is ruined, that he been stuff . . . sluff . . . stuffering.'

Alexey Alexandrovich was speaking so quickly that he stumbled and was quite unable to pronounce the word *suffering*. Eventually he came out with *stuffering*. She wanted to laugh, and was immediately ashamed that she could find anything funny at such a moment. And for a brief moment she felt for him, put herself in his shoes, and began to feel sorry for him for the first time. But what could she say or do? She bowed her head and was silent. He too was silent for a while, and then began speaking in a cold, less squeaky voice, emphasizing randomly chosen words that had no particular significance.

'I have come to tell you . . .' he said.

She looked at him. 'No, it was my imagination,' she thought, recalling the expression on his face when he floundered on the word *suffering*. 'No. Can a man with those dull eyes and that calm complacency really feel anything?'

'I cannot change anything,' she whispered.

'I have come to tell you that I am going to Moscow tomorrow and shall not return to this house any more, and you will be apprised of my decision through the lawyer I will appoint to start divorce proceedings. And my son will go and live with my sister,'* said Alexey Alexandrovich, making an effort to remember what he had wanted to say about his son.

'You just want Seryozha so you can hurt me,' she said, looking up at him from under her brows. 'You do not love him . . . Leave Seryozha!'

'Yes, I have even lost affection for my son, because he is associated with the repulsion I feel for you. But I shall still take him. Goodbye!'

And he was about to leave, but now she stopped him.

'Alexey Alexandrovich, leave Seryozha!' she whispered again. 'I have nothing else to say. Leave Seryozha until my . . . I will give birth soon, leave him!'

Alexey Alexandrovich flushed, snatched his hand from her, and left the room without a word.

5

THE waiting-room of the famous Petersburg lawyer was full when Alexey Alexandrovich entered it. Three ladies—an old woman, a young one, and a merchant's wife—and three gentlemen—one a German banker with a ring on his finger, the second a merchant with a beard, and the third an irate official in uniform with a decoration round his neck—had obviously already been waiting a long time. Two clerks were writing at desks, their pens rasping. The writing implements, objects for which Alexey Alexandrovich had a particular enthusiasm, were of an unusually fine quality, and he could not help noticing them. One of the clerks narrowed his eyes and turned to Alexey Alexandrovich without getting up.

'What do you want?'

'I have a matter to discuss with the lawyer.'

'The lawyer is busy,' the clerk replied sternly, indicating with his pen the people waiting, and he carried on writing.

'Could he not find the time?' said Alexey Alexandrovich.

'He has no free time, he is always busy. Be so kind as to wait.'

'Then if I might trouble you to give him my card,' Alexey Alexandrovich said with dignity, seeing the necessity of revealing his identity.

The clerk took the card and, clearly not approving of what he read on it, went through the door.

Alexey Alexandrovich was in favour of public trials in principle, but for purely professional reasons known to him, he was not fully in favour of certain aspects of their application in Russia, and condemned them, insofar as he could condemn anything endorsed at the highest level. His whole life had proceeded in administrative work, and so whenever he was not in favour of something, his disfavour was mitigated by an acknowledgement of the inevitability of mistakes and the possibility of correcting them in each case. In the new judicial institutions he did not approve of the circumstances in which lawyers had been placed. But until this point he had never dealt with lawyers, and so had disapproved of them only in theory; now, however, his disapproval was intensified by the unpleasant impression he received in the lawyer's waiting-room.

'He will be out in just a moment,' said the clerk; and indeed, two minutes later in the doorway appeared the long figure of an old jurist who had been conferring with the lawyer, and the lawyer himself.

The lawyer was a short, thickset, bald man, with a reddish-black beard, long, fair-haired eyebrows, and a bulging forehead. He was as smartly dressed as a bridegroom, from his cravat and double watch-chain to his patent-leather boots. He had an intelligent, peasant-like face, but his attire was flamboyant and in poor taste.

'Do come in,' said the lawyer, addressing Alexey Alexandrovich. And after gloomily ushering Karenin in, he closed the door.

'Won't you sit down?' He indicated an armchair by a desk strewn with papers and proceeded to sit down behind it, rubbing together his small hands with their stubby fingers covered with white hairs, and inclining his head to one side. But no sooner had he settled in this position than a moth flitted over the desk. With a celerity one would never have expected of him, the lawyer opened his hands wide, caught the moth, and resumed his former position.

'Before I start talking about my case,' said Alexey Alexandrovich, having watched the lawyer's movements with amazement, 'I must point out that the matter I have come to speak to you about must remain confidential.'

A barely perceptible smile parted the lawyer's drooping, reddish moustache.

'I should not be a lawyer if I could not keep the confidences entrusted to me. But if you would like confirmation . . .'

Alexey Alexandrovich glanced at his face, and saw that the shrewd, grey eyes were laughing and seemed to know everything already.

'You know my name?' continued Alexey Alexandrovich.

'I know you and the good'—he caught another moth—'work you are doing, like every Russian does,' said the lawyer, bowing.

Alexey Alexandrovich sighed, plucking up courage. But once he was resolved, he went on in his squeaky voice, boldly and without hesitation, emphasizing certain words.

'I have the misfortune', Alexey Alexandrovich began, 'to be a deceived husband, and I want to break off relations with my wife legally, that is, to divorce her, but in such a way that my son does not remain with his mother.'

The lawyer's grey eyes tried not to laugh, but they were dancing with irrepressible glee, and Alexey Alexandrovich saw not only the glee of a man receiving a profitable commission, but also triumph and delight, and a gleam similar to that malevolent gleam he had seen in his wife's eyes.

'You would like my assistance in obtaining a divorce?'

'Precisely, but I must warn you,' said Alexey Alexandrovich, 'that I may be wasting your time. I have just come for a preliminary consultation with you. I want a divorce, but the forms in which it is possible are important to me. It may well be that if the forms do not correspond with my requirements, I will relinquish legal proceedings.'

'Oh, that's always the case,' said the lawyer, 'and that's always for you to decide.'

The lawyer brought his eyes to rest on Alexey Alexandrovich's feet, feeling that their look of irrepressible glee might offend his client. He watched a moth fluttering in front of his nose, and his hand twitched, but out of deference to Alexey Alexandrovich's situation he did not catch it.

'Although I am familiar in general terms with our laws on this subject,' Alexey Alexandrovich continued, 'I should be glad to know about the form in which such matters proceed in practice.'

'You would like me', replied the lawyer without raising his eyes, and, not without pleasure, adopting his client's tone of speech, 'to set out for you the methods by which your wishes may be carried out?'

Receiving an affirmative nod from Alexey Alexandrovich, he went on, occasionally stealing a glance at Alexey Alexandrovich's face, on which red blotches had appeared.

'Divorce under our laws', he said with a slight note of disapproval for our laws, 'is possible, as you know, in the following cases . . . You'll have to wait!' he said to the clerk who had put his head round the door, but he nevertheless got up, said a few words, and sat down again. 'In the following cases: physical defects of the married partners; separation for five years without communication,' he said, crooking a stubby finger covered with hair, 'and adultery' (this word he pronounced with obvious relish). 'The subdivisions are as follows' (he continued to crook his fat fingers, although the cases and the subdivisions clearly could not be classified together): 'physical defects of the husband or wife; and adultery committed by the husband or the wife.' Since he had used all his fingers up, he unbent them all and continued: 'This is the theoretical view, but I imagine you have done me the honour of consulting me in order to find out about its practical application. Guided therefore by precedent, I have to tell you that cases of divorce are all reduced to the following—there are no physical defects, I take it, or absence without communication? . . .'

Alexey Alexandrovich inclined his head in affirmation.

'—are all reduced to the following: adultery by one of the married partners, exposure of the guilty party by mutual consent, or involuntary exposure when there is no such consent. I must say that the latter case is rarely met with in practice,' said the lawyer, and after stealing a glance at Alexey Alexandrovich, he paused, as a man selling pistols awaits his customer's choice after having described the advantages of particular weapons. But Alexey Alexandrovich said nothing, and so the lawyer went on: 'The most usual, straightforward, and sensible course, I consider, is adultery by mutual consent. I would not have permitted myself to express it in these terms if I was speaking to an uneducated person,' he said, 'but I am presuming this is evident to you.'

Alexey Alexandrovich, however, was so upset that he could not immediately grasp how adultery by mutual consent could be regarded as sensible, and he expressed this bewilderment in his look; but the lawyer promptly came to his assistance.

'People can no longer live together—that is a fact. And if both are in agreement on that, the details and formalities become irrelevant. And at the same time this is also the simplest and surest way.'

Alexey Alexandrovich now fully understood. But he had religious dictates which prevented him from accepting this course of action.

'This is out of the question in the present case,' he said. 'Only one circumstance is possible: involuntary exposure, confirmed by letters in my possession.'

At the mention of letters, the lawyer pursed his lips and produced a high-pitched sound of pity and contempt.

'Allow me to explain,' he began. 'Cases of this kind are decided by the ecclesiastical authorities, as you know; and the reverend fathers are great sticklers for the minutest details with cases of this kind,' he said with a smile which showed his predilection for the reverend fathers' tastes. 'Letters can, of course, provide partial confirmation; but evidence must be obtained directly, that is, by witnesses. In general, if you will do me the honour of entrusting me with your confidence, you should leave it to me to select the measures which need to be employed. He who wants the result must accept the means.'

'If that is so . . .' Alexey Alexandrovich began, suddenly turning pale, but at that moment the lawyer got up and went over to the door again to speak to the clerk who had interrupted.

'Tell her we don't haggle over fees!' he said, and returned to Alexey Alexandrovich.

As he came back to his chair he surreptitiously caught another moth. 'A fine state my upholstery will be in by summer!' he thought, frowning.

'So, as you were kindly saying . . .' he said.

'I will inform you of my decision in writing,' said Alexey Alexandrovich, getting up and grasping the desk. After standing for a moment in silence, he said: 'From what you have said, I can consequently conclude that divorce proceedings are possible. I would also like to ask you to inform me of your terms.'

'Everything is possible if you give me complete freedom of action,' said the lawyer, not answering his question. 'When may I expect to hear from you?' he asked, moving towards the door, his eyes and his patent-leather boots shining.

'In a week's time. And you will be so good as to inform me of your answer as to whether you will undertake the case, and on what terms.'

'Very good, sir.'

The lawyer bowed respectfully, showed his client out, and once alone, surrendered to his feeling of jubilation. He was in such good spirits that, contrary to his rules, he gave a discount to the lady who had been haggling and stopped catching moths, having firmly resolved that by next winter he would have his furniture upholstered in velvet, like at Sigonin's.

6

ALEXEY ALEXANDROVICH had won a brilliant victory at the meeting of the Commission of 17th of August, but the consequences of this victory proved to be his undoing. The new commission for a root-and-branch investigation into the lives of the ethnic minorities had been set up and dispatched to its place of operation with an extraordinary speed and energy inspired by Alexey Alexandrovich. Within three months a report was presented. The everyday lives of the ethnic minorities had been investigated in their political, administrative, economic, ethnographic, material, and religious aspects. All questions received finely articulated answers, and answers that were not open to doubt, since they were not the product of human thought, which is always liable to error, but were the product of professional administrative activity. The answers were all the result of official data, drawing on reports from provincial governors and bishops, which were based on reports from district commissioners and archpriests, which were in turn based on reports from rural authorities and parish priests; so all these answers were therefore indisputable. All those issues about why there were crop failures, for example, why inhabitants clung to their religious beliefs and so on, issues which for centuries would not and could not be resolved without the convenience of the administrative machine, had received a clear and unequivocal resolution. And the decision went in favour of Alexey Alexandrovich's opinion. But when Stremov, who had been grievously offended at the last session, received the Commission's reports, he deployed a tactic Alexey Alexandrovich was not expecting. Carrying certain other members with him, Stremov suddenly went over to Alexey Alexandrovich's side, and now not only vigorously defended the application of the measures proposed by Karenin, but proposed other extreme measures in the same spirit. These measures, which were far more radical than Alexey Alexandrovich's basic idea, were adopted, and then Stremov's tactics were laid bare. When taken to extremes, these measures suddenly turned out to be so stupid that government figures, public opinion, clever ladies, and newspapers all tore into them simultaneously, expressing indignation both with the measures themselves, and with their acknowledged progenitor, Alexey Alexandrovich. Stremov meanwhile stepped aside, pretending he had blindly followed Karenin's plan, and was himself now surprised and indignant about what had been done. This undermined Alexey Alexandrovich. But despite his faltering health, and despite his family woes, Alexey Alexandrovich did not give in. A split appeared in the Commission. Some members, with Stremov at their head, justified their mistake on the grounds that they had trusted the inspection Commission led by Alexey Alexandrovich, which had presented the report, and said that this Commission's report was a lot of nonsense, and not worth the paper it was written on. Alexey Alexandrovich, along with a group of people who saw the danger in such a revolutionary attitude to official documents, continued to support the data produced by the inspection Commission. This led to a great deal of confusion in higher spheres, and even in society at large, and although everyone was extremely interested, no one could work out whether the ethnic minorities were really in a state of poverty and decline, or flourishing. Alexey Alexandrovich's position as a result of this, and also partly as a result of the contempt which descended on him due to his wife's infidelity, became highly precarious. And in this position Alexey Alexandrovich made an important decision. To the surprise of the Commission, he announced that he was going to ask permission to go and investigate the matter on the spot himself. And after obtaining permission, Alexey Alexandrovich set off for the distant provinces.

Alexey Alexandrovich's departure caused a great stir, particularly since just before leaving he formally returned the travel expenses officially given to him for twelve horses to take him to his destination.

'I think that it's very noble,' Betsy said to Princess Myagkaya when talking about this. 'Why give money for post-horses when everyone knows there are railways everywhere now?'

But Princess Myagkaya did not agree, and Princess Tverskaya's opinion annoyed her.

'It's all very well for you to talk,' she said, 'when you have heaven knows how many millions, but I love it when my husband goes off to do his inspections in the summer. It's very salubrious and enjoyable for him to do all that travelling, and it's become my custom to use the money to keep a carriage and coachman.'

On his way to the distant provinces, Alexey Alexandrovich stopped for three days in Moscow.

The day after his arrival he went to pay a call on the Governor-General. At the crossroads by Gazetny Lane, a place always swarming with carriages and cabs, Alexey Alexandrovich suddenly heard his name called out in such a loud and cheerful voice that he could not help looking round. On the corner of the pavement, in a short, fashionable coat and a short, fashionable hat set at a tilt, beaming a smile showing white teeth between red lips, all cheerful, youthful, and glowing, stood Stepan Arkadyich, shouting and demanding with determination and insistence that he stop. He had one hand resting on the window of a carriage that had stopped at the corner, out of which peeped the head of a lady in a velvet hat and the heads of two small children, and he was smiling and with his other hand beckoning to his brother-in-law. The lady was smiling warmly, and also waving at Alexey Alexandrovich. It was Dolly with her children.

Alexey Alexandrovich did not want to see anyone in Moscow, least of all his wife's brother. He raised his hat and was about to drive on, but Stepan Arkadyich ordered the coachman to stop and ran over to him across the snow.

'Well, you could have let us know! Have you been here long? I was at Dusseaux's yesterday and saw "Karenin" on the board, but it never occurred to me that it was you,' said Stepan Arkadyevich, thrusting his head through the carriage window, 'or I would have dropped round. I am so glad to see you!' he said banging one foot against the other to shake off the snow. 'You could have let us know!' he repeated.

'I had no time, I am very busy,' replied Alexey Alexandrovich crisply.

'Come and speak to my wife, she is so anxious to see you.'

Alexey Alexandrovich removed the rug in which his chilly feet were wrapped, got out of the carriage, and made his way over the snow to Darya Alexandrovna.

'What's this all about, Alexey Alexandrovich, why are you avoiding us like this?' said Dolly, smiling wistfully.

'I've been very busy. Very glad to see you,' he said in a tone which clearly showed that he was distressed by this. 'How are you?'

'So, how is my dearest Anna?'

Alexey Alexandrovich mumbled something and was on the verge of leaving. But Stepan Arkadyich stopped him.

'Here's what we'll do tomorrow. Dolly, invite him to dinner! We'll ask Koznyshev and Pestsov, and treat him to the Moscow intelligentsia.'

'Yes, please do come,' said Dolly; 'we will expect you at five, or six o'clock, if you like. How is my dearest Anna? It's a long time . . .'

'She is well,' Alexey Alexandrovich mumbled, frowning. 'Very glad to see you!' and he headed for his carriage.

'You will come?' Dolly shouted out.

Alexey Alexandrovich said something which Dolly could not hear in the noise of the moving carriages.

'I will drop by tomorrow!' Stepan Arkadyich shouted out to him.

Alexey Alexandrovich got into his carriage, and buried himself in it so he could neither see nor be seen.

'Odd fellow!' said Stepan Arkadyich to his wife, and after glancing at his watch, he made a gesture with his hand in front of his face indicating affection for his wife and children, and walked jauntily along the pavement.

'Stiva! Stiva!' Dolly called out, blushing.

He turned round.

'I have to buy coats, you know, for Grisha and Tanya. Do give me some money!'

'Don't worry, just tell them I'll pay!' and after nodding genially to an acquaintance driving by, he vanished.

7

THE next day was Sunday. Stepan Arkadyich dropped in at a ballet rehearsal at the Bolshoi Theatre to give Masha Chibisova, a pretty dancer recently taken on through his patronage, the coral necklace he had promised her the previous day, and in the wings, in the daytime darkness of the theatre, managed to kiss her pretty little face, which was glowing with pleasure from the gift. Besides giving her the corals, he needed to arrange a meeting with her after the ballet. After explaining to her that he could not be there at the beginning of the ballet, he promised he would come for the last act and take her out for supper. From the theatre Stepan Arkadyich went on to Okhotny Row, picked out the fish and asparagus for dinner himself, and at twelve o'clock was already at Dusseaux's, where he had to see three people, who, luckily for him, were all staying at the same hotel: Levin, who had recently returned from abroad and was staying there; the new head of his department, just appointed to this lofty position and in Moscow on a tour of inspection; and his brother-in-law Karenin, whom he definitely had to bring home for dinner.

Stepan Arkadyich loved a good dinner, but what he liked even more was to host a dinner—small-scale, but refined as regards the food, the drink, and the selection of guests. He particularly liked the programme for that day's dinner: there would be live perch,* asparagus, and *la pièce de résistance*—a superb but simple roast beef, and wines to match: that was the food and drink. Amongst the guests would be Kitty and Levin, plus another female cousin and young Shcherbatsky to make it less obvious, while *la pièce de résistance* among the guests would be Sergey Koznyshev and Alexey Alexandrovich. Sergey Ivanovich was a Muscovite and a philosopher, while Alexey Alexandrovich was a practical man from Petersburg; and for good measure he was also going to invite the well-known eccentric and enthusiast Pestsov, who was a liberal, a chatterbox, a musician, a historian, and the most charming fifty-year-old young man, who would provide the sauce or the garnish for Koznyshev and Karenin. He would stir them up and pit them against each other.

The second instalment of money for the wood had been received from the merchant and was not yet spent, Dolly had been very sweet and kind of late, and the thought of this dinner delighted Stepan Arkadyich in all respects. He was in the most ebullient of spirits. There were two slightly disagreeable circumstances, but both these circumstances were drowned in the sea of good-natured jollity surging in Stepan Arkadyich's soul. These two circumstances were, firstly, that when he had met Alexey Alexandrovich on the street the day before he had noticed that he was stiff and unfriendly with him, and putting the expression on Alexey Alexandrovich's face together with the fact that he had not come to see them or let them know of his arrival, and the rumours he had heard about Anna and Vronsky, Stepan Arkadyich guessed that all was not well between husband and wife.

That was the first disagreeable thing. The other slightly disagreeable thing was that his new head of department, like all new heads, already had the reputation of being a terrifying person who got up at six o'clock in the morning, worked like a horse, and demanded the same from his subordinates. This new head also had a reputation for having the manners of a bear, moreover, and rumour had it that he was a person with diametrically opposed views to those held by the previous head and still held by Stepan Arkadyich himself. The previous day Stepan Arkadyich had turned up at the office in uniform, and the new head had been very amiable and chattered away to him as if they were acquaintances; Stepan Arkadyich therefore considered it his duty to call on him now in a frock-coat. The thought that the new head might give him a frosty reception was the other unpleasant circumstance. But Stepan Arkadyich instinctively felt that everything would *shape up* in splendid fashion. 'They're all people, all mortal, like us sinners: what is there to rage and wrangle about?' he thought as he walked into the hotel.

'Hello, Vasily,' he said to a footman he knew as he walked down the corridor with his hat at an angle, 'are you growing side-whiskers? Levin is in room seven, is he? Please escort me. And could you find out whether Count Anichkin'—this was the new head—'will receive me?'

'Yes, sir,' Vasily replied, smiling. 'It's a long time since you were last here.'

'I was here yesterday, but came in through the other entrance. Is this room seven?'

Levin was standing in the middle of the room with a peasant from Tver, measuring a fresh bearskin with a yardstick when Stepan Arkadyich came in.

'Ah, is this one you've shot?' cried Stepan Arkadyich. 'A fine specimen! A she-bear? Hello, Arkhip!'

He shook hands with the peasant and perched on the edge of a chair without taking off his coat and hat.

'Come on, take your coat off and sit down!' said Levin, taking his hat off him.

'No, I haven't got time, I've just popped in for a minute,' answered Stepan Arkadyich. He threw open his coat, but then took it off and sat for a whole hour talking to Levin about hunting and the most personal matters.

'So now, tell me, please, what did you do when you were abroad? Where did you go?' said Stepan Arkadyich when the peasant had left.

'Well, I was in Germany, in Prussia, in France, in England, but in the manufacturing towns, not in the capitals, and I saw a lot of new things. And I'm glad I went.'

'Yes, I know your idea about organizing the workers.'

'Not at all: in Russia there can be no issue about the workers. In Russia the issue is about the working people's relationship to the land; it exists there too, but it's a matter of repairing the damage there, while here . . .'

Stepan Arkadyich listened attentively to Levin.

'Yes, yes!' he said. 'It's quite possible you're right. But I'm glad you're in good spirits, that you are going bear-hunting, and working, and are caught up in things. Because Shcherbatsky told me—he met you—that you were in some kind of depression, and kept talking about death. . . .'

'Well, yes, I never stop thinking about death,' said Levin. 'It's true that it's time for me to die. And that all this is nonsense. I'll be honest with you: I set great store by my ideas and my work, but essentially—well, think about it: this whole world of ours is really just a spot of mildew which has formed on a tiny planet. And we think we can have something grand—thoughts, deeds! They are just grains of sand.'

'But that's as old as the hills, my friend!'

'It is, but you know, when you have a clear understanding of that, somehow everything becomes insignificant. When you understand that you might die today or tomorrow, and that nothing will remain, everything is so insignificant! I do think my ideas are very important, but even if they were to be put into practice, they would turn out to be just as insignificant as stalking this bear. And that's how you spend your life, distracting yourself with hunting, working—anything so as not to think about death.'

Stepan Arkadyich smiled perceptively and affectionately as he listened to Levin.

'Well, of course! See—you've come round to my point of view. Remember how you used to attack me for seeking enjoyment in life? *Oh moralist, do not be so severe! . . .**

'No, all the same, what is good in life is . . .' Levin became confused. 'Oh, I don't know. All I know is that we shall soon be dead.'

'But why soon?'

'And you know, life has less charm when one thinks about death, but it's more peaceful.'

'On the contrary, it gets even jollier toward the end. However, I must go,' said Stepan Arkadyich, getting up for the tenth time.

'No, don't go yet!' said Levin, trying to detain him. 'When are we going to see each other again? I'm leaving tomorrow.'

'I'm a fine one! I came expressly to . . . You have got to come to dinner with us this evening. Your brother will be there, and Karenin, my brother-in-law, will be there.'

'He's here, is he?' said Levin, and he wanted to ask about Kitty. He had heard that at the beginning of winter she had been staying in Petersburg with her sister, the wife of the diplomat, and he did not know whether she had returned or not, but he changed his mind about asking. 'It's all the same whether she is there or not,' he thought.

'So you'll come?'

'Well, of course.'

'At five o'clock, then, and it's frock-coats.'

And Stepan Arkadyich got up and went downstairs to see his new head of department. Instinct had not deceived Stepan Arkadyich. The terrifying new head turned out to be a thoroughly affable man, and Stepan Arkadyich lunched with him and stayed so long that it was well after three by the time he got to Alexey Alexandrovich.

8

AFTER returning from church, Alexey Alexandrovich spent the whole morning indoors. There were two things he had to do that morning: firstly, receive and send on its way a deputation of ethnic minorities which was bound for Petersburg and currently in Moscow, and secondly write the letter he had promised to the lawyer. The deputation presented many inconveniences and even dangers, despite having been summoned on Alexey Alexandrovich's initiative, and he was very glad their paths had crossed in Moscow. The members of this deputation did not have the slightest idea of their role or their responsibilities. They were naively convinced that, in asking the government for help, their task was to explain their needs and the reality of their situation, and they completely failed to understand that some of their statements and requests supported the opposition, thus ruining their whole case. Alexey Alexandrovich spent a long time going over things with them, drew up a programme for them from which they were not to deviate, and after letting them go, wrote letters to Petersburg about the direction the deputation should take. His main assistant in this matter was supposed to be Countess Lydia Ivanovna. She was a specialist in the business of deputations, and no one knew better than she how to set things up and steer deputations in the right direction. Having done this, Alexey Alexandrovich also wrote the letter to the lawyer. He had no hesitation in giving him permission to act at his own discretion. With the letter he enclosed three notes from Vronsky to Anna, which he had found in the folder he had taken.

Ever since Alexey Alexandrovich had left home with the intention of not going back to his family, ever since he had been to see the lawyer and told at least one person of his intention, and particularly ever since he had turned this real-life matter into a bureaucratic procedure, he had grown more and more used to his intention, and could now clearly see the possibility of carrying it out.

He was just sealing the envelope to the lawyer when he heard the booming tones of Stepan Arkadyich's voice. Stepan Arkadyich was arguing with Alexey Alexandrovich's servant, and insisting on being announced.

'It's all the same,' thought Alexey Alexandrovich, 'and so much the better: I will tell him now about my position with respect to his sister and explain why I can't come to dinner with him.'

'Show him in!' he said loudly as he gathered up his papers and filed them away in the blotter.

'There you are, you see, you are lying, and he's at home!' Stepan Arkadyich's voice replied to the servant who had not let him in, and Oblonsky walked into the room, taking his coat off as he went. 'Well, I'm very glad I've found you in! So I'm hoping . . .' Stepan Arkadyich began merrily.

'I cannot come,' Alexey Alexandrovich said coldly, standing and not asking his visitor to sit down.

Alexey Alexandrovich had been thinking of entering straight away into the frosty relations he ought to have with the brother of his wife, against whom he was starting divorce proceedings. But he had not reckoned on the ocean of goodwill spilling over the shores in Stepan Arkadyich's soul.

Stepan Arkadyich opened wide his bright, shining eyes.

'Why can't you? What do you mean?' he asked in French, bewildered. 'No, no, you've promised. And we're all counting on you to come.'

'I mean that I cannot come to your house, because the family relations which have existed between us must cease.'

'What? What do you mean? Why?' said Stepan Arkadyich with a smile.

'Because I am starting divorce proceedings against your sister, my wife. I have been obliged to . . .'

But before Alexey Alexandrovich had finished what he had to say, Stepan Arkadyich reacted in a way he had not at all expected. He groaned and sat down in an armchair.

'No, Alexey Alexandrovich, you can't mean it!' cried Oblonsky, the pain evident in his face.

'It is so.'

'I'm sorry, but I just can't, I can't believe it . . .'

Alexey Alexandrovich sat down, feeling that his words had not produced the effect he had anticipated, that he had no option but to explain everything, and that whatever explanation he gave, his relations with his brother-in-law would remain unchanged.

'Yes, I am faced with the painful necessity of seeking a divorce,' he said.

'I will say one thing, Alexey Alexandrovich. I know you to be an excellent and fair man, and I know Anna—I'm sorry, I can't change my opinion of her—to be a fine, excellent woman, and therefore I'm sorry, but I cannot believe this. There must be some misunderstanding,' he said.

'Yes, if it only were a misunderstanding . . .'

'Forgive me, I understand,' interrupted Stepan Arkadyich. 'But of course . . . One thing: you should not act in haste. You should definitely not act in haste!'

'I have not acted in haste,' Alexey Alexandrovich said coldly, 'but one cannot seek advice from anyone in a matter like this. My mind is made up.'

'This is awful!' said Stepan Arkadyich, sighing deeply. 'There is just one thing I would do, Alexey Alexandrovich. Do it, I beg you!' he said. 'The proceedings have not yet begun, if I understand correctly. Before you start the proceedings, go and see my wife and talk to her. She loves Anna like a sister, she loves you, and she's a wonderful woman. For God's sake, talk to her! Do me this favour, I beg you!'

Alexey Alexandrovich thought for a while, and Stepan Arkadyich looked at him in sympathy, without breaking his silence.

'Will you go and see her?'

'Oh, I don't know. This is why I have not called. I believe our relations must change.'

'Why on earth should they? I can't see why. Allow me to believe that apart from our family ties, you have the same friendly feelings for me, at least in part, as I have always had for you . . . And sincere respect,' said Stepan Arkadyich, pressing his hand. 'Even if your worst suppositions were correct, I could and never would presume to judge either one side or the other, and I see no reason why our relationship has to change. But do this now, come over and see my wife.'

'Well, we look at the matter differently,' said Alexey Alexandrovich coldly. 'However, let's not talk about it.'

'But why shouldn't you come over? At least for dinner tonight. My

wife is expecting you. Please, do come. And, above all, do have a talk
with her. She's a wonderful woman. For God's sake, I beg you on bended
knees!'

'If you really want me to come that much, I will,' said Alexey
Alexandrovich, sighing.

And anxious to change the subject, he enquired about something
which interested them both—Stepan Arkadyich's new head, a man
who was not yet old, who had suddenly been appointed to such a high
position.

Alexey Alexandrovich had disliked Count Anichkin even before, and
had always disagreed with him, but now he could not suppress the
hatred, understood by all civil servants, which a man who has suffered
a professional setback feels for the man who has received a promotion.

'Well, have you seen him?' said Alexey Alexandrovich with a malicious smile.

'Of course, he was at our office yesterday. He seems to know his job
extremely well, and he is very energetic.'

'Yes, but where are his energies directed?' said Alexey Alexandrovich.
'Towards getting things done, or changing what has been done? The
misfortune of our government is its administrative paperwork, of
which he's a worthy representative.'

'Really, I don't know what one could criticize about him. I don't
know what his views are, but I do know that he's a splendid fellow,'
answered Stepan Arkadyich. 'I've just been to see him, and really, he's
a splendid fellow. We had lunch together, and I taught him how to make
that drink, you know, wine with oranges. It's very refreshing. And he
didn't know it, surprisingly enough. He liked it a lot. No, really, he's
a very nice fellow.'

Stepan Arkadyich glanced at his watch.

'Oh, good heavens, it's after four already, and I still need to see
Dolgovushin! So please come over for dinner. You can't imagine how
my wife and I will be disappointed if you don't.'

Alexey Alexandrovich escorted his brother-in-law out in a very different manner to the one in which he had greeted him.

'I've promised, and I'll come,' he answered wearily.

'Believe me, I appreciate it, and I hope you won't regret it,' answered
Stepan Arkadyich, smiling.

And putting on his coat as he went, he tapped the servant on the
head, chuckled, and left.

'Five o'clock, and frock-coats, please,' he called out again, coming
back to the door.

9

It was past five, and some of the guests had already arrived, when the host also arrived himself. He came in together with Sergey Ivanovich Koznyshev and Pestsov, who had bumped into each other on the doorstep. They were the two main representatives of the Moscow intelligentsia, as Oblonsky called them. They were both people respected for their character and their intellect. They respected each other, but were in complete and hopeless disagreement about almost everything—not because they belonged to opposing schools of thought, but precisely because they belonged to the same camp (their enemies tarred them with the same brush), although each held his own nuanced opinion within this camp. And since nothing is less conducive to consensus than disagreement on semi-abstract matters, they not only never shared the same opinions, but had long since become used to making gentle fun of each other's incorrigible misapprehensions without getting angry.

They were going in through the door, talking about the weather, when Stepan Arkadyich caught up with them. Oblonsky's father-in-law, Prince Alexander Dmitrievich, young Shcherbatsky, Turovtsyn, Kitty, and Karenin were already sitting in the drawing room.

Stepan Arkadyich saw immediately that things were going badly in the drawing room without him. Darya Alexandrovna, in her best grey silk dress, clearly worried both about the children having to eat in the nursery on their own and the fact that her husband was still not home, had not succeeded in getting the guests to mingle without him. They were all sitting like priests' daughters on a visit (as the old Prince put it), clearly perplexed as to why they should be there, and making forced remarks in order not to be silent. The good-natured Turovtsyn clearly felt uncomfortable, and the smile on his thick lips with which he greeted Stepan Arkadyich said as plain as words: 'This is a clever lot you've put me with, my friend! A drink at the Château des Fleurs would be more in my line.' The old Prince was sitting in silence, his beady little eyes stealing furtive glances at Karenin, and Stepan Arkadyich realized that he had already thought up some catch-phrase with which to stamp this statesman, whom one invited one's friends over to feast on like some fine sturgeon. Kitty was watching the door, fortifying herself so as not to blush when Konstantin Levin came in. Young Shcherbatsky, who had not been introduced to Karenin, was trying to look as though he were not in the least embarrassed by this. Karenin himself had followed the Petersburg custom of wearing white tie and tails when dining with ladies, and Stepan Arkadyich could see from his face that he had come simply to keep his word, and was carrying out an onerous duty by being part of this company. He indeed was the chief cause of the chill which had frozen all the guests before Stepan Arkadyich's arrival.

Entering the drawing room, Stepan Arkadyich apologized, explaining that he had been held up by a particular prince who was the perennial scapegoat whenever he was late or failed to appear, and in a trice he had reintroduced everybody and, bringing Alexey Alexandrovich and Sergey Koznyshev together, broached with them the topic of the Russification of Poland,* which they and Pestsov immediately latched on to. Clapping Turovtsyn on the shoulder, he whispered something funny to him, and sat him down next to his wife and the old Prince. Then he told Kitty she was looking very pretty that evening, and introduced Shcherbatsky to Karenin. He kneaded together all that social dough so well that within one minute the drawing room was abuzz, and ringing with animated voices. Only Konstantin Levin was missing. But that was for the best, because when he went into the dining room Stepan Arkadyich was horrified to see that the port and the sherry had been procured from Depret and not from Levé,* and after arranging for the coachman to be sent as quickly as possible over to Levé, he headed back to the drawing room.

At the door he encountered Konstantin Levin.

'I'm not late?'

'As if you could be anything but!' said Stepan Arkadyich, taking his arm.

'Are there a lot of people here? Who are they?' asked Levin, unable to stop himself blushing as he tapped the snow off his hat with his glove.

'All our own crowd. Kitty's here. Come along, I'll introduce you to Karenin.'

Despite his liberal views, Stepan Arkadyich knew that it could not but be an honour to make Karenin's acquaintance, and therefore treated his best friends to it. But Konstantin Levin was not at that moment capable of fully appreciating the pleasure of this acquaintance. He had not seen Kitty since that memorable evening when he had met Vronsky, apart from the moment when he had caught sight of her on the highway. He had known in the depths of his soul that he would see her here today. But in order to maintain his freedom of thought he had been trying to persuade himself he did not know that. Now when he heard that she was here, though, he suddenly felt such joy, and at the same time such fear, that it took his breath away, and he could not articulate what he wanted to say.

'What will she be like? Like she was before, or like she was in the carriage? What if Darya Alexandrovna spoke the truth? And why should it not be the truth?' he thought.

'Oh, do please introduce me to Karenin,' he articulated with effort, then with a desperately determined step he walked into the drawing room and saw her.

She was neither how she was before nor how she had been in the carriage; she was quite different.

She was scared, timid, shamefaced, and all the more lovely for it. She saw him the minute he walked into the room. She had been waiting for him. She was filled with joy, and so embarrassed by her joy that there was a moment—the moment when he went up to the hostess and looked at her again—when it seemed to him, and to her, and also to Dolly, who saw everything, that she would break down and burst into tears. She blushed, turned pale, blushed again, then froze as she waited for him to approach, her lips trembling slightly. He came up to her, bowed, and silently extended his hand. Except for the slight tremble of her lips and the moisture covering her eyes and adding to their sparkle, her smile was almost calm when she said:

'How long it is since we've seen each other!' and with desperate determination she placed her cold hand in his and pressed it.

'You haven't seen me, but I have seen you,' said Levin, with a radiant smile of happiness. 'I saw you when you were driving from the railway station to Ergushovo.'

'When?' she asked in surprise.

'You were driving to Ergushovo,' said Levin, feeling that he was choking with the happiness that was flooding his soul. 'How could I dare to associate any less than innocent thoughts with this touching creature! And yes, it seems that what Darya Alexandrovna told me is true,' he thought.

Stepan Arkadyich took him by the arm and brought him over to Karenin.

'Let me introduce you.' He gave their names.

'Very pleased to meet you again,' said Alexey Alexandrovich coldly as he shook Levin's hand.

'You are acquainted?' Stepan Arkadyich asked in surprise.

'We spent three hours in the train together,' said Levin smiling, 'but got out feeling intrigued, like leaving a masked ball, or I did at any rate.'

'Well, well! This way, please,' said Stepan Arkadyich, showing the way to the dining room.

The men entered the dining room and went up to an hors d'oeuvres table on which were arranged six different sorts of vodka and as many sorts of cheese, with and without little silver scoops, caviar, herring, preserves of various kinds, and plates with thin slices of French bread.

The men stood around the fragrant vodkas and hors d'oeuvres, and the conversation between Koznyshev, Karenin, and Pestsov about the Russification of Poland started to flag in anticipation of dinner.

Sergey Ivanovich, who had an unrivalled ability to end the most abstract and serious argument by unexpectedly adding a pinch of Attic salt, and thus alter the mood of his interlocutors, did that now.

Alexey Alexandrovich was arguing that the Russification of Poland could only be achieved as a result of higher principles, which should be introduced by the Russian administration.

Pestsov was insisting that one nation can only absorb another when it is more densely populated.

Koznyshev accepted both arguments, but with reservations. And when they were leaving the drawing room, he said with a smile, in order to bring the conversation to a close:

'There is, therefore, only one means of Russifying ethnic minorities, and that is to rear as many children as possible. My brother and I are performing worse than anyone. But you married men, especially you, Stepan Arkadyich, are behaving like true patriots; how many do you have?' he said, turning with a friendly smile to their host and holding out to him a tiny glass.

Everyone laughed, and Stepan Arkadyich with particular mirth.

'Yes, that's the best way!' he said, munching on some cheese and pouring a special sort of vodka into the glass held out before him. The conversation really did end with that joke.

'This cheese is not bad. May I offer you some?' said the host. 'You haven't been doing gymnastics again, have you?' he said, turning to Levin and feeling his muscles with his left hand.

Levin smiled, crooked his arm, and a steely mound like a Dutch cheese rose up under Stepan Arkadyich's fingers beneath the fine cloth of his frock-coat.

'Those are proper biceps! A real Samson!'

'I imagine you need to have great strength for hunting bears,' said Alexey Alexandrovich, who had the vaguest notions about hunting, as he broke the gossamer-thin sliver of bread on which he was spreading some cheese.

Levin smiled.

'None at all. On the contrary, a child can kill a bear,' he said, stepping aside with a slight bow to the ladies, who were approaching the hors d'oeuvres table with the hostess.

'But you have killed a bear, I'm told?' said Kitty, trying vainly to apprehend an insubordinate, slippery mushroom with her fork and shaking the lace through which her white arm gleamed. 'Are there really bears in your neck of the woods?' she added, half-turning her lovely little head to him and smiling.

There did not seem to be anything unusual about what she said, but what meaning, impossible to put into words, there was for him in every sound, every movement of her lips, eyes, and hands as she said this! There was entreaty for forgiveness, trust in him, affection, tender, timid affection, commitment, hope, and also love for him, in which he could not but believe, and which suffocated him with happiness.

'No, we went to Tver province. As I was coming back on the train, I met your *beau-frère*, or your brother-in-law's brother-in-law,' he said with a smile. 'It was a funny meeting.'

And he told the merry and amusing story of how, after a sleepless night, he had burst into Alexey Alexandrovich's compartment in his sheepskin jacket.

'The conductor, contrary to the proverb,* wanted to throw me out on account of how I was dressed; but then I began speaking in a sophisticated way, and . . . you too,' he said, addressing Karenin and forgetting his name, 'you also wanted to turn me out on account of my sheepskin, but then you interceded, for which I am very grateful.'

'The rights of passengers in choosing seats are, in general, extremely unclear,' said Alexey Alexandrovich, as he wiped the tips of his fingers with a napkin.

'I saw you could not make up your mind about me,' said Levin with a good-natured smile, 'so I hastened to start a clever conversation to make amends for my sheepskin.'

Sergey Ivanovich continued his conversation with the hostess, and listening with one ear to his brother, cast a sidelong glance at him. 'What is going on with him today? Quite the conqueror,' he thought. He did not know that Levin felt he had grown wings. Levin knew she was listening to him speak, and was enjoying listening to him. And this was the only thing that concerned him. Having now invested himself with enormous significance and importance, he felt that he and Kitty were the only people who existed, not just in that room, but in the whole world. He felt he was at such a high altitude that his head was spinning, while somewhere far away down below were all those nice, good Karenins, Oblonskys, and the rest of the world.

Completely unobtrusively, without looking at them, and as if there were no other places available, Stepan Arkadyich seated Levin and Kitty next to each other.

'Why don't you sit here,' he said to Levin.

The meal was as good as the dinner service, which was something for which Stepan Arkadyich had a particular enthusiasm. The *soupe Marie-Louise* was a great success; the tiny little pies which melted in the mouth were flawless. Two footmen and Matvey, in white tie, performed their duties with the food and wines inconspicuously, quietly, and efficiently. The dinner was a success on the material side; and it was no less of a success on the non-material side. The conversation, sometimes general and sometimes private, never flagged, and had become so animated by the end of dinner that the men rose from the table still talking, and even Alexey Alexandrovich had livened up.

10

PESTSOV liked to bring arguments to their conclusion, and was not satisfied with Sergey Ivanovich's remarks, particularly as he felt his opinion was flawed.

'I never had in mind density of population on its own,' he said, addressing Alexey Alexandrovich over the soup, 'but in conjunction with firm foundations, rather than principles.'

'It seems to me that is one and the same thing,' replied Alexey Alexandrovich slowly and lethargically. 'In my opinion, only a nation with superior development can influence another, one which . . .'

'But that's precisely the issue,' interrupted Pestsov in his bass voice, always in a hurry to speak, and always seeming to put his heart and soul into whatever he said. 'How are we to define superior development? The English, the French, the Germans—which of them is at the highest level of development? Which one of them will nationalize another? We have seen the Rhine become French,* but the Germans are in no way inferior!' he exclaimed. 'There is another law at work here!'

'It seems to me that influence will always be on the side of true education,' said Alexey Alexandrovich, arching his eyebrows slightly.

'But what must we define as the signs of true education?' said Pestsov.

'I would argue that those signs are obvious,' said Alexey Alexandrovich.

'Are they completely obvious?' interjected Sergey Ivanovich, with a subtle smile. 'Nowadays it is accepted that a true education can only be a purely classical one; but we have been seeing fierce debates from both sides, and it is impossible to deny that the opposing camp has some strong arguments in its favour.'

'You are a classicist, Sergey Ivanovich. Will you have some red?' said Stepan Arkadyich.

'I am not expressing my own opinion of education,' Sergey Ivanovich said, smiling condescendingly, as if to a child, as he held out his glass. 'I am only saying that there are strong arguments on both sides,' he continued, addressing Alexey Alexandrovich. 'I received a classical education, but I am personally unable to find my own ground in this dispute. I do not see any clear arguments as to why classical subjects should take precedence over modern ones.'

'Natural sciences have just as much influence from the point of view of pedagogy and development,' put in Pestsov. 'Take astronomy alone, or botany, or zoology with its system of general laws!'

'I cannot fully agree with that,' replied Alexey Alexandrovich. 'It seems to me that it is impossible not to concede that the very process of studying the forms of languages has a particularly beneficial effect on spiritual development. It cannot be denied, moreover, that the influence of classical authors is moral in the highest degree, while the teaching of natural sciences is regrettably linked to those harmful and false doctrines which are the bane of our times.'

Sergey Ivanovich was about to say something, but Pestsov interrupted him in his thick bass. He began fervently demonstrating the error of this point of view. Sergey Ivanovich quietly bided his time to speak, clearly armed with an invincible rejoinder.

'But it must be agreed', said Sergey Ivanovich, addressing Karenin with a subtle smile, 'that it is difficult to weigh up fully all the benefits and shortcomings of different subjects, and that the question as to which should be preferred would not have been so quickly and conclusively resolved had there not been in favour of classical education that advantage which you mentioned just now: its moral, *disons le mot*,[1] anti-nihilist influence.'*

'Undoubtedly.'

'If it had not been for this advantage of anti-nihilist influence on the side of the classics, we might have given greater consideration to the issue, weighed up the arguments on both sides,' said Sergey Ivanovich with a subtle smile, 'and given full rein to both tendencies.

[1] 'let us be frank'.

But now that we know that these pills of classical education contain the healing power of anti-nihilism, we boldly prescribe them to our patients . . . But what if they had no such healing power?' he concluded with a sprinkle of Attic salt.

Everyone laughed at Sergey Ivanovich's pills, and Turovtsyn especially loudly and heartily after finally hearing something funny, which was the only thing he had been waiting for as he listened to the conversation. Stepan Arkadyich had not erred in inviting Pestsov. With Pestsov present, clever conversation could not flag for an instant. No sooner had Sergey Ivanovich concluded the conversation with his joke than Pestsov promptly started a new one.

'It is impossible even to concur that the government had that aim,' he said. 'The government is clearly guided by general considerations, and remains indifferent to the influence exerted by any of its adopted measures. The education of women, for instance, ought to be regarded as harmful, but the government has founded courses and universities for women.'

And the conversation immediately sprang on to the new topic of women's education.*

Alexey Alexandrovich expressed the idea that the question of women's education tended to be mixed up with that of women's emancipation, and could only be considered harmful for that reason.

'I would argue, on the contrary, that these two questions are inseparably linked,' said Pestsov. 'It is a vicious circle. Women are deprived of rights due to their lack of education, and their lack of education comes from them not having rights. We must not forget that the subjection of women is so great, and so deep-rooted, that we are often unwilling to comprehend the gulf that separates them from us,' he said.

'When you mentioned the word "rights",' said Sergey Ivanovich, who had been waiting for Pestsov to fall silent, 'you meant the right to occupy the position of jury member, councillor, chairman of a board, civil servant, member of parliament . . .'

'Absolutely.'

'But if women, as a rare exception, were able to occupy these positions, then it seems to me you are wrong to use the term "rights". It would be more accurate to say "duties". Everyone would agree that we feel we are performing a duty by taking up a post as a juror, councillor, or telegraph clerk. And therefore it would be more accurate to say that women are seeking duties, and quite legitimately. And one can only sympathize with their desire to assist men with their common toil.'

'Completely true,' Alexey Alexandrovich affirmed. 'The only question, I would submit, is whether they are capable of performing these duties.'

'They will probably be very capable when education becomes widespread amongst them,' Stepan Arkadyich put in. 'We see this . . .'

'What about that saying?' said the Prince, who had been following the conversation for a long time, his mischievous little eyes twinkling. 'I can say this in front of my daughters: long hair, but short . . .'*

'That is just what they thought about negroes before their emancipation!' said Pestsov angrily.

'I just find it strange that women are seeking new duties,' said Sergey Ivanovich, 'while we can unfortunately see that men usually avoid them.'

'Duties are bound up with rights—power, money, honour; these are what women are seeking,' said Pestsov.

'It would be exactly as if I sought the right to be a wet-nurse, and took offence that women got paid while I wasn't,' said the old Prince.

Turovtsyn burst out laughing loudly and Sergey Ivanovich regretted that he had not said this. Even Alexey Alexandrovich smiled.

'Yes, but a man can't feed a baby,' said Pestsov, 'while a woman . . .'

'No, there was an Englishman who brought up his baby on a ship once,' said the old Prince, allowing himself this licence in front of his daughters.

'There are as many Englishmen like that as there are women who will become civil servants,' said Sergey Ivanovich.

'Yes, but what is a girl without a family to do?' interjected Stepan Arkadyich, remembering Masha Chibisova, whom he had kept in mind all the time he had been sympathizing with Pestsov and supporting him.

'If you were to look closely into the story of that girl, you would find she had abandoned a family—either her own or a sister's, where she might have had a woman's work,' Darya Alexandrovna said irritably as she unexpectedly joined in the conversation, having probably guessed what girl Stepan Arkadyich had in mind.

'But we are defending a principle, an ideal!' countered Pestsov in his sonorous bass. 'Women want to have the right to be independent, educated. They are hampered and oppressed by their consciousness of this not being possible.'

'And I'm hampered and oppressed that I can't get a job at the Orphanage as a wet-nurse,' the old Prince said again, to the great glee of Turovtsyn, who laughed so much he dropped the plump tip of his asparagus into the sauce.

11

EVERYONE took part in the general conversation except Kitty and
Levin. At first, while they were discussing the influence of one nation
on another, things he had to say on this subject started involuntarily
coming into Levin's mind; but these thoughts, previously very
important to him, flashed through his mind as if in a dream and now
held not the slightest interest for him. It even seemed strange to him
that they should be so eager to talk about something which was no use
to anyone. One would have presumed that Kitty also should have been
interested in what they were saying about the rights and education of
women. How often indeed had she thought about this, remembering
Varenka, her friend abroad, and her painful state of dependence, and
how often had she thought about herself and what would happen to
her if she did not get married, and how often had she argued with her
sister about this! But now it did not interest her at all. She and Levin
were engaged in a conversation of their own, in fact not a conversation
but some kind of mysterious communication, which every moment
brought them closer and provoked in both a feeling of rapt awe before
the unknown realm they were entering.

At first, in answer to Kitty's question as to how he could have seen
her in the carriage last year, Levin told her how he had been coming
home from the mowing and had encountered her on the highway.

'It was very early in the morning. You must have just woken up.
Your *maman* was asleep in her corner. It was a glorious morning.
I was walking along and wondering who it could be in the coach
and four. It was a splendid team of horses with little bells, and for
a second you flashed into view, and I looked through the window—
you were sitting like this, holding the ribbons of your cap in both
hands, and thinking deeply about something,' he said, smiling. 'How
I would like to have known what you were thinking about! Was it
something important?'

'Wasn't I all dishevelled?' she thought; but seeing the rapturous
smile these details evoked in his memory, she felt that the impression
she had made must on the contrary have been a very good one. She
blushed and laughed with happiness.

'I honestly don't remember.'

'What a good laugh Turovtsyn has!' said Levin, admiring his moist
eyes and shaking body.

'Have you known him long?' asked Kitty.

'Who doesn't know him!'

'And I see that you think he's a bad person?'

'Not bad, but worthless.'

'That's not true! And you must stop thinking that straight away!' said Kitty. 'I used to have a low opinion of him too, but he—he is an exceedingly nice and remarkably kind man. He has a heart of gold.'

'How did you manage to find out about his heart?'

'We are great friends. I know him very well. Last winter, soon after . . . you came to see us,' she said, with a guilty but at the same time trusting smile, 'all Dolly's children had scarlet fever, and he came to see her one day. And can you imagine,' she said in a whisper, 'he felt so sorry for her that he stayed on, and began helping her look after the children. Yes, and he went on living with them for three weeks, and looked after the children like a nanny.'

'I am telling Konstantin Dmitrich about Turovtsyn during the scarlet fever,' she said, leaning over to her sister.

'Yes, it was remarkable, he was wonderful!' said Dolly, glancing at Turovtsyn, who sensed he was being talked about, and smiling at him gently. Levin cast Turovtsyn another glance, and was amazed he had not realized the extent of this man's charm before.

'I'm sorry, I'm sorry, I'll never think ill of people again!' he said merrily, expressing what he genuinely now felt.

12

IN the conversation that had been struck up about women's rights were certain issues about the inequality of rights in marriage which were sensitive topics to discuss with ladies present. Pestsov tried to tackle these issues several times during dinner, but Sergey Ivanovich and Stepan Arkadyich carefully warded him off.

When they got up from the table and the ladies left, however, instead of following them Pestsov turned to Alexey Alexandrovich and began expounding the main cause of inequality. In his opinion, inequality in marriage lay in the fact that a wife's infidelity and a husband's infidelity were not punished equally, either by the law or by public opinion.

Stepan Arkadyich hurried over to Alexey Alexandrovich and offered him a cigar.

'No, I don't smoke,' Alexey Alexandrovich answered calmly, and he turned to Pestsov with a cold smile, as if deliberately wishing to show that he was not afraid of this subject.

'I submit that the basis for such a view lies in the very nature of things,' he said, and was about to proceed into the drawing room; but just then Turovtsyn suddenly and unexpectedly started talking, addressing Alexey Alexandrovich.

'Did you happen to hear about Pryachnikov?' said Turovtsyn, stimulated by the champagne he had drunk, and having long waited for an opportunity to break the silence which oppressed him. 'Vasya Pryachnikov,' he said, with a good-natured smile on his moist, red lips, addressing himself primarily to the most important guest, Alexey Alexandrovich. 'I was told today that he fought a duel with Kvitsky in Tver, and killed him.'

Just as one always seems to bruise a sore spot, as if on purpose, so Stepan Arkadyich now felt that the conversation that evening kept unfortunately hitting Alexey Alexandrovich's sore spot. He again tried to draw his brother-in-law aside, but Alexey Alexandrovich himself asked with curiosity:

'What was Pryachnikov fighting about?'

'His wife. Behaved like a man! Called him out and shot him!'

'Ah!' said Alexey Alexandrovich indifferently and, raising his eyebrows, he proceeded into the drawing room.

'I am so glad you came,' Dolly said with a frightened smile, meeting him in the connecting drawing room. 'I need to talk to you. Let's sit down here.'

Alexey Alexandrovich sat down beside Darya Alexandrovna with the same expression of indifference lent by his raised eyebrows and feigned a smile.

'So much the better,' he said, 'as I was about to ask you to forgive me for taking my leave straight away. I must set off tomorrow.'

Darya Alexandrovna was firmly convinced of Anna's innocence, and she could feel herself going pale and her lips trembling with anger at this cold-blooded, heartless man, who so calmly intended to ruin her innocent friend.

'Alexey Alexandrovich,' she said, looking into his eyes with a desperate resolve. 'I asked you about Anna, and you did not give me an answer. How is she?'

'I believe she is well, Darya Alexandrovna,' replied Alexey Alexandrovich without looking at her.

'Alexey Alexandrovich, forgive me, I have no right . . . but I love and respect Anna as a sister; I beg you, I beseech you to tell me, what is going on between you? What do you accuse her of?'

Alexey Alexandrovich frowned and bowed his head, his eyes almost closed.

'I presume your husband has told you the reasons why I consider it necessary to change my former relations with Anna Arkadyevna,' he said, not looking at her, and casting a look of annoyance at Shcherbatsky, who was walking through the room.

'I don't believe it, I don't believe it, I simply can't believe it!' Dolly said, clasping her bony hands together in front of her with a vigorous gesture. She stood up quickly and placed her hand on Alexey Alexandrovich's sleeve. 'We shall be disturbed here. Come this way, please.'

Dolly's agitation affected Alexey Alexandrovich. He got up and followed her meekly into the schoolroom. They sat down at a table covered with an oilcloth cut all over by penknives.

'I don't believe it, I just don't believe it!' Dolly said, trying to meet his gaze, which was avoiding hers.

'One cannot disbelieve facts, Darya Alexandrovna,' he said, with an emphasis on the word *facts*.

'But what is it she has done? What? What?' said Darya Alexandrovna. 'What exactly has she done?'

'She has scorned her duties and betrayed her husband. That is what she has done,' he said.

'No, no, it can't be! No, for God's sake, you must be mistaken,' said Dolly, putting her hands to her temples and closing her eyes.

Alexey Alexandrovich smiled coldly with just his lips, wishing to show her and also himself the firmness of his conviction; but this passionate defence, though it did not unsettle him, rubbed salt in his wound. He began to speak with greater animation.

'It is extremely difficult to be mistaken when a wife informs her husband of it herself. Informs him that eight years of life together and a son—that it was all a mistake and that she wants to begin life again,' he said angrily, snorting.

'Anna and vice—I cannot put them together, I cannot believe that!'

'Darya Alexandrovna!' he said, now looking straight into Dolly's kind, upset face, and feeling his tongue involuntarily loosening. 'I would give a great deal for doubt still to be possible. When I doubted, I was miserable, but it was easier than it is now. When I doubted, there was hope; but now there is no hope, and I still doubt everything. I doubt everything, I hate my son, and I sometimes do not believe he is my son. I am very unhappy.'

He did not need to say that. Darya Alexandrovna realized it as soon as he looked into her face; and she began to feel sorry for him, and her belief in her friend's innocence began to falter.

'Oh, this is terrible, terrible! But can it really be true that you have made up your mind to divorce?'

'I have made up my mind to take the final step. There is nothing else for me to do.'

'Nothing else to do, nothing else to do . . .' she said with tears in her eyes. 'No, there must be something to do!' she said.

'That is what is so awful about this kind of misfortune, that one cannot bear one's cross as in any other calamity—a loss, or a death—but must act,' he said, as if guessing her thoughts. 'It is necessary to extract oneself from the humiliating position in which one has been placed; it is not possible to live *à trois*.'

'I understand that, I understand that very well,' said Dolly, and she bowed her head. She was silent for a moment, thinking of herself, of her own domestic troubles, then suddenly she raised her head impulsively and brought her hands together in a gesture of supplication. 'But wait! You are a Christian. Think of her! What will become of her, if you cast her aside?'

'I have thought, Darya Alexandrovna, I have thought a great deal,' said Alexey Alexandrovich. Red blotches had appeared on his face, and his dull eyes were looking straight at her. By now Darya Alexandrovna pitied him with all her heart. 'That is exactly what I did after she herself informed me of my humiliation; I left everything as it was. I gave her the chance to reform, I tried to save her. And what was the result? She failed to carry out the easiest of requirements—the observation of propriety,' he said, becoming heated. 'One can save a person who does not want to be ruined; but when her whole nature is so corrupt and so depraved that she actually perceives ruin as salvation, what is to be done?'

'Anything, only not divorce!' answered Darya Alexandrovna.

'But what is "anything"?'

'No, it is awful! She will be nobody's wife, she will be ruined!'

'But what can I do?' said Alexey Alexandrovich, shrugging his shoulders and raising his eyebrows. Recollection of his wife's latest misdemeanour had so annoyed him that he again became cold, as at the beginning of the conversation. 'I am very grateful for your sympathy, but I must be going,' he said, getting up.

'No, wait! You must not ruin her. Wait, I will tell you about myself. I married. My husband was unfaithful to me, and in anger and jealousy, I was about to abandon everything, I was on the verge myself of . . . But I came to my senses, and who was it but Anna who saved me? And here I am living on. The children are growing up, my husband is returning to his family and is aware he has done wrong, he is becoming purer and better, and I live on . . . I have forgiven, and you must forgive!'

Alexey Alexandrovich listened to her, but her words no longer had any effect on him. All the rage he had felt on the day he had decided on divorce rose up again in his soul. He shook himself, and said in a shrill, loud voice:

'I cannot forgive, I do not wish to, and consider it wrong. I have done everything for this woman, and she has trampled everything into the mud. Which is her natural milieu. I am not a spiteful man, I have never hated anyone before, but I hate her with every fibre of my being, and cannot even forgive her, because I hate her too much for all the wrong she has done me!' he said, with tears of anger in his voice.

'Love them that hate you . . .' Darya Alexandrovna whispered shamefacedly.

Alexey Alexandrovich smirked contemptuously. He had known this for a long time, but it could not be applied to his case.

'Love them that hate you, but loving those whom one hates is impossible. Forgive me for upsetting you. Each person has enough grief of his own!' And having regained his composure, Alexey Alexandrovich calmly said goodbye and left.

13

WHEN everyone rose from the table, Levin wanted to follow Kitty into the drawing room; but he was afraid she might be displeased by his too obvious courtship of her. He remained in the company of the men, taking part in the general conversation, and without looking at Kitty, was aware of her movements, her glances, and of where she was in the drawing room.

He had already begun, and without the slightest effort, to keep the promise he had made her, of always thinking well about everybody, and of always liking everybody. The conversation turned to the village commune, in which Pestsov saw some special principle, which he called the choral principle.* Levin agreed neither with Pestsov, nor with his brother, who in his idiosyncratic way both acknowledged and did not acknowledge the significance of the Russian commune. But he talked to them, trying only to reconcile them and moderate their arguments. He was not remotely interested in what he himself was saying, and even less in what they were saying, and wanted only one thing—that they and everyone else should feel happy and enjoy themselves. He now knew what was the one thing that mattered. And that one thing had first been there in the drawing room, and then had begun moving about and stopped at the door. Without turning round he felt a gaze and a smile directed at him, and he could not help turning round. She was standing in the doorway with Shcherbatsky and looking at him.

'I thought you were going over to the piano,' he said as he came up to her. 'That's what I miss in the country: music.'

'No, we were only coming to fetch you, and also,' she said, rewarding him with a smile as if it was a gift, 'I want to thank you for coming. Why do people love arguing? After all, no one ever succeeds in convincing anyone else.'

'Yes, it's true,' said Levin. 'It's invariably the case that you end up in a vociferous argument because you can't understand exactly what it is your opponent is trying to prove.'

Levin had often noticed in arguments between the most intelligent people that after an enormous expenditure of effort, and an enormous quantity of logical subtleties and words, the adversaries would finally come to the realization that what they had long been battling to prove to one another had been known to both of them for a very long time, from the outset of the argument, but that they liked different things, and did not want to articulate what they liked lest it be called into question. It was often his experience during an argument that you would sometimes fathom what it was your opponent held dear, and suddenly start liking the same thing yourself and immediately concur, and then all arguments would fall away as superfluous; while sometimes he experienced the opposite: you would finally state what it was you held dear yourself, and for the sake of which you were thinking up arguments, and if you happened to state your case well and sincerely, then your opponent would suddenly agree and stop arguing. This is what he wanted to say.

She wrinkled her forehead, trying to understand. But as soon as he began to explain, she understood.

'I see: one must find out what a person is arguing in favour of, what he holds dear, then one can . . .'

She had grasped and expressed perfectly his badly expressed idea. Levin smiled in delight, so astonished was he by this transition from the convoluted, verbose argument with Pestsov and his brother to this laconic and clear, almost wordless communication of the most complex ideas.

Shcherbatsky left them, and Kitty went over to the card table that had been set up, sat down, picked up the chalk, and proceeded to draw concentric circles on the new green cloth.

They resumed the conversation that had proceeded at dinner about freedom and occupations for women. Levin was in agreement with Darya Alexandrovna's view that a girl who had not married should find woman's work within the family. He supported this view by saying that no family could manage without female help, and that there were, and had to be, nannies in every family, rich and poor, whether they were hired or were relatives.

'No,' said Kitty, blushing, but looking at him all the more boldly with her truthful eyes, 'a girl may be placed in such a situation that she cannot join a family without humiliation, while she herself . . .'

He understood what she was alluding to.

'Oh, yes!' he said. 'Yes, yes, yes—you're right, you're right!'

And he understood everything that Pestsov had been trying to prove at dinner about freedom for women, simply by seeing the fear of spinsterhood and humiliation in Kitty's heart, and, loving her, he began to feel that fear and humiliation and immediately renounced his argument.

A silence ensued. She continued to draw on the table with the chalk. Her eyes shone with a soft light. Surrendering to her mood, he felt throughout his whole being the ever-mounting tension of happiness.

'Ah! I've scribbled all over the table!' she said, and, putting down the chalk, she made a movement as if she was about to get up.

'How can I stay here on my own . . . without her?' he thought with horror, and he picked up the chalk. 'Wait a minute,' he said, sitting down at the table. 'There is one thing I have long wanted to ask you.'

He looked straight into her affectionate but frightened eyes.

'Please, ask it.'

'Here,' he said, and he wrote the initial letters: *w, y, a, m, t, c, b, d, t, m, n, o, t.* These letters meant: 'When you answered me "that cannot be", did that mean never or then?' There was no likelihood that she could make out this complicated sentence; but he looked at her as though his life depended on her understanding these words.

She looked at him earnestly, then rested her furrowed forehead on her hand and began to read. Occasionally she glanced up at him, asking him with her look, 'Is this what I think it is?'

'I've understood,' she said, blushing.

'What is this word?' he said, pointing to the *n* which stood for *never*.

'This word means *never*,' she said, 'but it's not true!'

He quickly rubbed out what he had written, gave her the chalk, and stood up. She wrote: *t, i, c, n, a, o.*

Dolly found complete consolation from the sorrow caused by her conversation with Alexey Alexandrovich when she caught sight of the two figures: Kitty with the chalk in her hand, looking up at Levin with a shy and happy smile, and his handsome figure bending over the table, with shining eyes focused one minute on the table and the next on her. Suddenly he beamed: he had understood. It meant: 'Then I could not answer otherwise.'

He glanced at her questioningly, timidly.

'Only then?'

'Yes,' her smile answered.

'And n . . . And now?' he asked.

'Well, read this then. I'll tell you what I would like. What I would really like!' She wrote the initial letters: *t, y, c, f, a, f, w, h.* This meant: 'that you could forget and forgive what happened.'

He seized the chalk with tense, trembling fingers, broke it, and wrote the initial letters of the following phrase: 'I have nothing to forget and forgive, I have never ceased loving you.'

She glanced at him with a steady smile.

'I have understood,' she said in a whisper.

He sat down and wrote a long phrase. She understood everything and, without asking if she was right, took the chalk and immediately replied.

For a long while he was unable to understand what she had written, and kept looking into her eyes. He was dazed with happiness. He just could not summon up the words she had in mind; but in her lovely eyes, beaming with happiness, he understood everything he needed to know. And he wrote three letters. But he had not finished writing when she started reading over his hand, finished them off herself, and wrote the answer: 'Yes.'

'Playing *secrétaire*?' said the old Prince as he approached. 'We must be off, though, if you want to get to the theatre in time.'

Levin stood up and escorted Kitty to the door.

In their conversation everything had been said; what was said was that she loved him, and would tell her father and mother that he would come the following morning.

14

WHEN Kitty left and Levin remained on his own, he began to feel such restlessness without her, and such an impatient desire for time to pass quickly, as quickly as possible, until the following morning, when he would see her again and be forever united with her, that he feared like death those fourteen hours he faced spending without her. It was vital for him to be with and talk to someone, so as not to have to remain alone, and so as to kill time. Stepan Arkadyich would have been the most congenial person for him to talk to, but he was going off, so he said, to a soirée, although actually to the ballet. Levin only managed to tell him he was happy, and that he loved him, and would never, ever forget what he had done for him. Stepan Arkadyich's eyes and smile showed Levin that he understood this feeling in the right way.

'So, it's not time to die yet?' said Stepan Arkadyich, pressing Levin's hand warmly.

'Oh, no-o-o!' said Levin.

Darya Alexandrovna also seemed to be congratulating him when she bid him goodbye, saying,

'I am so glad you have met Kitty again; one must cherish old friends.'

But Levin did not like what Darya Alexandrovna said. She could not understand how sublime and inaccessible this all was to her, and she should not have dared mention it.

Levin said goodbye to them, but attached himself to his brother so as not to be left alone.

'Where are you going?'

'I'm going to a meeting.'

'Well, I'll come with you. May I?'

'Why not? Let's go,' said Sergey Ivanovich, smiling. 'What has happened to you today?'

'What's happened to me? Happiness has happened to me!' said Levin, lowering the window of the carriage in which they were riding. 'You don't mind? It's stuffy otherwise. Happiness has happened to me! Why have you never got married?'

Sergey Ivanovich smiled.

'I am very glad, she seems like a lovely gi . . .' began Sergey Ivanovich.

'Don't say anything! Don't say anything!' exclaimed Levin, seizing the collar of his brother's fur coat with both hands, and encasing him in it. 'She's a lovely girl' were such simple, mundane words, so unequal to his feelings.

Sergey Ivanovich burst out laughing merrily, which was a rare occurrence with him.

'Well, I can still say that I'm very happy about it.'

'You can do that tomorrow, tomorrow, but nothing more now! Nothing, nothing, silence!' said Levin, and muffling him up again in his fur coat, he added: 'I love you very much! So, can I be at the meeting?'

'Of course you can.'

'What is on your agenda today?' asked Levin, unable to stop smiling.

They arrived at the meeting. Levin listened to the secretary haltingly read the minutes, which he obviously did not understand himself; but Levin could see from this secretary's face what a nice, kind-hearted, splendid person he was. This was clear from the way he became confused and embarrassed reading the minutes. Then the deliberations began. They argued about the allocation of certain sums, and about the laying of certain pipes, and Sergey Ivanovich slighted two members and spoke gloatingly about something for a long time; then another member, who had written something on a bit of paper, started out timidly, but then countered him in the most cordial but venomous terms. And Sviyazhsky (he was there too) also said something in such an eloquent and noble way. Levin listened to them and saw clearly that none of these allocated sums and pipes really existed, and that they were not really angry at all, but were all such nice, kind people, and were conducting their business so smoothly and cordially. They were not doing any harm to anyone, and everyone was happy. What Levin found remarkable was that he could see through all of them that night, and by means of little signs he had never noticed before he was able to look into the soul of each one and clearly see that they were all good people. And they all seemed extremely fond of Levin in particular that night. This was evident from the way they spoke to him, and from the friendly, affectionate way in which even people he did not know looked at him.

'So, are you happy you came?' Sergey Ivanovich asked him.

'Very. I never thought it would be so interesting! It's wonderful, splendid!'

Sviyazhsky went up to Levin and invited him to come home and have tea with him. Levin was at a loss to understand and remember what it was he did not like about Sviyazhsky, and what he had found wanting in him. He was a clever and remarkably kind man.

'I should be delighted,' he said, and asked after his wife and sister-in-law. And by a strange sequence of thoughts, since in his imagination the thought of Sviyazhsky's sister-in-law was connected with marriage, it seemed to him that there could be no better people to whom he could talk of his happiness than Sviyazhsky's wife and sister-in-law, and he was very glad to go and see them.

Sviyazhsky questioned him about his work in the country, as always discounting the possibility of discovering anything not already discovered in Europe, and now Levin was not in the least bit put out by this. On the contrary, he felt that Sviyazhsky was right about all this work being of no value, and saw the amazing gentleness and delicacy with which Sviyazhsky avoided declaring that he was right. Sviyazhsky's ladies were particularly amiable. It seemed to Levin that they already knew everything and approved, but refrained from saying anything only out of tact. He sat there for one hour, two, three, talking about various topics, but with his mind only on the one thing which filled his soul, and did not notice that he was boring them dreadfully, and that it was long past their bedtime. Sviyazhsky escorted him into the hall, yawning and wondering about the strange state his friend was in. It was past one o'clock. Levin went back to his hotel and was frightened by the thought of how, left alone with his impatience, he was going to spend the remaining ten hours. The servant on duty, who was not asleep, lit candles for him and was about to leave, but Levin stopped him. This servant, Yegor, whom Levin had not noticed before, turned out to be a very intelligent, nice, and above all kind man.

'So, do you find it hard staying awake, Yegor?'

'Can't be helped! It's my job. It's easier in a gentleman's house; but the pay is better here.'

It turned out that Yegor had a family—three boys and a seamstress daughter, whom he wanted to marry off to a clerk in a saddler's shop.

This prompted Levin to share with Yegor his idea that the main thing in marriage was love, and that with love one would always be happy, because happiness only resides within oneself.

Yegor listened attentively, and obviously fully grasped Levin's idea, but confirmed it in a way Levin was not expecting, by remarking that when he had been in service with good folk, he had always been happy with his masters, and was thoroughly happy with his master now, although he was a Frenchman.

'What a wonderfully kind man,' Levin thought.

'And you, Yegor, when you got married, did you love your wife?'

'Of course I did,' replied Yegor.

And Levin saw that Yegor was also in a euphoric state, and on the point of divulging all his most intimate thoughts.

'My life has also been surprising. Ever since I was a child . . .' he began with shining eyes, clearly infected by Levin's euphoria in the same way that people are infected by yawning.

But at that moment a bell rang; Yegor left, and Levin remained alone. He had scarcely eaten anything at dinner, and had refused tea and supper at Sviyazhsky's, but he could not think about supper. He had not slept the previous night, but he could not think about sleeping either. His room was chilly, but he felt suffocated by the heat. He opened both the casement windows and sat down on the table in front of them. Peeping out behind the snow-covered roof he could see a cross adorned with chains and above it the rising triangle of the Charioteer constellation and bright yellow Capella. He stared at the cross, then at the star, breathed in the fresh frosty air which was streaming steadily into the room and, as if he was in a dream, followed the images and memories arising in his imagination. Some time after three o'clock he heard steps in the corridor and poked his head round the door. It was his gambler friend Myaskin returning from the club. He was shuffling along dolefully, scowling and trying to clear his throat. 'Poor, unhappy fellow!' thought Levin, and love and pity for this man made his eyes brim with tears. He was about to go and talk to him and comfort him, but when he remembered that he had nothing on but his shirt, he changed his mind and went to sit down again by the casement window, so he could wallow in the cold air and gaze at the wondrous silhouette of the cross, which was silent but full of meaning for him, and at the bright yellow star as it rose. After six the floor-polishers began to make a noise, the bells started ringing for a service, and Levin felt that he was beginning to catch cold. He shut the casement window, washed, dressed, and went out into the street.

15

THE streets were still empty. Levin walked over to the Shcherbatskys' house. The front door was locked and everyone was asleep. He retraced his steps, went back to his room, and ordered coffee. It was brought to him by a daytime waiter, who was no longer Yegor. Levin was about to engage him in conversation, but the waiter was called away by the bell, and he left. Levin tried to sip the coffee and put the roll into his mouth, but his mouth had absolutely no idea what to do with the roll. Levin spat the roll out, put on his coat, and went out for another walk. It was after nine when he arrived at the Shcherbatskys' porch for the second time. The occupants were only just up, and the cook was going out to buy provisions. He had to endure at least another two hours.

Levin had lived completely unconsciously all that night and morning, and he felt completely detached from the conditions of material life. He not eaten for a whole day, he had not slept for two nights, he had spent several hours undressed, exposed to the frost, and he felt not only fresher and healthier than ever, but also as if he was completely independent of his body: he was moving about without exerting his muscles and felt he could do anything. He was sure he could take flight or move the corner of a house if necessary. He spent the remaining time walking in the streets, constantly glancing at his watch and looking around him.

And what he saw then, he never saw again. He was particularly moved by the sight of children going to school, blue-grey pigeons swooping down to the pavement from a roof, and rolls dusted with flour being put out by an unseen hand. These rolls, the pigeons, and the two boys were ethereal creatures. All of this happened at the same time: a boy ran towards a pigeon and glanced up at Levin with a smile; the pigeon beat its wings and flew off, sparkling in the sun amidst particles of snow shimmering in the air, while from a window came the smell of freshly baked bread, and rolls were put out. All this together was so exceptionally good that Levin started laughing and crying with happiness. After completing a big circuit along Gazetny Lane and Kislovka, he went back again to the hotel, placed his watch in front of him, and sat down to wait for twelve o'clock. In the room next door they were talking about machines and fraud, and having a bout of morning coughing. They did not realize that the hand was already approaching twelve. The hand reached twelve. Levin went out on to the porch. The cab drivers obviously knew everything. They surrounded Levin with happy faces, arguing with each other as they offered their services. Trying not to offend the other cabbies and promising he would hire them another time, Levin picked one and told him to drive to the Shcherbatskys'. The cabby was resplendent in a white shirt collar sticking out from under his kaftan which fitted tightly round his corpulent, red, sturdy neck. This cabby's sleigh was high and nimble, the likes of which Levin never rode in again, and the horse was good and tried to go at a fast pace but did not seem to be moving at all. The cabby knew the Shcherbatskys' house, and after rounding his arms and saying 'whoa' with particular deference to his fare, he drew up at the porch. The Shcherbatskys' doorman definitely knew everything. This was clear from the twinkle in his eyes and the way he said:

'You haven't been here in a long while, Konstantin Dmitrich!'

Not only did he know everything, but it was obvious to Levin that he was thrilled, and was making an effort to conceal his jubilation. Looking into his kindly old eyes, Levin even apprehended something new about his happiness.

'Are they up?'

'Come in, please! You can leave that here,' he said with a smile when Levin was about to go back for his hat. That meant something.

'To whom shall I announce you?' asked the footman.

The footman, although young, one of the new school of footmen and a sharp dresser, was a very kind and good man and he also understood everything.

'The Princess . . . the Prince . . . the young Princess . . .' said Levin.

The first person he saw was Mademoiselle Linon. She was walking through the ballroom, her ringlets and her face shining. He had just started talking to her when suddenly footsteps and the rustle of a dress could be heard behind the door, and Mademoiselle Linon disappeared from Levin's sight, and he was enveloped with a joyous terror at the proximity of his happiness. Mademoiselle Linon hastened to leave him and went towards the other door. As soon as she had left, the swiftest of light steps could be heard on the parquet, and his happiness, his life, his own self—the best part of his own self, and that which he had sought and desired for so long—was coming swiftly towards him. She was not walking, but being transported towards him by some kind of invisible force.

He saw nothing but her clear, truthful eyes, frightened by the same joy of love that filled his heart. These eyes shone nearer and nearer, dazzling him with their bright light of love. She stopped close to him, touching him. Her arms rose and came down to rest on his shoulders.

She had done all she could—she had run up to him and surrendered herself completely, shy and happy. He put his arms round her and pressed his lips to her mouth, which sought his kiss.

She also had not slept all night, and had been waiting for him all morning. Her mother and father had given their consent without demur, and were happy in her happiness. She had been waiting for him. She wanted to be the first to inform him of his and her own happiness. She had been preparing to meet him alone and was excited at the prospect, but also shy and diffident, and she did not know herself what she would do. She had heard his steps and his voice and had waited behind the door for Mademoiselle Linon to leave. Mademoiselle Linon had left. Without thinking or asking herself how and what, she had gone up to him and acted as she did.

'Let us go to Mama!' she said, taking him by the hand. For a long time he could not say anything, not so much because he was afraid of tainting the loftiness of his feelings with words, as because every time he was about to say something he felt that tears of happiness would come pouring out instead of words. He took her hand and kissed it.

'Can this really be true?' he said at last in a muffled voice. 'I cannot believe you love me!'

She smiled at his switch to this more intimate form of address and the timid way he looked at her.

'Yes!' she said, meaningfully and slowly. 'I am so happy!'

She went into the drawing room without letting go of his hand. When she saw them, the Princess began breathing quickly and immediately started crying and laughing at the same time, and now she came running up to them with a vigour Levin had not expected, took his head in her hands, kissed him, and wet his cheeks with her tears.

'So it is all settled! I am happy. Love her. I am happy . . . Kitty!'

'You settled things quickly!' said the old Prince, trying to appear nonchalant; but Levin noticed that his eyes were moist when he addressed him.

'I have long, in fact always, wanted this!' he said, taking Levin by the arm and drawing him closer. 'Even when this featherbrain conceived the idea . . .'

'Papa!' cried Kitty, and closed his mouth with her hands.

'Very well, I won't!' he said. 'I'm very, very . . . happ . . . Oh, what a fool I am . . .'

He embraced Kitty, kissed her face, her hand, and her face again, then made the sign of the cross over her.

And Levin was filled with a new feeling of love for the old Prince, this man who had previously been a stranger to him, when he saw how long Kitty spent tenderly kissing his chubby hand.

16

THE Princess sat smiling silently in an armchair; the Prince sat down next to her. Kitty stood by her father's armchair, still holding his hand. Everyone was silent.

The Princess was the first to put everything into words and translate all thoughts and feelings into real-life questions. And they all found this equally strange and even painful to begin with.

'When is it to be then? We must give our blessing and make an announcement. But when is the wedding going to be? What do you think, Alexander?'

'Here's the man,' said the old Prince, pointing to Levin. 'He's the main person in this.'

'When?' said Levin, blushing. 'Tomorrow. If you ask me, I think we should have the blessing today and the wedding tomorrow.'

'Come, come, *mon cher*, that's absurd!'

'Well, in a week then.'

'He's quite mad.'

'No, why?'

'Heavens!' said the mother, smiling gleefully at this haste. 'But what about the trousseau?'

'Does there really have to be a trousseau and all that?' thought Levin with horror. 'However, a trousseau and a blessing and all that—could it really spoil my happiness? Nothing can spoil it!' He glanced at Kitty and noticed that she was not in the slightest bit perturbed by the idea of a trousseau. 'Then it must be necessary,' he thought.

'I don't know anything, you see, I just expressed my wish,' he said apologetically.

'We'll discuss it then. The blessing and the announcement can be made now. That's fine.'

The Princess went up to her husband, kissed him, and was about to leave; but he held her back to embrace her, smiling as he kissed her tenderly several times like a young lover. The old people were obviously confused for a brief moment, and did not quite know whether it was they who were in love again or just their daughter. When the Prince and the Princess had gone, Levin went up to his fiancée and took her hand. He had now regained his composure and could speak, and there was a lot he needed to say to her. But what he said was completely different to what was needed.

'I knew it would be like this! I never had any hope; but in my soul I was always sure,' he said. 'I believe this was predestined.'

'And me?' she said. 'Even back then . . .' She stopped and then continued, looking at him resolutely with her truthful eyes, 'even then, when I spurned my happiness. I have always only loved you, but I got carried away. I have to say . . . Can you forget that?'

'Maybe it was for the best. You will have to forgive me a great deal. I have to tell you . . .'

This was one of the things he had decided to tell her. He had resolved to tell her two things at the outset—that he was not pure as she was, and that he was not a believer. It was painful, but he believed he should tell her both things.

'No, not now, later!' he said.

'Very well, later, but you must definitely tell me. I'm not afraid of anything. I need to know everything. Things are settled now.'

He finished the sentence. 'What is settled is that you'll take me, however I am, and you won't reject me? Yes?'

'Yes, yes.'

Their conversation was interrupted by Mademoiselle Linon, who came to congratulate her favourite pupil with a forced but affectionate smile. Before she had left, the servants came in to offer their congratulations. Then members of the family arrived, and there began that blessed confusion from which Levin would not emerge until the day after his wedding. Levin constantly felt awkward and bored, but the intense happiness continued and kept increasing. He constantly felt that a great deal was expected of him that he knew nothing about, but he did everything he was told, and it all brought him happiness. He thought that his engagement would be nothing like other people's, and that the usual routine of being engaged would spoil his special happiness; but he ended up doing what other people did, and this made his happiness only increase and become more and more special, quite unlike any that had ever been before.

'Now we will have some sweets,' said Mademoiselle Linon, and Levin went off to buy sweets.

'Well, I'm very pleased,' said Sviyazhsky. 'I advise you to get flowers from Fomin's.'

'I need to get flowers?' And he drove off to Fomin's.

His brother told him he should borrow some money, as there would be many expenses, presents . . .

'I need to give presents?' And he trotted off to Fulde's.*

At the confectioner's, at Fomin's, and at Fulde's he saw that they were expecting him, were pleased for him and keen to celebrate his happiness, like everyone else with whom he had dealings during these days. The extraordinary thing was not only that everyone treated him with affection, but that everyone who had previously been unfriendly, cold, and indifferent now admired him and deferred to him in everything, attended to his feelings with sensitivity and tact, and shared his conviction that he was the happiest man in the world because his fiancée was the pinnacle of perfection. Kitty felt the same way. When Countess Nordston had the temerity to hint that she had hoped for something better, Kitty became so incensed and proved so conclusively that there could be no one in the world better than Levin that Countess Nordston had to acknowledge this, and thereafter never encountered Levin in Kitty's presence without an admiring smile.

The serious discussion he had promised was the one difficult episode during this time. He consulted the old Prince and, after receiving his permission, handed Kitty his diary, in which he had written down what troubled him. When he had written this diary it had actually been with his future fiancée in mind. Two things troubled him: his lack of chastity and his lack of faith. The admission of his lack of faith passed unnoticed. She was devout and had never doubted the truths of religion, but his outward lack of faith gave her no qualms. Her love enabled her to know his soul completely, and in his soul she saw what she wanted, so it was a matter of indifference to her that this state of the soul was equated with not being a believer. The other confession made her weep bitterly, however.

It was not without an inner struggle that Levin handed her his diary. He knew that there could be and should be no secrets between them, and so he decided this was the right thing to do; but he had not fully thought through the effect it might have, or put himself in her shoes. It was only when he came to their house that evening before going to the theatre, went to her room, and saw her tear-stained, pitiful, sweet face, made unhappy by the irreparable pain he had caused, that he understood the abyss which separated his shameful past from her dove-like purity, and was horrified by what he had done.

'Take these dreadful books, take them!' she said, pushing away the notebooks that lay on the table in front of her. 'Why did you give them to me? . . . No, all the same it's better you did,' she added, taking pity on his despairing face. 'But it's awful, awful!'

His bowed his head, and was silent. There was nothing he could say.

'You won't forgive me,' he whispered.

'No, I have forgiven you, but it's awful!'

His happiness was so great, however, that this confession did not shatter it, but merely gave it another nuance. She forgave him; but from that time on he considered himself even more unworthy of her, felt even more abject before her morally, and valued even more highly his undeserved happiness.

17

UNCONSCIOUSLY sifting through the impressions of the conversations held during and after dinner in his mind, Alexey Alexandrovich returned to his lonely hotel room. What Darya Alexandrovna had said about forgiveness merely annoyed him. Whether or not to apply this Christian rule in his case was too difficult a question to be discussed lightly, and this question had long ago been answered by Alexey

Alexandrovich in the negative. Of all the things that had been said, the words spoken by the silly, kind-hearted Turovtsyn were most deeply etched in his imagination: *acted like a man*; *challenged him to a duel and killed him*. They obviously all agreed with this, although were too polite to say so.

'Anyway, the matter is settled, there is no point thinking about it,' Alexey Alexandrovich told himself. And thinking only of his impending departure and the matter of the inspection, he went into his room and asked the porter who had escorted him where his valet was; the porter said his valet had just gone out. Alexey Alexandrovich gave an order for some tea, sat down at the table, picked up Froom's railway guide,* and began planning his journey.

'Two telegrams,' said his valet as he came into the room after returning. 'Excuse me, Your Excellency, I had only just gone out.'

Alexey Alexandrovich took the telegrams and opened them. The first telegram was the announcement of Stremov's appointment to the very post Karenin had coveted. Alexey Alexandrovich threw down the telegram and began pacing up and down the room, red in the face. '*Quos vult perdere dementat*,'* he said, meaning by *quos* those who had engineered this appointment. It was not so much that he was annoyed he had not been appointed and had obviously been passed over; but he found it incomprehensible, indeed astounding, they could not see that windbag and phrasemonger Stremov was least of all competent to do the job. How could they not see that they were fatally undermining themselves and their prestige with this appointment?

'This will be more of the same,' he said to himself biliously as he opened the second telegram. The telegram was from his wife. Her signature 'Anna', written in blue pencil, was the first thing to catch his eye. 'Am dying, beg, implore you come. Will die more peacefully with forgiveness,' he read. He smiled contemptuously, and flung down the telegram. That this was a deception and a trick, which was his first thought, there could be no shadow of a doubt.

'There is no deception she would stop short of. She is due to give birth. Maybe she has fallen ill giving birth. But what is their goal? To legitimize the child, compromise me, and prevent a divorce,' he thought. 'But there was something it said: "I am dying . . ."' He reread the telegram; and he was suddenly struck by the literal meaning of what it said. 'But what if it is true?' he said to himself. 'What if it's true that during her moment of suffering at the point of death she is genuinely repenting, and I take it as a trick and refuse to go? That would not only be cruel, and everyone would condemn me, but it would be stupid on my part.'

'Pyotr, stop the carriage. I am going to Petersburg,' he said to his valet.

Alexey Alexandrovich decided that he would go to Petersburg and see his wife. If her illness was a trick, he would say nothing and leave. If she really was ill, close to death and anxious to see him before she died, then he would forgive her, if he found her alive, and he would perform his final duty if he arrived too late.

At no point on his journey did he think further about what he would do.

Feeling tired and grimy after spending the night in the train, Alexey Alexandrovich drove down the deserted Nevsky Prospect in the early morning Petersburg fog and stared straight in front him, not thinking about what awaited him. He could not think about it, because when he imagined what might happen, he could not dispel the idea that her death would at one stroke undo all the difficulty of his position. Bakers, closed-up shops, night cabbies, street-cleaners sweeping the pavements flashed in front of his eyes, and he observed all of this, trying to stifle within himself the thought of what awaited him and what he dared not wish for, but nevertheless did wish for. He drove up to the porch. A cabby and a carriage with a sleeping coachman stood by the front door. As he went into the lobby, Alexey Alexandrovich retrieved a decision from, as it were, the far recesses of his brain, and processed it. Its import was: 'If it's a trick, then calm contempt and departure. If it's true, then observe proprieties.'

The porter opened the door even before Alexey Alexandrovich rang. Petrov the porter, otherwise known as Kapitonich, cut a strange figure, dressed in an old frock-coat without a tie and slippers.

'How is the mistress?'

'Safely delivered yesterday.'

Alexey Alexandrovich stopped and turned pale. He now clearly understood how intensely he had wanted her to die.

'And how is she?'

Korney came running down the stairs in his morning apron.

'Very poorly,' he answered. 'There was a doctors' consultation yesterday, and the doctor is here now.'

'Take my things,' said Alexey Alexandrovich, and feeling slightly relieved at the news that there was still a hope she might die, he went into the hall.

There was a military overcoat hanging up. Alexey Alexandrovich noticed it and asked:

'Who is here?'

'The doctor, the midwife, and Count Vronsky.'

Alexey Alexandrovich went through into the inner rooms. There was no one in the drawing room; the midwife, wearing a cap with lilac ribbons, came out of Anna's boudoir at the sound of his steps.

She went up to Alexey Alexandrovich and, with the familiarity conferred by the proximity of death, took him by the arm and ushered him into the bedroom.

'Thank God you've come! She keeps on about you all the time, only you,' she said.

'Bring me some ice, quick!' came the doctor's imperious voice from the bedroom.

Alexey Alexandrovich went into her boudoir. Sitting by her desk, sideways against the back of a low chair, was Vronsky, who had covered his face with his hands and was crying. He jumped up at the sound of the doctor's voice, took his hands away from his face, and saw Alexey Alexandrovich. The sight of the husband made him feel so uncomfortable that he sat down again and drew his head into his shoulders as if wishing to disappear somewhere; but he made a concerted effort, stood up, and said:

'She is dying. The doctors have said there is no hope. I am entirely in your hands, but allow me to be here . . . I am at your mercy, however, I . . .'

When he saw Vronsky's tears, Alexey Alexandrovich felt a rush of the emotional distress which the sight of other people's suffering always provoked in him and, averting his eyes, he walked hurriedly over to the door without hearing him out. From the bedroom came the sound of Anna's voice saying something. Her voice was cheerful and lively, with extremely precise intonation. Alexey Alexandrovich went into the bedroom and approached the bed. She was lying with her face turned towards him. Her cheeks were flushed crimson, her eyes were shining, and the small white hands sticking out from the sleeves of her bed-jacket were playing with the corner of the blanket, twisting it. She seemed not only to be fit and well, but in the best of spirits. She was talking rapidly in a resonant voice, with unusually correct and deeply felt intonation.

'Because Alexey, I am talking about Alexey Alexandrovich (what a strange, terrible fate that they both are Alexey, isn't it?), Alexey would not refuse me. I would forget, he would forgive . . . But why doesn't he come? He is kind, he doesn't know himself how kind he is. Oh, goodness, what heartache! Give me some water, quick, quick! Oh, that will be bad for her, my little girl! Well, all right, give her to the wet-nurse. Yes, I agree, that would be better actually. He'll arrive and it will be painful for him to see her. Take her away.'

'Anna Arkadyevna, he has come. Here he is!' said the midwife, trying to draw her attention to Alexey Alexandrovich.

'Oh, what nonsense!' Anna continued, not seeing her husband. 'Oh, give her to me, give me my little girl! He still has not come. You say he won't forgive, because you don't know him. No one knew him. Only I did, and even so it was difficult for me. His eyes, you need to know, Seryozha's are just the same, and I can't bear to see them because of it. Has Seryozha had his dinner? I know they will all forget, you see. He would not have forgotten. Seryozha must be moved into the corner room, and Mariette must be asked to sleep with him.'

Suddenly she recoiled, fell silent, and raised her hands to her face in fear, as if defending herself from the blow she seemed to be expecting. She had seen her husband.

'No, no!' she began. 'I am not afraid of him, I am afraid of death. Alexey, come here. I am in a hurry, because I have no time, I don't have long to live, I'll be feverish soon, and then I won't understand anything. I do understand things now, I understand everything, I see everything!'

Alexey Alexandrovich's crumpled face took on a harrowed look; he took her hand and tried to speak, but was incapable of saying anything; his lower lip trembled, but he was still struggling with his emotions and only glanced at her occasionally. And every time he did glance at her, he saw her eyes, which were looking at him with a tender and rapturous affection such as he had never seen in them before.

'Just a minute, you don't know . . . Wait, wait! . . .' She stopped, as if gathering her thoughts. 'Yes,' she began. 'Yes, yes, yes. This is what I wanted to say. Don't be surprised at me. I'm still the same . . . But there is someone else inside me, I'm afraid of her—she fell in love with that man, and I wanted to hate you and couldn't forget the woman I used to be. That person is not me. Now I am the real one, all of me. I'm dying now, I know I will die, ask him. Even now, look, here they are, I can feel huge weights on my hands, on my feet, on my fingers. See how huge my fingers are! But it will end soon . . . There is just one thing I need: you must forgive me, forgive me completely! I am awful, but my nanny used to tell me: the holy martyr*—what was she called?—she was worse. And I'll go to Rome, there are cloisters there, and I won't be in anyone's way, I'll just take Seryozha and the little girl . . . No, you cannot forgive me! I know, this can't be forgiven! No, no, go away, you're too good!' With one feverish hand she held on to his arm, while with the other she pushed him away.

Alexey Alexandrovich's emotional distress had been continually increasing and had now reached the point where he had given up struggling with it; he suddenly began to feel that what he had considered emotional distress was in fact a blessed spiritual state giving him a sudden new happiness he had never experienced before. He did not think that the Christian law which he had wanted to follow all his life ordained that he should forgive and love his enemies; but a joyous feeling of love and forgiveness of his enemies was filling his heart. He got down on his knees, put his head in the crook of her arm, whose raging heat burned him through her bed-jacket, and sobbed like a child. She put her arm around his balding head, moved closer to him, and raised her eyes with a defiant pride.

'Here he is, I knew it! Farewell now everyone, farewell! . . . They've come again, why won't they leave? . . . Oh, take these furs off me!'

The doctor put down her arms, laid her carefully on the pillow, and covered her shoulders. She lay meekly on her back, and looked straight ahead with shining eyes.

'Remember one thing, that all I needed was forgiveness, and there is nothing else I want . . . But why won't *he* come?' she said, addressing Vronsky through the door. 'Come here, come here! Give him your hand.'

Vronsky came up to the edge of the bed, and when he saw her he hid his face in his hands again.

'Uncover your face, look at him. He's a saint,' she said. 'Come on, uncover your face!' she said angrily. 'Alexey Alexandrovich, uncover his face! I want to see him.'

Alexey Alexandrovich took Vronsky's hands and drew them away from his face, which was terrible in its expression of suffering and shame.

'Give him your hand. Forgive him.'

Alexey Alexandrovich gave him his hand without holding back the tears which were streaming down his face.

'Thank God, thank God,' she said, 'now everything is ready. Just stretch my legs a bit. That's it, that's wonderful. How tastelessly those flowers were done, they're not at all like violets,' she said, pointing to the wallpaper. 'Oh my God, oh my God! When will it end? Give me some morphine. Doctor! Give me some morphine! Oh my God, oh my God!'

And she started tossing and turning on the bed.

The doctor and the other doctors said that it was puerperal fever, which in ninety-nine cases out of a hundred ends in death. All day there was fever, delirium, and unconsciousness. By midnight the patient was lying insensible and almost without a pulse.

The end was expected any moment.

Vronsky went home, but in the morning he came to enquire, and Alexey Alexandrovich, meeting him in the hall, said:

'Stay, she might ask for you,' and showed him into his wife's boudoir himself.

Towards morning the agitation, feverishness, rapid thoughts, and speech began again, and again ended in unconsciousness. On the third day it was the same thing, and the doctor said there was hope. That day Alexey Alexandrovich went out into the boudoir, where Vronsky was sitting, closed the door, and sat down opposite him.

'Alexey Alexandrovich,' said Vronsky, feeling that this was going to be a frank conversation, 'I cannot speak, I cannot make any sense. Spare me! However hard it is for you, believe me, it is more terrible for me.'

He wanted to get up, but Alexey Alexandrovich took him by the hand.

'I beg you to listen to me, this is crucial. I need to explain my feelings, those which have guided me in the past and will continue to guide me, so that you do not misunderstand me. You know that I had decided on a divorce, and had even begun proceedings. I will not conceal from you that I was in a dilemma when I began proceedings, and was in agony about it; I confess that I was obsessed with a desire to take revenge on you and her. When I received the telegram, I came here with the same feelings, and I'll go further: I wanted her to die. But . . .' He paused to consider whether he should reveal his feelings to him or not. 'But I saw her and forgave her. And the happiness of forgiveness has revealed to me what my duty is. I have forgiven her completely. I want to turn the other cheek, I want to give my shirt when my coat is taken from me, and I pray only that God does not take from me the happiness of forgiveness!' There were tears in his eyes, and Vronsky was astonished by his radiant, serene expression. 'That is my position. You can trample me into the mud, make me the laughing-stock of society, but I will not abandon her, and will never utter a word of reproach to you,' he continued. 'My duty is clearly marked out for me: I must be with her, and I will be. If she wishes to see you, I will let you know, but now I believe it would be best for you to leave.'

He got up, and sobs prevented him from speaking further. Vronsky got up and looked at him uneasily from his stooping, hunched state. He was downcast. He did not understand Alexey Alexandrovich's feelings, but he felt that there was something exalted and even inaccessible to him in his outlook.

18

AFTER his conversation with Alexey Alexandrovich, Vronsky went out on to the porch of the Karenins' house and stopped, finding it hard to remember where he was and where he needed to go. He felt ashamed, humiliated, guilty, and divested of any possibility of washing away his humiliation. He felt he had been thrown off the path he had been walking along so proudly and easily until now. All the habits and rules of his life that had seemed so unshakeable suddenly turned out to be false and inapplicable. The deceived husband, who until now had seemed like a pathetic creature, an unexpected and slightly comic obstacle to his happiness, had suddenly been summoned by Anna herself, elevated to an awe-inspiring height, and had shown himself at this height to be neither vindictive nor false nor ridiculous, but kind, straightforward, and dignified. Vronsky could not help but feel this. The roles had suddenly been reversed. Vronsky felt Karenin's towering stature and his own humiliation, Karenin's righteousness and his own falsehood. He felt that the husband was magnanimous even in his sorrow, while he had been mean and petty in his deceit. But this perception of his shabbiness before the man he had unjustly despised made up only a small part of his misery. He felt unimaginably wretched now because his passion for Anna, which he had recently imagined was starting to cool, had grown more intense than ever now that he knew he had lost her for ever. He had seen all of her during her illness, he had come to see right into her soul, and it seemed to him that he had never really loved her until that point. But now, when he had come to know her and love her properly, he had been humiliated before her and had lost her for ever, leaving her nothing but a shameful memory of him. Most terrible of all had been his ludicrous, shameful predicament when Alexey Alexandrovich drew his hands away from his mortified face. He stood on the porch of the Karenins' house like someone lost, not knowing what to do.

'A cab, sir?' asked the porter.

'Yes, a cab.'

Upon his return home after three sleepless nights, Vronsky lay face-down on the sofa without undressing, and lay his head on his crossed arms. His head was heavy. The strangest images, recollections, and thoughts followed one after the other with extraordinary speed and clarity: one moment it was the medicine he was dispensing for the patient, and spilling over the edge of the spoon, the next it was the midwife's white arms, then Alexey Alexandrovich's strange position on the floor in front of the bed.

'Sleep! Forget!' he said to himself with the serene confidence of a healthy man who believes in his ability to nod off at once if he is tired and sleepy. And indeed, his thoughts became muddled at that very moment, and he began to tumble into the abyss of oblivion. The waves of the sea of unconsciousness had already started to close over his head when suddenly—it was as if he had received a powerful electric shock—he gave himself such a start that his whole body bounced on the springs of the sofa, and he leapt up on to his knees in fright, bracing himself with his hands. His eyes were wide open, as if he had never been asleep. The heaviness of his head and the weariness in his limbs he had experienced a moment earlier had suddenly gone.

'You may trample me into the mud,' he heard Alexey Alexandrovich saying and saw him in front of him, and he saw Anna's face with its feverish flush and shining eyes, gazing with love and tenderness not at him but at Alexey Alexandrovich; he saw his own foolish and ludicrous figure when Alexey Alexandrovich took his hands away from his face. He stretched his legs out again, flung himself on the sofa in the same position as before, and shut his eyes.

'Sleep! Sleep!' he repeated to himself. But with his eyes shut he could see more clearly than ever Anna's face as it had been on that fateful evening before the races.

'It is not to be and never will be, and she wants to erase it from her memory. But I cannot live without it. So how can we be reconciled, how on earth can we be reconciled?' he said aloud and started unconsciously repeating these words. The repetition held back the apparition of new images and recollections he could feel clustering in his brain. But repeating words did not hold his imagination back for long. The best moments, and along with them his recent humiliation, started appearing again with extraordinary speed, one after the other. 'Take away his hands,' Anna's voice says. Her husband takes his hands away and he feels the mortified and stupid expression on his face.

He went on lying there, trying to fall asleep, although he did not feel there was the remotest chance that he would, and kept repeating random words from some thought or other in a whisper, hoping this would prevent new images from appearing. He listened keenly and heard words being repeated in a strange, mad whisper: 'Wasn't able to appreciate, wasn't able to make the most, wasn't able to appreciate, wasn't able to make the most.'

'What is this? Or am I going mad?' he said to himself. 'Maybe I am. Why else do people go mad, why else do they shoot themselves?' he answered himself, and when he opened his eyes, he was surprised to see by his head an embroidered cushion, which had been worked by Varya, his brother's wife. He touched the tassel on the cushion and tried to think about Varya, and about when he had last seen her. But thinking of anything else was agonizing. 'No, I must sleep!' He moved the cushion, and pressed his head against it, but he had to make an effort to keep his eyes shut. He jumped up and then sat down. 'It's over for me,' he said to himself. 'I must think what to do. What is left?' He ran over in his mind everything in his life that lay beyond his love for Anna.

'Ambition? Serpukhovskoy? Society? The Court?' He was unable to dwell on anything. It all had meaning before, but not any longer. He got up from the sofa, took off his coat, loosened his belt, and baring his hairy chest so he could breathe more freely, walked up and down the room. 'This is how people go mad,' he repeated, 'and how they shoot themselves . . . to escape the shame,' he added slowly.

He went to the door and shut it; then, with a glassy stare and his teeth firmly clenched, he went over to the table, picked up his revolver, inspected it, turned it to a chamber which was loaded, and became lost in thought. With his head bowed and an expression of intense concentration on his face, he stood motionless for about two minutes with the revolver in his hands, thinking. 'Of course,' he said to himself, as if a logical, sustained, and clear pattern of thought had brought him to an incontrovertible conclusion. In reality, however, this emphatic 'of course' was only the consequence of going through exactly the same circle of memories and images he had already gone through dozens of times within the past hour. The same memories of happiness lost for ever, the same perception that whatever life might bring now was meaningless, the same consciousness of his humiliation. Even the sequence of these images and feelings was the same.

'Of course,' he repeated, when his mind embarked for the third time on the same vicious circle of memories and thoughts, and pressing the revolver to the left side of his chest, and gripping it strongly with his whole hand, as if he was clenching his fist, he pulled the trigger. He did not hear the sound of the shot, but a powerful blow to the chest knocked him off his feet. He tried to hold on to the edge of the table, dropped the revolver, lurched and collapsed on to the floor, looking about in surprise. He did not recognize his room as he looked up at the curved table-legs, the wastepaper basket, and the tiger-skin rug. The squeaky steps of his servant hurrying through the drawing room brought him to his senses. He made an effort to think, and realized that he was on the floor, and when he saw blood on the tiger-skin and on his hand, he realized he had shot himself.

'Stupid! I missed,' he said as he groped for the revolver with his hand. The revolver was beside him, but he was looking further away. Still on the hunt for it, he stretched out to the other side, and as he was unable to keep his balance, he toppled over, bleeding profusely.

The elegant servant with sideburns, who was always complaining to his acquaintances about his delicate nerves, suffered such a fright when he saw his master lying on the floor that he left him bleeding to death while he ran off to get help. An hour later his brother's wife Varya had arrived, and with the assistance of the three doctors present, whom she had summoned from every quarter, and who all arrived at the same time, she got the wounded man into bed, and stayed to look after him.

19

THE error committed by Alexey Alexandrovich while preparing to see his wife, in not considering the possibility that her repentance might be sincere, that he might forgive her, and that she might not die—this error became glaringly evident to him two months after his return from Moscow. But the error he had committed had come about not only because he had not considered this possibility, but also because until that day when he had come face to face with his dying wife he had not known his own heart. At his sick wife's bedside he had for the first time in his life surrendered to that feeling of tender compassion which the sufferings of others always aroused in him, and which he had previously been ashamed of as a harmful weakness; and pity for her, and remorse at having wished for her death, and above all the very joy of forgiveness meant that he suddenly felt not only relief from his sufferings, but also an inner peace which he had never experienced before. He suddenly felt that the very thing which had been the source of his sufferings had become the source of his spiritual joy, and that what had seemed insoluble when he was engaged in condemning, chastising, and hating became simple and clear when he forgave and loved.

He forgave his wife and pitied her for her sufferings and remorse. He forgave Vronsky and pitied him, especially after rumours reached him of his desperate act. He also pitied his son more than before, and now reproached himself for taking so little interest in him. But for the newborn baby girl he experienced feelings not just of pity, but of tenderness. At first it was a feeling of pure compassion which led him to devote himself to the frail little baby girl who was not his daughter and had been neglected during her mother's illness, and who would probably have died if he had not taken care of her—and he did not notice himself how attached to her he became. He would go into the nursery several times a day and sit there for long periods, so that the wet-nurse and the nanny, who were at first shy with him, eventually got used to him. Sometimes he would sit there for a good half-hour, gazing silently at the sleeping baby's saffron-red, downy, puckered little face, and observing the movements of her wrinkled forehead and the backs of her chubby little hands with their curled fingers as they rubbed her little eyes and the bridge of her nose. It was at such moments in particular that Alexey Alexandrovich felt completely calm and at peace with himself, and saw nothing unusual about his situation, nothing that needed to be changed.

But the more time passed, the more clearly he saw that however natural this situation was for him now, he would not be allowed to remain in it. He felt that, in addition to the benign force ruling his soul, there was another primitive force ruling his life which was as powerful, if not more powerful, and that this force was not going to give him that meek tranquillity he craved. He felt that everyone was looking at him with quizzical surprise, that they did not understand him, and were expecting something from him. He particularly felt the fragility and artificiality of his relationship with his wife.

When the softness caused by her proximity to death had worn off, Alexey Alexandrovich began to notice that Anna feared him, felt ill at ease with him, and could not look him straight in the eye. It was as if there was something she wanted, but could not bring herself to tell him, and also, somehow foreseeing that their current relations could not continue, as if she was expecting something from him.

At the end of February, Anna's baby daughter, who was also called

Anna, happened to fall ill. Alexey Alexandrovich was in the nursery in the morning, and after arranging to send for the doctor, he went to the ministry. After finishing his work, he returned home some time after three. As he went into the hall, he saw a handsome footman in braided livery and a bearskin cape, holding a white fur cloak made of American arctic fox.

'Who is here?' asked Alexey Alexandrovich.

'Princess Elizaveta Fyodorovna Tverskaya,' the footman answered, with what appeared to Alexey Alexandrovich to be a smile.

Throughout this difficult time Alexey Alexandrovich had noticed that his society acquaintances, especially the women amongst them, were taking a particular interest in him and his wife. He observed in all these acquaintances a thinly disguised feeling of glee about something, the same glee he had seen in the lawyer's eyes and now in the footman's eyes. It was as if they were all thrilled, as if they had succeeded in marrying someone off. Whenever they met him, they asked about his wife's health with a scarcely disguised glee.

Alexey Alexandrovich was not happy about the presence of Princess Tverskaya, both because of the memories associated with her, and also because he generally disliked her, so he went straight to the nursery. In the first nursery Seryozha was lying face-down on the table, his legs on a chair, chattering merrily while he drew something. The English governess who had replaced the French one during Anna's illness, and who was sitting next to the boy doing *mignardise* crochet-work*, stood up hurriedly, curtsied, and tugged at Seryozha's sleeve.

Alexey Alexandrovich stroked his son's hair, answered the governess's enquiries about his wife's health and asked what the doctor had said about *the baby*.[1]

'The doctor said it was nothing serious, and prescribed baths, sir.'

'But she is still suffering,' said Alexey Alexandrovich, listening to the baby crying in the next room.

'I don't think the wet-nurse is suitable, sir,' said the Englishwoman firmly.

'Why do you think that?' he asked, stopping for a moment.

'It was the same thing at Countess Paul's, sir. The baby was given treatment, but it turned out the baby was just hungry: the wet-nurse had no milk, sir.'

Alexey Alexandrovich stood there for a few seconds thinking, then went through the other door. The little girl was lying with her head

---

[1] [English in the original.]

thrown back, writhing in the wet-nurse's arms, and was refusing either to take the plump breast offered her or to quieten down, despite attempts to hush her by both the wet-nurse and the nanny bending over her.

'Still no better?' said Alexey Alexandrovich.

'She's very restless,' answered the nanny in a whisper.

'Miss Edwards says that perhaps the wet-nurse has no milk,' he said.

'I think so too, Alexey Alexandrovich.'

'Then why didn't you say so?'

'Whom could I say it to? With Anna Arkadyevna still ill . . .' said the nanny indignantly.

The nanny was an old family servant. And Alexey Alexandrovich felt there was an allusion to his situation in her simple words.

The baby was screaming louder than ever, spluttering and wheezing. With a wave of her hand, the nanny went over and took the child from the wet-nurse's arms and began rocking her as she walked up and down.

'The doctor must be asked to examine the wet-nurse,' said Alexey Alexandrovich.

Scared that she might be dismissed, the smartly dressed wet-nurse, who certainly looked healthy, muttered something to herself under her breath and, as she tucked away her large breast, smiled disdainfully at the doubt expressed about her capacity to produce milk. In that smile Alexey Alexandrovich also detected a mockery of his situation.

'Poor baby!' said the nanny, hushing the baby while she continued to walk with her.

Alexey Alexandrovich sat down on a chair, and watched the nanny walking up and down with a pained and dejected expression.

After the baby had at last quietened down and been lowered into her deep cot, and after the nanny had smoothed her pillow and left her, Alexey Alexandrovich got up and tiptoed clumsily over to the baby. For a minute or so he was silent, staring at the baby with the same dejected air; but suddenly his face was lit up by a smile which moved his hair and the skin on his forehead, and he left the room just as quietly.

In the dining room he rang the bell and told the servant who appeared to send for the doctor again. He was annoyed with his wife for not taking care of this beautiful baby, and he had no desire to go in and see her while he was in this state of irritation with her, nor did he have any desire to see Princess Betsy; but his wife might be wondering why he had not come in to see her as usual, so he braced himself and headed for the bedroom. As he padded over the soft carpet towards the door, he could not help overhearing a conversation he did not want to hear.

'If he wasn't going away, I could understand your refusal, and his too. But your husband ought to be above that,' Betsy was saying.

'It's for my sake that I don't want to, not for my husband's. Don't say that!' answered Anna's agitated voice.

'Yes, but you can't not want to say goodbye to a man who tried to shoot himself because of you . . .'

'That's precisely why I don't want to.'

Alexey Alexandrovich stopped with a frightened and guilty expression, and was on the verge of quietly retreating. But reflecting that this would be unworthy of him, he turned round again, coughed, and walked up to the bedroom. The voices fell silent, and he went in.

Anna was sitting on the couch in a grey dressing-gown, her close-cropped black hair growing back in a thick brush on her round head. The animation in her face immediately vanished, as it always did when she saw her husband; she bowed her head and glanced round anxiously at Betsy. Betsy, dressed according to the very latest fashion, in a hat that hovered somewhere above her head like the shade on a lampstand, and a dove-grey dress with garish diagonal stripes going one way on the bodice and another on the skirt, was sitting next to Anna, holding her flat, tall figure erect, and inclining her head, she greeted Alexey Alexandrovich with a withering smile.

'Ah!' she said, as if surprised. 'I'm very glad you're at home. You never put in an appearance anywhere, and I haven't seen you since Anna's illness. I have heard all about it—about your solicitude. Yes, you're a wonderful husband!' she said with a meaningful and affectionate expression, as if bestowing on him an order of magnanimity for his conduct towards his wife.

Alexey Alexandrovich bowed coldly, kissed his wife's hand, and asked after her health.

'I'm feeling better, I think,' she said, avoiding his glance.

'But you have a rather feverish complexion,' he said, stressing the word 'feverish'.

'We've been talking too much,' said Betsy. 'It's selfishness on my part, I am afraid, and I am going.'

She stood up, but Anna, suddenly blushing, quickly seized her hand. 'No, please stay. I need to tell you . . . no, you,' she said, turning to Alexey Alexandrovich, the colour spreading to her neck and forehead. 'I do not want, nor am I able to keep anything secret from you,' she said.

Alexey Alexandrovich cracked his fingers and bowed his head.

'Betsy was saying that Count Vronsky wishes to call on us so he can say goodbye before his departure for Tashkent.'* She did not look at her husband, and was clearly hurrying to get everything out, however hard she found it. 'I told her I could not receive him.'

'You said, my friend, that it would depend on Alexey Alexandrovich,' Betsy corrected her.

'No, no, I cannot receive him, and there would be no . . .' She stopped suddenly and looked searchingly at her husband (he was not looking at her). 'In short, I don't want . . .'

Alexey Alexandrovich moved closer so he could take her hand.

Her first impulse was to withdraw her hand from the clammy hand with large swollen veins seeking hers; but, clearly making a concerted effort, she pressed his hand.

'I am very grateful to you for your confidence, but . . .' he said, feeling embarrassed and annoyed that what he could easily and simply decide on his own was not something which could be discussed in front of Princess Tverskaya, whom he saw as the personification of that primitive force which was destined to rule his life in the eyes of society, preventing him from surrendering to his feelings of love and forgiveness. He paused and looked at Princess Tverskaya.

'Well, goodbye, my dearest,' said Betsy, getting up. She kissed Anna, and left. Alexey Alexandrovich escorted her out.

'Alexey Alexandrovich! I know you to be a truly magnanimous man,' said Betsy, stopping in the small drawing room and pressing his hand again with particular vigour. 'I am an outsider, but I have so much affection for her and respect for you that I will take the liberty of offering some advice. Receive him. Alexey Vronsky is honour personified, and he is going away to Tashkent.'

'Thank you, Princess, for your concern and advice. But the question of whether my wife can or cannot receive anyone is one she must decide for herself.'

He said this with his usual dignified raising of the eyebrows, then immediately surmised that, no matter what he said, there could be no dignity in his position. He saw this in the subtle and malicious, taunting smile with which Betsy looked at him after he uttered this phrase.

20

ALEXEY ALEXANDROVICH took his leave of Betsy in the ballroom and went to his wife. She was lying down, but she hurriedly sat up in her previous position when she heard his steps and looked at him with trepidation. He saw she had been crying.

'I am very grateful for your confidence in me,' he said, meekly repeating in Russian the phrase he had spoken in French in Betsy's presence, and he sat down beside her. Whenever he spoke to her in Russian and used the intimate form of address, that intimate form of address intensely irritated Anna. 'And I am very grateful for your decision. I also believe that, since he is going away, there is absolutely no need for Count Vronsky to come here. However . . .'

'But I've already said that, so why repeat it?' Anna suddenly interrupted him with an irritation she could not manage to suppress. 'There is no need at all', she thought, 'for a man to come and say goodbye to the woman he loves, for whom he was ready to ruin himself and has ruined himself, and who cannot live without him. No need at all!' She pursed her lips, and lowered her blazing eyes to his swollen-veined hands, which he was slowly rubbing together.

'Let us never talk about this,' she added more calmly.

'I left it to you to decide this question, and I am very glad to see . . .' began Alexey Alexandrovich.

'That my wish coincides with yours,' she finished quickly, irritated that he was speaking so slowly when she knew beforehand everything he was going to say.

'Yes,' he confirmed, 'and it is completely inappropriate for Princess Tverskaya to meddle with the most difficult family matters. In particular, she . . .'

'I don't believe anything they say about her,' said Anna quickly. 'I know she is genuinely fond of me.'

Alexey Alexandrovich sighed and fell silent. She played nervously with the tassels of her dressing-gown, glancing at him with that ghastly feeling of physical revulsion for which she reproached herself but could not overcome. There was only one thing she wanted now—to be rid of his odious presence.

'By the way, I have just sent for the doctor,' said Alexey Alexandrovich.

'I am well; why do I need a doctor?'

'No, the little one keeps crying, and apparently the wet-nurse doesn't have enough milk.'

'So why didn't you let me feed her when I was begging to do it? It is all the same,'—Alexey Alexandrovich knew what was meant by this 'it's all the same'—'she's a baby, and they will kill her.' She rang the bell and ordered the baby to be brought to her. 'I asked to feed her, I wasn't allowed to, and now I'm the one who is blamed.'

'I'm not blaming . . .'

'Yes, you are! Oh God! Why didn't I die!' And she burst out sobbing.

'Forgive me, I'm irritable, I'm being unfair,' she said, collecting her-self. 'But just go away . . .'

'No, it can't go on like this,' Alexey Alexandrovich said to himself firmly as he left his wife.

Never had the impossibility of his position in the eyes of society, his wife's hatred of him, and the general power of that primitive mysterious force ruling his life, in opposition to his emotional needs, demanding the execution of its will and a change in his relations with his wife, never had this appeared so manifestly obvious to him as at this moment. He saw clearly that all of society and his wife were expect-ing something from him, but what exactly it was he could not make out. He felt a mounting anger in his soul on account of this, which was destroying his peace of mind and all the rewards of his selfless behaviour. He believed that it would be better for Anna to break off relations with Vronsky, but if they all thought this was not possible, he was even prepared to allow these relations to be resumed, as long as the children were not disgraced, he was not deprived of them, and did not have to change his situation. However bad this would be, it was still better than a separation, which would place her in a hopeless, shameful position and deprive him of everything he loved. But he felt helpless; he knew in advance that everyone was against him, and that he would not be allowed to do what now seemed to him to be so natural and good, but that he would be forced to do what was wrong, but what they considered to be correct.

21

BETSY had not yet managed to leave the ballroom when in the doorway she ran into Stepan Arkadyich, who had just arrived from Yeliseyev's, where they had just received a consignment of fresh oysters.

'Ah, Princess! Now this is a pleasant meeting!' he began. 'I have just been to your house.'

'It will have to be a one-minute meeting, because I am on my way out,' said Betsy, smiling and putting on her glove.

'Don't put on your glove yet, Princess, let me kiss your lovely hand. There's nothing about the revival of old fashions that gratifies me more than the kissing of hands.' He kissed Betsy's hand. 'When are we going to see each other?'

'You are not worthy,' answered Betsy, smiling.

'No, I am very worthy, because I've become a highly serious person.

I don't only sort out my own family affairs, but other people's too,' he said with a meaningful look.

'Oh, I'm very glad!' answered Betsy, immediately realizing that he was talking about Anna. And they went back into the ballroom and stood in a corner. 'He's killing her,' said Betsy in a meaningful whisper. 'It's impossible, impossible . . .'

'I'm glad you think so,' said Stepan Arkadyich, shaking his head with a serious expression of pained sympathy. 'That's why I've come to Petersburg.'

'The whole city is talking about it,' she said. 'It's an impossible position. She is just wasting away. He doesn't understand that she's one of those women who can't trifle with their feelings. There are two options: either he acts decisively and takes her away, or he gives her a divorce. But this is suffocating her.'

'Yes, yes . . . exactly . . .' Oblonsky said, sighing. 'That's the reason I've come. Well, not actually for that . . . I've been made court chamberlain, well, I had to register my gratitude. But the main thing is to sort this out.'

'Well, God help you!' said Betsy.

After accompanying Betsy into the lobby, kissing her hand once again above the glove, where the pulse beats, and spinning her a yarn of such prurient nonsense that she no longer knew whether to be angry or to laugh, Stepan Arkadyich went to see his sister. He found her in tears.

Despite being in exuberant high spirits, Stepan Arkadyich naturally shifted at once to a sympathetic and poetically anxious tone which suited her mood. He asked after her health, and how she had spent the morning.

'Very, very badly. The afternoon, the morning, and every day in the past and the future,' she said.

'It seems to me you're succumbing to gloominess. You have to shake yourself out of it, you have to look at life pragmatically. I know it's hard, but . . .'

'I have heard that women love men even for their vices,' Anna began suddenly, 'but I hate him for his virtues. I can't live with him. You've got to understand, his appearance affects me physically, I'm at my wit's end. I cannot, cannot live with him. So what am I to do? I was unhappy and did not think it was possible to be more unhappy, but I could not have imagined the awful state I'm in now. Can you believe, even though I know he's a kind and excellent man, and that I'm not worth one his fingernails, I still hate him. I hate him for his magnanimity. And there's nothing left for me except . . .'

She was about to say death, but Stepan Arkadyich would not let her finish.

'You're unwell and irritable,' he said. 'Believe me, you're exaggerating terribly. Nothing is that dreadful.'

And Stepan Arkadyich smiled. No one else in Stepan Arkadyich's place would have allowed himself to smile when dealing with such despair (a smile would have seemed uncouth), but there was so much kindness and almost feminine tenderness in his smile that it was not offensive, but soothing and comforting. His gentle, comforting words and smiles had a soothingly comforting effect, like almond oil. And Anna soon felt this.

'No, Stiva,' she said, 'I'm completely ruined, ruined! Worse than ruined! I'm not quite ruined yet, because I can't say that it is all over, on the contrary, I feel that it is not all over. I'm like a taut string which is about to break. But it is not over yet . . . and the end will be ghastly.'

'Don't worry, the string can be unwound gently. There is no situation from which there is no way out.'

'I have thought and thought. There is only one . . .'

He again realized from her frightened expression that this one way out in her opinion was death, and he would not let her finish.

'Not at all,' he said. 'Let me say something. You can't see your own position as I can. Let me give you my frank opinion.' He cautiously smiled his almond smile again. 'I'll begin from the beginning: you married a man twenty years older than you. You married him without love or without having known love. That was a mistake, let's admit that.'

'A terrible mistake!' said Anna.

'But I repeat: it's an accomplished fact. Then you had, let us say, the misfortune to fall in love with a man who was not your husband. It is a misfortune; but it is also an accomplished fact. And your husband has accepted and forgiven this.' He paused after every sentence, expecting her to object, but she did not respond. 'This is so. Now the question is: can you go on living with your husband? Do you wish this? Does he wish this?'

'I don't know anything, anything.'

'But you said yourself that you can't stand him.'

'No, I didn't. I take it back. I don't know anything, and I don't understand anything.'

'Yes, but let . . .'

'You can't understand. I feel like I'm flying head-first down into some kind of abyss, but I must not save myself. And I can't.'

'Don't worry, we'll spread something out and catch you. I understand you, I understand that you can't bring yourself to voice your
wishes, your feelings.'

'There is nothing I wish, nothing . . . except for it all to be over.'

'But he sees this and he knows. And do you think he is finding this
any less difficult than you? You're suffering, he's suffering, and what
good can that possibly do? While a divorce would solve everything,'
said Stepan Arkadyich, expressing his main idea not without effort,
and giving her a meaningful look.

She made no reply and just shook her cropped head. But from the
expression on her face, which all of a sudden began to glow with its
former beauty, he could see that she did not want that, only because it
seemed to her like an impossible happiness.

'I'm awfully sorry for you both! And how happy I would be if I could
sort this out!' said Stepan Arkadyich, smiling more boldly now. 'Don't,
don't say anything! God grant only that I may be able to speak as I feel.
I'm going to go and see him.'

Anna looked at him with wistful, shining eyes, and said nothing.

22

STEPAN ARKADYICH entered Alexey Alexandrovich's study with
the same slightly solemn face with which he would sit down in the
chairman's seat at his board. Alexey Alexandrovich was walking around
the room with his hands clasped behind his back, thinking about the
very thing that Stepan Arkadyich and his wife had been talking about.

'I'm not disturbing you?' said Stepan Arkadyich, suddenly experiencing an unaccustomed feeling of embarrassment at the sight of his
brother-in-law. To conceal this embarrassment he took out a newly
purchased cigarette case which opened in a novel way, sniffed the
leather, and took out a cigarette.

'No. Is there something you need?' Alexey Alexandrovich replied
reluctantly.

'Yes, I would like . . . I need to . . . yes, I need to talk to you,' said
Stepan Arkadyich, taken aback by the unaccustomed timidity he was
feeling.

This feeling was so unexpected and strange that Stepan Arkadyich
did not believe it was the voice of his conscience telling him that what
he was about to do was wrong. Stepan Arkadyich made an effort to
conquer the timidity that had come over him.

'I hope you believe in my love for my sister and in my sincere affection and respect for you,' he said, blushing.

Alexey Alexandrovich stopped and did not answer, but Stepan Arkadyich was struck by the expression of meek victimhood on his face.

'I was intending . . . I wanted to talk about my sister and your mutual situation,' said Stepan Arkadyich, still struggling with his unaccustomed shyness.

Alexey Alexandrovich smiled sadly, looked at his brother-in-law, and without answering went over to his desk, took from it an unfinished letter, and handed it to him.

'I think constantly about the same thing. And this is what I have begun to write, believing that I could put it better in writing, and that my presence would irritate her,' he said, handing over the letter.

Stepan Arkadyich took the letter, looked with befuddled surprise at the dull eyes fixed immovably on him, and began reading.

'I can see that my presence is irksome to you. However painful it is for me to acknowledge this, I see that it is so, and cannot be otherwise. I don't blame you, and God is my witness that I made a wholehearted decision after seeing you during your illness to forget all that had passed between us and begin a new life. I do not regret, and shall never regret what I did; but I desired one thing, which was your well-being and the well-being of your soul, and now I see I have not achieved that. Tell me yourself what will give you true happiness and peace of mind. I entrust myself fully to your wishes and to your sense of justice.'

Stepan Arkadyich handed back the letter and continued to look at his brother-in-law with the same bewilderment, not knowing what to say. This silence was so awkward for both of them that Stepan Arkadyich's lips began twitching nervously as he sat there silently with his eyes glued to Karenin's face.

'That is what I wanted to say to her,' said Alexey Alexandrovich, turning away.

'Yes, yes . . .' said Stepan Arkadyich, unable to answer because of the tears which were choking him. 'Yes, yes, I understand you,' he managed to say finally.

'I wish to know what she wants,' said Alexey Alexandrovich.

'I am afraid that she does not understand her position herself. She is no judge,' said Stepan Arkadyich, regaining his composure. 'She is crushed, literally crushed, by your magnanimity. If she reads this letter she will be incapable of saying anything, she will only hang her head lower.'

'Yes, but what's to be done in that case? How can one explain . . . how can one find out her wishes?'

'If you will allow me to express my opinion, I think that it is up to you to be clear in specifying the measures you consider necessary to end this situation.'

'You consider it necessary to end it then?' Alexey Alexandrovich interrupted him. 'But how?' he added, making an unusual gesture with his hands in front of his eyes. 'I do not see any possible way out.'

'There is a way out of every situation,' said Stepan Arkadyich, perking up as he got to his feet. 'There was a time when you wanted to sever . . . If you now come to the conclusion that you cannot make each other happy . . .'

'Happiness may be variously understood. But let us suppose I agree to everything, that I want nothing. What is the way out of our situation then?'

'If you want to know my opinion . . .' began Stepan Arkadyich with the same soothing smile of almond tenderness with which he had talked to Anna. His kind smile was so persuasive that Alexey Alexandrovich, sensing his weakness and succumbing to it, unconsciously found himself ready to believe what Stepan Arkadyich had to say. 'She would never say this out loud. But one thing is possible, one thing she might desire,' Stepan Arkadyich went on, 'and that is the breaking off of relations and all memories associated with them. In my opinion, what you need in your situation is to work out a new relationship with each other. And that relationship can only be established if both parties are free.'

'Divorce,' interrupted Alexey Alexandrovich with revulsion.

'Yes, I believe it means divorce. Yes, divorce,' Stepan Arkadyich repeated, blushing. 'It is the most sensible solution in all respects for a married couple who find themselves in the situation you are in. What is there to be done if a married couple find that life is impossible for them together? That can always happen.' Alexey Alexandrovich heaved a heavy sigh and closed his eyes. 'There's only one point to consider: does either party wish to enter into another marriage? If not, it is very simple,' said Stepan Arkadyich, feeling increasingly liberated from his embarrassment.

Alexey Alexandrovich, frowning with agitation, muttered something to himself and did not reply. Everything that turned out to be very simple for Stepan Arkadyich had been thought over by Alexey Alexandrovich thousands and thousands of times. And not only did it not seem very simple to him, but completely impossible. Divorce, the details of which he was already familiar with, now seemed impossible to him, because his own sense of dignity and respect for religion would not allow him to take upon himself a fictitious accusation of adultery and still less permit his wife, whom he loved and had forgiven, to be exposed and disgraced. Divorce also seemed impossible for other, even more important reasons.

What would become of his son if there was a divorce? To leave him with his mother was out of the question. The divorced mother would have her own illegitimate family, in which the position and upbringing of a stepson would in all likelihood be undesirable. Should the boy be left with him? He knew this would be vindictive on his part, and he did not want that. But over and above all that, the main reason why divorce seemed impossible to Alexey Alexandrovich was that, by agreeing to a divorce, he would be the agent of Anna's ruin. What Darya Alexandrovna had said in Moscow, that he was only thinking about himself when he made up his mind to divorce, without considering that it would lead to her irrevocable ruin, had imprinted itself deeply on his soul. And connecting what she said with his forgiveness and his attachment to the children, he now understood it in his own way. Consenting to a divorce and giving her freedom, as he understood it, meant he would lose his last tie to the lives of the children he loved, while she would lose her last foothold on the path of goodness and be plunged into ruin. If she became a divorced wife, he knew she would form a liaison with Vronsky, and their union would be unlawful and criminal, because according to ecclesiastical law, a wife cannot marry again while her husband is alive. 'She will form a union with him, and in a year or two he will leave her, or she will enter into a new liaison,' thought Alexey Alexandrovich. 'And by agreeing to an unlawful divorce, I shall be to blame for her ruin.' He had thought it all over hundreds of times, and was convinced that not only was a divorce not as simple as his brother-in-law said, but completely impossible. He did not believe a single word Stepan Arkadyich said, and had a thousand arguments to refute it all, but he listened to him, feeling that his words were an expression of that powerful primitive force which ruled his life, and to which he would have to submit.

'The only question is on what terms you will agree to grant her a divorce. She does not want or dare to ask for anything, she is content to rely on your magnanimity.'

'Oh God! Oh God! Why this?' thought Alexey Alexandrovich, remembering the details of a divorce in which the husband had taken the blame, and he covered his face with his hands in shame, just as Vronsky had done.

'You are upset, I understand. But if you think it over . . .'

'And whosoever shall smite thee on thy right cheek, turn to him the other also, and if any man take away thy coat, let him have thy cloak also,'* thought Alexey Alexandrovich.

'Yes, yes!' he cried in a shrill voice. 'I will take the disgrace on myself, I will even give up my son, but . . . but is it not better just to leave it? However, you do what you want . . .'

And turning away so that his brother-in-law could not see him, he sat down on a chair by the window. He felt bitter, he felt ashamed; but alongside this bitterness and shame he felt joy and awe at his supreme humility.

Stepan Arkadyich was moved. He was silent for a while.

'Alexey, believe me, she will appreciate your generosity,' he said. 'But it was clearly God's will,' he added, and as soon as he said this he realized it was stupid, and had difficulty restraining himself from smiling at his own stupidity.

Alexey Alexandrovich wanted to say something in reply, but was prevented by tears.

'This is a misfortune ordained by fate, and we have to recognize that. I recognize this misfortune as an accomplished fact and am just trying to help both you and her,' said Stepan Arkadyich.

When Stepan Arkadyich left his brother-in-law's room he felt moved, but that did not prevent him from being pleased that he had successfully accomplished his task, for he felt certain Alexey Alexandrovich would not go back on his words. Mingling with his feeling of pleasure was an idea for a question he would ask his wife and close friends when the matter was settled: 'What is the difference between me and the Tsar? When the Tsar annuls something no one benefits, while I have annulled something, and three people have benefited . . .* Or: what do I and the Tsar have in common? When . . . Anyway, I'll think of something better,' he said to himself with a smile.

23

VRONSKY'S wound was dangerous, even though it had missed his heart. And for several days he lay suspended between life and death. When he was able to speak for the first time, only his brother's wife Varya was in his room.

'Varya!' he said, looking at her sternly, 'I shot myself by accident.

And please, don't ever talk about it, and tell that to everyone. Otherwise it's too ridiculous!'

Not responding to what he said, Varya bent over him and looked into his face with a delighted smile. His eyes were bright, not feverish, but their expression was stern.

'Well, thank God!' she said. 'You're not in pain?'

'A little, here.' He pointed to his chest.

'Then let me change the dressing.'

He looked at her in silence while she bandaged him, his broad jaws firmly clenched. When she finished he said:

'I'm not delirious; please make sure there aren't any conversations about me shooting myself on purpose.'

'No one is saying that. I just hope you won't shoot yourself by accident again,' she said with a quizzical smile.

'I'm sure I won't, but it would have been better . . .'

And he smiled dolefully.

In spite of these words and the smile, which Varya found so alarming, when the inflammation stopped and he began to recover, he felt that he had completely liberated himself from one part of his grief. With this action it was as if he had somehow washed away the shame and humiliation he had felt before. He could now think calmly about Alexey Alexandrovich. He acknowledged the extent of his magnanimity, but no longer felt humiliated. Furthermore, his life resumed its old pattern again. He saw the possibility of looking people in the eye without shame, and could live in accordance with his habits. The one thing he could not tear from his heart, despite never ceasing to struggle with this feeling, was the regret, bordering on despair, that he had lost her for ever. The idea that he now, having atoned for his guilt before her husband, had to renounce her and never again stand between her and her remorse and her husband, had been firmly decided in his heart; but he could not tear from his heart his regrets about losing her love, nor could he erase from his memory those moments of happiness he had enjoyed with her, which he had so little valued at the time and which now haunted him in all their loveliness.

Serpukhovskoy had thought up an appointment for him in Tashkent, and Vronsky had agreed to the proposition without the slightest hesitation. But the nearer the time of his departure approached, the harder he found it to carry out the sacrifice he was making to what he regarded as his duty.

His wound had healed, and he was already out and about, making preparations for his departure to Tashkent.

'To see her once and then bury myself and die,' he thought, and he expressed this thought to Betsy when he was paying his farewell visits. Betsy had gone to see Anna with this mission and brought him back a refusal.

'So much the better,' thought Vronsky when he received this news. 'This was a weakness which would have sapped my last strength.'

The following morning Betsy came to see him herself, and announced that she had received, through Oblonsky, the good news that Alexey Alexandrovich had agreed to a divorce, and that he could therefore see her.

Without even troubling to show Betsy out, forgetting all his resolutions, and without asking when he could see her, or where her husband was, Vronsky drove straight round to the Karenins'. He bolted up the stairs without seeing anyone or anything and, barely able to restrain himself from running, walked with rapid steps into her room. And without thinking or noticing whether there was anyone else in the room or not, he threw his arms round her and began covering her face, her hands, and her neck with kisses.

Anna had been preparing herself for this meeting, and thinking about what she would say to him, but she did not manage to say any of it: his passion overwhelmed her. She wanted to calm him down, to calm herself, but it was already too late. His feelings communicated themselves to her. Her lips were trembling so much that for a long time she was unable to speak.

'Yes, you have taken possession of me, and I am yours,' she said at last, pressing his hand to her breast.

'It had to be!' he said. 'So long as we are alive, it has to be. I know that now.'

'It's true,' she said, growing ever paler and clasping his head in her hands. 'All the same, there is something terrible in this, after all that has happened.'

'It will all pass, it will all pass, we shall be so happy! Our love, if it could become stronger, will become stronger by having something terrible in it,' he said, lifting his head and revealing his strong teeth in a smile.

And she could not help but respond with a smile—not to his words, but to his lovestruck eyes. She took his hand and with it stroked her cropped hair and her cheeks, which had grown cold.

'I don't recognize you with this short hair. You've become even prettier. Like a boy. But how pale you are!'

'Yes, I'm very weak,' she said, smiling. And her lips began trembling again.

'We'll go to Italy, you will get better,' he said.

'Is it really possible that we could be like husband and wife, by ourselves, as a family?' she said, looking deep into his eyes.

'I'm only surprised that it could ever have been otherwise.'

'Stiva says that *he* has agreed to everything, but I can't accept his generosity,' she said, looking wistfully past Vronsky's face. 'I don't want a divorce, it's all the same to me now. Only I don't know what he will decide about Seryozha.'

He simply could not understand how at this point in their meeting she could remember or think about her son, or a divorce. Did any of that really matter?

'Don't speak about it, don't think,' he said, turning her hand over in his and trying to attract her attention; but she still would not look at him.

'Oh, why didn't I die, it would have been better!' she said, and silent tears streamed down her cheeks; but she tried to smile, so as not to upset him.

To turn down a flattering and dangerous appointment in Tashkent would have been shameful and inconceivable according to Vronsky's previous ideas. But now he turned it down without a moment's thought, and when he noticed disapproval of his action amongst his superiors, he immediately resigned his commission.

A month later Alexey Alexandrovich was left alone with his son in his house, while Anna went abroad with Vronsky, without having obtained a divorce and having firmly decided against one.

PART FIVE

I

PRINCESS SHCHERBATSKAYA found that it would be impossible to arrange the wedding before Lent, which was five weeks away, as half the trousseau would not be ready by then; but she could not help agreeing with Levin that after Lent would be too late, as Prince Shcherbatsky's old aunt was very ill and might die soon, and then the mourning would delay the wedding still further. And so, having decided to divide the trousseau into two parts, a large and a small trousseau, the Princess consented to have the wedding before Lent. She decided that she would get all of the small trousseau ready now, but send the large one on later, and she became very cross with Levin for being completely incapable of giving her a serious answer as to whether he was happy with this or not. This arrangement was all the more convenient as the young couple were going to the country immediately after the wedding, where the things in the big trousseau would not be needed.

Levin continued to be in that same state of madness in which he imagined that he and his happiness constituted the one and only aim of all existence, and that he now had no need to think or worry about anything, since everything was being, and would be, done for him by others. He did not even have any plans and aims for the future; he left all that to be decided by others, knowing that everything would be wonderful. His brother Sergey Ivanovich, Stepan Arkadyich, and the Princess guided him in what he ought to do. He merely agreed wholeheartedly with everything that was suggested to him. His brother borrowed money for him, the Princess recommended leaving Moscow after the wedding. Stepan Arkadyich recommended going abroad. He agreed to everything. 'Do whatever you want, if it gives you enjoyment. I'm happy, and my happiness cannot be enhanced or diminished by anything you do,' he thought. When he told Kitty that Stepan Arkadyich had recommended they go abroad, he was very surprised that she did not agree to this, and had some clear-cut wishes of her own about their future life. She knew that Levin had work in the country which he loved. As he could see, she not only did not understand this work, but did not even want to understand it. This did not prevent her from regarding this work as very important, however. And because she knew their home would be in the country, she therefore did not want to go abroad, where she was not going to live, but to the place where they would be making their home. This clearly expressed intent surprised Levin. But since it was all the same to him, he immediately asked Stepan Arkadyich, as if it was his responsibility, to go down to the country and arrange everything there as he saw fit, with that good taste for which he was renowned.

'Listen, I've just had a thought,' Stepan Arkadyich said to Levin one day after his return from the country, where he had arranged everything in preparation for the young couple's arrival, 'do you have a certificate showing you have been to confession?'

'No. Why?'

'You can't be married without it.'

'Oh, no!' exclaimed Levin. 'It must be about nine years since I last prepared for Communion. It never even occurred to me.'

'You're a fine one!' said Stepan Arkadyich, laughing; 'and you call me a nihilist! However, there is no getting round it, you know. You need to prepare for Communion.'

'But when? There are only four days left.'

Stepan Arkadyich arranged this too. And Levin began to prepare for Communion. As someone who did not believe, but who nevertheless had respect for other people's religious beliefs, Levin found attending and taking part in any kind of church service very difficult. In that state of mind he found himself in now, however, softened and sensitive to everything, this obligation to pretend seemed not only burdensome to Levin but downright impossible. Now that he was in his state of glory, in full bloom, he would have to either lie or blaspheme. He did not feel capable of doing either. But no matter how persistently he quizzed Stepan Arkadyich as to whether he could obtain the certificate without preparing for Communion, Stepan Arkadyich was adamant that it was impossible.

'But anyway, what will it cost you—two days? And he's a terribly nice, clever old man. He'll pull that tooth out for you so that you even won't notice it.'

While he was standing through the first liturgy, Levin tried to revive his youthful memories of the fervent religious feelings he had experienced between the ages of sixteen and seventeen. But he discovered straight away that this was completely impossible for him to do. He tried to look at it all as an empty, meaningless custom, like the custom of paying calls, but he felt quite incapable of doing that either. Like the majority of his contemporaries, Levin's position was highly ambiguous where religion was concerned. He could not believe, yet at the same time he was not wholly convinced that it was all untrue. And since he was neither able to believe in the significance of what he was doing nor look at it dispassionately as an empty formality, he felt throughout this preparation for Communion a sense of awkwardness and shame about doing something he did not himself understand, and something which was therefore, as an inner voice told him, false and wrong.

During the service he either listened to the prayers, trying to ascribe to them a meaning which would not differ from his own views, or did his best not to listen to them, feeling he could not understand them and should condemn them, and instead became wrapped up in his own thoughts, observations, and memories, which were rambling around in his head with extraordinary vividness during this idle standing in church.

He stood through the liturgy, vespers, and the vigil, and the next day, after getting up earlier than usual and going without tea, he arrived at church at eight in the morning for morning prayers and confession.

There was no one in the church but a destitute soldier, two old women, and the clergy.

A young deacon, the two halves of his long back clearly discernible under his thin cassock, greeted him and went straight over to the little table by the wall to begin reading the prayers. As the reading proceeded, especially during the frequent and rapid repetition of the same words: 'Lord, have mercy,' which sounded like 'lormers, lormers,' Levin felt that his critical faculties were locked and sealed, and that he should not disturb or stimulate them now as that would produce confusion, and so he continued standing behind the deacon, not listening or paying attention, and thinking his own thoughts. 'There's an extraordinary amount of expression in her hand,' he thought, remembering how they had sat at the corner table the previous evening. They had nothing to talk about, as was almost always the case at that time, and she had placed her hand on the table and kept opening and shutting it, and laughing herself as she watched her movements. He remembered how he had kissed that hand and then examined the converging lines on its pink palm. 'Lormers again,' thought Levin, crossing himself, bowing, and looking at the supple movement of the deacon's back as he bowed. 'Then she took my hand and examined the lines on it. "You've got a nice hand," she said.' And he looked at his hand, and at the deacon's stubby hand. 'Yes, it will be over soon,' he was thinking. 'No, we seem to have gone back to the beginning,' was his next thought as he listened more closely to the prayers. 'No, it is ending; he is bowing down to the ground. That always comes just before the end.'

After surreptitiously receiving a three-rouble note in his velveteen-cuffed hand, the deacon said he would put Levin's name down and headed for the sanctuary, his new boots squeaking loudly on the flag-stones of the empty church. A moment later he peered out and beck-oned Levin over. Levin's critical faculties, which were still locked up inside his head, began to stir, but he hurriedly shut them down. 'It will all work out somehow or other,' he thought, and walked towards the ambo.* He went up the steps, turned to the right, and saw the priest. The little old man, with a thin, grizzled beard and tired, kind eyes, was standing at the lectern, leafing through a prayer-book. After making a slight bow to Levin, he immediately began reading the prayers in his customary voice. When he finished them, he bowed down to the ground and turned to face Levin.

'Christ is invisibly present here, receiving your confession,' he said, pointing to the crucifix. 'Do you believe in all that the holy apostolic church teaches us?' the priest went on, averting his eyes from Levin's face and folding his hands under his stole.

'I have doubted, I doubt everything,' said Levin in a voice he did not like, and fell silent.

The priest waited a few seconds to see if he would say anything else, then closed his eyes and said quickly with his strong Vladimir pronunciation:*

'Human weakness is prone to doubt, but we must pray that our merciful Lord will strengthen us. What particular sins do you have?' he added without pausing for breath, as if endeavouring not to waste time.

'My chief sin is doubt. I doubt everything, and am in a state of doubt most of the time.'

'Human weakness is prone to doubt,' said the priest, repeating the same words. 'Where do your greatest doubts lie?'

'I doubt everything. I sometimes even doubt the existence of God,' Levin said reluctantly, and was appalled at the impropriety of what he was saying. But Levin's words did not seem to make any impression on the priest.

'What doubt can there be in the existence of God?' he said hur-riedly, with a faint smile.

Levin remained silent.

'What doubt can you have about the Creator when you behold His creation?' the priest continued in his rapid, customary patter. 'Who then decked the heavenly firmament with stars? Who clothed the earth with its beauty? How could it all happen without the Creator?' he said, looking enquiringly at Levin.

Levin felt that it would be improper to enter into a philosophical debate with the priest, and so he merely gave a reply which related directly to the question.

'I don't know,' he said.

'You don't know? Then how can you doubt that God created it all?' the priest said with amused bewilderment.

'I don't understand anything,' said Levin, blushing, and feeling what he was saying was stupid, and could not but be stupid in such circumstances.

'Pray to God and beseech Him. Even the Holy Fathers had doubts, and they beseeched God to strengthen their faith. The devil has great power, and we must not surrender to him. Pray to God and beseech Him. Pray to God,' he repeated hurriedly.

The priest was then silent for a while, as if in deep thought.

'I hear you are about to enter into matrimony with the daughter of my parishioner and spiritual son, Prince Shcherbatsky?' he added with a smile. 'A lovely girl!'

'Yes,' answered Levin, blushing for the priest. 'Why does he need to ask about this at confession?' he thought.

And as if answering his thought, the priest said to him:

'You are about to enter into matrimony, and God will perhaps reward you with descendants, is that not so? Well, what sort of upbringing can you give your little ones if you do not vanquish within yourself the temptation of the devil, luring you into unbelief?' he said in mild reproach. 'If you love your offspring, then as a good father you will not desire only wealth, luxury, and honours for your child; you will desire his salvation, and for his spiritual enlightenment to be guided by the light of truth. Is that not so? What then will you answer when the innocent little one asks you: "Papa! Who made everything that enchants me in this world—the earth, the waters, the sun, the flowers, the grass?" Surely you won't say to him: "I don't know"? You can't not know, when the Lord God in His great mercy has revealed it to you. Or your child will ask you: "What awaits me in the life beyond the grave?" What will you tell him if you don't know anything? How will you answer him? Leave him to worldly pleasures and the devil? That is wrong!' he said and paused, inclining his head to one side and looking at Levin with kind, gentle eyes.

Levin could give no answer now—not because he did not want to enter into an argument with the priest, but because no one had ever asked him such questions; and there would be plenty of time to think about what to answer when his little ones asked him these questions.

'You are entering into a time of life', the priest continued, 'when you need to choose your path and keep to it. Pray to God that He may in His goodness help you and have mercy upon you,' he concluded. 'May our Lord God Jesus Christ, with the grace and munificence of His love for mankind, pardon thee . . .' And when he had finished the prayer of absolution, the priest blessed and dismissed him.

When he returned home that day, Levin experienced an exultant feeling that the awkward situation had come to an end, and had come to an end without his having to lie. He was also left with a vague recollection that what that nice, kind old man had said was not at all as stupid as he had at first imagined, and that there was something in it that he needed to unravel.

'Not now, of course,' thought Levin, 'another time.' Levin now felt more than ever that there was something unclear and impure in his soul, and that he was in exactly the same position regarding religion which he saw so clearly and disliked in others, and for which he reproached his friend Sviyazhsky.

Levin was in particularly high spirits while spending that evening with his fiancée at Dolly's, and in explaining his state of exhilaration to Stepan Arkadyich he said he was as happy as a dog taught to jump through a hoop which, when it finally understands and does what it has been asked to do, yelps and jumps up in excitement on to tables and window-ledges, wagging its tail.

2

ON the day of the wedding, in accordance with custom (the Princess and Darya Alexandrovna insisted on strict observance of all the customs), Levin did not see his fiancée and dined at his hotel with three bachelor friends who had happened to gather with him there: Sergey Ivanovich, Katavasov, a university friend, now a professor of natural sciences, whom Levin had dragged back to the hotel after they met on the street, and Chirikov, his best man,* a Moscow magistrate and his companion on bear hunts. The dinner was very convivial. Sergey Ivanovich was in an exceptionally good mood and found Katavasov's originality very entertaining. Katavasov, sensing that his originality was appreciated and understood, made a great show of it. The good-natured Chirikov was happy to sustain any conversation.

'Just think, after all, what a talented fellow our friend Konstantin Dmitrich used to be,' said Katavasov, drawing out his words in a habit he had picked up while lecturing. 'I'm talking about absent friends, as he is no longer with us. He used to love science back then, when he left university, and he had normal human interests; but now half his talents are devoted to deceiving himself, while the other half have to justify the deceit.'

'A more implacable foe of marriage than you I've yet to clap eyes on,' said Sergey Ivanovich.

'No, I'm not a foe. I'm a friend of the division of labour. People who can do nothing else should manufacture people, while the rest should contribute to their enlightenment and happiness. That's how I see things. There are a whole host of people eager to mix these two trades up, but I'm not among them.'

'How happy I will be when I find out that you have fallen in love!' said Levin. 'Please invite me to the wedding.'

'I'm already in love.'

'Yes, with a cuttlefish. You know,' Levin turned to his brother, 'Mikhail Semyonich is writing a study about the nutrition and . . .'

'Now, don't confuse things! It doesn't matter what it's about. As it happens, I do actually love cuttlefish.'

'But that shouldn't be an obstacle to you loving a wife.'

'It's not the cuttlefish which is the obstacle, but the wife.'

'Why?'

'Oh, you'll see. You love farming and hunting, for example—well, you'd better watch out!'

'Arkhip was here today, and he said there were lots of elk in Prudno, and two bears,' said Chirikov.

'Well, you'll have to get them without me.'

'That's the hard truth,' said Sergey Ivanovich. 'You'll have to wave goodbye to bear-hunting in the future too—your wife won't let you go!'

Levin smiled. The notion that his wife would not let him go seemed so appealing to him, he was ready to renounce the pleasure of ever seeing bears again.

'Still, it's a pity they will get those two bears without you. Do you remember that last time at Khapilovo? It would be great hunting!' said Chirikov.

Levin did not want to disabuse him of the notion that there could be anything good without her somewhere, so he said nothing.

'There is a good reason why this custom of saying farewell to one's bachelor life became established,' said Sergey Ivanovich. 'However happy you might be, it's still a shame to lose your freedom.'

'Come on, admit it, do you feel like that bridegroom in Gogol's play who wants to jump out of the window?'*

'He probably does, but he won't admit it,' said Katavasov, bursting out laughing loudly.

'Well, the window's open . . . Let's go to Tver now! One of them is a she-bear, we can go up to her lair. Seriously, we can go on the five o'clock train! And they can do what they like here,' said Chirikov, smiling.

'Well, I swear to God,' said Levin, smiling, 'that I can't find in my heart any regret for my freedom!'

'But there's such chaos in your heart at the moment, you're not going to find anything,' said Katavasov. 'Wait until you have sorted yourself out a bit, then you'll find it!'

'No, because apart from my feelings . . .' (he did not want say the word 'love' in front of him) 'and my happiness, I would surely feel at least a twinge of regret about losing my freedom . . . On the contrary, I am actually happy about this loss of freedom.'

'It's bad! A hopeless case!' said Katavasov. 'Well, let's drink to his recovery, or simply wish that at least a hundredth part of his dreams may come true. And even then that would be happiness never before seen on earth!'

The guests left soon after dinner so there would be time to get changed for the wedding.

When he was left on his own and was recalling the conversations of those bachelors, Levin asked himself again: did he have in his heart that feeling of regret at losing his freedom which they had talked about? He smiled at the question. 'Freedom? Why do I need freedom? Happiness only consists of loving, wishing, and thinking her wishes and thoughts, in other words, there is no freedom—that's what happiness is!'

'But do I know her thoughts, her wishes, her feelings?' a voice suddenly whispered to him. The smile vanished from his face, and he became lost in thought. And then a strange feeling suddenly overwhelmed him. He was overwhelmed by fear and doubt—doubt about everything.

'What if she does not love me? What if she's marrying me only in order to get married? What if she doesn't know herself what she's doing?' he asked himself. 'She may come to her senses, and only realize after she is married that she does not and cannot love me.' And strange, contemptible thoughts about her started coming into his head. He was jealous of Vronsky, as he had been a year ago, as if that evening when he had seen her with Vronsky was yesterday. He suspected she had not told him everything.

He jumped up quickly. 'No, this won't do!' he told himself in despair. 'I'll go to her and I'll ask her and say for the last time: we are free, and wouldn't it be better to stay that way? Anything is better than endless unhappiness, disgrace, and infidelity!' With despair in his heart and ill-feelings towards all people, to himself, and to her, he left the hotel and drove to her house.

No one was expecting him. He found her in one of the back rooms. She was sitting on a trunk and giving instructions to a maid as she sorted through heaps of different-coloured dresses, which were spread out over the backs of chairs and on the floor.

'Ah!' she cried out when she saw him, beaming all over with happiness. 'What are you . . . why are you . . . ?' (she was alternating even now between the polite and familiar form of address with him). 'I wasn't expecting you! I've been going through the dresses I wore as a girl, working out whom . . .'

'Ah! That's very good!' he said, looking darkly at the maid.

'You can go, Dunyasha, I'll call you later,' said Kitty.

'What is the matter with you?' she asked, decisively using the familiar form of address as soon as the maid had gone out. She had noticed his strange, agitated, and gloomy expression, and was scared.

'Kitty! I'm in agony. I can't tolerate this agony alone,' he said with despair in his voice as he stopped in front of her and looked imploringly into her eyes. He could already see from her loving, truthful face that nothing could come of what he intended to say, but he still needed her to make the disavowal herself. 'I've come to say that there is still time. It can all be undone and put right.'

'What? I don't understand anything. What is bothering you?'

'What I have said a thousand times and can't help thinking . . . that I'm not worthy of you. You couldn't have agreed to marry me. Think about it. You made a mistake. Think hard. You cannot love me . . . If . . . it's better to tell me,' he said, not looking at her. 'I will be miserable. Let people say what they like; anything's better than unhappiness . . . It's better now while there's still time . . .'

'I don't understand,' she answered, terrified, 'you mean you want to break it off . . . that we shouldn't go through with it?'

'Yes, if you don't love me.'

'You've gone mad!' she cried, flushing with exasperation.

But his face was so pitiful that she curbed her exasperation, threw the clothes off the armchair, and sat down closer to him.

'What are you thinking? Tell me everything.'

'I am thinking that you cannot love me. What is there to love about me?'

'Good God! What on earth can I do? . . .' she said and burst into tears.

'Oh, what have I done!' he exclaimed, and got down on to his knees in front of her and started kissing her hands.

When the Princess came into the room five minutes later she found them already completely reconciled. Kitty had not only assured him that she loved him, but in answer to his question as to why she loved him, had even told him why. She told him that she loved him because she completely understood him, because she knew what he was bound to love, and because everything he loved was good. And this seemed to make perfect sense to him. When the Princess came in they were sitting side by side on the trunk, sorting out the dresses and arguing, because Kitty wanted Dunyasha to have the brown dress she had been wearing when Levin proposed to her, while he was insisting that dress should never be given away, and that Dunyasha should be given the blue one.

'Why can't you understand? She's a brunette, and it won't suit her . . . I've got it all worked out.'

When she discovered why he had come, the Princess became angry, half in jest and half in earnest, and packed him off home to get dressed and not interfere with Kitty having her hair done, since Charles was about to arrive.

'As it is, she hasn't eaten anything for days, and is not looking her best, and then you come along and upset her even more with your nonsense,' she said to him. 'Off you go, my dear, off you go.'

Levin went back to his hotel feeling guilty and ashamed, but reassured. His brother, Darya Alexandrovna, and Stepan Arkadyich, all in evening dress, were already waiting for him so that they could bless him with the icon. There was no time to lose. Darya Alexandrovna still had to drive home to fetch her pomaded and ringleted son, who was to carry the icon in the bride's carriage. Then one carriage had to be sent for the best man, while the one that would take Sergey Ivanovich would have to be sent back . . . Altogether there were a great many extremely complicated arrangements. One thing that was certain was that there could be no dawdling, as it was already half-past six.

The blessing with the icon was not a huge success. Stepan Arkadyich assumed a comically solemn pose next to his wife, took the icon, and after telling Levin to bow to the ground, blessed him with his kind, wry smile, and kissed him three times; Darya Alexandrovna did the same, then immediately had to hurry off, and again got in a muddle about where all the carriages were going.

'Look, this is what we will do: you drive in our carriage to fetch him, and Sergey Ivanovich, if he would be so kind, could go on and then send the carriage back.'

'Of course, I'd be very happy to.'

'And we'll come with him shortly. Have your things been sent off?' said Stepan Arkadyich.

'They have,' answered Levin, and he told Kuzma to put out his clothes so he could get dressed.

3

A CROWD of people, mostly women, had surrounded the church, which was lit up for the wedding. Those who had not managed to get into the middle of the throng were crowding round the windows, pushing, arguing, and peering in through the grilles.

More than twenty carriages had already been lined up by the police along the street. A police officer, disregarding the frost, was standing by the entrance, resplendent in his uniform. More carriages kept arriving, and a steady stream of ladies in flowers, holding up their trains, and men removing their caps or black hats, were entering the church. Inside the church itself both candelabra and all the candles by the icons were already lit. The golden glow on the red background of the iconostasis, the gilded carving of the icons, the silver of the chandelier and the candlesticks, the flagstones, the mats, the banners above the choir-stands,* the steps of the ambo, the old blackened books, the cassocks and the surplices—everything was flooded with light. On the right-hand side of the warm church, amongst the crowd of tailcoats and white ties, uniforms and damask, velvet, satin, hair, flowers, bare shoulders and arms and long gloves, the hushed but lively sound of voices could be heard, reverberating strangely in the high cupola. Each time the door gave a squeak as it was being opened, the murmuring voices in the crowd fell silent, and everybody looked round, expecting to see the bride and bridegroom enter. But the door had already opened more than ten times, and each time it was one or other of the late-arriving guests joining the group of those who had been invited on the right, or a female onlooker who had managed to deceive or win over the police officer, and joined the crowd of strangers on the left. Both relatives and strangers had now passed through every stage of anticipation.

At first they thought the bride and bridegroom were about to arrive at any moment and did not attach any importance to the delay. Then they began looking round to the door more and more often, and discussing whether anything might have happened. Then the delay became distinctly awkward, and both relatives and guests tried to look as if they were not thinking about the bridegroom and were engrossed in their conversation.

The archdeacon, as if to remind people that his time was valuable, coughed impatiently from time to time, making the glass in the windows rattle. In the choir-stand bored choristers could be heard trying out their voices and blowing their noses. The priest kept dispatching first the sacristan and then the deacon to find out whether the bridegroom had arrived, while he himself, in his purple cassock and embroidered belt, went with increasing frequency over to the side door in expectation of the bridegroom. Eventually one of the ladies looked at her watch and said: 'Well, this is a bit odd!' and then all the guests became restless and started loudly giving vent to their surprise and displeasure. One of the ushers went to find out what had happened. Kitty, meanwhile, who had long been completely ready in her white dress, long veil, and garland of orange blossoms, was standing in the ballroom of the Shcherbatskys' house with her sponsor and sister Natalya, looking out of the window, having vainly waited for over half an hour for her best man to bring her the news that the bridegroom had arrived at the church.

Levin, meanwhile, wearing his trousers but neither waistcoat nor tails, was pacing back and forth in his hotel room, continually poking his head round the door and scouring the corridor. But the person he was expecting in the corridor was nowhere to be seen, and he kept coming back in despair to throw up his hands and address Stepan Arkadyich, who was calmly smoking.

'Has there ever been a man in such an unbelievably idiotic situation?' he said.

'Yes, it is stupid,' acknowledged Stepan Arkadyich with a soothing smile. 'But don't worry, they'll soon be here with it.'

'How can I not worry?' said Levin with suppressed rage. 'And these idiotic open waistcoats! Impossible!' he said, looking at his crumpled shirt-front. 'And what if they have already taken the things to the railway station?' he exclaimed in despair.

'Then you can wear mine.'

'I should have done that a long time ago.'

'It's not good to look ridiculous . . . Just wait! *It will all shape up.*'

The fact of the matter was that when Levin had decided to get dressed, his old servant Kuzma had brought him his waistcoat and tails and everything else necessary.

'But what about my shirt?' Levin had exclaimed.

'You're wearing it,' Kuzma had answered with a tranquil smile.

Kuzma had not thought of leaving out a clean shirt, and having received instructions to pack everything up and take it to the Shcherbatskys' house, from where the young couple were to leave that evening, he had done just that, packing everything except the dress suit. The shirt, worn since morning, was crumpled, and inconceivable with the fashionable open waistcoat. It was a long way to send to the Shcherbatskys'. They sent out a servant to buy a shirt. The servant came back: everything was closed—it was Sunday. They sent to Stepan Arkadyich's and brought a shirt; it was impossibly wide and short. Finally they sent to the Shcherbatskys' to unpack his things. The bridegroom was expected at the church, while he was walking round his room like a caged animal, looking out into the corridor, and recalling with horror and despair what he had said to Kitty, and what she might be thinking now.

At last the guilty Kuzma, gasping for breath, charged into the room with the shirt.

'Only just in time. They were already loading up the cart,' said Kuzma.

Three minutes later, not looking at his watch to avoid rubbing salt into the wound, Levin was sprinting down the corridor.

'That won't help matters,' said Stepan Arkadyich with a smile as he set off in unhurried pursuit of him. 'I'm telling you, *it will shape up, it will all shape up . . .*'

4

'THEY'VE arrived!' 'There he is!' 'Which one?' 'The younger one, you mean?' 'But look at her, poor dear, she looks more dead than alive!' people in the crowd were saying when Levin met his bride at the doorway and walked with her into the church.

Stepan Arkadyich told his wife the reason for the delay, and the guests whispered to one another, smiling. Levin was unable to notice anyone or anything; he was looking at his bride and could not take his eyes off her.

Everyone was saying that she had not looked her best during the last few days and was nowhere near as pretty as usual under her veil; but Levin did not think so. He looked at her tall hair-arrangement with the long white veil and white flowers, at her high, gathered collar, so chastely covering the sides of her long neck but opening out in the front, and at her strikingly slender waist, and it seemed to him that she looked better than ever—not because her beauty was enhanced by the flowers, the veil, or the dress ordered from Paris, but because, despite the studied splendour of her attire, the expression of her sweet face, eyes, and her lips was still her own unique expression of innocent truthfulness.

'I was beginning to think you wanted to run away,' she said and smiled at him.

'It was so stupid, what happened to me, I'm ashamed to talk about it!' he said, blushing, then had to turn to Sergey Ivanovich, who was coming up to him.

'That was quite a story about your shirt!' said Sergey Ivanovich, shaking his head and smiling.

'Yes, yes,' answered Levin, who had no clue what people were talking to him about.

'Now look, Kostya,' said Stepan Arkadyich with an expression of mock alarm. 'We have an important question which needs answering. You are exactly in the right state of mind now to appreciate its full importance. They are asking me whether they should light used candles or new ones? It's a difference of ten roubles,' he added, bringing his lips together into a smile. 'I have made a decision, but I'm afraid you might not give your consent.'

Levin realized this was a joke, but he could not smile.

'So what is it to be then? Used candles or new? That's the question.'

'Yes, yes! New ones.'

'Well, I'm very glad. That's settled then!' said Stepan Arkadyich, smiling. 'It's astonishing how people lose their wits at this point,' he said to Chirikov after Levin gave him a blank look and moved towards his bride.

'Make sure you're the first to step on the mat, Kitty,' said Countess Nordston as she approached. 'You're a fine one!' she said to Levin.

'So, you're not scared?' said Marya Dmitrievna, an old aunt.

'You're not feeling chilly? You look pale. Just a minute, bend over!' said Kitty's sister Natalya, and making a circle with her lovely plump arms, she adjusted the flowers on her head with a smile.

Dolly came up and tried to say something but could not speak, and she burst into tears and started laughing unnaturally.

Kitty was looking at everybody with glazed eyes, just like Levin. She could only respond to everything that was being said to her with the happy smile that was now so natural to her.

Meanwhile, the clergy had donned their vestments, and the priest and the deacon had come out to the lectern which stood in the vestibule of the church. The priest turned to Levin and said something. Levin did not hear what the priest said.

'Take the bride's hand and lead her,' the best man said to Levin.

It took Levin a long time to work out what was required of him. They spent ages correcting him and were on the verge of giving up—because he kept extending the wrong hand or taking the wrong hand—when he at last understood that he needed to take her right hand in his right hand without changing position. When he had at last taken the bride's hand in the correct way, the priest walked a few steps in front of them and stopped at the lectern. The crowd of relatives and friends moved after them, voices buzzing and trains swishing. Someone bent over and straightened the bride's train. It became so quiet in the church that you could hear the drops of wax falling.

The little old priest, wearing a *kamilavka*,* the grey locks of his silver-gleaming hair parted down the middle and tucked behind his ears, freed his small, wizened hands from his heavy silver chasuble with a gold cross on the back, and fumbled with something at the lectern.

Stepan Arkadyich approached him cautiously, whispered something, then stepped back again, after winking at Levin.

The priest lit two candles festooned with flowers, and holding them sideways in his left hand so that the wax would drip from them slowly, he turned to face the bridal couple. It was the same priest who had heard Levin's confession. He looked with weary and sad eyes at the bride and groom, let out a sigh, extricated his right hand from his chasuble and blessed the bridegroom with it, then similarly laid his clasped fingers on Kitty's bowed head, but with a hint of cautious tenderness. Then he gave them the candles, picked up the censer, and moved slowly away from them.

'Can this really be true?' thought Levin, and he looked round at his bride. He could just glimpse her profile slightly below him, and from the barely perceptible movement of her lips and eyelashes he knew she was aware of his eyes on her. She did not look round, but her high gathered collar moved, rising towards her pink little ear. He saw a sigh stop in her breast and the small hand in the long glove holding the candle started to tremble.

All the fuss about the shirt, about being late, the conversations with friends and relations, their displeasure, his ridiculous situation—all that had suddenly vanished, and he was filled with joy and trepidation.

The handsome, burly archdeacon in a silver surplice, whose tight curls stuck up on either side of his parting, stepped forward briskly and, lifting his stole with two fingers in a practised gesture, stopped in front of the priest.

'Bless us, Father!' The solemn sounds rang out slowly one after the other, making the air vibrate.

'Blessed is our God always, now and for ever and unto ages of ages,' responded the old priest humbly and melodiously as he continued to fumble with something at the lectern. And harmoniously and sonorously, filling the whole church from the windows to the vaulted ceiling, the invisible choir's full chord rose, grew louder, hung for a second, and quietly died away.

They prayed, as always, for peace and salvation from on high, for the Synod, and for the Sovereign; and they prayed for God's servants Konstantin and Ekaterina, that day entering into holy matrimony.

'Let us pray to the Lord that He might grant them perfect love, peace, and help'—the whole church seemed to breathe with the voice of the archdeacon.

Levin heard the words, and they astonished him. 'How did they guess that it's help, precisely help, that one needs?' he thought, recalling all his recent fears and doubts. 'What do I know? What can I achieve in this fearful business,' he thought, 'without help? Yes, it is precisely help that I need now.'

When the deacon had finished the litany, the priest turned to the bridal couple with a book:

'Eternal God, who hast joined those who were separate,' he read in a meek, melodious voice, 'in a union of love which cannot be sundered; Thou who didst bless Isaac and Rebecca and their heirs, according to Thy holy Covenant, bless now Thy servants Konstantin and Ekaterina, and lead them on to the path of righteousness. For Thou art a merciful and compassionate God, and we glorify Thee, the Father, the Son, and the Holy Ghost, now and always and unto ages of ages.' 'Aa-men,' the invisible choir again permeated the air.

' "Joined those who were separate in a union of love which cannot be

sundered." How profound these words are, and how well they correspond to what one feels at this moment!' thought Levin. 'Is she feeling
what I am feeling?'

And when he looked round their eyes met.

And he concluded from the expression in her eyes that she understood what he did. But that was not true; she had understood almost
none of the words of the service and had not even listened to them during the betrothal ceremony. She was unable to listen or to understand
them, so powerful was the one single emotion filling her heart and
becoming ever more intense. That feeling was joy at the culmination
of what had already taken place in her heart a month and a half ago,
and which throughout those six weeks had brought her both joy and
pain. What had taken place in her soul that day when she had silently
gone up to him in her brown dress in the ballroom of the house on the
Arbat* and given herself to him—what had taken place in her soul
on that day and at that hour was a complete break with all her former
life, and a completely different, new, and completely unknown life had
begun, although in reality her old life had continued. Those six weeks
had been the most blissful and agonizing time for her. Her whole life
and all her desires and hopes were focused on this one man whom she
still found incomprehensible, and to whom she was joined by alternate
feelings of attraction and aversion which were even more incomprehensible than the man himself, while all the while she continued living in the conditions of her former life. Living her old life, she was
appalled at herself and her complete and overwhelming indifference to
everything in her past: to things, habits, people who had loved her and
those who loved her now, her mother, who was distressed by this indifference, and her dear, affectionate father, whom she used to love more
than anyone in the world. She was both appalled by this indifference
and thrilled by what had caused it. She could not conceive of or wish
for anything beyond life with this man; but this new life did not yet
exist, and she could not even picture it clearly in her mind. There was
only anticipation—fear and joy of the new and unknown. And now, in
just a few moments, the anticipation, the unknown, and the remorse
at renouncing her old life was about to come to an end, and something
new would begin. This new thing could not but be frightening as it
was unknown; but frightening or not, it had already taken place six
weeks earlier in her soul; today they were merely sanctifying what had
happened a long time ago in her soul.

Turning again to the lectern, the priest with some difficulty picked
up Kitty's little ring, asked for Levin's hand, and slid it down to the first

joint of his finger. 'God's servant Konstantin is joined in matrimony to God's servant Ekaterina.' And after putting the big ring on Kitty's pink, pitifully delicate little finger, the priest said the same thing.

The bridal couple tried several times to work out what they were supposed to do, but got it wrong each time, and the priest corrected them in a whisper. After finally doing what was required and making the sign of the cross over them with the rings, he again gave Kitty the big ring and Levin the small one; once again they got in a muddle and twice handed the rings back to each other, and still they ended up not doing what was required.

Dolly, Chirikov, and Stepan Arkadyich came forward to sort them out. There was confusion, whispering, and smiles, but the solemn and emotional expression on the faces of the bridal couple did not change: on the contrary, they looked even more serious and solemn while they were getting their hands muddled than before, and the smile with which Stepan Arkadyich whispered that they should each now put on their own rings instinctively faded from his lips. He sensed that any smile would offend them.

'For Thou didst in the beginning create them male and female,' read the priest after the exchange of rings, 'and Thou hast joined woman to man, as a helpmeet and for the procreation of the human race. O Lord our God, who hast sent down Thy truth upon Thy heritage, and given Thy promise to our fathers from generation to generation of Thy chosen people, bless Thy servant Konstantin and Thy servant Ekaterina, and make stable their betrothal in faith, in oneness of mind, in truth, and in love . . .'

Levin was increasingly feeling that all his ideas about marriage, his dreams about how he would organize his life—that all this had been childish and that it was something he had not yet understood and now understood even less, even though it was happening to him; there were shudders rising higher and higher in his chest, and unruly tears springing into his eyes.

5

ALL Moscow, including relatives and friends, was in the church. And during the betrothal ceremony, in the brilliant illumination of the church, there was an unceasing, decorously hushed conversation amongst the group of elegantly dressed women and girls and men in white ties, tails, and uniforms, which was mostly conducted by the men, while the women were absorbed in observing every detail of the sacred rite they always find so moving.

In the group nearest the bride were her two sisters: Dolly and the eldest, the serenely beautiful Natalya Lvova, who had come from abroad.

'Why is Marie wearing purple at a wedding? You might as well be wearing black,' said Madame Korsunskaya.

'With a complexion like that, it's her one saving grace . . .' replied Madame Drubetskaya. 'I'm surprised they are having the wedding in the evening. Like merchants . . .'

'It's more beautiful. I was also married in the evening,' answered Madame Korsunskaya, and she sighed, remembering how nice she had looked that day, and how absurdly in love her husband had been, and how different it all was now.

'They say that whoever is a best man more than ten times will never get married; I wanted to be best man for the tenth time as insurance, but the post was taken,' said Count Sinyavin to the pretty Princess Charskaya, who had designs on him.

Princess Charskaya answered only with a smile. She was looking at Kitty, thinking about how and when she would stand beside Count Sinyavin in Kitty's place, and how she would remind him then of the joke he had just cracked.

Shcherbatsky was telling the old Lady-in-Waiting, Madame Nikolayeva, that he intended putting the crown on Kitty's chignon, so she would be happy.

'She shouldn't have worn a chignon,' answered Madame Nikolayeva, who had long ago decided that if the elderly widower she was trying to catch were to marry her, the wedding would be of the utmost simplicity. 'I don't like all this *faste*.'[1]

Sergey Ivanovich was talking to Darya Dmitrievna,* jokingly assuring her that the custom of going away after the wedding was spreading because newlyweds always felt rather sheepish.

'Your brother can feel proud. She's absolutely lovely. I wonder if you're envious?'

'I'm past all that, Darya Dmitrievna,' he replied, and his face unexpectedly took on a sad and serious expression.

Stepan Arkadyich was telling his sister-in-law his pun about annulments.

'The garland needs adjusting,' she answered, not listening to him.

[1] 'splendour'.

'What a pity she's not looking her best,' Countess Nordston said to Natalya Lvova. 'He's still not worth her little finger though, is he?'

'No, I like him very much. And not just because he's my future *beau-frère*,'[1]

Natalya Lvova answered. 'And how well he is conducting himself! It's so difficult to conduct oneself well in that situation and not be ridiculous. And he's not ridiculous, he's not putting on an act, it's clear he is moved.'

'It seems that you were expecting this?'

'Almost. She was always fond of him.'

'Well, let's see who steps on the mat first. I told Kitty she should.'

'It will make no difference,' said Natalya Lvova, 'as we're all submissive wives, it runs in the family.'

'Well, I made sure I stepped on it before Vasily. What about you, Dolly?'

Dolly was standing next to them and she heard them, but she did not answer.

She was deeply moved. There were tears in her eyes, and she could not have said anything without bursting out crying. She was happy for Kitty and Levin; as her thoughts went back to her own wedding, she glanced at the beaming Stepan Arkadyich, forgot all about the present, and remembered only her first innocent love. She was remembering not only herself, but all the women she knew and was close to; she recalled them at that uniquely solemn time in their lives, when, like Kitty, they had stood under the crown with love, hope, and fear in their hearts, renouncing their past, and stepping into a mysterious future. Among all those brides who came into her mind, she also recalled her dear Anna, the details of whose proposed divorce she had recently heard. She too had stood there just as purely, adorned with orange-blossoms and a veil. And now?

'It's terribly strange,' she murmured.

It was not only the sisters, female friends, and relatives who were following every detail of the sacred rite; other women, onlookers, were also following avidly with bated breath, afraid to miss a single gesture or expression of the bride and groom, and peevishly did not answer and often did not hear what was being said by the indifferent men who were making droll or irrelevant remarks.

'Why is she so tearful? Or is she marrying against her will?'

'Against her will to such a fine fellow? A prince, isn't he?'

---

[1] 'brother-in-law'.

'Is that her sister in the white satin? Well, listen out for how the deacon bellows: "And obey thy husband".'

'Is it the Chudov choir?'

'No, the Synodal.'

'I was asking the footman. He says he's going to take her straight home to his country estate. Filthy rich, they say. That's why she's being married off to him.'

'No, they're a fine couple.'

'Marya Vasilievna, it was you who were arguing that no one is wearing flyaway crinolines. Have a look at that one on the woman in the puce dress, an ambassador's wife they say, and look at how it's gathered . . . It goes this way, and that.'

'What a sweet little thing the bride is—like a lamb dressed for slaughter! Whatever you say, you have to feel sorry for the girl.'

Such were the comments being made in the crowd of women onlookers who had managed to slip in through the church door.

6

WHEN the ceremony of betrothal was over, a clergyman spread out a piece of pink silk cloth in front of the lectern in the middle of the church, the choir sang an elaborate and complicated psalm, in which the bass and the tenor sang responses to one another, and then the priest turned round and beckoned the betrothed pair on to the outspread piece of pink cloth. No matter how much and how often they had heard about the old saying which deemed that the first person to step on the mat would be head of the family, neither Levin nor Kitty were able to remember it when they took those few steps. They also did not hear the loud remarks and arguments between those who insisted he had stepped first and others who thought they had both stepped together.

After the usual questions about whether they desired to enter into matrimony or were pledged to anyone else, and their replies, which sounded strange even to them, a new ceremony began. Kitty listened to the words of the prayer, wanting to understand their meaning, but she could not. As the service moved towards its conclusion, an ever greater feeling of jubilation and radiant joy filled Kitty's soul and made it impossible for her to concentrate.

They prayed 'that they be granted chastity for the good of the fruits of the womb, and find joy in their sons and daughters'. There was mention of God creating woman from Adam's rib, that 'for this cause a man shall leave his father and mother, and cleave unto his wife, and they two shall be one flesh', and that 'this is a great mystery'; they prayed that God would make them fruitful and bless them, as he had Isaac and Rebecca, Joseph, Moses, and Zipporah, and that they might see their children's children.

'It's all been lovely,' thought Kitty as she listened to these words, 'and it could not be any other way,' and a smile of joy, which unconsciously transmitted itself to everyone looking at her, shone on her radiant face.

'Put it right on!' came the advice when the priest put the crowns on them and Shcherbatsky, his hand trembling in its three-button glove, held the crown high above her head.

'Put it on!' she whispered, smiling.

Levin looked round at her and was struck by the joyful radiance in her face; and this feeling was unconsciously transmitted to him. He began to feel, just as she did, elated and euphoric.

They enjoyed listening to the Epistle being read, and to the archdeacon's voice reverberating in the last verse, which had been awaited with such anticipation by the public onlookers. They enjoyed drinking the warm red wine and water from the shallow chalice, and it became even more enjoyable when the priest threw back his chasuble, took both their hands in his, and led them round the lectern, while a bass voice boomed: 'Isaiah, rejoice!' Shcherbatsky and Chirikov, who were holding up the crowns and getting caught in the bride's train, were also smiling and rejoicing about something as they kept falling behind or bumping into the bridal pair whenever the priest stopped. The spark of joy ignited in Kitty seemed to have transmitted itself to everyone in the church. It seemed to Levin that both the priest and the deacon wanted to smile just as he did.

After removing the crowns from their heads, the priest read the last prayer and congratulated the young couple. Levin glanced at Kitty and had never seen her looking that way before. She was quite enchanting with that new glow of happiness on her face. Levin wanted to say something to her, but he did not know whether it was all over yet. The priest helped him out of his difficulty. His kind mouth stretched into a smile and he said quietly:

'Kiss your wife, and you kiss your husband,' and he took the candles from their hands.

Levin carefully kissed her smiling lips, gave her his arm, and sensing a strange, new intimacy, walked out of the church. He did not believe, and could not believe, that it was true. It was only when their surprised and timid eyes met that he believed it, because he felt that they were already one.

After supper that same night, the young people left for the country.

7

VRONSKY and Anna had been travelling together in Europe for three months now. They had visited Venice, Rome, and Naples, and had just arrived in a small Italian town where they intended to settle for a while.

A handsome maître d'hôtel with thick, pomaded hair parted from the nape, dressed in a tailcoat and an expansive white cambric shirt-front, with a bundle of seals hanging from the watch-chain on his rounded paunch and his hands in his pockets, was looking disdainfully through narrowed eyes as he responded curtly to a gentleman who had stopped to ask something. Hearing someone walking up the steps from the other side of the entrance, the maître d'hôtel turned round, and when he saw the Russian count who was occupying their best rooms, he respectfully removed his hands from his pockets and explained with a bow that a messenger had come, and that the business of renting the palazzo had been settled. The general manager was ready to sign the agreement.

'Ah! I'm very glad to hear that,' said Vronsky. 'Is Madame in or out?'

'Madame went out for a walk but has now returned,' answered the maître d'hôtel.

Vronsky took off his soft, broad-brimmed hat and passed a handkerchief over his perspiring brow and his hair, which he had let grow half-way down his ears and combed back to cover his bald patch. Glancing absently at the gentleman, who was still standing there and scrutinizing him, he was about to go on in.

'This gentleman is Russian, and was enquiring after you,' said the maître d'hôtel.

With a feeling of annoyance at never being able to get away from his acquaintances mingling with a yearning to find at least some distraction from the monotony of his life, Vronsky glanced back again at the gentleman who was standing a few paces away, and their eyes lit up at the same moment.

'Golenishchev!'

'Vronsky!'

It really was Golenishchev—Vronsky's comrade in the Page Corps.

Golenishchev had belonged to the liberal party in the Corps; he had graduated with a civil rank and never served anywhere. The two comrades had gone their separate ways when they left the Corps, and had only met once since then.

During that meeting Vronsky grasped that Golenishchev was pursuing some high-minded liberal profession, and consequently felt inclined to look down on Vronsky's profession and rank. Vronsky had therefore rebuffed Golenishchev during their meeting with that cool and arrogant manner he was capable of mustering with people, and which meant: 'You may or may not like my way of life, it is of no concern to me, but you do have to respect me if you want to know me.' Golenishchev had countered Vronsky's tone with supercilious indifference. That meeting, one would have thought, ought to have estranged them still further. But now they beamed and cried out with delight upon recognizing one another. Vronsky would never have expected to be so pleased to see Golenishchev, but he was probably unaware himself how bored he was. He forgot the unpleasant impression of their last meeting, and held out his hand to his former comrade with an expression of unalloyed delight. The same expression of delight replaced the look of unease on Golenishchev's face.

'How glad I am to see you!' said Vronsky, displaying his strong white teeth in a friendly smile.

'I heard the name Vronsky, but I didn't know which one. I'm very, very glad to see you!'

'Let's go in. So what are you doing?'

'I've been living here for two years. Working.'

'Ah!' said Vronsky solicitously. 'Come on, let's go in.'

And following the usual habit of Russians, instead of saying in Russian what he wanted to conceal from the servants, he began speaking in French.

'Do you know Madame Karenina? We are travelling together. I am going to see her now,' he said in French, examining Golenishchev's face closely.

'Ah! I didn't know' (although he did know), Golenishchev answered impassively. 'Have you been here long?' he added.

'What, me? Oh, three days,' Vronsky answered, closely examining his friend's face again.

'Yes, he's a decent person, and he understands the situation in the right way,' Vronsky said to himself, taking note of Golenishchev's expression and his change of subject. 'I can introduce him to Anna, he sees things in the right way.'

When meeting new people during those three months which he had spent with Anna abroad, Vronsky always asked himself what kind of attitude the new person would adopt towards his relationship with Anna, and he mostly encountered men who understood in the *right way*. But if he and all those people who understood things in the 'right way' had been asked what exactly it implied, both he and they would have been hard-pressed to know how to answer.

In actual fact, those people who in Vronsky's opinion understood things in the 'right' way did not understand them at all, but behaved as well-bred people generally do behave with regard to all the complex and insoluble problems impinging on life from every quarter—they behaved with decorum, avoiding insinuations and unpleasant questions. They pretended that they completely understood the significance and meaning of the situation, and accepted and even approved of it, but considered it inappropriate and superfluous to explain it all.

Vronsky immediately guessed that Golenishchev was one of those people, and was therefore doubly glad to see him. And when Golenishchev was introduced to Anna, his behaviour with her was indeed all that Vronsky could have wished. He avoided, clearly without the slightest effort, any conversation which might lead to awkwardness.

He had not known Anna before, and was struck by her beauty and even more by the simplicity with which she accepted her situation. She blushed when Vronsky brought Golenishchev in, and he found that childlike colour which spread over her open and beautiful face tremendously appealing. But what he particularly liked was the fact that straight away, so there could be no misunderstandings in the presence of a stranger, she seemed to make a point of calling Vronsky simply Alexey and said that they were moving into a house they had just rented, which people called a palazzo there. Golenishchev liked this straightforward and simple attitude to her situation. Observing Anna's light-hearted, amiable, and vivacious manner, and knowing Alexey Alexandrovich and Vronsky, Golenishchev felt he could understand her completely. He felt he could understand what she could not possibly understand: how exactly she could feel so ebulliently cheerful and happy after bringing misfortune on her husband, abandoning him and her son, and losing her good name.

'It's in the guide-book,' said Golenishchev, referring to the palazzo Vronsky had rented. 'There's a wonderful Tintoretto there. From his late period.'

'Do you know what? It's a lovely day, let's go there and have another look round,' said Vronsky, turning to Anna.

'I would love to, I'll just go and put on my hat. You say it's hot?' she said, stopping at the door and looking inquiringly at Vronsky. And again a deep blush spread over her face.

Vronsky realized from her look that she did not know on what terms he wished to be with Golenishchev, and was afraid of not having behaved as he would have wished.

He gave her a long, tender look.

'No, not very,' he said.

And she felt that she had understood everything, and principally that he was pleased with her; and smiling at him, she walked with a brisk step out through the door.

The friends glanced at one another and a look of embarrassment appeared on both their faces, as if Golenishchev, who clearly admired her, wanted to say something about her but could not think what, while Vronsky was both hopeful and fearful that he would.

'So then,' Vronsky began, in order to start some kind of conversation. 'So you're settled here? So you're still working on the same thing?' he went on, recalling that he had been told Golenishchev was writing something . . .

'Yes, I'm writing the second part of *The Two Principles*,' said Golenishchev, flushing with pleasure at the question, 'or rather, I am not writing yet, to be exact, but I am laying the groundwork, gathering materials. It's going to be much more substantial, and will cover almost all the issues. No one in Russia wants to understand that we are the heirs to Byzantium,' and he launched into a long and heated explanation.

Vronsky initially felt uncomfortable about not even knowing the first part of *The Two Principles*, which the author was describing to him as something well known. But later on, when Golenishchev began to set out his ideas and Vronsky was able to follow them, even without knowing *The Two Principles*, he listened with a certain degree of interest, as Golenishchev spoke well. But Vronsky was surprised and disheartened by the nervous irascibility with which Golenishchev talked about the subject which absorbed him. The longer he talked, the more his eyes blazed, the quicker he was to parry imaginary opponents, and the more apprehensive and wounded the expression on his face became. Remembering Golenishchev as a scrawny but lively, good-natured, principled boy, always top of the class in the Corps, Vronsky just could not understand the reason for this irritation, and he did not approve of it. What he particularly disliked was that Golenishchev, a man from a good social circle, was stooping to the level of a bunch of hacks who irritated him, and getting angry with them. Was it worth it? Vronsky disliked it, but nonetheless he sensed that Golenishchev was unhappy, and felt sorry for him. An unhappiness bordering on mental derangement was visible on his animated, rather handsome face as he ploughed on hurriedly and fervently with the exposition of his ideas, oblivious even to Anna's appearance.

When Anna appeared in her hat and cape and came to stand next to him, toying with her parasol with rapid movements of her beautiful hand, Vronsky turned with a feeling of relief from Golenishchev's plaintive, staring eyes and looked with renewed love at his enchanting companion, who was brimming with life and happiness. Golenishchev found it difficult to regain his composure and was at first despondent and gloomy, but Anna, being warmly disposed to everyone (as she was at that time), soon revived him with her ingenuous, light-hearted manner. After trying various topics of conversation, she steered him on to painting, about which he spoke very well, and she listened to him attentively. They went on foot to the house they had rented and had a look round.

'There is one thing I am glad about,' said Anna to Golenishchev when they were already on their way back. 'Alexey will have a good *atelier.*[1] You must definitely take that room,' she said to Vronsky in Russian, using the familiar form of address, since she had already realized that Golenishchev would become a close friend to them in their isolation and that there was no need to conceal anything in his presence.

'Do you paint then?' said Golenishchev, turning round quickly to Vronsky.

'Yes, I used to a long time ago, and I have begun to dabble again,' said Vronsky, blushing.

'He is very talented,' said Anna with a blithe smile. 'I'm no judge, of course. But people who know have said the same.'

8

DURING that first period of her liberation and rapid recovery, Anna felt unpardonably happy and full of the joys of life. Recollection of her husband's unhappiness did not spoil her happiness. On the one hand that recollection was too terrible to contemplate. On the other, her husband's unhappiness had brought her too much happiness to

---

[1] 'studio'.

cause her remorse. The recollection of everything that happened to her after her illness—the reconciliation with her husband, the rift, the news of Vronsky's wound, his appearance, the preparations for the divorce, the departure from her husband's house, the parting from her son—all that seemed to her like a delirious dream, from which she had woken up alone with Vronsky abroad. The recollection of the damage inflicted on her husband aroused in her a feeling akin to repugnance, such as a drowning man might feel after shaking off a person clinging to him. That person had drowned. That had been bad, of course, but it had been the sole means of salvation, and it was better not to dwell on those terrible details.

One consoling reflection about her conduct had occurred to her then, at the first moment of the rift, and now when she recalled everything that had happened, she remembered that one reflection. 'I could not avoid bringing misfortune upon this person,' she thought, 'but I don't want to take advantage of that misfortune; I am also suffering, and will go on suffering; I am forfeiting what I valued above all else—I am forfeiting my good name and my son. I have done wrong, and for that reason I don't want happiness, I don't want a divorce, and will go on suffering from the disgrace and the separation from my son.' But however sincerely Anna wanted to suffer, she was not suffering. There was no disgrace at all. With the abundance of tact common to both of them, they never placed themselves in a false position while they were abroad, by avoiding Russian ladies and always meeting people who pretended they fully understood their mutual position, and far better than they did themselves. Even separation from the son she loved did not cause her pain to begin with. The baby girl, his child, was so sweet, and had so endeared herself to Anna since the time when she became the only child left to her, that Anna rarely thought about her son.

The thirst for life, intensified by her recovery, was so powerful, and her living conditions so new and pleasant, that Anna felt unpardonably happy. The better she got to know Vronsky, the more she loved him. She loved him for himself, and because of his love for her. Complete possession of him gave her constant joy. His proximity was always a pleasure to her. The traits in his character, which she was coming to know better and better, were all ineffably dear to her. She found his appearance, altered by civilian dress, as attractive as if she was a love-sick girl. In everything he said, thought, and did, she saw something especially noble and elevated. Her awe of him often alarmed even her; she sought and could not find anything unappealing about him. She did not dare reveal to him any awareness of her own insignificance beside him. She felt that he might stop loving her sooner if he knew of it; and there was nothing she feared more now, although she had no reason to fear losing his love. But she could not help being grateful to him for the way he behaved towards her, and showing how much she appreciated it. Despite having, in her opinion, such a clear aptitude for public service, in which he should have played a prominent role, he had sacrificed his ambition for her without the slightest sign of regret. He was more lovingly respectful of her than before, and the thought that she should never feel the awkwardness of her position never left him for a moment. He was such a virile man, but where she was concerned, he not only never contradicted her, but had no will of his own and seemed only concerned with anticipating her wishes. And she could not help appreciating this, although the very intensity of his attention to her, and the atmosphere of care with which he surrounded her, sometimes oppressed her.

Vronsky, meanwhile, despite the complete fulfilment of what he had desired for so long, was not completely happy. He soon began to feel that the fulfilment of his desires had given him no more than a grain of sand from the mountain of happiness he had been expecting. This fulfilment had shown him the error people invariably make when they imagine happiness to be the fulfilment of desires. In the initial period after joining his life to hers and putting on civilian clothes, he experienced the full delights of freedom in general, which he had not known before, and also the freedom of love, and he was content, but not for long. He soon felt desires for desires, and tedium arising in his soul. Independent of his will, he began grasping at every passing whim, perceiving it as a desire and a purpose. Sixteen hours of the day needed to be filled with something, as they were living a life of complete freedom abroad, and one which lay outside that round of conventional social activities which filled the time in Petersburg. There could be no question of even thinking about the pleasures of bachelor life which had occupied Vronsky on previous trips abroad, since his one foray of that kind had provoked an unexpected depression in Anna which was incommensurate with a late supper with acquaintances. Fraternizing with local and Russian society was also out of the question due to the ambivalence of their position. Sightseeing, apart from the fact that they had already seen everything, did not have for him, a Russian and intelligent man, that unaccountable importance which the English are able to attach to this activity.

And like a hungry animal will pounce on every object it comes across, hoping to find food in it, Vronsky quite unconsciously pounced first on politics, then on new books, then on paintings.

Since he had possessed an aptitude for painting from childhood, and since, not knowing what to spend his money on, he had begun to collect engravings, he settled on painting, started to devote his energies to it, and invested in it that unused stock of desires which demanded satisfaction.

He had an aptitude for understanding art and also for imitating it faithfully, and with taste, and he thought he possessed what was needed to be an artist; and after hesitating for a while about which style of painting he would choose—religious, historical, genre, or realistic—he started to paint. He understood all of these styles and could have found inspiration in any one of them; but he could not imagine that it could be possible not to know what styles of painting there were, and to be inspired directly by what resides in the soul, without worrying whether what he would paint would belong to a particular style of painting. Since he did not know this, and was not inspired directly by life but indirectly by life already embodied in art, he found his inspiration very quickly and easily, and just as quickly and easily succeeded in painting something very similar to the style of painting he was trying to imitate.

He liked the graceful, showy French style more than any other, and it was in this style that he began to paint a portrait of Anna in Italian costume, and the portrait seemed to him and everyone who saw it to be very successful.

9

THE old, neglected palazzo, with its high stucco ceilings and frescos on the walls, mosaic floors, heavy yellow damask curtains at the high windows, vases on consoles and mantelpieces, carved doors, and sombre rooms hung with paintings—this palazzo, after they had moved into it, by its very appearance nurtured in Vronsky the pleasant illusion that he was not so much a Russian landowner and unemployed equerry as an enlightened amateur and patron of the arts, and himself a modest artist who had renounced society, connections, and ambition for the woman he loved.

The role chosen by Vronsky upon moving into the palazzo was a resounding success, and having met some interesting people through Golenishchev, he was calm to begin with. He painted sketches from nature under the tutelage of an Italian professor of painting, and studied medieval Italian life. Vronsky had in fact become so captivated with medieval Italian life lately that he had even started wearing a hat and cloak over his shoulder in the medieval manner, which greatly became him.

'We live without knowing anything, you know,' said Vronsky to Golenishchev when he came to see him one morning. 'Have you seen Mikhailov's painting?' he said, handing him a Russian newspaper just received that morning and pointing to an article about a Russian artist living in the same town, who had finished a painting which had long been the subject of rumours, and which had been bought in advance. The article contained reproaches that a remarkable artist was being deprived of encouragement and support from the government and the Academy.*

'I have,' answered Golenishchev. 'Of course, he's not without talent, but the direction is all wrong. It's the same old Ivanov–Strauss–Renan* attitude to Christ and to religious painting.'

'What is the subject of the painting?' asked Anna.

'Christ before Pilate. Christ is depicted as a Jew, with all the realism of the new school.'*

And having been steered on to one of his favourite topics by the painting's content, Golenishchev began to state his case:

'I can't understand how they can make such a gross mistake. Christ already has a well-defined incarnation in the art of the old masters. Therefore, if they want to depict a revolutionary or a wise man rather than a God, let them take someone from history—Socrates, Franklin, or Charlotte Corday,* but just not Christ. They take the one individual who cannot be taken as an artistic subject, and then . . .'

'But this Mikhailov, is it true he is so poverty-stricken?' asked Vronsky, thinking that, as a Russian Maecenas, he ought to help the artist regardless of whether his painting was good or bad.

'Hardly. He's a remarkable portrait painter. Have you seen his portrait of Madame Vasilchikova? But it seems he does not want to paint any more portraits, and maybe that is why he is in such dire straits. I would say that . . .'

'Couldn't we ask him to paint a portrait of Anna Arkadyevna?' said Vronsky.

'Why mine?' said Anna. 'After yours I don't want any other portrait. It would be better to paint Annie' (as she called her baby girl). 'And here she is,' she added, glancing out of the window at the beautiful Italian wet-nurse who had carried the baby out into the garden, and then immediately stealing a furtive glance at Vronsky. This beautiful wet-nurse, whose head Vronsky had painted for his picture, was the one secret heartache in Anna's life. Vronsky had admired her beauty and medieval quality while painting her, and Anna did not dare admit to herself that she was afraid of becoming jealous of this wet-nurse, and for that reason was particularly kind to both her and her little boy and spoiled them.

Vronsky also glanced out of the window and into Anna's eyes, and turning round immediately to Golenishchev, he said:

'So do you know this Mikhailov?'

'I have met him. But he's eccentric and completely uneducated. You know, one of those wild new men who are often to be encountered these days; you know, one of those freethinkers brought up *d'emblée*[1] on ideas of atheism, negation, and materialism. It used to be the case,' said Golenishchev, not noticing, or not wishing to notice, that both Anna and Vronsky wished to speak, 'it used to be the case that a freethinker was someone brought up on ideas of religion, law, and morality, who came to freethinking by dint of struggle and hard work; but now there is a new breed of unorthodox freethinkers growing up who have never even heard of laws of morality or religion, or authorities, and who are growing up from the very beginning with ideas of negating everything, as savages, in other words. Well, he's one of those. He's the son, it seems, of a senior court footman from Moscow and did not receive any education. Being no fool, when he entered the Academy and made his reputation, he naturally started wanting to educate himself. And he turned to what he thought was the fount of education—journals. And a person wanting to educate himself in the old days, you understand, a Frenchman, let's say, would start by studying all the classics: the theologians, the tragedians, the historians, and the philosophers, and you can imagine the sheer intellectual hard work he would have in prospect. But in our country these days he will head straight for the literature of negation, rapidly master the whole essence of the science of negation, and leave it at that. And that's not all: about twenty years ago he would have found in that literature signs of a struggle with authorities, with age-old views, and he would have realized from this struggle that there was something else possible; but nowadays he will come straight to a literature in which old-fashioned attitudes are not even dignified with an argument, and which says straight out: there is nothing but evolution, natural selection, the struggle for existence—and that's all. In my article I . . .'

---

[1] 'from the beginning'.

'Do you know what,' said Anna, who had for some time been exchanging cautious glances with Vronsky, knowing that he was not interested in the education of this artist, but was only concerned with the idea of helping him and commissioning a portrait from him. 'Do you know what,' she said, resolutely interrupting Golenishchev while he was in full flow, 'let's go and see him!'

Golenishchev pulled himself together and readily agreed. But as the artist lived in a remote quarter, they decided to take the carriage.

An hour later, Anna, with Golenishchev beside her and Vronsky on the front seat of the carriage, drove up to an unattractive new building in the remote quarter. Learning from the doorman's wife, who came out to meet them, that Mikhailov did receive visitors at his studio, but was at that moment at home in his apartment round the corner, they sent her to him with their cards, asking permission to see his pictures.

10

THE artist Mikhailov was, as always, at work when the cards of Count Vronsky and Golenishchev were brought to him. He had spent the morning working in his studio on the big painting. When he returned home he lost his temper with his wife because she had not been able to take care of the landlady, who was demanding money.

'I've told you twenty times, don't get into explanations. You're already a fool, but when you start explaining things in Italian, you're a fool three times over,' he said to her after a long argument.

'Then you shouldn't be so neglectful, it's not my fault. If I had any money . . .'

'Leave me in peace, for God's sake!' Mikhailov exclaimed with tears in his voice, and, stopping up his ears, he went off into his workroom behind the partition and locked the door behind him. 'Brainless woman!' he said to himself as he sat down at the table, opened a portfolio, and immediately started working with peculiar ardour on an unfinished drawing.

He never worked more ardently and productively than when his life was going badly, and especially when he had quarrelled with his wife. 'Oh, if I could only disappear somewhere!' he thought as he went on working. He was making a sketch for the figure of a man in a fit of rage. The sketch had been done before, but he had not been happy with it. 'No, the other one was better . . . Where is it?' He went to his wife, and scowling, not looking at her, asked their eldest girl what had happened to the piece of paper he had given them. The paper with the discarded sketch on it was found, but was smudged and spotted with candle-grease. He nevertheless took the sketch back to his room, laid it on the table, stepped back, screwed up his eyes, and started looking at it. Suddenly he smiled and threw up his hands in delight.

'That's it! that's it!' he said, and picking up the pencil, he immediately began drawing rapidly. A spot of candle-grease had given the man a new pose.

He was drawing this new pose when he suddenly recalled the animated face of a shopkeeper with a prominent chin from whom he bought cigars, and he gave that same face and chin to the figure of the man he was drawing. He chuckled with delight. From being lifeless and contrived, the figure had suddenly come alive, in such a way that it could not now be changed. This figure lived and had been given clear and unmistakable form. It was possible to correct the sketch in accordance with the demands of this figure, it was possible, and indeed even necessary, to arrange the feet in a different way, completely change the position of the left hand, and throw back the hair. But in making these corrections he was not altering the figure, merely removing what concealed it. It was as if he was removing the veils which prevented it from being completely visible; each new feature only revealed more of the whole figure in all its dynamic force, as it had suddenly appeared to him as a result of the spot of candle-grease. He was carefully putting the finishing touches to the figure when the visiting-cards were brought to him.

'Just a moment, just a moment!'

He went in to his wife.

'Come on now, Sasha, don't be cross!' he said, with a sheepish, tender smile. 'You were to blame. I was to blame. I'll sort it all out.' And after making peace with his wife, he put on an olive-green coat with a velvet collar and a hat, and set off to his studio. He had already forgotten the successful figure. What thrilled and excited him now was the visit to his studio by these important Russians, who had come in a carriage.

About his painting, the one now standing on his easel, he had in the depths of his soul just one assessment—that no one had ever painted a picture like it. He did not think his painting was better than anything by Raphael, but he knew that no one ever had conveyed what he wanted to convey and had conveyed in this painting. He was quite sure of this and had been sure for a long time, ever since he had begun painting it; but other people's assessments, whatever they might be, nevertheless had immense significance for him and affected him profoundly.

Any remark, even the most trivial, showing that his judges saw even a fraction of what he saw in this painting, affected him profoundly. He always credited his judges with a deeper understanding than he had himself, and always expected from them something he did not see in the painting himself. And he often thought he found this in his viewers' assessments.

He strode quickly up to the door of his studio and, in spite of his excitement, was struck by the way Anna's figure was softly lit up as she stood in the shadow of the porch, listening to Golenishchev ardently telling her something while at the same time clearly wanting to look round at the approaching artist. He himself did not notice how he seized and assimilated this impression as he approached them, just like the chin of the shopkeeper who sold cigars, and buried it away in a place where he could later retrieve it when he needed it. The visitors, disillusioned in advance by what Golenishchev had told them about the artist, were even more disillusioned by his appearance. Of medium height, heavily built, with a jittery gait, Mikhailov made an unfavourable impression in his brown hat, olive-green coat, and narrow trousers (when wide ones had long been the fashion), and particularly with the nondescript appearance of his broad face, whose expression combined timidity with a desire to maintain his dignity.

'Do come in,' he said, trying to appear indifferent, and going into the passage he took a key out of his pocket and unlocked the door.

11

As he went into the studio, Mikhailov scrutinized his visitors once again and this time took note in his imagination of Vronsky's facial expression, particularly his cheekbones. Despite the fact that his artistic sense was constantly at work gathering material, and despite the fact that he was feeling increasingly nervous as the moment of judgement about his work approached, he rapidly and astutely formed an idea about these three people from inconspicuous signs. That man (Golenishchev) was a local Russian. Mikhailov could remember neither his surname nor where he had met him and what he had talked to him about. He only remembered his face, as he remembered every face he had ever seen, but he also remembered it being one of those faces filed away in his imagination in the vast category of those with falsely important and impoverished expressions. The mass of hair and very open forehead lent a superficial gravity to his face, in which there was one small, childish, worried expression concentrated on the narrow bridge of his nose. According to Mikhailov's calculations, Vronsky and Karenina had to be eminent and wealthy Russians who knew nothing about art, like all those wealthy Russians, but pretended they were enthusiasts and connoisseurs. 'They've probably already examined all the old stuff and now they're doing the rounds of studios of new artists, such as that German charlatan and the cretinous English Pre-Raphaelite, and have come to me just to complete the picture,' he thought. He was well acquainted with the way dilettantes (the cleverer they were, the worse it was) looked round the studios of contemporary artists with the sole objective of having the right to say that art was in decline, and that the more one looked at modern art, the more one saw how incomparable the great masters still were. He expected all this and saw it all in their faces, in the offhand and aloof way they talked amongst themselves, looked at the mannequins and busts, and casually strolled about while they waited for him to uncover the painting. But despite this, while he was turning over his sketches, pulling up the blinds, and removing the dust-sheet he felt a great excitement, which was all the more intense because, although all eminent rich Russians were bound to be brutes and idiots in his estimation, he liked both Vronsky and, especially, Anna.

'Here, would you care to have a look?' he said, stepping to one side in his jittery way and indicating his painting. 'It's *The Admonition of Pilate*. Matthew, chapter 27,' he said, feeling his lips beginning to tremble with emotion. He stepped back and stood behind them.

During those few seconds while the visitors were silently looking at the painting, Mikhailov also looked at it, with the dispassionate eye of an outsider. For those few seconds he believed in advance that the most just and supreme judgement would be pronounced by them, the very visitors whom he had so despised a moment ago. He forgot everything he had thought about his painting before, during the three years he had spent painting it; he forgot all of those qualities he felt were indisputable—he saw the painting with their dispassionate outsider's new eye and saw nothing good about it. He saw Pilate's angry face and Christ's serene face in the foreground, and the figures of Pilate's servants and the face of John surveying what was happening in the background. Every face that he had nurtured with such soul-searching, and so many mistakes and corrections, each with its own particular character, every face which had given him such pain and joy, and all those faces which had been moved around so many times for the sake of the whole, and all those nuances of colour and tone which had cost him so much effort—when all this was put together now and seen through their eyes, it seemed trite, done a thousand times before. The face that meant most to him, the face of Christ, the focus of the painting, which had brought him such elation when he had revealed it, was also lost for him when he looked at the painting with their eyes. He saw a well-painted (actually not even all that well-painted, as he could clearly see a mass of defects now) reprise of those endless Christs by Titian, Raphael, Rubens, and the same soldiers and Pilate. It was all trite, mediocre, and stale and even badly painted—it was lurid and second-rate. They would be right to mouth falsely polite phrases in the artist's presence, and pity him and laugh at him when they were on their own.

The silence (though it lasted no more than a minute) became too painful for him to bear. To break it and show he was not nervous, he braced himself and turned to Golenishchev.

'I believe I've had the pleasure of meeting you before,' he said to him, glancing uneasily first at Anna then at Vronsky, so as not to miss a single detail in the expressions on their faces.

'Of course! We met at Rossi's, you remember, the evening when that young Italian lady, the new Rachel,* did a reading,' Golenishchev answered fluently, withdrawing his gaze from the painting without the slightest regret and turning to the artist.

Noticing, however, that Mikhailov was awaiting judgement on his painting, he said:

'Your painting has come on a great deal since I saw it last. What I find particularly striking, as I did back then, is the figure of Pilate. One can understand the man so well as a good, kind man, but a functionary to his fingertips, who knows not what he does. But it seems to me . . .'

The whole of Mikhailov's mobile face suddenly lit up: his eyes began to sparkle. He wanted to say something, but was too emotional to speak and had to pretend he was coughing. However low his opinion of Golenishchev's ability to understand art, however worthless that valid comment about the truth of Pilate's expression as an official, and however offensive he might find voicing such a worthless observation without saying anything about what was really important, Mikhailov was delighted by it. He himself felt what Golenishchev had said about the figure of Pilate. The fact that this opinion was one of a million other opinions which would all be valid, as Mikhailov well knew, did not diminish the significance of Golenishchev's observation for him. He warmed to Golenishchev for making this observation, and was suddenly transported from a state of dejection to one of elation. His whole painting immediately came to life before him with all the ineffable complexity of everything living. Mikhailov again tried to say that this was how he understood Pilate, but his lips refused to stop trembling, and he could not get the words out. Vronsky and Anna were also saying something in that hushed tone which people usually use at exhibitions of paintings, partly so as not to offend the artist and partly to avoid saying anything stupid out loud, which is so easy to do when talking about art. Mikhailov sensed that the painting had also made an impression on them. He went up to them.

'How wonderful Christ's expression is!' said Anna. She liked this expression more than anything else she had seen, and she felt that it was the centre of the painting, and that praise of it would therefore please the artist. 'You can see he feels sorry for Pilate.'

This was another of the million valid opinions that could be formed about his painting and the figure of Christ. She had said that he felt sorry for Pilate. There indeed had to be pity in Christ's expression, because it contained love, otherworldly peace, readiness for death, and an awareness of the futility of words. There was naturally something of the functionary in Pilate's expression and pity in Christ, since one was the incarnation of the life of the flesh, while the other represented spiritual life. All this and many other things flashed through Mikhailov's mind. And his face lit up again with elation.

'Yes, and how well that figure is done, so much air. One can walk round it,' said Golenishchev, clearly showing by this remark that he did not approve of the content or the idea of the figure.

'Yes, amazing mastery!' said Vronsky. 'How those figures in the background stand out! There is technique for you,' he said to Golenishchev in an allusion to a previous conversation of theirs in which Vronsky had despaired of acquiring this technique.

'Yes, yes, amazing!' confirmed Golenishchev and Anna. In spite of his excited state, the remark about technique grated painfully on Mikhailov and, glancing angrily at Vronsky, he suddenly scowled. He often heard this word 'technique', and he had absolutely no idea what was meant by it. He knew that people used this word to imply a mechanical ability to paint or draw, quite independent of content. Often he noticed, as in the praise he had just received, that people contrasted technique to inner qualities, as though it were possible to paint something bad well. He knew that a great deal of attention and care was needed in order to remove a veil without damaging the work itself, and in order to remove all the veils; but there was no technique to the art of painting. If what he saw had been revealed to a small child or to his cook, they too would be able to remove the husk from what they were seeing. And even the most experienced and skilled painter-technician would not be able to paint anything with mechanical ability alone if an outline of the content had not been revealed to him first. Besides, he saw that when it came to talking about technique, he could not be praised for it. In everything he was painting or had painted he could see glaring faults which were the result of his lack of care in removing the veils, and which he could not now correct without spoiling the whole work. And in almost all of his figures and faces he could still see the remnants of veils which had not been fully removed and spoilt the painting.

'There is one thing which could be said, if you will allow me to make an observation . . .' remarked Golenishchev.

'Oh, please do, I'd be very glad,' said Mikhailov with a feigned smile.

'It is that you have made Him a man-God, and not a God-man. However, I know this is what you intended.'

'I could not paint a Christ who was not in my soul,' said Mikhailov despondently.

'Yes, but in that case, if you will allow me to express my idea . . . Your painting is so good that my observation cannot detract from it, and, anyway, this is just my personal opinion. It is different for you. The theme itself is different. Take Ivanov, for example. I believe that if Christ is to be reduced to the level of a historical figure, then it would have been better for Ivanov to have selected some other historical subject, something fresh, untouched.'

'But what if this is the greatest subject available to art?'

'Others can be found if you look. But the fact is that art does not brook argument and debate. And with Ivanov's painting, the question for the believer and the unbeliever arises as to whether this is God or not, and the integrity of the impression is destroyed.'

'But why should that be so? I think that for educated people,' said Mikhailov, 'there can no longer be any debate.'

Golenishchev did not agree with this and, abiding by his initial idea about the unity of impression necessary in art, he quashed Mikhailov.

Mikhailov was agitated, but unable to say anything in defence of his ideas.

12

ANNA and Vronsky had long been exchanging glances by this stage, regretting their friend's loquacity, and finally Vronsky went over to another small painting without waiting for their host.

'Oh, how charming, how charming! It's wonderful! How charming!'
they began saying with one voice.

'What is it they like so much?' thought Mikhailov. He had forgotten
about that picture he had painted three years earlier. He had forgotten
all the suffering and elation he had gone through with that painting,
when it was his sole obsession day and night for several months, he had
forgotten it as he always forgot about paintings he had finished. He did
not even like looking at it, and had only put it on display because he
was expecting an Englishman who wanted to buy it.

'Oh, that's just an old study,' he said.

'How good it is!' said Golenishchev, who clearly had also genuinely
succumbed to the painting's charm.

Two boys were fishing in the shade of a willow tree. One of them, the
elder one, had just cast his line and was carefully extracting the float
from behind a bush, completely absorbed in this activity; the other,
younger boy was lying face-down in the grass, his tousled, fair head
propped in his hands, staring at the water with dreamy blue eyes. What
was he thinking about?

The admiration expressed for this painting of his rekindled in
Mikhailov his previous excitement, but he feared and disliked this
pointless feeling for the past, and for that reason, even though he was
delighted by these words of praise, he wanted to draw his visitors away
to a third painting.

But Vronsky asked whether the painting was for sale. For Mikhailov
now, unsettled by his visitors, talk about money matters was extremely
distasteful.

'It has been put out for sale,' he answered with a gloomy scowl.

When the visitors had gone, Mikhailov sat opposite the painting
of Pilate and Christ and went over in his mind what had been said
and, if not actually said, implied by these visitors. And it was strange:
what had carried such weight with him when they had been there and
when he had looked at things from their point of view, suddenly lost all
significance for him. He began to focus intently on his painting with
his comprehensive artist's eye, and arrived at that state of confidence
in the perfection, and therefore importance, of his painting that was
required for the intense concentration, excluding all other interests,
without which he could not work.

Christ's foreshortened foot was still not quite right. He picked up
his palette and set to work. As he corrected the foot, he kept a close
eye on the figure of John in the background, which his visitors had not
even noticed, but which he knew was the height of perfection. When

he finished the foot, he wanted to start working on this figure, but he felt he was too agitated for that. He could work neither when he was detached, nor when he was too emotional and his vision was too acute. There was only one stage in this transition from detachment to inspiration when work was possible. But today he was too agitated. He was about to cover up the painting, but paused and spent a long time gazing at the figure of John, with the sheet in his hand and a beatific smile on his face. Eventually, as if sad to tear himself away, he lowered the sheet and set off home, tired but happy.

Vronsky, Anna, and Golenishchev were particularly lively and high-spirited during their journey home. They talked about Mikhailov and his paintings. The word *talent*, by which they meant an innate, almost physical ability independent of mind and heart, and which they wanted to apply to everything experienced by the artist, cropped up particularly often in their conversation, since they needed to have a name for something about which they had not the first idea, but wanted to discuss. They said that there was no denying he had talent, but that his talent could not develop due to his lack of education—the common misfortune of our Russian artists. But the painting of those boys had impressed itself on their memory, and they kept coming back to it.

'So charming! How well he has executed it, and so simply! He doesn't even realize how good it is. Yes, we mustn't let the opportunity pass and should buy it,' said Vronsky.

13

MIKHAILOV sold Vronsky his little painting and agreed to paint a portrait of Anna. On the appointed day he came and started work.

From the fifth sitting onwards the portrait astonished everyone, and Vronsky in particular, not only with its likeness but also its special beauty. It was uncanny how Mikhailov had been able to uncover her special beauty. 'One would have had to know and love her as I have loved her to uncover that most endearing heartfelt expression of hers,' thought Vronsky, although he had only discovered this most endearing heartfelt expression of hers from the portrait. But this expression was so truthful that he and others felt they had known it for a long time.

'I have been battling away for ages and have not achieved anything,' he said of his own portrait, 'and he just looked and started painting. That's what technique is all about.'

'It will come,' Golenishchev reassured him, believing that Vronsky had both talent and, most importantly, the education which gives an exalted view on art. Golenishchev's faith in Vronsky's talent was also bolstered by the fact that he needed Vronsky's sympathy and praise for his articles and ideas, and he felt that praise and support ought to be reciprocal.

In someone else's house, and especially in Vronsky's palazzo, Mikhailov was a completely different person compared with how he was in his own studio. He was icily deferential, as though he were afraid of intimacy with people he did not respect. He called Vronsky 'Your Eminence', and he never stayed to lunch, despite Anna's and Vronsky's invitations, nor did he ever visit except when there was a sitting. Anna was more friendly to him than to other people and was grateful for her portrait. Vronsky was more than courteous with him, and was obviously interested in the artist's opinion of his own picture. Golenishchev never missed an opportunity to instil in Mikhailov proper ideas about art. But Mikhailov remained equally unfriendly to all of them. Anna could see in his eyes that he liked looking at her, but he avoided conversation with her. He maintained a stubborn silence when Vronsky talked about his painting, maintained the same stubborn silence when he was shown Vronsky's picture, and clearly found it tiresome listening to Golenishchev talk and never contradicted him.

Generally speaking, they thoroughly disliked Mikhailov and his reticent and unpleasant, almost hostile attitude when they got to know him better. And they were glad when the sittings came to an end, they were left with a marvellous portrait, and he stopped coming.

Golenishchev was the first to express the thought they all had— namely, that Mikhailov was simply envious of Vronsky.

'Well, perhaps he is not envious, since he has *talent*; but it annoys him that a wealthy man from the court, who is also a count (they hate all that, you know), can without any particular effort do exactly, if not better, what he has devoted all his life to achieving. The main thing is education, which he lacks.'

Vronsky defended Mikhailov, but in the depths of his soul he believed this, because in his view a person from a different, lower social order had to be envious.

Anna's portrait—the same subject painted from life by him and Mikhailov, ought to have shown Vronsky the difference which lay between himself and Mikhailov; but he did not see it. He merely stopped painting his portrait of Anna after Mikhailov had finished, having decided that it was now superfluous. He continued with his picture drawn from medieval life, however. And he himself, along with Golenishchev, and, in particular, Anna, thought it was very good, because it had a far greater resemblance to famous paintings than Mikhailov's picture did.

Mikhailov, meanwhile, despite having been captivated by the portrait of Anna, was even more glad than they were when the sittings came to an end, and he no longer had to listen to Golenishchev prattling on about art and could forget about Vronsky's painting. He knew that Vronsky could not be forbidden from indulging in painting; he knew that he and every other dilettante had a perfect right to paint whatever they liked, but it was distasteful to him. One cannot forbid a person from making himself a big wax doll and kissing it. But if this person were to come with his doll, sit down in front of a man in love, and begin caressing his doll in the way a man in love caresses his beloved, the man in love would find it distasteful. Mikhailov experienced the same kind of unpleasant sensation when he saw Vronsky's painting: he found it ridiculous, and annoying, and pathetic, and offensive.

Vronsky's enthusiasm for painting and the Middle Ages did not last long. He had sufficient taste in painting to be unable to finish his picture. The painting came to a halt. He was vaguely aware that its defects, inconspicuous at first, would be starkly apparent if he were to continue. What happened to him was the same thing that had happened to Golenishchev, who sensed he had nothing to say and continually deluded himself into thinking that his ideas had not yet matured, that he was developing them and gathering materials. But while this left Golenishchev feeling embittered and tormented, Vronsky was incapable of deceiving and tormenting himself, and in particular of becoming embittered. In keeping with his resolute character, he stopped painting without any explanation or excuse.

But without this occupation, his life, and also that of Anna, who was surprised by his disenchantment, seemed so boring in the Italian town, the palazzo suddenly seemed so manifestly old and dirty, the stains on the curtains, the cracks in the floors, and the chipped stucco on the cornices palled so disagreeably, and the endless, unchanging company of Golenishchev, the Italian professor, and the German traveller became so tedious, that it was necessary to change their lifestyle. They decided to go to Russia, to the country. In Petersburg Vronsky planned to divide up his property with his brother, while Anna would see her son. But they planned to spend the summer on Vronsky's large family estate.

14

LEVIN had been married for over two months. He was happy, but not at all in the way he had expected. At every step he encountered disenchantment with his old dreams and unexpected new enchantment. Levin was happy, but after embarking on family life, he saw at every step that it was completely unlike what he had imagined. At every step he experienced what would be experienced by a man who has admired the smooth, happy progress of a little rowing-boat across a lake and has got into that little boat himself. He saw that it was not enough to sit straight without rocking the boat—he also had to keep his wits about him, not for one moment forgetting where he was heading, or that there was water beneath his feet and he had to row, that it was painful for his unaccustomed hands, and that watching it was easy, while actually doing it, although very enjoyable, was very difficult.

When, as a bachelor he used to observe other people's married life, their petty worries, quarrels, and jealousy, he would just smile contemptuously in his soul. He was convinced that not only could there be nothing of that sort in his future married life, but he also believed that it would be completely and utterly unlike the life of other people even in all its outward forms. And instead of that, he suddenly found that not only had his life with his wife not formed into something special, but, on the contrary, was entirely formed of those same trifling details which he had so despised before, but which were now against his will acquiring an extraordinary and unassailable significance. And Levin saw that working out all these details was by no means as easy as he had thought before. Although Levin believed he had a crystal-clear idea of family life, like all men, he could not help construing family life exclusively as the enjoyment of love, which nothing should obstruct, and from which petty cares should not detract. As he understood it, he needed to get on with his work and rest from it in the happiness of love. She should be loved, and that was all. But like all men, he forgot that she too needed to work. And he was amazed at how his poetic, lovely Kitty, not just in the first weeks, but in the first days of their family life, could think, remember, and fuss about tablecloths, furniture, mattresses for visitors, a tray, the cook, the dinner, and so on. When they were still engaged, he had been astonished by how emphatically she had declined a trip abroad in favour of going to the country, as though she knew what was needed, and could also think about things above and beyond her love. He had felt hurt by this then, and there had also been several occasions when he had felt hurt by her petty concerns and worries now. But he saw they were necessary to her. And although he did not understand the point of them, and teased her about them, he could not fail to admire these worries because he loved her. He chuckled about the way she arranged the furniture they had brought from Moscow, reorganized his and her rooms, hung up curtains, allocated rooms for future visitors and for Dolly, organized a room for her new maid, gave the old cook orders for dinner, and had an altercation with Agafya Mikhailovna when she dismissed her from overseeing the pantry. He saw how the old cook smiled admiringly as he listened to her inept, impossible orders; he saw how Agafya Mikhailovna shook her head thoughtfully and kindly at the young mistress's new arrangements for the pantry; he saw how unbelievably endearing Kitty was when she came to tell him, laughing and crying, that her maid Masha was used to seeing her as a young girl and so no one was obeying her. He found this endearing but strange, and he thought it would have been better without it.

He did not know the feeling of change she was experiencing after having sometimes wanted cabbage with kvass or sweets at home and never being able to have either, whereas she could now order whatever she wanted, buy mounds of sweets, spend as much money as she wished, and order whatever cakes she wanted.

She was now dreaming fervently of Dolly arriving with the children, particularly because she was going to order each child's favourite cake, and Dolly would appreciate all her new arrangements. She herself did not understand the whys or wherefores of it, but housekeeping held an irresistible attraction for her. Instinctively feeling the approach of spring, and knowing that there would also be rainy days, she was building her nest as best she could, hurrying both to build it and learn how to at the same time.

This preoccupation Kitty had with small details, which was so at odds with Levin's ideal of sublime happiness in the early days, was one of his disenchantments; but this endearing preoccupation, the point of which he could not understand but which he could not help loving, was one of his new enchantments.

Their quarrels were another source of disenchantment and enchantment. Levin could never have imagined that relations between himself and his wife could be anything other than affectionate, respectful, and loving, and then suddenly they had quarrelled in the first few days, to the extent that she told him that he did not love her and loved only himself, burst into tears, and flung her arms about.

This first quarrel of theirs arose as a result of Levin going to a new farm and being away for half an hour longer than planned, because he wanted to take a short-cut and lost his way. He rode home thinking only about her, her love, and his happiness, and the nearer he drew, the warmer his feeling of tenderness for her became. He had run into the room with this same feeling, which was even more intense than when he had gone to the Shcherbatskys to propose. And then suddenly he was greeted by a glowering expression he had never encountered before. He tried to kiss her but she pushed him away.

'What is the matter?'

'You've been enjoying yourself . . .' she began, wanting to be coolly venomous.

But no sooner had she opened her mouth than a torrent of reproach driven by meaningless jealousy, and everything that had been tormenting her during that half-hour she had spent sitting motionless on the window-ledge, burst out of her. It was only then that he clearly understood for the first time what he had not understood when he led her out of the church after the wedding. He realized that he was not just close to her, but did not know where she ended and he began. He realized this from the agonizing feeling of being split in two he experienced at that moment. He felt hurt during that first moment, but at the same time he felt that he could not be hurt by her, that she was himself. He experienced during that first moment a feeling similar to that which would be experienced by a man who has suddenly received a violent blow from behind, turns round angrily to find the culprit so he can retaliate, only to discover he has accidentally hit himself, that there is no one to be angry with, and that he must endure and try to ease the pain.

Never again did he feel this quite so powerfully, but on this first occasion it took him a long time to regain his composure. His natural instinct demanded that he justify himself and prove to her she was wrong; but proving that she was wrong would mean aggravating her further and widening the breach that was the cause of all of the trouble. One ingrained instinct urged him to shift the blame from himself on to her; another, stronger instinct urged him to heal the breach quickly, as quickly as possible, before it widened any further. Having to endure such an unjust accusation was painful, but justifying himself and causing her pain was even worse. Like a man half-asleep who is racked by pain, he wanted to tear off and throw away the painful spot, and when he came to his senses, he felt that the painful spot was actually himself. He simply had to try and help the painful spot to endure, and this he tried to do.

They made up. Aware that she had been in the wrong, but not acknowledging it, she became more affectionate towards him, and they experienced a new, redoubled happiness in their love. But that did not prevent these conflicts from recurring, and also with great frequency, for the most unexpected and trivial reasons. These conflicts often happened because they did not yet know what was important to each other, and also because they were both often in a bad mood throughout this early period. When one was in a good mood and the other in a bad mood, the peace was not broken, but when both happened to be in a bad mood, conflicts would occur for such incomprehensibly trivial reasons that they could not remember afterwards what they had quarrelled about. It is true that when they were both in a good mood their enjoyment of life doubled. All the same, this early period was a difficult time for them.

Throughout this early period they were acutely conscious of a feeling of tension, as if the chain which bound them was being pulled in opposite directions. Generally speaking, the honeymoon, that is to say, the month after the wedding from which, by tradition, Levin expected so much, was not only devoid of honey, but remained in both their memories as the most painful and humiliating time of their lives. They both tried equally in later life to erase from their memories all the hideous and shameful circumstances of that unhealthy time, when they both were rarely in a normal frame of mind, and rarely themselves.

It was only in the third month of their marriage, after their return from Moscow, where they had gone to stay for a month, that their life began to proceed more smoothly.

15

THEY had just arrived back from Moscow and were relishing their solitude. He was sitting at the desk in his study, writing. She, in that dark mauve gown she had worn in the first days of their marriage and put on again today, and which held particularly fond memories for him, was sitting doing *broderie anglaise** on the sofa, the same ancient leather sofa which had always stood in Levin's father's and grandfather's study. As he thought and wrote, he was constantly and joyously aware of her presence. He had not relinquished his work on the estate and on the book in which he planned to set out the principles of the new farming system; but just as these pursuits and ideas had seemed trivial and insignificant by comparison with the gloom into which all of existence had been plunged before, now they seemed just as trivial and insignificant by comparison with the bright light of happiness flooding his life ahead. He had resumed his activities, but he felt now that his attention's centre of gravity had transferred to something else, and that consequently he looked at his work quite differently, and with greater lucidity. This work had been an escape from life for him before. He used to feel before that his life would be too miserable without this work. Now, however, he needed these pursuits to prevent his life from becoming too uniformly bright. As he took up his papers again and reread what he had written, he was pleased to find that the work was worth doing. It was new and useful. Many of his previous ideas seemed superfluous and extreme, but many gaps were clarified for him when he refreshed his memory about the whole project. He was now writing a new chapter on the reasons why agriculture was unprofitable in Russia. He was arguing that Russia's poverty was due not only to incorrect distribution of landed property and misguided policies, but that this had recently been abetted by the foreign civilization which had been abnormally grafted on to Russia, in particular by means of communication, namely railways, which gave rise to centralization in towns, the growth of luxury, and as a consequence of that, to the detriment of agriculture, the growth of industrial manufacturing, credit, and its accessory—speculation on the stock exchange. It seemed to him that when a nation's wealth increased in a normal way, all these phenomena arose only when significant work had already been invested in agriculture and it ran along the correct, or at least well-defined lines; that the wealth of a country should increase in a consistent way, and, in particular, in such a way that other branches of wealth should not outstrip agriculture; that means of communication should be appropriate to the given state of agriculture, and that railways, which were the product of political rather than economic expediency, were premature while the land was being used incorrectly, since instead of boosting agriculture, as was expected of them, they had brought agriculture to a halt by outstripping it and promoting the development of industry and credit; and that therefore, just as the one-sided and premature development of a single organ in an animal would hinder its overall growth, so credit, transport, and the development of manufacturing, certainly necessary in Europe where they were timely, had only caused harm to the general growth of wealth in Russia by displacing the principal and immediate issue of the organization of agriculture.

While he was writing out his ideas, she was thinking how unnaturally attentive her husband had been to young Prince Charsky, who had flirted with her very tactlessly on the eve of their departure. 'Why, he's jealous,' she thought. 'Goodness, how sweet and silly he is! He's jealous of me! If he only knew that none of them mean any more to me than Pyotr the cook,' she thought, looking at the back of his head and red neck with a proprietory feeling she found strange. 'Although it would be a pity to tear him away from his work (but he'll get it done!), I need to look at his face; will he sense that I'm looking at him, I wonder? I want him to turn round . . . Come on, turn round!' And she opened her eyes wider, in order to try and intensify the effect of her gaze.

'Yes, they siphon off all the juices and give off a false glitter,' he muttered, and feeling that she was looking at him and smiling, he stopped writing and looked round.

'What is it?' he asked with a smile as he got up.

'He looked round,' she thought.

'Nothing, I just wanted you to look round,' she said, looking at him and trying to work out whether he was annoyed that she had distracted him.

'How lovely it is when we are on our own! It is for me, at any rate,' he said, going up to her with a radiant smile of happiness.

'It is for me too. I'm never going to go anywhere, especially not to Moscow.'

'But what were you thinking about?'

'Me? I was thinking . . . No, no, you go on writing, don't get distracted,' she said, pursing her lips, 'and I now have to cut out these little holes, do you see?'

She picked up her scissors and began cutting.

'No, tell me, what was it?' he said, sitting down beside her and watching the small scissors make a circle.

'Oh, what was it I was thinking? I was thinking about Moscow, about the back of your head.'

'What have I done to deserve such happiness? It's not natural. It's too good,' he said, kissing her hand.

'I feel, on the contrary, that the better it is, the more natural it is.'

'You've got a little curl,' he said, carefully turning her head round. 'A little curl. Look, here. No, no, we have serious business to attend to.'

Work was not resumed, and they sprang apart from one another like guilty parties when Kuzma came in to announce that tea was served.

'Have they arrived from town?' Levin asked Kuzma.

'They arrived just now, they're unpacking.'

'Don't be long,' she said to him as she was walking out of the study, 'or I will read the letters without you. And then let's play duets.'

Once on his own, and having put his notebooks away in the new briefcase she had bought him, he started washing his hands at the new washstand with the elegant toiletries that had all made their appearance with her. Levin's thoughts made him smile and shake his head disapprovingly at the same time; a feeling akin to remorse was tormenting him. There was something shameful, over-indulgent, and Capuan,* as he called it privately, about his present life. 'It's not good to live like this,' he thought. 'It'll soon be three months, and I'm hardly doing anything. I sat down to some serious work today for about the first time, and what happened? All I did was begin and then give up. Even my usual activities—I have practically abandoned them too. And the estate as well—I've barely walked or ridden round it. Either I don't want to leave her, or I see that she's bored. And there I was, thinking that life before marriage was nothing special, that it somehow didn't count, and that real life began after marriage. But it will be three months soon, and I have never spent time so idly and unprofitably. No, I can't go on this way, I've got to make a start. It's not her fault, obviously. I can't hold anything against her. I ought to have been tougher myself, and safeguarded my masculine independence. Otherwise I might develop bad habits and pass them on to her . . . It's not her fault, obviously,' he told himself.

But it is hard for someone who is dissatisfied not to reproach another person, especially the person to whom they are closest, with being the cause of their dissatisfaction. And it vaguely occurred to Levin that it was not she herself who was to blame (she could not possibly be blamed for anything), but her upbringing, which was too superficial and frivolous ('that fool Charsky; she wanted to stop him, I know, but didn't know how to'). 'Yes, apart from her interest in the household (which she does have), and apart from her clothes and her *broderie anglaise*, she doesn't have any serious interests. No interest in my work, in the estate, in the peasants, nor in music, which she's quite good at, nor in reading. She doesn't do anything and is perfectly contented.' Levin condemned this deep down, and did not yet understand that she was preparing for the period of activity which was bound to ensue for her, when at one and the same time she would be the wife of her husband, mistress of the house, and would bear, nurse, and raise children. He did not know that she was instinctively aware of this and, while preparing herself for this formidable task, did not reproach herself for the moments she could enjoy now of being carefree and happy in love as she merrily built her future nest.

16

WHEN Levin went upstairs, his wife was sitting next to the new silver samovar by the new tea service and, having seated old Agafya Mikhailovna at the little table and poured her a cup of tea, was reading a letter from Dolly, with whom she kept up a frequent and regular correspondence.

'See, your lady sat me down here, told me to sit with her,' said Agafya Mikhailovna, casting a friendly smile at Kitty.

In these words spoken by Agafya Mikhailovna, Levin read the denouement of the drama which had recently been unfolding between Agafya Mikhailovna and Kitty. He saw that in spite of all the hurt caused to Agafya Mikhailovna by the new mistress taking the reins of government away from her, Kitty had nevertheless emerged victorious and made herself loveable.

'Here, I've opened your letter too,' said Kitty, handing him an illiterate letter. 'It's from that woman of your brother's, I think . . .' she said. 'I haven't read it. And this one is from my parents and from Dolly. Imagine! Dolly took Tanya and Grisha to a children's ball at the Sarmatskys'; Tanya was a marquise.'

But Levin was not listening to her; blushing, he took the letter from Marya Nikolayevna, his brother Nikolay's former mistress, and started reading it. This was already the second letter from Marya Nikolayevna. In the first letter, Marya Nikolayevna had written that his brother had driven her out though she had done nothing wrong, and with touching naivety had added that although she was destitute again, there was nothing she needed or was asking for, but was just worried sick by the thought of Nikolay Dmitrievich wasting away without her because of his poor health, and asked his brother to keep an eye on him. Now she wrote differently. She had found Nikolay Dmitrievich, had gone to live with him again in Moscow, and had travelled with him to a provincial town, where he had obtained a post in the local administration. But she wrote that he had quarrelled with his superior there and had set off back to Moscow, but had fallen so ill during the journey that he was unlikely to rise from his bed again. 'He keeps mentioning you and now he has run out of money.'

'Read what Dolly writes about you,' Kitty began with a smile, but she stopped suddenly when she noticed the changed expression on her husband's face.

'What is the matter? What has happened?'

'She has written to tell me my brother Nikolay is dying. I have to go.'

Kitty's face changed in an instant. Thoughts of Tanya as a marquise, and of Dolly all evaporated.

'But when are you going to go?' she said.

'Tomorrow.'

'And may I go with you?' she said.

'Kitty! What has got into you?' he said reproachfully.

'What do you mean?' she replied, hurt by the reluctance and irritation with which he seemed to receive her suggestion. 'Why shouldn't I go? I won't get in your way. I . . .'

'I'm going because my brother is dying,' said Levin. 'Why should you . . .'

'Why should I want to go? For the same reason as you.'

'Such a critical moment for me, and all she can think about is being bored on her own,' thought Levin. And this feeble excuse in such a grave matter angered him.

'It's impossible,' he said sternly.

Agafya Mikhailovna, seeing a quarrel brewing, quietly put down her cup and went out. Kitty did not even notice her. The tone in which her husband had said those last words offended her, particularly because he clearly did not believe what she said.

'But I'm telling you that if you go, I will go with you, I will definitely go,' she said impulsively and furiously. 'Why is it impossible? Why do you say it's impossible?'

'Because God knows where I'll have to go and what kind of roads and inns I will have to deal with. You will get in my way,' said Levin, trying to retain his composure.

'I won't get in your way at all. I don't need anything. Wherever you can go, I can go too. . . .'

'Well, the fact that there is this woman there with whom you can't associate is reason enough.'

'I don't know and don't want to know who or what is there. I just know that my husband's brother is dying, that my husband is going to him, and that I am going with my husband so that . . .'

'Kitty! Don't be angry. But think about it, this is such an important matter that it's painful for me to think about you muddling it up with your feeling of weakness and your reluctance to be left on your own. If you're bored on your own, well, you can go to Moscow.'

'There you are, you are *always* attributing horrid, low-minded motives to me,' she said with tears of outrage and anger. 'It's not weakness or anything like that . . . I feel that it's my duty to be with my husband when he is stricken by sorrow, but you deliberately want to hurt me, you're trying deliberately not to understand. . . .'

'No, this is awful! To be some kind of slave!' cried Levin as he got up, no longer able to contain his irritation. But at that same moment he felt he was injuring himself.

'Then why did you get married? You would be free. Why did you, if you regret it?' she said, then leapt up and ran into the drawing room.

When he came to find her, she was sobbing.

He began to speak, hoping to find the words which might at least calm her down, if not actually dissuade her. But she would not listen to him and would not agree to anything. He bent over her and took her resistant hand. He kissed her hand, kissed her hair, and kissed her hand again while she maintained a stony silence. But when he took her face in both his hands and said 'Kitty!' she suddenly came to her senses and shed a few tears, and they made up.

It was decided they would go together the next day. Levin told his wife that he believed she wanted to go simply in order to be useful, and agreed that there was nothing improper about Marya Nikolayevna's presence at his brother's bedside; but deep down he set off feeling displeased both with her and with himself. He was displeased with her that she could not bring herself to let him go when it was necessary (and how strange it was for him to think that, having so recently still not dared to believe in the good fortune that she might love him, he now felt unhappy because she loved him too much!), and he was displeased with himself for not standing his ground. Deep down he even more seriously disagreed with the idea that she need not have anything to do with that woman who was with his brother, and he thought with horror of all the possible conflicts that might arise. The mere thought of his wife, his Kitty, being in the same room as a whore made him shudder with disgust and horror.

17

THE hotel in the provincial town in which Nikolay Levin was laid up was one of those provincial hotels established according to new, improved specifications, with the very best intentions of cleanliness, comfort, and even elegance, but which, due to the public which frequents them, are turned with extraordinary speed into dirty taverns with pretensions to modern improvements, these very pretensions making them even worse than old-fashioned, merely dirty hotels. This hotel had already reached that state; the soldier in the dirty uniform smoking a cigarette by the main entrance who was supposed to represent a porter, the draughty, dark, and unpleasant iron staircase, the overly familiar waiter in the dirty frock-coat, the public dining room with the dusty bouquet of wax flowers decorating the table, the dirt, dust, and slovenliness everywhere, combined with this hotel's strange kind of new, up-to-the-minute, smug, railway station-like bustle—all this made a most dispiriting impression on the Levins after their young life together, particularly since the artificial air of the hotel could in no way be reconciled with what awaited them.

As always, after the question about how much they wanted to pay for a room, it turned out that there was not a single good room available: one good room was occupied by an inspector of railways, another by a lawyer from Moscow, and a third by Princess Astafieva travelling from the country. There remained one dirty room, next to another which they were promised would be vacated by the evening. Annoyed with his wife that what he had expected had happened, namely, that when they had arrived, and when he was beside himself with anxiety about how his brother was, he had to take care of her instead of rushing straight away to see his brother, Levin showed her into the room allocated to them.

'Go, go!' she said, looking at him with timid, guilty eyes.

He walked silently through the door and immediately bumped into Marya Nikolayevna, who had found out about his arrival and did not dare enter his room. She was just the same as she had been when he saw her in Moscow: the same woollen dress and bare arms and neck, and the same kindly, albeit dim-witted, slightly plumper, pitted face.

'So what is the latest? How is he?'

'Very bad. He can't get up. He has been waiting and waiting for you to arrive. He . . . You . . . are with your wife.'

Levin did not at first understand the source of her embarrassment, but she immediately explained.

'I'll go off, I'll go to the kitchen,' she said. 'He will be happy. He heard about it and knows her, and he remembers seeing her abroad.'

Levin realized that she meant his wife, and did not know how to reply.

'Come, let's go!' he said.

But as soon as he set off, the door of his room opened and Kitty peered out. Levin blushed both with shame and anger at his wife for putting herself and him in this difficult position; but Marya Nikolayevna blushed even more. She cowered and blushed to the point of tears, and clutching the ends of her headscarf in both hands, she twisted them in her red fingers without knowing what to say or do.

During that first moment, Levin saw an expression of eager curiosity in the gaze Kitty fixed on this awful woman she could not fathom; but that lasted only an instant.

'Well, what is the news? How is he?' she said, turning to her husband and then to her.

'We can't hold a conversation in the corridor!' Levin said, looking round with annoyance at a gentleman who was just then walking unsteadily down the corridor, supposedly on business of his own.

'Well, come in then,' said Kitty, turning to Marya Nikolayevna, who had by now recovered; but when she noticed the alarm on her husband's face, she said 'or else go, go off and then send for me,' and went back into the room. Levin went off to see his brother.

He certainly had not anticipated what he saw and felt in his brother's room. He had anticipated finding that same state of self-deception to which he had heard consumptives so often succumb, and which he had found so shocking during his brother's visit in the autumn. He had been anticipating the physical signs of approaching death to be more marked—greater weakness, greater emaciation, but for his condition nevertheless to be more or less the same. He had anticipated feeling the same pity at losing a beloved brother and the same horror of death that he had felt then, only to a greater degree. And he had prepared himself for this; but he found something quite different.

In a small, dirty room, the painted panels of its walls smeared with spittle, conversation audible behind its thin partition, and the air filled with a suffocating smell of excrement, a body covered with a blanket lay on a bed moved away from the wall. One hand belonging to this body was on top of the blanket, and the huge, rake-like wrist of this hand was inexplicably attached to a long, thin spindle which was flat from middle to end. The head lay sideways on the pillow. Levin could see sweat-laden, sparse hairs on the temples and a hollow, almost transparent forehead.

'It cannot be that this dreadful body is my brother Nikolay,' thought Levin. But he went closer, saw the face, and doubt could no longer be entertained. In spite of the terrible change to the face, Levin had only to glance at those lively eyes which had looked up towards the person entering, and notice the faint movement of the mouth beneath the matted moustache, to realize the terrible truth that this dead body was indeed his living brother.

The feverishly bright eyes looked sternly and reproachfully at the brother coming in. And this look instantly established a living relationship between living people. Levin instantly also felt both the reproach in the look levelled at him and remorse for his happiness.

When Konstantin took him by the hand, Nikolay smiled. The smile was faint and barely noticeable, and the stern expression of the eyes did not change, despite the smile.

'You did not expect to find me like this,' he managed to say with difficulty.

'Yes . . . no,' said Levin, getting his words confused. 'Why on earth didn't you let me know earlier, at the time of my wedding, I mean? I made enquiries everywhere.'

It was necessary to talk so as not to be silent, but he did not know what to say, particularly since his brother made no response but just kept on staring at him and was evidently pondering the meaning of each word. Levin told his brother that his wife had come with him. Nikolay expressed pleasure, but said he was afraid of frightening her with his condition. Silence followed. Suddenly Nikolay stirred and began saying something. Judging from the expression on his face, Levin expected it to be something particularly significant and important, but Nikolay started talking about his health. He blamed the doctor, lamented that the famous doctor from Moscow was not there, and Levin realized that he still had hope.

Seizing the first moment of silence and wanting respite from his agonizing emotions, if only for a minute, Levin got up and said that he would go and fetch his wife.

'Well, all right, and I'll get this place cleaned up. It's dirty here and it stinks, I'm sure. Masha! Come and clear up,' the sick man said with effort. 'And when you've tidied up, you can make yourself scarce,' he added, looking quizzically at his brother.

Levin did not reply. As he went out into the corridor, he stopped. He had said he would fetch his wife, but now that he was aware of the emotions he was going through, he decided that he would, on the contrary, try and persuade her not to go and see the sick man. 'Why should she have to suffer what I am going through?' he thought.

'Well, how is he?' Kitty asked with a frightened face.

'Oh, it's awful, it's awful! Why did you come?' said Levin.

Kitty was silent for a few seconds as she looked timidly and pityingly at her husband, then she went up and took hold of his elbow with both her hands.

'Kostya! Take me to him, it will be easier for us to do this together. You just take me, please, just take me and then leave,' she said. 'You must understand that for me to see you and not see him is far more painful. I may be useful to you and to him there. Please, let me!' she implored her husband, as if her life's happiness depended on it.

Levin had to agree, and after tidying himself up, and having by this stage completely forgotten about Marya Nikolayevna, he set off to see to his brother again with Kitty.

Treading softly and continually glancing at her husband, showing him a brave and sympathetic face, she went into the sick man's room and, taking her time to turn round, noiselessly closed the door. With silent steps she went quickly over to the sick man's bed and, going round it so that he did not have to turn his head, she immediately took his huge, skeletal hand in her sprightly young hand, pressed it, and began talking to him in that gentle, compassionate, and quietly animated way of which only women are capable.

'We met in Soden, although we were not acquainted,' she said. 'You never thought that I would one day be your sister.'

'You wouldn't have recognized me, would you?' he said, with a smile that had lit up his face when she came in.

'Oh yes, I would. What a good thing you let us know! There hasn't been a day that Kostya hasn't remembered you and been worried.'

But the sick man's animation did not last long.

The stern, reproachful expression of the dying man's envy of the living had settled on his face again before she had finished speaking.

'I am afraid you are not quite comfortable here,' she said, diverting her gaze from his penetrating stare and looking around the room. 'We must ask the landlord for another room,' she said to her husband, 'also so we can be nearer.'

18

LEVIN could not look calmly at his brother, and could not himself be natural and calm in his presence. When he went in to the sick man, his eyes and his attention unconsciously clouded over, and he could neither see nor distinguish the details of his brother's condition. He registered the terrible smell, saw the dirt, the mess, the agonizing condition and the groaning, and felt that nothing could be done to help. It did not occur to him to think about trying to understand all the details of the sick man's condition, to think about how that body was lying under the blanket, how those emaciated shins, haunches, and back lay there all contorted and whether they could not somehow be positioned in a better way, and whether something could be done which might make the situation, if not actually better, at least less bad. A shiver ran down his spine when he began to think about all these details. He was absolutely convinced that nothing could be done to prolong his brother's life or relieve his suffering. But the sick man could sense his realization that he considered all help to be ineffective, and it irritated him. And this made it even more painful for Levin. To be in the sick man's room was agonizing for him, but not to be there was even worse. And so he kept going out and coming in on various pretexts, unable to remain alone.

Kitty, however, thought, felt, and acted quite differently. When she saw the sick man she felt pity for him. And pity certainly did not produce in her woman's heart that feeling of horror and disgust which it produced in her husband, but rather a need to take action, to find out all the details of his condition and remedy them. And since she had not the slightest doubt that she should help him, she also had no doubt that it was possible to do so, and she immediately set to work. Those very same details, the mere thought of which horrified her husband, immediately engaged her attention. She sent for the doctor, sent for things from the chemist, ordered the maid who had come with her and Marya Nikolayevna to sweep, dust, and scrub, while she busied herself with rinsing and bathing, and putting something under the blanket. On her instructions things were brought in and taken out of the sick man's room. She herself, meanwhile, made several trips back to her own room, paying no attention to the people she met on the way, so she could get sheets, pillowcases, towels, and shirts to bring back.

The waiter, who was serving lunch to some engineers in the public dining room, responded several times to her summons with a scowl on his face, and yet he could not help carrying out her orders, since she gave them with such gentle insistence there was simply no way of evading her. Levin did not approve of all this; he did not believe the patient might derive any benefit from it. Above all, he feared the patient might become angry. But although the sick man seemed to be indifferent to it, he did not become angry but just embarrassed, and generally appeared to be rather curious about what she was doing to him. When Levin returned from seeing the doctor to whom Kitty had sent him, and opened the door, he found the sick man in the middle of having his nightshirt changed on Kitty's instructions. The long, white, skeletal frame of his spine, with huge, protruding shoulderblades and jutting ribs and vertebrae, was bare, and Marya Nikolayevna and the waiter had got the sleeve of the nightshirt tangled up and could not get the long, limp arm to go into it. Kitty, hurriedly closing the door after Levin, was not looking in that direction; but the sick man started groaning, and she swiftly headed over to him.

'Hurry up,' she said.

'Don't come near me,' mumbled the sick man angrily. 'I can do it myself. . . .'

'What was that?' asked Marya Nikolayevna.

But Kitty heard and understood that he felt ashamed and uncomfortable at being naked in front of her.

'I'm not looking, I'm not looking!' she said as she directed his arm. 'Marya Nikolayevna, you go round to the other side and sort things out,' she added.

'Could you please go and fetch the vial I have in my little bag,' she said, turning to her husband, 'you know, the one in the side pocket—if you could bring it, please, while they finish clearing up in here.'

When he returned with the vial, Levin found the sick man already settled and everything around him completely changed. The ghastly smell had been replaced by the smell of scented vinegar, which Kitty, pushing out her lips and puffing up her rosy cheeks, was spraying via a little tube. There was no dust to be seen anywhere, and a rug had been placed beneath the bed. Neatly arranged on the table were vials and a carafe, and folded up next to them were all the linen that was needed and Kitty's *broderie anglaise*. On the other table, by the sick man's bed, there was something to drink, a candle, and powders. The sick man himself, washed and combed, lay on clean sheets and high, raised pillows, in a clean nightshirt with a white collar around his unnaturally thin neck, and he was looking intently at Kitty with a new expression of hope.

The doctor brought by Levin, who had been tracked down at the club, was not the one who had been treating Nikolay Levin, and with whom he had not been happy. The new doctor took out a stethoscope to sound the patient, shook his head, prescribed medicine, and went into painstaking detail to explain first how to take the medicine and then what diet to follow. He advised raw or lightly boiled eggs, and seltzer water with fresh milk at a particular temperature. When the doctor had left, the sick man said something to his brother, of which Levin only caught the last words: 'Your Katya,' but from the way he was looking at her, Levin realized he was praising her. He now summoned Katya, as he called her, over to him.

'I'm feeling much better already,' he said. 'I can see that with you I would have recovered long ago. How nice this is!' He took her hand

and drew it towards his lips, but as if fearing she would find this unpleasant, he changed his mind, let it go, and only stroked it. Kitty took this hand with both of hers and pressed it.

'Now just turn me over on to my left side and go to bed,' he said.

No one could make out what he said; Kitty alone understood. She could understand because she was constantly keeping a mental note of what he needed.

'On to the other side,' she said to her husband, 'he always sleeps on that side. Turn him over, it's not nice to have to call the servants. I can't do it. Maybe you could?' she said, turning to Marya Nikolayevna.

'I'm afraid to,' replied Marya Nikolayevna.

However terrible it was for Levin to put his arms round that terrible body and take hold of those parts under the blanket he did not want to know about, he submitted to his wife's influence, donned that resolute expression of his which she knew well, and, thrusting his hands in, did take hold of them, but despite his strength he was struck by the strange heaviness of those wasted limbs. While he turned him over, conscious of the huge emaciated arm around his neck, Kitty swiftly and noiselessly turned over the pillow and plumped it up, then adjusted the sick man's head and the wisps of hair once again sticking to his forehead.

The sick man still was gripping his brother's hand in his own. Levin could feel that he wanted to do something with his hand and was pulling it somewhere. Levin yielded, his heart sinking. Yes, he drew it to his mouth and kissed it. Racked with sobs and unable to articulate a word, Levin left the room.

19

'YOU have hidden things from the most wise and revealed them to children and the foolish.'* So Levin thought about his wife as he talked to her that evening.

It was not because he considered himself one of the most wise that Levin thought of this passage from the Gospel, but he could not help knowing that he was cleverer than his wife and Agafya Mikhailovna, and he also could not help knowing that whenever he thought about death, he thought about it with all the strength of his soul. He also knew that a great many male intellects, whose thoughts about it he had read, had ruminated about it without knowing a fraction of what his wife and Agafya Mikhailovna knew about it. However different those two women were, in this Agafya Mikhailovna and Katya, as his brother

Nikolay called her and as Levin now took particular pleasure in calling her, were completely as one. They both knew without a shadow
of a doubt what life was, and what death was, and although neither of
them could have begun to answer or even understand the questions
which occurred to Levin, neither had any doubt as to the significance of
this phenomenon, and their attitude to it, which was not just exclusive
to them but shared with millions of people, was completely identical.
The proof that they really did know what death was lay in the fact that
they knew without a moment's hesitation how to deal with people who
were dying, and were not frightened of them. Levin and others, on the
other hand, although they could say a lot about death, clearly did not
know, because they were afraid of death and did not have the faintest
idea what to do when people were dying. If Levin had been alone with
his brother Nikolay now, he would have looked at him in terror and sat
there waiting with still greater terror, unable to do anything else.

He did not know, moreover, what to say, how to look, or how to walk.
Talking about anything else seemed offensive to him, out of the question; talking about death, about gloomy things—also out of the question. Saying nothing—also out of the question. 'If I look at him, I'm
afraid he will think I am examining him; if I don't look at him, he'll
think I'm thinking about other things. He'll be displeased if I walk
about on tiptoe; but I would feel embarrassed treading normally.' Kitty,
however, clearly did not think about herself and had no time to; she
was thinking about him because she knew something, and everything
turned out well. She told him about herself and about her wedding,
she smiled, she sympathized, she was affectionate with him, she talked
about cases where people recovered, and everything turned out well, so
she had to know. The proof that her and Agafya Mikhailovna's activity
was not instinctive, animal, or irrational was that, apart from the physical care and the relief of suffering, both Agafya Mikhailovna and Kitty
insisted that a dying man should also receive something which was
more important than physical care, and which had nothing in common
with his physical condition. Agafya Mikhailovna had said about an old
man who had died: 'Well, thank heavens, he took Communion and
received Holy Unction,* God grant that we all die like that.' Besides
all her cares about linen, bedsores, and things to drink, Katya managed
on the very first day to convince the sick man of the necessity of taking
Communion and being anointed in just the same way.

After returning from the sick man to their two rooms for the night,
Levin sat with his head bowed, not knowing what to do. Quite apart
from having supper, getting ready for bed, and thinking over what they

were going to do, he could not even talk to his wife: he felt ashamed. Kitty, by contrast, was busier than usual. She was even livelier than usual. She ordered supper to be brought, unpacked their things herself, helped to make the beds herself, and did not forget to sprinkle them with insect powder. She was in that heightened and mentally alert state one finds in men before combat, a battle, or at dangerous and decisive moments in life—those moments when for once and for all a man proves his worth, and that the whole of his previous life has not been spent in vain, but has been a preparation for these moments.

Everything she did turned out well, and it was not yet midnight when all their things had been arranged neatly and tidily, and in such a special sort of way that the room seemed more like home, and like her rooms: the beds were made up, brushes, combs, mirrors had been laid out, and little cloths spread over the tables.

Levin considered that it was unforgiveable to eat, sleep, or talk even now, and felt that his every movement was indecent. She was busy arranging the brushes, but was doing it all in such a way that there was nothing offensive about it.

They could not eat anything, however, and could not fall asleep for a long time, indeed they did not even go to bed for a long time.

'I am very glad I persuaded him to receive Holy Unction tomorrow,' she said, sitting in her dressing-jacket before her travelling mirror, and combing her soft, fragrant hair with a fine comb. 'I have never seen it being done, but I know that there are prayers for recovery, Mama told me.'

'Surely you don't think he can recover?' said Levin, watching the narrow parting at the back of her round little head being continually covered up whenever she brought the comb forward.

'I asked the doctor: he said he couldn't live more than three days. But can they really know? I'm very glad, anyway, that I persuaded him,' she said, casting a sideways glance at her husband through her hair. 'Anything is possible,' she added with that particular, slightly artful expression her face always bore when she talked about religion.

Following their conversation about religion while they were still engaged, neither he nor she had broached the subject again, but she carried out the rites of going to church and saying prayers, always with the same calm awareness that this was what was necessary. Despite his assurances to the contrary, she was firmly convinced that he was just as much a Christian as she was, indeed a better one, and that everything he said about it was just one of his funny male quirks, like what he used to say about her *broderie anglaise*: that good people darned holes, while she cut them out on purpose, and so on.

'Yes, well, that woman, Marya Nikolayevna, was not capable of arranging all that,' said Levin. 'And . . . I must confess, I'm very, very glad you came. You are so pure, that . . .' He took her hand and did not kiss it (to kiss her hand in such proximity to death seemed obscene to him), but just squeezed it with a guilty expression, looking at her brightening eyes.

'It would have been so ghastly for you on your own,' she said, and raising aloft her arms which had been hiding her cheeks, which were now flushed pink with pleasure, she twisted the braids on the nape of her neck and pinned them. 'No,' she went on, 'she did not know . . . I was lucky to learn a great deal in Soden.'

'Surely there weren't any people there who were so ill?'

'Worse.'

'What's so awful for me is that I can't help seeing him as he was when he was young . . . You wouldn't believe how charming he was as a boy, but I didn't understand him then.'

'Oh, I can believe it very well. I feel so sure we *would* have been friends!' she said, and frightened by what she had said, she looked round at her husband, and tears sprang into her eyes.

'Yes, *would have* been,' he said sadly. 'He is a prime example of those people about whom one says that they're not for this world.'

'We have many days ahead of us, however, so we must go to bed,' said Kitty, glancing at her tiny watch.

20

DEATH

THE next day the sick man took communion and received Holy Unction. Nikolay Levin prayed fervently during the service. There was such passionate entreaty and hope expressed in his large eyes, which were fixed on an icon set up on a card-table covered with a coloured napkin, that Levin found it terrible to watch. Levin knew that this passionate entreaty and hope would only make his parting from life, which he so loved, more painful. Levin knew his brother and the workings of his mind; he knew that his loss of faith had not come about because he found it easier to live without faith, but because contemporary scientific explanations of the phenomena of the world had driven out his beliefs one by one; thus he knew that his present return was not a legitimate one, accomplished by means of the same thought-processes, but only temporary and self-interested, and accompanied by an insane hope of recovery. Levin also knew that Kitty had bolstered this hope with stories of the extraordinary recoveries she had heard about. Levin knew all this, and it was as exquisitely painful for him to see that imploring look, full of hope, and the emaciated wrist of his hand rise with effort to make the sign of the cross on the tautly stretched skin of his brow, as it was to see those protruding shoulders and hollow, wheezing chest, which could no longer house the life for which the sick man was begging. During the sacrament Levin also prayed, doing what he had done a thousand times as an unbeliever. He said, addressing God: 'If you exist, make this man recover (this has happened many times after all), and you will save him and me.'

After being anointed, the sick man suddenly felt much better. He did not cough for a whole hour, smiled, kissed Kitty's hand as he thanked her with tears in his eyes, and said he was comfortable, free from pain, and could feel his appetite and his energy returning. He even sat up by himself when he was brought some soup, and asked for another cutlet. However hopeless his condition, and however obvious it was to see by just glancing at him that he could not recover, Levin and Kitty spent that hour in the same state of happy and cautious (lest they were mistaken) excitement.

'Is he better?' 'Yes, much.' 'It's remarkable.' 'There's nothing remarkable about it.' 'Anyway, he's better,' they said in a whisper, smiling to each other.

This delusion was short-lived. The sick man quietly fell asleep, but was woken half an hour later by coughing. And then suddenly all the hopes which those around him, and he himself, had harboured disappeared. The reality of suffering, allowing for no doubt, nor memories of former hopes, obliterated them for Levin and Kitty and for the sick man himself.

Without even mentioning what he had believed half an hour earlier, as if it was embarrassing enough just to recall it, he demanded to be given iodine to inhale in a glass jar covered with perforated paper. Levin gave him the jar, and the same look of passionate hope with which he had received the sacrament was now fixed on his brother, as he demanded from him confirmation of what the doctor had said about the inhalation of iodine working wonders.

'Katya's not here?' he wheezed, looking round while Levin reluctantly confirmed what the doctor had said. 'Well, then I can say it . . . It was for her sake that I staged that comedy. She's so sweet, but you and I can't deceive ourselves. This is what I believe in,' he said, and, gripping the jar in his bony hand, he began breathing over it.

At eight o'clock in the evening Levin and his wife were drinking tea in their room when Marya Nikolayevna came running in to them, out of breath. She was pale, and her lips were trembling.

'He is dying!' she whispered. 'I'm afraid he will die any minute.'

They both rushed to him. He had raised himself and was sitting propped up on one elbow on the bed, his long back bent, and his head hanging low.

'What do you feel?' Levin asked in a whisper, after a silence.

'I feel that I'm departing,' Nikolay said with difficulty but with extraordinary precision, slowly squeezing the words out of himself. He did not lift his head, but just turned his eyes upwards, although they did not reach his brother's face. 'Katya, go away!' he added.

Levin jumped up, and with a peremptory whisper made her go out.

'I'm going,' he said again.

'Why do you think so?' said Levin, in order to say something.

'Because I'm departing,' he repeated, as if he had taken a liking to the phrase. 'It's the end.'

Marya Nikolayevna went over to him.

'You should lie down, you'd feel more comfortable,' she said.

'I'll soon be lying down quietly,' he mumbled, 'dead,' he added scornfully, angrily. 'Well, lay me down if you want.'

Levin laid his brother on his back, sat down beside him, and peered at his face, holding his breath. The dying man lay with his eyes shut, but the muscles on his forehead twitched occasionally, as with a man in deep and intense thought. Levin involuntarily started thinking with him about what was going on inside him now, but despite all his efforts to keep pace, he could see from the expression of that calm, stern face and the quivering of the muscle above his eyebrow, that what was becoming clearer and clearer for the dying man was still as obscure as ever for Levin.

'Yes, yes, that's it,' said the dying man, pronouncing the words slowly. 'Wait.' He fell silent again. 'That's it!' he suddenly drawled in a soothing voice, as if everything had been resolved for him. Then he said 'Oh God!' and sighed deeply.

Marya Nikolayevna felt his feet.

'They're growing cold,' she whispered.

For a long time, for a very long time, it seemed to Levin, the sick man lay motionless. But he was still alive, and from time to time he sighed. Levin was now exhausted from the mental exertion. He felt that despite all his mental exertion, he could not understand what *it* was. He felt he had long stopped keeping up with the dying man. He could no longer think about the question of death itself, but he could not prevent himself thinking of what he would have to do next: close his eyes, dress him, order a coffin. And, strangely enough, he felt completely detached, and experienced neither grief nor loss, and still less pity for his brother. If he had any feeling for his brother now, it was envy for the knowledge the dying man now possessed, but which he could not possess.

He went on sitting beside him in that way for a long time, constantly expecting the end. But the end did not come. The door opened and Kitty appeared. Levin got up in order to stop her. But just as he was getting up, he heard the dying man move.

'Don't leave,' said Nikolay, and he held out his hand. Levin gave him his hand and gesticulated angrily at his wife to go away.

Holding the dying man's hand in his, he sat for half an hour, then an hour, then another hour. He was no longer thinking about death at all now. He was wondering what Kitty was doing, who was staying in the next room, and whether the doctor owned the house he lived in. He wanted to eat and sleep. He carefully extracted his hand and felt his brother's feet. The feet were cold, but the sick man was breathing. Levin tried again to leave on tiptoe, but again the sick man stirred and said:

'Don't leave.'

.   .   .   .

Dawn broke; the sick man's condition was unchanged. Levin surreptitiously withdrew his hand without looking at the dying man, went back to his room, and fell asleep. When he woke up, instead of receiving news of his brother's death, which he was expecting, he learned that the sick man had returned to his earlier condition. He had started sitting up again and coughing, he had started to eat and talk again, he had once again stopped talking about death and was again expressing hope of recovery, and he had become even more irritable and gloomy than before. No one, neither his brother nor Kitty, could pacify him. He was angry with everyone and saying unpleasant things to everyone, reproaching everyone for his suffering, and demanding that they bring the famous doctor from Moscow. Whenever he was asked how he felt, he gave the same reply, with an expression of anger and reproach:

'I'm suffering horribly, it's unbearable!'

The sick man was suffering more and more, especially from bedsores, which could not now be treated, and was growing more and more irate with everyone around him, blaming them for everything, and particularly for not having brought the doctor from Moscow. Kitty did all she could to help him and calm him down; but it was all to no avail, and Levin saw that she herself was both physically and emotionally exhausted, although she would not admit to it. The feeling of death, which had been aroused in all of them by his farewell to life on the night when he had summoned his brother, had been eradicated. They all knew that he would inevitably die soon, that he was half-dead already. They all desired only one thing—that he should die as soon as possible and, concealing this, they all went on giving him medicine from bottles, looking for remedies and doctors, and deceiving him, themselves, and one another. It was all a lie, a disgusting, offensive, and blasphemous lie. And because of the nature of his character, and the fact that he loved the dying man more than anyone else, Levin found this lie particularly hard to bear.

Having long been occupied by the idea of reconciling his brothers, even if only on the brink of death, Levin had written to his brother Sergey Ivanovich, and after receiving an answer from him, now read this letter out to the sick man. Sergey Ivanovich wrote that he could not come in person, but begged his brother's forgiveness in touching terms.

The sick man said nothing.

'So what should I write to him?' said Levin. 'I hope you are not angry with him?'

'No, not at all!' Nikolay answered, irritated to be asked this question. 'Write and ask him to send me a doctor.'

Three more agonizing days went by; the sick man was still in the same condition. Everyone who set eyes on him now experienced the feeling of wishing for his death: the servants at the hotel and its proprietor, the hotel residents, the doctor, Marya Nikolayevna, Levin, and Kitty. The sick man was the only one not to manifest this feeling, but on the contrary was angry that the doctor had not been brought, and he went on taking medicine and talking about life. Only on rare occasions, when the opium induced him to find a moment's oblivion from his unending suffering, and he was half-asleep, did he sometimes express what was felt more powerfully in his heart than in everyone else's: 'Oh, if only the end would come!' Or: 'When will this end?'

The suffering, which steadily increased, did its work and prepared him for death. There was no position in which he did not suffer, there was no moment when he might have attained oblivion, there was no part or limb of his body that did not ache and cause him agony. By now even this body's memories, impressions, and thoughts aroused in him the same revulsion as the body itself. The sight of other people, their talk, his own memories—all this was sheer agony for him. Those around him could sense this and they unconsciously held themselves back from moving about freely, talking, or expressing their wishes in front of him. His whole life coalesced into a single feeling of suffering and the desire to be rid of it.

He was clearly undergoing the transformation that would contrive to make him see death as the satisfaction of his desires, as happiness. Previously each individual desire aroused by suffering or privation, such as hunger, tiredness, or thirst, could be relieved by some bodily function which brought pleasure; but suffering and privation now received no relief, and any attempt to find relief brought on new suffering. And so all desires coalesced into one—the desire to be rid of all suffering and its source, the body. But he had no words to express this desire for deliverance, and so did not talk about it, but from force of habit kept demanding the satisfaction of those desires that could no longer be fulfilled. 'Turn me over on to my other side,' he would say, and immediately afterwards demand to be turned back to how he had been before. 'Give me some broth. Take away the broth. Talk to me about something, why are you silent?' And as soon as they began to talk he would close his eyes and show tiredness, indifference, and revulsion.

On the tenth day after their arrival in the town, Kitty fell ill. She had developed a headache and nausea, and could not get out of bed all morning.

The doctor explained that the illness was the result of tiredness and stress, and prescribed rest.

After dinner, however, Kitty got up and went as usual to the sick man, taking her needlework. He looked at her sternly when she came in, and smiled contemptuously when she said she had been unwell. He had spent the day continually blowing his nose and groaning piteously.

'How do you feel?' she asked him.

'Worse,' he pronounced with difficulty. 'It hurts!'

'Where does it hurt?'

'Everywhere.'

'It will be over today, you'll see,' whispered Marya Nikolayevna, but so loudly that the sick man, who was very perceptive, as Levin had noticed, was bound to have heard her. Levin hissed at her to be quiet, and looked round to the sick man. Nikolay had heard, but these words made absolutely no impression on him. He still had the same intense, accusatory look.

'Why do you think so?' Levin asked her, when she followed him out into the corridor.

'He has begun picking at himself,' said Marya Nikolayevna.

'What do you mean?'

'Like this,' she said, tugging at the folds of her woollen skirt. He had noticed that the sick man had indeed been snatching at himself all day, as if there was something he wanted to pull off.

Marya Nikolayevna's prediction was accurate. By nightfall the sick man was no longer able to lift his arms and could only look straight ahead, not changing the intensely concentrated expression of his gaze. Even when his brother or Kitty bent over him so that he could see them, his look was just the same. Kitty sent for the priest to read the prayers for the dying.

While the priest was reading the prayers, the dying man did not show any sign of life: his eyes were closed. Levin, Kitty, and Marya Nikolayevna stood by the bed. The priest had not finished reading the concluding prayer when the dying man stretched, sighed, and opened his eyes. When he finished the prayer, the priest placed the cross on the cold forehead, then slowly wrapped it up in his stole, and after standing for a couple more minutes in silence, touched the huge, bloodless hand that was growing cold.

'He has gone,' said the priest, and was about to walk away; but suddenly there was a faint movement in the dead man's matted moustache, and ringing out clearly in the silence from the depths of his ribcage came the distinctly crisp sounds:

'Not quite . . . Soon.'

And a minute later the face brightened, a smile appeared beneath the moustache, and the women who had gathered round began carefully laying out the dead body.

The sight of his brother and the proximity of death revived in Levin's heart that feeling of horror at the combined unfathomability, proximity, and inevitability of death which had overwhelmed him that autumn evening when his brother came to visit. This feeling was now even stronger than before, while he felt even less capable of understanding the meaning of death, and its inevitability seemed even more ghastly; but now, thanks to his wife being close by, that feeling did not reduce him to despair; he felt the need for life and love in spite of death. He felt that love had saved him from despair, and that this love had become even stronger and purer in the face of despair.

Scarcely had the still-unfathomed mystery of death unfolded before his eyes when there materialized another equally unfathomable mystery which was a call to love and life.

The doctor confirmed his hypothesis with regards to Kitty. Her ill-health was pregnancy.

21

FROM the moment Alexey Alexandrovich grasped from his discussions with Betsy and Stepan Arkadyich that all that was required of him was that he should leave his wife in peace and not trouble her with his presence, and that his wife desired this herself, he felt so lost he could not decide anything himself, nor did he himself know what he wanted now, and putting himself in the hands of those who took such pleasure in taking care of his affairs, he gave his consent to everything. It was only when Anna had already left his house and the English governess sent to ask him whether she should dine with him or separately that he grasped his position clearly for the first time, and was appalled by it.

What was most difficult about this position was the fact that he simply could not connect and reconcile his past with what was going on now. It was not the past when he had lived happily with his wife that troubled him. He had already experienced the agonizing transition from that past to knowledge of his wife's infidelity; that state had been painful, but comprehensible to him. If his wife had left him after confessing her infidelity back then, he would have been devastated and unhappy, but he would not have been in the hopeless and incomprehensible position he felt himself to be in now. He simply could not reconcile his recent forgiveness, his tenderness, and his love for his sick wife and another man's child with what was going on now, that is, with the fact that, as if in recompense for all of this, he now found himself alone, pilloried, ridiculed, not needed by anyone and despised by everyone.

For the first two days after his wife's departure Alexey Alexandrovich received petitioners and his private secretary, attended committee meetings, and went to have dinner in the dining room as usual. Without accounting to himself why he was doing so, he strained every nerve of his being during those two days just to maintain a calm and even indifferent air. When answering questions as to what should be done with Anna Arkadyevna's rooms and belongings, he made a supreme effort to give the impression of a man for whom what had happened had not been unforeseen and was in no way out of the ordinary, and he achieved his aim: no one could have detected in him any signs of despair. But on the third day after her departure, when Korney gave him a bill from a milliner's shop which Anna had forgotten to pay, and announced that the shopkeeper himself had come in person, Alexey Alexandrovich instructed him to be shown in.

'Excuse me, Your Excellency, for taking the liberty of troubling you. But if you wish us to approach Her Excellency, then please be so kind as to provide her address.'

Alexey Alexandrovich seemed to the shopkeeper to be deliberating, and then all of a sudden he turned round and sat down at his desk. Letting his head sink into his hands, he sat in this position for a long time, making several attempts to speak and coming to a halt each time.

Understanding what his master was feeling, Korney asked the shopkeeper to call another time. Left alone again, Alexey Alexandrovich realized he did not have the strength to maintain the pretence of calmness and resolve. He dismissed the carriage that was waiting for him, gave instructions that he would receive no one, and did not emerge for dinner.

He sensed he would not be capable of enduring the full brunt of the contempt and vitriol he had clearly seen on the faces of both the shopkeeper and Korney, indeed every person without exception whom he had encountered during those two days. He felt he could not repulse people's hatred of him, because this hatred did not come from his being bad (he could then have tried to be better), but from his being shamefully and repulsively unhappy. He felt that because of this, precisely because his heart was torn to shreds, they would be merciless to him. He felt that people would destroy him as dogs savage an injured dog, howling in pain. Hiding his wounds from people was his only way of escaping from them, and he had unconsciously tried to do that for two days, but now he no longer felt capable of prolonging this unequal battle.

His despair was increased still further by the awareness that he was completely alone in his grief. It was not just that he did not have a single person in all of Petersburg to whom he could talk about everything he was going through, who might pity him, not as a senior official, or as a member of society, but simply as a suffering human being; he did not have such a person anywhere.

Alexey Alexandrovich had grown up as an orphan. There were two brothers. They did not remember their father, and their mother had died when Alexey Alexandrovich was ten years old. They had small means. Their uncle Karenin, a prominent official and one-time favourite of the late Tsar, had brought them up.

After finishing high school and university with medals, Alexey
Alexandrovich had, with his uncle's help, embarked straight away on
a prominent civil-service career, and since then he had exclusively
dedicated himself to professional ambition. Neither at school nor at
university, nor subsequently at work, had Alexey Alexandrovich struck
up friendly relations with anyone. His brother had been the closest
person to him, but he worked for the Ministry of Foreign Affairs,
and had always lived abroad, where he had died shortly after Alexey
Alexandrovich's marriage.

During his term as a provincial governor, Anna's aunt, a wealthy
provincial lady, had acquainted the no-longer-youthful but still young
governor with her niece, and placed him in such a position that he was
obliged either to declare himself or leave town. Alexey Alexandrovich
had vacillated for a long time. There were then as many reasons for this
step as against it, and there was no single, decisive argument which
would have impelled him to alter his general rule of abstaining when
in doubt;* but Anna's aunt intimated to him through an acquaintance
that he had already compromised the girl, and that he was honour-
bound to propose. He did propose, and lavished on his betrothed and
on his wife all the feeling he could muster.

His attachment to Anna eliminated in his heart any remaining need
for affectionate relations with other people. And now, amongst all his
acquaintances, there was not one person to whom he was close. He
had many so-called contacts, but there were no friendships. Alexey
Alexandrovich knew many people whom he could invite to dinner,
ask to become involved in a matter which interested him or to give
preferential treatment to one or another petitioner, and with whom he
could openly discuss the actions of other people and senior government;
but his relations with these people were confined to one area clearly
defined by custom and habit, beyond which it was impossible to move.
There was one university comrade with whom he had later become
friendly, and with whom he could have spoken about the misfortune
which had befallen him; but this comrade was Head of Education in
a remote region. Of the people in Petersburg, the closest to him and
the most likely candidates were his private secretary and his doctor.

Mikhail Vasilievich Slyudin, the private secretary, was an intelligent,
kind, and decent man, and Alexey Alexandrovich could feel that he
was well disposed towards him; but their five-year professional relationship had placed a barrier between them where heart-to-heart talks
were concerned.

After signing papers, Alexey Alexandrovich fell into a long silence during which he repeatedly glanced at Mikhail Vasilievich and several times endeavoured, but failed, to start speaking. He had prepared a phrase: 'You've heard of my misfortune?' But he ended by saying the customary: 'If you'll get this ready for me then,' and with that dismissed him.

The other person was the doctor, who was also well disposed towards him; but there had long been a tacit understanding between them that they were both overwhelmed with work and had no time to spare.

To his women friends, chief amongst them the Countess Lydia Ivanovna, Alexey Alexandrovich gave no thought. All women, simply as women, frightened and repelled him.

22

ALEXEY ALEXANDROVICH had forgotten about Countess Lydia Ivanovna, but she had not forgotten him. At this most painful moment of his solitary despair she had come to his house and walked into his study without being announced. She found him in the position in which he was still sitting, with his head in his hands.

'*J'ai forcé la consigne*,'[1] she said, coming in with rapid steps and breathing heavily from agitation and rapid movement. 'I have heard everything! Alexey Alexandrovich! Dear friend!' she continued, firmly clasping his hand in both of hers and fixing her beautiful, wistful eyes on his.

Frowning, Alexey Alexandrovich got up, and after disengaging his hand, he proffered her a chair.

'Won't you sit down, Countess? I'm not receiving anyone because I'm unwell, Countess,' he said, and his lips started to tremble.

'Dear friend!' repeated Countess Lydia Ivanovna without taking her eyes off him, and suddenly the inner edges of her eyebrows rose, forming a triangle on her forehead; her unattractive, sallow face became even more unattractive, but Alexey Alexandrovich sensed she felt sorry for him and was on the verge of tears. And he too was overcome with emotion: he grasped her plump hand and began kissing it.

'Dear friend!' she said in a voice breaking with emotion. 'You must not succumb to grief. Your sorrow is great, but you must find consolation.'

'I am broken, I am crushed, I am no longer a man!' said Alexey

[1] 'I've forced my way in.'

Alexandrovich, letting go of her hand, but continuing to look into her tear-filled eyes. 'What is awful about my position is that I cannot find any firm ground anywhere, or within myself.'

'You will find firm ground; do not look for it in me, although I beseech you to believe in my friendship,' she said with a sigh. 'Our firm ground is love, that love which He bequeathed us. His burden is an easy one,' she said with the ecstatic look which Alexey Alexandrovich knew so well. 'He will help you and give you sustenance.'

Despite these words, manifesting both the emotion wrought by her lofty feelings and the ecstatic new mystical fervour that had lately been spreading throughout Petersburg,* which Alexey Alexandrovich found excessive, he was pleased to hear them now.

'I am weak. I am destroyed. I did not foresee anything, and now I don't understand anything.'

'My friend,' repeated Lydia Ivanovna.

'It's not the loss of what no longer exists, it's not that,' Alexey Alexandrovich continued. 'I do not lament that. But I cannot help feeling humiliated in front of people because of the position I am in. It is bad, but I can't help it, I just can't.'

'It was not you who performed that noble act of forgiveness which I and everyone else marvelled at, but He who dwells within your heart,' said Countess Lydia Ivanovna, looking up ecstatically, 'and for that reason you cannot be ashamed of what you did.'

Alexey Alexandrovich frowned, flexed his hands, and started cracking his fingers.

'One has to know all the details,' he said in a high-pitched voice. 'There is a limit to a person's strength, Countess, and I have reached the limits of mine. I have had to spend the whole day today making arrangements, domestic arrangements, arising'—he emphasized the word *arising*—'from my new, solitary situation. The servants, the governess, bills . . . I have been consumed by these petty flames, and did not have the strength to endure. At dinner . . . I almost had to leave the table yesterday. I could not bear the way my son looked at me. He did not ask me the meaning of all this, but he wanted to ask, and I could not bear the look in his eyes. He was afraid to look at me, but that is not all . . .'

Alexey Alexandrovich was about to mention the bill that had been brought to him, but his voice started shaking and he stopped. He could not think about that bill on blue paper for a hat and ribbons without feeling sorry for himself.

'I understand, my friend,' said Lydia Ivanovna. 'I understand everything. You will not find help and comfort in me, but I have come to see you with the sole aim of helping you if I can. If I could only relieve you of these humiliating petty worries . . . I understand that a woman's word and a woman's authority is needed. Will you entrust this to me?'

Alexey Alexandrovich pressed her hand silently and gratefully.

'We will take care of Seryozha together. Practical affairs are not my strong suit. But I will take this on and be your housekeeper. Don't thank me. I'm not doing it myself . . .'

'I can't help thanking you.'

'But, my friend, do not give in to that feeling of which you were speaking—do not be ashamed of what is for a Christian the loftiest pinnacle: *he that humbleth himself shall be exalted.* And you cannot thank me. You must thank Him, and pray to Him for help. In Him alone we will find peace, comfort, salvation, and love,' she said and, turning her eyes towards heaven, she began to pray, as Alexey Alexandrovich gathered from her silence.

Alexey Alexandrovich listened to her now, and those expressions which he had previously found if not exactly distasteful, then certainly excessive, now seemed natural and comforting. Alexey Alexandrovich did not like this new ecstatic fervour. He was a believer interested in religion primarily in the political sense, while the new teaching, which permitted certain new interpretations, was abhorrent to him on principle, precisely because it opened the door to argument and analysis. He had previously maintained a cold and even hostile attitude to this new teaching, and had never argued with Countess Lydia Ivanovna, who was an enthusiastic adherent, but had studiously evaded her challenges with silence. Now for the first time, however, he enjoyed listening to what she was saying and did not mentally object.

'I am very, very grateful to you, both for your deeds and for your words,' he said, when she had finished praying.

Countess Lydia Ivanovna pressed both her friend's hands once more.

'Now I will set to work,' she said with a smile after a moment's silence, wiping away the traces of tears. 'I will go to Seryozha. I will turn to you only if it's really necessary.' And she got up and went out.

Countess Lydia Ivanovna went off to Seryozha's part of the house, and there, spilling tears on to the frightened boy's cheeks, she told him that his father was a saint and that his mother had died.

Countess Lydia Ivanovna kept her promise. She really did take upon herself all the cares of the organization and the running of Alexey

Alexandrovich's household. But she had not exaggerated when she said that practical matters were not her strong suit. All her instructions had to be changed, because they were impossible to carry out, and they were changed by Korney, Alexey Alexandrovich's valet, who unbeknownst to everybody had now taken charge of Karenin's entire household, and would quietly and prudently inform his master what he needed to know while he was dressing. But Lydia Ivanovna's help was nevertheless highly effective: she gave Alexey Alexandrovich moral support through the perception of her affection and respect for him, and particularly, as it comforted her to believe, by nearly converting him to Christianity, that is, converting him from an indifferent and apathetic believer into an ardent and steadfast adherent of the new interpretation of Christian teaching which had lately been spreading through Petersburg. It was easy for Alexey Alexandrovich to be won over. Like Lydia Ivanovna and others who shared their views, Alexey Alexandrovich was completely lacking in any depth of imagination, that spiritual capacity by which ideas engendered by the imagination become so real that they have to be brought into line with other ideas and with reality. He saw nothing impossible and incongruous in the idea that death, which existed for non-believers, did not exist for him, and that, since he had complete faith, the measure of which he himself was the judge, there was no longer any sin in his soul, and he was already experiencing complete salvation here on earth.

It is true that Alexey Alexandrovich vaguely sensed that this idea of his faith was shallow and erroneous, and he knew that when he surrendered to the direct feeling of forgiveness without thinking at all about it being effected by a higher power, he felt a greater happiness than when he was thinking every minute, as he was now, that Christ resided in his heart, and that he was doing His will when he signed documents; but it was crucial for Alexey Alexandrovich to think this, indeed it was so crucial for him in his humiliation to have this lofty height, however contrived, from which he, despised by everyone, could despise others, that he clung to his illusory salvation as if it was true salvation.

23

COUNTESS LYDIA IVANOVNA had been married off when she was a very young and ecstatic girl to a rich, aristocratic, extremely kind, and extremely dissipated *bon-viveur*. In the second month of the marriage her husband had abandoned her, responding to her ecstatic assurances of affection with a constant stream of sarcasm and even hostility, which people who knew the Count's good heart and saw no flaws in the ecstatic Lydia were quite unable to fathom. Since then they had lived apart, although they were not divorced, and whenever husband and wife happened to meet, he would always treat her with an unwavering vicious sarcasm, the cause of which was impossible to understand.

Countess Lydia Ivanovna had long ago ceased to be in love with her husband, but from that time on she had never ceased to be in love with someone. She would be in love with several people at once, with both men and women; she would be in love with almost every single person who had achieved particular distinction in something. She was in love with all the new princes and princesses who married into the Imperial family, she was in love with a Metropolitan, a bishop, and a priest. She was in love with a journalist, three Slavs, and Komisarov;* with a government minister, a doctor, an English missionary, and Karenin. Whether waxing or waning, all these passions filled her heart, gave her something to do, and did not prevent her from conducting the most diverse and complex relationships at court and in society. But ever since she had taken Karenin under her special protection following the misfortune which had befallen him, and ever since she had started work in the Karenin household and concerned herself with his welfare, she had felt that all the other passions were not real, and that she was truly in love only with Karenin. The feelings she now experienced for him seemed to her to be stronger than any of her previous feelings. Analysing her feelings, and comparing them with previous ones, she saw clearly that she would not have been in love with Komisarov if he had not saved the life of the Tsar, and would not have been in love with Ristich-Kudzhitsky* if there had been no Slav question, but Karenin she loved for himself, for his noble, misunderstood soul, for his high-pitched voice with its drawn-out cadences, which she found endearing, for his tired demeanour, his character, and his soft white hands with their swollen veins. She was not only happy to see him, but would search his face for signs of the impression she was making on him. She wanted him to find her whole person attractive, not just her words. On his account she now took greater care with her appearance than ever before. She caught herself dreaming about what might have been if she had not been married and he had been free. She blushed with excitement whenever he came into the room, and she could not repress a smile of delight whenever he said something nice to her.

Countess Lydia Ivanovna had been in a state of extreme agitation for several days now. She had found out that Anna and Vronsky were in Petersburg. Alexey Alexandrovich had to be saved from seeing her, he had to be saved even from the painful knowledge that this dreadful woman was in the same city, and that he might meet her at any moment.

Through her acquaintances Lydia Ivanovna was able to establish what those *vile people*, as she called Anna and Vronsky, intended to do, and she tried to direct all her friend's movements during those days so that he would not meet them. The young aide-de-camp from whom she had received her information, a friend of Vronsky's who was hoping to obtain a concession through Countess Lydia Ivanovna, told her that they had finished their business and were leaving the next day. Lydia Ivanovna had already begun to calm down when, the very next morning, she was brought a note whose handwriting she was horrified to recognize. The handwriting was Anna Karenina's. The envelope was as thick as bark; there was a huge monogram on the rectangular yellow paper, and the letter exuded a delightful fragrance.

'Who brought this?'

'A commissionaire from the hotel.'

It was a long time before Countess Lydia Ivanovna was able to sit down and read the letter. Her agitation brought on an attack of shortness of breath, which she suffered from. When she had calmed down, she read the following letter written in French:

'Madame la Comtesse,

The Christian feelings which fill your heart give me what I feel to be the unpardonable temerity of writing to you. I am unhappy about being separated from my son. I beg you to allow me to see him once before my departure. Forgive me for reminding you of myself. I'm addressing myself to you and not to Alexey Alexandrovich, simply because I do not wish to inflict suffering on that magnanimous man by having him remember me. Knowing your friendship for him, you are bound to understand me. Will you send Seryozha to me, or should I come to the house at some appointed time, or will you let me know when and where I might see him away from home? I do not anticipate a refusal, knowing the magnanimity of the person on whom this depends. You cannot imagine the longing I have to see him, and therefore you cannot imagine the gratitude that your help will inspire in me.

                                                              Anna.'

Everything in this letter annoyed Countess Lydia Ivanovna: its contents, the allusion to magnanimity, and especially what she perceived to be its overly familiar tone.

'Say there will be no answer,' said Countess Lydia Ivanovna, immediately opening her blotter to write to Alexey Alexandrovich that she hoped to see him some time after twelve at the Birthday Reception at the Palace.

'I need to discuss an important and sad matter with you,' she wrote. 'We can arrange where to meet when we are there. It would be best at my house, where I will order tea to be served the way you like it. It is essential. He gives us the burden of the cross. He also gives us the strength to bear it,' she added, so as to prepare him a little.

Countess Lydia Ivanovna usually wrote two or three notes a day to Alexey Alexandrovich. She loved this means of communication, since it had an elegance and mystery that her personal interactions with him lacked.

24

THE reception was coming to an end. As people met each other on their way out, they chatted about the latest news, the honours that had been newly awarded, and transfers for senior officials.

'Imagine the Countess Marya Borisovna as Minister of War and Princess Vatkovskaya as Chief-of-Staff,' said a little old man with grey hair in a gold-embroidered uniform addressing a tall, beautiful Lady-in-Waiting who had asked him about the transfers.

'And me as aide-de-camp,' said the Lady-in-Waiting with a smile.

'You already have an appointment. In the Ecclesiastical Department. With Karenin as your assistant.'

'Good afternoon, Prince!' said the little old man, shaking the hand of the person who had approached.

'What were you saying about Karenin?' said the Prince.

'He and Putyatov have received the Order of Alexander Nevsky.'*

'I thought he had it already.'

'No. Just look at him,' said the little old man, gesturing with his embroidered hat to Karenin, who was dressed in court uniform with the new red sash across his shoulder and standing next to an influential member of the State Council in the doorway of the hall. 'As pleased and as proud as a copper farthing,' he added, stopping to shake hands with a handsome, athletically built chamberlain.

'No, he has aged,' said the chamberlain.

'From stress. He's always drafting projects these days. He won't let that poor devil go now until he has explained everything point by point.'

'What do you mean, he has aged? *Il fait des passions.*[1] I think Countess Lydia Ivanovna is jealous of his wife now.'

'Oh, come now! Please don't say anything bad about Countess Lydia Ivanovna.'

'But what is bad about her being in love with Karenin?'

'Is it true that Madame Karenina's here?'

'She isn't here in the Palace, but she's in Petersburg. I met her yesterday with Alexey Vronsky, *bras dessus, bras dessous,*[2] on Morskaya.'

'*C'est un homme qui n'a pas . . .*'[3] the chamberlain began saying, but stopped to make way and bow as a member of the Imperial family walked past.

So people went on talking incessantly about Alexey Alexandrovich, castigating him and laughing at him, while he was setting out his financial project point by point to the member of the Imperial Council he had buttonholed, not pausing his exposition for an instant so as not to let him out of his grasp.

Almost at the same time that Alexey Alexandrovich's wife left him, he also suffered the bitterest moment possible in the life of an official—his professional career stopped advancing. That it had stopped advancing was an accomplished fact, and everyone saw this clearly, but Alexey Alexandrovich himself did not realize his career was over. Whether it was his clash with Stremov, or the misfortune with his wife, or simply that Alexey Alexandrovich had reached his predestined limit, it had become apparent to everyone that year that his professional career was at an end. He still occupied an important post, he was a member of many commissions and committees, but he was a spent force, and nothing more was expected of him. Regardless of what he said, regardless of what he proposed, people listened to him as though what he was proposing had long been known about and was exactly what was not needed.

But Alexey Alexandrovich did not sense this and, on the contrary, by being excluded from direct participation in the activities of the government, he could now see more clearly than before the defects and errors in the activities of others, and considered it his duty to point out ways of rectifying them. Shortly after separating from his wife he began writing a memorandum about the new legal procedures, the first of an innumerable number of pointless memoranda he was destined to write about all branches of the administration.

Alexey Alexandrovich not only failed to notice his hopeless position

---

[1] 'People fall in love with him.'

[2] 'arm in arm.'   [3] 'That's a man who has not . . .'

in the civil service, and not only failed to be discouraged by it, but was more pleased with his activities than ever before.

'He who is married cares for the things of the world, how he may please his wife, but he who is unmarried cares for the things that belong to the Lord, how to please the Lord,'* says the Apostle Paul, and Alexey Alexandrovich, who was now guided in all he did by the Scriptures, often recalled this passage. It seemed to him that ever since he had been left without a wife, he had been serving the Lord better than before with these very projects of his.

The obvious impatience of the Member of Council who wanted to get away from him did not perturb Alexey Alexandrovich; he stopped expatiating only when the councillor profited from a member of the Imperial family walking past to slip away.

Left alone, Alexey Alexandrovich bowed his head while he gathered his thoughts, then looked about absent-mindedly and headed towards the door, where he hoped to meet Countess Lydia Ivanovna.

'And how strong they all are, and physically healthy,' thought Alexey Alexandrovich, looking at a sturdy chamberlain with his combed and perfumed whiskers, and the red neck, wedged into its uniform, of a prince, whom he had to walk past. 'Truly is it said that everything in the world is evil,' he thought as he cast another sidelong glance at the chamberlain's calves.

Shifting his feet slowly, Alexey Alexandrovich bowed with his customary air of weariness and dignity to these gentlemen who had been talking about him, then looked towards the door, his eyes searching for Countess Lydia Ivanovna.

'Ah! Alexey Alexandrovich!' said the little old man with a malicious glint in his eye, just as Karenin drew level and nodded coldly to them. 'I haven't congratulated you yet,' he said, pointing to his newly received ribbon.

'Thank you,' Alexey Alexandrovich replied. 'What a *lovely* day this is,' he added, placing particular emphasis on the word 'lovely', as was his habit.

That they were laughing at him he was well aware, but then he did not expect anything but hostility from them; he was already used to it.

Catching sight of Lydia Ivanovna's sallow shoulders surging from her bodice, and her beautiful, wistful eyes beckoning him to her as she went out the door, Alexey Alexandrovich smiled, revealing his impeccably white teeth, and he went over to her.

Lydia Ivanovna's outfit had cost her a great deal of trouble, as indeed had all her outfits of late. Her goal in dressing was now quite the reverse of the one she had pursued thirty years earlier. Then her desire had been to adorn herself in some way, and the more adornments the better. Now, on the contrary, she was obliged to deck herself out in a way that was so inconsistent with her age and her figure that her one concern was that the contrast between these adornments and her appearance should not be too shocking. And as far as Alexey Alexandrovich was concerned, she succeeded and seemed attractive to him. For him, she was the solitary island, not only of goodwill but of love, in the sea of hostility and mockery which surrounded him.

As he ran the gauntlet of mocking glances, he was as naturally drawn to her enamoured look as a plant is drawn to the light.

'Congratulations,' she said to him as she eyed his ribbon.

Suppressing a smile of pleasure, he closed his eyes and shrugged his shoulders, as if to say that it could not make him happy. Countess Lydia Ivanovna was well aware that it was one of his main sources of happiness, although he would never admit it.

'How is our angel?' said Countess Lydia Ivanovna, meaning Seryozha.

'I cannot say that I am wholly satisfied with him,' said Alexey Alexandrovich, raising his eyebrows and opening his eyes. 'And Sitnikov is not satisfied with him either.' (Sitnikov was the tutor to whom Seryozha's secular education had been entrusted.) 'As I have told you, there's a sort of coldness in him when it comes to those fundamental questions which ought to touch the heart of every man and every child,' Alexey Alexandrovich said, as he began expounding his ideas on the one subject which interested him apart from his job—the education of his son.

When Alexey Alexandrovich had returned to life and work again with the help of Lydia Ivanovna, he felt it was his duty to concern himself with the education of the son left on his hands. Having never before concerned himself with questions of education, Alexey Alexandrovich devoted some time to a theoretical study of the subject. And after reading many books on anthropology, education, and pedagogy, Alexey Alexandrovich drew up an educational plan, engaged the best tutor in Petersburg to implement it, and got down to business. And this business constantly occupied him.

'Yes, but what about his heart? I see in him his father's heart, and no child with a heart like that can be bad,' said Lydia Ivanovna rapturously.

'Yes, perhaps . . . As far as I am concerned, I am doing my duty. It is all I can do.'

'Come to my house,' said Countess Lydia Ivanovna after a pause; 'we must address something you will find painful. I would give anything to spare you certain memories, but others think differently. I have received a letter from *her*. *She* is here, in Petersburg.'

Alexey Alexandrovich shuddered at the mention of his wife, but his expression immediately assumed that deathly rigidity which expressed utter impotence in this matter.

'I was expecting this,' he said.

Countess Lydia Ivanovna looked at him ecstatically, and tears of rapt admiration at the greatness of his soul sprang into her eyes.

25

WHEN Alexey Alexandrovich entered Countess Lydia Ivanovna's cosy little study, which was chock-full of old china and hung with portraits, the hostess herself had not yet appeared. She was changing.

The round table was covered with a cloth, and on it stood a Chinese tea-service, a silver tea-kettle, and a spirit lamp. Alexey Alexandrovich cast an absent-minded eye over the innumerable familiar portraits that decorated the study, and after sitting down at the table, opened the New Testament which was lying on it. The rustle of the Countess's silk dress distracted him.

'Well, now we can sit quietly,' said Countess Lydia Ivanovna with an anxious smile as she hastened to squeeze herself in between the table and the sofa, 'and talk while we are drinking our tea.'

After a few words of preparation, Countess Lydia Ivanovna, flushed and breathing heavily, placed into Alexey Alexandrovich's hands the letter she had received.

After reading the letter, he was silent for a long while.

'I don't suppose I have the right to refuse her,' he said timidly, raising his eyes.

'You never see evil in anyone, my friend!'

'On the contrary, I see that everything is evil. But would this be fair? . . .'

His face expressed indecision and a search for advice, support, and guidance in a matter he did not understand.

'No,' interrupted Countess Lydia Ivanovna. 'There are limits to everything. I can understand immorality,' she said, not altogether truthfully, since she never could understand what led women to immorality, 'but I don't understand cruelty, and to whom after all? To you! How can she stay in the city where you are? No, the longer one lives, the more one learns. And I'm learning to understand your nobility of spirit and her iniquity.'

'But who will cast a stone?' said Alexey Alexandrovich, clearly pleased with his allotted role. 'I have forgiven everything, so I cannot deprive her of what is a requirement of love for her—love for her son . . .'

'But is that love, my friend? Is it sincere? Supposing you have forgiven, that you do forgive . . . But do we have the right to affect the feelings of that angel? He thinks she is dead. He prays for her and asks God to forgive her sins . . . And it is better that way. Otherwise, what is he going to think?'

'I had not thought of that,' said Alexey Alexandrovich, evidently agreeing.

Countess Lydia Ivanovna hid her face in her hands and fell silent. She was praying.

'If you ask my advice,' she said, uncovering her face after she had finished praying, 'then I do not advise you to do this. Do you think I cannot see how you are suffering, how this has opened up all your wounds? But supposing you do not think about yourself, as usual. What can it lead to? To fresh suffering for you, and torture for the child? If there is a trace of humanity left in her, she herself would not wish this. No, I have no hesitation in advising against it, and if you give me permission, I will write to her.'

Alexey Alexandrovich agreed, and Countess Lydia Ivanovna wrote the following letter in French:

'Dear Madam,

Reminding your son about you might lead to questions on his part which cannot be answered without instilling in the child's heart a spirit of condemnation of what for him should be sacred, and I therefore beg you to understand your husband's refusal in the spirit of Christian love. I pray that Almighty God might have mercy upon you.

Countess Lydia'

This letter achieved that covert aim which Countess Lydia Ivanovna had been hiding even from herself. It wounded Anna to the depths of her soul.

After returning home from Lydia Ivanovna's, Alexey Alexandrovich was for his part unable that day to devote himself to his usual pursuits and find the spiritual serenity of the believer who has found salvation, which he had experienced before.

The reminder of his wife, who was guilty of so much before him, and before whom he had been so saintly, as Countess Lydia Ivanovna rightly told him, ought not to have troubled him; but he was not at ease: he could not understand the book he was reading, could not drive away the tortuous memories of his relations with her, and the mistakes which he now felt he had made with regard to her. The memory of how he had received her confession of infidelity as they returned from the races (particularly the fact that he had only required her to maintain outward appearances, but had not challenged Vronsky to a duel) tortured him as if with remorse. He was also tortured by the memory of the letter he had written her; in particular, his forgiveness, which no one wanted, and his care for another man's child made his heart burn with shame and remorse.

And it was exactly the same feeling of shame and remorse that he was experiencing now, as he went over all his past life with her and recalled the clumsy words with which, after long hesitation, he had proposed to her.

'But what am I guilty of?' he kept asking himself. And this question always prompted another question—about whether those other people, those Vronskys and Oblonskys . . . those chamberlains with fat calves, felt differently, loved differently, married differently. And he imagined a whole row of those vibrant, strong, self-confident men, who instinctively aroused his curiosity always and everywhere. He tried to dispel these thoughts, he tried to persuade himself that he was not living for this temporal, transient life but for life eternal, and that there was peace and love in his soul. But the fact that he believed he had made a few trivial errors in this transient, trivial life tormented him as though the eternal salvation in which he believed did not exist. But this temptation did not last long, and soon Alexey Alexandrovich's soul was again filled with the serenity and loftiness which enabled him to forget what he did not want to remember.

26

'WELL, Kapitonich?' said Seryozha, returning from his walk on the eve of his birthday red-cheeked and in high spirits, and handing his pleated coat to the tall, elderly doorman smiling down at the little person from his great height. 'Did the bandaged official come today? Did Papa see him?'

'He did. The minute the secretary came out, I announced him,' said the doorman with a cheery wink. 'Here, let me take that off.'

'Seryozha!' said his Slav tutor,* who had stopped in the doorway leading into the rooms of the house. 'Take it off yourself.'

Seryozha heard his tutor's frail voice, but did not pay him any attention. He was standing hanging on to the doorman's shoulder-strap, looking up into his face.

'So, and did Papa do what he needed him to do?'

The doorman nodded his head affirmatively.

Both Seryozha and the doorman were interested in the bandaged official, who had already called seven times to ask Alexey Alexandrovich about something. Seryozha had come across him in the entrance hall one day, and heard him pleading with the doorman to announce him, saying that he and his children were at death's door.

Since then, having met the official a second time in the entrance hall, Seryozha had taken an interest in him.

'So was he very pleased?' he asked.

'I should say so! He was almost jumping for joy when he left.'

'And has anyone brought anything?' asked Seryozha after a pause.

'Well, sir,' said the doorman in a whisper, shaking his head, 'there is something from the Countess.'

Seryozha immediately realized that the doorman was talking about a birthday present from Countess Lydia Ivanovna.

'Really? Where is it?'

'Korney took it to your Papa. It must be something nice!'

'How big is it? Like this?'

'Smaller, but very nice.'

'A book?'

'No, it's a thing. Run along, run along now, Vasily Lukich is calling you,' said the doorman as he heard the tutor's approaching footsteps and, carefully disengaging the little hand in the half-pulled-off glove which was holding on to his shoulder-strap, and winking, he indicated Vunic with his head.

'Vasily Lukich, just a minute!' answered Seryozha with that cheery and affectionate smile which always managed to win the industrious Vasily Lukich over.

Seryozha was in too high spirits, and having too happy a time, not to share with his friend the doorman another piece of family good fortune which he had heard about from Lydia Ivanovna's niece during his walk in the Summer Garden. This piece of good fortune seemed to him particularly important, since it coincided with the bandaged official's good fortune and his own good fortune that some toys had arrived for him. Seryozha felt this was a day when everyone should be happy and in good spirits.

'Did you know that Papa has received the Order of St Alexander Nevsky?'

'Of course! People have already come to congratulate him.'

'So, is he pleased?'

'How could you not be pleased at the Tsar's favour! It means he's deserved it,' said the doorman sternly and seriously.

Seryozha became pensive as he perused the face of the doorman that he had studied in minute detail, especially the chin hanging down between grey whiskers, which no one had seen except Seryozha, who only ever looked up at him from below.

'Well, and has your daughter been to see you lately?'

The doorman's daughter was a ballet dancer.

'When does she have time to come on a weekday? They have to study too. And you have to study, sir, so run along now.'

Instead of sitting down to his lessons when he came into the room, Seryozha told his tutor his theory that the parcel that had been delivered had to be a locomotive. 'What do you think?' he asked.

But Vasily Lukich was only thinking about their needing to prepare the grammar lesson for the teacher who was coming at two o'clock.

'But can you just tell me, Vasily Lukich,' he suddenly asked when he was already sitting at his desk holding a book, 'what is greater than the Alexander Nevsky? Did you know Papa's received the Alexander Nevsky?'

Vasily Lukich replied that the Order of St Vladimir was greater than the Alexander Nevsky.

'And what's higher than that?'

'The Order of St Andrew the First-Called is highest of all.'*

'And higher than the St Andrew?'

'I don't know.'

'What, even you don't know?' And propping himself up on his elbows, Seryozha became lost in thought.

His musings were of the most complex and varied kind. He imagined his father suddenly receiving the St Vladimir and the St Andrew, and how much nicer he would be at his lesson that day as a result, and how when he was grown up he would himself receive all the orders, and how they would invent one even higher than the St Andrew. As soon as they invented it, he would be awarded it. Then they would invent an even higher one, and he would immediately be awarded that.

In such musings the time went by, and when the teacher arrived, the lesson about adverbs of time and place and manner of action had not been prepared, so the teacher was not only displeased, but upset. Seryozha was touched that his teacher should be upset. He did not feel he was to blame for not having learned the lesson; however hard

he tried, he was just incapable of doing it: as long as his teacher was
explaining things to him he believed him and sort of understood,
but as soon as he was left on his own he was completely incapable of
remembering and understanding that such a short and familiar word
as 'suddenly' was an *adverb of manner of action*. All the same, he was
sorry he had upset his teacher and wanted to console him.

He chose a moment when the teacher was staring silently at the book.

'Mikhail Ivanich, when is your name-day?' he asked suddenly.

'You'd do better to think about your work, because a name-day
should not hold any importance for a rational being. It is a day just like
any other, when one has to work.'

Seryozha looked intently at his teacher, at his wispy beard, and at
his spectacles, which had slipped below the ridge on his nose, and he
became so lost in daydreams that he did not hear anything the teacher
was explaining to him. He realized that the teacher was not thinking
about what he was saying, he could feel that from the tone in which the
words were spoken. 'But why have they all plotted to say everything the
same way, and always the most boring and useless things? Why does he
push me away, why doesn't he like me?' he wondered sadly, unable to
think of an answer.

27

AFTER the lesson with the teacher came one with his father. Before his
father arrived, Seryozha sat down at his desk, playing with a penknife,
and started thinking. Amongst Seryozha's favourite occupations was
looking for his mother during his walks. He generally did not believe
in death, and in her death in particular, despite what Lydia Ivanovna
had told him and his father confirmed, and so even after they had
told him she was dead, he would look for her during his walks. Every
plump, graceful woman with dark hair was his mother. Whenever he
saw a woman of that description, a feeling of such tenderness arose in
his soul that he became choked up and tears came into his eyes. And he
would expect her to come up to him any minute and lift her veil. Her
whole face would be visible, she would smile, hug him, he would catch
her fragrance, feel the softness of her arms, and burst into tears with
happiness, just as when he had lain at her feet one evening and she had
tickled him, and he had laughed and bit her white hand with the rings.
When he then found out by chance from his nanny that his mother
had not died, and that his father and Lydia Ivanovna had explained

to him that she was dead because she was bad (which he could not possibly believe, because he loved her), he carried on looking and waiting for her. In the Summer Gardens that day there had been a lady in a mauve veil whom he had watched with bated breath, expecting it to be her, as she walked towards them on the path. The lady had not come up to them and had disappeared somewhere. That day Seryozha felt a stronger rush of love for her than ever before, and now, lost in thought as he waited for his father, he cut all around the edge of the desk with his penknife while staring straight ahead with shining eyes, thinking about her.

'Papa is coming!' said Vasily Lukich, rousing him.

Seryozha jumped up, went over to his father, kissed his hand, and carefully scrutinized him, looking for signs of joy at receiving the Alexander Nevsky.

'Did you have a good walk?' said Alexey Alexandrovich as he sat down in his armchair, drew the Old Testament towards him, and opened it. Although Alexey Alexandrovich repeatedly told Seryozha that every Christian ought to have a thorough knowledge of biblical history, he himself often had to consult the Bible about the Old Testament, and Seryozha had noticed this.

'Yes, Papa, it was very enjoyable,' said Seryozha, sitting sideways on his chair and rocking it, which was forbidden. 'I saw Nadenka' (Nadenka was Lydia Ivanovna's niece, and was being brought up by her). 'She told me you'd been given a new star. Are you pleased, Papa?'

'First of all, do not rock your chair, please,' said Alexey Alexandrovich. 'And secondly, it's not the reward but the work which is of value. And I would like you to understand that. You see, if you are going to work or study in order to receive a reward, then you will find the work difficult; but if you love what you are doing when you work'—Alexey Alexandrovich was remembering as he spoke how he had sustained himself with a sense of duty during the tedious work that morning, which consisted of signing one hundred and eighteen documents—'you will find your own reward in it.'

The affectionate and lively sparkle in Seryozha's eyes faded and went out under his father's gaze. It was the same, long-familiar tone his father always adopted with him and which Seryozha had already learned to imitate. His father always spoke to him—so Seryozha felt—as though he were addressing some imaginary boy such as one finds in books, who was utterly unlike Seryozha. And Seryozha always pretended to be that boy out of a book when he was with his father.

'You understand that, I hope?' said his father.

'Yes, Papa,' answered Seryozha, pretending to be the imaginary boy.

The lesson consisted of learning some verses from the Gospel by heart and repeating the beginning of the Old Testament. Seryozha knew the verses from the Gospel fairly well, but while he was saying them he became so transfixed with how sharply the bone of his father's forehead bent at his temples that he lost his train of thought and muddled the end of one verse with the beginning of another one which had the same word in it. To Alexey Alexandrovich it was obvious he did not understand what he was saying, and that irritated him.

He frowned and began explaining something Seryozha had heard many times before and could never remember, because he understood it too clearly—like 'suddenly' being an adverb of manner of action. Seryozha looked at his father with alarm and could think of only one thing: whether or not his father would make him repeat what he had just said, as he sometimes did. And this thought so terrified Seryozha that he no longer understood anything. But his father did not make him repeat it, and passed on to the lesson from the Old Testament. Seryozha recounted the events themselves well, but when it came to answering questions as to what certain events foreshadowed, he did not know anything, despite having already been punished for this lesson. The point at which he was unable to say anything and was left dithering, carving the desk and rocking on his chair, was where he had to talk about the patriarchs before the Flood. He did not know any of them except Enoch,* who had been taken up to heaven alive. He used to remember their names, but now he had completely forgotten them, mainly because Enoch was his favourite person in the whole of the Old Testament, and the story of Enoch being taken up to heaven alive was connected in his mind to a whole long train of thought which is what absorbed him now, while his eyes were fastened on his father's watch-chain and a button that was half-undone on his waistcoat.

Death, which people talked to him about so often, was something Seryozha did not believe in at all. He did not believe that the people he loved could die, and particularly that he himself would die. That seemed completely impossible and incomprehensible to him. But he was told that everyone died; he had even asked people he trusted, and they too had confirmed this; his old nanny also said the same thing, although reluctantly. But Enoch had not died, so that meant not everyone did die. 'Why shouldn't any person be able to serve God like he did and be taken up to heaven alive?' thought Seryozha. Bad people, that is, the people whom Seryozha did not like, they could die, but the good ones could all be like Enoch.

'Well, who were the patriarchs then?'

'Enoch, Enos.'

'Yes, but you have already said that. This is bad, Seryozha, very bad. If you don't try to learn what is the most vital thing of all for a Christian,' said his father, getting up, 'then what on earth can engage you? I am not happy with you, and Pyotr Ignatich' (his principal teacher) 'is not happy with you. I shall have to punish you.'

Both his father and his teacher were dissatisfied with him, and it was true that he was a very poor pupil. But there was no way it could be said that he was a slow-witted boy. On the contrary, he was far more quick-witted than those boys his teacher held up as an example to him. It was his father's view that he did not want to learn what he was taught. But the truth was that he could not learn it. The reason he could not was because there were demands in his heart which were more pressing than those made by his father and his teacher. These demands conflicted with each other, and so he was locked in a struggle with those educating him.

He was nine years old; he was a child; but he knew his own soul, it was precious to him, he protected it as the eyelid protects the eye, and he let no one into his soul without the key of love. His teachers complained that he did not want to learn, but his soul was filled with an abundant thirst for knowledge. He learned from Kapitonich, from his nanny, from Nadenka, from Vasily Lukich, but not from his teachers. The water that his father and his teacher were expecting to turn the wheels of their mill had long ago leaked away and was working elsewhere.

His father punished Seryozha by not letting him see Nadenka, Lydia Ivanovna's niece; but this punishment turned out to Seryozha's advantage. Vasily Lukich was in a good mood, and showed him how to make windmills. He spent the whole evening working on them and dreaming up how to make a windmill on which he could go round: by clutching at the blades or tying himself on and spinning round. Seryozha did not think about his mother all evening, but when he was tucked up in bed he suddenly remembered her and prayed in his own words that tomorrow, on his birthday, his mother would stop hiding and come to him.

'Vasily Lukich, do you know the extra thing I prayed for tonight, besides the usual things?'

'To be a better pupil?'

'No.'

'Toys?'

'No. You'll never guess. It's something wonderful, but it's a secret. When it happens I'll tell you. Have you guessed?'

'No, I can't guess. Tell me,' said Vasily Lukich with a smile, which was rare for him. 'Come on, lie down, I'm putting out the candle.'

'But what I can see and what I prayed for is clearer without the candle. Now I've almost told you my secret!' said Seryozha with a merry laugh.

When the candle was taken away, Seryozha heard and felt his mother. She was standing over him and caressing him with loving eyes. But then came windmills, a penknife, everything became mixed up, and he fell asleep.

28

WHEN they arrived in Petersburg, Vronsky and Anna stayed at one of the best hotels, Vronsky separately on the ground floor and Anna upstairs with the baby, the wet-nurse, and the maid, in a large suite consisting of four rooms.

On the day of their arrival Vronsky went to see his brother. There he found his mother, who had come from Moscow on business. His mother and sister-in-law greeted him in the usual way; they asked him about his trip abroad, and talked about mutual acquaintances, but did not say a single word about his relationship with Anna. His brother asked about her himself when he came the next morning to see Vronsky, however, and Alexey Vronsky told him frankly that he saw his relationship with Anna as a marriage; that he hoped to arrange a divorce and would then marry her, but until then he considered her his wife like any other wife, and asked him to convey this to their mother and his wife.

'If society does not approve of this, it is all the same to me,' Vronsky said, 'but if my relatives want to be on a family footing with me, they will have to be on the same footing with my wife.'

The elder brother, who had always respected his younger brother's judgement, could not be completely sure whether he was right or not until society had decided this question; for his part, however, he himself had nothing against it and went to see Anna with Alexey.

Vronsky used the formal mode of address with Anna in front of his brother, as he did with everyone, and spoke to her as if she were a close acquaintance, but it was assumed that his brother knew about their relationship, and they talked about Anna going to Vronsky's estate.

Despite all his experience of society, Vronsky succumbed to a strange state of delusion as a result of the new situation in which he found himself. He ought perhaps to have understood that society was closed to him and Anna; but he had conceived some vague notions in his head that it was only like that in the old days, and that with the rapid progress that was being made these days (he had unconsciously become a supporter of any kind of progress), the views of society had now changed and the issue as to whether they would be received in society had not yet been decided. 'Of course she will not be received at court,' he thought, 'but people close to us can and must understand things in the right way.'

It is possible to sit crossed-legged in the same position for several hours on end if you know there is nothing to prevent you changing position; but if a person knows that he must sit like that with crossed legs, he will experience cramps, and his legs will twitch and strain towards the place where he would like to stretch them. This was what Vronsky was experiencing with regard to society. Although he knew in the depths of his soul that society was closed to them, he was probing to see whether society would be different now and would receive them. But he very quickly realized that although society was open to him personally, it was closed to Anna. As in the game of cat and mouse, the arms raised for him were immediately lowered in front of Anna.

One of the first ladies in Petersburg society whom Vronsky saw was his cousin Betsy.

'At last!' she greeted him joyfully. 'And Anna? How glad I am! Where are you staying? I can imagine how awful old Petersburg must seem after your wonderful travels; I'm imagining your honeymoon in Rome. What about the divorce? Is that all arranged?'

Vronsky noticed that Betsy's exaltation decreased when she found out there was still no divorce.

'They will cast stones at me, I know,' she said, 'but I shall come and see Anna; yes, I will certainly come. You are not staying here long?'

And she did indeed come to see Anna that same day; but her tone was now completely different to what it had been before. She was clearly proud of her boldness and wanted Anna to appreciate the loyalty of her friendship. She stopped for no more than ten minutes to talk about society news, and as she was leaving she said:

'You haven't told me when the divorce will be. Let us just say that I have thrown my bonnet over the windmill, but all the other strait-laced people will give you the cold shoulder until you are married. And it's so simple nowadays. *Ça se fait.*[1] So you're leaving on Friday? It is a shame we won't see each other again.'

Vronsky might have realized from Betsy's tone what he was bound to expect from society; but he made another effort with his family. He had no confidence in his mother. He knew that his mother, who had been so delighted by Anna when they first met, was now implacably opposed to her for ruining her son's career. But he did place great hopes on Varya, his brother's wife. He believed she would not cast stones and would make a point of going to see Anna and receiving her without fuss.

Vronsky went to see her the very next day after their arrival and, finding her alone, was frank about expressing his wishes.

'Alexey,' she said after hearing him out, 'you know how fond of you I am and how ready I am to do anything for you; but I remained silent because I knew there was nothing I could do for you and Anna Arkadyevna,' she said, taking particular care to say 'Anna Arkadyevna'. 'Please do not think that I am passing judgement. I would never do that; I might have acted the same way if I had been in her position. I can't and won't go into details,' she said, peering timidly into his gloomy face. 'But one must call a spade a spade. You want me to go and see her, with the idea of receiving her and thus rehabilitating her in society; but you must understand that I *cannot* do that. I have daughters growing up, and I must move in society for the sake of my husband. Suppose I do visit Anna Arkadyevna; she will understand that I cannot invite her here or else will have do so in such a way that she does not encounter those who see things differently; that would deeply offend her. I cannot raise her . . .'

'But I don't consider that she has fallen any lower than hundreds of women whom you do receive!' broke in Vronsky even more despondently, and he got up in silence, realizing his sister-in-law's decision was irrevocable.

'Alexey! Don't be angry with me. Please understand that I'm not to blame,' Varya began, looking at him with a timid smile.

'I'm not angry with you,' he said just as despondently, 'but I am doubly pained. I'm also pained that this means breaking off our friendship. Well, perhaps not breaking it off, but weakening it. You will understand that it cannot be otherwise for me either.'

And with that he left her.

Vronsky realized that any further efforts would be in vain and that he would have to spend these few days in Petersburg as if in a foreign

---

[1] 'It is a thing that is done.'

city, avoiding any contact with his previous society acquaintances so as not to suffer the unpleasantnesses and insults which he found so harrowing. One of the most unpleasant aspects of the situation in Petersburg was that Alexey Alexandrovich and his name seemed to be everywhere. It was impossible to start talking about anything without the conversation turning to Alexey Alexandrovich; it was impossible to go anywhere without running into him. At least this is how it seemed to Vronsky, just as it seems to a man with a sore finger that he keeps brushing against everything with this sore finger, as if on purpose.

Vronsky found the stay in Petersburg even more difficult because throughout this period he saw in Anna a new mood which he did not understand. One moment she seemed to be in love with him, while the next she would become cold, irritable, and inscrutable. She was tormented by something and hiding something from him, and did not seem to notice the insults which were poisoning his life, and which, with her sensitivity of perception, should have been even more agonizing for her.

29

ONE of the goals of the trip to Russia for Anna was a meeting with her son. From the day she had left Italy the thought of this meeting had not ceased to agitate her. And the nearer she drew to Petersburg, the greater the joy and significance of this meeting became for her. She did not even ask herself how this meeting would be arranged. She felt it would be natural and straightforward to see her son when she was in the same city as him; but upon arrival in Petersburg her current position in society suddenly became clear to her, and she realized that arranging the meeting would be difficult.

She had already been in Petersburg for two days. The thought of her son had not left her for one moment, but she had not yet seen him. She felt she did not have the right to go directly to the house, where she might meet Alexey Alexandrovich. She might be refused entrance and be humiliated. Writing and entering into contact with her husband was excruciating even to contemplate; she could be calm only when she did not think about her husband. To catch a glimpse of her son when he was out for a walk, having found out where and when he went, was not enough for her: she had been so looking forward to this meeting, there was so much she needed to say to him, she so wanted to embrace and kiss him. Seryozha's old nanny could help and advise her. But the nanny was no longer living in Alexey Alexandrovich's house. Two days were taken up by these hesitations and the search for the nanny.

Having heard about Alexey Alexandrovich's close relations with Countess Lydia Ivanovna, Anna decided on the third day to write to her a letter that cost her a great deal of effort, in which she deliberately said that permission to see her son must depend on her husband's magnanimity. She knew that if the letter were shown to her husband, he would maintain his role of magnanimity and not refuse her.

The commissionaire who delivered the letter brought her the most cruel and unexpected answer that there would be no answer. She had never felt so humiliated as at the moment when, after summoning the commissionaire, she heard his detailed account of how he had waited and then been told: 'There will be no answer.' Anna felt humiliated and insulted, but she saw that, looking at things from her point of view, Countess Lydia Ivanovna was right. Her grief was all the more intense for being suffered in solitude. She could not and did not want to share it with Vronsky. She knew that despite the fact that he was the main cause of her unhappiness, the issue of the meeting with her son would seem to him to be of trifling importance. She knew that he would never be capable of understanding the depth of her suffering; she knew she would hate him for the cold tone he would adopt at the mere mention of it. And she feared this more than anything in the world, so hid from him everything that concerned her son.

After spending the whole day in the hotel, she had thought up a way of seeing her son and had resolved to write to her husband. She was already composing this letter when Lydia Ivanovna's letter was brought to her. The Countess's silence had humbled and subdued her, but the letter and everything she read between the lines so infuriated her, so outrageous did this vindictiveness seem to her in comparison with her passionate and legitimate affection for her son, that she was filled with indignation against others and stopped blaming herself.

'That coldness—that pretence at feeling!' she said to herself. 'They just want to hurt me and torture the child, and I am supposed to submit to them! Absolutely not! She is worse than I am. At least I don't lie.' And she decided then and there that the very next day, on Seryozha's actual birthday, she would go straight to her husband's house, bribe the servants, engage in deception, but would see her son at all costs and destroy the monstrous deception with which they had surrounded the unfortunate child.

She drove to a toy-shop, bought some toys, and thought through a plan of action. She would arrive early in the morning, at eight o'clock, when Alexey Alexandrovich would in all likelihood not yet be up. She would have money in her hand which she would give to the doorman and the footman so they would let her in, and, without raising her veil, she would say that she had come from Seryozha's godfather to wish him many happy returns, and that she had been asked to put the toys by his bed. The only thing she did not prepare was what she would say to her son. No matter how much thought she gave to this, she could not think of anything.

The next day, at eight o'clock in the morning, Anna got out of a hired carriage and rang at the front entrance of her former home.

'Go and see what they want. It's some lady,' said Kapitonich in his overcoat and galoshes, still not dressed, after peering through the window at the lady in a veil standing right by the door.

The doorman's assistant, a young lad Anna did not know, had barely opened the door when she had already walked through it, and, taking a three-rouble note out of her muff, she hurriedly thrust it into his hand.

'Seryozha . . . Sergey Alexeyich,' she said, and was about to proceed inside. After examining the note, the doorman's assistant stopped her by the other glass door.

'Whom is it you wish you see?' he asked.

She did not hear his words and did not reply.

Noticing the stranger's confusion, Kapitonich himself came out to let her in through the door and ask what she wanted.

'I've come from Prince Skorodumov to see Sergey Alexeyich,' she said.

'He is not up yet,' said the doorman, studying her carefully.

Anna had certainly not expected that the utterly unchanged decor of the hall in the house where she had lived for nine years would affect her so strongly. Memories, both happy and painful, rose up one after another in her soul, and for a moment she forgot why she was there.

'Would you care to wait?' said Kapitonich, helping her off with her fur coat.

After removing her coat, Kapitonich glanced at her face, recognized her, and silently made a low bow to her.

'Please come in, Your Excellency,' he said to her.

She tried to say something, but her voice refused to produce any sounds; casting a guilty look of entreaty at the old man, she went with swift, light steps up the stairs. Hunched over and tripping up on the stairs with his galoshes, Kapitonich chased after her, trying to get ahead of her.

'The tutor's there and he may not be dressed. I'll announce you.'

Anna carried on going up the familiar staircase, not understanding what the old man was saying.

'This way, to the left, please. I'm sorry it is not tidy. He is in the old sitting room now,' the doorman said, out of breath. 'If you could kindly wait a moment, Your Excellency; I'll take a peep,' he said, and going ahead of her, he half-opened the tall door and disappeared behind it. Anna stood waiting. 'He's just woken up,' said the doorman as he came out again.

And just as the doorman said this, Anna heard the sound of a child yawning. She could recognize her son from the sound of this yawning alone, and pictured him vividly before her.

'Let me in, let me in, you can go!' she said, and went in through the tall door. To the right of the door stood a bed, and sitting up in the bed was a boy wearing nothing but an unbuttoned nightshirt; his little body arched back, he was stretching and finishing his yawn. The minute his lips came together, they formed a blissful sleepy smile, and with that smile he slowly and sweetly sank back down again.

'Seryozha!' she whispered, going up to him without a sound.

During her separation from him, and amid the outpouring of love she had been feeling throughout this recent time, she had imagined him as he was when she had loved him the most, as a four-year-old boy. Now he was not even the same as he was when she had left him; he had left his four-year-old self even further behind, he had grown taller and lost weight. What was this? His face was so thin, and his hair so short! His arms were so long! He had changed so much since she had left him! But it was still him, with that particular shape of his head, his lips, his soft little neck and broad little shoulders.

'Seryozha!' she repeated just above the child's ear.

He raised himself again on his elbow, turned his tousled head from side to side as if looking for something, and opened his eyes. For a few seconds he looked quietly and questioningly at his mother standing there motionless before him, then suddenly he smiled a blissful smile and, closing his sleepy, stuck-together eyes again, he tumbled not backwards but forwards into her arms.

'Seryozha! My darling boy!' she said in a choked voice as she wrapped her arms round his plump body.

'Mama!' he said, wriggling about in her arms so that different parts of his body came into contact with them.

With a sleepy smile, his eyes still closed, he transferred his chubby little arms from the back of the bed to her shoulders, cuddled up to her, enveloping her with the wonderful sleepy smell and warmth that only children exude, and began rubbing his face against her neck and shoulders.

'I knew it,' he said, opening his eyes. 'It's my birthday today. I knew you would come. I'll get up straight away.'

And saying this, he fell asleep.

Anna ran her eyes over him hungrily; she saw how much he had grown and changed in her absence. She recognized and did not recognize his bare legs sticking out from under the blanket, which were now so long, those thinned-out cheeks and those close-cropped curls on the nape of his neck where she had so often kissed him. She felt all these parts of him and was unable to say anything; she was choked by tears.

'But what are you crying about, Mama?' he said, now completely awake. 'Mama, what are you crying about?' he exclaimed in a tearful voice.

'What am I crying about? I'm not going to cry . . . I'm crying with happiness. I haven't seen you for such a long time. I'm not going to, I promise,' she said, fighting back tears and turning away. 'Well, it's time for you to get dressed now,' she added after a moment's silence when she had regained her composure, and without letting go of his hand, she sat down by his bed on the chair on which his clothes had been laid out.

'How do you get dressed without me? How . . .' She wanted to start talking simply and cheerfully, but she could not and turned away again.

'I don't wash with cold water, Papa told me not to. You haven't seen Vasily Lukich, have you? He'll come in soon. But you sat down on my clothes!' And Seryozha burst out laughing.

She looked at him and smiled.

'Dear, darling Mama!' he shouted, throwing himself on her again and hugging her. It was as if he only clearly understood what had happened now, after seeing her smile. 'You don't need this,' he said, taking off her hat. And as if seeing her afresh without her hat, he again started showering her with kisses.

'But what did you think about me? You didn't think I was dead?'

'I never believed it.'

'You didn't believe it, my love?'

'I knew, I knew!' he said, repeating his favourite phrase and, seizing her hand, which was stroking his hair, he started pressing her palm to his mouth and kissing it.

30

VASILY LUKICH, meanwhile, not having understood at first who this lady was, and discovering in conversation that this was the very mother who had left her husband and whom he did not know, since he had joined the household after her departure, was in a quandary as to whether to go in or inform Alexey Alexandrovich. Finally concluding that his duty was to get Seryozha up at the appointed hour and that he was therefore not required to investigate who was there, be it the mother or some other person, but should instead do his duty, he dressed, went to the door, and opened it.

But the caresses of mother and son, the sound of their voices and what they were saying, made him change his mind. He shook his head, sighed, and closed the door. 'I'll wait another ten minutes,' he said to himself, clearing his throat and wiping away tears.

At the same time there was great commotion amongst the servants in the house. They had all heard that the mistress had come, that Kapitonich had let her in, and that she was now in the nursery, but they also knew that the master always made a personal visit to the nursery before nine o'clock, and they all understood that a meeting of husband and wife was out of the question and must be prevented. Korney, the valet, had gone down to the doorman's room to ask how she had been let in and by whom, and he reprimanded Kapitonich when he found out that the old man had received her and shown her in. The doorman remained stubbornly tight-lipped, but when Korney told him he ought to be dismissed for what he had done, Kapitonich made a lunge towards him and, shaking his hands in Korney's face, he began to speak out:

'Yes, I'm sure you wouldn't have let her in! In service here ten years and seen nothing but kindness, but you would have gone just now and said, "Off you go, please!" You know how to play your cards right! You certainly do! You should be looking out for yourself, so you can fleece the master and filch his fur coats!'

'Soldier!' said Korney contemptuously, and he turned to the nanny who was just coming in. 'You be the judge, Marya Efimovna: he let her in and didn't tell anyone,' said Korney, addressing her. 'Alexey Alexandrovich will be out in a minute and he will go into the nursery.'

'Dear me, what a business!' said the nanny. 'Korney Vasilyevich, you should try and detain him somehow, the master I mean, and I'll run up and take her away somehow. Dear me, what a business!'

When the nanny went into the nursery, Seryozha was telling his mother how he and Nadenka had taken a tumble together when they

were out tobogganing, and had done three somersaults. She was listening to the sound of his voice, looking at his face and its changing
expressions, and touching his hand, but she did not understand what
he was saying. She had to go, she had to leave him—that was the only
thing she could think and feel. She heard Vasily Lukich's steps as he
came up to the door, coughing, and she also heard the nanny's steps
when she approached; but she sat there as if turned to stone, incapable
of uttering a word or getting up.

'Madam, sweetheart!' began the nanny, going up to Anna and kissing her hands and shoulders. 'What joy God has brought our birthday
boy. You haven't changed one bit.'

'Oh nanny, dearest, I didn't know you were in the house,' said Anna,
coming to her senses for a moment.

'I don't live here, I live with my daughter. I've come to wish him
a happy birthday, Anna Arkadyevna, sweetheart!'

The nanny suddenly burst into tears, and began kissing her hand
again.

Seryozha, his eyes and face beaming as he held his mother with one
hand and his nanny with the other, was stamping on the carpet with
his chubby, bare little feet. He was thrilled by the affection his beloved
nanny was showing his mother.

'Mama! She often comes to see me, and when she comes . . .' he
began, but he stopped after noticing that the nanny had whispered
something to his mother, and that a look of fear and something resembling shame had appeared on his mother's face, which did not suit her
at all.

She went up to him.

'My darling!' she said.

She could not say *goodbye*, but the expression on her face said it, and
he understood.

'Darling, darling Kutik!' she said, using the name she had called
him when he was little, 'you won't forget me? You . . .' but she could
not say anything more.

She later thought of so many things she could have said to him!
But now she could not think of anything and could not speak. But
Seryozha understood everything she wanted to say to him. He understood she was unhappy and that she loved him. He even understood
what the nanny had whispered. He heard the words 'always before nine
o'clock,' and he understood that this referred to his father, and that
his father and mother must not meet. This he understood, but there
was one thing he could not understand: why did her face show fear

and shame? . . . She had not done anything wrong, yet she was afraid of him and ashamed of something. He wanted to ask a question that would clarify his doubts, but he did not dare; he saw she was suffering, and felt sorry for her. He nestled up to her silently and whispered:

'Don't go yet. He won't come for a while.'

His mother held him at arm's length to see if he was thinking about what he saying, and she could read in the frightened expression on his face that he was not only speaking about his father, but, as it were, asking her what he ought to think about his father.

'Seryozha, my darling,' she said, 'you must love him. He's better and kinder than I am, and I have done him wrong. When you grow up you will be able to judge.'

'There's no one better than you! . . .' he cried out tearfully in despair, and, clasping her by the shoulders, he began pressing her to him with all his might, his arms trembling from the intensity of the effort.

'My darling, little one!' said Anna, and she started crying in the same helpless, childlike way in which he was crying.

At that moment the door opened and Vasily Lukich came in. Footsteps could be heard at the other door, and the nanny said in a frightened whisper:

'He's coming,' and gave Anna her hat.

Seryozha collapsed on to his bed and started sobbing, covering his face with his hands. Anna removed his hands, kissed his wet face again, and headed for the door with rapid steps. Alexey Alexandrovich was coming towards her in the opposite direction. When he saw her, he stopped and bowed his head.

Although she had just said that he was better and kinder than she was, the rapid glance she gave him, taking in his whole figure down to the last detail, caused her to be overcome by feelings of revulsion and anger towards him and jealousy over her son. She swiftly lowered her veil and, quickening her step, almost ran out of the room.

She had not even managed to take out the toys she had picked out with such love and sorrow in the shop the previous day, and she took them home.

31

HOWEVER intensely Anna had desired a meeting with her son, and however long she had thought about it and prepared for it, she had definitely not expected this meeting to have such a powerful effect on her. For a long time after she returned to her lonely suite in the hotel, she could not understand why she was there. 'Yes, it's all over, and I am alone again,' she said to herself and, without taking off her hat, she sat down in an armchair by the fireplace. Fixing her motionless gaze on a bronze clock standing on a table between the windows, she started thinking.

The French maid brought from abroad came in to suggest that she dress. She looked at her in stupefaction and said:

'Later.'

The footman offered her coffee.

'Later,' she said.

The Italian wet-nurse, after tidying the baby, came in with her and carried her over to Anna. As she always did when she saw her mother, the chubby, well-fed baby twisted her bare little hands, wound round with threads, so that their palms faced downwards, and, smiling with her toothless little mouth, began to paddle with her little hands like a fish undulates its fins, making the starched folds of her embroidered little dress rustle. It was impossible not to smile and kiss the little girl, impossible not to offer her a finger which she seized hold of, squealing and wriggling with her whole body; it was impossible not to offer her a lip, which she sucked into her little mouth by way of a kiss. And Anna did all of these things. She took her in her arms and bounced her up and down, and she kissed her fresh little cheek and bare little elbows, but seeing this child had made it even clearer to her that the feelings she experienced for her did not even amount to love when compared to what she felt for Seryozha. Everything about this little girl was adorable, but for some reason none of it tugged at her heartstrings. On her first child, despite being by a man she did not love, had been bestowed all the powers of love which had not found fulfilment; the little girl had been born in the most difficult circumstances and had not received even a hundredth part of the care bestowed on her first child. Besides, in the little girl everything was still to come, while Seryozha was almost a person already, and a beloved person; within him there were already thoughts and feelings doing battle; he understood, loved, and judged her, she thought, recalling his words and his looks. And she was forever separated from him, not only physically but spiritually, and it was impossible to remedy this.

She gave the little girl back to the wet-nurse, dismissed her, and opened a locket containing a portrait of Seryozha when he was almost the same age as the little girl. She got up, took off her hat, and picked up an album from a small table in which there were photographic portraits of her son at different ages. She wanted to compare the photographs and began taking them out of the album. She took them all out. One remained, which was the most recent and best photograph. He was sitting astride a chair in a white shirt, his eyes glowering and his mouth smiling. This was his most characteristic and best expression. She tried several times to take hold of a corner of the photograph with her small, deft hands, whose slender white fingers were particularly tense that day, but the photograph had become dislodged, and she could not reach it. There was no paper-knife on the table, and so she removed the photograph next to it (a photograph of Vronsky with long hair in a round hat taken in Rome) and pushed out her son's photograph with it. 'Yes, there he is!' she said, glancing at the portrait of Vronsky and suddenly remembering who was the cause of her present misery. She had not thought of him once all that morning. But suddenly now, seeing that manly, noble, so familiar and so beloved face, she felt an unexpected rush of love for him.

'But where is he? How can he leave me alone with my suffering?' she thought with a sudden feeling of reproach, forgetting it was she herself who had concealed everything concerning her son from him. She sent to ask him to come to her immediately and, with her heart in her mouth, conjuring up the phrases she would use to tell him everything, and the expressions of his love which would comfort her, she awaited him. The messenger returned with the answer that he had a visitor, but that he would come straight away and wanted to know whether she could also receive Prince Yashvin, who had arrived in Petersburg. 'He's not coming on his own, but he hasn't seen me since dinner yesterday,' she thought; 'he's not coming on his own so I can tell him everything, but he's coming with Yashvin.' And a strange thought suddenly occurred to her: what if he had stopped loving her?

And as she went over the events of the last few days, it seemed to her that she could see confirmation of this terrible thought in everything: in the fact that he had not dined at home the day before, in the fact that he had insisted on their taking separate rooms in Petersburg, and that even now he was not coming to her on his own, as if wanting to avoid meeting her face to face.

'But he must tell me this. I need to know it. If I know it, then I will know what to do,' she said to herself, unable to imagine the position she should be in if she were convinced of his indifference. She thought he had stopped loving her, she felt close to despair, and as a result of that she felt particularly overwrought. She rang for her maid and went into the dressing room. As she dressed, she took greater care with her appearance than she had done throughout the last few days, as if, having fallen out of love with her, he might fall in love with her again, because she was wearing the dress and hairstyle that most became her.

She heard the bell ring before she was ready.

When she went into the drawing room it was Yashvin, not he, who met her gaze. Vronsky was looking through the photographs of her son that she had left on the table, and was in no hurry to look at her.

'We have met before,' she said, placing her small hand in the huge hand of Yashvin, who was embarrassed (which was strange, given his immense height and rough features). 'We met last year at the races. Give them to me,' she said, with a rapid movement taking from Vronsky the photographs of her son that he was looking at, her sparkling eyes flashing a meaningful look at him. 'Were the races good this year? I watched the races on the Corso in Rome instead. You don't care for life abroad, though,' she said with a warm smile. 'I know you and I know all your tastes, even though we have rarely met.'

'I'm very sorry to hear that, as my tastes are mostly bad,' said Yashvin, chewing the left side of his moustache.

After talking for a while, and noticing Vronsky glance at the clock, Yashvin asked her whether she would be staying in Petersburg for long, then straightened his huge frame and picked up his cap.

'Not long, it seems,' she said with consternation, glancing at Vronsky.

'So we won't meet again?' said Yashvin, turning to Vronsky as he stood up. 'Where are you dining?'

'Come and dine with me,' said Anna resolutely, as if angry with herself for her embarrassment, yet blushing as she always did when she had to make her position manifest to a new person. 'The dinner here is not good, but at least you will see each other. There is no one from the regiment whom Alexey likes as much as you.'

'I'd be delighted,' said Yashvin with a smile, from which Vronsky could see that he liked Anna very much.

Yashvin bowed and left. Vronsky stayed behind.

'Are you going out too?' she said to him.

'I'm already late,' he answered. 'You go on! I'll catch you up in a moment,' he called out to Yashvin.

She took his hand and racked her brains for something to say to keep him from going.

'Wait, there's something I need to say,' she said and, taking his stubby hand, she pressed it against her neck. 'So, was it all right that I asked him to dinner?'

'It was a wonderful thing to do,' he said with a calm smile, revealing his even teeth and kissing her hand.

'Alexey, you haven't changed towards me?' she said, pressing his hand in both of hers. 'Alexey, I am miserable here. When are we going away?'

'Soon, soon. You wouldn't believe how difficult I'm also finding our life here,' he said and withdrew his hand.

'Well, go then, off you go!' she said in an aggrieved tone and walked quickly away from him.

32

WHEN Vronsky returned home, Anna was not yet back. Soon after he left, he was told, a lady had come to see her, and she had gone out with her. The fact that she had gone off without saying where she was going, and was still not back, and the fact that she had also gone out somewhere that morning without saying anything to him—all this, together with the strangely overwrought expression on her face that morning, and the recollection of the hostile manner with which she had almost snatched the photographs of her son out of his hands in front of Yashvin, forced him to reflect. He decided that it was vital to have things out with her. And so he waited for her in her drawing room. But Anna did not come back alone, but brought her old maiden aunt, Princess Oblonskaya, along with her. This was the same lady who had come that morning and with whom Anna had gone shopping. Anna seemed not to notice Vronsky's worried and questioning expression as she blithely told him about what she had bought that morning. He saw that something strange was taking place within her: there was a strained attentiveness in her shining eyes when they briefly rested on him, while in her speech and in her movements there was that nervous quickness and grace he had found so captivating at the beginning of their relationship, but which now caused him worry and alarm.

The table was laid for four. They had already assembled and were about to go into the little dining room when Tushkevich arrived with a message for Anna from Princess Betsy. Princess Betsy sent apologies for not having come to say goodbye; she was unwell, but asked Anna to come and see her between half-past six and nine. Vronsky glanced at Anna upon mention of this specific time, which showed that measures had been taken to prevent her meeting anyone; but Anna seemed not to notice this.

'It's a great shame that between half-past six and nine is exactly when I cannot come,' she said with a faint smile.

'The Princess will be very sorry.'

'And I too.'

'You're going to hear Patti,* I expect?' said Tushkevich.

'Patti? Now that's an idea. I would go if it were possible to get a box.'

'I can get one,' Tushkevich offered.

'I would be very, very grateful to you,' said Anna. 'Would you care to dine with us?'

Vronsky gave a slight shrug of the shoulders. He had no clue what Anna was up to. Why had she brought over the old Princess, why had she asked Tushkevich to stay for dinner, and, most startling of all, why was she sending him to get a box? In her position, could she possibly be thinking of going to Patti's subscription performance, when all her society acquaintances would be there? He gave her a serious look, but she responded with that same provocative, half-ebullient, half-desperate look, the meaning of which he could not fathom. At dinner Anna was in aggressive high spirits—she seemed to be flirting with both Tushkevich and Yashvin. When they got up from the table and Tushkevich drove off to get the box, while Yashvin went to smoke, Vronsky went down with him to his rooms. After sitting there for a while he ran back upstairs. Anna was already dressed in a light silk-and-velvet gown, which had been made for her in Paris, with a low-cut neckline, and with costly white lace on her head which framed her face and showed off her striking beauty to particular advantage.

'Are you really going to the theatre?' he said, trying not to look at her.

'Why do you ask in such a scared way?' she said, hurt all over again that he was not looking at her. 'Why should I not go?'

She appeared not to understand the meaning of his words.

'Of course, there's no reason whatsoever,' he said, frowning.

'That's exactly what I say,' she said, deliberately failing to understand the irony of his tone and calmly rolling up a long, scented glove.

'Anna, for heaven's sake, what is the matter with you?' he said, trying to bring her to her senses exactly as her husband once used to do.

'I don't understand what you mean.'

'You know you cannot go.'

'Why not? I'm not going alone. Princess Varvara has gone to dress, she is coming with me.'

He shrugged his shoulders with a bewildered and despairing look.

'But do you not know? . . .' he began.

'I don't want to know!' she almost shouted. 'I don't. Do I regret what I have done? No, no, and no. And if I had to do it all over again, it would be the same. There is only one thing which matters for us, for you and for me: whether we love each other or not. There are no other considerations. Why are we living here separately and not seeing each other? Why can't I go? I love you, and I don't care about anything else,' she said in Russian, looking at him with a particular gleam in her eyes which he did not understand, 'as long as you have not changed. Why won't you look at me?'

He looked at her. He saw all the beauty of her face and her attire, which always suited her so well. But it was precisely her beauty and elegance that irritated him now.

'My feelings cannot change, you know that, but I beg you not to go, I implore you,' he said, speaking again in French with tender supplication in his voice, but with coldness in his eyes.

She did not hear his words, but she saw the coldness of his look, and answered irritably:

'And I'm asking you to explain why I should not go.'

'Because it might cause you . . .' he faltered.

'I don't understand. Yashvin *n'est pas compromettant*,[1] and Princess Varvara is no worse than anyone else. And here she is.'

33

VRONSKY for the first time experienced a feeling of vexation, almost anger, towards Anna for her deliberate refusal to understand her position. This feeling was aggravated by the fact that he had been unable to tell her the reason for his vexation. If he had told her exactly what he was thinking, he would have said: 'To show up at the theatre in that outfit, with a Princess who is known to everyone, not only means acknowledging your position as a fallen woman, but throwing down the gauntlet to society, that is, renouncing it for ever.'

He could not say that to her. 'But how can she not understand this, and what is going on with her?' he wondered. He felt his respect for her was diminishing at the same time as his consciousness of her beauty was increasing.

He returned to his rooms grim-faced and, sitting down beside Yashvin, who had stretched out his long legs on a chair and was drinking brandy-and-soda, ordered the same for himself.

'You were talking about Lankovsky's Mighty. He's a fine horse, and I would advise you to buy him,' said Yashvin, glancing at his comrade's

---

[1] 'Yashin is not compromising'.

gloomy face. 'He has a steep croup, but as far as his legs and his head are concerned one couldn't wish for anything better.'

'I think I will get him,' answered Vronsky.

The conversation about horses interested him, but he did not forget Anna for a single moment, could not help listening out for the sound of footsteps in the corridor, and kept glancing at the clock on the mantelpiece.

'Anna Arkadyevna requested to let you know that she has gone to the theatre,' announced a servant.

Yashvin emptied another glass of brandy into the sparkling water, drank it, and got up, buttoning his coat.

'Well, shall we go?' he said, smiling wanly under his moustache, and showing by this smile that he understood the reason for Vronsky's despondency, but did not attach any importance to it.

'I'm not going,' Vronsky answered despondently.

'I have to go though, I promised. Well goodbye. You could come to the stalls and take Krasinsky's seat,' added Yashvin as he went out.

'No, I'm busy.'

'A wife is a worry, but it's worse when she isn't your wife,' thought Yashvin as he left the hotel.

Once alone, Vronsky got up from his chair and started pacing around the room.

'What is it tonight? The fourth subscription . . . Yegor and his wife will be there, and probably my mother. That means the whole of Petersburg will be there. She will have gone in by now, taken off her coat, and made her appearance. Tushkevich, Yashvin, Princess Varvara . . .' he pictured it in his mind. 'And what about me? Am I scared, or have I handed over her protection to Tushkevich? Whichever way you look at it, it's stupid, stupid . . . And why is she putting me in this position?' he said with a wave of his hand.

As he made this gesture, he caught the edge of the little table on which stood the bottle of soda water and the decanter of brandy, and almost knocked it over. He tried to catch it, lost his grip, then kicked the table angrily and rang the bell.

'If you want to work for me,' he said to the valet who came in, 'you had better keep your eye on the job. This shouldn't happen. You must clear up.'

Feeling he was innocent of any wrongdoing, the valet was about to defend himself, but glancing at his master and seeing from his face that he should just keep quiet, he hurriedly crouched down on to the carpet and started sorting out the broken and unbroken glasses and bottles.

'That's not your job; send a waiter to clear up and get my dress coat ready.'

Vronsky entered the theatre at half-past eight. The performance was in full swing. The old usher helped Vronsky off with his fur coat, called him 'Your Eminence' when he recognized him, and suggested he just shout for Fyodor rather than taking a tag. There was no one in the brightly lit corridor except for the ushers and two footmen with fur coats over their arms, who were listening at the door. Through the partly open door came the sounds of a delicate staccato orchestral accompaniment and a solo female voice carefully articulating a musical phrase. The door opened to let an usher slip in, and Vronsky now clearly heard the musical phrase nearing its conclusion. But the door immediately closed again, and Vronsky did not hear the end of the phrase or the cadenza, but realized from the thunder of applause behind the door that the cadenza had finished. When he entered the auditorium, which was brilliantly lit up by chandeliers and bronze gas-brackets, the din was still going on. Onstage, bowing and smiling, the singer, her bare shoulders and diamonds glittering, was gathering the bouquets flying clumsily over the footlights with the assistance of the tenor holding her hand, and going up to a gentleman with glossy pomaded hair parted down the middle who was stretching his long arms across the footlights to hand her something—and the entire audience in the stalls as well as in the boxes was jostling, craning forward, shouting and clapping. The conductor was helping to pass the bouquets from his raised seat and straightening his white tie. Vronsky walked into the middle of the stalls, then stopped to look around. This evening he paid less attention than ever to the familiar, accustomed surroundings, to the stage, the din, and the whole familiar, uninteresting, motley herd of spectators in the packed theatre.

As always, there were the same nameless ladies in the boxes with the same nameless officers at the back of the boxes; the same brightly coloured women, uniforms, and frock-coats, heaven knows who they were; the same grubby crowd in the gods; and out of that entire crowd in the boxes and the front rows there were about forty *real* men and women. And it was to these oases that Vronsky at once directed his attention and at once made contact with them.

The act had finished when he came in, so instead of going to his brother's box he went up to the front row to stand by the stage with Serpukhovskoy, who had caught sight of him in the distance and had been beckoning him with a smile while he stood with his knee bent, tapping the wall of the orchestra pit with his heel.

Vronsky had not yet seen Anna, and was purposely not looking in her direction. But he knew from the direction of people's glances where she was. He looked round discreetly, but not looking for her; expecting the worst, his eyes sought Alexey Alexandrovich. Fortunately for him, Alexey Alexandrovich was not in the theatre that evening.

'There's so little of the military man about you now!' Serpukhovskoy said to him. 'A diplomat, or an artist would be nearer the mark.'

'Yes, as soon as I returned home I put on tails,' answered Vronsky, smiling and slowly taking out his opera glasses.

'Well, I envy you there, I have to confess. When I come back from abroad and put on these,'—he touched his aiguillettes—'I miss my freedom.'

Serpukhovskoy had long since given up on Vronsky's career, but was still just as fond of him as before and was now particularly friendly to him.

'It's a shame you missed the first act.'

Vronsky, listening with one ear, transferred his opera glasses from the stalls circle to the dress circle and examined the boxes. Near a lady in a turban and a bald old man blinking angrily in the lens of the roving opera glasses, Vronsky suddenly caught sight of Anna's head, proud, strikingly beautiful, and smiling in its frame of lace. She was in the fifth box in the stalls circle, twenty paces from him. She was sitting at the front, and had turned round slightly to say something to Yashvin. The poise of her head on her beautiful, broad shoulders, and the glow of restrained excitement in her eyes and her entire face reminded him of her being exactly like this when he had seen her at the ball in Moscow. But he perceived this beauty in a completely different way now. There was no longer anything mysterious in his feelings for her now, so while her beauty attracted him even more powerfully than before, it also offended him now. She was not looking in his direction, but Vronsky sensed that she had already seen him.

When Vronsky pointed his opera glasses in that direction again, he noticed that Princess Varvara was particularly red in the face, laughing unnaturally and continually looking round into the neighbouring box; Anna, meanwhile, was tapping her closed fan on the red velvet as she stared at something in the distance, but did not see, and clearly did not wish to see, what was taking place in the neighbouring box. On Yashvin's face was his habitual expression when he was losing at cards. Frowning, he was sucking the left end of his moustache further and further into his mouth and casting sidelong glances at the same neighbouring box.

In this box to the left were the Kartasovs. Vronsky knew them, and knew that Anna was acquainted with them. The wife, a thin little woman, was standing up in her box and, with her back to Anna, was putting on a stole that her husband was handing her. Her face was pale and angry, and she was agitatedly saying something. Kartasov, a stout, balding man, was trying to pacify his wife while continually looking round at Anna. When the wife had gone out, the husband loitered behind, trying to catch Anna's eye, and obviously wishing to bow to her. But Anna, who was deliberately not taking any notice of him, had turned right round and was saying something to Yashvin, whose cropped head was inclined towards her. Kartasov went out without bowing, and the box was left empty.

Vronsky did not understand what exactly had taken place between the Kartasovs and Anna, but he understood that it was something humiliating for Anna. He understood this both from what he had seen, and above all from Anna's face, as he knew she had summoned every last strength to maintain the role she had taken on. And she was completely successful in preserving this role of outward tranquillity. Those who did not know her and her circle, who had not heard all the women's expressions of condolence, indignation, and amazement that she had taken the liberty of making an appearance in society, and such an ostentatious appearance in her lace headdress and all her beauty, admired the composure and beauty of this woman, and did not suspect that she was experiencing the feelings of someone being pilloried.

Knowing that something had happened, but not knowing precisely what, Vronsky experienced an agonizing sense of alarm and, hoping to find something out, he went to his brother's box. He deliberately chose the gangway on the opposite side of the stalls to Anna's box, and on his way out bumped into the Commanding Officer of his old regiment, who was talking to two acquaintances. Vronsky heard the name of Karenina being mentioned, and noticed how the Commanding Officer hastened to address him loudly, glancing meaningfully at his companions.

'Ah, Vronsky! So when are you coming to the regiment? We can't let you go without a bash. You're our greatest stalwart,' said the Commanding Officer.

'I won't be able to manage it, very sorry, another time,' said Vronsky, and he ran up the stairs to his brother's box.

The old Countess, Vronsky's mother, with her steel-grey ringlets, was in his brother's box. Varya and Princess Sorokina encountered him in the dress-circle corridor.

After taking Princess Sorokina to Vronsky's mother, Varya held out her hand to her brother-in-law and immediately began talking to him about the subject which interested him. He had rarely seen her so agitated.

'I think it's mean and despicable, and Madame Kartasova had no right. Madame Karenina . . .' she began.

'But what happened? I don't know.'

'What, you haven't heard?'

'You must understand that I would be the last person to hear about it.'

'Can there be a more spiteful creature than that Madame Kartasova?'

'But what did she do?'

'My husband told me . . . She insulted Madame Karenina. Her husband began talking to her across the box, and Madame Kartasova made a scene. She apparently said something insulting in a loud voice and walked out.'

'Count, your *maman* is asking for you,' said Princess Sorokina, peering round the door of the box.

'I've been waiting for you all this time,' said his mother, smiling sarcastically. 'You've been invisible.'

Her son saw that she could not repress a gleeful smile.

'Good evening, *Maman*. I was just on my way to find you,' he said coldly.

'Why don't you go *faire la cour à Madame Karenina*?' she added, when Princess Sorokina had stepped aside. '*Elle fait sensation. On oublie la Patti pour elle.*'[1]

'*Maman*, I asked you not to talk about that to me,' he answered with a frown.

'I'm only saying what everyone's saying.'

Vronsky did not reply, and left after saying a few words to Princess Sorokina. At the door he met his brother.

'Ah, Alexey!' said his brother. 'What a horrible thing to do! She's a fool, nothing more . . . I was just about to go to her. Let's go together.'

Vronsky did not hear him. He had set off quickly down the stairs: he felt that he had to do something, but he did not know what. Vexation with her for having put herself and him in such a false position, together with pity for her suffering, gave him anxiety. He went down into the stalls and headed straight for Anna's box. Stremov was standing by the box and talking to her.

---

[1] 'and pay court to Madame Karenina? . . . She is causing a sensation. People are forgetting Patti because of her.'

'There are no more tenors. *Le moule en est brisé.*'[1]

Vronsky bowed to her and stopped to greet Stremov.

'You came in late, I think, and missed the best aria,' Anna said to Vronsky, giving him what he perceived to be an arch look.

'I am a poor judge,' he said, looking at her sternly.

'Like Prince Yashvin,' she said, smiling, 'who thinks that Patti sings too loudly.'

'Thank you,' she said, taking into her small hand in its long glove the programme Vronsky had picked up, and right at that moment her beautiful face suddenly trembled. She got up and went to the back of the box.

When he noticed during the next act that her box was empty, Vronsky left the stalls, provoking hisses from the audience which had fallen silent at the first notes of the cavatina, and drove home.

Anna was already home. When Vronsky went in to see her, she was alone, still dressed in the same outfit she had worn to the theatre. She was sitting in the first armchair by the wall and looking straight ahead. She glanced at him, then immediately resumed her previous posture.

'Anna,' he said.

'You are to blame for everything, you are!' she cried with tears of despair and rage in her voice as she got up.

'I asked you, I begged you not to go, I knew it would be unpleasant for you . . .'

'Unpleasant!' she cried. 'It was awful! I shall never forget it as long as I live. She said it was a disgrace to sit next to me.'

'They are the words of a silly woman,' he said, 'but what is the point of taking the risk, provoking . . .'

'I hate your calmness. You shouldn't have driven me to it. If you loved me . . .'

'Anna! I don't understand what the question of my love has to do with it . . .'

'Well, if you loved me as I love you, if you suffered as I do . . .' she said, looking at him with a frightened expression.

He felt sorry for her, but he was still angry. He assured her of his love because he saw this was the only thing that could calm her down now, and he did not reproach her with words, but he reproached her in his soul.

And she drank in those assurances of love he found so trite he was ashamed to utter them, and gradually calmed down. The following day they left for the country, fully reconciled.

---

[1] 'The mould for them is broken.'

PART SIX

I

DARYA ALEXANDROVNA was spending the summer with her children in Pokrovskoye, at her sister Kitty Levina's. The house on her own estate had completely fallen apart, and Levin and his wife had persuaded her to spend the summer with them. Stepan Arkadyich greatly approved of this arrangement. He said that he much regretted that his official duties prevented him from spending the summer in the country with his family, which would have been the greatest happiness for him, and remained in Moscow, coming occasionally to the country for a day or two. Apart from the Oblonskys with all the children and a governess, another guest of the Levins that summer was the old Princess, who considered it her duty to watch over her inexperienced daughter, as she was in a *certain condition*. And there was also Varenka, Kitty's friend from abroad, who had kept her promise to come and visit Kitty when she was married, and was staying with her friend. All these people were friends or relations of Levin's wife. And although he was fond of them all, he felt a bit sorry for his own Levin world and routine, which had been smothered by this influx of the 'Shcherbatsky element', as he referred to it privately. There was only Sergey Ivanovich from his family staying with them that summer, but even he was a man of the Koznyshev rather than the Levin mould, so that the Levin spirit had been completely obliterated.

There were now so many people in Levin's long-uninhabited house that nearly all the rooms were occupied, and nearly every day when sitting down to table the old Princess was obliged to count everyone all over again, and seat the thirteenth grandson or granddaughter at a special little table. And for Kitty, diligently running the household, there was a good deal of trouble involved in procuring chickens, turkeys, and ducks, a great number of which were consumed due to the summer appetites of the guests and the children.

The whole family was sitting at dinner. Dolly's children were making plans with the governess and Varenka about where they would go to gather mushrooms. Sergey Ivanovich, for whom all the guests harboured a respect bordering on adulation for his intellect and learning, surprised everyone by joining in the conversation about mushrooms.

'Take me along with you too. I am very fond of gathering mushrooms,' he said, looking at Varenka; 'I consider it a very good occupation.'

'Of course, we would be delighted,' answered Varenka, blushing. Kitty exchanged meaningful glances with Dolly. The learned and intellectual Sergey Ivanovich's proposal to go and gather mushrooms with Varenka confirmed for Kitty certain suppositions which had been greatly preoccupying her of late. She hurriedly began talking to her mother so that her glance would not be noticed. After dinner Sergey Ivanovich sat down by the drawing-room window with his cup of coffee, resuming a conversation that had been initiated with his brother and keeping an eye on the door through which would emerge the children, who were getting ready to go mushroom-gathering. Levin sat down on the windowsill next to his brother.

Kitty stood near her husband, clearly waiting for the end of this uninteresting conversation so that she could tell him something.

'You have changed a great deal since you got married, and for the better,' said Sergey Ivanovich, smiling at Kitty, clearly little interested in the conversation that had been initiated, 'but you have remained true to your passion for defending the most paradoxical ideas.'

'Katya, it's not good for you to stand,' her husband said to her, pulling up a chair for her and giving her a meaningful look.

'Yes, well, there's no time now anyway,' added Sergey Ivanovich, seeing the children come running out.

Ahead of all of them, in her tightly pulled-up stockings, waving a basket and Sergey Ivanovich's hat, came Tanya, running straight at him in a sideways gallop.

Running boldly up to Sergey Ivanovich with shining eyes which were so like her father's beautiful eyes, she handed him his hat and made it clear she wanted to put it on for him, moderating her impertinence with a shy and gentle smile.

'Varenka's waiting,' she said, carefully putting his hat on, after seeing from Sergey Ivanovich's smile that this was permissible.

Varenka was standing in the doorway, having changed into a yellow printed cotton dress, with a white scarf tied on her head.

'I'm coming, I'm coming, Varvara Andreyevna,' said Sergey Ivanovich, finishing his cup of coffee and putting his handkerchief and cigar-case into different pockets.

'What a delight my Varenka is! Don't you think?' said Kitty to her husband as soon as Sergey Ivanovich got up. She said this in such a way that Sergey Ivanovich would overhear her, which was obviously her intention. 'And she possesses such beauty, such noble beauty! Varenka!' Kitty shouted. 'Are you going to be in the wood by the mill? We'll come and join you.'

'You're completely forgetting your condition, Kitty,' said the old Princess, scurrying through the door. 'You mustn't shout like that.'

When she heard Kitty's call and her mother's reprimand, Varenka went up to Kitty with quick, light steps. The swiftness of her move-ments and the colour suffusing her animated face all indicated that something unusual was going on inside her. Kitty knew what this unusual thing was, and was watching her intently. She had only called out to Varenka just now in order to bestow on her a mental blessing for the important event which Kitty reckoned was bound to take place after dinner that day in the wood.

'Varenka, I am very happy, but I might be even happier if a certain thing happens,' she whispered as she kissed her.

'So are you going to come with us?' Varenka said to Levin in embar-rassment, pretending she had not heard what had been said to her.

'I will, but only as far as the threshing floor, and I'll stay there.'

'Why do you want to go there?' said Kitty.

'I have to go and look at the new wagons and take stock,' said Levin. 'And where will you be?'

'On the veranda.'

2

THE women of the household had all gathered on the veranda. They generally liked to sit there after dinner, but that day there was also work to do. Besides the sewing of baby vests and the knitting of swaddling clothes, with which they were all busy, that day they were making jam using a method new to Agafya Mikhailovna, that did not require the addition of water. Kitty was introducing this new method, which they used in her family. Agafya Mikhailovna, to whom this task had previously been entrusted, and who considered that nothing done in the Levin household could be wrong, had nevertheless been adding water to the wild and cultivated strawberries, maintaining that it was the only way; she had been caught out doing this, and now the raspberries were being boiled up in front of everyone, and Agafya

Mikhailovna had to be brought round to the idea that jam could also be made perfectly well without water.

With an aggrieved expression on her flushed face, her hair dishevelled and her thin arms bare to the elbows, Agafya Mikhailovna was shaking the preserving pan over the brazier with a circular movement, looking despondently at the raspberries and hoping with all her heart they would set without boiling properly. Conscious that Agafya Mikhailovna's anger was bound to be directed at her as the main adviser on making raspberry jam, the Princess tried to pretend she was busy doing something else and was not interested in the raspberries, so she talked about other matters, but kept looking at the brazier out of the corner of her eye.

'I always buy dresses for the maids myself, at discounted prices,' the Princess said, resuming their conversation. '. . . Isn't it time to skim off the froth, my dear?' she added, addressing Agafya Mikhailovna. 'There's absolutely no need for you to do it yourself, and it's hot,' she said, stopping Kitty.

'I'll do it,' said Dolly, getting up, and she carefully started to pass a spoon across the foaming sugar, from time to time tapping it, in order to remove what had stuck to the spoon, on a plate already covered with yellow-pink froth, underneath which trickled the blood-red syrup. 'How they'll enjoy licking this up with their tea!' she thought about her children, remembering how amazed she had been herself as a child that grown-ups did not eat the froth, which was the best part.

'Stiva says it's much better to give money,' said Dolly meanwhile, continuing the absorbing conversation about how best to give presents to servants, 'but . . .'

'You can't give money!' exclaimed the Princess and Kitty in one voice. 'That puts a price on it.'

'Well, last year, for example, I bought our Matryona Semyonovna something that was not poplin, but very like it,' said the Princess.

'I remember, she was wearing it on your name-day.'

'It had the most adorable pattern; so simple and refined. I would have had something made from it myself, if she hadn't had it. It was a bit like what Varenka's wearing. So pretty and inexpensive.'

'Well, I think it's done now,' said Dolly, letting the syrup drop from the spoon.

'When it forms threads it's ready. Boil it a bit longer, Agafya Mikhailovna.'

'These flies!' said Agafya Mikhailovna crossly. 'It'll be just the same,' she added.

'Ah, how sweet he is, don't frighten him!' Kitty said suddenly, look-ing at a sparrow that had perched on the balustrade and was pecking at the core of a raspberry it had turned over.

'Yes, but you should keep away from the brazier,' said her mother.

'*A propos de* Varenka,' said Kitty in French, which they had been speaking all this time so that Agafya Mikhailovna would not under-stand them. 'You know, *Maman*, for some reason I'm expecting a deci-sion today. You understand what kind. How nice it would be!'

'Hark at what an expert matchmaker she is!' said Dolly. 'How care-fully and cunningly she brings them together . . .'

'No, but tell me, *Maman*, what do you think?'

'But what is there to think about? He'—they were talking about Sergey Ivanovich—'could have always made the best match in Russia; these days he is of course not so young, but all the same, I know there are many who would marry him even now . . . She's very good-natured, but he could . . .'

'No, you have to understand, Mama, why it's impossible to think of anything better either for him or for her. In the first place, she is lovely!' said Kitty, crooking one finger.

'He does like her very much, that's true,' confirmed Dolly.

'Then secondly: the position he occupies in society is such that he has absolutely no need of a wife with money or a position in society. He just needs one thing: a good, sweet, wife, someone quiet.'

'Well, yes, with her it would certainly be quiet,' confirmed Dolly.

'Thirdly, she must love him. And she does . . . In other words, it would be such a good thing! I'm waiting for the moment when they come out of the wood and it will all be settled. I will see straight away from their eyes. I would be so glad! What do you think, Dolly?'

'But you mustn't get excited. You really shouldn't get excited,' said her mother.

'But I'm not excited, Mama. I have a feeling he will propose today.'

'Ah, it's so strange how and when a man proposes . . . There is some kind of barrier, then suddenly it's broken down,' said Dolly with a pen-sive smile as she recalled her past with Stepan Arkadyich.

'Mama, how did Papa propose to you?' Kitty asked suddenly.

'There was nothing special about it, it was very simple,' answered the Princess, but her face completely lit up at the memory.

'But how did he propose? All the same, you did love him before you were allowed to speak, didn't you?'

Kitty felt a particular delight now in being able to talk to her mother on equal terms about these pivotal questions in a woman's life.

'Of course I loved him; he used to come and visit us in the country.'

'But how was it decided, Mama?'

'You no doubt think you both invented something quite new? It's always the same thing: it was decided with looks and smiles . . .'

'How well you put it, Mama! It is exactly looks and smiles,' confirmed Dolly.

'But what words did he say?'

'What words did Kostya say to you?'

'He wrote them in chalk. It was wonderful . . . How long ago it seems!' she said.

And the three women started pondering the same thing. Kitty was the first to break the silence. She had been remembering all of that last winter before her marriage, and her infatuation with Vronsky.

'There is just one thing . . . and that's Varenka's old flame,' she said, a natural train of thought reminding her of this. 'I wanted to say something to Sergey Ivanovich somehow, to prepare him. They are terribly jealous of our past,' she added, 'all men are.'

'Not all of them,' said Dolly. 'You're judging that by your own husband. He is still plagued by the memory of Vronsky, isn't he? It's true, isn't it?'

'Yes,' Kitty answered, a pensive smile in her eyes.

'It is just that I do not know', said the Princess in defence of her maternal supervision of her daughter, 'what exactly in your past could have bothered him? The fact that Vronsky courted you? That happens to every girl.'

'But that's not what we are talking about,' Kitty said, blushing.

'No, excuse me,' her mother continued, 'and then you yourself would not allow me to talk it over with Vronsky. Remember?'

'Oh, Mama!' said Kitty with an agonized expression.

'There's no restraining you girls these days . . . Your relationship could not have gone further than it ought to have done or I would have summoned him myself. Anyway, my love, it's not good for you to be getting excited. Please remember that and calm down.'

'I'm perfectly calm, *Maman.*'

'How fortunate it turned out for Kitty then that Anna came,' said Dolly, 'and how unfortunate for her. It has turned out quite the opposite,' she added, struck by her thought. 'Anna was so happy back then, and Kitty considered herself to be unhappy. Now it is just the opposite! I often think about her.'

'What a person to think about! Disgusting, horrible, heartless woman,' said her mother, unable to forget that Kitty had married Levin, not Vronsky.

'What is the point of talking about that?' Kitty said with annoyance. 'I don't think about it and don't want to think about it . . . I don't want to think about it,' she repeated, hearing her husband's familiar footfall on the steps of the veranda.

'What is it you don't want to think about?' asked Levin as he walked on to the veranda.

But no one answered him, and he did not repeat the question.

'I'm sorry to barge in on your woman's kingdom,' he said, surveying them all grumpily and realizing they had been talking about something they would not have talked about in front of him.

For a brief moment he felt he shared Agafya Mikhailovna's feeling of resentment about them making raspberry jam without water, and about the alien Shcherbatsky influence in general. He smiled, however, and went up to Kitty.

'So, how are things?' he asked her, looking at her with the same expression with which everyone addressed her now.

'Fine,' said Kitty, smiling, 'and how are things with you?'

'The wagons hold three times more than the carts. Well, shall we go and fetch the children? I've ordered the horses to be harnessed.'

'What? Are you planning to take Kitty in the trap?' her mother said reprovingly.

'Only at a walking pace, Princess.'

Levin never called the Princess *Maman* as sons-in-law do, and this displeased her. But despite his fondness and respect for the Princess, Levin could not call her that without dishonouring his feelings for his dead mother.

'Come with us, *Maman*,' said Kitty.

'I don't wish to observe such recklessness.'

'Well, I'll walk then. It's good for me after all.' Kitty rose, went up to her husband, and took his arm.

'It may be good for you, but everything in moderation,' said the Princess.

'So, Agafya Mikhailovna, is the jam ready?' said Levin, smiling at Agafya Mikhailovna and wishing to cheer her up. 'Is it good the new way?'

'It ought to be good. Our way it would be overboiled.'

'It'll be all the better for it, Agafya Mikhailovna, because it won't ferment, and now that our ice has melted, we've nowhere to store it,' said Kitty, immediately cottoning on to her husband's intention and addressing the old woman in the same tone. 'You know, your pickles are so good that Mama says she never tasted anything like them,' she added, smiling as she straightened her kerchief for her.

Agafya Mikhailovna looked angrily at Kitty.

'You don't need to console me, ma'am. I just have to look at you with him and I feel jolly,' she said, and Kitty was touched by her crude way of saying 'with him' rather than 'with the master'.

'Come along with us to look for mushrooms, and you can show us the best places.' Agafya Mikhailovna smiled and shook her head, as if to say: 'I'd like to be angry with you too, but I can't.'

'Please follow my advice,' said the old Princess. 'Cover the jam with a piece of paper soaked in rum, then it will never go mouldy even without ice.'

3

KITTY was particularly glad of the chance to be alone with her husband, because when he came on to the veranda, asked what they were talking about, and received no answer, she noticed a shadow of consternation flitting across his face, which always registered everything so vividly.

After they had walked on ahead of the others and disappeared from view of the house on to the flattened, dusty road, which was strewn with ears of rye and grain kernels, she leaned more heavily on his arm and pressed it to her. He had already forgotten that fleetingly disagreeable impression, and alone with her now, with the thought of her pregnancy never leaving him for an instant, he experienced the radiant pleasure, still novel to him, of an intimacy with the woman he loved which was completely free of sensuality. There was nothing to say, but he wanted to hear the sound of her voice, which had modified during her pregnancy, as her look had. There was in both her voice and her look a softness and a seriousness such as are to be found in people who are constantly focused on a single beloved pursuit.

'Are you sure you won't get tired? Lean on me some more,' he said.

'No, I'm so glad of a chance of being alone with you, and I must admit that as much as I like being with them all, I do miss our winter evenings alone together.'

'That was good, but this is even better. Both are better,' he said, squeezing her arm.

'Do you know what we were talking about when you appeared?'

'About the jam?'

'About the jam as well, yes; but then about how men propose.'

'Ah!' said Levin, listening more to the sound of her voice than to what she was saying while he thought constantly about the road, which was now leading through a wood, so as to avoid places where she might stumble.

'And about Sergey Ivanovich and Varenka. Have you noticed? . . . I would so like it to happen,' she continued. 'What do you think about it?' And she looked into his face.

'I don't know what to think,' Levin answered with a smile. 'I find Sergey very strange in that regard. I think I told you . . .'

'Yes, that he was in love with that girl who died . . .'

'It was when I was a child; I know about it only from hearsay. I remember him then. He was extraordinarily charming. But I've watched him with women since then: he is amiable, and he likes some of them, but you feel that for him they're just people, not women.'

'Yes, but with Varenka now . . . I think there's something . . .'

'Maybe there is . . . But you have to know him . . . He's an unusual, remarkable person. He leads an exclusively spiritual life. He's too pure and high-minded a person.'

'What do you mean? Would it really lower him?'

'No, but he's so used to leading an exclusively spiritual life that he cannot adjust to reality, and Varenka is after all reality.'

Levin was used by now to blurting out his thoughts boldly, without bothering to put them into precise words; he knew that at loving moments such as this one his wife would grasp what he meant to say from a mere hint, and she did.

'Yes, but there is none of that reality in her as there is in me; I can understand why he would never have come to love me. She is completely spiritual . . .'

'No, he is so fond of you, and it is always so nice for me that my family is fond of you . . .'

'Yes, he's kind to me, but . . .'

'But it's not like how it was with our late lamented Nikolenka . . . you did come to love one another,' said Levin, finishing her sentence. 'Why shouldn't we talk about him?' he added. 'I sometimes reproach myself with the thought that I will end up forgetting him. Ah, what an awful and wonderful person he was . . . Now, what was it we were we talking about?' Levin said after a pause.

'You think he cannot fall in love,' said Kitty, translating into her own language.

'It's not so much that he can't fall in love,' Levin said, smiling, 'but that he doesn't have the necessary weakness . . . I've always envied him, and even now, when I'm so happy, I still envy him.'

'You envy him because he cannot fall in love?'

'I envy him for being better than I am,' said Levin. 'He does not live for himself. His whole life is subordinated to duty. And that is why he can be calm and contented.'

'And you?' said Kitty with a teasing, loving smile.

She would have been quite incapable of articulating the train of thought which had made her smile; but the ultimate conclusion was that by exalting his brother and abasing himself before him, her husband was being insincere. Kitty knew that this insincerity of his stemmed from love for his brother, from the pangs of his conscience at being too happy, and in particular from his never-ending desire to be better—she loved this about him, and that was why she smiled.

'And you? What is it you are dissatisfied with?' she asked with the same smile.

Her scepticism about his dissatisfaction with himself gladdened him, and he unconsciously wanted to provoke her into declaring the reasons for her scepticism.

'I am happy, but dissatisfied with myself . . .' he said.

'So how can you be dissatisfied if you are happy?'

'Well, how can I explain it to you? . . . Deep down, there is nothing I really care about except making sure you are not about to trip up. Look, you really shouldn't leap about like that you know!' he exclaimed, breaking off to scold her for making too rapid a movement when stepping over a branch lying on the path. 'But when I analyse myself and compare myself with others, particularly with my brother, I feel I'm bad.'

'But in what way?' continued Kitty with the same smile. 'Don't you also do things for others? What about your farmsteads, and your estate, and your book? . . .'

'No, I feel it, particularly now: it's your fault', he said, squeezing her arm, 'that things are not right. I'm doing everything in a perfunctory way, casually. If I could love all that work like I love you . . . but lately I've been doing it as if I have been set some homework; I'm pretending . . .'

'Well, what would you say about Papa?' asked Kitty. 'Is he bad too, because he has not done anything for the common good?'

'Your Papa? No. But you need to have the simplicity, the clarity, and the kindness of your father, and do you think I have that? I don't do anything, and I feel terrible about it. It's all your doing. When you weren't here and before there was *this*,' he said with a glance at her stomach which she understood, 'I put all my energy into work; but now I can't, and I feel ashamed; it's just as if I was doing homework, I'm pretending . . .'

'I see, but would you want to change places now with Sergey Ivanich?' said Kitty. 'Would you want to do all that work for the common good and love all that homework like he does, and be content with just that?'

'Of course not,' said Levin. 'Actually, I'm so happy that I don't understand anything. But do you really think he'll propose today?' he added after a brief silence.

'I do and I don't. It's just that I would really like it to happen. Here, wait a minute.' She bent down and picked an ox-eye daisy from the edge of the road. 'Come on now, count: he will propose, he won't propose,' she said, handing him the flower.

'He will, he won't,' said Levin, tearing off the slender, white-grooved petals.

'No, no!' Kitty had been anxiously watching his fingers, and she seized his hand and stopped him. 'You tore off two.'

'Yes, but this little one doesn't count,' said Levin, tearing off a short petal that was only half-grown. 'Now the trap has caught up with us.'

'Aren't you tired, Kitty?' the Princess called out.

'Not in the slightest.'

'Otherwise you could get in, as long as the horses are quiet and go at a walking pace.'

But it was not worth getting in. It was not far off now, and they all walked.

4

VARENKA, with her white kerchief covering her black hair, surrounded by the children, good-naturedly and happily busy with them, and clearly excited by the possibility of receiving a declaration of love from a man she liked, was extremely attractive. Sergey Ivanovich walked beside her and constantly admired her. As he looked at her, he remembered all the charming things he had heard her say and all the good things he knew about her, and became increasingly aware that the feelings he was experiencing for her were something special, which he had experienced only once before and long, long ago, when he was very young. The feeling of happiness at being close to her kept intensifying until it got to the point that he looked into her eyes while putting into her basket a huge birch mushroom with a thin stalk and curled-up edges which he had found and, noticing the flush of happy and timorous excitement suffusing her face, he became embarrassed himself and smiled to her silently with the kind of smile which said too much.

'If that is how things are,' he said to himself, 'I must reflect and make up my mind, and not get carried away in the heat of the moment like a boy.'

'I'm going to go and gather mushrooms on my own now, otherwise what I have collected won't be noticed,' he said, and he set off by himself from the edge of the wood, where they had been walking on short, silky grass between sparse old birch trees, into the middle of the wood, where there were grey aspen trunks and dark hazel bushes standing between the white birch trunks. After walking about forty paces away and going behind a spindle bush in full flower with its pinkish-red catkins, Sergey Ivanovich stopped, knowing he could not be seen. It was perfectly still all around him. All he could hear were flies buzzing incessantly like a swarm of bees, high up in the birch trees under which he was standing, and the children's voices which occasionally wafted over. Varenka's contralto voice calling Grisha suddenly rang out not far from the edge of the wood, and a radiant smile appeared on Sergey Ivanovich's face. Conscious of this smile, he shook his head disapprovingly at his state of mind, took out a cigar, and tried to light it. For a long time he could not get a match to strike against the trunk of a birch tree. The soft layer of white bark stuck to the phosphorous, and the light kept going out. Eventually one of his matches ignited, and the pungent cigar smoke, billowing like an outspread tablecloth, was drawn firmly forward and upwards over the bush beneath the branches of the birch tree. Following the ribbon of smoke with his eyes, Sergey Ivanovich walked quietly on, pondering his state of mind.

'Why on earth not?' he thought. 'If this were a sudden outburst or passion, if all I felt was this attraction—this mutual attraction (I can say *mutual*), but felt that it ran counter to my whole way of life, if I felt that I would be betraying my vocation and my duty by surrendering to this attraction . . . but that's not the case. The only thing I can say against it is that when I lost Marie, I told myself I would remain faithful to her memory. That is the only thing I can say against my feelings . . . It's important,' Sergey Ivanovich said to himself, feeling at the same time that this consideration could be of no importance to him personally, apart from possibly spoiling his romantic persona in the eyes of others. 'But apart from that, I am not going to find anything else to say against my feelings, however hard I look. If I were making a choice based on reason alone, I could not do better.'

When he scoured his memory of all the women and girls he had known, he could not recall a single one of them who could unite to such a degree all, literally all, the qualities he wished to find in his wife when reasoning coolly. She had all the charm and freshness of youth, but was not a child, and if she loved him, she loved him consciously, as a woman ought to love: that was one thing. Another: she was not only far from the world of high society, but was clearly repelled by it, while at the same time she was familiar with high society and had all the manners of a woman of good breeding, without which a life partner would be unthinkable for Sergey Ivanovich. Thirdly: she was religious, and not unreflectingly religious and good like a child, in the way that Kitty was, for example; but her life was founded on religious conviction. Even when it came down to the fine details, Sergey Ivanovich found in her everything he wanted in a wife: she was poor and alone, so she would not bring in her wake a cluster of relatives and their influence into her husband's house, as he saw Kitty had, but would be totally beholden to her husband, which he had also always wished for his future family life. And this girl, who united all these qualities, loved him. He was modest, but he could not help seeing this. And he loved her. The one factor against it was his age. But he came from long-living stock, did not have a single grey hair, no one would have taken him for forty, and he remembered Varenka saying that it was only in Russia that men of fifty saw themselves as old men, while in France a man of fifty would consider himself *dans la force de l'âge*,[1] and a forty year-old *un jeune homme*.[2] But what did his accumulation of years matter when he felt as young in spirit as he had been twenty years earlier? Was it not a feeling of youth he was experiencing now, when he came out to the edge of the wood again from the other side and saw against the bright light of the slanting rays of the sun the graceful figure of Varenka in her yellow dress, stepping lightly past the trunk of an old birch tree with her basket, and when the impression made by this vision of Varenka coalesced with the strikingly beautiful vision of the field of yellow oats bathed in the slanting rays, and beyond the field the distant old forest, speckled with yellow and melting into the blue distance? His heart missed a beat. A feeling of tender emotion came over him. He felt he

---

[1] in the prime of life.   [2] a young man.

had made up his mind. Varenka, who had just crouched down to pick
a mushroom, stood up with a lissom movement and looked round.
Throwing away his cigar, Sergey Ivanovich advanced with resolute
step towards her.

5

'VARVARA ANDREYEVNA, when I was still very young I formed my
ideal of the woman I would love and whom I would be happy to call
my wife. I have lived a long life, and now for the first time I have found
what I was searching for in you. I love you, and offer you my hand.'

Sergey Ivanovich was saying this to himself when he was already
within ten paces of Varenka. She had got down on to her knees to protect a mushroom from Grisha, and was calling to little Masha.

'Over here, over here! There are little ones! Lots of them!' she was
saying in her lovely, resonant voice.

She did not get up when she saw Sergey Ivanovich approaching, nor
did she change her position; but everything told him that she felt his
approach and was glad of it.

'Well, did you find any?' she asked, turning her pretty, gently smiling face towards him from under her white kerchief.

'Not one,' said Sergey Ivanovich. 'And you?'

She did not answer, as she was busy with the children flocking round
her.

'There's this one too, near the branch,' she said to little Masha,
pointing out a small russula mushroom, its spongy pink cap cut in
half by a dry blade of grass from under which it had pushed its way
up. Varenka stood up when Masha had picked the mushroom, breaking
it into two white halves. 'This takes me back to my childhood,' she
added, walking by Sergey Ivanovich's side, away from the children.

They took a few steps in silence. Varenka saw that he wanted to
speak; she guessed what about, and felt weak with the excitement of
joy and trepidation. They had walked so far off that no one could hear
them by now, but he still had not begun to speak. It would have been
better if Varenka had remained silent. It would have been easier to say
what they wanted to say after a silence, rather than after talking about
mushrooms; but against her will, as though by accident, Varenka said:

'So you didn't find any? There are always fewer in the middle of the
wood, though.'

Sergey Ivanovich sighed and did not reply. He was annoyed that she had started talking about mushrooms. He wanted to bring her back to her first remarks, when she had spoken about her childhood; but after remaining silent for a while, as if against his own will, he commented on what she had just said.

'I have only heard that white mushrooms are mostly found on the edges of woods, although I wouldn't even know how to identify one.'

A few more minutes passed, they walked even further away from the children, and were quite alone. Varenka's heart was beating so hard she could hear it thumping and she felt she was blushing, turning pale, then blushing again.

To be the wife of a man like Koznyshev after her position with Madame Stahl seemed to her the pinnacle of happiness. Besides, she was almost certain she was in love with him. And now it was about to be decided. She was frightened—frightened both of what he would say and what he would not say.

The declaration had to be made now or never: Sergey Ivanovich felt this too. Everything in Varenka's look, her flushed face and her downcast eyes, betrayed painful expectation. Sergey Ivanovich saw this and felt sorry for her. He even felt that to say nothing now would be to insult her. He quickly went over in his mind again all the arguments in favour of his decision. He also rehearsed the words with which he wanted to make his proposal; but instead of those words, he was struck by some unexpected consideration and suddenly asked:

'What is the difference between a white and a birch mushroom?'

Varenka's lips were quivering with emotion when she answered:

'There isn't any difference in the caps, it's in the stalks.'

And as soon as these words were uttered, both he and she realized that it was all over, that what should have been said would not be said, and their emotion, which just before had reached a point of extreme intensity, began to subside.

'The stalk of a birch mushroom reminds me of the beard of a man with dark hair who hasn't shaved for two days,' said Sergey Ivanovich, speaking quite calmly now.

'Yes, that's true,' answered Varenka, smiling, and the direction of their walk involuntarily changed. They began to draw closer towards the children. Varenka felt hurt and ashamed, but at the same time she experienced a sense of relief.

Returning home, and going over all the arguments again, Sergey Ivanovich found that his deliberations had been wrong. He could not have betrayed Marie's memory.

*

'Quiet, children, quiet!' shouted Levin with a touch of anger as he stood in front of his wife to protect her when the mob of children came rushing to meet them with whoops of delight.

Sergey Ivanovich and Varenka came out of the wood after the children. Kitty did not have to ask Varenka; she saw from the calm and somewhat shamefaced expressions on both their faces that her plans had not materialized.

'Well?' asked her husband when they were on their way home again.

'Won't take hold,' said Kitty, her smile and manner of speaking reminiscent of her father, which was something Levin often took pleasure in noticing about her.

'What do you mean, won't take hold?'

'I'll show you,' she said, taking her husband's hand, raising it to her mouth, and grazing it with closed lips. 'Like people kissing a bishop's hand.'

'Who won't take hold?' he said, laughing.

'Neither of them. You see, it needs to be like this . . .'

'There are peasants coming . . .'

'No, they didn't see.'

6

DURING the children's tea, the grown-ups sat on the balcony and chatted as if nothing had happened, although all of them, especially Sergey Ivanovich and Varenka, knew very well that something very important, albeit negative, had taken place. They were both experiencing the same feeling, like that experienced by a schoolboy who has failed an examination, and has to remain in the same class or be expelled from the school altogether. Also sensing that something had happened, everyone else present talked animatedly about unrelated matters. Levin and Kitty felt particularly happy and in love that evening. But the fact that they were happy in their love contained an unpleasant reminder of those who wanted but could not have the same thing—and that pricked their consciences.

'You mark my words, Alexandre will not come,' said the old Princess.

That evening they were expecting Stepan Arkadyich off the train, and the old Prince had written that he might come too.

'And I know why,' the Princess went on, 'because he says that young couples ought to be left alone at first.'

'Yes, Papa has certainly left us alone. We haven't seen him at all,' said Kitty. 'But how can we be regarded as young? We're already so old now.'

'Only if he doesn't come, I shall say goodbye to you children too,' said the Princess with a mournful sigh.

'Mama, you can't mean that!' Both daughters fell on her.

'But what do you think it's like for him? After all, now . . .'

And completely unexpectedly the old Princess's voice suddenly began to tremble. Her daughters fell silent and exchanged glances. '*Maman* will always find something to be sad about,' is what they said with that glance. What they did not know was that, however much the Princess was enjoying staying with her daughter, and however much she felt she was needed there, she had been feeling an unbearable sadness on both her and her husband's part since they had given away in marriage their last beloved daughter and the nest had completely emptied.

'What is it, Agafya Mikhailovna?' Kitty suddenly asked Agafya Mikhailovna, who had come in and was standing there with a mysterious look and a significant expression.

'About supper.'

'Ah yes, very good,' said Dolly. 'You go and see about that, and I'll go off with Grisha and help him with his schoolwork. Otherwise he won't have done anything all day.'

'That's a lesson for me! No, Dolly, I'll go,' said Levin, jumping up.

Grisha, who was already in high school, had homework to do during the summer. Darya Alexandrovna had been learning Latin with her son back in Moscow and, after arriving at the Levins, had made it a rule to go over the most difficult lessons in Latin and arithmetic with him at least once a day. Levin had volunteered to take her place; but the mother, after hearing Levin take a lesson one day and noticing that his coaching was unlike that of the teacher in Moscow, while embarrassed and anxious not to offend Levin, had told him firmly that they had to go through the textbook like the teacher did, and that she had better take over again herself. Levin was cross, both with Stepan Arkadyich for being so lackadaisical that it was not he but the mother who was supervising the teaching, which she had not the faintest idea about, and also with the teachers for teaching the children so badly; but he promised his sister-in-law to organize the teaching in the way she wanted. And he went on coaching Grisha by the book, rather in his own way, thus without any enthusiasm and often forgetting the time of the lesson. So it was that day.

'No, I'll go, Dolly, you sit still,' he said. 'We'll do it all properly, by the book. But look, when Stiva comes, we're going to go shooting, and that's when I'll miss a lesson.'

And Levin went off to find Grisha.

Varenka said the same thing to Kitty. Varenka had managed to make herself useful even in the happy, well-run Levin household.

'I'll see to the supper, you sit still,' she said, and got up to accompany Agafya Mikhailovna.

'Oh yes, they probably couldn't get any chickens. In which case, there are ours . . .' said Kitty.

'Agafya Mikhailovna and I will sort things out.' And Varenka vanished with her.

'What a nice girl!' said the Princess.

'Not nice, *Maman*, but so enchanting there is no one like her.'

'So you are expecting Stepan Arkadyich today?' said Sergey Ivanovich, clearly not wishing to continue the conversation about Varenka. 'It would be difficult to find two brothers-in-law less alike than your husbands,' he said with a thin-lipped smile. 'One always on the move, living only in society like a fish in water; the other, our Kostya, lively, quick, sensitive to everything, but as soon as he is in company he either clams up or flails about wildly like a fish on dry land.'

'Yes, he's very irresponsible,' said the Princess, turning to Sergey Ivanovich. 'I've actually been meaning to ask you to tell him that she—Kitty—cannot stay here, but absolutely must come to Moscow. He is talking about sending for a doctor . . .'

'*Maman*, he will do everything, he will agree to everything,' Kitty said, annoyed with her mother for inviting Sergey Ivanovich to be a judge in this matter.

In the middle of their conversation they heard the snorting of horses and the sound of wheels on gravel in the drive.

Before Dolly had managed to get up in order to go and greet her husband, Levin had leapt out of the window of the room downstairs where Grisha was doing his schoolwork and had helped Grisha down.

'It's Stiva!' Levin called out from under the balcony. 'We've finished, Dolly, don't worry!' he added, and ran off like a boy to meet the carriage.

'*Is ea id, eius, eius, eius!*'* yelled Grisha, skipping along the avenue.

'And there's someone else as well. It must be Papa!' shouted Levin, stopping at the top of the drive. 'Kitty, don't come down those steep steps, go round.'

But Levin had been mistaken in thinking the person sitting in the carriage with Oblonsky was the old Prince. As he approached the carriage, he saw beside Stepan Arkadyich not the Prince, but a handsome, plump young man in a Scotch cap* with long trailing ribbons at the back. This was Vasenka Veslovsky, a second cousin of the Shcherbatskys, a brilliant young man at home both in Petersburg and Moscow, 'a most excellent fellow and a passionate sportsman,' as Stepan Arkadyich introduced him.

Completely unabashed by the disappointment he had caused by taking the place of the old Prince, Veslovsky greeted Levin cheerily, reminding him of their previous acquaintance and, bundling Grisha into the carriage, lifted him over the pointer which Stepan Arkadyich had brought with him.

Levin did not get into the carriage, but walked behind. He was slightly peeved that the old Prince, for whom his affection was growing the more he got to know him, had not come, and that this Vasenka Veslovsky, a completely alien and superfluous person, had come instead. He seemed even more alien and superfluous when Levin approached the steps where the whole eager crowd of grown-ups and children had gathered, and saw Vasenka Veslovsky kiss Kitty's hand in a particularly affectionate and gallant manner.

'Your wife and I are cousins, as well as being old acquaintances,' said Vasenka Veslovsky, shaking Levin's hand again vigorously.

'Well, is there any game?' Stepan Arkadyich asked, turning to Levin almost before he had greeted everyone. 'He and I have the cruellest of intentions. Of course, *Maman*, they have not been in Moscow since then. Now, Tanya, I've got something for you! Get it out from the back of the carriage, please,' he said, talking in all directions. 'How well-rested you look, Dolly darling,' he said to his wife, kissing her hand again, holding it in his, and patting it with the other.

Levin, who a moment earlier had been in the best of spirits, now looked darkly at everyone, and everything displeased him.

'Who was he kissing yesterday with those lips?' he thought, observing Stepan Arkadyich's tenderness with his wife. He looked at Dolly and was also displeased with her.

'She doesn't believe in his love after all. So what is she so happy about? Disgusting!' thought Levin.

He looked at the Princess, whom he had found so endearing a minute earlier, and he did not like the manner in which she welcomed this Vasenka with his ribbons, as if into her own home.

Even Sergey Ivanovich, who had also come out on to the porch, seemed unpleasant to him as a result of the feigned friendliness with which he greeted Stepan Arkadyich, when Levin knew that his brother neither liked nor respected Oblonsky.

And Varenka too, he found offensive for making the acquaintance of this gentleman with her *sainte nitouche*[1] air, while all she could think about was how she could contrive to get married.

And Kitty was the most offensive of all for surrendering to the air of jollity with which this gentleman regarded his arrival in the country as a festive occasion for himself and for everyone else, and that special smile with which she responded to his smile was particularly offensive.

Talking noisily, they all went into the house; but the instant they had all sat down, Levin turned on his heel and left.

Kitty saw something was wrong with her husband. She tried to find a moment to speak to him alone, but he hastened away from her, saying he needed to go to the office. It had been a long time since his farm-work had seemed as important as it did on that day. 'It's all one long holiday for them,' he thought, 'but this is not holiday work, it won't wait, and life can't go on without it.'

7

LEVIN only came home when they sent to call him in to supper. Kitty and Agafya Mikhailovna were standing on the stairs, discussing the wines for supper.

'Why are you making such a *fuss*?[2] Serve the same ones as usual.'

'No, Stiva won't drink . . . Kostya, wait, what's the matter?' Kitty began, hurrying after him, but he strode heartlessly into the dining room without waiting for her and immediately launched into the general, lively conversation being maintained there by Vasenka Veslovsky and Stepan Arkadyich.

'So, are we going shooting tomorrow?' said Stepan Arkadyich.

'Oh please, do let's go,' said Veslovsky, moving to another chair, where he sat down sideways, with one fat leg crossed under him.

'Yes, let's go, I'd be delighted. So have you done any shooting yet this year?' said Levin to Veslovsky, but with that feigned bonhomie Kitty knew so well and which so ill-suited him, as he made a detailed examination of his leg. 'I don't know that we will find any great snipe, but there are plenty of common snipe. We would need to start early though. You won't be tired? Aren't you tired, Stiva?'

---

[1] holier than thou.   [2] [English in the original.]

'Me tired? I've never been tired in my life. Let's stay up all night! Let's go for a walk.'

'Yes, let's really stay up! Excellent!' Veslovsky agreed.

'Oh, we all know you can do without sleep, and keep other people up too,' Dolly said to her husband, with that faint note of irony with which she almost always addressed her husband now. 'But I think it's high time already . . . I'm off, I won't have any supper.'

'No, do stay for a while, Dolly darling,' he said, going round to her side of the big table at which they were having supper. 'I've got so much more to tell you!'

'Nothing, probably.'

'You know, Veslovsky has been to stay with Anna. And he's going to visit them again. They're only about fifty miles from you here, after all. I am definitely going to go over too. Veslovsky, come here!'

Vasenka moved over to the ladies and sat down next to Kitty.

'Oh, do tell me, please, you've been to see her? How is she?' Darya Alexandrovna said, turning to him.

Levin remained at the other end of the table and, while keeping up an unflagging conversation with the Princess and Varenka, he saw that there was a lively and mysterious conversation going on between Dolly, Kitty, and Veslovsky. A mysterious conversation was bad enough, but he also saw on his wife's face an expression of deep emotion when she fastened her eyes on Vasenka's handsome face while he was giving a lively account of something.

'It's very nice at their place,' Vasenka was saying about Vronsky and Anna. 'Obviously it's not for me to judge, but you feel part of the family in their house.'

'But what do they intend to do?'

'It seems they want to spend the winter in Moscow.'

'Wouldn't it be good if we all went over and visited them! When are you going?' Stepan Arkadyich asked Vasenka.

'I'm spending July with them.'

'And will you go?' said Stepan Arkadyich, turning to his wife.

'I've been wanting to for a long time and I definitely will go,' said Dolly. 'I am sorry for her, and I know her. She's a wonderful woman. I will go on my own, when you leave, and then I won't be in anyone's way. It will actually be better without you.'

'That sounds fine to me,' said Stepan Arkadyich. 'What about you, Kitty?'

'Me? Why should I go?' Kitty said, blushing furiously. And she glanced round at her husband.

'Do you know Anna Arkadyevna?' Veslovsky asked her. 'She's a very attractive woman.'

'Yes,' she replied to Veslovsky, blushing even more, and she stood up and went over to her husband.

'So are you going shooting tomorrow?' she said.

His jealousy had gone far during those few minutes, especially when he saw that crimson colour spreading over her cheeks while she was talking to Veslovsky. As he listened to the words she was speaking now, he was already interpreting them in his own way. However strange he found it to recall later, it now seemed clear to him that if she was asking whether he was going shooting, it was because she was only interested in finding out whether he was going to bestow that pleasure on Vasenka Veslovsky, with whom, he imagined, she was already in love.

'Yes, I am,' he answered her in an unnatural voice that he himself found odious.

'No, it would be better if you spent the day here tomorrow, as Dolly hasn't seen her husband at all, and then go the day after tomorrow,' said Kitty.

The meaning of Kitty's words was now already being translated by Levin thus: 'Don't separate me from *him*. I don't care if you go, but let me enjoy the company of this delightful young man.'

'Oh, we can stay here tomorrow if you wish,' Levin answered, with studied congeniality.

Vasenka, meanwhile, not remotely suspecting all the suffering caused by his presence, had got up from the table after Kitty and followed her, fixing her with a smiling, affectionate gaze.

Levin saw that look. He turned pale and for a moment could not draw breath. 'How dare he look at my wife like that!' was the thought seething inside him.

'Tomorrow then? Please let's go,' said Vasenka, sitting down on a chair and tucking his leg up under him again.

Levin's jealousy went even further. He already saw himself as a deceived husband, needed by his wife and her lover solely to provide them with material comforts and entertainment . . . But he nevertheless questioned Vasenka politely and hospitably about his shooting, his gun, and his boots, and agreed to go the next day.

Fortunately for Levin, the old Princess curtailed his suffering by getting up herself and advising Kitty to go to bed. But even at this point Levin could not escape another agony. As he took his leave of his hostess, Vasenka again tried to kiss her hand, but Kitty, blushing, withdrew her hand and said, with a naive rudeness for which the old Princess reproved her afterwards:

'That is not customary in our house.'

In Levin's eyes she was to blame for allowing such behaviour, even more so for showing so clumsily that she did not like it.

'Well, who could want to sleep!' said Stepan Arkadyich, who was now in his most likeable and romantic mood after drinking several glasses of wine at supper. 'Look, Kitty, look,' he said, pointing to the moon rising behind the linden trees. 'How lovely! Veslovsky, this is the moment for a serenade. You know, he has a wonderful voice. We did a bit of singing on our way here. He has brought some marvellous songs with him, two new ones. He should sing with Varvara Andreyevna.'

After everyone had dispersed, Stepan Arkadyich spent a long time walking along the drive with Veslovsky, and their voices could be heard trying out one of the new songs.

As he listened to these voices, Levin was sitting scowling in an armchair in his wife's bedroom and responding to her questions about what was wrong with a stubborn silence; but when she herself at last asked with a timid smile: 'Was there something you didn't like about Veslovsky?' he exploded, and told her everything: what he had to tell her was humiliating, which consequently annoyed him all the more.

He stood in front of her with his eyes blazing frighteningly from under scowling brows and with his hefty arms clamped to his chest, as if he was exerting every muscle in order to restrain himself. The expression on his face would have been harsh and even cruel, if it did not at the same time express suffering, and that touched her. His cheekbones were quivering, and his voice faltered.

'You must understand that I'm not jealous; that's a vile word. I can't be jealous and believe that . . . I can't say what I feel, but this is awful . . . I'm not jealous, but I feel insulted, humiliated that anybody could dare think, dare look at you with such eyes . . .'

'But with what eyes?' said Kitty, trying as diligently as possible to recall every word and gesture that evening and all their nuances.

She did think in the depths of her soul that there had been something, right at the moment when he had followed her and crossed over to the other end of the table, but she did not dare admit it even to herself, let alone tell him and thus increase his suffering.

'And what on earth could possibly be attractive about me looking the way I do? . . .'

'Ah!' he cried, clutching his head. 'You shouldn't say that! . . . So, if you had been attractive . . .'

'No, Kostya, just wait a minute and listen!' she said, looking at him with an expression of pained sympathy. 'Whatever can you be thinking! When you know full well that other people do not exist for me! . . . Well, would you rather I saw no one?'

She had initially been offended by his jealousy; she was vexed that she should be barred from the slightest and most innocent amusement; but now she would have willingly sacrificed not just such trifles, but everything for his peace of mind, to save him from the agony he was suffering.

'You must understand the horror and absurdity of my position,' he went on in a desperate whisper, 'which is that he's in my house, and that he's actually done nothing improper except for being unduly familiar and sitting with his leg tucked up under him. He regards it as the height of good form, and so I must be polite to him.'

'But, Kostya, you're exaggerating,' said Kitty, rejoicing in the depths of her soul at the intensity of his love for her, which was now being expressed in his jealousy.

'The worst thing is that you are just as you always are, and now when you're so sacred to me, we're so happy, so incredibly happy, and then suddenly a scoundrel like that . . . He's not a scoundrel, why am I abusing him? He is nothing to do with me. But why should your happiness and mine . . . ?'

'I understand what brought this on, you know,' Kitty began.

'What? What?'

'I saw you watching while we were talking at supper.'

'Well, yes, it's true!' Levin said in alarm.

She told him what they had been talking about. And as she told him, she became choked up with emotion. Levin was silent, then peered closely at her pale, frightened face and suddenly clutched at his head.

'Katya, I've been torturing you! Darling, forgive me! It's madness! Katya, it's all my fault. How could I have suffered agonies over such idiocy?'

'No, I feel sorry for you.'

'For me? Me? What am I? I'm a madman! . . . But why make you miserable? It's awful to think that any stranger could ruin our happiness.'

'Of course, that's what is so insulting . . .'

'Well, in that case I'll go out of my way to make him stay here all summer and will shower him with compliments,' said Levin, kissing her hands. 'You'll see. Tomorrow . . . Although tomorrow we are actually heading off.'

8

THE next day, the ladies had not yet risen before the trap and the little cart which made up the two hunting vehicles were standing by the front steps, and Laska, aware since early morning that they were going shooting, and having yelped and leapt about to her heart's content, was sitting next to the coachman in the trap and looking anxiously and with disapproval, due to the delay, at the door, through which the sportsmen had still not emerged. The first to appear was Vasenka Veslovsky, wearing new high boots which reached halfway up his thick thighs, a green smock round which was tied a new cartridge-belt smelling of leather, his cap with the ribbons, and a brand-new English gun without bracket or sling. Laska came bounding up to greet him and, after leaping about, asked him in her own way whether the others were going to come out soon, but when she received no reply from him she returned to her waiting-post and again sat stock still, with her head cocked to one side and one ear pricked. At last the door opened with a crash and Stepan Arkadyich's gold-brindle pointer Krak flew out, spinning round and turning over in the air, followed by Stepan Arkadyich himself, with a gun in his hand and a cigar in his mouth. 'Down, Krak, get down!' he reprimanded the dog affectionately when it thrust its paws on his stomach and chest, and got them caught up in his game-bag. Stepan Arkadyich was wearing light peasant moccasins and foot-bindings,* torn trousers, and a short coat. On his head were the remnants of some kind of hat, but his new-style gun was a gem, and his game-bag and cartridge-belt, though well worn, were of the very best quality.

Vasenka Veslovsky had not understood before that true style for the sportsman meant dressing in rags but having shooting equipment of the best quality. He understood it now, looking at the radiant Stepan Arkadyich, who cut an elegant, well-nourished, and jaunty seigneurial figure in these rags, and decided that he would definitely kit himself out like that the next time he went shooting.

'Well, what about our host?' he asked.

'Young wife,' said Stepan Arkadyich, smiling.

'Yes, and such a charming one.'

'He was already dressed. He's probably run up to her again.'

Stepan Arkadyich guessed right. Levin had dashed back to his wife to ask her again whether she forgave him for the previous day's idiocy, and also to ask her for the love of God to be more careful. The main thing was for her to keep away from the children—they could knock into her at any time. Then he also had to obtain yet another assurance from her that she was not angry with him for going away for two days, and ask her to make sure she sent him a note with a servant on horseback the next day, even if it meant writing only two words, just so he could know she was all right.

As always, Kitty found it painful to be parted from her husband for two days, but when she encountered his sprightly figure, looking particularly big and strong in his shooting-boots and white smock, and exuding a curious aura of excitement about shooting which she did not understand, she forgot her dejection on account of his exhilaration and said a merry goodbye to him.

'Sorry, gentlemen!' he said, running out onto the steps. 'Have you put the lunch in? Why is the chestnut on the right? Well, it doesn't matter. Stop it, Laska, go and sit down!'

'Put them in with the yearling flock,' he said turning to the herdsman, who had been waiting for him on the steps with a question about the wether sheep.* 'Sorry, here comes another miscreant.'

Levin jumped down from the trap, in which he had already taken his seat, to meet the carpenter, who was walking up to the steps with a ruler in his hand.

'Look, you didn't come to the office yesterday, and now you're holding me up. Well, what is it?'

'If you could just order another turn to be made. It would only add three more little steps. And then it will all fit. It'll be much easier.'

'You should have listened to me,' Levin answered with annoyance. 'I said: sort out the stringers and then cut the steps. You can't adjust things now. Do as I told you, and make a new one.'

What had happened was that the carpenter had botched the staircase in the wing that was being built, having built it separately without calculating the elevation so that all the steps ended up being slanted when it was put in position. Now the carpenter wanted to add three steps, using the same staircase.

'It will be much better.'

'But where's your staircase going to end up with these three steps?'

'If you will excuse me, sir,' the carpenter said with a scornful smile. 'It will end up where it should. So it'll start at the bottom,' he said with an emphatic gesture, 'then it will go up, and up, until it arrives.'

'But those three steps will add to the length . . . So where exactly will it arrive?'

'It'll arrive the same way it goes up from the bottom,' the carpenter said stubbornly and emphatically.

'It'll arrive under the ceiling and in the wall.'

'If you'll excuse me. It'll go up from the bottom, you see. It will go up and up and then arrive.'

Levin got out a ramrod and started drawing the staircase for him in the dust.

'So, now do you see?'

'As you wish,' said the carpenter, his eyes suddenly brightening, as he had obviously finally grasped what the problem was. 'Seems we'll have to cut a new one.'

'Well then, go off and do as you were instructed!' Levin shouted as he sat down in the trap. 'Drive on! Hold the dogs, Filip!'

Having left all his family and farming worries behind, Levin was now experiencing such an intense feeling of the joy of life and anticipation that he did not want to talk. He was also experiencing that feeling of concentrated excitement which every sportsman experiences upon approaching the field of action. If there was anything on his mind now, it was only questions about whether they would find anything in the Kolpensky marsh, how Laska would compare with Krak, and how well he himself would shoot that day. How to avoid disgracing himself in front of someone new, and how not to let Oblonsky outshoot him were also thoughts which occurred to him.

Oblonsky was experiencing similar feelings and was also taciturn. Only Vasenka Veslovsky kept up a ceaseless flow of merry chatter. As he listened to him now, Levin felt ashamed to recall how unjust to him he had been the day before. Vasenka really was a nice fellow—simple, kind-hearted, and very jolly. If Levin had come across him when he was a bachelor, he would have made friends with him. Levin did find the way he treated life like a holiday and his rather casual idea of elegance slightly unappealing. It was as if he automatically claimed an elevated importance for himself because he had long nails, a hat, and all the accoutrements that went with them; but this could be forgiven due to his good nature and decorum. Levin liked him for his manners, his excellent French and English pronunciation, and because he was a person from his own background.

Vasenka was greatly taken with the left trace-horse, which came from the Don Steppe. He kept admiring it.

'Galloping over the steppes on a steppe horse is so good. Eh? Don't you think?' he said.

He imagined there was something wild and romantic about riding a steppe horse, which he had never actually done; but his naivety, particularly in conjunction with his good looks, his winsome smile, and graceful movements, was very attractive. Either because his nature was congenial to Levin, or because Levin was trying to atone for his sin of the previous evening by only seeing good things in him, Levin enjoyed his company.

After they had driven about two miles, Veslovsky suddenly mislaid his cigars and wallet, and did not know whether he had lost them or left them on the table. There were three hundred and seventy roubles in the wallet, therefore the matter could not simply be dropped.

'Do you know what, Levin, I'll gallop home on this Don trace-horse. It would be marvellous, wouldn't it?' he said, preparing to mount.

'No, why should you have to do that?' answered Levin, calculating that Vasenka had to weigh no less than fifteen stone. 'I'll send the coachman.'

The coachman rode back on the trace-horse, while Levin himself drove the pair.

9

'WELL, so what's our route? Tell us all about it,' said Stepan Arkadyich.

'This is the plan: at the moment we're driving to Gvozdevo. On this side of Gvozdevo there's a marsh with great snipe, and beyond Gvozdevo there are some superb marshes for common snipe and sometimes great snipe too. It's hot now, and we'll arrive towards evening (it's fifteen miles or so), so we can do some evening shooting; we'll spend the night there and go on to the big marshes tomorrow.'

'But isn't there anything on the way?'

'There is, but it would hold us up, and it's hot. There are two nice little places, but I doubt there would be anything there.'

Levin wanted to stop off at these little places himself, but these little places were close to home, he could shoot there any time, and they were small—there was not room for three people to shoot. And so he was being disingenuous by saying he doubted there was anything there. When they drew level with a small marsh, Levin wanted to drive past, but Stepan Arkadyich's experienced sportsman's eye immediately spotted the patch of wetland that was visible from the road.

'How about stopping off here?' he said, pointing to the little marsh.

'Levin, do let's! How wonderful!' Vasenka Veslovsky began pleading, and Levin had no choice but to agree.

They had barely managed to stop before the dogs were already haring off towards the marsh, racing one another.

'Krak! Laska! . . .'

The dogs came back.

'Not enough room for three people. I'll stay here,' said Levin, hoping they would not find anything other than the lapwings, which had soared up away from the dogs and were crying plaintively above the marsh, wavering as they flew.

'No! Come along, Levin, let's go together!' Veslovsky called.

'Really, there won't be room. Laska, come back! Laska! You won't need another dog, will you?'

Levin remained with the trap and looked enviously at the sportsmen. The sportsmen went all over the little marsh. Apart from waterfowl and lapwings, one of which was killed by Vasenka, there was nothing in the marsh.

'So you see, I wasn't grudging you the marsh,' said Levin, 'it was just a waste of time.'

'No, it was still fun. Did you see?' said Vasenka Veslovsky, clambering awkwardly into the trap with his gun and the lapwing in his hands. 'How well I shot this one! Don't you think? Well, will we be getting to the real thing soon?'

The horses suddenly lurched forwards, Levin hit his head on the barrel of someone's gun, and a shot resounded. It was actually the shot which resounded first, but that is not how it seemed to Levin. What had happened was that while Vasenka Veslovsky was uncocking his gun, he had pressed one trigger while holding the other. The shot was fired into the ground without doing anyone any harm. Stepan Arkadyich shook his head and laughed reprovingly at Veslovsky. But Levin did not have the heart to scold him. Firstly, any reproach would seem to have been provoked by the danger which was now past and the bump which had sprung up on Levin's forehead; and secondly, Veslovsky was so naively upset to begin with and then laughed so good-naturedly and infectiously at their general panic that he could not help laughing himself.

When they reached the second marsh, which was fairly large and bound to take a good deal of time, Levin tried to persuade them not to get out, but Veslovsky again talked him round. Since the marsh was narrow, Levin remained with the vehicles again like a good host.

Krak went straight for the tussocks. Vasenka Veslovsky was the first to run after the dog. Stepan Arkadyich had barely time to approach before a great snipe flew out. Veslovsky missed and the snipe flew over into an unmown meadow. This snipe was left to Veslovsky. Krak found it again and pointed; Veslovsky shot it and went back to the vehicles.

'Now you go, and I'll stay with the horses,' he said.

Levin was beginning to be consumed with huntsman's envy. He handed the reins to Veslovsky and walked into the marsh.

Laska, who had long been whining pitifully and complaining about the injustice, sped off ahead, straight to a reliable patch of boggy ground covered with tussocks which Levin knew, where Krak had not yet been.

'Why don't you stop her?' shouted Stepan Arkadyich.

'She won't scare them off,' answered Levin, pleased with his dog and hurrying after her.

As Laska grew closer and closer to the familiar tussocks, her search became more and more serious. A small marsh bird only distracted her for a moment. She circled once in front of the tussocks, began to circle a second time, then suddenly gave a shudder and stood stock still.

'Stiva, come over here!' shouted Levin, feeling his heart beginning to beat faster, and then all of a sudden, as if some sort of bolt had been drawn back in his keen hearing, and having lost all measure of distance, every sound began to strike him randomly but distinctly. When he heard Stepan Arkadyich's footsteps, he took them for the distant sound of horses' hooves, and when he heard the delicate sound of the grass on the clump of tussock he had trodden on breaking off at the roots, he took this to be the sound of a great snipe on the wing. He also heard not far behind him a strange splashing sound in the water, which he could not account for.

Carefully choosing where to place his feet, he advanced towards the dog.

'Fetch!'

It was not a great snipe but a common snipe that flew up from under the dog. Levin raised his gun, but just at the moment when he was taking aim, that same sound of splashing in the water grew closer and more intense, and was joined by Veslovsky's voice shouting something strangely and loudly. Levin saw that he was aiming behind the snipe, but fired anyway.

After making sure he had missed, Levin looked round and saw that the horses and the trap were no longer on the road but in the marsh.

Eager to see the shooting, Veslovsky had driven into the marsh and got the horses stuck.

'Damn him!' Levin said to himself as he returned to the trap stuck in the mire. 'Why did you drive off?' he said to him brusquely and, after calling the coachman, he began getting the horses out.

Levin was cross that he had been put off his shot, he was cross that his horses had got stuck, and above all he was cross because neither Stepan

Arkadyich nor Veslovsky helped him and the coachman to unharness the horses in order to get them out, since neither of them had the slightest idea of how harnessing worked. Without saying a word in reply to Vasenka's assurances that it had been quite dry there, Levin worked silently with the coachman to extricate the horses. But later on, when he had been warmed up by the work and had watched Veslovsky pulling the trap by the mudguard so vigorously and earnestly that he even broke it off, Levin reproached himself for being under the influence of the previous day's feelings and treating Veslovsky with excessive coldness, so he tried to smooth over his brusqueness by being especially civil. When everything had been sorted out and the vehicles had been brought back on to the road, Levin ordered lunch to be served.

'*Bon appétit—bonne conscience! Ce poulet va tomber jusqu'au fond de mes bottes*,'[1] said the once-again cheerful Vasenka, quoting a French saying as he finished his second chicken. 'Well, our troubles are over now, and everything will go well. Only, for my sins I'm now duty bound to sit on the box. Don't you think? Eh? No, no, I'm Automedon.* You watch how I get you there!' he answered, not letting go of the reins when Levin asked him to let the coachman drive. 'No, I must atone for my sins, and I'm very comfortable on the box.' And he drove.

Levin was a little afraid he would tire the horses out, especially the chestnut on the left, which he did not know how to control; but he could not help succumbing to Veslovsky's high spirits as he listened to the songs he sang all the way while he was sitting on the box, or to his stories and impersonations of how to drive an English four-in-hand; and after lunch they all reached the Gvozdevo marsh in an exceptionally jolly frame of mind.

10

VASENKA drove the horses so hard that they arrived at the marsh too early, when it was still hot.

Having driven up to the real marsh, the main object of their trip, Levin could not help thinking about how to get rid of Vasenka so he would be able to move around without hindrance. Stepan Arkadyich clearly had the same idea, and on his face Levin could see that preoccupied look which a true sportsman always has before the start of shooting, as well as a degree of his characteristic good-natured cunning.

[1] 'A good appetite means a clear conscience. This chicken will go down to the bottom of my boots.'

'So how shall we proceed? It's a splendid marsh, I can see, and there are hawks,' said Stepan Arkadyich, pointing to two great birds hovering over the sedges. 'Where there are hawks, there is sure to be game.'

'Now look, gentlemen,' said Levin with a slightly dour expression as he pulled up his boots and examined the hammers on his gun. 'Do you see that sedge?' He pointed to a dark little island of black vegetation in the huge half-mown water meadow which stretched along the right bank of the river. 'The marsh begins here, right in front of us, do you see—where it is greener. From here it goes to the right where the horses are; there are tussocks there, and sometimes great snipe; and it goes round these sedges as far as those alders and right up to the mill. Over there, see, where the bay is. That's the best place. I shot seventeen snipe there once. We'll go our separate ways with the two dogs and meet up there at the mill.'

'Well, who is going left and who is going right?' asked Stepan Arkadyich. 'There's more room to the right, so you two go that way and I'll go to the left,' he said with apparent nonchalance.

'Excellent! We'll outshoot him! Well, come on, let's go!' Vasenka chimed in.

Levin had no option but to agree, and they split up.

As soon as they entered the marsh, both dogs set off hunting together and were drawn towards a patch of rust-coloured water. Levin knew this careful and indefinite method Laska had; he knew the place too and was expecting a wisp of snipe.

'Veslovsky, walk beside me. Beside me!' he said in a halting voice to his companion who was splashing through the water behind him, Levin now involuntarily taking an interest in the direction of his gun after that accidental shot in the Kolpensky marsh.

'No, I won't get in your way, don't worry about me.'

But Levin could not help worrying and remembering Kitty's parting words: 'Be careful you don't shoot each other.' The dogs were getting nearer and nearer, keeping out of each other's way as they followed their own trail; the expectation of snipe was so intense that Levin thought the squelching sound of his heel as he pulled it out of the bog was the call of a snipe, and he clutched the butt of his gun and held it tight.

'Bang! bang!' rang out above his ear. It was Vasenka shooting a flock of ducks that had been circling over the marsh and just then flying towards the sportsmen far out of range. A snipe squelched* before Levin had time to look round, followed by a second and a third, and then about eight more rose one after the other.

Stepan Arkadyich cut one down at the very moment it was beginning its zigzag flight, and the snipe fell into the bog in a little bundle. Oblonsky aimed unhurriedly at another which was still flying low towards the sedges and, together with the sound of the shot fired, that snipe also fell; it could be seen bouncing up from the mown sedges, flapping its uninjured wing and exposing the white underside.

Levin was not so lucky: he fired too near the first snipe and missed; he took aim at it when it started rising, but just at that moment another flew out from under his feet and distracted him, so he missed again.

While they were loading their guns, another snipe rose, and Veslovsky, who had finished reloading, fired two charges of birdshot across the water. Stepan Arkadyich collected his snipe, and looked at Levin with shining eyes.

'Well, let's separate now,' said Stepan Arkadyich and, limping with his left foot, holding his gun at the ready and whistling to his dog, he walked off in one direction. Levin and Veslovsky went in the other.

It always happened with Levin that whenever his first shots were unsuccessful, he would become cross and irritable and shoot badly all day. So it was that day. There turned out to be a great many snipe. They kept flying up from under the dogs, and from under the sportsmen's feet, and Levin could have recovered his form; but the more he shot, the more he brought shame on himself in front of Veslovsky, who kept merrily firing away, in range and out of range, never killing anything and not in the slightest abashed by it. Levin was over-hasty and rash, and he became more and more flustered until it got to the point where he was shooting almost without any hope of killing anything. It seemed that Laska also understood this. She became more languid about searching and looked round at the sportsmen as if with bewilderment or reproach. Shot followed shot. Gunpowder smoke hung about the sportsmen, but the large and capacious net in the game-bag contained only three slender little snipe. And even then, one had been killed by Veslovsky and another by both of them. Meanwhile from the other side of the marsh came the sound of sporadic, but what seemed to Levin to be effective, shots from Stepan Arkadyich's gun, almost every one followed by: 'Krak, Krak, go fetch!'

This upset Levin even more. There were snipe constantly circling in the air above the sedges. Their squelching down on the ground and their cawing up in the sky could be heard incessantly on all sides; the snipe flushed earlier which had been on the wing were landing in front of the sportsmen. Instead of two hawks there were now dozens of them screeching as they hovered over the marsh.

After walking through more than half the marsh, Levin and Veslovsky reached the place where the peasants' meadow was divided into long strips bordered by the sedges and either trodden down or mown. Half of these strips had already been mown.

Although there was not much hope of finding as many birds in the unmown areas as in the mown ones, Levin had promised to join up with Stepan Arkadyich, and he walked on further with his companion along the mown and unmown strips.

'Hey, huntsmen!' one of the peasants sitting on an unharnessed cart shouted out to them. 'Come and eat with us! Have something to drink!'

Levin looked round.

'Come on, it's good!' shouted a jovial, bearded peasant with a red face, baring his white teeth in a grin and holding up a greenish bottle which glinted in the sunlight.

'*Qu'est-ce qu'ils disent?*'[1] asked Veslovsky.

'They're inviting us to have some vodka. They've probably been dividing up the meadow. I'd have a drink,' said Levin, not without guile, hoping Veslovsky would be tempted by the vodka and go and join them.

'Why are they inviting us?'

'Oh, they are just enjoying themselves. Really, you should join them. You'd find it interesting.'

'*Allons, c'est curieux.*'[2]

'Off you go, you'll find the way to the mill!' Levin shouted, and when he looked round he was pleased to see Veslovsky, hunched over and stumbling on his tired legs, and holding his gun at arm's length, making his way out of the marsh towards the peasants.

'You come too!' the peasant shouted to Levin. 'Don't stand back! Have a bite of pie! Here!'

Levin was longing to drink some vodka and eat a piece of bread. He was exhausted, and felt he could only just pull his tottering legs out of the quagmire, so for a moment he hesitated. But Laska was pointing. All his tiredness vanished in an instant, and he walked easily through the quagmire towards his dog. A snipe flew out from under his feet; he fired and killed it, but the dog continued to point. 'Fetch!' Another bird flew up from under the dog. Levin fired. But it was not his lucky day; he missed, and when he went to look for the one he had killed, he could not find that either. He trawled through all the sedges, but Laska did not believe he had shot anything, and when

---

[1] 'What are they saying?'   [2] 'Let's go, it's interesting.'

he sent her to search, she pretended she was searching, but was not really searching.

Even without Vasenka, whom Levin blamed for his bad luck, things did not improve. There were plenty of snipe here too, but Levin missed one after another.

The slanting rays of the sun were still hot; his clothes, drenched with sweat, clung to his body; his left boot, which was full of water, was heavy and squelched; there were beads of sweat rolling down his gunpowder-smeared face; there was a bitter taste in his mouth, a smell of powder and the marsh in his nose, and an incessant sound of snipe squelching in his ears; the barrels of his gun had grown too hot to handle; his heart was thumping with rapid, short beats; his hands were trembling with the tension, and his weary legs were stumbling and getting in the way of each other on the tussocks and in the bog; but he carried on walking and shooting. Finally, after one disgraceful miss, he flung his gun and his hat on the ground.

'No, I must pull myself together!' he said to himself. He picked up his gun and his hat, called Laska to heel, and left the marsh. When he got out on to dry ground he sat down on a tussock, took off his boots and poured out the water, then walked over to the marsh, slaked his thirst with rusty-tasting water, wet the scorching-hot barrels of his gun, and washed his face and hands. After freshening up, he went back to the spot where a snipe had landed, with the firm intention of not losing his temper.

He wanted to remain calm, but it was the same as before. His finger pressed the trigger before he had taken aim at the bird. Things just got worse and worse.

He only had five birds in his game-bag when he headed towards the alder grove where he was to meet up with Stepan Arkadyich.

Before he saw Stepan Arkadyich he saw his dog. Completely black from the stinking mud from the bog, Krak leapt out from behind the upturned root of an alder and began sniffing Laska with the air of a conqueror. The imposing figure of Stepan Arkadyich materialized behind Krak in the shade of the alders. Red-faced and sweaty, his collar unbuttoned, he walked towards him, limping as before.

'Well, how did you get on? You were doing a lot of shooting!' he said, smiling merrily.

'And what about you?' asked Levin. But there was no need to ask, because he had already seen the full game-bag.

'Oh, it wasn't too bad.'

He had fourteen birds.

'Nice marsh! I'm sure Veslovsky got in your way. It's awkward having one dog for two people,' said Stepan Arkadyich, trying to tone down his triumph.

11

WHEN Levin and Stepan Arkadyich arrived at the peasant's hut where Levin always stayed, Veslovsky was already there. He was sitting in the middle of the hut, gripping a bench with both hands and laughing his infectiously merry laugh, while a soldier, the brother of the peasant's wife, tugged at his slime-covered boots.

'I've just arrived. *Ils ont été charmants.*[1] Can you imagine, they gave me drink and fed me. What bread, it was wonderful! *Delicieux!* And the vodka—I've never tasted anything better! And they absolutely refused to take any money. And they kept saying: "no offence" or something like that.'

'Why would they take any money? It means they were entertaining you. Do you suppose they keep vodka for sale?' said the soldier, succeeding at last in pulling off a sodden boot along with a blackened sock.

Despite the lack of cleanliness in the hut, which had been dirtied by the sportsmen's boots and the muddy dogs who were licking themselves, and despite the boggy, gunpowdery smell pervading it, and the absence of knives and forks, the sportsmen gulped down their tea and ate their supper with a relish known only to those who have been out shooting. Washed and clean, they went into the freshly swept hay barn, where the coachmen had made up beds for the gentlemen.

Although it was already growing dark, none of the sportsmen wanted to sleep.

After wavering between reminiscences and stories about guns, dogs, and previous shooting parties, the conversation settled on a topic that interested them all. Prompted by Vasenka's expressions of rapture, already reiterated several times, over the charm of the night's lodging and the smell of the hay, over the charm of the broken cart (which he thought was broken because its fore-wheels had been taken out), and over the kindliness of the peasants who had given him vodka, and the dogs, each lying at his master's feet, Oblonsky began telling them about the delights of the shooting party Malthus had invited him to join the previous summer. Malthus was a famous railway tycoon.

---

[1] 'They were charming.'

Stepan Arkadyich described the marshes this Malthus had bought in Tver province, and how they were protected, and about the vehicles called dogcarts used to transport the sportsmen, and the marquee that had been put up next to the marsh with lunch laid out.

'What I don't understand,' said Levin, sitting up in the hay, 'is how you can fail to find these people odious. I can understand that lunch with a glass of Lafite is very pleasant, but do you really not find all that luxury horrible? These people all make money in ways that garner people's contempt, just like our vodka monopolists used to do; they thumb their noses at this contempt, and then with their dishonest earnings they buy the contempt off.'

'Perfectly true!' chimed in Vasenka Veslovsky. 'Perfectly true! Oblonsky, of course, does it out of *bonhomie*, and then other people say: "Well, Oblonsky goes . . ." '

'Not at all.' Levin could hear Oblonsky smiling as he said this. 'I simply don't consider him in any way more dishonest than any other rich merchant or nobleman. They've all made their money by dint of hard work and intelligence.'

'Yes, but what sort of hard work? Is obtaining a concession and selling it really hard work?'

'Of course it's hard work. Hard work in the sense that if it were not for him and others like him, there would be no railways.'

'But that's not the same as the hard work of a peasant or a scholar.'

'Granted, but it's hard work in the sense that his activity produces a result—the railways. But then you think the railways are useless.'

'No, that's another issue; I am prepared to admit that they are useful. But any acquisition disproportionate to the amount of work invested is dishonest.'

'But who can possibly determine the proportion?'

'Acquisition by dishonest means, by trickery,' said Levin, conscious that he was unable to define a clear boundary between what was honest and what was dishonest, 'such as the acquisition of banking establishments,' he went on. 'It's evil, this acquisition of huge fortunes without work, just as it was with the vodka monopolies, except the form has changed. *Le roi est mort, vive le roi!*[1] No sooner were the vodka monopolies abolished than railways and banks materialized: that's also money-making without work.'

'Yes, all that might be true and clever . . . Lie down, Krak!' Stepan Arkadyich shouted at his dog, which was scratching itself and turning

---

[1] 'The king is dead, long live the king!'

all the hay upside down, otherwise speaking in calm and measured tones, clearly convinced of the validity of his point of view. 'But you have not defined the boundary between honest and dishonest work. Is it dishonest, for example, that I draw a bigger salary than my chief clerk, even though he knows the work better than I do?'

'I don't know.'

'Well, let me tell you: the fact that you clear about five thousand from your agricultural work, let's say, while our peasant host here will never earn more than fifty roubles, no matter how hard he works, is just as dishonest as my earning more than my chief clerk, and Malthus earning more than a railway engineer. On the contrary, I see that society has some kind of hostile attitude to these people which is entirely without foundation, and I think it's envy . . .'

'No, that's unfair,' said Veslovsky. 'It can't be envy, and there is something unsavoury about all of this.'

'No, excuse me,' Levin went on. 'You say that it's unfair that I get five thousand, while a peasant only gets fifty roubles: it's true. It is unfair, and I feel that, but . . .'

'It is indeed. Why should we be eating, drinking, shooting, or doing nothing, while he is always, always working?' said Vasenka with complete sincerity, obviously having thought clearly about this for the first time.

'Yes, you feel that, but you won't give away your estate to him,' said Stepan Arkadyich, as if deliberately goading Levin.

A kind of covert friction had lately established itself between the two brothers-in-law: ever since they had been married to sisters, it was as if a rivalry had sprung up between them over who had organized his life better, and now this friction was expressing itself in the way this conversation was beginning to acquire a personal flavour.

'I don't give it away because no one is demanding that I should, and even if I wanted to, I couldn't give it away,' answered Levin, 'nor is there anyone to give it to.'

'Give it away to this peasant; he won't refuse.'

'Yes, but how am I to give it away to him? Go off with him and have a deed of conveyance drawn up?'

'I don't know; but if you are convinced that you don't have the right . . .'

'I'm not at all convinced. On the contrary, I don't feel I have the right to give it away, and that I have responsibilities, both to the land and to my family.'

'No, excuse me; but if you consider this inequality is unjust, why don't you act accordingly? . . .'

'I do act, only negatively, in the sense that I will never try to increase the discrepancy that exists between his position and mine.'

'No, I'm sorry; that's a paradox.'

'Yes, there is a touch of sophistry in that explanation,' asserted Veslovsky. 'Ah! Our host,' he said to the peasant who was opening the creaking doors and coming into the barn. 'You're not asleep yet?'

'Oh no, not tonight! I was thinking our gentlemen would be asleep, but I heard you nattering. There's a crook I need from here. She won't bite?' he added, stepping forward gingerly in his bare feet.

'So where are you going to sleep?'

'We are going out to night pasture.'

'Ah, what a night!' said Veslovsky, looking at the edge of the hut and the unharnessed trap which the dim light of dusk had made visible in the large frame of the now open doors. 'But listen, there are women's voices singing, and they are really not at all bad. Who's singing, landlord?'

'Oh that's the servant girls next door.'

'Let's go for a walk! We won't fall sleep anyway. Oblonsky, let's go!'

'If only one could lie down and go at the same time,' answered Oblonsky, stretching. 'It's marvellous, lying down.'

'Well, I will go on my own then,' said Veslovsky, getting up briskly and putting on his boots. 'Goodbye, gentlemen. If it's fun, I'll call you. You've treated me to game, and I won't forget you.'

'He is a nice fellow, isn't he?' said Oblonsky when Veslovsky had gone out and the peasant had closed the door behind him.

'Yes, very nice,' answered Levin, still thinking about the subject of the conversation that had just taken place. It seemed to him that he had expressed his thoughts and feelings as clearly as he possibly could, yet both of them—and they were intelligent and sincere people—had said with one voice that he was taking comfort in sophistry. This disturbed him.

'So that is how it is, my friend. You must choose one of two things: either admit that the existing order of society is fair and then stand up for your rights; or acknowledge that you have unfair advantages, as I do, and enjoy having them.'

'No, if it was unfair, you would not be able to take pleasure in having these privileges, or I couldn't at any rate. The main thing I need to feel is that I'm not to blame.'

'Do you think we should actually go after all?' said Stepan Arkadyich, clearly tired from the mental exertion. 'We aren't going to fall asleep, you know. Come on, let's go!'

Levin did not answer. He was preoccupied by what he had said in their conversation about acting fairly only in a negative way. 'Is it really only possible to be fair in a negative way?' he was wondering.

'Goodness, how strong the smell of fresh hay is!' said Stepan Arkadyich, sitting up. 'I'll never fall asleep. Vasenka has got something going over there. Can you hear the laughter and his voice? What about going over? Let's go!'

'No, I'm not going,' answered Levin.

'Surely that's not down to a matter of principle too?' said Stepan Arkadyich, smiling as he felt about in the dark for his cap.

'No, it's not a matter of principle, but what would be the point of me going?'

'You know, you are going to make trouble for yourself,' said Stepan Arkadyich, finding his cap and getting up.

'How?'

'Do you think I can't see how you have set yourself up with your wife? I heard how you debated whether or not you would go shooting for a couple of days as an issue of prime importance. That's all very well as an idyll, but it won't last a whole lifetime. A man has to be independent, he has his own masculine interests. A man has to be manly,' said Oblonsky, opening the door.

'Which means what exactly? Running after servant girls?' said Levin.

'Why on earth not, if it is fun? *Ça ne tire pas à conséquence.*[1] My wife won't be the worse for it, and I'll have fun. The main thing is to respect the sanctity of the home. There should be nothing untoward at home. But don't tie your hands.'

'Maybe,' said Levin drily, and he turned on to his side. 'We need to make an early start tomorrow, and I won't wake anyone, but I'm going at dawn.'

'*Messieurs, venez vite!*[2] came the voice of Veslovsky as he returned. '*Charmante!* It's my discovery. *Charmante,* a perfect Gretchen,* and we've already got to know each other. She really is extremely pretty!' he recounted, with such an approving air as if she had been made pretty especially for him, and he was pleased with whoever was responsible for arranging this for him.

Levin pretended to be asleep, but Oblonsky walked out of the barn after putting on his slippers and lighting a cigar, and soon their voices died away.

Levin could not get to sleep for a long time. He heard his horses munching hay, then their host and his eldest boy getting ready and

---

[1] 'It's of no consequence.'   [2] 'Gentlemen, come quickly!'

leaving for the night pasture; then he heard the soldier going to bed on the other side of the barn with his nephew, their host's young son; he heard the boy in his high-pitched little voice relaying to his uncle his impression of the dogs, which he found huge and frightening; then the boy asking what these dogs were going to hunt, and the soldier in a hoarse and sleepy voice telling him the sportsmen were going to go to the marsh the next day and fire their guns; and then, to put a stop to the boy's questions, he said, 'Go to sleep, Vaska, go to sleep, or you'd better watch out,' and soon he himself began snoring and everything fell silent; all he could hear were the horses neighing and a snipe drumming. 'Do I really only act negatively?' he repeated to himself. 'Well, so what? I'm not to blame.' And he started thinking about the following day.

'Tomorrow I'll set off early, and make a point of keeping my head. There are masses of snipe. And great snipe. And when I come back there'll be a note from Kitty. Yes, Stiva may be right: I'm not manly with her, I've become effeminate . . . But there's nothing to be done about it! Negative again!'

Through his sleep, he heard the laughter and merry voices of Veslovsky and Stepan Arkadyich. He opened his eyes for a moment: the moon had risen, and they were standing talking by the open doors, which were brightly lit up by the moonlight. Stepan Arkadyich was saying something about a girl's freshness, comparing it to a freshly shelled nut, and Veslovsky, with his infectious laugh, was repeating something a peasant had probably told him: 'You should woo a wife of your own!' Levin mumbled in his sleep:

'Tomorrow at daybreak, gentlemen!' and fell asleep.

12

WAKING in the early dawn, Levin tried to rouse his companions. Vasenka, lying on his stomach with one stockinged leg stretched out, was sleeping so deeply it was impossible to get a response from him. Oblonsky, half-asleep, refused to go out so early. And even Laska, who had been asleep curled up in a ball on the edge of the hay, got up reluctantly, and stretched and straightened out her hind legs languidly one at a time. After putting on his boots, picking up his gun, and carefully opening the creaking barn doors, Levin went out on to the road. The coachmen were sleeping by the vehicles, the horses were dozing. There was just one of them lazily eating oats, scattering them all over the trough as it snorted. It was still grey outside.

'What are you up so early for, my dear?' said their elderly hostess as she came out of the hut, addressing him as warmly as if he were some cherished old acquaintance.

'Going shooting, auntie. Can I get to the marsh this way?'

'Straight along the backs, past our threshing floors, my dear, and the hemp fields; that's where the path is.'

Treading carefully with her bare, sunburnt feet, the old woman showed Levin the way, and held open the fence of the threshing floor for him.

'Straight on and the path will bring you to the marsh. Our lads drove the horses there last night.'

Laska scampered merrily on ahead along the path; Levin followed her at a brisk, light step, constantly glancing up at the sky. He did not want the sun to come up before he reached the marsh. But the sun did not dally. The moon, which had still been shining when he went out, now only glimmered like a piece of quicksilver; the morning star, which he could not help seeing before, now had to be sought out; the fuzzy dots in a distant field were now clearly visible. They were shocks of rye. Still invisible without sunlight, the dew on the tall, fragrant hemp, from which the male plants had already been removed, wet Levin's legs and his blouse up to above his belt. The smallest sounds could be heard in the transparent stillness of the morning. A bee flew past Levin's ear, whistling like a bullet. He looked around carefully and saw a second and a third. They were all flying out from behind the wattle fence of an apiary and disappearing as they flew over the hemp in the direction of the marsh. The path led straight into the marsh. The marsh could be recognized from the mist rising from it, which was thicker in some places and thinner in others, so that the sedges and willow bushes looked like little islands shimmering in this mist. The young boys and peasants who had been keeping watch during the night pasture were lying at the edge of the marsh and the road, having all fallen asleep under their kaftans before dawn. Three hobbled horses were grazing near them. One of them was clanking its chain. Laska walked beside her master, straining to go ahead and looking round. Once they were past the sleeping peasants and had reached the first patch of bog, Levin examined his gun caps and let the dog go. One of the horses, a sleek, three-year-old chestnut, shied when it saw the dog, lifted its tail, and snorted. The other horses also took fright and began springing out of the marsh, splashing through the water with their hobbled legs and making a squelching sound as they pulled their hooves out of the thick clay. Laska stopped, looking disparagingly at the horses and enquiringly at Levin. Levin patted Laska and whistled to let her know she could start.

Laska ran with rapt glee over the soft, swampy ground.

Amongst the familiar smells of roots, marsh grasses, rusty water, and the foreign smell of horse dung, Laska immediately detected the scent of a bird pervading this whole area as she ran into the marsh—that very bird whose smell excited her more than any other. Here and there amongst the moss and marsh burdocks this smell was very strong, but it was impossible to determine in which direction it grew stronger or weaker. To find the direction, she needed to go further downwind. Without feeling the movement in her legs, and setting off at a stiff gallop so that she could pull herself up at each bound if need be, Laska raced off to the right, turning away from the early morning breeze blowing from the east and into the wind. As she drew in air through her dilated nostrils, she immediately sensed that not only their tracks but *they* themselves were right there in front of her, and not just one, but many of them. Laska decreased her running-speed. They were here, but where exactly she could not yet determine. She had already begun to circle in order to find the exact spot when her master's voice suddenly distracted her. 'Laska! Here!' he said, pointing her in a different direction. She stood still, asking him whether it would not be better to carry on as she had started, but he repeated his command in an angry voice, pointing to a waterlogged patch of marsh covered with tussocks where there could not be anything. Pretending to search in order to give him pleasure, she obeyed him by scouring that patch of marsh, then headed back to her previous place and picked up their scent straight away. Now that he was not hindering her she knew what to do, and although she did not see what was underfoot and was annoyed at stumbling on the high tussocks and landing in the water, her strong, supple legs carried her, and she began to make the circle which would make everything clear to her. She was picking up *their* scent with ever greater intensity and precision, and suddenly it became perfectly clear to her that one of them was there, behind that tussock, five paces in front of her, and so she stopped and her whole body froze. She could not see anything in front of her on her short legs, but she knew from the scent that it was sitting no further than five paces away. She stood still, becoming more and more aware of it and enjoying the anticipation. Her outstretched tail was taut and quivering only at the very tip. Her mouth was slightly open, her ears pricked. One ear had turned back while she was running, and she was breathing heavily but cautiously, and she now glanced round with even greater caution, more with her eyes than her head, at her master. He was coming along with his usual face but ever terrifying eyes, stumbling over the tussocks and walking exceptionally slowly, it seemed to her. It seemed to her that he was walking slowly, but he was actually running.

Having noticed that particular manner of searching Laska had of pressing her body close to the ground, making wide raking kinds of movements with her hind paws, and opening her mouth slightly, Levin realized she was pointing at snipe and, praying inwardly to God for success, especially with the first bird, he ran up to her. When he was up close to her, he looked straight ahead from his height and saw with his eyes what she saw with her nose. In the narrow gap between two tussocks a few feet away there was a great snipe. It had turned its head and was listening. Then, after spreading its wings slightly and folding them again, it fluttered its tail awkwardly and disappeared round a corner.

'Fetch, fetch!' shouted Levin, pushing Laska from behind.

'But I can't move,' thought Laska. 'Where am I supposed to go? I can feel them from here, but if I move forward I won't be able to work out where they are or what they are.' But here he was, nudging her with his knee, and saying in an excited whisper, 'Fetch, Laska, good dog, fetch!'

'Well, if that's what he wants, I'll do it, but I can't answer for myself any longer,' she thought, and she raced off ahead at full pelt between the tussocks. She could no longer smell anything now and could only see and hear without understanding anything.

Ten paces away from the previous place, one great snipe flew up with a guttural croak, its wings producing the great-snipe sound of rushing air. And following the shot fired, it plopped heavily on its white breast into the wet bog. Another did not wait and flew up behind Levin without the dog.

It was already far away when Levin turned towards it. But his shot caught it. After flying for about twenty paces, the second snipe rose vertically upwards, spinning like a pitched ball, and fell heavily on to a dry patch.

'Now that's more like it!' thought Levin, as he tucked the warm, plump snipe into his game-bag. 'Don't you think, Laska, my beauty?'

When Levin moved on after loading his gun, the sun had already risen, although it was not visible behind the clouds. The moon had lost all its brightness and was like a little white cloud in the sky; by now not a single star could be seen. The sedges, which had been silver with dew before, had now turned gold. The rusty patches were all amber. The blue tinge to the grass had changed to a yellowish green. Small marsh birds were swarming about the low bushes, which were glistening with dew and casting long shadows by the stream. A hawk had woken up and was perched on a haycock, turning its head from side to side and looking sullenly at the marsh. Jackdaws were flying in the fields, and a barefooted young boy was already driving the horses over to an old man, who was getting up from under his coat and scratching himself. The smoke from the gunfire was as white as milk against the green of the grass.

One of the young boys ran up to Levin.

'There were ducks here yesterday, uncle!' he shouted to him, and he started following him at a distance.

And Levin was doubly pleased when, in full view of this boy who had expressed his approval, he immediately killed another three snipe, one after the other.

13

THE huntsman's saying that you will be lucky in the field if you do not miss your first beast or bird turned out to be true.

Tired, hungry, and happy after tramping about twenty miles, Levin returned to his lodgings towards ten o'clock with nineteen fine head of game and one duck, which he had tied to his belt since it would not fit into his game-bag. His companions had woken up long before and had grown hungry and eaten breakfast in the meantime.

'Wait, wait, I know there are nineteen,' said Levin, counting up a second time the common and great snipe, which did not look as impressive as when they were flying, now that they were all bunched up together, shrivelled and caked with blood, with their heads lolling to one side.

The counting was correct, and Levin was pleased that Stepan Arkadyich was envious. He was also pleased that the messenger Kitty had dispatched with a note was already there when he returned to their lodgings.

'I am quite well and happy. If you are fretting about me, you can be even calmer than before. I have a new bodyguard, Marya Vlasyevna' (this was the midwife, a new and important person in Levin's family life.). 'She came to see how I was. She found me to be in excellent health, and we are keeping her here until you are back. Everyone is happy and well, so please don't feel you need to hurry back, and stay another day if the shooting is good.'

These two joys, his successful shooting and the note from his wife, were so great that Levin barely registered the two minor disagreeable things which happened after this. One was that the chestnut trace-horse, which had clearly been worked too hard the previous day, was not eating its feed and was lethargic. The coachman said it had been over-strained.

'She was driven too hard yesterday, Konstantin Dmitrich,' he said. 'Did her no good being driven like that for seven miles!'

The other disagreeable thing, which did for a minute upset his good mood, but which he later had a good laugh about, was finding that nothing remained of the provisions that Kitty had supplied in such abundance that it had seemed impossible to consume them in a week. As he was returning tired and hungry from shooting, Levin was dreaming so specifically about the pies that he could already smell them and taste them in his mouth as he approached their lodgings, like Laska scenting game, and he straight away told Filip to serve him some. It turned out that not only were there no pies left, but no chicken either.

'That's some appetite!' said Stepan Arkadyich, laughing and pointing at Vasenka Veslovsky. 'I don't exactly suffer from loss of appetite myself, but this is remarkable . . .'

'*Mais c'était délicieux*,'[1] said Veslovsky in praise of the beef he had eaten.

'Well, it can't be helped!' said Levin, looking despondently at Veslovsky. 'Give me some beef then, Filip.'

'The beef has been eaten, I gave the bone to the dogs,' answered Filip.

Levin was so affronted he said with chagrin:

'You might have left me something!' and was on the verge of tears.

'Well, draw the birds,' he said in a trembling voice to Filip, trying not to look at Vasenka, 'and layer them with nettles. And at least get some milk for me.'

It was only later, when he had drunk his fill of milk, that he felt ashamed at having exhibited his vexation to a stranger, and he began laughing about his hunger-induced exasperation.

In the evening they ventured into another field, in which Veslovsky also shot a few birds, and they returned home later that night.

Their return journey was as jolly as their outward journey. Veslovsky either sang or enjoyed recalling his adventures with the peasants who

---

[1] 'But it was delicious.'

had treated him to vodka and said 'No offence'; and he also recalled his night-time adventures with the nuts and the servant girl and the peasant, who had asked him if he was married, and on learning that he was not, had told him, 'Well, mind you don't make eyes at other men's wives—you'd best get one of your own.' Veslovsky had found these words particularly amusing.

'All in all, I'm terribly pleased with our trip. What about you, Levin?'

'I'm very pleased,' Levin said with sincerity, particularly glad not only to feel none of the hostility he had experienced towards Vasenka Veslovsky at home but, on the contrary, the utmost friendliness.

14

THE next day at ten o'clock, having already been round the estate, Levin knocked at the room in which Vasenka was staying.

'*Entrez,*' Veslovsky called out to him. 'You must excuse me, I've only just finished my ablutions,' he said, smiling as he stood there before him in just his underwear.

'Please, don't mind me.' Levin sat down by the window. 'Did you sleep well?'

'Like the dead. What a splendid day for shooting!'

'Yes. Would you like tea or coffee?'

'Neither. I'll wait for lunch. I feel ashamed of myself, I really do. The ladies, I presume, are up already? A walk would be excellent now. You must show me your horses.'

After strolling round the garden, visiting the stables, and even doing some gymnastics together on the parallel bars, Levin returned to the house with his guest, and went into the drawing room with him.

'We had a splendid time shooting, and so many impressions!' said Veslovsky as he went up to Kitty, who was sitting by the samovar. 'What a pity that ladies are deprived of such pleasures!'

'Well, I suppose he has to say something to the lady of the house,' Levin said to himself. He again felt there was something in the smile, in that triumphant expression with which his guest addressed Kitty . . .

The Princess, who was sitting on the other side of the table with Marya Vlasyevna and Stepan Arkadyich, called Levin over and began talking to him about moving to Moscow for Kitty's confinement and preparing somewhere to stay. Just as Levin had found all the preparations for his wedding distasteful, their insignificance an insult to the solemnity of the occasion, so the preparations for the coming birth, the date of which they were somehow calculating on their fingers, seemed even more insulting. He made a concerted effort not to hear those conversations about the best way to swaddle the future baby, and he tried to turn away and not see endless numbers of some kind of mysterious knitted strips and linen triangles, to which Dolly attached special importance, and so on. The birth of a son (he was certain it would be a son), which he had been promised, but in which he still could not believe, so extraordinary did it seem, appeared to him on the one hand such an immense and therefore impossible happiness, and on the other such a mysterious event, that this fanciful knowledge of what would happen, and consequent preparation for it as if it were some ordinary thing manufactured by people, seemed outrageous and humiliating to him.

But the Princess did not understand his feelings, and attributed his reluctance to think and talk about it to thoughtlessness and indifference, and so she gave him no peace. She had entrusted Stepan Arkadyich with sorting out somewhere to stay, and she now summoned Levin over to her.

'I don't know anything, Princess. Do as you see fit,' he said.

'You must decide when you are going to move.'

'I really don't know. I know millions of babies are born without Moscow and doctors . . . so why . . .'

'Well, if that's how . . .'

'No, it's whatever Kitty wants.'

'I can't talk to Kitty about this! Do you really want me to frighten her? This spring Natalya Golitsyna died because she had a bad *accoucheur*.'[1]

'I'll do whatever you say,' he said gloomily.

The Princess began talking to him, but he did not listen to her. Although the conversation with the Princess did upset him, it was not this conversation that was causing him to feel despondent, but what he was now observing by the samovar.

'No, this is impossible,' he thought, glancing periodically at Vasenka as he leaned over towards Kitty, telling her something with his attractive smile, and at her flushed and agitated features.

There was something impure in Vasenka's demeanour, in his eyes, in his smile. Levin even saw something impure in Kitty's demeanour and look. And once again the light in his eyes grew dim. Again, as on the previous day, he suddenly felt he had been cast down without

---

[1] 'obstetrician'.

the slightest transition from the height of happiness, tranquillity, and dignity into an abyss of despair, rage, and humiliation. Everyone and everything again became loathsome to him.

'Just do as you think fit, Princess,' he said, looking round again.

'Heavy is the hat of Monomakh!'* Stepan Arkadyich said to him in jest, clearly alluding not just to the conversation with the Princess, but to the cause of Levin's agitation, which he had noticed. 'You are very late today, Dolly!'

Everyone rose to greet Darya Alexandrovna. Vasenka stood up only for a moment, made a slight bow, with that lack of courtesy to ladies typical of the new breed of young men, and resumed his conversation, laughing about something.

'Masha has been wearing me out. She slept badly and she has been terribly naughty today,' said Dolly.

The conversation Vasenka had struck up with Kitty was on the same subject as the previous one, which was Anna, and whether love can rise above social convention. Kitty found this conversation distasteful, and she was perturbed both by its content and the manner in which it was conducted, and in particular by the fact that she knew full well what effect it would have on her husband. But she was too naive and innocent to know how to curtail this conversation, or even to conceal the superficial pleasure she received from this young man's obvious attention. She wanted to stop this conversation, but she did not know what she should do. Whatever she did, she knew it would be noticed by her husband, and everything would be interpreted in a bad way. And indeed, when she asked Dolly what was wrong with Masha, and Vasenka started gazing indifferently at Dolly while he waited for the conclusion of a conversation he found boring, Levin perceived this question as an unnatural, disgusting ploy.

'So, shall we go and look for mushrooms today?' asked Dolly.

'Yes, please let's go, and I will come too,' said Kitty, and she blushed. Out of politeness she had intended asking Vasenka whether he would go, but did not. 'Where are you going, Kostya?' she asked her husband with a guilty look as he strode resolutely past her. This guilty expression confirmed all his doubts.

'The mechanic came when I was away, and I haven't seen him yet,' he said without looking at her.

He went downstairs, but before he had time to leave his study he heard the familiar footsteps of his wife coming towards him with incautious haste.

'What is it?' he said to her curtly. 'We are busy.'

'Excuse me,' she said to the German mechanic, 'I need to have a few words with my husband.'

The German was about to leave, but Levin said to him:

'Don't worry.'

'Is the train at three?' the German asked. 'I don't want to miss it.'

Levin did not answer him and himself left the room with his wife.

'Well, what is it you have to tell me?' he said in French.

He was not looking at her face and did not want to see that, in her condition, her whole face was trembling and she looked pitiful and crushed.

'I . . . I want to tell you that we can't live like this, that it's torture . . .' she said.

'There are servants here in the pantry,' he said angrily; 'don't make a scene.'

'Well, let's go in here!'

They were standing in a connecting room. She wanted to go through into the next room. But the English governess was giving Tanya a lesson in there.

'Well, let's go into the garden!'

In the garden they came across a peasant weeding the path. And no longer concerned that the peasant could see her tear-stained and his flustered face, no longer concerned that they looked like people running away from some misfortune, they kept walking on briskly, feeling that they needed to speak out and disabuse each other, be alone with each other and thus escape from the misery they were both experiencing.

'We can't live like this, it's torture! I am suffering, you are suffering. What is it in aid of?' she said when they had at last reached a secluded bench in a corner of the lime-tree avenue.

'But just tell me one thing: was there anything improper, impure, or humiliatingly awful in his tone?' he said, standing in front of her again in the same position in which he had stood before her the other night, with his fists clamped to his chest.

'There was,' she said in a trembling voice. 'But, Kostya, you do believe it's not my fault, don't you? I've been trying all morning to set a certain tone, but these people . . . Why did he come? We were so happy!' she said, breathless with the sobs that were racking her now plump body.

The gardener saw with surprise that although nothing had been pursuing them, there was nothing to run away from, and there was nothing they could have found particularly heart-warming on the bench, they walked past him back to the house with tranquil, beaming faces.

15

AFTER escorting his wife upstairs, Levin went to Dolly's part of the house. That day Darya Alexandrovna was in a state of great distress on her own account. She was pacing about the room and saying angrily to the little girl standing howling in the corner:

'And you'll stand in the corner all day and have your dinner on your own, and you won't see any of your dolls, and I won't make you a new dress,' she was saying, no longer knowing how she should punish her.

'Oh, she is a horrible child!' She turned to Levin. 'Where does she get such vile inclinations from?'

'But what has she done?' said Levin rather indifferently, as he wanted advice about his own situation and so felt annoyed that he had come at an inopportune moment.

'She and Grisha went into the raspberry bushes, and there . . . I can't even bring myself to tell you what she did. Vile things. It's a thousand pities Miss Elliot left. The new one doesn't supervise at all, she's a machine . . . *Figurez-vous qu'elle* . . .'[1]

And Darya Alexandrovna recounted Masha's crime.

'That doesn't prove anything, it's not vile inclinations at all, just mischievousness,' Levin reassured her.

'But are you upset about something? Why have you come?' asked Dolly. 'What is going on there?'

And from the tone of this question Levin realized it would be easy for him to say what he intended to say.

'I haven't been there, I've been alone in the garden with Kitty. We had a quarrel for the second time since . . . Stiva arrived.'

Dolly looked at him with intelligent, perceptive eyes.

'Well, tell me, hand on heart, has there been . . . not in Kitty's, but in that gentleman's manner, anything which could be unpleasant, or rather not unpleasant, but awful or insulting to a husband?'

'What I mean is, how shall I put it . . . You, stay there in the corner!' she said to Masha, who had been about to turn round after seeing a faint smile on her mother's face. 'Society opinion would hold that he is behaving like all young men behave. *Il fait la cour à une jeune et jolie femme*,[2] and a society husband can only be flattered by it.'

'Yes, yes,' said Levin gloomily, 'but did you notice it?'

---

[1] 'Can you imagine, she . . .'
[2] 'He is paying court to a young and pretty woman'.

'Not only I, but Stiva noticed it. He said to me straight after tea: *Je crois que Veslovsky fait un petit brin de cour à Kitty*.'[1]

'Well, that's excellent, my mind is at rest now. I'm going to throw him out,' said Levin.

'Good gracious, have you taken leave of your senses?' Dolly cried out in horror. 'Good gracious, Kostya, think about what you are saying!' she said, laughing. 'You can go to Fanny now,' she said to Masha. 'No, if that's really what you want, I'll tell Stiva. He'll take him away. We can say you're expecting guests. He doesn't really fit in here anyway.'

'No, no, I'll do it myself.'

'But are you going to pick a fight with him? . . .'

'Not at all. I will enjoy it immensely,' said Levin, his eyes really twinkling merrily. 'Now come on, Dolly, forgive her! She won't do it again,' he said about the young delinquent, who had not gone off to Fanny and was standing hesitantly opposite her mother, waiting uneasily and trying to catch her eye.

The mother glanced at her. The little girl burst out sobbing, hid her face in her mother's lap, and Dolly laid a thin, tender hand on her head.

'What do we have in common with him anyway?' thought Levin and he set off to find Veslovsky.

As he crossed the hall, he gave instructions for the carriage to be harnessed in order to drive to the station.

'A spring broke yesterday,' the footman replied.

'Well, the wagon, then, but be quick about it. Where's the guest?'

'He's gone to his room.'

Levin found Veslovsky just at the moment when he had finished unpacking the things in his suitcase and laid out his new songs, and was trying on some leggings to go out riding.

Whether there was something particular in Levin's face, or whether Vasenka himself had begun to feel that the *petit brin de coeur* he had embarked on was out of place in this family, he was slightly disconcerted (as much as a society man can be) by Levin's entrance.

'You ride in leggings?'

'Yes, it's much cleaner,' said Vasenka, putting a fat leg on to a chair and fastening the bottom hook with a merry, genial smile.

He was undoubtedly a nice fellow, and Levin felt sorry for him and ashamed of himself as head of the household when he observed a diffidence in Vasenka's look.

---

[1] 'I believe Veslovsky is courting Kitty a little bit.'

On the table lay part of a stick they had broken together that morning during their gymnastics while they were trying to raise the warped parallel bars. Levin picked up this piece of stick and began breaking splinters off the end, not knowing how to begin.

'I wanted . . .' He was about to lapse into silence, but suddenly, remembering Kitty and everything that had happened, he looked him square in the eye and said: 'I have ordered the horses to be harnessed for you.'

'What do you mean?' Vasenka began with surprise. 'To go where?'

'To take you to the station,' said Levin grimly, splintering the end of the stick.

'Are you going away or has something happened?'

'What has happened is that I am expecting guests,' said Levin, his strong fingers breaking off the splintered ends of the stick more and more quickly. 'Or rather, I'm not expecting guests, and nothing has happened, but I must ask you to leave. You can interpret my discourtesy as you like.'

Vasenka drew himself up.

'I must ask *you* to explain to me . . .' he said with dignity, understanding at last.

'I can't explain to you,' said Levin softly and slowly, trying to conceal the trembling of his jaw. 'And it would be better for you not to ask.'

And since the split ends had now all been broken off, Levin gripped the thick ends with his fingers, broke the stick in two, and carefully caught one end as it fell.

The sight of those nervously tensed arms, the same muscles he had felt that morning during their gymnastics, and the blazing eyes, quiet voice, and quivering jaw no doubt convinced Vasenka more than the words. Shrugging his shoulders and smiling scornfully, he bowed.

'Can I not see Oblonsky?'

Levin was not annoyed by the shrug of the shoulders and the smile. 'What else can he do?' he thought.

'I'll send him to you straight away.'

'What nonsense!' said Stepan Arkadyich after hearing from his friend that he was being thrown out of the house, and finding Levin in the garden, where he was perambulating while waiting for his guest's departure. '*Mais c'est ridicule*! What fly has bitten you? *Mais c'est du dernier ridicule*![1] What did you imagine, if a young man . . .'

But the spot where the fly had bitten Levin was evidently still

[1] 'But it's ridiculous! . . . It's the height of absurdity!'

painful, because he turned pale again when Stepan Arkadyich wanted to explain the reason, and hastily cut him short:

'Please don't explain the reasons! There is nothing else I can do! I feel very ashamed before both you and him. But I don't think it will cause him great sorrow to leave, and my wife and I find his presence disagreeable.'

'But it's insulting to him! *Et puis c'est ridicule*.'[1]

'And for me it's insulting and also agonizing! I'm not in any way to blame, and there's no reason for me to suffer!'

'Well, I never expected this of you! *On peut être jaloux, mais à ce point, c'est du dernier ridicule!*'[2]

Levin turned on his heels and walked away from him down to the end of the avenue, where he continued to walk up and down alone. Soon he heard the rattle of the wagon and from behind the trees he saw Vasenka in his Scotch cap sitting in the hay (there being unfortunately no seating in the wagon), and bouncing up and down on the bumps as he made his way along the drive.

'What's this now?' Levin thought when a servant ran out of the house and stopped the wagon. It was the mechanic, whom Levin had completely forgotten. The mechanic bowed as he said something to Veslovsky; then he climbed into the wagon, and they drove off together.

Stepan Arkadyich and the Princess were incensed by Levin's behaviour. And he himself felt not only in the highest degree *ridicule*, but also thoroughly at fault and covered in ignominy; but when he remembered what he and his wife had put up with, and wondered how he would have acted on another occasion, he told himself he would have done exactly the same thing.

Despite all this, by the end of the day everyone, with the exception of the Princess, who would not forgive Levin's behaviour, became unusually lively and high-spirited, like children after being punished or grown-ups after an onerous official reception, so that Vasenka's expulsion was talked about that evening, in the absence of the Princess, as if it had happened long ago. And Dolly, who had inherited her father's gift for telling funny stories, set Varenka rolling with laughter when she recounted for the third and fourth time, always with humorous new embellishments, how she had just got round to putting on new ribbons in the guest's honour and was already on her way into the drawing room when she suddenly heard the rattle of the old wagon. And who

---

[1] 'And then it's ridiculous.'

[2] 'One may be jealous, but when it gets to this point it's the height of absurdity.'

should be in the old wagon but Vasenka himself, sitting in the hay with his Scotch cap, his songs, and his leggings.

'You might at least have had the carriage harnessed! But no, and then I hear: "Wait!" Ah, I think, they've relented. Then I see that they've parked that fat German beside him and are taking them both off . . . And my ribbons were all in vain! . . .'

16

DARYA ALEXANDROVNA carried out her intention and went to visit Anna. She was sorry to upset her sister and displease her husband; she understood that the Levins were right in not wanting to have anything to do with Vronsky; but she considered it her duty to visit Anna and show her that her feelings could not change, despite the change in her situation.

In order not to depend on the Levins for this journey, Darya Alexandrovna sent to the village to hire horses; but Levin came to scold her when he found out about this.

'Why on earth do you think that I'm unhappy about you making this trip? Even if I were unhappy about it, I would be even more unhappy if you didn't take my horses,' he said. 'You never once told me you were definitely going. For one thing, I'm unhappy about you hiring horses in the village, but more importantly, they'll take the job on but they won't get you there. I've got horses. And if you don't want to upset me, you'll take mine.'

Darya Alexandrovna had to consent, and on the appointed day Levin had four horses and a relay ready for his sister-in-law, having assembled a team for her of dray and riding horses which was far from attractive, but capable of taking Darya Alexandrovna all the way in one day. This was difficult for Levin just now, when horses were needed for the Princess, who was leaving, and the midwife, but the obligations of hospitality dictated that he could not allow Darya Alexandrovna to hire horses while she was staying with him, and he knew, moreover, that the twenty roubles that they were asking from Darya Alexandrovna for the journey meant a great deal to her; and the Levins related to Darya Alexandrovna's financial affairs, which were in a very poor state, as if they were their own.

Following Levin's advice, Darya Alexandrovna set off before dawn. The road was good, the carriage comfortable, the horses ran along well, and on the box beside the coachman sat the clerk whom Levin had sent instead of a servant for safety. Darya Alexandrovna dozed off and woke up only when they were drawing up to the inn where the horses needed to be changed.

After drinking tea with the same wealthy peasant landlord with whom Levin had stopped off on the way to Sviyazhsky's, and chatting with the women about their children, and with the old man about Count Vronsky, whom he praised very highly, at ten o'clock Darya Alexandrovna continued her journey. At home she never had time to think, due to having to care for the children. But now, during this four-hour journey, all the thoughts that had previously been suppressed suddenly started crowding into her mind, and she thought over the whole of her life as she never had before, and from the most diverse angles. Her thoughts seemed strange even to herself. At first she thought about the children, whom the Princess, and mainly Kitty (she had greater faith in her), had promised to look after, but whom she nevertheless worried about. 'As long as Masha doesn't start being naughty again, and Grisha isn't kicked by a horse, and Lily's stomach isn't upset again.' But questions about the present then started to be replaced by questions about the immediate future. She began thinking about how she would have to find a new place for them to live in Moscow that winter, replace the furniture in the drawing room, and make her eldest daughter a fur coat. Then questions of the more distant future started looming: about how she would raise the children to adulthood. 'It will be all right with the girls,' she thought; 'but what about the boys?'

'All right, I'm teaching Grisha now, but that's only because I am free now, and not having a baby. Obviously I can't count on Stiva for anything. And I will raise them, with the help of kind people; but if there's another baby . . .' And the thought occurred to her about how inaccurately it had been said that a curse was laid on woman so that she would bring forth children in pain.* 'Giving birth is all right, but carrying them—that is what is painful,' she thought, picturing to herself her last pregnancy and the death of that last child. And she recalled her conversation with a young peasant woman at the inn. When asked whether she had any children, the attractive young woman had answered cheerfully:

'I had a little girl, but God set me free, I buried her in Lent.'

'So, do you miss her a lot?' Darya Alexandrovna had asked.

'What is there to miss? The old man has grandchildren enough as it is. They're just trouble. You can't work or do anything. They just tie you down.'

This answer had seemed abhorrent to Darya Alexandrovna, despite the kind-hearted, pretty appearance of the young woman; but now she could not help remembering those words. There was indeed a grain of truth in those cynical words.

'Yes, generally,' thought Darya Alexandrovna as she looked back over her whole life during the fifteen years she had been married, 'it's just been pregnancy, nausea, dull-wittedness, indifference to everything, and above all looking hideous. Even Kitty, young and pretty Kitty, has lost her looks, but when I'm pregnant I become hideous, I know. Labour, suffering, hideous suffering, that last moment . . . then the feeding, those sleepless nights, that dreadful pain . . .'

Darya Alexandrovna shuddered at the mere recollection of the pain from the cracked nipples she had experienced with almost every child. 'Then there are the children's illnesses to contend with, the constant anxiety; then bringing them up, revolting tendencies' (she remembered little Masha's crime amongst the raspberry bushes), 'lessons, Latin—it is all so perplexing and difficult. And if that was not enough, the death of those same children.' And again in her imagination arose the cruel memory, weighing eternally on her mother's heart, of the death of her last baby boy from croup, his funeral, the general indifference before that small pink coffin, and her heart-rending, solitary pain before that pale little forehead with the curls at the temples, and the open, surprised little mouth she had glimpsed in the coffin just as they were closing the pink lid with a gold braid cross.

'And what is it all for? What will it all lead to? To me living out my life without a moment's peace, either pregnant or breastfeeding, permanently cross, grumpy, worn out myself and wearing other people out, repulsive to my husband, while the children will grow up unhappy, badly brought up, and poor. And I don't know how we would have got by now if we weren't spending the summer at the Levins'. Of course, Kostya and Kitty are so tactful it is almost unnoticeable; but it can't go on. Once they have children, they won't be able to help; they are in straitened circumstances even now. Does that mean that Papa, who has left hardly anything for himself, will have to help? So I cannot even bring the children up by myself, but only with the help of others, which is humiliating. Well, all right, let's suppose the happiest outcome: the children will stop dying, and I manage to bring them up somehow. At best they simply won't end up as good-for-nothings. That's all I can hope for. And so much agony and hard work for that . . . A whole life ruined!' She once more recalled what the young peasant woman had said, and once more found it vile to remember; but she could not help agreeing that there was a grain of unvarnished truth in those words.

'Have we far to go, Mikhail?' Darya Alexandrovna asked the clerk, to take her mind off thoughts that were frightening her.

'They say it's about five miles from this village.'

The carriage drove along the village street on to a little bridge. Crossing the bridge and chattering with merry, sonorous voices was a crowd of jolly peasant women with lengths of coiled straw for tying sheaves flung over their shoulders. The women stopped for a moment on the bridge and examined the carriage with curiosity. The faces turned to Darya Alexandrovna all seemed to her to be healthy and cheerful, taunting her with the joys of life. 'They're all living, they're all enjoying life,' Darya Alexandrovna continued to reflect after they had passed the peasant women and were driving up a hill, and she was swaying pleasantly on the soft springs of the old carriage as they went back to a trot, 'while I, let out of a world which has been slowly killing me with worries, as if released from prison, have only now been able to come to my senses for a moment. They're all alive: those peasant women, my sister Natalya, Varenka, and Anna, whom I am on my way to see—everyone except me.

'And they attack Anna. Why? Am I any better? I at least have a husband I love. Not in the way I would like to love him, but I do love him, and Anna did not love hers. What is she guilty of? She wants to live. God has put that into our hearts. It could well be that I would have done the same. And I still don't know whether I was right to listen to her during that terrible time when she came to visit me in Moscow. I should have left my husband then and have begun my life anew. I could have loved and been loved properly. Because is it really any better now? I don't respect him. I need him,' she thought about her husband, 'and I put up with him. Is that any better? Back then I could still be attractive, I still had my beauty,' Darya Alexandrovna went on thinking, and she had an urge to look at herself in a mirror. She had a travelling mirror in her bag, and she wanted to get it out; but after looking at the backs of the coachman and the swaying clerk, she felt she would be embarrassed if either of them were to look round, so she did not take the mirror out.

But even without looking in the mirror, she thought it was still not too late, and she remembered Sergey Ivanovich, who was always particularly attentive to her, and Stiva's friend, the kind-hearted Turovtsyn, who had helped her care for the children when they had scarlet fever and who was in love with her. And there was also one much younger man who, as her husband told her jokingly, viewed her as the most beautiful of all the sisters. And Darya Alexandrovna began imagining the most passionate and impossible love affairs. 'Anna behaved admirably, and I am definitely not going to reproach her in any way. She is happy, she is making another person happy and she's not browbeaten like I am, but is no doubt just as vibrant, clever, and open to everything as ever,' thought Darya Alexandrovna, and a roguish smile of contentment wrinkled her lips, mainly because while she was thinking about Anna's love affair, Darya Alexandrovna had conjured up a parallel and almost identical love affair of her own with an imaginary composite man who was in love with her. Like Anna, she had confessed everything to her husband. And the astonishment and consternation with which Stepan Arkadyich greeted this news made her smile.

It was in the midst of such daydreams that she reached the turn from the main road that led to Vozdvizhenskoye.

17

THE coachman pulled up the four-in-hand and looked round to the right, to a field of rye in which some peasants were sitting by a cart. The clerk was about to jump down but then changed his mind and shouted imperiously to one of the peasants, beckoning him over. The breeze they had felt while travelling died down when they came to a halt; horseflies swarmed all over the sweating horses, which angrily tried to fend them off. The metallic sound coming from the cart of a scythe being whetted also died down. One of the peasants got up and walked towards the carriage.

'What an idler!' the clerk shouted angrily to the peasant, who was taking slow steps with his bare feet along the unflattened ruts of the dry road. 'Get a move on!'

The curly-haired old man, his hair tied back with a piece of bast and his hunched back dark with sweat, quickened his step, came up to the carriage, and took hold of the mudguard with his sunburnt hand.

'Vozdvizhenskoye, to the master's place? To the Count?' he repeated. 'You've just got to go over that hillock. There's a turning on the left. Straight down the drive and you can't miss it. But who do you want? The Count himself?'

'So are they at home, old fellow?' Darya Alexandrovna said vaguely, not even knowing how to ask a peasant about Anna.

'They ought to be at home,' said the peasant, shifting from one bare foot to the other, and leaving a clear footprint with five toes in the dust. 'They ought to be at home,' he repeated, clearly eager to get into conversation. 'More guests arrived yesterday. Tons of guests . . . What do you want?' He turned round to the lad shouting something to him from the cart. 'Oh, yes! A while back they all came up here on horses to look at the harvester. They ought to be home by now. And who do you work for? . . .'

'We've come from a long way away,' said the coachman, climbing on to the box. 'So it's not far?'

'As I said, you're almost there. As soon as you go over . . .' he said, as he ran his hand over the mudguard of the carriage.

The strapping, healthy-looking young lad came up too.

'So, will there be any work during the harvesting?' he asked.

'I don't know, lad.'

'Anyway, keep to the left and you'll run into it,' said the peasant, who was clearly reluctant to let the travellers go, and keen to talk.

The coachman started off, but no sooner had they turned round when the peasant shouted out:

'Stop! Hey, friend! Wait!' shouted two voices.

The coachman stopped.

'It's them coming! They're over there!' shouted the peasant. 'Look, it's quite a turnout!' he said, pointing to the four people on horseback and two in a *char-à-banc** coming down the road.

It was Vronsky with a jockey, Veslovsky and Anna on horseback, and Princess Varvara and Sviyazhsky in the *char-à-banc*. They had gone for a ride and to look at some newly imported reaping machines in action.

When the carriage stopped, the riders went on at a walking pace. In front was Anna, riding next to Veslovsky. Anna was riding at a quiet pace on a short, sturdy English cob with a cropped mane and docked tail. Her beautiful head, with her black hair escaping from under her top hat, her full shoulders, slender waist in her black riding habit, and the whole of her calm and graceful posture astonished Dolly.

For the first moment it seemed improper to her that Anna was riding a horse. The idea of horseback riding for a lady was associated in Darya Alexandrovna's mind with the idea of youthful mild flirtation, which was not becoming to Anna's position, in her opinion; but when she examined her closer she was at once reconciled to her riding a horse. Despite the elegance, everything in Anna's bearing, dress, and movements was so simple, calm, and dignified that nothing could have been more natural.

Beside Anna, on an overheated grey cavalry horse, stretching his fat legs out in front and clearly preening himself, rode Vasenka Veslovsky in his Scotch cap with the trailing ribbons, and Darya Alexandrovna could not suppress a bright smile when she recognized him. Vronsky was riding behind them. He was mounted on a dark bay thoroughbred that had obviously become overheated from galloping. He was working the reins, trying to restrain it.

Behind him rode a small man wearing a jockey's outfit. Sviyazhsky and the Princess were bringing up the rear in a brand-new *char-à-banc* drawn by a large black trotter.

Anna's face instantly lit up with a joyful smile the moment she recognized the small figure huddled in the corner of the old carriage. She let out a cry, adjusted her position in the saddle, and nudged her horse into a gallop. Riding up to the carriage, she jumped down without assistance and, holding up her riding habit, ran over to greet Dolly.

'I thought so and did not dare believe it. What joy! You can't imagine my joy!' she said, one moment pressing her face to Dolly and kissing her, and the next stepping back and examining her with a smile.

'What joy, Alexey!' she said, looking round at Vronsky, who had dismounted his horse and was walking towards them.

Vronsky removed his grey top hat and came up to Dolly.

'You can't believe how pleased we are by your arrival,' he said, attaching particular importance to his words and revealing his strong white teeth in a smile.

Without getting off his horse, Vasenka Veslovsky took off his cap and waved it joyfully over his head, ribbons flying, as he greeted the newly arrived guest.

'That's Princess Varvara,' Anna replied to Dolly's enquiring look when the *char-à-banc* drove up.

'Ah!' said Darya Alexandrovna, and her face involuntarily expressed displeasure.

Princess Varvara was her husband's aunt, and she had known her for a long time and did not respect her. She knew that Princess Varvara had spent her whole life as a dependant of wealthy relatives; but the fact that she was now living with Vronsky, to whom she was not related, offended Dolly on behalf of her husband's family. Anna noticed the expression on Dolly's face and became embarrassed; she blushed, let go of her riding habit, and tripped up on it.

Darya Alexandrovna went up to the *char-à-banc*, which had stopped, and greeted Princess Varvara coldly. Sviyazhsky was also an acquaintance. He asked after his eccentric friend and young wife, and after passing a quick eye over the mismatched horses and the carriage with its patched mudguards, proposed that the ladies should ride in the *char-à-banc*.

'And I'll go in this *véhicule*,' he said. 'The horse is quiet, and the Princess is an excellent driver.'

'No, stay as you are,' said Anna as she came over, 'and we'll go in the carriage,' and taking Dolly's arm, she led her away.

Darya Alexandrovna was bowled over by the elegant *équipage*, the likes of which she had never seen before, the splendid horses, and the elegant and extremely smart people surrounding her. But she was struck most of all by the change that had taken place in her familiar and beloved Anna. Another, less perceptive woman, who had not known Anna before, and who in particular had not been pondering the thoughts which Darya Alexandrovna had been pondering on the way over, would not have noticed anything special about Anna. But Dolly was struck now by that transient beauty which women only have in moments of love, and which she now detected in Anna's face. Everything in her face—the clearly defined dimples in her cheeks and chin, the outline of her lips, the smile which seemed to flutter about her face, the sparkle of her eyes, the grace and alacrity of her movements, the rich tones of her voice, even the half-angry, half-affectionate manner with which she answered Veslovsky when he asked permission to ride her cob, so he could teach it to gallop from the right leg—everything possessed a particular charm, and it seemed she herself knew this and was pleased by it.

When the two women were seated in the carriage, a sudden embarrassment came over them both. Anna was embarrassed by the intent look of enquiry Dolly had focused on her; Dolly was embarrassed because, after Sviyazhsky's words about the *véhicule*, she could not help feeling ashamed of the dirty old carriage in which Anna had sat down with her. Filip the coachman and the clerk were experiencing the same feeling. The clerk fussed about as he seated the ladies in order to hide his embarrassment, but Filip the coachman became downcast, and was girding himself in advance not to submit to this outward superiority. He smiled ironically as he looked at the black trotter, having already made up his mind that this black horse in the *char-à-banc* was good only for *promenages*, as he put it, and would never manage thirty miles on a hot day in one stretch.

The peasants had all got up from the cart and were watching the guest being greeted with amused curiosity, passing comments of their own.

'They look pleased too, haven't seen each other for a long time,' said the old man with curly hair tied back with bast.

'Hey, Uncle Gerasim, if we had that black stallion to cart sheaves, it would be quick work!'

'Hey, look. Over there in breeches, is that a woman?' said one of them, pointing to Vasenka Veslovsky, who was mounting sidesaddle.

'No, it's a man. See how nimbly he jumped up!'

'Well, lads, looks like we won't get our nap.'

'No chance of a nap today!' said the old man, squinting up at the sun. 'Look, it's after midday! Come on, pick up your crooks!'

18

ANNA looked at Dolly's thin, worn-out face with its little wrinkles lined with dust, and was about to say what she thought—which was that Dolly had lost weight; but remembering that she herself had grown prettier and that Dolly's look told her this, she sighed and began talking about herself.

'You are looking at me,' she said, 'and wondering if I can be happy in my situation? Well! It's shameful to admit it, but I . . . I am unforgivably happy. Something magical has happened to me, like a dream, when everything becomes awful and frightening, and suddenly you wake up and feel that all those fears are gone. I have woken up. I've survived the agonizing, awful period and I have been so happy for such a long time now, particularly since we've been here! . . .' she said, looking at Dolly with a timid, questioning smile.

'I am so glad!' said Dolly with a smile that was involuntarily colder than she would have liked. 'I'm very glad for you. Why didn't you write to me?'

'Why? . . . Because I didn't dare . . . you are forgetting my position . . .'

'Didn't dare? Write to me? If you only knew how I . . . I think . . .'

Darya Alexandrovna wanted to divulge her thoughts from that morning, but for some reason she felt it would be out of place now.

'Anyway, let's talk about that later. What are all these buildings?' she asked, wanting to change the conversation and pointing to some red and green roofs which could be seen behind the greenery of acacia and lilac hedges. 'Just like a little town.'

But Anna did not answer her.

'No, no! What is it that you think about my situation, what do you think about it, what?' she asked.

'I suppose . . .' Darya Alexandrovna began, but just at that moment

Vasenka Veslovsky, thudding heavily against the chamois leather of the lady's saddle in his short jacket, galloped past them, having managed to lead the cob into a gallop from the right leg.

'He's doing it, Anna Arkadyevna!' he shouted.

Anna did not even glance at him; but Darya Alexandrovna again felt awkward about beginning this long conversation in the carriage, and so she cut things short.

'I don't think anything,' she said, 'but I have always loved you, and if you love someone, you love the whole person, as they are, and not as you would like them to be.'

Averting her gaze from her friend's face and screwing up her eyes (this was a new habit which Dolly had not known her to have before), Anna paused to think, wanting to comprehend the full meaning of these words. And when she had evidently understood them in the way that she wished, she looked at Dolly.

'If you have any sins,' she said, 'they ought to all be forgiven you for coming here and saying those words.'

And Dolly saw that tears had sprung into her eyes. She silently pressed Anna's hand.

'So what are these buildings? There are so many of them!' she said, repeating her question after a moment's silence.

'They are the servants' houses, the stud farm, and the stables,' answered Anna. 'And that's where the park begins. It was all very neglected, but Alexey has revived everything. He is very fond of this estate, and has developed a passionate interest in farming, which I never expected from him. But then there are so many sides to his personality! Whatever he turns his hand to, he does superbly. Not only is he not bored, but he works with passion. As far as I can see, he has become expert at running the estate, and is even stingy. But only on the estate. When it comes to tens of thousands, he doesn't count,' she said with that gleeful, crafty smile with which women often talk about the secret qualities of their beloved, to which only they are privy. 'Do you see that big building? It's the new hospital. I think it will cost more than a hundred thousand. That's his *dada*[1] at the moment. And do you know how it all came about? Apparently the peasants asked him to reduce the rent for the meadow, and he refused, and I accused him of being stingy. Obviously it was not just that, but everything together, but he began building this hospital to show that he is not stingy, you see. *C'est une petitesse*,[2] if you like, but I love him all the more for it. And

---

[1] 'hobby'.   [2] 'It is pettiness'.

in a minute you'll see the house. It was his grandfather's house, and nothing on the outside has been altered.'

'How lovely!' said Dolly, looking with involuntary surprise at the splendid, columned house emerging from the variegated foliage of the old trees in the garden.

'It is lovely, isn't it? And there is a wonderful view from the top of the house.'

They drove into a courtyard strewn with gravel and decorated with shrubs, where two labourers were placing rough, porous stones round a well-turned flower-bed, and drew up under a covered porch.

'Ah, they're already here!' said Anna, looking at the riding horses, which were just being led away from the porch. 'Don't you think that's a lovely horse? It's a cob. My favourite. Bring her here and give me some sugar. Where is the Count?' she asked the two liveried footmen who sprang out. 'Ah, here he is!' she said, catching sight of Vronsky and Veslovsky coming out to meet her.

'Which room are you going to put the Princess in?' said Vronsky in French, turning to Anna, and without waiting for a reply, he greeted Darya Alexandrovna again and now kissed her hand. 'I was thinking, in the big room with the balcony?'

'Oh, no, that's too far away! It would be better in the corner room, so we will see each other more. Well, let's go,' said Anna, after giving her favourite horse the sugar which the footman had brought her.

'*Et vous oubliez votre devoir*,'[1] she said to Veslovsky, who had also come out into the porch.

'*Pardon, j'en ai tout plein les poches*,'[2] he answered, smiling, as he put his fingers into his waistcoat pocket.

'*Mais vous venez trop tard*,'[3] she said, using a handkerchief to wipe her hand, which the horse had got wet when it took the sugar. Anna turned to Dolly. 'Have you come to stay for a while? For only one day? That's impossible!'

'That's what I promised, and the children . . .' said Dolly, feeling embarrassed both because she had to get her bag out of the carriage, and because she knew her face must be covered with dust.

'No, Dolly, darling . . . Well, we'll see. Come on, let's go!' and Anna led Dolly to her room.

This room was not the smart one which Vronsky had suggested, but

---

[1] 'And you are forgetting your duty.'
[2] 'Pardon me, my pockets are full of it.'
[3] 'But you have come too late.'

one which Anna said Dolly would have to excuse her for. And even this room, for which excuses had to be made, was filled with more luxury than Dolly had ever encountered and reminded her of the best hotels abroad.

'Well, darling, how happy I am!' Anna said, sitting down in her riding habit for a moment beside Dolly. 'Tell me about everyone in your family. I did see Stiva briefly. But he cannot talk about the children. How is Tanya, my favourite? She must be a big girl by now, I suppose?'

'Yes, very big,' Darya Alexandrovna answered in clipped tones, surprised herself that she should answer so coldly about her children. 'We are having a lovely time staying with the Levins,' she added.

'Oh, if only I had known', said Anna, 'that you do not despise me . . . You could have all come to visit us. Stiva's an old and close friend of Alexey's, you know,' she added, and suddenly blushed.

'Yes, but we are having such a good . . .' replied Dolly with embarrassment.

'Yes, forgive me, I'm burbling nonsense out of sheer happiness. The one thing that matters, darling, is how happy I am to see you!' said Anna, kissing her again. 'You still haven't told me yet how and what you think about me, and I want to know everything. But I'm glad you will see me as I am. The most important thing for me is that I wouldn't like people to think there was something I wanted to prove. I don't want to prove anything, I just want to live, and do no harm to anyone but myself. I have the right to that, don't I? However, that's a long conversation, and we'll have a proper talk about everything later. I'm going to get dressed now, and I'll send a maid to you.'

19

LEFT alone, Darya Alexandrovna inspected her room with a housewifely eye. Everything she had seen driving up to the house and walking through it, and now in her room, gave her the impression of abundance and splendour and that new European opulence she had read about only in English novels, but had never before seen in Russia, let alone in the country. Everything was new, from the new French wallpaper to the carpet that covered the whole floor. The bed had a sprung mattress, a special kind of headboard, and silk pillowcases on the little pillows. The marble washstand, the dressing-table, the settee, the tables, the bronze clock on the mantelpiece, the drapery and door-curtains—all of it was new and expensive.

The fashionable maid who came in to offer her services, whose hair-style and dress were more fashionable than Dolly's, was as new and costly as the whole room. Darya Alexandrovna liked her courtesy, her neatness, and her obliging manner, but she felt awkward with her; she felt embarrassed about her patched bed-jacket which unfortunately had been packed for her by mistake. She was ashamed of the very patches and darned areas she was so proud of at home. At home it went without saying that six bed-jackets required over eighteen yards of nainsook at eighty-five kopecks a yard, which worked out at more than fifteen roubles, not counting the trimmings and the work involved, and that these fifteen roubles had to be saved up. But she felt awkward in front of the maid, if not exactly ashamed.

Darya Alexandrovna felt a great sense of relief when her old acquaintance Annushka came into the room. The fashionable maid was needed by her mistress, so Annushka remained with Darya Alexandrovna.

Annushka was clearly very glad that Dolly had arrived, and she kept up an unbroken stream of chatter. Dolly noticed that she was keen to express her opinion about her mistress's situation, particularly about the Count's love and devotion to Anna Arkadyevna, but Dolly made a point of checking her whenever she began talking about it.

'I grew up with Anna Arkadyevna, she's dearer to me than anything. Well, it's not for us to judge. But you'd think to love like that . . .'

'So if you would, please hand this to be washed, if that's possible,' Darya Alexandrovna said, interrupting her.

'Yes, ma'am. We have got two women specially in charge of washing small things, but the linen is all done by a machine. The Count sees to everything himself. Now what husband . . .'

Dolly was glad when Anna came in, her arrival putting a stop to Annushka's chatter.

Anna had changed into a very simple batiste gown. Dolly examined this simple gown closely. She knew what it meant, and how much money had to be spent on acquiring this simplicity.

'An old acquaintance,' said Anna about Annushka.

Anna was no longer embarrassed now. She was perfectly calm and at ease. Dolly saw that she had by this time fully recovered from the impression her arrival had made on her, and had assumed a superficial, detached tone, as if the door to the compartment containing her feelings and intimate thoughts was locked.

'Well, how is Anna, your little girl?' asked Dolly.

'Annie?' (This was what she called her daughter Anna.) 'She's well. She has put on a lot of weight. Do you want to see her? Come on, I'll show her to you. We had such a lot of trouble with nannies,' she began recounting. 'We took on an Italian wet-nurse. She was good, but so stupid! We wanted to send her home, but the child is so used to her that we've kept her on.'

'But how have you arranged? . . .' Dolly started to ask what name the little girl would have; but when she noticed the sudden frown on Anna's face, she changed the meaning of her question. 'How have you arranged things? Have you weaned her yet?'

But Anna had understood.

'You didn't mean to ask that, did you? You meant to ask about her surname. Am I right? Alexey has been agonizing about it. She doesn't have a surname. Or rather it's Karenina,' said Anna, screwing up her eyes so that you could only see the point where her eyelashes met. 'Anyway,' she said, her face suddenly brightening, 'we'll talk about all that later. Come on, I'll show her to you. *Elle est très gentille.*[1] She is already crawling.'

The opulence that had struck Dolly throughout the whole house struck her even more painfully in the nursery. There were little carts ordered from England, apparatuses for learning to walk, a couch deliberately set up like a billiard table for crawling, baby rocking-chairs, and special new bathtubs. All this was English, solidly built and of good quality, and obviously very expensive. The room was large and bright, with a very high ceiling.

When they went in, the little girl, dressed in just a smock, was sitting in a high chair at the table, having her dinner of bouillon, which she had spilled all down her front. The baby was being fed by the Russian servant who worked in the nursery and was herself clearly eating too. Neither the wet-nurse nor the nanny were there; they were in the next room, and from there came the sound of their conversation in a strange French in which only they could make themselves understood.

Hearing Anna's voice, a smart, tall Englishwoman with an unappealing face and a devious expression walked in through the door and immediately started making excuses, hurriedly shaking her fair curls, although Anna had not accused her of anything. The Englishwoman hurriedly said 'Yes, my lady' several times to everything Anna said.

Darya Alexandrovna greatly liked the black-browed, black-haired, rosy-cheeked little girl with the sturdy, red little body covered with gooseflesh, despite the stern expression with which she stared at the new person; she even envied her healthy appearance. She also greatly

---

[1] 'She is very sweet.'

liked the way the litle girl crawled. None of her own children had crawled like that. The little girl was quite adorable when she was put on the carpet with her little dress tucked up at the back. Looking round like a little animal at the grown-ups with her shining black eyes, obviously delighted to be admired, and smiling as she kept her feet turned out, she pressed down energetically on her hands, quickly drew up the whole of her little posterior, before reaching forwards again with her little hands.

But Darya Alexandrovna greatly disliked the general atmosphere of the nursery, and the Englishwoman in particular. Only by being aware that a good nanny would not have gone to work in such an irregular family as Anna's could Darya Alexandrovna explain to herself how Anna, with her knowledge of people, could have taken on such an unappealing, disreputable Englishwoman for her little girl. Moreover, with the exchange of only a few words, it immediately became apparent to Darya Alexandrovna that Anna, the wet-nurse, the nanny, and the child were not accustomed to being together, and that the mother's visit was an unusual occurrence. Anna wanted to give the little girl her toy and could not find it.

Most surprising of all was the fact that when asked how many teeth she had, Anna made a mistake and did not even know about the last two teeth.

'Sometimes it makes me sad that I seem to be superfluous here,' said Anna, leaving the nursery and lifting up the train of her dress in order to avoid the toys standing by the door. 'It was not like this with my first child.'

'I thought it would have been the opposite,' said Darya Alexandrovna timidly.

'Oh no! You know, I did see him, Seryozha,' said Anna, screwing up her eyes as if looking at something far away. 'Anyway, we'll talk about that later. You wouldn't believe, I'm like a starving person suddenly served a full dinner, who does not know what to tuck into first. The full dinner is you and the conversations I am going to have with you, which I could not have with anyone else, and I don't know which conversation to tackle first. *Mais je ne vous ferai grâce de rien.*[1] I need to talk about everything. Oh yes, I need to give you a sketch of the company you will find here,' she began. 'I'll begin with the ladies. Princess Varvara. You know her, and I know your and Stiva's opinion of her. Stiva says the sole aim of her existence is to prove her superiority over Aunt Katerina

---

[1] 'But I shall not let you off anything.'

Pavlovna: that's all true; but she's kind, and I am so grateful to her. There was a moment in Petersburg when it was essential for me to have a chaperone. And she just turned up. But she is kind, she really is. She did a great deal to make my situation easier. I can see you don't understand the full gravity of my situation . . . there in Petersburg,' she added. 'Here I'm completely happy and calm. Well, that's for later on. I need to list everybody. Then there is Sviyazhsky—he's a Marshal of the Nobility, and a very decent person, but he needs something from Alexey. Now that we have settled in the country, you see, Alexey can exert great influence with his wealth. Then there's Tushkevich—you saw him when he was with Betsy. Now he's been dropped and he's come to us. As Alexey says, he's one of those people who are very pleasant if you take them as they wish to appear, *et puis, il est comme il faut*,[1] as Princess Varvara says. Then there is Veslovsky . . . you know him. He's a very nice boy,' she said, and a mischievous smile wrinkled her lips. 'What's this wild story with Levin? Veslovsky told Alexey about it, and we don't believe it. *Il est tres gentil et naif*,'[2] she said again with the same smile. 'Men need distraction and Alexey needs an audience, so I value all these people. We need things to be lively and jolly here, and so that Alexey won't wish for something new. Then there is the steward, a German, who is very good, and knows his business. Alexey has a very high opinion of him. Then there is the doctor, a young man, not exactly a complete nihilist, but you know, he eats off his knife . . . but he's a very good doctor. Then there is the architect . . . *Une petite cour*.'[3]

20

'WELL, here's Dolly for you, Princess, you were so anxious to see her,' said Anna, coming out with Darya Alexandrovna on to the large stone terrace where Princess Varvara was sitting in the shade with an embroidery frame, working on an antimacassar for Count Alexey Kirillovich's armchair. 'She says she doesn't want anything before dinner, but please order some lunch for her, and I'll go and look for Alexey and gather everyone up.'

Princess Varvara received Dolly affectionately and slightly patronizingly, and immediately began explaining to her that she had settled at Anna's because she had always loved her more than did her sister

---

[1] 'and then, he is polite and well-bred'.
[2] 'He is very nice and naive.'
[3] 'A little court.'

Katerina Pavlovna, who had been the one to bring Anna up, and that now, when every one had abandoned Anna, she thought it her duty to help her in this most difficult period of transition.

'Her husband will grant her a divorce, and then I shall go back to my solitary life, but I can be useful now and am carrying out my duty, however difficult it might be for me, unlike some others. And what a dear you are, what a good deed you have done in coming! They live absolutely like the very best married couples; it is for God to judge them, not us. Think about Biryuzovsky and Madame Avenieva . . . Then even Nikandrov himself, and Vasiliev and Madame Mamonova, and Liza Neptunova . . . After all no one said anything, did they? And it has ended with them being received by everyone. And then, *c'est un intérieur si joli, si comme il faut. Tout-à-fait à l'anglaise. On se réunit le matin au breakfast, et puis on se sépare.*[1] Everyone does as he pleases till dinner. Dinner is at seven o'clock. Stiva did very well to send you. He must stand by them. You know, he can do anything through his mother and brother. Then they are doing so much good. He didn't tell you about his hospital? *Ce sera admirable*[2]—everything is from Paris.'

Their conversation was interrupted by Anna, who had found the men of the party in the billiard room and returned with them to the terrace. There was still a long time before dinner, the weather was lovely, and so several different ways of spending those two remaining hours were proposed. There were a great many ways to pass the time at Vozdvizhenskoye, and they all differed from those on offer at Pokrovskoye.

'*Une partie de lawn-tennis*,'[3] suggested Veslovsky, beaming his handsome smile. 'We can be partners again, Anna Arkadyevna.'

'No, it's too hot; it would be better to go for a walk round the garden and a row in the boat, to show Darya Alexandrovna the banks.' Vronsky suggested.

'I'll agree to anything,' said Sviyazhsky.

'I think that Dolly would most enjoy going for a walk, wouldn't you? And then we can go in the boat,' said Anna.

That is what was decided. Veslovsky and Tushkevich went off to the bathing place, promising to get the boat ready there and wait for them.

They set off along the path in two couples, Anna with Sviyazhsky, and Dolly with Vronsky. Dolly felt slightly uncomfortable and anxious

---

[1] 'It's such a pretty, such a refined home. Quite in the English style. We assemble for breakfast, and then we separate.'
[2] 'It will be admirable.'
[3] 'A game of lawn tennis.'

in the completely new surroundings in which she found herself.
She not only defended, but even approved of Anna's conduct at an
abstract, theoretical level. As is often the case with virtuous women
who weary of the monotony of a virtuous life, she was able not only
to excuse illicit love from afar, but even envy it. Besides, she loved
Anna with all her heart. But the reality of seeing Anna amongst these
people she found alien, whose idea of good taste was new to her, made
Darya Alexandrovna feel uncomfortable. She particularly disliked seeing Princess Varvara, who forgave them everything for the sake of the
comforts she enjoyed there.

In the abstract, Dolly generally approved of what Anna had done,
but she did not enjoy seeing the man for whom she had done it. Besides,
she had never liked Vronsky. She thought him very arrogant, and could
perceive no justification for his arrogance except his wealth. But here in
his own home, against her will, he overawed her even more than before,
and she was unable to feel at ease with him. She experienced the same
feeling with him as she had experienced with the maid because of her
bed-jacket. Just as she had felt uncomfortable if not exactly ashamed
about the patches in front of the maid, so she felt permanently uncomfortable if not exactly ashamed about who she was when with him.

Dolly felt embarrassed, and was trying to think of a topic of conversation. Although she thought he was bound, with his arrogance, to
dislike praise of his house and garden, she nevertheless did tell him
that she liked his house very much, as she could find no other topic of
conversation.

'Yes, it's a very beautiful building and in the good old-fashioned
style,' he said.

'I like the courtyard in front of the porch very much. Was it like that
before?'

'Oh no!' he said, and his face lit up with pleasure. 'You should have
seen that courtyard back in the spring!'

And he began, cautiously at first, but then with more and more
enthusiasm, to draw her attention to various details in the decoration
of his house and garden. Having devoted a great deal of trouble to
improving and beautifying his estate, Vronsky evidently felt it incumbent upon him to boast about it to someone new, and he was sincerely
delighted by Darya Alexandrovna's praise.

'If you would like to take a look at the hospital and are not tired, it's
not far off. Let's go,' he said, looking into her face to make sure that
she really was not bored.

'Are you coming, Anna?' he said, turning to her.

'Yes, we'll come, won't we?' she said, turning to Sviyazhsky. '*Mais il ne faut pas laisser le pauvre Veslovsky et Tushkevich se morfondre là dans le bateau.*[1] We must send someone to let them know. Yes, it's a monument he will be leaving behind here,' said Anna, turning to Dolly with that artful, knowing smile with which she had talked about the hospital earlier.

'Yes, it's a major project!' said Sviyazhsky. But in order not to appear too deferential to Vronsky, he promptly added a slightly critical remark. 'I'm surprised, however, Count,' he said, 'that while doing so much for public health, you take so little interest in schools.'

'*C'est devenu tellement commun, les écoles,*[2] said Vronsky. 'That's not the reason, you understand, I just got carried away somehow. Now, we need to go this way to the hospital,' he said to Darya Alexandrovna, pointing to a turning off the side of the avenue.

The ladies opened their parasols and set off down the side path. After making several turns and going through a gate, Darya Alexandrovna saw on high ground in front of her a large, red, elaborately designed building which was almost complete. The still-unpainted iron roof shone dazzlingly in the bright sunshine. Near the finished building was another being constructed that was surrounded by scaffolding, and workmen in aprons standing on the planks were laying bricks, pouring mortar from tubs, and smoothing it with trowels.

'How quickly you get the work done!' said Sviyazhsky. 'When I was here last time the roof was not on yet.'

'By the autumn it will all be ready. Nearly everything is finished now,' said Anna.

'And what's this new building?'

'This is where the doctor and the dispensary will be accommodated,' answered Vronsky, who had seen the architect coming towards him in his short coat, and, after making his apologies to the ladies, he went to meet him.

Walking around the pit from which the workmen were taking lime, he stopped and began saying something vehemently to the architect.

'The pediment is still too low,' he replied to Anna, who had asked what the matter was.

'I said the foundation needed to be raised,' said Anna.

'Yes, of course it would have been better, Anna Arkadyevna,' said the architect, 'but we've missed the boat now.'

---

[1] 'But we must not leave poor Veslovsky and Tushkevich moping in the boat.'
[2] 'Schools have become so common.'

'Yes, I'm very interested in it,' Anna replied to Sviyazhsky, who had expressed surprise at her knowledge of architecture. 'The new building needs to be in keeping with the hospital. But it was an afterthought, and begun without a plan.'

After finishing his conversation with the architect, Vronsky joined the ladies and took them inside the hospital.

Although they were still finishing the cornices outside and painting on the ground floor, nearly everything was finished upstairs. After going up the broad flight of iron stairs to the landing, they went into the first large room. The walls were stuccoed to look like marble, the huge plate-glass windows had already been mounted, only the parquet floor was not finished, and the carpenters, who had been planing a raised square block, left their work and removed the bands holding back their hair in order to greet the ladies and gentlemen.

'This will be the reception room,' said Vronsky. 'There will be a desk, a table, and a cupboard here, and nothing else.'

'This way, let us go through here. Don't go near the window,' said Anna, testing to see if the paint was dry. 'Alexey, the paint is already dry,' she added.

From the reception room they went into the corridor. Here Vronsky showed them the new ventilation system that had been installed. Then he showed them the marble baths and the beds with unusual springs. Then he showed them in succession the wards, the storeroom, and the linen room, then the new type of stove, then the trolleys which would not make any noise while transporting necessary items along the corridor, and many other things. Sviyazhsky appraised everything as someone familiar with all the latest improvements. Dolly was simply amazed by things she had never seen before, and in her desire to understand it all she asked detailed questions about everything, which gave Vronsky evident pleasure.

'Yes, I think that this will be the only properly equipped hospital in Russia,' said Sviyazhsky.

'But won't you have a maternity ward?' asked Dolly. 'It's so much needed in the country. I often . . .'

In spite of his courtesy, Vronsky interrupted her.

'This is not a maternity home, but a hospital, and is intended for all illnesses except infectious ones,' he said. 'Now, have a look at this . . .' and he wheeled over to Darya Alexandrovna a chair for convalescents that he had just acquired. 'Watch this.' He sat down in the chair and began moving it. 'The patient can't walk, he is still weak or his illness has affected his legs, but he needs fresh air, and so now he can get about, go for a spin . . .'

Darya Alexandrovna was interested in everything, and she liked everything very much, but most of all she liked Vronsky himself with his ingenuous, naive enthusiasm. 'Yes, he's a very nice, good man,' she thought at several points, not listening to what he was saying, but looking at him, trying to penetrate his expression, and mentally putting herself in Anna's shoes. She liked him so much now in his state of animation that she understood how Anna could have fallen in love with him.

21

'No, I think the Princess is tired, and horses don't interest her,' Vronsky said to Anna, who had suggested that they go on to the stud farm, where Sviyazhsky wanted to see the new stallion. 'You go on, and I will escort the Princess home and we can have a talk,' he said, turning to her, 'if you would like.'

'I know nothing about horses, and I should be delighted,' answered Darya Alexandrovna, slightly taken aback.

She could see from Vronsky's face that he wanted something from her. She was not mistaken. As soon as they had gone through the gate back into the garden, he looked over in the direction Anna had gone, and having made sure that she could neither hear nor see them, he began:

'You guessed that I wanted to have a talk with you?' he said, looking at her with twinkling eyes. 'I am not erring in believing you are Anna's friend.' He took off his hat, and taking out a handkerchief, wiped his balding head with it.

Darya Alexandrovna did not reply, and only cast a frightened glance at him. When she was left alone with him she suddenly started to feel afraid; his twinkling eyes and stern expression scared her.

The most diverse conjectures as to what he was planning to talk to her about flashed through her mind. 'He is going to ask me to move here with the children and stay with them, and I will have to refuse; or he's going to ask me to put together a social set for Anna in Moscow . . . Or will it be about Vasenka Veslovsky and his relations with Anna? Or perhaps it will be about Kitty, about the fact that he feels guilty?' She foresaw nothing but unpleasantness, but did not guess what he actually wanted to discuss with her.

'You have so much influence over Anna, she is so fond of you,' he said, 'help me.'

Darya Alexandrovna looked searchingly yet timidly at his lively face, which kept coming fully, then partially, into the shaft of sunlight in the shadow of the lime trees and being obscured by shadow again, and she waited to hear what he would say next, but he carried on walking silently beside her, his stick catching on the gravel.

'If you have come to visit us, and you are the only woman amongst Anna's former friends who has—I don't count Princess Varvara—then I understand that you have done this not because you regard our situation as normal, but because you understand all the difficulty of the situation but nevertheless love her and want to help her. Have I understood you correctly?' he asked, looking round at her.

'Oh yes,' answered Darya Alexandrovna, closing her parasol, 'but . . .'

'No,' he interrupted and involuntarily came to a halt, forgetting that he was thereby placing his companion in an awkward position so that she had to come to a halt too. 'No one feels all the difficulty of Anna's position more keenly and intensely than I do. And that is understandable if you can do me the honour of regarding me as a person with a heart. I am the cause of that position, and that is why I feel it.'

'I understand,' said Darya Alexandrovna, involuntarily admiring him for saying this so sincerely and firmly. 'But precisely because you feel you are the cause, I fear you exaggerate,' she said. 'Her position in society is difficult, I do understand that.'

'It is hell in society!' he shot back, frowning darkly. 'It is impossible to imagine worse moral agony than what she went through during those two weeks in Petersburg . . . and I beg you to believe that.'

'Yes, but here, as long as neither Anna . . . nor you feel a need for society . . .'

'Society!' he said scornfully. 'What need can I have for society?'

'As long as you are happy and at peace—and that might be for ever. I can see that Anna is happy, completely happy, she has already managed to tell me that,' said Darya Alexandrovna, smiling; and as she said this, an involuntary doubt now crept into her mind as to whether Anna really was happy.

But Vronsky seemed to have no doubts on that score.

'Yes, yes,' he said. 'I know that she has come back to life after all her sufferings; she is happy. She is happy in the present. But I? . . . I am afraid of what awaits us . . . I'm sorry, would you like to walk on?'

'No, I don't mind.'

'Well then, let us sit here.'

Darya Alexandrovna sat down on a garden bench in a corner of the avenue. He stood before her.

'I can see that she is happy,' he repeated, and Darya Alexandrovna was assailed by an even greater doubt as to whether she was happy. 'But can it go on like this? Whether we have acted rightly or wrongly is another question; but the die is cast,' he said, switching from Russian to French, 'and we are bound together for life. We are united by what we hold to be the most sacred bonds of love. We have a child, and we may have more children. But the law and all the circumstances of our position are such that thousands of complications arise which she does not see and does not want to see while she is still resting her spirit after all her sufferings and ordeals. And that's understandable. But I can't help seeing them. By law my daughter is not my daughter, but Karenin's. I don't want this deception!' he said, making a vigorous gesture of refusal and casting a woeful, enquiring glance at Darya Alexandrovna.

She made no reply and only looked at him. He went on:

'In time a son may be born, my son, and by law he will be a Karenin, he will not be the heir of my name or my estate, and however happy we may be in our family life and however many children we may have, there will be no tie between them and me. They will be Karenins. You can understand the burden and horror of this situation! I have tried talking about it to Anna. It irritates her. She does not understand, and I cannot unburden myself completely to *her*. Now look at it from another angle. I am happy in her love, but I must have an occupation. I have found that occupation and am proud of that occupation, and I consider it nobler than the occupations of my former comrades at court and in the army. And I would certainly not change my work for theirs. I am working here, I don't have to go anywhere, I am happy and contented, and we do not need anything else to be happy. I love what I do. *Ce n'est pas un pis-aller*,[1] on the contrary . . .'

Darya Alexandrovna noticed that at this point in his explanation he grew confused, and she did not quite understand this digression, but she felt that once he had begun to talk about his intimate feelings, which he could not talk about with Anna, he was now unburdening himself of everything, and that the question of his occupation in the country belonged to the same category of intimate thoughts as the question of his relationship with Anna.

---

[1] 'This is not a last resort'.

'So, to continue,' he said, coming back to his senses. 'The main thing I need while I am working is the conviction that what I am doing will not die with me, that I will have descendants—and this is what I don't have. Imagine the position of a man who knows in advance that the children he has with the woman he loves will not belong to him but to someone else, someone who hates them and does not want to know them. It is awful, you know!'

He fell silent, clearly in a state of great agitation.

'Yes, of course, I understand that. But what can Anna do?' said Darya Alexandrovna.

'Yes, that brings me to the purpose of my conversation,' he said, making a concerted effort to collect himself. 'Anna can, it depends on her . . . Even to petition the Tsar for adoption, a divorce is essential. And that depends on Anna. Her husband did agree to a divorce—your husband had almost everything arranged back then. And I know he would not refuse it now. Anna simply needs to write to him. He said plainly at the time that if she expressed the wish, he would not refuse. Of course,' he said gloomily, 'it is one of those Pharisaical cruelties of which only such heartless people are capable. He knows the agony any reminder of him affords her, and knowing her, he demands a letter from her. I can understand it is agonizing for her. But the reasons for it are so important that one must *passer pardessus toutes ces finesses de sentiment. Il y va du bonheur et de l'existence d'Anne et de ses enfants.*[1] I'm not talking about myself, though it's hard for me, very hard,' he said, looking as if he was threatening someone because they had made it hard for him. 'So you see, Princess, I am shamelessly clutching at you as my last hope. Help me to persuade her to write to him and demand a divorce.'

'Yes, of course,' Darya Alexandrovna said pensively, vividly recalling her last meeting with Alexey Alexandrovich. 'Yes, of course,' she repeated emphatically, remembering Anna.

'Use your influence with her, do what you can to make her write. I do not want and am scarcely able to talk to her about this.'

'Very well, I will talk to her. But why has she not thought of it herself?' said Darya Alexandrovna, for some reason suddenly remembering just then Anna's strange new habit of screwing up her eyes. And she recollected that Anna screwed up her eyes precisely when the intimate side of life came into question. 'It is as if she screws her eyes up

[1] 'One must brush aside all these refinements of feeling. The happiness and existence of Anna and her children depend on it.'

where her life is concerned, so as not to see everything,' thought Dolly. 'I will definitely speak to her, for my own sake and for hers,' Dolly said in reply to his expression of gratitude.

They stood up and walked towards the house.

22

FINDING Dolly had already returned, Anna looked intently into her eyes, as if asking about her conversation with Vronsky, but did not put her question into words.

'It seems it's already time for dinner,' she said. 'We haven't seen each other at all yet. I am counting on this evening. I need to go and dress now. I expect you need to as well. We all got dirty at the building site.'

Dolly went to her room and felt like laughing. She had nothing to change into, because she had already put on her best dress; but in order to signal her preparation for dinner in some way she asked the maid to brush her dress, while she changed her cuffs and bow and put some lace on her head.

'This is all I could do,' she said with a smile to Anna, who came in to her wearing a third gown, which was again of exceptional simplicity.

'Yes, we are very formal here,' she said, as if to apologize for her smart attire. 'Alexey is rarely so pleased with anything as he is with your visit. He is completely smitten with you,' she added. 'But are you not tired?' There was no time to talk about anything before dinner. When they went into the drawing room they found Princess Varvara and the men in black frock-coats already there. The architect was wearing tails. Vronsky introduced the doctor and the steward to his guest. He had already introduced the architect to her at the hospital.

The fat butler, with his round shaven face and starched bow of his white tie gleaming, announced that dinner was served, and the ladies rose. Vronsky asked Sviyazhsky to offer his arm to Anna Arkadyevna, while he himself went over to Dolly. Veslovsky offered his arm to Princess Varvara before Tushkevich did, so Tushkevich, the steward, and the doctor went in by themselves.

The dinner, the dining room, the dinner service, the servants, the wine, and the food were not just in keeping with the general tone of modern luxury in the house, but seemed even more luxurious and modern than everything else. Darya Alexandrovna observed this luxury which was new to her, and although she had no hope of applying anything she saw to her own home, since the luxury of everything was far superior to her own way of life, as the mistress of a household she automatically scrutinized every detail and wondered who had done it all and how. Vasenka Veslovsky, her husband, and even Sviyazhsky and many people she knew never thought about this, but took for granted what every respectable host wishes his guests to feel, which is that everything he has managed to arrange so well has cost him, the host, no effort at all, and happened all by itself. Darya Alexandrovna, however, knew that even porridge for the children's breakfast does not happen by itself, and that such a sophisticated and splendid operation must therefore have required someone's concentrated attention. And from the way in which Alexey Kirillovich inspected the table, made a sign with his head to the butler, and offered Darya Alexandrovna a choice of cold or hot soup, she realized that all of this was organized and maintained through the efforts of the host himself. Clearly all this depended no more on Anna than it did on Veslovsky. She, Sviyazhsky, the Princess, and Veslovsky were all guests in the same way, blithely consuming what had been provided for them.

Anna was the hostess only in conducting the conversation. And this conversation—which was a highly difficult one for the mistress of the house at a small dinner table, in the presence of people like the steward and the architect, people from a completely different world trying not to be abashed by the unaccustomed opulence and unable to sustain prolonged participation in the general conversation—this difficult conversation was conducted by Anna with her usual tact, and with naturalness and even enjoyment, as Darya Alexandrovna noted.

The conversation touched on the fact that Tushkevich and Veslovsky had gone out in the boat on their own, and Tushkevich started to talk about the latest races at the Yacht Club in Petersburg. But after waiting for a pause in the conversation, Anna immediately turned to the architect to draw him out of his silence.

'Nikolay Ivanich', she said, meaning Sviyazhsky, 'was astonished at how much the new building has shot up since he was here last; but I am there every day myself, and every day I am amazed at how rapidly the work is progressing.'

'It's pleasant working with His Eminence,' said the architect with a smile (he was a deferential and calm man with a sense of his own worth). 'It's not like dealing with the provincial authorities. Where they would use up reams of paper, I just report to the Count, we talk it over, and it is settled in a trice.'

'American methods,' said Sviyazhsky with a smile.

'Yes, sir, buildings get put up there in a rational fashion . . .'

The conversation moved on to the abuse of power by the United States government, but Anna immediately steered it to another topic, in order to draw the steward out of his silence.

'Have you ever seen a reaping machine?' she said, addressing Darya Alexandrovna. 'We had been to look at one when we met you. It was the first time I had seen one myself.'

'How do they work?' asked Dolly.

'Exactly like scissors. There is a board and a lot of little scissors. Like this.'

Anna took a small knife and fork in her beautiful white hands, which were covered with rings, and began to demonstrate. It was clear she could see that nothing would be understood from her explanation, but she continued on with this explanation in the knowledge that she was talking in an engaging way and that her hands were beautiful.

'It's more like little penknives,' Veslovsky said flirtatiously, not taking his eyes off her.

Anna smiled faintly, but made no reply.

'Karl Fyodorich, they are like scissors, aren't they?' she said, turning to the steward.

'*O ja*,' answered the German. '*Es it ein ganz einfaches Ding*,'[1] and he began to explain how the machine worked.

'It's a pity it doesn't bind too. I saw one at the Vienna exhibition which binds with a wire,' said Sviyazhsky. 'That would be more profitable.'

'*Es kommt drauf an . . . Der Preis vom Draht muss ausgerechnet werden.*'[2] And roused out of his silence, the German turned to Vronsky: '*Das lässt sich ausrechnen, Erlaucht.*'[3] The German had already started to feel in his pocket for his pencil and the notebook in which he always made all his calculations, but remembering he was sitting at the dinner table, and noticing Vronsky's cold stare, he restrained himself. '*Zu kompliziert, macht zu viel Klopot*,'[4] he concluded.

'*Wünscht man Dochots, so hat man auch Klopots*,'[5] said Vasenka Veslovsky, making fun of the German. '*J'adore l'allemand*,'[6] he said, turning to Anna again with the same smile.

---

[1] 'Oh yes, it is a quite simple thing.'

[2] 'It all depends . . . the price of the wire must be allowed for.'

[3] 'It can be estimated, Your Eminence.'

[4] 'Too complicated, too much trouble.' ('Klopot' is a Germanized form of the Russian *khlopoty*, meaning 'trouble'.)

[5] 'If one wants an income, one must also have trouble.' ('Dochots' is a Germanized form of the Russian *dokhod*, meaning 'income'.)

[6] 'I adore German.'

'*Cessez*,'[1] she said with mock severity.

'You know, we expected to find you out in the field, Vasily Semyonich,' she said, turning to the doctor, a sickly-looking man. 'Were you there?'

'I was there, but I bolted,' the doctor answered with doleful humour.

'Then you must have got some good exercise?'

'Splendid!'

'Well, and how is the old woman? I hope it's not typhus?'

'Whether it's typhus or not, there is no amelioration in her condition.'

'What a shame!' said Anna, and having thus paid her dues of courtesy to the members of the household, she turned to her friends.

'All the same, it would be tricky to construct a machine from your description, Anna Arkadyevna,' Sviyazhsky quipped.

'Oh, why do you think so?' said Anna with a smile which showed that she knew there had been something endearing in her explanation of the workings of the machine which Sviyazhsky had also noticed. Dolly was unpleasantly surprised by this new trait of youthful coquetry.

'But Anna Arkadyevna has a remarkable knowledge about architecture on the other hand,' said Tushkevich.

'I'll say; I heard Anna Arkadyevna talking yesterday about damp-courses and plinths,' said Veslovsky. 'Have I got that right?'

'There's nothing remarkable about it when you see and hear so much,' said Anna. 'But I suppose you probably don't even know what houses are made of?'

Darya Alexandrovna could see that Anna was uneasy about the flirtatious tone between her and Veslovsky, but involuntarily succumbed to it herself.

Vronsky behaved quite differently to Levin in this matter. He clearly attached no significance at all to Veslovsky's banter and, on the contrary, encouraged these jokes.

'Well, come on then, Veslovsky, can you tell us what joins the stones together?'

'Cement, of course.'

'Bravo! And what is cement?'

'Well, it's a sort of paste . . . no, purée,' said Veslovsky, provoking general laughter.

The conversation among those dining, with the exception of the doctor, the architect, and the steward, who were sunk in glum silence, did not let up, at times flowing smoothly, and at others catching on

[1] 'Stop.'

something and hitting a raw nerve with someone. There was one point when something hit a raw nerve with Darya Alexandrovna, and she grew so heated she even blushed, and afterwards tried to remember whether she had said anything gratuitous or unpleasant. Sviyazhsky had started talking about Levin, relaying his outlandish idea that machines could only bring harm to Russian agriculture.

'I do not have the pleasure of knowing this Mr Levin,' Vronsky said smiling, 'but he has probably never seen the machines he condemns. And if he has seen them and tried them out, he can't have been very thorough, and it wouldn't have been a foreign machine but some Russian one. And what kind of views can there be about this subject anyway?'

'Generally Turkish views,' Veslovsky said, turning to Anna with a smile.

'I can't defend his ideas,' Darya Alexandrovna said, colouring, 'but I can say that he is a very educated man, and if he were here he would know how to respond to you, but I can't.'

'I am very fond of him, and we are great friends,' Sviyazhsky said, smiling genially. '*Mais pardon, il est un petit peu toqué*;[1] for example, he maintains that there is no need for either the zemstvo or Justices of the Peace, and does not want to participate in anything.'

'It's typical of our Russian apathy,' said Vronsky, pouring water from an ice-cold decanter into a slender glass on a stem, 'not to feel the responsibilities our rights impose on us, and to deny those responsibilities.'

'I know no one more assiduous about fulfilling his responsibilities,' said Darya Alexandrovna, irritated by Vronsky's superior tone.

'I, on the other hand,' continued Vronsky, for whom this conversation had evidently hit a raw nerve for some reason, 'I, on the other hand, such as I am, feel very grateful for the honour bestowed on me, thanks to Nikolay Ivanich here'—he indicated Sviyazhsky—'when I was elected an honorary Justice of the Peace. I consider that the duty of going off to sessions and discussing a case a peasant has brought about a horse is just as important as everything else I might do. And I will regard it as an honour if I am elected to be a member of the zemstvo. It is the only way I can repay the advantages I enjoy as a landowner. Unfortunately people do not understand the role major landowners ought to play in the state.'

It was strange for Darya Alexandrovna to hear how calmly dogmatic he was sitting at his own table. She recalled how Levin, who thought

---

[1] 'But excuse me, he is a bit touched [in the head]'.

the opposite, was just as adamant in his opinions when he was at his own table. But she loved Levin, and was therefore on his side.

'So we can rely upon you, Count, for the next session?' said Sviyazhsky. 'But you will have to set off earlier, so you can already be there on the eighth. Perhaps you would do me the honour of staying with me?'

'Well, I rather agree with your *beau-frère*,'[1] said Anna, 'though not quite to the same degree,' she added with a smile. 'I'm afraid we've been saddled with too many of these public duties lately. Just as in the old days, when there were so many officials that one needed an official for every procedure, now it is all public figures. Alexey has been here now for six months, and he's a member of, I think, five or six different public bodies—he's a trustee, a Justice of the Peace, a councillor, and something to do with horses. *Du train que cela va*,[2] all his time will be taken up with this. And I'm afraid one runs the risk of merely paying lip-service with the sheer number of these duties. How many bodies are you a member of, Nikolay Ivanich?' she turned to Sviyazhsky. 'More than twenty, isn't it?'

Anna was joking, but irritation could be detected in her tone. Darya Alexandrovna, who had been watching Anna and Vronsky closely, noticed it immediately. She also noticed Vronsky's face immediately assuming a serious and stubborn expression. Noticing this together with the fact that Princess Varvara had immediately started talking about Petersburg acquaintances in order to change the subject, and recalling the extraneous things Vronsky had said in the garden about how he was spending his time, Dolly realized that this issue of public activity was connected to some intimate quarrel between Anna and Vronsky.

The dinner, the wine, and the service were all very good, but it was all the kind of thing Darya Alexandrovna had encountered at the grand formal dinners and balls she had grown unaccustomed to, with the same impersonal and strained character; and so on an ordinary day and at a small gathering it all made a disagreeable impression on her.

After dinner they sat for a while on the terrace. Then they started playing lawn tennis. The players, having split into two parties, took up position on either side of a net stretched between two gilt posts on the meticulously levelled and rolled croquet lawn. Darya Alexandrovna would have tried to play, but it took her a long time to understand the game, and when she finally did she was so tired that she sat down with Princess Varvara and just watched those playing. Her partner

---

[1] 'brother-in-law'.   [2] 'At this rate'.

Tushkevich also gave up; but the others carried on playing for a long time. Sviyazhsky and Vronsky both played very well and seriously. They kept an eagle eye on the ball served to them, ran lithely up to it, neither hurrying nor dragging their feet, waited for it to bounce, then hit it skilfully and accurately with the racket and dispatched it over the net. Veslovsky did not play as well as the others. He became overexcited, but on the other hand his exuberance inspired the players. He never let up with his laughter and shouting. Like the other men, he had taken off his jacket with the ladies' permission, and his large, handsome figure in his white shirt-sleeves, his red, perspiring face, and his impulsive movements etched themselves into the memory.

When Darya Alexandrovna went to bed that night, as soon as she closed her eyes she saw Vasenka Veslovsky charging all over the croquet lawn.

But Darya Alexandrovna had not enjoyed herself during the game. She did not like the playful relationship maintained throughout by Vasenka Veslovsky and Anna, or the general unnaturalness of grown-up people playing a children's game alone without children. But in order not to upset the others and to find some way of passing the time, she had joined the game again after having a rest, and had pretended to enjoy it. All that day she had felt she was acting in a theatre with actors who were better than she was, and that her bad acting was ruining the whole show.

She had come with the intention of staying two days, if all went well. But that evening, during the game, she decided she would leave the next day. Those agonizing maternal worries she had found so intolerable during her journey already appeared to her in a different light now, after a day spent without them, and were luring her home.

When, after evening tea and a nocturnal trip in the boat, Darya Alexandrovna went into her room alone, took off her dress, and began tidying her thin hair for the night, she felt a great sense of relief.

She even found it unpleasant to think that Anna was about to come to her. She wanted be alone with her thoughts.

23

DOLLY was about to get into bed when Anna came in to her, already in her nightgown.

Anna had begun talking about intimate matters several times over the course of the day, and each time she had stopped after saying a few words. 'We'll talk everything over later, when we are on our own. There is so much I need to tell you,' she had said.

Now they were on their own, and Anna did not know what to talk about. She was sitting by the window, looking at Dolly and trawling through all the stocks of intimate conversations in her mind that she thought were inexhaustible, but not finding anything. At that moment it seemed to her that everything had already been said.

'Well, how's Kitty?' she said with a heavy sigh, looking guiltily at Dolly. 'Tell me the truth, Dolly, isn't she angry with me?'

'Angry? No,' said Darya Alexandrovna, smiling.

'But doesn't she hate and despise me?'

'Oh, no! But you know, that sort of thing can't be forgiven.'

'Yes, I know,' said Anna, turning away and looking out of the open window. 'But I was not to blame. Who was to blame? And what does blame mean anyway? Could it have been different? Well, what do you think? Could it have happened that you didn't become Stiva's wife?'

'I really don't know. But what I want you to tell me is . . .'

'Yes, yes, but we haven't finished with Kitty. Is she happy? He's a wonderful man, they say.'

'Describing him as wonderful does not do him justice. I don't know a better man.'

'Oh, I am so glad! I'm very glad! Describing him as wonderful does not do him justice,' she repeated.

Dolly smiled.

'But tell me about yourself. We need to have a long conversation. And I've had a talk with . . .' Dolly did not know what to call him. She felt equally awkward calling him the Count and Alexey Kirillych.

'With Alexey,' said Anna, 'I know you did. But I wanted to ask you directly: what do you think about me, about my life?'

'How can you expect me to answer that straight away? I really don't know.'

'No, but tell me all the same . . . You can see my life. But you mustn't forget that you're seeing us in the summer, when you have come to visit, we are not on our own . . . But we came here in early spring when we were living completely on our own, and we will be living on our own in the future, and I don't wish for anything else. But imagine me living on my own without him, all alone, and it is going to happen . . . All the signs are that it will happen often, and that he will spend half his time away from home,' she said, getting up and sitting down closer to Dolly.

'Of course,' she interrupted Dolly, who was about to remonstrate, 'of course, I won't force him to stay. I don't make him stay now. The races are coming up, his horses are competing, he will go, and I'm very glad. But think about me, and imagine my position ... But there is no point talking about this!' She smiled. 'So what did he talk to you about?'

'He talked about what I want to talk about myself, so it is easy for me to be his advocate: about whether it would be possible and whether you might be able to . . .' Darya Alexandrovna faltered, 'remedy, improve your position . . . You know how I look at . . . But all the same, if you can, you should get married . . .'

'You mean get a divorce?' said Anna. 'Do you know, the only woman who came to see me in Petersburg was Betsy Tverskaya? You know her, don't you? *Au fond, c'est la femme la plus dépravée qui existe.*[1] She had a liaison with Tushkevich and deceived her husband in the most abominable way. And she told me she did not want to know me as long as my position was irregular. Don't think I am comparing . . . I know you, my darling. But I could not help remembering . . . Well, so what did he say to you?' she repeated.

'He said he was suffering for you, and on his account. Maybe you will say it's selfishness, but what legitimate and noble selfishness! He wants to legitimize his daughter and be your husband, have a right to you.'

'What wife, what slave, could be more of a slave than I am in my situation?' she interrupted despondently.

'But the main thing he wants . . . is that you should not suffer.'

'That's impossible! Well?'

'Well, his most legitimate wish is that your children should have a name.'

'Which children?' Anna said, not looking at Dolly and screwing up her eyes.

'Annie and those to come . . .'

'He need not worry on that count, as I won't have any more children.'

'How can you possibly say that you won't?'

'I won't, because I don't want any more.'

And in spite of all her agitation, Anna smiled when she noticed the naive expression of curiosity, surprise, and horror on Dolly's face.

'The doctor told me after my illness . . . .

. . . .'

'It can't be true!' said Dolly, opening her eyes wide. For her, this was one of those discoveries whose ramifications and inferences are so enormous that one feels only the impossibility of grasping it all in the

---

[1] 'Really, she is the most depraved woman in existence.'

first moment, while aware of the need to devote a very great deal of time thinking about it.

This discovery, which suddenly explained to her all those families she had previously found incomprehensible in which there were only one or two children, aroused in her so many thoughts, ideas, and contradictory feelings that she was unable to say anything and could only stare at Anna in wide-eyed amazement. This was the very thing she had been dreaming about during her journey earlier in the day, but now that she had learnt that it was possible, she was horrified. She felt that this was an excessively simple solution to an excessively complicated problem.

'*N'est-ce pas immoral?*'[1] was all she said, after a pause.

'What's immoral about it? Think about it, I am faced with two alternatives: either to be pregnant, in other words, ill, or to be the friend and companion of my husband, well, practically my husband,' Anna said in a deliberately superficial and glib tone.

'Well, yes, I see,' said Darya Alexandrovna, hearing the very arguments she had mustered herself, and no longer finding them as convincing as before.

'For you and for other people,' said Anna, as if guessing her thoughts, 'there might still be doubts; but for me . . . You have to understand that I am not his wife; he loves me as long as he loves me. So how am I supposed to keep his love? Like this?'

She held out her white arms in front of her stomach.

Thoughts and memories crowded into Darya Alexandrovna's mind with extraordinary rapidity, as often happens at moments of agitation. 'I did not make myself attractive to Stiva,' she thought; 'he abandoned me for others, and that first one he betrayed me for certainly did not keep him by always being beautiful and vivacious. He dropped her and took up with another. And surely Anna isn't going to be able to attract and keep Count Vronsky in this way? If that is what he is after, he will find outfits and manners which are even more alluring and vivacious. And however white and lovely her bare arms are, however beautiful her whole shapely figure and flushed face amongst all that black hair, he will find something even better, just as my disgusting, pathetic, dear husband does whenever he goes looking.'

Dolly made no reply and just sighed. Anna noticed this sigh, signifying disagreement, and continued. She had other arguments in reserve which were so powerful it would be utterly impossible to counter them.

'You say it is wrong? But one has to be rational,' she went on. 'You

---

[1] 'Isn't it immoral?'

are forgetting my situation. How can I want children? I'm not talking about the suffering, as I'm not afraid of that. But think about it, who are my children going to be? Unfortunate children who will bear some-one else's name. They will be obliged to be ashamed of their mother, their father, and their birth just by virtue of being born.'

'But that is why you need a divorce.'

But Anna was not listening to her. She wanted to enumerate all the arguments with which she had convinced herself on so many occasions.

'Why have I been given reason if not to use it to avoid bringing unfortunate children into the world?'

She looked at Dolly, but went on without waiting for a reply:

'I would always feel guilty towards these unfortunate children,' she said. 'If they do not exist, they are at least not unfortunate, but if they are unfortunate, then I alone am to blame.'

These were the very arguments Darya Alexandrovna had marshalled herself; but now she was listening to them and not understanding them. 'How can I feel guilty towards non-existent beings?' she thought. And an idea suddenly occurred to her: could it have been better for Grisha, her favourite, if he had never existed? And this seemed so outlandish to her, so strange, that she shook her head to disperse this jumble of whirling, mad thoughts.

'No, I don't know, it's not right,' was all she said, with an expression of disgust on her face.

'Yes, but you mustn't forget what you are, and what I am . . . And besides,' Anna added, seemingly acknowledging that it was nevertheless not right, despite the wealth of her arguments and the poverty of Dolly's, 'you mustn't forget the main thing, which is that I am not in the same situation as you are now. For you the question is whether you want not to have any more children, whereas for me it is whether I want to have children. It is a big difference. You have to understand that I can't want them in my situation.'

Darya Alexandrovna did not object. She suddenly felt that such a distance had opened up between her and Anna that there were issues between them on which they would never agree, and about which it was better not to speak.

24

'THEN there is all the more need for you to regularize your position, if possible,' said Dolly.

'Yes, if possible,' said Anna in a suddenly completely different, quiet and sad voice.

'A divorce is not impossible, is it? I was told your husband had consented.'

'Dolly! I don't want to talk about it.'

'Well, we won't then,' said Darya Alexandrovna hurriedly, noticing the expression of anguish on Anna's face. 'All I see is that you look at things too morbidly.'

'I do? Not at all. I'm very cheerful and contented. You saw, *je fais des passions.*[1] Veslovsky . . .'

'Yes, to tell the truth, I didn't like Veslovsky's tone,' said Darya Alexandrovna, keen to change the subject.

'Oh, it's nothing! Alexey is tickled by it and that's all; but he's a boy and putty in my hands; I steer him in the direction I want, you know. He's just like your Grisha . . . Dolly!' she said, suddenly changing tack, 'you say I look morbidly at things. You can't understand. It's too awful. I try not to look at all.'

'But I think you need to. You need to do all you can.'

'But what can I do? Nothing. You tell me to marry Alexey, and that I don't think about it. I don't think about it!!' she repeated, and the colour rose in her face. She got to her feet, drew herself up, sighed heavily, and started pacing up and down the room with her light step, stopping occasionally. 'I don't think about it? There isn't a day or an hour when I don't think about it and reproach myself for thinking about it . . . because thinking about it could drive me mad. Drive me mad!' she repeated. 'Whenever I think about it, I cannot go to sleep without morphine. Well, all right. Let us talk calmly. People tell me—divorce. In the first place, *he* won't grant me one. *He* is now under the influence of Countess Lydia Ivanovna.'

Darya Alexandrovna, sitting up straight on her chair with an expression of pained sympathy on her face, had to keep swivelling her head as she followed Anna walking up and down.

'You need to try,' she said quietly.

'Let's suppose I do try. What does that mean?' she said, giving voice to thoughts mulled over a thousand times and learned by heart. 'It means that while hating him, but nevertheless acknowledging being guilty before him—and I do consider him magnanimous—I have to humiliate myself by writing to him . . . Well, suppose I make the effort and do that. I will either receive an insulting answer or his consent . . .

[1] 'people fall in love with me'.

All right, say I receive his consent . . .' Anna was at this moment at the other end of the room and had stopped there to fiddle with the curtain at the window. 'I receive his consent, but what about my . . . my son? They won't give him back to me, you know. He will grow up, despising me, with his father, whom I left. You must understand that there are two beings I believe I love equally, but both more than myself—Seryozha and Alexey.'

She came into the middle of the room and stood in front of Dolly, with her hands pressed tightly to her chest. Her figure seemed particularly imposing and broad in her white dressing-gown. She bent her head and looked out from under her brows with shining, wet eyes at the small, thin, and pitiful-looking Dolly, who was trembling all over with emotion in her patched bed-jacket and nightcap.

'These are the only two beings I love, and the one excludes the other. I can't unite them, and that's the only thing I want. And if I can't have that, I don't care about anything. Anything at all. It will come to an end one way or another, and that is why I cannot and don't want to talk about it. So don't reproach me, don't pass judgement about me in anything. You, in your purity, cannot understand all that I'm suffering.'

She went and sat down beside Dolly and took her hand, looking into her face with a guilty expression.

'What do you think? What do you think about me? Don't despise me. I don't deserve contempt. I'm simply unhappy. If anyone is unhappy, I am,' she declared and, turning away, she burst into tears.

Left alone, Darya Alexandrovna said her prayers and got into bed. She had felt sorry for Anna with all her heart while she was talking to her; but she could not compel herself to think about her now. Memories of home and her children were springing up in her imagination with a particular new charm, shining with a new brightness. This world of hers now seemed to her so precious and lovely that she did not under any circumstance want to spend an extra day away from it, and she decided she would definitely leave the next day.

Anna, meanwhile, after returning to her boudoir, took a wine glass and poured into it a few drops of medicine, a key ingredient of which was morphine, and after drinking it and sitting still for a little while, she went into the bedroom with her composure regained, in a serene and cheerful state of mind.

When she went into the bedroom, Vronsky examined her carefully. He was looking for signs of the conversation he knew she must have had with Dolly, having stayed so long in her room. But in her expression of subdued excitement, in which something was concealed, he found nothing except that still-captivating, albeit familiar beauty, her awareness of it, and a desire for it to have an effect on him. He did not want to ask her what they had talked about, but was hoping she would say something herself. But she only said:

'I am glad you like Dolly. You do, don't you?'

'But I've known her a long time, you know. She seems very kind, it seems, *mais excessivement terre-à-terre*.[1] All the same I'm very glad to see her.'

He took Anna's hand and looked searchingly into her eyes.

Understanding this look to mean something else, she smiled at him.

The following morning, despite the entreaties of her hosts, Darya Alexandrovna prepared to leave. Levin's coachman, in his far-from-new kaftan and vaguely postilion-style hat, drove the carriage with the patched mudguards and the mismatched horses with grim deliberation up to the covered, sand-strewn porch.

Darya Alexandrovna did not enjoy taking leave of Princess Varvara and the men. After one day, both she and her hosts clearly sensed that they did not suit each other and that it was better for them not to spend time together. Only Anna was sad. She knew that with Dolly's departure there would now be no one to stir up in her soul the feelings which this meeting had aroused in her. She found it painful for these feelings to be stirred up, but she nevertheless knew that this was the best part of her soul, and that this part of her soul was rapidly being smothered in the life she was leading.

When they had driven out into the country, Darya Alexandrovna experienced a pleasant sense of relief, and she was about to ask the servants how they had liked it at Vronsky's when Filip the coachman suddenly began talking himself:

'They might be rolling in money, but they only gave us three measures of oats. They had got right through it before cockcrow. What's three measures? Just a nibble. You can get oats from innkeepers for forty-five kopecks these days. When people come to us, their horses can have as much as they can eat.'

'Stingy gentleman,' confirmed the clerk.

'Well, and did you like their horses?' asked Dolly.

'Beautiful horses. And the food was good. But it did seem a bit boring there, Darya Alexandrovna, I don't know how you found it,' he said, turning his handsome, kind face round towards her.

---

[1] 'but excessively down to earth'.

'Yes, I thought the same. So, will we be home by evening?'

'We should be.'

After arriving home and finding everyone in fine form and particularly endearing, Darya Alexandrovna gave a very lively account of her visit, in which she talked about how warmly she had been received, and about the luxury and good taste with which the Vronskys lived, and about their pastimes, and she would not let anyone say a word against them.

'You have to know Anna and Vronsky—I have got to know him better now—in order to understand how nice they are, and how touching,' she said now with complete sincerity, forgetting the vague feeling of disquiet and awkwardness she had experienced there.

25

VRONSKY and Anna spent the whole summer and part of the autumn in the country, still living in the same way, and still not taking any steps to obtain a divorce. It was settled between them that they would not go anywhere; but they both felt the longer they lived alone, especially in the autumn and without any guests, that they would not be able to endure this life and would have to change it.

Their life seemed to lack for nothing: they had ample means, they had good health, they had a child, and both had occupations. Anna devoted just as much care to her appearance when they had no visitors and read a great deal—both novels and the serious books that were in fashion. She ordered all the books greeted with acclaim in the foreign papers and journals she received, and read them with the kind of attention only possible when reading in solitude. She also studied books and specialist journals on every subject with which Vronsky was involved, so that he often turned straight to her with questions relating to agriculture, architecture, and sometimes even horse-breeding and sport. He was amazed at her knowledge and her memory, and, being doubtful at first, would ask for confirmation; and she would find what he was asking about in the books, and show him.

The organization of the hospital also occupied her. She not only helped, but organized and thought up many things herself. But her chief concern was nevertheless herself—specifically, how much Vronsky cherished her, and how much she could replace for him everything he had left behind. Vronsky appreciated this desire, which had become the sole aim of her existence, not just to please him but also to serve him, but at the same time he felt oppressed by those nets of love in which she tried to entangle him. The more time went on, the more frequently he saw himself entangled in these nets, and the more he wanted not so much to escape them, but to test whether they restricted his freedom. Had it not been for this growing desire to be free and not have a scene every time he wanted to go to town for a meeting or to the races, Vronsky would have been perfectly happy with his life. The role he had selected, the role of wealthy landowner, whose sort ought to constitute the very core of the Russian aristocracy, was not only entirely to his taste but now, having spent six months living in this way, brought him increasing pleasure. And his work, which occupied and absorbed him more and more as time went on, was going extremely well. Despite the immense sums he was paying out for the hospital, the machinery, the cows ordered from Switzerland, and much else besides, he was convinced he was not squandering but increasing his assets. Vronsky was as hard as nails where income was concerned, whether from the sale of timber, wheat, wool, or the leasing of land, and knew how to hold out for his price. In large-scale deals on this and his other estates he stuck to the simplest and most risk-free methods, and was extremely frugal and economical when it came to petty matters. Despite all the cunning and ingenuity of the German steward, who would lure him into making purchases by presenting every estimate in such a way that a far greater outlay seemed necessary, but having calculated that it was possible to do the same thing cheaper and make an immediate profit, Vronsky never gave in to him. He heard his steward out and questioned him, and agreed with him only when whatever was being ordered or organized was brand new, still unknown in Russia, and capable of provoking amazement. He would only commit to a major expenditure, moreover, when there were surplus funds, and would go into all the details and insist on getting the very best for his money when making this expenditure. So it was clear from the way he managed his affairs that he was not squandering but increasing his assets.

In October, elections for the nobility were held in Kashin Province, which incorporated the estates of Vronsky, Sviyazhsky, Koznyshev, Oblonsky, and a small part of Levin's land.

Due to various circumstances and the people taking part in them, these elections had attracted public attention. They had been much talked about, and preparations for them were under way. People who lived in Moscow, Petersburg, and abroad, who never attended elections, were assembling for these elections.

Vronsky had long ago promised Sviyazhsky he would go to them.

Before the elections, Sviyazhsky, who often visited Vozdvizhenskoye, drove over to fetch Vronsky.

The day before there had almost been a quarrel between Vronsky and Anna on account of this proposed trip. It was autumn, the dullest and most difficult time in the country, and so, bracing himself for a confrontation, Vronsky told Anna about his departure in stern, cold terms such as he had never used to speak to her before. But to his surprise, Anna received this news very calmly and merely asked when he would return. He looked at her carefully, not understanding this calmness. She responded to his look with a smile. He knew this capacity of hers for withdrawing into herself, and knew it only occurred when she had made some private decision without telling him of her plans. He was afraid of this; but he was so anxious to avoid a scene that he pretended to believe in, and partly genuinely did believe in, what he wished to believe—her good sense.

'I hope you won't be bored?'

'I hope not,' said Anna. 'I received a box of books yesterday from Gautier.* No, I won't be bored.'

'If she wants to adopt that tone then so much the better,' he thought, 'otherwise we will just be going over the same old ground.'

And so he left for the elections without challenging her to a frank discussion. It was the first time since the beginning of their relationship that he had parted from her without talking things through thoroughly. On the one hand this bothered him, but on the other, he felt this was better. 'At first there will be something vague, something suppressed, like now, but then she will get used to it. In any case, I can give her everything, but not my male independence,' he thought.

26

In September Levin moved to Moscow for Kitty's confinement. He had already spent a whole month in Moscow without doing anything when Sergey Ivanovich, who had property in Kashin Province and took an active interest in the question of the forthcoming elections, started making preparations to go and take part in them. He invited his brother, who had a vote in the Seleznev district, to come along with him. Levin also had some extremely important business he needed to attend to in Kashin for his sister who lived abroad, concerning a trusteeship and the receipt of some redemption payments.

Levin was still in a state of indecision, but Kitty, who could see he was bored in Moscow and advised him to go, went ahead without telling him and ordered him the requisite nobleman's uniform, costing eighty roubles. And those eighty roubles paid out for the uniform were the main reason that prompted Levin to go. He made the journey to Kashin.

Levin had now been in Kashin for five days, going to the assembly every day and embroiling himself in his sister's business, which was still not proceeding smoothly. The Marshals of the Nobility were all busy with the elections, and it was impossible to sort out the one very simple matter that depended on the trusteeship. The other matter— the receipt of the money—also met with obstacles. After going through the rigmarole required to remove the embargo, the money was ready to be paid out; but the notary, a most obliging man, could not issue the payment order because the signature of the chairman was needed, and the chairman, who had not appointed a delegate, was in session. All this fuss and bother, the endless going from one place to another, the conversations with very kind, good people, who completely understood the unpleasantness of the petitioner's position but could not assist him—all this effort without any result produced in Levin a ghastly feeling which was akin to that exasperating sense of powerlessness experienced in dreams when one wants to apply physical force. He felt this frequently when talking to his exceptionally good-natured lawyer. It seemed this lawyer was doing all he could, and exerting all his intellectual powers, in order to extricate Levin from his predicament. 'Here's what I suggest you try,' he said more than once; 'go off to such-and-such a place and such-and-such a place,' and the lawyer would draw up a whole plan for circumventing the one crucial element that was hindering everything. But he would immediately add: 'They will still hold you up; but try it anyway.' And Levin kept trying, and paying all the necessary visits. Everyone was kind and obliging, but what was being circumvented would inevitably end up looming into view again, and would again block his progress. What was particularly annoying was that Levin just could not understand whom he was battling against, and who stood to profit from his business being unfinished. No one seemed to know that; nor did the lawyer know. If Levin could have understood that, as he understood why one cannot go up to the ticket-office of a railway station without joining the queue, he would not have felt so annoyed and cross; but no one could actually explain to him why the obstacles he kept encountering with regard to his business existed.

But Levin had changed a great deal since his marriage; he was patient, and told himself that if he did not understand why everything was organized in this way, then without knowing all the details he was not in a position to judge, and that probably this was the way it had to be, so he tried not to be angry.

He was also trying not to criticize or take issue now that he was attending and taking part in the elections, but instead acquire as full an understanding as possible of the activity with which the honest and good people he respected were so seriously and passionately engaged. Since his marriage, Levin had discovered so many new and serious perspectives that he had previously considered trivial due to his frivolous attitude, that he now assumed and searched for serious significance in the matter of the elections as well.

Sergey Ivanovich explained to him the meaning and importance of the radical changes that the elections were expected to bring. The Provincial Marshal of the Nobility, in whose hands the law had placed so much important public business—not only trusteeships (such as the one now causing Levin grief), and the nobility's extensive funds, but also high schools for boys, girls, and the military, popular education according to the new model, and, finally, the zemstvo—this Provincial Marshal Snetkov was a nobleman of the old school who had squandered a huge fortune, a good man who was honest after his own fashion, but he did not understand the needs of the new age at all. He perennially took the side of the nobility in everything, he directly opposed the spread of popular education, and he belittled the zemstvo, which was supposed to have such enormous importance, by characterizing it in terms of social class. He needed to be replaced by a modern, practical, and completely new person with a fresh approach, who would run things in such a way as to elicit from all the rights granted to the nobility, not as the nobility, but as a constituent element of the zemstvo, every advantage of self-government that could be elicited. Such forces had now gathered in the wealthy Kashin Province, which was always so ahead of other provinces in everything, that whatever was properly put into place there could serve as a model for other provinces, and for the whole of Russia. The whole undertaking, therefore, had great significance. In place of Snetkov as Marshal, they were proposing to install either Sviyazhsky or, even better, Nevedovsky, a former professor, a remarkably clever man and a great friend of Sergey Ivanovich.

The assembly was opened by the Governor, who made a speech to the nobles in which he urged them to elect officials on merit and for the good of the fatherland, rather than on personal preference, and expressed the hope that the honourable Kashin nobility would perform its duty scrupulously as in past elections, and justify the supreme confidence of the monarch.

When he finished his speech, the Governor left the hall and the nobles followed him out and thronged round him noisily and eagerly, some even rapturously, while he was putting on his fur coat and chatting amicably to the Marshal of the Province. In his desire to immerse himself in everything and not miss anything, Levin stood there in the crowd and heard the Governor say: 'Please tell Marya Ivanovna my wife is very sorry, she has to go to the orphanage.' Then the nobles merrily grabbed their fur coats and they all drove off to the cathedral.

As he raised his hand along with the others in the cathedral and repeated the words of the priest, Levin swore by the most terrifying oaths to carry out everything hoped for by the Governor. Church services always affected Levin, and as he uttered the words, 'I kiss the cross,' and glanced round at that crowd of young and old men repeating the same words, he felt moved.

On the agenda for the second and third days were items to do with the nobility's funds and the high school for girls, which Sergey Ivanovich explained were of no importance, and Levin did not bother following them since he was busy traipsing from office to office on his own business. On the fourth day the audit of the province's funds was carried out at the Marshal's table. And this was when the first conflict between the new and the old parties arose. The committee charged with auditing the funds reported to the assembly that the funds were all present and correct. The Marshal of the Province got up, thanked the nobility for their confidence, and shed a few tears. The nobles gave him a rousing reception and shook his hand. But it was at that juncture that a noble from Sergey Ivanovich's party said that he had heard that the committee had not actually audited the funds, considering an audit to be an insult to the Marshal of the Province. One of the members of the committee foolishly confirmed this. Then a small, very young-looking, but very malevolent gentleman began to say that the Marshal of the Province would probably be pleased to give an account of the funds, and that the committee members' excessive tact was depriving him of that moral satisfaction. The members of the committee then withdrew their declaration, and Sergey Ivanovich pursued a logical line of argument to the effect that they had to confess whether the funds were audited or not, and he pursued the ramifications of this dilemma in some detail. A garrulous member from the opposing party countered Sergey Ivanovich. Then Sviyazhsky spoke, and the malevolent gentleman spoke again. The debate went on for a long time without reaching any conclusion. Levin was surprised that they argued about it for such a long time, particularly in view of the fact that when he asked Sergey Ivanovich whether he supposed that the funds had been spent, Sergey Ivanovich answered:

'Oh no! He's an honest man. But we needed to shake up that age-old, patriarchal, family way of managing the nobility's affairs.'

On the fifth day the elections of the District Marshals took place. It was quite a turbulent day in some districts. In the Seleznev district Sviyazhsky was elected unanimously without a ballot, and he hosted a dinner that evening.

27

THE elections for the province were scheduled for the sixth day. The large and small halls were full of noblemen in various uniforms. Many had come just for this day. Acquaintances who had not seen each other for a long time, some of whom had come from the Crimea, some from Petersburg, and some from abroad, were greeting each other in the halls. Discussions were being conducted at the Marshal's table under the portrait of the Tsar.

The nobles in both the large and the small halls were grouped into parties, and from their hostile and suspicious glances, from the way they fell silent whenever a stranger approached, and from the way that some of them went out whispering into a distant corridor, it was clear that each side was keeping secrets from the other. In their external appearance the nobles divided sharply into two types: the old and the new. The old were for the most part either wearing the old buttoned-up uniforms of the nobility with swords and hats, or the special navy, cavalry, or infantry uniforms to which they were entitled. The uniforms of the old nobility, which were gathered at the shoulders, were cut in the old-fashioned way; they were clearly too small, short in the waist and narrow, as if their wearers had grown out of them. The young, on the other hand, were wearing unbuttoned nobles' uniforms which were low-waisted and broad in the shoulders, with white waistcoats, or uniforms with black collars embroidered with laurel leaves, the insignia of the Ministry of Justice. The court uniforms that here and there added lustre to the crowd also belonged to the young nobles.

But the division into young and old did not correspond with the division into parties. Some of the young nobility belonged to the old party, as Levin observed, and some of the very oldest nobles, by contrast, were whispering with Sviyazhsky, and were clearly ardent supporters of the new party.

Levin was standing in the small hall, where people were smoking and taking refreshments, near those from his circle, and he was listening to what they were saying and exerting all his intellectual powers in a vain attempt to understand what was being said. Sergey Ivanovich was the centre around whom the others were clustered. He was now listening to Sviyazhsky and Khlyustov, the Marshal of another district who belonged to their party. Khlyustov was refusing to go along with his district in asking Snetkov to stand, while Sviyazhsky was trying to persuade him to do so, and Sergey Ivanovich approved this plan. Levin could not understand why the opposition party was going to ask the Marshal to stand when they wanted to defeat him.

Stepan Arkadyich, who had just had something to eat and drink, came up to them in his Court Chamberlain's uniform, wiping his mouth with a scented and bordered lawn handkerchief.

'We are taking up positions, Sergey Ivanovich!' he said, smoothing his whiskers.

And after listening to the conversation, he endorsed Sviyazhsky's viewpoint.

'One district's enough, and Sviyazhsky has obviously already become the opposition,' he said, with everyone except Levin understanding what he meant.

'So, Kostya, have you also developed a liking for all this?' he added, turning to Levin and taking him by the arm. Levin would have been glad to develop a liking for it, but he could not understand what was going on and, after taking a few steps away from the people talking, he expressed to Stepan Arkadyich his confusion as to why they should want to ask the Marshal of the Province to stand for election.

'*O sancta simplicitas!*' said Stepan Arkadyich, and he gave Levin a succinct and lucid explanation of what was going on.

If all the districts nominated the Marshal of the Province, as at the previous elections, he would be elected unanimously with white balls. They did not need that. Eight districts had now agreed to nominate him; but if two refused to nominate him, Snetkov might refuse to stand. Then the old party might choose another of their members, since their calculations would have come to nothing. But if it was only Sviyazhsky's district which did not nominate him, Snetkov would stand. They would even vote for him and make a point of switching over to him so that the opposition party would be misled, but when one of their candidates was put forward, they would then switch to him.

Levin understood, but not completely, and was about to ask a few questions when everyone suddenly began talking, making a commotion, and moving into the large hall.

'What is going on? What? Who? A mandate? To whom? What? They're rejecting it? There is no mandate. Flerov is not being admitted. What if he is being prosecuted? That means they won't admit anyone. It's despicable. It's the law!' heard Levin on all sides, and along with everyone else who had hurried off, fearing they might miss something, he headed into the large hall and jostled with the nobles to get close to the Marshal's table, where the Marshal of the Province, Sviyazhsky, and the other leaders were having a heated argument about something.

28

LEVIN was standing some way off. He was prevented from hearing clearly by one nobleman standing near him whose breathing was hoarse and heavy, and by another whose thick soles squeaked. From a distance he could only hear the Marshal's soft voice, then the malevolent nobleman's shrill voice, then Sviyazhsky's voice. As far as he could make out, they were arguing about an article of the law, and about the meaning of the words: 'under criminal investigation'.

The crowd parted to make way for Sergey Ivanovich, who was approaching the table. After waiting for the malevolent nobleman to finish speaking, Sergey Ivanovich said that he thought the most correct thing to do would be to consult this particular article of the law, and he asked the secretary to find it. The article stated that in the case of a difference of opinion, there should be a ballot.

Sergey Ivanovich read the article and had just started to explain its meaning when he was interrupted by a tall, plump, stooping landowner with dyed whiskers, in a tight uniform, whose collar was propping up the back of his neck. He came up to the table, struck it with his signet ring, and shouted loudly:

'A ballot! Put it to the vote! There is nothing to talk about! Put it to the vote!'

Then several voices began speaking, and the tall nobleman with the signet ring, who was getting more and more exasperated, started shouting louder and louder. But it was impossible to make out what he was saying.

He was saying exactly the same thing that Sergey Ivanovich had proposed; but he obviously hated him and his whole party, and this feeling of hatred spread to the whole party, provoking the other side to retaliate with equal, albeit more dignified, exasperation. Shouts went up, and for a moment all was confusion, so that the Marshal of the Province had to call for order.

'A ballot, a ballot! Any nobleman will understand that. We are shedding blood . . . The confidence of the monarch . . . The Marshal shouldn't be audited, he's not a shopkeeper . . . But that's not the point . . . Let's vote, please! An abomination! . . .'—exasperated and irate shouting could be heard on all sides. The looks and expressions betrayed even more exasperation and fury than the words. They expressed implacable hatred. Levin had absolutely no idea what was going on, and he was amazed at the sheer vehemence with which they were deliberating over the issue of whether the opinion about Flerov should be put to the vote or not. He had forgotten, as Sergey Ivanovich explained to him afterwards, the syllogism which reasoned that it was necessary to unseat the Marshal of the Province for the common good; to unseat the Marshal they needed to gain a majority of the votes; to gain a majority of the votes they needed to give Flerov the right to vote; and to give Flerov the right to vote they needed to explain how to interpret the relevant article of the law.

'A single vote could decide everything, so one needs to be serious and consistent if one wants to serve the common good,' concluded Sergey Ivanovich.

But Levin had forgotten that, and he found it harrowing to see these good people he respected in such unpleasant, vindictive ferment. To escape from this harrowing feeling, and without waiting for the end of the debate, he walked into a hall where there was no one but waiters near the buffet. When he saw the waiters busily wiping crockery and putting out plates and wine glasses, and when he saw their calm but lively faces, Levin felt an unexpected sense of relief, as if he had come out of a stuffy room into the fresh air. He began walking up and down, enjoying watching the waiters. He greatly liked the way one waiter with grey whiskers poured scorn on the other younger waiters who were poking fun at him while he taught them how to fold napkins. Levin was just about to enter into conversation with the old waiter when he was diverted by the secretary of the nobility's board of trustees, a little old man whose speciality was knowing all the noblemen of the province by name and patronymic.

'Please come, Konstantin Dmitrich,' he said, 'your brother's look-ing for you. They are voting on the opinion.'

Levin walked into the hall, received a small white ball, and followed his brother Sergey Ivanovich up to the table where Sviyazhsky was standing with a meaningful and ironic expression on his face while gathering his beard into his fist and sniffing it. Sergey Ivanovich put his hand into the box, put his ball somewhere, made room for Levin, and then stood still. Levin came up, but having completely forgotten what it was all about and overcome with embarrassment, he turned to Sergey Ivanovich with the question: 'Where do I put it?' He asked this quietly when there were people talking around him, in the hope that his question would not be overheard. But the people talking fell silent, and his scandalous question was heard. Sergey Ivanovich frowned.

'It is a matter of individual conviction,' he said severely.

Several people smiled. Levin turned crimson, hurriedly slipped his hand under the cloth, and placed it to the right, as it was in his right hand. Having placed his ball, he remembered that he needed to slip his left hand in too, so he did, but too late, and now feeling even more embarrassed, he beat a hasty retreat to the back rows.

'A hundred and twenty-six for! Ninety-eight against!' rang out the voice of the secretary, who could not pronounce the letter *r*. Then there was the sound of laughter; a button and two nuts had been found in the ballot box. Flerov was given the right to vote, and the new party had scored a victory.

But the old party did not consider itself defeated. Levin heard that they were asking Snetkov to stand, and he saw a crowd of nobles thronging round the Marshal, who was saying something. Levin went up closer. In his reply to the nobles, Snetkov spoke about the nobility's trust and its affection for him, which he did not deserve, as his only merit had been his devotion to the nobility, to which he had dedicated twelve years of service. Several times he repeated the words: 'I have served to the best of my powers, truthfully and faithfully, and I appre-ciate and thank'—then suddenly he broke off due to the tears which were choking him, and left the hall. Whether those tears stemmed from a sense of the injustice being done to him, or his love for the nobility, or the stressful situation he found himself in, in which he felt he was surrounded by enemies, most of the nobility were moved, and Levin felt a rush of affection for Snetkov.

The Marshal of the Province bumped into Levin in the doorway.

'I beg your pardon, excuse me, please,' he said as if to a stranger; but when he recognized Levin, he smiled gingerly. It seemed to Levin that he wanted to say something, but was too flustered to do so. The expression in his face and whole figure, as he scurried on past in his uniform adorned with crosses and white trousers with the gold brocade, reminded Levin of a hunted animal which can see the game is up. Levin found this expression on the Marshal's face all the more poignant because he had visited him at home about the business of the trusteeship only the day before, and had seen him as a kind-hearted, family man in all his splendour. The big house with the old family furniture; the rather shabby and grimy but respectful old footmen, obviously former serfs who had stayed with their master; the plump, good-natured wife in the lacy cap and Turkish shawl, caressing her pretty grandchild, the daughter of her daughter; the strapping son, in his sixth year at high-school, who had come home from school and greeted his father after kissing his large hand; the host's stirring and affectionate words and gestures—all this had garnered Levin's involuntary respect and sympathy the day before. Levin found the old man a touching and sorry figure now, and he wanted to say something nice to him.

'So you're going to be our Marshal again,' he said.

'Hardly,' said the Marshal, looking round timorously. 'I'm tired and old already. If there are others who are younger and more deserving than me, let them serve.'

And the Marshal disappeared through a side door.

The most solemn moment had arrived. They had to proceed with the election straight away. The leaders of both parties were counting white and black balls on their fingers.

The debate about Flerov had given the new party not only Flerov's vote, but also won them some time, so that they could go and collect three noblemen who had been deprived of the possibility of taking part in the election by the machinations of the other party. Two nobles with a weakness for the bottle had been made drunk by Snetkov's minions, while a third discovered his uniform had been taken away.

When they found out about this, the new party contrived during the debate about Flerov to dispatch some of its members in a hired cab to kit the nobleman out in a uniform and bring one of the two who were inebriated to the assembly.

'I've brought one of them and doused him with water,' said the land-owner who had gone to fetch him as he went up to Sviyazhsky. 'He's all right, he'll do.'

'You're sure he's not too drunk and won't fall over?' said Sviyazhsky, shaking his head.

'No, he's fine. As long as no one plies him with drink here . . . I told the man at the bar not to give him anything on any account.'

29

THE narrow hall in which people were smoking and taking refreshments was full of noblemen. The excitement kept mounting, and tension was discernible in every face. The leaders, who knew all the details and the total number of votes, were particularly tense. They were the commanders of the approaching battle. Although the others were also getting ready for the fight, like rank-and-file soldiers before a battle, they were seeking diversion in the meantime. Some were having a bite to eat standing up or seated at table; others were walking up and down the long room, smoking cigarettes and talking to friends they had not seen for a long time.

Levin did not feel like eating, and he did not smoke; nor did he have any desire to join his own crowd, that is to say, Sergey Ivanovich, Stepan Arkadyich, Sviyazhsky, and the others, because Vronsky, dressed in his equerry's uniform, was standing there engrossed in a lively conversation with them. Levin had caught sight of him at the elections the previous day and had studiously avoided him, as he did not want to meet him. He went over to the window and sat down, observing the groups and listening to what was being said around him. He felt particularly sad, because he could see that everyone was lively, preoccupied, and busy, and only he and a mumbling, ancient, toothless little old man in a naval uniform who had sat down beside him were uninterested and had nothing to do.

'He's such a blackguard! I told him, but it made no difference. It's appalling! He couldn't collect it in three years!' a squat, round-shouldered landowner with pomaded hair that lay on the embroidered collar of his uniform was saying vociferously, stamping the heels of the new boots which had obviously been put on for the elections. And casting a disgruntled glance at Levin, the landowner abruptly turned his back on him.

'Yes, it's a dirty business, there's no denying,' said a small landowner in a reedy voice.

A whole mob of landowners surrounding an overweight general came bearing down on Levin after that. The landowners were clearly looking for somewhere they could talk without being overheard.

'How dare he say that I gave the order for his trousers to be stolen!

Pawned them for drink, I bet. I couldn't care less about him and his princely title! He has no right to say that, it's outrageous!'

'Excuse me! They are going by the article of the law, after all,' they were saying in another group, 'the wife has to be registered as a noble.'

'To hell with the law! I am speaking frankly. That is why the nobility are noble. You must have trust.'

'Your Excellency, come, how about some *fine champagne*?'[1]

Another group was following a noble who was shouting something in a loud voice; it was one of the three who had been plied with drink.

'I've always advised Marya Semyonovna to let it, as she will never make it pay,' resounded the pleasant voice of a landowner with grey whiskers wearing the regimental uniform of a colonel in the old General Staff. It was the same landowner Levin had met at Sviyazhsky's. He recognized him straight away. The landowner also stared at Levin, and they exchanged greetings.

'Very nice to see you. Of course I do! I remember you very well. Last year at our Marshal Nikolay Ivanovich's place.'

'Well, and how is your farming going?' asked Levin.

'Oh, just the same, still making a loss,' answered the landowner as he drew up with a resigned smile, but also an expression of calm conviction that this was precisely the way things had to be. 'And how did you come to end up in our province?' he asked. 'Have you come to take part in our *coup d'état*?' he said, pronouncing the French words firmly but badly. 'All Russia's here: even chamberlains, and pretty well everyone but ministers.' He indicated the imposing figure of Stepan Arkadyich in his white trousers and Court Chamberlain's uniform, walking beside a general.

'I have to confess that I have a very poor idea of what these nobility elections mean,' said Levin.

The landowner looked at him.

'But what is there to understand? There's no meaning whatsoever. It's a superannuated institution which continues to function only through force of inertia. Just look at the uniforms, and they alone will tell you that this is an assembly of Justices of the Peace, Permanent Members, and so on, but not noblemen.'

'Then why do you come?' asked Levin.

'From habit, for one thing. Then there are connections one needs to keep up. There's also a kind of moral obligation. And then, to tell the truth, there are private reasons. My son-in-law wants to stand as

---

[1] 'cognac'.

a Permanent Member. They're not well off, and he needs a helping hand. But why do these gentlemen come?' he said, indicating the malevolent gentleman who had talked at the Marshal's table.

'That's the new generation of the nobility.'

'They might be new. They aren't nobility, though. They might own property, but we're the ancestral landowners. As noblemen, they're cutting their own throats.'

'But you say it's an institution that has outlived itself.'

'It might have outlived itself, but it still ought to be treated a little more respectfully. Take Snetkov . . . Whether we are a good thing or not, we've been around a thousand years. You know, if you needed to cultivate a garden in front of your house, and were planning it, and had a hundred-year-old tree growing there . . . It might be gnarled and old, but you still wouldn't cut that old fellow down for the sake of a few flowerbeds, you'd plan your beds to take advantage of the tree. You can't grow a tree like that in a year,' he said circumspectly, then immediately changed the subject. 'So, how is your farming going?'

'Oh, not too well. I make about five per cent.'

'Yes, but you aren't taking your own input into account. You are worth something too, aren't you? I'll tell you how it's been with me. Before I took up farming, I had a salary of three thousand from the civil service. Now I work more than I did in the service, and like you, get five per cent, and then only if I am lucky. But my labour counts for nothing.'

'Then why on earth do you do it? If there is a straight loss?'

'You just do it! What do you expect? It's a habit, and you know that is the way it has to be. And what's more,' the landowner went on, warming to his theme as he leant his elbow against the window, 'my son has no desire to farm. He's obviously going to be a scholar. So there will be no one to carry on. But you still do it. I've just gone and planted an orchard.'

'Yes, yes,' said Levin, 'that's quite right. I always feel there's no real economic basis to my farming, but you just go on doing it . . . You feel a kind of duty to the land.'

'And here's another thing,' the landowner continued. 'I had my neighbour over, he's a merchant. We walked through the farmlands and through the garden. "You know, Stepan Vasilich," he said, "everything is in good order, but that garden of yours needs some work." Actually my garden is in good order. "If you take my advice, I'd cut down those lime trees. But make sure you do it when the sap is rising. You've got thousands of these limes after all, and you could get two good lots of bast from each one of them. These days you can get a good price for bast, and you chop up the timber for huts." '

'And he'd buy up a load of cattle with the money, or buy some land for next to nothing and lease it to the peasants,' Levin finished the story with a smile, having clearly encountered such calculations more than once. 'And he would make his fortune. But you and I have to pray we can just hold on to what we've got so we can leave it to our children.'

'You've got married, I hear?' said the landowner.

'I have,' Levin answered, with proud contentment. 'Yes, it's rather strange,' he went on. 'We go on living without any hope of making a profit as if we were designated to guard some sacred fire like ancient vestals.'

The landowner chortled under his white moustache.

'Then there are some of us, such as our friend Nikolay Ivanovich, for example, or Count Vronsky, who has settled here recently, who want to farm along industrial lines; but apart from burning money, so far that is leading nowhere.'

'But why don't we behave like the merchants? And cut down our orchards for bast?' said Levin, returning to the thought that had struck him.

'Well, it's as you said, we have to guard the fire. And that is not a nobleman's work. A nobleman's work is not done here at the elections, but back at home. There's also our class instinct about what we should or should not do. And I can see it's the same thing with the peasants: a hard-working peasant will try to rent as much land as he can. He'll plough it, however bad the soil is. Also without profit. Straight into the red.'

'Just like with us,' said Levin. 'Very, very nice to see you,' he added, seeing Sviyazhsky approaching him.

'This is the first time we two have seen each other since we met at your place,' said the landowner, 'and we got quite carried away.'

'I suppose you've been railing against the new order?' said Sviyazhsky with a smile.

'A bit of that.'

'Letting off steam.'

30

SVIYAZHSKY took Levin's arm, and they went to join his friends.

It was now impossible to escape Vronsky. He was standing with Stepan Arkadyich and Sergey Ivanovich, and looking straight at Levin as he walked over.

'Very good to see you. I believe I had the pleasure of meeting you . . . at Princess Shcherbatskaya's,' he said, holding his hand out to Levin.

'Yes, I remember our meeting very well,' said Levin and, blushing crimson, he immediately turned and started talking to his brother.

Vronsky smiled faintly and went on talking to Sviyazhsky, clearly lacking any desire to enter into conversation with Levin; but Levin kept looking round at Vronsky while he was talking to his brother, trying to think of something he could talk to him about in order to smooth over his rudeness.

'What are we waiting for now?' asked Levin, looking at Sviyazhsky and Vronsky.

'For Snetkov. He had either to refuse or agree to stand,' answered Sviyazhsky.

'So has he agreed or not?'

'Well, that's the point—he's done neither,' said Vronsky.

'But if he refuses, who will stand?' asked Levin, looking at Vronsky.

'Whoever wants to,' said Sviyazhsky.

'Will you?' asked Levin.

'Not if I can help it,' said Sviyazhsky in embarrassment, casting an alarmed glance at the malevolent gentleman standing beside Sergey Ivanovich.

'Who will then? Nevedovsky?' said Levin, sensing that he was getting into hot water.

But this was even worse. Nevedovsky and Sviyazhsky were the two candidates.

'Not under any circumstances,' answered the malevolent gentleman. This was Nevedovsky himself. Sviyazhsky introduced Levin to him.

'So, are you on tenterhooks too?' said Stepan Arkadyich, winking at Vronsky. 'It's like the races. We could bet on it.'

'Yes, you do end up on tenterhooks,' said Vronsky. 'Once you get involved, you want a result. It's a battle!' he said, frowning and clenching his powerful jaws.

'How dynamic Sviyazhsky is! Everything is so clear with him.'

'Oh, yes,' Vronsky said absent-mindedly.

A silence ensued, during which Vronsky, since he had to look at something, looked at Levin—at his feet, at his uniform, then at his face, and noticing the doleful eyes fixed on him, said, in order to say something:

'How is it that, as someone who lives permanently in the country, you aren't a magistrate? You are not wearing a magistrate's uniform.'

'Because I consider that the magistrate's court is an idiotic institution,' Levin answered gloomily, having been waiting all this time for an opportunity to enter into conversation with Vronsky, in order to smooth over his rudeness when they had exchanged greetings.

'I don't think that's true, quite the contrary,' Vronsky said, with calm surprise.

'It's inane,' Levin said, interrupting him. 'We don't need magistrates. I've not had one case in the last eight years. And the only time I did, the wrong decision was made. The nearest magistrate is about thirty miles from me. I have to send a lawyer who costs me fifteen roubles for a dispute over two roubles.'

And he related how a peasant had stolen flour from a miller, and when the miller accused him of it, the peasant had taken him to court for slander. All this was beside the point and stupid, and Levin was aware of it as he spoke.

'Ah, what a character!' said Stepan Arkadyich with his most emollient almond smile. 'But let's go; I think the voting has begun . . .'

And they separated.

'I can't understand it,' said Sergey Ivanovich, who had noticed his brother's clumsy antics, 'I just can't understand how it is possible to be so devoid of political tact. That's what we Russians don't have. The Provincial Marshal is our opponent, but you're on *ami cochon*[1] terms with him, and are asking him to stand. As for Count Vronsky . . . I'll never be friends with him; he's asked me to dinner, and I won't go; but he's on our side, so why on earth make an enemy of him? Then asking Nevedovsky if he's going to stand. It's just not done.'

'Oh, I don't understand anything! And it's all so trivial anyway,' Levin answered gloomily.

'You say it's all so trivial, but as soon as you wade in, you muddle everything up.'

Levin fell silent, and they walked together into the big hall.

Despite sensing that a dirty trick was about to be played on him, and despite the fact that not everyone had asked him to stand, the Provincial Marshal had nevertheless made up his mind that he would stand. The hall fell silent and the secretary announced in a loud voice that Captain of the Guards Mikhail Stepanovich Snetkov was standing for election as Provincial Marshal.

The District Marshals carried the little dishes with the balls for voting from their tables to the Provincial Marshal's table, and the election began.

'Put it on the right,' Stepan Arkadyich whispered to Levin when he

---

[1] 'very thick with him'.

and his brother came up to the table behind the Marshal. But Levin had by now forgotten the strategy that had been explained to him, and was wondering whether Stepan Arkadyich had made a mistake when he said 'on the right'. Snetkov was the opponent, after all. As he went up to the box, he was holding the ball in his right hand but, thinking he was mistaken, when he was standing in front of the box itself he transferred the ball into his left hand, and obviously then put the ball on the left. The pundit standing by the box, who could tell from the mere movement of an elbow who was placing his ball where, frowned disapprovingly. There was no need for him to exercise any of his acumen.

Silence descended, and the counting of balls could be heard. Then a solitary voice proclaimed the numbers of votes for and against.

The Marshal had received a considerable majority of votes. There was a great commotion as everyone rushed towards the door. Snetkov came in, and the nobles thronged round him, offering their congratulations.

'So is it over now?' Levin asked Sergey Ivanovich.

'It's only just beginning,' Sviyazhsky said, replying for Sergey Ivanovich with a smile. 'Another candidate for Marshal may receive more votes.'

Levin had quite forgotten about that. He only now remembered there was some kind of subtlety that came into play at this point, but he was too bored to remember exactly what it consisted of. He felt utterly despondent, and yearned to escape the crowd.

Since no one was paying him any attention, and he did not seem to be needed by anyone, he surreptitiously made his way to the small hall, where people were having refreshments, and felt a great sense of relief when he saw the waiters again. The old waiter invited him to have something to eat, and Levin assented. After eating a cutlet and beans and talking to the waiter about his former masters, and reluctant to go back into the hall where he felt so ill at ease, Levin set off to walk through the gallery.

The gallery was full of smartly dressed ladies leaning over the balustrade, anxious not to miss a single word of what was being said below. Sitting or standing near the ladies were elegant lawyers, bespectacled high-school teachers, and officers. Everyone was talking about the elections, about how overwrought the Marshal was, and how good the debates had been; in one group Levin heard his brother being praised. A lady was telling a lawyer:

'I am so glad I heard Koznyshev! He's worth going hungry for.

Marvellous stuff! So clear. And completely audible! You don't have anyone who speaks like that at court.

There is just Maidel, and he is not nearly so eloquent.'

After finding a free spot at the balustrade, Levin leant over and began watching and listening.

The noblemen were all sitting behind the low partitions that marked off their districts. In the middle of the hall stood a man in a uniform who proclaimed in a loud, piercing voice:

'Staff Cavalry Captain Evgeny Ivanovich Opukhtin is nominated to stand as candidate for Provincial Marshal of the Nobility!'

A deathly silence followed, then a feeble, senile voice was heard: 'Declines!'

'Court Councillor Pyotr Petrovich Bohl is nominated to stand,' the voice began again.

'Declines!' resounded a shrill young voice. The same thing started up again, and again was followed by 'declines'. And so it went on for about an hour. Levin watched and listened, leaning his elbows on the balustrade. At first he was surprised and wanted to understand what this meant; then once he was sure he could not understand it, he started to become bored. Then, when he recalled the tension and animosity he had seen on everybody's faces, he felt sad; he made up his mind to leave, and set off to go back downstairs. As he walked through the lobby leading to the galleries he ran into a dejected schoolboy with bloodshot eyes, who was pacing up and down. And then on the stairs he ran into a couple: a lady running swiftly on high heels and the leisurely Deputy Public Prosecutor.

'I did tell you that you wouldn't be late,' said the Prosecutor as Levin stood aside to let the lady pass.

Levin was already on the stairs leading to the exit and getting the tag for his fur coat out of his waistcoat pocket when the Secretary buttonholed him. 'If you please, Konstantin Dmitrich, they are voting.'

The candidate up for election was Nevedovsky, who had so emphatically declined to stand.

Levin went up to the door of the hall; it was locked. The Secretary knocked, the door opened, and Levin was confronted by two red-faced landowners darting out.

'Can't stand any more,' said one red-faced landowner.

After the landowner, the Provincial Marshal poked his head round the door. The exhaustion and fear on his face were terrible to behold.

'I told you not to let anyone out!' he cried to the doorman.

'I was letting someone in, Your Excellency!'

'Oh, good gracious!' said the Provincial Marshal with a heavy sigh, and with his head bowed, he shuffled wearily in his white trousers over to the large table in the middle of the hall.

People transferred their votes to Nevedovsky, as had been calculated, and he became Provincial Marshal. Many were jubilant, many were pleased and happy, many were euphoric, and many were displeased and unhappy. The Provincial Marshal was plunged into a despair he could not hide. When Nevedovsky left the hall, the crowd thronged round him and followed after him enthusiastically, as it had followed the Governor when he had inaugurated the elections, and as it had followed Snetkov when he was elected.

31

THE newly elected Provincial Marshal and many of the victorious new party dined that day with Vronsky.

Vronsky had come to the elections partly because he was bored in the country and wanted to assert his right to freedom before Anna, partly to repay Sviyazhsky by supporting him at the elections after all the trouble he had gone to on Vronsky's behalf at the zemstvo elections, and above all to perform to the letter all the duties of the position of nobleman and landowner he had marked out for himself. But he had certainly not expected that he would be quite so absorbed and enthralled by the business of the elections, and that he would be so good at this kind of thing. He was a completely new face amongst the local nobility, but he had clearly scored a success, and he was not mistaken in thinking that he had already acquired influence amongst the nobles. This influence was boosted by his wealth and social position, the splendid residence in town lent to him by his old acquaintance Shirkov, a financier who had established a flourishing bank in Kashin; the excellent chef Vronsky had brought from the country; his friendship with the Governor, who was an old army comrade, and a comrade under Vronsky's protection to boot; and above all, his straightforward, level-headed manner with everyone, which had very quickly induced most of the nobility to change their opinion of his supposed arrogance. He himself felt that, with the exception of the demented gentleman married to Kitty Shcherbatskaya, who had with ridiculous bile subjected him to a stream of arrant nonsense *à propos de bottes*,[1] every nobleman with whom he had

---

[1] 'quite irrelevantly'.

become acquainted was now his ally. He could see clearly, and others acknowledged this, that he had done a great deal to secure Nevedovsky's success. And now at his own table, celebrating Nevedovsky's election, he was experiencing a pleasant sense of triumph on behalf of his candidate. The elections themselves exerted such an allure that he was thinking about standing himself if he could be married within the next three years, rather in the same way that he wanted to race himself whenever one of his jockeys won a prize.

They were now celebrating the success of his jockey. Vronsky sat at the head of the table, with the young Governor, a general of the Imperial Retinue, on his right. To everyone else he was the head of the province, who had solemnly inaugurated the elections, given a speech, and aroused both respect and obsequiousness in some people, as Vronsky observed; to Vronsky, however, he was still the same old Katka Maslov—as he had been nicknamed at the Corps of Pages— who felt inhibited in his presence, and whom he tried to *mettre à son aise.*[1] On his left sat Nevedovsky with his youthful, intransigent, and malevolent face. Vronsky was straightforward and respectful with him.

Sviyazhsky bore his defeat cheerfully. As he said himself, turning with glass in hand to Nevedovsky, it was not even a defeat for him: they could not have found a better representative of the new direction for the nobility to follow. And so everything honest, as he put it, was on the side of the day's success and was celebrating it.

Stepan Arkadyich was also glad that he was having a jolly time, and that everyone was happy. During the course of a superb dinner they went over episodes from the elections. Sviyazhsky gave a comic account of the Marshal's tearful speech, and remarked, addressing Nevedovsky, that His Excellency would have to choose another, more complicated method of auditing the accounts than tears. Another quick-witted noble recounted how footmen in stockings had been engaged for the provincial Marshal's ball, who would now have to be sent back unless the new Marshal decided to give a ball with footmen in stockings.

During dinner they continually addressed Nevedovsky as: 'our Provincial Marshal' and 'Your Excellency'.

These titles were spoken with the same pleasure with which a bride is called 'Madame', and by her husband's name. Nevedovsky pretended to be not only indifferent but contemptuous of this title, but it was

---

[1] 'put at ease'.

obvious that he was thrilled and keeping himself on a tight rein so as not to express his delight, which would not have suited the new liberal milieu in which they all found themselves.

During dinner several telegrams were sent to people interested in the progress of the election. And Stepan Arkadyich, who was in very high spirits, sent Darya Alexandrovna a telegram with the following words: 'Nevedovsky elected majority of twelve. Congratulations. Pass on.' He dictated it aloud, saying: 'Got to cheer them up.' Darya Alexandrovna, however, merely sighed over the rouble spent on the telegram when she received it, and realized that it must have been sent at the end of a dinner. She knew that Stiva had a weakness for *faire jouer le télégraphe*[1] at the end of good dinners.

Along with the excellent dinner and the wines, which did not come from Russian wine merchants but directly from foreign vintners, everything was very dignified, simple, and jolly. The party of twenty had been hand-picked by Sviyazhsky from like-minded new liberal activists who were also possessed of wit and respectability. They drank toasts, also half in jest, to the new Provincial Marshal, to the Governor, to the director of the bank, and to 'our amiable host'.

Vronsky was pleased. He had never expected to find such good taste in the provinces.

At the end of the dinner things became even merrier. The Governor asked Vronsky to go to a concert in aid of the *brethren** which was being organized by his wife, who was keen to meet him.

'There'll be a ball and you'll see our local beauty. It really will be wonderful.'

'*Not in my line*,'[2] replied Vronsky, who was fond of that English expression, but he smiled and promised to come.

Just before they got up from the table, when they had all started smoking, Vronsky's valet came up to him with a letter on a tray.

'From Vozdvizhenskoye by special messenger,' he said with a significant expression.

'It's extraordinary how much he resembles our Deputy Prosecutor Sventitsky,' said one of the guests in French about the valet, while Vronsky read the letter with a frown.

The letter was from Anna. Even before he had read the letter, he already knew what its contents were. Expecting the elections to be over in five days, he had promised to be back on Friday. Today was Saturday, and he knew that the letter contained reproaches that he had

---

[1] set the telegraph going.   [2] [English in the original.]

not returned on time. The letter he had sent the previous evening had probably not arrived yet.

The contents of the letter were what he expected, but the form of it was unexpected, and particularly disagreeable to him. 'Annie is very ill, the doctor says it might be pneumonia. I am tearing my hair out on my own. Princess Varvara is a hindrance rather than a help. I expected you the day before yesterday, and then yesterday, and now am sending to find out where you are and what you are doing. I was planning to come myself, but changed my mind, knowing you would not like that. Send some answer, that I may know what to do.'

The child was ill, but she thought of coming herself. Their daughter was ill, and this hostile tone.

Vronsky was struck by the contrast between the innocent fun of the elections and this depressing, burdensome love to which he had to return. But he had to go, and he took the first train home that night.

32

BEFORE Vronsky's departure for the elections, having thought about the fact that the scenes that always took place between them every time he left home could only estrange him rather than draw him closer to her, Anna resolved to make every effort to bear the separation from him with equanimity. But she was hurt by that cold, severe look he had fixed her with when he came to tell her he was leaving, and her equanimity had disintegrated even before he had left.

When she later reflected in solitude on that look, which had expressed his right to freedom, she came, as always, to one thing—consciousness of her humiliation. 'He has the right to go away when and where he wants. Not just to go away, but to leave me. He has all the rights, and I have none. Knowing that, he shouldn't have done it. But what has he done? . . . He looked at me with a cold, stern expression. Of course it is indefinable, intangible, but it wasn't there before, and that look is very significant,' she thought. 'That look shows he is beginning to cool.'

And although she was convinced he was beginning to cool, there was nevertheless nothing she could do, as she could not in any way change her relationship with him. Just as before, she could hold on to him only with love and physical attraction. And just as before, she could only suppress terrible thoughts about what would happen if he stopped loving her with activities during the day and morphine at night. It is true there was one other course of action, which would require her not holding on to him—and for that she wanted nothing except his love—but drawing closer to him, so as to be in such a position that he would not leave her. That course of action was divorce and marriage. And she began to wish for that, and made up her mind to agree to it the first time either he or Stiva broached the subject with her.

Absorbed in such thoughts, she spent five days without him—the five days he was supposed to be away.

Walks, conversations with Princess Varvara, visits to the hospital, and above all reading, one book after another, occupied her time. But on the sixth day, when the coachman returned without him, she no longer felt able to suppress thoughts about him and about what he was doing. It was just then that her daughter fell ill. Anna took on the job of nursing her, but that did not distract her either, especially as the illness was not serious. Try as she might, she could not love this little girl, and she could not pretend to love her either. Towards the evening of that day, when she was alone, Anna started to feel such panic about him that she decided to set off for town, but after thinking things over carefully, wrote the contradictory letter that Vronsky received, and sent it off by a special messenger without reading it through. The next morning she received his letter and repented her own. She dreaded a repetition of the severe look he gave her at his departure, especially when he discovered that the little girl was not dangerously ill. But she was still glad she had written to him. Anna now acknowledged to herself that he had tired of her, and would regret giving up his freedom in order to return to her, but in spite of that she was glad he was coming. Let him be tired of her, but at least he would be there with her, where she could see him and be aware of his every movement.

She was sitting under a lamp in the drawing room with a new volume of Taine,* and reading while she listened to the sound of the wind outside, expecting the carriage to arrive any minute. Several times she thought she heard the sound of its wheels, but she was mistaken; at last she heard not only the sound of wheels but the coachman shouting and a muffled sound in the covered porch. Even Princess Varvara, who was playing patience, confirmed this, and Anna stood up, blushing profusely, but instead of going downstairs, as she had done twice before, she stood still. She suddenly felt ashamed of her deception, but she was even more afraid of how he would receive her. The feeling of hurt had passed now; she was only afraid of the expression of his displeasure. She remembered that her daughter had been quite well for two days now. She was even annoyed with her for recovering just when the letter had been sent. Then she remembered him, that he was here, all of him, his eyes, and his hands. She heard his voice. And forgetting everything, she ran joyfully to meet him.

'Well, how is Annie?' he said timidly from below, looking up at Anna as she came running to meet him.

He was sitting on a chair, and the footman was pulling off his warm boot.

'All right, she is better.'

'And you?' he said, shaking himself.

She took his hand in both of hers, and drew it towards her waist, not taking her eyes off him.

'Well, I'm very glad,' he said, coldly surveying her, her hair, her dress, which he knew she had put on for him.

He found it all attractive, but he had found it attractive so many times before! And that severe, stony expression she had dreaded so much settled on his face.

'Well, I'm very glad. And are you well?' he said, wiping his damp beard with a handkerchief and kissing her hand.

'Never mind,' she thought, 'just as long as he is here, as once he's here he cannot, and dare not, stop loving me.'

The evening was spent happily and enjoyably in the company of Princess Varvara, who complained to him that Anna had taken morphine during his absence.

'What could I do? I couldn't sleep . . . My thoughts kept me awake. When he's here I never take it. Hardly ever.'

He told her about the elections, and Anna knew how to prod him with questions into talking about what he had most enjoyed—his own success. She told him about everything that interested him at home. And all her news was extremely cheerful.

But late in the evening, when they were on their own, and Anna saw that she had again regained complete possession of him, she wanted to erase the painful impression of the look he had given her because of the letter. She said:

'Tell me honestly, you were cross when you got my letter, and didn't believe me?'

As soon as she had said this, she realized that however loving he was being to her now, he had not forgiven her for that.

'Yes,' he said. 'It was such a strange letter. First Annie was ill, then you wanted to come yourself.'

'It was all true.'

'I don't doubt it.'

'But you do doubt it. I can see you are displeased.'

'Not at all. I'm only displeased, it is true, by the fact that you some-how seem unwilling to admit that there are duties . . .'

'The duties of going to a concert . . .'

'But let's not talk about it,' he said.

'Why not talk about it though?' she said.

'I only want to say that there might be business to attend to, that is unavoidable. Look, I will have to go to Moscow now to see about the house . . . Oh, Anna, why do you get so annoyed? Don't you know I can't live without you?'

'If that is so,' said Anna, her voice suddenly changing, 'it means that you are tired of this life . . . Yes, you will come here for a day and go away again, like men who . . .'

'Anna, that's cruel. I am ready to give up my whole life . . .'

But she did not hear him.

'If you go to Moscow, I will go too. I will not stay here. Either we must separate or live together.'

'Well, you know that's the single thing I desire. But in order for that . . .'

'We need a divorce? I will write to him. I see that I cannot go on like this . . . But I will go with you to Moscow.'

'It is as if you are threatening me. Why, there is nothing I wish more than never to be parted from you,' said Vronsky, smiling.

But it was not just the cold and angry look of a hounded and embit-tered man which flashed in his eyes as he spoke those tender words.

She saw that look and correctly divined its meaning.

'If that is so, then it's a misfortune!' that look told her. It was a fleet-ing impression, but she would never forget it.

Anna wrote to her husband to ask him for a divorce, and at the end of November, after saying goodbye to Princess Varvara, who had to go to Petersburg, she and Vronsky moved to Moscow. As they were daily expecting an answer from Alexey Alexandrovich, followed by a divorce, they now set up house together like a married couple.

PART SEVEN

I

THE Levins had been living in Moscow for over two months. The date had long since passed when Kitty ought to have given birth, according to the most reliable calculations of people expert in these matters; but she was still expecting, and there was no sign that the time was any nearer now than it had been two months earlier. The doctor, the midwife, Dolly, her mother, and particularly Levin, who could not think of what was looming without terror, began to feel impatient and worried; only Kitty felt perfectly calm and happy.

She was now acutely conscious of having conceived a new feeling of love for her future, already partially real, child, and she found pleasure in heeding this feeling. Her child was no longer completely a part of her, but sometimes lived its own life independently of her. Often this caused her pain, but at the same time this strange new joy also made her want to laugh.

Everyone she loved was with her, everyone was so kind to her and took such good care of her, everything was presented to her in so pleasant a light, that if she had not known and did not feel that it had to end soon, she could not have wished for a better and pleasanter life. The one thing that spoiled the charm of this life was the fact that her husband was not as she loved him to be and not as he was when they were in the country.

She liked his calm, affectionate, and hospitable manner in the country. In town, though, he seemed endlessly anxious and wary, as if he was afraid someone might offend him or, more importantly, her. Back in the country, where he clearly knew he was in the right place, he never hurried anywhere and was never at a loss for something to do. Here in town he was constantly in a hurry, as if afraid of missing something, and he had nothing to do. And she pitied him. She knew he did not seem pitiable to others; on the contrary, whenever Kitty looked at him during social engagements, as people sometimes do look at those they love, trying to see them as strangers in order to gauge the impression they make on others, she saw, with a jealousy that even alarmed her, that not only was he not pitiable, but that his sense of decorum, his slightly old-fashioned, diffident courtesy with women, his imposing figure, and, in her view, particularly expressive face made him very attractive. But she saw him from within rather than from the outside; she could see he was not authentic there; there was no other way she could define his current state. Sometimes she reproached him inwardly for not being capable of living in town; but at other times she recognized that it really was difficult for him to organize his life there in a way that satisfied him.

And indeed, what was there for him to do? He did not like playing cards. He did not go to a club. She already knew by now what keeping company with jovial gentlemen like Oblonsky entailed . . . it entailed drinking and going on somewhere else after drinking. She was horrified at the thought of where men went on such occasions. Attend society functions? But she knew that would require him to enjoy intimate contact with young women, and she could not wish for that. Stay at home with her, her mother, and her sisters? But however pleasant and amusing she found the same old conversations—'all those Alines and Nadines,' as the old Prince called these conversations between the sisters—she knew it had to be boring for him. What was there left for him to do? Go on writing his book? He had actually tried to do that, and at first regularly took himself off to the library to make notes and conduct the research for his book; but, as he said to her, the more time he spent doing nothing, the less time he had. He complained to her furthermore that he had talked too much about his book there, and that consequently all his ideas about it were muddled and had ceased to be interesting.

One advantage of this town life was that they never had any quarrels there. Whether it was because conditions in town were different, or because they had both become more careful and sensible in this respect, in Moscow they had none of the quarrels caused by jealousy that they had so dreaded when they moved to town.

In this respect there even took place one event which was of great importance to both of them, namely Kitty's meeting with Vronsky.

The old Princess Marya Borisovna, Kitty's godmother, who had always been very fond of her, had insisted on seeing her. Although Kitty had not been going out anywhere because of her condition, she went to see this venerable old lady with her father, and encountered Vronsky there.

The only thing for which Kitty could reproach herself during this meeting was that for a brief moment, when she recognized in civilian dress those features that had once been so familiar to her, she gasped, the blood rushed to her heart, and a vivid colour—she could feel it happening—suffused her face. But this lasted only a few seconds. Her father, who had deliberately started talking to Vronsky in a loud voice, had not even finished what he wanted to say when she was already quite prepared to look at Vronsky and to talk to him if necessary, in just the same way as she was talking to Princess Marya Borisovna, and, most importantly, in such a way that everything, right down to the last inton-ation and smile, would be approved by her husband, whose invisible presence she seemed to sense above her at that moment.

She said a few words to him, even smiled serenely at his joke about the elections, which he called 'our parliament'. (She had to smile in order to show that she understood the joke.) But she immediately turned away to Princess Marya Borisovna and did not glance at him once until he stood up to leave; she did look at him then, but obviously only because it was discourteous not to look at a man when he was bowing to you.

She was grateful to her father for not saying anything to her about the meeting with Vronsky; but after the visit, during their usual walk, she could tell he was pleased with her from his particular tenderness. She was pleased with herself too. She had certainly not expected she would find this reserve of strength to repress somewhere deep in her soul all the memories of her former feelings for Vronsky, and not only appear to be, but actually be completely detached and calm with him.

Levin blushed much more profusely than she had done when she told him she had encountered Vronsky at Princess Marya Borisovna's. It was very difficult for her to tell him this, but it was even more dif-ficult to give him further details of the meeting, since he did not ques-tion her but simply looked at her with a frown on his face.

'I'm very sorry you weren't there,' she said. 'Not that you weren't in the room . . . I wouldn't have been so natural in front of you . . . I am blushing much more now—much, much more,' she said, blushing to the point of tears. 'I'm just sorry you couldn't have looked through a crack.'

The truthful eyes told Levin that she was pleased with herself, and although she was blushing, he immediately calmed down and began asking her questions, which was all she wanted. When he had found out everything, right down to the fact that it was only during the first moment that she could not prevent herself from blushing, but that afterwards she had found it as straightforward and easy as if she was meeting someone for the first time, Levin cheered up completely and said he was glad this had happened, and that he would not now behave as stupidly as he had at the elections, and would try to be as friendly as possible the next time he met Vronsky.

'It's so agonizing to think there's a person out there, almost an enemy, whom it is difficult to meet,' said Levin. 'I'm very, very glad.'

2

'So please call on the Bohls,' Kitty said to her husband when he came in to see her at eleven o'clock before going out. 'I know you are dining at the club, Papa has signed you in. But what are you doing this morning?'

'I am just going to see Katavasov,' answered Levin.

'Why so early?'

'He promised to introduce me to Metrov. I wanted to talk to him about my work, as he's a famous Petersburg scholar,' said Levin.

'Oh yes, it was his article you were speaking of so highly, wasn't it? Well, and after that?' said Kitty.

'I may also call in at the court about my sister's business.'

'What about the concert?' she asked.

'I'm hardly likely to go on my own!'

'No, you should go; they're playing those new things . . . You used to be so interested in all that. I would definitely go.'

'Well, I will come home before dinner anyway,' he said, looking at his watch.

'But put on your frock-coat, so that you can go straight to call on Countess Bohl.'

'But is it absolutely necessary?'

'Yes, it absolutely is! He has been to call on us. How hard can it be? You drop by, sit down, talk for five minutes about the weather, get up and leave.'

'Well, you won't believe it, I've got so out of the habit of all that I'm actually quite embarrassed about it. How does it go? A stranger turns up, sits down, carries on sitting there without doing anything, is a nuisance to his hosts, upsets himself, and leaves.'

Kitty laughed:

'But surely you used to pay calls when you were a bachelor?' she said.

'I did, but I always used to feel embarrassed, and now I'm so out of the habit that I swear I'd rather go without dinner for two days than pay this call. It's so embarrassing! I keep thinking they will take offence and say: why have you come to visit for no good reason?'

'No, they won't take offence. I can assure you of that,' said Kitty, laughing as she looked into his face. She took his hand. 'Well, bye-bye . . . Please do make that call.'

He was on the point of leaving after kissing his wife's hand when she stopped him.

'Kostya, you know, I've only got fifty roubles left.'

'Well, I'll stop off at the bank and make a withdrawal. How much?' he said, with a disgruntled expression she was familiar with.

'No, wait.' She took hold of his arm. 'Let's talk, because I'm worried about this. I don't seem to be buying anything unnecessary, but the money still seems to disappear. There is something we are not doing right.'

'Not at all,' he said, coughing and looking at her with a scowl.

She knew that cough well. It was a sign that he was extremely displeased, not with her, but with himself. He really was displeased, not because a lot of money had been spent, but because he was reminded of something he wanted to forget which he knew was amiss.

'I told Sokolov to sell the wheat and get an advance on the mill. There will be money, in any case.'

'Yes, but I'm afraid that there are generally rather a lot . . .'

'Not at all, not at all,' he repeated. 'Well, bye-bye, darling.'

'No, really, I sometimes regret that I listened to Mama. How nice it would have been in the country! Instead I've been wearing you all out, and we're spending money . . .'

'Not at all, not at all. There hasn't been one time since I've been married when I would have said that things could have been better than they are. . . .'

'Truly?' she said, looking into his eyes.

He said it without thinking, simply to console her. But when he glanced at her and saw those truthful, sweet eyes fastened enquiringly on him, he said it again with his whole heart. 'I've definitely been neglecting her,' he thought. And he remembered what so soon awaited them.

'Do you think it will be soon? How do you feel?' he whispered, taking hold of both her hands.

'I have thought about it so often that I don't think or know anything now.'

'And you're not afraid?'

She let out a contemptuous laugh.

'Not in the slightest,' she said.

'Well, if anything happens, I will be at Katavasov's.'

'No, nothing will happen, and don't think about it. I am going to drive up to the boulevard for a walk with Papa. We'll drop in on Dolly. I will expect you before dinner. Oh, yes! You know that Dolly's position is becoming completely impossible? She's up to her ears in debt, and she doesn't have any money. I was talking yesterday to Mama and Arseny' (as she called her sister Natalya Lvova's husband), 'and we decided to set you and him on Stiva. It's quite impossible. We can't talk to Papa about it. . . . But if you and he . . .'

'But what can we do?' said Levin.

'You'll be at Arseny's anyway, so have a word with him; he will tell you what we decided.'

'Well, I'll agree to anything with Arseny in advance. I'll call round and see him. By the way, if I do go to the concert, I'll go with Natalya. Well, goodbye.'

In the porch Levin was stopped by Kuzma, the old servant from his bachelor days who ran the household in town.

'Beauty' (this was the left shaft-horse brought up from the country) 'has been re-shod, but he's still lame,' he said. 'What would you like done?'

When they first arrived in Moscow, the horses brought from the country took up Levin's time. He had wanted to organize that side of things in the best and cheapest way possible; but it turned out to cost more using their horses than hired ones, and they ended up using cabs anyway.

'Send for the vet, maybe there is a bruise.'

'But what about for Katerina Alexandrovna?' asked Kuzma.

Levin was now no longer shocked, as he had been when he was first in Moscow, that getting from Vozdvizhenka to Sivtsev Vrazhek necessitated harnessing a pair of sturdy horses to a heavy carriage, driving this carriage half a mile through the snow and slush, and keeping it there four hours, having paid five roubles for the privilege. This already seemed natural to him now.

'Get a cabby to bring over a pair of horses for our carriage,' he said. 'Yes, sir.'

And having so simply and easily resolved a problem which would have demanded so much personal effort and attention in the country, thanks to the conditions in town, Levin went out on to the porch, hailed a cab, got in, and drove to Nikitskaya Street. On his way over he was no longer thinking about money but mulling over what it would be like meeting the Petersburg scholar who studied sociology, and what he would say to him about his book.

It had only been during those first few days in Moscow that Levin had been shocked by those pointless but inevitable expenses, strange to a country-dweller, that assailed him from all directions. But he was already used to them now. What happened to him in this respect was what they say happens to drunkards: the first glass sticks in the throat, the second swoops down like a falcon, while the third goes down like tiny birds.* When Levin changed his first hundred-rouble note to pay for liveries for the footman and the doorman, he could not help thinking that these liveries, which were of no use to anyone but vitally necessary, to judge from the Princess's and Kitty's surprise at the mere suggestion that it would be possible to dispense with them—these liveries would cost as much as two summer labourers, that is, about three hundred days' work from Easter to Michaelmas, and hard grind every day from early morning to late in the evening, so that hundred-rouble note definitely did stick in the throat. But the next note, changed to buy provisions for a family dinner costing twenty-eight roubles, even though it provoked Levin to remember that twenty-eight roubles was nine measures of oats which men, sweating and groaning, had reaped, bound, threshed, winnowed, sifted, and bagged—this next note was nevertheless spent more easily. The notes he changed now, however, had long since ceased to provoke such reflections and flew away like tiny birds. Whether the labour expended in the acquisition of the money corresponded to the pleasure afforded by what was purchased with it was a consideration that had long ago been dispensed with. His economic calculation that there was a certain price below which one could not sell a certain amount of grain was also forgotten. The rye, whose price he had maintained for so long, was sold for fifty kopecks a measure less than it had fetched a month earlier. Even the calculation that their current expenses would make it impossible for them to live for a whole year without getting in debt no longer had any meaning. Only one thing was obligatory: to have money in the bank without asking where it came from, so one could always know there would be enough to buy the next day's beef. And until now he had been able to abide by that calculation; he always had money in the bank. But now the money in the bank had run out, and he was not at all sure where he might get more. And it was this that had upset him momentarily when Kitty had reminded him about the money; but he did not have time to think about this. As he was driving along he was ruminating about Katavasov and his forthcoming meeting with Metrov.

3

DURING this stay Levin had once again become close to his old
university friend Professor Katavasov, whom he had not seen since
getting married. What he liked about Katavasov was the clarity and
simplicity of his outlook on life. Levin thought that the clarity of
Katavasov's outlook on life was due to his arid nature, while Katavasov
thought that the incoherence of Levin's thought was due to his having
insufficient mental discipline; but Levin found Katavasov's clarity
appealing, Katavasov found Levin's profusion of undisciplined ideas
appealing, and they enjoyed meeting up and having arguments.

Katavasov had liked the extracts that Levin had read out to him
from his book. When he had met Levin at a public lecture the day
before, Katavasov told him that the celebrated Metrov, whose article
Levin had liked so much, was not only in Moscow and very interested
in what Katavasov had told him about Levin's work, but was coming
to see him tomorrow at eleven and would be very pleased to meet him.

'You've definitely turned over a new leaf, old fellow, it's good to see,'
said Katavasov, greeting Levin in the small drawing room. 'I heard the
bell and thought: he can't possibly be on time . . . Well, what do you
think about the Montenegrins?* They're born warriors.'

'What's happened?' asked Levin.

Katavasov gave him a summary of the latest news and, after they
had gone into his study, introduced Levin to a short, stocky man with
a very pleasant appearance. This was Metrov. The conversation lingered briefly on politics and on how the latest events were viewed in the
upper echelons of Petersburg. Metrov relayed the opinion supposedly
voiced on this matter by the Tsar and one of the ministers, which he
had heard from a reliable source. Katavasov, however, had also heard
from a reliable source that the Tsar had said something completely different. Levin tried to conjure up a situation in which both opinions
might have been expressed, and the subject was dropped.

'He has gone and written almost a whole book about the labourer's
natural state in relation to the land,' said Katavasov. 'I'm not a specialist, but as a natural scientist I like the fact that he does not discuss
mankind as being outside zoological laws, but on the contrary, sees it
as being dependent on the environment, and is trying to identify laws
of development within that state of dependency.'

'That's very interesting,' said Metrov.

'I actually started writing a book about agriculture, but when
I focused on the main instrument in agriculture, the labourer,' said

Levin, going red, 'I could not help coming to completely unexpected conclusions.'

And Levin began tentatively to expound his ideas, as if feeling his way. He knew Metrov had written an article in which he had argued against generally accepted doctrines of political economy, but he did not know to what extent he could hope for a sympathetic response to his new views, nor could he guess from the scholar's intelligent, phlegmatic face.

'But where exactly do you see the particular characteristics of the Russian labourer?' said Metrov. 'In his, so to speak, zoological characteristics, or in the conditions of his environment?'

Levin saw that there was already a thought expressed in this question with which he did not agree; but he went on explaining his idea, which posited that the Russian labourer has a completely different attitude to the land than that of other nations. And in order to prove his point, he hastened to add that, in his opinion, this attitude proceeded from the Russian people's consciousness of having a mission to settle the vast, unpopulated territories in the East.

'One can easily be led into error by drawing a conclusion about a nation's general mission,' said Metrov, interrupting Levin. 'The state of a labourer will always depend on his relationship to land and capital.'

And without allowing Levin to finish articulating his idea, Metrov began setting out the distinguishing features of his own doctrine.

Levin did not understand what the distinguishing features of his doctrine were, because he did not make any effort to understand them: he saw that Metrov, despite having refuted in his article what the economists taught, nevertheless looked at the position of the Russian peasant exclusively from the point of view of capital, wages, and rent just as they did. Although he had to admit that rent was still non-existent in the eastern and largest region of Russia, that wages for nine-tenths of the eighty million who made up the Russian population barely covered their own basic subsistence, and that capital did not yet exist except in the form of the most primitive tools, he still could only examine the labourer from this point of view, despite disagreeing with the economists about a great deal, and having developed a new theory of his own about wages which he propounded to Levin.

Levin listened reluctantly and at first raised objections. He wanted to interrupt Metrov so that he could state his own idea, which in his opinion ought to make any further exposition superfluous. But when he later came to realize that they looked at the matter so differently that they would never understand one another, he stopped remonstrating and simply listened. Despite the fact that he was no longer at all interested in what Metrov was saying, he did nevertheless experience a certain pleasure in listening to him. His vanity was flattered that such a learned man should be so keen to explain his ideas to him with such care, and with such confidence in Levin's knowledge of the subject, sometimes referring to a whole aspect of the matter with a mere allusion. He put this down to his own merit, not knowing that Metrov was particularly keen to talk about this subject to every new person, having already discussed it with everyone in his circle, and indeed was generally keen to speak to everyone on the subject that absorbed him, but which was still not clear to him.

'However, we are late,' said Katavasov, looking at his watch as soon as Metrov had finished expounding his ideas.

'Yes, there's a meeting at the Society of Amateurs today in honour of Svintich's fiftieth anniversary,' said Katavasov in answer to Levin's question. 'Pyotr Ivanovich and I have arranged to go. I've promised to deliver a talk on his zoological writings. Come with us, it will be very interesting.'

'Yes, it really is time to go,' said Metrov. 'Come along with us, and from there, if you would care to, come back to my place. I would very much like to hear your work.'

'Oh, I'm not sure. It's not really finished, you know. But I would be very glad to go to the meeting.'

'By the way, old man, have you heard? I've submitted a separate proposal,' said Katavasov as he put on his tails in the next room.

And they embarked on a conversation about the University Question.* This University Question was a very important concern in Moscow that winter. Three old professors on the Council had not accepted the proposals of the younger faculty; the young professors had submitted a separate proposal. In the judgement of some, this proposal was terrible, while in the judgement of others it was a most straightforward and reasonable proposal, and the professors had split into two camps.

Some, including Katavasov, perceived duplicity, denunciation, and treachery in the opposing camp; others imputed immaturity and a lack of respect for authority. Although he did not belong to the university, Levin had already heard about and discussed this affair at length several times during his stay in Moscow, and had formed his own opinion about it; he took part in the conversation, which continued in the street until all three had walked to the old university buildings.

The meeting had already begun . . . There were six people sitting around the cloth-covered table at which Katavasov and Metrov sat down, and one of them was reading something aloud, his head bent over a manuscript. Levin sat down on one of the empty chairs arranged around the table, and in a whisper asked a student sitting there what was being read. Eying Levin with disapproval, the student said:

'The biography.'

Although Levin was not interested in the scholar's biography, he could not help listening and discovered some new and interesting things about the famous scholar's life.

When the speaker had finished, the chairman thanked him and proceeded to read some poems the poet Ment had sent him on the occasion of the anniversary, and a few words of thanks to the poet. Then Katavasov gave his address about the academic writings of the man being honoured, in his loud, shrill voice.

When Katavasov finished, Levin looked at his watch, saw that it was already past one and realized he would not manage to read his study to Metrov before the concert, but he no longer had any desire to do so in any case. During the reading he had also thought about their conversation. It was clear to him now that although Metrov's ideas perhaps had some significance, his own ideas also had significance; these ideas could only be elucidated and lead to something if each of them ploughed his own furrow, but nothing could come from a simple exchange of these ideas. And having made up his mind to decline Metrov's invitation, Levin went up to him at the end of the meeting. Metrov introduced Levin to the chairman, with whom he was discussing the political news. This involved Metrov relating to the chairman the very same thing he had earlier related to Levin, and Levin made the same remarks he had already made that morning, but for the sake of variety he also voiced a new opinion that had just entered his head. After that the conversation turned again to the University Question. Since Levin had already heard enough of that, he hastened to tell Metrov that he regretted not being able to accept his invitation, took his leave, and drove over to see Lvov.

4

Lvov, who was married to Kitty's sister Natalya, had spent all his life either in Moscow and Petersburg or abroad, where he had been educated and served as a diplomat.

The previous year he had left the diplomatic service, although not on account of any unpleasant business (he never had unpleasant business with anyone), and had transferred to a post in the palace administration in Moscow, in order to give his two boys the best possible education.

Despite their habits and views being diametrically opposed, and despite Lvov being older than Levin, they had become great friends that winter and grown fond of each other.

Lvov was at home, and Levin went in to him unannounced.

Dressed in a long, belted frock-coat and suede shoes, Lvov was sitting in an armchair, holding a half-smoked cigar carefully at arm's length in his elegant hand, and reading a book placed on a lectern through blue-tinted pince-nez.

His handsome, sensitive, and still youthful face, its air of fine breeding further enhanced by his glossy curls of silver hair, lit up with a smile when he saw Levin.

'Excellent! I was just about to send you a note. Well, how's Kitty? Come and sit here, you'll find it more relaxing . . .' He rose and pulled up a rocking-chair. 'Have you read the latest circular in the *Journal de St Pétersbourg*?* I think it's splendid,' he said with a slight French accent.

Levin told him what he had heard from Katavasov about what was being said in Petersburg and, after discussing politics for a while, told him about making Metrov's acquaintance and going to the meeting. This was of great interest to Lvov.

'I do envy you having entrées into this interesting academic world,' he said. And as usual, once he had begun talking he promptly switched to French, with which he was more comfortable. 'It's true that I don't have the time for it though. My job and looking after the children put an end to that; and I'm also not ashamed to say that my education is too deficient.'

'I don't believe that,' said Levin with a smile, touched, as always, by his low opinion of himself, which was not in any way born of a desire to seem or even be modest, but was completely sincere.

'Oh no, it is! I am aware now how poorly educated I am. There is a lot I have to brush up on and learn from scratch, even for my children's education. Because it's not enough to have teachers, you need a supervisor, just as you need labourers and an overseer on your estate. Look at what I'm reading'—he indicated Buslayev's grammar* on the lectern—'Misha is expected to know it, and it's so difficult. . . . Now you explain to me. He says here . . .'

Levin wanted to explain to him that it was impossible to understand, and just needed to be learnt by heart; but Lvov did not agree with him.

'So you're just poking fun at it!'

'On the contrary, you can't imagine how I am always learning what lies ahead for me by looking at you—that is, bringing up children.'

'Well, there's nothing much to learn,' said Lvov.

'I only know', said Levin, 'that I have never seen better brought-up children than yours, and couldn't wish for better children than yours.'

Lvov clearly wished to refrain from expressing how pleased he was, but he still beamed a radiant smile.

'Just as long as they turn out better than I have. That's all I ask for. You don't know yet how much work there is', he began, 'with boys like mine who have been neglected because of this life abroad.'

'You'll catch up on all of that. They're such clever children. The main thing is moral education. That's what I learn when I look at your children.'

'You say moral education. You can't imagine how difficult it is! You've barely managed to conquer one tendency when others spring up, and you have another battle on your hands. If we didn't have our mainstay in religion—you remember we talked about that—no father could bring children up on his own without help from that source.'

This conversation, which always interested Levin, was cut short by the appearance of the beautiful Natalya Alexandrovna, already dressed to go out.

'I didn't know you were here,' she said, clearly not only not regretting but actually glad to have interrupted this deeply familiar conversation she found boring. 'Well, how is Kitty? I am dining with you today. Now listen, Arseny,' she turned to her husband, 'you take the carriage . . .'

And husband and wife began to deliberate about how they would spend the day. Since the husband had to go and meet someone on official business, and the wife had to go to the concert and to a public meeting of the South-Eastern Committee,* there was much to decide and think through. As one of the family, Levin had to be part of these plans. It was decided that Levin would go with Natalya to the concert and the public meeting, and from there they would send the carriage to the office for Arseny, and he would call round for her and take her on to Kitty's; or if he had not finished his business, he would send the carriage, and Levin would go with her.

'He's been spoiling me,' Lvov said to his wife, 'by assuring me our children are wonderful, when I know how much bad there is in them.'

'Arseny goes to extremes, I always say,' said his wife. 'If you look for perfection, you will never be satisfied. And it's true what Papa says, that there was one extreme when we were being brought up—we were kept in the attic, while our parents lived on the first floor; now it's the opposite—the parents are in the box-room, and the children are on the first floor. Parents aren't supposed to have a life now, as everything is for the children.'

'Why not, if it is more pleasant?' Lvov said, smiling his handsome smile and touching her hand. 'Anyone who didn't know you would think you were a stepmother rather than a mother.'

'No, extremes are never a good thing,' Natalya said calmly, putting the paper-knife back in its proper place on the desk.

'Well, come here, you perfect children,' Lvov said to the two hand-some boys who came in, bowed to Levin, and went up to their father, obviously wanting to ask him something.

Levin wanted to talk to them and hear what they were going to say to their father, but Natalya began talking to him, and right at that moment Lvov's colleague Makhotin, dressed in court uniform, came into the room so they could go off together for a meeting with someone, and an endless conversation ensued about Herzegovina, Princess Korzinskaya, the city council, and Countess Apraksina's untimely death.

Levin completely forgot about the instructions he had been given. He only remembered when he was already going into the hall.

'Oh yes, Kitty instructed me to talk to you about Oblonsky,' he said, when Lvov stopped on the stairs while seeing him and his wife out.

'Yes, yes, *Maman* wants us, *les beaux-frères*,[1] to pounce on him,' he said, blushing and smiling. 'But why should I?'

'Well, I will pounce on him then,' said Natalya with a smile as she waited in her cloak of white arctic fox for the conversation to end. 'Well, let us go.'

5

Two very interesting things were performed at the matinée concert.

One was a fantasia, *King Lear on the Heath*, and the other was a quar-tet dedicated to Bach's memory.* Both were new and in the new style, and Levin wanted to form his own opinions about them. After escort-ing his sister-in-law to her seat, he went to stand next to a column and

---

[1] 'brothers-in-law'.

resolved to listen as attentively and conscientiously as possible. He tried not to be distracted and spoil his impressions by looking at the white-tied conductor waving his arms, which was always an unpleasant distraction from the music, at the ladies in hats who had methodically tied ribbons over their ears for the concert, or at all those people who were either not engrossed in anything or engrossed in any number of things except the music. He tried to avoid meeting music experts and chatterboxes, but stood there looking down straight ahead of him and listening.

But the more he listened to the *King Lear* fantasia, the further he felt from the possibility of forming any kind of definite opinion about it. The musical expression of a feeling kept endlessly beginning, as if ready to expand, but would then immediately disintegrate into snatches of new beginnings of musical expressions, or sometimes merely into exceedingly complex sounds which had nothing in common except the whim of the composer. But even these fragments of musical expressions, although occasionally beautiful, were themselves unpleasant, because they were completely unexpected and unmotivated. Gaiety, sadness, despair, tenderness, and triumph alternated without any rationale, like the feelings of a madman. And these feelings then unexpectedly evaporated, also just like those of a madman.

Throughout the whole performance Levin felt like a deaf man watching people dance. He was in complete bewilderment when the piece finished, and felt considerable exhaustion from all that concentrated but unrewarded attention. Loud applause resounded on all sides. Everyone rose, started moving about and talking. Anxious to clarify his own bewilderment by comparing it with other people's impressions, Levin went off in search of experts, and was glad to see one of the well-known experts having a conversation with Pestsov, whom he knew.

'Wonderful!' Pestsov was saying in his deep bass. 'Hello, Konstantin Dmitrich. What was particularly imaginative and sculptural, so to speak, and rich in colour, was that point when you sense the arrival of Cordelia, the point where woman, *das ewig Weibliche*,[1] comes into conflict with fate. Don't you think?'

'But why is Cordelia involved in this?' Levin asked timidly, having completely forgotten that the fantasia represented King Lear on the heath.

'Cordelia comes in . . . here!' said Pestsov, his fingers stabbing at the glossy programme he was holding, which he handed to Levin.

---

[1] 'the Eternal Feminine'.

Only now did Levin remember the title of the fantasia, and hastened to read the Russian translation of the lines from Shakespeare printed on the back of the programme.

'You can't follow it without that,' said Pestsov addressing Levin, since the person he had been speaking to had gone, and there was no one else for him to talk to.

In the interval Levin and Pestsov fell into an argument about the merits and defects of the Wagnerian tendency in music. Levin argued that the mistake Wagner and all his followers made was in wanting music to cross over into the sphere of another art form,* and that poetry was equally mistaken when describing the features of a face, which is what painting ought to do, and as an example of this mistake he cited the sculptor* who had the idea of carving in marble the shadows of poetic images springing up around the figure of a poet on the pedestal. 'These sculptor's shadows are so far from being shadows that they are even clinging to steps,' said Levin. He liked this phrase, but he could not remember whether he had not actually used this exact phrase before, and to Pestsov too, and he felt embarrassed as soon as he said it.

Pestsov argued, on the other hand, that art was one, and that it could reach its greatest expression only when all its forms combined.

Levin was now unable to listen to the second work in the concert. Pestsov, who came to stand next to him, talked to him almost the whole time, censuring the piece for its excessive, cloying, false simplicity and comparing it with the simplicity of the Pre-Raphaelites in painting. On his way out Levin met many more acquaintances with whom he talked about politics, music, and mutual acquaintances; amongst them he met Count Bohl, whom he had completely forgotten to call on.

'Well, you should go over now,' said Natalya Lvova whom he told about this; 'Perhaps they won't receive you, and then you can come to the meeting to fetch me. I'll still be there.'

6

'PERHAPS they're not receiving?' said Levin as he entered the hall of Countess Bohl's house.

'They are receiving, please come in,' said the doorman, purposefully helping him off with his fur coat.

'What a nuisance,' thought Levin, taking off a glove with a sigh and smoothing his hat. 'Why have I come? What am I going to say to them?'

As he passed through the first drawing room, Levin encountered

Countess Bohl in the doorway, a preoccupied and stern expression discernible on her face as she instructed a servant to do something. When she saw Levin, she smiled and invited him into the next small drawing room, from which came the sound of voices. Seated in this drawing room in armchairs were the Countess's two daughters and a Moscow colonel of Levin's acquaintance. Levin went up to greet them and sat down next to the sofa, holding his hat on his knee.

'How is your wife? Were you at the concert? We couldn't go. Mama had to go to a requiem service.'

'Yes, I heard . . . What an untimely death,' said Levin.

The Countess came in, sat down on the sofa, and also asked about his wife and about the concert.

Levin replied and repeated his remark about Countess Apraksina's untimely death.

'Her health was always delicate, however.'

'Were you at the opera yesterday?'

'Yes, I was.'

'Lucca was very good.'*

'Yes, very good,' he said, and began repeating what he had heard hundreds of times about the particularities of the singer's talent, since he did not care in the slightest what they thought about him. Countess Bohl pretended to listen. And then when he had said enough and fell silent, the colonel, who had been silent until then, began to speak. The colonel also talked about the opera, and about the lighting. Finally, after talking about the *folle journeé*[1] that Tyurin was planning, the colonel started laughing and making a great commotion, then he got up and left. Levin also got up, but he noted from the Countess's face that it was not yet time for him to go. About two more minutes were required. He sat down.

But since he kept thinking how stupid this was, he could not find a subject for conversation and remained silent.

'Are you not going to the public meeting? They say it will be very interesting,' began the Countess.

'No, but I promised my *belle-soeur*[2] I would stop by to pick her up,' said Levin.

A silence ensued. Mother and daughter exchanged glances again.

'Well, now it seems it's time to go,' thought Levin, and he got up. The ladies shook hands with him and asked him to pass on *mille choses*[3] to his wife.

---

[1] 'mad day'. [2] 'sister-in-law'. [3] 'cordial regards'.

'Where are you staying, sir?' the doorman asked him as he held out his fur coat, and immediately noted it down in a large, handsomely bound book.

'It's all the same to me, of course, but it's still embarrassing and terribly stupid,' thought Levin, consoling himself with the fact that everyone did it, before driving off to the public meeting, where he had to find his sister-in-law so they could travel home together.

There was a large number of people and almost all of society in attendance at the Committee's public meeting. Levin was in time for the report which, as everyone had said, was very interesting. When the reading of the report came to an end, the society people started mingling and Levin ran into Sviyazhsky, who urged him to go at all costs that evening to the Agricultural Society, where an eminent lecture was to be given; he also ran into Stepan Arkadyich, who had just come from the races, and many other acquaintances, and Levin proffered and listened to still more opinions about the meeting, the new musical work, and a court case. But no doubt as a result of the mental fatigue he was beginning to feel, he made a mistake when he was talking about the court case, and he later recalled that mistake several times with annoyance. While talking about the impending punishment of a foreigner being tried in Russia,* and about how wrong it would be to punish him by expelling him abroad, Levin repeated what he had heard from an acquaintance during a conversation the day before.

'I think that sending him abroad would be like punishing a pike by dropping it into the water,' said Levin. It was only later that he remembered that this idea, which he seemed to be passing off as his own but had heard from an acquaintance, was from a Krylov fable,* and that his acquaintance had repeated this phrase from a newspaper article.

After calling in at home with his sister-in-law and finding Kitty in good cheer and feeling well, Levin drove to the club.

7

LEVIN arrived at the club at its busiest time. Guests and members were driving up alongside him. Levin had not been to the club for a very long time, not since he had been living in Moscow after leaving university and was going into society. He remembered the club and the external details of its layout, but he had completely forgotten the sensations he used to experience in the club back in the old days. But as soon as he stepped into the porch after driving into the spacious semicircular courtyard and getting out of the cab, and a porter in a shoulder-belt had noiselessly opened the door for him and bowed; as soon as he caught sight in the porter's lodge of the galoshes and fur coats of members who realized it would be less trouble to remove their galoshes downstairs rather than go upstairs in them; as soon as he heard the mysterious bell which preceded him and, as he went up the shallow carpeted steps, saw on the landing the statue and the familiar, aged, third porter in club livery in the doorway upstairs, promptly but unhurriedly opening the door and inspecting the new guest, Levin was imbued with the sensations he used to experience at the club in the old days—of relaxation, contentment, and decorum.

'Your hat, please,' the porter said to Levin, who had forgotten the club rule about leaving hats in the porter's lodge. 'You haven't been here in a long while. The Prince signed you in yesterday. Prince Stepan Arkadyich is not here yet.'

The porter not only knew Levin, but also all his acquaintances and relations, and immediately mentioned people close to him.

After going through the first connecting room with screens and an area partitioned off to the right where fruit was served, Levin overtook an old man slowly shuffling along and entered the crowded, noisy dining room.

He walked along the tables, already nearly fully occupied, perusing the guests. Wherever he looked, he encountered the most diverse array of people, old and young, slight acquaintances and good friends. There was not one angry or anxious face. They all seemed to have left their troubles and cares behind in the porter's lodge along with their hats, and were intending to take their time in enjoying life's material comforts. Sviyazhsky was there, and so was Shcherbatsky, Nevedovsky, the old Prince, Vronsky, and Sergey Ivanovich.

'Ah! Why are you late?' said the Prince with a smile as he proffered him a hand over his shoulder. 'How's Kitty?' he added while he straightened his napkin, which he had tucked in behind a button on his waistcoat.

'She's fine; the three of them are having dinner at home.'

'Ah, it's the Alines and Nadines. Well, we don't have any room. But go off to that table and get a place quick,' said the Prince, and he turned away and carefully received a plate of fish soup made with burbot.

'Levin, over here!' shouted a warm-hearted voice a little further off. It was Turovtsyn. He was sitting with a young officer, and next to them were two upturned chairs. Levin went over to them happily. He had always retained a soft spot for the good-natured sybarite Turovtsyn— he was associated with the memory of proposing to Kitty—but he was particularly glad to see Turovtsyn's good-natured face that evening, after the strain of all those clever conversations.

'These are for you and Oblonsky. He'll be here any minute.'

The officer holding himself ramrod-straight, with a constant merry twinkle in his eyes, was Gagin from Petersburg. Turovtsyn introduced them.

'Oblonsky's always late.'

'Ah, here he is.'

'Have you just arrived?' said Oblonsky as he walked briskly over to them. 'Greetings. Have you had a vodka? Well, let's go then.'

Levin got up and went off with him to a big table laid out with different kinds of vodkas and the widest possible selection of appetizers. It ought to have been possible to choose something to one's taste amongst the two-dozen appetizers on offer, but Stepan Arkadyich demanded something special, and one of the liveried waiters in attendance brought it immediately. They each downed a glass and returned to their table.

Gagin was straight away served champagne while they were still having their fish soup, and he ordered four glasses to be poured. Levin did not refuse the glass he was offered and ordered another bottle. He was ravenous, so ate and drank with great relish, and he took part in his companions' lively and down-to-earth conversations with even greater relish. Gagin lowered his voice to tell a new Petersburg joke, and although it was rude and stupid, the joke was so funny that Levin burst out laughing so loudly that the people nearby turned round to look at him.

'It's like the "That's just what I can't bear!" joke. Do you know it?' asked Stepan Arkadyich. 'Oh, it's delightful! Bring us another bottle,' he said to the waiter and started telling the joke.

'With Pyotr Ilyich Vinovsky's compliments,' interrupted a small, elderly waiter carrying two delicate glasses of still-effervescent champagne and addressing Stepan Arkadyich and Levin. Stepan Arkadyich took a glass, and after making eye-contact with a balding red-haired man with a moustache at the other end of the table, nodded to him with a smile.

'Who is that?' asked Levin.

'You met him once at my place, remember? Nice fellow.'

Levin did the same as Stepan Arkadyich and took the other glass.

Stepan Arkadyich's joke was also very amusing. And Levin told a joke which also went down well. Then they started talking about horses, about the races that day, and about the dashing way in which Vronsky's Satin had won first prize. Levin did not notice what the dinner was like.

'Ah, here they are!' said Stepan Arkadyich after they had finished dinner, leaning over the back of his chair and stretching out his hand to Vronsky, who was coming towards him with a tall colonel from the Guards. Vronsky's face also radiated the club's general jovial good humour. He rested his elbow jauntily on Stepan Arkadyich's shoulder, whispered something to him, and held out his hand to Levin with the same good-humoured smile.

'Very good to see you,' he said. 'You know, I was looking for you back at the elections, but I was told you had already left.'

'Yes, I left the same day. We've just been talking about your horse. Congratulations,' said Levin. 'That was a very fast ride.'

'But you have horses too, I believe.'

'No, it was my father who did; but I still remember and know about them.'

'Where have you been sitting?' asked Stepan Arkadyich.

'We were at the second table, behind the columns.'

'He has been receiving congratulations,' said the tall colonel. 'It's his second Imperial prize; if only I had the luck at cards he has with horses.'

'Well, no point wasting precious time. I'm off to the inferno,'* said the colonel, and he left the table.

'That's Yashvin,' Vronsky said in reply to Turovtsyn and perched on the now-empty chair beside them. After drinking the glass offered him, he ordered a bottle. Whether it was the influence of the club's atmosphere or the wine he had drunk, Levin got into conversation with Vronsky about the best breed of cattle, and was very glad he did not feel any hostility towards this man. He even mentioned to him in passing that he had heard from his wife that she had met him at Princess Marya Borisovna's.

'Ah, Princess Marya Borisovna, she's delightful!' said Stepan Arkadyich, and he told a joke about her which amused them all. Vronsky in particular burst out laughing in such a good-humoured way that Levin felt completely reconciled with him.

'Well, have we finished?' said Stepan Arkadyich, getting up with a smile. 'Let's go!'

8

AFTER getting up from the table, Levin set off with Gagin through the lofty rooms to the billiard room, feeling his arms were swinging with a particular regularity and lightness as he walked. As he was walking through the main lounge, he bumped into his father-in-law.

'Well? How do you like our temple of idleness?' said the Prince, taking his arm. 'Come on, let's take a stroll.'

'I was just wanting to go and have a look around actually. It's interesting.'

'Yes, it's interesting for you. But it's interesting for me in a different way than it is for you. You'll be looking at these old fellows now,' he said, indicating a hunched-up club member with a sagging lip coming towards them, who was barely able to move his feet in his soft boots, 'and thinking they've been *shlyupiks** from the day they were born.'

'*Shlyupiks?*'

'You see, you don't even know this name. It's a term we have in the club. You know, like in that game of rolling hard-boiled eggs, when an egg is rolled a lot and it becomes a *shlyupik*. It's the same with our members: you keep rolling up to the club year in, year out, and you become a *shlyupik*. Yes, you may well laugh, but we are always keeping an eye out for the day when we become *shlyupiks*. You know Prince Chechensky?' asked the Prince, and Levin saw from his face that he was going to tell a funny story.

'No, I don't.'

'You can't be serious! Everyone knows Prince Chechensky. Well, never mind. He's the one always playing billiards. Three years ago he wasn't a *shlyupik* yet and was keeping up appearances. He'd even call other people *shlyupiks*. Well, there was one day he turned up, and our porter . . . you know, Vasily? That fat one. He's a great one for the *bon mots*. And so Prince Chechensky asks him, "Well, Vasily, who's here then? Any *shlyupiks?*" And he says to him, "You're the third." Yes, my boy, that's how it is!'

Chatting and greeting the acquaintances they ran into, Levin and the Prince walked through all the rooms: the main one, where tables had already been set up and the usual partners were playing for small stakes; the lounge, where people were playing chess and Sergey Ivanovich was sitting talking to somebody; the billiard room, where in a recess by the sofa there was a lively game going on, accompanied by champagne, in which Gagin was taking part; and they also peeped into the inferno, where many people who had placed bets were crowding round one table at which Yashvin was already seated. Trying not to make any noise, they also went into the dark reading room, where under shaded lamps sat a young man with an angry face, who was picking up one journal after another, and a bald general, engrossed in his reading. They also went into what the Prince called the clever room. In this room three gentlemen were having a heated discussion about the latest political news.

'If you could come now please, Prince, we're ready,' said one of his partners, finding him there, and the Prince went off. Levin sat down for a while to listen, but when he remembered all the conversations that morning, he suddenly felt terribly bored. He got up hurriedly and went off to look for Oblonsky and Turovtsyn, who were good company.

Turovtsyn was sitting with a tankard of drink on a high sofa in the billiard room, and Stepan Arkadyich and Vronsky were talking about something by the door in the far corner of the room.

'It's not that she's bored, but this lack of certainty and resolution in her situation,' Levin heard, and was about to walk away hastily; but Stepan Arkadyich called him over.

'Levin!' said Stepan Arkadyich, and Levin noticed that while his eyes were not teary, they were moist, as was always the case when he had been drinking, or when he gave in to his feelings. Now it was both. 'Levin, don't go away,' he said, and clasped him tightly by the elbow, clearly not wanting to let him go for anything.

'This is my true, and maybe best friend,' he said to Vronsky. 'You have also become even more precious and dear to me. And I want and know you have to be friends and close to each other, because you're both good people.'

'Well, then, we just have to exchange kisses,' Vronsky said in good-natured jest, holding out his hand.

He quickly took the outstretched hand and pressed it warmly.

'I'm very, very glad,' said Levin, pressing his hand in return.

'Waiter, a bottle of champagne,' said Stepan Arkadyich.

'And I'm very glad,' said Vronsky.

But in spite of Stepan Arkadyich's wish, and their shared wish, they had nothing to talk about and they both felt it.

'Do you know, he has never met Anna?' Stepan Arkadyich said to Vronsky. 'And I definitely want to take him over to see her. Let's go, Levin!'

'Really?' said Vronsky. 'She will be very glad. I would go home now,' he added, 'but I'm worried about Yashvin, and I want to stay put until he finishes.'

'Are things going badly?'

'He keeps losing, and I'm the only one who can restrain him.'

'Well, what about a game of pyramids? Levin, will you play? Well, that is excellent!' said Stepan Arkadyich. 'Get the table ready,' he said to the marker.

'It's been ready for ages,' answered the marker, who had already arranged the balls in a triangle and was rolling the red one about for amusement.

'Well, let's start.'

After the game, Vronsky and Levin sat down at Gagin's table, and at Stepan Arkadyich's suggestion Levin started betting on aces. Vronsky divided his time between sitting at the table, surrounded by acquaintances who kept coming up to him, and going into the inferno to keep an eye on Yashvin. Levin was experiencing a pleasant respite from the mental exertion of the morning. He was glad that the antagonism with Vronsky was at an end, and the sensation of calmness, decorum, and pleasure did not leave him.

When the game was over, Stepan Arkadyich took Levin's arm.

'Well, so let's go over and see Anna. Right now? Shall we? She is at home. I promised her ages ago that I would bring you over. Where were you planning to go this evening?'

'Oh, nowhere special. I promised Sviyazhsky I'd go to the Agricultural Society. We could go if you like,' said Levin.

'Excellent, let's go! Find out if my carriage has come,' Stepan Arkadyich said, turning to a waiter.

Levin went over to the table, paid the forty roubles he had lost on aces, paid his club expenses to the old waiter standing in the doorway, who mysteriously knew what they amounted to, and swinging his arms in an exaggerated fashion, strode through all the rooms towards the exit.

9

'OBLONSKY's carriage!' the porter shouted out in an angry bass. The carriage drew up and they both got in. It was only for the first few moments while the carriage was driving out through the club gates that Levin continued to experience the sensation of the club's tranquillity and comfort, and the impeccable decorum of its surroundings; for as soon as they drove out on to the street and he felt the carriage jolting on the uneven road, heard the angry shout of a cabby coming towards them, and saw the red sign of a tavern and a shop in the dim light, that impression was obliterated and he began to ponder his actions and wonder whether it was a good thing for him to be going to see Anna. What would Kitty say? But Stepan Arkadyich did not give him time to reflect, and as if detecting his doubts, set out to dispel them.

'I am so glad', he said, 'that you will meet her. Dolly has been want-ing this for a long time, you know. And Lvov has been over and calls on her. Although she is my sister,' Stepan Arkadyich continued, 'I can boldly say that she's a remarkable woman. As you will see. Her position is very hard, especially now.'

'Why especially now?'

'We are having discussions with her husband about a divorce. And he has given his consent; but a difficulty has arisen with regard to the son, and this business, which ought to have been settled long ago, has been dragging on for three months now. As soon as we have the divorce, she will marry Vronsky. How stupid it is, that old custom of going round singing "Rejoice, Isaiah",* which no one believes in and which pre-vents people being happy!' Stepan Arkadyich added. 'Anyway, their position will then be as clear-cut as mine and as yours.'

'So where does the difficulty lie?' said Levin.

'Oh, it's a long and boring story! Everything is so indefinite in our country. But the fact is that for the past three months, while she has been waiting for the divorce, she has been living here in Moscow, where everyone knows him, and her; she never goes out, she does not see any women friends except for Dolly, because as you can understand, she doesn't want people calling on her out of charity; that fool Princess Varvara—even she has left, because she considers it improper. The thing is, another woman in this position would not have been able to find inner resources. But she—well, you'll see how she has organized her life, and how calm and dignified she is. On the left, in the lane, opposite the church!' shouted Stepan Arkadyich, leaning out of the window of the carriage. 'Phew, I'm so hot!' he said, loosening his already unfastened fur coat still further, despite the twelve-degree frost.

'But she has a daughter, after all; she must be busy with her?' said Levin.

'You seem to imagine every woman is just a mother hen, *une cou-veuse*,'[1] said Stepan Arkadyich. 'If she is to have an occupation, it must be with children. No, she seems to be doing a wonderful job of bring-ing her up, but we do not hear about her. Her occupations are, firstly, writing. I can see you are smiling ironically, but you're wrong. She has been writing a children's book and hasn't talked about it to anyone, but she read it to me and I gave the manuscript to Vorkuyev . . . you know, that publisher . . . he is also a writer himself, it seems. He knows his stuff, and he says it's remarkable. But you're thinking she is one of

---

[1] 'broody hen'.

those women authoresses? Absolutely not. She is first and foremost
a woman with a heart, as you will see. She has a little English girl and
a whole household she is occupied with at the moment.'

'So is this some kind of philanthropic venture?'

'You just want to see the bad side of everything. It's not philanthropy,
but compassion. They, or rather Vronsky, had an English trainer who
was superb at his job, but a drunkard. He drank himself into a state of
delirium tremens and deserted his family. She saw them, lent a helping
hand, got involved, and now she has taken the whole family in hand,
but not in a condescending way, with money, and she herself is coaching the boys in Russian in preparation for high school, and she has
taken in the little girl to live with her. And now you'll see her.'

The carriage drove into the courtyard and Stepan Arkadyich rang
loudly at the porch, where a sleigh was standing.

And without asking the factotum who opened the door whether
Anna was at home, Stepan Arkadyich marched into the lobby. Levin
followed him, beset by more and more doubts as to whether what he
was doing was right or wrong.

When he looked at himself in the mirror, Levin noticed that he was
red in the face; but he was sure he was not drunk, and he followed
Stepan Arkadyich up the carpeted staircase. On the landing Stepan
Arkadyich asked the servant, who bowed to him as if he was someone
he knew well, who was with Anna Arkadyevna, and received the answer
that it was Mr Vorkuyev.

'Where are they?'

'In the study.'

After going through a small dining room with dark, wood-panelled
walls, Stepan Arkadyich and Levin stepped on to soft carpet as they
entered the semi-dark study, which was lit by a single lamp with a large
dark shade. Another lamp with a reflector was burning on the wall and
illuminating a large full-length portrait of a woman, which involuntarily drew Levin's attention. It was the portrait of Anna that Mikhailov
had painted in Italy. While Stepan Arkadyich went behind the lattice
screen and the man's voice which had been speaking fell silent, Levin
gazed at the portrait, which stood out from the frame in the gleaming
light, and could not tear himself away from it. With his eyes riveted
on the remarkable portrait and not listening to what was being said,
he even forgot where he was. This was not a painting but an enchanting living woman with curly black hair, bare arms and shoulders, and
a pensive half-smile on lips covered with soft down, looking at him
triumphantly and tenderly with eyes which unnerved him. The only

thing which showed she was not alive was that she was more beautiful than a living woman could be.

'I am very glad,' he suddenly heard a voice saying, which was clearly addressed to him and was the voice of the same woman he had been admiring in the portrait. Anna had emerged from behind the screen to greet him, and Levin saw in the dim light of the study the very same woman of the portrait, in a dark dress of different shades of blue, not in the same posture or with the same expression, but with the same supreme beauty with which the artist had captured her in the portrait. She was less dazzling in reality, but in the flesh there was also something new and alluring about her that was not in the portrait.

10

SHE had risen to greet him without concealing her pleasure at seeing him. And in the composure with which she extended her energetic small hand to him, introduced him to Vorkuyev, and indicated a pretty girl with reddish hair she called her ward, who was sitting there with some work, Levin recognized the pleasant and familiar manners of a woman of high society who was always composed and natural.

'I am very, very glad,' she repeated, and for some reason these simple words, coming from her lips, acquired a particular significance for Levin. 'I have known and liked you for a long while, both through your friendship with Stiva and on account of your wife . . . I knew her for a very short time, but the impression she made on me was of a delightful flower, truly, a flower. And now she is soon going to be a mother!'

She spoke freely and without haste, occasionally transferring her glance from Levin to her brother, and Levin felt he was making a good impression, and he immediately found it easy, straightforward, and enjoyable being with her, as if he had known her from childhood.

'Ivan Petrovich and I settled in Alexey's study', she said in answer to Stepan Arkadyich's question about whether he could smoke, 'precisely so we could smoke,' and glancing at Levin instead of asking him whether he smoked, she drew a tortoiseshell cigar-case towards her and took out a cigarette.

'How are you feeling today?' her brother asked.

'All right. Nerves as usual.'

'It's extraordinarily good, isn't it?' said Stepan Arkadyich, noticing Levin glancing at the portrait.

'I have never seen a better portrait.'

'And an extraordinary likeness, don't you think?' said Vorkuyev.

Levin looked from the portrait to the original. A particular radiance lit up Anna's face while she felt his eyes on her. Levin blushed, and was about to ask whether she had seen Darya Alexandrovna lately in order to cover up his embarrassment; but just at that moment Anna said:

'Ivan Petrovich and I have just been talking about Vashchenkov's latest paintings. Have you seen them?'

'Yes, I have,' answered Levin.

'But forgive me, I interrupted, there was something you wanted to say . . .'

Levin asked if she had seen Dolly lately.

'She came to see me yesterday; she's very angry with the high school on Grisha's account. The Latin teacher has been unfair to him, it seems.'

'Yes, I have seen his paintings. I didn't like them very much,' said Levin, returning to the conversation she had initiated.

Levin was certainly no longer talking in the perfunctory, mechanical way in which he had spoken that morning. Each word in his conversation with her acquired a special significance. And while it was enjoyable talking to her, it was even more enjoyable listening to her.

Anna not only talked in a natural, clever way, but in a clever and nonchalant way, attaching no value to her own ideas, but ascribing great value to the ideas of the person to whom she was talking.

The conversation touched on the new movement in art, and a French artist's new illustrations of the Bible.* Vorkuyev accused the artist of taking realism to the point of coarseness. Levin said that the French had taken stylization in art further than anyone, and so consequently saw a great merit in returning to realism. They saw poetry in the fact that they were no longer lying.

Never had Levin produced a clever remark that gave him as much pleasure as this one. Anna's face suddenly completely lit up when she grasped the import of this idea. She burst out laughing.

'I am laughing', she said, 'in the way that one laughs when one sees a very true likeness in a portrait. What you have said perfectly characterizes French art at the moment, certainly painting and even literature: Zola, Daudet.* But maybe that is the way it always is—that first of all people mould their *conceptions* from contrived, stylized figures, and then they get to the point when all the *combinaisons*[1] have been tried out, the contrived figures have begun to pall, and they begin to think up more natural, accurate figures.'

---

[1] 'combinations'.

'Now that's absolutely true!' said Vorkuyev.

'So you've been at the club?' she asked, turning to her brother.

'Yes, yes, what a woman!' thought Levin, who was now in a state of oblivion and was staring fixedly at her beautiful, mobile face, which was now suddenly completely transformed. Levin did not hear what she was talking about while she leaned over towards her brother, but he was struck by the change in her expression. Her face, which had previously been so lovely in its composure, suddenly expressed a strange curiosity, anger, and pride. But this lasted only for a moment. She narrowed her eyes, as if trying to remember something.

'Well, yes, anyway, that's not of any interest to anyone,' she said and turned to the English girl:

'*Please, order the tea in the drawing room.*'[1]

The girl got up and went out.

'Well, did she pass her examination?' asked Stepan Arkadyich.

'With flying colours! She's a very clever girl, and she has a sweet nature.'

'You will end up loving her more than your own daughter.'

'There speaks a man. In love there is no more or less. I love my daughter with one kind of love, and her with another.'

'I was just telling Anna Arkadyevna', said Vorkuyev, 'that if she were to devote one per cent of the energy she invests in this English girl to the general cause of educating Russian children, she would be doing a great and useful thing.'

'Yes, but whatever you say, I still couldn't do it. Count Alexey Kirillych strongly encouraged me;'—as she uttered the words *Count Alexey Kirillych* she looked beseechingly and timidly at Levin, and he involuntarily responded with a deferential and affirmative look—'he encouraged me to get involved with the school in the village. I did go several times. They are very sweet, but I just couldn't develop an attachment to that kind of work. You talk about energy. Energy is based on love. And love is not something you can get from somewhere, it is not something you can summon up. I have developed an affection for this girl, for example, but I myself don't know why.'

And she glanced again at Levin. Both her smile and her glance told him that she was addressing him alone, and valued his opinion, at the same time knowing in advance that they understood each other.

'I completely understand that,' Levin answered. 'It's impossible to

---

[1] [English in the original.]

put one's heart into a school or a similar institution, and that is why, I think, these philanthropic institutions always yield such poor results.'

She was silent for a while, then smiled.

'Yes, exactly,' she confirmed. 'I never could. *Je n'ai pas le cœur assez large* to love a whole orphanage of horrid little girls. *Cela ne m'a jamais réussi.*[1] But there are so many women who create *une position sociale*[2] for themselves in this way. And now more than ever,' she said with a sad, trusting expression, ostensibly addressing her brother, but clearly only speaking to Levin, 'now, when I have such need for some kind of occupation, I find I can't do it.' And with a sudden frown (Levin realized she was actually frowning at herself because she was talking about herself), she changed the subject. 'I know about you,' she said to Levin, 'that you are a bad citizen, and I have defended you to the best of my ability.'

'How exactly have you defended me?'

'It depends on the attacks. However, wouldn't you like some tea?' She rose and picked up a book with a morocco binding.

'Do give it to me, Anna Arkadyevna,' said Vorkuyev, indicating the book. 'It certainly merits it.'

'Oh, no, it's all so unpolished.'

'I told him,' Stepan Arkadyich said to his sister, indicating Levin.

'You shouldn't have. My writing is like those little fretwork baskets that Liza Mertsalova used to sell me from the prisons. She used to run the prisons in our society,' she said, turning to Levin. 'And those unfortunate people performed miracles of forbearance.'

And Levin saw yet another new quality in this woman to whom he had taken such an extraordinary liking. Apart from intelligence, grace, and beauty, she possessed truthfulness. She had no desire to conceal all the difficulty of her position from him. When she stopped speaking, she sighed and her face suddenly took on a severe expression, as if it had turned to stone. With this expression on her face she was even more beautiful than before; but this expression was new; it lay beyond the range of expressions radiating and transmitting happiness that had been captured by the painter in the portrait. Levin looked again at the portrait and at her figure as she took her brother's arm and proceeded through the tall doors with him, and he felt a tenderness and pity for her that took him quite by surprise.

She asked Levin and Vorkuyev to go through into the drawing room, while she stayed behind to talk about something with her brother.

[1] 'I've never had a large enough heart . . . I have never managed to do it.'
[2] 'a social position'.

'About the divorce, about Vronsky, about what he gets up to at the club, about me?' Levin wondered. And he was so anxious to know what she was discussing with Stepan Arkadyich that he barely heard what Vorkuyev was telling him about the qualities of the children's novel which Anna Arkadyevna had written.

The same enjoyable and absorbing conversation was resumed over tea. Not only was there not a single moment when it became necessary to find a topic of conversation but, on the contrary, it felt as though there was not enough time to say all one wanted while willingly holding back to hear what someone else was saying. And whatever was said, not only by her, but also by Vorkuyev and Stepan Arkadyich—it all seemed to Levin to acquire particular significance as a result of her attention and her observations.

While following this interesting conversation, Levin constantly admired her—her beauty, her intelligence, her learning, and also her straightforwardness and sincerity. He listened and spoke, all the while thinking about her and her inner life, trying to fathom her feelings. And having judged her so severely before, he now found himself, as a result of some strange thought-process, defending her and at the same time feeling sorry for her and fearing that Vronsky did not fully understand her. At eleven o'clock, when Stepan Arkadyich got up to leave (Vorkuyev had left earlier), Levin felt that he had only just arrived. Regretfully, Levin also stood up.

'Goodbye,' she said, holding on to his hand and fixing him with a beguiling look. 'I am very glad *que la glace est rompue*.'[1]

She let go of his hand and narrowed her eyes.

'Tell your wife that I am as fond of her as before, and that if she cannot forgive me my situation, then I would rather she never forgave me. To forgive, it would be necessary to live through what I have lived through, and may God save her from that.'

'Yes, absolutely, I will tell her . . .' said Levin, blushing.

11

'What a wonderful, sweet, and pitiful woman!' he was thinking as he and Stepan Arkadyich stepped out into the frosty air.

'Well, what did I tell you?' said Stepan Arkadyich, seeing that Levin had been completely won over.

[1] 'the ice is broken'.

'Yes,' Levin replied pensively, 'an extraordinary woman! Not so much clever as wonderfully sincere. I feel terribly sorry for her!'

'God willing, everything will soon be settled now. Well, next time maybe don't judge people in advance,' said Stepan Arkadyich, opening the carriage door. 'Goodbye. We aren't going the same way.'

Thinking incessantly about Anna and all those perfectly straightforward conversations with her, all the while recalling every detail in the expression of her face as he entered more and more into her position and sympathized with her, Levin arrived home.

At home Kuzma informed Levin that Katerina Alexandrovna was well and that her sisters had only recently left, and handed him two letters. Levin read them straight away in the hall, so as not to be distracted later. One was from Sokolov, his steward. Sokolov wrote that the wheat could not be sold as they were only offering five and a half roubles, but there was no money to be got anywhere else. The other letter was from his sister. She reproached him for not having sorted out her affairs yet.

'Well, we'll sell it for five and a half if they won't give any more,' thought Levin, with extraordinary ease promptly resolving the first problem, which previously had seemed so intractable. 'It's remarkable how all one's time is taken up here,' he thought with regard to the second letter. He felt guilty on his sister's account that he had still not done what she had asked him to do. 'I failed to go to the court again today, but there was absolutely no time today.' And deciding that he would definitely attend to it the next day, he set off to find his wife. On his way to her Levin quickly went over the whole of that day again in his mind. All the events of that day had been conversations: conversations to which he had listened or taken part in. All the conversations had been about the sorts of subjects he would never have got embroiled in if he had been on his own and in the country, but here they had been very interesting. And all the conversations had been good; there were just two points that had not been altogether satisfactory. One was what he had said about the pike, the other was that something was *not right* about the tender feelings of pity he experienced for Anna.

Levin found his wife miserable and bored. The dinner of the three sisters would have been a resounding success, but then they had ended up waiting and waiting for him, they had all grown bored, the sisters had departed, and she had been left alone.

'Well, what have you been doing?' she asked, looking straight into his eyes, which for some reason had a particularly suspicious glitter. But in order not to prevent him from telling her everything, she masked her attentiveness and listened to his account of how he had spent the evening with an approving smile.

'Well, I'm very glad I met Vronsky. I found it very easy and straightforward being with him. I will try to avoid ever seeing him now, you understand, but we had to put an end to this awkwardness,' he said, and when he remembered that *trying to avoid ever seeing him* had resulted in him immediately going to visit Anna, he blushed. 'Now, we're always saying that the peasants drink; I don't know who drinks more, the peasants or our own class; the peasants at least drink on holidays, but . . .'

But Kitty was not interested in discussing the drinking habits of the peasants. She saw him blush, and she wanted to know why.

'Well, and where did you go next?'

'Stiva pleaded with me to go and visit Anna Arkadyevna.'

And Levin blushed even more when he said this, and his doubts about whether it was good or bad that he had gone to see Anna were resolved once and for all. He now knew that he should not have gone.

Kitty's eyes opened wide and glistened more than usual at the mention of Anna's name, but she made an effort to conceal her disquiet and so deceived him.

'Ah!' was all she said.

'I can't imagine you will be angry that I went. Stiva asked me to go, and Dolly was keen that I should,' Levin went on.

'Oh no,' she said, but in her eyes he saw the effort she was making to control herself, which did not augur at all well for him.

'She is a very nice and extremely pitiable, good woman,' he said, telling her about Anna, her occupations, and what she had ordered him to say.

'Yes, of course, she is very much to be pitied,' said Kitty, when he had finished. 'Who did you receive a letter from?'

He told her and, convinced by her calm tone, went to undress.

He came back to find Kitty in the same armchair. When he went up to her, she looked at him and burst out sobbing.

'What is it? What is it?' he asked, knowing full well what *it* was.

'You've fallen in love with that nasty woman, she has bewitched you. I saw it in your eyes. Yes, yes! What can come of this? You were drinking at the club, drinking and gambling, and then you went off . . . to go and see whom? No, we have to leave . . . I'm leaving tomorrow.'

It was a long while before Levin could calm his wife down. When he did finally calm her down, it was only by confessing that a feeling of pity combined with the wine had led him astray, leading him to succumb to Anna's cunning influence, and that he would avoid her in the future. The one thing he was able to confess to with the greatest sincerity was that living so long in Moscow, with nothing to do but talk, eat, and drink, had made him go soft in the head. They talked until three o'clock in the morning. Only at three o'clock were they sufficiently reconciled to be able to fall asleep.

12

AFTER seeing her guests out Anna did not sit down, but started pacing about the room. Although she had unconsciously spent the whole evening doing all she could to arouse in Levin a feeling of love for her (as she did with all young men lately), and although she knew she had succeeded, so far as that was possible with an honourable married man in a single evening, and although she had taken a great liking to him—despite the stark difference between Vronsky and Levin from a man's point of view, as a woman she could see what it was they had in common that had made Kitty fall in love with both Vronsky and Levin—as soon as he left the room she stopped thinking about him.

One single thought pursued her relentlessly in various guises. 'If I have this much effect on others, and on this devoted family man, why is *he* so cold to me? It's not exactly that he is cold, as he loves me, I know that. But something new has come between us. Why has he been out all evening? He told Stiva to let me know that he could not leave Yashvin and had to keep an eye on his gambling. Is Yashvin a child? But let's suppose it's the truth. He never tells lies. But there's something else within that truth. He is glad of the chance to show me he has other responsibilities. I know that, and I am happy about it. But why does he have to prove it to me? He wants to prove to me that his love for me should not interfere with his freedom. But I don't need proofs, I need love. He ought to understand all the difficulties of my life here in Moscow. Can I call this living? I am not living, but awaiting an outcome which keeps being protracted. There's no answer again! And Stiva says he cannot go and see Alexey Alexandrovich. But I can't write again. I can't do anything, can't start anything, can't change anything, I'm restraining myself, waiting, thinking up amusements for myself, such as the Englishman's family, writing, and reading, but it's all just a deception, it's all just morphine under another name. He ought to feel sorry for me,' she said, feeling tears of self-pity springing into her eyes.

She heard Vronsky's insistent ringing and hurriedly wiped away these tears, indeed not only wiped away her tears, but sat down by the lamp and opened a book, pretending to be calm. She needed to show him she was displeased he had not come home as he had promised, just displeased, but not under any circumstances show him her misery, let alone her self-pity. She could pity herself, but he should not pity her. She did not want a fight, and blamed him for wanting a fight, yet she was involuntarily taking up position for a fight.

'Well, you've not been bored, I hope?' he said, coming up to her in high spirits and full of good cheer. 'What a terrible passion gambling is!'

'No, I haven't been bored, and I learnt how not to be bored a long time ago. Stiva and Levin were here.'

'Yes, they were planning to come and see you. Well, how did you like Levin?' he said, sitting down beside her.

'I liked him very much. They left a short while ago. What has Yashvin done?'

'He was on a winning streak, seventeen thousand. I called him away. He was on the verge of leaving. But then he went back, and now he's on a losing streak.'

'So why on earth did you stay?' she asked, suddenly raising her eyes to him. The expression on her face was cold and hostile. 'You told Stiva you were staying so you could take Yashvin away. But you have left him.'

The same expression of cold readiness for a fight appeared on his face too.

'In the first place, I did not ask him to tell you anything, and in the second, I never tell lies. But mostly I stayed because I wanted to,' he said, frowning. 'Anna, what is this all for?' he said after a moment's silence as he leant towards her and opened his hand, hoping she would place hers in it.

She welcomed this appeal for tenderness. But some strange, evil force would not allow her to give in to her inclinations, as if the rules of the fight did not allow her to submit.

'Of course you wanted to stay, so you stayed. You do everything you want. But why do you have to tell me that? What is the point?' she said, growing increasingly angry. 'Is anyone questioning your rights? But you want to be right, so be right then.'

His hand closed, he turned aside, and his face assumed an even more stubborn expression than before.

'For you it's a question of obstinacy,' she said, studying him closely and suddenly finding the right word for the expression on his face that irritated her, 'sheer obstinacy. For you it's a question of whether you will be victorious over me, while for me . . .' She began to feel sorry for herself again, and almost burst into tears. 'If you knew what this means for me! When I feel, as I do now, that you are being hostile to me, yes, exactly that, if you only knew what it means for me! If you knew how close I feel to disaster at these moments, and how afraid I am, afraid of myself!' And she turned away, hiding her sobs.

'But what is this about?' he said, appalled at her expression of despair, and he leant over to her again, took her hand, and kissed it. 'What have I done? Do I seek amusements away from home? Don't I avoid the company of women?'

'I should certainly hope so!' she said.

'Well then, tell me, what is it I need to do in order to put your mind at rest? I am ready to do anything to make you happy,' he said, touched by her despair, 'there is nothing I wouldn't do to spare you from any kind of pain, like that which you are suffering now, Anna!' he said.

'It's nothing, nothing!' she said. 'I don't know myself whether it's this lonely life or nerves . . . Well, let's not talk about it. How did the races go? You haven't told me,' she asked, trying to conceal the triumph of victory, which was after all on her side.

He asked for supper and began telling her in detail about the races; but in his tone, and in the looks he gave her, which were becoming ever colder, she saw that he had not forgiven her for her victory, and that the feeling of obstinacy she had battled against had taken hold of him again. He was colder to her than before, as if he repented having surrendered. And when she recalled the words that had brought her victory, 'I am close to a terrible disaster and am afraid of myself,' she realized they were a dangerous weapon and could not be used a second time. And she felt that alongside the love which bound them, an evil spirit of some kind of conflict had installed itself between them, which she was unable to expunge from his heart, let alone her own.

13

THERE are no circumstances to which a man cannot accustom himself, especially if he sees that *everyone* around him lives in the same way. Levin would not have believed three months earlier that he could have calmly fallen asleep in the circumstances in which he found himself that evening; that after leading an aimless, stupid life, a life moreover which was beyond his means, and after the drunkenness (there was no other way he could describe what had happened at the club), the inappropriate friendly relations with a man with whom his wife had once been in love, and even more inappropriate visit to a woman who could only be described as fallen, and having been attracted to this woman and upset his wife—that he was able in such circumstances to fall fast asleep. But as a result of weariness, a sleepless night, and the wine he had drunk, he slept soundly and peacefully.

At five in the morning he was woken by the creak of a door being opened. He sat up and looked round. Kitty was not in bed beside him. But there was a light moving behind the screen, and he heard her steps.

'What is it? . . . What is it?' he mumbled, half-asleep. 'Kitty! What is it?'

'Nothing,' she said, emerging from behind the screen with a candle in her hand. 'It's nothing. I just felt a little unwell,' she said with a particularly winsome and meaningful smile.

'What? Has it started? Has it?' he said in alarm. 'We must send . . .' and he began hurriedly getting dressed.

'No, no,' she said, smiling and stopping him with her hand. 'I'm sure it's nothing. I just felt slightly unwell. But it's gone now.'

And she came back to bed, put out the candle, lay down, and was still. Although he was suspicious both of the stillness, as if she were holding her breath, and above all of the particular tenderness and excitement with which she had told him 'it's nothing' as she emerged from behind the screen, he felt so sleepy that he immediately nodded off. It was only later that he remembered the stillness of her breathing and understood everything that had been going on in her dear, sweet heart while she lay next to him without moving, awaiting the greatest event in a woman's life. At seven o'clock he was woken by the touch of her hand on his shoulder and a gentle whisper. She seemed to be torn between regret at waking him and the desire to speak to him.

'Kostya, don't be alarmed. I'm all right. But I think . . . We need to send for Lizaveta Petrovna.'

The candle had been lit again. She was sitting on the bed, holding some knitting she had been doing in the last few days.

'Please, don't be alarmed, I'm all right. I'm not at all scared,' she said, seeing his alarmed face, and she pressed his hand to her breast and then to her lips.

He quickly leapt up, mechanically put on his dressing-gown without taking his eyes off her, then stopped, still looking at her. He had to go, but he could not tear himself away from her gaze. No matter how much he loved her face, and no matter how well he knew her expressions and her looks, he had never seen her like this. Remembering how upset she had been the day before, how vile and awful he seemed to himself before her as she was now! Her flushed face, framed by the soft hair that had escaped from under her nightcap, shone with joy and determination.

However little artificiality and conventionality there was in Kitty's general character, Levin was nevertheless astonished by what was now revealed to him when all the veils were suddenly removed and the very core of her being shone in her eyes. And she, the very person he loved, was even more visible in this stark and exposed state. She was looking at him, smiling; but suddenly her brow became furrowed, she lifted her head, rushed over to him, took hold of his hand, and clung to him, enveloping him with her hot breath. She was suffering and seemed to be complaining to him about her suffering. And from habit, he felt he was to blame to begin with. But in her eyes there was a tenderness which told him that not only did she not reproach him, but actually loved him for this suffering. 'But if I am not to blame for this, who is?' was his involuntary thought as he sought to identify the perpetrator of this suffering so he could mete out punishment; but there was no perpetrator. Even though there was no perpetrator, surely it was possible simply to help her and ease her suffering, but it turned out to be neither possible nor necessary. She was suffering, complaining, and she was exulting in this suffering, revelling in it, and loving it. He saw that something wonderful was taking place in her soul, but what it was he could not fathom. It was beyond his understanding.

'I've sent for Mamma. But you should now go as quickly as you can to fetch Lizaveta Petrovna . . . Kostya! . . . It's all right, it's gone.'

She detached herself from him and went to ring the bell.

'Look, you can go now, Pasha's coming. I am all right.'

And Levin saw with amazement that she had taken up the knitting she had brought in that night and begun knitting again.

As Levin was going out of one door, he heard the maid coming in through the other. He stood by the door and heard Kitty giving the maid detailed instructions then start moving the bed with her herself.

He got dressed, and while they were harnessing the horses, since there were no cabbies about yet, he rushed back up to the bedroom, and not on tiptoe but on wings, it seemed to him. Two maids were busy moving something in the bedroom. Kitty was walking about knitting, rapidly casting off loops, and giving instructions.

'I'm going over to the doctor now. They have gone off to fetch Lizaveta Petrovna, but I'll stop by there too. There isn't anything you need? Yes, should I go to Dolly's?'

She looked at him, obviously not listening to what he was saying.

'Yes, yes. Off you go,' she murmured quickly, frowning and waving her hand at him.

He was already in the drawing room when suddenly out of the bedroom came the sound of a piteous moan that immediately abated. He stopped and took a long time to understand what was going on.

'Yes, it's her,' he said to himself and, clutching his head, he ran downstairs.

'Lord, have mercy! Forgive us and help us!' he kept saying, repeating words which had suddenly come to his lips unexpectedly for some reason. And he, a non-believer, was not merely mouthing these words with his lips. He now knew at that moment that not only his doubts, but also the impossibility of believing rationally, which he knew resided in him, did not in any way prevent him from turning to God. All that was now swept out of his soul like dust. To whom was he supposed to turn if not to Him in whose hands he felt himself, his soul, and his love to be?

The horse was not ready yet, but feeling a particularly intense concentration within himself of both physical energy and attentiveness to what needed to be done, he set off on foot without waiting for the horse in order not to waste a single moment, and told Kuzma to catch him up.

At the corner he encountered a night-cab hurrying along. Sitting in the small sleigh in a velvet cloak, wrapped up in a scarf, was Lizaveta Petrovna. 'Thank God, thank God!' he murmured, overjoyed to recognize her small blonde head and face, which now bore a particularly serious, even stern expression. Without bothering to tell the driver to stop, he ran back alongside her.

'So about two hours, then? Not more than that?' she enquired. 'You will find Pyotr Dmitrich at home, but make sure you don't hurry him. And pick up some opium at the chemist's.'

'So you think it might all turn out well? Lord, forgive us and help us!' Levin murmured when he saw his horse driving out through the gate. After jumping into the sleigh beside Kuzma, he told him to drive to the doctor's.

14

THE doctor was not yet up, and the footman said that he 'had gone to bed late and asked not to be woken, but would be up soon'. The footman was cleaning the glass lampshades and seemed very preoccupied with this. The footman's absorption with the glass lampshades and indifference to what was going on with him astounded Levin at first, but when he thought about it, he immediately realized that no one knew or had any obligation to know what he was feeling, so it was even more incumbent on him to act calmly, deliberately, and decisively, in order to break down this wall of indifference and attain his goal. 'Don't hurry and don't leave anything out,' Levin said to himself, feeling an ever greater increase in his physical energy and attentiveness to everything that needed to be done.

When he learnt that the doctor had still not got up, Levin settled on the following of the various options available to him: Kuzma would go with a note to another doctor, while he himself would go to the chemist for the opium, and if the doctor was still not up when he returned, he would bribe the footman or, if the latter refused, use force to wake the doctor, come what may.

At the chemist's a gaunt pharmacist was sealing a packet of powders for a waiting coachman with the same indifference with which the footman had cleaned the glass lampshades, and refused to dispense any opium. Endeavouring not to be impatient or lose his temper, Levin started trying to persuade him by supplying the names of the doctor and midwife, and explaining why the opium was needed. The pharmacist asked for advice in German on whether he could dispense it and, receiving permission from behind the partition, he took a bottle and a funnel, slowly poured the opium from the large bottle into a small one, affixed a label, sealed it, despite Levin's request to the contrary, and was about to wrap it up. This was more than Levin could bear; he snatched the bottle firmly from his hands and ran out through the big glass doors. The doctor had still not got up, and the footman, who was now busy with laying a carpet, refused to wake him. Without hurrying, Levin took out a ten-rouble note and, articulating his words slowly but also not wasting any time, handed him the note and explained that Pyotr Dmitrich (how great and important the formerly insignificant Pyotr Dmitrich seemed to Levin now!) had promised to come at any time, that he definitely would not be angry, and therefore should be woken at once.

The footman agreed and went upstairs, asking Levin to go into the waiting room.

Through the door Levin could hear the doctor coughing, walking about, washing, and saying something. About three minutes went by; it seemed to Levin that more than an hour had gone by. He could not wait any longer.

'Pyotr Dmitrich, Pyotr Dmitrich!' he said in an imploring voice through the open door. 'Forgive me, for God's sake. Receive me just as you are. It's been two hours already.'

'Just a minute, just a minute!' answered a voice, and to his amazement Levin could hear that the doctor was smiling as he said this.

'I only need a moment . . .'

'Just a minute.'

Two more minutes went by while the doctor put on his boots, followed by a further two minutes while the doctor finished dressing and combed his hair.

'Pyotr Dmitrich!' Levin began again in a plaintive voice, but just at that moment the doctor came out, dressed and combed. 'These people have no shame,' thought Levin. 'Combing their hair while we're at death's door!'

'Good morning!' the doctor said to him, holding out his hand and appearing to tease him with his calm demeanour. 'There's no hurry. Well, what can I do for you?'

Trying to be as comprehensive as possible, Levin began recounting every unnecessary detail of his wife's condition, constantly interrupting himself to ask the doctor to set off with him straight away.

'Now there is no need to hurry. You must know that I am probably not needed, but I promised, and will come if you like. But there's no urgency. Please sit down. Won't you have some coffee?'

Levin gave him a look as if to ask whether he was laughing at him. But the doctor had no thought of laughing.

'I know, I know,' the doctor said, smiling, 'I'm a family man myself; but we husbands are the most pathetic people at these moments. I have one patient whose husband always runs off into the stables when this happens.'

'But what do you think, Pyotr Dmitrich? Do you think it might go well?'

'Everything points to a successful outcome.'

'So you'll come now?' said Levin, glaring angrily at the servant who was bringing in the coffee.

'In about an hour.'

'For God's sake, no!'

'Well, let me at least drink my coffee.'

The doctor began drinking his coffee. They both fell silent.

'Well, those Turks are getting a proper hammering. Did you read yesterday's dispatch?' said the doctor as he chewed a roll.

'No, I can't bear this!' said Levin, leaping up. 'So you'll be with us in a quarter of an hour?'

'In half an hour.'

'You promise?'

Levin's return home coincided with the Princess's arrival, and they went up to the bedroom door together. The Princess had tears in her eyes and her hands were shaking. When she saw Levin, she embraced him and burst into tears.

'So, my dear Lizaveta Petrovna, tell us all,' she said, clasping the midwife's hand as Lizaveta Petrovna came out to meet them, her face glowing but preoccupied.

'It's going well,' she said, 'but see if you can persuade her to lie down. It will be easier for her.'

From the moment he had woken up and realized what was going on, and having suppressed all thoughts and feelings, Levin had steeled himself to endure what lay in store for him unflinchingly, not pondering or anticipating anything, and not upsetting his wife but, on the contrary, reassuring her and bolstering her courage. Not even allowing himself to think about what lay ahead or what the result would be, but judging from his enquiries as to how long it usually lasted, in his imagination Levin steeled himself to endure and wait with his heart in his mouth for about five hours, and that seemed feasible to him. But when he returned from the doctor and saw her suffering again, he began repeating 'Lord, forgive us and help us' more and more often, sighing, and lifting up his head; and he began to fear that he would not be able to endure this, that he would burst out crying or run away. It was that agonizing for him. And only one hour had gone by.

But after that hour another hour went by, then two, three, all five of the hours he had set himself as the extreme limit of his endurance went by, and the situation was unchanged; and he had to go on enduring, because there was nothing to do except endure, every moment thinking that he had reached the utmost limits of his capacity to endure and that his heart was about to burst with compassion.

But more minutes and hours went by, then still more hours, and his feelings of suffering and horror increased and became even more intense.

None of life's usual conditions, without which it is impossible to imagine anything, existed for Levin any more. He lost awareness of time. Either the minutes—those minutes when she summoned him to her side, and he held her clammy hand, which one moment gripped his with extraordinary strength and the next pushed it away—seemed like hours to him, or the hours seemed like minutes. He was surprised when Lizaveta Petrovna asked him to light the candle behind the screens and he discovered that it was already five o'clock in the evening. He would have been just as surprised if he had been told it was only ten o'clock in the morning. He had as little idea of where he was during this time as he did of when exactly things were going on. He saw her swollen face, at times bewildered and suffering, at others smiling and reassuring him. He saw the old Princess, looking red-faced and tense, with loose curls of straggling grey hair, shedding tears she was making herself swallow, biting her lip; he saw Dolly, and the doctor smoking fat cigarettes, and he saw Lizaveta Petrovna, whose face bore a firm, determined, reassuring expression, and the old Prince who was walking up and down the ballroom frowning. But how they came in and went out or where they were, he did not know. At one moment the Princess was with the doctor in the bedroom, at another she was in the study, where there turned out to be a table set for dinner; and then at another point she was not there, but Dolly was. Then Levin remembered he had been sent somewhere. One time he was sent to move a table and sofa. He did this conscientiously, thinking it was needed for her, and only later did he find out he had been preparing his own bed for the night. Then he was sent to the study to ask the doctor something. The doctor answered and then started talking about the disturbances at the Duma.* Then he was sent to the Princess's bedroom to fetch an icon in a silver-gilt frame, and with the help of the Princess's old maid he had clambered up on to a cabinet to get it and had broken the icon lamp, and the Princess's maid had reassured him about the lamp and about his wife, and he had taken the icon and placed it at the head of Kitty's bed, carefully slipping it in behind the pillow. But where, when, and why all this happened, he did not know. He also did not understand why the Princess took his hand and looked at him solicitously, begging him to calm down, or why Dolly persuaded him to eat something and led him out of the room, or why even the doctor looked at him gravely and with compassion, and offered him some drops.

He knew and felt only that what was taking place was similar to what had taken place the previous year at the deathbed of his brother Nikolay in the hotel of the provincial town. But that had been grief, whereas this was joy. But that grief and this joy both lay equally outside all of life's usual conditions, and were like apertures in this ordinary life through which something higher could be glimpsed. What was taking place was proceeding equally painfully and agonizingly and, as it perceived this higher something, his soul was ascending equally incomprehensibly to a height it had never understood before and with which his intellect could no longer keep pace.

'Lord, forgive us and help us!' he kept repeating to himself constantly, despite such a long and supposedly complete estrangement, feeling he was turning to God just as trustingly and simply as in the days of his childhood and early youth.

All this time he had two distinct states of mind. One was when he was out of her presence, with the doctor, who was smoking one fat cigarette after another and extinguishing them on the edge of a full ashtray, or with Dolly and the old Prince, when there was talk about dinner, politics, and Marya Petrovna's illness, and when Levin would suddenly forget for a minute what was happening and feel as if he had woken up, and the other state of mind was when he was in her presence, at her bedside, when his heart wanted to burst with compassion and kept not bursting, and he prayed unceasingly to God. And every time that he was brought back from a moment of oblivion by a scream coming from the bedroom, he succumbed to the same strange delusion which had taken hold of him in that first moment; each time he heard a shriek he would leap up and rush off to justify himself, then remember on the way that he was not to blame, and he would want to offer protection and help. But when he looked at her, he would see again that there was nothing he could do to help, and he would be horrified and say: 'Lord, forgive us and help us.' And the more time went by, the more intense both states of mind became, the calmer he became out of her presence, when he completely forgot about her, and the more agonizing both her suffering and his feeling of helplessness became. He would leap up, wanting to run away somewhere, but would run to her.

Sometimes, when she kept summoning him to her again and again, he would reproach her. But as soon as he saw her meek, smiling face and heard her say, 'I've worn you out,' he would blame God, and when he remembered about God he would immediately pray for forgiveness and mercy.

15

He did not know whether it was late or early. The candles had all burned down already. Dolly had just come into the study and suggested to the doctor that he lie down for a while. Levin was sitting listening to the doctor's stories about a quack hypnotist, and watching the ash of his cigarette. It was a moment of respite and he was lost in a daydream. He had completely forgotten what was going on at this point. He was listening to the doctor's story and taking it in. Suddenly an unearthly scream rang out. The scream was so awful that Levin did not even jump up, but cast a frightened and questioning look at the doctor, holding his breath. The doctor put his head to one side as he listened, and then smiled approvingly. Everything was so out of the ordinary that nothing could surprise Levin by now. 'No doubt that is how it has to be,' he thought, and carried on sitting there. Who was it who was screaming? He jumped up, ran on tiptoe into the bedroom, skirted round Lizaveta Petrovna and the Princess, and took up his position at the head of the bed. The screaming had stopped, but something had changed now. What it was he could not see or understand, and had no wish to see or understand. But he could see it by looking at Lizaveta Petrovna's face: Lizaveta Petrovna's face was stern and pale, and just as determined, although her jaw was trembling a little, and her eyes were trained on Kitty. Kitty's swollen, worn-out face, a strand of hair clinging to her clammy brow, was turned towards him and seeking his gaze. Her raised hands were seeking his. Seizing his cold hands in her clammy ones, she began pressing them to her face.

'Don't go, don't go! I'm not afraid, I'm not afraid!' she said quickly. 'Mama, take my earrings. They're getting in the way. You're not afraid, are you? Soon, Lizaveta Petrovna, soon . . .'

She was talking rapidly and trying to smile. But suddenly her face became distorted and she pushed him away.

'No, this is awful! I shall die, I shall die! Go away, go away!' she cried out, and that unearthly scream could be heard again.

Levin clutched at his head and ran out of the room.

'It's all right, it's all right, everything is fine!' Dolly called after him.

But whatever they might say, he knew now that all was lost. He stood in the next room leaning his head against the door-frame and heard something he had never heard before—shrieks and howls, and he knew that what had previously been Kitty was producing these screams. He had stopped wanting the child a long time ago. He hated this child now. He did not even wish her to live now, he wished only for this dreadful suffering to end.

'Doctor! What is this? What is this? My God!' he said, seizing the doctor's hand as he came in.

'The end is near,' said the doctor. And the doctor's face was so serious when he said this that Levin took *the end is near* to mean *dying*.

Beside himself, he ran into the bedroom. The first thing he saw was Lizaveta Petrovna's face. It was even more grim and stern. Kitty's face was not there. In the place where it used to be was something frightful, to judge from the visible strain and the sound coming from it.

He collapsed with his head resting on the wooden bed-frame, feeling that his heart was breaking. The frightful screaming did not let up, but became even more frightful until suddenly it stopped, as if it had reached the extreme limit of frightfulness. Levin could not believe his ears, but there could be no doubt: the screaming had stopped and he heard a quiet bustling about, some rustling and rapid breathing, then her halting, vibrant, tender, and happy voice say gently: 'It's over.'

He lifted his head. Looking extraordinarily lovely and serene, her arms lowered limply on to the eiderdown, she was gazing at him mutely, and trying but not managing to smile.

And all of a sudden, from that mysterious and awful, unearthly world he had inhabited for the past twenty-two hours, Levin felt himself instantly transported back to the former, ordinary world, but which now glowed with such a new light of happiness that he could not withstand it. The taut strings all snapped. Sobs and tears of joy, which he had not in any way foreseen, welled up in him with such force, shaking his whole body, that for a long time they prevented him from speaking.

Falling on to his knees in front of the bed, he held his wife's hand to his lips and kissed it, and the hand responded to his kiss with a feeble movement of the fingers. Meanwhile, down at the foot of the bed, the life of a human being who had never existed before, and who would go on in just the same way to live and reproduce others like himself, with the same rights, with the same degree of significance to himself, flickered in Lizaveta Petrovna's deft hands like the flame above a lamp.

'The baby's alive! Alive! And a boy too! Don't worry!' Levin heard Lizaveta Petrovna saying as she slapped the baby on the back with a trembling hand.

'Mama, is it true?' said Kitty's voice.

The Princess could only sob in reply.

And in the midst of the silence, like an unequivocal answer to the mother's question, came the sound of a voice that was completely unlike all the hushed voices that had been speaking in the room. It was the bold, impudent, heedless scream of the new human being which had mysteriously materialized from somewhere.

If Levin had been told before that Kitty was dead, that he had died with her, that their children were angels, and that God was right there in front of them, he would not have been at all surprised; but now, after returning to the world of reality, he had to make a great mental effort to comprehend that she was alive and well, and that the creature wailing so desperately was his son. Kitty was alive and her suffering was over. And he was unspeakably happy. This he understood, and it made him completely happy. But the baby boy? Where had he come from, why, and who was he? . . . He was quite unable to understand or become accustomed to this idea. It seemed somehow excessive to him, an over-abundance to which he took a long time to become accustomed.

16

SOME time after nine o'clock the old Prince, Sergey Ivanovich, and Stepan Arkadyich were sitting with Levin and, having talked about the new mother, chatting about other things. Involuntarily recalling the past during this conversation, what there had been before that morning, Levin was listening to them and also remembering himself, how he had been the previous day before this. It was as if a hundred years had gone by since then. He felt he was on some unattainable summit, from which he had to descend with great care so as not to offend the people he was talking to. As he talked, he thought constantly about his wife, the intricacies of her current condition, and about his son, trying to accustom himself to the idea of his existence. The whole woman's world, which had acquired for him a new, hitherto unknown significance since his marriage, had now risen so high in his estimation that he could not encompass it with his imagination. He listened to a conversation about the dinner at the club the previous evening and thought: 'I wonder what is she doing now, and whether she has fallen asleep? How is she feeling? What is she thinking? Is our son Dmitry crying?' And in the middle of the conversation, he jumped up mid-sentence and headed out of the room.

'Send to let me know if I can go and see her,' said the Prince.

'I will, in just a minute,' answered Levin, and he went straight in to see her without stopping.

She was not asleep, but talking quietly with her mother, making plans for the christening.

Tidied up, her hair brushed, wearing a smart nightcap with something blue in it, and resting her arms on the eiderdown, she was lying on her back, and greeted his look with a look which drew him to her. Her already radiant look became even more radiant as he came up to her. On her face was that same transition from the earthly to the unearthly to be found on the faces of the deceased; but while that was a farewell, this was a greeting. Once again his heart was filled with an anxiety similar to that which he had felt at the moment when she gave birth. She took his hand and asked him if he had slept. He could not answer, and turned away, conscious of his weakness.

'Well, I had a doze, Kostya!' she said to him. 'And I feel so well now.' She looked at him, but suddenly her expression changed.

'Give him to me,' she said, hearing the baby squeal. 'Give him to me, Lizaveta Petrovna, and he can have a look.'

'Well, yes, let Papa have a look,' said Lizaveta Petrovna, lifting up and carrying something red, strange, and quivering. 'Wait, we'll tidy ourselves up first,' and Lizaveta Petrovna laid this quivering red thing on the bed and began unswaddling and swaddling the baby, lifting him up and turning him over with one finger and sprinkling him with something.

As he gazed at this tiny, pathetic creature, Levin tried vainly to find some signs of paternal feeling in his heart. He felt only disgust for it. But when it was undressed and he caught a glimpse of tiny, tiny little arms and saffron-coloured little legs, complete with fingers and toes, and even a big toe different from the rest, and when he saw Lizaveta Petrovna squeeze those little arms as if they were soft little springs and enclose them in linen garments, he was overcome with such pity for this creature, and such fear that she would hurt it, that he took hold of her arm.

Lizaveta Petrovna laughed.

'Don't be afraid, don't be afraid!'

When the baby had been tidied up and transformed into a firm doll, Lizaveta Petrovna turned him over, as if proud of her work, and stepped aside so that Levin could see his son in all his glory.

Kitty looked on sideways, unable to take her eyes off him.

'Give him to me, give him to me!' she said, and even tried to sit up.

'Good heavens, Katerina Alexandrovna, you mustn't move around like that! Wait a minute and I'll give him to you. We just have to show Papa what a fine fellow we are!'

And Lizaveta Petrovna lifted up for Levin on one hand (while propping up the wobbling back of its head with just the fingers of the other) this strange, wobbling red creature which had buried its head in the swaddling clothes. But there was also a nose, squinting eyes, and smacking lips.

'A beautiful baby!' said Lizaveta Petrovna.

Levin sighed with dismay. This beautiful baby only inspired feelings of disgust and pity in him. These were not at all the feelings he had expected.

He turned away while Lizaveta Petrovna put the baby to the unaccustomed breast.

Laughter suddenly made him lift his head. It was Kitty laughing. The baby had taken the breast.

'Now, now, that's enough!' said Lizaveta Petrovna, but Kitty would not let him go. He fell asleep in her arms.

'Look now,' said Kitty, turning the baby towards him so that he could see it. The wizened little face suddenly wrinkled up even more, and the baby sneezed.

Smiling and barely able to hold back tears of tenderness, Levin kissed his wife and went out of the dark room.

What he felt for this little creature was not at all what he had expected. There was nothing jubilant or happy about this feeling; on the contrary, it was an agonizing new fear. It was the consciousness of a new area of vulnerability. And this consciousness was indeed so agonizing at first, and the fear that this helpless creature might suffer so intense, that he failed to notice the strange feeling of absurd joy and even pride he experienced when the baby sneezed.

17

STEPAN ARKADYICH'S affairs were in a bad way.

Two-thirds of the money for the wood had already been spent and, with a ten-per-cent deduction, he had obtained almost all of the remaining third from the merchant in advance. The merchant would not give any more money, particularly since Darya Alexandrovna had refused to sign the contract acknowledging receipt of the last third of the money for the wood, having for the first time directly asserted the rights to her assets that winter. All his salary went on household expenses and the settlement of urgent small debts. He had no money at all.

This was an unpleasant, awkward situation which in Stepan Arkadyich's opinion ought not to continue. The reason for it, in his estimation, was that his salary was too small. The post he occupied had obviously been very good five years ago, but it certainly was not now. Petrov, the bank director, received twelve thousand a year; Sventitsky, a company director, got seventeen thousand; Mitin, who had founded a bank, got fifty thousand. 'I've obviously been half-asleep, and they've forgotten about me,' Stepan Arkadyich thought about himself. So he began keeping his ear to the ground and his eyes open, and by the end of winter had scouted out a very good position and launched his assault on it, first from Moscow through aunts, uncles, and friends, and then in the spring, when the matter was suitably advanced, he went to Petersburg himself. It was one of those positions whose number now exceeded the previous cosy positions obtained through bribery at every level of the scale, from one thousand to fifty thousand roubles a year; it was the post of Member of the Commission of the United Agency of the Mutual Credit Balance of the Southern Railways and Banking Offices. Like all such positions, this position called for immense expertise and experience, which were difficult to find combined in one person. And since there was no one person who combined both these qualities, it was at least better that the position be filled by an honest rather than a dishonest man. And Stepan Arkadyich was not only a man who was honest (no emphasis intended), but he was also an *honest* man (emphasis intended), in the sense of the special meaning attached to this word in Moscow when they say: an *honest* politician, an *honest* writer, an *honest* journal, an *honest* institution, or an *honest* current of thought, and which not only implies that the man or the institution is not dishonest, but that they are capable of needling the government on occasion. Stepan Arkadyich moved in those Moscow circles where this word had been introduced, was regarded there as an *honest* man, and therefore had a greater claim to this position than others.

This position paid between seven and ten thousand a year, and Oblonsky could hold it without resigning his government position. It depended on two ministers, one lady, and two Jews; and Stepan Arkadyich needed to see all these people in Petersburg, even though they had already been primed. Stepan Arkadyich had promised his sister Anna, moreover, that he would obtain a definitive answer about the divorce from Karenin. After coaxing fifty roubles from Dolly, he left for Petersburg.

As he sat in Karenin's study listening to the draft of his paper on the causes of the poor state of Russian finances, Stepan Arkadyich could not wait for him to finish so he could start talking about his own business and about Anna.

'Yes, that's very true,' he said, when Alexey Alexandrovich took off the pince-nez without which he now was unable to read and looked enquiringly at his former brother-in-law, 'that's very true when it comes to the detail, but the principle of our day is nonetheless freedom.'

'Yes, but I am setting out another principle which embraces the principle of freedom,' said Alexey Alexandrovich, emphasizing the word 'embraces' and putting on his pince-nez again in order to reread to him the passage in which this very thing was spelled out.

And after sorting through the beautifully written manuscript with its huge margins, Alexey Alexandrovich once again read the cogent passage.

'I do not want a protective mechanism for the benefit of private individuals, but for the common good, and for the lower and upper classes equally,' he said, looking at Oblonsky over the top of his pince-nez. 'But *they* cannot understand that, because *they* are only concerned with personal interests and are carried away by verbiage.'

Stepan Arkadyich knew that whenever Karenin started talking about what *they* were doing and thinking—those same people who did not want to implement his proposals and were the cause of all the evil in Russia—then the end was not far off; so he now willingly relinquished the principle of freedom and heartily agreed. Alexey Alexandrovich fell silent as he leafed through his manuscript.

'Oh, by the way,' said Stepan Arkadyich, 'I wanted to ask if you could mention to Pomorsky, the next time you see him, that I would very much like to get the vacant position of Member of the Commission of the United Agency of the Mutual Credit Balance of the Southern Railways and Banking Offices.'

By now Stepan Arkadyich was familiar with the title of this position which was so close to his heart, and he rattled it off without error.

Alexey Alexandrovich enquired about the activities of this new commission, and paused to consider. He was trying to work out whether there was anything in the activities of this new commission that would run counter to his proposals. But since the activities of this new commission were very complex, and his proposals encompassed a very large area, he could not immediately work this out and, taking off his pince-nez, he said:

'I can certainly mention it to him; but why do you actually want this position?'

'It's a good salary, up to nine thousand, and my means . . .'

'Nine thousand,' repeated Alexey Alexandrovich, and he frowned. The high figure of this salary reminded him that, in this respect, Stepan Arkadyich's proposed activities were at variance with the main purpose of his proposals, which always tended towards economy.

'I find—and I have written a memorandum about this—that now-adays these huge salaries are a symptom of the unsound economic *assiette*[1] of our administration.'

'But what do you expect?' said Stepan Arkadyich. 'The director of

---

[1] 'policy'.

a bank, say, gets ten thousand—he's worth it, after all. Or an engineer gets twenty thousand. It's a lively business, whatever you say!'

'I consider that a salary is payment for a commodity, and should be subject to the law of supply and demand. If the fixing of salaries contravenes this law, however, as, for instance, when I see two engineers graduating from the institute, both equally knowledgeable and capable, and one gets forty thousand while the other is happy with two thousand; or when lawyers and hussars are appointed without any particular qualifications as directors of banks, with enormous salaries, I conclude that salaries are not being fixed in accordance with the law of supply and demand, but through blatant personal interest. And this is an abuse, serious in itself, with a detrimental impact on government service. I consider . . .'

Stepan Arkadyich hurried to interrupt his brother-in-law.

'Yes, but you must agree that this is a new and undoubtedly useful institution which is being set up. Whatever you say, it's a lively business! They are making a particular point of conducting their business in an *honest* way,' said Stepan Arkadyich with emphasis.

But the Moscow meaning of the word *honest* was lost on Alexey Alexandrovich.

'Honesty is only a negative quality,' he said.

'But you'll be doing me a great favour anyway,' said Stepan Arkadyich, 'by putting in a word with Pomorsky. And, while we are talking. . . .'

'But you know, I think it depends more on Bolgarinov,*' said Alexey Alexandrovich.

'Bolgarinov is in complete agreement, for his part,' said Stepan Arkadyich, going red.

Stepan Arkadyich went red at the mention of Bolgarinov, because he had been to see the Jew Bolgarinov that morning, and the visit had left him with unpleasant memories. Stepan Arkadyich knew full well that the business to which he wanted to devote himself was a new, lively, and honest business; but that morning, when Bolgarinov, with clear intent, had made him wait for two hours with the other petitioners in his waiting room, he had suddenly started to feel uncomfortable.

Whether he was uncomfortable that he, Prince Oblonsky, a descendant of Ryurik, had to wait for two hours in a Jew's waiting room, or that for the first time in his life he was not following the example of his ancestors and serving the government but was embarking on a new career, he certainly did feel very uncomfortable. During those two

hours in which he sat waiting for Bolgarinov, Stepan Arkadyich carefully concealed from others and even himself what he was feeling by
pacing nonchalantly about the waiting room, smoothing his whiskers,
entering into conversation with the other petitioners, and thinking up
a pun about having *wait-yid* to see a yid.*

But all this time he felt uncomfortable and aggravated, without
knowing why: either it was because he was not happy with his pun—
'I had some business with a yid and I *wait-yid* to see him'—or for some
other reason. When Bolgarinov finally received him with excessive
courtesy, clearly gloating over his humiliation, and then almost refused
him, Stepan Arkadyich was anxious to forget it as quickly as possible.
And he now blushed at the mere recollection.

18

'Now there is something else I want to talk about, and you know what
it is. It's about Anna,' Stepan Arkadyich said, having paused briefly
and shaken off the unpleasant impression.

As soon as Oblonsky uttered Anna's name, Alexey Alexandrovich's
face completely changed; it showed weariness and lethargy in place of
its previous vigour.

'What exactly do you want from me?' he said, swivelling round in
his chair and clicking his pince-nez shut.

'A decision, Alexey Alexandrovich, some sort of decision. I'm
appealing to you now'—'not as an injured husband,' Stepan Arkadyich
was going to say, but fearing this would ruin his prospects, he changed
the words to: 'not as a statesman' (which sounded inappropriate), 'but
simply as a man, a good man and a Christian. You must have pity on
her,' he said.

'But for what exactly?' Karenin said quietly.

'Yes, have pity on her. If you had seen her as I have—I have spent
the whole winter with her—you would take pity on her. Her situation
is terrible, absolutely terrible!'

'I was under the impression', answered Alexey Alexandrovich in
a more high-pitched, almost shrill, voice, 'that Anna Arkadyevna has
everything that she herself wanted.'

'Oh, Alexey Alexandrovich, for heaven's sake, let's not have recrim-
inations! What is done is done, and you know what she wants and is
waiting for—a divorce.'

'But it was my understanding that Anna Arkadyevna declined a divorce if I stipulated that she leave our son with me. That is how I responded, and I thought the matter was closed. I consider it closed,' shrieked Alexey Alexandrovich.

'But for heaven's sake, let's not get hot under the collar,' said Stepan Arkadyich, touching his brother-in-law's knee. 'The matter is not closed. If you will allow me to recapitulate, this is how things stood: when you parted, you were as magnanimous as anyone could possibly be; you were ready to give her everything—freedom, a divorce even. She valued this. No, don't think otherwise. She truly did. To such a degree that, feeling her guilt before you in those first moments, she did not and could not think everything through. She renounced everything. But reality and time have shown that her position is agonizing and impossible.'

'Anna Arkadyevna's life can be of no interest to me,' Alexey Alexandrovich interrupted, raising his eyebrows.

'Allow me not to believe that,' Stepan Arkadyich replied gently. 'Her position is agonizing for her and of no benefit to anyone at all. She has deserved it, you will say. She knows that and is not asking you for anything; she says outright that she does not dare ask you for anything. But I, all of us relatives, everyone who loves her, are asking and imploring you. What is the point of her suffering? Who gains from it?'

'Excuse me, but you seem to be putting me in the position of the guilty party,' observed Alexey Alexandrovich.

'Oh no, no, not at all, you have to understand me,' said Stepan Arkadyich, touching his arm again, as if convinced that this contact would soften his brother-in-law. 'All I am saying is that her position is agonizing, and can be eased by you, and you won't forfeit anything. I will arrange it all for you so that you won't even notice. You did promise, after all.'

'The promise was given before. And I assumed the issue over my son settled the matter. Apart from that, I was hoping Anna Arkadyevna would find the magnanimity . . .' Alexey Alexandrovich pronounced with difficulty, his lips trembling and his face pale.

'She leaves everything to your magnanimity. She is asking, begging, for only one thing—to be extricated from the impossible position she finds herself in. She is no longer asking for her son. Alexey Alexandrovich, you are a good man. Put yourself in her position for a moment. The question of divorce for her is a question of life and death in her position. If you had not promised before, she would have reconciled herself to her position and lived in the country. But you did promise, she wrote to you and moved to Moscow. And for six months now she has been living in Moscow, where every meeting is like a knife in the heart for her, expecting a decision every day. It's just like keeping a condemned man with a noose around his neck for months on end, promising maybe death, maybe a reprieve. Take pity on her, and then I'll undertake to arrange everything . . . *Vos scrupules* . . .'[1]

'I am not talking about that, about that . . .' Alexey Alexandrovich interrupted in a disgusted tone. 'But perhaps I promised what I did not have the right to promise.'

'So are you refusing to do what you promised?'

'I have never refused to do what was possible, but I wish to have time to consider how far what I promised is possible.'

'No, Alexey Alexandrovich!' Oblonsky exclaimed, jumping up, 'I won't believe that! She's as unhappy as a woman can be, and you cannot refuse in such . . .'

'How far what I promised is possible. *Vous professez d'être libre penseur.*[2] But as a man of faith I cannot act against Christian law in such an important matter.'

'But in Christian societies and in ours too, as far as I know, divorce is permitted,' said Stepan Arkadyich. 'Divorce is also permitted by our Church. And we see . . .'

'It is permitted, but not in this sense.'

'Alexey Alexandrovich, I do not recognize you,' said Oblonsky after a pause. 'Was it not you (and did we not appreciate it?) who forgave everything and, motivated precisely by Christian sentiment, were ready to sacrifice everything? You said yourself: give your coat away when they take your shirt, and now . . .'

'I must ask you,' said the ashen-faced Alexey Alexandrovich in a shrill voice, with his jaw trembling, as he suddenly got to his feet, 'I must ask you to stop, stop . . . this conversation.'

'Oh no! Well, forgive me, please forgive me if I have upset you,' said Stepan Arkadyich, holding out his hand with an embarrassed smile, 'anyway, I was simply delivering my message, as an envoy.'

Alexey Alexandrovich proffered his hand, thought for a while, and said:

'I must think it over and seek guidance. I will give you a final answer the day after tomorrow,' he added, having considered something.

---

[1] 'Your scruples . . .'   [2] 'You profess to be a freethinker.'

19

STEPAN ARKADYICH was on the verge of leaving when Korney came in to announce:

'Sergey Alexeyich!'

'Who is this Sergey Alexeyich?' Stepan Arkadyich was about to ask, but immediately remembered.

'Ah, Seryozha!' he said. 'I thought "Sergey Alexeyich" was the director of some department.' 'Anna also asked me to see him,' he recalled.

And he recalled the timid, pitiful expression with which Anna had said while seeing him off: 'Anyway, make sure you see him. Find out all you can about where he is, who is with him. And Stiva . . . if it might be possible! It might be possible, mightn't it?' Stepan Arkadyich understood what that 'if it might be possible' meant—if it might be possible to arrange the divorce so that she could be given her son . . . Stepan Arkadyich saw there was no point even thinking about that now, but he was nevertheless glad to see his nephew.

Alexey Alexandrovich reminded his brother-in-law that they never spoke to the boy about his mother, and asked him not to say a word about her.

'He was very ill after that meeting with his mother which we had not *an-ti-ci-pated*,' said Alexey Alexandrovich. 'We even feared for his life. But sensible treatment and sea-bathing in the summer have restored his health, and on the doctor's advice I have now sent him to school. The influence of his classmates has indeed had a good effect on him, and he is completely well and making good progress with his schoolwork.'

'What a fine fellow he has become! And no Seryozha indeed, but the fully fledged Sergey Alexeyich!' said Stepan Arkadyich with a smile as he looked at the handsome, broad-shouldered boy in a blue jacket and long trousers sauntering in breezily. The boy had a healthy and cheerful appearance. He bowed to his uncle as if to a stranger, but blushed when he recognized him and, as if offended and angered by something, hurriedly turned away from him. The boy went up to his father and handed him his school report.

'Well, this is respectable,' said his father, 'you can go.'

'He's grown thinner and taller, and has stopped being a child and become a proper boy; I like that,' said Stepan Arkadyich. 'So do you remember me?'

The boy looked round to his father.

'I do, *mon oncle*,' he answered, glancing at his uncle before lowering his eyes again.

His uncle called him over and took his hand.

'Well, how are things?' he said, wanting to get into conversation and not knowing what to say.

Blushing and not answering, the boy cautiously started withdrawing his hand from his uncle's grasp. As soon as Stepan Arkadyich let go of his hand, he cast a questioning glance at his father and swiftly left the room like a bird set free.

A year had passed since the last time Seryozha had seen his mother. Since then he had not heard anything more about her. And during that year he had been sent to school and had got to know and become fond of his classmates. The dreams and memories of his mother that had made him ill after he had seen her no longer bothered him. Whenever they loomed, he studiously drove them away, regarding them as shameful and befitting only girls, not a boy and the friend of his classmates. He knew there had been a quarrel between his father and mother which had separated them, knew he was destined to remain with his father, and had been trying to accustom himself to this idea.

Seeing his uncle, who was like his mother, was unpleasant for him because it awakened in him the very memories he regarded as shameful. What made it all the more unpleasant for him was that, to judge from certain words he overheard while he was waiting by the study door, and in particular the expressions on the faces of his father and uncle, he guessed they must have been talking about his mother. And in order not to find fault with his father, with whom he lived and on whom he depended, and, above all, not to succumb to the sentimentality he considered so humiliating, Seryozha tried not to look at this uncle who had come to disturb his peace of mind, nor to think about the memories he prompted.

But when Stepan Arkadyich saw him on the stairs after following him out, he beckoned him over and asked how he spent his time at school between classes, and Seryozha became talkative out of his father's presence.

'We have got a railway-line going at the moment,' he said in answer to his question. 'It's like this, you see: two of us sit down on a bench. They're the passengers. And one person stands up on the bench. And then everyone links up. You can do that either with arms or with belts, and then you go through all the rooms. The doors are opened in advance. Well, it's very hard being the guard!'

'He's the one standing up?' Stepan Arkadyich asked with a smile.

'Yes, you need courage and skill, especially when there is a sudden stop, or someone falls off.'

'Yes, it's a serious business,' said Stepan Arkadyich, looking wistfully into those eager eyes, so like his mother's, which now were no longer childlike, no longer completely innocent. And although he had promised Alexey Alexandrovich not to talk about Anna, he could not restrain himself.

'So do you remember your mother?' he asked suddenly.

'No, I don't,' Seryozha said quickly and, blushing crimson, he lowered his gaze. And his uncle could get nothing more out of him.

The Slav tutor found his pupil on the stairs half an hour later, and for a long time could not make out whether he was in a temper or crying.

'You must have hurt yourself when you fell down, I suppose?' said the tutor. 'I told you it was a dangerous game. And the headmaster must be told.'

'Even if I did hurt myself, nobody would have noticed. That's for sure.'

'Well, what is the matter, then?'

'Leave me alone! Maybe I remember, maybe I don't . . . What's it got to do with him? Why do I have to remember? Leave me alone!' he said, no longer addressing his tutor, but the whole world.

20

STEPAN ARKADYICH, as always, did not spend his time in Petersburg idly. Apart from tending to the business of his sister's divorce and the position, in Petersburg he needed, as always, to freshen up, as he put it, after the fustiness of Moscow.

Despite its *cafés chantants** and omnibuses, Moscow was still a stagnant backwater. Stepan Arkadyich always felt that. After living for a while in Moscow, particularly cooped up with his family, he would feel his spirits beginning to flag. When he lived in Moscow for long, uninterrupted stretches, he would reach a point where he would begin worrying about his wife's ill-humour and reproaches, the health and education of his children, and the petty concerns of his job; even the fact that he was in debt worried him. But he only had to come to Petersburg and spend some time in the company of the circle in which he moved, where people lived, truly lived, rather than vegetating like they did in Moscow, and immediately all those thoughts would vanish and melt away like wax before the fire.*

Wife? . . . Only that day he had been talking to Prince Chechensky. Prince Chechensky had a wife and family, with grown-up children in the Corps of Pages, and he had another, illegitimate family in which he also had children. Although there was nothing wrong with his first family, Prince Chechensky felt happier with his second family. He was in the habit of taking his eldest son along to visit his second family, and told Stepan Arkadyich that he considered it beneficial and edifying for his son. What would they say about that in Moscow?

Children? In Petersburg children did not stop their fathers from living. Children were brought up in institutions, and no one believed in the ludicrous idea circulating in Moscow—by Lvov, for example—that children should have all the luxuries of life, while parents should just have hard work and worry. They understood here that a person had to live for himself, as indeed every educated person should.

Work? Work here was also not the gruelling, unrewarding drudgery it was in Moscow; people were interested in their work here. A meeting, a favour, a well-judged remark, an ability to mimic others—and in a flash a person could make a career, like Bryantsev, whom Stepan Arkadyich had met the day before, and who was now a top-ranking official. This work was of interest.

But it was the Petersburg attitude to financial matters that had a particularly calming effect on Stepan Arkadyich. Bartnyansky, who had to be spending at least fifty thousand a year to judge from the kind of life he led, had said something remarkable to him on that score the day before.

While they were in conversation before dinner, Stepan Arkadyich had said to Bartnyansky:

'I believe you're on close terms with Mordvinsky; you can do me a favour by kindly putting in a good word for me with him. There's a position I should like to get. Member of the Agency . . .'

'Well, I won't remember that anyway . . . Only what makes you want to get involved in those railway businesses with yids? . . . It's abominable, whatever you might say!'

Stepan Arkadyich did not tell him it was a lively business; Bartnyansky would not have understood that.

'Need the money, I've got nothing to live on.'

'You are managing to live though?'

'Yes, but I have debts.'

'Really? A lot?' said Bartnyansky sympathetically.

'Massive, about twenty thousand's worth.'

Bartnyansky burst out into gleeful laughter.

'Lucky you!' he said. 'Mine are a million and a half, and I don't have anything, but as you see, one can still live!'

And Stepan Arkadyich saw how true this was, not just on paper but in practice. Zhivakhov had debts of three hundred thousand and not a penny to his name, yet he managed to live, and in some style! People had given up on Count Krivtsov a long time ago, yet he kept two mistresses. Petrovsky had squandered five million, yet carried on living in just the same way, indeed he even ran a finance department and drew a salary of twenty thousand. But apart from this, Petersburg had a beneficial physical effect on Stepan Arkadyich. It made him younger. In Moscow he would sometimes notice grey hairs, doze off after lunch, stretch, go upstairs one step at a time, breathing heavily, grow bored in the company of young women, and not dance at balls. In Petersburg, however, he always felt he had shed ten years.

His experience in Petersburg was exactly what the sixty-year-old Prince Pyotr Oblonsky, who had just returned from abroad, had described to him the previous day.

'We don't know how to live here,' said Pyotr Oblonsky. 'Can you believe it, I spent the summer in Baden, and, well, I felt like a completely young man, I really did. I'd see a nice young woman, and start having ideas . . . You have dinner and a few drinks, and your strength and energy come back. Then I came back to Russia—I had to go and see my wife, and in the country too—well, you wouldn't believe it, after a fortnight I had put on my dressing-gown and stopped dressing for dinner. As for thinking about nice young women! I became a complete old man. There was nothing left for me to do but save my soul. Then I went off to Paris, and that put me to rights again.'

Stepan Arkadyich experienced exactly the same difference as Pyotr Oblonsky. He went into such decline in Moscow that if he were to live there long, for all one knew it might indeed come to saving his soul; in Petersburg, however, he felt like a respectable man again.

Between Princess Betsy Tverskaya and Stepan Arkadyich there had long been extremely strange relations. Stepan Arkadyich always paid court to her in jest and said the most indecent things to her, also in jest, knowing there was nothing she liked more. When he went to visit her the day after his conversation with Karenin, Stepan Arkadyich felt so young he inadvertently went too far with this mock courtship and prattle, to the point that he was at a loss to know how to beat a retreat, since he unfortunately not only did not find her attractive, but actually repellent. This manner had become established because she was very attracted to him. So he was very gratified by the arrival of Princess Myagkaya, who promptly brought their tête-à-tête to an end.

'Ah, you're here too,' said she when she saw him. 'Well, how is your poor sister? Now don't you look at me like that,' she added. 'Ever since everyone turned on her, all those people who are a hundred thousand times worse than she is, I have felt she has behaved magnificently. I cannot forgive Vronsky for not letting me know when she was in Petersburg. I would have gone to see her and gone everywhere with her. Please send her my love. So come, do tell me about her.'

'Well, her situation is very difficult, she . . .' Stepan Arkadyich began, in his ingenuous way taking Princess Myagkaya's words 'tell me about your sister' for genuine currency. Princess Myagkaya immediately interrupted him according to her usual habit, however, and began talking herself.

'She has done what everyone except me does, although behind closed doors; but she did not want to behave deceitfully and acted magnificently. And she did even better because she left that half-witted brother-in-law of yours. You must excuse me. Everybody used to say how frightfully clever he was, and I was the only one who said he was stupid. Now that he is associating with Lydia and Landau, everyone says he is half-witted, and I would be happy not to agree with everybody, but on this occasion I can't.'

'But please could you explain', said Stepan Arkadyich, 'what this all means? I went to see him yesterday about my sister's business and asked for a final answer. He didn't give me an answer and said he would think about it, but this morning, instead of an answer, I received an invitation for this evening from Countess Lydia Ivanovna.'

'Well, of course, of course!' said Princess Myagkaya gleefully. 'They're going to ask Landau and see what he says.'

'What do you mean, ask Landau? Why? Who is Landau?'*

'You mean you don't know Jules Landau, *le fameux Jules Landau*, *le clairvoyant?*[1] He's also half-witted, but your sister's fate depends on him. That's what comes of living in the provinces, you don't know anything. Landau was a *commis*[2] in a shop in Paris, you see, and he went to see a doctor. He fell asleep in the doctor's waiting room, and while he was asleep he began giving advice to all the patients. And it was remarkable advice. Then the wife of Yury Meledinsky—you know, the one who is ill?—heard about this Landau, and took him to see her husband. He is treating her husband now. And he hasn't done him

---

[1] 'the famous Jules Landau, the clairvoyant?'   [2] 'clerk'.

any good, as far as I can see, because he's just as feeble as before, but they believe in him and take him everywhere. And they've brought him to Russia. He's been besieged by everyone here, and he has started treating everybody. He cured Countess Bezzubova, and she became so attached to him that she has adopted him.'

'What do you mean, adopted him?'

'Exactly that. He's now no longer Landau, but Count Bezzubov.* Anyway, that is beside the point, as Lydia—I'm very fond of her, but her head is not screwed on properly—has naturally pounced on this Landau now, and neither she nor Alexey Alexandrovich can make any decisions without him, so your sister's fate is now in the hands of this Landau, otherwise known as Count Bezzubov.'

21

AFTER a splendid dinner and a large quantity of cognac drunk at Bartnyansky's, Stepan Arkadyich arrived at Countess Lydia Ivanovna's only a little after the appointed time.

'Who else is with the Countess? The Frenchman?' Stepan Arkadyich asked the hall-porter as he observed Alexey Alexandrovich's familiar overcoat and a strange kind of homespun overcoat with clasps.

'Alexey Alexandrovich Karenin and Count Bezzubov,' the porter answered dourly.

'Princess Myagkaya's hunch was correct,' thought Stepan Arkadyich as he went upstairs. 'Strange! It would be good to be on friendly terms with her, though. She has immense influence. If she could put in a word with Pomorsky, I'd have it in the bag.'

It was still completely light outside, but the lamps had already been lit in Countess Lydia Ivanovna's little drawing room with the lowered blinds. The Countess and Alexey Alexandrovich were seated at a round table under a lamp, talking about something. At the other end of the room, examining the portraits on the wall, was a short, skinny man with feminine hips who was knock-kneed, very pale, handsome, with beautiful shining eyes and long hair falling over the collar of his frock-coat. After greeting his hostess and Alexey Alexandrovich, Stepan Arkadyich could not help casting another glance at the stranger.

'*Monsieur Landau!*' said the Countess, addressing him with a gentleness and circumspection that astonished Oblonsky. And she introduced them.

Landau hurriedly looked round, walked over, smiled as he placed his clammy, inert hand into Stepan Arkadyich's outstretched hand, then immediately walked off again to go and look at the portraits. The Countess and Alexey Alexandrovich exchanged knowing looks.

'I am very glad to see you, especially today,' said Countess Lydia Ivanovna, ushering Stepan Arkadyich to a seat next to Karenin.

'I introduced you to him as Landau,' she said quietly, glancing at the Frenchman then immediately at Alexey Alexandrovich, 'but he is really Count Bezzubov, as you probably know. Only he does not like that title.'

'Yes, I have heard,' replied Stepan Arkadyich. 'They say he completely cured Countess Bezzubova.'

'She was here today, poor thing!' the Countess said, turning to Alexey Alexandrovich. 'This separation is dreadful for her. For her it's such a blow!'

'And he is definitely going?' asked Alexey Alexandrovich.

'Yes, he's going to Paris. He heard a voice yesterday,' said Countess Lydia Ivanovna, looking at Stepan Arkadyich.

'Ah, a voice!' repeated Oblonsky, feeling it was vital to be as cautious as possible in this company, where something special, to which he had not yet found the key, was either taking place or about to take place.

A moment's silence ensued, after which Countess Lydia Ivanovna said with a thin smile to Oblonsky, as if she was now broaching the main topic of conversation:

'I've known you for a long time and I'm very glad of the opportunity to get to know you better. *Les amis de nos amis sont nos amis.*[1] But one needs to gain insight into a friend's spiritual state in order to be a friend, and I fear you are not doing that with relation to Alexey Alexandrovich. You understand what I mean,' she said, lifting her lovely dreamy eyes.

'I do partly understand, Countess, that Alexey Alexandrovich's situation . . .' said Oblonsky, not fully understanding what this was about, and therefore wishing to stick to generalities.

'The change is not in his external situation,' Countess Lydia Ivanovna said sternly, while following Alexey Alexandrovich with a besotted gaze as he got up and went over to Landau. 'His heart has changed, he has been given a new heart, and I fear you haven't completely acquired insight into this change that has taken place in him.'

'Well, I can imagine this change in general terms. We have always been friendly, and now . . .' said Stepan Arkadyich, responding to the Countess's look with a tender look as he tried to determine to which of

---

[1] 'The friends of our friends are our friends too.'

the two ministers she was closest, in order to know which of the two he would have to ask her to intercede with on his behalf.

'The change which has taken place in him cannot weaken the love he feels for his neighbour; on the contrary, the change which has taken place in him ought to increase his love. But I fear you do not understand me. Won't you have some tea?' she said, her eyes indicating a footman who was serving tea on a tray.

'Not quite, Countess. Of course, his misfortune . . .'

'Yes, a misfortune which became an event of the greatest fortune, when his heart became new and was filled with Him,' she said, looking ardently at Stepan Arkadyich.

'I suppose I could ask her to put in a word with both of them,' thought Stepan Arkadyich.

'Oh, of course, Countess,' he said, 'but these changes are so intimate that I cannot imagine anyone, not even one's closest friend, wanting to talk about them.'

'On the contrary! We must talk and help one another.'

'Yes, undoubtedly, but there tends to be such a difference between people's convictions, and then . . .' said Oblonsky with a gentle smile.

'There can be no difference in the matter of sacred truth.'

'Oh yes, of course, but . . .' and Stepan Arkadyich clammed up in embarrassment. He had grasped that they were talking about religion.

'I think he is about to fall asleep,' said Alexey Alexandrovich in a significant whisper as he came up to Lydia Ivanovna.

Stepan Arkadyich looked round. Landau was sitting by the window, leaning against the arm and back of an armchair, his head drooping. When he became conscious of being looked at, he raised his head and smiled a childishly naive smile.

'Don't pay any attention,' said Lydia Ivanovna, and with a nimble movement she drew up a chair for Alexey Alexandrovich. 'I have noticed . . .' she started saying, when a footman entered the room with a letter. Lydia Ivanovna ran her eye swiftly over the note, excused herself, wrote and handed over a reply with extraordinary rapidity, then returned to the table. 'I have noticed,' she said, resuming the sentence she had begun, 'that Muscovites, particularly the men, are supremely indifferent to religion.'

'Oh, no, Countess, I think Muscovites have a reputation for being the most devout,' answered Stepan Arkadyich.

'But as far as I can make out, you are unfortunately one of those who are indifferent,' said Alexey Alexandrovich, turning to him with a weary smile.

'How can one be indifferent!' said Lydia Ivanovna.

'I am not so much indifferent in this respect as in a state of anticipation,' said Stepan Arkadyich, with his most conciliatory smile. 'I don't think the time for these questions has come for me yet.'

Alexey Alexandrovich and Lydia Ivanovna exchanged glances.

'We can never know whether the time has come for us or not,' said Alexey Alexandrovich sternly. 'We should not be thinking about whether we are ready or not: grace is not guided by human considerations; sometimes it does not descend on those who are diligent, but does descend on those who are unprepared, like Saul.'*

'No, I don't think it is going to happen quite yet,' said Lydia Ivanovna, who had meanwhile been watching the Frenchman's movements.

Landau got up and came over to them.

'Will you allow me to listen?' he asked.

'Yes, by all means, I did not want to disturb you,' said Lydia Ivanovna, gazing at him tenderly; 'sit down here with us.'

'In order not to deprive oneself of the light one need only keep one's eyes open,' Alexey Alexandrovich continued.

'Ah, if you knew the happiness we experience by feeling His constant presence in our souls!' said Countess Lydia Ivanovna with a beatific smile.

'But a person may sometimes feel incapable of rising to this height,' said Stepan Arkadyich, conscious of being hypocritical in acknowledging a religious height, but at the same time unable to risk confessing his freethinking views to an individual who, with a single word to Pomorsky, could procure him the position he coveted.

'You mean, in other words, that sin holds him back?' said Lydia Ivanovna. 'But that view is wrong. There is no sin for believers, as sin has already been redeemed. *Pardon*,' she added, looking at the footman, who had come in again with another note. She read it and gave a verbal answer: 'Tomorrow at the Grand Duchess's, please say. For a believer there is no sin,' she said, continuing the conversation.

'Yes, but faith without works is dead,'* said Stepan Arkadyich, recalling this phrase from the catechism, and maintaining his independence now solely with a smile.

'There you are, from the Epistle of St James,' said Alexey Alexandrovich, turning to Lydia Ivanovna with a degree of reproach, this obviously being a subject they had already discussed on frequent occasions. 'So much harm has been done by the false interpretation of this passage! Nothing turns people away from faith so much as this interpretation. "I have no works, so I cannot have faith," while that is not said anywhere. What is said is just the opposite.'

'Doing good works for God, saving one's soul by fasting,' said Countess Lydia Ivanovna with fastidious disdain, 'these are the outlandish ideas of our monks . . . When that is not said anywhere. It is much simpler and easier than that,' she added, looking at Oblonsky with the same encouraging smile with which at court she encouraged young Ladies-in-Waiting flustered by their new surroundings.

'We are saved by Christ who suffered for us. We are saved by faith,' said Alexey Alexandrovich, confirming her words with an approving look.

'*Vous comprenez l'anglais?*'[1] asked Lydia Ivanovna and, receiving an affirmative answer, she got up and began looking through the books on a shelf.

'I want to read you *Safe and Happy*, or should it be *Under the Wing*?'[2]* she said, looking enquiringly at Karenin. And after finding the book and sitting back down again, she opened it. 'It's very short. It describes the path to acquiring faith, and the happiness above all earthly things that fills the soul when that happens. A person who has faith cannot be unhappy, because he is not alone. Well, you'll see.' She was just about to start reading when the footman came in again. 'Madame Borozdina? Tomorrow at two o'clock, please say. Yes,' she said, marking the place in the book with a finger, sighing, and staring straight ahead with her beautiful dreamy eyes. 'This is how true faith works. You know Marie Sanina? You know about her misfortune? She lost her only child. She was in despair. Well, what do you think happened? She found this friend, and now she thanks God for the death of her child. This is the happiness that faith provides!'

'Oh yes, it is very . . .' said Stepan Arkadyich, pleased they were going to read and give him the chance to collect himself. 'No, it would clearly be better not to ask her about anything today,' he thought, 'as I will have my work cut out getting out of here without making a mess of things.'

'It will be boring for you,' said Countess Lydia Ivanovna, turning to Landau, 'as you don't know English, but it's short.'

'Oh, I'll understand,' said Landau with the same smile, and he closed his eyes.

Alexey Alexandrovich and Lydia Ivanovna exchanged meaningful glances, and the reading began.

---

[1] 'Do you understand English?'   [2] [Titles in English in the original.]

22

STEPAN ARKADYICH felt completely perplexed by the strange new discourses he heard. The sophistication of Petersburg life generally had an invigorating effect on him, drawing him out of his Moscow lethargy; but he only liked and understood this sophistication in the spheres he knew well or was familiar with; in this alien environment, on the other hand, he felt perplexed and dumbfounded, and unable to grasp it all. Listening to Countess Lydia Ivanovna and feeling Landau's beautiful, naive or sly—he could not tell—eyes trained on him, Stepan Arkadyich began to feel a particular kind of heaviness in his head.

The most diverse thoughts were jumbled up in his head. 'Marie Sanina is glad her child died . . . Wouldn't mind a smoke now . . . To be saved, one need only have faith, and monks don't know how you should do that, but Countess Lydia Ivanovna does . . . And why does my head feel so heavy? Is it from the cognac or because all this is decidedly odd? I don't think I've done anything improper yet anyway. All the same, it would be out of the question to ask her now. I've heard they make you pray. They had better not try that with me. That would be just too silly. And what nonsense she is reading, but she has good diction. Landau—Bezzubov. Why is he Bezzubov?' Stepan Arkadyich suddenly became aware of his lower jaw beginning inexorably to relax into a yawn. He smoothed his whiskers to cover up the yawn, and shook himself. But the next thing he knew, he felt he was already sleeping and about to snore. He woke up just at the point when Countess Lydia Ivanovna's voice said 'he's asleep'.

Stepan Arkadyich woke up with a start, feeling guilty and exposed. But he was immediately consoled when he saw that the words 'he's asleep' referred not to him, but to Landau. The Frenchman had fallen asleep just like Stepan Arkadyich. But whereas Stepan Arkadyich would have offended them by falling asleep, so he thought (although he found everything so decidedly odd he did not even think that), they were absolutely delighted that Landau was asleep, especially Countess Lydia Ivanovna.

'*Mon ami*,' said Lydia Ivanovna, carefully holding the folds of her silk dress so they would not rustle, and in her excitement calling Karenin '*mon ami*' now rather than Alexey Alexandrovich, '*donnez-lui la main. Vous voyez?*[1] Sshh!' she hissed at the footman who had come in again. 'I'm not at home.'

---

[1] 'give him your hand. Do you see?'

The Frenchman was sleeping, or pretending to be asleep, with his head resting on the back of the armchair, and he was making feeble movements with the clammy hand lying in his lap as if trying to catch something. Alexey Alexandrovich got up and tried to be careful, but bumped into the table as he went over and placed his hand in the Frenchman's. Stepan Arkadyich also got up, and opening his eyes wide in order to rouse himself in case he was asleep, looked from one to the other. This was all really happening. Stepan Arkadyich felt his head getting worse and worse.

'*Que la personne qui est arrivée la dernière, celle qui demande, qu'elle sorte! Qu'elle sorte!*'[1] pronounced the Frenchman without opening his eyes.

'*Vous m'excuserez, mais vous voyez . . . Revenez vers dix heures, encore mieux demain.*'[2]

'*Qu'elle sorte!*'[3] repeated the Frenchman impatiently.

'*C'est moi, n'est-ce pas?*'[4]

And after receiving an answer in the affirmative, and forgetting both the favour he wanted to ask of Lydia Ivanovna, and his sister's business in his overwhelming desire to get away from the place as quickly as possible, Stepan Arkadyich crept out on tiptoe, then ran out into the street as if from a plague-stricken house, and spent a good while chatting and cracking jokes with the cab-driver in order to bring himself round.

At the French Theatre, where he caught the last act, and afterwards over champagne at the Tatar restaurant, Stepan Arkadyich caught his breath a little in surroundings more congenial to him. But he nevertheless did not feel at all himself that evening.

When he arrived back at the house of Pyotr Oblonsky, with whom he was staying, Stepan Arkadyich found a note from Betsy. She wrote that she was very keen to finish the conversation they had started and asked him to call the next day. He scarcely had time to read this note and frown about it when down below he heard the heavy steps of the servants carrying something heavy.

Stepan Arkadyich went out to look. It was the rejuvenated Pyotr Oblonsky. He was so drunk he could not walk up the stairs; but he ordered the servants to stand him on his feet when he saw Stepan

---

[1] 'The person who arrived last, who asks questions, must leave!'
[2] 'You must excuse me, but you can see . . . Come back towards ten o'clock, or better still, tomorrow.'
[3] 'He must leave!'
[4] 'That's me, isn't it?'

Arkadyich, and clinging to him, walked with him to his room, where he started telling him about how he had spent the evening, and instantly fell asleep.

Stepan Arkadyich was in low spirits, which rarely happened to him, and he took a long time to fall sleep. Whatever he recalled, it was all loathsome, but the most loathsome thing of all that he recalled, as if it was something shameful, was the evening at Countess Lydia Ivanovna's.

The following day he received Alexey Alexandrovich's definite refusal to grant Anna a divorce, and realized that this decision was based on what the Frenchman had said in his real or feigned trance the previous evening.

23

UNDERTAKING something in family life requires either outright discord between husband and wife or loving harmony. When marital relations are ill-defined and neither the former nor the latter exists, however, nothing can be undertaken.

Many families remain for years stuck in old ruts which are hateful to both husband and wife, simply because there is neither outright discord nor harmony.

Both Vronsky and Anna found Moscow life unbearable in the heat and dust, with the summer rather than the spring sun shining, all the trees on the boulevards long in leaf, and the leaves already covered with dust; but instead of moving to Vozdvizhenskoye, as had been decided long ago, they went on living in Moscow, which they both found ghastly, because there had been no harmony between them lately.

The aggravation dividing them had no external cause, and all attempts at talking things through had not only failed to eliminate it, but had exacerbated it. It was an inner aggravation, which on her part stemmed from him loving her less, and on his part from his regret at placing himself in a difficult position for her sake, which she was making even more difficult instead of easing. Neither of them had voiced the reason for their sense of aggravation, but each considered the other to be in the wrong, and used every pretext to try and prove it to the other.

For her, the whole of him, all his habits, thoughts, and desires, and his entire emotional and physical temperament consisted of one thing: love for women, and this love, which she felt ought to be concentrated exclusively on her alone, had diminished; according to her reasoning, therefore, he must have transferred part of his love to others or to one other woman—and she was jealous. She was not jealous of any woman in particular, but of the decline in his love. Not yet having an object for her jealousy, she sought one out. At the slightest hint she transferred her jealousy from one object to another. One moment she was jealous of those coarse women with whom he could so easily enter into a liaison thanks to his bachelor connections; the next she was jealous of the society women he might meet; or she was jealous of the imaginary girl he might want to marry after breaking off with her. And this last jealousy tormented her more than anything, particularly because he himself had rashly told her in a moment of frankness that his mother had so little understanding of him that she had taken the liberty of trying to persuade him to marry Princess Sorokina.

And jealousy of him led Anna to resenting him and seeking grounds for her resentment in everything. She blamed him for everything that was difficult about her situation. The agonizing state of suspense between heaven and earth which she had to endure in Moscow, Alexey Alexandrovich's slowness and indecision, her isolation—she put it all down to him. If he had loved her, he would have understood all the difficulty of her situation and extricated her from it. And he was the one to blame for the fact that she was living in Moscow and not in the country. He could not live buried in the country as she would have liked. He needed society, and he had put her in this dreadful situation, the difficulty of which he did not want to understand. And he was likewise to blame for the fact that she was forever separated from her son.

Even those rare moments of tenderness which arose between them did not reassure her: in his tenderness she now saw an element of composure and self-assurance which had not been there before, and which irritated her.

It was already dusk. As she waited on her own for him to return from a bachelor dinner he had gone to, Anna paced up and down in his study (the room in which the noise from the street was least audible) and went over in her mind every detail of what they had said in their quarrel the previous day. By continually going back from the memorably offensive words of their argument to what had provoked them, she eventually reached the beginning of their conversation. It took her a long time to believe that their bickering had begun with such an innocuous conversation about something close to neither of their hearts. But it really was so. It had all begun with his laughing at girls' high schools, which he did not consider to be necessary, while she had defended them. He was disparaging about women's education in general, and said that Hannah, Anna's English protégée, certainly did not need to have any knowledge of physics.

This annoyed Anna. She saw in it a contemptuous allusion to her own activities. And she formulated and uttered a phrase to pay him back for the pain he had caused her.

'I don't expect you to think about me or my feelings, as someone who loved me might, but I did expect some sensitivity,' she said.

And he had in fact flushed with irritation and said something unpleasant. She could not remember how she had replied to him, but just at that point he had said, with the obvious intent of also causing her pain:

'It's true that I have no interest in your partiality for this girl, because I can see it is not natural.'

The cruelty with which he destroyed the world she had taken such pains to construct for herself in order to endure her hard life, and the injustice with which he accused her of being affected and unnatural, infuriated her.

'I am very sorry that you only find coarse and material things comprehensible and natural,' she said and left the room.

When he came to her that evening they did not mention the quarrel, but both felt that the quarrel had been smoothed over but had not been resolved.

Today he had been out all day, and she had felt so lonely and wretched about quarrelling with him that she wanted to forget everything, to forgive and make up with him, she wanted to take the blame and exonerate him.

'It's my own fault. I'm irritable, I'm absurdly jealous. I will make up with him, and we'll leave for the country, I will be calmer there,' she told herself.

'Unnatural.' She suddenly recalled what had hurt her most of all, which was not so much the word as the intention to cause her pain.

'I know what he meant to say; he meant to say that it was unnatural to love someone else's child and not love my own daughter. What does he understand about love for children, about my love for Seryozha, whom I have sacrificed for him? But that desire to hurt me! No, he loves another woman, it can't be otherwise.'

And when she saw that in her desire to calm herself she had again completed the circle she had been round so many times before and had come back to her previous irritation, she was horrified at herself. 'Is it really impossible? Can I really not take it on myself?' she said to herself, and she began again from the beginning. 'He is truthful, he is honest, he loves me. I love him, and any day now the divorce will come through. What more do I need? I need peace and trust, and I will take the blame. Yes, as soon as he arrives now, I will say it was my fault, although it wasn't, and we will go away.'

And in order not to think any more and not to succumb to irritation, she rang and ordered the trunks to be brought in so their things could be packed for the country.

At ten o'clock Vronsky returned.

24

'So, did you enjoy yourself?' she asked as she came out to meet him with a guilty and meek expression on her face.

'The same as usual,' he replied, immediately realizing from one look at her that she was in one of her good moods. He had already grown used to these transitions and was particularly glad of it today, because he was in an extremely good mood himself.

'What do I see! Now that's good!' he said, pointing to the trunks in the hall.

'Yes, we must leave. I went for a drive, and it was so lovely I longed to be in the country. There's nothing to keep you, is there?'

'It's the one thing I want. I'll come in shortly and we'll talk about it, but I just want to go and change. Order some tea.'

And he went into his study.

There was something offensive in the fact that he had said 'Now that's good', as one might address a child who has stopped misbehaving; even more offensive was that contrast between her guilty and his self-confident tone; and for a moment she felt the desire for a fight rising within her; but by making an effort she was able to suppress it and greeted Vronsky as cheerfully as before.

When he came in to her, she told him about her day and about her plans for their departure, partly repeating words she had prepared earlier.

'You know, it came to me almost like an inspiration,' she said. 'Why should we wait here for the divorce? It would be just the same in the country, wouldn't it? I can't wait any longer. I don't want to hope, I don't want to hear anything about the divorce. I have decided it is not going to have any more influence on my life. And do you agree?'

'Oh, yes!' he said, glancing uneasily at her excited face.

'So what did you do there, who came?' she said, after a pause.

Vronsky named the guests.

'The dinner was excellent, and the boat-race and all that was quite pleasant, but in Moscow they can never quite manage without *ridicule*.[1] Some lady or other appeared who was the Queen of Sweden's swimming instructor, and she demonstrated her expertise.'

'What? You mean she swam?' asked Anna with a frown.

'In some absurd red *costume de natation*,[2] she was old and hideous. So when shall we leave?'

'What a stupid idea! So did she swim in some special way?' said Anna, not replying.

'There was absolutely nothing special about it. As I said, it was awfully stupid. So when do you think we should go?'

Anna shook her head as though trying to drive away some unpleasant thought.

'When should we go? Why, the sooner the better. We won't manage it tomorrow. The day after tomorrow.'

'Yes . . . no, wait. The day after tomorrow is Sunday, and I need to go and see *Maman*,' said Vronsky, embarrassed, because as soon as he mentioned his mother he became aware of a suspicious gaze fixed intently on him. His embarrassment confirmed her suspicions. She flushed scarlet and turned away from him. Now it was no longer the Queen of Sweden's swimming instructor whom Anna was imagining, but Princess Sorokina, who was staying with Countess Vronskaya on her estate outside Moscow.

'Can you go tomorrow?' she said.

'No, I can't! The authorization and the money for the business I have there won't have arrived by tomorrow,' he replied.

'In that case, we won't go at all.'

'But why not?'

'I won't go later. It's either Monday or not at all!'

'But why?' said Vronsky, as if surprised. 'That doesn't make any sense!'

'It doesn't make any sense to you, because you don't care about me. You don't want to understand my life. The one thing that has occupied me here has been Hannah. You say it's all pretence. You did, after all, say yesterday that I don't love my daughter but that I am pretending to love this English girl, and that it is unnatural; I would like to know how life for me here could be natural!'

---

[1] 'absurdity'.   [2] 'swimming-costume'.

For a moment she came to her senses and was aghast that she had broken her resolution. But even though she knew she was destroying herself, she could not restrain herself, she could not refrain from showing him how wrong he was, she could not give in to him.

'I never said that; I said that I do not approve of this sudden love.'

'As someone who boasts of being straightforward, why won't you tell the truth?'

'I never boast and I never tell lies,' he said quietly, curbing his mounting anger. 'It is a great pity if you cannot respect . . .'

'Respect was invented to cover up the empty place where there should be love. And if you don't love me, it would be better and more honest to say so.'

'No, this is becoming unbearable!' Vronsky exclaimed, getting up from his chair. 'Why are you trying my patience?' he said slowly, standing in front of her, looking as though he might have said much more but was holding himself back. 'It has its limits.'

'What do you mean by that?' she exclaimed, looking with dread at the clear expression of hatred which was in his whole face, and particularly in his cruel, threatening eyes.

'I mean . . .' he began, but stopped. 'I must ask what it is you want of me.'

'What can I want? All I can want is for you not to leave me, as you are thinking of doing,' she said, understanding everything he had left unsaid. 'But that's not what I want, that's secondary. I want love, and it's not there. Therefore it is all over!'

She headed towards the door.

'Wait! W-a-i-t!' said Vronsky, not changing the furrowed expression of his brows, but taking hold of her arm to stop her. 'What is the matter? I said that we must put off going for three days, and you told me I was lying and was a dishonest man.'

'Yes, and I repeat that a man who reproaches me by saying he has sacrificed everything for me', she said, recalling the words of an earlier quarrel, 'is worse than a dishonest man—he's a man without a heart.'

'No, there are limits to one's patience!' he cried, and quickly let go of her arm.

'He hates me, that's obvious,' she thought, and without looking round, she walked silently out of the room with faltering steps.

'He loves another woman, that's even more patently obvious,' she said to herself as she went into her room. 'I want love, and it is not there. Therefore it is all over,' she said, repeating her own words, 'and it must be ended.'

'But how?' she asked herself, and she sat down in the armchair in front of the mirror.

Thoughts about where she would go now—to the aunt who had brought her up, to Dolly, or simply abroad on her own, about what *he* was doing now alone in his study, about whether this was the final quarrel or whether reconciliation was still possible, about what all her former friends in Petersburg would say about her now, and about how Alexey Alexandrovich would look at it, started coming into her mind, along with many other thoughts about what would happen after their separation, but she did not surrender totally to these thoughts. There was some kind of vague thought in her soul which was the only thing that interested her, but she could not identify it. Thinking again about Alexey Alexandrovich, she also recalled the time of her illness after she had given birth, and the feeling which had never left her then. 'Why didn't I die?'—both her words and her feelings back then now came flooding back to her. And she suddenly understood what it was which was in her soul. Yes, this was the one thought which could resolve everything. 'Yes, to die! . . .'

'Alexey Alexandrovich's shame and disgrace, and Seryozha's, and my dreadful shame—all will be redeemed by death. If I die, he will feel remorse, he will be filled with pity and love, he will suffer on my account.' With a fixed smile of compassion for herself she sat in the armchair, taking off and putting on the rings on her left hand, and vividly imagining his feelings after her death from different points of view.

The sound of approaching steps, his steps, distracted her. Pretending to be busy with putting her rings away, she did not even turn to face him.

He came up to her, took her by the hand, and said softly:

'Anna, let's go the day after tomorrow, if you want. I agree to everything.'

She remained silent.

'What is it?' he asked.

'You know very well,' she said, and at the same moment, unable to restrain herself any longer, she burst into sobs.

'Leave me, leave me!' she pronounced between sobs. 'I'll go away tomorrow . . . I'll do more. What am I? A depraved woman. A millstone round your neck. I don't want to torment you, I don't! I'll release you. You don't love me, you love someone else!'

Vronsky begged her to calm down and assured her there was not even the shadow of grounds for her jealousy, that he had never stopped and would never stop loving her, and that he loved her more than ever.

'Anna, why must you torment yourself and me like this?' he said, kissing her hands. There was tenderness in his face now, and she thought she could hear the sound of tears in his voice and feel them wetting her hand. And in an instant Anna's desperate jealousy changed into a desperate, passionate tenderness; she put her arms round him and covered his head, his neck, and his hands with kisses.

25

FEELING that the reconciliation was complete, Anna threw herself energetically into preparations for their departure in the morning. Although it had not been decided whether they would go on the Monday or the Tuesday, since both had given way to each other the night before, Anna prepared busily for their departure, by this stage feeling completely indifferent about whether they went a day earlier or later. She was standing in her room over an open trunk, sorting things out, when he came in to see her earlier than usual, already dressed.

'I'm going off to see *Maman* now, as she can send me the money care of Yegorov. And tomorrow I will be ready to go,' he said.

No matter how good her mood was, mention of the visit to his mother's country house stung her.

'No, I won't be ready myself,' she said, and immediately thought: 'so it was possible to arrange things so we could do what I wanted.' 'No, you do as you wanted. Go into the dining room—I'll join you in a minute, I just need to sort out the things we don't need,' she said, handing one more item to Annushka, on whose arm already lay a mountain of clothes.

Vronsky was eating his beefsteak when she came into the dining room.

'You wouldn't believe how fed up I am with these rooms,' she said, sitting down to her coffee next to him. 'There's nothing worse than these *chambres garnies*.[1] They have no individuality, no soul. The clock, the curtains, and particularly the wallpaper—they are all a nightmare. I think of Vozdvizhenskoye as the promised land. You're not sending the horses off yet, are you?'

'No, they will come after us. Are you going somewhere?'

'I wanted to go and see Wilson. There are some dresses I need to take her. So we are definitely going tomorrow?' she said in a cheerful voice; but suddenly her face changed.

Vronsky's valet had come in to ask about a receipt for a telegram from Petersburg. There was nothing unusual about Vronsky receiving

---

[1] 'furnished rooms'.

a telegram, but he said that the receipt was in his study, as if wanting to hide something from her, and hurriedly turned to her.

'I will definitely have everything finished tomorrow.'

'Who was the telegram from?' she asked, not listening to him.

'From Stiva,' he answered reluctantly.

'Why didn't you show it to me? What possible secret could there be between Stiva and me?'

Vronsky called the valet back, and told him to bring the telegram.

'I didn't want to show it to you, because Stiva has a mania for sending telegrams: why send a telegram when nothing is settled?'

'About the divorce?'

'Yes, but he writes: have not achieved anything yet. Has promised final answer soon. But look, you read it.'

Anna took the telegram with trembling hands and read the same words that Vronsky had spoken. At the end was added: 'Few hopes, but will do everything possible and impossible.'

'I said yesterday that I couldn't care less when or even if I get a divorce,' she said, going red. 'There was absolutely no need to hide it from me.' 'This is how he might hide or is hiding his correspondence with women,' she thought.

'Yashvin wanted to come over this morning with Voitov,' said Vronsky; 'It seems he's won from Pevtsov all that he can pay out, even more—about sixty thousand.'

'No, wait,' she said, irritated that he was so obviously showing her with this change of subject that she was irritated; 'why do you think this news would be of such interest to me that you even had to conceal it? I said that I don't want to think about it, and I would have hoped you would be as little interested in it as I am.'

'I'm interested in it because I like clarity,' he said.

'Clarity is not a matter of form but of love,' she said, becoming more and more irritated, not by his words, but by the tone of cool composure with which he was speaking. 'What do you want it for?'

'Oh God, not love again,' he thought, frowning.

'You know very well what for: for your sake and for the children we will have.'

'There won't be any children.'

'That's a great pity,' he said.

'You want it for the children, but you don't think of me, do you?' she said, having completely forgotten or failed to hear that he had said, '*for your sake* and for the children'.

The question about the possibility of having children had long been a vexed one, and it irritated her. She explained his desire to have children as stemming from the fact that he did not cherish her beauty.

'Oh, I said: for your sake. Most of all for your sake,' he repeated, frowning as if in pain, 'because I am sure that a large part of your irritation stems from the uncertainty of your situation.'

'Yes, he has stopped pretending now, and all of his cold hatred for me has come to the fore,' she thought, not hearing what he was saying, but gazing in horror at the cold, cruel judge who was looking out of his eyes and taunting her.

'That is not the reason,' she said, 'and I don't even understand how the cause of my irritation, as you call it, can be the fact that I am completely in your power. What uncertainty is there in this situation? On the contrary . . .'

'I am very sorry that you don't want to understand,' he interrupted, with a stubborn desire to get his idea across. 'The uncertainty consists in your imagining that I am free.'

'You can rest assured on that account,' she said, and she turned away from him and began drinking her coffee.

She picked up her cup, sticking out her little finger, and brought it up to her mouth. After drinking a few sips, she glanced at him, and understood clearly from the expression on his face that he was repulsed by her hand, her gesture, and the sound she made with her lips.

'I could not care less what your mother thinks, and whom she wants to marry you off to,' she said, putting the cup down with a shaking hand.

'But we are not talking about that.'

'No, that is what we are talking about. And let me tell you, a woman without a heart, whether she's old or young, be it your mother or someone else's, has no appeal to me, and is not someone I want to know.'

'Anna, I must ask you not to speak disrespectfully about my mother.'

'A woman who has not gauged with her heart where her son's happiness and honour lie, does not have a heart.'

'I must repeat my request that you do not speak disrespectfully about my mother, whom I do respect,' he said, raising his voice and looking at her sternly.

She did not answer. As she gazed intently at him, at his face and his hands, she recalled every detail of the scene of their reconciliation the previous day, and his passionate caresses. 'Those are exactly the caresses he has lavished, and will lavish, and wants to lavish on other women!' she thought.

'You don't love your mother. It's all talk, talk, talk!' she said, looking at him with hatred.

'If that is the case, then we must . . .'

'We must make a decision, and I have made a decision,' she said, and was about to leave, but at that moment Yashvin walked into the room. Anna greeted him and stopped.

Why, when there was a storm raging in her soul and she felt she was standing at a turning-point in her life which might have terrible consequences, why she felt a need at that moment to keep up appearances in front of a stranger who would anyway know everything sooner or later, she did not know; but she immediately calmed the storm within her, sat down, and began talking to their guest.

'Well, what about that business of yours? Have you received what you are owed?' she asked Yashvin.

'Oh, things are going all right; it seems I won't get it all, and I have to leave on Wednesday. But when are you off?' said Yashvin, looking at Vronsky through narrowed eyes, and obviously guessing a quarrel had taken place.

'The day after tomorrow, I think,' said Vronsky.

'Well, you've been planning to go for a long time.'

'But now it's fixed,' said Anna, looking Vronsky straight in the eye with a look which told him he should not even think about the possibility of reconciliation.

'But don't you feel sorry for poor old Pevtsov?' she asked, continuing the conversation with Yashvin.

'I've never asked myself whether I feel sorry for him or not, Anna Arkadyevna. Just as in war you don't ask whether you are sorry or not. After all, my entire fortune is in here,' he said, indicating a side-pocket, 'and now I'm a wealthy man; but I'm going to the club today, and might leave penniless. Whoever sits down to play with me, after all, will also want to leave me without a stitch, and I will want to do the same. So we fight it out, and that's where the pleasure is.'

'Well, supposing you were married,' said Anna, 'what would your wife think about it?'

Yashvin laughed.

'That's presumably why I haven't got married and have never had any intention of doing so.'

'But what about Helsingfors?' said Vronsky, joining in the conversation and glancing at Anna's smiling face.

As their eyes met, Anna's face instantly assumed a coldly severe expression, as though she were saying to him: 'It is not forgotten. Everything is just the same.'

'Have you really been in love?' she said to Yashvin.

'Oh heavens! So many times! You see, there are some men for whom it is possible to sit down to cards provided they can always get up when the time comes for a *rendezvous*.[1] I, on the other hand, can dabble with love, but only so long as I am not late for my game in the evening. That's how I arrange things.'

'No, I wasn't asking about that, but the real thing.' She was going to say *Helsingfors*, but she did not want to repeat the word spoken by Vronsky.

Voitov, who was buying the stallion, arrived; Anna rose and left the room.

Before leaving the house, Vronsky came in to see her. She wanted to pretend she was looking for something on the table but, ashamed of the pretence, she looked straight at him with a cold expression.

'What do you want?' she asked in French.

'I need Gambetta's certificate, I've sold him,' he said, in a tone that said more clearly than words: 'I've no time for explanations, and they would be pointless.'

'I have nothing to feel guilty about before her,' he thought. 'If she wants to punish herself, *tant pis pour elle*.'[2] But as he was leaving he thought she said something, and his heart suddenly trembled with compassion for her.

'What is it, Anna?' he asked.

'Nothing,' she answered just as coldly and calmly.

'If it's nothing, then *tant pis*,'[3] he thought, becoming cold-hearted again, and he turned and went. As he was going out he caught sight of her pale face and trembling lips in the mirror. He wanted to stop and say something comforting to her, but his legs had carried him out of the room before he could think what to say. He spent the whole day away from home, and when he arrived back late in the evening, the maid told him that Anna Arkadyevna had a headache and asked him not to go in to her.

26

NEVER before had a quarrel lasted a whole day. Today it had happened for the first time. And it was not a quarrel. It was a clear admission that his feelings had completely cooled. Was it possible to look at her in the

---

[1] 'assignation'.
[2] 'so much the worse for her.'
[3] 'so much the worse.'

way that he had when he came into the room for the certificate? Look at her, see her heart breaking in despair, and leave in silence with that expression of calm indifference? It was not that his feelings had cooled towards her, but that he hated her because he loved another woman—that was clear.

And remembering all the cruel words he had spoken, Anna thought up all those other words which he had clearly wanted to say and could have said to her, and became more and more irritated.

'I won't stop you,' he might say. 'You can go wherever you like. You probably did not want to be divorced from your husband, so you could go back to him. Go back to him. If you need money, I'll give it to you. How many roubles do you need?'

All the cruellest words a coarse man could say, he said to her in her imagination, and she could not forgive him for them, as if he had actually said them.

'But didn't he, a truthful and honourable man, swear only yesterday that he loved me? Haven't I despaired for nothing many times already?' she said to herself afterwards.

Apart from the visit to Mrs Wilson, which took up two hours, Anna spent all that day vacillating about whether it was all over or whether there was a hope of reconciliation, and whether she should leave straight away or see him again. She waited for him all day and, as she went to her room that evening after leaving instructions that he should be told she had a headache, she thought to herself: 'If he comes in spite of what the maid says, it means that he loves me still. But if not, it means everything is over, and then I will decide what to do! . . .'

In the evening she heard the sound of his carriage as it came to a halt, his ringing, his footsteps and conversation with the maid; he believed what he was told, did not want to know any more, and went to his room. So that meant everything was over.

And death appeared clearly and vividly in her imagination as the only way to revive the love for her in his heart, punish him, and score a victory in the battle being waged with him by the evil spirit which had lodged in her heart.

Nothing mattered now: whether or not they went to Vozdvizhenskoye, whether or not she obtained a divorce from her husband—none of that mattered. The only thing that mattered was to punish him.

When she poured herself out her usual dose of opium and reflected that she only needed to drink the whole bottle in order to die, it seemed to her so easy and straightforward that she again began thinking with relish about how he would suffer, feel remorse, and revere her memory when it was too late. She lay in bed with her eyes open, staring by the light of a single burned-down candle at the stuccoed cornice of the ceiling and at the shadow cast on part of it by the screen, and vividly imagined what he would feel when she was gone, and was only a memory to him. 'How could I say those cruel words to her?' he would say. 'How could I leave the room without saying anything to her? But now she is no more. She has gone from us for ever. She is there . . .' Suddenly the shadow of the screen quivered, then enveloped the whole cornice and the whole ceiling; other shadows raced forwards to meet it from the other side; for a moment the shadows retreated, then advanced with renewed speed, quivered, merged, and all became dark. 'Death!' she thought. And she was so horror-stricken that it took her a long time to work out where she was, and for her shaking hands to find the matches and light another candle in place of the one that had burned down and gone out. 'No, anything—just as long as I can live! I love him after all. And he loves me after all! This has happened before and it will pass,' she said, feeling tears of joy at the return to life running down her cheeks. And she went quickly to find him in his study to escape from her fear.

He was sound asleep in his study. She went up to him and spent a long time gazing at him, holding the light above his face. She loved him so much now while he was sleeping that she could not hold back tears of tenderness at the sight of him; but she knew that if he woke up, he would fix her with his cold, self-righteous look, and that before telling him about her love she would have to prove to him how much he had wronged her. She went back to her room without waking him, and after a second dose of opium she fell towards morning into a heavy, fitful sleep, during which she never lost consciousness of herself.

In the morning she again experienced a terrible nightmare which had recurred several times in her dreams, even before her relationship with Vronsky, and which now woke her up. A little old peasant with a dishevelled beard, bent over some iron, was doing something while muttering meaningless words in French and, as always in this nightmare (which is what made it so terrifying), she felt that this little peasant was not paying any attention to her, but was doing some dreadful thing with the iron above her, there was something dreadful he was doing over her. And she woke up in a cold sweat.

When she got up, she recalled the events of the previous day as if in a fog.

'There was a quarrel, something which has happened several times before. I said I had a headache, and he did not come in to see me. We're leaving tomorrow so I must see him and prepare for our departure,' she said to herself. And learning that he was in his study, she went to find him. As she was walking through the drawing room, she heard a carriage stop at the front door, and looking out of the window she saw a young girl in a lilac hat leaning out of the carriage window and giving instructions to the footman ringing the bell. After a discussion in the hall, someone came upstairs, and Vronsky's footsteps could be heard outside the drawing room. He was walking quickly down the stairs. Anna went up to the window again. Now he had gone out on to the porch without a hat and had walked over to the carriage. The young girl in the lilac hat handed him a package. Vronsky said something to her with a smile. The carriage drove off; he quickly ran back up the stairs.

The fog shrouding everything in her soul suddenly lifted. Yesterday's feelings wrung her ailing heart with fresh pain. She now could not understand how she could have stooped to the point of spending a whole day with him in his house. She went into his study to inform him of her decision.

'That was Madame Sorokina and her daughter dropping by to bring me the money and the documents from *Maman*. I couldn't get them yesterday. How is your head—better?' he said calmly, not wanting to see or understand the gloomy, solemn expression on her face.

She stood in the middle of the room, staring at him in silence. He glanced at her, frowned briefly, and continued reading a letter. She turned and started slowly walking out of the room. He still could have brought her back, but she reached the door, he was still silent, and the only sound to be heard was the rustle of the piece of paper being turned over.

'Oh, by the way,' he said when she was already in the doorway, 'we're definitely going tomorrow, aren't we?'

'You are. I'm not,' she said, turning to face him.

'Anna, we can't live like this . . .'

'You are. I'm not,' she repeated.

'This is becoming unbearable!'

'You . . . you will regret this,' she said and walked out.

Alarmed by the desperate expression with which those words were uttered, he jumped up and was about to run after her but, collecting himself, he sat down again and frowned, his teeth firmly clenched. This, to his mind, unseemly threat of something irritated him. 'I've tried everything,' he thought, 'and the only thing left to do is not pay any attention,' so he began getting ready to drive into town and then again see his mother, whose signature he needed for the document of authorization.

She heard the sound of his steps in the study and the dining room. He stopped by the drawing room. But he did not turn towards her, and merely gave an order to let Voitov have the stallion in his absence. Then she heard the carriage drive up and the door open, and he went out again. But now he had come back into the hall, and someone was running upstairs. It was the valet running back for the gloves he had forgotten. She went over to the window and saw him take the gloves without looking, touch the coachman's back, and say something to him. Then, without glancing up at the windows, he sat down in the carriage in his usual posture, crossing his legs, and, putting on a glove, disappeared round the corner.

27

'He's gone! It's over!' said Anna to herself, standing by the window; and in answer to this conjecture, the impressions of darkness made by the candle going out and the terrible dream fused into one and filled her heart with cold terror.

'No, it can't be!' she exclaimed and, crossing the room, she rang the bell loudly. She was so frightened of being alone now that she went out to meet the servant before he arrived.

'Find out where the Count has gone,' she said.

The servant replied that the Count had gone to the stables.

'The Count instructed me to tell you that the carriage would return shortly, should you wish to go out.'

'Good. Wait. I'm just going to write a note. Send Mikhail with the note to the stables. Be quick.'

She sat down and wrote:

'It's all my fault. Come back home, as we need to talk things over. For heaven's sake come—I'm frightened.'

She sealed the note up and gave it to the servant.

She was afraid of being left alone now, and followed the servant out of the room and went into the nursery.

'Wait, this isn't right, it is not him! Where are his blue eyes and his sweet, shy smile?' was her first thought when she saw her chubby, pink-cheeked little girl with black hair instead of Seryozha, whom, amid the confusion of her thoughts, she was expecting to see in the nursery. Seated at the table, the little girl was stubbornly and loudly banging on it with the stopper from a carafe, and looking blankly at her mother with the two currants that were her black eyes. After answering the English governess that she was quite well and would be going to the country the following day, Anna sat down next to the little girl and began spinning the stopper in front of her. But the child's loud, ringing laughter and the movement she made with her eyebrows were such a vivid reminder of Vronsky that she got up hurriedly and went out, stifling her sobs. 'Can it really be over? No, it can't be,' she thought. 'He'll come back. But how will he explain that smile to me, and that excitement after speaking to her? But I'll believe him even if he doesn't explain. If I don't believe him, there's only one thing left for me—and I don't want that.'

She looked at her watch. Twenty minutes had passed. 'He must have received the note by now and will be driving back. It won't be long, another ten minutes . . . But what if he doesn't come? No, that is impossible. He mustn't see me with tear-stained eyes. I'll go and wash. Oh yes, is my hair brushed or not?' she asked herself. And she could not remember. She felt her head with her hand. 'Yes, I did have my hair brushed, but I have no idea when.' She could not even trust her hand, and went up to the mirror on the wall to see whether her hair really had been brushed or not. She had brushed her hair, but she could not remember when she had done it. 'Who is that?' she thought, looking in the mirror at the swollen face with the strangely shining eyes which were looking fearfully at her. 'Oh, it's me,' she suddenly realized, and as she looked herself up and down, she felt his kisses on her, and shuddered as she twitched her shoulders. Then she raised a hand to her lips and kissed it.

'What is this, I'm going out of my mind,' and she went into the bedroom, where Annushka was tidying up.

'Annushka,' she said, stopping in front of her maid and staring at her, not knowing what to say to her.

'You were going to see Darya Alexandrovna,' the maid said, as if she understood.

'Darya Alexandrovna? Yes, I'm going.'

'Fifteen minutes there, fifteen minutes back. He's already on his way and he'll be here any minute.' She took out her watch and looked at it. 'But how could he go off and leave me in such a state? How can he live without being reconciled with me?' She went over to the window and began looking down into the street. There had been enough time for him to return by now. But her calculation might have been wrong, and she again tried to remember when it was he had left and count the minutes.

Just as she was going over to the clock so she could check her watch, someone drove up. Glancing out of the window, she saw his carriage. But no one came up the stairs, and voices could be heard down below. It was the messenger who had returned in the carriage. She went down to him.

'I didn't find the Count. He had left for the Nizhny Novgorod station.'*

'What do you want? What is this? . . .' she said, addressing the ruddy-faced, jovial Mikhail as he handed her back her note.

'Oh, of course, he never got it,' she recollected.

'Take this same note to Countess Vronskaya out in the country, you know where I mean? And bring back an answer immediately,' she said to the messenger.

'But what on earth am I going to do in the meantime?' she thought. 'Yes, I'm going to Dolly's, that's right, otherwise I shall go mad. Oh, and I can wire too.' And she wrote out a telegram:

'I must talk to you, come at once.'

After sending off the telegram, she went to get dressed. When she was dressed and had her hat on, she gazed again into the eyes of the placid Annushka, who had put on weight. Evident sympathy could be seen in those small, kind, grey eyes.

'Annushka, dear, what am I to do?' said Anna, sobbing as she sank helplessly into an armchair.

'You shouldn't worry so much, Anna Arkadyevna! These things always happen. You go out now and take your mind off things,' said the maid.

'Yes, that's right, I'm going,' said Anna, coming to her senses and getting up. 'And if a telegram comes while I'm gone, send it on to Darya Alexandrovna's . . . No, I will come back myself.'

'Yes, I mustn't think, I must do something, go somewhere, and most important of all leave this house,' she said, listening with terror to the strange turmoil going on inside her heart, and she hurried out and got into the carriage.

'Where to?' asked Pyotr before sitting down on the box.

'Znamenka, to the Oblonskys.'

28

THE weather was clear. A fine, light drizzle had been falling all morning, and had just now cleared up. The iron roofs, the flagstones of the pavements, the cobblestones of the road, the wheels and leather, and the brass and tinplate of the carriages—everything gleamed brightly in the May sunshine. It was three o'clock, and the liveliest time out in the streets.

Sitting in a corner of the comfortable carriage, which was rocking slightly on its resilient springs to the fast trot of the greys, and amid the unceasing rattle of the wheels and the rapidly changing impressions in the fresh air, Anna saw her position in a completely different light to what it had seemed at home, as she once again went over the events of the last days. Even the thought of death did not seem so terrible and clear to her now, and death itself no longer appeared inevitable. She reproached herself now for the humiliation to which she had submitted. 'I am entreating him to forgive me. I have given in to him. I have taken the blame. Why? Can I not live without him?' And without answering the question of how she was going to live without him, she started reading the signboards. 'Office and warehouse. Dental surgeon. Yes, I'll tell Dolly everything. She has no great fondness for Vronsky. It will be embarrassing and painful, but I'll tell her everything. She is fond of me, and I'll follow her advice. I won't give in to him; I won't let him educate me. Filippov, bread loaves. Apparently they take their dough to Petersburg. The Moscow water is so good. And then there are the Mytishchi wells and pancakes.' And she remembered how, long, long ago, when she was seventeen, she had gone with her aunt to the Trinity Monastery.* 'On horses too. Was that really me, with the red hands? To think how much of what seemed so wonderful and inaccessible to me back then has become insignificant, while what there was back then is now inaccessible for ever. Would I have ever believed back then that I could submit to such humiliation? How proud and pleased he will be when he gets my note! But I'll show him . . . What an awful smell that paint has. Why are they always painting and building? Dressmaking and millinery,' she read. A man bowed to her. It was Annushka's husband. 'Our parasites,' she remembered Vronsky saying. 'Our parasites? Why ours? It is terrible that you cannot pull up the past by its roots. You can't pull it up, but you can blot out one's memory of it. And that's what I am going to do.' And she promptly recalled her past with Alexey Alexandrovich, and how she had erased it from her memory. 'Dolly will think I'm leaving a second husband and that I must therefore surely be in the wrong. As if I wanted to be in the right! I can't!' she said to herself, feeling that she was about to start crying. But she immediately started wondering what those two girls could be smiling so gleefully about. 'Love, I suppose? They don't know how grim and sordid it is . . . The boulevard and children. Three boys running about, playing at horses. Seryozha! And I'll lose everything and not get him back. Yes, I will lose everything if he doesn't come back. Perhaps he missed the train and is already back by now. You want humiliation again!' she said to herself. 'No, I'll go in to Dolly, and tell her straight out: I'm unhappy, I deserve to be, it's my fault, but I'm unhappy all the same, please help me. These horses, this carriage—how hateful I am to myself in this carriage—it's all his; but I won't see them again.'

Thinking up the phrases with which she would tell Dolly everything, and deliberately aggravating the pain in her heart, Anna went up the steps

'Is there anyone here?' she asked in the hall.

'Katerina Alexandrovna Levina,' answered the footman.

'Kitty! The same Kitty whom Vronsky fell in love with!' thought Anna. 'The same girl he remembers with love. He regrets not marrying her. Whereas he remembers me with loathing, and regrets getting involved with me.'

The sisters were having a consultation about breastfeeding when Anna arrived. Dolly went out on her own to greet the visitor whose arrival had interrupted their conversation.

'So you haven't left yet? I wanted to come and see you myself,' she said; 'I received a letter from Stiva today.'

'We also received a telegram,' answered Anna, looking round so she would be able to see Kitty.

'He writes that he can't understand exactly what it is that Alexey Alexandrovich wants, but that he won't leave before he has an answer.'

'I thought you had someone with you. May I read the letter?'

'Yes, Kitty,' said Dolly, embarrassed. 'She has stayed in the nursery. She has been very ill.'

'So I heard. May I read the letter?'

'I'll fetch it straight away. But he is not refusing; on the contrary, Stiva has hopes,' said Dolly, lingering in the doorway.

'I don't have hopes, and don't want it anyway,' said Anna.

'What's going on—does Kitty consider it degrading to meet me?' thought Anna when she was left alone. 'Maybe she's right. But it's not for her, the one who was in love with Vronsky, it's not for her to show me that, even if it is true. I know there is a not a single respectable woman who can receive me in my position. I know that I sacrificed everything to him from that first moment! And here is my reward! Oh, how I hate him! And why did I come here? It's worse for me, even more difficult.' She heard the voices of the sisters conferring in the next room. 'And what on earth am I going to tell Dolly now? Am I supposed to reassure Kitty with the fact that I am unhappy, and submit to her patronage? No, and Dolly won't understand anything anyway. And I've got nothing to say to her. It would only be interesting to see Kitty, to show her how I despise everyone and everything, how nothing matters to me now.'

Dolly came in with the letter. Anna read it and silently handed it back.

'I knew all that,' she said, 'and it doesn't interest me at all.'

'But why? I, on the other hand, am hopeful,' said Dolly, looking at Anna with curiosity. She had never seen her in such a strange, irascible state. 'When are you leaving?' she asked.

Anna screwed up her eyes and looked straight ahead without answering.

'Why is Kitty hiding from me?' she said, looking at the door and blushing.

'Oh, what nonsense! She's feeding the baby, and having a few difficulties, so I've been giving her some advice . . . She's very pleased. She'll come any minute,' said Dolly awkwardly, unskilled at lying. 'Here she is.'

When she learned that Anna had come, Kitty had not wanted to appear; but Dolly persuaded her. Mustering her courage, Kitty came out and, blushing, she went up to her and held out her hand.

'I am very pleased to see you,' she said in a quavering voice.

Kitty was torn by the struggle going on inside her between hostility towards this bad woman and a desire to be charitable; but as soon as she saw Anna's beautiful, likeable face, all the hostility immediately evaporated.

'But I wouldn't have been surprised if you hadn't wanted to meet me. I'm used to everything. You have been ill? Yes, you have changed,' said Anna.

Kitty felt that Anna was looking at her with hostility. She attributed this hostility to the awkward position Anna now felt she was in before her, having previously been the one bestowing patronage, and she felt sorry for her.

They talked about Kitty's illness, about the baby, about Stiva, but it was clear that nothing interested Anna.

'I came to say goodbye to you,' she said, getting up.

'So when are you leaving?'

But Anna turned to Kitty again without replying.

'Yes, I am very glad I have seen you,' she said with a smile. 'I have

heard so much about you from everyone, even from your husband. He
came to visit, and I liked him very much,' she added, with obvious
ill-intent. 'Where is he?'

'He has gone to the country,' said Kitty, blushing.

'Do remember me to him, be sure you don't forget.'

'I'll be sure to!' Kitty said naively, looking with compassion into her
eyes.

'Farewell then, Dolly!' And after kissing Dolly and shaking hands
with Kitty, Anna hurried out.

'She's just the same and as attractive as ever! Very beautiful!' said
Kitty, when she was alone with her sister. 'But there is something pitiful about her! Something terribly pitiful!'

'Yes, there was something odd about her today,' said Dolly. 'When
I was seeing her into the hall, I thought she was about to cry.'

29

ANNA got into the carriage in an even worse state than when she had
left home. To her previous agonies was now added the feeling of being
insulted and rejected, which she had clearly felt during the meeting
with Kitty.

'Where to? Home?' asked Pyotr.

'Yes, home,' she said, not even thinking now about where she was
going.

'How they looked at me, as if I was something terrible, unfathomable, and peculiar. What can he be talking about so fervently to that
other person?' she thought, looking at two pedestrians. 'Is it possible
to tell another person what you are feeling? I wanted to tell Dolly, and
it's a good thing I didn't. How gleeful she would have been about my
misfortune! She would have hidden it; but her main feeling would have
been glee that I am being punished for the pleasures she envied me for.
As for Kitty, she would have been even more gleeful. How I can see
straight through her! She knows I was more than usually hospitable to
her husband. And she's jealous and hates me. And she despises me too.
I'm an immoral woman in her eyes. If I were an immoral woman I could
have made her husband fall in love with me . . . if I had wanted to. And
I did want to. That man looks pleased with himself,' she thought about
a fat, ruddy-cheeked gentleman driving towards her, who had taken her
for an acquaintance and was lifting his shiny hat above his bald, shiny
head, and then realized he had made a mistake. 'He thought he knew

me. But he knows me as little as anyone in the world knows me. I don't know myself. I know my appetites, as the French say. Now these two want that filthy ice-cream. They know that for sure,' she thought, looking at two boys who had stopped an ice-cream seller; he had taken the tub down from his head and was wiping his sweaty face with the end of a towel. 'We all want delicious sweet things. If we can't have confectionery, then filthy ice cream. And Kitty's the same: if not Vronsky, then Levin. And she envies me. And hates me. And we all of us hate each other. I Kitty, Kitty me. That's the truth. *Tyutkin, coiffeur. Je me fais coiffer par Tyutkin . . .*[1]* I'll tell him that when he comes back,' she thought and smiled. But at that same moment she remembered she did not have someone to tell funny things to now. 'There's nothing funny or jolly anyway. Everything is vile. They're ringing for vespers, and how diligently that merchant is crossing himself—as if he were afraid of dropping something! What is the point of these churches, this bell-ringing, and these lies? Just to hide the fact that we all hate each other, like these cabbies who are swearing at each other so violently. Yashvin says, "He wants to strip me of my shirt, and I want to do the same to him." That is the truth!'

She was still wrapped up in these thoughts, which so engrossed her that she even stopped thinking about her situation, when the carriage pulled up at the porch of her house. Only when she saw the doorman coming out to meet her did she remember she had sent a note and a telegram.

'Is there an answer?' she asked.

'I'll just have a look,' answered the porter, and glancing at his desk, he picked up and handed her the thin square envelope of a telegram. 'I cannot come before ten o'clock. Vronsky,' she read.

'And the messenger has not come back?'

'No, ma'am,' answered the porter.

'Well, if that is the way it is, I know what I have to do,' she said, and feeling an inchoate anger and a need for vengeance welling up within her, she ran upstairs. 'I'll go to him myself. Before leaving for ever, I'll tell him everything. I have never, ever hated anyone as much as I hate this man!' she thought. Seeing his hat on the coat-stand, she shuddered with revulsion. She did not realize that his telegram was an answer to her telegram, and that he had not received her note yet. She pictured him now talking calmly to his mother and Princess Sorokina and revelling in her suffering.

---

[1] 'Tyutkin, hairdresser. I have my hair done by Tyutkin . . .'

'Yes, I must be off as soon as possible,' she said to herself, still not knowing where to go. She wanted to get away as quickly as possible from the feelings she had experienced in that awful house. The servants, the walls, the things in the house—everything provoked revulsion and rage in her and pressed down on her with some kind of weight.

'Yes, I must drive to the railway station, and if I don't find him, I'll go there and catch him out.' Anna looked at the railway timetable in the newspapers. There was an evening train leaving at two minutes past eight. 'Yes, I will make it.' She ordered the other horses to be harnessed and busied herself packing a travelling-bag with the things she would need for a few days. She knew she would never come back there. Out of the plans that came into her head she made a vague decision that, after whatever happened there at the station or at the Countess's estate, she would take the Nizhny Novgorod line as far as the first town and stay there.

Dinner was on the table; she went up, sniffed the bread and cheese, and after realizing that she was disgusted by the smell of anything edible, she ordered the carriage to be brought round and went out. The house was already casting a shadow across the whole street, and it was a clear evening, still warm in the sun. Annushka, who came out with her things, Pyotr, who put the things into the carriage, and the coachman, who was clearly disgruntled—they all disgusted her and she was irritated by everything they said and did.

'I don't need you, Pyotr.'

'But what about the ticket?'

'Well, as you like, I don't care,' she said with vexation.

Pyotr jumped up on to the box and, with his arms akimbo, told the coachman to drive to the station.

30

'Here it is again! I understand everything again!' said Anna to herself as soon as the carriage moved off, rocking as it clattered over the small cobbles, and different impressions started again coming into her mind, one after the other.

'Yes, what was it I was having such good thoughts about just now?' she tried to remember. 'Tyutkin, *coiffeur*? No, that was not it. Oh yes, it was about what Yashvin says: that hatred and the struggle to survive are the only things that connect people. "There is no point in you going, you know."' She was mentally addressing a party of people in a coach and four who were obviously going on a jaunt out of town. 'And the dog you are taking with you won't help you. You can't escape from yourselves.' Casting her gaze in the direction in which Pyotr had turned, she saw a half dead-drunk factory-worker with a lolling head being led off somewhere by a policeman. 'Although he might,' she thought. 'Count Vronsky and I also never experienced that pleasure, although we expected a lot from it.' And now for the first time Anna trained that bright light in which she saw everything on to her relations with him, which she had hitherto avoided thinking about. 'What was he looking for in me? It was not so much love as the satisfaction of his vanity.' She remembered his words when they were first together, and the expression on his face, which was reminiscent of an obedient setter. And now everything confirmed it. 'Yes, he gloried in his success. There was love too, of course, but mostly it was pride in his success. He flaunted me. Now that has gone. There's nothing to be proud of. Ashamed rather than proud. He took everything he could from me, and now he doesn't need me. He has grown tired of me and is trying not to act dishonourably with me. He gave himself away yesterday. He wants a divorce and marriage because he wants to burn his boats. He loves me, but how? *The zest is gone.*[1] This man wants to impress everyone and is very pleased with himself,' she thought, looking at a red-cheeked shop-assistant on a hired horse. 'Yes, I no longer have that zest for him. Deep down he will be glad if I leave him.'

This was not just a conjecture—she saw it all clearly in that penetrating light that now revealed to her the meaning of life and human relations.

'My love is becoming more and more passionate and selfish, while his is growing dimmer and dimmer, and that is why we are separating,' her thoughts continued. 'And there is nothing that can be done. I've invested everything in him, and I've been demanding more and more that he devote himself completely to me. But he wants to get away from me more and more. Before our relationship we really were moving towards each other, but since then we have inexorably been drifting apart. And that cannot be changed. He tells me I have no reason to be jealous, and I've told myself that I have no reason to be jealous; but it's not true. It's not that I'm jealous, I am discontented. But . . .' She opened her mouth, and the agitation caused by the thought that suddenly occurred to her made her change her position in the carriage. 'If only I could be something other than a mistress, passionately

---

[1] [English in the original.]

loving only his caresses; but I cannot and do not want to be anything else. And I provoke revulsion in him with this desire of mine, while he provokes anger in me, and it cannot be any other way. Don't I know that he would never betray me, that he has no designs on Sorokina, that he is not in love with Kitty, and that he would not be unfaithful to me? I do know all that, but that does not make it easier for me. If he is going to be kind and affectionate to me out of a sense of *duty*, without loving me, and there won't be what I want, that would be worse than anger, a thousand times worse! It would be hell! And that is indeed what it is. He has not loved me for a long time. And hatred begins where love ends. I don't know these streets at all. Some hills or other and houses, endless houses . . . And in the houses people, endless people . . . No end to how many of them there are, and they all hate each other. Well, suppose I imagine I get what I want, in order to be happy. Well? I get a divorce, Alexey Alexandrovich gives me Seryozha, and I marry Vronsky.' As she recalled Alexey Alexandrovich, she immediately had an exceptionally vivid image of him standing there before her in the flesh, with his meek, lifeless, dull eyes, blue-veined white hands, distinctive intonation, and cracking fingers, and the memory of the feeling which had existed between them and which was also called love made her shudder with revulsion. 'Well, imagine I get a divorce and become Vronsky's wife. Does that mean Kitty is going to stop looking at me the way she looked at me today? No. And is Seryozha going to stop asking or thinking about my two husbands? And what kind of new feeling am I going to dream up between Vronsky and myself? If no longer happiness, is at least some kind of an absence of torture possible? No, no, and no!' She answered herself without the slightest doubt now. 'It's inconceivable. Life is driving us apart—I am the cause of his unhappiness, and he of mine, and it is impossible to change either him or me. Everything has been tried, and the screw has lost its thread. A beggar-woman with a child, yes. She thinks she is to be pitied. But weren't we all cast into the world just to hate each other and thus torment ourselves and others? Look at those laughing schoolboys going by. And what about Seryozha?' she remembered. 'I also thought I loved him, and was moved by my own tenderness. But I lived without him, and exchanged him for another love, and while I was satisfied with that love I made no complaint about it.' And she remembered with revulsion what she had called that love. And the clarity with which she now saw her life and that of other people gladdened her. 'It is the same for me, and Pyotr, and Fyodor the coachman, and that merchant, and all those people who live along the Volga, where those advertisements invite you to go, and everywhere and always,' she thought as she drove up to the low building of the Nizhny Novgorod station and porters came running out to meet her.

'Shall I buy a ticket to Obiralovka?'* said Pyotr.

She had completely forgotten where and why she was going, and only by making a great deal of effort could she understand the question.

'Yes,' she said to him, handing over her purse and then getting out of the carriage, with her little red bag on her arm.

As she negotiated her way through the crowd to the first-class waiting room, she began to recall little by little all the details of her predicament and the courses of action she was prevaricating between. And once again the hope and despair alternately chafing the old sores began to aggravate the wounds of her tormented, violently trembling heart. As she sat waiting for the train on the star-shaped couch, looking with distaste at the people coming in and out (they were all loathsome to her), she thought first about how she would arrive at the station and write him a note, and about what she would write to him, and then she thought about how he was now complaining to his mother about his situation (not understanding her suffering), and how she would come into the room, and what she would say to him. And then she thought about how life could still be happy, and how agonizingly she loved and hated him, and how dreadfully her heart was pounding.

31

THE bell rang; some ugly, brazen-faced young men walked past, hurrying yet also attentive to the impression they were making; Pyotr in his livery and gaiters also crossed the hall with a dim-witted, brutish face, and came up to her in order to escort her to the carriage. The noisy young men fell silent when she walked past them on the platform, and one of them whispered something about her to another, something horrible, obviously. She climbed the high step and went to sit alone in the compartment on a soiled sprung seat that had once been white. Her bag bounced on the springs before coming to rest. Smiling inanely, Pyotr raised his gold-braided hat by the window as a gesture of farewell, and a brazen-faced guard slammed the door and the latch shut. An ugly lady with a bustle (Anna mentally undressed her and was shocked by her hideousness) and a girl who was laughing affectedly, ran past below.

'Katerina Andreyevna has it, she's got everything, *ma tante*!' the girl called out.

'A young girl—and even she is disfigured and giving herself airs,' thought Anna. In order not to see anyone, she swiftly got up and sat down at the opposite window of the empty carriage. A grimy, ugly peasant, with matted hair sticking out of his cap, walked past this window, bending down towards the wheels of the carriage. 'There is something familiar about that hideous peasant,' Anna thought. And remembering her dream, she went over to the opposite door, shaking with fear. The guard opened the door to let a man and his wife in.

'Would you like to get out?'

Anna did not reply. The guard and the people entering did not notice the horror on her face under the veil. She returned to her corner and sat down. The couple sat down opposite, making a thorough but furtive inspection of her dress. Both husband and wife seemed repellent to Anna. The husband asked whether she would allow him to smoke, obviously not in order to smoke, but in order to start a conversation with her. Receiving her permission, he talked to his wife in French about something he needed to talk about even less than he needed to smoke. Putting on a show, they talked nonsense, just so she would hear. Anna could clearly see that they were bored with each other and hated each other. And it was impossible not to hate such pitiful, ugly creatures.

The second bell rang, followed by the shunting of luggage, noise, shouting, and laughter. It was so clear to Anna that no one had any reason to be happy that this laughter irritated her to the point of physical pain, and she wanted to block her ears in order not to hear it. Finally the third bell rang, followed by the sound of the whistle and the screeching of the engine: the chain gave a jerk, and the husband crossed himself. 'It would be interesting to ask him what he means by that,' Anna thought, looking at him spitefully. She was looking past the lady through the window, at the people standing on the platform seeing the train off, who looked as if they were travelling backwards. Juddering evenly on the joints between the rails, the carriage in which Anna was sitting trundled past the platform, the brick wall, the signal, past other carriages; the wheels began to make a quiet ringing sound as they glided more effortlessly and smoothly over the rails; the window was flooded with bright evening sunshine, and a light breeze began playing with the curtain. Anna forgot about her fellow passengers and, breathing in fresh air to the gentle rocking of the train, she started thinking again.

'Yes, where did I leave off? On the fact that I cannot imagine a situation where life would not be a torment, that we are all created in order to suffer, and that we all know this and are continually thinking up ways of deceiving ourselves. But when you see the truth, what is to be done?'

'Man has been given reason so that he may free himself from his troubles,' said the lady in French, clearly pleased with her phrase and pulling a face as she articulated it.

These words seemed to respond to Anna's thoughts.

'Free himself from his troubles,' Anna repeated. And as she looked at the red-cheeked man and his thin wife, she could see that the sickly wife considered herself to be a misunderstood woman and the husband deceived her and encouraged this opinion she had about herself. Turning the beam of her light on to them, it was as if Anna could see their whole story and all the nooks and crannies of their souls. But there was nothing interesting there, so she continued her thoughts.

'Yes, I have many troubles, and if one has been given reason in order to free oneself from them, it follows that I must free myself from them. Why not put out the candle if there is nothing more to look at, when it is so loathsome looking at all of this? But how? Why did that guard run along the footboard, why are they shouting, those young people in that carriage? Why are they talking, why are they laughing? It's all a lie, it's all falsehood, all a deception, all evil! . . .'

When the train pulled into the station, Anna got out with the crowd of other passengers and, avoiding them as if they were lepers, stopped on the platform, trying to remember why she had come there and what she intended to do. Everything that had seemed possible to her before was now so difficult to grasp, especially in the noisy crowd of all these hideous people who would not leave her in peace. First there were the porters running up to offer her their services, then there were the young men clacking their heels on the boards of the platform and chattering loudly while they looked her up and down, and then there were the people coming towards her who kept making way on the wrong side. Remembering that she had planned to continue her journey if there was no answer, she stopped a porter and asked if there was a coachman there with a note from Count Vronsky.

'Count Vronsky? There was someone who came from him just now. Meeting Princess Sorokina and her daughter. What does the coachman look like?'

While she was talking to the porter, Mikhaila the coachman, ruddy-faced and jolly in his smart blue coat and watch-chain, clearly proud to have carried out his errand so well, came up to her and gave her a note. She unsealed it and her heart sank even before she read it.

'Very sorry your note did not reach me in time. I will be back at ten,' Vronsky had written in a careless hand.

'So! Just what I was expecting!' she said to herself with a malevolent smile.

'All right, you may go home,' she said quietly, turning to Mikhaila. She was speaking quietly because she found it difficult to breathe, her heart was beating so fast. 'No, I am not going to let you torment me,' she thought, addressing her threat not to him, or to herself, but to the one who was making her suffer, and she set off along the platform past the station.

Two maids who were walking along the platform turned their heads round to look at her, thinking something out loud about her clothes. 'It's real,' they said about the lace she was wearing. The young men would not leave her alone. Looking straight at her, laughing and shouting out something in unnatural voices, they walked past her again. The stationmaster, as he walked past, asked her if she was continuing her journey. The boy selling kvass could not take his eyes off her. 'Oh God, where should I go?' she thought, as she walked further and further down the platform. At the end she stopped. Some ladies and children meeting a gentleman in spectacles, and laughing and talking loudly, fell silent and turned their eyes on her as she came level with them. She quickened her pace and walked away from them to the edge of the platform. A goods-train was approaching. The platform shook and she felt she was on the train again.

And suddenly, remembering the man who had been crushed on the day she had first met Vronsky, she realized what she had to do. Treading quickly and lightly, she went down the steps which led from the water-tank* down to the rails, and stopped near the train as it passed right in front of her. She looked at the bottom of the wagons, at the screws and chains and the tall iron wheels of the first wagon as it rolled slowly along, and tried to gauge with her eye the midpoint between the front and back wheels and the moment when it would be opposite her.

'There!' she said to herself, looking down into the wagon's shadow at the mixture of sand and coal sprinkled on the sleepers; 'there, right at the midpoint, and I'll punish him and be rid of everybody and myself.'

She wanted to fall under the midpoint of the first wagon as it drew level with her. But she was held up by the little red bag which she started to remove from her arm, and then it was too late: she had missed the midpoint. She had to wait for the next wagon. She was overcome by a feeling akin to the one she used to experience when she went bathing and was about to enter the water, and she crossed herself. Making the familiar sign of the cross summoned up in her soul a whole host of childhood and youthful memories, and suddenly the darkness shrouding everything for her was rent, and for a moment life and all its radiant past joys appeared before her. But she did not take her eyes off the wheels of the approaching second goods-wagon. And just at the moment when the midpoint between the wheels came level with her, she threw away the little red bag and, drawing her head into her shoulders, fell under the wagon on to her hands and, with a light movement, as if preparing to stand up again straight away, dropped to her knees. And at that same instant she was horrified by what she was doing. 'Where am I? What am I doing? Why?' She wanted to get to her feet, hurl herself out of the way; but something huge and inexorable hit her on the head and pulled her along by her back. 'Lord, forgive me for everything!' she murmured, feeling the impossibility of struggling. The little peasant was working over the iron, muttering something. And the candle by which she had been reading that book full of anxiety, deceptions, grief, and evil flared up more brightly than at any other time, illuminated for her everything that had previously been in darkness, spluttered, grew dim, and went out for ever.

PART EIGHT

ALMOST two months had passed. It was already the middle of the hot summer, but Sergey Ivanovich was only now ready to leave Moscow.

Some important events had taken place in Sergey Ivanovich's life during this time. His book, entitled *Towards a Survey of the Principles and Forms of Government in Europe and Russia*, the fruit of six years' labour, had been completed about a year ago. Certain sections of the book and the introduction had appeared in periodical publications, and other parts had been read out by Sergey Ivanovich to people in his circle, so the ideas in this work could no longer be a complete novelty for the public; Sergey Ivanovich still had the expectation, however, that the appearance of his book was bound to make a serious impression on people, and at the very least cause a great stir in the academic world, if not a revolution in scholarship.

After careful polishing, the book had been published the previous year and distributed to booksellers.

Not asking anyone about it, answering his friends' questions about how his book was doing with reluctance and feigned indifference, and not even asking the booksellers how it was selling, Sergey Ivanovich kept an eagle-eyed and vigilant lookout for the first impression his book made on the public and in the press.

But a week went by, then another, and a third, and no impression whatsoever was noticeable amongst the public; his friends, who were specialists and scholars, would sometimes bring it up, but clearly just to be polite. The rest of his acquaintances, however, who had no interest in reading a scholarly book, did not talk to him about it at all. And the general public, whose attention was now particularly taken up with something else, was completely indifferent. A whole month went by without a word being said about his book in the press either.

Sergey Ivanovich had calculated with great precision the time needed to write a review, but a month went by, then a second, and there was the same silence.

Only in the *Northern Beetle*,* in a humorous squib about the singer Drabanti, who had lost his voice, were a few contemptuous remarks made in the same vein about Koznyshev's book, which showed that the book had long ago been condemned by everyone, and consigned to general ridicule.

A critical article finally appeared in a serious journal in the third month after publication. Sergey Ivanovich even knew the author of the article. He had met him once at Golubtsov's.

The author of the article was a very young and sickly newspaper satirist, who was incisive as a writer, but extremely uneducated and shy when it came to personal relations.

Despite his complete contempt for the author, Sergey Ivanovich sat down to read the article with complete respect. The article was terrible.

The journalist had clearly deliberately understood the entire book in a way in which it was impossible to understand it. But his selection of quotations was so skilful that for those who had not read the book (and it was clear that almost no one had read it), it was patently obvious that the whole book was nothing but a conglomeration of bombastic phrases, which were used inappropriately to boot (as the question-marks showed), and that the author of the book was a person who was completely ignorant. And all this was done so wittily that Sergey Ivanovich would not have baulked at such wit himself; but that was precisely what was so awful about it.

Despite the completely conscientious way in which Sergey Ivanovich tested the validity of the critic's arguments, he did not dwell for one moment on the faults and mistakes which were pilloried—it was too obvious they had all been deliberately singled out—but he at once involuntarily began to recall every last detail of his meeting and conversation with the author of the article.

'Have I offended him in some way?' Sergey Ivanovich wondered.

And when he remembered that during their meeting he had corrected a word the young man had used which betrayed his ignorance, Sergey Ivanovich found an explanation for the article's slant.

This article was followed by a deadly silence about the book, both in print and in conversation, and Sergey Ivanovich saw that his work of six years, in which he had invested so much love and effort, had passed without trace.

What made Sergey Ivanovich's situation even more painful was the fact that, having finished his book, which previously had taken up most of his time, he now had no other work to do in his study.

Sergey Ivanovich was clever, well-educated, healthy, and active, and he did not know how to channel his energies. Conversations in drawing rooms, assemblies, meetings, committees, and anywhere else where one could talk took up a part of his time; but as a long-term city-dweller he did not allow himself to become totally engrossed in conversations, as his less experienced brother did when he was in Moscow; that still left him with a lot of leisure and intellectual energy.

At this most difficult time for him, due to the failure of his book, it was his good fortune that questions about adherents of other faiths,* American friends,* the Samara famine,* the Exhibition,* and spiritualism, were succeeded by the Slav Question,* which had previously only smouldered in the public imagination, and Sergey Ivanovich, who had also been one of prime instigators of this question earlier, threw himself into it body and soul.

People in the circle in which Sergey Ivanovich moved were talking and writing at this time about nothing but the Slav Question and the Serbian War.* Everything that the idle crowd usually does to kill time was now done for the benefit of the Slavs. Balls, concerts, dinners, speeches, ladies' dresses, beer, taverns—everything bore witness to sympathy for the Slavs.

Sergey Ivanovich did not agree with the details of much of what was spoken and written on this subject. He saw that the Slav Question had become one of those fashionable, ever-changing enthusiasms which always serve the public as a focus for activity; and he also saw that a great number of people had become involved in it for selfish and egotistical reasons. He acknowledged that the newspapers published a great deal that was unnecessary and exaggerated, with the sole aim of drawing attention to themselves and shouting down all the others. He saw amid this general public clamour that it was all the losers and malcontents who were thrusting themselves forward and shouting louder than anyone else—commanders without armies, ministers without ministries, journalists without newspapers, party leaders without supporters. He saw that there was a great deal about it that was frivolous and ridiculous; but he also saw and acknowledged an unmistakable, ever-growing enthusiasm uniting all classes of society, with which it was impossible not to sympathize. The slaughter of fellow Orthodox Christians and brother Slavs aroused sympathy for the victims, and indignation against their oppressors. And the heroism of the Serbs and Montenegrins fighting for a great cause provoked amongst the entire nation a desire to help their brothers, no longer just in word but in deed.

But there was also something else about all this that made Sergey

Ivanovich rejoice: this was the manifestation of public opinion. The public had definitely expressed its wishes. The soul of the nation had found expression, as Sergey Ivanovich put it. And the more he involved himself with this cause, the more evident it seemed to him that this was a cause which was bound to assume enormous dimensions and become a major watershed.

He dedicated himself totally to the service of this great cause and forgot to think about his book.

All his time was taken up now, which meant he was unable to answer all the letters and requests addressed to him.

After working all spring and part of the summer, it was only in July that he was ready to go and visit his brother in the country.

He was going both to have a fortnight's rest and, in the holy of holies of the people, the depths of the countryside, to enjoy seeing that upsurge of national spirit in which he, along with residents in all the major cities and towns, fully believed. Katavasov, who had long been planning to keep his promise to go and visit Levin, went with him.

2

SERGEY IVANOVICH and Katavasov barely had time to drive up to the Kursk railway station,* which was particularly bustling with people that day, get out of their carriage, and look round for the servant following with the luggage, when some volunteers* also drove up in four cabs. Ladies met them with bouquets and they went into the station, accompanied by a crowd which came streaming after them.

One of the ladies who had met the volunteers addressed Sergey Ivanovich as she came out of the waiting room.

'Have you also come to see them off?' she asked in French.

'No, I'm travelling myself, Princess. To my brother's, for a holiday. So do you always see them off?' said Sergey Ivanovich with a barely perceptible smile.

'Oh, that would be impossible!' replied the Princess. 'Is it true that we have sent eight hundred already? Malvinsky wouldn't believe me.'

'More than eight hundred. And if you count those who weren't sent directly from Moscow, it's over a thousand,' said Sergey Ivanovich.

'There you are then. That's just what I said!' exclaimed the Princess. 'And it's true, isn't it, that about a million has been donated by now?'

'More, Princess.'

'And what about today's dispatch? They beat the Turks again.'

'Yes, I read it,' answered Sergey Ivanovich. They were talking about the latest dispatch, which confirmed that the Turks had been beaten on all fronts for three days in a row and were in flight, and that a decisive battle was expected the following day.

'Oh yes, you know, there is one young man, a splendid young man, who wants to volunteer. I don't know why they're making difficulties. I meant to ask you, as I know him; do please write a note. He was sent by Countess Lydia Ivanovna.'

After finding out from the Princess what she knew about the young man who wanted to volunteer, Sergey Ivanovich went into the first-class waiting-room, wrote out a note to the person in charge of such matters, and handed it to the Princess.

'You know, Count Vronsky, the famous one . . . is travelling on this train,' said the Princess with a solemn and meaningful smile when he found her again and handed her the note.

'I heard he was going, but didn't know when. On this train?'

'I've seen him. He's here; only his mother is seeing him off. All the same, it's the best thing he could have done.'

'Oh yes, of course.'

While they were talking, a crowd of people streamed past them towards the lunch table. They also moved in that direction and heard the loud voice of a gentleman who was giving a speech to the volunteers, with a glass in his hand. 'To serve for our faith, for mankind, for our brothers,' the gentleman said, continually raising his voice. 'Mother Moscow blesses you in this great undertaking. *Zhivio!*[1] he concluded in a loud and tearful voice.

Everyone shouted *Zhivio!* and then a new crowd streamed into the room and almost knocked the Princess off her feet.

'Ah, Princess, how about that!' said Stepan Arkadyich, who had suddenly appeared in the middle of the crowd, beaming his radiant smile. 'Wasn't that a splendid, warm speech? Bravo! And Sergey Ivanich is here! You should chip in with a few words of your own now, to bolster morale; you do that sort of thing so well,' he added with a warm, deferential, and cautious smile as he tugged at Sergey Ivanovich's arm.

'No, I'm about to leave.'

'Where are you going?'

'To the country, to my brother's,' answered Sergey Ivanovich.

'Then you'll see my wife. I've written to her, but you'll see her

---

[1] 'Hurrah!' [Croatian.]

first; please tell her that you've seen me and that it's *all right*.[1] She'll understand. Actually, tell her, if you would be so kind, that I've been appointed as a member of the Commission of the United . . . Well, anyway, she'll understand! You know, *les petites misères de la vie humaine*,'[2] he said, turning to the Princess as if apologizing. 'And Princess Myagkaya—not Liza, but Bibish—really is sending a thousand rifles and twelve nurses. Did I tell you?'

'Yes, I heard,' answered Koznyshev reluctantly.

'It's a pity you're going away, you know,' said Stepan Arkadyich. 'Tomorrow we're giving a dinner for two departing soldiers—Dimer-Bartnyansky from Petersburg and our own Grisha Veslovsky. They're both going. Veslovsky got married recently. What a marvellous fellow he is! Don't you think so, Princess?' he said, turning to the lady.

The Princess looked at Koznyshev without replying. But Stepan Arkadyich was not in the least bit perturbed by the fact that Sergey Ivanovich and the Princess appeared to want to shake him off. Smiling, his gaze kept darting from the feather on the Princess's hat to what was going on around him, as if he was trying to remember something. When he caught sight of a lady with a collecting-box walking by, he called her over and put in a five-rouble note.

'I can't look calmly at those collecting-boxes while I've got money,' he said. 'And what about today's dispatch? Well done those Montenegrins!'

'You don't say!' he exclaimed when the Princess told him that Vronsky was going on this train. For a brief moment Stepan Arkadyich's face expressed sadness, but a minute later, when, with a slight spring in his step and smoothing his whiskers, he went into the room where Vronsky was, he had already completely forgotten his desperate sobbing over his sister's dead body, and saw in Vronsky only a hero and an old friend.

'Despite all his faults, you have to give him his due,' the Princess said to Sergey Ivanovich as soon as Oblonsky had left them. 'There's a truly Russian, Slav nature for you! I'm just afraid that Vronsky will find it upsetting to see him. Say what you will, I'm moved by that man's fate. Have a chat with him during the journey,' said the Princess.

'Yes, maybe, if the occasion arises.'

'I never liked him. But this redeems a great deal. He's not only going himself, but taking a squadron at his own expense.'

'Yes, I heard.'

---

[1] [English in the original.]   [2] 'the small miseries of human life'.

The bell sounded. Everyone rushed towards the doors.

'There he is!' said the Princess, indicating Vronsky in a long over-coat and a black, wide-brimmed hat, walking along with his mother on his arm. Oblonsky was walking beside him, talking avidly about something.

Frowning, Vronsky was looking straight in front of him, as if not hearing what Stepan Arkadyich was saying.

Probably because Oblonsky had pointed them out, he looked round in the direction where the Princess and Sergey Ivanovich were stand-ing and silently raised his hat. His face, which had aged and expressed suffering, seemed to have turned to stone.

Stepping on to the platform, Vronsky allowed his mother to pass, then quietly disappeared into a compartment of the carriage.

'God save the Tsar' rang out on the platform, followed by shouts of 'Hurrah!' and '*Zhivio!*' One of the volunteers, a tall, very young man with a hollow chest, bowed in a particularly conspicuous way, waving a felt hat and a bouquet of flowers over his head. Poking their heads out behind him, also bowing, were two officers and an elderly man with a big beard, in a greasy cap.

3

AFTER taking leave of the Princess, Sergey Ivanovich got into the overcrowded carriage with Katavasov, who had joined him, and the train departed.

At Tsaritsyno station the train was met by a harmonious choir of young men singing 'Glory'.* The volunteers poked their heads out and bowed again, but Sergey Ivanovich did not pay any attention to them; he had so many dealings with the volunteers that he was by now familiar with their general type, and it did not interest him. Katavasov, on the other hand, had not had an opportunity of observing the vol-unteers due to his scholarly activities, was very interested in them, and plied Sergey Ivanovich with questions about them.

Sergey Ivanovich advised him to go along to the second-class car-riage and talk to them himself. At the next station Katavasov followed this piece of advice.

At the first stop he transferred to second class and made the acquaintance of the volunteers. They were sitting separately in a corner of the carriage, talking loudly and obviously aware that the attention of the passengers and Katavasov, who had just entered, was focused on them. The tall youth with the hollow chest was talking loudest of all. He was clearly drunk, and was telling the story of something that had happened at their establishment. An officer dressed in the military jacket of the Austrian Guards, who was getting on in years, was seated opposite him. He was listening with a smile to the raconteur and occasionally butting in. A third, wearing an artillery uniform, was sitting on a suitcase beside them. A fourth was asleep.

Entering into conversation with the youth, Katavasov learned that he was a wealthy Moscow merchant who had frittered away a large fortune before he was twenty-two. Katavasov did not like him, as he was effeminate, spoilt, and of delicate constitution; he was obviously convinced, especially now he had been drinking, that he was performing a heroic act, and was bragging in a most distasteful manner.

The second man, a retired officer, also made an unpleasant impression on Katavasov. He was evidently someone who had tried his hand at everything. He had worked on the railways, had been a manager, and had himself started up factories, and he talked about it all, needlessly and inappropriately using technical terms.

By contrast, Katavasov greatly liked the third volunteer, an artilleryman. He was a modest, quiet person, clearly in awe of the retired guards officer's knowledge and the heroic self-sacrifice of the merchant, and was not saying anything about himself. When Katavasov asked him what had made him want to go to Serbia, he answered modestly:

'Well, everybody is going. We have to help the Serbs too. You feel sorry for them.'

'Yes, artillerymen like you are in particularly short supply there,' said Katavasov.

'But I didn't serve very long in the artillery; they might assign me to the infantry or the cavalry.'

'Why put you in the infantry when it's artillerymen they need most of all?' said Katavasov, reckoning from the artilleryman's age that he must already have attained a high rank.

'I only served for a short time in the artillery, I retired as a cadet,' he said, and began to explain why he had not passed the examination.

All this combined to make a disagreeable impression on Katavasov, and when the volunteers got out at a station for a drink, he wanted to verify his unfavourable impression by talking to someone else. One old man in the carriage who was wearing a military overcoat had been listening throughout Katavasov's conversation with the volunteers. Once he was left alone with him, Katavasov turned to him.

'Yes, what a variety of situations they all have, these people who are setting off there,' Katavasov said vaguely, wanting to express his own opinion but at the same time elicit the opinion of the old man.

The old fellow was a military man who had completed two campaigns. He knew what a military man was, and he deemed these gentlemen, judging from their appearance and conversation, and the swashbuckling way in which they applied themselves to the flask during the journey, to be poor military men. He lived, moreover, in a provincial town, and was keen to recount how only one discharged soldier had joined up from his town, a drunkard and a thief whom no one would even employ as a labourer any more. But knowing from experience that it would be dangerous to express an opinion that ran contrary to the prevailing one, given the current public mood, and in particular to criticize the volunteers, he was also sounding Katavasov out.

'Well, they need people there,' he said. 'Apparently the Serbian officers are hopeless.'

'Oh yes, and this lot will certainly be gallant,' said Katavasov, his eyes twinkling. And they started discussing the latest news from the war, each concealing from the other his puzzlement about who would be the opponents in the following day's confrontation, when, according to the latest reports, the Turks had been beaten on all fronts. And so they parted, neither having expressed his opinion.

Coming back into his carriage, Katavasov involuntarily dissembled when he passed on to Sergey Ivanovich his observations about the volunteers, thus giving the impression that they were an excellent bunch.

Singing and cheers again greeted the volunteers at the main station in the city, women and men again appeared with collecting-boxes, and ladies from the provincial capital presented the volunteers with bouquets and followed them into the buffet; but it was all on a much more muted and smaller scale than in Moscow.

4

DURING the stop in the provincial capital, Sergey Ivanovich did not go to the buffet but instead started walking up and down the platform.

The first time he walked past Vronsky's compartment he noticed the curtains were drawn. But as he passed it the second time he saw the old Countess at the window. She beckoned Koznyshev over.

'I'm travelling too, accompanying him as far as Kursk,' she said.

'Yes, I'd heard,' said Sergey Ivanovich, pausing by her window and peering in. 'What a fine thing this is on his part!' he added, noticing that Vronsky was not in the compartment.

'But after his misfortune what else was there for him to do?'

'Such a terrible event!' said Sergey Ivanovich.

'Ah, what I have endured! But do come inside . . . Ah, the things I have been through!' she repeated when Sergey Ivanovich had come in and sat down beside her on the seat. 'You couldn't imagine! For six weeks he spoke to no one, and would only eat when I begged him to. And he could not be left alone for a single minute. We removed everything he might have used to kill himself; we were living on the ground floor, but it was impossible to predict anything. You know, of course, that he had already shot himself once on her account,' she said, and the old lady's brow furrowed at the recollection. 'Yes, she met her end in the way a woman like that had to meet her end. Even the death she chose was ignoble and sordid.'

'It's not for us to judge, Countess,' said Sergey Ivanovich with a sigh; 'but I can understand how hard it was for you.'

'Ah, you don't have to tell me! I was staying at my estate, and he was with me. A note was brought. He wrote a reply and sent it off. We had no idea she was right there at the station. That evening I had only just retired when my Mary told me a lady had thrown herself under a train at the station. It was as if I had received a blow! I knew it was her. The first thing I said was: don't tell him. But they had already told him. His coachman was there and saw it all. By the time I had rushed into his room he was already beside himself—it was terrible to see him. He didn't say a word, and galloped off to the station. I don't know what happened, but they brought him back like a corpse. I would not have recognized him. *Prostration complète,*[1] the doctor said. Then he almost went out of his mind.

'Oh, it's impossible to talk about!' said the Countess with a wave of her hand. 'A terrible time! No, whatever you may say, she was a bad woman. Well, what were those desperate passions all about? It was all about trying to prove something particular. Well, she certainly proved it. She destroyed herself and two fine people—her husband and my unfortunate son.'

'And what about her husband?' asked Sergey Ivanovich.

'He has taken her daughter. Alyosha consented to everything at first. But now he is in terrible anguish that he gave his daughter away to a stranger. But he can't take back his word. Karenin came to

---

[1] 'complete prostration'.

the funeral. But we tried to make sure he and Alyosha did not meet. For him, her husband that is, it has been easier after all. She released him. But my poor son had devoted himself to her utterly. He gave up everything—his career, me, and even then she did not spare him, but set out to destroy him completely. No, whatever you may say, even her death was that of a vile woman without religion. God forgive me, but I can't help hating her memory when I look at my son's ruin.'

'But how is he now?'

'It's a godsend for us, this Serbian war. I'm an old person who doesn't understand anything about it, but it's a godsend for him. Of course for me, as his mother, it's terrifying; and the main thing is that apparently *ce n'est pas très bien vu a Pétersbourg.*[1] But it can't be helped! This has been the only thing that has got him back on his feet. Yashvin—his friend—he lost everything gambling and decided to go to Serbia. He called round and persuaded him to go. Now it's keeping him occupied. Do please go and talk to him, as I would like to distract him. He's so sad. And to make things worse, he has toothache too. But he'll be very glad to see you. Please do go and talk to him, he's walking along the other side.'

Sergey Ivanovich said he would be only too glad, and crossed to the other side of the train.

5

IN his long coat and pulled-down hat, with his hands in his pockets, Vronsky was walking along in the slanting evening shadow of some sacks piled up on the platform like a caged animal, turning round smartly every twenty paces. It seemed to Sergey Ivanovich, when he approached, that Vronsky could see him but was pretending not to. Sergey Ivanovich did not mind. He was above any such personal scores with Vronsky.

At that moment Vronsky was an important figure working for a great cause in Sergey Ivanovich's eyes, and Koznyshev considered it his duty to encourage him and show his approval. He went up to him.

Vronsky stopped, looked intently, recognized him, and taking a few steps towards Sergey Ivanovich, shook his hand vigorously.

'You maybe didn't even want to see me,' said Sergey Ivanovich, 'but can I not be of some use to you?'

---

[1] 'It is not seen very well in Petersburg.'

'There is no one whom it would be less unpleasant for me to see than you,' said Vronsky. 'Forgive me. There is nothing pleasant in life for me.'

'I understand, and just wanted to offer you my services,' said Sergey Ivanovich, studying Vronsky's patently suffering face. 'You don't need a letter to Ristić or Milan?'*

'Oh no!' Vronsky said, as if he had difficulty understanding him. 'If you don't mind, let's walk. It's sweltering in the carriages. A letter? No, thank you; one doesn't need letters of introduction in order to die. Except to the Turks . . .' he said, smiling with only his lips. His eyes retained their look of angry suffering.

'Yes, but it may be easier for you to establish relations, which are nevertheless unavoidable, with someone who has been primed. As you wish, however. I was very glad to hear of your decision. The volunteers have been subject to so many attacks that a person like you will enhance their public standing.'

'What is good about me as a person', said Vronsky, 'is that I do not value my life. Also that I have enough physical energy to slash my way into a *carré** and smite or be slain—that I do know. I'm glad there is something for which I can give up my life, which, if not exactly redundant, has certainly become loathsome to me. It will be of use to somebody.' And he made an impatient movement with his jaw, due to the incessant, gnawing ache in his tooth, which prevented him even from speaking with the expression he wished.

'I predict that you will be reborn,' said Sergey Ivanovich, feeling moved. 'To free one's brothers from the yoke is an aim worthy of both death and life. May God grant you outward success—and inner peace,' he added and held out his hand.

Vronsky shook Sergey Ivanovich's outstretched hand vigorously.

'Yes, as an instrument I may be of some use. But as a man, I'm a wreck,' he pronounced slowly.

The throbbing pain in his strong tooth, which had filled his mouth with saliva, was making it difficult for him to speak. He fell silent and stared at the wheels of the tender as they trundled slowly and smoothly along the rails.

And suddenly a completely different sensation, not of pain, but of a general agonizing inner discomfort, made him forget his toothache for a moment. As he looked at the tender and at the rails, under the influence of his conversation with an acquaintance he had not seen since his misfortune, he suddenly remembered *her*, that is, what still remained of her when he had run like a madman into the railway shed:

her bloodstained body still full of recent life, stretched out shamelessly among strangers on a table in the shed; her thrown-back intact head with its heavy plaits and curls round the temples, and on the lovely face with its half-open, red mouth a strange frozen expression which was pitiful on the lips and awful in the fixed, staring eyes, as if she were pronouncing the dreadful words—about how he would come to repent—that she had uttered during their quarrel.

And he tried to remember her as she had been when he met her for the first time, also at a railway station, when she was mysterious, enchanting, loving, seeking and bestowing happiness, rather than cruel and vengeful, as he recalled her being at that last moment. He tried to remember his best moments with her, but those moments were poisoned for ever. He could only remember her triumphantly carrying out her totally pointless threat of provoking everlasting remorse. He stopped feeling the pain in his tooth, and his face was distorted by sobs.

After silently walking up and down past the sacks twice and regaining his composure, he turned calmly to Sergey Ivanovich:

'You haven't had a new telegram since yesterday? Yes, routed a third time, but the decisive battle is expected tomorrow.'

And after talking further about the proclamation of Milan as king and the enormous repercussions this might have, they each went to their respective carriages after the second bell.

6

NOT knowing when he would be able to leave Moscow, Sergey Ivanovich had not wired his brother to arrange for someone to meet them. Levin was not at home when, towards midday, Katavasov and Sergey Ivanovich, covered with dust and looking like blackamoors, drove up to the porch of the Pokrovskoye house in a little wagon hired at the station. Kitty, who was sitting on the balcony with her father and sister, recognized her brother-in-law and ran down to greet him.

'It's shameful of you not to have let us know,' she said, holding out her hand to Sergey Ivanovich and proffering him her forehead for him to kiss.

'We've had a splendid journey and didn't want to trouble you,' Sergey Ivanovich replied. 'I'm so dusty I'm afraid to touch you. I've been so busy I didn't know when I could tear myself away. But here you are as ever,' he said, smiling, 'enjoying your quiet happiness in your quiet backwater away from the currents. And our friend Fyodor Vasilievich here has finally managed to come.'

'But I'm not a negro—I will look like a human being once I have washed,' said Katavasov in his usual droll way, holding out his hand and smiling with unusually gleaming teeth because of his black face.

'Kostya will be very glad. He went off to the farmstead. It's about time for him to come back.'

'Still busy with his farming. You really are in a backwater,' said Katavasov. 'While in town we have nothing in our field of vision except the Serbian war. Well, how does my friend view it? No doubt a bit differently to other people?'

'Oh, I don't know, like everybody else I think,' Kitty answered with slight embarrassment, looking round at Sergey Ivanovich. 'I'll send for him now. We have Papa staying with us. He's recently returned from abroad.'

And after arranging for Levin to be sent for, and for the dusty guests to be taken in to wash, one in the study, the other in Dolly's former room, and for lunch to be served to the guests, she ran up on to the balcony, exercising the right of rapid movement which had been denied her during her pregnancy.

'It's Sergey Ivanovich and Katavasov, the professor,' she said.

'Oh, that's all we need in this heat!' said the Prince.

'No, Papa, he's very nice, and Kostya is very fond of him,' said Kitty with a smile, as if trying to convince him of something, after noticing the withering expression on her father's face.

'Oh, I didn't mean it.'

'You go and keep them entertained, darling,' said Kitty to her sister. 'They saw Stiva at the station, he is well. And I'll run along to Mitya. It's terrible, I haven't fed him since tea this morning. He is awake now, and is bound to be crying.' And feeling the flow of milk, she scurried off to the nursery.

Indeed, she did not so much guess (the bond with her baby was not yet broken) as know for certain from the flow of her milk that he needed to be fed.

She knew he was crying even before she reached the nursery. And indeed he was crying. She heard his voice and quickened her step. But the faster she walked, the louder he cried. His voice was fine and healthy, just hungry and impatient.

'How long has this being going on, nanny, how long?' said Kitty hurriedly, as she sat down on the chair and prepared herself for feeding.

'Do hurry up and give him to me. Oh, nanny, how tiresome you are, come on, you can tie on his bonnet afterwards!'

The baby was wearing itself out with its ravenous screaming.

'No, that won't do, my dear,' said Agafya Mikhailovna, who was almost always to be found in the nursery. 'He must be properly tidied up. Goo, goo!' she cooed over him, ignoring his mother.

The nanny brought the baby to his mother. Agafya Mikhailovna followed them, her face dissolving into tenderness.

'He knows me, he does. Honest to God, Katerina Alexandrovna, my dear, he recognized me!' Agafya Mikhailovna shouted over the baby's screams.

But Kitty was not listening to what she was saying. Her impatience was mounting, along with that of her baby.

Due to the impatience, things took a long time to settle down. The baby did not take hold in the right way, and was angry.

Eventually, after desperate, breathless screaming and ineffectual sucking, things did settle down, and mother and child simultaneously experienced a sense of calm, and they both quietened down.

'But poor little thing, he's all sweaty too,' said Kitty in a whisper, as she felt the baby. 'What makes you think he recognizes you?' she added, casting a sidelong glance at the baby's eyes, which seemed to her to be peeping out impishly from under his pulled-down bonnet, at his little cheeks with their steady puffing, and at his little hand with its red palm, with which he was making circular movements.

'That can't be right! If he was going to recognize anyone, it would be me,' said Kitty in response to Agafya Mikhailovna's claim, and she smiled.

She smiled, because although she had said he could not recognize anyone yet, she knew in her heart that not only did he recognize Agafya Mikhailovna, but that he knew and understood everything, and also knew and understood a great deal that no one else knew, which she, his mother, had discovered and come to understand purely thanks to him. For Agafya Mikhailovna, his nanny, his grandfather, and even his father, Mitya was a living creature who only required material care; but for his mother he had long been a moral creature, with whom she already had a whole history of spiritual relations.

'Well, as soon as he wakes up, you'll see for yourself, God willing. I just do this, and he beams all over, the little darling. Beams all over like a sunny day,' said Agafya Mikhailovna.

'Well, all right, all right, let's see what happens then,' whispered Kitty. 'But go now, he's falling asleep.'

7

AGAFYA MIKHAILOVNA went out on tiptoe; the nanny let down the blind, drove out the flies from under the muslin canopy of the cot, and a hornet that was beating against the windowpane, and sat down, waving a wilting birch branch over mother and baby.

'Dear me, this heat! If the good Lord would only send a drop of rain,' she said.

'Yes, yes, sh-sh . . .' was Kitty's only reply as she rocked herself gently and tenderly squeezed the plump little hand that seemed to be tied at the wrist with a thread, and which Mitya was still waving feebly while he opened and shut his eyes. That little hand was bothering Kitty: she wanted to kiss that little hand, but was afraid to do so lest she wake the baby. At last the little hand stopped moving, and the eyes closed. Just occasionally, as he continued feeding, the baby raised his long, curly eyelashes and gazed at his mother with moist eyes which seemed black in the half-light. The nanny stopped her fanning and dozed off. From upstairs came the sound of the old Prince's booming voice and Katavasov's hearty laughter.

'They seem to have struck up a conversation without my help,' thought Kitty, 'but all the same, it's annoying Kostya is not here. He must have stopped by the apiary again. It makes me sad he's there so often,* but I'm glad too. It is a distraction for him. He's become much more cheerful, much better now, compared to how he was in the spring. Back then he was so tormented and miserable, I began to fear for him. And how funny he is!' she whispered, smiling.

She knew what was tormenting her husband. It was his lack of faith. Despite the fact that, if asked whether she supposed he would be damned in the next life if he did not believe, she would have to concur that he would, his lack of faith caused her no unhappiness, so while acknowledging there can be no salvation for an unbeliever and loving her husband's soul more than anything in the world, she smiled as she thought about his lack of faith, and told herself he was funny.

'Why has he spent the whole year reading all that philosophy?' she thought. 'If it is all written in these books, then he can understand it. But if what is in them is untrue, why read them? He says himself that he would like to believe. So why doesn't he believe? It must be because he thinks so much. And he thinks so much because of his seclusion. He's always, always alone. He can't tell us all about it. I think he'll welcome these visitors, especially Katavasov. He likes arguing with him,' she thought, which immediately prompted her to think about where it would be most comfortable for Katavasov to sleep—in a separate room or with Sergey Ivanich. And then a thought suddenly occurred to her that made her shudder with alarm and even disturb Mitya, who looked at her sternly for it. 'I don't think the laundrywoman has brought the clean linen back yet, and all the bed linen for guests has been used. If I don't see to it, Agafya Mikhailovna will give Sergey Ivanovich used sheets,' and the blood rushed to Kitty's face at the mere thought of it.

'Yes, I will see to it,' she decided, and going back to her previous thoughts, she remembered that some important matter close to her heart had not been fully thought through and she began trying to remember what it was. 'Yes, Kostya does not believe,' she thought again with a smile.

'Well, so what if he does not believe? Better to let him always be like that than like Madame Stahl, or how I wanted to be when I was abroad. No, he is never going to pretend.'

And a recent example of his kindness came vividly into her mind. Two weeks earlier a penitent letter from Stepan Arkadyich had arrived for Dolly. He begged her to save his honour by selling her estate to pay his debts. Dolly was in despair, she hated her husband, despised him, pitied him, made up her mind to obtain a divorce and refuse him, but she ended up agreeing to sell part of her estate. After that Kitty remembered with an involuntary tender smile her husband's embarrassment, his repeated clumsy attempts to broach a subject which was of concern to him, and how, after thinking up the one sole means of helping Dolly without offending her, he had finally suggested to Kitty that she give up her share of the estate, which had not previously occurred to her.

'How can anyone say he does not believe? With that heart of his, and that fear of upsetting anyone, even a child! Everything for others, nothing for himself. Sergey Ivanovich plainly thinks it's Kostya's duty to be his steward. And so does his sister. Now Dolly and her children have been taken under his wing. And all those peasants who come to see him every day, as if it were his duty to serve them.'

'Yes, you be just like your father, just like him,' she said, handing Mitya to the nanny and brushing his cheek with her lips.

8

FROM the moment when the sight of his beloved dying brother had caused Levin to look for the first time at the issues of life and death through the prism of those new convictions, as he called them, which between the ages of twenty and thirty-four had imperceptibly replaced the beliefs he had held in his childhood and youth, he had been horrified not so much by death as by life, lacking the slightest knowledge about where it came from, what it was for, why it existed, and what it was. The human organism, its destruction, the ineradicability of matter, the law of the conservation of energy, and evolution were the terms which had replaced his former beliefs. These words and the concepts associated with them were very good for intellectual purposes, but as a guide to life they offered nothing, and Levin suddenly felt like a man who has exchanged his warm fur coat for a muslin garment, and who, the first time he is out in the frost, unequivocally establishes with his whole being rather than with his intellect that he is as good as naked and must inexorably suffer an agonizing death.

From that moment, although he was not aware of it and went on living as before, Levin did not cease to experience this fear on account of his ignorance.

He had a vague sense, moreover, that what he called his convictions constituted not just ignorance, but the kind of cast of mind which made knowledge of what he needed to know impossible.

Marriage and the new joys and duties it brought had completely suppressed these thoughts to begin with; but lately, while he had been living in Moscow with nothing to do after his wife's confinement, a question requiring an answer had started presenting itself to him with ever greater frequency and urgency.

The question for him consisted of the following: 'If I do not accept the answers Christianity gives to the problems of my life, then what answers do I accept?' And not only was he unable to find any answers amongst the whole arsenal of his convictions, but he could not find anything even approaching an answer.

He was in the position of someone looking for food in shops selling toys and guns.

He now involuntarily and unconsciously sought a connection and a solution to these questions in every book, every conversation, every person.

What most astonished and disconcerted him in this regard was that the majority of people in his circle and age-group who had replaced their previous beliefs as he had, and acquired the same new convictions as he had, saw nothing untoward about this, and were completely contented and calm. So that, apart from the main question, Levin was tormented by still other questions. Were these people sincere? Were they not putting on an act? Or did they understand in a different or clearer way the answers which science gives to the questions that preoccupied him? And he diligently studied both these people's opinions and the books that articulated these answers.

One thing he had discovered since these questions first started to absorb him was that he was mistaken in presuming on the basis of memories of his youthful university circle that religion had become obsolete and no longer existed. All the people close to him who led good lives believed. The old Prince, and Lvov, of whom he had grown so fond, and Sergey Ivanovich, and all the women believed, and his wife believed in the way that he had believed in early childhood, and ninety-nine out of a hundred Russian peasants—all the people whose lives inspired him with the most respect—also believed.

Another thing was that he came to the conclusion, after reading a great many books, that people who shared identical views with him did not give them a second thought, and that they simply dismissed without explanation those questions he felt he could not live without answering, and tried instead to solve completely different problems which could not be of any interest to him, such as the evolution of organisms, the materialistic explanation of the soul, and so on.

During his wife's confinement, moreover, something extraordinary had happened to him. He, a person who did not believe, had started to pray, and in the moment when he was praying he had believed. But that moment had passed, and he was unable to allocate any place in his life to the state of mind he had been in then.

He could not admit that he had known the truth then and was mistaken now, because as soon as he began to think calmly about it, everything shattered into little pieces; nor could he admit that he was mistaken then, because he cherished that spiritual state of mind, and admitting it to be the result of weakness would have resulted in him desecrating those moments. He was in painful disharmony with himself and mustering all his emotional energy in order to find a way out of it.

9

THESE thoughts taxed and tormented him with varying degrees of intensity, but they never left him. He went on reading and thinking, and the more he read and thought, the further he felt from the goal he was pursuing.

Having come to the conclusion during the latter part of his stay in Moscow and in the country that he would not find the answer from the materialists, he read and reread Plato, Spinoza, Kant, Schelling, Hegel, and Schopenhauer—the philosophers who provided a non-materialistic explanation of life.

Ideas seemed productive to him when he was either reading or thinking up his own refutations of other doctrines, especially those of the materialists; but as soon as he read or himself thought up solutions to problems, the same thing always happened. By following the given definitions of nebulous words such as *spirit, will, freedom, substance*, and deliberately falling into the verbal trap the philosophers or he himself had set, he began somehow to understand something. But he had only to forget the artificial train of thought, returning from real life to the thoughts that had satisfied him while he was following the given line of reasoning, for this entire artificial edifice to collapse at once like a house of cards, making it clear that the edifice had been constructed from the same words, but simply transposed, and without regard for anything more important in life than reason.

At one point, while reading Schopenhauer, he had replaced the word *will** with the word *love*, and this new philosophy gave him solace for those few days while he adhered to it; but then when he looked at it from the vantage-point of real life, it collapsed in just the same way, and turned out to be a muslin garment providing no warmth.

His brother Sergey Ivanovich advised him to read the theological works of Khomyakov.* Levin read the second volume of Khomyakov's works, and despite their polemical, elegant, and witty tone, which repelled him at first, he was struck by the teaching he found in them about the Church. He was struck first of all by the idea that it is not given to the individual person to perceive divine truths, but to the sum of people joined together in love—the Church. He was gratified by the idea that it was easier to believe in the present, living Church, comprising all peoples' beliefs, with God at its head and therefore holy and infallible, and from there derive one's belief in God, creation, the fall, and redemption, rather than take as the starting point a distant, mysterious God, the creation, etc. But when he went on to read a Catholic writer's history of the Church and an Orthodox writer's history of the Church, and saw that each Church, infallible by its very nature, repudiated the other, he became disillusioned by Khomyakov's teaching about the Church too, and this building crumbled into dust just as the philosophical edifices had done.

All that spring he was not himself, and he experienced some terrible moments.

'It is impossible to live without knowing what I am and why I am here. But I can't know that, so therefore it is impossible to live,' Levin said to himself.

'An organism like a bubble will emerge out of infinite time, infinite matter, and infinite space, and that bubble will last for a while and burst, and that bubble is me.'

This was an agonizing untruth, but it was the sole, ultimate conclusion of the work of centuries of human thought in this direction.

This was the ultimate belief upon which had been built all investigations in almost every branch of human thought. This was the reigning dogma, and without knowing when or how, this was the explanation Levin involuntarily adopted out of all the other explanations, as the one that was nevertheless the most lucid.

But it was not only an untruth; it was also cruel mockery on the part of some kind of evil power—evil and reprehensible, and of a kind to which one could not surrender.

It was necessary to free himself of this power.* And deliverance was in the hands of every person. It was necessary to put an end to this dependence on evil. And there was one means—death.

And Levin, the happy family man in good health, was on several occasions so close to suicide that he hid a rope so he could not hang himself with it, and was afraid to go out with a gun lest he shoot himself.

But Levin did not shoot or hang himself, and he went on living.

10

WHEN Levin thought about what he was and what he was living for, he could find no answer and was driven to despair; but when he stopped questioning himself about this, he seemed to know what he was and what he was living for, because he acted and lived in a resolute and definite way; and even during this recent time he lived in a far more resolute and definite way than before.

When he returned to the country at the beginning of June, he resumed his usual activities. Farming, relations with the peasants and his neighbours, running the household, the affairs of his sister and brother which were under his jurisdiction, relations with his wife and relatives, concerns over the baby, and the new bee-keeping hobby he had developed a passion for that spring occupied all his time.

These matters occupied him not because he could justify them to himself with some or other general views as he used to do before; on the contrary, his disappointment on the one hand about the failure of previous projects undertaken for the common good, and on the other, his preoccupation with his own thoughts, and the sheer quantity of things converging on him from all sides, had led him to put all thoughts about the common good, completely to one side and so these things occupied him simply because he felt he had to do what he was doing, and could not do otherwise.

Previously (this had started almost in childhood and had continued to increase until full adulthood), whenever he had tried to do something that would be of benefit to everybody, to mankind, to Russia, to the province, or to the whole village, he had noticed that while thinking about it was pleasant, the activity itself was always ineffective, he lacked complete confidence that the thing was strictly necessary, and the activity itself, which initially had seemed so significant, would shrink until it was reduced to nothing; now, however, when after his marriage he had begun increasingly to restrict himself to living for himself, although he no longer experienced any pleasure at the thought of what he was doing, he felt confident that his work was vitally important, saw that it was going much better than before, and that it kept on expanding.

Now, as if against his will, he was cutting ever deeper into the soil like a plough, so that he could no longer extract himself without turning over the furrow.

For his family to live in the manner to which his father and forefathers had grown accustomed, that is, with the same level of education, and to bring up his children in the same way was without question a necessity. It was just as necessary as sitting down to dinner when one is hungry; and for that, just as it is necessary to prepare dinner, it was equally necessary to run the estate at Pokrovskoye in a way that provided an income. Just as it was without question necessary to repay a debt, so it was necessary to maintain the family property in a condition such that his son would thank his father when he inherited it, as Levin had thanked his grandfather for everything he had built and planted. And for that, it was necessary for him not to lease the land out but farm it himself, by keeping cattle, spreading manure over the fields, and planting trees.

It was impossible not to do things for Sergey Ivanovich, his sister, and all the peasants who came for advice and had a habit of doing so, just as it is impossible to let go of a baby you are already holding in your arms. It was necessary to see to the comfort of his sister-in-law, who had been invited to stay with her children, and that of his wife and baby, and it was impossible not to spend at least a small part of the day with them.

And all this, together with shooting for game and the new bee-keeping hobby, filled up all that part of Levin's life which had no meaning for him when he was thinking.

But apart from the fact that Levin knew precisely *what* he had to do, he also knew precisely *how* he needed to do everything, and which job was more important than others.

He knew that he should hire labourers as cheaply as possible, but also that he should not reduce them to bondage by paying them in advance less than they were worth, even though it was very profitable. He could sell straw to the peasants when there was a shortage of fodder, although he felt sorry for them; but the inn and the tavern had to be closed down, even though they provided revenue. He had to impose the strictest possible penalty for the illegal felling of timber, but he could not extract fines when cattle were driven on to his land, and although this angered the watchmen and eliminated fear of reprisal, he had to let those straying cattle go.

He needed to give a loan to Pyotr, who was paying a moneylender ten per cent a month, so his debt could be redeemed; but he could not lower or defer the rent for peasants who had fallen into arrears. He could not let the steward get away with not having mown the meadow and letting the grass go to waste; but the two hundred acres sown with young trees could not be mown. He could not excuse a labourer who had gone home during the peak work season because his father had died, however sorry he felt for him, and he had to dock him for the costly months he had been absent; but he also could not refrain from paying monthly wages to the old servants who were of no use for anything.

Levin also knew that when he got home he first of all had to go and see his wife, who was unwell; but the peasants who had already been waiting for him for three hours could wait a bit longer; and he knew that despite all the pleasure he derived in capturing a swarm, he had to forgo that pleasure and let the old man capture the swarm without him, while he went and talked to the peasants who had found him at the apiary.

Whether he was acting rightly or wrongly he did not know, and not only was he not disposed to argument now, but avoided talking and thinking about this.

Reasoning had led him into doubt, and prevented him from seeing what should and should not be done. When he did not think, however, but lived, he was constantly aware in his soul of the presence of an infallible judge determining which of two possible courses of action was better and which was worse; and as soon as he did not act as he should have done, he was immediately aware of it.

Thus he lived, neither knowing nor seeing any possibility of knowing what he was and what the point of his life on earth was, and while he was tormented by this lack of knowledge to such a degree that he was afraid of committing suicide, he was at the same time resolutely carving his own particular decisive path in life.

I I

THE day on which Sergey Ivanovich arrived in Pokrovskoye was one of Levin's most harrowing days.

It was the most frenetic period of work, when the peasants all display an extraordinary intensity of self-sacrifice such as they never display in any other circumstances in life, and which would be highly valued if the people displaying these qualities themselves placed a value on them, if it were not repeated every year, and if the results of this intensity of effort were not so simple.

To reap and bind the rye and oats and cart them all off, finish mowing the meadows, re-plough the fallow land, thresh the seed, and sow the winter crops—all this might seem simple and ordinary; but in order to manage to do all this it is imperative that every person in the village, from the oldest to the youngest, works three times harder than usual and without a break during these three or four weeks, living on kvass, onions, and black bread, threshing and carting the sheaves at night, and not relinquishing more than two or three hours out of twenty-four to sleep. And this happens every year all over Russia.

Having spent most of his life living in the country and in close contact with the peasants, Levin always felt during the working period that this general exhilaration amongst the peasantry also communicated itself to him.

In the early morning he rode over to the first sowing of the rye, and to the oats, which were being carted and stacked, and after returning home to be there when his wife and sister-in-law got up, he drank coffee with them before setting off on foot to the farm buildings, where they were due to start up the newly installed threshing machine for the preparation of the seed corn.

All that day, while he was talking to the steward and the peasants, and while he was talking to his wife, Dolly, her children, and his father-in-law at home, Levin kept thinking about the one single thing that occupied him apart from the farm-work, and in everything he searched for some perspective on his question: 'What am I, and where am I? And why am I here?'

Standing in the cool of the newly roofed threshing barn, the hazel laths with their fragrant, still unshed leaves pressed against the freshly stripped aspen poles of the thatch roof, Levin looked out through the open doorway, in which the dry and acrid chaff from the threshing danced and sparkled, at the grass on the threshing floor lit by the hot sun and the fresh straw just brought over from the shed, at the white-breasted swallows with brightly coloured heads, whistling as they flew in under the roof to hover, wings fluttering, in the shafts of light created by the doors, and at the peasants bustling about in the dark and dusty threshing barn, and he thought strange thoughts.

'Why is all this being done?' he thought. 'Why am I standing here, making them work? What are they bustling about for, trying to show how diligent they are in front of me? What is my good friend old Matryona slaving away for? (I treated her when a beam fell on her during the fire)' he thought, looking at a thin woman who was treading painfully with her bare, sun-blackened feet over the uneven, hard threshing floor as she raked the grain. 'She recovered then, but today or tomorrow, or in ten years' time they'll be burying her, and nothing will be left of her, nor of that fashionable girl in the red skirt winnowing the chaff with such a deft and gentle movement. They'll bury her very soon, and that piebald gelding,' he thought, gazing at the horse dragging its belly and taking short breaths through flared nostrils as it walked on the inclined wheel moving underneath it. 'They will bury him, and they'll bury Fyodor the machine-feeder, with his curly beard full of chaff and his shirt torn on his white shoulder. But he's loosening the sheaves, and giving orders, and shouting at the women, and adjusting the belt on the flywheel with a quick movement. And the main thing is that they will be burying not just them but me, and nothing will be left. What is the point?'

This is what he thought, but at the same time he was looking at his watch to work out how much threshing they would get through in an hour. He needed to know this so he could set the quota for the day by it.

'We're coming up to an hour now, and they've only just begun the third sheaf,' thought Levin and, going up to the man doing the feeding, he shouted over the roar of the machine to tell him to thin it out.

'You're feeding it too much, Fyodor! You see—it gets stuck, and that's why it's not going better. Level it out!'

Black from the chaff sticking to his sweaty face, Fyodor shouted something in reply, but still did not do it in the way Levin wanted.

Levin went up to the drum, moved Fyodor aside, and started doing the feeding himself.

After working until the peasants' dinner-time, which was not long in coming, he left the barn with the machine-feeder and got into conversation with him, stopping beside the neat yellow stack of harvested rye arranged on the threshing floor for seed.

The machine-feeder was from a distant village, the one where Levin had previously let land on a cooperative basis. Now the land was being let to an innkeeper.

Levin got talking to Fyodor the machine-feeder about this land, and asked whether Platon, a rich and well-liked peasant from the same village, would not take over the land the following year.

'The rent is high, and Platon couldn't make it pay, Konstantin Dmitrich,' answered the peasant, picking the ears of corn off his clammy shirt.

'But how does Kirillov make it pay?'

'Mityukha'—as the peasant called the innkeeper, witheringly—'he'll always make things pay, Konstantin Dmitrich! That man will squeeze you, and he'll make sure he gets what he is due. He won't take pity on a peasant. But Uncle Fokanych'—as he called the old man Platon—'do you think he'd skin a man alive? Sometimes he'll lend, and other times he'll let you off. And he doesn't always get it back. He's a good man.'

'But why would he let people off?'

'Well, you know—people are different; one man lives just for his own needs, like Mityukha, who only stuffs his belly, but Fokanych—he's a righteous old man. He lives for his soul. Remembers God.'

'How does he remember God? How does he live for his soul?' asked Levin, almost shouting.

'You know, in the usual way, obeying the truth, obeying God's will. People are different, after all. Take you, for instance, you also wouldn't want to hurt someone . . .'

'Yes, yes, goodbye!' said Levin, breathless with excitement, and he turned round to pick up his stick then walked off quickly towards home.

Levin was overcome by a joyous new feeling. While the peasant had talked about Fokanych living for his soul by obeying the truth and

God's will, a throng of vague but significant thoughts seemed to break loose from wherever they had been locked up and, all rushing towards the same goal, they started spinning round in his head, blinding him with their light.

12

LEVIN strode along the highway, heedful not so much of his thoughts (he could not decipher them yet) as of a spiritual state that he had never experienced before.

The words spoken by the peasant had produced in his soul the effect of an electric spark, transforming and fusing in an instant a whole swarm of isolated, powerless, separate thoughts that had never ceased to engage him. Without realizing it, these thoughts had also been engaging him while he was talking about letting the land.

He sensed something new in his soul, and took pleasure in exploring this new thing, without yet knowing what it was.

'To live not according to one's needs, but for God. For what God? For God. And what could be more meaningless than what he said? He said that one should not live according to one's needs, in other words, we should not live for what we understand, what we are attracted by, or what we want, but we should live for something we do not under-stand—for God, whom no one can understand or define. So what then? Did I misunderstand those meaningless things Fyodor said? Or did I understand them but doubt their truth, or find them stupid, unclear, or imprecise?

'No, I did understand him, and in exactly the same way he does; I understood him completely and more clearly than I've understood anything else in life, and never in my life have I doubted this, nor can I ever doubt it. And I am not alone in this, as everyone, the whole world, completely understands this one thing, and it is the one thing they do not doubt and always agree on.

'Fyodor says that Kirillov the innkeeper lives for his belly. That's understandable and rational. As rational beings, none of us can do other than live for our belly. But then this same Fyodor suddenly says that it is bad living for one's belly, and that one must live for truth, for God, and I understand him at the first inkling! I and millions of people who lived centuries ago and who are living now, from peasants and the poor in spirit to wise men who have thought and written about this, saying the same thing in their opaque language—we are all agreed about this one thing: what we should live for and what is good. Along with everyone else, I have solid, irrefutable, and clear knowledge of only one thing, and that one thing cannot be explained by reason—it lies beyond it and has no causes, nor can it have any effects.

'If goodness has a cause, it is no longer goodness, and if it has a consequence in the form of a reward, it is also not goodness. Goodness must therefore lie outside the chain of cause and effect.

'I know that, and we all know that.

'But I was looking for miracles and regretting that I did not see a miracle which might have convinced me. But here is one—the only possible miracle which surrounds me on all sides and exists in perpetuity, and I failed to notice it!

'What could be a greater miracle than that?

'Can I really have found the solution to everything, can my sufferings really be over now?' thought Levin as he paced along the dusty road, noticing neither the heat nor his tiredness, and experiencing a feeling of deliverance after prolonged suffering. This feeling was so joyous that it seemed scarcely credible. He was now breathless with excitement and, incapable of going further, he turned off the road into the wood and sat down on the uncut grass in the shade of some aspen trees. He took his hat off his perspiring head and lay down in the lush, feathery, woodland grass, propped up on his elbow.

'Yes, I need to collect myself and think this through,' he thought, staring at the untrampled grass in front of him and following the movements of a small green insect which was climbing up a stalk of couch-grass and being impeded in its ascent by a leaf of ground-elder. 'Everything from the beginning,' he told himself, moving the ground-elder leaf out of the way so it did not obstruct the insect, and bending another blade of grass over so the insect could cross over on to it. 'What gives me joy? What have I discovered?

'I used to say that there was an exchange of matter taking place in my body, and in the body of this grass and this insect (turns out it didn't want to go on to that bit of grass, as it has spread its wings and flown off), in accordance with physical, chemical, and physiological laws. And that there was a process of evolution taking place in all of us, along with the aspens and the clouds and the patches of mist. Evolution from what? Into what? Infinite evolution and struggle? . . . As if there could be any sort of direction and struggle in infinity! And I used to be surprised that the meaning of life, and the meaning of my motives and aspirations, were still not revealed to me despite the intense concentration of thought focused along these lines. But the meaning of my motives is so clear within me that I permanently live in harmony with it, and I was surprised and overjoyed when the peasant articulated it to me: to live for God, for one's soul.

'I haven't discovered anything. I have just found out what I know. I have understood that power which has not only given me life in the past, but is giving me life now. I have freed myself from deception and have discovered the master.'

And he briefly went over in his mind the whole sequence of his thoughts over the previous two years, which had begun with the clear and obvious thought of death at the sight of his beloved, hopelessly ill brother.

After grasping clearly for the first time back then that there was nothing ahead but suffering, death, and eternal oblivion for every person, including himself, he had made up his mind that he could not live like that, and that he must either explain his life in such a way that it did not appear to be the evil mockery of some kind of devil, or shoot himself.

But he had done neither, and had instead gone on living, thinking, and feeling, and had even gone and got married during that very time and experienced many joys, and was happy when he was not thinking about the meaning of his life.

What did this mean? It meant that he had been living well, but thinking badly.

He had been living (without being aware of it) by those spiritual truths he had imbibed with his mother's milk, and not only thinking without acknowledging these truths, but studiously ignoring them.

It was now clear to him that he could only live thanks to the beliefs in which he had been raised.

'What would I have been, and how would I have spent my life, if I did not have these beliefs, and did not know that one must live for God and not for one's needs? I would have robbed, lied, and murdered. Nothing of what constitutes the main joys in my life would have existed for me.' And despite the best efforts of his imagination, he still could not picture the brutal creature he himself would have been had he not known what he was living for.

'I looked for an answer to my question. But rational thought could not give me an answer to my question, as it is incommensurate with the question. The answer has been given to me by life itself, in my knowledge of what is good and what is bad. But there was no way that I could acquire this knowledge; it was given to me as it is to all people—*given*, because there was nowhere that I could have taken it from.

'Where did I get it from? Was it through reason that I came to know one must love one's neighbour and not strangle him? They told me that in my childhood, and I believed it gladly, because they told me what was in my soul. But who discovered that? It was not reason. What reason discovered was the struggle for existence, and the law demanding that I strangle all those who obstruct the satisfaction of my desires. That is the conclusion of reason. But reason could never discover loving one's neighbour, because that is something unreasonable.

'Yes, pride,' he said to himself, turning over on to his stomach and beginning to tie some blades of grass into a knot, trying not to break them.

'And not just intellectual pride, but intellectual idiocy. And above all, trickery, yes, intellectual trickery. Intellectual dishonesty, that's what it is,' he repeated.

13

AND Levin remembered a recent scene with Dolly and her children. Left to their own devices, the children had started cooking raspberries over candles and pouring streams of milk into each other's mouths. After catching them at it, their mother began impressing upon them in front of Levin how much effort it had cost the grown-ups to provide what they were destroying, and that this effort was being made for their benefit, so if they broke the cups they would have nothing from which to drink their tea, and if they spilt the milk they would have nothing to eat and would die of hunger.

And Levin was struck by the impassive, forlorn disbelief with which the children listened to what their mother was saying. They were only annoyed that their entertaining game had been stopped, and did not believe a word of what their mother was saying. They could not believe it, because they could not imagine the totality of everything that they used, and so could not imagine they were destroying the very things they lived by.

'All that happens anyway,' they thought, 'and there is nothing interesting or important about it because it has always been there and always will be. And it is always the same. There is no need for us to think about it, as it's just there; but we want to think up something of our own that is new. So we thought of putting raspberries in a cup and cooking them over a candle, and pouring streams of milk straight into each other's mouths. It is fun and new, and no worse than drinking out of cups.'

'Don't we do the same thing, as I did, by using reason to search for the meaning of the forces of nature and the purpose of human life?' he went on thinking.

'And don't all philosophical theories do the same, by means of the kind of thought which is strange and unnatural to man, leading him to knowledge of what he has known for a long time, and knows so well to be true that he could not live without it? Is it not patently obvious in the development of each philosopher's theory that he knows in advance the main purpose of life with as much certainty as the peasant Fyodor, and certainly with no greater clarity, and just wants to come back to what everyone knows by means of a dubious intellectual process?

'Well then, suppose the children were left alone to fend for themselves by having to make crockery and milk the cows and so on. Would they get up to mischief? They would die of hunger. And try leaving us with our passions and our thoughts, without a concept of the one God and Creator! Or without a concept of what is good, or an explanation of moral evil.

'Just see if you can build something without these concepts!

'We only destroy because we are spiritually replete. Just like children!

'Where did I derive that joyous knowledge I share with the peasants, which alone gives me peace of mind? Where did I get it from?

'After being brought up with an understanding of God, as a Christian, and having filled my whole life with the spiritual blessings given to me by Christianity, to the point where I am awash with these blessings and live by them, but, like the children, do not understand them, I have ended up destroying, or rather wanting to destroy that by which I live. But I turn to it the moment an important event in life comes along, like children when they are cold and hungry, and I feel that my childish attempts at waywardness are held against me even less than children scolded by their mother for their childish pranks.

'Yes, what I know, I don't know through reason, but because it was given to me, revealed to me, and I know it with my heart, with faith in the main idea professed by the Church.

'The Church? The Church!' Levin repeated to himself as he rolled on to his other side and, leaning on his elbow, started gazing into the distance, at a herd of cattle coming down towards the river from the opposite direction.

'But can I believe in everything the Church professes?' he thought, testing himself and trying to think of everything that could destroy his current peace of mind. He deliberately started recalling all those teachings of the Church which had always seemed the strangest to him and had tempted him. 'The Creation? But how on earth did I explain existence? With existence? With nothing? The devil and sin? But how do I explain evil? . . . The Redeemer? . . .

'But I know absolutely nothing and can know nothing other than what I and everybody else have been told.'

And it now seemed to him that there was not a single doctrine of the Church which could violate the fundamental thing, which was faith in God, in good as the sole purpose of mankind.

Each doctrine of the Church could be replaced by the doctrine of serving truth rather than one's own needs. And not only did none of these doctrines destroy this, but each was essential to the accomplishment of the main miracle constantly unfolding on earth, which consisted in the possibility of each individual, along with millions of the most diverse people, from sages to holy fools, children to old men, everyone—a peasant, Lvov, Kitty, beggars and Tsars—unequivocally understanding one and the same thing and piecing together that life of the soul which is the one thing worth living for, and the one thing we value.

Lying on his back, he was now looking up at the lofty, cloudless sky. 'Don't I know that this is infinite space and not a rounded vault? But however much I squint and strain my eyes, I cannot see it except as rounded and finite, and despite knowing about infinite space, I am manifestly right when I see a solid blue vault, I'm more right than when I strain to see beyond it.'

Levin had now stopped thinking, and only seemed to be listening to the mysterious voices that were joyfully and ardently discussing something amongst themselves.

'Can this really be faith?' he thought, afraid to believe in his happiness. 'My God, thank you!' he said, stifling the sobs rising within him and wiping away with both hands the tears that had filled his eyes.

14

LEVIN looked straight ahead and saw the herd of cattle, then he saw his trap drawn by Raven, and the coachman, who drove up to the cattle and spoke to the herdsman; then he heard the sound of wheels and the snort of a well-fed horse close by; but he was so engrossed in his thoughts that he did not even wonder why the coachman was driving towards him.

He only thought of that when the coachman had driven right up and called out to him.

'The mistress sent me. Your brother has arrived, and some gentleman too.'

Levin got into the trap and took the reins.

As if waking from a dream, Levin took a long while to come to his senses. He spent some time gazing at the sleek horse, lathering between its haunches and on its neck where the reins chafed, then spent some time gazing at Ivan the coachman sitting beside him, and remembered that he had been expecting his brother, and that his wife was probably worried at his long absence, and he tried to guess who the visitor who had come with his brother might be. He now perceived his brother and his wife and the unknown visitor in a different way than before. It seemed to him that his relations with everyone would be altered.

'With my brother there won't be that feeling of distance which always used to come between us—there won't be any arguments; I'll never have any arguments with Kitty; I'll be friendly and kind to the visitor, whoever he is; and everything will be different with the servants, and with Ivan.'

Holding back his trusty horse on taut reins as it lunged forward, snorting with impatience, Levin kept glancing round and trying to find a pretext to start a conversation with Ivan sitting next to him, who was continually trying to smooth out his shirt, at a loss to know what to do with his unoccupied hands. He wanted to say that Ivan did not need to have pulled the saddle-girth so tight, but that would have sounded like a rebuke, and he wanted the conversation to be affable. But nothing else came to mind.

'Best keep to the right, sir, there's a stump,' said the coachman, pulling on the rein to correct Levin.

'Please let go and don't teach me!' said Levin, angered by this interference from the coachman. This sort of interference riled him just as much as it always did, and it was with sadness that he immediately recognized how mistaken he had been in presuming that his spiritual state of mind could instantly change him when he came back into contact with reality.

When they were a few hundred yards away from the house, Levin saw Grisha and Tanya running towards him.

'Uncle Kostya! Mama's coming, and grandfather, and Sergey Ivanich, and someone else,' they said, clambering up into the trap.

'Who is it?'

'Someone awfully terrible! And he does this with his hands,' said Tanya, standing up in the trap and mimicking Katavasov.

'But is he old or young?' asked Levin, laughing as he wondered who Tanya's mimicry reminded him of.

'Just as long as it is not someone disagreeable!' thought Levin.

As soon as they turned the bend in the road and saw the people coming towards them, Levin recognized Katavasov in a straw hat, who was walking along gesticulating with his hands just as Tanya had demonstrated.

Katavasov was very fond of talking about philosophy, having acquired his understanding of it from natural scientists who had never studied philosophy; and Levin had lately frequently argued with him in Moscow.

And one of those discussions, from which Katavasov clearly believed he had emerged victorious, was the first thing Levin remembered when he recognized him.

'No, I will not on any account get into an argument and express my ideas in a casual way,' he thought.

After getting out of the trap and greeting his brother and Katavasov, Levin asked about his wife.

'She has taken Mitya to the Grove' (this was a wood near the house). 'She wanted to get him settled there because it's hot in the house,' said Dolly.

Levin had always advised his wife against taking the baby into the wood, believing it to be dangerous, and he was not pleased by this news.

'She is always carrying him about from place to place,' said the Prince, smiling. 'I advised her to try taking him to the ice-house.'

'She wanted to come to the apiary. She thought you would be there. That is where we are going,' said Dolly.

'Well, what have you been doing?' said Sergey Ivanovich, dropping back from the others to walk beside his brother.

'Oh, nothing special. I've been busy with the estate as usual,' Levin replied. 'And what about you, can you stay for a while? We have been expecting you for such a long time.'

'About two weeks or so. There is a lot to do in Moscow.'

At these words the brothers' eyes met, and despite Levin's constant and now particularly strong desire to be on affectionate and, most importantly, straightforward terms with his brother, he felt uncomfortable looking at him. He lowered his gaze and did not know what to say.

After going over in his mind the topics of conversation which might interest Sergey Ivanovich, and which might draw him away from a conversation about the Serbian war and the Slav Question, to which he had alluded with mention of his activities in Moscow, Levin began to talk about Sergey Ivanovich's book.

'So, have there been any reviews of your book?' he asked.

Sergey Ivanovich smiled at the contrived question.

'No one is interested in that, and I least of all,' he said. 'Darya Alexandrovna, look, we'll have a bit of rain,' he added, pointing with his umbrella to the white clouds that had appeared above the aspen tops.

And these words were enough to re-establish the not-exactly hostile but certainly chilly relations between the brothers that Levin had so wanted to avoid.

Levin went up to Katavasov.

'What a good idea of yours it was to come,' he said to him.

'I've been meaning to for ages. Now we can have some proper discussions and see where they take us. Did you read Spencer?'

'No, I didn't finish,' said Levin. 'Anyway, I don't need him now.'

'How so? That's interesting. What prompted that?'

'What I mean is that I'm now firmly convinced that I will never find the solutions to the problems that occupy me in him or his like. Now . . .'

But Katavasov's calm and cheery expression had suddenly confounded him, and made him feel such regret about his own mood, which he was clearly ruining with this conversation, that he remembered his intentions and stopped.

'Let's talk later, however,' he added. 'If we're going to the apiary, it's this way, along this path,' he said, addressing them all.

After following the narrow path to a small unmown clearing, covered on one side by a bright carpet of wild pansies with many tall clumps of dark-green hellebores growing amongst them, Levin settled his guests in the dense, cool shade of some young aspens, on a bench and some tree-stumps which had been specially arranged for visitors to the apiary who were afraid of bees, while he himself went off to the hut to fetch bread, cucumbers, and fresh honey for the children and the grown-ups.

Trying to make as few rapid movements as possible, and listening carefully to the bees which were flying past him with ever-increasing frequency, he walked along the path until he reached the hut. One bee started buzzing loudly right in the entrance after becoming entangled in his beard, but he carefully freed it. After going into the shady hallway, he took down his veil, which was hanging from a peg on the wall, put it on, thrust his hands in his pockets, and went out into the enclosed apiary, where the old hives, all familiar to him, and each with its own history, stood in regular rows in the middle of a mown area, tied with bast to stakes, while along the wattle fence were the young ones, established that year. In front of the entrances to the hives his eyes were dazzled by playful bees and drones as they circled and bumped into each other on one spot, and amongst them, continually plying the same route to the blossoming lime trees in the wood and back towards the hives, flew worker bees with their spoils and in pursuit of their spoils.

His ears reverberated with the varied sounds of one moment a busy worker bee flying swiftly past, the next a low-humming, jubilant drone, and the next apprehensive sentry bees protecting their property from the enemy, ready to sting. On the other side of the fence the old man was planing a hoop, and did not see Levin. Levin stood in the middle of the apiary and did not call out to him.

He was glad of the chance to be alone, so as to recover from reality, which had already managed to dampen his spirits considerably.

He recalled that he had already managed to lose his temper with Ivan, treat his brother coldly, and talk in an offhand manner to Katavasov.

'Was that really just an ephemeral state of mind which will vanish without trace?' he thought.

But at that very moment when he went back to his state of mind, he perceived with joy that something new and important had taken place within him. Reality had for a while obscured the spiritual calm he had found, but it was still intact within him.

Just as the bees now circling round him, threatening and distracting him, depriving him of complete physical calm, forced him to recoil in order to avoid them, so the cares that had clustered round him from the moment he sat down in the trap restricted his emotional freedom; but that lasted only while he was in the midst of them. Just as his physical strength was intact within him despite the bees, so too was his newly acknowledged spiritual strength.

15

'Kostya, do you know who Sergey Ivanovich travelled with on his way here?' said Dolly, after she had doled out cucumbers and honey to the children. 'Vronsky! He's going to Serbia.'

'And not alone either; he's taking a squadron with him at his own expense!' said Katavasov.

'That's like him,' said Levin. 'Are there volunteers still going out then?' he added, glancing at Sergey Ivanovich.

With the blunt edge of a knife Sergey Ivanovich was carefully extracting a still-live bee which had got stuck in the honey running from a corner of white honeycomb lying in a bowl, and so did not reply.

'I'll say! You should have seen what was going on at the station yesterday!' said Katavasov, noisily biting into a cucumber.

'Well, how is one to understand this? For the love of God, will you explain to me, Sergey Ivanovich, where all those volunteers are going and whom they are fighting?' asked the old Prince, clearly continuing a conversation that had begun in Levin's absence.

'With the Turks,' Sergey Ivanovich answered, smiling calmly after freeing the bee, which was black from the honey and helplessly moving its legs, and then transferring it from the knife to a sturdy aspen leaf.

'But who has declared war on the Turks? Ivan Ivanich Ragozov and Countess Lydia Ivanovna, together with Madame Stahl?'

'No one has declared war, but people sympathize with the sufferings of their neighbours and wish to help them,' said Sergey Ivanovich.

'But the Prince is not speaking about help,' said Levin, standing up for his father-in-law, 'but about war. The Prince is saying that private individuals cannot take part in a war without the permission of the government.'

'Kostya, look, it's a bee! We really are going to get stung!' said Dolly, waving away a wasp.

'But that's not a bee, it's a wasp,' said Levin.

'Come along then, what's your theory?' Katavasov said to Levin with a smile, clearly challenging him to a debate. 'Why do private individuals not have the right?'

'My theory is this: war is on the one hand such a bestial, cruel, and awful thing that no single person, let alone a Christian, can personally take on the responsibility for starting a war; only a government can do that, being duty-bound to do so and being inevitably drawn into war. On the other hand, both science and common sense tell us that in matters of state, and particularly in matters of war, citizens renounce their personal will.'

Sergey Ivanovich and Katavasov began voicing their objections at the same time.

'But the whole point, my dear fellow, is that there may be a case when the government does not carry out the will of its citizens and society then asserts its will,' said Katavasov.

But Sergey Ivanovich clearly did not approve of this objection. He frowned at Katavasov's remarks and said something else.

'You are not stating the issue in the right way. There is no declaration of war in this case, but simply the expression of human, Christian feeling. Our brothers by blood and faith are being killed. Well, let us suppose they are not even our brothers, nor share our faith, but simply children, women, old people; feelings have been outraged and the Russian people have been charging in to help stop these atrocities. Imagine you were walking down a street and saw drunks beating up a woman or a child; I don't think you would stop to ask whether war had been declared on that person, but would rush in to offer protection.'

'But I wouldn't kill,' said Levin.

'No, you would kill.'

'I don't know. If I saw that, I would give in to my spontaneous feelings; but I can't say in advance. And there are no such spontaneous feelings about the oppression of the Slavs, nor can there be.'

'Not for you perhaps. But there are for others,' said Sergey Ivanovich with a disgruntled frown. 'Amongst the people, legends about Orthodox Christians suffering under the yoke of the 'ungodly Hagarians'* are very much alive. The people have heard about the sufferings of their brethren and have spoken up.'

'Perhaps so,' said Levin evasively; 'but I don't see that; I'm one of the people myself, and I don't feel that.'

'Nor do I,' said the Prince. 'I was living abroad, reading the newspapers, and even before the Bulgarian atrocities I have to confess it was simply beyond my comprehension why all Russians should suddenly have become so fond of their brother Slavs, while I didn't feel the slightest affection for them. I was very distressed and thought I was a monster, or that Carlsbad was having an effect on me. But I calmed down when I came here and saw that there are other people besides me who are only interested in Russia, and not in their brother Slavs. Konstantin here is one of them.'

'Personal opinions are irrelevant in this case,' said Sergey Ivanovich. 'There is no room for personal opinions when all Russia—the people— has expressed its will.'

'Excuse me, but I don't see that. The people don't know anything about it,' said the Prince.

'No, Papa . . . how can you say that? What about in church on Sunday?' said Dolly, who was listening keenly to the conversation. 'Give me a towel please,' she said to the old man, who was looking at the children with a smile. 'It cannot be that all . . .'

'But what actually happened in church on Sunday? The priest was ordered to read. He did the reading. They didn't understand a word of it and sighed like they do during every sermon,' continued the Prince. 'Then they were told that there was to be a collection for a beneficial cause in church, so they all got out a kopeck and gave. But they don't know themselves what it was for.'

'The people cannot help knowing; the people always have a consciousness of their destiny, and at times like the present it is revealed to them,' said Sergey Ivanovich, glancing at the old bee-keeper.

The handsome old man with his grizzled black beard and thick silver hair was standing motionless, holding a bowl of honey, as he looked down kindly and imperturbably from his height at the gentry, clearly not understanding anything and not wanting to understand.

'That's quite right,' he said, nodding his head meaningfully at what Sergey Ivanovich was saying.

'Well, just go ahead and ask him. He doesn't know anything about it and doesn't think about it,' said Levin. 'Have you heard about the war, Mikhailych?' he said, turning to him. 'That thing they read in church? What do you think? Should we be fighting for the Christians?'

'What is there for us to think about? Alexander Nikolayich, the Emperor, has thought for us, and he thinks for us in all things. Things are clearer to him . . . Shall I bring a bit more bread? Give the little lad some more?' he said, addressing Darya Alexandrovna and pointing to Grisha, who was finishing his crust.

'I don't need to ask,' said Sergey Ivanovich. 'We have seen and are seeing hundreds and hundreds of people giving up everything to serve a just cause, coming from all corners of Russia, and plainly and clearly expressing their thoughts and objectives. They bring their coppers or else they go themselves and say plainly why. So what does this mean?'

'It means, in my opinion,' said Levin, who was beginning to grow angry, 'that in a nation of eighty million there will always be not hundreds, as is the case now, but tens of thousands of people who have lost their social standing, reckless types, who are always ready for anything, whether it's joining Pugachev's mob, or going to Khiva* or Serbia . . .'

'I tell you it's not hundreds, and they are not reckless types, but the best representatives of the people!' said Sergey Ivanovich, with as much irritation as if he were defending his last possession. 'And what about the donations? That really is the entire people directly expressing its will.'

'This word "people" is so vague,' said Levin. 'District clerks, teachers, and one out of a thousand peasants perhaps know what it is all about. But the remaining eighty million, like Mikhailych, are not only not expressing their will, but do not have the faintest idea what they should be expressing their will about. What right do we have to say that this is the will of the people?'

16

BEING an experienced dialectician, Sergey Ivanovich did not remonstrate, but promptly steered the conversation into another area.

'Yes, if you want to determine the spirit of the people by arithmetical means, that is of course very difficult to do. Voting has not been introduced in our country and cannot be introduced, because it does not express the will of the people; but there are other means. You can feel it in the air, you can feel it in your heart. And that is without even mentioning the undercurrents which have been stirring in the stagnant sea of the people, and which are evident to every unprejudiced person; look at society in the narrow sense. All the most diverse factions in the world of the intelligentsia, previously so antagonistic, have merged into one. All discord is at an end, all the public organs are saying the same thing over and over, they have all sensed the elemental force that has overtaken them and is carrying them in the same direction.'

'Yes, the newspapers do all say the same thing,' said the Prince. 'That's true. So much the same thing that they are just like frogs before a storm. You can't hear anything because of them.'

'I don't know whether they are like frogs or not—I don't publish newspapers and don't want to defend them, but I am talking about consensus in the world of the intelligentsia,' said Sergey Ivanovich, addressing his brother.

Levin was about to reply, but the old Prince interrupted him.

'Well, there's another thing one could say about that consensus,' said the Prince. 'I have a son-in-law, Stepan Arkadyich, whom you know. He's now getting a post as committee member of a commission and something else that I don't remember. But there's nothing to do there—well, Dolly, it's not a secret!—and it comes with a salary of eight thousand. Try asking him whether his work will be useful and he'll prove to you that it's indispensable. And he's a truthful man too, but it's impossible not to believe in the usefulness of eight thousand roubles.'

'Yes, he asked me to let Darya Alexandrovna know he got the post,' said Sergey Ivanovich irritably, thinking that the Prince was speaking out of turn.

'And so it is with the consensus in the press. It was explained to me: as soon as there is war, their revenue is doubled. How on earth can they not consider that the destinies of the people and the Slavs . . . and all that?'

'There are many papers I don't like, but that's unfair,' said Sergey Ivanovich.

'I would impose just one condition,' the Prince continued. 'Alphonse Karr* expressed it very well before the war with Prussia: "You consider war is necessary? Excellent. Whoever preaches war should join a special front-line legion and lead the assault into the attack in front of everyone else!"'

'The editors would cut fine figures,' said Katavasov, laughing loudly as he pictured the editors he knew in this hand-picked legion.

'Oh, they'd run away,' said Dolly, 'and just be a hindrance.'

'Well, if they start running, you could have them followed by grape-shot or Cossacks with whips,' said the Prince.

'But this is a joke, and not a very good one either, if you'll excuse my saying so, Prince,' said Sergey Ivanovich.

'I don't see it as a joke, it's . . .' began Levin, but Sergey Ivanovich interrupted him.

'Every member of society is called upon to do their part in their own way,' he said. 'And thinking people are doing their part when they express public opinion. The unanimous and full expression of public opinion is a tribute to the press, and at the same time it is a gratifying phenomenon. Twenty years ago we would have been silent, but now you can hear the voice of the Russian people, who are ready to stand up as one person, and ready to sacrifice themselves for our oppressed brethren; it is a great step and a mark of strength.'

'But it's not just a question of making a sacrifice, but of killing Turks,' said Levin timidly. 'The people do make sacrifices and they are always ready to make sacrifices for their soul, but not for murder,' he added, instinctively linking the conversation to the ideas that had been absorbing him.

'What do you mean, for their soul? That's a tricky expression for a natural scientist, you understand. What is this soul?' said Katavasov, smiling.

'Oh, you know!'

'I swear to God, I haven't the faintest idea!' said Katavasov with a roar of laughter.

' "I have brought not peace, but a sword,"* says Christ,' Sergey Ivanovich countered for his part, quoting as simply as if it was the easiest thing to understand, the very passage from the Gospels which had always puzzled Levin the most.

'That's quite right,' repeated the old man, who was standing near them, in response to a glance casually thrown in his direction.

'I'm afraid you've been beaten, old boy, soundly beaten!' exclaimed Katavasov jovially.

Levin flushed with vexation, not because he had been beaten, but because he had been unable to restrain himself from arguing.

'No, it's impossible for me to argue with them,' he thought; 'they're wearing impenetrable armour, but I'm naked.'

He saw that it was impossible to convince his brother and Katavasov, and he saw even less possibility of being able to agree with them himself. What they were advocating was that same intellectual pride which had almost been his ruin. He could not agree that dozens of people, including his brother, had the right to say, on the basis of what they were told by the hundreds of smooth-tongued volunteers arriving in Moscow and Petersburg, that they and the newspapers were expressing the will and ideas of the people, ideas which were expressed through vengeance and murder. He could not agree with this, both because he did not see the expression of these thoughts in the people amongst whom he lived, and because he did not find these thoughts in himself (and he could not consider himself other than as one of the individuals who made up the Russian people), but mainly because, along with the people, he did not know, nor could he know, what constituted the common good, but he was firmly convinced that this common good could only be attained through strict observance of that law of goodness which is available to every person, and therefore he could neither desire war nor advocate it for any shared goals. He spoke with Mikhailych and the people, whose views were expressed in the legend about the mission of the Varangians: 'Reign and rule over us.* We are happy to promise complete obedience. We will take on all the labouring, all the humiliations, and all the sacrifices; but we will not be the ones to judge and take decisions.' According to Sergey Ivanovich's account, however, the people had now renounced this right which they had bought at such a high cost.

He also wanted to say that if public opinion was such an infallible judge, then why were not revolution and the commune as legitimate as the movement in favour of the Slavs? But these were all just ideas which could not resolve anything. The one incontrovertible thing which could be seen was that the argument was irritating Sergey Ivanovich right now, and it was therefore bad to argue; so Levin fell silent and drew the attention of his guests to the fact that the clouds were gathering, and that it would be better to go home before it rained.

17

THE old Prince and Sergey Ivanich got into the trap and drove off; the rest of the party set off home on foot, quickening their pace.

But the clouds, white one minute and black the next, were gathering so rapidly that it was necessary to quicken their pace still further in order to arrive home before the rain. The clouds in front, low and black, like soot-laden smoke, were racing across the sky with extraordinary speed. There were still about two hundred paces to go before they reached home, but the wind had already risen, and a downpour could be expected any minute.

The children ran on ahead with frightened and gleeful shrieks. Darya Alexandrovna, battling with her skirts, which were clinging to her legs, was no longer walking but running, with her eyes fixed on the children. The men, holding on to their hats, were taking big strides. They had just reached the porch when a big drop hit and splashed against the edge of the iron gutter. The children, followed by the grown-ups, ran under the shelter of the roof, chattering merrily.

'Katerina Alexandrovna?' Levin enquired of Agafya Mikhailovna, who met them with shawls and rugs in the hall.

'We thought she was with you,' she said.

'And Mitya?'

'He must be in the Grove, and the nanny is with them.'

Levin grabbed the rugs and ran off to the Grove.

In that short space of time, the middle of the cloud had moved so far over the sun that it became as dark as in an eclipse. The wind stubbornly held Levin back, as if insisting on having its way, and as it tore leaves and blossom from the lime trees and savagely and strangely stripped white branches from the birches, it bent everything in one direction: acacias, flowers, burdocks, grass, and the tops of trees. The peasant girls working in the garden ran shrieking under the roof of the servants' quarters. A white curtain of torrential rain had already completely enveloped the distant wood and half of the nearby field, and was rapidly encroaching on the Grove. The dampness of the rain could be felt in the air as it disintegrated into fine drops.

Bowing his head and battling with the wind, which was trying to wrench the shawls from him, Levin had almost run as far as the Grove and could already see something white behind the oak tree, when all of a sudden everything flashed, the whole earth lit up, and it seemed as if the vault of heaven was cracking overhead. To his horror, after opening his dazzled eyes, the first thing Levin saw through the thick curtain of rain that now separated him from the Grove was the strangely altered position of the green top of a familiar oak in the middle of the wood. Levin hardly had time to think, 'Has it really been struck?' when, rapidly picking up speed, the top of the oak disappeared behind the other trees, and he heard the crash of the big tree falling on to the others.

The flash of lightning, the sound of thunder, and the sensation of a chill running through his body all fused for Levin into a single impression of horror.

'Oh God! Oh God, as long as it was not on them!' he murmured.

And although he immediately thought how pointless was his entreaty that they should not have been killed by the oak which had now fallen, he repeated it, knowing that he could do no better than utter this pointless prayer.

He ran up to the place where they usually went, but he did not find them there.

They were at the other side of the wood under an old lime tree, and were calling out to him. Two figures in dark clothes (which had been light-coloured) stood bending over something. It was Kitty and the nanny. When Levin ran over to them the rain was already easing off and it was beginning to brighten up. The hem of the nanny's skirt was not wet, but Kitty's clothes were soaked right through, and were clinging to her. Although the rain had stopped, they were still standing in the same position they had been in when the storm had broken. Both stood bent over the perambulator with a green parasol.

'Safe? And sound? Thank God!' he said, splashing through the puddles with one shoe half-off and full of water as he ran up to them. Kitty's pink, wet face was turned towards him and smiling timidly from under her misshapen hat.

'Well, you should be ashamed of yourself! I can't understand how you can be so irresponsible!' he said, turning angrily on his wife.

'It wasn't my fault, really. We were just about to leave when he started kicking up a fuss. We had to change him. We had just . . .' Kitty began excusing herself.

Mitya was alive and well, and dry, and he continued to sleep soundly.

'Well, thank God! I don't know what I'm saying!'

They gathered up the wet swaddling-clothes; the nanny took the baby out and carried him in her arms. Levin walked beside his wife, feeling guilty at having been angry, and out of the view of the nanny surreptitiously squeezed her hand.

18

DURING the course of the whole day, and throughout the most varied conversations, in which he participated with, as it were, only the outer part of his mind, Levin did not cease to be joyously aware of the fullness of his heart, despite the disappointment about the change which was supposed to have taken place within him.

It was too wet to go for a walk after the rain; besides, storm-clouds still lingered on the horizon, and here and there they were moving, black and thundery, along the edges of the sky. The whole party spent the rest of the day indoors.

No more arguments were started as, on the contrary, after dinner every one was in the very best of spirits.

Katavasov began by amusing the ladies with his quirky jokes, which always went down so well on first acquaintance with him, but at Sergey Ivanovich's bidding he then recounted his very interesting observations about the differences in character, and even physiognomy, of male and female houseflies, and about their lives. Sergey Ivanovich was also in a genial mood and, at his brother's request, over tea set out his views about the future of the Eastern Question,* which he did so simply and so well that everyone listened with rapt attention.

Only Kitty could not hear it all—she was called to go and give Mitya his bath.

A few minutes after Kitty left, Levin was also summoned to her in the nursery.

Leaving his tea and also regretting the break in the interesting conversation, while at the same time worrying why he had been summoned, since this only happened on important occasions, Levin went to the nursery.

Although he was very interested in what he had so far heard of Sergey Ivanovich's plan for the liberated world of forty million Slavs to usher in a new epoch in history in conjunction with Russia, as it was something completely new to him, and although curiosity and worry about why he had been summoned filled him with trepidation, as soon as he was alone after leaving the drawing room, he immediately remembered what he had been thinking about that morning. And all those conjectures about the significance of the Slav element in world history seemed to him so paltry in comparison with what was going on in his own soul that he promptly forgot all about them and was transported back to the same mood he had been in that morning.

He did not now recall the whole train of his thought, as he used to before (he had no need to). He was immediately transported back to the feeling which had guided him and which was connected with those thoughts, and he found that this feeling was even stronger and more firmly established in his soul than before. What was happening to him now was not like what had gone on with his previous states of contrived serenity, when it was necessary to retrace his entire train of thought in order locate the feeling. On the contrary, the feeling of joy and serenity was now more vivid than before, and his thoughts could not keep up with his feelings.

He was walking across the veranda and looking at two stars that had appeared in the already darkening sky when he suddenly remembered: 'Yes, when I was looking at the sky, I thought I was not wrong to see a vault, and at the same time there was something I did not think through, something I hid from myself,' he thought. 'But whatever it was, there can be no objection. I just need to think about it, and everything will be unravelled!'

Just as he was going into the nursery, he remembered what it was that he had hidden from himself. It was that, if the main proof of the existence of God is His revelation of what is good, then why is this revelation confined solely to the Christian Church? What relation is there between this revelation and the beliefs of Buddhists and Muslims, who are also reverent and do good?

He felt he had an answer to this question; but before he could manage to articulate it to himself he had gone into the nursery.

Kitty was standing with her sleeves rolled up over the bath, in which the baby was splashing about, and when she heard her husband's footsteps she turned her face towards him and beckoned him with a smile. With one hand she was supporting the chubby baby's head while he floated on his back and kicked his little legs, while with the other, tensing her muscles evenly, she was squeezing the sponge over him.

'There you are, look, look!' she said when her husband came up to her. 'Agafya Mikhailovna's right. He does know us.'

The point was that Mitya had clearly and unmistakably begun to recognize his own family that day.

As soon as Levin had come up to the bath an experiment was carried out in front of him, and the experiment was a complete success. The cook, who had been specially summoned for this, replaced Kitty and bent over the baby. He frowned and started shaking his head. Then when Kitty bent over him, his face lit up with a smile, and he pushed his little hands into the sponge and burbled with his lips, making such a happy and strange sound that not just Kitty and the nanny but also Levin were lost in unexpected admiration.

The baby was taken out of the bath on one hand, doused with water, wrapped in a towel, dried, and after some piercing screams, handed to his mother.

'Well, I am glad you are beginning to love him,' said Kitty to her husband after she had settled down calmly in her usual place, with the baby at her breast. 'I am very glad. Because it was beginning to upset me. You said you had no feelings for him.'

'No, did I really say I had no feelings? I just said I was disappointed.'

'What do you mean—disappointed in him?'

'Not so much disappointed in him as in my own feelings; I expected more. I was expecting pleasant new feelings to blossom in me, like a surprise. And suddenly, instead of that, there was disgust and pity . . .'

She listened attentively, looking at him over the baby, while putting back on her slender fingers the rings she had taken off in order to wash Mitya.

'And mainly, there has been far more fear and pity than pleasure. After that scare during the storm today, I realized how much I love him.'

Kitty's face was wreathed with smiles.

'Were you very scared?' she said. 'I was too, but it seems more frightening now that it's over. I'm going to go and look at the oak. How nice Katavasov is! And generally the whole day has been so enjoyable. And you can be so good with Sergey Ivanovich when you want to be . . . Well, you should go back to them. Because it's always so hot and steamy here after the bath . . .'

19

ONCE he had left the nursery and was alone, Levin immediately recalled the thought in which there had been something unclear.

Instead of going into the drawing room, from where voices could be heard, he stopped on the veranda and, leaning on the balustrade, started looking up at the sky.

It was already quite dark and there were no clouds in the south, where he was looking. The clouds were in the opposite direction. Flashes of lightning and the sound of distant thunder were coming from that direction. Levin listened to the raindrops falling steadily from the lime trees in the garden and gazed at the familiar triangle of stars, with the Milky Way and its spiral arms running through the middle. Every time there was a flash of lightning, not just the Milky Way but even the bright stars vanished, only to reappear in their usual places as soon as the lightning faded, as if thrown there by some deft hand.

'So, what is it that is bothering me?' Levin said to himself, feeling in advance that the solution to his doubts, although he did not know it yet, was already in his soul.

'Yes, the one clear, unquestionable manifestation of divinity are the laws of goodness, which have been presented to the world through revelation, which I feel within myself, and through recognition of which I do not so much unite, but am united with, other people, whether I like it or not, in a congregation of believers which is called the Church. Well, what about Jews, Muslims, Confucians, Buddhists—what are they?' he pondered, putting to himself the very question he found dangerous.

'Surely it can't be the case that all these hundreds of millions of people are deprived of that greatest of blessings, without which life has no meaning?' He thought for a moment, but immediately corrected himself. 'But what exactly am I asking about?' he said to himself. 'I am asking about the relation to divinity of all the different faiths of mankind. I am asking about God's general manifestation to the whole world, with all these nebulous areas. What is it that I am doing, then? Knowledge unattainable through reason has incontrovertibly been revealed to me personally, to my heart, yet I am stubbornly trying to use reason so I can express this knowledge in words.

'Don't I know that the stars don't move?' he asked himself, gazing at a bright planet which had already shifted its position up to the topmost branch of a birch tree. 'But I can't picture to myself the rotation of the earth when I look at the movement of the stars, and I'm right in saying that the stars move.

'And could astronomers have understood and calculated anything if they had taken into account all the complicated and varied motions of the earth? All their astounding conclusions about the distances, weight, movements, and perturbations of heavenly bodies are based purely on the visible movements of stars round a motionless earth, on that very movement which is in front of me now, and which has been the same for millions of people over the course of centuries and was and will always be the same and can always be verified. And just as the conclusions of the astronomers would have been pointless and unreliable if they had not been based on observations of the visible sky in relation to one meridian and one horizon, so my conclusions would be pointless and unreliable if they were not based on that understanding of goodness which always has been and always will be the same for everyone, which has been revealed to me through Christianity, and which can always be verified in my soul. I do not have either the right or the possibility to resolve the question about other religions and their relation to divinity.'

'Oh, you haven't gone?' suddenly came the voice of Kitty, who was going the same way to the drawing room. 'You're not upset about anything, are you?' she said, carefully examining his face by the light of the stars.

But she would have been unable to discern his expression had not another flash of lightning concealed the stars and revealed it. With the flash of lightning she could discern his expression fully, and when she saw that he was calm and happy, she smiled at him.

'She understands,' he thought; 'she knows what I'm thinking about. Should I tell her or not? Yes, I will tell her.' But just at the moment when he was about to start speaking, she began speaking too.

'Kostya! Do me a favour, please,' she said; 'go into the corner room and see how they have set up everything for Sergey Ivanovich. I can't very well myself. Did they put in the new washstand?'

'Yes, certainly I'll do that,' said Levin, standing up and kissing her.

'No, I shouldn't tell her,' he thought, as she went in before him. 'It is a secret which is only necessary and important to me, and can't be expressed in words.

'This new feeling has not changed me, made me happy, or suddenly enlightened me as I dreamed it would, just as with my feelings towards my son. It also has not brought a surprise. Whether this is faith or not—I don't know what it is—but this feeling has just as imperceptibly, and with suffering, entered and lodged firmly in my soul.

'I will continue to lose my temper with Ivan the coachman, and I will continue to argue and express my thoughts out of turn; there will still be the same wall between the holy of holies of my soul and other people, even my wife, and I will continue to blame her for my own fear and later repent of it; I will continue to fail to understand with my mind why I pray, and I will continue to pray, but my life now—my whole life, irrespective of everything that might happen to me, every minute of it—is not only not meaningless like it was before, but has the indisputable meaning of goodness, which I have the power to instil in it!'

THE END

EXPLANATORY NOTES

The following notes draw on those compiled by W. Gareth Jones for the 1995 edition of the Louise and Aylmer Maude translation in Oxford World's Classics; the notes on Part One of the novel compiled by Vladimir Nabokov, which are included in his *Lectures on Russian Literature* (London, 1981), 210–36; the notes by V. F. Savodnik in volume 8 of the 22-volume edition of Tolstoy's works (Moscow, 1981–2); and the notes compiled by C. J. G. Turner in *A Karenina Companion* (Waterloo, Ont., 1993), 123–86. References to the Bible are to the King James Version.

1 *[Epigraph] Vengeance is mine; I will repay*: the epigraph, quoted in biblical Church Slavonic, is taken from Romans 12: 17–19, in which St Paul quotes from Deuteronomy 32: 35: 'Recompense to no man evil for evil. Provide things honest in the sight of all men. If it be possible, as much as lieth in you, live peaceably with all men. Dearly beloved, avenge not yourselves, but *rather* give place unto wrath: for it is written, Vengeance *is* mine; I will repay, saith the Lord.' Its appearance in modern Russian in an earlier draft of the novel, however, suggests it was taken originally from Arthur Schopenhauer's central work, *The World as Will and Representation* (1818), and seems to be a direct translation of 'Mein ist die Rache'. Tolstoy became a devotee of Schopenhauer in 1869.

PART ONE

3 *the Oblonskys' house*: the word *house* ('dom') and variations of it, are deliberately repeated eight times in the novel's first six sentences in Russian.

Darmstadt: as noted by Vladimir Nabokov, the Darmstadt-based *Cologne Gazette* was devoting much space in February 1872 to the 'Alabama Claims', made by the United States against Great Britain in respect of damage to shipping during the American Civil War.

Il mio tesoro: aria from Mozart's *Don Giovanni* (1787) sung by the noble Don Ottavio in Act II, in which he swears vengeance on Don Giovanni for murdering his betrothed's father.

5 *'reflexes of the brain'*: Stepan Arkadyich is thinking of Ivan Sechenov's book of the same name, a classic of Russian physiology, first published in a medical journal in 1863, having been censored earlier that year for the literary journal the *Contemporary* for 'propaganda of materialism'.

8 *'After the feast. . .'*: '. . . comes the reckoning', the English equivalent of *Lyubish katat'sya, lyubi i sanochki vozit*—'He who likes going for a ride should like dragging his sleigh.'

8   *seals*: the Russian word *breloki* is a transliteration of the French *breloques*, and denotes seals or charms attached to a watch-chain.

    a liberal newspaper: Stepan Arkadyich most likely reads *Russian News* (*Russkie vedomosti*), a Moscow daily founded in 1868. Given where he lives, it is less likely, despite the views of some critics, that he reads the *Voice* ('Golos'), another liberal paper founded during the permissive atmosphere of the Great Reforms in 1863 in St Petersburg.

9   *Ryurik*: the Viking who in 862 founded Russia's first ruling dynasty, which survived until 1598, and in 1613 was eventually succeeded by the Romanovs. Only sixty families could claim descent from Ryurik, including the Obolenskys, cousins of the Tolstoys, whose name 'Oblonsky' closely imitates.

    repudiate our original ancestor—the ape: the first Russian translation, by Ivan Sechenov, of Charles Darwin's ground-breaking study of human evolution, *On the Origin of Species* (1859), was first published in 1871, and stimulated much debate on the pages of all the monthly 'thick' journals in subsequent years. Tolstoy approved of the critical article his friend Strakhov published in 1872, and voices his scepticism through his alter ego Levin in *Anna Karenina*.

    Bentham and Mill: the jurist Jeremy Bentham (1748–1832) was the founder of Utilitarianism, a philosophy subsequently developed by his pupil John Stuart Mill (1806–73), which argues that an action is right if it is useful or benefits the majority. Utilitarian ideas enjoyed popularity amongst the radical intelligentsia in Russia, and are parodied in Dostoevsky's *Crime and Punishment* (1866).

10   *Count Beust*: Count Ferdinand von Beust (1809–86) was a German politician who became Austrian Foreign Minister in 1866 and Austrian Ambassador to the Court of St James in 1871. Oblonsky's paper reported him making a visit to Italy and stopping in Wiesbaden during his return journey to London, where he was to attend a service of thanksgiving in St Paul's Cathedral for the recovery from typhoid of the Prince of Wales on 27 February 1872. This suggests the action of the novel begins in February 1872.

    roll: the word in Russian is *kalach*, a popular small loaf in the shape of a padlock, and the oldest form of white bread in Russia. Those produced by the Moscow baker Filippov were the most famous, and sent daily to the imperial household in St Petersburg. To Russians, the distinctive form of a *kalach* was reminiscent of parts of the body, with a 'stomach' and a 'lip'.

13   *What do you want?*: Dolly addresses her husband here as *vy*, the polite form of 'you' in Russian, requiring a plural verb, a distinction lost in English.

14   *You think about the children*: Stiva immediately realizes Dolly is beginning to soften by addressing him here as *ty*, the more usual familiar pronoun, followed by a single verb, but then immediately reverts again to *vy* when she next tells him: 'You are loathsome . . .'

16   *government institutions*: Tolstoy does not specify which part of the civil service Oblonsky works in, and later reference to the symbol of imperial

justice does not necessarily mean he was employed by the Ministry of Justice, although this is likely.

18 *Penza*: provincial capital located nearly 400 miles south-east of Moscow.

symbol of imperial justice: the *zertsalo* was a triangular prism introduced by Peter I which stood on the desk of all government institutions in the Russian empire. Crowned with a two-headed eagle, its three sides bore three Petrine decrees—the 17 April 1722 decree on the observance of civil rights, the 21 January 1724 decree on honest service in court, and the 22 January 1724 decree on the importance of government regulations.

Gentleman of the Bedchamber: the most junior honorary court title (eleventh in the Table of Ranks established in 1722 by Peter the Great), entitling Grinevich to attend occasions such as court balls, with the implication being that he is of higher social standing than his colleague Nikitin. The Russian *kamer-yunker*, dating from 1722, was derived from the German *Kammerjunker*. A title usually awarded to young men in their twenties, the poet Alexander Pushkin was insulted to be given it in 1833, when he was thirty-four. Oblonsky is thirty-four at the start of the novel, and this is probably also the age of his colleague Grinevich.

20 *zemstvo*: the *zemstvo* was the name for the first forms of local self-government in imperial Russia. These nationwide elected assemblies were introduced at the district and provincial level in 1864 as part of Alexander II's 'great reforms', and consisted of a representative council and an executive board, in which the majority of members were from the nobility.

22 *Karazin district*: this is an imaginary place, like most of the rural locations in *Anna Karenina*. In 1874 Tolstoy chopped down some of his own forest and sold the wood in order to buy land adjacent to the estate he inherited from his brother.

26 *Kharkov*: second largest city in Ukraine, located some 500 miles south of Moscow. Its university, founded in 1804 by Alexander I, was one of the first in Russia.

psychological and physiological phenomena: this is a reference to a real-life polemic on this topic which sprang up on the pages of the journal *Messenger of Europe* (*Vestnik Evropy*) in 1872 between the historian and sociologist Konstantin Kavelin and the above-mentioned Ivan Sechenov.

27 *Keiss . . . Wurst, and Knaust, and Pripasov*: fictitious and lightly satirical names of materialist philosophers highly suggestive of 'Cheese . . . Sausage, Bread, and Provisions', the first three derived from the German words *Käse*, *Wurst*, and *Knaust* and the last from the Russian *pripasy*.

35 *Angleterre or the Hermitage*: the Hermitage, at the top of Neglinnaya Street, was Moscow's best restaurant in the late nineteenth century, owned by Lucien Olivier, inventor of the 'Russian Salad'. There was also

a hotel of somewhat dubious reputation called the 'Angliya' on Petrovka Street, but the restaurant Oblonsky has in mind was most probably invented by Tolstoy.

35 *Tatars*: a term used interchangeably with 'Mongol' in Russia. Mongols were often employed as waiters in restaurants, since their Islamic beliefs prohibited them from consuming alcohol, thus reassuring proprietors they would remain sober.

36 *kasha à la russe*: buckwheat porridge (*grechnevaya kasha*) and cabbage soup (*shchi*) were staples of the Russian peasant diet.

37 *Would you like your cheese?*: cheese was eaten as an hors d'oeuvre and between courses.

38 *You Levins are all peculiar*: the Russian word Tolstoy uses for what has been translated here as 'peculiar' is *dikii*, meaning 'wild', 'unsociable', 'weird', or 'eccentric', depending on the context. Levin has just used this same word to describe his reaction, as a country-dweller, to the opulence and modernity of his surroundings in the sophisticated restaurant, and also to the long fingernails of Oblonsky's colleague Grinevich. Tolstoy further identified *dikost'* with independence and originality, and defined it as the cardinal trait of his eccentric family. He took pride in being 'peculiar'.

39 *'Spirited steeds . . . love-sick youths by their eyes'*: inaccurate quotation of the Greek poet Anacreon's 55th Ode, as translated by Pushkin. In Nabokov's more accurate translation of Pushkin, the lines read: 'Gallant steeds one recognizes | By the marking branded on them; | Uppish Parthians one can tell | By their elevated mitres; | As to me I recognize | Happy lovers by their eyes . . .'

41 *"as I with loathing behold my life, I tremble and curse, and bitterly lament"*: quotation from Pushkin's 1828 poem 'Remembrance' (*Vospominanie*), which Tolstoy was particularly fond of.

not according to my deserts, but according to God's mercy: a paraphrase of the first verse of Psalm 51.

Tver: important provincial town about 100 miles north of Moscow, on the road to St Petersburg.

42 *when the woodcock are roding*: Levin uses the specific word *tyaga*, denoting the spring courtship flight at dawn and dusk of the male woodcock, which is known in English as 'roding'.

43 *Himmlisch ist's . . . Hatt' ich auch recht hübsch Plaisir*: inaccurate quotation of a short poem by Heinrich Heine from his 1823 sequence 'Die Heimkehr' ('The Homecoming'). Many commentators have attributed these lines to the (originally French) libretto of Johann Strauss's operetta *Die Fledermaus* (1874), where they do not actually exist. Heine's poem actually reads: 'Himmlisch wars, wenn ich bezwang | Meine sündige Begier, | Aber wenns mir nicht gelang, | Hatt ich doch ein groß Pläsier.' Tolstoy was quoting a friend's rendition of the poem when he

used it here, and was apparently unaware himself of its inaccuracy until informed by a correspondent.

lovely fallen creatures: paraphrase of a line in Pushkin's verse drama *Feast in the Time of Plague* (1830).

Christ would have never said . . . misused: a reference to Jesus's words in Luke 7: 47 about the sinful woman who pours perfume on his feet: 'Wherefore I say unto thee, Her sins, which are many, are forgiven; for she loved much: but to whom little is forgiven, the same loveth little.'

that gentleman in Dickens . . . with his left hand: a typically inaccurate reference by Oblonsky to the pompous John Podsnap in *Our Mutual Friend* (1865), who 'even acquired a peculiar flourish of the right arm in often clearing the world of its most difficult questions by sweeping them behind him'.

44 *both kinds of love, which you remember Plato defines in his Symposium*: Pausanias, one of the diners who discuss love in Plato's dialogue *Symposium*, distinguishes 'earthly' (physical) from 'heavenly' (what we would now call 'platonic') love.

45 *She had come out for her first season that winter*: the winter social season for Russian high society traditionally lasted from Christmas to the beginning of Lent.

46 *the matchmaking aunt*: Russian marriages were traditionally arranged through the agency of a matchmaker, who would liaise with both sets of parents, but this practice had been abandoned in high society.

47 *enrolled in courses*: the first higher-education courses for women were founded in St Petersburg and Moscow in 1869, and established on a more permanent and official footing in Moscow in 1872 by the historian Professor Vladimir Guerrier.

52 *Kaluga*: city on the Oka river, nearly 100 miles south-west of Moscow.

53 *bast shoes*: simple peasant footwear made of plaited birch or linden bark.

54 *classical and modern education and universal military service*: a 'classical' (*klassicheskoe*) education at a high school or gymnasium (*gimnaziya*) in Russia led to university entrance, and focused on the study of Greek and Latin. The inferior 'modern' (*real'noe*) education taught at the *real'noe uchilishche* (based on the German *Realschule*), established in 1872, signified modern languages, and scientific subjects more suitable for a career in commerce and industry. In 1874 a reform reduced the liability of all social classes, rather than just the lower ones, to conscription for up to six rather than the previous twenty-five years.

table-turning and spirits: spiritualism was very fashionable in high society in Russia in the 1870s, and was written about in 1875 in the *Russian Messenger*. Tolstoy was, naturally, highly critical.

house-spirits: the house-spirit (*domovoi*) was an age-old figure from Russian folklore; all houses were supposed to have their own house-spirits, who acted like guardians and lived either under the stove or under the front door.

56   *I'm very glad to see you*: the old Prince uses both the informal *ty* and the formal *vy* in one sentence.

   playing hide the ring: *kolechko* is a traditional Russian game with many variations. In one, the players (usually girls) first sit in a row, then the leader surreptitiously places a ring or a coin in the hands of another player, who becomes leader if successful in breaking free of the others. Nabokov describes a version in which a ring is passed along a string held by all players, who sit in a circle, and the player in the middle has to guess who has the ring.

58   *Corps of Pages*: his Imperial Majesty's 'Corps des Pages', founded in 1802 in St Petersburg, and re-formed in 1865, was an elite school of military cadets. Pupils were sons of noblemen and high-ranking officers from the top three levels of the Table of Ranks, who were generally admitted by examination and then assigned to the regiment of their choice.

60   *bezique*: a seventeenth-century French card game which became fashionable in Russia in the 1870s.

   Château des Fleurs . . . can-can: this was an establishment in Moscow's Petrovsky Park based on the Parisian *café-chantant*, where dancers and gymnasts performed. The can-can, a risqué dance which originated in working-class ballrooms in Paris in the 1830s, was later danced by courtesans as entertainment, and retained its louche associations when it transferred to Russia.

   Dusseaux's: a fashionable French hotel and restaurant in Moscow where both Karenin and Levin stay in the novel. Tolstoy stayed there in February 1873.

75   *enfilade*: a suite of rooms with interconnecting doors formally aligned with each other, found typically in grand palaces, and in old-style Russian houses, particularly on country estates.

81   *I will not cast the first stone*: this refers to the passage in St John's Gospel in which Jesus refuses to condemn an adulterous woman (John 8: 7: 'So when they continued asking him, he lifted up himself, and said unto them, He that is without sin among you, let him first cast a stone at her'). This phrase, which reminds us of the novel's epigraph, is reproduced by Vronsky, Karenin, and Dolly at subsequent points of the novel.

82   *projected public theatre*: a professional 'people's theatre' (*narodnyi teatr*) operated for the first time during the Moscow Polytechnical Exhibition in the summer of 1872 (held in honour of the bicentenary of Peter the Great's birth), and generated hopes for the abolition of the imperial monopoly on theatrical performance in St Petersburg and Moscow, but it remained in force until 1882.

87   *Western Territory*: western and southern territories, comprising much of present-day Lithuania, Belorussia, and Ukraine, which had been

absorbed into the Russian empire between the middle of the seventeenth and the end of the eighteenth century, and represented nine provinces.

'the monk': Tolstoy's brother Dmitry, on whom Levin's brother Nikolay seems to be modelled, was also called 'the monk' by his brothers during his religious period. Tolstoy was not present when Dmitry died of tuberculosis in 1856, but he was present at the death of his eldest brother Nikolay from the same disease in 1860.

88   *short kaftan . . . without cuffs or collar*: Dmitry's friend Kritsky wears a *poddevka*, a traditional Russian short kaftan, a coat-like garment which was tight-fitting, waisted, fastened at the side, with a tall collar and usually worn under a full-length kaftan or fur coat. The Slavophile Konstantin Aksakov was the first Slavophile to wear a *poddevka* in the 1830s, but in the cities it was a garment mostly worn by the lower classes. Unlike Dmitry's companion Masha, respectable women would always wear dresses with collars and cuffs.

89   *Sunday schools*: non-official schools operated by the mostly young liberal intelligentsia for illiterate working people in Russian cities between 1859 and 1862 on their only free day in the week. There were twenty-three in St Petersburg by the end of 1860, but amidst widespread disappointment about the terms of the Emancipation of Serfdom act, all were then shut down by the government, which believed they were being used by revolutionaries to distribute seditious propaganda. In the 1870s it became possible for secular Sunday schools to open again. Tolstoy was very active in rural peasant education, having started a school on his estate in 1859, but he had his own views about education and did not collaborate with anyone, except to hire young students to teach at the new schools he opened in neighbouring villages between 1860 and 1862. He abruptly dropped his school activities soon after the secret police raided his estate. Tolstoy taught peasants again briefly in 1872, before beginning work on *Anna Karenina*.

good riddance: Nikolay uses the traditional Russian expression *vot Bog, vot i porog*, meaning 'there is God [i.e. the icon corner], and there is the threshold [of the door]'.

90   *Kazan Province*: the Tatar khanate of Kazan, about 500 miles east of Moscow, was conquered by Ivan the Terrible in 1552, and later became the capital city in the province formed in 1708 as part of Peter the Great's administrative reforms.

97   *Tyndall's book about heat*: a Russian translation of John Tyndall's work on thermodynamics, *Heat Considered as a Mode of Motion* (1863), was published in 1864. Tolstoy read it in 1872.

101   *third bell*: the first bell would ring fifteen minutes before a train's departure, the second ten minutes before, and the third bell meant departure was imminent.

107   *Bologovo*: real-life Bologoe was a junction roughly halfway between Moscow and St Petersburg, where there would be a twenty-minute stop for refreshments.

110 *Pan-Slavist*: an adherent of the movement which sought the liberation
of Slav nations from Ottoman or Habsburg rule, and ultimately advo-
cated the political and spiritual union of all Slavs under the leadership
of Russia. The Slavonic Benevolent Committees (Moscow 1858, St
Petersburg 1869) were private organizations which sought to give help to
subjugated Slavs outside Russia, and were the only legal means for helping Southern Slavs resist the Ottoman empire in the early 1870s. The
South Slav theme is resumed later on in the novel.

111 *his two stars*: insignia worn on the chest indicating Karenin's high ministerial ranking in the civil service as an Actual Privy Councillor.

113 *Duc de Lille's Poésie des enfers*: an invented poet, reminiscent of Leconte
de Lisle (1818–94), and an invented collection, reminiscent of the work
of Baudelaire, author of *Les Fleurs du mal* (1857).

114 *Morskaya Street*: Vronsky probably lives on the fashionable and expensive
Bolshaya Morskaya ('Great Sea') Street, in the centre of St Petersburg,
rather than the nearby Malaya Morskaya ('Small Sea') Street.

116 *French Theatre*: the Imperial Mikhailovsky Theatre was the home of a
celebrated French drama troupe, which also started staging operettas in
1866, but Vronsky is here referring to the round wooden circus building of
the 'Theatre Bouffe', opposite the Imperial Alexandrinsky Theatre, where
French operetta was staged between 1870 and 1878. Renamed the 'Opera
Bouffe' in 1873, it became very fashionable amongst the aristocracy, who
came to hear French stars perform in the latest operettas from Paris.

117 *Rebecca-the-slave-girl genre*: possibly an allusion to the beautiful Rebecca
of Genesis 24, but she was not a slave-girl. Probably Petritsky simply has
in mind a Middle Eastern kind of beauty.

PART TWO

119 *'What a babbler'*: Tolstoy uses the term *pustobrekh*, denoting both someone who talks too much and needlessly, and, in hunting, a dog which
barks too much and needlessly in the field. The English word has the
same joint meaning.

120 *Yauza bridge*: a wooden bridge over a tributary of the Moskva river in
the eastern city centre, dismantled during icy weather or high waters.
Probably this is the 'Ust'inskii' bridge, at the mouth of the Yauza
where it flows into the Moskva river, linking the Moskvoretskaya and
Kotel'nicheskaya embankments. The first permanent metal bridge was
built in 1883.

121 *Soden waters*: Soden is a German spa town situated between Frankfurt
and Wiesbaden. Tolstoy visited it in 1860.

123 *Alexander Andreyich*: in Part 4, Chapter 9, p. 384, Tolstoy refers to the old
Prince as 'Alexander Dmitrievich'.

125 *vieux Saxe*: a type of porcelain from Saxony.

128   *Lent*: 'Great Lent' marked the end of the winter social season and the beginning of seven weeks of austerity, leading up to Easter.

130   *famous prima donna*: we learn subsequently from Betsy Tverskaya that this is Christina Nilsson (1843–1921), a celebrated Swedish soprano with an admired range and *bel canto* technique who enjoyed great success as a guest soloist with the Imperial Italian Opera at the Bolshoi Theatre between 1872 and 1885, rivalled only by Adelina Patti.

131   *French Theatre*: see note to p. 116.

     Blessed are the peacemakers: Betsy misquotes Matthew 5: 9, which reads: 'Blessed are the peacemakers: for they shall be called the children of God.'

132   *Titular Councillor*: the ninth out of fourteen ranks in the civil service Table of Ranks.

     Talleyrand: the diplomat Charles de Talleyrand-Périgord (1754–1838) represented France after the Napoleonic Wars at the Congress of Vienna (1814–15).

133   *fast cab*: there was a significant difference in price and quality of ride between hiring a *Van'ka* (diminutive of 'Ivan'), whose cab and horse would be very shabby, and a *likhach* (a daring, fast driver), as in this case.

135   *Kaulbach*: Wilhelm von Kaulbach (1805–74), a German painter whose illustrations of Shakespeare and Goethe assisted Nilsson in creating the roles of Ophelia (in Thomas's *Hamlet*, 1868) and Marguerite in Gounod's *Faust* (1859). It is the latter which is clearly being discussed here. Nilsson concluded her first Russian tour in March 1873 in this role. When she opened the jewel-box in the garden scene in Act 3, she found real jewels, gifts from the Tsar. After the performance, students lay down on the snow to create a living carpet for her.

     Princess Myagkaya: an ironic name, in view of her waspish comments— *myagkaya* means soft.

136   *Louis Quinze*: King Louis XV of France (1715–74) earned a notorious reputation for the debauchery of his court at the end of his reign, and is associated with the phrase *Après moi, le déluge* ('After me, the deluge').

     diable rose outfit: a reference to the comedy *Les Diables roses* ('The Pink Devils') by Grange and Thiboux, which was performed at the French Theatre in St Petersburg in 1874.

137   *man who is deprived of his shadow*: Tolstoy must actually have in mind Adalbert von Chamisso's *Peter Schlemihls wundersame Geschichte* ('Peter Schlemihl's Strange Adventure', 1814), as Grimm wrote no such tale. 'The Shadow' by Hans Christian Andersen appeared in an anthology of *Best Tale*s for the first time in Russian translation in 1870.

138   *every person is happy with his wits . . . French saying*: adaptation of Le Rochefoucauld's *Maximes*, no. 89: 'Tout le monde se plaint de sa mémoire, et personne ne se plaint de son jugement' ('Everyone complains about their memory, and no one complains about their judgement').

139   *Sir John*: a fictional character clearly modelled on Granville Waldegrave, 3rd Baron Radstock, whose first missionary activities in St Petersburg in 1874 were welcomed by many Russian aristocrats, who were receptive to his message of personal salvation through independent Bible study. The New Testament only became widely available in modern Russian translation in 1876, the Russian Orthodox Church having earlier suppressed it for political reasons. Radstock was banned from Russia in 1878.

140   *Vlasieva*: it is perfectly polite in Russian in this kind of social setting to refer to women simply by their surname, unlike in English—in most cases in the current translation, therefore, surnames are preceded by 'Madame'.

142   *Rambouillet . . . the graces and the muses*: the Marquise de Rambouillet (1588–1665) created the first literary salon at her Parisian residence, the Hôtel de Rambouillet, and was instrumental in defining taste and public opinion. The three Graces were goddesses of beauty who lived on Olympus with the Muses, inspiration to each art form.

155   *minus nine*: this is Celsius; in the novel the temperature is recorded at minus 7 degrees Réamur.

      Thomas Sunday: the first Sunday after Easter, referred to in the text as 'Red Hill' (*Krasnaya Gorka*), a popular folk holiday of pagan origin celebrating the arrival of spring which was assigned after the adoption of Christianity to 'Thomas Sunday', so-called because of the reading from John 20: 19–31 set for that day. The 'Red Hill' name perhaps derives from the custom of playing games on this day on the first patches of raised ground clear of snow, 'red' in Russian (*krasnyi*) being synonymous with 'beautiful' (*prekrasnyi*).

      first spring flight from their new home: Tolstoy, a keen bee-keeper, uses here two words linked to specialized terms in the Russian apiarist's lexicon which are impossible to translate succinctly into English. The first, *vystavlennaya*, denotes the transfer of beehives from their winter to their summer resting-place; *obletavshayasya* relates to the first spring flight bees make once their hives have been moved. This is one of several instances in Tolstoy's writing where he uses the singular 'bee' to describe bees collectively.

165   *Ossian's type of woman*: the mysterious and tragic heroines in the poems of James Macpherson (1738–96), who masqueraded as Ossian, a third-century Gaelic bard. The poems were very popular in Russia.

166   *croaking sound*: the woodcock's roding call during the mating season consists of several frog-like croaks, alternating with a higher-frequency whistle.

169   *It's not young-growth*: Tolstoy uses the word *obidnoi* from his local Tula dialect, meaning 'young wood', therefore of inferior quality to mature timber.

      'Although a lofty mind . . . planet's rays': a quotation from the second stanza of the ode 'God' (1784) by the distinguished poet and statesman Gavriila Derzhavin (1743–1816).

170 *searching for the icon*: it was traditional, particularly for Russian merchants, who were especially devout, to make the sign of the cross in front of the icon corner when entering the reception room in someone's house.

171 *open legal proceedings for absolutely everything nowadays*: courts in Russia were not open to the public until the Judicial Reforms of 1864.

174 *Electric light everywhere*: electric light was still a rarity in 1870s Russia, except in establishments of public entertainment such as the Château des Fleurs, which adopted it in 1873 in order to attract custom.

175 *even the walls help when you are at home*: a Russian proverbial saying (*doma stena pomogayut*—'at home the walls help').

176 *Woodcock roding in the morning can be good*: woodcock are traditionally hunted either at dawn or dusk during their spring mating season in Russia.

177 *Werther-like*: a reference to the hero of Goethe's *The Sorrows of Young Werther* (1774), who kills himself for love of Lotte, married to his friend.

178 *Krasnoye Selo races*: from 1824, the Imperial army was permanently transferred from St Petersburg and garrisoned during the summer months, in preparation for annual military manoeuvres in the presence of the Tsar, at Krasnoye Selo, a village outside St Petersburg. It is situated close to the former imperial summer residence at Tsarskoye Selo, now renamed Pushkin in honour of the poet's school years spent there. The first horse races were held at the Krasnoye Selo racetrack in July 1872, then almost annually until 1897. Restricted to officers of guards, cavalry, or horse artillery regiments, they were very popular with the court, for whom a spectators' pavilion was erected at the finish. The 2.5-mile 'Emperor's Cup' steeplechase was the main race, held at the end of the day. In 1872 it had twelve obstacles, and fifteen of the twenty-seven officers competing managed to stay the course. Tolstoy was never a spectator at any of these races himself, but his friend and neighbour Dmitry Obolensky gave him an eyewitness account of the 1872 Emperor's Cup steeplechase.

dacha: usually a rustic vacation house, typically lived in during the summer months.

179 *Krasnoye Theatre*: a summer theatre was established during the army's residency at Krasnoye Selo.

181 *'There was a King in Th-u-u-le'*: first line of Marguerite's aria 'Il était un roi de Thulé' from Act III, scene 6 of Gounod's *Faust*.

Peterhof: another popular summer vacation resort close to St Petersburg, on the Gulf of Finland, now named Petrodvorets in honour of the palace built there by Peter the Great.

182 *Tsarskoye*: abbreviation for the village of Tsarskoye Selo.

183 *Frou-Frou*: a popular comic play in five acts by Meilhac and Halévy entitled *Froufrou* (1869) was performed in Russian translation in St Petersburg in 1872. It tells of a woman who leaves her husband and son

to run off with her lover. Tolstoy bought a horse of this name in 1873 from his friend Dmitry Obolensky.

184	*serious sweating*: sweating is the most common way to reduce parts of the neck between the poll and withers of a horse to enhance its conformation, and is also used to reduce a horse's body mass artificially by eliminating excess water.

190	*'I did not expect . . . you'*: the hesitation is due to Anna deciding to address Vronsky with the familiar pronoun *ty*.

195	*Cossack Horse Guards' race*: His Majesty's Life-Guards Cossack Regiment formed the Third Brigade of the First Cavalry Divison of the Imperial Guard.

207	*Marshal of the Nobility*: elected office for an administrative district in imperial Russia.

209	*nightingales don't live on fables*: one of the many Russian proverbs featuring a nightingale.

218	*Carlsbad*: a popular spa, now called Karlovy Vary, in the Czech Republic.

223	*daughter of a court chef*: this story reflects that of Pasha, the ward taken in by Tolstoy's aunt Alexandra.

227	*Widows' Home*: charitable institution in Moscow and St Petersburg founded in 1803.

228	*give up your tunic if someone takes your cloak*: Luke 6: 29.

232	*Pietists*: adherents of a Protestant movement begun in the late seventeenth century which advocated Bible study and personal piety.

237	*they've conquered everybody*: between 1863 and 1870, under Prime Minister Otto von Bismarck, Prussia was victorious in the Schleswig, Austro-Prussian, and Franco-Prussian wars, paving the way for the Prussian King Wilhelm I to become the first Emperor of a united Germany in 1871.

PART THREE

241	*Sergei Ivanovich's attitude to the peasantry*: the word used here is *narod*, meaning variously 'people' in a general sense as well as 'the common people', who in Russia are the peasants.

244	*zemstvo doctor*: the reforms of the 1860s led to the establishment of a free public health care service administered by the zemstvo. Until then medical provision in rural areas had been primitive, with one doctor to tens of thousands of patients, so the influx of doctors, who had hitherto occupied a very low social status, and the building of clinics and hospitals funded by the zemstvo was a major step forward.

245	*skep*: a straw or wicker beehive.

246	*St Peter's Day*: 29 June. This was traditionally the day to begin mowing in central Russia.

The grass says to the water: we will sway and sway: Tolstoy included the complete riddle in his ABC book (1872). The first says, 'We will run and run.' The second says, 'We will stand and stand.' The third says, 'We will sway and sway.' The answer is: a river, its banks, the grass growing on them.

249   *the emancipation of the serfs*: the serf became a free citizen as a result of the Act of Emancipation (1861), able to marry, own property, take legal action, and engage in trade, but landowners' privileges were preserved.

250   *birch trees we stick in the ground on Trinity Sunday*: the birch tree was traditionally considered the most venerated symbol of fertility and the renewal of life during Russian Trinity Week (Pentecost). Russians would celebrate Trinity Sunday on the fiftieth day after Easter by decorating homes and churches with flowers and greenery.

256   *kvass*: traditional non-alcoholic Russian drink made from fermented black bread.

258   *corvée*: before the Emancipation, serfs had to work on their owners' land for a set number of days per week.

259   *wood cow-wheat*: the plant *Melampyrum nemorosum*, annual with yellow flowers and purple upper leaves, which grows on the edges of forests and in wooded meadows, usually in the shade. It is called 'wood cow-wheat' in English due to its use as cattle fodder, and the supposed resemblance of its seeds to wheat. In Russian its popular name of 'Ivan-and-Marya' (*Ivan-da-Marya*) is derived from the folk-tale of a young couple who, after falling in love and marrying, discover they are brother and sister. They decide to turn into a flower with two contrasting colours in order not to have to part.

262   *wooden rattle*: a percussive folk instrument rather than a toy, the *treshchotka* consists of a set of wooden plates threaded together on a string that are 'clapped' together.

263   *annexe*: most Russian estate houses had a wing (known by the German word *Flügel*) on either side. At Tolstoy's estate, Yasnaya Polyana, the main house was also absent (as he'd been forced to sell it to pay gambling debts), and his family lived in one of the wings, which was extended as his family grew.

266   *metempsychosis*: the idea that the soul can migrate from one body to another.

268   *birch mushroom*: the specific word for mushroom used here is *shlyupik*, which is later used to describe a superannuated member of the English Club in Moscow in Part Seven, chapter 8, but given a different etymology there.

270   *petticoat*: a reference to the contemporary fashion for hoop petticoats, which would have to be bunched up into a flat disc, stepped into, and pulled to the waist, after which the wearer would spin round so that the hoops descended properly.

278 *St Philip's Day*: commemorated by the Orthodox Church on 14
     November. The forty-day Christmas Fast lasts from 15 November to 24
     December.

283 *La Belle Hélène*: the title of Offenbach's 1864 operetta, which tells the story
     of how Paris causes the Trojan War by carrying off Menelaus' wife Helen.

285 *crude proof the law required*: in Russia at this time ocular evidence of adul-
     tery was required in order to obtain a divorce, after which the guilty party
     could not remarry.

288 *Eugubine Tables*: an article on these inscribed bronze tablets, discovered
     in Umbria in 1444, was published in the *Revue des Deux Mondes* in 1874.

290 *settlement of minorities*: a reference to the disturbances in the 1870s
     caused by the illegal expropriation of Bashkir lands by Russian settlers
     in the newly colonized provinces of Ufa and Orenburg. The Bashkirs,
     originally nomadic horsemen from the southern Urals, were a Turkic-
     speaking Muslim people who had been subjugated by the Russians by the
     middle of the eighteenth century, and had gradually found themselves
     becoming a minority. Tolstoy himself purchased property in Bashkir
     territory near Samara, where he regularly took summer holidays in the
     1870s, so was highly conscious of this issue.

298 *croquet*: the English game had been imported to Russia by 1869, when the
     All-England Croquet and Lawn Tennis Club was founded, and become
     fashionable.

301 *They've thrown their caps over the windmill*: a translation of the French
     expression 'ils ont jeté ses bonnets par-dessus les moulins'.

307 *Decembrist*: one of the idealistic aristocrats involved in the abortive upris-
     ing of 14 December 1825, which sought to introduce democratic reforms
     at the time of Nicholas I's accession. Those not executed were exiled to
     Siberia, and amnestied in 1856, after the death of Nicholas I. Tolstoy's
     War and Peace originated with his interest in the amnestied Decembrists,
     one of whom was his distant relative.

310 *Central Asia*: the 1870s was a time of intense imperial expansion into
     Central Asia. The Khiva Khanate was annexed to Russia in 1873.

314 *Russian communists*: there were no political parties in Russia at this time,
     so the reference is not specific, but many members of the radical intel-
     ligentsia, such as Nikolay Chernyshevsky (1828–89), author of the incen-
     diary novel *What Is To Be Done?* (1863), advocated communism under
     the influence of French utopian socialists such as Charles Fourier (1772–
     1837) and Saint-Simon (1760–1825), whose ideas were very popular in
     Russia.

325 *hay-tedder*: a machine with rotating forks used to loosen the hay for
     drying.

327 *tarantass*: a four-wheeled vehicle without springs or seats, but lined with
     straw.

     troika: Russian carriage or sleigh pulled by three horses abreast.

330 *cap with the red band and cockade*: insignia for a district Marshal of the Nobility.

336 *Percherons*: breed of dray-horse originating in France.

338 *primitive commune*: the Russian village gathering (*obshchina*), which operated on a principle of shared responsibility.

Schulze-Delitzsch movement . . . the Mulhausen system: Hermann Schultze-Delitzsch (1808–83), a German economist, founded mutual savings societies. Ferdinand Lasalle (1825–64) led the German workers' movement campaigning for universal suffrage. Jean Dollfus (1800–87), factory owner and mayor of Mulhouse in Alsace, founded the Mulhausen system in 1853, which enabled workers to buy the houses they were renting.

339 *not Frederick at all*: Poland was partitioned in 1772, 1793, and 1795 by Russia, Austria, and Prussia, which was ruled at that time by Frederick the Great.

341 *Spencer*: the English sociologist and philosopher Herbert Spencer (1820–1903) sought to apply Darwin's ideas about evolution to sociology.

346 *Kauffmann . . . Jones . . . Dubois . . . Micelli*: fictional names.

348 *Franklin*: the American scientist and statesman Benjamin Franklin (1706–90), whom Tolstoy revered.

351 *ancient legends*: the warriors here are *bogatyri*, the semi-mythical heroes of Russian medieval epics.

354 *métayers*: farmers who paid rent in kind.

PART FOUR

358 *bliny*: Russian pancakes, made with yeast and buckwheat, and traditionally served as part of the festive fare during Shrovetide.

359 *peasant stalker*: the word *obkladchik* here denotes in bear hunting someone who tracks the animal down, then drives it in the direction of those hunting.

366 *Italian Opera*: the Imperial Italian Opera had been the main resident company at the St Petersburg Bolshoi Theatre since 1843, and the most prestigious in Russia, although its popularity began to wane after the opening of the Mariinsky Theatre in 1860.

368 *And my son will go and live with my sister*: Karenin's sister is not mentioned elsewhere, which leads one to assume she was posited as a character only in early drafts. The novel is not free from gaps and inconsistencies, related to the passing of time, and to minor details which are subsequently contradicted, such as the heating of Levin's house. In Part One, chapter 27, we learn that he heats his whole house, and then in Part Three, chapter 31, we read that he heats only one room.

377 *live perch*: the custom was for the host to keep the fish alive in a tank until immediately before cooking.

379 *Oh moralist, do not be so severe!*: paraphrase of the first line of a poem
by the fourteenth-century Persian poet and mystic Hafiz, translated into
Russian from a German translation by Afanasy Fet (1859).

385 *Russification of Poland*: during the 1870s the Tsarist government followed
a policy of promoting Russian institutions in Poland with the aim of
eradicating Polish nationalism.

Depret . . . Levé: leading French wine merchants in Moscow.

388 *contrary to the proverb*: 'People greet you according to your cap; they part
with you according to your wit.'

389 *the Rhine become French*: Alsace and Lorraine were ceded to Germany in
1871, but in elections in 1873–4 voters registered their protest against
this.

390 *anti-nihilist influence*: the term 'nihilist' first gained currency in Turgenev's
Fathers and Sons (1862), and denotes a radical young intellectual of the
1860s who rejects all authorities, like his hero Bazarov.

391 *women's education*: a government commission discussed the question of
higher education for women between 1873 and 1875, leading to official
authorization the following year.

392 *long hair, but short . . .*: the full proverb is 'long hair, short wit'.

398 *choral principle*: a term used by the writer Konstantin Aksakov (1817–60)
to denote the fundamental Slavophile concept of spiritual community
(*sobornost'*). The radical Populist intelligentsia believed the peasant commune contained the seeds of an innate Russian form of socialism because
of this inherent 'choral principle', in which the individual is not suppressed but is devoid of ego.

410 *Fulde's*: a Moscow jeweller established in 1823, which had a shop on the
fashionable Kuznetsky Most.

412 *Froom's railway guide*: a guide to Russian and European railways published in 1870.

'Quos vult perdere dementat': 'those whom [a God] wishes to destroy he
sends mad'.

415 *martyr*: St Mary of Egypt, a former prostitute who spent forty-seven
years in the desert after converting to Christianity.

423 *crochet-work*: *mignardise* is a type of narrow braid on which a crochet
design is worked.

425 *Tashkent*: now capital of Uzbekistan, annexed by Russia in 1865.

435 *and if any man take away thy coat, let him have thy cloak also*: Matthew 5:
39. Compare with the note to p. 228 and the reference to Luke 6: 29: 'give
up your tunic if someone takes your cloak.'

and three people have benefited: in the text, Oblonsky's untranslatable pun
plays on the Russian word *razvod*, meaning both divorce and the posting
[of sentries].

PART FIVE

442   *ambo*: raised platform in front of the iconostasis in a Russian Orthodox church.

      Vladimir pronunciation: with a particular stress on the 'o'. Vladimir is an ancient Russian city located 120 miles east of Moscow.

444   *best man*: the Russian *shafer* has a different function from the 'best man' in a Western wedding ceremony; the bride also has one. Their chief duty is to hold crowns over the bride and groom during the marriage service.

446   *Gogol's play . . . window*: the character Podkolesin in *Marriage* (1842).

449   *choir-stands*: there is a special place (*kliros*) on both the right and left sides of a Russian Orthodox church so the choir can sing antiphonally.

453   *kamilavka*: the Russianized (and inaccurate) name for the Greek *kali-mavkion*, denoting the cylindrical brimless hat worn by some Orthodox clergy.

455   *Arbat*: well-appointed street in a residential area of central Moscow (which gives its name to that particular district of the city).

457   *Darya Dmitrievna*: presumably Tolstoy meant to write Darya Alexandrovna here.

469   *Academy*: the St Petersburg Imperial Academy of Fine Arts was founded in 1757.

      Ivanov–Strauss–Renan: Alexander Ivanov (1806–58) completed his most famous painting, *Christ's Appearance to the People* (1837–57), in Italy. Influenced by the German theologian David-Friedrich Strauss (1808–74), author of a highly controversial 'historical' life of Jesus (1835–6), Ivanov inspired other Russian artists to depict Jesus as a historical figure. Ernest Renan's equally controversial *Life of Jesus* (1863), which denied Christ's divinity, was banned in Russia.

      realism of the new school: Mikhailov bears a resemblance to Ivan Kramskoy (1837–87), who in 1863 led an historic rebellion against the conservative strictures of the Imperial Academy and founded an artists' cooperative. It was succeeded in 1871 by the progressive Society of Itinerant Exhibitions whose adherents (the 'Wanderers') promoted Russian art and a realistic technique. Kramskoy's *Christ in the Wilderness* (1872) and these new developments were topics of conversation with Tolstoy at Yasnaya Polyana the following year, when the writer sat for his portrait.

      Charlotte Corday: (1768–93), the French assassin of the revolutionary Jean-Paul Marat.

475   *new Rachel*: Elisa Rachel (1820–58) was a renowned French classical actress.

485   *broderie anglaise*: a type of open, patterned embroidery on fine white linen which became particularly popular in England in the nineteenth century.

488 *Capuan*: a neologism derived from Capua, a town north of Naples, where
     the excessive indolence of Hannibal's troops during their winter stay
     there in 216 BC during the Punic Wars proved fateful. Parallels were
     drawn in Russian journals in the 1870s with the Paris of Napoleon III,
     and Tolstoy coins an adjective here which means self-indulgent and
     sybaritic.

498 *revealed them to children and the foolish*: inaccurate quotation from
     Matthew 11: 25, which reads: 'Thou hast hidden from the wise and
     revealed to children and those without understanding.'

499 *Holy Unction*: in the Orthodox Church, *Soborovanie*, known as 'Extreme
     Unction' in the West, is the Sacrament by means of which a sick person is
     anointed with holy oil. Ideally this is done by seven priests, in accordance
     with the seven candles symbolizing the seven gifts of the Holy Spirit,
     seven Gospel readings, seven prayers, and seven anointments of the sick
     person's body.

510 *abstaining when in doubt*: a translation of the French phrase 'dans le doute,
     abstiens-toi', which Tolstoy was fond of.

512 *lately been spreading through Petersburg*: this relates to the Evangelical
     Christianity preached by visiting aristocratic English Protestant mis-
     sionaries like the 'Sir John' mentioned earlier, and the real-life Baron
     Radstock.

515 *Komisarov*: the Kostroma peasant Osip Komissarov knocked a pistol
     from the hand of the revolutionary Dmitry Karakozov in 1866, thus sav-
     ing Alexander II's life during the first assassination attempt on the life of
     a Tsar. For a while he was lionized by high society, but then faded from
     view when he began to drink heavily. The 'Slavs' with whom Countess
     Lydia Ivanovna is in love may well be Serbs, who entered into war with
     the Ottoman empire in 1876.

     Ristich-Kudzhitsky: Jovan Ristić (1831–99) was a Russophile Serbian
     politician who acted as Foreign Minister during the Serbo-Turkish War
     of 1876, but Tolstoy adds another name to differentiate his character. In
     Part Eight, chapter 4, his name recurs without this addition.

517 *Alexander Nevsky*: the Order of St Alexander Nevsky, a red-enamelled
     gold cross worn at the hip on a scarlet sash across the left shoulder, was
     first bestowed in 1725 for distinguished state service.

519 *'He who is married . . . how to please the Lord'*: 1 Corinthians 7: 32–3.

523 *Slav tutor*: he is pointedly described as a 'Slav' (so possibly not Russian),
     which is unusual, since most tutors were French or German.

525 *The Order of St Andrew the First-Called*: worn on a blue sash over the
     right shoulder, the Order of St Andrew was the first and most prestigious
     Russian decoration, named after Russia's patron saint, and Jesus' first
     apostle, and founded by Peter the Great in 1698 after he witnessed award
     ceremonies in England and Austria during his 'Great Embassy'. The

Order of St Vladimir, which had four classes, was established in 1782 by Catherine the Great in honour of the Grand Prince of Kiev who brought Christianity to Rus in the tenth century.

528 *Enoch*: Enoch is the great-grandfather of Noah. In Genesis, we read about the ten patriarchs before the Flood who live for several centuries before dying. Enoch, who does not experience death, is the exception (Genesis 5: 24: 'Enoch walked faithfully with God; then he was no more, because God took him away').

545 *Patti*: the Italian soprano Carlotta Patti (1835–89) sang in Russia between 1872 and 1875 and was very popular. Her more celebrated sister Adelina (1840–89) sang in Russia in 1874.

PART SIX

570 *'Is ea id, eius, eius, eius!'*: the nominative declension of the demonstrative third-person pronoun ('he, she, it') in Latin, followed by the genitive case.

571 *Scotch cap*: Veslovsky presumably wears either a Balmoral bonnet or a glengarry bonnet, both traditional Scottish hats which can be worn as part of highland dress.

577 *light peasant moccasins and foot-bindings*: Tolstoy uses two colloquial Russian words here. *Porshni* denotes primitive, light peasant shoes made out of one piece of leather which are drawn tight with a string or cord threaded through holes along the edges—very like native American moccasins. They are particularly well suited for hunting in marshes, both because they are light and also because they can dry out quickly. *Podvertki* relates to the cloths wound around the foot and lower leg which all peasants wore, and were also a standard part of Russian army uniform instead of socks.

578 *wether sheep*: castrated male sheep.

583 *Automedon*: the name of Achilles' charioteer in Homer's *Iliad*.

584 *squelched*: Tolstoy deliberately and imaginatively uses the same onomatopoeic verb *chmokat'* to denote both the sucking sound made by Levin's heel as he extracts it from the bog and the 'scape' call made by the common snipe (*Gallinago gallinago*) when flushed, typically described in contemporary Russian ornithology as *chvek* or *zhvyak*. Also characteristic for male common snipe is the distinctive 'drumming' or 'bleating' sound produced by its vibrating tail feathers in flight during the mating season.

592 *a perfect Gretchen*: diminutive of Margareta, Faust's love in Goethe's *Faust* and Gounod's opera of the same name.

601 *'Heavy is the hat of Monomakh!'*: inaccurate quotation from Pushkin's play *Boris Godunov* (1825), which refers to the gold filigree skull-cap encrusted with precious stones and trimmed with sable, which was passed

to Vladimir II Monomakh by his maternal grandfather, the Byzantine Emperor Constantine IX Monomachus.

608 *bring forth children in pain*: Genesis 3: 16.

612 *char-à-banc*: usually open-topped horse-drawn carriage with benches.

647 *Gautier*: a well-known bookshop in Moscow run by a family of French origin.

667 *brethren*: a reference to the Balkan Slavs currently engaged in asserting their independence from the Turks.

669 *Taine*: the French historian, philosopher, and critic Hippolyte Taine (1828–93) published *L'Ancien Régime* in 1875, the first volume of his magnum opus *L'Origine de la France contemporaine*.

PART SEVEN

679 *tiny birds*: proverbial expression reliant on its rhyme: *pervaya kolom, vtoraya sokolom, tret'ya melkimi ptashechkami*.

680 *Montenegrins*: the principality of Montenegro also rose up against the Turks in 1876, and had more success than the Serbs.

682 *University Question*: a debate about university autonomy as opposed to the unpopular state control imposed in 1875.

684 *Journal de St Pétersbourg*: a semi-official, French-language Russian publication founded in 1842, which reflected the conservative political views of the aristocracy.

Buslayev's grammar: the philologist Fyodor Buslayev published a *Textbook of Russian Grammar compared with Church Slavonic* in 1869.

685 *South-Eastern Committee*: probably what is intended is an organization committed to supporting the Southern Slavs against the Turks.

686 *quartet dedicated to Bach's memory*: like the other piece Levin hears, this is an invention of Tolstoy's. Leading exponent of the Baroque musical style, and champion of counterpoint, J. S. Bach (1685–1750) was a neglected composer until Mendelssohn conducted an historic performance of the *St Matthew Passion* in 1829, despite the reverence Mozart and Beethoven both showed for his music in their own compositions. By the 1870s, however, when Levin goes to his concert, at the height of the Romantic movement in music, the 'Bach revival' was well under way. In December 1876, while he was working on Part Seven of *Anna Karenina*, Tolstoy requested a meeting with Tchaikovsky, whom he harangued about Beethoven's failings as a composer. He was given a private performance of Tchaikovsky's First Quartet (1871), in which he was moved to tears by the Russian folk song in its second movement.

688 *Wagner . . . sphere of another art form*: Levin generalizes and oversimplifies the aim of Richard Wagner (1813–83) to revive the spirit of ancient tragedy by combining poetry with the expressive power of symphonic

music to transform opera into 'music drama'. Levin mistakenly believes Wagner sought for music and poetry to stray into each other's territory, whereas Wagner's stated goal was for them to be combined in an organic way. Wagner's *Ring* cycle was first performed in Bayreuth in 1876, and was hotly discussed throughout Europe, including Russia, where very little of his music had yet been heard at that point. Tolstoy's knowledge of Wagner's music at this time was probably close to non-existent, but later on his partial attendance of a performance of *Siegfried* in 1896 would lead to a blistering critique in his treatise *What is Art?* (1897).

sculptor: in 1875, Mark Antokolsky (1843–1902) entered the competition to create a memorial for the 1880 celebrations of the national poet Pushkin. The design he submitted to the Academy of Arts showed Pushkin sitting on a rock, and was intended to evoke lines from his poem 'Autumn' (1830), in which he speaks of an 'invisible swarm' of familiar guests from his dreams coming towards him.

689 *'Lucca was very good'*: the soprano Pauline Lucca (1841–98) gave successful performances in St Petersburg and Moscow in 1869 and in 1877.

690 *foreigner being tried in Russia*: a reference to the German industrialist and railway entrepreneur Bethel Strousberg (1823–84) who, after going into business with Samuil Polyakov (see note to p. 724), in October 1875 went bankrupt and was arrested for defrauding a Moscow bank. The trial continued until November 1876 and aroused widespread indignation when Strousberg was deported rather than made to serve his sentence in Siberia.

Krylov fable: Ivan Krylov (1769–1844) is Russia's best-known author of fables, written in verse. In 'The Pike', a Fox, secretary to a panel of judges, is bribed by the Pike with fish, and suggests his sentence of hanging should instead be death by drowning.

693 *the inferno*: the non-Slavic word *infernal'naya* used here, based on the Latin *infernalis* (belonging to the lower regions, or hell), implies the club's gambling room.

694 *shlyupiks*: this word denotes a kind of birch mushroom, which is referred to as such in Part Six, chapter 8 (see note to p. 268).

697 *"Rejoice, Isaiah"*: a reference to a part of the Russian Orthodox wedding service.

700 *new illustrations of the Bible*: the French artist is Gustave Doré (1832–83), whose illustrated edition (1865) was published in Russia in 1875.

Zola, Daudet: the novelists Émile Zola (1840–1902) and Alphonse Daudet (1840–97), both associated with French Naturalism.

715 *Duma*: the Moscow Duma (municipal council) was first elected in 1863, and strongly supported the Balkan Slavs.

724 *Bolgarinov*: a clear reference to the Jewish industrialist Samuil Polyakov (1837–88), christened the 'king of the railways' for having built a quarter of Russia's railways. Tolstoy's invented name of Bolgarinov ('son of a Bulgarian') is close to Polyakov ('son of a Pole').

725 *wait-yid to see a yid*: the practice of referring to a Jew as a 'Yid' (*zhid*) was widespread in nineteenth-century Russia, and not perceived as necessarily pejorative. Oblonsky's pun relies on the resemblance to *zhid* in the Russian verb 'to wait' (*bylo delo do* zhida *i ya do* zhida-*lsya*).

730 *cafés chantants*: literally 'singing cafés', these establishments, where light music was performed for the public, originated in Paris in the eighteenth century, and became particularly popular throughout Europe in the late nineteenth century, including in the more permissive Russian cities such as Moscow and Odessa.

wax before the fire: a citation from Psalm 68: 2: 'May you blow them away like smoke—as wax melts before the fire, may the wicked perish before God.'

733 *Who is Landau?*: to some extent he is modelled on the celebrated Scottish medium Daniel Dunglas Home (1833–86), whom Tolstoy saw in Paris in 1857, and who held seances for Alexander II in St Petersburg and lectured on spiritualism in 1871. Another source was the Parisian medium of humble origins Camille Brédif, who came to St Petersburg in 1875.

734 *Count Bezzubov*: Home came to Russia in 1859 with Count Kushelev-Bezborodko, and made an advantageous marriage with his sister-in-law, a goddaughter of Nicholas I, and became a Count. Bezzubov ('toothless') is Tolstoy's humorous variation on Bezborodko ('beardless').

737 *like Saul*: a reference to St Paul's 'Damascene' conversion and subsequent mission, as outlined in Acts 9.

faith without works is dead: James 2: 26.

738 *Safe and Happy . . . Under the Wing*: invented titles of tracts written by visiting English evangelicals such as Lord Radstock. Tolstoy's source of intelligence about Radstock's activities amongst the Petersburg high aristocracy was his distant cousin Alexandra, a Lady-in-Waiting at court, who provided him with full details by letter at his request in March 1876. She also informed him that his caricature provided much mirth when these chapters were read out to the Empress and her entourage in May 1877.

758 *Nizhny Novgorod station*: this was the second station to be built in Moscow after the grandiose Nikolayevsky Station (from which trains departed for St Petersburg), but despite widespread expectation that it would be equally impressive, the modest wooden building which was completed in 1862 remained in place until 1896. The platform was particularly low, causing inconvenience for ladies boarding trains. After the inauguration of the railway line to Nizhny Novgorod, 250 miles east of Moscow, three passenger- and four goods-trains operated daily between the cities. The line was single-track until 1877.

759 *Trinity Monastery*: the Trinity Lavra of St Sergius, the most important monastery of the Russian Orthodox Church, north-east of Moscow.

763 *Tyutkin*: the name is reminiscent of the word *tyutki* ('young pups'), as the old Prince Shcherbatsky refers to eligible Muscovite men in Part One, chapter 15.

767 *Obiralovka*: the second stop on the line after Kuskovo, situated about fifteen miles east of Moscow. From 1877 Obiralovka was the final station for the three daily 'dacha trains' which operated from Moscow, with a journey-time of fifty minutes. The name of the station, which occupied a small, one-storey wooden building, comes from the verb 'to rob' (*obirat*), apparently because so many merchants passing through the village on their way to and from Moscow were robbed. In the 1870s only about twenty-five passengers a day would get off at Obiralovka, whereas 70,000 now pass through the station daily. It was renamed Zheleznodorozhnaya ('Railway') in 1939.

770 *water-tank*: this was situated in a pentagonal-shaped tower about thirty metres down the line from the station, and used when Obiralovka was the end of the line. Trains would load up with water from it before using the turning circle and then making the return journey to Moscow, travelling no faster than about twelve miles per hour.

PART EIGHT

774 *Northern Beetle*: Tolstoy has in mind here the *Northern Bee*, a reactionary St Petersburg newspaper.

775 *adherents of other faiths*: there was much debate when Uniate Christians in Western Ukraine who resisted the official conversion to Orthodoxy in 1875 were persecuted by the Russian Church. Uniates, who lived in former Orthodox areas subsequently taken over by the Poles or the Habsburgs, whose faith was Catholicism, followed the Eastern rite, but with allegiance to the Pope.

775 *American friends*: Russia had supported the federal cause in the American Civil War and received a delegation from the United States in 1866, and relations had continued to be friendly. Grand Duke Alexey visited the United States in 1871–2, and Russia participated in the Philadelphia Fair of 1876.

Samara famine: in 1873 Tolstoy played an important role in drawing public attention and raising money for relief-work when he discovered the extent of the disaster during a vacation on his property in the Samara area that summer.

the Exhibition: presumably the 1872 Polytechnical exhibition in Moscow.

Slav Question: debates concerning the liberation of the Slav peoples still under Ottoman rule in the Balkans and possible capture of Constantinople. Following uprisings in Bosnia-Herzegovina and Montenegro, Serbia declared war in 1876. Atrocities committed against the Bulgarians in 1876 aroused widespread support for their cause, and an intense upsurge in patriotic feeling. Russia declared war on Turkey in April 1877.

Serbian War: the Serbo-Turkish War of 1876.

776 *Kursk railway station*: situated in the east of Moscow close to the Nizhny

Novgorod station, with which it was later merged, this was the main railway going south from Moscow, via Tula and Oryol to Kursk. Tolstoy would use this railway line to travel home by train to Yasnaya Polyana.

volunteers: enthusiasm for the Pan-Slavic cause led many to join the Serbians in their war against Turkey in 1876. The merchant Alexander Porokhovshchikov organized the recruitment of volunteers in Moscow from the Slavyansky ('Slavonic') Bazaar Hotel, founded by him in 1873 to embody his vision of Slavonic brotherhood.

779 *'Glory'*: the rousing finale to Glinka's patriotic opera *A Life for the Tsar* (1836), 'Glory, Glory to you, Holy Rus', served as an unofficial national anthem.

784 *Ristić or Milan*: unlike the earlier reference in Part Five, chapter 23, Tolstoy unequivocally has the historical figure of Ristić in mind here (see note to p. 515). Milan Obrenović (1852–1901) declared himself Prince of Serbia in 1868 and became King in 1882.

carré: a close order infantry formation in the shape of a square used to defend against cavalry attack.

788 *It makes me sad he's there so often*: Tolstoy's wife used to lament that her husband spent so much time in his apiary during the early years of their marriage.

792 *will*: the fundamental force driving our lives, and central to the philosophical system put forward by Schopenhauer in *The World as Will and Representation*. See note to the Epigraph.

Khomyakov: Alexey Khomyakov (1804–60) was a prominent Slavophile who placed great store on the Russian Orthodox Church as instrumental to national destiny.

793 *free himself of this power*: there is an echo here with Anna's thoughts prior to her suicide at the end of Part Seven, chapter 31. Levin, also close to suicide, uses the same verb *izbavit'sya*—to free oneself.

810 *'ungodly Hagarians'*: descendants of Abraham's concubine Hagar (Genesis 16, 21), and here a way of referring to Muslims.

811 *Pugachev's mob . . . Khiva*: the Cossack Emelyan Pugachev (1742–75) led a popular revolt in 1773–4, for which he was executed by Catherine the Great. Khiva, a city south of the Aral Sea, was captured by the Russians during their Central Asian campaigns of 1871–5.

813 *Alphonse Karr*: French journalist and writer (1808–90), who printed pamphlets excoriating the Franco-Prussian War of 1870.

814 *"I have brought not peace, but a sword"*: inaccurate citation of Matthew 10: 34 ('Think not that I am come to send peace on earth: I came not to send peace, but a sword').

Reign and rule over us: the medieval *Primary Chronicle* relates that the Russians invited the Varangians, Norsemen who had entered the service of the Byzantine emperor, to become their leaders in the ninth century.

817 *Eastern Question*: the problems posed from the late eighteenth century onwards by the impending collapse of the Ottoman empire, which became acute after the revolt of its Christian subjects in the Balkans. The question dominated foreign-policy debates from the 1870s, with France and Britain wishing to bring an end to Turkish corruption and brutality but also resist Russian expansionism.

The Oxford World's Classics Website

www.worldsclassics.co.uk

- Browse the full range of Oxford World's Classics online

- Sign up for our monthly e-alert to receive information on new titles

- Read extracts from the Introductions

- Listen to our editors and translators talk about the world's greatest literature with our Oxford World's Classics audio guides

- Join the conversation, follow us on Twitter at OWC_Oxford

- Teachers and lecturers can order inspection copies quickly and simply via our website

www.worldsclassics.co.uk

	Eirik the Red and Other Icelandic Sagas
	The Kalevala
	The Poetic Edda
LUDOVICO ARIOSTO	Orlando Furioso
GIOVANNI BOCCACCIO	The Decameron
GEORG BÜCHNER	Danton's Death, Leonce and Lena, and Woyzeck
LUIS VAZ DE CAMÕES	The Lusiads
C. P. CAVAFY	The Collected Poems
MIGUEL DE CERVANTES	Don Quixote
	Exemplary Stories
CARLO COLLODI	The Adventures of Pinocchio
DANTE ALIGHIERI	The Divine Comedy
	Vita Nuova
J. W. VON GOETHE	Elective Affinities
	Erotic Poems
	Faust: Part One and Part Two
	The Sorrows of Young Werther
JACOB and WILHELM GRIMM	Selected Tales
E. T. A. HOFFMANN	The Golden Pot and Other Tales
HENRIK IBSEN	An Enemy of the People, The Wild Duck, Rosmersholm
	Four Major Plays
	Peer Gynt
FRANZ KAFKA	The Castle
	A Hunger Artist and Other Stories
	The Man who Disappeared (America)
	The Metamorphosis and Other Stories
	The Trial
LEONARDO DA VINCI	Selections from the Notebooks
LOPE DE VEGA	Three Major Plays